SIGMUND FREUD

EX LIBRIS

D.H. LAWRENCE

D.H. LAWRENCE

Selected Works

SONS AND LOVERS

THE PRUSSIAN OFFICER
AND OTHER STORIES

LADY CHATTERLEY'S LOVER

GRAMERCY BOOKS
NEW YORK • AVENEL

This 1994 edition is published by Gramercy Books,
distributed by Random House Value Publishing, Inc.,
40 Engelhard Avenue,
Avenel, New Jersey 07001.

Random House
New York • Toronto • London • Sydney • Auckland

Printed and bound in the United States

Library of Congress Cataloging-in-Publication Data

Lawrence, D.H. (David Herbert), 1885–1930
[Selections. 1994]
Selected works / D.H. Lawrence.
p. cm.
Contents: Sons and Lovers—Lady Chatterley's Lover—
The Prussian officer and other stories.
ISBN 0-517-10124-6
I. Title
PR6023.A93A6 1994
823'.912–dc20 93–44691 CIP

10 9 8 7 6 5 4 3 2 1

Contents

INTRODUCTION

Throughout his career, David Herbert Lawrence as a writer was a rebel. He consciously pushed accepted boundaries to attain his own vision and paid a high price. During his lifetime he had continual financial problems, and had to cope with public ostracism, and, many times, persecution. It was not until after World War II that his work began to be studied seriously and appreciated. Now, more than sixty years after his death, D.H. Lawrence is considered one of the twentieth-century's greatest and most visionary English novelists.

Lawrence was born in 1885 in Eastwood, a mining community in Nottinghamshire. His father Arthur Lawrence was a miner; his mother, Lydia Beardsall, had been a schoolteacher before she married. His mother came from a lower-middle-class family and her marriage to a miner was considered a step down in the eyes of those who adhered to England's rigid class system.

Lawrence was a sickly child, but encouraged by his mother—to whom he was very close—he was a good student. When he was twenty-one, he won a King's Scholarship competition and was able to attend Nottingham University College to study for a teacher's certificate. Two years later he began teaching at the Davidson Road School in Croydon, a London suburb. In 1909, several of his poems were published in the *English Review*. Then in 1911, his first novel, *The White Peacock*, was published, followed a year later by *The Trespasser*. About this time, because of illness and to concentrate more on his writing, he gave up teaching. In April 1912, he met Frieda Weekley, the German wife of one of his former professors and the daughter of the Baron Friederich von Richtoven. A month later they eloped to Italy.

It was in Italy that Lawrence finished what would become his first great novel, the autobiographical *Sons and Lovers*, which he had begun working on years earlier. The death of his mother in 1910 freed him to write truthfully and fearlessly about his own life. In a letter to a friend, Lawrence described the book as the story of a woman whose possessive love for her sons hinders their ability to achieve fulfilling relationships with other women. While the novel is a depiction of the destructive qualities of a mother's love—reflecting Freud's theory of the Oedipus complex—it is also the first great novel of the working class, as Lawrence said himself, "probably the only one written completely from the inside." Set in a town similar to the one where he was born and using the experience of his own family, Lawrence gives a detailed and realistic portrayal of the hardships and conflicts of the Morels, a mining family.

Gertrude Morel, the character based on his mother, is a woman who has married below her station. A religious woman from the lower-middle class she is serious, productive, and reveres hard work and adherence to a strict code of morals. Physical attraction led her to marriage with Walter Morel, who is from a mining family. When that attraction no longer exists the class difference becomes more important and results in a stormy marriage. Morel is a simple man, a coal miner with uncomplicated tastes and no real ambition, which is reflected in the family's frequent financial difficulties. His inability to live up to his wife's bourgeois expectations forces her to invest her ambitions in her two eldest sons, William and Paul, and live vicariously through them. Therefore the sons "love the mother—all the sons hate and are jealous of the father." William finds a lucrative job in London, but dies soon after marrying a frivolous woman. The mother then turns all her attentions upon Paul—the character based on Lawrence himself—in an abnormally close relationship.

For Lawrence, the mother and father represent the two conflicting sides of modern industrial England. Greatly influenced by William Wordsworth, the English poet who revered nature, Lawrence was essentially a romantic. He believed the pre-industrial society was superior to the mechanized and dehumanizing modern civilization. Walter Morel, the father, represents the pre-industrial man: simple, honest, and physical. But modern society has robbed him of his dignity and vitality. The mother, with her strong Protestant work ethic, represents the forces that built the industrial society. Her spirit, energy, and force of will—the things that make her an appealing person—are the attributes that made England a prosperous nation. But while materially successful, the mercantile spirit of English society is destructive to the soul. Mrs. Morel, by directing her attentions to her sons and treating her husband as a failure, is also partly the cause of his becoming an irresponsible drunk. The battle that takes place in the Morel home is symbolic of the struggle taking place in England. Industrial British society, by turning away from its agrarian roots, was destroying England to its very core, eradicating the old way of life which was more vibrant and complete.

This conflict is also represented by Lawrence in the actual landscape. In the opening chapter of *Sons and Lovers*, Lawrence describes the encroachment of industrial society upon the idyllic pastoral England: "six mines like black studs on the countryside, linked by a loop of fine chain, the railway." Industrialism for Lawrence was a physical and spiritual blight and he wrote "The real tragedy of England, as I see it, is the tragedy of ugliness. The country is so lovely: the man-made England is so vile."

Paul Morel—and Lawrence himself—in a sense, is a union and a product of these two opposing forces: the agrarian and the industrial. He embodies and personifies the conflict. Paul sides with his mother and views life from her point of view. He hates his father and rejects everything that his father is. He wants to be an artist and avoids working in the coal mine by taking a job in a surgical supply factory. But his closeness to his mother inhibits him from forming lasting relationships with other women. His first lover, Miriam, is, in many ways, like his mother—religious, pure, and possessive. Miriam helps and encourages Paul, but their relationship cannot be truly fulfilling because he is still attached to his mother, and Miriam is afraid of sex and wants an almost unreasonable spiritual communion which he cannot give. Lacking in Paul are the very qualities that he has rejected in his father. Lawrence believed that the "intellect is only a bit and a bridle," and is harmful if it alone rules a person's life as it does Paul's, who lives a dominantly conscious and ultimately unfulfilling life. To become whole he must free the natural part of himself, the part that is the physical and instinctive. His next lover, the buxom Clara Dawes, has the positive qualities of Paul's father. She possesses a sensuous and intuitive consciousness that Miriam lacks. She fulfills Paul's sexual desires, and, in a sense, makes him a true man, but the relationship ends because, again, of Paul's attachment to his mother and because Clara lacks the spiritual dimension of Miriam.

When his mother dies Paul is devastated. He is free of her possessive tyranny, but he misses the safety of the relationship. The challenge facing Paul—and symbolic of England's—is to become whole again by healing the split in himself and finding the way back to a more natural state. This was also Lawrence's goal as a writer and as a man: "To be alive, to be a man alive, to be whole man alive: that is the point."

In his first collection of short stories, *The Prussian Officer and Other Stories*, published in 1914, Lawrence pursues many of the same themes found in *Sons and Lovers*. In "Odor of Chrysanthemums," a miner's wife, modeled after Lawrence's mother, realizes when her husband dies that they "had denied each other in life." In "Daughters of the Vicar," two sisters choose very different husbands. One sister, in trying to improve her family's fortunes, allows herself to marry a man by whom she is physically repelled. The other sister, following her instincts, chooses a physically robust miner and bravely bears the burden of being a social outcast. Although "The Prussian Officer," which takes place in a military setting, appears on the surface to be unrelated to the other stories set in provincial England, it also explores the theme of the repressive and destructive qualities of modern civilization. In the story a captain's erotic desires are at odds with the repressive and controlled military society he is forced to live in.

Lawrence and his wife Frieda returned to England shortly before World War I. His next novel, *The Rainbow*—considered to be one of his finest—was published in 1915. The novel was officially banned in England as immoral on political as well as sexual grounds and marked the beginning of his battle with censors and an outraged public. *Women in Love*, the continuation of the story begun in *The Rainbow*, was completed in 1917, but was not published until 1920. The delay was caused by the difficulty in finding a publisher after the reception to the earlier book.

At the same time, because of Lawrence's outspoken antiwar views and Frieda's nationality, the couple were persecuted and harassed as possible enemy spies. Lawrence became very disillusioned with his native England. He dreamed of founding a utopian community he called Rananim, his "colony of lost souls," and tried, unsuccessfully, to convince his friends to join him.

The first World War was a major turning point in his life. Except for a few brief visits to England, Lawrence lived the rest of his life abroad, a self-imposed exile living on loans from friends and the precarious income from his writing. The foreign locales inspired his writings and also served as settings for his novels and short stories. He wrote *Kangaroo*, published in 1923, in six weeks during a visit to Australia. His novel about Mexico, *The Plumed Serpent*, published in 1926, was written while he was living in New Mexico, and was based on his trips into Mexico as well as his study of Aztec history and archaeology. He also wrote several nonfiction travel books, among them *Twilight in Italy*, *Mornings in Mexico*, and *Etruscan Places*.

In late 1925, the Lawrences returned to Europe and settled in Italy. By this time the tuberculosis that would kill Lawrence was already debilitating. But nevertheless he began work on his last and most famous novel, *Lady Chatterley's Lover*, which he set in England. In 1928 he had the book privately printed in a little shop in Florence and published it himself. It was declared obscene and was banned in the United States until 1959 and in England until 1960. Lawrence knew the book would cause a stir and even enjoyed the prospect: "like a bomb . . . they're still suffering from shell-shock."

Lawrence's use of four-letter words and his frank depiction of sexual activity are the controversial aspects of *Lady Chatterley's Lover*. The stated rationale behind the use of "obscenity" in the novel was that he was trying to free these words from their offensive connotations and restore them to decent usage in the English language. Lawrence knew the words were of Saxon origin and believed that they were suppressed and perverted from their honest and true meanings by aristocratic Norman conquerors.

Lawrence's use of sex is more important and crucial to the meaning of the novel as well as understanding his beliefs. To him sex was a fundamental fact of life that he concluded was being corrupted by modern Western society. He reviled what he called "sex in the head"—the modern degradation of the sex act which to him was attraction and copulation based on personality and thus superficial, not lasting, and ultimately unfulfilling because it was performed merely for momentary pleasure or social purposes. To Lawrence, sex was not a social function, but a natural manifestation of the primal force of the universe. Lawrence believed that through sex a man and a woman could go beyond their conscious personalities. It was a union that obliterated the barriers of their individuality and connected them with their transcendent, true selves in a marriage of the physical and the spiritual. Sex in Lawrence's view was a mystic ritual to integrate humans to a higher and more complete state of awareness through a merging with what he defined as "blood consciousness":

> There is another seat of consciousness which exists in us independently of the ordinary mental consciousness. One lives, knows, and has one's being in the blood, without any reference to nerves and brain. This is one half of life belonging to the darkness. When I take a woman, then the blood-precept is supreme. My blood-knowing is overwhelming. We should realize that we have a blood-being, a blood-consciousness, a blood-soul complete and apart from a mental and nervous consciousness.

This is exactly what the characters in *Lady Chatterley's Lover* are lacking as the novel begins. Sir Clifford Chatterley, personifies what Lawrence believed to be wrong with modern Western society and England in particular. He is crippled and impotent as a result of combat injuries sustained in World War I—a war Lawrence believed to be the apotheosis of the destructive powers of industrial civilization. He lives a totally mental existence, writing witty stories for upper-class readers. He is a successful industrialist who revitalizes the economic success of his family's coal mine, but has no connection with his workers, who, to him, are a lower form of life. His life lacks vitality as does his marriage to Connie. Lawrence stresses that the marriage never had a firm sexual foundation, and that Clifford considers sex necessary only for the procreation of heirs, and that the bond between he and his wife was formed on a "superior" intellectual plane. The shallow and empty life Connie leads at Wragby Hall with Clifford, however, is destroying her physical and spiritual vitality—"old at twenty-seven, with no gleam and sparkle in the flesh."

When Connie first meets the new gamekeeper, Oliver Mellors, she is frightened by him—"he seemed to emerge with such menace . . . like the sudden rush of a threat out of nowhere." She unconsciously perceives that he is a hazard to her present existence. He stirs something deep within her being, which she finally realizes is sexual attraction. For Connie to begin an affair with a servant meant that she was breaking a taboo of the rigid English class system and revolting against the ultimately false social structures of society.

The sex scenes are integral to the book. The critic Edmund Wilson, referring to the book, commended Lawrence by saying that he wrote "the best descriptions of sexual experience which have yet been done in English." They are lyrical and beautiful, but also show Connie's emotional growth and fulfillment.

Mellors was meant to represent the "natural" man, but he is not an ignorant brute. A bit like Lawrence himself, Mellors is the son of a miner, is educated, and is worldly. But he, too, has been damaged as a result of a bad marriage and upper-class snobbery. He has retreated from the world by becoming a gamekeeper and seeks refuge from the turmoils of modern existence within the remnants of pastoral England. Lawrence wrote this novel as his final declaration of faith, a sign of the possibility of future hope in humanity. Connie and Mellors are, in a way, a new Adam and Eve, Lawrence's ideal of a new covenant between the sexes, and perhaps, a new developing social order.

When D.H. Lawrence died in Vence, France in 1930, at the age of forty-four, he left behind a large and diverse body of work including novels, short stories, poetry, essays, and travel books. The works included in this collection—*Sons and Lovers*, *The Prussian Officer and Other Stories*, and *Lady Chatterley's Lover* (including Lawrence's defense of the book, "A Propos of *Lady Chatterley's Lover*")—rank among his finest accomplishments and will serve as a excellent introduction to one of the most visionary novelists of the twentieth century.

CHRISTOPHER MOORE

New York
1994

Sons and Lovers

PART ONE

❖ 1 ❖

THE EARLY MARRIED LIFE OF THE MORELS

The Bottoms succeeded to "Hell Row." Hell Row was a block of thatched, bulging cottages that stood by the brookside on Greenhill Lane. There lived the colliers who worked in the little gin pits two fields away. The brook ran under the alder trees, scarcely soiled by these small mines, whose coal was drawn to the surface by donkeys that plodded wearily in a circle round a gin. And all over the countryside were these same pits, some of which had been worked in the time of Charles II, the few colliers and the donkeys burrowing down like ants into the earth, making queer mounds and little black places among the cornfields and the meadows. And the cottages of these coal miners, in blocks and pairs here and there, together with odd farms and homes of the stockingers, straying over the parish, formed the village of Bestwood.

Then, some sixty years ago, a sudden change took place. The gin pits were elbowed aside by the large mines of the financiers. The coal and iron field of Nottinghamshire and Derbyshire was discovered. Carston, Waite and Co. appeared. Amid tremendous excitement, Lord Palmerston formally opened the company's first mine at Spinney Park, on the edge of Sherwood Forest.

About this time the notorious Hell Row, which through growing old had acquired an evil reputation, was burned down, and much dirt was cleansed away.

Carston, Waite and Co. found they had struck on a good thing, so, down the valleys of the brooks from Selby and Nuttall, new mines were sunk, until soon there were six pits working. From Nuttall, high up on the sandstone among the woods, the railway ran, past the ruined priory of the Carthusians and past Robin Hood's Well, down to Spinney Park, then on to Minton, a large mine among cornfields; from Minton across the farmlands of the valley-side to Bunker's Hill, branching off there, and running north to Beggarlee and Selby, that looks over at Crich and the hills of Derbyshire; six mines like black studs on the countryside, linked by a loop of fine chain, the railway.

To accommodate the regiments of miners, Carston, Waite and Co. built the Squares, great quadrangles of dwellings on the hillside of Bestwood, and then, in the brook valley, on the site of Hell Row, they erected the Bottoms.

The Bottoms consisted of six blocks of miners' dwellings, two rows of three, like the dots on a blank-six domino, and twelve houses in a block. This double row of dwellings sat at the foot of the rather sharp slope from Bestwood, and looked out, from the attic windows at least, on the slow climb of the valley towards Selby.

The houses themselves were substantial and very decent. One could walk all round, seeing little front gardens with auriculas and saxifrage in the shadow of the bottom block, sweet-williams and pinks in the sunny top block; seeing neat front windows, little porches, little privet hedges, and dormer windows for the attics. But that was outside; that was the view on to the uninhabited parlors of all the colliers' wives. The dwelling-room, the kitchen, was at the back of the house, facing inward between the blocks, looking at a scrubby back garden, and then at the ash pits. And between the rows, between the long lines of ash pits, went the alley, where the children played and the women gossiped and the men smoked. So, the actual conditions of living in the Bottoms, that was so well built and that looked so nice, were quite unsavory because people must live in the kitchen, and the kitchens opened on to that nasty alley of ash pits.

Mrs. Morel was not anxious to move into the Bottoms, which was already twelve years old and on the downward path, when she descended to it from Bestwood. But it was the best she could do. Moreover, she had an end house in one of the top blocks, and thus had only one neighbor; on the other side an extra strip of garden. And, having an end house, she enjoyed a kind of aristocracy among the other women of the "between" houses, because her rent was five shillings and sixpence instead of five shillings a week. But this superiority in station was not much consolation to Mrs. Morel.

She was thirty-one years old, and had been married eight years. A rather small woman, of delicate mold but resolute bearing, she shrank a little from the first contact with the Bottoms women. She came down in the July, and in the September expected her third baby.

Her husband was a miner. They had only been in their new home three weeks when the wakes, or fair, began. Morel, she knew, was sure to make a holiday of it. He went off early on the Monday morning, day of the fair. The two children were highly excited. William, a boy of seven, fled off immediately after breakfast, to prowl round the wakes ground, leaving Annie, who was only five, to whine all morning to go also. Mrs. Morel did her work. She scarcely knew her neighbors yet, and knew no one with whom to trust the little girl. So she promised to take her to the wakes after dinner.

William appeared at half-past twelve. He was a very active lad, fair-haired, with a touch of the Dane or Norwegian about him.

"Can I have my dinner, mother?" he cried, rushing in with his cap on. " 'Cause it begins at half-past one, the man says so."

"You can have your dinner as soon as it's done," replied the mother.

"Isn't it done?" he cried, his blue eyes staring at her in indignation. "Then I'm goin' be-out it."

"You'll do nothing of the sort. It will be done in five minutes. It is only half-past twelve."

"They'll be beginnin'," the boy half cried, half shouted.

"You won't die if they do," said the mother. "Besides, it's only half-past twelve, so you've a full hour."

The lad began hastily to lay the table, and directly the three sat down. They were eating batter-pudding and jam, when the boy jumped off his chair and stood perfectly still. Some distance away could be heard the first small braying of a merry-go-round, and the tooting of a horn. His face quivered as he looked at his mother.

"I told you!" he said, running to the dresser for his cap.

"Take your pudding in your hand—and it's only five past one, so you were wrong—you haven't got your twopence," cried the mother in a breath.

The boy came back, bitterly disappointed, for his twopence; then went off without a word.

"I want to go, I want to go," said Annie, beginning to cry.

"Well, and you shall go, whining, wizzening little stick!" said the mother. And later in the afternoon she trudged up the hill under the tall hedge with her child. The hay was gathered from the fields, and cattle were turned on to the eddish. It was warm, peaceful.

Mrs. Morel did not like the wakes. There were two sets of horses, one going by steam, one pulled round by a pony; three organs were grinding, and there came odd cracks of pistol shots, fearful screeching of the coconut man's rattle, shouts of the Aunt Sally man, screeches from the peep-show lady. The mother perceived her son gazing enraptured outside the Lion Wallace booth, at the pictures of this famous lion that had killed a Negro and maimed for life two white men. She left him alone, and went to get Annie a spin of toffee. Presently the lad stood in front of her, wildly excited.

"You never said you was coming—isn't the' a lot of things?—that lion's killed three men—I've spent my tuppence—an' look here."

He pulled from his pocket two egg cups, with pink moss roses on them.

"I got these from that stall where y'ave ter get them marbles in them holes. An' I got these two in two goes—'aepenny a go—they've got moss roses on, look here, I wanted these."

She knew he wanted them for her.

"H'm!" she said, pleased. "They *are* pretty!"

"Shall you carry 'em,'cause I'm frightened o' breakin' 'em?"

He was tipful of excitement now she had come, led her about the ground, showed her everything. Then, at the peep show, she explained the pictures, in a sort of story, to which he listened as if spellbound. He would not leave her. All the time he stuck close to her, bristling with a small boy's pride of her. For no other woman looked such a lady as she did, in her little black bonnet and her cloak. She smiled when she saw women she knew. When she was tired she said to her son:

"Well, are you coming now, or later?"

"Are you goin' a'ready?" he cried, his face full of reproach.

"Already? It is past four, *I* know."

"What are you goin' a'ready for?" he lamented.

"You needn't come if you don't want," she said.

And she went slowly away with her little girl, whilst her son stood watching her, cut to the heart to let her go, and yet unable to leave the wakes. As she crossed the open ground in front of the Moon and Stars she heard men shouting, and smelled the beer, and hurried a little, thinking her husband was probably in the bar.

At about half-past six her son came home, tired now, rather pale, and somewhat wretched. He was miserable, though he did not know it, because he had let her go alone. Since she had gone, he had not enjoyed his wakes.

"Has my dad been?" he asked.

"No," said the mother.

"He's helping to wait at the Moon and Stars. I seed him through that black tin stuff wi' holes in, on the window, wi' his sleeves rolled up."

"Ha!" exclaimed the mother shortly. "He's got no money. An' he'll be satisfied if he gets his 'lowance, whether they give him more or not."

When the light was fading, and Mrs. Morel could see no more to sew, she rose and went to the door. Everywhere was the sound of excitement, the restlessness of the holiday, that at last infected her. She went out into the side garden. Women were coming home from the wakes, the children hugging a white lamb with green legs, or a wooden horse. Occasionally a man lurched past, almost as full as he could carry. Sometimes a good husband came along with his family, peacefully. But usually the women and children were alone. The stay-at-home mothers stood gossiping at the corners of the alley, as the twilight sank, folding their arms under their white aprons.

Mrs. Morel was alone, but she was used to it. Her son and her little girl slept upstairs; so, it seemed, her home was there behind her, fixed and stable. But she felt wretched with the coming child. The world seemed a dreary place, where nothing else would happen for her—at least until William grew up. But for herself, nothing but this dreary endurance—till the children grew up. And the children! She could not afford to have this third. She did not want it. The father was serving beer in a public house, swilling himself drunk. She despised him, and was tied to him. This coming child was too much for her. If it were not for William and Annie, she was sick of it, the struggle with poverty and ugliness and meanness.

She went into the front garden, feeling too heavy to take herself out, yet unable to stay indoors. The heat suffocated her. And looking ahead, the prospect of her life made her feel as if she were buried alive.

The front garden was a small square with a privet hedge. There she stood, trying to soothe herself with the scent of flowers and the fading, beautiful evening. Opposite her small gate was the stile that led uphill, under the tall hedge, between the burning glow of the cut pastures. The sky overhead throbbed and pulsed with light. The glow sank quickly off the field; the earth and the hedges smoked dusk. As it grew dark, a ruddy glare came out on the hilltop, and out of the glare the diminished commotion of the fair.

Sometimes, down the trough of darkness formed by the path under the hedges, men came lurching home. One young man lapsed into a run down the steep bit that ended the hill, and went with a crash into the stile. Mrs. Morel shuddered. He picked himself up, swearing viciously, rather pathetically, as if he thought the stile had wanted to hurt him.

She went indoors, wondering if things were never going to alter. She was beginning by now to realize that they would not. She seemed so far away from her girlhood, she wondered if it were the same person walking heavily up the back garden at the Bottoms as had run so lightly on the breakwater at Sheerness ten years before.

"What have *I* to do with it?" she said to herself. "What have I to do with all this? Even the child I am going to have! It doesn't seem as if *I* were taken into account."

Sometimes life takes hold of one, carries the body along, accomplishes one's history, and yet is not real, but leaves oneself as it were slurred over.

"I wait," Mrs. Morel said to herself—"I wait, and what I wait for can never come."

Then she straightened the kitchen, lit the lamp, mended the fire, looked out the washing for the next day, and put it to soak. After which she sat down to her sewing. Through the long hours her needle flashed regularly through the stuff. Occasionally she sighed, moving to relieve herself. And all the time she was thinking how to make the most of what she had, for the children's sakes.

At half-past eleven her husband came. His cheeks were very red and very shiny above his black moustache. His head nodded slightly. He was pleased with himself.

"Oh! Oh! waitin' for me, lass? I've bin 'elpin' Anthony, an' what's think he's gen me? Nowt b'r a lousy hae'fcrown, an' that's ivry penny——"

"He thinks you've made the rest up in beer," she said shortly.

"An' I 'aven't—that I 'aven't. You b'lieve me, I've 'ad very little this day, I have an' all." His voice went tender. "Here, an' I browt thee a bit o' brandysnap, an' a coconut for th' children." He laid the gingerbread and the coconut, a hairy object, on the table. "Nay, tha niver said thankyer for nowt i' thy life, did ter?"

As a compromise, she picked up the coconut and shook it, to see if it had any milk.

"It's a good 'un, you may back yer life o' that. I got it fra' Bill Hodgkisson. 'Bill,' I says, 'tha non wants them three nuts, does ter? Arena ter for gi'ein' me one for my bit of a lad an' wench?' 'I ham, Walter, my lad,' 'e says; 'ta'e which on 'em ter's a mind.' An' so I took one, an' thanked 'im. I didn't like ter shake it afore 'is eyes, but 'e says, 'Tha'd better ma'e sure it's a good un, Walt.' An' so, yer see, I knowed it was. He's a nice chap, is Bill Hodgkisson,'e's a nice chap!"

"A man will part with anything so long as he's drunk, and you're drunk along with him," said Mrs. Morel.

"Eh, tha mucky little 'ussy, who's drunk, I sh'd like ter know?" said Morel. He was extraordinarily pleased with himself, because of his day's helping to wait in the Moon and Stars. He chattered on.

Mrs. Morel, very tired, and sick of his babble, went to bed as quickly as possible, while he raked the fire.

Mrs. Morel came of a good old burgher family, famous independents who had fought with Colonel Hutchinson, and who remained stout Congregationalists. Her grandfather had gone bankrupt in the lace market at a time when so many lace manufacturers were ruined in Nottingham. Her father, George Coppard, was an engineer—a large, handsome, haughty man, proud of his fair skin and blue eyes, but more proud still of his integrity. Gertrude resembled her mother in her small build. But her temper, proud and unyielding, she had from the Coppards.

George Coppard was bitterly galled by his own poverty. He became foreman of the engineers in the dockyard at Sheerness. Mrs. Morel—Gertrude—was the second daughter. She favored her mother, loved her mother best of all; but she had the Coppards' clear, defiant blue eyes and their broad brow. She remembered to have hated her father's overbearing manner towards her gentle, humorous, kindly souled mother. She remembered running over the breakwater at Sheerness and finding the boat. She remembered to have been petted and flattered by all the men when she had gone to the dockyard, for she was a delicate, rather proud child. She remembered the funny old mistress, whose assistant she had become, whom she had loved to help in the private school. And she still had the Bible that John Field had given her. She used to walk home from chapel with John Field when she was nineteen. He was the son of a well-to-do tradesman, had been to college in London, and was to devote himself to business.

She could always recall in detail a September Sunday afternoon, when they had sat under the vine at the back of her father's house. The sun came through the chinks in the vine leaves and made beautiful patterns, like a lace scarf, falling on her and on him. Some of the leaves were clean yellow, like yellow flat flowers.

"Now sit still," he had cried. "Now your hair, I don't know what it *is* like! It's as bright as copper and gold, as red as burnt copper, and it has gold threads where the sun shines on it. Fancy their saying it's brown. Your mother calls it mouse color."

She had met his brilliant eyes, but her clear face scarcely showed the elation which rose within her.

"But you say you don't like business," she pursued.

"I don't. I hate it!" he cried hotly.

"And you would like to go into the ministry," she half implored.

"I should. I should love it, if I thought I could make a first-rate preacher."

"Then why don't you—why *don't* you?" Her voice rang with defiance. "If *I* were a man, nothing would stop me."

She held her head erect. He was rather timid before her.

"But my father's so stiff-necked. He means to put me into the business, and I know he'll do it."

"But if you're a *man*?" she had cried.

"Being a man isn't everything," he replied, frowning with puzzled helplessness.

Now, as she moved about her work at the Bottoms, with some experience of what being a man meant, she knew that it was *not* everything.

At twenty, owing to her health, she had left Sheerness. Her father had retired home to Nottingham. John Field's father had been ruined; the son had gone as a teacher in Norwood. She did not hear of him until, two years later, she made determined inquiry. He had married his landlady, a woman of forty, a widow with property.

And still Mrs. Morel preserved John Field's Bible. She did not now believe him to be—Well, she understood pretty well what he might or might not have been. So she preserved his Bible, and kept his memory intact in her heart, for her own sake. To her dying day, for thirty-five years, she did not speak of him.

When she was twenty-three years old, she met, at a Christmas party, a young man from the Erewash Valley. Morel was then twenty-seven years old. He was well set-up, erect, and very smart. He had wavy black hair that shone again, and a vigorous black beard that had never been shaved. His cheeks were ruddy, and his red, moist mouth was noticeable because he laughed so often and so heartily. He had that rare thing, a rich, ringing laugh. Gertrude Coppard had watched him, fascinated. He was so full of color and animation, his voice ran so easily into comic grotesque, he was so ready and so pleasant with everybody. Her own father had a rich fund of humor, but it was satiric. This man's was different: soft, nonintellectual, warm, a kind of gamboling.

She herself was opposite. She had a curious, receptive mind, which found much pleasure and amusement in listening to other folk. She was clever in leading folk on to talk. She loved ideas, and was considered very intellectual. What she liked most of all was an argument on religion or philosophy or politics with some educated man. This she did not often enjoy. So she always had people tell her about themselves, finding her pleasure so.

In her person she was rather small and delicate, with a large brow, and dropping bunches of brown silk curls. Her blue eyes were very straight, honest, and searching. She had the beautiful hands of the Coppards. Her dress was always subdued. She wore dark blue silk, with a peculiar silver chain of silver scallops. This, and a heavy brooch of twisted gold, was her only ornament. She was still perfectly intact, deeply religious, and full of beautiful candor.

Walter Morel seemed melted away before her. She was to the miner that thing of mystery and fascination, a lady. When she spoke to him, it was with a southern pronunciation and a purity of English which thrilled him to hear. She watched him. He danced well, as if it were natural and joyous in him to dance. His grandfather was a French refugee who had married an English barmaid—if it had been a marriage. Gertrude Coppard watched the young miner as he danced, a certain subtle exultation like glamor in his movement, and his face the flower of his body, ruddy, with tumbled black hair, and laughing alike whatever partner he bowed above. She thought him rather wonderful, never having met anyone like him. Her father was to her the type of all men. And George Coppard, proud in his bearing, handsome, and rather bitter; who preferred theology in reading, and who drew near in sympathy only to one man, the Apostle Paul; who was harsh in government, and in familiarity ironic; who ignored all sensuous pleasure;—he was very different from the miner. Gertrude herself was rather contemptuous of dancing; she had not the slightest inclination towards that accomplishment, and had never learned even a Roger de Coverley. She was a puritan, like her father, high-minded, and really stern. Therefore the dusky, golden softness of this man's sensuous flame of life, that flowed off his flesh like the flame from a candle, not baffled and gripped into incandescence by thought and spirit as her life was, seemed to her something wonderful, beyond her.

He came and bowed above her. A warmth radiated through her as if she had drunk wine.

"Now do come and have this one wi' me," he said caressively. "It's easy, you know. I'm pining to see you dance."

She had told him before she could not dance. She glanced at his humility and smiled. Her smile was very beautiful. It moved the man so that he forgot everything.

"No, I won't dance," she said softly. Her words came clean and ringing.

Not knowing what he was doing—he often did the right thing by instinct—he sat beside her, inclining reverentially.

"But you mustn't miss your dance," she reproved.

"Nay, I don't want to dance that—it's not one as I care about."

"Yet you invited me to it."

He laughed very heartily at this.

"I never thought o' that. Tha'rt not long in taking the curl out of me."

It was her turn to laugh quickly.

"You don't look as if you'd come much uncurled," she said.

"I'm like a pig's tail, I curl because I canna help it," he laughed, rather boisterously.

"And you are a miner!" she exclaimed in surprise.

"Yes. I went down when I was ten."

She looked at him in wondering dismay.

"When you were ten! And wasn't it very hard?" she asked.

"You soon get used to it. You live like th' mice, an' you pop out at night to see what's going on."

"It makes me feel blind," she frowned.

"Like a moudiwarp!" he laughed. "Yi, an' there's some chaps as does go round like moudiwarps." He thrust his face forward in the blind, snout-like way of a mole, seeming to sniff and peer for direction. "They dun though!" he protested naively. "Tha niver seed such a way they get in. But tha mun let me ta'e thee down some time, an' tha can see for thysen."

She looked at him, startled. This was a new tract of life suddenly opened before her. She realized the life of the miners, hundreds of them toiling below earth and coming up at evening. He seemed to her noble. He risked his life daily, and with gaiety. She looked at him, with a touch of appeal in her pure humility.

"Shouldn't ter like it?" he asked tenderly. " 'Appen not, it 'ud dirty thee."

She had never been "thee'd" and "thou'd" before.

The next Christmas they were married, and for three months she was perfectly happy: for six months she was very happy.

He had signed the pledge, and wore the blue ribbon of a teetotaler: he was nothing if not showy. They lived, she thought, in his own house. It was small, but convenient enough, and quite nicely furnished, with solid, worthy stuff that suited her honest soul. The women, her neighbors, were rather foreign to her, and Morel's mother and sisters were apt to sneer at her ladylike ways. But she could perfectly well live by herself, so long as she had her husband close.

Sometimes, when she herself wearied of love-talk, she tried to open her heart seriously to him. She saw him listen deferentially, but without understanding. This killed her efforts at a finer intimacy, and she had flashes of fear. Sometimes he was restless of an evening: it was not enough for him just to be near her, she realized. She was glad when he set himself to little jobs.

He was a remarkably handy man—could make or mend anything. So she would say:

"I do like that coal rake of your mother's—it is small and natty."

"Does ter, my wench? Well, I made that, so I can make thee one."

"What! why it's a steel one!"

"An' what if it is! Tha s'lt ha'e one very similar, if not exactly same."

She did not mind the mess, nor the hammering and noise. He was busy and happy.

But in the seventh month, when she was brushing his Sunday coat, she felt papers in the breast-pocket, and, seized with a sudden curiosity, took them out to read. He very rarely wore the frockcoat he was married in: and it had not occurred to her before to feel curious concerning the papers. They were the bills of the household furniture, still unpaid.

"Look here," she said at night, after he was washed and had had his dinner. "I found these in the pocket of your wedding coat. Haven't you settled the bills yet?"

"No. I haven't had a chance."

"But you told me all was paid. I had better go into Nottingham on Saturday and settle them. I don't like sitting on another man's chairs and eating from an unpaid table."

He did not answer.

"I can have your bankbook, can't I?"

"Tha can ha'e it, for what good it'll be to thee."

"I thought—" she began. He had told her he had a good bit of money left over. But she realized it was no use asking questions. She sat rigid with bitterness and indignation.

The next day she went down to see his mother.

"Didn't you buy the furniture for Walter?" she asked.

"Yes, I did," tartly retorted the elder woman.

"And how much did he give you to pay for it?"

The elder woman was stung with fine indignation.

"Eighty pound, if you're so keen on knowin'," she replied.

"Eighty pounds! But there are forty-two pounds still owing!"

"I can't help that."

"But where has it all gone?"

"You'll find all the papers, I think, if you look—beside ten pound as he owed me, an' six pound as the wedding cost down here."

"Six pounds!" echoed Gertrude Morel. It seemed to her monstrous that, after her own father had paid so heavily for her wedding, six pounds more should have been squandered in eating and drinking at Walter's parents' house, at his expense.

"And how much has he sunk in his houses?" she asked,

"His houses—which houses?"

Gertrude Morel went white to the lips. He had told her the house he lived in, and the next one, were his own.

"I thought the house we live in—" she began.

"They're my houses, those two," said the mother-in-law. "And not clear either. It's as much as I can do to keep the mortgage interest paid."

Gertrude sat white and silent. She was her father now.

"Then we ought to be paying you rent," she said coldly.

"Walter is paying me rent." replied the mother.

"And what rent?" asked Gertrude.

"Six-and-six a week," retorted the mother.

It was more than the house was worth. Gertrude held her head erect, looked straight before her.

"It is lucky to be you," said the elder woman, bitingly, "to have a husband as takes all the worry of the money, and leaves you a free hand."

The young wife was silent.

She said very little to her husband, but her manner had changed towards him. Something in her proud, honorable soul had crystallized out hard as rock.

When October came in, she thought only of Christmas. Two years ago, at

Christmas, she had met him. Last Christmas she had married him. This Christmas she would bear him a child.

"You don't dance yourself, do you, missis?" asked her nearest neighbor, in October, when there was great talk of opening a dancing class over the Brick and Tile Inn at Bestwood.

"No—I never had the least inclination to," Mrs. Morel replied.

"Fancy! An' how funny as you should ha' married your Mester. You know he's quite a famous one for dancing."

"I didn't know he was famous," laughed Mrs. Morel.

"Yea, he is though! Why, he run that dancing class in the Miners Arms clubroom for over five year."

"Did he?"

"Yes, he did." The other woman was defiant. "An' it was thronged every Tuesday, and Thursday, an' Sat'day—an' there *was* carryin's-on, accordin' to all accounts."

This kind of thing was gall and bitterness to Mrs. Morel, and she had a fair share of it. The women did not spare her, at first; for she was superior, though she could not help it.

He began to be rather late in coming home.

"They're working very late now aren't they?" she said to her washerwoman.

"No later than they allers do, I don't think. But they stop to have their pint at Ellen's, an' they get talkin', an' there you are! Dinner stone cold—an' it serves 'em right."

"But Mr. Morel does not take any drink."

The woman dropped the clothes, looked at Mrs. Morel, then went on with her work, saying nothing.

Gertrude Morel was very ill when the boy was born. Morel was good to her, as good as gold. But she felt very lonely, miles away from her own people. She felt lonely with him now, and his presence only made it more intense.

The boy was small and frail at first, but he came on quickly. He was a beautiful child, with dark gold ringlets, and dark-blue eyes which changed gradually to a clear gray. His mother loved him passionately. He came just when her own bitterness of disillusion was hardest to bear; when her faith in life was shaken, and her soul felt dreary and lonely. She made much of the child, and the father was jealous.

At last Mrs. Morel despised her husband. She turned to the child; she turned from the father. He had begun to neglect her; the novelty of his own home was gone. He had no grit, she said bitterly to herself. What he felt just at the minute, that was all to him. He could not abide by anything. There was nothing at the back of all his show.

There began a battle between the husband and wife—a fearful, bloody battle that ended only with the death of one. She fought to make him undertake his own responsibilities, to make him fulfill his obligations. But he was too different from her. His nature was purely sensuous, and she strove to make him moral, religious. She tried to force him to face things. He could not endure it—it drove him out of his mind.

While the baby was still tiny, the father's temper had become so irritable that it was not to be trusted. The child had only to give a little trouble when the man began to bully. A little more, and the hard hands of the collier hit the baby. Then Mrs. Morel loathed her husband, loathed him for days; and he went out and drank; and she cared very little what he did. Only, on his return, she scathed him with her satire.

The estrangement between them caused him, knowingly or unknowingly, grossly to offend her where he would not have done.

William was only one year old, and his mother was proud of him, he was so pretty. She was not well off now, but her sisters kept the boy in clothes. Then, with his little white hat curled with an ostrich feather, and his white coat, he was a joy to her, the twining wisps of hair clustering round his head. Mrs. Morel lay listening, one Sunday morning, to the chatter of the father and child downstairs. Then she dozed off. When she came downstairs, a great fire glowed in the grate, the room was hot, the breakfast was roughly laid, and seated in his armchair, against the chimney piece, sat Morel, rather timid; and standing between his legs, the child—cropped like a sheep, with such an odd round poll—looking wondering at her; and on a newspaper spread out upon the hearthrug, a myriad of crescent-shaped curls, like the petals of a marigold scattered in the reddening firelight.

Mrs. Morel stood still. It was her first baby. She went very white, and was unable to speak.

"What dost think o' 'im?" Morel laughed uneasily.

She gripped her two fists, lifted them, and came forward. Morel shrank back.

"I could kill you, I could!" she said. She choked with rage, her two fists uplifted.

"Yer non want ter make a wench on 'im," Morel said, in a frightened tone, bending his head to shield his eyes from hers. His attempt at laughter had vanished.

The mother looked down at the jagged, close-clipped head of her child. She put her hands on his hair, and stroked and fondled his head.

"Oh—my boy!" she faltered. Her lip trembled, her face broke, and, snatching up the child, she buried her face in his shoulder and cried painfully. She was one of those women who cannot cry; whom it hurts as it hurts a man. It was like ripping something out of her, her sobbing.

Morel sat with his elbows on his knees, his hands gripped together till the knuckles were white. He gazed in the fire, feeling almost stunned, as if he could not breathe.

Presently she came to an end, soothed the child and cleared away the breakfast table. She left the newspaper, littered with curls, spread upon the hearthrug. At last her husband gathered it up and put it at the back of the fire. She went about her work with closed mouth, and very quiet. Morel was subdued. He crept about wretchedly, and his meals were a misery that day. She spoke to him civilly, and never alluded to what he had done. But he felt something final had happened.

Afterwards she said she had been silly, that the boy's hair would have had to be cut, sooner or later. In the end, she even brought herself to say to her husband it was just as well he had played barber when he did. But she knew, and Morel knew, that that act had caused something momentous to take place in her soul. She remembered the scene all her life, as one in which she had suffered the most intensely.

This act of masculine clumsiness was the spear through the side of her love for Morel. Before, while she had striven against him bitterly, she had fretted after after him, as if he had gone astray from her. Now she ceased to fret for his love: he was an outsider to her. This made life much more bearable.

Nevertheless, she still continued to strive with him. She still had her high moral sense, inherited from generations of Puritans. It was now a religious instinct, and she was almost a fanatic with him, because she loved him, or had loved him. If he sinned, she tortured him. If he drank, and lied, was often a poltroon, sometimes a knave, she wielded the lash unmercifully.

The pity was, she was too much his opposite. She could not be content with the little he might be; she would have him the much that he ought to be. So, in seeking to make him nobler than he could be, she destroyed him. She injured and hurt and scarred herself, but she lost none of her worth. She also had the children.

He drank rather heavily, though not more than many miners, and always beer, so that whilst his health was affected, it was never injured. The weekend was his chief carouse. He sat in the Miners' Arms until turning-out time every Friday, every Saturday, and every Sunday evening. On Monday and Tuesday he had to get up and reluctantly leave towards ten o'clock. Sometimes he stayed at home on Wednesday and Thursday evenings, or was only out for an hour. He practically never had to miss work owing to his drinking.

But although he was very steady at work, his wages fell off. He was blabmouthed, a tongue wagger. Authority was hateful to him, therefore he could only abuse the pit managers. He would say, in the Palmerston:

"Th' gaffer come down to our stal this morning, an' 'e says, 'You know, Walter, this 'ere'll not do. What about these props?' An' I says to him, 'Why, what art talkin' about? What d'st mean about th' props?' 'It'll never do, this 'ere,' 'e says. 'You'll be havin' th' roof in, one o' these days.' An' I says, 'Tha'd better stan' on a bit o' clunch, then, an' hold it up wi' thy 'ead.' So 'e wor that mad,'e cossed an' 'e swore, an' t'other chaps they did laugh." Morel was a good mimic. He imitated the manager's fat, squeaky voice, with its attempt at good English.

" 'I shan't have it, Walter. Who knows more about it, me or you?' So I says, 'I've niver fun out how much tha' knows, Alfred. It'll 'appen carry thee ter bed an' back.' "

So Morel would go on to the amusement of his boon companions. And some of this would be true. The pit manager was not an educated man. He had been a boy along with Morel, so that, while the two disliked each other, they more or less took each other for granted. But Alfred Charlesworth did not forgive the butty these public-house sayings. Consequently, although Morel was a good miner, sometimes earning as much as five pounds a week when he married, he came gradually to have worse and worse stalls, where the coal was thin, and hard to get, and unprofitable.

Also, in summer, the pits are slack. Often, on bright sunny mornings, the men are seen trooping home again at ten, eleven, or twelve o'clock. No empty trucks stand at the pit-mouth. The women on the hillside look across as they shake the hearthrug against the fence, and count the wagons the engine is taking along the line up the valley. And the children, as they come from school at dinnertime, looking down the fields and seeing the wheels on the headstocks standing, say:

"Minton's knocked off. My dad'll be at home."

And there is a sort of shadow over all, women and children and men, because money will be short at the end of the week.

Morel was supposed to give his wife thirty shillings a week, to provide everything—rent, food, clothes, clubs, insurance, doctors. Occasionally, if he were flush, he gave her thirty-five. But these occasions by no means balanced those when he gave her twenty-five. In winter, with a decent stall, the miner might earn fifty or fifty-five shillings a week. Then he was happy. On Friday night, Saturday, and Sunday, he spent royally, getting rid of his sovereign or thereabouts. And out of so much, he scarcely spared the children an extra penny or bought them a pound of apples. It all went in drink. In the bad times, matters were more worrying, but he was not so often drunk, so that Mrs. Morel used to say:

"I'm not sure I wouldn't rather be short, for when he's flush, there isn't a minute of peace."

If he earned forty shillings he kept ten; from thirty-five he kept five; from thirty-two he kept four; from twenty-eight he kept three; from twenty-four he kept two; from twenty he kept one-and-six; from eighteen he kept a shilling; from sixteen he kept sixpence. He never saved a penny, and he gave his wife no opportunity of saving; instead, she had occasionally to pay his debts; not public-house debts, for those never were passed on to the women, but debts when he had bought a canary, or a fancy walking stick.

At the wakes time, Morel was working badly, and Mrs. Morel was trying to save against her confinement. So it galled her bitterly to think he should be out taking his pleasure and spending money, whilst she remained at home, harassed. There were two days' holiday. On the Tuesday morning Morel rose early. He was in good spirits. Quite early, before six o'clock, she heard him whistling away to himself downstairs. He had a pleasant way of whistling, lively and musical. He nearly always whistled hymns. He had been a choirboy with a beautiful voice, and had taken solos in Southwell cathedral. His morning whistling alone betrayed it.

His wife lay listening to him tinkering away in the garden, his whistling ringing out as he sawed and hammered away. It always gave her a sense of warmth and peace to hear him thus as she lay in bed, the children not yet awake, in the bright early morning, happy in his man's fashion.

At nine o'clock, while the children with bare legs and feet were sitting playing on the sofa, and the mother was washing up, he came in from his carpentry, his sleeves rolled up, his waistcoat hanging open. He was still a good-looking man, with black, wavy hair, and a large black moustache. His face was perhaps too much inflamed, and there was about him a look almost of peevishness. But now he was jolly. He went straight to the sink where his wife was washing up.

"What, are thee there!" he said boisterously. "Sluther off an' let me wesh mysen."

"You may wait till I've finished," said his wife.

"Oh, mun I? An' what if I shonna?"

This good-humored threat amused Mrs. Morel.

"Then you can go and wash yourself in the soft-water tub."

"Ha! I can an' a', tha mucky little 'ussy."

With which he stood watching her a moment, then went away to wait for her.

When he chose he could still make himself again a real gallant. Usually he preferred to go out with a scarf round his neck. Now, however, he made a toilet. There seemed so much gusto in the way he puffed and swilled as he washed himself, so much alacrity with which he hurried to the mirror in the kitchen, and bending because it was too low for him, scrupulously parted his wet black hair, that it irritated Mrs. Morel. He put on a turndown collar, a black bow, and wore his Sunday tail coat. As such, he looked spruce, and what his clothes would not do, his instinct for making the most of his good looks would.

At half-past nine Jerry Purdy came to call for his pal. Jerry was Morel's bosom friend, and Mrs. Morel disliked him. He was a tall, thin man, with a rather foxy face, the kind of face that seems to lack eyelashes. He walked with a stiff, brittle dignity, as if his head were on a wooden spring. His nature was cold and shrewd. Generous where he intended to be generous, he seemed to be very fond of Morel and more or less to take charge of him.

Mrs. Morel hated him. She had known his wife, who had died of consumption, and who had, at the end, conceived such a violent dislike of her husband, that if he came into her room it caused her hemorrhage. None of which Jerry had seemed to mind. And now his eldest daughter, a girl of fifteen, kept a poor house for him, and looked after the two younger children.

"A mean, wizzen-hearted stick!" Mrs. Morel said of him.

"I've never known Jerry mean in *my* life," protested Morel. "A opener-handed and more freer chap you couldn't find anywhere, accordin' to my knowledge."

"Openhanded to you," retorted Mrs. Morel. "But his fist is shut tight enough to his children, poor things."

"Poor things! And what for are they poor things, I should like to know?"

But Mrs. Morel would not be appeased on Jerry's score.

The subject of argument was seen, craning his thin neck over the scullery curtain. He caught Mrs. Morel's eye.

"Mornin', missis! Mester in?"

"Yes—he is."

Jerry entered unasked, and stood by the kitchen doorway.

He was not invited to sit down, but stood there, coolly asserting the rights of men and husbands. "A nice day," he said to Mrs. Morel.

"Yes."

"Grand out this morning—grand for a walk."

"Do you mean *you're* going for a walk?" she asked.

"Yes. We mean walkin' to Nottingham," he replied.

"H'm!"

The two men greeted each other, both glad: Jerry, however, full of assurance, Morel rather subdued, afraid to seem too jubilant in presence of his wife. But he laced his boots quickly, with spirit. They were going for a ten-mile walk across the fields to Nottingham. Climbing the hillside from the Bottoms, they mounted gaily into the morning. At the Moon and Stars they had their first drink, then on to the Old Spot. Then a long five miles of drought to carry them into Bulwell to a glorious pint of bitter. But they stayed in a field with some haymakers whose gallon bottle was full, so that, when they came in sight of the city, Morel was sleepy. The town spread upwards before them, smoking vaguely in the midday glare, fridging the crest away to the south with spires and factory bulks and chimneys. In the last field Morel lay down under an oak tree and slept soundly for over an hour. When he arose to go forward he felt queer.

The two had dinner in the Meadows, with Jerry's sister, then repaired to the Punch Bowl, where they mixed in the excitement of pigeon racing. Morel never in his life played cards, considering them as having some occult, malevolent power—"the devil's pictures," he called them! But he was a master of skittles and of dominoes. He took a challenge from a Newark man, on skittles. All the men in the old, long bar took sides, betting either one way or the other. Morel took off his coat. Jerry held the hat containing the money. The men at the tables watched. Some stood, with their mugs in their hands. Morel felt his big wooden ball carefully, then launched it. He played havoc among the ninepins, and won half-a-crown, which restored him to solvency.

By seven o'clock the two were in good condition. They caught the 7:30 train home.

In the afternoon the Bottoms was intolerable. Every inhabitant remaining was out of doors. The women, in twos and threes, bareheaded and in white aprons, gossiped in the alley between the blocks. Men, having a rest between drinks, sat on their heels and talked. The place smelled stale; the slate roofs glistered in the arid heat.

Mrs. Morel took the little girl down to the brook in the meadows, which were not more than two hundred yards away. The water ran quickly over stones and broken pots. Mother and child leaned on the rail of the old sheep-bridge, watching. Up at the dipping-hole, at the other end of the meadow, Mrs. Morel could see the naked forms of boys flashing round the deep yellow water, or an occasional bright figure dart glittering over the blackish stagnant meadow. She knew William was at the dipping-hole, and it was the dread of her life lest he should get drowned. Annie played under the tall old hedge, picking up alder cones, that she called currants. The child required much attention, and the flies were teasing.

The children were put to bed at seven o'clock. Then she worked awhile.

When Walter Morel and Jerry arrived at Bestwood they felt a load off their minds; a railway journey no longer impended, so they could put the finishing touches to a glorious day. They entered the Nelson with the satisfaction of returned travelers.

The next day was a workday, and the thought of it put a damper on the men's spirits. Most of them, moreover, had spent their money. Some were already rolling dismally home, to sleep in preparation for the morrow. Mrs. Morel, listening to their mournful singing, went indoors. Nine o'clock passed, and ten, and still "the pair" had not returned. On a doorstep somewhere a man was singing loudly, in a drawl, "Lead, kindly Light." Mrs. Morel was always indignant with drunken men that they must sing that hymn when they got maudlin.

"As if 'Genevieve' weren't good enough," she said.

The kitchen was full of the scent of boiled herbs and hops. On the hob a large black saucepan steamed slowly. Mrs. Morel took a panchion, a great bowl of thick red earth, streamed a heap of white sugar into the bottom, and, then, straining herself to the weight, was pouring in the liquor.

Just then Morel came in. He had been very jolly in the Nelson, but coming home had grown irritable. He had not quite got over the feeling of irritability and pain, after having slept on the ground when he was so hot; and a bad conscience afflicted him as he neared the house. He did not know he was angry. But when the garden gate resisted his attempts to open it, he kicked it and broke the latch. He entered just as Mrs. Morel was pouring the infusion of herbs out of the saucepan. Swaying slightly, he lurched against the table. The boiling liquor pitched. Mrs. Morel started back.

"Good gracious," she cried, "coming home in his drunkenness!"

"Comin' home in his what?" he snarled, his hat over his eye.

Suddenly her blood rose in a jet.

"Say you're *not* drunk!" she flashed.

She had put down her saucepan, and was stirring the sugar into the beer. He dropped his two hands heavily on the table, and thrust his face forward at her.

" 'Say you're not drunk,' " he repeated. "Why, nobody but a nasty little bitch like you 'ud 'ave such a thought."

He thrust his face forward at her.

"There's money to bezzle with, if there's money for nothing else."

"I've not spent a two-shillin' bit this day," he said.

"You don't get as drunk as a lord on nothing," she replied. "And," she cried, flashing into sudden fury, "if you've been sponging on your beloved Jerry, why, let him look after his children, for they need it."

"It's a lie, it's a lie. Shut your face, woman."

They were now at battle-pitch. Each forgot everything save the hatred of the other and the battle between them. She was fiery and furious as he. They went on till he called her a liar.

"No," she cried, starting up, scarce able to breathe. "Don't call me that—you, the most despicable liar that ever walked in shoe leather." She forced the last words out of suffocated lungs.

"You're a liar!" he yelled, banging the table with his fist. "You're a liar, you're a liar."

She stiffened herself, with clenched fists.

"The house is filthy with you," she cried.

"Then get out on it—it's mine. Get out on it!" he shouted. "It's me as brings th' money whoam, not thee. It's my house, not thine. Then ger out on't—ger out on't!"

"And I would," she cried, suddenly shaken into tears of impotence. "Ah, wouldn't I, wouldn't I have gone long ago, but for those children. Ay, haven't I repented not going years ago, when I'd only the one"—suddenly drying into rage. "Do you think it's for *you* I stop—do you think I'd stop one minute for *you*?"

"Go, then," he shouted, beside himself. "Go!"

"No!" she faced round. "No," she cried loudly, "you shan't have it *all* your own way; you shan't do *all* you like. I've got those children to see to. My word," she laughed, "I should look well to leave them to you."

"Go," he cried thickly, lifting his fist. He was afraid of her. "Go!"

"I should be only too glad. I should laugh, laugh, my lord, if I could get away from you," she replied.

He came up to her, his red face, with its bloodshot eyes, thrust forward, and gripped her arms. She cried in fear of him, struggled to be free. Coming slightly to himself, panting, he pushed her roughly to the outer door, and thrust her forth, slotting the bolt behind her with a bang. Then he went back into the kitchen, dropped into his armchair, his head, bursting full of blood, sinking between his knees. Thus he dipped gradually into a stupor, from exhaustion and intoxication.

The moon was high and magnificent in the August night. Mrs. Morel, seared with passion, shivered to find herself out there in a great white light, that fell cold on her, and gave a shock to her inflamed soul. She stood for a few moments helplessly staring at the glistening great rhubarb leaves near the door. Then she got the air into her breast. She walked down the garden path, trembling in every limb, while the child boiled within her. For a while she could not control her consciousness; mechanically she went over the last scene, then over it again, certain phrases, certain moments coming each time like a brand red-hot down on her soul; and each time she enacted again the past hour, each time the brand came down at the same points, till the mark was burnt in, and the pain burnt out, and at last she came to herself. She must have been half an hour in this delirious condition. Then the presence of the night came again to her. She glanced round in fear. She had wandered to the side garden, where she was walking up and down the path beside the currant bushes under the long wall. The garden was a narrow strip, bounded from the road, that cut transversely between the blocks, by a thick thorn hedge.

She hurried out of the side garden to the front, where she could stand as if in an immense gulf of white light, the moon streaming high in face of her, the moonlight standing up from the hills in front, and filling the valley where the Bottoms crouched, almost blindingly. There, panting and half weeping in reaction from the stress, she murmured to herself over and over again: "The nuisance! the nuisance!"

She became aware of something about her. With an effort she roused herself to see what it was that penetrated her consciousness. The tall white lilies were reeling in the moonlight, and the air was charged with their perfume, as with a presence. Mrs. Morel gasped slightly in fear. She touched the big, pallid flowers on their petals, then shivered. They seemed to be stretching in the moonlight. She put her hand into one white bin: the gold scarcely showed on her fingers by moonlight. She bent down to look at the binful of yellow pollen; but it only appeared dusky. Then she drank a deep draught of the scent. It almost made her dizzy.

Mrs. Morel leaned on the garden gate, looking out, and she lost herself awhile. She did not know what she thought. Except for a slight feeling of sickness, and her consciousness in the child, herself melted out like scent into the shiny, pale air. After a time the child, too, melted with her in the mixing-pot of moonlight, and she rested with the hills and lilies and houses, all swum together in a kind of swoon.

When she came to herself she was tired for sleep. Languidly she looked about her; the clumps of white phlox seemed like bushes spread with linen; a moth ricocheted over them, and right across the garden. Following it with her eye roused her. A few whiffs of the raw, strong scent of phlox invigorated her. She passed along the path, hesitating at the white rosebush. It smelled sweet and simple. She touched the white ruffles of the roses. Their fresh scent and cool, soft leaves reminded her of the morning-time and sunshine. She was very fond of them. But she was tired, and wanted to sleep. In the mysterious out-of-doors she felt forlorn.

There was no noise anywhere. Evidently the children had not been awakened, or had gone to sleep again. A train, three miles away, roared across the valley. The night was very large, and very strange, stretching its hoary distances infinitely. And out of the silver-gray fog of darkness came sounds vague and hoarse: a corncrake not far off, sound of a train like a sigh, and distant shouts of men.

Her quietened heart beginning to beat quickly again, she hurried down the side garden to the back of the house. Softly she lifted the latch; the door was still bolted, shut hard against her. She rapped gently, waited, then rapped again. She must not rouse the children, nor the neighbors. He must be asleep, and he would not wake easily. Her heart began to burn to be indoors. She clung to the door handle. Now it was cold; she would take a chill, and in her present condition!

Putting her apron over her head and her arms, she hurried again to the side garden, to the window of the kitchen. Leaning on the sill, she could just see, under the blind, her husband's arms spread out on the table, and his black head on the board. He was sleeping with his face lying on the table. Something in his attitude made her feel tired of things. The lamp was burning smokily; she could tell by the copper color of the light. She tapped at the window more and more noisily. Almost it seemed as if the glass would break. Still he did not wake up.

After vain efforts, she began to shiver, partly from contact with the stone, and from exhaustion. Fearful always for the unborn child, she wondered what she could do for warmth. She went down to the coal house, where was an old hearthrug she had carried out for the ragman the day before. This she wrapped over her shoulders. It was warm, if grimy. Then she walked up and down the garden path, peeping every now and then under the blind, knocking, and telling herself that in the end the very strain of his position must wake him.

At last after about an hour, she rapped long and low at the window. Gradually the sound penetrated to him. When, in despair, she had ceased to tap, she saw him stir, then lift his face blindly. The laboring of his heart hurt him into consciousness. She rapped imperatively at the window. He started awake. Instantly she saw his fists set and his eyes glare. He had not a grain of physical fear. If it had been twenty burglars, he would have gone blindly for them. He glared round, bewildered, but prepared to fight.

"Open the door, Walter," she said coldly.

His hands relaxed. It dawned on him what he had done. His head dropped, sullen and dogged. She saw him hurry to the door, heard the bolt chock. He tried the latch. It opened—and there stood the silver-gray night, fearful to him, after the tawny light of the lamp. He hurried back.

When Mrs. Morel entered, she saw him almost running through the door to the stairs. He had ripped his collar off his neck in his haste to be gone ere she came in, and there it lay with bursten buttonholes. It made her angry.

She warmed and soothed herself. In her weariness forgetting everything, she moved about at the little tasks that remained to be done, set his breakfast, rinsed his pit-bottle, put his pit-clothes on the hearth to warm, set his pit-boots beside them, put him out a clean scarf and snap-bag and two apples, raked the fire, and went to bed. He was already dead asleep. His narrow black eyebrows were drawn up in a sort of peevish misery into his forehead, while his cheeks' downstrokes, and his sulky mouth, seemed to be saying: "I don't care who you are nor what you are, I *shall* have my own way."

Mrs. Morel knew him too well to look at him. As she unfastened her brooch at the mirror, she smiled faintly to see her face all smeared with the yellow dust of lilies. She brushed it off, and at last lay down. For some time her mind continued snapping and jetting sparks, but she was asleep before her husband awoke from the first sleep of his drunkenness.

2

The Birth of Paul, and Another Battle

After such a scene as the last, Walter Morel was for some days abashed and ashamed, but he soon regained his old bullying indifference. Yet there was a slight shrinking, a diminishing in his assurance. Physically even, he shrank, and his fine full presence waned. He never grew in the least stout, so that, as he sank from his erect, assertive bearing, his physique seemed to contract along with his pride and moral strength.

But now he realized how hard it was for his wife to drag about at her work, and, his sympathy quickened by penitence, hastened forward with his help. He came straight home from the pit, and stayed in at evening till Friday, and then he could not remain at home. But he was back again by ten o'clock, almost quite sober.

He always made his own breakfast. Being a man who rose early and had plenty of time he did not, as some miners do, drag his wife out of bed at six o'clock. At five, sometimes earlier, he woke, got straight out of bed, and went downstairs. When she could not sleep, his wife lay waiting for this time, as for a period of peace. The only real rest seemed to be when he was out of the house.

He went downstairs in his shirt and then struggled into his pit-trousers, which were left on the hearth to warm all night. There was always a fire, because Mrs. Morel raked. And the first sound in the house was the bang, bang of the poker against the raker, as Morel smashed the remainder of the coal to make the kettle, which was filled and left on the hob, finally boil. His cup and knife and fork, all he wanted except just the food, was laid ready on the table on a newspaper. Then he got his breakfast, made the tea, packed the bottom of the doors with rugs to shut out the draught, piled a big fire, and sat down to an hour of joy. He toasted his bacon on a fork and caught the drops of fat on his bread; then he put the rasher on his thick slice of bread, and cut off chunks with a clasp knife, poured his tea into his saucer, and was happy. With his family about, meals were never so pleasant. He loathed a fork; it is a modern introduction which has still scarcely reached common people. What Morel preferred was a clasp knife. Then, in solitude, he ate and drank, often sitting, in cold weather, on a little stool with his back to the warm chimney piece, his food on the fender, his cup on the hearth. And then he read the last night's newspaper—what of it he could—spelling it over laboriously. He preferred to keep the blinds down and the candle lit even when it was daylight; it was the habit of the mine.

At a quarter to six he rose, cut two thick slices of bread-and-butter, and put them in the white calico snap bag. He filled his tin bottle with tea. Cold tea without milk or sugar was the drink he preferred for the pit. Then he pulled off his shirt, and put on his pit-singlet, a vest of thick flannel cut low round the neck, and with short sleeves like a chemise.

Then he went upstairs to his wife with a cup of tea because she was ill, and because it occurred to him.

"I've brought thee a cup o' tea, lass," he said.

"Well, you needn't, for you know I don't like it," she replied.

"Drink it up; it'll pop thee off to sleep again."

She accepted the tea. It pleased him to see her take it and sip it.

"I'll back my life there's no sugar in," she said.

"Yi—there's one big un," he replied, injured.

"It's a wonder," she said, sipping again.

She had a winsome face when her hair was loose. He loved her to grumble at him in this manner. He looked at her again, and went, without any sort of leave-taking. He never took more than two slices of bread-and-butter to eat in the pit, so an apple or an orange was a treat to him. He always liked it when she put one out for him. He tied a scarf round his neck, put on his great, heavy boots, his coat, with the big pocket, that carried his snap bag and his bottle of tea, and went forth into the fresh morning air, closing, without locking, the door behind him. He loved the early morning, and the walk across the fields. So he appeared at the pit-top, often with a stalk from the hedge between his teeth, which he chewed all day to keep his mouth moist, down the mine, feeling quite as happy as when he was in the field.

Later, when the time for the baby grew nearer, he would bustle round in his slovenly fashion, poking out the ashes, rubbing the fireplace, sweeping the house before he went to work. Then, feeling very self-righteous, he went upstairs.

"Now I'm cleaned up for thee; tha's no 'casions ter stir a peg all day, but sit and read thy books."

Which made her laugh, in spite of her indignation.

"And the dinner cooks itself?" she answered.

"Eh, I know nowt about th' dinner."

"You'd know if there weren't any."

"Ay,'appen so," he answered, departing.

When she got downstairs, she would find the house tidy, but dirty. She could not rest until she had thoroughly cleaned; so she went down to the ash pit with her dustpan. Mrs. Kirk, spying her, would contrive to have to go to her own coal-place at that minute. Then, across the wooden fence, she would call:

"So you keep wagging on, then?"

"Ay," answered Mrs. Morel deprecatingly. "There's nothing else for it."

"Have you seen Hose?" called a very small woman from across the road. It was Mrs. Anthony, a black-haired, strange little body, who always wore a brown velvet dress, tight fitting.

"I haven't," said Mrs. Morel.

"Eh, I wish he'd come. I've got a copperful of clothes, an' I'm sure I heered his bell."

"Hark! He's at the end."

The two women looked down the alley. At the end of the Bottoms a man stood in a sort of old-fashioned trap, bending over bundles of cream-colored stuff; while a cluster of women held up their arms to him, some with bundles. Mrs. Anthony herself had a heap of creamy, undyed stockings hanging over her arm.

"I've done ten dozen this week," she said proudly to Mrs. Morel.

"T-t-t!" went the other. "I don't know how you can find time."

"Eh!" said Mrs. Anthony. "You can find time if you make time."

"I don't know how you do it," said Mrs. Morel. "And how much shall you get for those many?"

"Tuppence-ha'penny a dozen," replied the other.

"Well," said Mrs. Morel, "I'd starve before I'd sit down and seam twenty-four stockings for twopence ha'penny."

"Oh, I don't know," said Mrs. Anthony. "You can rip along with 'em."

Hose was coming along, ringing his bell. Women were waiting at the yard-ends with their seamed stockings hanging over their arms. The man, a common fellow, made jokes with them, tried to swindle them, and bullied them. Mrs. Morel went up her yard disdainfully.

It was an understood thing that if one woman wanted her neighbor, she should put the poker in the fire and bang at the back of the fireplace, which, as the fires were back to back, would make a great noise in the adjoining house. One morning Mrs. Kirk, mixing a pudding, nearly started out of her skin as she heard the thud, thud, in her grate. With her hands all floury, she rushed to the fence.

"Did you knock, Mrs. Morel?"

"If you wouldn't mind, Mrs. Kirk."

Mrs. Kirk climbed on to her copper, got over the wall on to Mrs. Morel's copper, and ran in to her neighbor.

"Eh, dear, how are you feeling?" she cried in concern.

"You might fetch Mrs. Bower," said Mrs. Morel.

Mrs. Kirk went into the yard, lifted up her strong, shrill voice, and called:

"Ag-gie—Ag-gie!"

The sound was heard from one end of the Bottoms to the other. At last Aggie came running up, and was sent for Mrs. Bower, whilst Mrs. Kirk left her pudding and stayed with her neighbor.

Mrs. Morel went to bed. Mrs. Kirk had Annie and William for dinner. Mrs. Bower, fat and waddling, bossed the house.

"Hash some cold meat up for the master's dinner, and make him an apple-charlotte pudding," said Mrs. Morel.

"He may go without pudding *this* day," said Mrs. Bower.

Morel was not as a rule one of the first to appear at the bottom of the pit, ready to come up. Some men were there before four o'clock, when the whistle blew loose-all; but Morel, whose stall, a poor one, was at this time about a mile and a half away from the bottom, worked usually till the first mate stopped, then he finished also. This day, however, the miner was sick of the work. At two o'clock he looked at his watch, by the light of the green candle—he was in a safe working—and again at half-past two. He was hewing at a piece of rock that was in the way for the next day's work. As he sat on his heels, or kneeled, giving hard blows with his pick, "Uszza-uszza!" he went.

"Shall ter finish, Sorry?"[1] cried Barker, his fellow butty.

"Finish? Niver while the world stands!" growled Morel. And he went on striking. He was tired.

"It's a heartbreaking job," said Barker.

But Morel was too exasperated, at the end of his tether, to answer. Still he struck and hacked with all his might.

"Tha might as well leave it, Walter," said Barker. "It'll do tomorrow, without thee hackin' thy guts out."

"I'll lay no b——finger on this tomorrow, Isr'el!" cried Morel.

"Oh, well, if tha wunna, someb'dy else'll ha'e to," said Israel.

Then Morel continued to strike.

"Hey-up there—*loose-a*!" cried the men, leaving the next stall.

Morel continued to strike.

"Tha'll happen catch me up," said Barker, departing.

When he had gone, Morel, left alone, felt savage. He had not finished his job. He had overworked himself into a frenzy. Rising, wet with sweat, he threw his tool down, pulled on his coat, blew out his candle, took his lamp, and went. Down the main road the lights of the other men went swinging. There was a hollow sound of many voices. It was a long, heavy tramp underground.

He sat at the bottom of the pit, where the great drops of water fell plash. Many colliers were waiting their turns to go up, talking noisily. Morel gave his answers short and disagreeable.

"It's rainin', Sorry," said old Giles, who had had the news from the top.

Morel found one comfort. He had his old umbrella, which he loved, in the lamp cabin. At last he took his stand on the chair, and was at the top in a moment. Then he handed in his lamp and got his umbrella, which he had bought at an auction for one-and-six. He stood on the edge of the pit-bank for a moment, looking out over the fields; gray rain was falling. The trucks stood full of wet, bright coal. Water ran down the sides of the wagons, over the white "C. W. and Co." Colliers, walking indifferent to the rain, were streaming down the line and up the field, a gray, dismal host. Morel put up his umbrella, and took pleasure from the peppering of the drops thereon.

All along the road to Bestwood the miners tramped, wet and gray and dirty, but their red mouths talking with animation. Morel also walked with the gang, but he said nothing. He frowned peevishly as he went. Many men passed into the Prince of Wales or into Ellen's. Morel, feeling sufficiently disagreeable to resist temptation, trudged along under the dripping trees that overhung the park wall, and down the mud of Greenhill Lane.

Mrs. Morel lay in bed, listening to the rain, and the feet of the colliers from Minton, their voices, and the bang, bang of the gates as they went through the stile up the field.

"There's some herb beer behind the pantry door," she said. "Th' master'll want a drink, if he doesn't stop."

But he was late, so she concluded he had called for a drink, since it was raining. What did he care about the child or her?

She was very ill when her children were born.

"What is it?" she asked, feeling sick to death.

"A boy."

And she took consolation in that. The thought of being the mother of men was warming to her heart. She looked at the child. It had blue eyes, and a lot of fair hair, and was bonny. Her love came up hot, in spite of everything. She had it in bed with her.

Morel, thinking nothing, dragged his way up the garden path, wearily and angrily. He closed his umbrella, and stood it in the sink; then he sluthered his heavy boots into the kitchen. Mrs. Bower appeared in the inner doorway.

"Well," she said, "she's about as bad as she can be. It's a boy childt."

The miner grunted, put his empty snap bag and his tin bottle on the dresser, went back into the scullery and hung up his coat, then came and dropped into his chair.

"Han yer got a drink?" he asked.

The woman went into the pantry. There was heard the pop of a cork. She set the mug, with a little, disgusted rap, on the table before Morel. He drank, gasped, wiped his big moustache on the end of his scarf, drank, gasped, and lay back in his chair. The woman would not speak to him again. She set his dinner before him, and went upstairs.

"Was that the master?" asked Mrs. Morel.

"I've gave him his dinner," replied Mrs. Bower.

After he had sat with his arms on the table—he resented the fact that Mrs. Bower put no cloth on for him, and gave him a little plate, instead of a full-sized dinner plate—he began to eat. The fact that his wife was ill, that he had another boy, was nothing to him at that moment. He was too tired; he wanted his dinner; he wanted to sit with his arms lying on the board; he did not like having Mrs. Bower about. The fire was too small to please him.

After he had finished his meal, he sat for twenty minutes; then he stoked up a big fire. Then, in his stockinged feet, he went reluctantly upstairs. It was a struggle to face his wife at this moment, and he was tired. His face was black, and smeared with sweat. His singlet had dried again, soaking the dirt in. He had a dirty woollen scarf round his throat. So he stood at the foot of the bed.

"Well, how are ter, then?" he asked.

"I s'll be all right," she answered.

"H'm!"

He stood at a loss what to say next. He was tired, and this bother was rather a nuisance to him, and he didn't quite know where he was.

"A lad, tha says," he stammered.

She turned down the sheet and showed the child.

"Bless him!" he murmured. Which made her laugh, because he blessed by rote—pretending paternal emotion, which he did not feel just then.

"Go now," she said.

"I will, my lass," he answered, turning away.

Dismissed, he wanted to kiss her, but he dared not. She half wanted him to kiss her, but could not bring herself to give any sign. She only breathed freely when he was gone out of the room again, leaving behind him a faint smell of pit-dirt.

Mrs. Morel had a visit every day from the Congregational clergyman. Mr. Heaton was young, and very poor. His wife had died at the birth of his first baby, so he remained alone in the manse. He was a Bachelor of Arts of Cambridge, very shy, and no preacher. Mrs. Morel was fond of him, and he depended on her. For hours he talked to her, when she was well. He became the godparent of the child.

Occasionally the minister stayed to tea with Mrs. Morel. Then she laid the cloth early, got out her best cups, with a little green rim, and hoped Morel would not come too soon; indeed, if he stayed for a pint, she would not mind this day. She had always two dinners to cook, because she believed children should have their chief meal at midday, whereas Morel needed his at five o'clock. So Mr. Heaton would hold the baby, whilst Mrs. Morel beat up a batter-pudding or peeled the potatoes, and he, watching her all the time, would discuss his next sermon. His ideas were quaint and fantastic. She brought him judiciously to earth. It was a discussion of the wedding at Cana.

"When He changed the water into wine at Cana," he said, "that is a symbol that the ordinary life, even the blood, of the married husband and wife, which had before been uninspired, like water, became filled with the Spirit, and was as wine, because, when love enters, the whole spiritual constitution of a man changes, is filled with the Holy Ghost, and almost his form is altered."

Mrs. Morel thought to herself:

"Yes, poor fellow, his young wife is dead; that is why he makes his love into the Holy Ghost."

They were halfway down their first cup of tea when they heard the sluther of pit-boots.

"Good gracious!" exclaimed Mrs. Morel, in spite of herself.

The minister looked rather scared. Morel entered. He was feeling rather savage. He nodded a "How d'yer do" to the clergyman, who rose to shake hands with him.

"Nay," said Morel, showing his hand, "look thee at it! Tha niver wants ter shake hands wi' a hand like that, does ter? There's too much pick-haft and shovel-dirt on it."

The minister flushed with confusion, and sat down again. Mrs. Morel rose, carried out the steaming saucepan. Morel took off his coat, dragged his armchair to table, and sat down heavily.

"Are you tired?" asked the clergyman.

"Tired? I ham that," replied Morel. "*You* don't know what it is to be tired, as *I'm* tired."

"No," replied the clergyman.

"Why, look yer 'ere," said the miner, showing the shoulders of his singlet. "It's a bit dry now, but it's wet as a clout with sweat even yet. Feel it."

"Goodness!" cried Mrs. Morel. "Mr. Heaton doesn't want to feel your nasty singlet."

The clergyman put out his hand gingerly.

"No, perhaps he doesn't," said Morel; "but it's all come out of *me*, whether or not. An' ivry day alike my singlet's wringin' wet. 'Aven't you got a drink, Missis, for a man when he comes home barkled up from the pit?"

"You know you drank all the beer," said Mrs. Morel, pouring out his tea.

"An' was there no more to be got?" Turning to the clergyman—"A man gets that caked up wi' th' dust, you know—that clogged up down a coal mine, he *needs* a drink when he comes home."

"I am sure he does," said the clergyman.

"But it's ten to one if there's owt for him."

"There's water—and there's tea," said Mrs. Morel.

"Water! It's not water as'll clear his throat."

He poured out a saucerful of tea, blew it, and sucked it up through his great black moustache, sighing afterwards. Then he poured out another saucerful, and stood his cup on the table.

"My cloth!" said Mrs. Morel, putting it on a plate.

"A man as comes home as I do 's too tired to care about cloths," said Morel.

"Pity!" exclaimed his wife, sarcastically.

The room was full of the smell of meat and vegetables and pit-clothes.

He leaned over to the minister, his great moustache thrust forward, his mouth very red in his black face.

"Mr. Heaton," he said, "a man as has been down the black hole all day, dingin' away at a coal face, yi, a sight harder than that wall—"

"Needn't make a moan of it," put in Mrs. Morel.

She hated her husband because, whenever he had an audience, he whined and played for sympathy. William, sitting nursing the baby, hated him, with a boy's hatred for false sentiment, and for the stupid treatment of his mother. Annie had never liked him; she merely avoided him.

When the minister had gone, Mrs. Morel looked at her cloth.

"A fine mess!" she said.

"Dos't think I'm goin' to sit wi' my arms danglin', cos tha's got a parson for tea wi' thee?" he bawled.

They were both angry, but she said nothing. The baby began to cry, and Mrs. Morel, picking up a saucepan from the hearth, accidentally knocked Annie on the head, where upon the girl began to whine, and Morel to shout at her. In the midst of this pandemonium, William looked up at the big glazed text over the mantelpiece and read distinctly:

"God Bless Our Home!"

Whereupon Mrs. Morel, trying to soothe the baby, jumped up, rushed at him, boxed his ears, saying:

"What are *you* putting in for?"

And then she sat down and laughed, till tears ran over her cheeks, while William kicked the stool he had been sitting on, and Morel growled:

"I canna see what there is so much to laugh at."

One evening, directly after the parson's visit, feeling unable to bear herself after another display from her husband, she took Annie and the baby and went out. Morel had kicked William, and the mother would never forgive him.

She went over the sheep-bridge and across a corner of the meadow to the cricket-ground. The meadows seemed one space of ripe, evening light, whispering with the distant millrace. She sat on a seat under the alders in the cricket-ground, and fronted the evening. Before her, level and solid, spread the big green cricket-field like the bed of a sea of light. Children played in the bluish shadow of the pavilion. Many rooks, high up, came cawing home across the softly woven sky. They stooped in a long curve down into the golden glow, concentrating, cawing, wheeling, like black flakes on a slow vortex, over a tree-clump that made a dark boss among the pasture.

A few gentlemen were practicing, and Mrs. Morel could hear the chock of the ball, and the voices of men suddenly roused; could see the white forms of men shifting silently over the green, upon which already the under shadows were smoldering. Away at the grange, one side of the haystack was lit up, the other sides blue-gray. A wagon of sheaves rocked small across the melting yellow light.

The sun was going down. Every open evening, the hills of Derbyshire were blazed over with red sunset. Mrs. Morel watched the sun sink from the glistening sky, leaving a soft flower-blue overhead, while the western space went red, as if all the fire had swum down there, leaving the bell cast flawless blue. The mountain ash berries across the field stood fierily out from the dark leaves, for a moment. A few shocks of corn in a corner of the fallow stood up as if alive; she imagined them bowing; perhaps her son would be a Joseph. In the east, a mirrored sunset floated pink opposite the west's scarlet. The big haystacks on the hillside, that butted into the glare, went cold.

With Mrs. Morel it was one of those still moments when the small frets vanish, and the beauty of things stands out, and she had the peace and the strength to see herself. Now and again, a swallow cut close to her. Now and again, Annie came up with a handful of alder currants. The baby was restless on his mother's knee, clambering with his hands at the light.

Mrs. Morel looked down at him. She had dreaded this baby like a catastrophe, because of her feeling for her husband. And now she felt strangely towards the infant. Her heart was heavy because of the child, almost as if it were unhealthy, or malformed. Yet it seemed quite well. But she noticed the peculiar knitting of the baby's brows, and the peculiar heaviness of its eyes, as if it were trying to understand something that was pain. She felt, when she looked at the child's dark, brooding pupils, as if a burden were on her heart.

"He looks as if he was thinking about something—quite sorrowful," said Mrs. Kirk.

Suddenly, looking at him, the heavy feeling at the mother's heart melted into passionate grief. She bowed over him, and a few tears shook swiftly out of her very heart. The baby lifted his fingers.

"My lamb!" she cried softly.

And at that moment she felt, in some far inner place of her soul, that she and her husband were guilty.

The baby was looking up at her. It had blue eyes like her own, but its look was heavy, steady, as if it had realized something that had stunned some point of its soul.

In her arms lay the delicate baby. Its deep blue eyes, always looking up at her unblinking, seemed to draw her innermost thoughts out of her. She no longer loved her husband; she had not wanted this child to come, and there it lay in her arms and pulled at her heart. She felt as if the navel string that had connected its frail little body with hers had not been broken. A wave of hot love went over her to the infant. She held it close to her face and breast. With all her force, with all her soul she would make up to it for having brought it into the world unloved. She would love it all the more now it was here; carry it in her love. Its clear, knowing eyes gave her pain and fear. Did it know all about her? When it lay under her heart, had it been listening then? Was there a reproach in the look? She felt the marrow melt in her bones, with fear and pain.

Once more she was aware of the sun lying red on the rim of the hill opposite. She suddenly held up the child in her hands.

"Look!" she said. "Look, my pretty!"

She thrust the infant forward to the crimson, throbbing sun, almost with relief. She saw him lift his little fist. Then she put him to her bosom again, ashamed almost of her impulse to give him back again whence he came.

"If he lives," she thought to herself, "what will become of him—what will he be?"

Her heart was anxious.

"I will call him 'Paul,' " she said suddenly; she knew not why.

After a while she went home. A fine shadow was flung over the deep green meadow, darkening all.

As she expected, she found the house empty. But Morel was home by ten o'clock, and that day, at least, ended peacefully.

Walter Morel was, at this time, exceedingly irritable. His work seemed to exhaust him. When he came home he did not speak civilly to anybody. If the fire were rather low he bullied about that; he grumbled about his dinner; if the children made a chatter he shouted at them in a way that made their mother's blood boil, and made them hate him.

On the Saturday, he was not home by eleven o'clock. The baby was unwell, and was restless, crying if he were put down. Mrs. Morel, tired to death, and still weak, was scarcely under control.

"I wish the nuisance would come," she said wearily to herself.

The child at last sank down to sleep in her arms. She was too tired to carry him to the cradle.

"But I'll say nothing, whatever time he comes," she said. "It only works me up; I won't say anything. But I know if he does anything it'll make my blood boil," she added to herself.

She sighed, hearing him coming, as if it were something she could not bear. He, taking his revenge, was nearly drunk. She kept her head bent over the child as he entered, not wishing to see him. But it went through her like a flash of hot fire when, in passing, he lurched against the dresser, setting the tins rattling, and clutched at the white pot knobs for support. He hung up his hat and coat, then returned, stood glowering from a distance at her, as she sat bowed over the child.

"Is there nothing to eat in the house?" he asked, insolently, as if to a servant. In certain stages of his intoxication he affected the clipped, mincing speech of the towns. Mrs. Morel hated him most in this condition.

"You know what there is in the house," she said, so coldly, it sounded impersonal.

He stood and glared at her without moving a muscle.

"I asked a civil question, and I expect a civil answer," he said affectedly.

"And you got it," she said, still ignoring him.

He glowered again. Then he came unsteadily forward. He leaned on the table with one hand, and with the other jerked at the table drawer to get a knife to cut bread. The drawer stuck because he pulled sideways. In a temper he dragged it, so that it flew out bodily, and spoons, forks, knives, a hundred metallic things, splashed with a clatter and a clang upon the brick floor. The baby gave a little convulsed start.

"What are you doing, clumsy, drunken fool?" the mother cried.

"Then tha should get the flamin' thing thysen. Tha should get up, like other women have to, an' wait on a man."

"Wait on you—wait on you?" she cried. "Yes, I see myself."

"Yis, an' I'll learn thee tha's got to. Wait on *me*, yes, tha sh'lt wait on me——"

"Never, milord. I'd wait on a dog at the door first."

"What—what?"

He was trying to fit in the drawer. At her last speech he turned round. His face was crimson, his eyes bloodshot. He stared at her one silent second in threat.

"P-h!" she went quickly, in contempt.

He jerked at the drawer in his excitement. It fell, cut sharply on his shin, and on the reflex he flung it at her.

One of the corners caught her brow as the shallow drawer crashed into the fireplace. She swayed, almost fell stunned from her chair. To her very soul she was sick; she clasped the child tightly to her bosom. A few moments elapsed; then, with an effort, she brought herself to. The baby was crying plaintively. Her left brow was bleeding rather profusely. As she glanced down at the child, her brain reeling, some drops of blood soaked into its white shawl; but the baby was at least not hurt. She balanced her head to keep equilibrium, so that the blood ran into her eye.

Walter Morel remained as he had stood, leaning on the table with one hand, looking blank. When he was sufficiently sure of his balance, he went across to her, swayed, caught hold of the back of her rocking chair, almost tipping her out; then, leaning forward over her, and swaying as he spoke, he said, in tone of wondering concern:

"Did it catch thee?"

He swayed again, as if he would pitch onto the child. With the catastrophe he had lost all balance.

"Go away," she said, struggling to keep her presence of mind.

He hiccoughed. "Let's—let's look at it," he said, hiccoughing again.

"Go away!" she cried.

"Lemme—lemme look at it, lass."

She smelled him of drink, felt the unequal pull of his swaying grasp on the back of her rocking chair.

"Go away," she said, and weakly she pushed him off.

He stood, uncertain in balance, gazing upon her. Summoning all her strength she rose, the baby on one arm. By a cruel effort of will, moving as if in sleep, she went across to the scullery, where she bathed her eye for a minute in cold water; but she was too dizzy. Afraid lest she should swoon, she returned to her rocking chair, trembling in every fiber. By instinct, she kept the baby clasped.

Morel, bothered, had succeeded in pushing the drawer back into its cavity, and was on his knees, groping, with numb paws, for the scattered spoons.

Her brow was still bleeding. Presently Morel got up and came craning his neck towards her.

"What has it done to thee, lass?" he asked, in a very wretched, humble tone.

"You can see what it's done," she answered.

He stood, bending forward, supported on his hands, which grasped his legs just above the knee. He peered to look at the wound. She drew away from the thrust of his face with its great moustache, averting her own face as much as possible. As he looked at her, who was cold and impassive as stone, with mouth shut tight, he sickened with feebleness and hopelessness of spirit. He was turning drearily away, when he saw a drop of blood fall from the averted wound into the baby's fragile, glistening hair. Fascinated, he watched the heavy dark drop hang in the glistening cloud, and pull down the gossamer. Another drop fell. It would soak through to the baby's scalp. He watched, fascinated, feeling it soak in; then, finally, his manhood broke.

"What of this child?" was all his wife said to him. But her low, intense tones brought his head lower. She softened: "Get me some wadding out of the middle drawer," she said.

He stumbled away very obediently, presently returning with a pad, which she singed before the fire, then put on her forehead, as she sat with the baby on her lap.

"Now that clean pit-scarf."

Again he rummaged and fumbled in the drawer, returning presently with a red, narrow scarf. She took it, and with trembling fingers proceeded to bind it round her head.

"Let me tie it for thee," he said humbly.

"I can do it myself," she replied. When it was done she went upstairs, telling him to rake the fire and lock the door.

In the morning Mrs. Morel said:

"I knocked against the latch of the coal-place, when I was getting a raker in the dark, because the candle blew out." Her two small children looked up at her with wide, dismayed eyes. They said nothing, but their parted lips seemed to express the unconscious tragedy they felt.

Walter Morel lay in bed next day until nearly dinnertime. He did not think of the previous evening's work. He scarcely thought of anything, but he would not think of that. He lay and suffered like a sulking dog. He had hurt himself most; and he was the more damaged because he would never say a word to her, or express his sorrow. He tried to wriggle out of it. "It was her own fault," he said to himself. Nothing, however, could prevent his inner consciousness inflicting on him the punishment which ate into his spirit like rust, and which he could only alleviate by drinking.

He felt as if he had not the initiative to get up, or to say a word, or to move, but could only lie like a log. Moreover, he had himself violent pains in the head. It was Saturday. Towards noon he rose, cut himself food in the pantry, ate it with his head dropped, then pulled on his boots, and went out, to return at three o'clock slightly tipsy and relieved: then once more straight to bed. He rose again at six in the evening, had tea and went straight out.

Sunday was the same: bed till noon, the Palmerston Arms till 2:30, dinner, and bed; scarcely a word spoken. When Mrs. Morel went upstairs, towards four o'clock, to put on her Sunday dress, he was fast asleep. She would have felt sorry for him, if he had once said, "Wife, I'm sorry." But no; he insisted to himself it was her fault. And so he broke himself. So she merely left him alone. There was this deadlock of passion between them, and she was stronger.

The family began tea. Sunday was the only day when all sat down to meals together.

"Isn't my father going to get up?" asked William.

"Let him lie," the mother replied.

There was a feeling of misery over all the house. The children breathed the air that was poisoned, and they felt dreary. They were rather disconsolate, did not know what to do, what to play at.

Immediately Morel woke he got straight out of bed. That was characteristic of him all his life. He was all for activity. The prostrated inactivity of two mornings was stifling him.

It was near six o'clock when he got down. This time he entered without hesitation, his wincing sensitiveness having hardened again. He did not care any longer what the family thought or felt.

The tea-things were on the table. William was reading aloud from "The Child's Own," Annie listening and asking eternally "Why?" Both children hushed into silence as they heard the approaching thud of their father's stockinged feet, and shrank as he entered. Yet he was usually indulgent to them.

Morel made the meal alone, brutally. He ate and drank more noisily than he had need. No one spoke to him. The family life withdrew, shrank away, and became hushed as he entered. But he cared no longer about his alienation.

Immediately he had finished tea he rose with alacrity to go out. It was this alacrity, this haste to be gone, which so sickened Mrs. Morel. As she heard him sousing heartily in cold water, heard the eager scratch of the steel comb on the side of the bowl, as he wetted his hair, she closed her eyes in disgust. As he bent over, lacing his boots, there was a certain vulgar gusto in his movement that divided him from the reserved, watchful rest of the family. He always ran away from the battle with himself. Even in his own heart's privacy, he excused himself, saying, "If she hadn't said so-and-so, it would never have happened. She asked for what she's got." The children waited in restraint during his preparations. When he had gone, they sighed with relief.

He closed the door behind him, and was glad. It was a rainy evening. The Palmerston would be the cosier. He hastened forward in anticipation. All the slate roofs of the Bottoms shone black with wet. The roads, always dark with coal dust, were full of blackish mud. He hastened along. The Palmerston windows were steamed over. The passage was paddled with wet feet. But the air was warm, if foul, and full of the sound of voices and the smell of beer and smoke.

"What shollt ha'e, Walter?" cried a voice, as soon as Morel appeared in the doorway.

"Oh, Jim, my lad, wheriver has thee sprung frae?"

The men made a seat for him, and took him in warmly. He was glad. In a minute or two they had thawed all responsibility out of him, all shame, all trouble, and he was clear as a bell for a jolly night.

On the Wednesday following, Morel was penniless. He dreaded his wife. Having hurt her, he hated her. He did not know what to do with himself that evening, having not even twopence with which to go to the Palmerston, and being already rather deeply in debt. So, while his wife was down the garden with the child, he hunted in the top drawer of the dresser where she kept her purse, found it, and looked inside. It contained a half-crown, two half-pennies, and a sixpence. So he took the sixpence, put the purse carefully back, and went out.

The next day, when she wanted to pay the greengrocer, she looked in the purse for her sixpence, and her heart sank to her shoes. Then she sat down and thought: "*Was* there a sixpence? I hadn't spent it, had I? And I hadn't left it anywhere else?"

She was much put about. She hunted round everywhere for it. And, as she thought, the conviction came into her heart that her husband had taken it. What she had in her purse was all the money she possessed. But that he should sneak it from her thus was unbearable. He had done so twice before. The first time she had not accused him, and at the weekend he had put the shilling again into her purse. So that was how she had known he had taken it. The second time he had not paid back.

This time she felt it was too much. When he had had his dinner—he came home early that day—she said to him coldly:

"Did you take sixpence out of my purse last night?"

"Me!" he said, looking up in an offended way. "No, I didna! I niver clapped eyes on your purse."

But she could detect the lie.

"Why, you know you did," she said quietly.

"I tell you I didna," he shouted. "Yer at me again, are yer? I've had about enough on't."

"So you filch sixpence out of my purse while I'm taking the clothes in."

"I'll make yer pay for this," he said, pushing back his chair in desperation. He bustled and got washed, then went determinedly upstairs. Presently he came down dressed, and with a big bundle in a blue-checked, enormous handkerchief.

"And now," he said, "you'll see me again when you do."

"It'll be before I want to," she replied; and at that he marched out of the house with his bundle. She sat trembling slightly, but her heart brimming with contempt. What would she do if he went to some other pit, obtained work, and got in with another woman? But she knew him too well—he couldn't. She was dead sure of him. Nevertheless her heart was gnawed inside her.

"Where's my dad?" said William, coming in from school.

"He says he's run away," replied the mother.

"Where to?"

"Eh, I don't know. He's taken a bundle in the blue handkerchief, and says he's not coming back."

"What shall we do?" cried the boy.

"Eh, never trouble, he won't go far."

"But if he doesn't come back," wailed Annie.

And she and William retired to the sofa and wept. Mrs. Morel sat and laughed.

"You pair of gabeys!" she exclaimed. "You'll see him before the night's out."

But the children were not to be consoled. Twilight came on. Mrs. Morel grew anxious from very weariness. One part of her said, it would be a relief to see the last of him; another part fretted because of keeping the children; and inside her, as yet, she could not quite let him go. At the bottom, she knew very well he could *not* go.

When she went down to the coal-place at the end of the garden, however, she felt something behind the door. So she looked. And there in the dark lay the big blue bundle. She sat on a piece of coal in front of the bundle and laughed. Every time she saw it, so fat and yet so ignominious, slunk into its corner in the dark, with its ends flopping like dejected ears from the knots, she laughed again. She was relieved.

Mrs. Morel sat waiting. He had not any money, she knew, so if he stopped he was running up a bill. She was very tired of him—tired to death. He had not even the courage to carry his bundle beyond the yard-end.

As she meditated, at about nine o'clock, he opened the door and came in, slinking, and yet sulky. She said not a word. He took off his coat, and slunk to his armchair, where he began to take off his boots.

"You'd better fetch your bundle before you take your boots off," she said quietly.

"You may thank your stars I've come back tonight," he said, looking up from under his dropped head, sulkily, trying to be impressive.

"Why, where should you have gone? You daren't even get your parcel through the yard-end," she said.

He looked such a fool she was not even angry with him. He continued to take his boots off and prepare for bed.

"I don't know what's in your blue handkerchief," she said. "But if you leave it the children shall fetch it in the morning."

Whereupon he got up and went out of the house, returning presently and crossing the kitchen with averted face, hurrying upstairs. As Mrs. Morel saw him slink quickly through the inner doorway, holding his bundle, she laughed to herself; but her heart was bitter, because she had loved him.

❖ 3 ❖

THE CASTING OFF OF MOREL— THE TAKING ON OF WILLIAM

During the next week Morel's temper was almost unbearable. Like all miners, he was a great lover of medicines, which strangely enough, he would often pay for himself.

"You mun get me a drop o' laxy vitral," he said. "It's a winder as we canna ha'e a sup i'th' 'ouse."

So Mrs. Morel bought him elixir of vitriol, his favorite first medicine. And he made himself a jug of wormwood tea. He had hanging in the attic great bunches of dried herbs: wormwood, rue, horehound, elder-flowers, parsley-purt, marshmallow, hyssop, dandelion, and centuary. Usually there was a jug of one or other decoction standing on the hob, from which he drank largely.

"Grand!" he said, smacking his lips after wormwood. "Grand!" And he exhorted the children to try.

"It's better than any of your tea or your cocoa stews," he vowed. But they were not to be tempted.

This time, however, neither pills nor vitriol nor all his herbs would shift the "nasty peens in his head." He was sickening for an attack of an inflammation of the brain. He had never been well since his sleeping on the ground when he went with Jerry to Nottingham. Since then he had drunk and stormed. Now he fell seriously ill, and Mrs. Morel had him to nurse. He was one of the worst patients imaginable. But, in spite of all, and putting aside the fact that he was breadwinner, she never quite wanted him to die. Still there was one part of her wanted him for herself.

The neighbors were very good to her: occasionally some had the children in to meals, occasionally some would do the downstairs work for her, one would mind the baby for a day. But it was a great drag, nevertheless. It was not every day the neighbors helped. Then she had nursing of baby and husband, cleaning and cooking, everything to do. She was quite worn out, but she did what was wanted of her.

And the money was just sufficient. She had seventeen shillings a week from clubs, and every Friday Barker and the other butty put by a portion of the stall's profits for Morel's wife. And the neighbors made broths, and gave eggs, and such invalids' trifles. If they had not helped her so generously in those times, Mrs. Morel would never have pulled through, without incurring debts that would have dragged her down.

The weeks passed. Morel, almost against hope, grew better. He had a fine constitution, so that, once on the mend, he went straight forward to recovery. Soon he was pottering about downstairs. During his illness his wife had spoilt him a little. Now he wanted her to continue. He often put his hand to his head, pulled down the corners of his mouth, and shammed pains he did not feel. But there was no deceiving her. At first she merely smiled to herself. Then she scolded him sharply.

"Goodness, man, don't be so lachrymose."

That wounded him slightly, but still he continued to feign sickness.

"I wouldn't be such a mardy baby," said his wife shortly.

Then he was indignant, and cursed under his breath, like a boy. He was forced to resume a normal tone, and to cease to whine.

Nevertheless, there was a state of peace in the house for some time. Mrs. Morel was more tolerant of him, and he, depending on her almost like a child, was rather happy. Neither knew that she was more tolerant because she loved him less. Up till this time, in spite of all, he had been her husband and her man. She had felt that, more or less, what he did to himself he did to her. Her living depended on him. There were many, many stages in the ebbing of her love for him, but it was always ebbing.

Now, with the birth of this third baby, her self no longer set towards him, helplessly, but was like a tide that scarcely rose, standing off from him. After this she scarcely desired him. And, standing more aloof from him, not feeling him so much part of herself, but merely part of her circumstances, she did not mind so much what he did, could leave him alone.

There was the halt, the wistfulness about the ensuing year, which is like autumn in a man's life. His wife was casting him off, half regretfully, but relentlessly; casting him off and turning now for love and life to the children. Henceforward he was more or less a husk. And he half acquiesced, as so many men do, yielding their place to their children.

During his recuperation, when it was really over between them, both made an effort to come back somewhat to the old relationship of the first months of their marriage. He sat at home and, when the children were in bed, and she was sewing—she did all her sewing by hand, made all shirts and children's clothing—he would read to her from the newspaper, slowly pronouncing and delivering the words like a man pitching quoits. Often she hurried him on, giving him a phrase in anticipation. And then he took her words humbly.

The silences between them were peculiar. There would be the swift, slight "cluck" of her needle, the sharp "pop" of his lips as he let out the smoke, the warmth, the sizzle on the bars as he spat in the fire. Then her thoughts turned to William. Already he was getting a big boy. Already he was top of the class, and the master said he was the smartest lad in the school. She saw him a man, young, full of vigor, making the world glow again for her.

And Morel sitting there, quite alone, and having nothing to think about, would be feeling vaguely uncomfortable. His soul would reach out in its blind way to her and find her gone. He felt a sort of emptiness, almost like a vacuum in his soul. He was unsettled and restless. Soon he could not live in that atmosphere, and he affected his wife. Both felt an oppression on their breathing when they were left together for some time. Then he went to bed and she settled down to enjoy herself alone, working, thinking, living.

Meanwhile another infant was coming, fruit of this little peace and tenderness between the separating parents. Paul was seventeen months old when the new baby was born. He was then a plump, pale child, quiet, with heavy blue eyes, and still the peculiar slight knitting of the brows. The last child was also a boy, fair and bonny. Mrs. Morel was sorry when she knew she was with child, both for economic reasons and because she did not love her husband; but not for the sake of the infant.

They called the baby Arthur. He was very pretty, with a mop of gold curls, and he loved his father from the first. Mrs. Morel was glad this child loved the father. Hearing the miner's footsteps, the baby would put up his arms and crow. And if Morel were in a good temper, he called back immediately, in his hearty, mellow voice:

"What then, my beauty? I sh'll come to thee in a minute."

And as soon as he had taken off his pit-coat, Mrs. Morel would put an apron round the child, and give him to his father.

"What a sight the lad looks!" she would exclaim sometimes, taking back the baby, that was smutted on the face from his father's kisses and play. Then Morel laughed joyfully.

"He's a little collier, bless his bit o' mutton!" he exclaimed.

And these were the happy moments of her life now, when the children included the father in her heart.

Meanwhile William grew bigger and stronger and more active, while Paul, always rather delicate and quiet, got slimmer, and trotted after his mother like her shadow. He was usually active and interested, but sometimes he would have fits of depression. Then the mother would find the boy of three or four crying on the sofa.

"What's the matter?" she asked, and got no answer.

"What's the matter?" she insisted, getting cross.

"I don't know," sobbed the child.

So she tried to reason him out of it, or to amuse him, but without effect. It made her feel beside herself. Then the father, always impatient, would jump from his chair and shout:

"If he doesn't stop, I'll smack him till he does."

"You'll do nothing of the sort," said the mother coldly. And then she carried the child into the yard, plumped him into his little chair, and said: "Now cry there, Misery!"

And then a butterfly on the rhubarb leaves perhaps caught his eye, or at last he cried himself to sleep. These fits were not often, but they caused a shadow in Mrs. Morel's heart, and her treatment of Paul was different from that of the other children.

Suddenly one morning as she was looking down the alley of the Bottoms for the barm man, she heard a voice calling her. It was the thin little Mrs. Anthony in brown velvet.

"Here, Mrs. Morel, I want to tell you about your Willie."

"Oh, do you?" replied Mrs. Morel. "Why, what's the matter?"

"A lad as gets 'old of another an' rips his clothes off'n 'is back," Mrs. Anthony said, "wants showing something."

"Your Alfred's as old as my William," said Mrs. Morel.

" 'Appen 'e is, but that doesn't give him a right to get hold of the boy's collar, an' fair rip it clean off his back."

"Well," said Mrs. Morel, "I don't thrash my children, and even if I did, I should want to hear their side of the tale."

"They'd happen be a bit better if they did get a good hidin'," retorted Mrs. Anthony. "When it comes ter rippin' a lad's clean collar off'n 'is back a-purpose——"

"I'm sure he didn't do it on purpose," said Mrs. Morel.

"Make me a liar!" shouted Mrs. Anthony.

Mrs. Morel moved away and closed her gate. Her hand trembled as she held her mug of barm.

"But I s'll let your mester know," Mrs. Anthony cried after her.

At dinnertime, when William had finished his meal and wanted to be off again—he was then eleven years old—his mother said to him:

"What did you tear Alfred Anthony's collar for?"

"When did I tear his collar?"

"I don't know when, but his mother says you did."

"Why—it was yesterday—an' it was torn a'ready."

"But you tore it more."

"Well, I'd got a cobbler as 'ad licked seventeen—an' Alfy Ant'ny says:

Adam an' Eve an' pinch-me,
    Went down to a river to bade.
Adam an' Eve got drownded,
    Who do yer think got saved?

An' so I says, 'Oh, Pinch-*you*,' an' so I pinched 'im, an' 'e was mad, an' so he snatched my cobbler an' run off with it. An' so I run after 'im, an' when I was gettin' hold of him,'e dodged, an' it ripped 'is collar. But I got my cobbler——"

He pulled from his pocket a black old horse chestnut hanging on a string. This old cobbler had "cobbled"—hit and smashed—seventeen other cobblers on similar strings. So the boy was proud of his veteran.

"Well," said Mrs. Morel, "you know you've got no right to rip his collar."

"Well, our mother!" he answered. "I never meant tr'a done it—an' it was on'y an old indirubber collar as was torn a'ready."

"Next time," said his mother, "*you* be more careful. I shouldn't like it if you came home with *your* collar torn off."

"I don't care, our mother; I never did it a-purpose."

The boy was rather miserable at being reprimanded.

"No—well, you be more careful."

William fled away, glad to be exonerated. And Mrs. Morel, who hated any bother with the neighbors, thought she would explain to Mrs. Anthony, and the business would be over.

But that evening Morel came in from the pit looking very sour. He stood in the kitchen and glared round, but did not speak for some minutes. Then:

"Wheer's that Willy?" he asked.

"What do you want *him* for?" asked Mrs. Morel, who had guessed.

"I'll let 'im know when I get him," said Morel, banging his pit-bottle on to the dresser.

"I suppose Mrs. Anthony's got hold of you and been yarning to you about their Alfy's collar," said Mrs. Morel, rather sneering.

"Niver mind who's got hold of me," said Morel. "When I get hold of *'im* I'll make his bones rattle."

"It's a poor tale," said Mrs. Morel, "that you're so ready to side with any snipey vixen who likes to come telling tales against your own children."

"I'll learn 'im!" said Morel. "It none matters to me whose lad 'e is; 'e's non goin' rippin' an' tearin' about just as he's a mind."

" 'Ripping and tearing about'!" repeated Mrs. Morel. "He was running after that Alfy, who'd taken his cobbler, and he accidentally got hold of his collar, because the other dodged—as an Anthony would."

"I know!" shouted Morel threateningly.

"You would, before you're told," replied his wife bitingly.

"Niver you mind," stormed Morel. "I know my business."

"That's more than doubtful," said Mrs. Morel, "supposing some loud-mouthed creature had been getting you to thrash your own children."

"I know," repeated Morel.

And he said no more, but sat and nursed his bad temper. Suddenly William ran in, saying:

"Can I have my tea, mother?"

"Tha can ha'e more than that!" shouted Morel.

"Hold your noise, man," said Mrs. Morel; "and don't look so ridiculous."

"He'll look ridiculous before I've done wi' him!" shouted Morel, rising from his chair and glaring at his son.

William, who was a tall lad for his years, but very sensitive, had gone pale, and was looking in a sort of horror at his father.

"Go out!" Mrs. Morel commanded her son.

William had not the wit to move. Suddenly Morel clenched his fist, and crouched.

"I'll *gi'e* him 'go out'!" he shouted like an insane thing.

"What!" cried Mrs. Morel, panting with rage. "You shall not touch him for *her* telling, you shall not!"

"Shonna I?" shouted Morel. "Shonna I?"

And, glaring at the boy, he ran forward. Mrs. Morel sprang in between them, with her fist lifted.

"Don't you *dare*!" she cried.

"What!" he shouted, baffled for the moment. "What!"

She spun round to her son.

"*Go* out of the house!" she commanded him in fury.

The boy, as if hypnotized by her, turned suddenly and was gone. Morel rushed to the door, but was too late. He returned, pale under his pit-dirt with fury. But now his wife was fully roused.

"Only dare!" she said in a loud, ringing voice. "Only dare, milord, to lay a finger on that child! You'll regret it forever."

He was afraid of her. In a towering rage, he sat down.

When the children were old enough to be left, Mrs. Morel joined the Women's Guild. It was a little club of women attached to the Cooperative Wholesale Society, which met on Monday night in the long room over the grocery shop of the Bestwood "Co-op." The women were supposed to discuss the benefits to be derived from cooperation, and other social questions. Sometimes Mrs. Morel read a paper.

It seemed queer to the children to see their mother, who was always busy about the house, sitting writing in her rapid fashion, thinking, referring to books, and writing again. They felt for her on such occasions the deepest respect.

But they loved the Guild. It was the only thing to which they did not grudge their mother—and that partly because she enjoyed it, partly because of the treats they derived from it. The Guild was called by some hostile husbands, who found their wives getting too independent, the "clat-fart" shop—that is, the gossip shop. It is true, from off the basis of the Guild, the women could look at their homes, at the conditions of their own lives, and find fault. So the colliers found their women had a new standard of their own, rather disconcerting. And also, Mrs. Morel always had a lot of news on Monday nights, so that the children liked William to be in when their mother came home, because she told him things.

Then, when the lad was thirteen, she got him a job in the Co-op office. He was a very clever boy, frank, with rather rough features and real viking blue eyes.

"What dost want ter ma'e a stool-harsed Jack on 'im for?" said Morel. "All he'll do is to wear his britches behind out, an' earn nowt. What's 'e startin' wi'?"

"It doesn't matter what he's starting with," said Mrs. Morel.

"It wouldna! Put 'im i' th' pit wi' me, an' 'e'll earn a easy ten shillin' a wik from th' start. But six shillin' wearin' his truck-end out on a stool's better than ten shillin' i' th' pit wi' me, I know."

"He is *not* going in the pit," said Mrs. Morel, "and there's an end of it."

"It wor good enough for me, but it's non good enough for 'im."

"If your mother put you in the pit at twelve, it's no reason why I should do the same with my lad."

"Twelve! It wor a sight afore that!"

"Whenever it was," said Mrs. Morel.

She was very proud of her son. He went to the night school, and learned shorthand, so that by the time he was sixteen he was the best shorthand clerk and bookkeeper on the place, except one. Then he taught in the night school. But he was so fiery that only his good nature and his size protected him.

All the things that men do—the decent things—William did. He could run like the wind. When he was twelve he won a first prize in a race—an inkstand of glass, shaped like an anvil. It stood proudly on the dresser, and gave Mrs. Morel a keen pleasure. The boy only ran for her. He flew home with his anvil, breathless, with a "Look, mother!" That was the first real tribute to herself. She took it like a queen.

"How pretty!" she exclaimed.

Then he began to get ambitious. He gave all his money to his mother. When he earned fourteen shillings a week, she gave him back two for himself, and, as he never drank, he felt himself rich. He went about with the bourgeois of Bestwood. The townlet contained nothing higher than the clergyman. Then came the bank manager, then the doctors, then the tradespeople, and after that the hosts of colliers. William began to consort with the sons of the chemist, the schoolmaster, and the tradesmen. He played billiards in the Mechanics Hall. Also he danced—this in spite of his mother. All the life that Bestwood offered he enjoyed, from the sixpenny-hops down Church Street, to sports and billiards.

Paul was treated to dazzling descriptions of all kinds of flowerlike ladies, most of whom lived like cut blooms in William's heart for a brief fortnight.

Occasionally some flame would come in pursuit of her errant swain. Mrs. Morel would find a strange girl at the door, and immediately she sniffed the air.

"Is Mr. Morel in?" the damsel would ask appealingly.

"My husband is at home," Mrs. Morel replied.

"I—I mean *young* Mr. Morel," repeated the maiden painfully.

"Which one? There are several."

Whereupon much blushing and stammering from the fair one.

"I—I met Mr. Morel—at Ripley," she explained.

"Oh—at a dance!"

"Yes."

"I don't approve of the girls my son meets at dances. And he is *not* at home."

Then he came home angry with his mother for having turned the girl away so rudely. He was a careless, yet eager-looking fellow, who walked with long strides, sometimes frowning, often with his cap pushed jollily to the back of his head. Now he came in frowning. He threw his cap on to the sofa, and took his strong jaw in his hand, and glared down at his mother. She was small, with her hair taken straight back from her forehead. She had a quiet air of authority, and yet of rare warmth. Knowing her son was angry, she trembled inwardly.

"Did a lady call for me yesterday, mother?" he asked.

"I don't know about a lady. There was a girl came."

"And why didn't you tell me?"

"Because I forgot, simply."

He fumed a little.

"A good-looking girl—seemed a lady?"

"I didn't look at her."

"Big brown eyes?"

"I did *not* look. And tell your girls, my son, that when they're running after you, they're not to come and ask your mother for you. Tell them that—brazen baggages you meet at dancing classes."

"I'm sure she was a nice girl."

"And I'm sure she wasn't."

There ended the altercation. Over the dancing there was a great strife between the mother and the son. The grievance reached its height when William said he was going to Hucknall Torkard—considered a low town—to a fancy-dress ball. He was to be a Highlander. There was a dress he could hire, which one of his friends had had, and which fitted him perfectly. The Highland suit came home. Mrs. Morel received it coldly and would not unpack it.

"My suit come?" cried William.

"There's a parcel in the front room."

He rushed in and cut the string.

"How do you fancy your son in this!" he said, enraptured, showing her the suit.

"You know I don't want to fancy you in it."

On the evening of the dance, when he had come home to dress, Mrs. Morel put on her coat and bonnet.

"Aren't you going to stop and see me, mother?" he asked.

"No; I don't want to see you," she replied.

She was rather pale, and her face was closed and hard. She was afraid of her son's going the same way as his father. He hesitated a moment, and his heart stood still with anxiety. Then he caught sight of the Highland bonnet with its ribbons. He picked it up gleefully, forgetting her. She went out.

When he was nineteen he suddenly left the Co-op office and got a situation in Nottingham. In his new place he had thirty shillings a week instead of eighteen. This was indeed a rise. His mother and his father were brimmed up with pride. Everybody praised William. It seemed he was going to get on rapidly. Mrs. Morel hoped, with his aid, to help her younger sons. Annie was now studying to be a teacher. Paul, also very clever, was getting on well, having lessons in French and German from his godfather, the clergyman who was still a friend to Mrs. Morel. Arthur, a spoilt and very good-looking boy, was at the Board-school, but there was talk of his trying to get a scholarship for the High School in Nottingham.

William remained a year at his new post in Nottingham. He was studying hard, and growing serious. Something seemed to be fretting him. Still he went out to the dances and the river parties. He did not drink. The children were all rabid teetotalers. He came home very late at night, and sat yet longer studying. His mother implored him to take more care, to do one thing or another.

"Dance, if you want to dance, my son; but don't think you can work in the office, and then amuse yourself, and *then* study on top of all. You can't; the human frame won't stand it. Do one thing or the other—amuse yourself or learn Latin; but don't try to do both."

Then he got a place in London, at a hundred and twenty a year. This seemed a fabulous sum. His mother doubted almost whether to rejoice or to grieve.

"They want me in Lime Street on Monday week, mother," he cried, his eyes blazing as he read the letter. Mrs. Morel felt everything go silent inside her. He read the letter: " 'And will you reply by Thursday whether you accept. Yours faithfully—' They want me, mother, at a hundred and twenty a year, and don't even ask to see me. Didn't I tell you I could do it! Think of me in London! And I can give you twenty pounds a year, mater. We s'll all be rolling in money."

"We shall, my son," she answered sadly.

It never occurred to him that she might be more hurt at his going away than glad of his success. Indeed, as the days drew near for his departure, her heart began to close and grow dreary with despair. She loved him so much! More than that, she hoped in him so much. Almost she lived by him. She liked to do things for him; she liked to put a cup for his tea and to iron his collar, of which he was so proud. It was a joy to her to have him proud of his collars. There was no laundry. So she used to rub away at them with her little convex iron, to polish them, till they shone from the sheer pressure of her arm. Now she would not do it for him. Now he was going away. She felt almost as if he were going as well out of her heart. He did not seem to leave her inhabited with himself. That was the grief and the pain to her. He took nearly all himself away.

A few days before his departure—he was just twenty—he burned his love letters. They had hung on a file at the top of the kitchen cupboard. From some of them he had read extracts to his mother. Some of them she had taken the trouble to read herself. But most were too trivial.

Now, on the Saturday morning he said:

"Come on, 'Postle, let's go through my letters, and you can have the birds and flowers."

Mrs. Morel had done her Saturday's work on the Friday, because he was having a last day's holiday. She was making him a rice cake, which he loved, to take with him. He was scarcely conscious that she was so miserable.

He took the first letter off the file. It was mauve-tinted, and had purple and green thistles. William sniffed the page.

"Nice scent! Smell."

And he thrust the sheet under Paul's nose.

"Um!" said Paul, breathing in. "What d'you call it? Smell, mother."

His mother ducked her small, fine nose down to the paper.

"*I* don't want to smell their rubbish," she said, sniffing.

"This girl's father," said William, "is as rich as Crœsus. He owns property without end. She calls me Lafayette, because I know French. 'You will see, I've forgiven you'—I like *her* forgiving me. 'I told mother about you this morning, and she will have much pleasure if you come to tea on Sunday, but she will have to get father's consent also. I sincerely hope he will agree. I will let you know how it transpires. If, however, you——' "

" 'Let you know how it' what?" interrupted Mrs. Morel.

" 'Transpires'—oh yes!"

" 'Transpires'!" repeated Mrs. Morel mockingly. "I thought she was so well educated!"

William felt slightly uncomfortable, and abandoned this maiden, giving Paul the corner with the thistles. He continued to read extracts from his letters, some of which amused his mother, some of which saddened her and made her anxious for him.

"My lad," she said, "they're very wise. They know they've only got to flatter your vanity, and you press up to them like a dog that has its head scratched."

"Well, they can't go on scratching forever," he replied. "And when they've done, I trot away."

"But one day you'll find a string round your neck that you can't pull off," she answered.

"Not me! I'm equal to any of 'em, mater, they needn't flatter themselves."

"You flatter *yourself*," she said quietly.

Soon there was a heap of twisted black pages, all that remained of the file of scented letters, except that Paul had thirty or forty pretty tickets from the corners of the notepaper—swallows and forget-me-nots and ivy sprays. And William went to London, to start a new file.

4

THE YOUNG LIFE OF PAUL

Paul would be built like his mother, slightly and rather small. His fair hair went reddish, and then dark brown; his eyes were gray. He was a pale, quiet child, with eyes that seemed to listen, and with a full, dropping underlip.

As a rule he seemed old for his years. He was so conscious of what other people felt, particularly his mother. When she fretted he understood, and could have no peace. His soul seemed always attentive to her.

As he grew older he became stronger. William was too far removed from him to accept him as a companion. So the smaller boy belonged at first almost entirely to Annie. She was a tomboy and a "flybie-skybie," as her mother called her. But she was intensely fond of her second brother. So Paul was towed round at the heels of Annie, sharing her game. She raced wildly at lerky with the other young wildcats of the Bottoms. And always Paul flew beside her, living her share of the game, having as yet no part of his own. He was quiet and not noticeable. But his sister adored him. He always seemed to care for things if she wanted him to.

She had a big doll of which she was fearfully proud, though not so fond. So she laid the doll on the sofa, and covered it with an antimacassar, to sleep. Then she forgot it. Meantime Paul must practice jumping off the sofa arm. So he jumped crash into the face of the hidden doll. Annie rushed up, uttered a loud wail, and sat down to weep a dirge. Paul remained quite still.

"You couldn't tell it was there, mother; you couldn't tell it was there," he repeated over and over. So long as Annie wept for the doll he sat helpless with misery. Her grief wore itself out. She forgave her brother—he was so much upset. But a day or two afterwards she was shocked.

"Let's make a sacrifice of Arabella," he said. "Let's burn her."

She was horrified, yet rather fascinated. She wanted to see what the boy would do. He made an altar of bricks, pulled some of the shavings out of Arabella's body, put the waxen fragments into the hollow face, poured on a little paraffin, and set the whole thing alight. He watched with wicked satisfaction the drops of wax melt off the broken forehead of Arabella, and drop like sweat into the flame. So long as the stupid big doll burned he rejoiced in silence. At the end he poked among the embers with a stick, fished out the arms and legs, all blackened, and smashed them under stones.

"That's the sacrifice of Missis Arabella," he said. "An' I'm glad there's nothing left of her."

Which disturbed Annie inwardly, although she could say nothing. He seemed to hate the doll so intensely, because he had broken it.

All the children, but particularly Paul, were peculiarly *against* their father, along with their mother. Morel continued to bully and to drink. He had periods, months at a time, when he made the whole life of the family a misery. Paul never forgot coming home from the Band of Hope one Monday evening and finding his mother with her eye swollen and discolored, his father standing on the hearthrug, feet astride, his head down, and William, just home from work, glaring at his father. There was a silence as the young children entered, but none of the elders looked round.

William was white to the lips, and his fists were clenched. He waited until the children were silent, watching with children's rage and hate; then he said:

"You coward, you daren't do it when I was in."

But Morel's blood was up. He swung round on his son. William was bigger, but Morel was hard-muscled, and mad with fury.

"Dossn't I?" he shouted. "Dossn't I? Ha'e much more o' thy chelp, my young jockey, an' I'll rattle my fist about thee. Ay, an' I sholl that, dost see."

Morel crouched at the knees and showed his fist in an ugly, almost beastlike fashion. William was white with rage.

"Will yer?" he said, quiet and intense. "It 'ud be the last time, though."

Morel danced a little nearer, crouching, drawing back his fist to strike. William put his fists ready. A light came into his blue eyes, almost like a laugh. He watched his father. Another word, and the men would have begun to fight. Paul hoped they would. The three children sat pale on the sofa.

"Stop it, both of you," cried Mrs. Morel in a hard voice. "We've had enough for *one* night. And *you*," she said, turning on to her husband, "look at your children!"

Morel glanced at the sofa.

"Look at the children, you nasty little bitch!" he sneered. "Why, what have *I* done to the children, I should like to know? But they're like yourself; you've put 'em up to your own tricks and nasty ways—you've learned 'em in it, you 'ave."

She refused to answer him. No one spoke. After a while he threw his boots under the table and went to bed.

"Why didn't you let me have a go at him?" said William, when his father was upstairs. "I could easily have beaten him."

"A nice thing—your own father," she replied.

" '*Father!*' " repeated William. "Call *him my* father!"

"Well, he is—and so——"

"But why don't you let me settle him? I could do, easily."

"The idea!" she cried. "It hasn't come to *that* yet."

"No," he said, "it's come to worse. Look at yourself. *Why* didn't you let me give it him?"

"Because I couldn't bear it, so never think of it," she cried quickly.

And the children went to bed, miserably.

When William was growing up, the family moved from the Bottoms to a house on the brow of the hill, commanding a view of the valley, which spread out like a convex cockleshell, or a clampshell, before it. In front of the house was a huge old ash tree. The west wind, sweeping from Derbyshire, caught the houses with full force, and the tree shrieked again. Morel liked it.

"It's music," he said. "It sends me to sleep."

But Paul and Arthur and Annie hated it. To Paul it became almost a demoniacal noise. The winter of their first year in the new house their father was very bad. The children played in the street, on the brim of the wide, dark valley, until eight o'clock. Then they went to bed. Their mother sat sewing below. Having such a great space in front of the house gave the children a feeling of night, of vastness, and of terror. This terror came in from the shrieking of the tree and the anguish of the home discord. Often Paul would wake up, after he had been asleep a long time, aware of thuds downstairs. Instantly he was wide awake. Then he heard the booming shouts of his father, come home nearly drunk, then the sharp replies of his mother, then the bang, bang of his father's fist on the table, and the nasty snarling shout as the man's voice got higher. And then the whole was drowned in a piercing medley of shrieks and cries from the great, wind-swept ash tree. The children lay silent in suspense, waiting for a lull in the wind to hear what their father was doing. He might hit their mother again. There was a feeling of horror, a kind of bristling in the darkness, and a sense of blood. They lay with their hearts in the grip of an intense anguish. The wind came through the tree fiercer and fiercer. All the cords of the great harp hummed, whistled, and shrieked. And then came the horror of the sudden silence, silence everywhere, outside and downstairs. What was it? Was it a silence of blood? What had he done?

The children lay and breathed the darkness. And then, at last, they heard their father throw down his boots and tramp upstairs in his stockinged feet. Still they listened. Then at last, if the wind allowed, they heard the water of the tap drumming into the kettle, which their mother was filling for morning, and they could go to sleep in peace.

So they were happy in the morning—happy, very happy playing, dancing at night round the lonely lamppost in the midst of the darkness. But they had one tight place of anxiety in their hearts, one darkness in their eyes, which showed all their lives.

Paul hated his father. As a boy he had a fervent private religion.

"Make him stop drinking," he prayed every night. "Lord, let my father die," he prayed very often. "Let him not be killed at pit," he prayed when, after tea, the father did not come home from work.

That was another time when the family suffered intensely. The children came from school and had their teas. On the hob the big black saucepan was simmering, the stew-jar was in the oven, ready for Morel's dinner. He was expected at five o'clock. But for months he would stop and drink every night on his way from work.

In the winter nights, when it was cold, and grew dark early, Mrs. Morel would put a brass candlestick on the table, light a tallow candle to save the gas. The children finished their bread-and-butter, or dripping, and were ready to go out to play. But if Morel had not come they faltered. The sense of his sitting in all his pit-dirt, drinking, after a long day's work, not coming home and eating and washing, but sitting, getting drunk, on an empty stomach, made Mrs. Morel unable to bear herself. From her the feeling was transmitted to the other children. She never suffered alone any more: the children suffered with her.

Paul went out to play with the rest. Down in the great trough of twilight, tiny clusters of lights burned where the pits were. A few last colliers straggled up the dim fieldpath. The lamplighter came along. No more colliers came. Darkness shut down over the valley; work was gone. It was night.

Then Paul ran anxiously into the kitchen. The one candle still burned on the table, the big fire glowed red. Mrs. Morel sat alone. On the hob, the saucepan steamed; the dinner plate lay waiting on the table. All the room was full of the sense of waiting, waiting for the man who was sitting in his pit-dirt, dinnerless, some mile away from home, across the darkness, drinking himself drunk. Paul stood in the doorway.

"Has my dad come?" he asked.

"You can see he hasn't," said Mrs. Morel, cross with the futility of the question.

Then the boy dawdled about near his mother. They shared the same anxiety. Presently Mrs. Morel went out and strained the potatoes.

"They're ruined and black," she said; "but what do I care?"

Not many words were spoken. Paul almost hated his mother for suffering because his father did not come home from work.

"What do you bother yourself for?" he said. "If he wants to stop and get drunk, why don't you let him?"

"Let him!" flashed Mrs. Morel. "You may well say 'let him.' "

She knew that the man who stops on the way home from work is on a quick way to ruining himself and his home. The children were yet young, and depended on the breadwinner. William gave her the sense of relief, providing her at last with someone to turn to if Morel failed. But the tense atmosphere of the room on these waiting evenings was the same.

The minutes ticked away. At six o'clock still the cloth lay on the table, still the dinner stood waiting, still the same sense of anxiety and expectation in the room. The boy could not stand it any longer. He could not go out and play. So he ran in to Mrs. Inger, next door but one, for her to talk to him. She had no children. Her husband was good to her, but was in a shop, and came home late. So, when she saw the lad at the door, she called:

"Come in, Paul."

The two sat talking for some time, when suddenly the boy rose, saying:

"Well, I'll be going and seeing if my mother wants an errand doing."

He pretended to be perfectly cheerful, and did not tell his friend what ailed him. Then he ran indoors.

Morel at these times came in churlish and hateful.

"This is a nice time to come home," said Mrs. Morel.

"Wha's it matter to yo' what time I come whoam?" he shouted.

And everybody in the house was still, because he was dangerous. He ate his food in the most brutal manner possible, and, when he had done, pushed all the pots in a heap away from him, to lay his arms on the table. Then he went to sleep.

Paul hated his father so. The collier's small, mean head, with its black hair slightly soiled with gray, lay on the bare arms, and the face, dirty and inflamed, with a fleshy nose and thin, paltry brows, was turned sideways, asleep with beer and weariness and nasty temper. If anyone entered suddenly, or a noise were made, the man looked up and shouted:

"I'll lay my fist about thy y'ead, I'm tellin' thee, if tha doesna stop that clatter! Dost hear?"

And the two last words, shouted in a bullying fashion, usually at Annie, made the family writhe with hate of the man.

He was shut out from all family affairs. No one told him anything. The children, alone with their mother, told her all about the day's happenings, everything. Nothing had really taken place in them until it was told to their mother. But as soon as the father came in, everything stopped. He was like the scotch in the smooth, happy machinery of the home. And he was always aware of this fall of silence on his entry, the shutting off of life, the unwelcome. But now it was gone too far to alter.

He would dearly have liked the children to talk to him, but they could not. Sometimes Mrs. Morel would say:

"You ought to tell your father."

Paul won a prize in a competition in a child's paper. Everybody was highly jubilant.

"Now you'd better tell your father when he comes in," said Mrs. Morel. "You know how he carries on and says he's never told anything."

"All right," said Paul. But he would almost rather have forfeited the prize than have to tell his father.

"I've won a prize in a competition, dad," he said.

Morel turned round to him.

"Have you, my boy? What sort of a competition?"

"Oh, nothing—about famous women."

"And how much is the prize, then, as you've got?"

"It's a book."

"Oh, indeed!"

"About birds."

"Hm—hm!"

And that was all. Conversation was impossible between the father and any other member of the family. He was an outsider. He had denied the God in him.

The only times when he entered again into the life of his own people was when he worked, and was happy at work. Sometimes, in the evening, he cobbled the boots or mended the kettle or his pit-bottle. Then he always wanted several attendants, and the children enjoyed it. They united with him in the work, in the actual doing of something, when he was his real self again.

He was a good workman, dexterous, and one who, when he was in a good humor, always sang. He had whole periods, months, almost years, of friction and nasty temper. Then sometimes he was jolly again. It was nice to see him run with a piece of red-hot iron into the scullery, crying:

"Out of my road—out of my road!"

Then he hammered the soft, red-glowing stuff on his iron goose, and made the shape he wanted. Or he sat absorbed for a moment, soldering. Then the children watched with joy as the metal sank suddenly molten, and was shoved about against the nose of the soldering iron, while the room was full of a scent of burnt resin and hot tin, and Morel was silent and intent for a minute. He always sang when he mended boots because of the jolly sound of hammering. And he was rather happy when he sat putting great patches on his moleskin pit trousers, which he would often do, considering them too dirty, and the stuff too hard, for his wife to mend.

But the best time for the young children was when he made fuses. Morel fetched a sheaf of long sound wheat-straws from the attic. These he cleaned with his hand, till each one gleamed like a stalk of gold, after which he cut the straws into lengths of about six inches, leaving, if he could, a notch at the bottom of each piece. He always had a beautifully sharp knife that could cut a straw clean without hurting it. Then he set in the middle of the table a heap of gunpowder, a little pile of black grains upon the white-scrubbed board. He made and trimmed the straws while Paul and Annie filled and plugged them. Paul loved to see the black grains trickle down a crack in his palm into the mouth of the straw, peppering jollily downwards till the straw was fill. Then he bunged up the mouth with a bit of soap—which he got on his thumbnail from a pat in a saucer—and the straw was finished.

"Look, dad!" he said.

"That's right, my beauty," replied Morel, who was peculiarly lavish of endearments to his second son. Paul popped the fuse into the powder tin, ready for the morning, when Morel would take it to the pit, and use it to fire a shot that would blast the coal down.

Meantime Arthur, still fond of his father, would lean on the arm of Morel's chair, and say:

"Tell us about down pit, daddy."

This Morel loved to do.

"Well, there's one little 'oss—we call 'im Taffy," he would begin. "An' he's a fawce un!"

Morel had a warm way of telling a story. He made one feel Taffy's cunning.

"He's a brown un," he would answer, "an' not very high. Well, he comes i' th' stall wi' a rattle, an' then yo' 'ear 'im sneeze.

" 'Ello, Taff,' you say, 'what art sneezin' for? Bin ta'ein' some snuff?'

"An' 'e sneezes again. Then he slives up an' shoves 'is 'ead on yer, that cadin'.

" 'What's want, Taff?' yo' say."

"And what does he?" Arthur always asked.

"He wants a bit o'bacca, my duckey."

This story of Taffy would go on interminably, and everybody loved it.

Or sometimes it was a new tale.

"An' what dost think, my darlin'? When I went to put my coat on at snap-time, what should go runnin' up my arm but a mouse.

" 'Hey up, theer!' I shouts.

"An' I wor just in time ter get 'im by th' tail."

"And did you kill it?"

"I did, for they're a nuisance. The place is fair snied wi' 'em."

"An' what do they live on?"

"The corn as the 'osses drops—an' they'll get in your pocket an' eat your snap, if you'll let 'em—no matter where yo' hing your coat—the slivin', nibblin' little nuisances, for they are."

These happy evenings could not take place unless Morel had some job to do. And then he always went to bed very early, often before the children. There was nothing remaining for him to stay up for, when he had finished tinkering, and had skimmed the headlines of the newspaper.

And the children felt secure when their father was in bed. They lay and talked softly awhile. Then they started as the lights went suddenly sprawling over the ceiling from the lamps that swung in the hands of the colliers tramping by outside, going to take the nine o'clock shift. They listened to the voices of the men, imagined them dipping down into the dark valley. Sometimes they went to the window and watched the three or four lamps growing tinier and tinier swaying down the fields in the darkness. Then it was a joy to rush back to bed and cuddle closely in the warmth.

Paul was rather a delicate boy, subject to bronchitis. The others were all quite strong; so this was another reason for his mother's difference in feeling for him. One day he came home at dinner-time feeling ill. But it was not a family to make any fuss.

"What's the matter with *you*?" his mother asked sharply.

"Nothing," he replied.

But he ate no dinner.

"If you eat no dinner, you're not going to school," she said.

"Why?" he asked.

"That's why."

So after dinner he lay down on the sofa, on the warm chintz cushions the children loved. Then he fell into a kind of doze. That afternoon Mrs. Morel was ironing. She listened to the small, restless noise the boy made in his throat as she worked. Again rose in her heart the old, almost weary feeling towards him. She had never expected him to live. And yet he had a great vitality in his young body. Perhaps it would have been a little relief to her if he had died. She always felt a mixture of anguish in her love for him.

He, in his semiconscious sleep, was vaguely aware of the clatter of the iron on the iron stand, of the faint thud, thud on the ironing board. Once roused, he opened his eyes to see his mother standing on the hearthrug with the hot iron near her cheek, listening, as it were, to the heat. Her still face, with the mouth closed tight from suffering and disillusion and self-denial, and her nose the smallest bit on one side, and her blue eyes so young, quick, and warm, made his heart contract with love. When she was quiet, so, she looked brave and rich with life, but as if she had been done out of her rights. It hurt the boy keenly, this feeling about her that she had never had her life's fulfillment: and his own incapability to make up to her hurt him with a sense of impotence, yet made him patiently dogged inside. It was his childish aim.

She spat on the iron, and a little ball of spit bounded, raced off the dark, glossy surface. Then, kneeling, she rubbed the iron on the sack lining of the hearthrug vigorously. She was warm in the ruddy firelight. Paul loved the way she crouched and put her head on one side. Her movements were light and quick. It was always a pleasure to watch her. Nothing she ever did, no movement she ever made, could have been found fault with by her children. The room was warm and full of the scent of hot linen. Later on the clergyman came and talked softly with her.

Paul was laid up with an attack of bronchitis. He did not mind much. What happened happened, and it was no good kicking against the pricks. He loved the evenings, after eight o'clock, when the light was put out, and he could watch the fire flames spring over the darkness of the walls and ceiling; could watch huge shadows waving and tossing, till the room seemed full of men who battled silently.

On retiring to bed, the father would come into the sickroom. He was always very gentle if anyone were ill. But he disturbed the atmosphere for the boy.

"Are ter asleep, my darlin'?" Morel asked softly.

"No; is my mother comin'?"

"She's just finishin' foldin' the clothes. Do you want any thing?" Morel rarely "thee'd" his son.

"I don't want nothing. But how long will she be?"

"Not long, my duckie."

The father waited undecidedly on the hearthrug for a moment or two. He felt his son did not want him. Then he went to the top of the stairs and said to his wife:

"This childt's axin' for thee; how long art goin' to be?"

"Until I've finished, good gracious! Tell him to go to sleep."

"She says you're to go to sleep," the father repeated gently to Paul.

"Well, I want *her* to come," insisted the boy.

"He says he can't go off till you come," Morel called, downstairs.

"Eh, dear! I shan't be long. And do stop shouting downstairs. There's the other children——"

Then Morel came again, and crouched before the bedroom fire. He loved a fire dearly.

"She says she won't be long," he said.

He loitered about indefinitely. The boy began to get feverish with irritation. His father's presence seemed to aggravate all his sick impatience. At last Morel, after having stood looking at his son awhile, said softly:

"Good-night, my darling."

"Good-night," Paul replied, turning round in relief to be alone.

Paul loved to sleep with his mother. Sleep is still most perfect, in spite of hygienists, when it is shared with a beloved. The warmth, the security and peace of soul, the utter comfort from the touch of the other, knits the sleep, so that it takes the body and soul completely in its healing. Paul lay against her and slept, and got better; whilst she, always a bad sleeper, fell later on into a profound sleep that seemed to give her faith.

In convalescence he would sit up in bed, see the fluffy horses feeding at the troughs in the field, scattering their hay on the trodden yellow snow; watch the miners troop home—small, black figures trailing slowly in gangs across the white field. Then the night came up in dark blue vapor from the snow.

In convalescence everything was wonderful. The snowflakes, suddenly arriving on the windowpane, clung there a moment like swallows, then were gone, and a drop of water was crawling down the glass. The snowflakes whirled round the corner of the house, like pigeons dashing by. Away across the valley the little black train crawled doubtfully over the great whiteness.

While they were so poor, the children were delighted if they could do anything to help economically. Annie and Paul and Arthur went out early in the morning, in summer, looking for mushrooms, hunting through the wet grass, from which the larks were rising, for the white-skinned, wonderful naked bodies crouched secretly in the green. And if they got half a pound they felt exceedingly happy: there was the joy of finding something, the joy of accepting something straight from the hand of Nature, and the joy of contributing to the family exchequer.

But the most important harvest, after gleaning for frumenty, was the blackberries. Mrs. Morel must buy fruit for puddings on the Saturdays; also she liked blackberries. So Paul and Arthur scoured the coppices and woods and old quarries, so long as a blackberry was to be found, every weekend going on their search. In that region of mining villages blackberries became a comparative rarity. But Paul hunted far and wide. He loved being out in the country, among the bushes. But he also could not bear to go home to his mother empty. That, he felt, would disappoint her, and he would have died rather.

"Good gracious!" she would exclaim as the lads came in, late, and tired to death, and hungry, "wherever have you been?"

"Well," replied Paul, "there wasn't any, so we went over Misk Hills. And look here, our mother!"

She peeped into the basket.

"Now, those are fine ones!" she exclaimed.

"And there's over two pounds—isn't there over two pounds?"

She tried the basket.

"Yes," she answered doubtfully.

Then Paul fished out a little spray. He always brought her one spray, the best he could find.

"Pretty!" she said in a curious tone, of a woman accepting a love token.

The boy walked all day, went miles and miles, rather than own himself beaten and come home to her empty-handed. She never realized this, whilst he was young. She was a woman who waited for her children to grow up. And William occupied her chiefly.

But when William went to Nottingham, and was not so much at home, the mother made a companion of Paul. The latter was unconsciously jealous of his brother, and William was jealous of him. At the same time, they were good friends.

Mrs. Morel's intimacy with her second son was more subtle and fine, perhaps not so passionate as with her eldest. It was the rule that Paul should fetch the money on Friday afternoons. The colliers of the five pits were paid on Fridays, but not individually. All the earnings of each stall were put down to the chief butty, as contractor, and he divided the wages again, either in the public house or in his own home. So that the children could fetch the money, school closed early on Friday afternoons. Each of the Morel children—William, then Annie, then Paul—had fetched the money on Friday afternoons, until they went themselves to work. Paul used to set off at half-past three, with a little calico bag in his pocket. Down all the paths, women, girls, children, and men were seen trooping to the offices.

These offices were quite handsome: a new, red-brick building, almost like a mansion, standing in its own well-kept grounds at the end of Greenhill Lane. The waiting room was the hall, a long, bare room paved with blue brick, and having a seat all round, against the wall. Here sat the colliers in their pit-dirt. They had come up early. The women and children usually loitered about on the red gravel paths. Paul always examined the grass border, and the big grass bank, because in it grew tiny pansies and tiny forget-me-nots. There was a sound of many voices. The women had on their Sunday hats. The girls chattered loudly. Little dogs ran here and there. The green shrubs were silent all around.

Then from inside came the cry "Spinney Park—Spinney Park." All the folk for Spinney Park trooped inside. When it was time for Bretty to be paid, Paul went in among the crowd. The pay room was quite small. A counter went across, dividing it into half. Behind the counter stood two men—Mr. Braithwaite and his clerk, Mr. Winterbottom. Mr. Braithwaite was large, somewhat of the stern patriarch in appearance, having a rather thin white beard. He was usually muffled in an enormous silk neckerchief, and right up to the hot summer a huge fire burned in the open grate. No window was open. Sometimes in winter the air scorched the throats of the people, coming in from the freshness. Mr. Winterbottom was rather small and fat, and very bald. He made remarks that were not witty, whilst his chief launched forth patriarchal admonitions against the colliers.

The room was crowded with miners in their pit-dirt, men who had been home and changed, and women, and one or two children, and usually a dog. Paul was quite small, so it was often his fate to be jammed behind the legs of the men, near the fire which scorched him. He knew the order of the names—they went according to stall number.

"Holliday," came the ringing voice of Mr. Braithwaite. Then Mrs. Holliday stepped silently forward, was paid, drew aside.

"Bower—John Bower."

A boy stepped to the counter. Mr. Braithwaite, large and irascible, glowered at him over his spectacles.

"John Bower!" he repeated.

"It's me," said the boy.

"Why, you used to 'ave a different nose than that," said glossy Mr. Winterbottom, peering over the counter. The people tittered, thinking of John Bower senior.

"How is it your father's not come?" said Mr. Braithwaite, in a large and magisterial voice.

"He's badly," piped the boy.

"You should tell him to keep off the drink," pronounced the great cashier.

"An' niver mind if he puts his foot through yer," said a mocking voice from behind.

All the men laughed. The large and important cashier looked down at his next sheet.

"Fred Pilkington!" he called, quite indifferent.

Mr. Braithwaite was an important shareholder in the firm.

Paul knew his turn was next but one, and his heart began to beat. He was pushed against the chimney piece. His calves were burning. But he did not hope to get through the wall of men.

"Walter Morel!" came the ringing voice.

"Here!" piped Paul, small and inadequate.

"Morel—Walter Morel!" the cashier repeated, his finger and thumb on the invoice, ready to pass on.

Paul was suffering convulsions of self-consciousness, and could not or would not shout. The backs of the men obliterated him. Then Mr. Winterbottom came to the rescue.

"He's here. Where is he? Morel's lad?"

The fat, red, bald little man peered round with keen eyes. He pointed at the fireplace. The colliers looked round, moved aside, and disclosed the boy.

"Here he is!" said Mr. Winterbottom.

Paul went to the counter.

"Seventeen pounds eleven and fivepence. Why don't you shout up when you're called?" said Mr. Braithwaite. He banged on to the invoice a five-pound bag of silver, then, in a delicate and pretty movement, picked up a little ten-pound column of gold, and plumped it beside the silver. The gold slid in a bright stream over the paper. The cashier finished counting off the money; the boy dragged the whole down the counter to Mr. Winterbottom, to whom the stoppages for rent and tools must be paid. Here he suffered again.

"Sixteen an' six," said Mr. Winterbottom.

The lad was too much upset to count. He pushed forward some loose silver and half a sovereign.

"How much do you think you've given me?" asked Mr. Winterbottom.

The boy looked at him, but said nothing. He had not the faintest notion.

"Haven't you got a tongue in your head?"

Paul bit his lip, and pushed forward some more silver.

"Don't they teach you to count at the Board-school?" he asked.

"Nowt but Algibbra an' French," said a collier.

"An' cheek an' impidence," said another.

Paul was keeping someone waiting. With trembling fingers he got his money into the bag and slid out. He suffered the tortures of the damned on these occasions.

His relief, when he got outside, and was walking along the Mansfield Road, was infinite. On the park wall the mosses were green. There were some gold and some white fowls pecking under the apple trees of an orchard. The colliers were walking home in a stream. The boy went near the wall, self-consciously. He knew many of the men, but could not recognize them in their dirt. And this was a new torture to him.

When he got down to the New Inn, at Bretty, his father was not yet come. Mrs. Wharmby, the landlady, knew him. His grandmother, Morel's mother, had been Mrs. Wharmby's friend.

"Your father's not come yet," said the landlady, in the peculiar half-scornful, half-patronizing voice of a woman who talks chiefly to grown men. "Sit you down."

Paul sat down on the edge of the bench in the bar. Some colliers were "reckoning"—sharing out their money—in a corner; others came in. They all glanced at the boy without speaking. At last Morel came; brisk, and with something of an air, even in his blackness.

"Hello!" he said rather tenderly to his son. "Have you bested me? Shall you have a drink of something?"

Paul and all the children were bred up fierce anti-alcoholists; and he would have suffered more in drinking a lemonade before all the men than in having a tooth drawn.

The landlady looked at him *de haut en bas*, rather pitying, and at the same time resenting his clear, fierce morality. Paul went home, glowering. He entered the house silently. Friday was baking day, and there was usually a hot bun. His mother put it before him.

Suddenly he turned on her in a fury, his eyes flashing:

"I'm *not* going to the office anymore," he said.

"Why, what's the matter?" his mother asked in surprise. His sudden rages rather amused her.

"I'm *not* going any more," he declared.

"Oh, very well, tell your father so."

He chewed his bun as if he hated it.

"I'm not—I'm not going to fetch the money."

"Then one of Carlin's children can go; they'd be glad enough of the sixpence," said Mrs. Morel.

This sixpence was Paul's only income. It mostly went in buying birthday presents; but it *was* an income, and he treasured it. But——

"They can have it, then!" he said. " I don't want it."

"Oh, very well," said his mother. "But you needn't bully *me* about it."

"They're hateful, and common, and hateful, they are, and I'm not going any more. Mr. Braithwaite drops his 'h's,' an' Mr. Winterbottom says 'You was.' "

"And is that why you won't go any more?" smiled Mrs. Morel.

The boy was silent for some time. His face was pale, his eyes dark and furious. His mother moved about at her work, taking no notice of him.

"They always stan' in front of me, so's I can't get out," he said.

"Well, my lad, you've only to *ask* them," she replied.

"An' then Alfred Winterbottom says, 'What do they teach you at the Board-school?' "

"They never taught *him* much," said Mrs. Morel, "that is a fact—neither manners nor wit—and his cunning he was born with."

So, in her own way, she soothed him. His ridiculous hypersensitiveness made her heart ache. And sometimes the fury in his eyes roused her, made her sleeping soul lift up its head a moment, surprised.

"What was the cheque?" she asked.

"Seventeen pounds eleven and fivepence, and sixteen and six stoppages," replied the boy. "It's a good week; and only five shillings stoppages for my father."

So she was able to calculate how much her husband had earned, and could call him to account if he gave her short money. Morel always kept to himself the secret of the week's amount.

Friday was the baking night and market night. It was the rule that Paul should stay at home and bake. He loved to stop in and draw or read; he was very fond of drawing. Annie always "gallivanted" on Friday nights; Arthur was enjoying himself as usual. So the boy remained alone.

Mrs. Morel loved her marketing. In the tiny marketplace on the top of the hill, where four roads, from Nottingham and Derby, Ilkeston and Mansfield, meet, many stalls were erected. Brakes ran in from surrounding villages. The market-place was full of women, the streets packed with men. It was amazing to see so many men everywhere in the streets. Mrs. Morel usually quarreled with her lace woman, sympathized with her fruit man—who was a gabey, but his wife was a bad un—laughed with the fish man—who was a scamp but so droll—put the linoleum man in his place, was cold with the odd-wares man, and only went to the crockery man when she was driven—or drawn by the cornflowers on a little dish; then she was coldly polite.

"I wondered how much that little dish was," she said.

"Sevenpence to you."

"Thank you."

She put the dish down and walked away; but she could not leave the marketplace without it. Again she went by where the pots lay coldly on the floor, and she glanced at the dish furtively, pretending not to.

She was a little woman, in a bonnet and a black costume. Her bonnet was in its third year; it was a great grievance to Annie.

"Mother!" the girl implored, "don't wear that nubbly little bonnet."

"Then what else shall I wear?" replied the mother tartly. "And I'm sure it's right enough."

It had started with a tip; then had had flowers; now was reduced to black lace and a bit of jet.

"It looks rather come down," said Paul. "Couldn't you give it a pick-me-up?"

"I'll jowl your head for impudence," said Mrs. Morel, and she tied the strings of the black bonnet valiantly under her chin.

She glanced at the dish again. Both she and her enemy, the pot man, had an uncomfortable feeling, as if there were something between them. Suddenly he shouted:

"Do you want it for fivepence?"

She started. Her heart hardened; but then she stooped and took up the dish.

"I'll have it," she said.

"Yer'll do me the favor, like?" he said. "Yer'd better spit in it, like yer do when y'ave something give yer."

Mrs. Morel paid him the fivepence in a cold manner.

"I don't see you give it me," she said. "You wouldn't let me have it for fivepence if you didn't want to."

"In this flamin', scrattlin' place you may count yerself lucky if you can give your things away," he growled.

But she had forgiven the pot man. They were friends. She dare now finger his pots. So she was happy.

Paul was waiting for her. He loved her homecoming. She was always her best so—triumphant, tired, laden with parcels, feeling rich in spirit. He heard her quick, light step in the entry and looked up from his drawing.

"Oh!" she sighed, smiling at him from the doorway.

"My word, you *are* loaded!" he exclaimed, putting down his brush.

"I am!" she gasped. "That brazen Annie said she'd meet me. *Such* a weight!"

She dropped her string bag and her packages on the table.

"Is the bread done?" she asked, going to the oven.

"The last one is soaking," he replied. "You needn't look. I've not forgotten it."

"Oh, that pot man!" she said, closing the oven door. "You know what a wretch I've said he was? Well, I don't think he's quite so bad."

"Don't you?"

The boy was attentive to her. She took off her little black bonnet.

"No. I think he can't make any money—well, it's everybody's cry alike nowadays—and it makes him disagreeable."

"It would *me*," said Paul.

"Well, one can't wonder at it. And he let me have—how much do you think he let me have *this* for?"

She took the dish out of its rag of newspaper, and stood looking on it with joy.

"Show me!" said Paul.

The two stood together gloating over the dish.

"I *love* cornflowers on things," said Paul.

"Yes, and I thought of the teapot you bought me——"

"One and three," said Paul.

"Fivepence!"

"It's not enough, mother."

"No. Do you know, I fairly sneaked off with it. But I'd been extravagant, I couldn't afford any more. And he needn't have let me have it if he hadn't wanted to."

"No, he needn't, need he?" said Paul, and the two comforted each other from the fear of having robbed the pot man.

"We e'n have stewed fruit in it," said Paul.

"Or custard, or a jelly," said his mother.

"Or radishes and lettuce," said he.

"Don't forget that bread," she said, her voice bright with glee.

Paul looked in the oven; tapped the loaf on the base.

"It's done," he said, giving it to her.

She tapped it also.

"Yes," she replied, going to unpack her bag. "Oh, and I'm a wicked, extravagant woman. I know I s'll come to want."

He hopped to her side eagerly, to see her latest extravagance. She unfolded another lump of newspaper and disclosed some roots of pansies and of crimson daisies.

"Four penn'orth!" she moaned.

"How *cheap*!" he cried.

"Yes, but I couldn't afford it *this* week of all weeks."

"But lovely!" he cried.

"Aren't they!" she exclaimed, giving way to pure joy. "Paul, look at this yellow one, isn't it—and a face just like an old man!"

"Just!" cried Paul, stooping to sniff. "And smells that nice! But he's a bit splashed."

He ran in the scullery, came back with the flannel, and carefully washed the pansy.

"*Now* look at him now he's wet!" he said.

"Yes!" she exclaimed, brimful of satisfaction.

The children of Scargill Street felt quite select. At the end where the Morels lived there were not many young things. So the few were more united. Boys and girls played together, the girls joining in the fights and the rough games, the boys taking part in the dancing games and rings and make-belief of the girls.

Annie and Paul and Arthur loved the winter evenings, when it was not wet. They stayed indoors till the colliers were all gone home, till it was thick dark, and the street would be deserted. Then they tied their scarves round their necks, for they scorned overcoats, as all the colliers' children did, and went out. The entry was very dark, and at the end the whole great night opened out, in a hollow, with a little tangle of lights below where Minton pit lay, and another far away opposite for Selby. The farthest tiny lights seemed to stretch out the darkness forever. The children looked anxiously down the road at the one lamppost, which stood at the end of the field path. If the little luminous space were deserted, the two boys felt genuine desolation. They stood with their hands in their pockets under the lamp, turning their backs on the night, quite miserable, watching the dark houses. Suddenly a pinafore under a short coat was seen, and a long-legged girl came flying up.

"Where's Billy Pillins an' your Annie an' Eddie Dakin?"

"I don't know."

But it did not matter so much—there were three now. They set up a game round the lamppost, till the others rushed up, yelling. Then the play went fast and furious.

There was only this one lamppost. Behind was the great scoop of darkness, as if all the night were there. In front, another wide, dark way opened over the hill brow. Occasionally somebody came out of this way and went into the field down the path. In a dozen yards the night had swallowed them. The children played on.

They were brought exceedingly close together, owing to their isolation. If a quarrel took place, the whole play was spoilt. Arthur was very touchy, and Billy Pillins—really Philips—was worse. Then Paul had to side with Arthur, and on Paul's side went Alice, while Billy Pillins always had Emmie Limb and Eddie Dakin to back him up. Then the six would fight, hate with a fury of hatred, and flee home in terror. Paul never forgot, after one of these fierce internecine fights, seeing a big red moon lift itself up, slowly, between the waste road over the hilltop, steadily, like a great bird. And he thought of the Bible, that the moon should be turned to blood. And the next day he made haste to be friends with Billy Pillins. And then the wild, intense games went on again under the lamppost, surrounded by so much darkness. Mrs. Morel, going into her parlor, would hear the children singing away:

My shoes are made of Spanish leather,
My socks are made of silk;
I wear a ring on every finger,
I wash myself in milk.

They sounded so perfectly absorbed in the game as their voices came out of the night, that they had the feel of wild creatures singing. It stirred the mother; and she understood when they came in at eight o'clock, ruddy, with brilliant eyes, and quick, passionate speech.

They all loved the Scargill Street house for its openness, for the great scallop of the world it had in view. On summer evenings the women would stand against the field fence, gossiping, facing the west, watching the sunsets flare quickly out, till the Derbyshire hills ridged across the crimson far away, like the black crest of a newt.

In this summer season the pits never turned full time particularly the soft coal. Mrs. Dakin, who lived next door to Mrs. Morel, going to the field fence to shake her hearth-rug, would spy men coming slowly up the hill. She saw at once they were colliers. Then she waited, a tall, thin shrew-faced woman, standing on the hill brow, almost like a menace to the poor colliers who were toiling up. It was only eleven o'clock. From the far-off wooded hills the haze that hangs like fine black crape at the back of a summer morning had not yet dissipated. The first man came to the stile. "Chock-chock!" went the gate under his thrust.

"What, han yer knocked off?" cried Mrs. Dakin.

"We han, missis."

"It's a pity as they letn yer goo," she said sarcastically.

"It is that," replied the man.

"Nay, you know you're flig to come up again," she said.

And the man went on. Mrs. Dakin, going up her yard, spied Mrs. Morel taking the ashes to the ash pit.

"I reckon Minton's knocked off, missis," she cried.

"Isn't it sickenin'!" exclaimed Mrs. Morel in wrath.

"Ha! But I'n just seed Jont Hutchby."

"They might as well have saved their shoe leather," said Mrs. Morel. And both women went indoors, disgusted.

The colliers, their faces scarcely blackened, were trooping home again. Morel hated to go back. He loved the sunny morning. But he had gone to pit to work, and to be sent home again spoilt his temper.

"Good gracious, at this time!" exclaimed his wife, as he entered.

"Can I help it, woman?" he shouted.

"And I've not done half enough dinner."

"Then I'll eat my bit o' snap as I took with me," he bawled pathetically. He felt ignominious and sore.

And the children, coming home from school, would wonder to see their father eating with his dinner the two thick slices of rather dry and dirty bread-and-butter that had been to pit and back.

"What's my dad eating his snap for now?" asked Arthur.

"I should ha'e it holled at me if I didna," snorted Morel.

"What a story!" exclaimed his wife.

"An' is it goin' to be wasted?" said Morel. "I'm not such a extravagant mortal as you lot, with your waste. If I drop a bit of bread at pit, in all the dust an' dirt, I pick it up an' eat it."

"The mice would eat it," said Paul. "It wouldn't be, wasted."

"Good bread-an'-butter's not for mice, either," said Morel. "Dirty or not dirty, I'd eat it rather than it should be wasted."

"You might leave it for the mice and pay for it out of your next pint," said Mrs. Morel.

"Oh, might I?" he exclaimed.

They were very poor that autumn. William had just gone away to London, and his mother missed his money. He sent ten shillings once or twice, but he had many things to pay for at first. His letters came regularly once a week. He wrote a good deal to his mother, telling her all his life, how he made friends, and was exchanging lessons with a Frenchman, how he enjoyed London. His mother felt again he was remaining to her just as when he was at home. She wrote to him every week her direct, rather witty letters. All day long, as she cleaned the house, she thought of him. He was in London: he would do well. Almost, he was like her knight who wore *her* favor in the battle.

He was coming at Christmas for five days. There had never been such preparations. Paul and Arthur scoured the land for holly and evergreens. Annie made the pretty paper hoops in the old-fashioned way. And there was unheard-of extravagance in the larder. Mrs. Morel made a big and magnificent cake. Then, feeling queenly, she showed Paul how to blanch almonds. He skinned the long nuts reverently, counting them all, to see not one was lost. It was said that eggs whisked better in a cold place. So the boy stood in the scullery, where the temperature was nearly at freezing point, and whisked and whisked, and flew in excitement to his mother as the white of egg grew stiffer and more snowy.

"Just look, mother! Isn't it lovely?"

And he balanced a bit on his nose, then blew it in the air.

"Now, don't waste it," said the mother.

Everybody was mad with excitement. William was coming on Christmas Eve. Mrs. Morel surveyed her pantry. There was a big plum cake, and a rice cake, jam tarts, lemon tarts, and mince pies—two enormous dishes. She was finishing cooking—Spanish tarts and cheese cakes. Everywhere was decorated. The kissing-bunch of berried holly hung with bright and glittering things, spun slowly over Mrs. Morel's head as she trimmed her little tarts in the kitchen. A great fire roared. There was a scent of cooked pastry. He was due at seven o'clock, but he would be late. The three children had gone to meet him. She was alone. But at a quarter to seven Morel came in again. Neither wife nor husband spoke. He sat in his armchair, quite awkward with excitement, and she quietly went on with her baking. Only by the careful way in which she did things could it be told how much moved she was. The clock ticked on.

"What time dost say he's coming?" Morel asked for the fifth time.

"The train gets in at half-past six," she replied emphatically.

"Then he'll be here at ten past seven."

"Eh, bless you, it'll be hours late on the Midland," she said indifferently. But she hoped, by expecting him late, to bring him early. Morel went down the entry to look for him. Then he came back.

"Goodness, man!" she said. "You're like an ill-sitting hen."

"Hadna you better be gettin' him summat t' eat ready?" asked the father.

"There's plenty of time," she answered.

"There's not so much as *I* can see on," he answered, turning crossly in his chair. She began to clear her table. The kettle was singing. They waited and waited.

Meantime the three children were on the platform at Sethley Bridge, on the Midland main line, two miles from home. They waited one hour. A train came—he was not there. Down the line the red and green lights shone. It was very dark and very cold.

"Ask him if the London train's come," said Paul to Annie, when they saw a man in a tip cap.

"I'm not," said Annie. "You be quiet—he might send us off."

But Paul was dying for the man to know they were expecting someone by the London train: it sounded so grand. Yet he was much too much scared of broaching any man, let alone one in a peaked cap, to dare to ask. The three children could scarcely go into the waiting room for fear of being sent away, and for fear something should happen whilst they were off the platform. Still they waited in the dark and cold.

"It's an hour an' a half late," said Arthur pathetically.

"Well," said Annie, "it's Christmas Eve."

They all grew silent. He wasn't coming. They looked down the darkness of the railway. There was London! It seemed the uttermost of distance. They thought anything might happen if one came from London. They were all too troubled to talk. Cold, and unhappy, and silent, they huddled together on the platform.

At last, after more than two hours, they saw the lights of an engine peering round, away down the darkness. A porter ran out. The children drew back with beating hearts. A great train, bound for Manchester, drew up. Two doors opened, and from one of them, William. They flew to him. He handed parcels to them cheerily, and immediately began to explain that this great train had stopped for *his* sake at such a small station as Sethley Bridge: it was not booked to stop.

Meanwhile the parents were getting anxious. The table was set, the chop was cooked, everything was ready. Mrs. Morel put on her black apron. She was wearing her best dress. Then she sat, pretending to read. The minutes were a torture to her.

"H'm!" said Morel. "It's an hour an' a ha'ef."

"And those children waiting!" she said.

"Th' train canna ha' come in yit," he said.

"I tell you, on Christmas Eve they're *hours* wrong."

They were both a bit cross with each other, so gnawed with anxiety. The ash tree moaned outside in a cold, raw wind. And all that space of night from London home! Mrs. Morel suffered. The slight click of the works inside the clock irritated her. It was getting so late; it was getting unbearable.

At last there was a sound of voices, and a footstep in the entry.

"Ha's here!" cried Morel, jumping up.

Then he stood back. The mother ran a few steps towards the door and waited. There was a rush and a patter of feet, the door burst open. William was there. He dropped his Gladstone bag and took his mother in his arms.

"Mater!" he said.

"My boy!" she cried.

And for two seconds, no longer, she clasped him and kissed him. Then she withdrew and said, trying to be quite normal:

"But how late you are!"

"Aren't I!" he cried turning to his father. "Well, dad!"

The two men shook hands.

"Well, my lad!"

Morel's eyes were wet.

"We thought tha'd niver be commin'," he said.

"Oh, I'd come!" exclaimed William.

Then the son turned round to his mother.

"But you look well," she said proudly, laughing.

"Well!" he exclaimed. "I should think so—coming home!"

He was a fine fellow, big, straight, and fearless-looking. He looked round at the evergreens and the kissing bunch, and the little tarts that lay in their tins on the hearth.

"By jove! mother, it's not different!" he said, as if in relief.

Everybody was still for a second. Then he suddenly sprang forward, picked a tart from the hearth, and pushed it whole into his mouth.

"Well, did iver you see such a parish oven!" his father exclaimed.

He had brought them endless presents. Every penny he had he had spent on them. There was a sense of luxury overflowing in the house. For his mother there was an umbrella with gold on the pale handle. She kept it to her dying day, and would have lost anything rather than that. Everybody had something gorgeous, and besides, there were pounds of unknown sweets: Turkish delight, crystallized pineapple, and such-like things which, the children thought, only the splendor of London could provide. And Paul boasted of these sweets among his friends.

"Real pineapple, cut off in slices, and then turned into crystal—fair grand!"

Everybody was mad with happiness in the family. Home was home, and they loved it with a passion of love, whatever the suffering had been. There were parties, there were rejoicings. People came in to see William, to see what difference London had made to him. And they all found him "such a gentleman, and *such* a fine fellow, my word!"

When he went away again the children retired to various places to weep alone. Morel went to bed in misery, and Mrs. Morel felt as if she were numbed by some drug, as if her feelings were paralyzed. She loved him passionately.

He was in the office of a lawyer connected with a large shipping firm, and at the midsummer his chief offered him a trip in the Mediterranean on one of the boats, for quite a small cost. Mrs. Morel wrote: "Go, go, my boy. You may never have a chance again, and I should love to think of you cruising there in the Mediterranean almost better than to have you at home." But William came home for his fortnight's holiday. Not even the Mediterranean, which pulled at all his young man's desire to travel, and at his poor man's wonder at the glamorous south, could take him away when he might come home. That compensated his mother for much.

❖ 5 ❖

PAUL LAUNCHES INTO LIFE

Morel was rather a heedless man, careless of danger. So he had endless accidents. Now, when Mrs. Morel heard the rattle of an empty coal cart cease at her entry-end, she ran into the parlor to look, expecting almost to see her husband seated in the wagon, his face gray under his dirt, his body limp and sick with some hurt or other. If it were he, she would run out to help.

About a year after William went to London, and just after Paul had left school, before he got work, Mrs. Morel was upstairs and her son was painting in the kitchen—he was very clever with his brush—when there came a knock at the door. Crossly he put down his brush to go. At the same moment his mother opened a window upstairs and looked down.

A pit lad in his dirt stood on the threshold.

"Is this Walter Morel's?" he asked.

"Yes," said Mrs. Morel. "What is it?"

But she had guessed already.

"Your mester's got hurt," he said.

"Eh, dear me!" she exclaimed. "It's a wonder if he hadn't, lad. And what's he done this time?"

"I don't know for sure, but it's 'is leg somewhere. They ta'ein' 'im ter th' 'ospital."

"Good gracious me!" she exclaimed. "Eh, dear, what a one he is! There's not five minutes of peace, I'll be hanged if there is! His thumb nearly better, and now—Did you see him?"

"I seed him at th' bottom. An' I seed 'em bring 'im up in a tub, an' 'e wor in a dead faint. But he shouted like anythink when Doctor Fraser examined him i' th' lamp cabin—an' cossed an' swore, an' said as 'e wor goin' to be ta'en whoam—'e worn't goin' ter th' 'ospital."

The boy faltered to an end.

"He *would* want to come home, so that I can have all the bother. Thank you, my lad. Eh, dear, if I'm not sick—sick and surfeited, I am!"

She came downstairs. Paul had mechanically resumed his painting.

"And it must be pretty bad if they've taken him to the hospital," she went on.

"But what a *careless* creature he is! *Other* men don't have all these accidents. Yes, he *would* want to put all the burden on me. Eh, dear, just as we *were* getting easy a bit at last. Put those things away, there's no time to be painting now. What time is there a train? I know I s'll have to go trailing to Keston. I s'll have to leave that bedroom."

"I can finish it," said Paul.

"You needn't. I shall catch the seven o'clock back, I should think. Oh, my blessed heart, the fuss and commotion he'll make! And those granite setts at Tinder Hill—he might well call them kidney pebbles—they'll jolt him almost to bits. I wonder why they can't mend them, the state they're in, an' all the men as go across in that ambulance. You'd think they'd have a hospital here. The men bought the ground, and, my sirs, there'd be accidents enough to keep it going. But no, they must trail them ten miles in a slow ambulance to Nottingham. It's a crying shame! Oh, and the fuss he'll make! I know he will! I wonder who's with him. Barker, I s'd think. Poor beggar, he'll wish himself anywhere rather. But he'll look after him, I know. Now there's no telling how long he'll be stuck in that hospital—and won't he hate it! But if it's only his leg it's not so bad."

All the time she was getting ready. Hurriedly taking off her bodice, she crouched at the boiler while the water ran slowly into her lading-can.

"I wish this boiler was at the bottom of the sea!" she exclaimed, wriggling the handle impatiently. She had very handsome, strong arms, rather surprising on a smallish woman.

Paul cleared away, put on the kettle, and set the table.

"There isn't a train till four-twenty," he said. "You've time enough."

"Oh no, I haven't!" she cried, blinking at him over the towel as she wiped her face.

"Yes, you have. You must drink a cup of tea at any rate. Should I come with you to Keston?"

"Come with me? What for, I should like to know? Now, what have I to take him? Eh, dear! His clean shirt—and it's a blessing *it is* clean. But it had better be aired. And stockings—he won't want them—and a towel, I suppose; and handkerchiefs. Now what else?"

"A comb, a knife and fork and spoon," said Paul. His father had been in the hospital before.

"Goodness knows what sort of state his feet were in," continued Mrs. Morel, as she combed her long brown hair, that was fine as silk, and was touched now with gray. "He's very particular to wash himself to the waist, but below he thinks doesn't matter. But there, I suppose they see plenty like it."

Paul had laid the table. He cut his mother one or two pieces of very thin bread-and-butter.

"Here you are," he said, putting her cup of tea in her place.

"I can't be bothered!" she exclaimed crossly.

"Well, you've got to, so there, now it's put out ready," he insisted.

So she sat down and sipped her tea, and ate a little, in silence. She was thinking.

In a few minutes she was gone, to walk the two and a half miles to Keston Station. All the things she was taking him she had in her bulging string bag. Paul watched her go up the road between the hedges—a little, quick-stepping figure, and his heart ached for her, that she was thrust forward again into pain and trouble. And she, tripping so quickly in her anxiety, felt at the back of her her son's heart waiting on her, felt him bearing what part of the burden he could, even supporting her. And when she was at the hospital, she thought: "It *will* upset that lad when I tell him how bad it is. I'd better be careful." And when she was trudging home again, she felt she was coming to share her burden.

"Is it bad?" asked Paul, as soon as she entered the house.

"It's bad enough," she replied.

"What?"

She sighed and sat down, undoing her bonnet strings. Her son watched her face as it was lifted, and her small, work-hardened hands fingering at the bow under her chin.

"Well," she answered, "it's not really dangerous, but the nurse says it's a dreadful smash. You see, a great piece of rock fell on his leg—here—and it's a compound fracture. There are pieces of bone sticking through——"

"Ugh—how horrid!" exclaimed the children.

"And," she continued, "of course he says he's going to die—it wouldn't be him if he didn't. 'I'm done for, my lass!' he said, looking at me. 'Don't be so silly,' I said to him. 'You're not going to die of a broken leg, however badly it's smashed.' 'I s'll niver come out of 'ere but in a wooden box,' he groaned. 'Well,' I said, 'if you want them to carry you into the garden in a wooden box, when you're better, I've no doubt they will.' 'If we think it's good for him,' said the Sister. She's an awfully nice Sister, but rather strict."

Mrs. Morel took off her bonnet. The children waited in silence.

"Of course, he *is* bad," she continued, "and he will be. It's a great shock, and he's lost a lot of blood; and, of course, it *is* a very dangerous smash. It's not at all sure that it will mend so easily. And then there's the fever and the mortification—if it took bad ways he'd quickly be gone. But there, he's a clean-blooded man, with wonderful healing flesh, and so I see no reason why it *should* take bad ways. Of course there's a wound——"

She was pale now with emotion and anxiety. The three children realized that it was very bad for their father, and the house was silent, anxious.

"But he always gets better," said Paul after a while.

"That's what I tell him," said the mother.

Everybody moved about in silence.

"And he really looked nearly done for," she said. "But the Sister says that is the pain."

Annie took away her mother's coat and bonnet.

"And he looked at me when I came away! I said: 'I s'll have to go now, Walter, because of the train—and the children.' And he looked at me. It seems hard."

Paul took up his brush again and went on painting. Arthur went outside for some coal. Annie sat looking dismal. And Mrs. Morel, in her little rocking chair that her husband had made for her when the first baby was coming, remained motionless, brooding. She was grieved, and bitterly sorry for the man who was hurt so much. But still, in her heart of hearts, where the love should have burned, there was a blank. Now, when all her woman's pity was roused to its full extent, when she would have slaved herself to death to nurse him and to save him, when she would have taken the pain herself, if she could, somewhere far away inside her, she felt indifferent to him and to his suffering. It hurt her most of all, this failure to love him, even when he roused her strong emotions. She brooded awhile.

"And there," she said suddenly, "when I'd got halfway to Keston, I found I'd come out in my working boots—and *look* at them." They were an old pair of Paul's, brown and rubbed through at the toes. "I didn't know what to do with myself, for shame," she added.

In the morning, when Annie and Arthur were at school, Mrs. Morel talked again to her son, who was helping her with her housework.

"I found Barker at the hospital. He did look bad, poor little fellow! 'Well,' I said to him, 'what sort of a journey did you have with him?' 'Dunna ax me, missis!' he said. 'Ay,' I said, 'I know what he'd be.' 'But it *wor* bad for him, Mrs. Morel, it *wor* that!' he said. 'I know,' I said. 'At ivry jolt I thought my 'eart would ha' flown clean out o' my mouth,' he said. 'An' the scream 'e give sometimes! Missis, not for a fortune would I go through wi' it again.' 'I can quite understand it,' I said. 'It's a nasty job, though,' he said, 'an' one as'll be a long while afore it's right again.' 'I'm afraid it will,' I said. I like Mr. Barker—I *do* like him. There's something so manly about him."

Paul resumed his task silently.

"And of course," Mrs. Morel continued, "for a man like your father, the hospital *is* hard. He *can't* understand rules and regulations. And he won't let anybody else touch him, not if he can help it. When he smashed the muscles of his thigh, and it had to be dressed four times a day, *would* he let anybody but me or his mother do it? He wouldn't. So, of course, he'll suffer in there with the nurses. And I didn't like leaving him. I'm sure, when I kissed him an' came away, it seemed a shame."

So she talked to her son, almost as if she were thinking aloud to him, and he took it in as best he could, by sharing her trouble to lighten it. And in the end she shared almost everything with him without knowing.

Morel had a very bad time. For a week he was in a critical condition. Then he began to mend. And then, knowing he was going to get better, the whole family sighed with relief, and proceeded to live happily.

They were not badly off whilst Morel was in the hospital. There were fourteen shillings a week from the pit, ten shillings from the sick club, and five shillings from the Disability Fund; and then every week the butties had something for Mrs. Morel—five or seven shillings—so that she was quite well to do. And whilst Morel was progressing favorably in the hospital, the family was extraordinarily happy and peaceful. On Saturdays and Wednesdays Mrs. Morel went to Nottingham to see her husband. Then she always brought back some little thing: a small tube of paints for Paul, or some thick paper; a couple of postcards for Annie, that the whole family rejoiced over for days before the girl was allowed to send them away; or a fret saw for Arthur, or a bit of pretty wood. She described her adventures into the big shops with joy. Soon the folk in the picture shop knew her, and knew about Paul. The girl in the bookshop took a keen interest in her. Mrs. Morel was full of information when she got home from Nottingham. The three sat round till bedtime, listening, putting in, arguing. Then Paul often raked the fire.

"I'm the man in the house now," he used to say to his mother with joy. They learned how perfectly peaceful the home could be. And they almost regretted—though none of them would have owned to such callousness—that their father was soon coming back.

Paul was now fourteen, and was looking for work. He was a rather small and rather finely made boy, with dark brown hair and light blue eyes. His face had already lost its youthful chubbiness, and was becoming somewhat like William's—rough-featured, almost rugged—and it was extraordinarily mobile. Usually he looked as if he saw things, was full of life, and warm; then his smile, like his mother's, came suddenly and was very lovable; and then, when there was any clog in his soul's quick running, his face went stupid and ugly. He was the sort of boy that becomes a clown and a lout as soon as he is not understood, or feels himself held cheap; and, again, is adorable at the first touch of warmth.

He suffered very much from the first contact with anything. When he was seven, the starting school had been a nightmare and a torture to him. But afterwards he liked it. And now that he felt he had to go out into life, he went through agonies of shrinking self-consciousness. He was quite a clever painter for a boy of his years, and he knew some French and German and mathematics that Mr.

Heaton had taught him. But nothing he had was of any commercial value. He was not strong enough for heavy manual work, his mother said. He did not care for making things with his hands, preferred racing about, or making excursions into the country, or reading, or painting.

"What do you want to be?" his mother asked.

"Anything."

"That is no answer," said Mrs. Morel.

But it was quite truthfully the only answer he could give. His ambition, as far as this world's gear went, was quietly to earn his thirty or thirty-five shillings a week somewhere near home, and then, when his father died, have a cottage with his mother, paint and go out as he liked, and live happy ever after. That was his program as far as doing things went. But he was proud within himself, measuring people against himself, and placing them, inexorably. And he thought that *perhaps* he might also make a painter, the real thing. But that he left alone.

"Then," said his mother, "you must look in the paper for the advertisements."

He looked at her. It seemed to him a bitter humiliation and an anguish to go through. But he said nothing. When he got up in the morning, his whole being was knotted up over this one thought:

"I've got to go and look for advertisements for a job."

It stood in front of the morning, that thought, killing all joy and even life, for him. His heart felt like a tight knot.

And then, at ten o'clock, he set off. He was supposed to be a queer, quiet child. Going up the sunny street of the little town, he felt as if all the folk he met said to themselves: "He's going to the Co-op reading room to look in the papers for a place. He can't get a job. I suppose he's living on his mother." Then he crept up the stone stairs behind the drapery shop at the Co-op, and peeped in the reading room. Usually one or two men were there, either old, useless fellows, or colliers "on the club." So he entered, full of shrinking and suffering when they looked up, seated himself at the table, and pretended to scan the news. He knew they would think, "What does a lad of thirteen want in a reading room with a newspaper?" and he suffered.

Then he looked wistfully out of the window. Already he was a prisoner of industrialism. Large sunflowers stared over the old red wall of the garden opposite, looking in their jolly way down on the women who were hurrying with something for dinner. The valley was full of corn, brightening in the sun. Two colliers, among the fields, waved their small white plumes of steam. Far off on the hills were the woods of Annesley, dark and fascinating. Already his heart went down. He was being taken into bondage. His freedom in the beloved home valley was going now.

The brewers' wagons came rolling up from Keston with enormous barrels, four a side, like beans in a burst bean pod. The wagoner, throned aloft, rolling massively in his seat, was not so much below Paul's eye. The man's hair, on his small, bullet head, was bleached almost white by the sun, and on his thick red arms, rocking idly on his sack apron, the white hairs glistened. His red face shone and was almost asleep with sunshine. The horses, handsome and brown, went on by themselves, looking by far the masters of the show.

Paul wished he were stupid. "I wish," he thought to himself, "I was fat like him, and like a dog in the sun. I wish I was a pig and a brewer's wagoner."

Then, the room being at last empty, he would hastily copy an advertisement on a scrap of paper, then another, and slip out in immense relief. His mother would scan over his copies.

"Yes," she said, "you may try."

William had written out a letter of application, couched in admirable business language, which Paul copied, with variations. The boy's handwriting was execrable, so that William, who did all things well, got into a fever of impatience.

The elder brother was becoming quite swanky. In London he found that he could associate with men far above his Bestwood friends in station. Some of the clerks in the office had studied for the law, and were more or less going through a kind of apprenticeship. William always made friends among men wherever he went, he was so jolly. Therefore he was soon visiting and staying in houses of men who, in Bestwood, would have looked down on the unapproachable bank manager, and would merely have called indifferently on the Rector. So he began to fancy himself as a great gun. He was, indeed, rather surprised at the ease with which he became a gentleman.

His mother was glad, he seemed so pleased. And his lodging in Walthamstow was so dreary. But now there seemed to come a kind of fever into the young man's letters. He was unsettled by all the change, he did not stand firm on his own feet, but seemed to spin rather giddily on the quick current of the new life. His mother was anxious for him. She could feel him losing himself. He had danced and gone to the theater, boated on the river, been out with friends; and she knew he sat up afterwards in his cold bedroom grinding away at Latin, because he intended to get on in his office, and in the law as much as he could. He never sent his mother any money now. It was all taken, the little he had, for his own life. And she did not want any, except sometimes, when she was in a tight corner, and when ten shillings would have saved her much worry. She still dreamed of William, and of what he would do, with herself behind him. Never for a minute would she admit to herself how heavy and anxious her heart was because of him.

Also he talked a good deal now of a girl he had met at a dance, a handsome brunette, quite young, and a lady, after whom the men were running thick and fast.

"I wonder if you would run, my boy," his mother wrote to him, "unless you saw all the other men chasing her too. You feel safe enough and vain enough in a crowd. But take care, and see how you feel when you find yourself alone, and in triumph."

William resented these things, and continued the chase. He had taken the girl on the river. "If you saw her, mother, you would know how I feel. Tall and elegant, with the clearest of clear, transparent olive complexions, hair as black as jet, and such gray eyes—bright, mocking, like lights on water at night. It is all very well to be a bit satirical till you see her. And she dresses as well as any woman in London. I tell you, your son doesn't half put his head up when she goes walking down Piccadilly with him."

Mrs. Morel wondered, in her heart, if her son did not go walking down Piccadilly with an elegant figure and fine clothes, rather than with a woman who was near to him. But she congratulated him in her doubtful fashion. And, as she stood over the washing tub, the mother brooded over her son. She saw him saddled with an elegant and expensive wife, earning little money, dragging along and getting draggled in some small, ugly house in a suburb. "But there," she told herself, "I am very likely a silly—meeting trouble halfway." Nevertheless, the load of anxiety scarcely ever left her heart, lest William should do the wrong thing by himself.

Presently, Paul was bidden call upon Thomas Jordan, Manufacturer of Surgical Appliances, at 21, Spaniel Row, Nottingham. Mrs. Morel was all joy.

"There, you see!" she cried, her eyes shining. "You've only written four letters, and the third is answered. You're lucky, my boy, as I always said you were."

Paul looked at the picture of a wooden leg, adorned with elastic stockings and other appliances, that figured on Mr. Jordan's notepaper, and he felt alarmed. He had not known that elastic stockings existed. And he seemed to feel the business world, with its regulated system of values, and its impersonality, and he dreaded it. It seemed monstrous also that a business could be run on wooden legs.

Mother and son set off together one Tuesday morning. It was August and blazing hot. Paul walked with something screwed up tight inside him. He would have suffered much physical pain rather than this unreasonable suffering at being exposed to strangers, to be accepted or rejected. Yet he chattered away with his mother. He would never have confessed to her how he suffered over these things, and she only partly guessed. She was gay, like a sweetheart. She stood in front of the ticket office at Bestwood, and Paul watched her take from her purse the money for the tickets. As he saw her hands in their old black kid gloves getting the silver out of the worn purse, his heart contracted with pain of love of her.

She was quite excited, and quite gay. He suffered because she *would* talk aloud in presence of the other travelers.

"Now look at that silly cow!" she said, "careering round as if it thought it was a circus."

"It's most likely a bottfly," he said very low.

"A what?" she asked brightly and unashamed.

They thought awhile. He was sensible all the time of having her opposite him. Suddenly their eyes met, and she smiled to him—a rare, intimate smile, beautiful with brightness and love. Then each looked out of the window.

The sixteen slow miles of railway journey passed. The mother and son walked down Station Street, feeling the excitement of lovers having an adventure together. In Carrington Street they stopped to hang over the parapet and look at the barges on the canal below.

"It's just like Venice," he said, seeing the sunshine on the water that lay between high factory walls.

"Perhaps," she answered, smiling.

They enjoyed the shops immensely.

"Now you see that blouse," she would say, "wouldn't that just suit our Annie? And for one-and-eleven-three. Isn't that cheap?"

"And made of needlework as well," he said.

"Yes."

They had plenty of time, so they did not hurry. The town was strange and delightful to them. But the boy was tied up inside in a knot of apprehension. He dreaded the interview with Thomas Jordan.

It was nearly eleven o'clock by St. Peter's Church. They turned up a narrow street that led to the Castle. It was gloomy and old-fashioned, having low dark shops and dark green house doors with brass knockers, and yellow-ochered door steps projecting on to the pavement; then another old shop whose small window looked like a cunning, half-shut eye. Mother and son went cautiously, looking everywhere for "Thomas Jordan and Son." It was like hunting in some wild place. They were on tiptoe of excitement.

Suddenly they spied a big, dark archway, in which were names of various firms, Thomas Jordan among them.

"Here it is!" said Mrs. Morel. "But now *where* is it?"

They looked round. On one side was a queer, dark, cardboard factory, on the other a Commercial Hotel.

"It's up the entry," said Paul.

And they ventured under the archway, as into the jaws of the dragon. They emerged into a wide yard, like a well, with buildings all round. It was littered with straw and boxes, and cardboard. The sunshine actually caught one crate whose straw was streaming on to the yard like gold. But elsewhere the place was like a pit. There were several doors, and two flights of steps. Straight in front, on a dirty glass door at the top of a staircase, loomed the ominous words "Thomas Jordan and Son—Surgical Appliances." Mrs. Morel went first, her son followed her. Charles I mounted his scaffold with a lighter heart than had Paul Morel as he followed his mother up the dirty steps to the dirty door.

She pushed open the door, and stood in pleased surprise. In front of her was a big warehouse, with creamy paper parcels everywhere, and clerks, with their shirtsleeves rolled back, were going about in an at-home sort of way. The light was subdued, the glossy cream parcels seemed luminous, the counters were of dark brown wood. All was quiet and very homely. Mrs. Morel took two steps forward, then waited. Paul stood behind her. She had on her Sunday bonnet and a black veil; he wore a boy's broad white collar and a Norfolk suit.

One of the clerks looked up. He was thin and tall, with a small face. His way of looking was alert. Then he glanced round to the other end of the room, where was a glass office. And then he came forward. He did not say anything, but leaned in a gentle, inquiring fashion towards Mrs. Morel.

"Can I see Mr. Jordan?" she asked.

"I'll fetch him," answered the young man.

He went down to the glass office. A red-faced, white-whiskered old man looked up. He reminded Paul of a Pomeranian dog. Then the same little man came up the room. He had short legs, was rather stout, and wore an alpaca jacket. So, with one ear up, as it were, he came stoutly and inquiringly down the room.

"Good-morning!" he said, hesitating before Mrs. Morel, in doubt as to whether she were a customer or not.

"Good-morning. I came with my son, Paul Morel. You asked him to call this morning."

"Come this way," said Mr. Jordan, in a rather snappy little manner intended to be businesslike.

They followed the manufacturer into a grubby little room, upholstered in black American leather, glossy with the rubbing of many customers. On the table was a pile of trusses, yellow wash-leather hoops tangled together. They looked new and living. Paul sniffed the odor of new wash leather. He wondered what the things were. By this time he was so much stunned that he only noticed the outside things.

"Sit down!" said Mr. Jordan, irritably pointing Mrs. Morel to a horsehair chair. She sat on the edge in an uncertain fashion. Then the little old man fidgeted and found a paper.

"Did you write this letter?" he snapped, thrusting what Paul recognized as his own notepaper in front of him.

"Yes," he answered.

At that moment he was occupied in two ways: first, in feeling guilty for telling a lie, since William had composed the letter; second, in wondering why his letter seemed so strange and different, in the fat, red hand of the man, from what it had been when it lay on the kitchen table. It was like part of himself, gone astray. He resented the way the man held it.

"Where did you learn to write?" said the old man crossly.

Paul merely looked at him shamedly, and did not answer.

"He *is* a bad writer," put in Mrs. Morel apologetically. Then she pushed up her veil. Paul hated her for not being prouder with this common little man, and he loved her face clear of the veil.

"And you say you know French?" inquired the little man, still sharply.

"Yes," said Paul.

"What school did you go to?"

"The Board-school."

"And did you learn it there?"

"No—I—" The boy went crimson and got no further.

"His godfather gave him lessons," said Mrs. Morel, half-pleading and rather distant.

Mr. Jordan hesitated. Then, in his irritable manner—he always seemed to keep his hands ready for action—he pulled another sheet of paper from his pocket, unfolded it. The paper made a crackling noise. He handed it to Paul.

"Read that," he said.

It was a note in French, in thin, flimsy foreign handwriting that the boy could not decipher. He stared blankly at the paper.

" 'Monsieur,' " he began; then he looked in great confusion at Mr. Jordan. "It's the—it's the——"

He wanted to say "handwriting," but his wits would no longer work even sufficiently to supply him with the word. Feeling an utter fool, and hating Mr. Jordan, he turned desperately to the paper again.

" 'Sir—Please send me'—er—er—I can't tell the—er—'two pairs—*gris fil bas*—gray thread—stockings'—er—er—'*sans*—without'—er—I can't tell the words—er—'*doigts*—fingers'—er—I can't tell the——"

He wanted to say "handwriting," but the word still refused to come. Seeing him stuck, Mr. Jordan snatched the paper from him.

" 'Please send by return two pairs gray thread stockings without *toes*.' "

"Well," flashed Paul, " '*doigts*' means 'fingers'—as well—as a rule——"

The little man looked at him. He did not know whether "*doigts*" meant "fingers"; he knew that for all *his* purposes it meant "toes."

"Fingers to stockings!" he snapped.

"Well, it *does* mean fingers," the boy persisted.

He hated the little man, who made such a clod of him. Mr. Jordan looked at the pale, stupid, defiant boy, then at the mother, who sat quiet and with that peculiar shut-off look of the poor who have to depend on the favor of others.

"And when could he come?" he asked.

"Well," said Mrs. Morel, "as soon as you wish. He has finished school now."

"He would live in Bestwood?"

"Yes; but he could be in—at the station—at quarter to eight."

"H'm!"

It ended by Paul's being engaged as junior spiral clerk, at eight shillings a week. The boy did not open his mouth to say another word, after having insisted that "*doigts*" meant "fingers." He followed his mother down the stairs. She looked at him with her bright blue eyes full of love and joy.

"I think you'll like it," she said.

" '*Doigts*' does mean 'fingers,' mother, and it was the writing. I couldn't read the writing."

"Never mind, my boy. I'm sure he'll be all right, and you won't see much of him. Wasn't that first young fellow nice? I'm sure you'll like him."

"But wasn't Mr. Jordan common, mother? Does he own it all?"

"I suppose he was a workman who has got on," she said. "You mustn't mind people so much. They're not being disagreeable to *you*—it's their way. You always think people are meaning things for you. But they don't."

It was very sunny. Over the big desolate space of the marketplace the blue sky shimmered, and the granite cobbles of the paving glistened. Shops down the Long Row were deep in obscurity, and the shadow was full of color. Just where the horse trams trundled across the market was a row of fruit stalls, with fruit blazing in the sun—apples and piles of reddish oranges, small greengage plums and bananas. There was a warm scent of fruit as mother and son passed. Gradually his feeling of ignominy and of rage sank.

"Where should we go for dinner?" asked the mother.

It was felt to be a reckless extravagance. Paul had only been in an eating-house once or twice in his life, and then only to have a cup of tea and a bun. Most of the people of Bestwood considered that tea and bread-and-butter, and perhaps potted beef, was all they could afford to eat in Nottingham. Real cooked dinner was considered great extravagance. Paul felt rather guilty.

They found a place that looked quite cheap. But when Mrs. Morel scanned the bill of fare, her heart was heavy, things were so dear. So she ordered kidney pies and potatoes as the cheapest available dish.

"We oughtn't to have come here, mother," said Paul.

"Never mind," she said. "We won't come again."

She insisted on his having a small currant tart, because he liked sweets.

"I don't want it, mother," he pleaded.

"Yes," she insisted; "you'll have it."

And she looked round for the waitress. But the waitress was busy, and Mrs. Morel did not like to bother her then. So the mother and son waited for the girl's pleasure, whilst she flirted among the men.

"Brazen hussy!" said Mrs. Morel to Paul. "Look now, she's taking that man *his* pudding, and he came long after us."

"It doesn't matter, mother," said Paul.

Mrs. Morel was angry. But she was too poor, and her orders were too meager, so that she had not the courage to insist on her rights just then. They waited and waited.

"Should we go, mother?" he said.

Then Mrs. Morel stood up. The girl was passing near.

"Will you bring one currant tart?" said Mrs. Morel clearly.

The girl looked round insolently.

"Directly," she said.

"We have waited quite long enough," said Mrs. Morel.

In a moment the girl came back with the tart. Mrs. Morel asked coldly for the bill. Paul wanted to sink through the floor. He marveled at his mother's hardness. He knew that only years of battling had taught her to insist even so little on her rights. She shrank as much as he.

"It's the last time I go *there* for anything!" she declared, when they were outside the place, thankful to be clear.

"We'll go," she said, "and look at Keep's and Boot's, and one or two places, shall we?"

They had discussions over the pictures, and Mrs. Morel wanted to buy him a little sable brush that he hankered after. But this indulgence he refused. He stood in front of milliners' shops and drapers' shops almost bored, but content for her to be interested. They wandered on.

"Now, just look at those black grapes!" she said. "They make your mouth water. I've wanted some of those for years, but I s'll have to wait a bit before I get them."

Then she rejoiced in the florists, standing in the doorway, sniffing.

"Oh! oh! Isn't it simply lovely!"

Paul saw, in the darkness of the shop, an elegant young lady in black peering over the counter curiously.

"They're looking at you," he said, trying to draw his mother away.

"But what *is* it?" she exclaimed, refusing to be moved.

"Stocks!" he answered, sniffing hastily. "Look there's a tubful."

"So there is—red and white. But really, I never knew stocks to smell like it!" And, to his great relief, she moved out of the doorway, but only to stand in front of the window.

"Paul!" she cried to him, who was trying to get out of sight of the elegant young lady in black—the shopgirl. "Paul! Just look here!"

He came reluctantly back.

"Now, just look at that fuchsia!" she exclaimed, pointing.

"H'm!" He made a curious, interested sound. "You'd think every second as the flowers was going to fall off, they hang so big an' heavy."

"And such an abundance!" she cried.

"And the way they drop downwards with their threads and knots!"

"Yes!" she exclaimed. "Lovely!"

"I wonder who'll buy it!" he said.

"I wonder!" she answered. "Not us."

"It would die in our parlor."

"Yes, beastly cold, sunless hole; it kills every bit of a plant you put in, and the kitchen chokes them to death."

They bought a few things, and set off towards the station. Looking up the canal, through the dark pass of the buildings, they saw the Castle on its bluff of brown, green-bushed rock, in a positive miracle of delicate sunshine.

"Won't it be nice for me to come out at dinnertimes?" said Paul. "I can go all round here and see everything. I s'll love it."

"You will," assented his mother.

He had spent a perfect afternoon with his mother. They arrived home in the mellow evening, happy, and glowing, and tired.

In the morning he filled in the form for his season-ticket and took it to the station. When he got back, his mother was just beginning to wash the floor. He sat crouched up on the sofa.

"He says it'll be here by Saturday," he said.

"And how much will it be?"

"About one pound eleven," he said.

She went on washing her floor in silence.

"Is it a lot?" he asked.

"It's no more than I thought," she answered.

"An' I s'll earn eight shillings a week," he said.

She did not answer, but went on with her work. At last she said:

"That William promised me, when he went to London, as he'd give me a pound a month. He has given me ten shillings—twice; and now I know he hasn't a farthing if I asked him. Not that I want it. Only just now you'd think he might be able to help with this ticket, which I'd never expected."

"He earns a lot," said Paul.

"He earns a hundred and thirty pounds. But they're all alike. They're large in promises, but it's precious little fulfillment you get."

"He spends over fifty shillings a week on himself," said Paul.

"And I keep this house on less than thirty," she replied: "and am supposed to find money for extras. But they don't care about helping you, once they've gone. He'd rather spend it on that dressed-up creature."

"She should have her own money if she's so grand," said Paul.

"She should, but she hasn't. I asked him. And *I* know he doesn't buy her a gold bangle for nothing. I wonder whoever bought *me* a gold bangle."

William was succeeding with his "Gypsy," as he called her. He asked the girl—her name was Louisa Lily Denys Western—for a photograph to send to his mother. The photo came—a handsome brunette, taken in profile, smirking slightly—and, it might be, quite naked, for on the photograph not a scrap of clothing was to be seen, only a naked bust.

"Yes," wrote Mrs. Morel to her son, "the photograph of Louie is very striking, and I can see she must be attractive. But do you think, my boy, it was very good taste of a girl to give her young man that photo to send to his mother—the first? Certainly the shoulders are beautiful, as you say. But I hardly expected to see so much of them at the first view."

Morel found the photograph standing on the chiffonier in the parlor. He came out with it between his thick thumb and finger.

"Who dost reckon this is?" he asked of his wife.

"It's the girl our William is going with," replied Mrs. Morel.

"Her name is Louisa Lily Denys Western."

"An' come again tomorrer!" exclaimed the miner. "An is 'er an actress?"

"She is not. She's supposed to be a lady."

"I'll bet!" he exclaimed, still staring at the photo. "A lady, is she? An' how much does she reckon ter keep up this sort o' game on?"

"On nothing. She lives with an old aunt, whom she hates, and takes what bit of money's given her."

"H'm!" said Morel, laying down the photograph. "Then he's a fool to ha' ta'en up wi' such a one as that."

"Dear Mater," William replied. "I'm sorry you didn't like the photograph. It never occurred to me when I sent it, that you mightn't think it decent. However, I told Gyp that it didn't quite suit your prim and proper notions, so she's going to send you another, that I hope will please you better. She's always being photographed; in fact, the photographers *ask* her if they may take her for nothing."

Presently the new photograph came, with a little silly note from the girl. This time the young lady was seen in a black satin evening bodice, cut square, with little puff sleeves, and black lace hanging down her beautiful arms.

"I wonder if she ever wears anything except evening clothes," said Mrs. Morel sarcastically. "I'm sure I *ought* to be impressed."

"You are disagreeable, mother," said Paul. "I think the first one with bare shoulders is lovely."

"Do you?" answered his mother. "Well, I don't."

On the Monday morning the boy got up at six to start work. He had the season-ticket, which had cost such bitterness, in his waistcoat pocket. He loved it with its bars of yellow across. His mother packed his dinner in a small, shut-up basket, and he set off at a quarter to seven to catch the 7:15 train. Mrs. Morel came to the entry-end to see him off.

It was a perfect morning. From the ash tree the slender green fruits that the children call "pigeons" were twinkling gaily down on a little breeze, into the front gardens of the houses. The valley was full of a lustrous dark haze, through which the ripe corn shimmered, and in which the steam from Minton pit melted swiftly. Puffs of wind came. Paul looked over the high woods of Aldersley, where the country gleamed and home had never pulled at him so powerfully.

"Good-morning, mother," he said, smiling, but feeling very unhappy.

"Good-morning," she replied cheerfully and tenderly.

She stood in her white apron on the open road, watching him as he crossed the field. He had a small, compact body that looked full of life. She felt, as she saw him trudging over the field, that where he determined to go he would get. She thought of William. He would have leaped the fence instead of going round to the stile. He was away in London, doing well. Paul would be working in Nottingham. Now she had two sons in the world. She could think of two places, great centers of industry, and feel that she had put a man into each of them, that these men would work out what *she* wanted; they were derived from her, they were of her, and their works also would be hers. All the morning long she thought of Paul.

At eight o'clock he climbed the dismal stairs of Jordan's Surgical Appliance Factory, and stood helplessly against the first great parcel rack, waiting for somebody to pick him up. The place was still not awake. Over the counters were great dust sheets. Two men only had arrived, and were heard talking in a corner, as they took off their coats and rolled up their shirtsleeves. It was ten past eight. Evidently there was no rush of punctuality. Paul listened to the voice of the two clerks. Then he heard someone cough, and saw in the office at the end of the room an old, decaying clerk, in a round smoking cap of black velvet embroidered with red and green, opening letters. He waited and waited. One of the junior clerks went to the old man, greeted him cheerily and loudly. Evidently the old "chief" was deaf. Then the young fellow came striding importantly down to his counter. He spied Paul.

"Hello!" he said. "You the new lad?"

"Yes," said Paul.

"H'm! What's your name?"

"Paul Morel."

"Paul Morel? All right, you come on round here."

Paul followed him round the rectangle of counters. The room was second storey. It had a great hole in the middle of the floor, fenced as with a wall of counters, and down this wide shaft the lifts went, and the light for the bottom storey. Also there was a corresponding big, oblong hole in the ceiling, and one could see above, over the fence of the top floor, some machinery; and right away overhead was the glass roof, and all light for the three storeys came downwards, getting dimmer, so that it was always night on the ground floor and rather gloomy on the second floor. The factory was the top floor, the warehouse the second, the storehouse the ground floor. It was an insanitary, ancient place.

Paul was led round to a very dark corner.

"This is the 'Spiral' corner," said the clerk. "You're Spiral, with Pappleworth. He's your boss, but he's not come yet. He doesn't get here till half-past eight. So you can fetch the letters, if you like, from Mr. Melling down there."

The young man pointed to the old clerk in the office.

"All right," said Paul.

"Here's a peg to hang your cap on. Here are your entry ledgers. Mr. Pappleworth won't be long."

And the thin young man stalked away with long, busy strides over the hollow wooden floor.

After a minute or two Paul went down and stood in the door of the glass office. The old clerk in the smoking cap looked down over the rim of his spectacles.

"Good-morning," he said, kindly and impressively. " You want the letters for the Spiral department, Thomas?"

Paul resented being called "Thomas." But he took the letters and returned to his dark place, where the counter made an angle, where the great parcel rack came to an end and where there were three doors in the corner. He sat on a high stool and read the letters—those whose handwriting was not too difficult. They ran as follows:

"Will you please send me at once a pair of lady's silk spiral thigh-hose, without feet, such as I had from you last year; length, thigh to knee," etc. Or, "Major Chamberlain wishes to repeat his previous order for a silk non-elastic suspensory bandage."

Many of these letters, some of them in French or Norwegian, were a great puzzle to the boy. He sat on his stool nervously awaiting the arrival of his "boss." He suffered tortures of shyness when, at half-past eight, the factory girls for upstairs trooped past him.

Mr. Pappleworth arrived, chewing a chlorodyne gum, at about twenty to nine, when all the other men were at work. He was a thin, sallow man with a red nose, quick, staccato, and smartly but stiffly dressed. He was about thirty-six years old. There was something rather "doggy," rather smart, rather 'cute and shrewd, and something warm, and something slightly contemptible about him.

"You my new lad?" he said.

Paul stood up and said he was.

"Fetched the letters?"

Mr. Pappleworth gave a chew to his gum.

"Yes."

"Copied 'em?"

"No."

"Well, come on then, let's look slippy. Changed your coat?"

"No."

"You want to bring an old coat and leave it here." He pronounced the last words with the chlorodyne gum between his side teeth. He vanished into darkness behind the great parcel rack, reappeared coatless, turning up a smart striped shirt cuff over a thin and hairy arm. Then he slipped into his coat. Paul noticed how thin he was, and that his trousers were in folds behind. He seized a stool, dragged it beside the boy's, and sat down.

"Sit down," he said.

Paul took a seat.

Mr. Pappleworth was very close to him. The man seized the letters, snatched a long entry book out of a rack in front of him, flung it open, seized a pen, and said:

"Now look here. You want to copy these letters in here." He sniffed twice, gave a quick chew at his gum, stared fixedly at a letter, then went very still and absorbed and wrote the entry rapidly, in a beautiful flourishing hand. He glanced quickly at Paul.

"See that?"

"Yes."

"Think you can do it all right?"

"Yes."

"All right then, let's see you."

He sprang off his stool. Paul took a pen. Mr. Pappleworth disappeared. Paul rather liked copying the letters, but he wrote slowly, laboriously, and exceedingly badly. He was doing the fourth letter, and feeling quite busy and happy, when Mr. Pappleworth reappeared.

"Now then, how'r' yer getting on? Done 'em?"

He leaned over the boy's shoulder, chewing, and smelling of chlorodyne.

"Strike my bob, lad, but you're a beautiful writer!" he exclaimed satirically. "Ne'er mind, how many h'yer done? Only three! I'd 'a' eaten 'em. Get on, my lad, an' put numbers on 'em. Here, look! Get on!"

Paul ground away at the letters, whilst Mr. Pappleworth fussed over various jobs. Suddenly the boy started as a shrill whistle sounded near his ear. Mr. Pappleworth came, took a plug out of a pipe, and said, in an amazingly cross and bossy voice:

"Yes?"

Paul heard a faint voice, like a woman's, out of the mouth of the tube. He gazed in wonder, never having seen a speaking tube before.

"Well," said Mr. Pappleworth disagreeably into the tube, "you'd better get some of your back work done, then."

Again the woman's tiny voice was heard, sounding pretty and cross.

"I've not time to stand here while you talk," said Mr. Pappleworth, and he pushed the plug into the tube.

"Come, my lad," he said imploringly to Paul, "there's Polly crying out for them orders. Can't you buck up a bit? Here, come out!"

He took the book, to Paul's immense chagrin, and began the copying himself. He worked quickly and well. This done, he seized some strips of long yellow paper, about three inches wide, and made out the day's orders for the work girls.

"You'd better watch me," he said to Paul, working all the while rapidly. Paul watched the weird little drawings of legs, and thighs, and ankles, with the strokes across and the numbers, and the few brief directions which his chief made upon the yellow paper. Then Mr. Pappleworth finished and jumped up.

"Come on with me," he said, and the yellow papers flying in his hands, he dashed through a door and down some stairs, into the basement where the gas was burning. They crossed the cold, damp storeroom, then a long, dreary room with a long table on trestles, into a smaller, cosy apartment, not very high, which had been built on to the main building. In this room a small woman with a red serge blouse, and her black hair done on top of her head, was waiting like a proud little bantam.

"Here y'are!" said Pappleworth.

"I think it is 'here you are'!" exclaimed Polly. "The girls have been here nearly half an hour waiting. Just think of the time wasted!"

"*You* think of getting your work done and not talking so much," said Mr. Pappleworth. "You could ha' been finishing off."

"You know quite well we finished everything off on Saturday!" cried Polly, flying at him, her dark eyes flashing.

"Tu-tu-tu-tu-terterter!" he mocked. "Here's your new lad. Don't ruin him as you did the last."

" 'As we did the last'!" repeated Polly. "Yes, *we* do a lot of ruining, we do. My word, a lad would *take* some ruining after he'd been with you."

"It's time for work now, not for talk," said Mr. Pappleworth severely and coldly.

"It was time for work some time back," said Polly, marching away with her head in the air. She was an erect little body of forty.

In that room were two round spiral machines on the bench under the window. Through the inner doorway was another, longer room, with six more machines. A little group of girls, nicely dressed and in white aprons, stood talking together.

"Have you nothing else to do but talk?" said Mr. Pappleworth.

"Only wait for you," said one handsome girl, laughing.

"Well, get on, get on," he said. "Come on, my lad. You'll know your road down here again."

And Paul ran upstairs after his chief. He was given some checking and invoicing to do. He stood at the desk, laboring in his execrable handwriting. Presently Mr. Jordan came strutting down from the glass office and stood behind him, to the boy's great discomfort. Suddenly a red and fat finger was thrust on the form he was filling in.

"*Mr.* J. A. Bates, Esquire!" exclaimed the cross voice just behind his ear.

Paul looked at "Mr. J. A. Bates, Esquire" in his own vile writing, and wondered what was the matter now.

"Didn't they teach you any better than *that* while they were at it? If you put 'Mr.' you don't put 'Esquire'—a man can't be both at once."

The boy regretted his too-much generosity in disposing of honors, hesitated, and with trembling fingers, scratched out the "Mr." Then all at once Mr. Jordan snatched away the invoice.

"Make another! Are you going to send *that* to a gentleman?" And he tore up the blue form irritably.

Paul, his ears red with shame, began again. Still Mr. Jordan watched.

"I don't know what they *do* teach in school. You'll have to write better than that. Lads learn nothing nowadays, but how to recite poetry and play the fiddle. Have you seen his writing?" he asked of Mr. Pappleworth.

"Yes; prime, isn't it?" replied Mr. Pappleworth indifferently.

Mr. Jordan gave a little grunt, not unamiable. Paul divined that his master's bark was worse than his bite. Indeed, the little manufacturer, although he spoke bad English, was quite gentleman enough to leave his men alone and to take no notice of trifles. But he knew he did not look like the boss and owner of the show, so he had to play his role of proprietor at first, to put things on a right footing.

"Let's see, *what's* your name?" asked Mr. Pappleworth of the boy.

"Paul Morel."

It is curious that children suffer so much at having to pronounce their own names.

"Paul Morel, is it? All right, you Paul-Morel through them things there, and then——"

Mr. Pappleworth subsided on to a stool, and began writing. A girl came up from out of a door just behind, put some newly pressed elastic web appliances on the counter, and returned. Mr. Pappleworth picked up the whitey-blue kneeband, examined it, and its yellow order paper quickly, and put it on one side. Next was a flesh-pink "leg." He went through the few things, wrote out a couple of orders, and called to Paul to accompany him. This time they went through the door whence the girl had emerged. There Paul found himself at the top of a little wooden flight of steps and below him saw a room with windows round two sides and at the farther end half a dozen girls sitting bending over the benches in the light from the window, sewing. They were singing together "Two Little Girls in Blue." Hearing the door opened, they all turned round, to see Mr. Pappleworth and Paul looking down on them from the far end of the room. They stopped singing.

"Can't you make a bit less row?" said Mr. Pappleworth. "Folk'll think we keep cats."

A hunchback woman on a high stool turned her long, rather heavy face towards Mr. Pappleworth, and said, in a contralto voice:

"They're all tomcats then."

In vain Mr. Pappleworth tried to be impressive for Paul's benefit. He descended the steps into the finishing-off room, and went to the hunchback Fanny. She had such a short body on her high stool that her head, with its great bands of bright brown hair, seemed over large, as did her pale, heavy face. She wore a dress of green-black cashmere, and her wrists, coming out of the narrow cuffs, were thin and flat, as she put down her work nervously. He showed her something that was wrong with a kneecap.

"Well," she said, "you needn't come blaming it on to me. It's not my fault." Her color mounted to her cheek.

"I never said it *was* your fault. Will you do as I tell you?" replied Mr. Pappleworth shortly.

"You don't say it's my fault, but you'd like to make out as it was," the hunchback woman cried, almost in tears. Then she snatched the kneecap from her "boss," saying: "Yes, I'll do it for you, but you needn't be snappy."

"Here's your new lad," said Mr. Pappleworth.

Fanny turned, smiling very gently on Paul.

"Oh!" she said.

"Yes; don't make a softy of him between you."

"It's not us as 'ud make a softy of him," she said indignantly.

"Come on then, Paul," said Mr. Pappleworth.

"*Au revoy*, Paul," said one of the girls.

There was a titter of laughter. Paul went out, blushing deeply, not having spoken a word.

The day was very long. All morning the work people were coming to speak to Mr. Pappleworth. Paul was writing or learning to make up parcels, ready for the midday post. At one o'clock, or, rather, at a quarter to one, Mr. Pappleworth disappeared to catch his train; he lived in the suburbs. At one o'clock, Paul, feeling very lost, took his dinner basket down into the stockroom in the basement, that had the long table on trestles, and ate his meal hurriedly, alone in that cellar of gloom and desolation. Then he went out of doors. The brightness and the freedom of the streets made him feel adventurous and happy. But at two o'clock he was back in the corner of the big room. Soon the work girls went trooping past, making remarks. It was the commoner girls who worked upstairs at the heavy tasks of truss-making and the finishing of artificial limbs. He waited for Mr. Pappleworth, not knowing what to do, sitting scribbling on the yellow order paper. Mr. Pappleworth came at twenty minutes to three. Then he sat and gossiped with Paul, treating the boy entirely as an equal, even in age.

In the afternoon there was never very much to do, unless it were near the weekend, and the accounts had to be made up. At five o'clock all the men went down into the dungeon with the table on trestles, and there they had tea, eating bread-and-butter on the bare, dirty boards, talking with the same kind of ugly haste and slovenliness with which they ate their meal. And yet upstairs the atmosphere among them was always jolly and clear. The cellar and the trestles affected them.

After tea, when all the gases were lighted, *work* went more briskly. There was the big evening post to get off. The hose came up warm and newly pressed from the workrooms. Paul had made out the invoices. Now he had the packing up and addressing to do, then he had to weigh his stock of parcels on the scales. Everywhere voices were calling weights, there was the chink of metal, the rapid snapping of string, the hurrying to old Mr. Melling for stamps. And at last the postman came with his sack, laughing and jolly. Then everything slacked off, and Paul took his dinner basket and ran to the station to catch the eight-twenty train. The day in the factory was just twelve hours long.

His mother sat waiting for him rather anxiously. He had to walk from Keston, so was not home until about twenty past nine. And he left the house before seven in the morning. Mrs. Morel was rather anxious about his health. But she herself had had to put up with so much that she expected her children to take the same odds. They must go through with what came. And Paul stayed at Jordan's, although all the time he was there his health suffered from the darkness and lack of air and the long hours.

He came in pale and tired. His mother looked at him. She saw he was rather pleased, and her anxiety all went.

"Well, and how was it?" she asked.

"Ever so funny, mother," he replied. "You don't have to work a bit hard, and they're nice with you."

"And did you get on all right?"

"Yes; they only say my writing's bad. But Mr. Pappleworth—he's my man—said to Mr. Jordan I should be all right. I'm Spiral, mother; you must come and see. It's ever so nice."

Soon he liked Jordan's. Mr. Pappleworth, who had a certain "saloon bar" flavor about him, was always natural, and treated him as if he had been a comrade. Sometimes the "Spiral boss" was irritable, and chewed more lozenges than ever. Even then, however, he was not offensive, but one of those people who hurt themselves by their own irritability more than they hurt other people.

"Haven't you done that *yet*?" he would cry. "Go on, be a month of Sundays."

Again, and Paul could understand him least then, he was jocular and in high spirits.

"I'm going to bring my little Yorkshire terrier bitch tomorrow," he said jubilantly to Paul.

"What's a Yorkshire terrier?"

"*Don't* know what a Yorkshire terrier is? *Don't know a Yorkshire*—" Mr. Pappleworth was aghast.

"Is it a little silky one—colors of iron and rusty silver?"

"*That's* it, my lad. She's a gem. She's had five pounds' worth of pups already, and she's worth over seven pounds herself; and she doesn't weigh twenty ounces."

The next day the bitch came. She was a shivering, miserable morsel. Paul did not care for her; she seemed so like a wet rag that would never dry. Then a man called for her, and began to make coarse jokes. But Mr. Pappleworth nodded his head in the direction of the boy and the talk went on *sotto voce*.

Mr. Jordan only made one more excursion to watch Paul, and then the only fault he found was seeing the boy lay his pen on the counter.

"Put your pen in your ear, if you're going to be a clerk. Pen in your ear!" And one day he said to the lad, "Why don't you hold your shoulders straighter? Come down here," when he took him into the glass office and fitted him with special braces for keeping the shoulders square.

But Paul liked the girls best. The men seemed common and rather dull. He liked them all, but they were uninteresting. Polly, the little brisk overseer downstairs, finding Paul eating in the cellar, asked him if she could cook him anything on her little stove. Next day his mother gave him a dish that could be heated up He took it into the pleasant, clean room to Polly. And very soon it grew to be an established custom that he should have dinner with her. When he came in at eight in the morning he took his basket to her, and when he came down at one o'clock she had his dinner ready.

He was not very tall, and pale, with thick chestnut hair, irregular features, and a wide, full mouth. She was like a small bird. He often called her a "robinet." Though naturally rather quiet, he would sit and chatter with her for hours, telling her about his home. The girls all liked to hear him talk. They often gathered in a little circle while he sat on a bench, and held forth to them, laughing. Some of them regarded him as a curious little creature, so serious, yet so bright and jolly, and always so delicate in his way with them. They all liked him, and he adored them. Polly he felt he belonged to. Then Connie, with her mane of red hair, her face of apple blossom, her murmuring voice, such a lady in her shabby black frock, appealed to his romantic side.

"When you sit winding," he said, "it looks as if you were spinning at a spinning wheel—it looks ever so nice. You remind me of Elaine in the *Idylls of the King*. I'd draw you if I could."

And she glanced at him blushing shyly. And later on he had a sketch he prized very much: Connie sitting on the stool before the wheel, her flowing mane of red hair on her rusty black frock, her red mouth shut and serious, running the scarlet thread off the hank on to the reel.

With Louie, handsome and brazen, who always seemed to thrust her hip at him, he usually joked.

Emma was rather plain, rather old, and condescending. But to condescend to him made her happy, and he did not mind.

"How do you put needles in?" he asked.

"Go away and don't bother."

"But I ought to know how to put needles in."

She ground at her machine all the while steadily.

"There are many things you ought to know," she replied.

"Tell me, then, how to stick needles in the machine."

"Oh, the boy, what a nuisance he is! Why, *this* is how you do it."

He watched her attentively. Suddenly a whistle piped. Then Polly appeared, and said in a clear voice:

"Mr. Pappleworth wants to know how much longer you're going to be down here playing with the girls, Paul."

Paul flew upstairs, calling "Good-bye!" and Emma drew herself up.

"It wasn't *me* who wanted him to play with the machine," she said.

As a rule, when all the girls came back at two o'clock, he ran upstairs to Fanny, the hunchback, in the finishing-off room. Mr. Pappleworth did not appear till twenty to three, and he often found his boy sitting beside Fanny, talking, or drawing, or singing with the girls.

Often, after a minute's hesitation, Fanny would begin to sing. She had a fine contralto voice. Everybody joined in the chorus, and it went well. Paul was not at all embarrassed, after a while, sitting in the room with the half a dozen work girls.

At the end of the song Fanny would say:

"I know you've been laughing at me."

"Don't be so soft, Fanny!" cried one of the girls.

Once there was mention of Connie's red hair.

"Fanny's is better, to my fancy," said Emma.

"You needn't try to make a fool of me," said Fanny, flushing deeply.

"No, but she has, Paul; she's got beautiful hair."

"It's a treat of a color," said he. "That coldish color, like earth, and yet shiny. It's like bog water."

"Goodness me!" exclaimed one girl, laughing.

"How I do but get criticized," said Fanny.

"But you should see it down, Paul," cried Emma earnestly. "It's simply beautiful. Put it down for him, Fanny, if he wants something to paint."

Fanny would not, and yet she wanted to.

"Then I'll take it down myself," said the lad.

"Well, you can if you like," said Fanny.

And he carefully took the pins out of the knot, and the rush of hair, of uniform dark brown, slid over the humped back.

"What a lovely lot! " he exclaimed.

The girls watched. There was silence. The youth shook the hair loose from the coil.

"It's splendid!" he said, smelling its perfume. "I'll bet it's worth pounds."

"I'll leave it you when I die, Paul," said Fanny, half joking.

"You look just like anybody else, sitting drying their hair," said one of the girls to the long-legged hunchback.

Poor Fanny was morbidly sensitive, always imagining insults. Polly was curt and businesslike. The two departments were for ever at war, and Paul was always finding Fanny in tears. Then he was made the recipient of all her woes, and he had to plead her cause with Polly.

So the time went along happily enough. The factory had a homely feel. No one was rushed or driven. Paul always enjoyed it when the work got faster, towards post time, and all the men united in labor. He liked to watch his fellow clerks at work. The man was the work and the work was the man, one thing, for the time being. It was different with the girls. The real woman never seemed to be there at the task, but as if left out, waiting.

From the train going home at night he used to watch the lights of the town, sprinkled thick on the hills, fusing together in a blaze in the valleys. He felt rich in life and happy. Drawing farther off, there was a patch of lights at Bulwell like myriad petals shaken to the ground from the shed stars; and beyond was the red glare of the furnaces, playing like hot breath on the clouds.

He had to walk two and more miles from Keston home, up two long hills, down two short hills. He was often tired, and he counted the lamps climbing the hill above him, how many more to pass. And from the hilltop, on pitch-dark nights, he looked round on the villages five or six miles away, that shone like swarms of glittering living things, almost a heaven against his feet. Marlpool and Heanor scattered the far-off darkness with brilliance. And occasionally the black valley space between was traced, violated by a great train rushing south to London or north to Scotland. The trains roared by like projectiles level on the darkness, fuming and burning, making the valley clang with their passage. They were gone, and the lights of the towns and villages glittered in silence.

And then he came to the corner at home, which faced the other side of the night. The ash tree seemed a friend now. His mother rose with gladness as he entered. He put his eight shillings proudly on the table.

"It'll help, mother?" he asked wistfully.

"There's precious little left," she answered, "after your ticket and dinners and such are taken off."

Then he told her the budget of the day. His life story, like an Arabian Nights, was told night after night to his mother. It was almost as if it were her own life.

❖ 6 ❖

DEATH IN THE FAMILY

Arthur Morel was growing up. He was a quick, careless, impulsive boy, a good deal like his father. He hated study, made a great moan if he had to work, and escaped as soon as possible to his sport again.

In appearance he remained the flower of the family, being well made, graceful, and full of life. His dark brown hair and fresh coloring, and his exquisite dark blue eyes shaded with long lashes, together with his generous manner and fiery temper, made him a favorite. But as he grew older his temper became uncertain. He flew into rages over nothing, seemed unbearably raw and irritable.

His mother, whom he loved, wearied of him sometimes. He thought only of himself. When he wanted amusement, all that stood in his way he hated, even if it were she. When he was in trouble, he moaned to her ceaselessly.

"Goodness, boy!" she said, when he groaned about a master who, he said, hated him, "if you don't like it, alter it, and if you can't alter it, put up with it."

And his father, whom he had loved and who had worshipped him, he came to detest. As he grew older Morel fell into a slow ruin. His body, which had been beautiful in movement and in being, shrank, did not seem to ripen with the years, but to get mean and rather despicable. There came over him a look of meanness and of paltriness. And when the mean-looking elderly man bullied or ordered the boy about, Arthur was furious. Moreover, Morel's manners got worse and worse, his habits somewhat disgusting. When the children were growing up and in the crucial stage of adolescence, the father was like some ugly irritant to their souls. His manners in the house were the same as he used among the colliers down pit.

"Dirty nuisance!" Arthur would cry, jumping up and going straight out of the house when his father disgusted him. And Morel persisted the more because his children hated it. He seemed to take a kind of satisfaction in disgusting them, and driving them nearly mad, while they were so irritably sensitive at the age of fourteen or fifteen. So that Arthur, who was growing up when his father was degenerate and elderly, hated him worst of all.

Then, sometimes, the father would seem to feel the contemptuous hatred of his children.

"There's not a man tries harder for his family!" he would shout. "He does his best for them, and then gets treated like a dog. But I'm not going to stand it, I tell you!"

But for the threat and the fact that he did not try so hard as he imagined, they would have felt sorry. As it was, the battle now went on nearly all between father and children, he persisting in his dirty and disgusting ways, just to assert his independence. They loathed him.

Arthur was so inflamed and irritable at last, that when he won a scholarship for the Grammar School in Nottingham, his mother decided to let him live in town, with one of her sisters, and only come home at weekends.

Annie was still a junior teacher in the Board-school, earning about four shillings a week. But soon she would have fifteen shillings, since she had passed her examination, and there would be financial peace in the house.

Mrs. Morel clung now to Paul. He was quiet and not brilliant. But still he stuck to his painting, and still he stuck to his mother. Everything he did was for her. She waited for his coming home in the evening, and then she unburdened herself of all she had pondered, or of all that had occurred to her during the day. He sat and listened with his earnestness. The two shared lives.

William was engaged now to his brunette, and had bought her an engagement ring that cost eight guineas. The children gasped at such a fabulous price.

"Eight guineas!" said Morel. "More fool him! If he'd gen me some on't, it 'ud ha' looked better on 'im."

"Given *you* some of it!" cried Mrs. Morel. "Why give *you* some of it!"

She remembered *he* had bought no engagement ring at all, and she preferred William, who was not mean, if he were foolish. But now the young man talked only of the dances to which he went with his betrothed, and the different resplendent clothes she wore; or he told his mother with glee how they went to the theater like great swells.

He wanted to bring the girl home. Mrs. Morel said she should come at the Christmas. This time William arrived with a lady, but with no presents. Mrs. Morel had prepared supper. Hearing footsteps, she rose and went to the door. William entered.

"Hello, mother!" He kissed her hastily, then stood aside to present a tall, handsome girl, who was wearing a costume of fine black-and-white check, and furs.

"Here's Gyp!"

Miss Western held out her hand and showed her teeth in a small smile.

"Oh, how do you do, Mrs. Morel!" she exclaimed.

"I am afraid you will be hungry," said Mrs. Morel.

"Oh, no, we had dinner in the train. Have you got my gloves, Chubby?"

William Morel, big and raw-boned, looked at her quickly.

"How should I?" he said.

"Then I've lost them. Don't be cross with me."

A frown went over his face, but he said nothing. She glanced round the kitchen. It was small and curious to her, with its glittering kissing-bunch, its evergreens behind the pictures, its wooden chairs and little deal table. At that moment Morel came in.

"Hello, dad!"

"Hello, my son! Tha's let on me!"

The two shook hands, and William presented the lady. She gave the same smile that showed her teeth.

"How do you do, Mr. Morel?"

Morel bowed obsequiously.

"I'm very well, and I hope so are you. You must make yourself very welcome."

"Oh, thank you," she replied, rather amused.

"You will like to go upstairs," said Mrs. Morel.

"If you don't mind; but not if it is any trouble to you."

"It is no trouble. Annie will take you. Walter, carry up this box."

"And don't be an hour dressing yourself up," said William to his betrothed.

Annie took a brass candlestick, and, too shy almost to speak, preceded the young lady to the front bedroom, which Mr. and Mrs. Morel had vacated for her. It, too, was small and cold by candlelight. The colliers' wives only lit fires in bedrooms in case of extreme illness.

"Shall I unstrap the box?" asked Annie.

"Oh, thank you very much!"

Annie played the part of maid, then went downstairs for hot water.

"I think she's rather tired, mother," said William. "It's a beastly journey, and we had such a rush."

"Is there anything I can give her?" asked Mrs. Morel.

"Oh, no, she'll be all right."

But there was a chill in the atmosphere. After half an hour Miss Western came down, having put on a purplish-colored dress, very fine for the collier's kitchen.

"I told you you'd no need to change," said William to her.

"Oh, Chubby!" Then she turned with that sweetish smile to Mrs. Morel. "Don't you think he's always grumbling, Mrs. Morel?"

"Is he?" said Mrs. Morel. "That's not very nice of him."

"It isn't, really!"

"You are cold," said the mother. "Won't you come near the fire?"

Morel jumped out of his armchair.

"Come and sit you here!" he cried. "Come and sit you here!"

"No, dad, keep your own chair. Sit on the sofa, Gyp," said William.

"No, no!" cried Morel. "This cheer's warmest. Come and sit here, Miss Wesson."

"Thank you *so* much," said the girl, seating herself in the collier's armchair, the place of honor. She shivered, feeling the warmth of the kitchen penetrate her.

"Fetch me a hanky, Chubby dear!" she said, putting up her mouth to him, and using the same intimate tone as if they were alone; which made the rest of the family feel as if they ought not to be present. The young lady evidently did not realize them as people: they were creatures to her for the present. William winced.

In such a household, in Streatham, Miss Western would have been a lady condescending to her inferiors. These people were, to her, certainly clownish—in short, the working classes. How was she to adjust herself?

"I'll go," said Annie.

Miss Western took no notice, as if a servant had spoken. But when the girl came downstairs again with the handkerchief, she said, "Oh, thank you!" in a gracious way.

She sat and talked about the dinner on the train, which had been so poor; about London, about dances. She was really very nervous, and chattered from fear. Morel sat all the time smoking his thick twist tobacco, watching her, and listening to her glib London speech, as he puffed. Mrs. Morel, dressed up in her best black silk blouse, answered quietly and rather briefly. The three children sat round in silence and admiration. Miss Western was the princess. Everything of the best was got out for her: the best cups, the best spoons, the best tablecloth, the best coffee jug. The children thought she must find it quite grand. She felt strange, not able to realize the people, not knowing how to treat them. William joked, and was slightly uncomfortable.

At about ten o'clock he said to her:

"Aren't you tired, Gyp?"

"Rather, Chubby," she answered, at once in the intimate tones and putting her head slightly on one side.

"I'll light her the candle, mother," he said.

"Very well," replied the mother.

Miss Western stood up, held out her hand to Mrs. Morel.

"Good-night, Mrs. Morel," she said.

Paul sat at the boiler, letting the water run from the tap into a stone beer bottle. Annie swathed the bottle in an old flannel pit-singlet, and kissed her mother good-night. She was to share the room with the lady, because the house was full.

"You wait a minute," said Mrs. Morel to Annie. And Annie sat nursing the hot-water bottle. Miss Western shook hands all round, to everybody's discomfort, and took her departure, preceded by William. In five minutes he was downstairs again. His heart was rather sore: he did not know why. He talked very little till everybody had gone to bed, but himself and his mother. Then he stood with his legs apart, in his old attitude on the hearthrug, and said hesitatingly:

"Well, mother?"

"Well, my son?"

She sat in her best silk blouse in the rocking chair, feeling somehow hurt and humiliated, for his sake.

"Do you like her?"

"Yes," came the slow answer.

"She's shy yet, mother. She's not used to it. It's different from her aunt's house, you know."

"Of course it is, my boy; and she must find it difficult."

"She does." Then he frowned swiftly. "If only she wouldn't put on her *blessed* airs!"

"It's only her first awkwardness, my boy. She'll be all right."

"That's it, mother," he replied gratefully. But his brow was gloomy. "You know, she's not like you, mother. She's not serious, and she can't think."

"She's young, my boy."

"Yes; and she's had no sort of show. Her mother died when she was a child. Since then she's lived with her aunt, whom she can't bear. And her father was a rake. She's had no love."

"No! Well, you must make up to her."

"And so—you have to forgive her a lot of things."

"*What* do you have to forgive her, my boy?"

"I dunno. When she seems shallow, you have to remember she's never had anybody to bring her deeper side out. And she's *fearfully* fond of me."

"Anybody can see that."

"But you know, mother—she's—she's different from us. Those sort of people, like those she lives amongst, they don't seem to have the same principles."

"You mustn't judge too hastily," said Mrs. Morel.

But he seemed uneasy within himself.

In the morning, however, he was up singing and larking round the house.

"Hello!" he called, sitting on the stairs. "Are you getting up?"

"Yes," her voice called faintly.

"Merry Christmas!" he shouted to her.

Her laugh, pretty and tinkling, was heard in the bedroom. She did not come down in half an hour.

"Was she *really* getting up when she said she was?" he asked of Annie.

"Yes, she was," replied Annie.

He waited awhile, then went to the stairs again.

"Happy New Year," he called.

"Thank you, Chubby dear!" came the laughing voice, far away.

"Buck up!" he implored.

It was nearly an hour, and still he was waiting for her. Morel, who always rose before six, looked at the clock.

"Well, it's a winder!" he exclaimed.

The family had breakfasted, all but William. He went to the foot of the stairs.

"Shall I have to send you an Easter egg up there?" he called, rather crossly. She only laughed. The family expected, after that time of preparation, something like magic. At last she came, looking very nice in a blouse and skirt.

"Have you *really* been all this time getting ready?" he asked.

"Chubby dear! That question is not permitted, is it, Mrs. Morel?"

She played the grand lady at first. When she went with William to chapel, he in his frock coat and silk hat, she in her furs and London-made costume, Paul and Arthur and Annie expected everybody to bow to the ground in admiration. And Morel, standing in his Sunday suit at the end of the road, watching the gallant pair go, felt he was the father of princes and princesses.

And yet she was not so grand. For a year now she had been a sort of secretary or clerk in a London office. But while she was with the Morels she queened it. She sat and let Annie or Paul wait on her as if they were her servants. She treated Mrs. Morel with a certain glibness and Morel with patronage. But after a day or so she began to change her tune.

William always wanted Paul or Annie to go along with them on their walks. It was so much more interesting. And Paul really *did* admire "Gypsy" wholeheartedly; in fact, his mother scarcely forgave the boy for the adulation with which he treated the girl.

On the second day, when Lily said, "Oh, Annie, do you know where I left my muff?" William replied.

"You know it is in your bedroom. Why do you ask Annie?"

And Lily went upstairs with a cross, shut mouth. But it angered the young man that she made a servant of his sister.

On the third evening William and Lily were sitting together in the parlor by the fire in the dark. At a quarter to eleven Mrs. Morel was heard raking the fire. William came out to the kitchen, followed by his beloved.

"Is it as late as that, mother?" he said. She had been sitting alone.

"It is not *late*, my boy, but it is as late as I usually sit up."

"Won't you go to bed, then?" he asked.

"And leave you two? No, my boy, I don't believe in it."

"Can't you trust us, mother?"

"Whether I can or not, I won't do it. You can stay till eleven if you like, and I can read."

"Go to bed, Gyp," he said to his girl. "We won't keep mater waiting."

"Annie has left the candle burning, Lily," said Mrs. Morel; "I think you, will see."

"Yes, thank you. Good-night, Mrs. Morel."

William kissed his sweetheart at the foot of the stairs, and she went. He returned to the kitchen.

"Can't you trust us, mother?" he repeated, rather offended.

"My boy, I tell you I don't *believe* in leaving two young things like you alone downstairs when everyone else is in bed."

And he was forced to take this answer. He kissed his mother good-night.

At Easter he came over alone. And then he discussed his sweetheart endlessly with his mother.

"You know, mother, when I'm away from her I don't care for her a bit. I shouldn't care if I never saw her again. But, then, when I'm with her in the evenings I am awfully fond of her."

"It's a queer sort of love to marry on," said Mrs. Morel, "if she holds you no more than that!"

"It *is* funny!" he exclaimed. It worried and perplexed him. "But yet—there's so much between us now I couldn't give her up."

"You know best," said Mrs. Morel. "But if it is as you say, I wouldn't call it *love*—at any rate, it doesn't look much like it."

"Oh, I don't know, mother. She's an orphan, and——"

They never came to any sort of conclusion. He seemed puzzled and rather fretted. She was rather reserved. All his strength and money went in keeping this girl. He could scarcely afford to take his mother to Nottingham when he came over.

Paul's wages had been raised at Christmas to ten shillings to his great joy. He was quite happy at Jordan's, but his health suffered from the long hours and the confinement. His mother, to whom he became more and more significant, thought how to help.

His half-holiday was on Monday afternoon. On a Monday morning in May, as the two sat alone at breakfast, she said:

"I think it will be a fine day."

He looked up in surprise. This meant something.

"You know Mr. Leivers has gone to live on a new farm. Well, he asked me last week if I wouldn't go and see Mrs. Leivers, and I promised to bring you on Monday if it's fine. Shall we go?"

"I say, little woman, how lovely!" he cried. "And we'll go this afternoon?"

Paul hurried off to the station jubilant. Down Derby Road was a cherry tree that glistened. The old brick wall by the Statutes ground burned scarlet, spring was a very flame of green. And the steep swoop of high road lay, in its cool morning dust, splendid with patterns of sunshine and shadow, perfectly still. The trees sloped their great green shoulders proudly; and inside the warehouse all the morning, the boy had a vision of spring outside.

When he came home at dinnertime his mother was rather excited.

"Are we going?" he asked.

"When I'm ready," she replied.

Presently he got up.

"Go and get dressed while I wash up," he said.

She did so. He washed the pots, straightened, and then took her boots. They were quite clean. Mrs. Morel was one of those naturally exquisite people who can walk in mud without dirtying their shoes. But Paul had to clean them for her. They were kid boots at eight shillings a pair. He, however, thought them the most dainty boots in the world, and he cleaned them with as much reverence as if they had been flowers.

Suddenly she appeared in the inner doorway rather shyly. She had got a new cotton blouse on. Paul jumped up and went forward.

"Oh, my stars!" he exclaimed. "What a bobby-dazzler!"

She sniffed in a little haughty way, and put her head up.

"It's not a bobby-dazzler at all!" she replied. "It's very quiet!"

She walked forward, whilst he hovered round her.

"Well," she asked, quite shy, but pretending to be high and mighty, "do you like it?"

"Awfully! You *are* a fine little woman to go jaunting out with!"

He went and surveyed her from the back.

"Well," he said, "if I was walking down the street behind you, I should say, 'Doesn't *that* little person fancy herself!' "

"Well, she doesn't," replied Mrs. Morel. "She's not sure it suits her."

"Oh no! she wants to be in dirty black, looking as if she was wrapped in burnt paper. It *does* suit you, and *I* say you look nice."

She sniffed in her little way, pleased, but pretending to know better.

"Well," she said, "it's cost me just three shillings. You couldn't have got it ready-made for that price, could you?"

"I should think you couldn't," he replied.

"And, you know, it's good stuff."

"Awfully pretty," he said.

The blouse was white, with a little sprig of heliotrope and black.

"Too young for me, though, I'm afraid," she said.

"Too young for you!" he exclaimed in disgust. "Why don't you buy some false white hair and stick it on your head?"

"I s'll soon have no need," she replied. "I'm going white fast enough."

"Well, you've no business to," he said. "What do I want with a white-haired mother?"

"I'm afraid you'll have to put up with one, my lad," she said rather strangely.

They set off in great style, she carrying the umbrella William had given her, because of the sun. Paul was considerably taller than she, though he was not big. He fancied himself.

On the fallow land the young wheat shone silkily. Minton pit waved its plumes of white steam, coughed, and rattled hoarsely.

"Now look at that!" said Mrs. Morel. Mother and son stood on the road to watch. Along the ridge of the great pit-hill crawled a little group in silhouette against the sky, a horse, a small truck, and a man. They climbed the incline against the heavens. At the end the man tipped the wagon. There was an undue rattle as the waste fell down the sheer slope of the enormous bank.

"You sit a minute, mother," he said, and she took a seat on a bank, whilst he sketched rapidly. She was silent whilst he worked, looking round at the afternoon, the red cottages shining among their greenness.

"The world is a wonderful place," she said, "and wonderfully beautiful."

"And so's the pit," he said. "Look how it heaps together, like something alive almost—a big creature that you don't know."

"Yes," she said. "Perhaps!"

"And all the trucks standing waiting, like a string of beasts to be fed," he said.

"And very thankful I am they *are* standing," she said, "for that means they'll turn middling time this week."

"But I like the feel of *men* on things, while they're alive. There's a feel of men about trucks, because they've been handled with men's hands, all of them."

"Yes," said Mrs. Morel.

They went along under the trees of the highroad. He was constantly informing her, but she was interested. They passed the end of Nethermere, that was tossing its sunshine like petals lightly in its lap. Then they turned on a private road, and in some trepidation approached a big farm. A dog barked furiously. A woman came out to see.

"Is this the way to Willey Farm?" Mrs. Morel asked.

Paul hung behind in terror of being sent back. But the woman was amiable, and directed them. The mother and son went through the wheat and oats, over a little bridge into a wild meadow. Peewits, with their white breasts glistening, wheeled and screamed about them. The lake was still and blue. High overhead a heron floated. Opposite, the wood heaped on the hill, green and still.

"It's a wild road, mother," said Paul. "Just like Canada."

"Isn't it beautiful!" said Mrs. Morel, looking round.

"See that heron—see—see her legs?"

He directed his mother, what she must see and what not. And she was quite content.

"But now," she said, "which way? He told me through the wood."

The wood, fenced and dark, lay on their left.

"I can feel a bit of a path this road," said Paul. "You've got town feet, somehow or other, you have."

They found a little gate, and soon were in a broad green alley of the wood, with a new thicket of fir and pine on one hand, an old oak glade dipping down on the other. And among the oaks the bluebells stood in pools of azure, under the new green hazels, upon a pale fawn floor of oak leaves. He found flowers for her.

"Here's a bit of new-mown hay," he said; then, again, he brought her forget-me-nots. And, again, his heart hurt with love, seeing her hand, used with work, holding the little bunch of flowers he gave her. She was perfectly happy.

But at the end of the riding was a fence to climb. Paul was over in a second.

"Come," he said, "let me help you."

"No, go away. I will do it in my own way."

He stood below with his hands up ready to help her. She climbed cautiously.

"What a way to climb!" he exclaimed scornfully, when she was safely to earth again.

"Hateful stiles!" she cried.

"Duffer of a little woman," he replied, "who can't get over 'em."

In front, along the edge of the wood, was a cluster of low red farm buildings. The two hastened forward. Flush with the wood was the apple orchard, where blossom was falling on the grindstone. The pond was deep under a hedge and overhanging oak trees. Some cows stood in the shade. The farm and buildings, three sides of a quadrangle, embraced the sunshine towards the wood. It was very still.

Mother and son went into the small railed garden, where was a scent of red gillivers. By the open door were some floury loaves, put out to cool. A hen was just coming to peck them. Then, in the doorway suddenly appeared a girl in a dirty apron. She was about fourteen years old, had a rosy dark face, a bunch of short black curls, very fine and free, and dark eyes; shy, questioning, a little resentful of the strangers, she disappeared. In a minute another figure appeared, a small, frail woman, rosy, with great dark brown eyes.

"Oh!" she exclaimed, smiling with a little glow, "you've come, then. I *am* glad to see you." Her voice was intimate and rather sad.

The two women shook hands.

"Now are you sure we're not a bother to you?" said Mrs. Morel. "I know what a farming life is."

"Oh, no! We're only too thankful to see a new face, it's so lost up here."

"I suppose so," said Mrs. Morel.

They were taken through into the parlor—a long, low room, with a great bunch of guelder roses in the fireplace. There the women talked, whilst Paul went out to survey the land. He was in the garden smelling the gillivers and looking at the plants, when the girl came out quickly to the heap of coal which stood by the fence.

"I suppose these are cabbage roses?" he said to her, pointing to the bushes along the fence.

She looked at him with startled, big brown eyes.

"I suppose they are cabbage roses when they come out?" he said.

"I don't know," she faltered. "They're white with pink middles."

"Then they're maiden-blush."

Miriam flushed. She had a beautiful warm coloring.

"I don't know," she said.

"You don't have *much* in your garden," he said.

"This is our first year here," she answered, in a distant, rather superior way, drawing back and going indoors. He did not notice, but went his round of exploration. Presently his mother came out, and they went through the buildings. Paul was hugely delighted.

"And I suppose you have the fowls and calves and pigs to look after?" said Mrs. Morel to Mrs. Leivers.

"No," replied the little woman. "I can't find time to look after cattle, and I'm not used to it. It's as much as I can do to keep going in the house."

"Well, I suppose it is," said Mrs. Morel.

Presently the girl came out.

"Tea is ready, mother," she said in a musical, quiet voice.

"Oh, thank you, Miriam, then we'll come," replied her mother, almost ingratiatingly. "Would you *care* to have tea now, Mrs. Morel?"

"Of course," said Mrs. Morel. "Whenever it's ready."

Paul and his mother and Mrs. Leivers had tea together. Then they went out into the wood that was flooded with bluebells, while fumy forget-me-nots were in the paths. The mother and son were in ecstasy together.

When they got back to the house, Mr. Leivers and Edgar, the eldest son, were in the kitchen. Edgar was about eighteen. Then Geoffrey and Maurice, big lads of twelve and thirteen, were in from school. Mr. Leivers was a good-looking man in the prime of life, with a golden-brown moustache, and blue eyes screwed up against the weather.

The boys were condescending, but Paul scarcely observed it. They went round for eggs, scrambling into all sorts of places. As they were feeding the fowls Miriam came out. The boys took no notice of her. One hen, with her yellow chickens, was in a coop. Maurice took his hand full of corn and let the hen peck from it.

"Durst you do it?" he asked of Paul.

"Let's see," said Paul.

He had a small hand, warm, and rather capable-looking. Miriam watched. He held the corn to the hen. The bird eyed it with her hard, bright eye, and suddenly made a peck into his hand. He started, and laughed. "Rap, rap, rap!" went the bird's beak in his palm. He laughed again, and the other boys joined.

"She knocks you, and nips you, but she never hurts," said Paul, when the last corn had gone.

"Now, Miriam," said Maurice, "you come an' 'ave a go."

"No," she cried, shrinking back.

"Ha! baby. The mardy-kid!" said her brothers.

"It doesn't hurt a bit," said Paul. "It only just nips rather nicely."

"No," she still cried, shaking her black curls and shrinking.

"She durstn't, " said Geoffrey. "She niver durst do anything except recite poitry."

"Dursn't jump off a gate, dursn't tweedle, dursn't go on a slide, dursn't stop a girl hittin' her. She can do nowt but go about thinkin' herself somebody. 'The Lady of the Lake.' Yah!" cried Maurice.

Miriam was crimson with shame and misery.

"I dare do more than you," she cried. "You're never anything but cowards and bullies."

"Oh, cowards and bullies!" they repeated, mincingly mocking her speech.

Not such a clown shall anger me,
A boor is answered silently

he quoted against her, shouting with laughter.

She went indoors. Paul went with the boys into the orchard, where they had rigged up a parallel bar. They did feats of strength. He was more agile than strong, but it served. He fingered a piece of apple blossom that hung low on a swinging bough.

"I wouldn't get the apple blossom," said Edgar, the eldest brother. "There'll be no apples next year."

"I wasn't going to get it," replied Paul, going away.

The boys felt hostile to him; they were more interested in their own pursuits. He wandered back to the house to look for his mother. As he went round the back, he saw Miriam kneeling in front of the hencoop, some maize in her hand, biting her lip, and crouching in an intense attitude. The hen was eyeing her wickedly. Very gingerly she put forward her hand. The hen bobbed for her. She drew back quickly with a cry, half of fear, half of chagrin.

"It won't hurt you," said Paul.

She flushed crimson and started up.

"I only wanted to try," she said in a low voice.

"See, it doesn't hurt," he said, and, putting only two corns in his palm, he let the hen peck, peck, peck at his bare hand. "It only makes you laugh," he said.

She put her hand forward, and dragged it away, tried again, and started back with a cry. He frowned.

"Why, I'd let her take corn from my face," said Paul, "only she bumps a bit. She's ever so neat. If she wasn't, look how much ground she'd peck up every day."

He waited grimly, and watched. At last Miriam let the bird peck from her hand. She gave a little cry—fear, and pain because of fear—rather pathetic. But she had done it, and she did it again.

"There, you see," said the boy. "It doesn't hurt, does it?"

She looked at him with dilated dark eyes.

"No," she laughed, trembling.

Then she rose and went indoors. She seemed to be in some way resentful of the boy.

"He thinks I'm only a common girl," she thought, and she wanted to prove she was a grand person like the "Lady of the Lake."

Paul found his mother ready to go home. She smiled on her son. He took the great bunch of flowers. Mr. and Mrs. Leivers walked down the fields with them. The hills were golden with evening; deep in the wood showed the darkening purple of bluebells. It was everywhere perfectly still, save for the rustling of leaves and birds.

"But it is a beautiful place," said Mrs. Morel.

"Yes," answered Mr. Leivers; "it's a nice little place, if only it weren't for the rabbits. The pasture's bitten down to nothing. I dunno if ever I s'll get the rent off it."

He clapped his hands, and the field broke into motion near the woods, brown rabbits hopping everywhere.

"Would you believe it!" exclaimed Mrs. Morel.

She and Paul went on alone together.

"Wasn't it lovely, mother?" he said quietly.

A thin moon was coming out. His heart was full of happiness till it hurt. His mother had to chatter, because she, too, wanted to cry with happiness.

"Now *wouldn't* I help that man!" she said. "*Wouldn't* I see to the fowls and the young stock! And *I'd* learn to milk, and *I'd* talk with him, and *I'd* plan with him. My word, if I were his wife, the farm would be run, I know! But there, she hasn't the strength—she simply hasn't the strength. She ought never to have been burdened like it, you know. I'm sorry for her, and I'm sorry for him too. My word, if *I'd* had him, I shouldn't have thought him a bad husband! Not that she does either; and she's very lovable."

William came home again with his sweetheart at the Whitsuntide. He had one week of his holidays then. It was beautiful weather. As a rule, William and Lily and Paul went out in the morning together for a walk. William did not talk to his beloved much, except to tell her things from his boyhood. Paul talked endlessly to both of them. They lay down, all three, in a meadow by Minton Church. On one side, by the Castle Farm, was a beautiful quivering screen of poplars. Hawthorn was dropping from the hedges; penny daisies and ragged robin were in the field, like laughter. William, a big fellow of twenty-three, thinner now and even a bit gaunt, lay back in the sunshine and dreamed, while she fingered with his hair. Paul went gathering the big daisies. She had taken off her hat; her hair was black as a horse's mane. Paul came back and threaded daisies in her jet-black hair—big spangles of white and yellow, and just a pink touch of ragged robin.

"Now you look like a young witch-woman," the boy said to her. "Doesn't she, William?"

Lily laughed. William opened his eyes and looked at her. In his gaze was a certain baffled look of misery and fierce appreciation.

"Has he made a sight of me?" she asked, laughing down on her lover.

"That he has!" said William, smiling.

He looked at her. Her beauty seemed to hurt him. He glanced at her flower-decked head and frowned.

"You look nice enough, if that's what you want to know," he said.

And she walked without her hat. In a little while William recovered, and was rather tender to her. Coming to a bridge, he carved her initials and his in a heart.

She watched his strong, nervous hand, with its glistening hairs and freckles, as he carved, and she seemed fascinated by it.

All the time there was a feeling of sadness and warmth, and a certain tenderness in the house, whilst William and Lily were at home. But often he got irritable. She had brought, for an eight-days' stay, five dresses and six blouses.

"Oh, would you mind," she said to Annie, "washing me these two blouses, and these things?"

And Annie stood washing when William and Lily went out the next morning. Mrs. Morel was furious. And sometimes the young man, catching a glimpse of his sweetheart's attitude towards his sister, hated her.

On Sunday morning she looked very beautiful in a dress of foulard, silky and sweeping, and blue as a jaybird's feather, and in a large cream hat covered with many roses, mostly crimson. Nobody could admire her enough. But in the evening, when she was going out, she asked again:

"Chubby, have you got my gloves?"

"Which?" asked William.

"My new black *suede*."

"No."

There was a hunt. She had lost them.

"Look here, mother," said William, "that's the fourth pair she's lost since Christmas—at five shillings a pair!"

"You only gave me *two* of them," she remonstrated.

And in the evening, after supper, he stood on the hearthrug whilst she sat on the sofa, and he seemed to hate her. In the afternoon he had left her whilst he went to see some old friend. She had sat looking at a book. After supper William wanted to write a letter.

"Here is your book, Lily," said Mrs. Morel. "Would you care to go on with it for a few minutes?"

"No, thank you," said the girl. "I will sit still."

"But it is so dull."

William scribbled irritably at a great rate. As he sealed the envelope he said:

"Read a book! Why, she's never read a book in her life!"

"Oh, go along!" said Mrs. Morel, cross with the exaggeration.

"It's true, mother—she hasn't," he cried, jumping up and taking his old position on the hearthrug. "She's never read a book in her life."

" 'Er's like me," chimed in Morel. " 'Er canna see what there is i' books, ter sit borin' your nose in 'em for, nor more can I."

"But you shouldn't say these things," said Mrs. Morel to her son.

"But it's true, mother—she *can't* read. What did you give her?"

"Well, I gave her a little thing of Annie Swan's. Nobody wants to read dry stuff on Sunday afternoon."

"Well, I'll bet she didn't read ten lines of it."

"You are mistaken," said his mother.

All the time Lily sat miserably on the sofa. He turned to her swiftly.

"*Did* you read any?" he asked.

"Yes, I did," she replied.

"How much?"

"I don't know how many pages."

"Tell me *one thing* you read."

She could not.

She never got beyond the second page. He read a great deal, and had a quick, active intelligence. She could understand nothing but lovemaking and chatter. He was accustomed to having all his thoughts sifted through his mother's mind; so, when he wanted companionship, and was asked in reply to be the billing and twittering lover, he hated his betrothed.

"You know, mother," he said, when he was alone with her at night, "she's no idea of money, she's so weasel-brained. When she's paid, she'll suddenly buy such rot as *marrrons glacés*, and then *I* have to buy her season-ticket, and her extras, even her underclothing. And she wants to get married, and I think myself we might as well get married next year. But at this rate——"

"A fine mess of a marriage it would be," replied his mother. "I should consider it again, my boy."

"Oh, well, I've gone too far to break off now," he said, "and so I shall get married as soon as I can."

"Very well, my boy. If you will, you will, and there's no stopping you; but I tell you, *I* can't sleep when I think about it."

"Oh, she'll be all right, mother. We shall manage."

"And she lets you buy her underclothing?" asked the mother.

"Well," he began apologetically, "she didn't ask me; but one morning—and it *was* cold—I found her on the station shivering, not able to keep still; so I asked her if she was well wrapped up. She said: 'I think so' So I said: 'Have you got warm underthings on?' And she said: 'No, they are cotton.' I asked her why on earth she hadn't got something thicker on in weather like that, and she said because she *had* nothing. And there she is—a bronchial subject! I *had* to take her and get some warm things. Well, mother, I shouldn't mind the money if we had any. And, you know, she *ought* to keep enough to pay for her season-ticket; but no, she comes to me about that, and I have to find the money."

"It's a poor lookout," said Mrs. Morel bitterly.

He was pale, and his rugged face, that used to be so perfectly careless and laughing, was stamped with conflict and despair.

"But I can't give her up now; it's gone too far," he said. "And, besides, for *some* things I couldn't do without her."

"My boy, remember you're taking your life in your hands," said Mrs. Morel. "*Nothing* is as bad as a marriage that's a hopeless failure. Mine was bad enough, God knows, and ought to teach you something; but it might have been worse by a long chalk."

He leaned with his back against the side of the chimney piece, his hands in his pockets. He was a big, raw-boned man, who looked as if he would go to the world's end if he wanted to. But she saw the despair on his face.

"I couldn't give her up now," he said.

"Well," she said, "remember there are worse wrongs than breaking off an engagement."

"I can't give her up *now*," he said.

The clock ticked on; mother and son remained in silence, a conflict between them; but he would say no more. At last she said:

"Well, go to bed, my son. You'll feel better in the morning, and perhaps you'll know better."

He kissed her, and went. She raked the fire. Her heart was heavy now as it had never been. Before, with her husband, things had seemed to be breaking down in her, but they did not destroy her power to live. Now her soul felt lamed in itself. It was her hope that was struck.

And so often William manifested the same hatred towards his betrothed. On the last evening at home he was railing against her.

"Well," he said, "if you don't believe me, what she's like, would you believe she has been confirmed three times?"

"Nonsense!" laughed Mrs. Morel.

"Nonsense or not, she *has*! That's what confirmation means for her—a bit of a theatrical show where she can cut a figure."

"I haven't, Mrs. Morel!" cried the girl—"I haven't! it is not true!"

"What!" he cried, flashing round on her. "Once in Bromley, once in Beckenham, and once somewhere else."

"Nowhere else!" she said, in tears—"nowhere else!"

"It *was*! And if it wasn't, why were you confirmed *twice*?"

"Once I was only fourteen, Mrs. Morel," she pleaded, tears in her eyes.

"Yes," said Mrs. Morel; "I can quite understand it, child. Take no notice of him. You ought to be ashamed, William, saying such things."

"But it's true. She's religious—she has blue velvet Prayer Books—and she's not as much religion, or anything else, in her than that table leg. Gets confirmed three times for show, to show herself off, and that's how she is in *everything—everything*!"

The girl sat on the sofa, crying. She was not strong.

"As for *love*!" he cried, "you might as well as a fly to love you! It'll love settling on you——"

"Now, say no more," commanded Mrs. Morel. "If you want to say these things, you must find another place than this. I am ashamed of you, William! Why don't you be more manly? To do nothing but find fault with a girl, and then pretend you're engaged to her!"

Mrs. Morel subsided in wrath and indignation.

William was silent, and later he repented, kissed and comforted the girl. Yet it was true, what he had said. He hated her.

When they were going away, Mrs. Morel accompanied them as far as

Nottingham. It was a long way to Keston station.

"You know, mother," he said to her, "Gyp's shallow. Nothing goes deep with her."

"William, I *wish* you wouldn't say these things," said Mrs. Morel, very uncomfortable for the girl who walked beside her.

"But it doesn't, mother. She's very much in love with me *now*, but if I died she'd have forgotten me in three months."

Mrs. Morel was afraid. Her heart beat furiously, hearing the quiet bitterness of her son's last speech.

"How do you know?" she replied. "You *don't* know, and therefore you've no right to say such a thing."

"He's always saying these things!" cried the girl.

"In three months after I was buried you'd have somebody else, and I should be forgotten," he said. "And that's your love!"

Mrs. Morel saw them into the train in Nottingham, then she returned home.

"There's one comfort," she said to Paul—"he'll never have any money to marry on, that I *am* sure of. And so she'll save him that way."

So she took cheer. Matters were not yet very desperate. She firmly believed William would never marry his Gypsy. She waited, and she kept Paul near to her.

All summer long William's letters had a feverish tone; he seemed unnatural and intense. Sometimes he was exaggeratedly jolly, usually he was flat and bitter in his letter.

"Ay," his mother said, "I'm afraid he's ruining himself against that creature, who isn't worthy of his love—no, no more than a rag doll."

He wanted to come home. The midsummer holiday was gone; it was a long while to Christmas. He wrote in wild excitement, saying he could come for Saturday and Sunday at Goose Fair, the first week in October.

"You are not well, my boy," said his mother, when she saw him.

She was almost in tears at having him to herself again.

"No, I've not been well," he said. "I've seemed to have a dragging cold all the last month, but it's going, I think."

It was sunny October weather. He seemed wild with joy, like a schoolboy escaped; then again he was silent and reserved. He was more gaunt than ever, and there was a haggard look in his eyes.

"You are doing too much," said his mother to him.

He was doing extra work, trying to make some money to marry on, he said. He only talked to his mother once on the Saturday night; then he was sad and tender about his beloved.

"And yet, you know, mother, for all that, if I died she'd be brokenhearted for two months, and then she'd start to forget me. You'd see, she'd never come home here to look at my grave, not even once."

"Why, William," said his mother, "you're not going to die, so why talk about it?"

"But whether or not—" he replied.

"And she can't help it. She is like that, and if you choose her—well, you can't grumble," said his mother.

On the Sunday morning, as he was putting his collar on:

"Look," he said to his mother, holding up his chin, "what a rash my collar's made under my chin!"

Just at the junction of chin and throat was a big red inflammation.

"It ought not to do that," said his mother. "Here, put a bit of this soothing ointment on. You should wear different collars."

He went away on Sunday midnight, seeming better and more solid for his two days at home.

On Tuesday morning came a telegram from London that he was ill. Mrs. Morel got off her knees from washing the floor, read the telegram, called a neighbor, went to her landlady and borrowed a sovereign, put on her things, and set off. She hurried to Keston, caught an express for London in Nottingham. She had to wait in Nottingham nearly an hour. A small figure in her black bonnet, she was anxiously asking the porters if they knew how to get to Elmers End. The journey was three hours. She sat in her corner in a kind of stupor, never moving. At King's Cross still no one could tell her how to get to Elmers End. Carrying her string bag, that contained her nightdress, comb and brush, she went from person to person. At last they sent her underground to Cannon Street.

It was six o'clock when she arrived at William's lodging. The blinds were not down.

"How is he?" she asked.

"No better," said the landlady.

She followed the woman upstairs. William lay on the bed, with bloodshot eyes, his face rather discolored. The clothes were tossed about, there was no fire in the room, a glass of milk stood on the stand at his bedside. No one had been with him.

"Why, my son!" said the mother bravely.

He did not answer. He looked at her, but did not see her. Then he began to say, in a dull voice, as if repeating a letter from dictation: "Owing to a leakage in the hold of this vessel, the sugar had set, and become converted into rock. It needed hacking——"

He was quite unconscious. It had been his business to examine some such cargo of sugar in the Port of London.

"How long has he been like this?" the mother asked the landlady.

"He got home at six o'clock on Monday morning, and he seemed to sleep all day; then in the night we heard him talking, and this morning he asked for you. So I wired, and we fetched the doctor."

"Will you have a fire made?"

Mrs. Morel tried to soothe her son, to keep him still.

The doctor came. It was pneumonia, and, he said, a peculiar erysipelas, which had started under the chin where the collar chafed, and was spreading over the face. He hoped it would not get to the brain.

Mrs. Morel settled down to nurse. She prayed for William, prayed that he would recognize her. But the young man's face grew more discolored. In the night she struggled with him. He raved, and raved, and would not come to consciousness. At two o'clock, in a dreadful paroxysm, he died.

Mrs. Morel sat perfectly still for an hour in the lodging bedroom; then she roused the household.

At six o'clock, with the aid of the charwoman, she laid him out; then she went round the dreary London village to the registrar and the doctor.

At nine o'clock to the cottage on Scargill Street came another wire:

"William died last night. Let father come, bring money."

Annie, Paul, and Arthur were at home; Mr. Morel was gone to work. The three children said not a word. Annie began to whimper with fear; Paul set off for his father.

It was a beautiful day. At Brinsley pit the white steam melted slowly in the sunshine of a soft blue sky; the wheels of the headstocks twinkled high up; the screen, shuffling its coal into the trucks, made a busy noise.

"I want my father; he's got to go to London," said the boy to the first man he met on the bank.

"Tha wants Walter Morel? Go in theer an' tell Joe Ward."

Paul went into the little top office.

"I want my father; he's got to go to London."

"Thy feyther? Is he down? What's his name?"

"Mr. Morel."

"What, Walter? Is owt amiss?"

"He's got to go to London."

The man went to the telephone and rang up the bottom office.

"Walter Morel's wanted. Number 42, Hard. Summat's amiss; there's his lad here."

Then he turned round to Paul.

"He'll be up in a few minutes," he said.

Paul wandered out to the pit-top. He watched the chair come up, with its wagon of coal. The great iron cage sank back on its rest, a full carfle was hauled off, an empty tram run on to the chair, a bell ting'ed somewhere, the chair heaved, then dropped like a stone.

Paul did not realize William was dead; it was impossible, with such a bustle going on. The puller-off swung the small truck on to the turntable, another man ran with it along the bank down the curving lines.

"And William is dead, and my mother's in London, and what will she be doing?" the boy asked himself, as if it were a conundrum.

He watched chair after chair come up, and still no father. At last, standing beside a wagon, a man's form! The chair sank on its rests, Morel stepped off. He was slightly lame from an accident.

"Is it thee, Paul? Is 'e worse?"

"You've got to go to London."

The two walked off the pit-bank, where men were watching curiously. As they came out and went along the railway, with the sunny autumn field on one side and a wall of trucks on the other, Morel said in a frightened voice:

" 'E's niver gone, child?"

"Yes."

"When wor't?"

The miner's voice was terrified.

"Last night. We had a telegram from my mother."

Morel walked on a few strides, then leaned up against a truck side, his hand over his eyes. He was not crying. Paul stood looking around, waiting. On the weighing machine a truck trundled slowly. Paul saw everything, except his father leaning against the truck as if he were tired.

Morel had only once before been to London. He set off, scared and peaked, to help his wife. That was on Wednesday. The children were left alone in the house. Paul went to work, Arthur went to school, and Annie had in a friend to be with her.

On Saturday night, as Paul was turning the corner, coming home from Keston, he saw his mother and father, who had come to Sethley Bridge Station. They were walking in silence in the dark, tired, straggling apart. The boy waited.

"Mother!" he said, in the darkness.

Mrs. Morel's small figure seemed not to observe. He spoke again.

"Paul!" she said, uninterestedly.

She let him kiss her, but she seemed unaware of him.

In the house she was the same—small, white, and mute. She noticed nothing, she said nothing, only:

"The coffin will be here tonight, Walter. You'd better see about some help." Then, turning to the children: "We're bringing him home."

Then she relapsed into the same mute looking into space, her hands folded on her lap. Paul, looking at her, felt he could not breathe. The house was dead silent.

"I went to work, mother," he said plaintively.

"Did you?" she answered dully.

After half an hour Morel, troubled and bewildered, came in again.

"Wheer s'll we ha'e him when he *does* come?" he asked his wife.

"In the front room."

"Then I'd better shift th' table?"

"Yes."

"An' ha'e him across th' chairs?"

"You know there—Yes, I suppose so."

Morel and Paul went, with a candle, into the parlor. There was no gas there. The father unscrewed the top of the big mahogany oval table, and cleared the middle of the room; then he arranged six chairs opposite each other, so that the coffin could stand on their beds.

"You niver seed such a length as he is!" said the miner, and watching anxiously as he worked.

Paul went to the bay window and looked out. The ash tree stood monstrous and black in front of the wide darkness. It was a faintly luminous night. Paul went back to his mother.

At ten o'clock Morel called:

"He's here!"

Everyone started. There was a noise of unbarring and unlocking the front door, which opened straight from the night into the room.

"Bring another candle," called Morel.

Annie and Arthur went. Paul followed with his mother. He stood with his arm round her waist in the inner doorway. Down the middle of the cleared room waited six chairs, face to face. In the window, against the lace curtains, Arthur held up one candle, and by the open door, against the night, Annie stood leaning forward, her brass candlestick glittering.

There was the noise of wheels. Outside in the darkness of the street below Paul could see horses and a black vehicle, one lamp, and a few pale faces; then some men, miners, all in their shirtsleeves, seemed to struggle in the obscurity. Presently two men appeared, bowed beneath a great weight. It was Morel and his neighbor.

"Steady!" called Morel, out of breath.

He and his fellow mounted the steep garden step, heaved into the candlelight with their gleaming coffin end. Limbs of other men were seen struggling behind. Morel and Burns, in front, staggered; the great dark weight swayed.

"Steady, steady!" cried Morel, as if in pain.

All the six bearers were up in the small garden, holding the great coffin aloft. There were three more steps to the door. The yellow lamp of the carriage shone alone down in the black road.

"Now then!" said Morel.

The coffin swayed, the men began to mount the three steps with their load. Annie's candle flickered, and she whimpered as the first men appeared, and the limbs and bowed heads of six men struggled to climb into the room, bearing the coffin that rode like sorrow on their living flesh.

"Oh, my son—my son!" Mrs. Morel sang softly, and each time the coffin swung to the unequal climbing of the men: "Oh, my son—my son—my son!"

"Mother!" Paul whimpered, his hand round her waist. "Mother!"

She did not hear.

"Oh, my son—my son!" she repeated.

Paul saw drops of sweat fall from his father's brow. Six men were in the room—six coatless men, with yielding, struggling limbs, filling the room and knocking against the furniture. The coffin veered, and was gently lowered on to the chairs. The sweat fell from Morel's face on its boards.

"My word, he's a weight!" said a man, and the five miners sighed, bowed, and, trembling with the struggle, descended the steps again, closing the door behind them.

The family was alone in the parlor with the great polished box. William, when laid out, was six feet four inches long. Like a monument lay the bright brown, ponderous coffin. Paul thought it would never be got out of the room again. His mother was stroking the polished wood.

They buried him on the Monday in the little cemetery on the hillside that looks over the fields at the big church and the houses. It was sunny, and the white chrysanthemums frilled themselves in the warmth.

Mrs. Morel could not be persuaded, after this, to talk and take her old bright interest in life. She remained shut off. All the way home in the train she had said to herself: "If only it could have been me!"

When Paul came home at night he found his mother sitting, her day's work done, with hands folded in her lap upon her coarse apron. She always used to have changed her dress and put on a black apron, before. Now Annie set his supper, and his mother sat looking blankly in front of her, her mouth shut tight. Then he beat his brains for news to tell her.

"Mother, Miss Jordan was down today, and she said my sketch of a colliery at work was beautiful."

But Mrs. Morel took no notice. Night after night he forced himself to tell her things, although she did not listen. It drove him almost insane to have her thus.

At last:

"What's a-matter, mother?" he asked.

She did not hear.

"What's a-matter?" he persisted. "Mother, what's a-matter?"

"You know what's the matter," she said irritably, turning away.

The lad—he was sixteen years old—went to bed drearily. He was cut off and wretched through October, November, and December. His mother tried, but she could not rouse herself. She could only brood on her dead son; he had been let to die so cruelly.

At last, on December 23, with his five shillings Christmas-box in his pocket, Paul wandered blindly home. His mother looked at him, and her heart stood still.

"What's the matter?" she asked.

"I'm badly, mother!" he replied. "Mr. Jordan gave me five shillings for a Christmas-box!"

He handed it to her with trembling hands. She put it on the table.

"You aren't glad!" he reproached her; but he trembled violently.

"Where hurts you?" she said, unbuttoning his overcoat.

It was the old question.

"I feel badly, mother."

She undressed him and put him to bed. He had pneumonia dangerously, the doctor said.

"Might he never have had it if I'd kept him at home, not let him go to Nottingham?" was one of the first things she asked.

"He might not have been so bad," said the doctor.

Mrs. Morel stood condemned on her own ground.

"I should have watched the living, not the dead," she told herself.

Paul was very ill. His mother lay in bed at nights with him; they could not afford a nurse. He grew worse, and the crisis approached. One night he tossed into consciousness in the ghastly, sickly feeling of dissolution, when all the cells in the boy seem in intense irritability to be breaking down and consciousness makes a last flare of struggle, like madness.

"I s'll die, mother!" he cried, heaving for breath on the pillow.

She lifted him up, crying in a small voice:

"Oh, my son—my son!"

That brought him to. He realized her. His whole will rose up and arrested him. He put his head on her breast, and took ease of her for love.

"For some things," said his aunt, "it was a good thing Paul was ill that Christmas. I believe it saved his mother."

Paul was in bed for seven weeks. He got up white and fragile. His father had bought him a pot of scarlet and gold tulips. They used to flame in the window in the March sunshine as he sat on the sofa chattering to his mother. The two knitted together in perfect intimacy. Mrs. Morel's life now rooted itself in Paul.

William had been a prophet. Mrs. Morel had a little present and a letter from Lily at Christmas. Mrs. Morel's sister had a letter at the New Year.

"I was at a ball last night. Some delightful people were there, and I enjoyed myself thoroughly," said the letter. "I had every dance—did not sit out one."

Mrs. Morel never heard any more of her.

Morel and his wife were gentle with each other for some time after the death of their son. He would go into a kind of daze, staring wide-eyed and blank across the room. Then he would get up suddenly and hurry out to the Three Spots, returning in his normal state. But never in his life would he go for a walk up Shepstone, past the office where his son had worked, and he always avoided the cemetery.

PART TWO

❖ 7 ❖

LAD-AND-GIRL LOVE

Paul had been many times up to Willey Farm during the autumn. He was friends with the two youngest boys, Edgar, the eldest, would not condescend at first. And Miriam also refused to be approached. She was afraid of being set at nought, as by her own brothers. The girl was romantic in her soul. Everywhere was a Walter Scott heroine being loved by men with helmets or with plumes in their caps. She herself was something of a princess turned into a swine-girl, in her own imagination. And she was afraid lest this boy, who, nevertheless, looked something like a Walter Scott hero, who could paint and speak French, and knew what algebra meant, and who went by train to Nottingham every day, might consider her simply as the swinegirl, unable to perceive the princess beneath; so she held aloof.

Her great companion was her mother. They were both brown-eyed, and inclined to be mystical, such women as treasure religion inside them, breathe it in their nostrils, and see the whole of life in a mist thereof. So to Miriam, Christ and God made one great figure, which she loved tremblingly and passionately when a tremendous sunset burned out the western sky, and Ediths, and Lucys, and Rowenas, Brian de Bois Guilberts, Rob Roys, and Guy Mannerings, rustled the sunny leaves in the morning, or sat in her bedroom aloft, alone, when it snowed. That was life to her. For the rest, she drudged in the house, which work she would not have minded had not her clean red floor been mucked up immediately by the trampling farm boots of her brothers. She madly wanted her little brother of four to let her swathe him and stifle him in her love; she went to church reverently, with bowed head, and quivered in anguish from the vulgarity of the other choirgirls and from the common-sounding voice of the curate; she fought with her brothers, whom she considered brutal louts; and she held not her father in too high esteem because he did not carry any mystical ideals cherished in his heart, but only wanted to have as easy a time as he could, and his meals when he was ready for them.

She hated her position as swinegirl. She wanted to be considered. She wanted to learn, thinking that if she could read, as Paul said he could read, *Colomba*, or the *Voyage autour de ma Chambre*, the world would have a different face for her and a deepened respect. She could not be princess by wealth or standing. So she was mad to have learning whereon to pride herself. For she was different from other folk, and must not be scooped up among the common fry. Learning was the only distinction to which she thought to aspire.

Her beauty—that of a shy, wild, quiveringly sensitive thing—seemed nothing to her. Even her soul, so strong for rhapsody, was not enough. She must have something to reinforce her pride, because she felt different from other people. Paul she eyed rather wistfully. On the whole, she scorned the male sex. But here was a new specimen, quick, light, graceful, who could be gentle and who could be sad, and who was clever, and who knew a lot, and who had a death in the family. The boy's poor morsel of learning exalted him almost sky-high in her esteem. Yet she tried hard to scorn him, because he would not see in her the princess but only the swinegirl. And he scarcely observed her.

Then he was so ill, and she felt he would be weak. Then she would be stronger than he. Then she could love him. If she could be mistress of him in his weakness, take care of him, if he could depend on her, if she could, as it were, have him in her arms, how she would love him!

As soon as the skies brightened and plum blossom was out, Paul drove off in the milkman's heavy float up to Willey Farm. Mr. Leivers shouted in a kindly fashion at the boy, then clicked to the horse as they climbed the hill slowly, in the freshness of the morning. White clouds went on their way, crowding to the back of the hills that were rousing in the springtime. The water of Nethermere lay below, very blue against the seared meadows and the thorn trees.

It was four and a half miles' drive. Tiny buds on the hedges, vivid as copper-green, were opening into rosettes; and thrushes called, and blackbirds shrieked and scolded. It was a new, glamorous world.

Miriam, peeping through the kitchen window, saw the horse walk through the big white gate into the farmyard that was backed by the oak-wood, still bare. Then a youth in a heavy overcoat climbed down. He put up his hands for the whip and the rug that the good-looking, ruddy farmer handed down to him.

Miriam appeared in the doorway. She was nearly sixteen, very beautiful, with her warm coloring, her gravity, her eyes dilating suddenly like an ecstasy.

"I say," said Paul, turning shyly aside, "Your daffodils are nearly out. Isn't it early? But don't they look cold?"

"Cold!" said Miriam, in her musical, caressing voice.

"The green on their buds—" and he faltered into silence timidly.

"Let me take the rug," said Miriam over-gently.

"I can carry it," he answered, rather injured. But he yielded it to her.

Then Mrs. Leivers appeared.

"I'm sure you're tired and cold," she said. "Let me take your coat. It *is* heavy. You mustn't walk far in it."

She helped him off with his coat. He was quite unused to such attention. She was almost smothered under its weight.

"Why, mother," laughed the farmer as he passed through the kitchen, swinging the great milk churns, "you've got almost more than you can manage there."

She beat up the sofa cushions for the youth.

The kitchen was very small and irregular. The farm had been originally a laborer's cottage. And the furniture was old and battered. But Paul loved it—loved the sack bag that formed the hearthrug, and the funny little corner under the stairs, and the small window deep in the corner, through which, bending a little, he could see the plum trees in the back garden and the lovely round hills beyond.

"Won't you lie down?" said Mrs. Leivers.

"Oh no; I'm not tired," he said. "Isn't it lovely coming out, don't you think? I saw a sloe bush in blossom and a lot of celandines. I'm glad it's sunny."

"Can I give you anything to eat or to drink?"

"No, thank you."

"How's your mother?"

"I think she's tired now. I think she's had too much to do. Perhaps in a little while she'll go to Skegness with me. Then she'll be able to rest. I s'll be glad if she can."

"Yes," replied Mrs. Leivers. "It's a wonder she isn't ill herself."

Miriam was moving about preparing dinner. Paul watched everything that happened. His face was pale and thin, but his eyes were quick and bright with life as ever. He watched the strange, almost rhapsodic way in which the girl moved about, carrying a great stew-jar to the oven, or looking in the saucepan. The atmosphere was different from that of his own home, where everything seemed so ordinary. When Mr. Leivers called loudly outside to the horse, that was reaching over to feed on the rose bushes in the garden, the girl started, looked round with dark eyes, as if something had come breaking in on her world. There was a sense of silence inside the house and out. Miriam seemed as in some dreamy tale, a maiden in bondage, her spirit dreaming in a land far away and magical. And her discolored, old blue frock and her broken boots seemed only like the romantic rags of King Cophetua's beggar maid.

She suddenly became aware of his keen blue eyes upon her, taking her all in. Instantly her broken boots and her frayed old frock hurt her. She resented his seeing everything. Even he knew that her stocking was not pulled up. She went into the scullery, blushing deeply. And afterwards her hands trembled slightly at her work. She nearly dropped all she handled. When her inside dream was shaken, her body quivered with trepidation. She resented that he saw so much.

Mrs. Leivers sat for some time talking to the boy, although she was needed at her work. She was too polite to leave him. Presently she excused herself and rose. After a while she looked into the tin saucepan.

"Oh *dear*, Miriam," she cried, "these potatoes have boiled dry!"

Miriam started as if she had been stung.

"*Have* they, mother?" she cried.

"I shouldn't care, Miriam," said the mother, "if I hadn't trusted them to you." She peered into the pan.

The girl stiffened as if from a blow. Her dark eyes dilated; she remained standing in the same spot.

"Well," she answered, gripped tight in self-conscious shame, "I'm sure I looked at them five minutes since."

"Yes," said the mother, "I know it's easily done."

"They're not much burned, " said Paul. "It doesn't matter, does it?"

Mrs. Leivers looked at the youth with her brown, hurt eyes.

"It wouldn't matter but for the boys," she said to him. "Only Miriam knows what a trouble they make if the potatoes are 'caught.' "

"Then," thought Paul to himself, "you shouldn't let them make a trouble."

After a while Edgar came in. He wore leggings, and his boots were covered with earth. He was rather small, rather formal, for a farmer. He glanced at Paul, nodded to him distantly, and said:

"Dinner ready?"

"Nearly, Edgar," replied the mother apologetically.

"I'm ready for mine," said the young man, taking up the newspaper and reading. Presently the rest of the family trooped in. Dinner was served. The meal went rather brutally. The over-gentleness and apologetic tone of the mother brought out all the brutality of manners in the sons. Edgar tasted the potatoes, moved his mouth quickly like a rabbit, looked indignantly at his mother, and said:

"These potatoes are burnt, mother."

"Yes, Edgar. I forgot them for a minute. Perhaps you'll have bread if you can't eat them."

Edgar looked in anger across at Miriam.

"What was Miriam doing that she couldn't attend to them?" he said.

Miriam looked up. Her mouth opened, her dark eyes blazed and winced, but she said nothing. She swallowed her anger and her shame, bowing her dark head.

"I'm sure she was trying hard," said the mother.

"She hasn't got sense even to boil the potatoes," said Edgar. "What is she kept at home for?"

"On'y for eating everything that's left in th' pantry," said Maurice.

"They don't forget that potato pie against our Miriam," laughed the father.

She was utterly humiliated. The mother sat in silence, suffering, like some saint out of place at the brutal board.

It puzzled Paul. He wondered vaguely why all this intense feeling went running because of a few burnt potatoes. The mother exalted everything—even a bit of housework—to the plane of a religious trust. The sons resented this; they felt themselves cut away underneath, and they answered with brutality and also with a sneering superciliousness.

Paul was just opening out from childhood into manhood. This atmosphere, where everything took a religious value, came with a subtle fascination to him. There was something in the air. His own mother was logical. Here there was something different, something he loved, something that at times he hated.

Miriam quarreled with her brothers fiercely. Later in the afternoon, when they had gone away again, her mother said:

"You disappointed me at dinnertime, Miriam."

The girl dropped her head.

"They are such *brutes*!" she suddenly cried, looking up with flashing eyes.

"But hadn't you promised not to answer them?" said the mother. "And I believed in you. I *can't* stand it when you wrangle."

"But they're so hateful!" cried Miriam, "and—and *low*."

"Yes, dear. But how often have I asked you not to answer Edgar back? Can't you let him say what he likes?"

"But why should he sày what he likes?"

"Aren't you strong enough to bear it, Miriam, if even for my sake? Are you so weak that you must wrangle with them?"

Mrs. Leivers stuck unflinchingly to this doctrine of "the other cheek." She could not instill it at all into the boys. With the girls she succeeded better, and Miriam was the child of her heart. The boys loathed the other cheek when it was presented to them. Miriam was often sufficiently lofty to turn it. Then they spat on her and hated her. But she walked in her proud humility, living within herself.

There was always this feeling of jangle and discord in the Leivers family. Although the boys resented so bitterly this eternal appeal to their deeper feelings of resignation and proud humility, yet it had its effect on them. They could not establish between themselves and an outsider just the ordinary human feeling and unexaggerated friendship; they were always restless for the something deeper. Ordinary folk seemed shallow to them, trivial and inconsiderable. And so they were unaccustomed, painfully uncouth in the simplest social intercourse, suffering, and yet insolent in their superiority. Then beneath was the yearning for the soul-intimacy to which they could not attain because they were too dumb, and every approach to close connection was blocked by their clumsy contempt of other people. They wanted genuine intimacy, but they could not get even normally near to anyone, because they scorned to take the first steps, they scorned the triviality which forms common human intercourse.

Paul fell under Mrs. Leivers' spell. Everything had a religious and intensified meaning when he was with her. His soul, hurt, highly developed, sought her as if for nourishment. Together they seemed to sift the vital fact from an experience.

Miriam was her mother's daughter. In the sunshine of the afternoon mother and daughter went down the fields with him. They looked for nests. There was a jenny wrens' in the hedge by the orchard.

"I *do* want you to see this," said Mrs. Leivers.

He crouched down and carefully put his finger through the thorns into the round door of the nest.

"It's almost as if you were feeling inside the live body of the bird," he said, "it's so warm. They say a bird makes its nest round like a cup with pressing its breast on it. Then how did it make the ceiling round, I wonder?"

The nest seemed to start into life for the two women. After that, Miriam came to see it every day. It seemed so close to her. Again, going down the hedgeside with the girl, he noticed the celandines, scalloped splashes of gold, on the side of the ditch.

"I like them," he said, "when their petals go flat back with the sunshine. They seem to be pressing themselves at the sun."

And then the celandines ever after drew her with a little spell. Anthropomorphic as she was, she stimulated him into appreciating things thus, and then they lived for her. She seemed to need things kindling in her imagination or in her soul before she felt she had them. And she was cut off from ordinary life by her religious intensity which made the world for her either a nunnery garden or a paradise, where sin and knowledge were not, or else an ugly, cruel thing.

So it was in this atmosphere of subtle intimacy, this meeting in their common feeling for something in nature, that their love started.

Personally, he was a long time before he realized her. For ten months he had to stay at home after his illness. For a while he went to Skegness with his mother, and was perfectly happy. But even from the seaside he wrote long letters to Mrs. Leivers about the shore and the sea. And he brought back his beloved sketches of the flat Lincoln coast, anxious for them to see. Almost they would interest the Leivers more than they interested his mother. It was not his art Mrs. Morel cared about; it was himself and his achievement. But Mrs. Leivers and her children were almost his disciples. They kindled him and made him glow to his work, whereas his mother's influence was to make him quietly determined, patient, dogged, unwearied.

He soon was friends with the boys, whose rudeness was only superficial. They had all, when they could trust themselves, a strange gentleness and lovableness.

"Will you come with me on to the fallow?" asked Edgar, rather hesitatingly.

Paul went joyfully, and spent the afternoon helping to hoe or to single turnips with his friend. He used to lie with the three brothers in the hay piled up in the barn, and tell them about Nottingham and about Jordan's. In return, they taught him to milk, and let him do little jobs—chopping hay or pulping turnips—just as much as he liked. At midsummer he worked all through hay harvest with them, and then he loved them. The family was so cut off from the world, actually. They seemed, somehow, like "les derniers fils d'une race épuisée." Though the lads were strong and healthy, yet they had all that over-sensitiveness and hanging back which made them so lonely, yet also such close, delicate friends once their intimacy was won. Paul loved them dearly, and they him.

Miriam came later. But he had come into her life before she made any mark on his. One dull afternoon, when the men were on the land and the rest at school, only Miriam and her mother at home, the girl said to him, after having hesitated for some time:

"Have you seen the swing?"

"No," he answered. "Where?"

"In the cowshed," she replied.

She always hesitated to offer or to show him anything. Men have such different standards of worth from women, and her dear things—the valuable things to her—her brothers had so often mocked or flouted.

"Come on, then," he replied, jumping up.

There were two cowsheds, one on either side of the barn. In the lower, darker shed there was standing for four cows. Hens flew scolding over the manger wall as the youth and girl went forward for the great thick rope which hung from the beam in the darkness overhead, and was pushed back over a peg in the wall.

"It's something like a rope!" he exclaimed appreciatively; and he sat down on it, anxious to try it. Then immediately he rose.

"Come on, then, and have first go," he said to the girl.

"See," she answered, going into the barn, "we put some bags on the seat"; and she made the swing comfortable for him. That gave her pleasure. He held the rope.

"Come on, then," he said to her.

"No, I won't go first," she answered.

She stood aside in her still, aloof fashion.

"Why?"

"You go," she pleaded.

Almost for the first time in her life she had the pleasure of giving up to a man, of spoiling him. Paul looked at her.

"All right," he said, sitting down. "Mind out!"

He set off with a spring, and in a moment was flying through the air, almost out of the door of the shed, the upper half of which was open, showing outside the drizzling rain, the filthy yard, the cattle standing disconsolate against the black cart shed, and at the back of all the gray-green wall of the wood. She stood below in her crimson tam-o'-shanter and watched. He looked down at her, and she saw his blue eyes sparkling.

"It's a treat of a swing," he said.

"Yes."

He was swinging through the air, every bit of him swinging, like a bird that swoops for joy of movement. And he looked down at her. Her crimson cap hung over her dark curls, her beautiful warm face, so still in a kind of brooding, was lifted towards him. It was dark and rather cold in the shed. Suddenly a swallow came down from the high roof and darted out of the door.

"I didn't know a bird was watching," he called.

He swung negligently. She could feel him falling and lifting through the air, as if he were lying on some force.

"Now I'll die," he said, in a detached, dreamy voice, as though he were the dying motion of the swing. She watched him, fascinated. Suddenly he put on the brake and jumped out.

"I've had a long turn," he said. "But it's a treat of a swing—it's a real treat of a swing!"

Miriam was amused that he took a swing so seriously and felt so warmly over it.

"No; you go on," she said.

"Why, don't you want one?" he asked, astonished.

"Well, not much. I'll have just a little."

She sat down, whilst he kept the bags in place for her.

"It's so ripping!" he said, setting her in motion. "Keep your heels up, or they'll bang the manger wall."

She felt the accuracy with which he caught her, exactly at the right moment, and the exactly proportionate strength of his thrust, and she was afraid. Down to her bowels went the hot wave of fear. She was in his hands. Again, firm and inevitable came the thrust at the right moment. She gripped the rope, almost swooning.

"Ha!" she laughed in fear. "No higher!"

"But you're not a *bit* high," he remonstrated.

"But no higher."

He heard the fear in her voice, and desisted. Her heart melted in hot pain when the moment came for him to thrust her forward again. But he left her alone. She began to breathe.

"Won't you really go any farther?" he asked. "Should I keep you there?"

"No; let me go by myself," she answered.

He moved aside and watched her.

"Why, you're scarcely moving," he said.

She laughed slightly with shame, and in a moment got down.

"They say if you can swing you won't be seasick," he said, as he mounted again. "I don't believe I should ever be seasick."

Away he went. There was something fascinating to her in him. For the moment he was nothing but a piece of swinging stuff; not a particle of him that did not swing. She could never lose herself so, nor could her brothers. It roused a warmth in her. It were almost as if he were a flame that had lit a warmth in her whilst he swung in the middle air.

And gradually the intimacy with the family concentrated for Paul on three persons—the mother, Edgar, and Miriam. To the mother he went for that sympathy and that appeal which seemed to draw him out. Edgar was his very close friend. And to Miriam he more or less condescended, because she seemed so humble.

But the girl gradually sought him out. If he brought up his sketchbook, it was she who pondered longest over the last picture. Then she would look up at him. Suddenly, her dark eyes alight like water that shakes with a stream of gold in the dark, she would ask:

"Why do I like this so?"

Always something in his breast shrank from these close, intimate, dazzled looks of hers.

"Why *do* you?" he asked.

"I don't know. It seems so true."

"It's because—it's because there is scarcely any shadow in it; it's more shimmery, as if I'd painted the shimmering protoplasm in the leaves and everywhere, and not the stiffness of the shape. That seems dead to me. Only this shimmeriness is the real living. The shape is a dead crust. The shimmer is inside really."

And she, with her little finger in her mouth, would ponder these sayings. They gave her a feeling of life again, and vivified things which had meant nothing to her. She managed to find some meaning in his struggling, abstract speeches. And they were the medium through which she came distinctly at her beloved objects.

Another day she sat at sunset whilst he was painting some pine trees which caught the red glare from the west. He had been quiet.

"There you are!" he said suddenly. "I wanted that. Now, look at them and tell me, are they pine trunks or are they red coals, standing-up pieces of fire in that darkness? There's God's burning bush for you, that burned not away."

Miriam looked, and was frightened. But the pine trunks were wonderful to her, and distinct. He packed his box and rose. Suddenly he looked at her.

"Why are you always sad?" he asked her.

"Sad!" she exclaimed, looking up at him with startled, wonderful brown eyes.

"Yes," he replied. "You are always, always sad."

"I am not—oh, not a bit!" she cried.

"But even your joy is like a flame coming off of sadness," he persisted. "You're never jolly or even just all right."

"No," she pondered. "I wonder—why."

"Because you're not; because you're different inside, like a pine tree, and then you flare up; but you're not just like an ordinary tree, with fidgety leaves and jolly——"

He got tangled up in his own speech; but she brooded on it, and he had a strange, roused sensation, as if his feelings were new. She got so near him. It was a strange stimulant.

Then sometimes he hated her. Her youngest brother was only five. He was a frail lad, with immense brown eyes in his quaint, fragile face—one of Reynold's "Choir of Angels," with a touch of elf. Often Miriam kneeled to the child and drew him to her.

"Eh, my Hubert!" she sang, in a voice heavy and surcharged with love. "Eh, my Hubert!"

And, folding him in her arms, she swayed slightly from side to side with love, her face half lifted, her eyes half closed, her voice drenched with love.

"Don't!" said the child, uneasy—"don't, Miriam!"

"Yes; you love me, don't you?" she murmured deep in her throat, almost as if she were in a trance, and swaying also as if she were swooned in an ecstasy of love.

"Don't!" repeated the child, a frown on his clear brow.

"You love me, don't you?" she murmured.

"What do you make such a *fuss* for?" cried Paul, all in suffering because of her extreme emotion. "Why can't you be ordinary with him?"

She let the child go, and rose, and said nothing. Her intensity, which would leave no emotion on a normal plane, irritated the youth into a frenzy. And this tearful, naked contact of her on small occasions shocked him. He was used to his mother's reserve. And on such occasions he was thankful in his heart and soul that he had his mother, so sane and wholesome.

All the life of Miriam's body was in her eyes, which were usually dark as a dark church, but could flame with light like a conflagration. Her face scarcely ever altered from its look of brooding. She might have been one of the women who went with Mary when Jesus was dead. Her body was not flexible and living. She walked with a swing, rather heavily, her head bowed forward, pondering. She was not clumsy, and yet none of her movements seemed quite *the* movement. Often, when wiping the dishes, she would stand in bewilderment and chagrin because she had pulled in two halves a cup or a tumbler. It was as if, in her fear and self-mistrust, she put too much strength into the effort. There was no looseness or abandon about her. Everything was gripped stiff with intensity, and her effort, overcharged, closed in on itself.

She rarely varied from her swinging, forward, intense walk. Occasionally she ran with Paul down the fields. Then her eyes blazed naked in a kind of ecstasy that frightened him. But she was physically afraid. If she were getting over a stile, she gripped his hands in a little hard anguish, and began to lose her presence of mind. And he could not persuade her to jump from even a small height. Her eyes dilated became exposed and palpitating.

"No!" she cried, half laughing in terror—"no!"

"You shall!" he cried, once, and, jerking her forward, he brought her falling from the fence. But her wild "Ah!" of pain, as if she were losing consciousness, cut him. She landed on her feet safely, and afterwards had courage in this respect.

She was very much dissatisfied with her lot.

"Don't you like being at home?" Paul asked her, surprised.

"Who would?" she answered, low and intense. "What is it? I'm all day cleaning what the boys make just as bad in five minutes. I don't *want* to be at home."

"What do you want, then?"

"I want to do something. I want a chance like anybody else. Why should I, because I'm a girl, be kept at home and not allowed to be anything? What chance *have* I?"

"Chance of what?"

"Of knowing anything—of learning, of doing anything. It's not fair, because I'm a woman."

She seemed very bitter. Paul wondered. In his own home Annie was almost glad to be a girl. She had not so much responsibility; things were lighter for her. She never wanted to be other than a girl. But Miriam almost fiercely wished she were a man. And yet she hated men at the same time.

"But it's as well to be a woman as a man," he said, frowning.

"Ha! Is it? Men have everything."

"I should think women ought to be as glad to be women as men are to be men," he answered.

"No!" she shook her head—"no! Everything the men have."

"But what do you want?" he asked.

"I want to learn. Why *should* it be that I know nothing?"

"What! such as mathematics and French?"

"Why *shouldn't* I know mathematics? Yes!" she cried, her eye expanding in a kind of defiance.

"Well, you can learn as much as I know," he said. "I'll teach you, if you like."

Her eyes dilated. She mistrusted him as teacher.

"Would you?" he asked.

Her head had dropped, and she was sucking her finger broodingly.

"Yes," she said hesitatingly.

He used to tell his mother all these things.

"I'm going to teach Miriam algebra," he said.

"Well," replied Mrs. Morel, "I hope she'll get fat on it."

When he went up to the farm on the Monday evening, it was drawing twilight. Miriam was just sweeping up the kitchen, and was kneeling at the hearth when he entered. Everyone was out but her. She looked round at him, flushed, her dark eyes shining, her fine hair falling about her face.

"Hello!" she said, soft and musical. "I knew it was you."

"How?"

"I knew your step. Nobody treads so quick and firm."

He sat down, sighing.

"Ready to do some algebra?" he asked, drawing a little book from his pocket.

"But——"

He could feel her backing away.

"You said you wanted," he insisted.

"Tonight, though?" she faltered.

"But I came on purpose. And if you want to learn it, you must begin."

She took up her ashes in the dustpan and looked at him, half tremulously, laughing.

"Yes, but tonight! You see, I haven't thought of it."

"Well, my goodness! Take the ashes and come."

He went and sat on the stone bench in the backyard, where the big milk cans were standing, tipped up, to air. The men were in the cowsheds. He could hear the little singsong of the milk spurting into the pails. Presently she came, bringing some big greenish apples.

"You know you like them," she said.

He took a bite.

"Sit down," he said, with his mouth full.

She was shortsighted, and peered over his shoulder. It irritated him. He gave her the book quickly.

"Here," he said. "It's only letters for figures. You put down '*a*' instead of '2' or '6.' "

They worked, he talking, she with her head down on the book. He was quick and hasty. She never answered. Occasionally, when he demanded of her, "Do you see?" she looked up at him, her eyes wide with the half-laugh that comes of fear. "Don't you?" he cried.

He had been too fast. But she said nothing. He questioned her more, then got hot. It made his blood rouse to see her there, as it were, at his mercy, her mouth open, her eyes dilated with laughter that was afraid, apologetic, ashamed. Then Edgar came along with two buckets of milk.

"Hello!" he said. "What are you doing?"

"Algebra," replied Paul.

"Algebra!" repeated Edgar curiously. Then he passed on with a laugh. Paul took a bite at his forgotten apple, looked at the miserable cabbages in the garden, pecked into lace by the fowls, and he wanted to pull them up. Then he glanced at Miriam. She was poring over the book, seemed absorbed in it, yet trembling lest she could not get at it. It made him cross. She was ruddy and beautiful. Yet her soul seemed to be intensely supplicating. The algebra book she closed, shrinking, knowing he was angered; and at the same instant he grew gentle, seeing her hurt because she did not understand.

But things came slowly to her. And when she held herself in a grip, seemed so utterly humble before the lesson, it made his blood rouse. He stormed at her, got ashamed, continued the lesson, and grew furious again, abusing her. She listened in silence. Occasionally, very rarely, she defended herself. Her liquid dark eyes blazed at him.

"You don't give me time to learn it," she said.

"All right," he answered, throwing the book on the table and lighting a cigarette. Then, after awhile, he went back to her repentant. So the lessons went. He was always either in a rage or very gentle.

"What do you tremble your *soul* before it for?" he cried. "You don't learn algebra with your blessed soul. Can't you look at it with your clear simple wits?"

Often, when he went again into the kitchen, Mrs. Leivers would look at him reproachfully, saying:

"Paul, don't be so hard on Miriam. She may not be quick, but I'm sure she tries."

"I can't help it," he said rather pitiably. "I go off like it."

"You don't mind me, Miriam, do you?" he asked of the girl later.

"No," she reassured him in her beautiful deep tones—"no, I don't mind."

"Don't mind me; it's my fault."

But, in spite of himself, his blood began to boil with her. It was strange that no one else made him in such fury. He flared against her. Once he threw the pencil in her face. There was a silence. She turned her face slightly aside.

"I didn't—" he began, but got no farther, feeling weak in all his bones. She never reproached him or was angry with him. He was often cruelly ashamed. But still again his anger burst like a bubble surcharged; and still, when he saw her eager, silent, as it were, blind face, he felt he wanted to throw the pencil in it; and still, when he saw her hand trembling and her mouth parted with suffering, his heart was scalded with pain for her. And because of the intensity to which she roused him, he sought her.

Then he often avoided her and went with Edgar. Miriam and her brother were naturally antagonistic. Edgar was a rationalist, who was curious, and had a sort of scientific interest in life. It was a great bitterness to Miriam to see herself deserted by Paul for Edgar, who seemed so much lower. But the youth was very happy with her elder brother. The two men spent afternoons together on the land or in the loft doing carpentry, when it rained. And they talked together, or Paul taught Edgar the songs he himself had learned from Annie at the piano. And often all the men, Mr. Leivers as well, had bitter debates on the nationalizing of the land and similar problems. Paul had already heard his mother's views, and as these were as yet his own, he argued for her. Miriam attended and took part, but was all the time waiting until it should be over and a personal communication might begin.

"After all," she said within herself, "if the land were nationalized, Edgar and Paul and I would be just the same." So she waited for the youth to come back to her.

He was studying for his painting. He loved to sit at home, alone with his mother, at night, working and working. She sewed or read. Then, looking up from his task, he would rest his eyes for a moment on her face, that was bright with living warmth, and he returned gladly to his work.

"I can do my best things when you sit there in your rocking chair, mother," he said.

"I'm sure!" she exclaimed, sniffing with mock skepticism. But she felt it was so, and her heart quivered with brightness. For many hours she sat still, slightly conscious of him laboring away, whilst she worked or read her book. And he, with all his soul's intensity directing his pencil, could feel her warmth inside him like strength. They were both very happy so, and both unconscious of it. These times, that meant so much, and which were real living, they almost ignored.

He was conscious only when stimulated. A sketch finished, he always wanted to take it to Miriam. Then he was stimulated into knowledge of the work he had produced unconsciously. In contact with Miriam he gained insight; his vision went deeper. From his mother he drew the life-warmth, the strength to produce; Miriam urged this warmth into intensity like a white light.

When he returned to the factory the conditions of work were better. He had Wednesday afternoon off to go to the Art School—Miss Jordan's provision—returning in the evening. Then the factory closed at six instead of at eight on Thursday and Friday evenings.

One evening in the summer Miriam and he went over the fields by Herod's Farm on their way from the library home. So it was only three miles to Willey Farm. There was a yellow glow over the mowing grass, and the sorrel heads burned crimson. Gradually, as they walked along the high land, the gold in the west sank down to red, the red to crimson, and then the chill blue crept up against the glow.

They came out upon the high road to Alfreton, which ran white between the darkening fields. There Paul hesitated. It was two miles home for him, one mile forward for Miriam. They both looked up the road that ran in shadow right under the glow of the northwest sky. On the crest of the hill, Selby, with its stark houses and the up-pricked headstocks of the pit, stood in black silhouette small against the sky.

He looked at his watch.

"Nine o'clock!" he said.

The pair stood, loath to part, hugging their books.

"The wood is so lovely now," she said. "I wanted you to see it."

He followed her slowly across the road to the white gate.

"They grumble so if I'm late," he said.

"But you're not doing anything wrong," she answered impatiently.

He followed her across the nibbled pasture in the dusk. There was a coolness in the wood, a scent of leaves, of honeysuckle, and a twilight. The two walked in silence. Night came wonderfully there, among the throng of dark tree trunks. He looked round, expectant.

She wanted to show him a certain wild rosebush she had discovered. She knew it was wonderful. And yet, till he had seen it, she felt it had not come into her soul. Only he could make it her own, immortal. She was dissatisfied.

Dew was already on the paths. In the old oak-wood a mist was rising, and he hesitated, wondering whether one whiteness were a strand of fog or only campion flowers pallid in a cloud.

By the time they came to the pine trees Miriam was getting very eager and very tense. Her bush might be gone. She might not be able to find it; and she wanted it so much. Almost passionately she wanted to be with him when he stood before the flowers. They were going to have a communion together—something that thrilled her, something holy. He was walking beside her in silence. They were very near to each other. She trembled, and he listened, vaguely anxious.

Coming to the edge of the wood, they saw the sky in front, like mother-of-pearl, and the earth growing dark. Somewhere on the outermost branches of the pine wood the honeysuckle was streaming scent.

"Where?" he asked.

"Down the middle path," she murmured, quivering.

When they turned the corner of the path she stood still. In the wide walk between the pines, gazing rather frightened, she could distinguish nothing for some moments; the graying light robbed things of their color. Then she saw her bush.

"Ah!" she cried, hastening forward.

It was very still. The tree was tall and straggling. It had thrown its briers over a hawthorn bush, and its long streamers trailed thick, right down to the grass, splashing the darkness everywhere with great spilt stars, pure white. In bosses of ivory and in large splashed stars the roses gleamed on the darkness of foliage and stems and grass. Paul and Miriam stood close together, silent, and watched. Point after point the steady roses shone out to them, seeming to kindle something in their souls. The dusk came like smoke around, and still did not put out the roses.

Paul looked into Miriam's eyes. She was pale and expectant with wonder, her lips were parted, and her dark eyes lay open to him. His look seemed to travel down into her. Her soul quivered. It was the communion she wanted. He turned aside, as if pained. He turned to the bush.

"They seem as if they walk like butterflies, and shake themselves," he said.

She looked at her roses. They were white, some incurved and holy, others expanded in an ecstasy. The tree was dark as a shadow. She lifted her hand impulsively to the flowers; she went forward and touched them in worship.

"Let us go," he said.

There was a cool scent of ivory roses—a white, virgin scent. Something made him feel anxious and imprisoned. The two walked in silence.

"Till Sunday," he said quietly, and left her; and she walked home slowly, feeling her soul satisfied with the holiness of the night. He stumbled down the path. And as soon as he was out of the wood, in the free open meadow, where he could breathe, he started to run as fast as he could. It was like a delicious delirium in his veins.

Always when he went with Miriam, and it grew rather late, he knew his mother was fretting and getting angry about him—why he could not understand. As he went into the house, flinging down his cap, his mother looked up at the clock. She had been sitting thinking, because a chill to her eyes prevented her reading. She could feel Paul being drawn away by this girl. And she did not care for Miriam. "She is one of those who will want to suck a man's soul out till he has none of his own left," she said to herself; "and he is just such a gaby as to let himself be absorbed. She will never let him become a man; she never will." So, while he was away with Miriam, Mrs. Morel grew more and more worked up.

She glanced at the clock and said, coldly and rather tired:

"You have been far enough tonight."

His soul, warm and exposed from contact with the girl, shrank.

"You must have been right home with her," his mother continued.

He would not answer. Mrs. Morel, looking at him quickly, saw his hair was damp on his forehead with haste, saw him frowning in his heavy fashion, resentfully.

"She must be wonderfully fascinating, that you can't get away from her, but must go trailing eight miles at this time of night."

He was hurt between the past glamor with Miriam and the knowledge that his mother fretted. He had meant not to say anything, to refuse to answer. But he could not harden his heart to ignore his mother.

"I *do* like to talk to her," he answered irritably.

"Is there nobody else to talk to?"

"You wouldn't say anything if I went with Edgar."

"You know I should. You know, whoever you went with, I should say it was too far for you to go trailing, late at night, when you've been to Nottingham. Besides"—her voice suddenly flashed into anger and contempt—"it is disgusting—bits of lads and girls courting."

"It is *not* courting," he cried.

"I don't know what else you call it."

"It's not! Do you think we *spoon* and do? We only talk."

"Till goodness knows what time and distance," was the sarcastic rejoinder.

Paul snapped at the laces of his boots angrily.

"What are you so mad about?" he asked. "Because you don't like her?"

"I don't say I don't like her. But I don't hold with children keeping company, and never did."

"But you don't mind our Annie going out with Jim Inger."

"They've more sense than you two."

"Why?"

"Our Annie's not one of the deep sort."

"Well," he said, "it's so pretty in the country. Mr. Sleath asked about you. He said he'd missed you. Are you a bit better?"

"I ought to have been in bed a long time ago," she replied.

"Why, mother, you know you wouldn't have gone before quarter-past ten."

"Oh yes, I should!"

"Oh, little woman, you'd say anything now you're disagreeable with me, wouldn't you?"

He kissed her forehead that he knew so well: the deep marks between the brows, the rising of the fine hair, graying now, and the proud setting of the temples. His hand lingered on her shoulder after his kiss. Then he went slowly to bed. He had forgotten Miriam; he only saw how his mother's hair was lifted back from her warm, broad brow. And somehow, she was hurt.

Then the next time he saw Miriam he said to her:

"Don't let me be late tonight—not later than ten o'clock. My mother gets so upset."

Miriam dropped her head, brooding.

"Why does she get upset?" she asked.

"Because she says I oughtn't to be out late when I have to get up early."

"Very well!" said Miriam, rather quietly, with just a touch of a sneer.

He resented that. And he was usually late again.

That there was any love growing between him and Miriam neither of them would have acknowledged. He thought he was too sane for such sentimentality, and she thought herself too lofty. They both were late in coming to maturity, and psychical ripeness was much behind even the physical. Miriam was exceedingly sensitive, as her mother had always been. The slightest grossness made her recoil almost in anguish. Her brothers were brutal, but never coarse in speech. The men did all the discussing of farm matters outside. But, perhaps because of the continual business of birth and of begetting which goes on upon every farm, Miriam was the more hypersensitive to the matter, and her blood was chastened almost to disgust of the faintest suggestion of such intercourse. Paul took his pitch from her, and their intimacy went on in an utterly blanched and chaste fashion. It could never be mentioned that the mare was in foal.

When he was nineteen, he was earning only twenty shillings a week, but he was happy. His painting went well, and life went well enough. On the Good Friday he organized a walk to the Hemlock Stone. There were three lads of his own age, then Annie and Arthur, Miriam and Geoffrey. Arthur, apprenticed as an electrician in Nottingham, was home for the holiday. Morel, as usual, was up early, whistling and sawing in the yard. At seven o'clock the family heard him buy threepennyworth of hot-cross buns; he talked with gusto to the little girl who brought them, calling her "my darling." He turned away several boys who came with more buns, telling them they had been "kested" by a little lass. Then Mrs. Morel got up, and the family straggled down. It was an immense luxury to everybody, this lying in bed just beyond the ordinary time on a weekday. And Paul and Arthur read before breakfast, and had the meal unwashed, sitting in their shirtsleeves. This was another holiday luxury. The room was warm. Everything felt free of care and anxiety. There was a sense of plenty in the house.

While the boys were reading, Mrs. Morel went into the garden. They were now in another house, an old one, near the Scargill Street home, which had been left soon after William had died. Directly came an excited cry from the garden:

"Paul, Paul! come and look!"

It was his mother's voice. He threw down his book and went out. There was a long garden that ran to a field. It was a gray, cold day, with a sharp wind blowing out of Derbyshire. Two fields away Bestwood began, with a jumble of roofs and red house-ends, out of which rose the church tower and the spire of the Congregational chapel. And beyond went woods and hills, right away to the pale gray heights of the Pennine Chain.

Paul looked down the garden for his mother. Her head appeared among the young currant bushes.

"Come here!" she cried.

"What for?" he answered.

"Come and see."

She had been looking at the buds on the currant trees. Paul went up.

"To think," she said, "that here I might never have seen them!"

Her son went to her side. Under the fence, in a little bed, was a ravel of poor grassy leaves, such as come from very immature bulbs, and three scyllas in bloom. Mrs. Morel pointed to the deep blue flowers.

"Now, just see those!" she exclaimed. "I was looking at the currant bushes, when, thinks I to myself, 'There's something very blue; is it a bit of sugar bag?' and there, behold you! Sugar bag! Three glories of the snow, and *such* beauties! But where on earth did they come from?"

"I don't know," said Paul.

"Well, that's a marvel, now! I *thought* I knew every weed and blade in this garden. But *haven't* they done well? You see, that gooseberry bush just shelters them. Not nipped, not touched!"

He crouched down and turned up the bells of the little blue flowers.

"They're a glorious color!" he said.

"Aren't they!" she cried. "I guess they come from Switzerland, where they say they have such lovely things. Fancy them against the snow! But where have they come from? They can't have *blown* here, can they?"

Then he remembered having set here a lot of little trash of bulbs to mature.

"And you never told me," she said.

"No; I thought I'd leave it till they might flower."

"And now, you see! I might have missed them. And I've never had a glory of the snow in my garden in my life."

She was full of excitement and elation. The garden was an endless joy to her. Paul was thankful for her sake at last to be in a house with a long garden that went down to a field. Every morning after breakfast she went out and was happy pottering about in it. And it was true, she knew every weed and blade.

Everybody turned up for the walk. Food was packed, and they set off, a merry, delighted party. They hung over the wall of the millrace, dropped paper in the water on one side the tunnel and watched it shoot out on the other. They stood on the footbridge over Boathouse Station and looked at the metals gleaming coldly.

"You should see the Flying Scotchman come through at half-past six!" said Leonard, whose father was a signalman. "Lad, but she doesn't half buzz!" and the little party looked up the lines one way, to London, and the other way, to Scotland, and they felt the touch of these two magical places.

In Ilkeston the colliers were waiting in gangs for the public houses to open. It was a town of idleness and lounging. At Stanton Gate the iron foundry blazed. Over everything there were great discussions. At Trowell they crossed again from Derbyshire into Nottinghamshire. They came to the Hemlock at dinnertime. Its field was crowded with folk from Nottingham and Ilkeston.

They had expected a venerable and dignified monument. They found a little, gnarled, twisted stump of rock, something like a decayed mushroom, standing out pathetically on the side of a field. Leonard and Dick immediately proceeded to carve their initials, "L. W." and "R. P.," in the old red sandstone; but Paul desisted, because he had read in the newspaper satirical remarks about initial-carvers, who could find no other road to immortality. Then all the lads climbed to the top of the rock to look round.

Everywhere in the field below, factory girls and lads were eating lunch or sporting about. Beyond was the garden of an old manor. It had yew hedges and thick clumps and borders of yellow crocuses round the lawn.

"See," said Paul to Miriam, "what a quiet garden!"

She saw the dark yews and the golden crocuses, then she looked at him gratefully. He had not seemed to belong to her among all these others; he was different then—not her Paul, who understood the slightest quiver of her innermost soul, but something else, speaking another language than hers. How it hurt her, and deadened her very perceptions. Only when he came right back to her, leaving his other, his lesser self, as she thought, would she feel alive again. And now he asked her to look at this garden, wanting the contact with her again. Impatient of the set in the field, she turned to the quiet lawn, surrounded by sheaves of shut-up crocuses. A feeling of stillness, almost of ecstasy, came over her. It felt almost as if she were alone with him in this garden.

Then he left her again and joined the others. Soon they started home. Miriam loitered behind, alone. She did not fit in with the others; she could very rarely get into human relations with anyone: so her friend, her companion, her lover, was Nature. She saw the sun declining wanly. In the dusky, cold hedgerows were some red leaves. She lingered to gather them, tenderly, passionately. The love in her fingertips caressed the leaves; the passion in her heart came to a glow upon the leaves.

Suddenly she realized she was alone in a strange road, and she hurried forward. Turning a corner in the lane, she came upon Paul, who stood bent over something, his mind fixed on it, working away steadily, patiently, a little hopelessly. She hesitated in her approach, to watch.

He remained concentrated in the middle of the road. Beyond, one rift of rich gold in that colorless gray evening seemed to make him stand out in dark relief. She saw him, slender and firm, as if the setting sun had given him to her. A deep pain took hold of her, and she knew she must love him. And she had discovered him, discovered him in him a rare potentiality, discovered his loneliness. Quivering as at some "annunciation," she went slowly forward.

At last he looked up.

"Why," he exclaimed gratefully, "have you waited for me!"

She saw a deep shadow in his eyes.

"What was it?" she asked.

"The spring broken here"; and he showed her where his umbrella was injured.

Instantly, with some shame, she knew he had not done the damage himself, but that Geoffrey was responsible.

"It is only an old umbrella, isn't it?" she asked.

She wondered why he, who did not usually trouble over trifles, made such a mountain of this molehill.

"But it was William's, an' my mother can't help but know," he said quietly, still patiently working at the umbrella.

The words went through Miriam like a blade. This, then, was the confirmation of her vision of him! She looked at him. But there was about him a certain reserve, and she dared not comfort him, not even speak softly to him.

"Come on," he said. "I can't do it"; and they went in silence along the road.

That same evening they were walking along under the trees by Nether Green. He was talking to her fretfully, seemed to be struggling to convince himself.

"You know," he said, with an effort, "if one person loves, the other does."

"Ah!" she answered. "Like mother said to me when I was little, 'Love begets love.' "

"Yes, something like that, I think it *must* be."

"I hope so, because, if it were not, love might be a very terrible thing," she said.

"Yes, but it *is*—at least with most people," he answered.

And Miriam, thinking he had assured himself, felt strong in herself. She always regarded that sudden coming upon him in the lane as a revelation. And this conversation remained graven in her mind as one of the letters of the law.

Now she stood with him and for him. When, about this time, he outraged the family feeling at Willey Farm by some overbearing insult, she stuck to him, and believed he was right. And at this time she dreamed dreams of him, vivid, unforgettable. These dreams came again later on, developed to a more subtle psychological stage.

On the Easter Monday the same party took an excursion to Wingfield Manor. It was great excitement to Miriam to catch a train at Sethley Bridge, amid all the bustle of the Bank Holiday crowd. They left the train at Alfreton. Paul was interested in the street and in the colliers with their dogs. Here was a new race of miners. Miriam did not live till they came to the church. They were all rather timid of entering, with their bags of food, for fear of being turned out. Leonard, a comic, thin fellow, went first; Paul, who would have died rather than be sent back, went last. The place was decorated for Easter. In the font hundreds of white narcissi seemed to be growing. The air was dim and colored from the windows, and thrilled with a subtle scent of lilies and narcissi. In that atmosphere Miriam's soul came into a glow. Paul was afraid of the things he mustn't do; and he was sensitive to the feel of the place. Miriam turned to him. He answered. They were together. He would not go beyond the Communion rail. She loved him for that. Her soul expanded into prayer beside him. He felt the strange fascination of shadowy religious places. All his latent mysticism quivered into life. She was drawn to him. He was a prayer along with her.

Miriam very rarely talked to the other lads. They at once became awkward in conversation with her. So usually she was silent.

It was past midday when they climbed the steep path to the manor. All things shone softly in the sun, which was wonderfully warm and enlivening. Celandines and violets were out. Everybody was tip-top full with happiness. The glitter of the ivy, the soft, atmospheric gray of the Castle walls, the gentleness of everything near the ruin, was perfect.

The manor is of hard, pale gray stone, and the outer walls are blank and calm. The young folk were in raptures. They went in trepidation, almost afraid that the delight of exploring this ruin might be denied them. In the first courtyard, within the high broken walls, were farm carts, with their shafts lying idle on the ground, the tires of the wheels brilliant with gold-red rust. It was very still.

All eagerly paid their sixpences, and went timidly through the fine clean arch of the inner courtyard. They were shy. Here on the pavement, where the hall had been, an old thorn tree was budding. All kinds of strange openings and broken rooms were in the shadow around them.

After lunch they set off once more to explore the ruin. This time the girls went with the boys, who could act as guides and expositors. There was one tall tower in a corner, rather tottering, where they say Mary Queen of Scots was imprisoned.

"Think of the Queen going up here,!" said Miriam in a low voice, as she climbed the hollow stairs.

"If she could get up," said Paul, "for she had rheumatism like anything. I reckon they treated her rottenly."

"You don't think she deserved it?" asked Miriam.

"No, I don't. She was only lively."

They continued to mount the winding staircase. A high wind, blowing through the loopholes, went rushing up the shaft, and filled the girl's skirts like a balloon, so that she was ashamed, until he took the hem of her dress and held it down for her. He did it perfectly simply, as he would have picked up her glove. She remembered this always.

Round the broken top of the tower the ivy bushed out, old and handsome. Also, there were a few chill gillivers, in pale cold bud. Miriam wanted to lean over for some ivy, but he would not let her. Instead, she had to wait behind him, and take from him each spray as he gathered it and held it to her, each one separately, in the purest manner of chivalry. The tower seemed to rock in the wind. They looked over miles and miles of wooded country, and country with gleams of pasture.

The crypt underneath the manor was beautiful, and in perfect preservation. Paul made a drawing: Miriam stayed with him. She was thinking of Mary Queen of Scots looking with her strained, hopeless eyes, that could not understand misery, over the hills whence no help came, or sitting in this crypt, being told of a God as cold as the place she sat in.

They set off again gaily, looking round on their beloved manor that stood so clean and big on its hill.

"Supposing you could have *that* farm," said Paul to Miriam.

"Yes!"

"Wouldn't it be lovely to come and see you!"

They were now in the bare country of stone walls, which he loved, and which, though only ten miles from home, seemed so foreign to Miriam. The party was straggling. As they were crossing a large meadow that sloped away from the sun, along a path embedded with innumerable tiny glittering points, Paul, walking alongside, laced his fingers in the strings of the bag Miriam was carrying, and instantly she felt Annie behind, watchful and jealous. But the meadow was bathed in a glory of sunshine, and the path was jeweled, and it was seldom that he gave her any sign. She held her fingers very still among the strings of the bag, his fingers touching, and the place was golden as a vision.

At last they came into the straggling gray village of Crich, that lies high. Beyond the village was the famous Crich Stand that Paul could see from the garden at home. The party pushed on. Great expanse of country spread around and below. The lads were eager to get to the top of the hill. It was capped by a round knoll, half of which was by now cut away, and on the top of which stood an ancient monument, sturdy and squat, for signaling in old days far down into the level lands of Nottinghamshire and Leicestershire.

It was blowing so hard, high up there in the exposed place, that the only way to be safe was to stand nailed by the wind to the wall of the tower. At their feet fell the precipice where the limestone was quarried away. Below was a jumble of hills and tiny villages—Matlock, Ambergate, Stoney Middleton. The lads were eager to spy out the church of Bestwood, far away among the rather crowded country on the left. They were disgusted that it seemed to stand on a plain. They saw the hills of Derbyshire fall into the monotony of the Midlands that swept away South.

Miriam was somewhat scared by the wind, but the lads enjoyed it. They went on, miles and miles, to Whatstandwell. All the food was eaten, everybody was hungry, and there was very little money to get home with. But they managed to procure a loaf and a currant loaf, which they hacked into pieces with shut knives, and ate sitting on the wall near the bridge, watching the bright Derwent rushing by, and the brakes from Matlock pulling up at the inn.

Paul was now pale with weariness. He had been responsible for the party all day, and now he was done. Miriam understood, and kept close to him, and he left himself in her hands.

They had an hour to wait at Ambergate Station. Trains came, crowded with excursionists returning to Manchester, Birmingham, and London.

"We might be going there—folk easily might think we're going that far," said Paul.

They got back rather late. Miriam, walking home with Geoffrey, watched the moon rise big and red and misty. She felt something was fulfilled in her.

She had an elder sister, Agatha, who was a schoolteacher. Between the two girls was a feud. Miriam considered Agatha worldly. And she wanted herself to be a schoolteacher.

One Saturday afternoon Agatha and Miriam were upstairs dressing. Their bedroom was over the stable. It was a low room, not very large, and bare. Miriam had nailed on the wall a reproduction of Veronese's "St. Catherine." She loved the woman who sat in the window, dreaming. Her own windows were too small to sit in. But the front one was dripped over with honeysuckle and Virginia creeper, and looked upon the treetops of the oak-wood across the yard, while the little back window, no bigger than a handkerchief, was a loophole to the east, to the dawn beating up against the beloved round hills.

The two sisters did not talk much to each other. Agatha, who was fair and small and determined, had rebelled against the home atmosphere, against the doctrine of "the other cheek." She was out in the world now, in a fair way to be independent. And she insisted on worldly values, on appearance, on manners, on position, which Miriam would fain have ignored.

Both girls liked to be upstairs, out of the way, when Paul came. They preferred to come running down, open the stairfoot door, and see him watching, expectant of them. Miriam stood painfully pulling over her head a rosary he had given her. It caught in the fine mesh of her hair. But at last she had it on, and the red-brown wooden beads looked well against her cool brown neck. She was a well-developed girl, and very handsome. But in the little looking glass nailed against the whitewashed wall she could only see a fragment of herself at a time. Agatha had bought a little mirror of her own, which she propped up to suit herself. Miriam was near the window. Suddenly she heard the well-known click of the chain, and she saw Paul fling open the gate, push his bicycle into the yard. She saw him look at the house, and she shrank away. He walked in a nonchalant fashion, and his bicycle went with him as if it were a live thing.

"Paul's come!" she exclaimed.

"Aren't you glad?" said Agatha cuttingly.

Miriam stood still in amazement and bewilderment.

"Well, aren't you?" she asked.

"Yes, but I'm not going to let him see it, and think I wanted him."

Miriam was startled. She heard him putting his bicycle in the stable underneath, and talking to Jimmy, who had been a pit-horse, and who was seedy.

"Well, Jimmy my lad, how are ter? Nobbut sick an' sadly, like? Why, then, it's a shame, my owd lad."

She heard the rope run through the hole as the horse lifted its head from the lad's caress. How she loved to listen when he thought only the horse could hear. But there was a serpent in her Eden. She searched earnestly in herself to see if she wanted Paul Morel. She felt there would be some disgrace in it. Full of twisted feeling, she was afraid she did want him. She stood self-convicted. Then came an agony of new shame. She shrank within herself in a coil of torture. Did she want Paul Morel, and did he know she wanted him? What a subtle infamy upon her! She felt as if her whole soul coiled into knots of shame.

Agatha was dressed first, and ran downstairs. Miriam heard her greet the lad gaily, knew exactly how brilliant her gray eyes became with that tone. She herself would have felt it bold to have greeted him in such wise. Yet there she stood under the self-accusation of wanting him, tied to that stake of torture. In bitter perplexity she kneeled down and prayed:

"O Lord, let me not love Paul Morel. Keep me from loving him, if I ought not to love him."

Something anomalous in the prayer arrested her. She lifted her head and pondered. How could it be wrong to love him? Love was God's gift. And yet it caused her shame. That was because of him, Paul Morel. But, then, it was not his affair, it was her own, between herself and God. She was to be a sacrifice. But it was God's sacrifice, not Paul Morel's or her own. After a few minutes she hid her face in the pillow again, and said:

"But, Lord, if it is Thy will that I should love him, make me love him—as Christ would, who died for the souls of men. Make me love him splendidly, because he is Thy son."

She remained kneeling for some time, quite still, and deeply moved, her black hair against the red squares and the lavender-sprigged squares of the patchwork quilt. Prayer was almost essential to her. Then she fell into that rapture of self-sacrifice, identifying herself with a God who was sacrificed, which gives to so many human souls their deepest bliss.

When she went downstairs Paul was lying back in an armchair, holding forth with much vehemence to Agatha, who was scorning a little painting he had brought to show her. Miriam glanced at the two, and avoided their levity. She went into the parlor to be alone.

It was teatime before she was able to speak to Paul, and then her manner was so distant he thought he had offended her.

Miriam discontinued her practice of going each Thursday evening to the library in Bestwood. After calling for Paul regularly during the whole spring, a number of trifling incidents and tiny insults from his family awakened her to their attitude towards her, and she decided to go no more. So she announced to Paul one evening she would not call at his house again for him on Thursday nights.

"Why?" he asked, very short.

"Nothing. Only I'd rather not."

"Very well."

"But," she faltered, "if you'd care to meet me, we could still go together."

"Meet you where?"

"Somewhere—where you like."

"I shan't meet you anywhere. I don't see why you shouldn't keep calling for me. But if you won't, I don't want to meet you."

So the Thursday evenings which had been so precious to her, and to him, were dropped. He worked instead. Mrs. Morel sniffed with satisfaction at this arrangement.

He would not have it that they were lovers. The intimacy between them had been kept so abstract, such a matter of the soul, all thought and weary struggle into consciousness, that he saw it only as a platonic friendship. He stoutly denied there was anything else between them. Miriam was silent, or else she very quietly agreed. He was a fool who did not know what was happening to himself. By tacit agreement they ignored the remarks and insinuations of their acquaintances.

"We aren't lovers, we are friends," he said to her. "*We* know it. Let them talk. What does it matter what they say?"

Sometimes, as they were walking together, she slipped her arm timidly into his. But he always resented it, and she knew it. It caused a violent conflict in him. With Miriam he was always on the high plane of abstraction, when his natural fire of love was transmitted into the fine stream of thought. She would have it so. If he were jolly and, as she put it, flippant, she waited till he came back to her, till the change had taken place in him again, and he was wrestling with his own soul, frowning, passionate in his desire for understanding. And in this passion for understanding her soul lay close to his; she had him all to herself. But he must be made abstract first.

Then, if she put her arm in his, it caused him almost torture. His consciousness seemed to split. The place where she was touching him ran hot with friction. He was one internecine battle, and he became cruel to her because of it.

One evening in midsummer Miriam called at the house, warm from climbing. Paul was alone in the kitchen; his mother could be heard moving about upstairs.

"Come and look at the sweet peas," he said to the girl.

They went into the garden. The sky behind the townlet and the church was orange-red; the flower garden was flooded with a strange warm light that lifted every leaf into significance. Paul passed along a fine row of sweet peas, gathering a blossom here and there, all cream and pale blue. Miriam followed, breathing the fragrance. To her, flowers appealed with such strength she felt she must make them part of herself. When she bent and breathed a flower, it was as if she and the flower were loving each other. Paul hated her for it. There seemed a sort of exposure about the action, something too intimate.

When he had got a fair bunch, they returned to the house. He listened for a moment to his mother's quiet movements upstairs, then he said:

"Come here, and let me pin them in for you." He arranged them two or three at a time in the bosom of her dress, stepping back now and then to see the effect. "You know," he said, taking the pin out of his mouth, "a woman ought always to arrange her flowers before her glass."

Miriam laughed. She thought flowers ought to be pinned in one's dress without any care. That Paul should take pains to fix her flowers for her was his whim.

He was rather offended at her laughter.

"Some women do—those who look decent," he said.

Miriam laughed again, but mirthlessly, to hear him thus mix her up with women in a general way. From most men she would have ignored it. But from him it hurt her.

He had nearly finished arranging the flowers when he heard his mother's footstep on the stairs. Hurriedly he pushed in the last pin and turned away.

"Don't let mater know," he said.

Miriam picked up her books and stood in the doorway looking with chagrin at the beautiful sunset. She would call for Paul no more, she said.

"Good evening, Mrs. Morel," she said, in a deferential way. She sounded as if she felt she had no right to be there.

"Oh, is it you, Miriam?" replied Mrs. Morel coolly.

But Paul insisted on everybody's accepting his friendship with the girl, and Mrs. Morel was too wise to have any open rupture.

It was not till he was twenty years old that the family could ever afford to go away for a holiday. Mrs. Morel had never been away for a holiday, except to see her sister, since she had been married. Now at last Paul had saved enough money, and they were all going. There was to be a party: some of Annie's friends, one friend of Paul's, a young man in the same office where William had previously been, and Miriam.

It was great excitement writing for rooms. Paul and his mother debated it endlessly between them. They wanted a furnished cottage for two weeks. She thought one week would be enough, but he insisted on two.

At last they got an answer from Mablethorpe, a cottage such as they wished for thirty shillings a week. There was immense jubilation. Paul was wild with joy for his mother's sake. She would have a real holiday now. He and she sat at evening picturing what it would be like. Annie came in, and Leonard, and Alice, and Kitty. There was wild rejoicing and anticipation. Paul told Miriam. She seemed to brood with joy over it. But the Morels' house rang with excitement.

They were to go on Saturday morning by the seven train. Paul suggested that Miriam should sleep at his house, because it was so far for her to walk. She came down for supper. Everybody was so excited that even Miriam was accepted with warmth. But almost as soon as she entered the feeling in the family became close and tight. He had discovered a poem by Jean Ingelow which mentioned Mablethorpe, and so he must read it to Miriam. He would never have got so far in the direction of sentimentality as to read poetry to his own family. But now they condescended to listen. Miriam sat on the sofa absorbed in him. She always seemed absorbed in him, and by him, when he was present. Mrs. Morel sat jealously in her own chair. She was going to hear also. And even Annie and the father attended, Morel with his head cocked on one side, like somebody listening to a sermon and feeling conscious of the fact. Paul ducked his head over the book. He had got now all the audience he cared for. And Mrs. Morel and Annie almost contested with Miriam who should listen best and win his favor. He was in very high feather.

"But," interrupted Mrs. Morel, "what *is* the 'Bride of Enderby' that the bells are supposed to ring?"

"It's an old tune they used to play on the bells for a warning against water. I suppose the Bride of Enderby was drowned in a flood," he replied. He had not the faintest knowledge what it really was, but he would have never sunk so low as to confess that to his womenfolk. They listened and believed him. He believed himself.

"And the people knew what that tune meant?" said his mother.

"Yes—just like the Scotch when they heard 'The Flowers o' the Forest'—and when they used to ring the bells backward for alarm."

"How?" said Annie. "A bell sounds the same whether it's rung backwards or forwards."

"But," he said, "if you start with the deep bell and ring up to the high one—der—der—der—der—der—der—der—der!"

He ran up the scale. Everybody thought it clever. He thought so too. Then, waiting a minute, he continued the poem.

"H'm!" said Mrs. Morel curiously, when he finished. "But I wish everything that's written weren't so sad."

"*I* canna see what they want drownin' theirselves for," said Morel.

There was a pause. Annie got up to clear the table.

Miriam rose to help with the pots.

"Let *me* help to wash up," she said.

"Certainly not," cried Annie. "You sit down again. There aren't many."

And Miriam, who could not be familiar and insist, sat down again to look at the book with Paul.

He was master of the party; his father was no good. And great tortures he suffered lest the tin box should be put out at Firsby instead of at Mablethorpe. And he wasn't equal to getting a carriage. His bold little mother did that.

"Here!" she cried to a man. "Here!"

Paul and Annie got behind the rest, convulsed with shamed laughter.

"How much will it be to drive to Brook Cottage?" said Mrs. Morel.

"Two shillings."

"Why, how far is it?"

"A good way."

"I don't believe it," she said.

But she scrambled in. There were eight crowded in one old seaside carriage.

"You see," said Mrs. Morel, "it's only threepence each, and if it were a tramcar——"

They drove along. Each cottage they came to, Mrs. Morel cried:

"Is it this? Now, this is it!"

Everybody sat breathless. They drove past. There was a universal sigh.

"I'm thankful it wasn't that brute," said Mrs. Morel. "I *was* frightened." They drove on and on.

At last they descended at a house that stood alone over the dyke by the high-road. There was wild excitement because they had to cross a little bridge to get into the front garden. But they loved the house that lay so solitary, with a sea meadow on one side, and immense expanse of land patched in white barley, yellow oats, red wheat, and green rootcrops, flat and stretching level to the sky.

Paul kept accounts. He and his mother ran the show. The total expenses—lodging, food, everything—was sixteen shillings a week per person. He and Leonard went bathing in the morning. Morel was wandering abroad quite early.

"You, Paul," his mother called from the bedroom, "eat a piece of bread-and-butter."

"All right," he answered.

And when he got back he saw his mother presiding in state at the breakfast table. The woman of the house was young. Her husband was blind, and she did laundry work. So Mrs. Morel always washed the pots in the kitchen and made the beds.

"But you said you'd have a real holiday," said Paul, "and now you work."

"Work!" she exclaimed. "What are you talking about!"

He loved to go with her across the fields to the village and the sea. She was afraid of the plank bridges, and he abused her for being a baby. On the whole he stuck to her as if he were *her* man.

Miriam did not get much of him, except, perhaps, when all the others went to the "Coons." Coons were insufferably stupid to Miriam, so he thought they were to himself also, and he preached priggishly to Annie about the fatuity of listening to them. Yet he, too, knew all their songs, and sang them along the roads roisterously. And if he found himself listening, the stupidity pleased him very much. Yet to Annie he said:

"Such rot! there isn't a grain of intelligence in it. Nobody with more gumption than a grasshopper could go and sit and listen." And to Miriam he said, with much scorn of Annie and the others: "I suppose they're at the 'Coons.'"

It was queer to see Miriam singing coon songs. She had a straight chin that went in a perpendicular line from the lower lip to the turn. She always reminded Paul of some sad Botticelli angel when she sang, even when it was:

> Come down lover's lane
> For a walk with me, talk with me.

Only when he sketched, or at evening when the others were at the "Coons," she had him to himself. He talked to her endlessly about his love of horizontals: how they, the great levels of sky and land in Lincolnshire, meant to him the eternality of the will, just as the bowed Norman arches of the church, repeating themselves, meant the dogged leaping forward of the persistent human soul, on and on, nobody knows where; in contradiction to the perpendicular lines and to the Gothic arch, which, he said, leapt up at heaven and touched the ecstasy and lost itself in the divine. Himself, he said, was Norman, Miriam was Gothic. She bowed in consent even to that.

One evening he and she went up the great sweeping shore of sand towards Theddlethorpe. The long breakers plunged and ran in a hiss of foam along the coast. It was a warm evening. There was not a figure but themselves on the far reaches of sand, no noise but the sound of the sea. Paul loved to see it clanging at the land. He loved to feel himself between the noise of it and the silence of the sandy shore. Miriam was with him. Everything grew very intense. It was quite dark when they turned again. The way home was through a gap in the sand hills, and then along a raised grass road between two dykes. The country was black and still. From behind the sand hills came the whisper of the sea. Paul and Miriam walked in silence. Suddenly he started. The whole of his blood seemed to burst into flame, and he could scarcely breathe. An enormous orange moon was staring at them from the rim of the sandhills. He stood still, looking at it.

"Ah!" cried Miriam, when she saw it.

He remained perfectly still, staring at the immense and ruddy moon, the only thing in the far-reaching darkness of the level. His heart beat heavily, the muscles of his arms contracted.

"What is it?" murmured Miriam, waiting for him.

He turned and looked at her. She stood beside him, forever in shadow. Her face, covered with the darkness of her hat, was watching him unseen. But she was brooding. She was slightly afraid—deeply moved and religious. That was her best state. He was impotent against it. His blood was concentrated like a flame in his chest. But he could not get across to her. There were flashes in his blood. But somehow she ignored them. She was expecting some religious state in him. Still yearning, she was half aware of his passion, and gazed at him, troubled.

"What is it?" she murmured again.

"It's the moon," he answered, frowning.

"Yes," she assented. "Isn't it wonderful?" She was curious about him. The crisis was past.

He did not know himself what was the matter. He was naturally so young, and their intimacy was so abstract, he did not know he wanted to crush her on to his breast to ease the ache there. He was afraid of her. The fact that he might want her as a man wants a woman had in him been suppressed into a shame. When she shrank in her convulsed coiled torture from the thought of such a thing, he had winced to the depths of his soul. And now this "purity" prevented even their first love-kiss. It was as if she could scarcely stand the shock of physical love, even a passionate kiss, and then he was too shrinking and sensitive to give it.

As they walked along the dark fen-meadow he watched the moon and did not speak. She plodded beside him. He hated her, for she seemed in some way to make him despise himself. Looking ahead—he saw the one light in the darkness, the window of their lamp-lit cottage.

He loved to think of his mother, and the other jolly people.

"Well, everybody else has been in long ago!" said his mother as they entered.

"What does that matter!" he cried irritably. "I can go a walk if I like, can't I?"

"And I should have thought you could get in to supper with the rest," said Mrs. Morel.

"I shall please myself," he retorted. "It's not *late*. I shall do as I like."

"Very well," said his mother cuttingly, "then *do* as you like." And she took no further notice of him that evening. Which he pretended neither to notice nor to care about, but sat reading. Miriam read also, obliterating herself. Mrs. Morel hated her for making her son like this. She watched Paul growing irritable, priggish, and melancholic. For this she put the blame on Miriam. Annie and all her friends joined against the girl. Miriam had no friend of her own, only Paul. But she did not suffer so much, because she despised the triviality of these other people.

And Paul hated her because, somehow, she spoilt his ease and naturalness. And he writhed himself with a feeling of humiliation.

❖ 8 ❖

STRIFE IN LOVE

Arthur finished his apprenticeship, and got a job on the electrical plant at Minton Pit. He earned very little, but had a good chance of getting on. But he was wild and restless. He did not drink nor gamble. Yet he somehow contrived to get into endless scrapes, always through some hotheaded thoughtlessness. Either he went rabbiting in the woods, like a poacher, or he stayed in Nottingham all night instead of coming home, or he miscalculated his dive into the canal at Bestwood, and scored his chest into one mass of wounds on the raw stones and tins at the bottom.

He had not been at his work many months when again he did not come home at night.

"Do you know where Arthur is?" asked Paul at breakfast.

"I do not," replied his mother.

"He is a fool," said Paul. "And if he *did* anything I shouldn't mind. But no, he simply can't come away from a game of whist, or else he must see a girl home from the skating rink—quite proprietously—and so can't get home. He's a fool."

"I don't know that it would make it any better if he did something to make us all ashamed," said Mrs. Morel.

"Well, *I* should respect him more," said Paul.

"I very much doubt it," said his mother coldly.

They went on with breakfast.

"Are you fearfully fond of him?" Paul asked his mother.

"What do you ask that for?"

"Because they say a woman always likes the youngest best."

"She may do—but I don't. No, he wearies me."

"And you'd actually rather he was good?"

"I'd rather he showed some of a man's common sense."

Paul was raw and irritable. He also wearied his mother very often. She saw the sunshine going out of him, and she resented it.

As they were finishing breakfast came the postman with a letter from Derby. Mrs. Morel screwed up her eyes to look at the address.

"Give it here, blind eye!" exclaimed her son, snatching it away from her.

She started, and almost boxed his ears.

"It's from your son Arthur," he said.

"What now—!" cried Mrs. Morel.

" 'My dearest Mother,' " Paul read, " 'I don't know what made me such a fool. I want you to come and fetch me back from here. I came with Jack Bredon yesterday, instead of going to work, and enlisted. He said he was sick of wearing the seat of a stool out, and, like the idiot you know I am, I came away with him.

" 'I have taken the King's shilling, but perhaps if you came for me they would let me go back with you. I was a fool when I did it. I don't want to be in the army. My dear mother, I am nothing but a trouble to you. But if you get me out of this, I promise I will have more sense and consideration . . .' "

Mrs. Morel sat down in her rocking chair.

"Well, *now*," she cried, "let him stop!"

"Yes," said Paul, "let him stop."

There was silence. The mother sat with her hands folded in her apron, her face set, thinking.

"If I'm not *sick*!" she cried suddenly. "Sick!"

"Now," said Paul, beginning to frown, "you're not going to worry your soul out about this, do you hear?"

"I suppose I'm to take it as a blessing," she flashed turning on her son.

"You're not going to mount it up to a tragedy, so there," he retorted.

"The *fool*!—the young fool!" she cried.

"He'll look well in uniform," said Paul irritatingly.

His mother turned on him like a fury.

"Oh, will he!" she cried. "Not in my eyes!"

"He should get in a cavalry regiment; he'll have the time of his life, and will look an awful swell."

"Swell!—*swell*!—a mighty swell indeed!—a common soldier!"

"Well," said Paul, "what am I but a common clerk?"

"A good deal, my boy!" cried his mother, stung.

"What?"

"At any rate, a *man*, and not a thing in a red coat."

"I shouldn't mind being in a red coat—or dark blue, that would suit me better—if they didn't boss me about too much."

But his mother had ceased to listen.

"Just as he was getting on, or might have been getting on, at his job—a young nuisance—here he goes and ruins himself for life. What good will he be, do you think, after *this*?"

"It may lick him into shape beautifully," said Paul.

"Lick him into shape!—lick what marrow there *was* out of his bones. A *soldier*!—and a common *soldier*!—nothing but a body that makes movements when it hears a shout! It's a fine thing!"

"I can't understand why it upsets you," said Paul.

"No, perhaps you can't. But *I* understand"; and she sat back in her chair, her chin in one hand, holding her elbow with the other, brimmed up with wrath and chagrin.

"And shall you go to Derby?" asked Paul.

"Yes."

"It's no good."

"I'll see for myself."

"And why on earth don't you let him stop? It's just what he wants."

"Of course," cried the mother, "*you* know what he wants!"

She got ready and went by the first train to Derby, where she saw her son and the sergeant. It was, however, no good.

When Morel was having his dinner in the evening, she said suddenly:

"I've had to go to Derby today."

The miner turned up his eyes, showing the whites in his black face.

"Has ter, lass? What took thee there?"

"That Arthur!"

"Oh—an' what's agate now?"

"He's only enlisted."

Morel put down his knife and leaned back in his chair.

"Nay," he said, "that he niver 'as!"

"And is going down to Aldershot tomorrow."

"Well!" exclaimed the miner. "That's a winder." He considered it a moment, said "H'm!" and proceeded with his dinner. Suddenly his face contracted with wrath. "I hope he may never set foot i' my house again," he said.

"The idea!" cried Mrs. Morel. "Saying such a thing!"

"I do," repeated Morel. "A fool as runs away for a soldier, let 'im look after 'issen; I s'll do no more for 'im."

"A fat sight you have done as it is," she said.

And Morel was almost ashamed to go to his public house that evening.

"Well, did you go?" said Paul to his mother when he came home.

"I did."

"And could you see him?"

"Yes."

"And what did he say?"

"He blubbered when I came away."

"H'm!"

"And so did I, so you needn't 'h'm'!"

Mrs. Morel fretted after her son. She knew he would not like the army. He did not. The discipline was intolerable to him.

"But the doctor," she said with some pride to Paul, "said he was perfectly proportioned—almost exactly; all his measurements were correct. He *is* good-looking, you know."

"He's awfully nice-looking. But he doesn't fetch the girls like William, does he?"

"No; it's a different character. He's a good deal like his father, irresponsible."

To console his mother, Paul did not go much to Willey Farm at this time. And in the autumn exhibition of students work in the Castle he had two studies, a landscape in watercolor and a still life in oil, both of which had first-prize awards. He was highly excited.

"What do you think I've got for my pictures, mother?" he asked, coming home one evening. She saw by his eye he was glad. Her face flushed.

"Now, how should I know, my boy!"

"A first prize for those glass jars——"

"H'm!"

"And a first prize for that sketch up at Willey Farm."

"Both first?"

"Yes."

"H'm!"

There was a rosy, bright look about her, though she said nothing.

"It's nice," he said, "isn't it?"

"It is."

"Why don't you praise me up to the skies?"

She laughed.

"I should have the trouble of dragging you down again," she said.

But she was full of joy, nevertheless. William had brought her his sporting trophies. She kept them still, and she did not forgive his death. Arthur was handsome—at least, a good specimen—and warm and generous, and probably would do well in the end. But Paul was going to distinguish himself. She had a great belief in him, the more because he was unaware of his own powers. There was so much to come out of him. Life for her was rich with promise. She was to see herself fulfilled. Not for nothing had been her struggle.

Several times during the exhibition Mrs. Morel went to the Castle unknown to Paul. She wandered down the long room looking at the other exhibits. Yes, they were good. But they had not in them a certain something which she demanded for her satisfaction. Some made her jealous, they were so good. She looked at them a long time trying to find fault with them. Then suddenly she had a shock that made her heart beat. There hung Paul's picture! She knew it as if it were printed on her heart.

"Name—Paul Morel—First Prize."

It looked so strange, there in public, on the walls of the Castle gallery, where in her lifetime she had seen so many pictures. And she glanced round to see if anyone had noticed her again in front of the same sketch.

But she felt a proud woman. When she met well-dressed ladies going home to the Park, she thought to herself:

"Yes, you look very well—but I wonder if *your* son has two first prizes in the Castle."

And she walked on, as proud a little woman as any in Nottingham. And Paul felt he had done something for her, if only a trifle. All his work was hers.

One day, as he was going up Castle Gate, he met Miriam. He had seen her on the Sunday, and had not expected to meet her in town. She was walking with a rather striking woman, blonde, with a sullen expression, and a defiant carriage. It was strange how Miriam, in her bowed, meditative bearing, looked dwarfed beside this woman with the handsome shoulders. Miriam watched Paul searchingly. His gaze was on the stranger, who ignored him. The girl saw his masculine spirit rear its head.

"Hello!" he said, "you didn't tell me you were coming to town."

"No," replied Miriam, half apologetically. "I drove in to Cattle Market with father."

He looked at her companion.

"I've told you about Mrs. Dawes," said Miriam huskily; she was nervous. "Clara, do you know Paul?"

"I think I've seen him before," replied Mrs. Dawes indifferently, as she shook hands with him. She had scornful gray eyes, a skin like white honey, and a full mouth, with a slightly lifted upper lip that did not know whether it was raised in scorn of all men or out of eagerness to be kissed, but which believed the former. She carried her head back, as if she had drawn away in contempt, perhaps from men also. She wore a large, dowdy hat of black beaver, and a sort of slightly affected simple dress that made her look rather sack-like. She was evidently poor, and had not much taste. Miriam usually looked nice.

"Where have you seen me?" Paul asked of the woman.

She looked at him as if she would not trouble to answer. Then:

"Walking with Louie Travers," she said.

Louie was one of the "spiral" girls.

"Why, do you know her?" he asked.

She did not answer. He turned to Miriam.

"Where are you going?" he asked.

"To the Castle."

"What train are you going home by?"

"I am driving with father. I wish you could come too. What time are you free?"

"You know not till eight tonight, damn it!"

And directly the two women moved on.

Paul remembered that Clara Dawes was the daughter of an old friend of Mrs. Leivers. Miriam had sought her out because she had once been spiral overseer at Jordan's, and because her husband, Baxter Dawes, was smith for the factory, making the irons for cripple instruments, and so on. Through her Miriam felt she got into direct contact with Jordan's, and could estimate better Paul's position. But Mrs. Dawes was separated from her husband, and had taken up Women's Rights. She was supposed to be clever. It interested Paul.

Baxter Dawes he knew and disliked. The smith was a man of thirty-one or thirty-two. He came occasionally through Paul's corner—a big, well-set man, also striking to look at, and handsome. There was a peculiar similarity between himself and his wife. He had the same white skin, with a clear, golden tinge. His hair was of soft brown, his moustache was golden. And he had a similar defiance in his bearing and manner. But then came the difference. His eyes, dark brown and quick-shifting, were dissolute. They protruded very slightly, and his eyelids hung over them in a way that was half hate. His mouth, too, was sensual. His whole manner was of cowed defiance, as if he were ready to knock anybody down who disapproved of him—perhaps because he really disapproved of himself.

From the first day he had hated Paul. Finding the lad's impersonal, deliberate gaze of an artist on his face, he got into a fury.

"What are yer lookin' at?" he sneered, bullying.

The boy glanced away. But the smith used to stand behind the counter and talk to Mr. Pappleworth. His speech was dirty, with a kind of rottenness. Again he found the youth with his cool, critical gaze fixed on his face. The smith started round as if he had been stung.

"What'r yer lookin' at, three hap'orth o' pap?" he snarled.

The boy shrugged his shoulders slightly.

"Why yer—!" shouted Dawes.

"Leave him alone," said Mr. Pappleworth, in that insinuating voice which means "he's only one of your good little sops who can't help it."

Since that time the boy used to look at the man every time he came through with the same curious criticism, glancing away before he met the smith's eyes. It made Dawes furious. They hated each other in silence.

Clara Dawes had no children. When she had left her husband the home had been broken up, and she had gone to live with her mother. Dawes lodged with his sister. In the same house was a sister-in-law, and somehow Paul knew that this girl, Louie Travers, was now Dawes's woman. She was a handsome, insolent hussy, who mocked at the youth, and yet flushed if he walked along to the station with her as she went home.

The next time he went to see Miriam it was Saturday evening. She had a fire in the parlor, and was waiting for him. The others, except her father and mother and the young children, had gone out, so the two had the parlor together. It was a long, low, warm room. There were three of Paul's small sketches on the wall, and his photo was on the mantelpiece. On the table and on the high old rosewood piano were bowls of colored leaves. He sat in the armchair, she crouched on the hearthrug near his feet. The glow was warm on her handsome, pensive face as she kneeled there like a devotee.

"What did you think of Mrs. Dawes?" she asked quietly.

"She doesn't look very amiable," he replied.

"No, but don't you think she's a fine woman?" she said, in a deep tone.

"Yes—in stature. But without a grain of taste. I like her for some things. *Is* she disagreeable?"

"I don't think so. I think she's dissatisfied."

"What with?"

"Well—how would *you* like to be tied for life to a man like that?"

"Why did she marry him, then, if she was to have revulsions so soon?"

"Ay, why did she!" repeated Miriam bitterly.

"And I should have thought she had enough fight in her to match him," he said.

Miriam bowed her head.

"Ay?" she queried satirically. "What makes you think so?"

"Look at her mouth—made for passion—and the very set-back of her throat—" He threw his head back in Clara's defiant manner.

Miriam bowed a little lower.

"Yes," she said.

There was a silence for some moments, while he thought of Clara.

"And what were the things you liked about her?" she asked.

"I don't know—her skin and the texture of her—and her—I don't know—there's a sort of fierceness somewhere in her. I appreciate her as an artist, that's all."

"Yes."

He wondered why Miriam crouched there brooding in that strange way. It irritated him.

"You don't really like her, do you?" he asked the girl.

She looked at him with her great, dazzled dark eyes.

"I do," she said.

"You don't—you can't—not really."

"Then what?" she asked slowly.

"Eh, I don't know—perhaps you like her because she's got a grudge against men."

That was more probably one of his own reasons for liking Mrs. Dawes, but this did not occur to him. They were silent. There had come into his forehead a knitting of the brows which was becoming habitual with him, particularly when he was with Miriam. She longed to smooth it away, and she was afraid of it. It seemed the stamp of a man who was not her man in Paul Morel.

There were some crimson berries among the leaves in the bowl. He reached over and pulled out a bunch.

"If you put red berries in your hair," he said, "why would you look like some witch or priestess, and never like a reveler?"

She laughed with a naked, painful sound.

"I don't know," she said.

His vigorous warm hands were playing excitedly with the berries.

"Why can't you laugh?" he said. "You never laugh laughter. You only laugh when something is odd or incongruous, and then it almost seems to hurt you."

She bowed her head as if he were scolding her.

"I wish you could laugh at me just for one minute—just for one minute. I feel as if it would set something free."

"But"—and she looked up at him with eyes frightened and struggling—"I do laugh at you—I *do*."

"Never! There's always a kind of intensity. When you laugh I could always cry; it seems as if it shows up your suffering. Oh, you make me knit the brows of my very soul and cogitate."

Slowly she shook her head despairingly.

"I'm sure I don't want to," she said.

"I'm so damned spiritual with *you* always!" he cried.

She remained silent, thinking, "Then why don't you be otherwise?" But he saw her crouching, brooding figure, and it seemed to tear him in two.

"But there, it's autumn," he said, "and everybody feels like a disembodied spirit then."

There was still another silence. This peculiar sadness between them thrilled her soul. He seemed so beautiful, with his eyes gone dark, and looking as if they were deep as the deepest well.

"You make me so spiritual!" he lamented. "And I don't want to be spiritual."

She took her finger from her mouth with a little pop, and looked up at him almost challenging. But still her soul was naked in her great dark eyes, and there was the same yearning appeal upon her. If he could have kissed her in abstract purity he would have done so. But he could not kiss her thus—and she seemed to leave no other way. And she yearned to him.

He gave a brief laugh.

"Well," he said, "get that French and we'll do some—some Verlaine."

"Yes," she said in a deep tone, almost of resignation. And she rose and got the books. And her rather red, nervous hands looked so pitiful, he was mad to comfort her and kiss her. But then he dared not—or could not. There was something prevented him. His kisses were wrong for her. They continued the reading till ten o'clock, when they went into the kitchen, and Paul was natural and jolly again with the father and mother. His eyes were dark and shining; there was a kind of fascination about him.

When he went into the barn for his bicycle he found the front wheel punctured.

"Fetch me a drop of water in a bowl," he said to her. "I shall be late, and then I s'll catch it."

He lighted the hurricane lamp, took off his coat, turned up the bicycle, and set speedily to work. Miriam came with the bowl of water and stood close to him, watching. She loved to see his hands doing things. He was slim and vigorous, with a kind of easiness even in his most hasty movements. And busy at his work, he seemed to forget her. She loved him absorbedly. She wanted to run her hands down his sides. She always wanted to embrace him, so long as he did not want her.

"There!" he said, rising suddenly. "Now, could you have done it quicker?"

"No!" she laughed.

He straightened himself. His back was towards her. She put her two hands on his sides, and ran them quickly down.

"You are so *fine*!" she said.

He laughed, hating her voice, but his blood roused to a wave of flame by her hands. She did not seem to realize *him* in all this. He might have been an object. She never realized the male he was.

He lighted his bicycle lamp, bounced the machine on the barn floor to see that the tires were sound, and buttoned his coat.

"That's all right!" he said.

She was trying the brakes, that she knew were broken.

"Did you have them mended?" she asked.

"No!"

"But why didn't you?"

"The back one goes on a bit."

"But it's not safe."

"I can use my toe."

"I wish you'd had them mended," she murmured.

"Don't worry—come to tea tomorrow, with Edgar."

"Shall we?"

"Do—about four. I'll come to meet you."

"Very well."

She was pleased. They went across the dark yard to the gate. Looking across, he saw through the uncurtained window of the kitchen the heads of Mr. and Mrs. Leivers in the warm glow. It looked very cosy. The road, with pine trees, was quite black in front.

"Till tomorrow," he said, jumping on his bicycle.

"You'll take care, won't you?" she pleaded.

"Yes."

His voice already came out of the darkness. She stood a moment watching the light from his lamp race into obscurity along the ground. She turned very slowly indoors. Orion was wheeling up over the wood, his dog twinkling after him, half smothered. For the rest, the world was full of darkness, and silent, save for the breathing of cattle in their stalls. She prayed earnestly for his safety that night. When he left her, she often lay in anxiety, wondering if he had got home safely.

He dropped down the hills on his bicycle. The roads were greasy, so he had to let it go. He felt a pleasure as the machine plunged over the second, steeper drop in the hill. "Here goes!" he said. It was risky, because of the curve in the darkness at the bottom, and because of the brewers' wagons with drunken wagoners asleep. His bicycle seemed to fall beneath him, and he loved it. Recklessness is almost a man's revenge on his woman. He feels he is not valued, so he will risk destroying himself to deprive her altogether.

The stars on the lake seemed to leap like grasshoppers, silver upon the blackness, as he spun past. Then there was the long climb home.

"See, mother!" he said, as he threw her the berries and leaves on to the table.

"H'm!" she said, glancing at them, then away again. She sat reading, alone, as she always did.

"Aren't they pretty?"

"Yes."

He knew she was cross with him. After a few minutes he said:

"Edgar and Miriam are coming to tea tomorrow."

She did not answer.

"You don't mind?"

Still she did not answer.

"Do you?" he asked.

"You know whether I mind or not."

"I don't see why you should. I have plenty of meals there."

"You do."

"Then why do you begrudge them tea?"

"I begrudge whom tea?"

"What are you so horrid for?"

"Oh, say no more! You've asked her to tea, it's quite sufficient. She'll come."

He was very angry with his mother. He knew it was merely Miriam she objected to. He flung off his boots and went to bed.

Paul went to meet his friends the next afternoon. He was glad to see them coming. They arrived home at about four o'clock. Everywhere was clean and still for Sunday afternoon. Mrs. Morel sat in her black dress and black apron. She rose to meet the visitors. With Edgar she was cordial, but with Miriam cold and rather grudging. Yet Paul thought the girl looked so nice in her brown cashmere frock.

He helped his mother to get the tea ready. Miriam would have gladly proffered, but was afraid. He was rather proud of his home. There was about it now, he thought, a certain distinction. The chairs were only wooden, and the sofa was old. But the hearthrug and cushions were cosy; the pictures were prints in good taste; there was a simplicity in everything, and plenty of books. He was never ashamed in the least of his home, nor was Miriam of hers, because both were what they should be, and warm. And then he was proud of the table; the china was pretty, the cloth was fine. It did not matter that the spoons were not silver nor the knives ivory-handled; everything looked nice. Mrs. Morel had managed wonderfully while her children were growing up, so that nothing was out of place.

Miriam talked books a little. That was her unfailing topic. But Mrs. Morel was not cordial, and turned soon to Edgar.

At first Edgar and Miriam used to go into Mrs. Morel's pew. Morel never went to chapel, preferring the public house. Mrs. Morel, like a little champion, sat at the head of her pew, Paul at the other end; and at first Miriam sat next to him. Then the chapel was like home. It was a pretty place, with dark pews and slim, elegant pillars, and flowers. And the same people had sat in the same places ever since he was a boy. It was wonderfully sweet and soothing to sit there for an hour and a half, next to Miriam, and near to his mother, uniting his two loves under the spell of the place of worship. Then he felt warm and happy and religious at once. And after chapel he walked home with Miriam, whilst Mrs Morel spent the rest of the evening with her old friend, Mrs. Burns. He was keenly alive on his walks on Sunday nights with Edgar and Miriam. He never went past the pits at night, by the lighted lamphouse, the tall black headstocks and lines of trucks, past the fans spinning slowly like shadows, without the feeling of Miriam returning to him, keen and almost unbearable.

She did not very long occupy the Morels' pew. Her father took one for themselves once more. It was under the little gallery, opposite the Morels'. When Paul and his mother came in the chapel the Leivers' pew was always empty. He was anxious for fear she would not come: it was so far, and there were so many rainy Sundays. Then, often very late indeed, she came in, with her long stride, her head bowed, her face hidden under her hat of dark green velvet. Her face, as she sat opposite, was always in shadow. But it gave him a very keen feeling, as if all his soul stirred within him, to see her there. It was not the same glow, happiness, and pride, that he felt in having his mother in charge: something more wonderful, less human, and tinged to intensity by a pain, as if there were something he could not get to.

At this time he was beginning to question the orthodox creed. He was twenty-one, and she was twenty. She was beginning to dread the spring: he became so wild, and hurt her so much. All the way he went cruelly smashing her beliefs. Edgar enjoyed it. He was by nature critical and rather dispassionate. But Miriam suffered exquisite pain, as, with an intellect like a knife, the man she loved examined her religion in which she lived and moved and had her being. But he did not spare her. He was cruel. And when they went alone he was even more fierce, as if he would kill her soul. He bled her beliefs till she almost lost consciousness.

"She exults—she exults as she carries him off from me," Mrs. Morel cried in her heart when Paul had gone. "She's not like an ordinary woman, who can leave me my share in him. She wants to absorb him. She wants to draw him out and absorb him till there is nothing left of him, even for himself. He will never be a man on his own feet—she will suck him up." So the mother sat, and battled and brooded bitterly.

And he, coming home from his walks with Miriam, was wild with torture. He walked biting his lips and with clenched fists, going at a great rate. Then, brought up against a stile, he stood for some minutes, and did not move. There was a great hollow of darkness fronting him, and on the black up-slopes patches of tiny lights, and in the lowest trough of the night, a flare of the pit. It was all weird and dreadful. Why was he torn so, almost bewildered, and unable to move? Why did his mother sit at home and suffer? He knew she suffered badly. But why should she? And why did he hate Miriam, and feel so cruel towards her, at the thought of his mother. If Miriam caused his mother suffering, then he hated her—and he easily hated her. Why did she make him feel as if he were uncertain of himself, insecure, an indefinite thing, as if he had not sufficient sheathing to prevent the night and the space breaking into him? How he hated her! And then, what a rush of tenderness and humility!

Suddenly he plunged on again, running home. His mother saw on him the marks of some agony, and she said nothing. But he had to make her talk to him. Then she was angry with him for going so far with Miriam.

"Why don't you like her, mother?" he cried in despair.

"I don't know, my boy," she replied piteously. "I'm sure I've tried to like her. I've tried and tried, but I can't—I can't!"

And he felt dreary and hopeless between the two.

Spring was the worst time. He was changeable, and intense, and cruel. So he decided to stay away from her. Then came the hours when he knew Miriam was expecting him. His mother watched him growing restless. He could not go on with his work. He could do nothing. It was as if something were drawing his soul out towards Willey Farm. Then he put on his hat and went, saying nothing. And his mother knew he was gone. And as soon as he was on the way he sighed with relief. And when he was with her he was cruel again.

One day in March he lay on the bank of Nethermere, with Miriam sitting beside him. It was a glistening, white-and-blue day. Big clouds, so brilliant, went by overhead, white shadows stole along on the water. The clear spaces in the sky were of clean, cold blue. Paul lay on his back in the old grass, looking up. He could not bear to look at Miriam. She seemed to want him, and he resisted. He resisted all the time. He wanted now to give her passion and tenderness, and he could not. He felt that she wanted the soul out of his body, and not him. All his strength and energy she drew into herself through some channel which united them. She did not want to meet him, so that there were two of them, man and woman together. She wanted to draw all of him into her. It urged him to an intensity like madness, which fascinated him, as drug taking might.

He was discussing Michaelangelo. It felt to her as if she were fingering the very quivering tissue, the very protoplasm of life, as she heard him. It gave her her deepest satisfaction. And in the end it frightened her. There he lay in the white intensity of his search, and his voice gradually filled her with fear, so level it was, almost inhuman, as if in a trance.

"Don't talk any more," she pleaded softly, laying her hand on his forehead.

He lay quite still, almost unable to move. His body was somewhere discarded.

"Why not? Are you tired?"

"Yes, and it wears you out."

He laughed shortly, realizing.

"Yet you always make me like it," he said.

"I don't wish to," she said, very low.

"Not when you've gone too far, and you feel you can't bear it. But your unconscious self always asks it of me. And I suppose I want it."

He went on, in his dead fashion:

"If only you could want *me*, and not want what I can reel off for you!"

"I!" she cried bitterly—"I! Why, when would you let me take you?"

"Then it's my fault," he said, and, gathering himself together, he got up and began to talk trivialities. He felt insubstantial. In a vague way he hated her for it. And he knew he was as much to blame himself. This, however, did not prevent his hating her.

One evening about this time he had walked along the home road with her. They stood by the pasture leading down to the wood, unable to part. As the stars came out the clouds closed. They had glimpses of their own constellation, Orion, towards the west. His jewels glimmered for a moment, his dog ran low, struggling with difficulty through the spume of cloud.

Orion was for them chief in significance among the constellations. They had gazed at him in their strange, surcharged hours of feeling, until they seemed themselves to live in every one of his stars. This evening Paul had been moody and perverse. Orion had seemed just an ordinary constellation to him. He had fought against his glamor and fascination. Miriam was watching her lover's mood carefully. But he said nothing that gave him away, till the moment came to part, when he stood frowning gloomily at the gathered clouds, behind which the great constellation must be striding still.

There was to be a little party at his house the next day, at which she was to attend.

"I shan't come and meet you," he said.

"Oh, very well; it's not very nice out," she replied slowly.

"It's not that—only they don't like me to. They say I care more for you than for them. And you understand, don't you? You know it's only friendship."

Miriam was astonished and hurt for him. It had cost him an effort. She left him, wanting to spare him any further humiliation. A fine rain blew in her face as she walked along the road. She was hurt deep down; and she despised him for being blown about by any wind of authority. And in her heart of hearts, unconsciously, she felt that he was trying to get away from her. This she would never have acknowledged. She pitied him.

At this time Paul became an important factor in Jordan's warehouse. Mr. Pappleworth left to set up a business of his own, and Paul remained with Mr. Jordan as spiral overseer. His wages were to be raised to thirty shillings at the year-end, if things went well.

Still on Friday night Miriam often came down for her French lesson. Paul did not go so frequently to Willey Farm, and she grieved at the thought of her education's coming to an end; moreover, they both loved to be together, in spite of discords. So they read Balzac, and did compositions, and felt highly cultured.

Friday night was reckoning night for the miners. Morel "reckoned"—shared up the money at the stall—either in the New Inn at Bretty or in his own house, according as his fellow butties wished. Barker had turned a non-drinker, so now the men reckoned at Morel's house.

Annie, who had been teaching away, was at home again. She was still a tomboy; and she was engaged to be married. Paul was studying design.

Morel was always in good spirits on Friday evening, unless the week's earnings were small. He bustled immediately after his dinner, prepared to get washed. It was decorum for the women to absent themselves while the men reckoned. Women were not supposed to spy into such a masculine privacy as the butties' reckoning, nor were they to know the exact amount of the week's earnings. So, whilst her father was spluttering in the scullery, Annie went out to spend an hour with a neighbor. Mrs. Morel attended to her baking.

"Shut that doo-er!" bawled Morel furiously.

Annie banged it behind her, and was gone.

"If tha oppens it again while I'm weshin' me, I'll ma'e thy jaw rattle," he threatened from the midst of his soapsuds. Paul and the mother frowned to hear him.

Presently he came running out of the scullery, with the soapy water dripping from him, dithering with cold.

"Oh, my sirs!" he said. "Wheer's my towel?"

It was hung on a chair to warm before the fire, otherwise he would have bullied and blustered. He squatted on his heels before the hot baking-fire to dry himself.

"F-ff-f!" he went, pretending to shudder with cold.

"Goodness, man, don't be such a kid!" said Mrs. Morel. "It's *not* cold."

"Thee strip thysen stark nak'd to wesh thy flesh i' that scullery," said the miner, as he rubbed his hair; "nowt b'r a ice-'ouse!"

"And I shouldn't make that fuss," replied his wife.

"No, tha'd drop down stiff, as dead as a doorknob, wi' thy nesh sides."

"Why is a doorknob deader than anything else?" asked Paul, curious.

"Eh, I dunno; that's what they say," replied his father. "But there's that much draught i' yon scullery, as it blows through your ribs like through a five-barred gate."

"It would have some difficulty in blowing through yours," said Mrs. Morel.

Morel looked down ruefully at his sides.

"Me!" he exclaimed. "I'm nowt b'r a skinned rabbit. My bones fair juts out on me."

"I should like to know where," retorted his wife.

"Iv'ry-wheer! I'm nobbut a sack o' faggots."

Mrs. Morel laughed. He had still a wonderfully young body, muscular, without any fat. His skin was smooth and clear. It might have been the body of a man of twenty-eight, except that there were, perhaps, too many blue scars, like tattoo marks, where the coal dust remained under the skin, and that his chest was too hairy. But he put his hand on his sides ruefully. It was his fixed belief that, because he did not get fat, he was as thin as a starved rat.

Paul looked at his father's thick, brownish hands all scarred, with broken nails, rubbing the fine smoothness of his sides, and the incongruity struck him. It seemed strange they were the same flesh.

"I suppose," he said to his father, "you had a good figure once."

"Eh!" exclaimed the miner, glancing round, startled and timid, like a child.

"He had," exclaimed Mrs. Morel, "if he didn't hurtle himself up as if he was trying to get in the smallest space he could."

"Me!" exclaimed Morel—"me a good figure! I wor niver much more n'r a skeleton."

"Man!" cried his wife, "don't be such a pulamiter!"

" 'Strewth!" he said. "Tha's niver knowed me but what I looked as if I wor goin' off in a rapid decline."

She sat and laughed.

"You've had a constitution like iron," she said; "and never a man had a better start, if it was body that counted. You should have seen him as a young man," she cried suddenly to Paul, drawing herself up to imitate her husband's once handsome bearing.

Morel watched her shyly. He saw again the passion she had had for him. It blazed upon her for a moment. He was shy, rather scared, and humble. Yet again he felt his old glow. And then immediately he felt the ruin he had made during these years. He wanted to bustle about, to run away from it.

"Gi'e my back a bit of a wesh," he asked her.

"Eh, tha mucky little 'ussy!" he cried. "Cowd as death!"

"You ought to have been a salamander," she laughed, washing his back. It was very rarely she would do anything so personal for him. The children did those things.

"The next world won't be half hot enough for you," she added.

"No," he said; "tha'lt see as it's draughty for me."

But she had finished. She wiped him in a desultory fashion, and went upstairs, returning immediately with his shifting-trousers. When he was dried he struggled into his shirt. Then, ruddy and shiny, with hair on end, and his flannelette shirt hanging over his pit-trousers, he stood warming the garments he was going to put on. He turned them, he pulled them inside out, he scorched them.

"Goodness, man!" cried Mrs. Morel; "get dressed!"

"Should thee like to clap thysen into britches as cowd as a tub o' water?" he said.

At last he took off his pit-trousers and donned decent black. He did all this on the hearthrug, as he would have done if Annie and her familiar friends had been present.

Mrs. Morel turned the bread in the oven. Then from the red earthenware panchion of dough that stood in a corner she took another handful of paste, worked it to the proper shape, and dropped it into a tin. As she was doing so Barker knocked and entered. Hs was a quiet, compact little man, who looked as if he would go through a stone wall. His black hair was cropped short, his head was bony. Like most miners, he was pale, but healthy and taut.

"Evenin', missis," he nodded to Mrs. Morel, and he seated himself with a sigh.

"Good evening," she replied cordially.

"Tha's made thy heels crack," said Morel.

"I dunno as I have," said Barker.

He sat, as the men always did in Mrs. Morel's kitchen, effacing himself rather.

"How's missis?" she asked of him.

He had told her some time back:

"We're expectin' us third just now, you see."

"Well," he answered, rubbing his head, "she keeps pretty middlin', I think."

"Let's see—when?" asked Mrs. Morel.

"Well, I shouldn't be surprised any time now."

"Ah! And she's kept fairly?"

"Yes, tidy."

"That's a blessing, for she's none too strong."

"No. An' I've done another silly trick."

"What's that?"

Mrs. Morel knew Barker wouldn't do anything very silly.

"I'm come be-out th' market bag."

"You can have mine."

"Nay, you'll be wantin' that yourself."

"I shan't. I take a string bag always."

She saw the determined little collier buying in the week's groceries and meat on the Friday nights, and she admired him. "Barker's little, but he's ten times the man you are," she said to her husband.

Just then Wesson entered. He was thin, rather frail-looking, with a boyish ingenuousness and a slightly foolish smile, despite his seven children. But his wife was a passionate woman.

"I see you've kested me," he said, smiling rather vapidly.

"Yes," replied Barker.

The newcomer took off his cap and his big wooden muffler. His nose was pointed and red.

"I'm afraid you're cold, Mr. Wesson," said Mrs. Morel.

"It's a bit nippy," he replied.

"Then come to the fire."

"Nay, I s'll do where I am."

Both colliers sat away back. They could not be induced to come on to the hearth. The hearth is sacred to the family.

"Go thy ways i' th' armchair," cried Morel cheerily.

"Nay, thank yer; I'm very nicely here."

"Yes, come, of course," insisted Mrs. Morel.

He rose and went awkwardly. He sat in Morel's armchair awkwardly. It was too great a familiarity. But the fire made him blissfully happy.

"And how's that chest of yours?" demanded Mrs. Morel.

He smiled again, with his blue eyes rather sunny.

"Oh, it's very middlin'," he said.

"Wi' a rattle in it like a kettledrum," said Barker shortly.

"T-t-t-t!" went Mrs. Morel rapidly with her tongue. "Did you have that flannel singlet made?"

"Not yet," he smiled.

"Then, why didn't you?" she cried.

"It'll come," he smiled.

"Ah, an' Doomsday!" exclaimed Barker.

Barker and Morel were both impatient of Wesson. But, then, they were both as hard as nails, physically.

When Morel was nearly ready he pushed the bag of money to Paul.

"Count it, boy," he asked humbly.

Paul impatiently turned from his books and pencil, tipped the bag upside down on the table. There was a five-pound bag of silver, sovereigns and loose money. He counted quickly, referred to the checks—the written papers giving amount of coal—put the money in order. Then Barker glanced at the checks.

Mrs. Morel went upstairs, and the three men came to table. Morel, as master of the house, sat in his armchair, with his back to the hot fire. The two butties had cooler seats. None of them counted the money.

"What did we say Simpson's was?" asked Morel; and the butties caviled for a minute over the dayman's earnings. Then the amount was put aside.

"An' Bill Naylor's?"

This money also was taken from the pack.

Then, because Wesson lived in one of the company's houses, and his rent had been deducted, Morel and Barker took four-and-six each. And because Morel's coals had come, and the leading was stopped, Barker and Wesson took four shillings each. Then it was plain sailing. Morel gave each of them a sovereign till there were no more sovereigns; each half a crown till there were no more half-crowns; each a shilling till there were no more shillings. If there was anything at the end that wouldn't split, Morel took it and stood drinks.

Then the three men rose and went. Morel scuttled out of the house before his wife came down. She heard the door close, and descended. She looked hastily at the bread in the oven. Then, glancing on the table, she saw her money lying. Paul had been working all the time. But now he felt his mother counting the week's money, and her wrath rising.

"T-t-t-t-t!" went her tongue.

He frowned. He could not work when she was cross. She counted again.

"A measly twenty-five shillings!" she exclaimed. "How much was the cheque?"

"Ten pounds eleven," said Paul irritably. He dreaded what was coming.

"And he gives me a scrattlin' twenty-five, an' his club this week! But I know him. He thinks because *you're* earning he needn't keep the house any longer. No, all he has to do with his money is to guttle it. But I'll show him!"

"Oh, mother, don't!" cried Paul.

"Don't what, I should like to know?" she exclaimed.

"Don't carry on again. I can't work."

She went very quiet.

"Yes, it's all very well," she said; "but how do you think I'm going to manage?"

"Well, it won't make it any better to whittle about it."

"I should like to know what you'd do if you had it to put up with."

"It won't be long. You can have my money. Let him go to hell."

He went back to his work, and she tied her bonnet strings grimly. When she was fretted he could not bear it. But now he began to insist on her recognizing him.

"The two loaves at the top," she said, "will be done in twenty minutes. Don't forget them."

"All right," he answered; and she went to market.

He remained alone working. But his usual intense concentration became unsettled. He listened for the yard gate. At a quarter-past seven came a low knock, and Miriam entered.

"All alone?" she said.

"Yes."

As if at home, she took off her tam-o'-shanter and her long coat, hanging them up. It gave him a thrill. This might be their own house, his and hers. Then she came back and peered over his work.

"What is it?" she asked.

"Still design, for decorating stuffs, and for embroidery."

She bent short-sightedly over the drawings.

It irritated him that she peered so into everything that was his, searching him out. He went into the parlor and returned with a bundle of brownish linen. Carefully unfolding it, he spread it on the floor. It proved to be a curtain or *portière*, beautifully stenciled with a design on roses.

"Ah, how beautiful!" she cried.

The spread cloth, with its wonderful reddish roses and dark green stems, all so simple, and somehow so wicked-looking, lay at her feet. She went on her knees before it, her dark curls dropping. He saw her crouched voluptuously before his work, and his heart beat quickly. Suddenly she looked up at him.

"Why does it seem cruel?" she asked.

"What?"

"There seems a feeling of cruelty about it," she said.

"It's jolly good, whether or not," he replied, folding up his work with a lover's hands.

She rose slowly, pondering.

"And what will you do with it?" she asked.

"Send it to Liberty's. I did it for my mother, but I think she'd rather have the money."

"Yes," said Miriam. He had spoken with a touch of bitterness, and Miriam sympathized. Money would have been nothing to *her*.

He took the cloth back into the parlor. When he returned, he threw to Miriam a smaller piece. It was a cushion cover with the same design.

"I did that for you," he said.

She fingered the work with trembling hands, and did not speak. He became embarrassed.

"By Jove, the bread!" he cried.

He took the top loaves out, tapped them vigorously. They were done. He put them on the hearth to cool. Then he went to the scullery, wetted his hands, scooped the last white dough out of the punchion, and dropped it in a baking tin. Miriam was still bent over her painted cloth. He stood rubbing the bits of dough from his hands.

"You do like it?" he asked.

She looked up at him, with her dark eyes one flame of love. He laughed uncomfortably. Then he began to talk about the design. There was for him the most intense pleasure in talking about his work to Miriam. All his passion, all his wild blood, went into this intercourse with her, when he talked and conceived his work. She brought forth to him his imaginations. She did not understand, any more than a woman understands when she conceives a child in her womb. But this was life for her and for him.

While they were talking, a young woman of about twenty-two, small and pale, hollow-eyed, yet with a relentless look about her, entered the room. She was a friend at the Morels'.

"Take your things off," said Paul.

"No, I'm not stopping."

She sat down in the armchair opposite Paul and Miriam, who were on the sofa. Miriam moved a little farther from him. The room was hot, with a scent of new bread. Brown, crisp loaves stood on the hearth.

"I shouldn't have expected to see you here tonight, Miriam Leivers," said Beatrice wickedly.

"Why not?" murmured Miriam huskily.

"Why, let's look at your shoes."

Miriam remained uncomfortably still.

"If tha doesna tha durs'na," laughed Beatrice.

Miriam put her feet from under her dress. Her boots had that queer, irresolute, rather pathetic look about them, which showed how self-conscious and self-mistrustful she was. And they were covered with mud.

"Glory! You're a positive muck heap," exclaimed Beatrice. "Who cleans your boots?"

"I clean them myself."

"Then you wanted a job," said Beatrice. "It would ha' taken a lot of men to ha' brought me down here tonight. But love laughs at sludge, doesn't it, 'Postle my duck?"

"*Inter alia*," he said.

"Oh, Lord! are you going to spout foreign languages? What does it mean, Miriam?"

There was a fine sarcasm in the last question, but Miriam did not see it.

" 'Among other things,' I believe," she said humbly.

Beatrice put her tongue between her teeth and laughed wickedly.

" 'Among other things,' 'Postle?" she repeated. "Do you mean love laughs at mothers, and fathers, and sisters, and brothers, and men friends, and lady friends, and even at the b'loved himself?"

She affected a great innocence.

"In fact, it's one big smile," he replied.

"Up its sleeve, 'Postle Morel—you believe me," she said; and she went off into another burst of wicked, silent laughter!

Miriam sat silent, withdrawn into herself. Every one of Paul's friends delighted in taking sides against her, and he left her in the lurch—seemed almost to have a sort of revenge upon her then.

"Are you still at school?" asked Miriam of Beatrice.

"Yes."

"You've not had your notice, then?"

"I expect it at Easter."

"Isn't it an awful shame, to turn you off merely because you didn't pass the exam?"

"I don't know," said Beatrice coldly.

"Agatha says you're as good as any teacher anywhere. It seems to me ridiculous. I wonder why you didn't pass."

"Short of brains, eh, 'Postle?" said Beatrice briefly.

"Only brains to bite with," replied Paul, laughing.

"Nuisance!" she cried; and, springing from her seat, she rushed and boxed his ears. She had beautiful small hands. He held her wrists while she wrestled with him. At last she broke free, and seized two handfuls of his thick, dark brown hair, which she shook.

"Beat!" he said, as he pulled his hair straight with his fingers. "I hate you!"

She laughed with glee.

"Mind!" she said. "I want to sit next to you."

"I'd as lief be neighbors with a vixen," he said, nevertheless making place for her between him and Miriam.

"Did it ruffle his pretty hair, then!" she cried; and, with her hair comb, she combed him straight. "And his nice little moustache!" she exclaimed. She tilted his head back and combed his young moustache. "It's a wicked moustache, 'Postle," she said. "It's a red for danger. Have you got any of those cigarettes?"

He pulled his cigarette case from his pocket. Beatrice looked inside it.

"And fancy me having Connie's last cig," said Beatrice, putting the thing between her teeth. He held a lit match to her, and she puffed daintily.

"Thanks so much, darling," she said mockingly.

It gave her a wicked delight.

"Don't you think he does it nicely, Miriam?" she asked.

"Oh, very!" said Miriam.

He took a cigarette for himself.

"Light, old boy?" said Beatrice, tilting her cigarette at him.

He bent forward to her to light his cigarette at hers. She was winking at him as she did so. Miriam saw his eyes trembling with mischief, and his full, almost sensual, mouth quivering. He was not himself, and she could not bear it. As he was now, she had no connection with him; she might as well not have existed. She saw the cigarette dancing on his full red lips. She hated his thick hair for being tumbled loose on his forehead.

"Sweet boy!" said Beatrice, tipping up his chin and giving him a little kiss on the cheek.

"I s'll kiss thee back, Beat," he said.

"Tha wunna!" she giggled, jumping up and going away. "Isn't he shameless, Miriam?"

"Quite," said Miriam. "By the way, aren't you forgetting the bread?"

"By Jove!" he cried, flinging open the oven door.

Out puffed the bluish smoke and a smell of burned bread.

"Oh, golly!" cried Beatrice, coming to his side. He crouched before the oven, she peered over his shoulder. "This is what comes of the oblivion of love, my boy."

Paul was ruefully removing the loaves. One was burnt black on the hot side; another was hard as a brick.

"Poor mater!" said Paul.

"You want to grate it," said Beatrice. "Fetch me the nutmeg grater."

She arranged the bread in the oven. He brought the grater, and she grated the bread on to a newspaper on the table. He set the doors open to blow away the smell of burned bread. Beatrice grated away, puffing her cigarette, knocking the charcoal off the poor loaf.

"My word, Miriam! you're in for it this time," said Beatrice.

"I!" exclaimed Miriam in amazement.

"You'd better be gone when his mother comes in. *I* know why King Alfred burned the cakes. Now I see it! 'Postle would fix up a tale about his work making him forget, if he thought it would wash. If that old woman had come in a bit sooner, she'd have boxed the brazen thing's ears who made the oblivion, instead of poor Alfred's."

She giggled as she scraped the loaf. Even Miriam laughed in spite of herself. Paul mended the fire ruefully.

The garden gate was heard to bang.

"Quick!" cried Beatrice, giving Paul the scraped loaf. "Wrap it up in a damp towel."

Paul disappeared into the scullery. Beatrice hastily blew her scrapings into the fire, and sat down innocently. Annie came bursting in. She was an abrupt, quite smart young woman. She blinked in the strong light.

"Smell of burning!" she exclaimed.

"It's the cigarettes," replied Beatrice demurely.

"Where's Paul?"

Leonard had followed Annie. He had a long comic face and blue eyes, very sad.

"I suppose he's left you to settle it between you," he said. He nodded sympathetically to Miriam, and became gently sarcastic to Beatrice.

"No," said Beatrice, "he's gone off with number nine."

"I just met number five inquiring for him," said Leonard.

"Yes—we're going to share him up like Solomon's baby," said Beatrice.

Annie laughed.

"Oh, ay," said Leonard. "And which bit should you have?"

"I don't know, " said Beatrice. "I'll let all the others pick first."

"An' you'd have the leavings, like?" said Leonard, twisting up a comic face.

Annie was looking in the oven. Miriam sat ignored. Paul entered.

"This bread's a fine sight, our Paul," said Annie.

"Then you should stop an' look after it," said Paul.

"You mean *you* should do what you're reckoning to do," replied Annie.

"He should, shouldn't he!" cried Beatrice.

"I s'd think he'd got plenty on hand," said Leonard.

"You had a nasty walk, didn't you, Miriam?" said Annie.

"Yes—but I'd been in all week——"

"And you wanted a bit of a change, like," insinuated Leonard kindly.

"Well, you can't be stuck in the house forever," Annie agreed. She was quite amiable. Beatrice pulled on her coat, and went out with Leonard and Annie. She would meet her own boy.

"Don't forget that bread, our Paul," cried Annie. "Good-night, Miriam. I don't think it will rain."

When they had all gone, Paul fetched the swathed loaf, unwrapped it, and surveyed it sadly.

"It's a mess!" he said.

"But," answered Miriam impatiently, "what is it, after all—twopence ha'penny."

"Yes, but—but it's the mater's precious baking, and she'll take it to heart. However, it's no good bothering."

He took the loaf back into the scullery. There was a little distance between him and Miriam. He stood balanced opposite her for some moments considering, thinking of his behavior with Beatrice. He felt guilty inside himself, and yet glad. For some inscrutable reason it served Miriam right. He was not going to repent. She wondered what he was thinking of as he stood suspended. His thick hair was tumbled over his forehead. Why might she not push it back for him, and remove the marks of Beatrice's comb? Why might she not press his body with her two hands? It looked so firm, and every whit living. And he would let other girls, why not her?

Suddenly he started into life. It made her quiver almost with terror as he quickly pushed the hair off his forehead and came towards her.

"Half-past eight!" he said. "We'd better buck up. Where's your French?"

Miriam shyly and rather bitterly produced her exercise book. Every week she wrote for him a sort of diary of her inner life, in her own French. He had found this was the only way to get her to do composition. And her diary was mostly a love letter. He would read it now; she felt as if her soul's history were going to be desecrated by him in his present mood. He sat beside her. She watched his hand, firm and warm, rigorously scoring her work. He was reading only the French, ignoring her soul that was there. But gradually his hand forgot its work. He read in silence, motionless. She quivered.

" 'Ce matin les oiseaux m'ont éveillé,' " he read. " 'Il faisait encore un crépuscule. Mais la petite fenêtre de ma chambre, était blême, et puis, jaûne, et tous les oiseaux du bois éclatèrent dans un chanson vif et résonnant. Toute l'aûbe tressaillit. J'avais rêvé de vous. Est-ce que vous voyez aussi l'aûbe? Les oiseaux m'éveillent presque tous les matins, et toujours il y a quelque chose de terreur dans le cri des grives. Il est si clair——' "

Miriam sat tremulous, half ashamed. He remained quite still, trying to understand. He only knew she loved him. He was afraid of her love for him. It was too good for him, and he was inadequate. His own love was at fault, not hers. Ashamed, he corrected her work, humbly writing above her words.

"Look," he said quietly, "the past participle conjugated with *avoir* agrees with the direct object when it precedes."

She bent forward, trying to see and to understand. Her free, fine curls tickled his face. He started as if they had been red hot, shuddering. He saw her peering forward at the page, her red lips parted piteously, the black hair springing in fine strands across her tawny, ruddy cheek. She was colored like a pomegranate for richness. His breath came short as he watched her. Suddenly she looked up at him. Her dark eyes were naked with their love, afraid, and yearning. His eyes, too, were dark, and they hurt her. They seemed to master her. She lost all her self-control, was exposed in fear. And he knew, before he could kiss her, he must drive something out of himself. And a touch of hate for her crept back again into his heart. He returned to her exercise.

Suddenly he flung down the pencil, and was at the oven in a leap, turning the bread. For Miriam he was too quick. She started violently, and it hurt her with real pain. Even the way he crouched before the oven hurt her. There seemed to be something cruel in it, something cruel in the swift way he pitched the bread out of the tins, caught it up again. If only he had been gentle in his movements she would have felt so rich and warm. As it was, she was hurt.

He returned and finished the exercise.

"You've done well this week," he said.

She saw he was flattered by her diary. It did not repay her entirely.

"You really do blossom out sometimes," he said. "You ought to write poetry."

She lifted her head with joy, then she shook it mistrustfully.

"I don't trust myself," she said.

"You should try!"

Again she shook her head.

"Shall we read, or is it too late?" he asked.

"It is late—but we can read just a little," she pleaded.

She was really getting now the food for her life during the next week. He made her copy Baudelaire's "Le Balcon." Then he read it for her. His voice was soft and caressing, but growing almost brutal. He had a way of lifting his lips and showing his teeth, passionately and bitterly, when he was much moved. This he did now. It made Miriam feel as if he were trampling on her. She dared not look at him, but sat with her head bowed. She could not understand why he got into such a tumult and fury. It made her wretched. She did not like Baudelaire, on the whole—nor Verlaine.

> Behold her singing in the field,
> Yon solitary highland lass.

That nourished her heart. So did "Fair Ines." And—

> It is a beauteous evening, calm and free,
> The holy time is quiet as a Nun.

These were like herself. And there was he, saying in his throat bitterly:

> "Tu te rappeleras la beauté des caresses."

The poem was finished; he took the bread out of the oven, arranging the burnt loaves at the bottom of the panchion, the good ones at the top. The desiccated loaf remained swathed up in the scullery.

"Mater needn't know till morning," he said. "It won't upset her so much then as at night."

Miriam looked in the bookcase, saw what postcards and letters he had received, saw what books were there. She took one that had interested him. Then he turned down the gas, and they set off. He did not trouble to lock the door.

He was not home again until a quarter to eleven. His mother was seated in the rocking chair. Annie, with a rope of hair hanging down her back, remained sitting on a low stool before the fire, her elbows on her knees, gloomily. On the table stood the offending loaf unswathed. Paul entered rather breathless. No one spoke. His mother was reading the little local newspaper. He took off his coat, and went to sit down on the sofa. His mother moved curtly aside to let him pass.

No one spoke. He was very uncomfortable. For some minutes he sat pretending to read a piece of paper he found on the table. Then——

"I forgot that bread, mother," he said.

There was no answer from either woman.

"Well," he said, "it's only twopence ha'penny. I can pay you for that."

Being angry he put three pennies on the table, and slid them towards his mother. She turned away her head. Her mouth was shut tightly.

"Yes," said Annie, "you don't know how badly my mother is!"

The girl sat staring glumly into the fire.

"Why is she badly?" asked Paul, in his overbearing way.

"Well!" said Annie. "She could scarcely get home."

He looked closely at his mother. She looked ill.

"*Why* could you scarcely get home?" he asked her, still sharply. She would not answer.

"I found her as white as a sheet sitting here," said Annie, with a suggestion of tears in her voice.

"Well, *why*?" insisted Paul. His brows were knitting, his eyes dilating passionately.

"It was enough to upset anybody," said Mrs. Morel, "hugging those parcels—meat, and green-groceries, and a pair of curtains——"

"Well, why *did* you hug them; you needn't have done."

"Then who would?"

"Let Annie fetch the meat."

"Yes, and I *would* fetch the meat, but how was I to know? You were off with Miriam, instead of being in when my mother came."

"And what was the matter with you?" asked Paul of his mother.

"I suppose it's my heart," she replied. Certainly she looked bluish round the mouth.

"And have you felt it before? "

"Yes—often enough."

"Then why haven't you told me?—and why haven't you seen a doctor?"

Mrs. Morel shifted in her chair, angry with him for his hectoring.

"You'd never notice anything," said Annie. "You're too eager to be off with Miriam."

"Oh, am I—and any worse than you with Leonard?"

"*I* was in at a quarter to ten."

There was silence in the room for a time.

"I should have thought," said Mrs. Morel bitterly, "that she wouldn't have occupied you so entirely as to burn a whole ovenful of bread."

"Beatrice was here as well as she."

"Very likely. But we know why the bread is spoilt."

"Why?" he flashed.

"Because you were engrossed with Miriam," replied Mrs. Morel hotly.

"Oh, very well—then it was *not*!" he replied angrily.

He was distressed and wretched. Seizing a paper, he began to read. Annie, her blouse unfastened, her long ropes of hair twisted into a plait, went up to bed, bidding him a very curt good-night.

Paul sat pretending to read. He knew his mother wanted to upbraid him. He also wanted to know what had made her ill, for he was troubled. So, instead of running away to bed, as he would have liked to do, he sat and waited. There was a tense silence. The clock ticked loudly.

"You'd better go to bed before your father comes in," said the mother harshly. "And if you're going to have anything to eat, you'd better get it."

"I don't want anything."

It was his mother's custom to bring him some trifle for supper on Friday night, the night of luxury for the colliers. He was too angry to go and find it in the pantry this night. This insulted her.

"If I *wanted* you to go to Selby on Friday night, I can imagine the scene," said Mrs. Morel. "But you're never too tired to go if *she* will come for you. Nay, you neither want to eat nor drink then."

"I can't let her go alone."

"Can't you? And why does she come?"

"Not because I ask her."

"She doesn't come without you want her——"

"Well, what if I *do* want her—" he replied.

"Why, nothing if it was sensible or reasonable. But to go traipsing up there miles and miles in the mud, coming home at midnight, and got to go to Nottingham in the morning——"

"If I hadn't, you'd be just the same."

"Yes, I should, because there's no sense in it. Is she *so* fascinating that you must follow her all that way?" Mrs. Morel was bitterly sarcastic. She sat still, with averted face, stroking with a rhythmic, jerked movement the black sateen of her apron. It was a movement that hurt Paul to see.

"I do like her," he said, "but——"

"*Like* her!" said Mrs. Morel, in the same biting tones. "It seems to me you like nothing and nobody else. There's neither Annie, nor me, nor anyone now for you."

"What nonsense, mother—you know I don't love her—I—I tell you I *don't* love her—she doesn't even walk with my arm, because I don't want her to."

"Then why do you fly to her so often!"

"I *do* like to talk to her—I never said I didn't. But I *don't* love her."

"Is there nobody else to talk to?"

"Not about the things we talk of. There's lots of things that you're not interested in, that——"

"What things?"

Mrs. Morel was so intense that Paul began to pant.

"Why—painting—and books. *You* don't care about Herbert Spencer."

"No," was the sad reply. "And *you* won't at my age."

"Well, but I do now—and Miriam does——"

"And how do you know," Mrs. Morel flashed defiantly, "that *I* shouldn't? Do you ever try me?"

"But you don't, mother, you know you don't care whether a picture's decorative or not; you don't care what *manner* it is in."

"How do you know I don't care? Do you ever try me? Do you ever talk to me about these things, to try?"

"But it's not that that matters to you, mother, you know it's not."

"What is it, then—what is it, then, that matters to me?" she flashed. He knitted his brows with pain.

"You're old, mother, and we're young."

He only meant that the interests of *her* age were not the interests of his. But he realized the moment he had spoke that he had said the wrong thing.

"Yes, I know it well—I am old. And therefore I may stand aside; I have nothing more to do with you. You only want me to wait on you—the rest is for Miriam."

He could not bear it. Instinctively he realized that he was life to her. And, after all, she was the chief thing to him, the only supreme thing.

"You know it isn't, mother, you know it isn't!"

She was moved to pity by his cry.

"It looks a great deal like it," she said, half putting aside her despair.

"No, mother—I really *don't* love her. I talk to her, but I want to come home to you."

He had taken off his collar and tie, and rose, bare-throated, to go to bed. As he stooped to kiss his mother, she threw her arms round his neck, hid her face on his shoulder, and cried in a whimpering voice, so unlike her own that he writhed in agony.

"I can't bear it. I could let another woman—but not her. She'd leave me no room, not a bit of room——"

And immediately he hated Miriam bitterly.

"And I've never—you know, Paul—I've never had a husband—not really——"

He stroked his mother's hair, and his mouth was on her throat.

"And she exults so in taking you from me—she's not like ordinary girls."

"Well, I don't love her, mother," he murmured, bowing his head and hiding his eyes on her shoulder in misery. His mother kissed him a long, fervent kiss.

"My boy!" she said, in a voice trembling with passionate love.

Without knowing, he gently stroked her face.

"There," said his mother, "now go to bed. You'll be *so* tired in the morning." As she was speaking she heard her husband coming. "There's your father—now go." Suddenly she looked at him almost as if in fear. "Perhaps I'm selfish. If you want her, take her, my boy."

His mother looked so strange, Paul kissed her, trembling.

"Ha—mother!" he said softly.

Morel came in, walking unevenly. His hat was over one corner of his eye. He balanced in the doorway.

"At your mischief again?" he said venomously.

Mrs. Morel's emotion turned into sudden hate of the drunkard who had come in thus upon her.

"At any rate, it is sober," she said.

"H'm—h'm! h'm—h'm!" he sneered. He went into the passage, hung up his hat and coat. Then they heard him go down three steps to the pantry. He returned with a piece of pork pie in his fist. It was what Mrs. Morel had bought for her son.

"Nor was that bought for you. If you can give me no more than twenty-five shillings, I'm sure I'm not going to buy you pork pie to stuff, after you've swilled a bellyful of beer."

"Wha-at—wha-at!" snarled Morel, toppling in his balance. "Wha-at—not for me?" He looked at the piece of meat and crust, and suddenly, in a vicious spurt of temper, flung it into the fire.

Paul started to his feet.

"Waste your own stuff!" he cried.

"What—what!" suddenly shouted Morel, jumping up and clenching his fist. "I'll show yer, yer young jockey!"

"All right!" said Paul viciously, putting his head on one side. "Show me!"

He would at that moment dearly have loved to have a smack at something. Morel was half crouching, fists up, ready to spring. The young man stood, smiling with his lips.

"Ussha!" hissed the father, swiping round with a great stroke just past his son's face. He dared not, even though so close, really touch the young man, but swerved an inch away.

"Right!" said Paul, his eyes upon the side of his father's mouth, where in another instant his fist would have hit. He ached for that stroke. But he heard a faint moan from behind. His mother was deadly pale, dark at the mouth. Morel was dancing up to deliver another blow.

"Father!" said Paul, so that the word rang.

Morel started, and stood at attention.

"Mother!" moaned the boy. "Mother!"

She began to struggle with herself. Her open eyes watched him, although she could not move. Gradually she was coming to herself. He laid her down on the sofa, and ran upstairs for a little whisky, which at last she could sip. The tears were hopping down his face. As he kneeled in front of her he did not cry, but the tears ran down his face quickly. Morel, on the opposite side of the room, sat with his elbows on his knees glaring across.

"What's a-matter with 'er?" he asked.

"Faint!" replied Paul.

"H'm!"

The elderly man began to unlace his boots. He stumbled off to bed. His last fight was fought in that home.

Paul kneeled there, stroking his mother's hand.

"Don't be poorly, mother—don't be poorly!" he said time after time.

"It's nothing, my boy," she murmured.

At last he rose, fetched in a large piece of coal, and raked the fire. Then he cleared the room, put everything straight, laid the things for breakfast, and brought his mother's candle.

"Can you go to bed, mother?"

"Yes, I'll come."

"Sleep with Annie, mother, not with him."

"No. I'll sleep in my own bed."

"Don't sleep with him, mother."

"I'll sleep in my own bed."

She rose, and he turned out the gas, then followed her closely upstairs, carrying her candle. On the landing he kissed her close.

"Good-night, mother."

"Good-night!" she said.

He pressed his face upon the pillow in a fury of misery. And yet, somewhere in his soul, he was at peace because he still loved his mother best. It was the bitter peace of resignation.

The efforts of his father to conciliate him next day were a great humiliation to him.

Everybody tried to forget the scene.

❖ 9 ❖

DEFEAT OF MIRIAM

Paul was dissatisfied with himself and with everything. The deepest of his love belonged to his mother. When he felt he had hurt her, or wounded his love for her, he could not bear it. Now it was spring, and there was battle between him and Miriam. This year he had a good deal against her. She was vaguely aware of it. The old feeling that she was to be a sacrifice to this love, which she had had when she prayed, was mingled in all her emotions. She did not at the bottom believe she ever would have him. She did not believe in herself primarily: doubted whether she could ever be what he would demand of her. Certainly she never saw herself living happily through a lifetime with him. She saw tragedy, sorrow, and sacrifice ahead. And in sacrifice she was proud, in renunciation she was strong, for she did not trust herself to support everyday life. She was prepared for the big things and the deep things, like tragedy. It was the sufficiency of the small day-life she could not trust.

The Easter holidays began happily. Paul was his own frank self. Yet she felt it would go wrong. On the Sunday afternoon she stood at her bedroom window, looking across at the oak trees of the wood, in whose branches a twilight was tangled, below the bright sky of the afternoon. Gray-green rosettes of honeysuckle leaves hung before the window, some already, she fancied, showing bud. It was spring, which she loved and dreaded.

Hearing the clack of the gate she stood in suspense. It was a bright gray day. Paul came into the yard with his bicycle, which glittered as he walked. Usually he rang his bell and laughed towards the house. Today he walked with shut lips and cold, cruel bearing, that had something of a slouch and a sneer in it. She knew him well by now, and could tell from that keen-looking, aloof young body of his what was happening inside him. There was a cold correctness in the way he put his bicycle in its place, that made her heart sink.

She came downstairs nervously. She was wearing a new net blouse that she thought became her. It had a high collar with a tiny ruff, reminding her of Mary, Queeen of Scots, and making her, she thought, look wonderfully a woman, and dignified. At twenty she was full-breasted and luxuriously formed. Her face was still like a soft rich mask, unchangeable. But her eyes, once lifted, were wonderful. She was afraid of him. He would notice her new blouse.

He, being in a hard, ironical mood, was entertaining the family to a description of a service given in the Primitive Methodist Chapel, conducted by one of the well-known preachers of the sect. He sat at the head of the table, his mobile face, with the eyes that could be so beautiful, shining with tenderness or dancing with laughter, now taking on one expression and then another, in imitation of various people he was mocking. His mockery always hurt her; it was too near the reality. He was too clever and cruel. She felt that when his eyes were like this, hard with mocking hate, he would spare neither himself nor anybody else. But Mrs. Leivers was wiping her eyes with laughter, and Mr. Leivers, just awake from his Sunday nap, was rubbing his head in amusement. The three brothers sat with ruffled, sleepy appearance in their shirt-sleeves, giving a guffaw from time to time. The whole family loved a "take-off" more than anything.

He took no notice of Miriam. Later, she saw him remark her new blouse, saw that the artist approved, but it won from him not a spark of warmth. She was nervous, could hardly reach the teacups from the shelves.

When the men went out to milk, she ventured to address him personally.

"You were late," she said.

"Was I?" he answered.

There was silence for a while.

"Was it rough riding?" she asked.

"I didn't notice it."

She continued quickly to lay the table. When she had finished——

"Tea won't be for a few minutes. Will you come and look at the daffodils?" she said.

He rose without answering. They went out into the back garden under the budding damson trees. The hills and the sky were clean and cold. Everything looked washed, rather hard. Miriam glanced at Paul. He was pale and impassive. It seemed cruel to her that his eyes and brows, which she loved, could look so hurting.

"Has the wind made you tired?" she asked. She detected an underneath feeling of weariness about him.

"No, I think not," he answered.

"It must be rough on the road—the wood moans so."

"You can see by the clouds it's a southwest wind; that helps me here."

"You see, I don't cycle, so I don't understand," she murmured.

"Is there need to cycle to know that?" he said.

She thought his sarcasms were unnecessary. They went forward in silence. Round the wild, tussocky lawn at the back of the house was a thorn hedge, under which daffodils were craning forward from among their sheaves of gray-green blades. The cheeks of the flowers were greenish with cold. But still some had burst, and their gold ruffled and glowed. Miriam went on her knees before one cluster, took a wild-looking daffodil between her hands, turned up its face of gold to her, and bowed down, caressing it with her mouth and cheeks and brow. He stood aside, with his hands in his pockets, watching her. One after another she turned up to him the faces of the yellow, bursten flowers appealingly, fondling them lavishly all the while.

"Aren't they magnificent?" she murmured.

"Magnificent! it's a bit thick—they're pretty!"

She bowed again to her flowers at his censure of her praise. He watched her crouching, sipping the flowers with fervid kisses.

"Why must you always be fondling things!" he said irritably.

"But I love to touch them," she replied, hurt.

"Can you never like things without clutching them as if you wanted to pull the heart out of them? Why don't you have a bit more restraint, or reserve, or something?"

She looked up at him full of pain, then continued slowly to stroke her lips against a ruffled flower. Their scent, as she smelled it, was so much kinder than he; it almost made her cry.

"You wheedle the soul out of things," he said. "I would never wheedle—at any rate, I'd go straight."

He scarcely knew what he was saying. These things came from him mechanically. She looked at him. His body seemed one weapon, firm and hard against her.

"You're always begging things to love you," he said, "as if you were a beggar for love. Even the flowers, you have to fawn on them——"

Rhythmically, Miriam was swaying and stroking the flower with her mouth, inhaling the scent which ever after made her shudder as it came to her nostrils.

"You don't want to love—your eternal and abnormal craving is to be loved. You aren't positive, you're negative. You absorb, absorb, as if you must fill yourself up with love, because you've got a shortage somewhere."

She was stunned by his cruelty, and did not hear. He had not the faintest notion of what he was saying. It was as if his fretted, tortured soul, run hot by thwarted passion, jetted off these sayings like sparks from electricity. She did not grasp anything he said. She only sat crouched beneath his cruelty and his hatred of her. She never realized in a flash. Over everything she brooded and brooded.

After tea he stayed with Edgar and the brothers, taking no notice of Miriam. She, extremely unhappy on this looked-for holiday, waited for him. And at last he yielded and came to her. She was determined to track this mood of his to its origin. She counted it not much more than a mood.

"Shall we go through the wood a little way?" she asked him, knowing he never refused a direct request.

They went down to the warren. On the middle path they passed a trap, a narrow horseshoe hedge of small fir boughs, baited with the guts of a rabbit. Paul glanced at it frowning. She caught his eye.

"Isn't it dreadful?" she asked.

"I don't know! Is it worse than a weasel with its teeth in a rabbit's throat? One weasel or many rabbits? One or the other must go!"

He was taking the bitterness of life badly. She was rather sorry for him.

"We will go back to the house," he said. "I don't want to walk out."

They went past the lilac tree, whose bronze leaf buds were coming unfastened. Just a fragment remained of the haystack, a monument squared and brown, like a pillar of stone. There was a little bed of hay from the last cutting.

"Let us sit here a minute," said Miriam.

He sat down against his will, resting his back against the hard wall of hay. They faced the amphitheater of round hills that glowed with sunset, tiny white farms standing out, the meadows golden, the woods dark and yet luminous, treetops folded over treetops, distinct in the distance. The evening had cleared, and the east was tender with a magenta flush under which the land lay still and rich.

"Isn't it beautiful?" she pleaded.

But he only scowled. He would rather have had it ugly just then.

At that moment a big bull terrier came rushing up, openmouthed, pranced his two paws on the youth's shoulders, licking his face. Paul drew back, laughing. Bill was a great relief to him. He pushed the dog aside, but it came leaping back.

"Get out," said the lad, "or I'll dot thee one."

But the dog was not to be pushed away. So Paul had a little battle with the creature, pitching poor Bill away from him, who, however, only floundered tumultuously back again, wild with joy. The two fought together, the man laughing grudgingly, the dog grinning all over. Miriam watched them. There was something pathetic about the man. He wanted so badly to love, to be tender. The rough way he bowled the dog over was really loving. Bill got up, panting with happiness, his brown eyes rolling in his white face, and lumbered back again. He adored Paul. The lad frowned.

"Bill, I've had enough o' thee," he said.

But the dog only stood with two heavy paws, that quivered with love, upon his thigh, and flickered a red tongue at him. He drew back.

"No," he said—"no—I've had enough."

And in a minute the dog trotted off happily to vary the fun.

He remained staring miserably across at the hills, whose still beauty he begrudged. He wanted to go and cycle with Edgar. Yet he had not the courage to leave Miriam.

"Why are you sad?" she asked humbly.

"I'm not sad; why should I be," he answered. "I'm only normal."

She wondered why he always claimed to be normal when he was disagreeable.

"But what is the matter?" she pleaded, coaxing him soothingly.

"Nothing!"

"Nay!" she murmured.

He picked up a stick and began to stab the earth with it.

"You'd far better not talk," he said.

"But I wish to know—" she replied.

He laughed resentfully.

"You always do," he said.

"It's not fair to me," she murmured.

He thrust, thrust, thrust at the ground with the pointed stick, digging up little clods of earth as if he were in a fever of irritation. She gently and firmly laid her hand on his wrist.

"Don't!" she said. "Put it away."

He flung the stick into the currant bushes, and leaned back. Now he was bottled up.

"What is it?" she pleaded softly.

He lay perfectly still, only his eyes alive, and they full of torment.

"You know," he said at length, rather wearily—"you know—we'd better break off."

It was what she dreaded. Swiftly everything seemed to darken before her eyes.

"Why!" she murmured. "What has happened?"

"Nothing has happened. We only realize where we are. It's no good——"

She waited in silence, sadly, patiently. It was no good being impatient with him. At any rate, he would tell her now what ailed him.

"We agreed on friendship," he went on in a dull, monotonous voice. "How often *have* we agreed for friendship! And yet—it neither stops there, nor gets anywhere else."

He was silent again. She brooded. What did he mean? He was so wearying. There was something he would not yield. Yet she must be patient with him.

"I can only give friendship—it's all I'm capable of—it's a flaw in my make-up. The thing overbalances to one side—I hate a toppling balance. Let us have done."

There was warmth of fury in his last phrases. He meant she loved him more than he her. Perhaps he could not love her. Perhaps she had not in herself that which he wanted. It was the deepest motive of her soul, this self-mistrust. It was so deep she dared neither realize nor acknowledge it. Perhaps she was sufficient. Like an infinitely subtle shame, it kept her always back. If it were so, she would do without him. She would never let herself want him. She would merely see.

"But what has happened?" she said.

"Nothing—it's all in myself—it only comes out just now. We're always like this towards Easter-time."

He groveled so helplessly, she pitied him. At least she never floundered in such a pitiable way. After all, it was he who was chiefly humiliated.

"What do you want?" she asked him.

"Why—I musn't come often—that's all. Why should I monopolize you when I'm not—You see, I'm deficient in something with regard to you——"

He was telling her he did not love her, and so ought to leave her a chance with another man. How foolish and blind and shamefully clumsy he was! What were other men to her! What were men to her at all! But he, ah! she loved his soul. Was *he* deficient in something? Perhaps he was.

"But I don't understand," she said huskily. "Yesterday——"

The night was turning jangled and hateful to him as the twilight faded. And she bowed under her suffering.

"I know," he cried, "you never will! You'll never believe that I can't—can't physically, anymore than I can fly up like a skylark——"

"What?" she murmured. Now she dreaded.

"Love you."

He hated her bitterly at that moment because he made her suffer. Love her! She knew he loved her. He really belonged to her. This about not loving her, physically, bodily, was a mere perversity on his part, because he knew she loved him. He was stupid like a child. He belonged to her. His soul wanted her. She guessed somebody had been influencing him. She felt upon him the hardness, the foreignness of another influence.

"What have they been saying at home?" she asked.

"It's not that," he answered.

And then she knew it was. She despised them for their commonness, his people. They did not know what things were really worth.

He and she talked very little more that night. After all he left her to cycle with Edgar.

He had come back to his mother. Hers was the strongest tie in his life. When he thought round, Miriam shrank away. There was a vague, unreal feel about her. And nobody else mattered. There was one place in the world that stood solid and did not melt into unreality: the place where his mother was. Everybody else could grow shadowy, almost nonexistent to him, but she could not. It was as if the pivot and pole of his life, from which he could not escape, was his mother.

And in the same way she waited for him. In him was established her life now. After all, the life beyond offered very little to Mrs. Morel. She saw that our chance for *doing* is here, and doing counted with her. Paul was going to prove that she had been right; he was going to make a man whom nothing should shift off his feet; he was going to alter the face of the earth in some way which mattered. Wherever he went she felt her soul went with him. Whatever he did she felt her soul stood by him, ready, as it were, to hand him his tools. She could not bear it when he was with Miriam. William was dead. She would fight to keep Paul.

And he came back to her. And in his soul was a feeling of the satisfaction of self-sacrifice because he was faithful to her. She loved him first; he loved her first. And yet it was not enough. His new young life, so strong and imperious, was urged towards something else. It made him mad with restlessness. She saw this, and wished bitterly that Miriam had been a woman who could take this new life of his, and leave her the roots. He fought against his mother almost as he fought against Miriam.

It was a week before he went again to Willey Farm. Miriam had suffered a great deal, and was afraid to see him again. Was she now to endure the ignominy of his abandoning her? That would only be superficial and temporary. He would come back. She held the keys to his soul. But meanwhile, how he would torture her with his battle against her. She shrank from it.

However, the Sunday after Easter he came to tea. Mrs. Leivers was glad to see him. She gathered something was fretting him, that he found things hard. He seemed to drift to her for comfort. And she was good to him. She did him that great kindness of treating him almost with reverence.

He met her with the young children in the front garden.

"I'm glad you've come," said the mother, looking at him with her great appealing brown eyes. "It is such a sunny day. I was just going down the fields for the first time this year."

He felt she would like him to come. That soothed him. They went, talking simply, he gentle and humble. He could have wept with gratitude that she was deferential to him. He was feeling humiliated.

At the bottom of the Mow Close they found a thrush's nest.

"Shall I show you the eggs?" he said.

"Do!" replied Mrs. Leivers. "They seem *such* a sign of spring, and so hopeful."

He put aside the thorns, and took out the eggs, holding them in the palm of his hand.

"They are quite hot—I think we frightened her off them," he said.

"Ay, poor thing!" said Mrs. Leivers.

Miriam could not help touching the eggs, and his hand which, it seemed to her, cradled them so well.

"Isn't it a strange warmth!" she murmured, to get near him.

"Blood heat," he answered.

She watched him putting them back, his body pressed against the hedge, his arm reaching slowly through the thorns, his hand folded carefully over the eggs. He was concentrated on the act. Seeing him so, she loved him; he seemed so simple and sufficient to himself. And she could not get to him.

After tea she stood hesitating at the bookshelf. He took *Tartarin de Tarascon*. Again they sat on the bank of hay at the foot of the stack. He read a couple of pages, but without any heart for it. Again the dog came racing up to repeat the fun of the other day. He shoved his muzzle in the man's chest. Paul fingered his ear for a moment. Then he pushed him away.

"Go away, Bill," he said. "I don't want you."

Bill slunk off, and Miriam wondered and dreaded what was coming. There was a silence about the youth that made her still with apprehension. It was not his furies, but his quiet resolutions that she feared.

Turning his face a little to one side, so that she could not see him, he began, speaking slowly and painfully:

"Do you think—if I didn't come up so much—you might get to like somebody else—another man?"

So this was what he was still harping on.

"But I don't know any other men. Why do you ask?" she replied, in a low tone that should have been a reproach to him.

"Why," he blurted, "because they say I've no right to come up like this—without we mean to marry——"

Miriam was indignant at anybody's forcing the issues between them. She had been furious with her own father for suggesting to Paul, laughingly, that he knew why he came so much.

"Who says?" she asked, wondering if her people had anything to do with it. They had not.

"Mother—and the others. They say at this rate everybody will consider me engaged, and I ought to consider myself so, because it's not fair to you. And I've tried to find out—and I don't think I love you as a man ought to love his wife. What do *you* think about it?"

Miriam bowed her head moodily. She was angry at having this struggle. People should leave him and her alone.

"I don't know," she murmured.

"Do you think we love each other enough to marry?" he asked definitely. It made her tremble.

"No," she answered truthfully. "I don't think so—we're too young."

"I thought perhaps," he went on miserably, "that you, with your intensity in things, might have given me more—than I could ever make up to you. And even now—if you think it better—we'll be engaged."

Now Miriam wanted to cry. And she was angry, too. He was always such a child for people to do as they liked with.

"No, I don't think so," she said firmly.

He pondered a minute.

"You see," he said, "with me—I don't think one person would ever monopolize me—be everything to me—I think never."

This she did not consider.

"No," she murmured. Then, after a pause, she looked at him and her dark eyes flashed.

"This is your mother," she said. "I know she never liked me."

"No, no, it isn't," he said hastily. "It was for your sake she spoke this time. She only said, if I was going on, I ought to consider myself engaged." There was a silence. "And if I ask you to come down any time, you won't stop away will you?"

She did not answer. By this time she was very angry.

"Well, what shall we do?" she said shortly. "I suppose I'd better drop French. I was just beginning to get on with it. But I suppose I can go on alone."

"I don't see that we need," he said. "I can give you a French lesson, surely."

"Well—and there are Sunday nights. I shan't stop coming to chapel, because I enjoy it, and it's all the social life I get. But you've no need to come home with me. I can go alone."

"All right," he answered, rather taken aback. "But if I ask Edgar, he'll always come with us, and then they can say nothing."

There was silence. After all, then, she would not lose much. For all their talk down at his home there would not be much difference. She wished they would mind their own business.

"And you won't think about it, and let it trouble you, will you?" he asked.

"Oh, no," replied Miriam, without looking at him.

He was silent. She thought him unstable. He had no fixity of purpose, no anchor of righteousness that held him.

"Because," he continued, "a man gets across his bicycle and goes to work—and does all sorts of things. But a woman broods."

"No, I shan't bother," said Miriam. And she meant it.

It had gone rather chilly. They went indoors.

"How white Paul looks!" Mrs. Leivers exclaimed. "Miriam, you shouldn't have let him sit out of doors. Do you think you've taken cold, Paul?"

"Oh no!" he laughed.

But he felt done up. It wore him out, the conflict in himself. Miriam pitied him now. But quite early, before nine o'clock, he rose to go.

"You're not going home, are you?" asked Mrs. Leivers anxiously.

"Yes," he replied. "I said I'd be early." He was very awkward.

"But this *is* early," said Mr. Leivers.

Miriam sat in the rocking chair, and did not speak. He hesitated, expecting her to rise and go with him to the barn as usual for his bicycle. She remained as she was. He was at a loss.

"Well—good-night all!" he faltered.

She spoke her good-night along with all the others. But as he went past the window he looked in. She saw him pale, his brows knit slightly in a way that had become constant with him, his eyes dark with pain.

She rose and went to the doorway to wave good-bye to him as he passed through the gate. He rode slowly under the pine trees, feeling a cur and a miserable wretch. His bicycle went tilting down the hills at random. He thought it would be a relief to break one's neck.

Two days later he sent her up a book and a little note, urging her to read and be busy.

At this time he gave all his friendship to Edgar. He loved the family so much, he loved the farm so much; it was the dearest place on earth to him. His home was not so lovable. It was his mother. But then he would have been just as happy with his mother anywhere. Whereas Willey Farm he loved passionately. He loved the little pokey kitchen, where men's boots tramped, and the dog slept with one eye open for fear of being trodden on; where the lamp hung over the table at night, and everything was so silent. He loved Miriam's long, low parlor, with its atmosphere of romance, its flowers, its books, its high rosewood piano. He loved the gardens and the buildings that stood with their scarlet roofs on the naked edges of the fields, crept towards the wood as if for cosiness, the wild country scooping down a valley and up the uncultured hills of the other side. Only to be there was an exhilaration and a joy to him. He loved Mrs. Leivers, with her unworldliness and her quaint cynicism; he loved Mr. Leivers, so warm and young and lovable; he loved Edgar, who lit up when he came, and the boys and the children and Bill—even the sow Circe and the Indian gamecock called Tippoo. All this besides Miriam. He could not give it up.

So he went as often, but he was usually with Edgar. Only all the family, including the father, joined in charades and games at evening. And later, Miriam drew them together, and they read *Macbeth* out of penny books, taking parts. It was great excitement. Miriam was glad, and Mrs. Leivers was glad, and Mr. Leivers enjoyed it. Then they all learned songs together from tonic sol-fa, singing in a circle round the fire. But now Paul was very rarely alone with Miriam. She waited.

When she and Edgar and he walked home together from chapel or from the literary society in Bestwood, she knew his talk, so passionate and so unorthodox nowadays, was for her. She did envy Edgar, however, his cycling with Paul, his Friday nights, his days working in the fields. For her Friday nights and her French lessons were gone. She was nearly always alone, walking, pondering in the wood, reading, studying, dreaming, waiting. And he wrote to her frequently.

One Sunday evening they attained to their old rare harmony. Edgar had stayed to Communion—he wondered what it was like—with Mrs. Morel. So Paul came on alone with Miriam to his home. He was more or less under her spell again. As usual, they were discussing the sermon. He was setting now full sail towards Agnosticism, but such a religious Agnosticism that Miriam did not suffer so badly. They were at the Renan *Vie de Jésus* stage. Miriam was the threshing floor on which he threshed out all his beliefs. While he trampled his ideas upon her soul, the truth came out for him. She alone was his threshing floor. She alone helped him towards realization. Almost impassive, she submitted to his argument and expounding. And somehow, because of her, he gradually realized where he was wrong. And what he realized, she realized. She felt he could not do without her.

They came to the silent house. He took the key out of the scullery window, and they entered. All the time he went on with his discussion. He lit the gas, mended the fire, and brought her some cakes from the pantry. She sat on the sofa, quietly, with a plate on her knee. She wore a large white hat with some pinkish flowers. It was a cheap hat, but he liked it. Her face beneath was still and pensive, golden-brown and ruddy. Always her ears were hid in her short curls. She watched him.

She liked him on Sundays. Then he wore a dark suit that showed the lithe movement of his body. There was a clean, clear-cut look about him. He went on with his thinking to her. Suddenly he reached for a Bible. Miriam liked the way he reached up—so sharp, straight to the mark. He turned the pages quickly, and read her a chapter of St. John. As he sat in the armchair reading, intent, his voice only thinking, she felt as if he were using her unconsciously as a man uses his tools at some work he is bent on. She loved it. And the wistfulness of his voice was like a reaching to something, and it was as if she were what he reached with. She sat back on the sofa away from him, and yet feeling herself the very instrument his hand grasped. It gave her great pleasure.

Then he began to falter and to get self-conscious. And when he came to the verse, "A woman, when she is in travail, hath sorrow because her hour is come," he missed it out. Miriam had felt him growing uncomfortable. She shrank when the well-known words did not follow. He went on reading, but she did not hear. A grief and shame made her bend her head. Six months ago he would have read it simply.

Now there was a scotch in his running with her. Now she felt there was really something hostile between them, something of which they were ashamed.

She ate her cake mechanically. He tried to go on with his argument, but could not get back the right note. Soon Edgar came in. Mrs. Morel had gone to her friends'. The three set off to Willey Farm.

Miriam brooded over his split with her. There was something else he wanted. He could not be satisfied; he could give her no peace. There was between them now always a ground for strife. She wanted to prove him. She believed that his chief need in life was herself. If she could prove it, both to herself and to him, the rest might go; she could simply trust to the future.

So in May she asked him to come to Willey Farm and meet Mrs. Dawes. There was something he hankered after. She saw him, whenever they spoke of Clara Dawes, rouse and get slightly angry. He said he did not like her. Yet he was keen to know about her. Well, he should put himself to the test. She believed that there were in him desires for higher things, and desires for lower, and that the desires for the higher would conquer. At any rate, he should try. She forgot that her "higher" and "lower" were arbitrary.

He was rather excited at the idea of meeting Clara at Willey Farm. Mrs. Dawes came for the day. Her heavy, dun-colored hair was coiled on top of her head. She wore a white blouse and navy skirt, and somehow, wherever she was, seemed to make things look paltry and insignificant. When she was in the room, the kitchen seemed too small and mean altogether. Miriam's beautiful twilighty parlor looked stiff and stupid. All the Leivers were eclipsed like candles. They found her rather hard to put up with. Yet she was perfectly amiable, but indifferent, and rather hard.

Paul did not come till afternoon. He was early. As he swung off his bicycle, Miriam saw him look round at the house eagerly. He would be disappointed if the visitor had not come. Miriam went out to meet him, bowing her head because of the sunshine. Nasturtiums were coming out crimson under the cool green shadow of their leaves. The girl stood, dark-haired, glad to see him.

"Hasn't Clara come?" he asked.

"Yes," replied Miriam in her musical tone. "She's reading."

He wheeled his bicycle into the barn. He had put on a handsome tie, of which he was rather proud, and socks to match.

"She came this morning?" he asked.

"Yes," replied Miriam, as she walked at his side. "You said you'd bring me that letter from the man at Liberty's. Have you remembered?"

"Oh dash, no!" he said. "But nag at me till you get it."

"I don't like to nag at you."

"Do it whether or not. And is she any more agreeable?" he continued.

"You know I always think she is quite agreeable."

He was silent. Evidently his eagerness to be early today had been the newcomer. Miriam already began to suffer. They went together towards the house. He took the clips off his trousers, but was too lazy to brush the dust from his shoes, in spite of the socks and tie.

Clara sat in the cool parlor reading. He saw the nape of her white neck, and the fine hair lifted from it. She rose, looking at him indifferently. To shake hands she lifted her arm straight, in a manner that seemed at once to keep him at a distance, and yet to fling something to him. He noticed how her breasts swelled inside her blouse, and how her shoulder curved handsomely under the thin muslin at the top of her arm.

"You have chosen a fine day," he said.

"It happens so," she said.

"Yes," he said; "I am glad."

She sat down, not thanking him for his politeness.

"What have you been doing all morning?" asked Paul of Miriam.

"Well, you see," said Miriam, coughing huskily, "Clara only came with father—and so—she's not been here very long."

Clara sat leaning on the table, holding aloof. He noticed her hands were large, but well kept. And the skin on them seemed almost coarse, opaque, and white, with fine golden hairs. She did not mind if he observed her hands. She intended to scorn him. Her heavy arm lay negligently on the table. Her mouth was closed as if she were offended, and she kept her face slightly averted.

"You were at Margaret Bonford's meeting the other evening," he said to her.

Miriam did not know this courteous Paul. Clara glanced at him.

"Yes," she said.

"Why," asked Miriam, "how do you know?"

"I went in for a few minutes before the train came," he answered.

Clara turned away again rather disdainfully.

"I think she's a lovable little woman," said Paul.

"Margaret Bonford!" exclaimed Clara. "She's a great deal cleverer than most men."

"Well, I didn't say she wasn't," he said, deprecating. "She's lovable for all that."

"And of course, that is all that matters," said Clara witheringly.

He rubbed his head, rather perplexed, rather annoyed.

"I suppose it matters more than her cleverness," he said; "which, after all, would never get her to heaven."

"It's not heaven she wants to get—it's her fair share on earth," retorted Clara. She spoke as if he were responsible for some deprivation which Miss Bonford suffered.

"Well," he said, "I thought she was warm, and awfully nice—only too frail. I wished she was sitting comfortably in peace——"

" 'Darning her husband's stockings,' " said Clara scathingly.

"I'm sure she wouldn't mind darning even my stockings," he said. "And I'm sure she'd do them well. Just as I wouldn't mind blacking her boots if she wanted me to."

But Clara refused to answer this sally of his. He talked to Miriam for a little while. The other woman held aloof.

"Well," he said, "I think I'll go and see Edgar. Is he on the land?"

"I believe," said Miriam, "he's gone for a load of coal. He should be back directly."

"Then," he said, "I'll go and meet him."

Miriam dared not propose anything for the three of them. He rose and left them.

On the top road, where the gorse was out, he saw Edgar walking lazily beside the mare, who nodded her white-starred forehead as she dragged the clanking load of coal. The young farmer's face lighted up as he saw his friend. Edgar was good-looking, with dark, warm eyes. His clothes were old and rather disreputable, and he walked with considerable pride.

"Hello!" he said, seeing Paul bareheaded. "Where are you going?"

"Came to meet you. Can't stand 'Nevermore.' "

Edgar's teeth flashed in a laugh of amusement.

"Who is 'Nevermore'?" he asked.

"The lady—Mrs. Dawes—it ought to be Mrs. The Raven that quothed 'Nevermore.' "

Edgar laughed with glee.

"Don't you like her?" he asked.

"Not a fat lot," said Paul. "Why, do you?"

"No!" The answer came with a deep ring of conviction. "No!" Edgar pursed up his lips. "I can't say she's much in my line." He mused a little. Then: "But why do you call her 'Nevermore'?" he asked.

"Well," said Paul, "if she looks at a man she says haughtily 'Nevermore,' and if she looks at herself in the looking glass she says disdainfully 'Nevermore,' and if she thinks back she says it in disgust, and if she looks forward she says it cynically."

Edgar considered this speech, failed to make much out of it, and said, laughing:

"You think she's a man-hater?"

"*She* thinks she is," replied Paul.

"But you don't think so?"

"No," replied Paul.

"Wasn't she nice with you, then?"

"Could you imagine her *nice* with anybody?" asked the young man.

Edgar laughed. Together they unloaded the coal in the yard. Paul was rather self-conscious, because he knew Clara could see if she looked out of the window. She didn't look.

On Saturday afternoons the horses were brushed down and groomed. Paul and Edgar worked together, sneezing with the dust that came from the pelts of Jimmy and Flower.

"Do you know a new song to teach me?" said Edgar.

He continued to work all the time. The back of his neck was sun-red when he bent down, and his fingers that held the brush were thick. Paul watched him sometimes.

" 'Mary Morrison'?" suggested the younger.

Edgar agreed. He had a good tenor voice, and he loved to learn all the songs his friend could teach him, so that he could sing whilst he was carting. Paul had a very indifferent baritone voice, but a good ear. However, he sang softly, for fear of Clara. Edgar repeated the line in a clear tenor. At times they both broke off to sneeze, and first one, then the other, abused his horse.

Miriam was impatient of men. It took so little to amuse them—even Paul. She thought it anomalous in him that he could be so thoroughly absorbed in a triviality.

It was teatime when they had finished.

"What song was that?" asked Miriam.

Edgar told her. The conversation turned to singing.

"We have such jolly times," Miriam said to Clara.

Mrs. Dawes ate her meal in a slow, dignified way. When ever the men were present she grew distant.

"Do you like singing?" Miriam asked her.

"If it is good," she said.

Paul, of course, colored.

"You mean if it is high-class and trained?" he said.

"I think a voice needs training before the singing is anything," she said.

"You might as well insist on having people's voices trained before you allowed them to talk," he replied. "Really, people sing for their own pleasure, as a rule."

"And it may be for other people's discomfort."

"Then the other people should have flaps to their ears," he replied.

The boys laughed. There was silence. He flushed deeply, and ate in silence.

After tea, when all the men had gone but Paul, Mrs. Leivers said to Clara:

"And you find life happier now?"

"Infinitely."

"And you are satisfied?"

"So long as I can be free and independent."

"And you don't *miss* anything in your life?" asked Mrs. Leivers gently.

"I've put all that behind me."

Paul had been feeling uncomfortable during this discourse. He got up.

"You'll find you're always tumbling over the things you've put behind you," he said. Then he took his departure to the cowsheds. He felt he had been witty, and his manly pride was high. He whistled as he went down the brick track.

Miriam came for him a little later to know if he would go with Clara and her for a walk. They set off down to Strelley Mill Farm. As they were going beside the brook, on the Willey Water side, looking through the brake at the edge of the wood, where pink campions glowed under a few sunbeams, they saw, beyond the tree trunks and the thin hazel bushes, a man leading a great bay horse through the gullies. The big red beast seemed to dance romantically through that dimness of green hazel drift, away there where the air was shadowy, as if it were in the past, among the fading bluebells that might have bloomed for Deidre of Iseult.

The three stood charmed.

"What a treat to be a knight," he said, "and to have a pavilion here."

"And to have us shut up safely?" replied Clara.

"Yes," he answered, "singing with your maids at your broidery. I would carry your banner of white and green and heliotrope. I would have 'W.S.P.U.' emblazoned on my shield, beneath a woman rampant."

"I have no doubt," said Clara, "that you would much rather fight for a woman than let her fight for herself."

"I would. When she fights for herself she seems like a dog before a looking glass, gone into a mad fury with its own shadow."

"And *you* are the looking glass?" she asked, with a curl of the lip.

"Or the shadow," he replied.

"I am afraid," she said, "that you are too clever."

"Well, I leave it to you to be *good*," he retorted, laughing. "Be good, sweet maid, and just let *me* be clever."

But Clara wearied of his flippancy. Suddenly, looking at her, he saw that the upward lifting of her face was misery and not scorn. His heart grew tender for everybody. He turned and was gentle with Miriam, whom he had neglected till then.

At the wood's edge they met Limb, a thin, swarthy man of forty, tenant of Strelley Mill, which he ran as a cattle-raising farm. He held the halter of the powerful stallion indifferently, as if he were tired. The three stood to let him pass over the steppingstones of the first brook. Paul admired that so large an animal should walk on such springy toes, with an endless excess of vigor. Limb pulled up before them.

"Tell your father, Miss Leivers," he said, in a peculiar piping voice, "that his young beas'es 'as broke that bottom fence three days an' runnin'."

"Which?" asked Miriam, tremulous.

The great horse breathed heavily, shifting round its red flanks, and looking suspiciously with its wonderful big eyes upwards from under its lowered head and falling mane.

"Come along a bit," replied Limb, "an' I'll show you."

The man and the stallion went forward. It danced sideways, shaking its white fetlocks and looking frightened, as it felt itself in the brook.

"No hanky-pankyin'," said the man affectionately to the beast.

It went up the bank in little leaps, then splashed finely through the second brook. Clara, walking with a kind of sulky abandon, watched it half-fascinated, half-contemptuous. Limb stopped and pointed to the fence under some willows.

"There, you see where they got through," he said. "My man's druv 'em back three times."

"Yes," answered Miriam, coloring as if she were at fault.

"Are you comin' in?" asked the man.

"No, thanks; but we should like to go by the pond."

"Well, just as you've a mind," he said.

The horse gave little whinnies of pleasure at being so near home.

"He is glad to be back," said Clara, who was interested in the creature.

"Yes—'e's been a tidy step today."

They went through the gate, and saw approaching them from the big farmhouse a smallish, dark, excitable-looking woman of about thirty-five. Her hair was touched with gray, her dark eyes looked wild. She walked with her hands behind her back. Her brother went forward. As it saw her, the big bay stallion whinnied again. She came up excitedly.

"Are you home again, my boy!" she said tenderly to the horse, not to the man. The great beast shifted round to her, ducking his head. She smuggled into his mouth the wrinkled yellow apple she had been hiding behind her back, then she kissed him near the eyes. He gave a big sigh of pleasure. She held his head in her arms against her breast.

"Isn't he splendid!" said Miriam to her.

Miss Limb looked up. Her dark eyes glanced straight at Paul.

"Oh, good-evening, Miss Leivers," she said. "It's ages since you've been down."

Miriam introduced her friends.

"Your horse *is* a fine fellow!" said Clara.

"Isn't he!" Again she kissed him. "As loving as any man!"

"More loving than most men, I should think," replied Clara.

"He's a nice boy!" cried the woman, again embracing the horse.

Clara, fascinated by the big beast, went up to stroke his neck.

"He's quite gentle," said Miss Limb. "Don't you think big fellows are?"

"He's a beauty!" replied Clara.

She wanted to look in his eyes. She wanted him to look at her.

"It's a pity he can't talk," she said.

"Oh, but he can—all but," replied the other woman.

Then her brother moved on with the horse.

"Are you coming in? *Do* come in, Mr.—I didn't catch it."

"Morel," said Miriam. "No, we won't come in, but we should like to go by the millpond."

"Yes—yes, do. Do you fish, Mr. Morel?"

"No," said Paul.

"Because if you do you might come and fish any time," said Miss Limb. "We scarcely see a soul from week's end to week's end. I should be thankful."

"What fish are there in the pond?" he asked.

They went through the front garden, over the sluice, and up the steep bank to the pond, which lay in shadow, with its two wooded islets. Paul walked with Miss Limb.

"I shouldn't mind swimming here," he said.

"Do," she replied. "Come when you like. My brother will be awfully pleased to talk with you. He is so quiet because there is no one to talk to. Do come and swim."

Clara came up.

"It's a fine depth," she said, "and so clear."

"Yes," said Miss Limb.

"Do you swim?" said Paul. "Miss Limb was just saying we could come when we liked."

"Of course there's the farmhands," said Miss Limb.

They talked a few moments, then went on up the wild hill, leaving the lonely, haggard-eyed woman on the bank.

The hillside was all ripe with sunshine. It was wild and tussocky, given over to rabbits. The three walked in silence. Then:

"She makes me feel uncomfortable," said Paul.

"You mean Miss Limb?" asked Miriam. "Yes."

"What's a matter with her? Is she going dotty with being too lonely?"

"Yes," said Miriam. "It's not the right sort of life for her. I think it's cruel to bury her there. *I* really ought to go and see her more. But—she upsets me."

"She makes me feel sorry for her—yes, and she bothers me," he said.

"I suppose," blurted Clara suddenly, "she wants a man."

The other two were silent for a few moments.

"But it's the loneliness sends her cracked," said Paul.

Clara did not answer, but strode on uphill. She was walking with her head hanging, her legs swinging as she kicked through the dead thistles and the tussocky grass, her arms hanging loose. Rather than walking, her handsome body seemed to be blundering up the hill. A hot wave went over Paul. He was curious about her. Perhaps life had been cruel to her. He forgot Miriam, who was walking beside him talking to him. She glanced at him, finding he did not answer her. His eyes were fixed ahead on Clara.

"Do you still think she is disagreeable?" she asked.

He did not notice that the question was sudden. It ran with his thoughts.

"Something's the matter with her," he said.

"Yes," answered Miriam.

They found at the top of the hill a hidden wild field, two sides of which were backed by the wood, the other sides by high loose hedges of hawthorn and elder bushes. Between these overgrown bushes were gaps that the cattle might have walked through had there been any cattle now. There the turf was smooth as velveteen, padded and holed by the rabbits. The field itself was coarse, and crowded with tall, big cowslips that had never been cut. Clusters of strong flowers rose everywhere above the coarse tussocks of bent. It was like a roadstead crowded with tall, fairy shipping.

"Ah!" cried Miriam, and she looked at Paul, her dark eyes dilating. He smiled. Together they enjoyed the field of flowers. Clara, a little way off, was looking at the cowslips disconsolately. Paul and Miriam stayed close together, talking in subdued tones. He kneeled on one knee, quickly gathering the best blossoms, moving from tuft to tuft restlessly, talking softly all the time. Miriam plucked the flowers lovingly, lingering over them. He always seemed to her too quick and almost scientific. Yet his bunches had a natural beauty more than hers. He loved them, but as if they were his and he had a right to them. She had more reverence for them: they held something she had not.

The flowers were very fresh and sweet. He wanted to drink them. As he gathered them, he ate the little yellow trumpets. Clara was still wandering about disconsolately. Going towards her, he said:

"Why don't you get some?"

"I don't believe in it. They look better growing."

"But you'd like some?"

"They want to be left."

"I don't believe they do."

"I don't want the corpses of flowers about me," she said.

"That's a stiff, artificial notion," he said. "They don't die any quicker in water than on their roots. And besides, they *look* nice in a bowl—they look jolly. And you only call a thing a corpse because it looks corpse-like."

"Whether it is one or not?" she argued.

"It isn't one to me. A dead flower isn't a corpse of a flower."

Clara now ignored him.

"And even so—what right have you to pull them?" she asked.

"Because I like them, and want them—and there's plenty of them."

"And that is sufficient?"

"Yes. Why not? I'm sure they'd smell nice in your room in Nottingham."

"And I should have the pleasure of watching them die."

"But then—it does not matter if they do die."

Whereupon he left her, and went stooping over the clumps of tangled flowers which thickly sprinkled the field like pale, luminous foam-clots. Miriam had come close. Clara was kneeling, breathing some scent from the cowslips.

"I think," said Miriam, "if you treat them with reverence you don't do them any harm. It is the spirit you pluck them in that matters."

"Yes," he said. "But no, you get 'em because you want 'em, and that's all." He held out his bunch.

Miriam was silent. He picked some more.

"Look at these!" he continued; "sturdy and lusty like little trees and like boys with fat legs."

Clara's hat lay on the grass not far off. She was kneeling, bending forward still to smell the flowers. Her neck gave him a sharp pang, such a beautiful thing, yet not proud of itself just now. Her breasts swung slightly in her blouse. The arching curve of her back was beautiful and strong; she wore no stays. Suddenly, without knowing, he was scattering a handful of cowslips over her hair and neck, saying:

Ashes to ashes, and dust to dust,
If the Lord won't have you the devil must.

The chill flowers fell on her neck. She looked up at him with almost pitiful, scared gray eyes, wondering what he was doing. Flowers fell on her face, and she shut her eyes.

Suddenly, standing there above her, he felt awkward.

"I thought you wanted a funeral," he said, ill at ease.

Clara laughed strangely, and rose, picking the cowslips from her hair. She took up her hat and pinned it on. One flower had remained tangled in her hair. He saw, but would not tell her. He gathered up the flowers he had sprinkled over her.

At the edge of the wood the bluebells had flowed over into the field and stood there like floodwater. But they were fading now. Clara strayed up to them. He wandered after her. The bluebells pleased him.

"Look how they've come out of the wood!" he said.

Then she turned with a flash of warmth and of gratitude.

"Yes," she smiled.

His blood beat up.

"It makes me think of the wild men of the woods, how terrified they would be when they got breast to breast with the open space."

"Do you think they were?" she asked.

"I wonder which was more frightened among old tribes—those bursting out of their darkness of woods upon all the space of light, or those from the open tiptoeing into the forests."

"I should think the second," she answered.

"Yes, you *do* feel like one of the open space sort, trying to force yourself into the dark, don't you?"

"How should I know?" she answered queerly.

The conversation ended there.

The evening was deepening over the earth. Already the valley was full of shadow. One tiny square of light stood opposite at Crossleigh Bank Farm. Brightness was swimming on the tops of the hills. Miriam came up slowly, her face in her big, loose bunch of flowers, walking ankle-deep through the scattered froth of the cowslips. Beyond her the trees were coming into shape, all shadow.

"Shall we go?" she asked.

And the three turned away. They were all silent. Going down the path they could see the light of home right across, and on the ridge of the hill a thin dark outline with little lights, where the colliery village touched the sky.

"It has been nice, hasn't it?" he asked.

Miriam murmured assent. Clara was silent.

"Don't you think so?" he persisted.

But she walked with her head up, and still did not answer. He could tell by the way she moved, as if she didn't care, that she suffered.

At this time Paul took his mother to Lincoln. She was bright and enthusiastic as ever, but as he sat opposite her in the railway carriage, she seemed to look frail. He had a momentary sensation as if she were slipping away from him. Then he wanted to get hold of her, to fasten her, almost to chain her. He felt he must keep hold of her with his hand.

They drew near to the city. Both were at the window looking for the cathedral.

"There she is, mother!" he cried.

They saw the great cathedral lying couchant above the plain.

"Ah!" she exclaimed. "So she is!"

He looked at his mother. Her blue eyes were watching the cathedral quietly. She seemed again to be beyond him. Something in the eternal repose of the uplifted cathedral, blue and noble against the sky, was reflected in her, something of the fatality. What was, *was*. With all his young will he could not alter it. He saw her face, the skin still fresh and pink and downy, but crow's-feet near her eyes, her eyelids steady, sinking a little, her mouth always closed with disillusion; and there was on her the same eternal look, as if she knew fate at last. He beat against it with all the strength of his soul.

"Look, mother, how big she is above the town! Think, there are streets and streets below her! She looks bigger than the city altogether."

"So she does!" exclaimed his mother, breaking bright into life again. But he had seen her sitting, looking steady out of the window at the cathedral, her face and eyes fixed, reflecting the relentlessness of life. And the crow's-feet near her eyes, and her mouth shut so hard, made him feel he would go mad.

They ate a meal that she considered wildly extravagant.

"Don't imagine I like it," she said, as she ate her cutlet. "I *don't* like it, I really don't! Just *think* of your money wasted!"

"You never mind my money," he said. "You forget I'm a fellow taking his girl for an outing."

And he bought her some blue violets.

"Stop it at once, sir!" she commanded. "How can I do it?"

"You've got nothing to do. Stand still!"

And in the middle of High Street he stuck the flowers in her coat.

"An old thing like me!" she said, sniffing.

"You see," he said, "I want people to think we're awful swells. So look ikey."

"I'll jowl your head," she laughed.

"Strut!" he commanded. "Be a fantail pigeon."

It took him an hour to get her through the street. She stood above Glory Hole, she stood before Stone Bow, she stood everywhere, and exclaimed.

A man came up, took off his hat, and bowed to her.

"Can I show you the town, madam?"

"No, thank you," she answered. "I've got my son."

Then Paul was cross with her for not answering with more dignity.

"You go away with you!" she exclaimed. "Ha! that's the Jew's House. Now, do you remember that lecture, Paul—?"

But she could scarcely climb the cathedral hill. He did not notice. Then suddenly he found her unable to speak. He took her into a little public house, where she rested.

"It's nothing," she said. "My heart is only a bit old; one must expect it."

He did not answer, but looked at her. Again his heart was crushed in a hot grip. He wanted to cry, he wanted to smash things in fury.

They set off again, pace by pace, so slowly. And every step seemed like a weight on his chest. He felt as if his heart would burst. At last they came to the top. She stood enchanted, looking at the castle gate, looking at the cathedral front. She had quite forgotten herself.

"Now *this* is better than I thought it could be!" she cried.

But he hated it. Everywhere he followed her, brooding. They sat together in the cathedral. They attended a little service in the choir. She was timid.

"I suppose it is open to anybody?" she asked him.

"Yes," he replied. "Do you think they'd have the damned cheek to send us away."

"Well, I'm sure," she exclaimed, "they would if they heard your language."

Her face seemed to shine again with joy and peace during the service. And all the time he was wanting to rage and smash things and cry.

Afterwards, when they were leaning over the wall, looking at the town below, he blurted suddenly:

"Why can't a man have a *young* mother? What is she old for?"

"Well," his mother laughed, "she can scarcely help it."

"And why wasn't I the oldest son? Look—they say the young ones have the advantage—but look, *they* had the young mother. You should have had me for your eldest son."

"*I* didn't arrange it," she remonstrated. "Come to consider, you're as much to blame as me."

He turned on her, white, his eyes furious.

"What are you old for!" he said, mad with his impotence. "*Why* can't you walk? *Why* can't you come with me to places?"

"At one time," she replied, "I could have run up that hill a good deal better than you."

"What's the good of that to *me*?" he cried, hitting his fist on the wall. Then he became plaintive. "It's too bad of you to be ill. Little, it is——"

"Ill!" she cried. "I'm a bit old, and you'll have to put up with it, that's all."

They were quiet. But it was as much as they could bear. They got jolly again over tea. As they sat by Brayford, watching the boats, he told her about Clara. His mother asked him innumerable questions.

"Then who does she live with?"

"With her mother, on Bluebell Hill."

"And have they enough to keep them?"

"I don't think so. I think they do lace work."

"And wherein lies her charm, my boy?"

"I don't know that she's charming, mother. But she's nice. And she seems straight, you know—not a bit deep, not a bit."

"But she's a good deal older than you."

"She's thirty, I'm going of twenty-three."

"You haven't told me what you like her for."

"Because I don't know—a sort of defiant way she's got—a sort of angry way."

Mrs. Morel considered. She would have been glad now for her son to fall in love with some woman who would—she did not know what. But he fretted so, got so furious suddenly, and again was melancholic. She wished he knew some nice woman—She did not know what she wished, but left it vague. At any rate she was not hostile to the idea of Clara.

Annie, too, was getting married. Leonard had gone away to work in Birmingham. One weekend when he was home she had said to him:

"You don't look very well, my lad."

"I dunno," he said. "I feel anyhow or nohow, ma."

He called her "ma" already in his boyish fashion.

"Are you sure they're good lodgings?" she asked.

"Yes—yes. Only—it's a winder when you have to pour your own tea out—an' nobody to grouse if you team it in your saucer and sup it up. It somehow takes a' the taste out of it."

Mrs. Morel laughed.

"And so it knocks you up?" she said.

"I dunno. I want to get married," he blurted, twisting his fingers and looking down at his boots. There was a silence.

"But," she exclaimed, "I thought you said you'd wait another year."

"Yes, I did say so," he replied stubbornly.

Again she considered.

"And you know," she said, "Annie's a bit of a spendthrift. She's saved no more than eleven pounds. And I know, lad, you haven't had much chance."

He colored up to the ears.

"I've got thirty-three quid," he said.

"It doesn't go far," she answered.

He said nothing, but twisted his fingers.

"And you know," she said, "I've nothing——"

"I didn't want, ma!" he cried, very red, suffering and remonstrating.

"No, my lad, I know. I was only wishing I had. And take away five pounds for the wedding and things—it leaves twenty-nine pounds. You won't do much on that."

He twisted still, impotent, stubborn, not looking up.

"But do you really want to get married?" she asked. "Do you feel as if you ought?"

He gave her one straight look from his blue eyes.

"Yes," he said.

"Then," she replied, "we must all do the best we can for it, lad."

The next time he looked up there were tears in his eyes.

"I don't want Annie to feel handicapped," he said, struggling.

"My lad," she said, "you're steady—you've got a decent place. If a man had *needed* me I'd have married him on his last week's wages. She may find it a bit hard to start humbly. Young girls *are* like that. They look forward to the fine home they think they'll have. But *I* had expensive furniture. It's not everything."

So the wedding took place almost immediately. Arthur came home, and was splendid in uniform. Annie looked nice in a dove-gray dress that she could take for Sundays. Morel called her a fool for getting married, and was cool with his son-in-law. Mrs. Morel had white tips in her bonnet, and some white on her blouse, and was teased by both her sons for fancying herself so grand. Leonard was jolly and cordial, and felt a fearful fool. Paul could not quite see what Annie wanted to get married for. He was fond of her, and she of him. Still, he hoped rather lugubriously that it would turn out all right. Arthur was astonishingly handsome in his scarlet and yellow, and he knew it well, but was secretly ashamed of the uniform. Annie cried her eyes up in the kitchen, on leaving her mother. Mrs. Morel cried a little, then patted her on the back and said:

"But don't cry, child, he'll be good to you."

Morel stamped and said she was a fool to go and tie herself up. Leonard looked white and overwrought. Mrs. Morel said to him:

"I s'll trust her to you, my lad, and hold you responsible for her."

"You can," he said, nearly dead with the ordeal. And it was all over.

When Morel and Arthur were in bed, Paul sat talking, as he often did, with his mother.

"You're not sorry she's married, mother, are you?" he asked.

"I'm not sorry she's married—but—it seems strange that she should go from me. It even seems to me hard that she can prefer to go with her Leonard. That's how mothers are—I know it's silly."

"And shall you be miserable about her?"

"When I think of my own wedding day," his mother answered, "I can only hope her life will be different."

"But you can trust him to be good to her?"

"Yes, yes. They say he's not good enough for her. But I say if a man is *genuine*, as he is, and a girl is fond of him—then—it should be all right. He's as good as she."

"So you don't mind?"

"I would *never* have let a daughter of mine marry a man I didn't *feel* to be genuine through and through. And yet, there's the gap now she's gone."

They were both miserable, and wanted her back again. It seemed to Paul his mother looked lonely, in her new black silk blouse with its bit of white trimming.

"At any rate, mother, I s'll never marry," he said.

"Ay, they all say that, my lad. You've not met the one yet. Only wait a year or two."

"But I shan't marry, mother. I shall live with you, and we'll have a servant."

"Ay, my lad, it's easy to talk. We'll see when the time comes."

"What time? I'm nearly twenty-three."

"Yes, you're not one that would marry young. But in three years' time——"

"I shall be with you just the same."

"We'll see, my boy, we'll see."

"But you don't want me to marry?"

"I shouldn't like to think of you going through your life without anybody to care for you and do—no."

"And you think I ought to marry?"

"Sooner or later every man ought."

"But you'd rather it were later."

"It would be hard—and very hard. It's as they say:

> A son's my son till he takes him a wife,
> But my daughter's my daughter the whole of her life.

"And you think I'd let a wife take me from you?"

"Well, you wouldn't ask her to marry your mother as well as you," Mrs. Morel smiled.

"She could do what she liked; she wouldn't have to interfere."

"She wouldn't—till she'd got you—and then you'd see."

"I never will see. I'll never marry while I've got you—I won't."

"But I shouldn't like to leave you with nobody, my boy," she cried.

"You're not going to leave me. What are you? Fifty-three! I'll give you till seventy-five. There you are, I'm fat and forty-four. Then I'll marry a staid body. See!"

His mother sat and laughed.

"Go to bed," she said—"go to bed."

"And we'll have a pretty house, you and me, and a servant, and it'll be just all right. I s'll perhaps be rich with my painting."

"Will you go to bed!"

"And then you s'll have a pony-carriage. See yourself—a little Queen Victoria trotting round."

"I tell you to go to bed," she laughed.

He kissed her and went. His plans for the future were always the same.

Mrs. Morel sat brooding—about her daughter, about Paul, about Arthur. She fretted at losing Annie. The family was very closely bound. And she felt she *must* live now, to be with her children. Life was so rich for her. Paul wanted her, and so did Arthur. Arthur never knew how deeply he loved her. He was a creature of the moment. Never yet had he been forced to realize himself. The army had disciplined his body, but not his soul. He was in perfect health and very handsome. His dark, vigorous hair sat close to his smallish head. There was something childish about his nose, something almost girlish about his dark blue eyes. But he had the full red mouth of a man under his brown moustache, and his jaw was strong. It was his father's mouth; it was the nose and eyes of her own mother's people—good-looking, weak-principled folk. Mrs. Morel was anxious about him. Once he had really run the rig he was safe. But how far would he go?

The army had not really done him any good. He resented bitterly the authority of the petty officers. He hated having to obey as if he were an animal. But he had too much sense to kick. So he turned his attention to getting the best out of it. He could sing, he was a boon-companion. Often he got into scrapes, but they were the manly scrapes that are easily condoned. So he made a good time out of it, whilst his self-respect was in suppression. He trusted to his good looks and handsome figure, his refinement, his decent education to get him most of what he wanted, and he was not disappointed. Yet he was restless. Something seemed to gnaw him inside. He was never still, he was never alone. With his mother he was rather humble. Paul he admired and loved and despised slightly. And Paul admired and loved and despised him slightly.

Mrs. Morel had had a few pounds left to her by her father, and she decided to buy her son out of the army. He was wild with joy. Now he was like a lad taking a holiday.

He had always been fond of Beatrice Wyld, and during his furlough he picked up with her again. She was stronger and better in health. The two often went long walks together, Arthur taking her arm in soldier's fashion, rather stiffly. And she came to play the piano whilst he sang. Then Arthur would unhook his tunic collar. He grew flushed, his eyes were bright, he sang in a manly tenor. Afterwards they sat together on the sofa. He seemed to flaunt his body: she was aware of him so—the strong chest, the sides, the thighs in their close-fitting trousers.

He liked to lapse into the dialect when he talked to her. She would sometimes smoke with him. Occasionally she would only take a few whiffs of his cigarette.

"Nay," he said to her one evening, when she reached for his cigarette. "Nay, tha doesna. I'll gi'e thee a smoke kiss if ter's a mind."

"I wanted a whiff, no kiss at all," she answered.

"Well, an' tha s'lt ha'e a whiff," he said, "along wi' t' kiss."

"I want a draw at thy fag," she cried, snatching for the cigarette between his lips.

He was sitting with his shoulder touching her. She was small and quick as lightning. He just escaped.

"I'll gi'e thee a smoke kiss," he said.

"Tha'rt a nivey nuisance, Arty Morel," she said, sitting back.

"Ha'e a smoke kiss?"

The soldier leaned forward to her, smiling. His face was near hers.

"Shonna!" she replied, turning away her head.

He took a draw at his cigarette, and pursed up his mouth, and put his lips close to her. His dark-brown cropped moustache stood out like a brush. She looked at the puckered crimson lips, then suddenly snatched the cigarette from his fingers and darted away. He, leaping after her, seized the comb from her back hair. She turned, threw the cigarette at him. He picked it up, put it in his mouth, and sat down.

"Nuisance!" she cried. "Give me my comb!"

She was afraid that her hair, specially done for him, would come down. She stood with her hands to her head. He hid the comb between his knees.

"I've non got it," he said.

The cigarette trembled between his lips with laughter as he spoke.

"Liar!" she said.

" 'S true as I'm here!" he laughed, showing his hands.

"You brazen imp!" she exclaimed, rushing and scuffling for the comb, which he had under his knees. As she wrestled with him, pulling at his smooth, tight-covered knees, he laughed till he lay back on the sofa shaking with laughter. The cigarette fell from his mouth, almost singeing his throat. Under his delicate tan the blood flushed up, and he laughed till his blue eyes were blinded, his throat swollen almost to choking. Then he sat up. Beatrice was putting in her comb.

"Tha tickled me, Beat," he said thickly.

Like a flash her small white hand went out and smacked his face. He started up, glaring at her. They stared at each other. Slowly the flush mounted her cheek, she dropped her eyes, then her head. He sat down sulkily. She went into the scullery to adjust her hair. In private there she shed a few tears, she did not know what for.

When she returned she was pursed up close. But it was only a film over her fire. He, with ruffled hair, was sulking upon the sofa. She sat down opposite, in the armchair, and neither spoke. The clock ticked in the silence like blows.

"You are a little cat, Beat," he said at length, half apologetically.

"Well, you shouldn't be brazen," she replied.

There was again a long silence. He whistled to himself, like a man much agitated but defiant. Suddenly she went across to him and kissed him.

"Did it, pore fing!" she mocked.

He lifted her face, smiling curiously.

"Kiss?" he invited her.

"Daren't I?" she asked.

"Go on!" he challenged, his mouth lifted to her.

Deliberately, and with a peculiar quivering smile that seemed to overspread her whole body, she put her mouth on his. Immediately his arms folded round her. As soon as the long kiss was finished she drew back her head from him, put her delicate fingers on his neck, through the open collar. Then she closed her eyes, giving herself up again in a kiss.

She acted of her own free will. What she would do she did, and made nobody responsible.

Paul felt life changing around him. The conditions of youth were gone. Now it was a home of grown-up people. Annie was a married woman, Arthur was following his own pleasure in a way unknown to his folk. For so long they had all lived at home, and gone out to pass their time. But now, for Annie and Arthur, life lay outside their mother's house. They came home for holiday and for rest. So there was that strange, half-empty feeling about the house, as if the birds had flown. Paul became more and more unsettled. Annie and Arthur had gone. He was restless to follow. Yet home was for him beside his mother. And still there was something else, something outside, something he wanted.

He grew more and more restless. Miriam did not satisfy him. His old mad desire to be with her grew weaker. Sometimes he met Clara in Nottingham, sometimes he went to meetings with her, sometimes he saw her at Willey Farm. But on these last occasions the situation became strained. There was a triangle of antagonism between Paul and Clara and Miriam. With Clara he took on a smart, worldly, mocking tone very antagonistic to Miriam. It did not matter what went before. She might be intimate and sad with him. Then as soon as Clara appeared, it all vanished, and he played to the newcomer.

Miriam had one beautiful evening with him in the hay. He had been on the horse-rake, and, having finished, came to help her to put the hay in cocks. Then he talked to her of his hopes and despairs, and his whole soul seemed to lie bare before her. She felt as if she watched the very quivering stuff of life in him. The moon came out: they walked home together: he seemed to have come to her because he needed her so badly, and she listened to him, gave him all her love and her faith. It seemed to her he brought her the best of himself to keep, and that she would guard it all her life. Nay, the sky did not cherish the stars more surely and eternally than she would guard the good in the soul of Paul Morel. She went on home alone feeling exalted, glad in her faith.

And then, the next day, Clara came. They were to have tea in the hayfield. Miriam watched the evening drawing to gold and shadow. And all the time Paul was sporting with Clara. He made higher and higher heaps of hay that they were jumping over. Miriam did not care for the game, and stood aside. Edgar and Geoffrey and Maurice and Clara and Paul jumped. Paul won, because he was light. Clara's blood was roused. She could run like an Amazon. Paul loved the determined way she rushed at the haycock and leaped, landed on the other side, her breasts shaken, her thick hair coming undone.

"You touched!" he cried. "You touched!"

"No!" she flashed, turning to Edgar. "I didn't touch, did I? Wasn't I clear?"

"I couldn't say," laughed Edgar.

None of them could say.

"But you touched," said Paul. "You're beaten."

"I did *not* touch!" she cried.

"As plain as anything," said Paul.

"Box his ears for me!" she cried to Edgar.

"Nay," Edgar laughed. "I darn't. You must do it yourself."

"And nothing can alter the fact that you touched," laughed Paul.

She was furious with him. Her little triumph before these lads and men was gone. She had forgotten herself in the game. Now he was to humble her.

"I think you are despicable!" she said.

And again he laughed, in a way that tortured Miriam.

"And I *knew* you couldn't jump that heap," he teased.

She turned her back on him. Yet everybody could see that the only person she listened to, or was conscious of, was he, and he of her. It pleased the men to see this battle between them. But Miriam was tortured.

Paul could choose the lesser in place of the higher, she saw. He could be unfaithful to himself, unfaithful to the real, deep Paul Morel. There was a danger of his becoming frivolous, of his running after his satisfactions like any Arthur, or like his father. It made Miriam bitter to think that he should throw away his soul for this flippant traffic of triviality with Clara. She walked in bitterness and silence, while the other two rallied each other, and Paul sported.

And afterwards, he would not own it, but he was rather ashamed of himself, and protested himself before Miriam. Then again he rebelled.

"It's not religious to be religious," he said. "I reckon a crow is religious when it sails across the sky. But it only does it because it feels itself carried to where it's going, not because it thinks it is being eternal."

But Miriam knew that one should be religious in everything, have God, whatever God might be, present in every thing.

"I don't believe God knows such a lot about Himself," he cried. "God doesn't *know* things. He *is* things. And I'm sure He's not soulful."

And then it seemed to her that Paul was arguing God on to his own side, because he wanted his own way and his own pleasure. There was a long battle between him and her. He was utterly unfaithful to her even in her own presence; then he was ashamed, then repentant; then he hated her, and went off again. Those were the ever-recurring conditions.

When she was twenty-one he wrote her a letter which could only have been written to her.

"May I speak of our old, worn love, this last time. It, too, is changing, is it not? Say, has not the body of that love died, and left you its invulnerable soul? You see, I can give you a spirit love, I have given it you this long, long time; but not embodied passion. See, you are a nun. I have given you what I would give a holy nun—as a mystic monk to a mystic nun. Surely you esteem it best. Yet you regret—no, have regretted—the other. In all our relations no body enters. I do not talk to you through the senses—rather through the spirit. That is why we cannot love in the common sense. Ours is not an everyday affection. As yet we are mortal, and to live side by side with one another would be dreadful, for somehow with you I cannot long be trivial, and, you know, to be always beyond this mortal state would be to lose it. If people marry, they must live together as affectionate humans, who may be commonplace with each other without feeling awkward—not as two souls. So I feel it.

"Ought I to send this letter—I doubt it. But there—it is best to understand. Au revoir."

Miriam read this letter twice, after which she sealed it up. A year later she broke the seal to show her mother the letter.

"You are a nun—you are a nun." The words went into her heart again and again. Nothing he ever had said had gone into her so deeply, fixedly, like a mortal wound.

She answered two days after the party.

" 'Our intimacy would have been all-beautiful but for one little mistake,' " she quoted. "Was the mistake mine?"

Almost immediately he replied to her from Nottingham, sending her at the same time a little "Omar Khayyám."

"I am glad you answered; you are so calm and natural you put me to shame. What a ranter I am! We are often out of sympathy. But in fundamentals we may always be together, I think.

"I must thank you for your sympathy with my painting and drawing. Many a sketch is dedicated to you. I do look forward to your criticisms, which, to my shame and glory, are always grand appreciations. It is a lovely joke, that. Au revoir."

This was the end of the first phase of Paul's love affair. He was now about twenty-three years old, and, though still virgin, the sex instinct that Miriam had over-refined for so long now grew particularly strong. Often, as he talked to Clara Dawes, came that thickening and quickening of his blood, that peculiar concentration in the breast, as if something were alive there, a new self or a new center of consciousness, warning him that sooner or later he would have to ask one woman or another. But he belonged to Miriam. Of that she was so fixedly sure that he allowed her right.

❖ 10 ❖

CLARA

When he was twenty-three years old Paul sent in a landscape to the winter exhibition at Nottingham Castle. Miss Jordan had taken a good deal of interest in him, had invited him to her house, where he met other artists. He was beginning to grow ambitious.

One morning the postman came just as he was washing in the scullery. Suddenly he heard a wild noise from his mother. Rushing into the kitchen, he found her standing on the hearthrug wildly waving a letter and crying "Hurrah!" as if she had gone mad. He was shocked and frightened.

"Why, mother!" he exclaimed.

She flew to him, flung her arms round him for a moment then waved the letter, crying:

"Hurrah, my boy! I knew we should do it!"

He was afraid of her—the small, severe woman with graying hair suddenly bursting out in such frenzy. The postman came running back, afraid something had happened. They saw his tipped cap over the short curtain. Mrs. Morel rushed to the door.

"His picture's got first prize, Fred," she cried, " and is sold for twenty guineas."

"My word, that's something like!" said the young postman, whom they had known all his life.

"And Major Moreton has bought it!" she cried.

"It looks like meanin' something, that does, Mrs. Morel," said the postman, his blue eyes bright. He was glad to have brought such a lucky letter. Mrs. Morel went indoors and sat down, trembling. Paul was afraid lest she might have misread the letter, and might be disappointed after all. He scrutinized it once, twice. Yes, he became convinced it was true. Then he sat down, his heart beating with joy.

"Mother!" he exclaimed.

"Didn't I *say* we should do it!" she said, pretending she was not crying.

He took the kettle off the fire and mashed the tea.

"You didn't think, mother—" he began tentatively.

"No, my son—not so much—but I expected a good deal."

"But not so much," he said.

"No—no—but I knew we should do it."

And then she recovered her composure, apparently at least. He sat with his shirt turned back, showing his young throat almost like a girl's, and the towel in his hand, his hair sticking up wet.

"Twenty guineas, mother! That's just what you wanted to buy Arthur out. Now you needn't borrow any. It'll just do."

"Indeed, I shan't take it all," she said.

"But why?"

"Because I shan't."

"Well—you have twelve pounds, I'll have nine."

They cavilled about sharing the twenty guineas. She wanted to take only the five pounds she needed. He would not hear of it. So they got over the stress of emotion by quarreling.

Morel came home at night from the pit, saying:

"They tell me Paul's got first prize for his picture, and sold it to Lord Henry Bentley for fifty pound."

"Oh, what stories people do tell!" she cried.

"Ha!" he answered. "I said I wor sure it wor a lie. But they said tha'd told Fred Hodgkisson."

"As if I would tell him such stuff!"

"Ha!" assented the miner.

But he was disappointed nevertheless.

"It's true he has got the first prize," said Mrs. Morel.

The miner sat heavily in his chair.

"Has he, beguy!" he exclaimed.

He stared across the room fixedly.

"But as for fifty pounds—such nonsense!" She was silent awhile. "Major Moreton bought it for twenty guineas, that's true."

"Twenty guineas! Tha niver says!" exclaimed Morel.

"Yes, and it was worth it."

"Ay!" he said. "I don't misdoubt it. But twenty guineas for a bit of a paintin' as he knocked off in an hour or two!"

He was silent with conceit of his son. Mrs. Morel sniffed, as if it were nothing.

"And when does he handle th' money?" asked the collier.

"That I couldn't tell you. When the picture is sent home I suppose."

There was silence. Morel stared at the sugar-basin instead of eating his dinner. His black arm, with the hand all gnarled with work, lay on the table. His wife pretended not to see him rub the back of his hand across his eyes, nor the smear in the coal dust on his black face.

"Yes, an' that other lad 'ud 'a done as much if they hadna ha' killed 'im," he said quietly.

The thought of William went through Mrs. Morel like a cold blade. It left her feeling she was tired, and wanted rest.

Paul was invited to dinner at Mr. Jordan's. Afterwards he said:

"Mother, I want an evening suit."

"Yes, I was afraid you would," she said. She was glad. There was a moment or two of silence. "There's that one of William's," she continued, "that I know cost four pounds ten and which he'd only worn three times."

"Should you like me to wear it, mother?" he asked.

"Yes. I think it would fit you—at least the coat. The trousers would want shortening."

He went upstairs and put on the coat and vest. Coming down, he looked strange in a flannel collar and a flannel shirt front, with an evening coat and vest. It was rather large.

"The tailor can make it right," she said, smoothing her hand over his shoulder. "It's beautiful stuff. I never could find in my heart to let your father wear the trousers, and very glad I am now."

And as she smoothed her hand over the silk collar she thought of her eldest son. But this son was living enough inside the clothes. She passed her hand down his back to feel him. He was alive and hers. The other was dead.

He went out to dinner several times in his evening suit that had been William's. Each time his mother's heart was firm with pride and joy. He was started now. The studs she and the children had bought for William were in his shirt front; he wore one of William's dress shirts. But he had an elegant figure. His face was rough but warm-looking and rather pleasing. He did not look particularly a gentleman, but she thought he looked quite a man.

He told her everything that took place, everything that was said. It was as if she had been there. And he was dying to introduce her to these new friends who had dinner at seven-thirty in the evening.

"Go along with you!" she said. "What do they want to know me for?"

"They do!" he cried indignantly. "If they want to know me—and they say they do—then they want to know you, because you are quite as clever as I am."

"Go along with you, child!" she laughed.

But she began to spare her hands. They, too, were work-gnarled now. The skin was shiny with so much hot water, the knuckles rather swollen. But she began to be careful to keep them out of soda. She regretted what they had been—so small and exquisite. And when Annie insisted on her having more stylish blouses to suit her age, she submitted. She even went so far as to allow a black velvet bow to be placed on her hair. Then she sniffed in her sarcastic manner, and was sure she looked a sight. But she looked a lady, Paul declared, as much as Mrs. Major Moreton, and far, far nicer. The family was coming on. Only Morel remained unchanged, or rather, lapsed slowly.

Paul and his mother now had long discussions about life. Religion was fading into the background. He had shoveled away all the beliefs that would hamper him, had cleared the ground, and come more or less to the bedrock of belief that one should feel inside oneself for right and wrong, and should have the patience to gradually realize one's God. Now life interested him more.

"You know," he said to his mother, "I don't want to belong to the well-to-do middle class. I like my common people best. I belong to the common people."

"But if anyone else said so, my son, wouldn't you be in a tear! *You* know you consider yourself equal to any gentleman."

"In myself," he answered, "not in my class or my education or my manners. But in myself I am."

"Very well, then. Then why talk about the common people?"

"Because—the difference between people isn't in their class, but in themselves. Only from the middle classes one gets ideas, and from the common people—life itself, warmth. You feel their hates and loves."

"It's all very well, my boy. But, then, why don't you go and talk to your father's pals?"

"But they're rather different."

"Not at all. They're the common people. After all, whom do you mix with now—

among the common people? Those that exchange ideas, like the middle classes. The rest don't interest you."

"But—there's the life——"

"I don't believe there's a jot more life from Miriam than you could get from any educated girl—say Miss Moreton. It is *you* who are snobbish about class."

She frankly *wanted* him to climb into the middle classes, a thing not very difficult, she knew. And she wanted him in the end to marry a lady.

Now she began to combat him in his restless fretting. He still kept up his connection with Miriam, could neither break free nor go the whole length of engagement. And this indecision seemed to bleed him of his energy. Moreover, his mother suspected him of an unrecognized leaning towards Clara, and, since the latter was a married woman, she wished he would fall in love with one of the girls in a better station of life. But he was stupid, and would refuse to love or even to admire a girl much, just because she was his social superior.

"My boy," said his mother to him, "all your cleverness your breaking away from old things, and taking life in your own hands, doesn't seem to bring you much happiness."

"What is happiness!" he cried. "It's nothing to me! How *am* I to be happy?"

The plump question disturbed her.

"That's for you to judge, my lad. But if you could meet some *good* woman who would *make* you happy—and you began to think of settling your life—when you have the means—so that you could work without all this fretting—it would be much better for you."

He frowned. His mother caught him on the raw of his wound of Miriam. He pushed the tumbled hair off his forehead, his eyes full of pain and fire.

"You mean easy, mother," he cried. "That's a woman's whole doctrine for life—ease of soul and physical comfort. And I do despise it."

"Oh, do you!" replied his mother. "And do you call yours a divine discontent?"

"Yes. I don't care about its divinity. But damn your happiness! So long as life's full, it doesn't matter whether it's happy or not. I'm afraid your happiness would bore me."

"You never give it a chance," she said. Then suddenly all her passion of grief over him broke out. "But it does matter!" she cried. "And you *ought* to be happy, you ought to try to be happy, to live to be happy. How could I bear to think your life wouldn't be a happy one!"

"Your own's been bad enough, mater, but it hasn't left you so much worse off than the folk who've been happier. I reckon you've done well. And I am the same. Aren't I well enough off?"

"You're not, my son. Battle—battle—and suffer. It's about all you do, as far as I can see."

"But why not, my dear? I tell you it's the best——"

"It isn't. And one *ought* to be happy, one *ought*."

By this time Mrs. Morel was trembling violently. Struggles of this kind often took place between her and her son, when she seemed to fight for his very life against his own will to die. He took her in his arms. She was ill and pitiful.

"Never mind, Little," he murmured. "So long as you don't feel life's paltry and a miserable business, the rest doesn't matter, happiness or unhappiness."

She pressed him to her.

"But I want you to be happy," she said pathetically.

"Eh, my dear—say rather you want me to live."

Mrs. Morel felt as if her heart would break for him. At this rate she knew he would not live. He had that poignant carelessness about himself, his own suffering, his own life, which is a form of slow suicide. It almost broke her heart. With all the passion of her strong nature she hated Miriam for having in this subtle way undermined his joy. It did not matter to her that Miriam could not help it. Miriam did it, and she hated her.

She wished so much he would fall in love with a girl equal to be his mate—educated and strong. But he would not look at anybody above him in station. He seemed to like Mrs. Dawes. At any rate that feeling was wholesome. His mother prayed and prayed for him, that he might not be wasted. That was all her prayer—not for his soul or his righteousness, but that he might not be wasted. And while he slept, for hours and hours she thought and prayed for him.

He drifted away from Miriam imperceptibly, without knowing he was going. Arthur only left the army to be married. The baby was born six months after his wedding. Mrs. Morel got him a job under the firm again, at twenty-one shillings a week. She furnished for him, with the help of Beatrice's mother, a little cottage of two rooms. He was caught now. It did not matter how he kicked and struggled, he was fast. For a time he chafed, was irritable with his young wife, who loved him; he went almost distracted when the baby, which was delicate, cried or gave trouble. He grumbled for hours to his mother. She only said, "Well, my lad, you did it yourself, now you must make the best of it." And then the grit came out in him. He buckled to work, undertook his responsibilities, acknowledged that he belonged to his wife and child, and did make a good best of it. He had never been very closely inbound into the family. Now he was gone altogether.

The months went slowly along. Paul had more or less got into connection with the Socialist, Suffragette, Unitarian people in Nottingham, owing to his acquaintance with Clara. One day a friend of his and of Clara's in Bestwood, asked him to take a message to Mrs. Dawes. He went in the evening across Sneinton Market to Bluebell Hill. He found the house in a mean little street paved with granite cobbles and having causeways of dark blue, grooved bricks. The front door went up a step from off this rough pavement, where the feet of the passersby rasped and clattered. The brown paint on the door was so old that the naked wood showed between the rents. He stood on the street below and knocked. There came a heavy footstep; a large, stout woman of about sixty towered above him. He looked up at her from the pavement. She had a rather severe face.

She admitted him into the parlor, which opened on to the street. It was a small, stuffy, defunct room, of mahogany, and deathly enlargements of photographs of departed people done in carbon. Mrs. Radford left him. She was stately, almost martial. In a moment Clara appeared. She flushed deeply, and he was covered with confusion. It seemed as if she did not like being discovered in her home circumstances.

"I thought it couldn't be your voice," she said.

But she might as well be hung for a sheep as for a lamb. She invited him out of the mausoleum of a parlor into the kitchen.

That was a little, darkish room too, but it was smothered in white lace. The mother had seated herself again by the cupboard, and was drawing thread from a vast web of lace. A clump of fluff and raveled cotton was at her right hand, a heap of three-quarter-inch lace lay on her left, whilst in front of her was the mountain of the lace web, piling the hearthrug. Threads of curly cotton, pulled out from between the lengths of lace, strewed over the fender and the fireplace. Paul dared not go forward, for fear of treading on piles of white stuff.

On the table was a jenny for carding the lace. There were a pack of brown cardboard squares, a pack of cards of lace, a little box of pins, and on the sofa lay a heap of drawn lace.

The room was all lace, and it was so dark and warm that the white, snowy stuff seemed the more distinct.

"If you're coming in you won't have to mind the work," said Mrs. Radford. "I know we're about blocked up. But sit you down."

Clara, much embarrassed, gave him a chair against the wall opposite the white heaps. Then she herself took her place on the sofa, shamedly.

"Will you drink a bottle of stout?" Mrs. Radford asked "Clara, get him a bottle of stout."

He protested, but Mrs. Radford insisted.

"You look as if you could do with it," she said. "Haven't you never any more color than that?"

"It's only a thick skin I've got that doesn't show the blood through," he answered.

Clara, ashamed and chagrined, brought him a bottle of stout and a glass. He poured out some of the black stuff.

"Well," he said, lifting the glass, "here's health!"

"And thank you," said Mrs. Radford.

He took a drink of stout.

"And light yourself a cigarette, so long as you don't set the house on fire," said Mrs. Radford.

"Thank you," he replied.

"Nay, you needn't thank me," she answered. "I s'll be glad to smell a bit of smoke in th' 'ouse again. A house o' women is as dead as a house wi' no fire, to my thinkin'. I'm not a spider as likes a corner to myself. I like a man about, if he's only something to snap at."

Clara began to work. Her jenny spun with a subdued buzz; the white lace hopped from between her fingers on to the card. It was filled; she snipped off the length, and pinned the end down to the banded place. Then she put a new card in her jenny. Paul watched her. She sat square and magnificent. Her throat and arms were bare. The blood still mantled below her ears; she bent her head in shame of her humility. Her face was set on her work. Her arms were creamy and full of life beside the white lace; her large, well-kept hands worked with a balanced movement, as if nothing would hurry them. He, not knowing, watched her all the time. He saw the arch of her neck from the shoulder, as she bent her head; he saw the coil of dun hair; he watched her moving, gleaming arms.

"I've heard a bit about you from Clara," continued the mother. "You're in Jordan's, aren't you?" She drew her lace unceasing.

"Yes."

"Ay, well, and I can remember when Thomas Jordan used to ask *me* for one of my toffies."

"Did he?" laughed Paul. "And did he get it?"

"Sometimes he did, sometimes he didn't—which was latterly. For he's the sort that takes all and gives naught, he is—or used to be."

"I think he's very decent," said Paul.

"Yes; well, I'm glad to hear it."

Mrs. Radford looked across at him steadily. There was something determined about her that he liked. Her face was falling loose, but her eyes were calm, and there was something strong in her that made it seem she was not old; merely her wrinkles and loose cheeks were an anachronism. She had the strength and sang-froid of a woman in the prime of life. She continued drawing the lace with slow, dignified movements. The big web came up inevitably over her apron; the length of lace fell away at her side. Her arms were finely shapen, but glossy and yellow as old ivory. They had not the peculiar dull gleam that made Clara's so fascinating to him.

"And you've been going with Miriam Leivers?" the mother asked him.

"Well—" he answered.

"Yes, she's a nice girl," she continued. "She's very nice, but she's a bit too much above this world to suit my fancy."

"She is a bit like that," he agreed.

"She'll never be satisfied till she's got wings and can fly over everybody's head, she won't," she said.

Clara broke in, and he told her his message. She spoke humbly to him. He had surprised her in her drudgery. To have her humble made him feel as if he were lifting his head in expectation.

"Do you like jennying?" he asked.

"What can a woman do!" she replied bitterly.

"Is it sweated?"

"More or less. Isn't *all* woman's work? That's another trick the men have played, since we force ourselves into the labor market."

"Now then, you shut up about the men," said her mother. "If the women wasn't fools, the men wouldn't be bad uns, that's what I say. No man was ever that bad wi' me but what he got it back again. Not but what they're a lousy lot, there's no denying it."

"But they're all right really, aren't they?" he asked.

"Well, they're a bit different from women," she answered.

"Would you care to be back at Jordan's?" he asked Clara.

"I don't think so," she replied.

"Yes, she would!" cried her mother; "thank her stars if she could get back. Don't you listen to her. She's forever on that 'igh horse of hers, an' its back's that thin an' starved it'll cut her i' two one of these days."

Clara suffered badly from her mother. Paul felt as if his eyes were coming very wide open. Wasn't he to take Clara's fulminations so seriously, after all? She spun steadily at her work. He experienced a thrill of joy, thinking she might need his help. She seemed denied and deprived of so much. And her arm moved mechanically, that should never have been subdued to a mechanism, and her head was bowed to the lace, that never should have been bowed. She seemed to be stranded there among the refuse that life has thrown away, doing her jennying. It was a bitter thing to her to be put aside by life, as if it had no use for her. No wonder she protested.

She came with him to the door. He stood below in the mean street, looking up at her. So fine she was in her stature and her bearing, she reminded him of Juno dethroned. As she stood in the doorway, she winced from the street, from her surroundings.

"And you will go with Mrs. Hodgkinson to Hucknall?"

He was talking quite meaninglessly, only watching her. Her gray eyes at last met his. They looked dumb with humiliation, pleading with a kind of captive misery. He was shaken and at a loss. He had thought her high and mighty.

When he left her, he wanted to run. He went to the station in a sort of dream, and was at home without realizing he had moved out of her street.

He had an idea that Susan, the overseer of the spiral girls, was about to be married. He asked her the next day.

"I say, Susan, I heard a whisper of your getting married. What about it?"

Susan flushed red.

"Who's been talking to you?" she replied.

"Nobody. I merely heard a whisper that you *were* thinking——"

"Well, I am, though you needn't tell anybody. What's more, I wish I wasn't!"

"Nay, Susan, you won't make me believe that."

"Shan't I? You *can* believe it, though. I'd rather stop here a thousand times."

Paul was perturbed.

"Why, Susan?"

The girl's color was high, and her eyes flashed.

"That's why!"

"And must you?"

For answer, she looked at him. There was about him a candor and gentleness which made the women trust him. He understood.

"Ah, I'm sorry," he said.

Tears came to her eyes.

"But you'll see it'll turn out all right. You'll make the best of it," he continued rather wistfully.

"There's nothing else for it."

"Yea, there's making the worst of it. Try and make it all right."

He soon made occasion to call again on Clara.

"Would you," he said, "care to come back to Jordan's?"

She put down her work, laid her beautiful arms on the table, and looked at him for some moments without answering. Gradually the flush mounted her cheek.

"Why?" she asked.

Paul felt rather awkward.

"Well, because Susan is thinking of leaving," he said.

Clara went on with her jennying. The white lace leaped in little jumps and bounds on to the card. He waited for her. Without raising her head, she said at last, in a peculiar low voice:

"Have you said anything about it?"

"Except to you, not a word."

There was again a long silence.

"I will apply when the advertisement is out," she said.

"You will apply before that. I will let you know exactly when."

She went on spinning her little machine, and did not contradict him.

Clara came to Jordan's. Some of the older hands, Fanny among them, remembered her earlier rule, and cordially disliked the memory. Clara had always been "ikey," reserved, and superior. She had never mixed with the girls as one of themselves. If she had occasion to find fault, she did it coolly and with perfect politeness, which the defaulter felt to be a bigger insult than crossness. Towards Fanny, the poor, overstrung hunchback, Clara was unfailingly compassionate and gentle, as a result of which Fanny shed more bitter tears than ever the rough tongues of the other overseers had caused her.

There was something in Clara that Paul disliked, and much that piqued him. If she were about, he always watched her strong throat or her neck, upon which the blonde hair grew low and fluffy. There was a fine down, almost invisible, upon the skin of her face and arms, and when once he had perceived it, he saw it always.

When he was at his work, painting in the afternoon, she would come and stand near to him, perfectly motionless. Then he felt her, though she neither spoke nor touched him. Although she stood a yard away he felt as if he were in contact with her. Then he could paint no more. He flung down the brushes, and turned to talk to her.

Sometimes she praised his work; sometimes she was critical and cold.

"You are affected in that piece," she would say; and, as there was an element of truth in her condemnation, his blood boiled with anger.

Again: "What of this?" he would ask enthusiastically.

"H'm!" She made a small doubtful sound. "It doesn't interest me much."

"Because you don't understand it," he retorted.

"Then why ask me about it?"

"Because I thought you would understand."

She would shrug her shoulders in scorn of his work. She maddened him. He was furious. Then he abused her, and went into passionate exposition of his stuff. This amused and stimulated her. But she never owned that she had been wrong.

During the ten years that she had belonged to the women's movement she had acquired a fair amount of education, and, having had some of Miriam's passion to be instructed, had taught herself French, and could read in that language with a struggle. She considered herself as a woman apart, and particularly apart, from her class. The girls in the spiral department were all of good homes. It was a small, special industry, and had a certain distinction. There was an air of refinement in both rooms. But Clara was aloof also from her fellow workers.

None of these things, however, did she reveal to Paul. She was not the one to give herself away. There was a sense of mystery about her. She was so reserved, he felt she had much to reserve. Her history was open on the surface, but its inner meaning was hidden from everybody. It was exciting. And then sometimes he caught her looking at him from under her brows with an almost furtive, sullen scrutiny, which made him move quickly. Often she met his eyes. But then her own were, as it were, covered over, revealing nothing. She gave him a little, lenient smile. She was to him extraordinarily provocative, because of the knowledge she seemed to possess, and gathered fruit of experience he could not attain.

One day he picked up a copy of *Lettres de mon Moulin* from her workbench.

"You read French, do you?" he cried.

Clara glanced round negligently. She was making an elastic stocking of heliotrope silk, turning the spiral machine with slow, balanced regularity, occasionally bending down to see her work or to adjust the needles; then her magnificent neck, with its down and fine pencils of hair, shone white against the lavender, lustrous silk. She turned a few more rounds, and stopped.

"What did you say?" she asked, smiling sweetly.

Paul's eyes glittered at her insolent indifference to him.

"I did not know you read French," he said, very polite.

"Did you not?" she replied, with a faint, sarcastic smile.

"Rotten swank!" he said, but scarcely loud enough to be heard.

He shut his mouth angrily as he watched her. She seemed to scorn the work she mechanically produced; yet the hose she made were as nearly perfect as possible.

"You don't like spiral work," he said.

"Oh, well, all work is work," she answered, as if she knew all about it.

He marveled at her coldness. He had to do everything hotly. She must be something special.

"What would you prefer to do?" he asked.

She laughed at him indulgently, as she said:

"There is so little likelihood of my ever being given a choice, that I haven't wasted time considering."

"Pah!" he said, contemptuous on his side now. "You only say that because you're too proud to own up what you want and can't get."

"You know me very well," she replied coldly.

"I know you think you're terrific great shakes, and that you live under the eternal insult of working in a factory."

He was very angry and very rude. She merely turned away from him in disdain. He walked whistling down the room, flirted and laughed with Hilda.

Later on he said to himself:

"What was I so impudent to Clara for?" He was rather annoyed with himself, at the same time glad. "Serve her right; she stinks with silent pride," he said to himself angrily.

In the afternoon he came down. There was a certain weight on his heart which he wanted to remove. He thought to do it by offering her chocolates.

"Have one?" he said. "I bought a handful to sweeten me up."

To his great relief, she accepted. He sat on the workbench beside her machine, twisting a piece of silk round his finger. She loved him for his quick, unexpected movements, like a young animal. His feet swung as he pondered. The sweets lay strewn on the bench. She bent over her machine, grinding rhythmically, then stooping to see the stocking that hung beneath, pulled down by the weight. He watched the handsome crouching of her back, and the apron strings curling on the floor.

"There is always about you," he said, "a sort of waiting. Whatever I see you doing, you're not really there: you are waiting—like Penelope when she did her weaving." He could not help a spurt of wickedness. "I'll call you Penelope," he said.

"Would it make any difference?" she said, carefully removing one of her needles.

"That doesn't matter, so long as it pleases me. Here, I say, you seem to forget I'm your boss. It just occurs to me."

"And what does that mean?" she asked coolly.

"It means I've got a right to boss you."

"Is there anything you want to complain about?"

"Oh, I say, you needn't be nasty," he said angrily.

"I don't know what you want," she said, continuing her task.

"I want you to treat me nicely and respectfully."

"Call you 'sir,' perhaps?" she asked quietly.

"Yes, call me 'sir.' I should love it."

"Then I wish you would go upstairs, sir."

His mouth closed, and a frown came on his face. He jumped suddenly down.

"You're too blessed superior for anything," he said.

And he went away to the other girls. He felt he was being angrier than he had any need to be. In fact, he doubted slightly that he was showing off. But if he were, then he would. Clara heard him laughing, in a way she hated, with the girls down the next room.

When at evening he went through the department after the girls had gone, he saw his chocolates lying untouched in front of Clara's machine. He left them. In the morning they were still there, and Clara was at work. Later on Minnie, a little brunette they called Pussy, called to him:

"Hey, haven't you got a chocolate for anybody?"

"Sorry, Pussy," he replied. "I meant to have offered them; then I went and forgot 'em."

"I think you did," she answered.

"I'll bring you some this afternoon. You don't want them after they've been lying about, do you?"

"Oh, I'm not particular," smiled Pussy.

"Oh no," he said. "They'll be dusty."

He went up to Clara's bench.

"Sorry I left these things littering about," he said.

She flushed scarlet. He gathered them together in his fist.

"They'll be dirty now," he said. "You should have taken them. I wonder why you didn't. I meant to have told you I wanted you to."

He flung them out of the window into the yard below. He just glanced at her. She winced from his eyes.

In the afternoon he brought another packet.

"Will you take some?" he said, offering them first to Clara. "These are fresh."

She accepted one, and put it onto the bench.

"Oh, take several—for luck," he said.

She took a couple more, and put them on the bench also. Then she turned in confusion to her work. He went on up the room.

"Here you are, Pussy," he said. "Don't be greedy!"

"Are they all for her?" cried the others, rushing up.

"Of course they're not," he said.

The girls clamored around. Pussy drew back from her mates.

"Come out!" she cried. "I can have first pick, can't I, Paul?"

"Be nice with 'em," he said, and went away.

"You *are* a dear," the girls cried.

"Tenpence," he answered.

He went past Clara without speaking. She felt the three chocolate creams would burn her if she touched them. It needed all her courage to slip them into the pocket of her apron.

The girls loved him and were afraid of him. He was so nice while he was nice, but if he were offended, so distant, treating them as if they scarcely existed, or not more than the bobbins of thread. And then, if they were impudent, he said quietly: "Do you mind going on with your work," and stood and watched.

When he celebrated his twenty-third birthday, the house was in trouble. Arthur was just going to be married. His mother was not well. His father, getting an old man, and lame from his accidents, was given a paltry, poor job. Miriam was an eternal reproach. He felt he owed himself to her, yet could not give himself. The house, moreover, needed his support. He was pulled in all directions. He was not glad it was his birthday. It made him bitter.

He got to work at eight o'clock. Most of the clerks had not turned up. The girls were not due until 8:30. As he was changing his coat, he heard a voice behind him say:

"Paul, Paul, I want you," she said.

It was Fanny, the hunchback, standing at the top of her stairs, her face radiant with a secret. Paul looked at her in astonishment.

"I want you," she said.

He stood, at a loss.

"Come on," she coaxed. "Come before you begin of the letters."

He went down the half-dozen steps into her dry, narrow, "finishing-off" room. Fanny walked before him: her black bodice was short—the waist was under her armpits—and her green-black cashmere skirt seemed very long, as she strode with big strides before the young man, himself so graceful. She went to her seat at the narrow end of the room, where the window opened on to chimney-pots. Paul watched her thin hands and her flat red wrists as she excitedly twitched her white apron, which was spread on the bench in front of her. She hesitated.

"You didn't think we'd forgot you?" she asked, reproachful.

"Why?" he asked. He had forgotten his birthday himself.

" 'Why,' he says! 'Why!' Why, look here!" She pointed to the calendar, and he saw, surrounding the big black number "21," hundreds of little crosses in blacklead.

"Oh, kisses for my birthday," he laughed. "How did you know?"

"Yes, you want to know, don't you?" Fanny mocked, hugely delighted. "There's one from everybody—except Lady Clara—and two from some. But I shan't tell you how many *I* put."

"Oh, I know, you're spooney," he said.

"There you *are* mistaken!" she cried indignant. "I could never be so soft." Her voice was strong and contralto.

"You always pretend to be such a hardhearted hussy," he laughed. "And you know you're as sentimental——"

"I'd rather be called sentimental than frozen meat," Fanny blurted. Paul knew she referred to Clara, and he smiled.

"Do you say such nasty things about me?" he laughed.

"No, my duck," the hunchback woman answered, lavishly tender. She was thirty-nine. "No, my duck, because you don't think yourself a fine figure in marble and us nothing but dirt. I'm as good as you, aren't I, Paul?" and the question delighted her.

"Why, we're not better than one another, are we?" he replied.

"But I'm as good as you aren't I, Paul?" she persisted daringly.

"Of course you are. If it comes to goodness, you're better."

She was rather afraid of the situation. She might get hysterical.

"I thought I'd get here before the others—won't they say I'm deep! Now shut your eyes—" she said.

"And open your mouth, and see what God sends you," he continued, suiting action to words, and expecting a piece of chocolate. He heard the rustle of the apron, and a faint clink of metal. "I'm going to look," he said.

He opened his eyes. Fanny, her long cheeks flushed, her blue eyes shining, was gazing at him. There was a little bundle of paint tubes on the bench before him. He turned pale.

"No, Fanny," he said quickly.

"From us all," she answered hastily.

"No, but——"

"Are they the right sort?" she asked, rocking herself with delight.

"Jove! they're the best in the catalogue."

"But they're the right sorts?" she cried.

"They're off the little list I'd made to get when my ship came in." He bit his lip.

Fanny was overcome with emotion. She must turn the conversation.

"They was all on thorns to do it; they all paid their shares, all except the Queen of Sheba."

The Queen of Sheba was Clara.

"And wouldn't she join?" Paul asked.

"She didn't get the chance; we never told her; we wasn't going to have *her* bossing *this* show. We didn't *want* her to join."

Paul laughed at the woman. He was much moved. At last he must go. She was very close to him. Suddenly she flung her arms round his neck and kissed him vehemently.

"I can give you a kiss today," she said apologetically. "You've looked so white, it's made my heart ache."

Paul kissed her, and left her. Her arms were so pitifully thin that his heart ached also.

That day he met Clara as he ran downstairs to wash his hands at dinner-time.

"You have stayed to dinner!" he exclaimed. It was unusual for her.

"Yes; and I seem to have dined on old surgical-appliance stock. I *must* go out now, or I shall feel stale india-rubber right through."

She lingered. He instantly caught at her wish.

They went together up to the Castle. Outdoors she dressed very plainly, down to ugliness; indoors she always looked nice. She walked with hesitating steps alongside Paul, bowing and turning away from him. Dowdy in dress, and drooping, she showed to great disadvantage. He could scarcely recognize her strong form, that seemed to slumber with power. She appeared almost insignificant, drowning her stature in her stoop, as she shrank from the public gaze.

The Castle grounds were very green and fresh. Climbing the precipitous ascent, he laughed and chattered, but she was silent, seeming to brood over something. There was scarcely time to go inside the squat, square building that crowns the bluff of rock. They leaned upon the wall where the cliff runs sheer down to the Park. Below them, in their holes in the sandstone, pigeons preened themselves and cooed softly. Away down upon the boulevard at the foot of the rock, tiny trees stood in their own pools of shadow, and tiny people went scurrying about in almost ludicrous importance.

"You feel as if you could scoop up the folk like tadpoles, and have a handful of them," he said.

She laughed, answering.

"Yes; it is not necessary to get far off in order to see us proportionately. The trees are much more significant."

"Bulk only," he said.

She laughed cynically.

Away beyond the boulevard the thin stripes of the metals showed upon the railway track, whose margin was crowded with little stacks of timber, beside which smoking toy engines fussed. Then the silver string of the canal lay at random among the black heaps. Beyond, the dwellings, very dense on the river flat, looked like black, poisonous herbage, in thick rows and crowded beds, stretching right away, broken now and then by taller plants, right to where the river glistened in a hieroglyph across the country. The steep scarp cliffs across the river looked puny. Great stretches of country darkened with trees and faintly brightened with corn-land, spread towards the haze, where the hills rose blue beyond gray.

"It is comforting," said Mrs. Dawes, "to think the town goes no farther. It is only a *little* sore upon the country yet."

"A little scab," Paul said.

She shivered. She loathed the town. Looking drearily across at the country which was forbidden her, her impassive face pale and hostile, she reminded Paul of one of the bitter, remorseful angels.

"But the town's all right," he said; "it's only temporary. This is the crude, clumsy makeshift we've practiced on, till we find out what the idea is. The town will come all right."

The pigeons in the pockets of rock, among the perched bushes, cooed comfortably. To the left the large church of St. Mary rose into space, to keep close company with the Castle, above the heaped rubble of the town. Mrs. Dawes smiled brightly as she looked across the country.

"I feel better," she said.

"Thank you," he replied. "Great compliment!"

"Oh, my brother!" she laughed.

"H'm! that's snatching back with the left hand what you gave with the right, and no mistake," he said.

She laughed in amusement at him.

"But what was the matter with you?" he asked. "I know you were brooding something special. I can see the stamp of it on your face yet."

"I think I will not tell you," she said.

"All right, hug it," he answered.

She flushed and bit her lip.

"No," she said, "it was the girls."

"What about 'em?" Paul asked.

"They have been plotting something for a week now, and today they seem particularly full of it. All alike; they insult me with their secrecy."

"Do they?" he asked in concern.

"I should not mind," she went on, in the metallic, angry tone, "if they did not thrust it into my face—the fact that they have a secret."

"Just like women," said he.

"It is hateful, their mean gloating," she said intensely.

Paul was silent. He knew what the girls gloated over. He was sorry to be the cause of this new dissension.

"They can have all the secrets in the world," she went on, brooding bitterly; "but they might refrain from glorying in them, and making me feel more out of it than ever. It is—it is almost unbearable."

Paul thought for a few minutes. He was much perturbed.

"I will tell you what it's all about," he said, pale and nervous. "It's my birthday, and they've bought me a fine lot of paints, all the girls. They're jealous of you"—he felt her stiffen coldly at the word "jealous"—"merely because I sometimes bring you a book," he added slowly. "But, you see, it's only a trifle. Don't bother about it, will you—because"—he laughed quickly—"well, what would they say if they saw us here now, in spite of their victory?"

She was angry with him for his clumsy reference to their present intimacy. It was almost insolent of him. Yet he was so quiet, she forgave him, although it cost her an effort.

Their two hands lay on the rough stone parapet of the Castle wall. He had inherited from his mother a fineness of mold, so that his hands were small and vigorous. Hers were large, to match her large limbs, but white and powerful looking. As Paul looked at them he knew her. "She is wanting somebody to take her hands—for all she is so contemptuous of us," he said to himself. And she saw nothing but his two hands, so warm and alive, which seemed to live for her. He was brooding now, staring out over the country from under sullen brows. The little, interesting diversity of shapes had vanished from the scene; all that remained was a vast, dark matrix of sorrow and tragedy, the same in all the houses and the river flats and the people and the birds; they were only shapen differently. And now that the forms seemed to have melted away, there remained the mass from which all the landscape was composed, a dark mass of struggle and pain. The factory, the girls, his mother, the large, uplifted church, the thicket of the town, merged into one atmosphere—dark, brooding, and sorrowful, every bit.

"Is that two o'clock striking?" Mrs. Dawes said in surprise.

Paul started, and everything sprang into form, regained its individuality, its forgetfulness, and its cheerfulness.

They hurried back to work.

When he was in the rush of preparing for the night's post, examining the work up from Fanny's room, which smelt of ironing, the evening postman came in.

"Mr. Paul Morel," he said smiling, handing Paul a package. "A lady's handwriting! Don't let the girls see it."

The postman, himself a favorite, was pleased to make fun of the girls' affection for Paul.

It was a volume of verse with a brief note: "You will allow me to send you this, and so spare me my isolation. I also sympathize and wish you well.—C. D." Paul flushed hot.

"Good Lord! Mrs. Dawes. She can't afford it. Good Lord, who ever'd have thought it!"

He was suddenly intensely moved. He was filled with the warmth of her. In the glow he could almost feel her as if she were present—her arms, her shoulders, her bosom, see them, feel them, almost contain them.

This move on the part of Clara brought them into closer intimacy. The other girls noticed that when Paul met Mrs. Dawes his eyes lifted and gave that peculiar bright greeting which they could interpret. Knowing he was unaware, Clara made no sign, save that occasionally she turned aside her face from him when he came upon her.

They walked out together very often at dinner-time; it was quite open, quite frank. Everybody seemed to feel that he was quite unaware of the state of his own feeling, and that nothing was wrong. He talked to her now with some of the old fervor with which he had talked to Miriam, but he cared less about the talk; he did not bother about his conclusions.

One day in October they went out to Lambley for tea. Suddenly they came to a halt on top of the hill. He climbed and sat on a gate, she sat on the stile. The afternoon was perfectly still, with a dim haze, and yellow sheaves glowing through. They were quiet.

"How old were you when you married?" he asked quietly.

"Twenty-two."

Her voice was subdued, almost submissive. She would tell him now.

"It is eight years ago?"

"Yes."

"And when did you leave him?"

"Three years ago."

"Five years! Did you love him when you married him?"

She was silent for some time; then she said slowly:

"I thought I did—more or less. I didn't think much about it. And he wanted me. I was very prudish then."

"And you sort of walked into it without thinking?"

"Yes. I seemed to have been asleep nearly all my life."

"Somnambule? But—when did you wake up?"

"I don't know that I ever did, or ever have—since I was a child."

"You went to sleep as you grew to be a woman? How queer! And he didn't wake you?"

"No; he never got there," she replied, in a monotone.

The brown birds dashed over the hedges where the rose hips stood naked and scarlet.

"Got where?" he asked.

"At me. He never really mattered to me."

The afternoon was so gently warm and dim. Red roofs of the cottages burned among the blue haze. He loved the day. He could feel, but he could not understand, what Clara was saying.

"But why did you leave him? Was he horrid to you?"

She shuddered lightly.

"He—he sort of degraded me. He wanted to bully me because he hadn't got me. And then I felt as if I wanted to run, as if I was fastened and bound up. And he seemed dirty."

"I see."

He did not at all see.

"And was he always dirty?" he asked.

"A bit," she replied slowly. "And then he seemed as if he couldn't get *at* me, really. And then he got brutal—he *was* brutal!"

"And why did you leave him finally?"

"Because—because he was unfaithful to me——"

They were both silent for some time. Her hand lay on the gatepost as she balanced. He put his own over it. His heart beat thickly.

"But did you—were you ever—did you ever give him a chance?"

"Chance? How?"

"To come near to you."

"I married him—and I was willing——"

They both strove to keep their voices steady.

"I believe he loves you," he said.

"It looks like it," she replied.

He wanted to take his hand away, and could not. She saved him by removing her own. After a silence, he began again:

"Did you leave him out of count all along?"

"He left me," she said.

"And I suppose he couldn't *make* himself mean everything to you?"

"He tried to bully me into it."

But the conversation had got them both out of their depth. Suddenly Paul jumped down.

"Come on," he said. "Let's go and get some tea."

They found a cottage, where they sat in the cold parlor. She poured out his tea. She was very quiet. He felt she had withdrawn again from him. After tea, she stared broodingly into her teacup, twisting her wedding ring all the time. In her abstraction she took the ring off her finger, stood it up, and spun it upon the table. The gold became a diaphanous, glittering globe. It fell, and the ring was quivering upon the table. She spun it again and again. Paul watched, fascinated.

But she was a married woman, and he believed in simple friendship. And he considered that he was perfectly honorable with regard to her. It was only a friendship between man and woman, such as any civilized persons might have.

He was like so many young men of his own age. Sex had become so complicated in him that he would have denied that he ever could want Clara or Miriam or any woman whom he *knew*. Sex desire was a sort of detached thing, that did not belong to a woman. He loved Miriam with his soul. He grew warm at the thought of Clara, he battled with her, he knew the curves of her breast and shoulders as if they had been molded inside him; and yet he did not positively desire her. He would have denied it forever. He believed himself really bound to Miriam. If ever he should marry, some time in the far future, it would be his duty to marry Miriam. That he gave Clara to understand, and she said nothing, but left him to his courses. He came to her, Mrs. Dawes, whenever he could. Then he wrote frequently to Miriam, and visited the girl occasionally. So he went on through the winter; but he seemed not so fretted. His mother was easier about him. She thought he was getting away from Miriam.

Miriam knew now how strong was the attraction of Clara for him; but still she was certain that the best in him would triumph. His feeling for Mrs. Dawes—who, moreover, was a married woman—was shallow and temporal, compared with his love for herself. He would come back to her, she was sure; with some of his young freshness gone, perhaps, but cured of his desire for the lesser things which other women than herself could give him. She could bear all if he were inwardly true to her and must come back.

He saw none of the anomaly of his position. Miriam was his old friend, lover, and she belonged to Bestwood and home and his youth. Clara was a newer friend, and she belonged to Nottingham, to life, to the world. It seemed to him quite plain.

Mrs. Dawes and he had many periods of coolness, when they saw little of each other; but they always came together again.

"Were you horrid with Baxter Dawes?" he asked her. It was a thing that seemed to trouble him.

"In what way?"

"Oh, I don't know. But weren't you horrid with him? Didn't you do something that knocked him to pieces?"

"What, pray?"

"Making him feel as if he were nothing—*I* know," Paul declared.

"You are so clever, my friend," she said coolly.

The conversation broke off there. But it made her cool with him for some time.

She very rarely saw Miriam now. The friendship between the two women was not broken off, but considerably weakened.

"Will you come in to the concert on Sunday afternoon?" Clara asked him just after Christmas.

"I promised to go up to Willey Farm," he replied.

"Oh, very well."

"You don't mind, do you?" he asked.

"Why should I?" she answered.

Which almost annoyed him.

"You know," he said, "Miriam and I have been a lot to each other ever since I was sixteen—that's seven years now."

"It's a long time," Clara replied.

"Yes; but somehow she—it doesn't go right——"

"How?" asked Clara.

"She seems to draw me and draw me, and she wouldn't leave a single hair of me free to fall out and blow away—she'd keep it."

"But you like to be kept."

"No," he said, "I don't. I wish it could be normal, give and take—like me and you. I want a woman to keep me, but not in her pocket."

"But if you love her, it couldn't be normal, like me and you."

"Yes; I should love her better then. She sort of wants me so much that I can't give myself."

"Wants you how?"

"Wants the soul out of my body. I can't help shrinking back from her."

"And yet you love her!"

"No, I don't love her. I never even kiss her."

"Why not?" Clara asked.

"I don't know."

"I suppose you're afraid," she said.

"I'm not. Something in me shrinks from her like hell—she's so good, when I'm not good."

"How do you know what she is?"

"I do! I know she wants a sort of soul union."

"But how do you know what she wants?"

"I've been with her for seven years."

"And you haven't found out the very first thing about her."

"What's that?"

"That she doesn't want any of your soul communion. That's your own imagination. She wants you."

He pondered over this. Perhaps he was wrong.

"But she seems—" he began.

"You've never tried," she answered.

❖ 11 ❖

THE TEST ON MIRIAM

With the spring came again the old madness and battle. Now he knew he would have to go to Miriam. But what was his reluctance? He told himself it was only a sort of overstrong virginity in her and him which neither could break through. He might have married her; but his circumstances at home made it difficult, and, moreover, he did not want to marry. Marriage was for life, and because they had become close companions, he and she, he did not see that it should inevitably follow they should be man and wife. He did not feel that he wanted marriage with Miriam. He wished he did. He would have given his head to have felt a joyous desire to marry her and to have her. Then why couldn't he bring it off? There was some obstacle; and what was the obstacle? It lay in the physical bondage. He shrank from the physical contact. But Why? With her he felt bound up inside himself. He could not go out to her. Something struggled in him, but he could not get to her. Why? She loved him. Clara said she even wanted him; then why couldn't he go to her, make love to her, kiss her? Why, when she put her arm in his, timidly, as they walked, did he feel he would burst forth in brutality and recoil? He owed himself to her; he wanted to belong to her. Perhaps the recoil and the shrinking from her was love in its first fierce modesty. He had no aversion for her. No, it was the opposite; it was a strong desire battling with a still stronger shyness and virginity. It seemed as if virginity were a positive force, which fought and won in both of them. And with her he felt it so hard to overcome; yet he was nearest to her, and with her alone could he deliberately break through. And he owed himself to her. Then, if they could get things right, they could marry; but he would not marry unless he could feel strong in the joy of it—never. He could not have faced his mother. It seemed to him that to sacrifice himself in a marriage he did not want would be degrading, and would undo all his life, make it a nullity. He would try what he *could* do.

And he had a great tenderness for Miriam. Always, she was sad, dreaming her religion; and he was nearly a religion to her. He could not bear to fail her. It would all come right if they tried.

He looked round. A good many of the nicest men he knew were like himself, bound in by their own virginity, which they could not break out of. They were so sensitive to their women that they would go without them forever rather than do them a hurt, an injustice. Being the sons of mothers whose husbands had blundered rather brutally through their feminine sanctities, they were themselves too diffident and shy. They could easier deny themselves than incur any reproach from a woman; for a woman was like their mother, and they were full of the sense of their mother. They preferred themselves to suffer the misery of celibacy, rather than risk the other person.

He went back to her. Something in her, when he looked at her, brought the tears almost to his eyes. One day he stood behind her as she sang. Annie was playing a song on the piano. As Miriam sang her mouth seemed hopeless. She sang like a nun singing to heaven. It reminded him so much of the mouth and eyes of one who sings beside a Botticelli Madonna, so spiritual. Again, hot as steel, came up the pain in him. Why must he ask her for the other thing? Why was there his blood battling with her? If only he could have been always gentle, tender with her, breathing with her the atmosphere of reverie and religious dreams, he would give his right hand. It was not fair to hurt her. There seemed an eternal maidenhood about her; and when he thought of her mother, he saw the great brown eyes of a maiden who was nearly scared and shocked out of her virgin maidenhood, but not quite, in spite of her seven children. They had been born almost leaving her out of count, not of her, but upon her. So she could never let them go, because she never had possessed them.

Mrs. Morel saw him going again frequently to Miriam, and was astonished. He said nothing to his mother. He did not explain nor excuse himself. If he came home late, and she reproached him, he frowned and turned on her in an overbearing way:

"I shall come home when I like," he said; "I am old enough."

"Must she keep you till this time?"

"It is I who stay," he answered.

"And she lets you? But very well, " she said.

And she went to bed, leaving the door unlocked for him; but she lay listening until he came, often long after. It was a great bitterness to her that he had gone back to Miriam. She recognized, however, the uselessness of any further interference. He went to Willey Farm as a man now, not as a youth. She had no right over him. There was a coldness between him and her. He hardly told her anything. Discarded, she waited on him, cooked for him still, and loved to slave for him; but her face closed again like a mask. There was nothing for her to do now but the housework; for all the rest he had gone to Miriam. She could not forgive him. Miriam killed the joy and the warmth in him. He had been such a jolly lad, and full of the warmest affection; now he grew colder, more and more irritable and gloomy. It reminded her of William; but Paul was worse. He did things with more intensity, and more realization of what he was about. His mother knew how he was suffering for want of a woman, and she saw him going to Miriam. If he had made up his mind, nothing on earth would alter him. Mrs. Morel was tired. She began to give up at last; she had finished. She was in the way.

He went on determinedly. He realized more or less what his mother felt. It only hardened his soul. He made himself callous towards her; but it was like being callous to his own health. It undermined him quickly; yet he persisted.

He lay back in the rocking chair at Willey Farm one evening. He had been talking to Miriam for some weeks, but had not come to the point. Now he said suddenly:

"I am twenty-four, almost."

She had been brooding. She looked up at him suddenly in surprise.

"Yes. What makes you say it?"

There was something in the charged atmosphere that she dreaded.

"Sir Thomas More says one can marry at twenty-four."

She laughed quaintly, saying:

"Does it need Sir Thomas More's sanction?"

"No; but one ought to marry about then."

"Ay," she answered broodingly; and she waited.

"I can't marry you," he continued slowly, "not now, because we've no money, and they depend on me at home."

She sat half-guessing what was coming.

"But I want to marry now——"

"You want to marry?" she repeated.

"A woman—you know what I mean."

She was silent.

"Now, at last, I must," he said.

"Ay," she answered.

"And you love me?"

She laughed bitterly.

"Why are you ashamed of it?" he answered. "You wouldn't be ashamed before your God, why are you before people?"

"Nay," she answered deeply, "I am not ashamed."

"You are," he replied bitterly; "and it's my fault. But you know I can't help being—as I am—don't you?"

"I know you can't help it," she replied.

"I love you an awful lot—then there is something short."

"Where?" she answered, looking at him.

"Oh, in me! It is I who ought to be ashamed—like a spiritual cripple. And I am ashamed. It is misery. Why is it?"

"I don't know," replied Miriam.

"And I don't know," he repeated. "Don't you think we have been too fierce in our what they call purity? Don't you think that to be so much afraid and averse is a sort of dirtiness?"

She looked at him with startled dark eyes.

"You recoiled away from anything of the sort, and I took the motion from you, and recoiled also, perhaps worse."

There was silence in the room for some time.

"Yes," she said, "it is so."

"There is between us," he said, "all these years of intimacy. I feel naked enough before you. Do you understand?"

"I think so," she answered.

"And you love me?"

She laughed.

"Don't be bitter," he pleaded.

She looked at him and was sorry for him; his eyes were dark with torture. She was sorry for him; it was worse for him to have this deflected love than for herself, who could never be properly mated. He was restless, forever urging forward and trying to find a way out. He might do as he liked, and have what he liked of her.

"Nay," she said softly, "I am not bitter."

She felt she could bear anything for him; she would suffer for him. She put her hand on his knee as he leaned forward in his chair. He took it and kissed it; but it hurt to do so. He felt he was putting himself aside. He sat there sacrificed to her purity, which felt more like nullity. How could he kiss her hand passionately, when it would drive her away, and leave nothing but pain? Yet slowly he drew her to him and kissed her.

They knew each other too well to pretend anything. As she kissed him, she watched his eyes; they were staring across the room, with a peculiar dark blaze in them that fascinated her. He was perfectly still. She could feel his heart throbbing heavily in his breast.

"What are you thinking about?" she asked.

The blaze in his eyes shuddered, became uncertain.

"I was thinking, all the while, I love you. I have been obstinate."

She sank her head on his breast.

"Yes," she answered.

"That's all," he said, and his voice seemed sure, and his mouth was kissing her throat.

Then she raised her head and looked into his eyes with her full gaze of love. The blaze struggled, seemed to try to get away from her, and then was quenched. He turned his head quickly aside. It was a moment of anguish.

"Kiss me," she whispered.

He shut his eyes, and kissed her, and his arms folded her closer and closer.

When she walked home with him over the fields, he said:

"I am glad I came back to you. I feel so simple with you—as if there was nothing to hide. We will be happy?"

"Yes," she murmured, and the tears came to her eyes.

"Some sort of perversity in our souls," he said, "makes us not want, get away from, the very thing we want. We have to fight against that."

"Yes," she said, and she felt stunned.

As she stood under the drooping thorn tree, in the darkness by the roadside, he kissed her, and his fingers wandered over her face. In the darkness, where he could not see her but only feel her, his passion flooded him. He clasped her very close.

"Sometime you will have me?" he murmured, hiding his face on her shoulder. It was so difficult.

"Not now," she said.

His hopes and his heart sunk. A dreariness came over him.

"No" he said.

His clasp of her slackened.

"I love to feel your arm *there!*" she said, pressing his arm against her back, where it went round her waist. "It rests me so."

He tightened the pressure of his arm upon the small of her back to rest her.

"We belong to each other," he said.

"Yes."

"Then why shouldn't we belong to each other altogether?"

"But—" she faltered.

"I know it's a lot to ask," he said; "but there's not much risk for you really—not in the Gretchen way. You can trust me there?"

"Oh, I can trust you." The answer came quick and strong. "It's not that—it's not that at all—but——"

"What?"

She hid her face in his neck with a little cry of misery.

"I don't know!" she cried.

She seemed slightly hysterical, but with a sort of horror. His heart died in him.

"You don't think it ugly?" he asked.

"No, not now. You have *taught* me it isn't."

"You are afraid?"

She calmed herself hastily.

"Yes, I am only afraid," she said.

He kissed her tenderly.

"Never mind," he said. "You shall please yourself."

Suddenly she gripped her arms round him, and clenched her body stiff.

"You *shall* have me," she said, through her shut teeth.

His heart beat up again like fire. He folded her close, and his mouth was on her throat. She could not bear it. She drew away. He disengaged her.

"Won't you be late?" she asked gently.

He sighed, scarcely hearing what she said. She waited, wishing he would go. At last he kissed her quickly and climbed the fence. Looking round he saw the pale blotch of her face down in the darkness under the hanging tree. There was no more of her but this pale blotch.

"Good-bye!" she called softly. She had no body, only a voice and a dim face. He turned away and ran down the road, his fists clenched; and when he came to the wall over the lake he leaned there, almost stunned, looking up the black water.

Miriam plunged home over the meadows. She was not afraid of people, what they might say; but she dreaded the issue with him. Yes, she would let him have her if he insisted; and then, when she thought of it afterwards, her heart went down. He would be disappointed, he would find no satisfaction, and then he would go away. Yet he was so insistent; and over this, which did not seem so all-important to her, was their love to break down. After all, he was only like other men, seeking his satisfaction. Oh, but there was something, more in him, something deeper! She could trust to it, in spite of all desires. He said that possession was a great moment in life. All strong emotions concentrated there. Perhaps it was so. There was something divine in it; then she would submit, religiously, to the sacrifice. He should have her. And at the thought her whole body clenched itself involuntarily, hard, as if against something; but Life forced her through this gate of suffering, too, and she would submit. At any rate, it would give him what he wanted, which was her deepest wish. She brooded and brooded and brooded herself towards accepting him.

He courted her now like a lover. Often, when he grew hot, she put his face from her, held it between her hands, and looked in his eyes. He could not meet her gaze. Her dark eyes, full of love, earnest and searching, made him turn away. Not for an instant would she let him forget. Back again he had to torture himself into a sense of his responsibility and hers. Never any relaxing, never any leaving himself to the great hunger and impersonality of passion; he must be brought back to a deliberate, reflective creature. As if from a swoon of passion she called him back to the littleness, the personal relationship. He could not bear it. "Leave me alone—leave me alone!" he wanted to cry; but she wanted him to look at her with eyes full of love. His eyes, full of the dark, impersonal fire of desire, did not belong to her.

There was a great crop of cherries at the farm. The trees at the back of the house, very large and tall, hung thick with scarlet and crimson drops, under the dark leaves. Paul and Edgar were gathering in the fruit one evening. It had been a hot day, and now the clouds were rolling in the sky, dark and warm. Paul climbed high in the tree, above the scarlet roofs of the buildings. The wind, moaning steadily, made the whole tree rock with a subtle, thrilling motion that stirred the blood. The young man, perched insecurely in the slender branches, rocked till he felt slightly drunk, reached down the boughs, where the scarlet beady cherries hung thick underneath, and tore off handful after handful of the sleek, cool-fleshed fruit. Cherries touched his ears and his neck as he stretched forward, their chill fingertips sending a flash down his blood. All shades of red, from a golden vermilion to a rich crimson, glowed and met his eyes under a darkness of leaves.

The sun, going down, suddenly caught the broken clouds. Immense piles of gold flared out in the southeast, heaped in soft, glowing yellow right up the sky.

The world, till now dusk and gray, reflected the gold glow, astonished. Everywhere the trees, and the grass, and the far-off water, seemed roused from the twilight and shining.

Miriam came out wondering.

"Oh!" Paul heard her mellow voice call, "isn't it wonderful?"

He looked down. There was a faint gold glimmer on her face, that looked very soft, turned up to him.

"How high you are!" she said.

Beside her, on the rhubarb leaves, were four dead birds, thieves that had been shot. Paul saw some cherry-stones hanging quite bleached, like skeletons, picked clear of flesh. He looked down again to Miriam.

"Clouds are on fire," he said.

"Beautiful!" she cried.

She seemed so small, so soft, so tender, down there. He threw a handful of cherries at her. She was startled and frightened. He laughed with a low, chuckling sound, and pelted her. She ran for shelter, picking up some cherries. Two fine red pairs she hung over her ears; then she looked up again.

"Haven't you got enough?" she asked.

"Nearly. It is like being on a ship up here."

"And how long will you stay?"

"While the sunset lasts."

She went to the fence and sat there, watching the gold clouds fall to pieces, and go in immense, rose-colored ruin towards the darkness. Gold flamed to scarlet, like pain in its intense brightness. Then the scarlet sank to rose, and rose to crimson, and, quickly the passion went out of the sky. All the world was dark gray. Paul scrambled quickly down with his basket, tearing his shirtsleeve as he did so.

"They are lovely," said Miriam, fingering the cherries.

"I've torn my sleeve," he answered.

She took the three-cornered rip, saying:

"I shall have to mend it." It was near the shoulder. She put her fingers through the tear. "How warm!" she said.

He laughed. There was a new, strange note in his voice, one that made her pant.

"Shall we stay out?" he said.

"Won't it rain?" she asked.

"No, let us walk a little way."

They went down the fields and into the thick plantation of fir trees and pines.

"Shall we go in among the trees?" he asked.

"Do you want to?"

"Yes."

It was very dark among the firs, and the sharp spines pricked her face. She was afraid. Paul was silent and strange.

"I like the darkness," he said. "I wish it were thicker—good, thick darkness."

He seemed to be almost unaware of her as a person: she was only to him then a woman. She was afraid.

He stood against a pine tree trunk and took her in his arms. She relinquished herself to him, but it was a sacrifice in which she felt something of horror. This thick-voiced, oblivious man was a stranger to her.

Later it began to rain. The pine trees smelled very strong. Paul lay with his head on the ground, on the dead pine needles, listening to the sharp hiss of the rain—a steady, keen noise. His heart was down, very heavy. Now he realized that she had not been with him all the time, that her soul had stood apart, in a sort of horror. He was physically at rest, but no more. Very dreary at heart, very sad, and very tender, his fingers wandered over her face pitifully. Now again she loved him deeply. He was tender and beautiful.

"The rain!" he said.

"Yes—is it coming on you?"

She put her hands over him, on his hair, on his shoulders, to feel if the raindrops fell on him. She loved him dearly. He, as he lay with his face on the dead pine leaves, felt extraordinarily quiet. He did not mind if the raindrops came on him: he would have lain and got wet through: he felt as if nothing mattered, as if his living were smeared away into the beyond, near and quite lovable. This strange, gentle reaching-out to death was new to him.

"We must go," said Miriam.

"Yes," he answered, but did not move.

To him now, life seemed a shadow, day a white shadow; night, and death, and stillness, and inaction, this seemed like *being*. To be alive, to be urgent and insistent—that was *not-to-be*. The highest of all was to melt out into the darkness and sway there, identified with the great Being.

"The rain is coming in on us," said Miriam.

He rose, and assisted her.

"It is a pity," he said.

"What?"

"To have to go. I feel so still."

"Still!" she repeated.

"Stiller than I have ever been in my life."

He was walking with his hand in hers. She pressed his fingers, feeling a slight fear. Now he seemed beyond her; she had a fear lest she should lose him.

"The fir trees are like presences on the darkness: each one only a presence."

She was afraid, and said nothing.

"A sort of hush: the whole night wondering and asleep: I suppose that's what we do in death—sleep in wonder."

She had been afraid before of the brute in him: now of the mystic. She trod beside him in silence. The rain fell with a heavy "Hush!" on the trees. At last they gained the cartshed.

"Let us stay here awhile," he said.

There was a sound of rain everywhere, smothering everything.

"I feel so strange and still," he said; "along with everything."

"Ay," she answered patiently.

He seemed again unaware of her, though he held her hand close.

"To be rid of our individuality, which is our will, which is our effort—to live effortless, a kind of conscious sleep—that is very beautiful, I think; that is our afterlife—our immortality."

"Yes?"

"Yes—and very beautiful to have."

"You don't usually say that."

"No."

In a while they went indoors. Everybody looked at them curiously. He still kept the quiet, heavy look in his eyes, the stillness in his voice. Instinctively, they all left him alone.

About this time Miriam's grandmother, who lived in a tiny cottage in Woodlinton, fell ill, and the girl was sent to keep house. It was a beautiful little place. The cottage had a big garden in front, with red brick walls, against which the plum trees were nailed. At the back another garden was separated from the fields by a tall old hedge. It was very pretty. Miriam had not much to do, so she found time for her beloved reading, and for writing little introspective pieces which interested her.

At the holiday-time her grandmother, being better, was driven to Derby to stay with her daughter for a day or two. She was a crotchety old lady, and might return the second day or the third; so Miriam stayed alone in the cottage, which also pleased her.

Paul used often to cycle over, and they had as a rule peaceful and happy times. He did not embarrass her much; but then on the Monday of the holiday he was to spend a whole day with her.

It was perfect weather. He left his mother, telling her where he was going. She would be alone all the day. It cast a shadow over him; but he had three days that were all his own, when he was going to do as he liked. It was sweet to rush through the morning lanes on his bicycle.

He got to the cottage at about eleven o'clock. Miriam was busy preparing dinner.

She looked so perfectly in keeping with the little kitchen, ruddy and busy. He kissed her and sat down to watch. The room was small and cosy. The sofa was covered all over with a sort of linen in squares of red and pale blue, old, much washed, but pretty. There was a stuffed owl in a case over a corner cupboard. The sunlight came through the leaves of the scented geraniums in the window. She was cooking a chicken in his honor. It was their cottage for the day, and they were man and wife. He beat the eggs for her and peeled the potatoes. He thought she gave a feeling of home almost like his mother; and no one could look more beautiful, with her tumbled curls, when she was flushed from the fire.

The dinner was a great success. Like a young husband, he carved. They talked all the time with unflagging zest. Then he wiped the dishes she had washed, and they went out down the fields. There was a bright little brook that ran into a bog at the foot of a very steep bank. Here they wandered, picking still a few marsh marigolds and many big blue forget-me-nots. Then she sat on the bank with her hands full of flowers, mostly golden water-blobs. As she put her face down into the marigolds, it was all overcast with a yellow shine.

"Your face is bright," he said, "like a transfiguration."

She looked at him, questioning. He laughed pleadingly to her, laying his hand on hers. Then he kissed her fingers, then her face.

The world was all steeped in sunshine, and quite still, yet not asleep, but quivering with a kind of expectancy.

"I have never seen anything more beautiful than this," he said. He held her hand fast all the time.

"And the water singing to itself as it runs—do you love it?" She looked at him full of love. His eyes were very dark, very bright.

"Don't you think it's a great day?" he asked.

She murmured her assent. She *was* happy, and he saw it.

"And our day—just between us," he said.

They lingered a little while. Then they stood up upon the sweet thyme, and he looked down at her simply.

"Will you come?" he asked.

Then went back to the house, hand-in-hand, in silence. The chickens came scampering down the path to her. He locked the door, and they had the little house to themselves.

He never forgot seeing her as she lay on the bed, when he was unfastening his collar. First he saw only her beauty, and was blind with it. She had the most beautiful body he had ever imagined. He stood unable to move or speak, looking at her, his face half smiling with wonder. And then he wanted her, but as he went forward to her, her hands lifted in a little pleading movement, and he looked at her face, and stopped. Her big brown eyes were watching him, still and resigned and loving; she lay as if she had given herself up to sacrifice: there was her body for him; but the look at the back of her eyes, like a creature awaiting immolation, arrested him, and all his blood fell back.

"You are sure you want me?" he asked, as if a cold shadow had come over him.

"Yes, quite sure."

She was very quiet, very calm. She only realized that she was doing something for him. He could hardly bear it. She lay to be sacrificed for him because she loved him so much. And he had to sacrifice her. For a second, he wished he were sexless or dead. Then she shut his eyes again to her, and his blood beat back again.

And afterwards he loved her—loved her to the last fiber of his being. He loved her. But he wanted, somehow, to cry. There was something he could not bear for her sake. He stayed with her till quite late at night. As he rode home he felt that he was finally initiated. He was a youth no longer. But why had he the dull pain in his soul? Why did the thought of death, the afterlife, seem so sweet and consoling?

He spent the week with Miriam, and wore her out with his passion before it was gone. He had always, almost willfully, to put her out of count, and act from the brute strength of his own feelings. And he could not do it often, and there remained afterwards always the sense of failure and of death. If he were really with her, he had to put aside himself and his desire. If he would have her, he had to put her aside.

"When I come to you," he asked her, his eyes dark with pain and shame, "you don't really want me, do you?"

"Ah, yes!" she replied quickly.

He looked at her.

"Nay," he said.

She began to tremble.

"You see," she said, taking his face and shutting it out against her shoulder—"you see—as we are—how can I get used to you? It would come all right if we were married."

He lifted her head and looked at her.

"You mean, now, it is always too much shock?"

"Yes—and——"

"You are always clenched against me."

She was trembling with agitation.

"You see," she said, "I'm not used to the thought——"

"You are lately," he said.

"But all my life. Mother said to me, 'There is one thing in marriage that is always dreadful, but you have to bear it.' And I believed it."

"And still believe," he said.

"No!" she cried hastily. "I believe, as you do, that loving, even in *that* way, is the high-water mark of living."

"That doesn't alter the fact that you never *want* it."

"No," she said, taking his head in her arms and rocking in despair. "Don't say so! You don't understand." She rocked with pain. "Don't I want your children?"

"But not me."

"How can you say so? But we must be married to have children——"

"Shall we be married, then? *I* want you to have my children."

He kissed her hand reverently. She pondered sadly, watching him.

"We are too young," she said at length.

"Twenty-four and twenty-three——"

"Not yet," she pleaded, as she rocked herself in distress.

"When you will," he said.

She bowed her head gravely. The tone of hopelessness in which he said these things grieved her deeply. It had always been a failure between them. Tacitly, she acquiesced in what he felt.

And after a week of love he said to his mother suddenly one Sunday night, just as they were going to bed:

"I shan't go so much to Miriam's, mother."

She was surprised, but she would not ask him anything.

"You please yourself," she said.

So he went to bed. But there was a new quietness about him which she had wondered at. She almost guessed. She would leave him alone, however. Precipitation might spoil things. She watched him in his loneliness, wondering where he would end. He was sick, and much too quiet for him. There was a perpetual little knitting of his brows, such as she had seen when he was a small baby, and which had been gone for many years. Now it was the same again. And she could do nothing for him. He had to go on alone, make his own way.

He continued faithful to Miriam. For one day he had loved her utterly. But it never came again. The sense of failure grew stronger. At first it was only a sadness. Then he began to feel he could not go on. He wanted to run, to go abroad, anything. Gradually he ceased to ask her to have him. Instead of drawing them together, it put them apart. And then he realized, consciously, that it was no good. It was useless trying: it would never be a success between them.

For some months he had seen very little of Clara. They had occasionally walked out for half an hour at dinner-time. But he always reserved himself for Miriam. With Clara, however, his brow cleared, and he was gay again. She treated him indulgently, as if he were a child. He thought he did not mind. But deep below the surface it piqued him.

Sometimes Miriam said:

"What about Clara? I hear nothing of her lately."

"I walked with her about twenty minutes yesterday," he replied.

"And what did she talk about?"

"I don't know. I suppose I did all the jawing—I usually do. I think I was telling her about the strike, and how the women took it."

"Yes."

So he gave the account of himself.

But insidiously, without his knowing it, the warmth he felt for Clara drew him away from Miriam, for whom he felt responsible, and to whom he felt he belonged. He thought he was being quite faithful to her. It is not easy to estimate exactly the strength and warmth of one's feelings for a woman till they have run away with one.

He began to give more time to his men friends. There was Jessop, at the Art School; Swain, who was chemistry demonstrator at the University; Newton, who was a teacher; besides Edgar and Miriam's younger brothers. Pleading work, he sketched and studied with Jessop. He called in the University for Swain, and the two went "down town" together. Having come home in the train with Newton, he called and had a game of billiards with him in the Moon and Stars. If he gave to Miriam the excuse of his men friends, he felt quite justified. His mother began to be relieved. He always told her where he had been.

During the summer Clara wore sometimes a dress of soft cotton stuff with loose sleeves. When she lifted her hands, her sleeves fell back, and her beautiful strong arms shone out.

"Half a minute," he cried. "Hold your arm still."

He made sketches of her hand and arm, and the drawings contained some of the fascination the real thing had for him. Miriam, who always went scrupulously through his books and papers, saw the drawings.

"I think Clara has such beautiful arms," he said.

"Yes! When did you draw them?"

"On Tuesday, in the workroom. You know, I've got a corner where I can work. Often I can do every single thing they need in the department, before dinner. Then I work for myself in the afternoon, and just see to things at night."

"Yes," she said, turning the leaves of his sketchbook.

Frequently he hated Miriam. He hated her as she bent forward and pored over his things. He hated her way of patiently casting him up, as if he were an endless psychological account. When he was with her, he hated her for having got him, and yet not got him, and he tortured her. She took all and gave nothing, he said. At least, she gave no living warmth. She was never alive, and giving off life. Looking for her was like looking for something which did not exist. She was only his conscience, not his mate. He hated her violently, and was more cruel to her. They dragged on till the next summer. He saw more and more of Clara.

At last he spoke. He had been sitting working at home one evening. There was between him and his mother a peculiar condition of people frankly finding fault with each other. Mrs. Morel was strong on her feet again. He was not going to stick to Miriam. Very well; then she would stand aloof till he said something. It had been coming a long time, this bursting of the storm in him, when he would come back to her. This evening there was between them a peculiar condition of suspense. He worked feverishly and mechanically, so that he could escape from himself. It grew late. Through the open door, stealthily, came the scent of madonna lilies, almost as if it were prowling abroad. Suddenly he got up and went out of doors.

The beauty of the night made him want to shout. A half-moon, dusky gold, was sinking behind the black sycamore at the end of the garden, making the sky dull purple with its glow. Nearer, a dim white fence of lilies went across the garden, and the air all round seemed to stir with scent, as if it were alive. He went across the bed of pinks, whose keen perfume came sharply across the rocking, heavy scent of the lilies, and stood alongside the white barrier of flowers. They flagged all loose, as if they were panting. The scent made him drunk. He went down to the field to watch the moon sink under.

A corncrake in the hay-close called insistently. The moon slid quite quickly downwards, growing more flushed. Behind him the great flowers leaned as if they were calling. And then, like a shock, he caught another perfume, something raw and coarse. Hunting round, he found the purple iris, touched their fleshy throats and their dark, grasping hands. At any rate, he had found something. They stood stiff in the darkness. Their scent was brutal. The moon was melting down upon the crest of the hill. It was gone; all was dark. The corncrake called still.

Breaking off a pink, he suddenly went indoors.

"Come, my boy," said his mother. "I'm sure it's time you went to bed."

He stood with the pink against his lips.

"I shall break off with Miriam, mother," he answered calmly.

She looked up at him over her spectacles. He was staring back at her, unswerving. She met his eyes for a moment, then took off her glasses. He was white. The male was up in him, dominant. She did not want to see him too clearly.

"But I thought—" she began.

"Well," he answered, "I don't love her. I don't want to marry her—so I shall have done."

"But," exclaimed his mother, amazed, "I thought lately you had made up your mind to have her, and so I said nothing."

"I had—I wanted to—but now I don't want. It's no good. I shall break off on Sunday. I ought to, oughtn't I?"

"You know best. You know I said so long ago."

"I can't help that now. I shall break off on Sunday."

"Well," said his mother, "I think it will be best. But lately I decided you had made up your mind to have her, so I said nothing, and should have said nothing. But I say as I have always said, I *don't* think she is suited to you."

"On Sunday I break off," he said, smelling the pink. He put the flower in his mouth. Unthinking, he bared his teeth, closed them on the blossom slowly, and had a mouthful of petals. These he spat into the fire, kissed his mother, and went to bed.

On Sunday he went up to the farm in the early afternoon. He had written Miriam that they would walk over the fields to Hucknall. His mother was very tender with him. He said nothing. But she saw the effort it was costing. The peculiar set look on his face stilled her.

"Never mind, my son," she said. "You will be so much better when it is all over."

Paul glanced swiftly at his mother in surprise and resentment. He did not want sympathy.

Miriam met him at the lane-end. She was wearing a new dress of figured muslin that had short sleeves. Those short sleeves, and Miriam's brown-skinned arms beneath them—such pitiful, resigned arms—gave him so much pain that they helped to make him cruel. She had made herself look so beautiful and fresh for him. She seemed to blossom for him alone. Every time he looked at her—a mature young woman now, and beautiful in her new dress—it hurt so much that his heart seemed almost to be bursting with the restraint he put on it. But he had decided, and it was irrevocable.

On the hills they sat down, and he lay with his head in her lap, whilst she fingered his hair. She knew that "he was not there," as she put it. Often, when she had him with her, she looked for him, and could not find him. But this afternoon she was not prepared.

It was nearly five o'clock when he told her. They were sitting on the bank of a stream, where the lip of turf hung over a hollow bank of yellow earth, and he was hacking away with a stick, as he did when he was perturbed and cruel.

"I have been thinking," he said, "we ought to break off."

"Why?" she cried in surprise.

"Because it's no good going on."

"Why is it no good?"

"It isn't. I don't want to marry. I don't want ever to marry. And if we're not going to marry, it's no good going on."

"But why do you say this now?"

"Because I've made up my mind."

"And what about these last months, and the things you told me then?"

"I can't help it; I don't want to go on."

"You don't want any more of me?"

"I want us to break off—you be free of me, I free of you."

"And what about these last months?"

"I don't know. I've not told you anything but what I thought was true."

"Then why are you different now?"

"I'm not—I'm the same—only I know it's no good going on."

"You haven't told me why it's no good."

"Because I don't want to go on—and I don't want to marry."

"How many times have you offered to marry me, and I wouldn't?"

"I know; but I want us to break off."

There was silence for a moment or two, while he dug viciously at the earth. She bent her head, pondering. He was an unreasonable child. He was like an infant which, when it has drunk its fill, throws away and smashes the cup.

She looked at him, feeling she could get hold of him and *wring* some consistency out of him. But she was helpless. Then she cried:

"I have said you were only fourteen—you are only *four!*"

He still dug at the earth viciously. He heard.

"You are a child of four," she repeated in her anger.

He did not answer, but said in his heart: "All right; if I'm a child of four, what do you want me for? *I* don't want another mother." But he said nothing to her, and there was silence.

"And have you told your people? " she asked.

"I have told my mother."

There was another long interval of silence.

"Then what do you *want?*" she asked.

"Why, I want us to separate. We have lived on each other all these years; now let us stop. I will go my own way without you, and you will go your way without me. You will have an independent life of your own then."

There was in it some truth that, in spite of her bitterness, she could not help registering. She knew she felt in a sort of bondage to him, which she hated because she could not control it. She had hated her love for him from the moment it grew too strong for her. And, deep down, she had hated him because she loved him and he dominated her. She had resisted his domination. She had fought to keep herself free of him in the last issue. And she *was* free of him, even more than he of her.

"And," he continued, "we shall always be more or less each other's work. You have done a lot for me, I for you. Now let us start and live by ourselves."

"What do you want to do?" she asked.

"Nothing—only be free," he answered.

She, however, knew in her heart that Clara's influence was over him to liberate him. But she said nothing.

"And what have I to tell my mother?" she asked.

"I told my mother," he answered, "that I was breaking off—clean and altogether."

"I shall not tell them at home," she said.

Frowning, "You please yourself," he said.

He knew he had landed her in a nasty hole, and was leaving her in the lurch. It angered him.

"Tell them you wouldn't and won't marry me, and have broken off," he said. "It's true enough."

She bit her finger moodily. She thought over their whole affair. She had known it would come to this; she had seen it all along. It chimed with her bitter expectation.

"Always—it has always been so!" she cried. "It has been one long battle between us—you fighting away from me."

It came from her unawares, like a flash of lightning. The man's heart stood still. Was this how she saw it?

"But we've had *some* perfect hours, *some* perfect times, when we were together!" he pleaded.

"Never!" she cried; "never! It has always been you fighting me off."

"Not always—not at first!" he pleaded.

"Always, from the very beginning—always the same!"

She had finished, but she had done enough. He sat aghast. He had wanted to say, "It has been good, but it is at an end." And she—she whose love he had believed in when he had despised himself—denied that their love had ever been love. "He had always fought away from her?" Then it had been monstrous. There had never been anything really between them; all the time he had been imagining something where there was nothing. And she had known. She had known so much, and had told him so little. She had known all the time. All the time this was at the bottom of her!

He sat silent in bitterness. At last the whole affair appeared in a cynical aspect to him. She had really played with him, not he with her. She had hidden all her condemnation from him, had flattered him, and despised him. She despised him now. He grew intellectual and cruel.

"You ought to marry a man who worships you," he said; "then you could do as you liked with him. Plenty of men will worship you, if you get on the private side of their natures. You ought to marry one such. They would never fight you off."

"Thank you!" she said. "But don't advise me to marry someone else any more. You've done it before."

"Very well," he said; "I will say no more."

He sat still, feeling as if he had had a blow, instead of giving one. Their eight years of friendship and love, *the* eight years of his life, were nullified.

"When did you think of this?" she asked.

"I thought definitely on Thursday night."

"I knew it was coming," she said.

That pleased him bitterly. "Oh, very well! If she knew, then it doesn't come as a surprise to her," he thought.

"And have you said anything to Clara?" she asked.

"No; but I shall tell her now."

There was a silence.

"Do you remember the things you said this time last year, in my grandmother's house—nay, last month even?"

"Yes," he said; "I do! And I meant them! I can't help that it's failed."

"It has failed because you want something else."

"It would have failed whether or not. *You* never believed in me."

She laughed strangely.

He sat in silence. He was full of a feeling that she had deceived him. She had despised him when he thought she worshipped him. She had let him say wrong things, and had not contradicted him. She had let him fight alone. But it stuck in his throat that she had despised him whilst he thought she worshipped him. She should have told him when she found fault with him. She had not played fair. He hated her. All these years she had treated him as if he were a hero, and thought of him secretly as an infant, a foolish child. Then why had she left the foolish child to his folly? His heart was hard against her.

She sat full of bitterness. She had known—oh, well she had known! All the time he was away from her she had summed him up, seen his littleness, his meanness, and his folly. Even she had guarded her soul against him. She was not overthrown, nor prostrated, not even much hurt. She had known. Only why, as he sat there, had he still this strange dominance over her? His very movements fascinated her as if she were hypnotized by him. Yet he was despicable, false, inconsistent, and mean. Why this bondage for her? Why was it the movement of his arm stirred her as nothing else in the world could? Why was she fastened to him? Why, even now, if he looked at her and commanded her, would she have to obey? She would obey him in his trifling commands. But once he was obeyed, then she had him in her power, she knew, to lead him where she would. She was sure of herself. Only, this new influence! Ah, he was not a man! He was a baby that cries for the newest toy. And all the attachment of his soul would not keep him. Very well, he would have to go. But he would come back when he had tired of his new sensation.

He hacked at the earth till she was fretted to death. She rose. He sat flinging lumps of earth in the stream.

"We will go and have tea here?" he asked.

"Yes," she answered.

They chattered over irrelevant subjects during tea. He held forth on the love of ornament—the cottage parlor moved him thereto—and its connexion with æsthetics. She was cold and quiet. As they walked home, she asked:

"And we shall not see each other?"

"No—or rarely," he answered.

"Nor write?" she asked, almost sarcastically.

"As you will," he answered. "We're not strangers—never should be, whatever happened. I will write to you now and again. You please yourself."

"I see!" she answered cuttingly.

But he was at that stage at which nothing else hurts. He had made a great cleavage in his life. He had had a great shock when she told him their love had been always a conflict. Nothing more mattered. If it never had been much, there was no need to make a fuss that it was ended.

He left her at the lane-end. As she went home, solitary, in her new frock, having her people to face at the other end, he stood still with shame and pain in the highroad, thinking of the suffering he caused her.

In a reaction towards restoring his self-esteem, he went into the Willow Tree for a drink. There were four girls who had been out for the day, drinking a modest glass of port. They had some chocolates on the table. Paul sat near with his whisky. He noticed the girls whispering and nudging. Presently one, a, bonny dark hussy, leaned to him and said:

"Have a chocolate?"

The others laughed loudly at her impudence.

"All right," said Paul, "Give me a hard one—nut. I don't like creams."

"Here you are, then," said the girl; "here's an almond for you."

She held the sweet between her fingers. He opened his mouth. She popped it in, and blushed.

"You *are* nice!" he said.

"Well," she answered, "we thought you looked overcast, and they dared me offer you a chocolate."

"I don't mind if I have another—another sort," he said.

And presently they were all laughing together.

It was nine o'clock when he got home, falling dark. He entered the house in silence. His mother, who had been waiting, rose anxiously.

"I told her," he said.

"I'm glad," replied the mother, with great relief.

He hung up his cap wearily.

"I said we'd have done altogether," he said.

"That's right, my son," said the mother. "It's hard for her now, but best in the long-run. I know. You weren't suited for her."

He laughed shakily as he sat down.

"I've had such a lark with some girls in a pub," he said.

His mother looked at him. He had forgotten Miriam now. He told her about the girls in the Willow Tree. Mrs. Morel looked at him. It seemed unreal, his gaiety. At the back of it was too much horror and misery.

"Now have some supper," she said very gently.

Afterwards he said wistfully:

"She never thought she'd have me, mother, not from the first, and so she's not disappointed."

"I'm afraid," said his mother, "she doesn't give up hopes of you yet."

"No," he said, "perhaps not."

"You'll find it's better to have done," she said.

"*I* don't know," he said desperately.

"Well, leave her alone," replied his mother.

So he left her, and she was alone. Very few people cared for her, and she for very few people. She remained alone with herself, waiting.

❖ 12 ❖

PASSION

He was gradually making it possible to earn a livelihood by his art. Liberty's had taken several of his painted designs on various stuffs, and he could sell designs for embroideries, for altar-cloths, and similar things, in one or two places. It was not very much he made at present, but he might extend it. He also had made friends with the designer for a pottery firm, and was gaining some knowledge of his new acquaintance's art. The applied arts interested him very much. At the same time he labored slowly at his pictures.

He loved to paint large figures, full of light, but not merely made up of lights and cast shadows, like the impressionists; rather definite figures that had a certain luminous quality, like some of Michael Angelo's people. And these he fitted into a landscape, in what he thought true proportion. He worked a great deal from memory, using everybody he knew. He believed firmly in his work, that it was good and valuable. In spite of fits of depression, shrinking, everything, he believed in his work.

He was twenty-four when he said his first confident thing to his mother.

"Mother," he said, "I s'll make a painter that they'll attend to."

She sniffed in her quaint fashion. It was like a half-pleased shrug of the shoulders.

"Very well, my boy, we'll see," she said.

"You shall see, my pigeon! You see if you're not swanky one of these days!"

"I'm quite content, my boy," she smiled.

"But you'll have to alter. Look at you with Minnie!"

Minnie was the small servant, a girl of fourteen.

"And what about Minnie?" asked Mrs. Morel, with dignity.

"I heard her this morning: "Eh, Mrs. Morel! I was going to do that,' when you went out in the rain for some coal," he said. "That looks a lot like your being able to manage servants!"

"Well, it was only the child's niceness," said Mrs. Morel.

"And you apologizing to her: "You can't do two things at once, can you?' "

"She *was* busy washing up," replied Mrs. Morel.

"And what did she say? "It could easy have waited a bit. Now look how your feet paddle!' "

"Yes—brazen young baggage!" said Mrs. Morel, smiling.

He looked at his mother, laughing. She was quite warm and rosy again with love of him. It seemed as if all the sunshine were on her for a moment. He continued his work gladly. She seemed so well when she was happy that he forgot her gray hair.

And that year she went with him to the Isle of Wight for a holiday. It was too exciting for them both, and too beautiful. Mrs. Morel was full of joy and wonder. But he would have her walk with him more than she was able. She had a bad fainting bout. So gray her face was, so blue her mouth! It was agony to him. He felt as if someone were pushing a knife in his chest. Then she was better again, and he forgot. But the anxiety remained inside him, like a wound that did not close.

After leaving Miriam he went almost straight to Clara. On the Monday following the day of the rupture he went down to the workroom. She looked up at him and smiled. They had grown very intimate unawares. She saw a new brightness about him.

"Well, Queen of Sheba!" he said, laughing.

"But why?" she asked.

"I think it suits you. You've got a new frock on."

She flushed, asking:

"And what of it?"

"Suits you—awfully! *I* could design you a dress."

"How would it be?"

He stood in front of her, his eyes glittering as he expounded. He kept her eyes fixed with his. Then suddenly he took hold of her. She half started back. He drew the stuff of her blouse tighter, smoothed it over her breast.

"More *so*!" he explained.

But they were both of them flaming with blushes, and immediately he ran away. He had touched her. His whole body was quivering with the sensation.

There was already a sort of secret understanding between them. The next evening he went into the cinematograph with her for a few minutes before train-time. As they sat, he saw her hand lying near him. For some moments he dared not touch it. The pictures danced and dithered. Then he took her hand in his. It was large and firm; it filled his grasp. He held it fast. She neither moved nor made any sign. When they came out his train was due. He hesitated.

"Good-night," she said. He darted away across the road.

The next day he came again, talking to her. She was rather superior with him.

"Shall we go a walk on Monday?" he asked.

She turned her face aside.

"Shall you tell Miriam?" she replied sarcastically.

"I have broken off with her," he said.

"When?"

"Last Sunday."

"You quarreled?"

"No! I had made up my mind. I told her quite definitely I should consider myself free."

Clara did not answer, and he returned to his work. She was so quiet and so superb!

On the Saturday evening he asked her to come and drink coffee with him in a restaurant, meeting him after work was over. She came, looking very reserved and very distant. He had three-quarters of an hour to train-time.

"We will walk a little while," he said.

She agreed, and they went past the Castle into the Park. He was afraid of her. She walked moodily at his side, with a kind of resentful, reluctant, angry walk. He was afraid to take her hand.

"Which way shall we go?" he asked as they walked in darkness.

"I don't mind."

"Then we'll go up the steps."

He suddenly turned round. They had passed the Park steps. She stood still in resentment at his suddenly abandoning her. He looked for her. She stood aloof. He caught her suddenly in his arms, held her strained for a moment, kissed her. Then he let her go.

"Come along," he said, penitent.

She followed him. He took her hand and kissed her fingertips. They went in silence. When they came to the light, he let go her hand. Neither spoke till they reached the station. Then they looked each other in the eyes.

"Good-night," she said.

And he went for his train. His body acted mechanically. People talked to him. He heard faint echoes answering them. He was in a delirium. He felt that he would go mad if Monday did not come at once. On Monday he would see her again. All himself was pitched there, ahead. Sunday intervened. He could not bear it. He could not see her till Monday. And Sunday intervened—hour after hour of tension. He wanted to beat his head against the door of the carriage. But he sat still. He drank some whisky on the way home, but it only made it worse. His mother must not be upset, that was all. He dissembled, and got quickly to bed. There he sat, dressed, with his chin on his knees, staring out of the window at the far hill, with its few lights. He neither thought nor slept, but sat perfectly still, staring. And when at last he was so cold that he came to himself, he found his watch had stopped at half-past two. It was after three o'clock. He was exhausted, but still there was the torment of knowing it was only Sunday morning. He went to bed and slept. Then he cycled all day long, till he was fagged out. And he scarcely knew where he had been. But the day after was Monday. He slept till four o'clock. Then he lay and thought. He was coming nearer to himself—he could see himself, real, somewhere in front. She would go a walk with him in the afternoon. Afternoon! It seemed years ahead.

Slowly the hours crawled. His father got up; he heard him pottering about. Then the miner set off to the pit, his heavy boots scraping the yard. Cocks were still crowing. A cart went down the road. His mother got up. She knocked the fire. Presently she called him softly. He answered as if he were asleep. This shell of himself did well.

He was walking to the station—another mile! The train was near Nottingham. Would it stop before the tunnels? But it did not matter; it would get there before dinner-time. He was at Jordan's. She would come in half an hour. At any rate, she would be near. He had done the letters. She would be there. Perhaps she had not come. He ran downstairs. Ah! he saw her through the glass door. Her shoulders stooping a little to her work made him feel he could not go forward; he could not stand. He went in. He was pale, nervous, awkward, and quite cold. Would she misunderstand him? He could not right his real self with this shell.

"And this afternoon," he struggled to say. "You will come?"

"I think so," she replied, murmuring.

He stood before her, unable to say a word. She hid her face from him. Again came over him the feeling that he would lose consciousness. He set his teeth and went upstairs. He had done everything correctly yet, and he would do so. All the morning things seemed a long way off, as they do to a man under chloroform. He himself seemed under a tight band of constraint. Then there was his other self, in the distance, doing things, entering stuff in a ledger, and he watched that far-off him carefully to see he made no mistake.

But the ache and strain of it could not go on much longer. He worked incessantly. Still it was only twelve o'clock. As if he had nailed his clothing against the desk, he stood there and worked, forcing every stroke out of himself. It was a quarter to one; he could clear away. Then he ran downstairs.

"You will meet me at the Fountain at two o'clock," he said.

"I can't be there till half-past."

"Yes!" he said.

She saw his dark, mad eyes.

"I will try at a quarter-past."

And he had to be content. He went and got some dinner. All the time he was still under chloroform, and every minute was stretched out indefinitely. He walked miles of street. Then he thought he would be late at the meeting-place. He was at the Fountain at five past two. The torture of the next quarter of an hour was refined beyond expression. It was the anguish of combining the living self with the shell. Then he saw her. She came! And he was there.

"You are late," he said.

"Only five minutes," she answered.

"I'd never have done it to you," he laughed.

She was in a dark blue costume. He looked at her beautiful figure.

"You want some flowers," He said, going to the nearest florists.

She followed him in silence. He bought her a bunch of scarlet, brick-red carnations. She put them in her coat, flushing.

"That's a fine color!" he said.

"I'd rather have had something softer," she said.

He laughed.

"Do you feel like a blot of vermilion walking down the street!" he said.

She hung her head, afraid of the people they met. He looked sideways at her as they walked. There was a wonderful close down on her face near the ear that he wanted to touch. And a certain heaviness, the heaviness of a very full ear of corn that dips slightly in the wind, that there was about her, made his brain spin. He seemed to be spinning down the street, everything going round.

As they sat in the tramcar, she leaned her heavy shoulder against him, and he took her hand. He felt himself coming round from the anesthetic, beginning to breathe. Her ear, half hidden among her blonde hair, was near to him. The temptation to kiss it was almost too great. But there were other people on top of the car. It still remained to him to kiss it. After all, he was not himself, he was some attribute of hers, like the sunshine that fell on her.

He looked quickly away. It had been raining. The big bluff of the Castle rock was streaked with rain, as it reared above the flat of the town. They crossed the wide, black space of the Midland Railway, and passed the cattle enclosure that stood out white. Then they ran down sordid Wilford Road.

She rocked slightly to the tram's motion, and as she leaned against him, rocked upon him. He was a vigorous, slender man, with exhaustless energy. His face was rough, with rough-hewn features, like the common people's; but his eyes under the deep brows were so full of life that they fascinated her. They seemed to dance, and yet they were still, trembling on the finest balance of laughter. His mouth the same was just going to spring into a laugh of triumph, yet did not. There was a sharp suspense about him. She bit her lip moodily. His hand was hard clenched over hers.

They paid their two halfpennies at the turnstile and crossed the bridge. The Trent was very full. It swept silent and insidious under the bridge, traveling in a soft body. There had been a great deal of rain. On the river levels were flat gleams of flood water. The sky was gray, with glisten of silver here and there. In Wilford Churchyard the dahlias were sodden with rain—wet black-crimson balls. No one was on the path that went along the green river meadow, along the elm-tree colonnade.

There was the faintest haze over the silvery-dark water and the green meadow banks, and the elm trees that were spangled with gold. The river slid by in a body, utterly silent and swift, intertwining among itself like some subtle, complex creature. Clara walked moodily beside him.

"Why," she asked at length, in rather a jarring tone, "did you leave Miriam?"

He frowned.

"Because I *wanted* to leave her," he said.

"Why?"

"Because I didn't want to go on with her. And I didn't want to marry."

She was silent for a moment. They picked their way down the muddy path. Drops of water fell from the elm trees.

"You didn't want to marry Miriam, or you didn't want to marry at all?" she asked.

"Both," he answered—"both!"

They had to maneuver to get to the stile, because of the pools of water.

"And what did she say?" Clara asked.

"Miriam? She said I was a baby of four, and that I always *had* battled her off."

Clara pondered over this for a time.

"But you have really been going with her for some time?" she asked.

"Yes."

"And now you don't want any more of her?"

"No. I know it's no good."

She pondered again.

"Don't you think you've treated her rather badly?" she asked.

"Yes; I ought to have dropped it years back. But it would have been no good going on. Two wrongs don't make a right."

"How old *are* you?" Clara asked.

"Twenty-five."

"And I am thirty," she said.

"I know you are."

"I shall be thirty-one—or *am* I thirty-one?"

"I neither know nor care. What does it matter it!"

They were at the entrance to the Grove. The wet, red track, already sticky with fallen leaves, went up the steep bank between the grass. On either side stood the elm trees like pillars along a great aisle, arching over and making high up a roof from which the dead leaves fell. All was empty and silent and wet. She stood on top of the stile, and he held both her hands. Laughing, she looked down into his eyes. Then she leaped. Her breast came against his; he held her, and covered her face with kisses.

They went on up the slippery, steep red path. Presently she released his hand and put it round her waist.

"You press the vein in my arm, holding it so tightly," she said.

They walked along. His fingertips felt the rocking of her breast. All was silent and deserted. On the left the red wet plough-land showed through the doorways between the elm-boles and their branches. On the right, looking down, they could see the treetops of elms growing far beneath them, hear occasionally the gurgle of the river. Sometimes there below they caught glimpses of the full, soft-sliding Trent, and of water-meadows dotted with small cattle.

"It has scarcely altered since little Kirke White used to come," he said.

But he was watching her throat below the ear, where the flush was fusing into the honey-white, and her mouth that pouted disconsolate. She, stirred against him as she walked, and his body was like a taut string.

Half-way up the big colonnade of elms, where the Grove rose highest above the river, their forward movement faltered to an end. He led her across to the grass, under the trees at the edge of the path. The cliff of red earth sloped swiftly down, through trees and bushes, to the river that glimmered and was dark between the foliage. The far-below water-meadows were very green. He and she stood leaning against one another, silent, afraid, their bodies touching all along. There came a quick gurgle from the river below.

"Why," he asked at length, "did you hate Baxter Dawes?"

She turned to him with a splendid movement. Her mouth was offered him, and her throat; her eyes were half shut; her breast was tilted as if it asked for him. He flashed with a small laugh, shut his eyes, and met her in a long, whole kiss. Her mouth fused with his; their bodies were sealed and annealed. It was some minutes before they withdrew. They were standing beside the public path.

"Will you go down to the river?" he asked.

She looked at him, leaving herself in his hands. He went over the brim of the declivity and began to climb down.

"It is slippery," he said.

"Never mind," she replied.

The red clay went down almost sheer. He slid, went from one tuft of grass to the next, hanging on to the bushes, making for a little platform at the foot of a tree. There he waited for her, laughing with excitement. Her shoes were clogged with red earth. It was hard for her. He frowned. At last he caught her hand, and she stood beside him. The cliff rose above them and fell away below. Her color was up, her eyes flashed. He looked at the big drop below them.

"It's risky," he said; "or messy, at any rate. Shall we go back?"

"Not for my sake," she said quickly.

"All right. You see, I can't help you; I should only hinder. Give me that little parcel and your gloves. Your poor shoes!"

They stood perched on the face of the declivity, under the trees.

"Well, I'll go again," he said.

Away he went, slipping, staggering, sliding to the next tree, into which he fell with a slam that nearly shook the breath out of him. She came after cautiously, hanging on to the twigs and grasses. So they descended, stage by stage, to the river's brink. There, to his disgust, the flood had eaten away the path, and the red decline ran straight into the water. He dug in his heels and brought himself up violently. The string of the parcel broke with a snap; the brown parcel bounded down, leaped into the water, and sailed smoothly away. He hung on to his tree.

"Well, I'll be damned!" he cried crossly. Then he laughed. She was coming perilously down.

"Mind!" he warned her. He stood with his back to the tree, waiting. "Come now," he called, opening his arms.

She let herself run. He caught her, and together they stood watching the dark water scoop at the raw edge of the bank. The parcel had sailed out of sight.

"It doesn't matter," she said.

He held her close and kissed her. There was only room for their four feet.

"It's a swindle!" he said. "But there's a rut where a man has been, so if we go on I guess we shall find the path again."

The river slid and twined its great volume. On the other bank cattle were feeding on the desolate flats. The cliff rose high above Paul and Clara on their right hand. They stood against the tree in the watery silence.

"Let us try going forward," he said; and they struggled in the red clay along the groove a man's nailed boots had made. They were hot and flushed. Their barkled shoes hung heavy on their steps. At last they found the broken path. It was littered with rubble from the water, but at any rate it was easier. They cleaned their boots with twigs. His heart was beating thick and fast.

Suddenly, coming on to the little level, he saw two figures of men standing silent at the water's edge. His heart leaped. They were fishing. He turned and put his hand up warningly to Clara. She hesitated, buttoned her coat. The two went on together.

The fishermen turned curiously to watch the two intruders on their privacy and solitude. They had had a fire, but it was nearly out. All kept perfectly still. The men turned again to their fishing, stood over the gray glinting river like statues. Clara went with bowed head, flushing; he was laughing to himself. Directly they passed out of sight behind the willows.

"Now they ought to be drowned," said Paul softly.

Clara did not answer. They toiled forward along a tiny path on the river's lip. Suddenly it vanished. The bank was sheer red solid clay in front of them, sloping straight into the river. He stood and cursed beneath his breath, setting his teeth.

"It is impossible!" said Clara.

He stood erect. looking round. Just ahead were two islets in the stream, covered with osiers. But they were unattainable. The cliff came down like a sloping wall from far above their heads. Behind, not far back, were the fishermen. Across the river the distant cattle fed silently in the desolate afternoon. He cursed again deeply under his breath. He gazed up the great steep bank. Was there no hope but to scale back to the public path?

"Stop a minute," he said, and, digging his heels sideways into the steep bank of red clay, he began nimbly to mount. He looked across at every tree-foot. At last he found what he wanted. Two beech trees side by side on the hill held a little level on the upper face between their roots. It was littered with damp leaves, but it would do. The fishermen were perhaps sufficiently out of sight. He threw down his rainproof and waved to her to come.

She toiled to his side. Arriving there, she looked at him heavily, dumbly, and laid her head on his shoulder. He held her fast as he looked round. They were safe enough from all but the small, lonely cows over the river. He sunk his mouth on her throat, where he felt her heavy pulse beat under his lips. Everything was perfectly still. There was nothing in the afternoon but themselves.

When she arose, he, looking on the ground all the time, saw suddenly sprinkled on the black, wet beech-roots many scarlet carnation petals, like splashed drops of blood; and red, small splashes fell from her bosom, streaming down her dress to her feet.

"Your flowers are smashed," he said.

She looked at him heavily as she put back her hair. Suddenly he put his fingertips on her cheek.

"Why dost look so heavy?" he reproached her.

She smiled sadly, as if she felt alone in herself. He caressed her cheek with his fingers, and kissed her.

"Nay!" he said. "Never thee bother!"

She gripped his fingers tight, and laughed shakily. Then she dropped her hand. He put the hair back from her brows, stroking her temples, kissing them lightly.

"But tha shouldna worrit!" he said softly, pleading.

"No, I don't worry!" she laughed tenderly and resigned.

"Yea, tha does! Dunna thee worrit," he implored, caressing.

"No!" she consoled him, kissing him.

They had a stiff climb to get to the top again. It took them a quarter of an hour. When he got on to the level grass, he threw off his cap, wiped the sweat from his forehead, and sighed.

"Now we're back at the ordinary level," he said.

She sat down, panting, on the tussocky grass. Her cheeks were flushed pink. He kissed her, and she gave way to joy.

"And now I'll clean thy boots and make thee fit for respectable folk," he said.

He kneeled at her feet, worked away with a stick and tufts of grass. She put her fingers in his hair, drew his head to her, and kissed it.

"What am I supposed to be doing," he said, looking at her laughing; "cleaning shoes or dibbling with love? Answer me that!"

"Just whichever I please," she replied.

"I'm your boot-boy for the time being, and nothing else!" But they remained looking into each other's eyes and laughing. Then they kissed with little nibbling kisses.

"T-t-t-t!" he went with his tongue, like his mother. "I tell you, nothing gets done when there's a woman about."

And he returned to his boot-cleaning, singing softly. She touched his thick hair, and he kissed her fingers. He worked away at her shoes. At last they were quite presentable.

"There you are, you see!" he said. "Aren't I a great hand at restoring you to respectability? Stand up! There, you look as irreproachable as Britannia herself!"

He cleaned his own boots a little, washed his hands in a puddle, and sang. They went on into Clifton village. He was madly in love with her; every movement she made, every crease in her garments, sent a hot flash through him and seemed adorable.

The old lady at whose house they had tea was roused into gaiety by them.

"I could wish you'd had something of a better day," she said, hovering round.

"Nay!" he laughed. "We've been saying how nice it is."

The old lady looked at him curiously. There was a peculiar glow and charm about him. His eyes were dark and laughing. He rubbed his moustache with a glad movement.

"Have you been saying *so*!" she exclaimed, a light rousing in her old eyes.

"Truly!" he laughed.

"Then I'm sure the day's good enough," said the old lady. She fussed about, and did not want to leave them.

"I don't know whether you'd like some radishes as well," she said to Clara; "but I've got some in the garden—*and* a cucumber."

Clara flushed. She looked very handsome.

"I should like some radishes," she answered.

And the old lady pottered off gleefully.

"If she knew!" said Clara quietly to him.

"Well, she doesn't know; and it shows we're nice in ourselves, at any rate. You look quite enough to satisfy an archangel, and I'm sure I feel harmless—so—if it makes you look nice, and makes folk happy when they have us, and makes us happy—why, we're not cheating them out of much!"

They went on with the meal. When they were going away, the old lady came timidly with three tiny dahlias in full blow, neat as bees, and speckled scarlet and white. She stood before Clara, pleased with herself, saying:

"I don't know whether—" and holding the flowers forward in her old hand.

"Oh, how pretty!" cried Clara, accepting the flowers.

"Shall she have them all?" asked Paul reproachfully of the old woman.

"Yes, she shall have them all," she replied, beaming with joy. "You have got enough for your share."

"Ah, but I shall ask her to give me one!" he teased.

"Then she does as she pleases," said the old lady, smiling. And she bobbed a little curtsey of delight.

Clara was rather quiet and uncomfortable. As they walked along, he said:

"You don't feel criminal, do you?"

She looked at him with startled gray eyes.

"Criminal!" she said. "No."

"But you seem to feel you have done a wrong?"

"No," she said. "I only think, "If they knew!' "

"If they knew, they'd cease to understand. As it is, they do understand, and they like it. What do they matter? Here, with only the trees and me, you don't feel not the least bit wrong, do you?"

He took her by the arm, held her facing him, holding her eyes with his. Something fretted him.

"Not sinners, are we?" he said, with an uneasy little frown.

"No," she replied.

He kissed her, laughing.

"You like your little bit of guiltiness, I believe," he said. "I believe Eve enjoyed it, when she went cowering out of Paradise."

But there was a certain glow and quietness about her that made him glad. When he was alone in the railway carriage, he found himself tumultuously happy, and the people exceedingly nice, and the night lovely, and everything good.

Mrs. Morel was sitting reading when he got home. Her health was not good now, and there had come that ivory pallor into her face which he never noticed, and which afterwards he never forgot. She did not mention her own ill health to him. After all, she thought, it was not much.

"You are late!" she said, looking at him.

His eyes were shining; his face seemed to glow. He smiled to her.

"Yes; I've been down Clifton Grove with Clara."

His mother looked at him again.

"But won't people talk?" she said.

"Why? They know she's a suffragette, and so on. And what if they do talk!"

"Of course, there may be nothing wrong in it," said his mother. "But you know what folk are, and if once she gets talked about——"

"Well, I can't help it. Their jaw isn't so almighty important, after all."

"I think you ought to consider *her*."

"So I *do*! What can people say?—that we take a walk together. I believe you're jealous."

"You know I should be *glad* if she weren't a married woman."

"Well, my dear, she lives separate from her husband, and talks on platforms; so she's already singled out from the sheep, and, as far as I can see, hasn't much to lose. No; her life's nothing to her, so what's the worth of nothing? She goes with me—it becomes something. Then she must pay—we both must pay! Folk are so frightened of paying; they'd rather starve and die."

"Very well, my son. We'll see how it will end."

"Very well, my mother. I'll abide by the end."

"We'll see!"

"And she's—she's *awfully* nice, mother; she is really! You don't know!"

"That's not the same as marrying her."

"It's perhaps better."

There was a silence for a while. He wanted to ask his mother something, but was afraid.

"Should you like to know her?" He hesitated.

"Yes," said Mrs. Morel coolly. "I should like to know what she's like."

"But she's nice, mother, she is! And not a bit common!"

"I never suggested she was."

"But you seem to think she's—not as good as—She's better than ninety-nine folk out of a hundred, I tell you! She's *better*, she is! She's fair, she's honest, she's straight! There isn't anything underhand or superior about her. Don't be mean about her!"

Mrs. Morel flushed.

"I am sure I am not mean about her. She may be quite as you say, but——"

"You don't approve," he finished.

"And do you expect me to?" she answered coldly.

"Yes!—yes!—if you'd anything about you, you'd be glad! Do you *want* to see her?"

"I said I did."

"Then I'll bring her—shall I bring her here?"

"You please yourself."

"Then I *will* bring her here—one Sunday—to tea. If you think a horrid thing about her, I shan't forgive you."

His mother laughed.

"As if it would make any difference!" she said. He knew he had won.

"Oh, but it feels so fine, mother, when she's there! She's such a queen in her way."

Occasionally he still walked a little way from chapel with Miriam and Edgar. He did not go up to the farm. She, however, was very much the same with him, and he did not feel embarrassed in her presence. One evening she was alone when he accompanied her. They began by talking books; it was their unfailing topic. Mrs. Morel had said that his and Miriam's affair was like a fire fed on books—if there were no more volumes it would die out. Miriam, for her part, boasted that she could read him like a book, could place her finger any minute on the chapter and the line. He, easily taken in, believed that Miriam knew more about him than anyone else. So it pleased him to talk to her about himself, like the simplest egoist. Very soon the conversation drifted to his own doings. It flattered him immensely that he was of such supreme interest.

"And what have you been doing lately?"

"I—oh, not much! I made a sketch of Bestwood from the garden, that is nearly right at last. It's the hundredth try."

So they went on. Then she said:

"You've not been out, then, lately?"

"Yes; I went up Clifton Grove on Monday afternoon with Clara."

"It was not very nice weather," said Miriam, "was it?"

"But I wanted to go out, and it was all right. The Trent *is* full."

"And did you go to Barton?" she asked.

"No; we had tea in Clifton."

"*Did* you! That would be nice."

"It was! The jolliest old woman! She gave us several pom-pom dahlias, as pretty as you like."

Miriam bowed her head and brooded. He was quite unconscious of concealing anything from her.

"What made her give them you?" she asked.

He laughed.

"Because she liked us—because we were jolly, I should think."

Miriam put her finger in her mouth.

"Were you late home?" she asked.

At last he resented her tone.

"I caught the seven-thirty."

"Ha!"

They walked on in silence, and he was angry.

"And how *is* Clara?" asked Miriam.

"Quite all right, I think."

"That's good!" she said, with a tinge of irony. "By the way, what of her husband? One never hears anything of him."

"He's got some other woman, and is also quite all right," he replied. "At least, so I think."

"I see—you don't know for certain. Don't you think a position like that is hard on a woman?"

"Rottenly hard!"

"It's so unjust!" said Miriam. "The man does as he likes——"

"Then let the woman also," he said.

"How can she? And if she does, look at her position!"

"What of it?"

"Why, it's impossible! You don't understand what a woman forfeits——"

"No, I don't. But if a woman's got nothing but her fair fame to feed on, why, it's thin tack, and a donkey would die of it!"

So she understood his moral attitude, at least, and she knew he would act accordingly.

She never asked him anything direct, but she got to know enough.

Another day, when he saw Miriam, the conversation turned to marriage, then to Clara's marriage with Dawes.

"You see," he said, "she never knew the fearful importance of marriage. She thought it was all in the day's march—it would have to come and Dawes—well, a good many women would have given their souls to get him; so why not him? Then she developed into the *femme incomprise*, and treated him badly, I'll bet my boots."

"And she left him because he didn't understand her?"

"I suppose so. I suppose she had to. It isn't altogether a question of understanding; it's a question of living. With him, she was only half alive; the rest was dormant, deadened. And the dormant woman was the *femme incomprise*, and she had to be awakened."

"And what about him?"

"I don't know. I rather think he loves her as much as he can, but he's a fool."

"It was something like your mother and father," said Miriam.

"Yes; but my mother, I believe, got *real* joy and satisfaction out of my father at first. I believe she had a passion for him; that's why she stayed with him. After all, they were bound to each other."

"Yes," said Miriam.

"That's what one *must have*, I think," he continued—"the real, real flame of feeling through another person—once, only once, if it only lasts three months. See, my mother looks as if she'd *had* everything that was necessary for her living and developing. There's not a tiny bit of a feeling of sterility about her."

"No," said Miriam.

"And with my father, at first, I'm sure she had the real thing. She knows; she has been there. You can feel it about her, and about him, and about hundreds of people you meet every day; and, once it has happened to you, you can go on with anything and ripen."

"What has happened, exactly?" asked Miriam.

"It's so hard to say, but the something big and intense that changes you when you really come together with somebody else. It almost seems to fertilize your soul and make it that you can go on and mature."

"And you think your mother had it with your father?"

"Yes; and at the bottom she feels grateful to him for giving it her, even now, though they are miles apart."

"And you think Clara never had it?"

"I'm sure."

Miriam pondered this. She saw what he was seeking—a sort of baptism of fire in passion, it seemed to her. She realized that he would never be satisfied till he had it. Perhaps it was essential to him, as to some men, to sow wild oats; and afterwards, when he was satisfied, he would not rage with restlessness any more, but could settle down and give her his life into her hands. Well, then, if he must go, let him go and have his fill—something big and intense, he called it. At any rate, when he had got it, he would not want it—that he said himself; he would want the other thing that she could give him. He would want to be owned, so that he could work. It seemed to her a bitter thing that he must go, but she could let him go into an inn for a glass of whisky, so she could let him go to Clara, so long as it was something that would satisfy a need in him, and leave him free for herself to possess.

"Have you told your mother about Clara?" she asked.

She knew this would be a test of the seriousness of his feeling for the other woman; she knew he was going to Clara for something vital, not as a man goes for pleasure to a prostitute, if he told his mother.

"Yes," he said, "and she is coming to tea on Sunday."

"To your house?"

"Yes; I want mater to see her."

"Ah!"

There was a silence. Things had gone quicker than she thought. She felt a sudden bitterness that he could leave her so soon and so entirely. And was Clara to be accepted by his people, who had been so hostile to herself?

"I may call in as I go to chapel," she said. "It is a long time since I saw Clara."

"Very well," he said, astonished, and unconsciously angry.

On the Sunday afternoon he went to Keston to meet Clara at the station. As he stood on the platform he was trying to examine in himself if he had a premonition.

"Do I *feel* as if she'd come?" he said to himself, and he tried to find out. His heart felt queer and contracted. That seemed like foreboding. Then he *had* a foreboding she would not come! Then she would not come, and instead of taking her over the fields home, as he had imagined, he would have to go alone. The train was late; the afternoon would be wasted, and the evening. He hated her for not coming. Why had she promised, then, if she could not keep her promise? Perhaps she had missed her train—he himself was always missing trains—but that was no reason why she should miss this particular one. He was angry with her; he was furious.

Suddenly he saw the train crawling, sneaking round the corner. Here, then, was the train, but of course she had not come. The green engine hissed along the platform, the row of brown carriages drew up, several doors opened. No; she had not come! No! Yes; ah, there she was! She had a big black hat on! He was at her side in a moment.

"I thought you weren't coming," he said.

She was laughing rather breathlessly as she put out her hand to him; their eyes met. He took her quickly along the platform, talking at a great rate to hide his feeling. She looked beautiful. In her hat were large silk roses, colored like tarnished gold. Her costume of dark cloth fitted so beautifully over her breast and shoulders. His pride went up as he walked with her. He felt the station people, who knew him, eyed her with awe and admiration.

"I was sure you weren't coming," he laughed shakily.

She laughed in answer, almost with a little cry.

"And I wondered, when I was in the train, what*ever* I should do if you weren't there!" she said.

He caught her hand impulsively, and they went along the narrow twitchel. They took the road into Nuttall and over the Reckoning House Farm. It was a blue, mild day. Everywhere the brown leaves lay scattered; many scarlet hips stood upon the hedge beside the wood. He gathered a few for her to wear.

"Though, really," he said, as he fitted them into the breast of her coat, "you ought to object to my getting them, because of the birds. But they don't care much for rose hips in this part, where they can get plenty of stuff. You often find the berries going rotten in springtime."

So he chattered, scarcely aware of what he said, only knowing he was putting berries in the bosom of her coat, while she stood patiently for him. And she watched his quick hands, so full of life, and it seemed to her she had never *seen* anything before. Till now, everything had been indistinct.

They came near to the colliery. It stood quite still and black among the cornfields, its immense heap of slag seen rising almost from the oats.

"What a pity there is a coal pit here where it is so pretty!" said Clara.

"Do you think so?" he answered. "You see, I am so used to it I should miss it. No; and I like the pits here and there. I like the rows of trucks, and the headstocks, and the steam in the daytime, and the lights at night. When I was a boy, I always thought a pillar of cloud by day and a pillar of fire by night was a pit, with its steam, and its lights, and the burning bank,—and I thought the Lord was always at the pit-top."

As they drew near home she walked in silence, and seemed to hang back. He pressed her fingers in his own. She flushed. but gave no response.

"Don't you want to come home?" he asked.

"Yes, I want to come," she replied.

It did not occur to him that her position in his home would be rather a peculiar and difficult one. To him it seemed just as if one of his men friends were going to be introduced to his mother, only nicer.

The Morels lived in a house in an ugly street that ran down a steep hill. The street itself was hideous. The house was rather superior to most. It was old, grimy, with a big bay window, and it was semi-detached; but it looked gloomy. Then Paul opened the door to the garden, and all was different. The sunny afternoon was there, like another land. By the path grew tansy and little trees. In front of the window was a plot of sunny grass, with old lilacs round it. And away went the garden, with heaps of disheveled chrysanthemums in the sunshine, down to the sycamore tree, and the field, and beyond one looked over a few red-roofed cottages to the hills with all the glow of the autumn afternoon.

Mrs. Morel sat in her rocking chair, wearing her black silk blouse. Her gray-brown hair was taken smooth back from her brow and her high temples; her face was rather pale. Clara, suffering, followed Paul into the kitchen. Mrs. Morel rose. Clara thought her a lady, even rather stiff. The young woman was very nervous. She had almost a wistful look, almost resigned.

"Mother—Clara," said Paul.

Mrs. Morel held out her hand and smiled.

"He has told me a good deal about you," she said.

The blood flamed in Clara's cheek.

"I hope you don't mind my coming," she faltered.

"I was pleased when he said he would bring you," replied Mrs. Morel.

Paul, watching, felt his heart contract with pain. His mother looked so small, and sallow, and done-for beside the luxuriant Clara.

"It's such a pretty day, mother!" he said. "And we saw a jay."

His mother looked at him; he had turned to her. She thought what a man he seemed, in his dark, well-made clothes. He was pale and detached-looking; it would be hard for any woman to keep him. Her heart glowed; then she was sorry for Clara.

"Perhaps you'll leave your things in the parlor," said Mrs. Morel nicely to the young woman.

"Oh, thank you," she replied.

"Come on," said Paul, and he led the way into the little front room, with its old piano, its mahogany furniture, its yellowing marble mantelpiece. A fire was burning; the place was littered with books and drawing boards. "I leave my things lying about," he said. "It's so much easier."

She loved his artist's paraphernalia, and the books, and the photos of people. Soon he was telling her: this was William, this was William's young lady in the evening dress, this was Annie and her husband, this was Arthur and his wife and the baby. She felt as if she were being taken into the family. He showed her photos, books, sketches, and they talked a little while. Then they returned to the kitchen. Mrs. Morel put aside her book. Clara wore a blouse of fine silk chiffon, with narrow black-and-white stripes; her hair was done simply, coiled on top of her head. She looked rather stately and reserved.

"You have gone to live down Sneinton Boulevard?" said Mrs. Morel. "When I was a girl—girl, I say!—when I was a young woman *we* lived in Minerva Terrace."

"Oh, did you!" said Clara. "I have a friend in Number 6."

And the conversation had started. They talked Nottingham and Nottingham people; it interested them both. Clara was still rather nervous; Mrs. Morel was still somewhat on her dignity. She clipped her language very clear and precise. But they were going to get on well together, Paul saw.

Mrs. Morel measured herself against the younger woman, and found herself easily stronger. Clara was deferential. She knew Paul's surprising regard for his mother, and she had dreaded the meeting, expecting someone rather hard and cold. She was surprised to find this little interested woman chatting with such readiness; and then she felt, as she felt with Paul, that she would not care to stand in Mrs. Morel's way. There was something so hard and certain in his mother, as if she never had a misgiving in her life.

Presently Morel came down, ruffled and yawning, from his afternoon sleep. He scratched his grizzled head, he podded in his stocking feet, his waistcoat hung open over his shirt. He seemed incongruous.

"This is Mrs. Dawes, father," said Paul.

Then Morel pulled himself together. Clara saw Paul's manner of bowing and shaking hands.

"Oh, indeed!" exclaimed Morel. "I am very glad to see you—I am, I assure you. But don't disturb yourself. No, no; make yourself quite comfortable, and be very welcome."

Clara was astonished at this flood of hospitality from the old collier. He was so courteous, so gallant! She thought him most delightful.

"And may you have come far?" he asked.

"Only from Nottingham," she said.

"From Nottingham! Then you have had a beautiful day for your journey."

Then he strayed into the scullery to wash his hands and face, and from force of habit came on to the hearth with the towel to dry himself.

At tea Clara felt the refinement and sang-froid of the household. Mrs. Morel was perfectly at her ease. The pouring out the tea and attending to the people went on unconsciously, without interrupting her in her talk. There was a lot of room at the oval table; the china of dark blue willow-pattern looked pretty on the glossy cloth. There was a little bowl of small, yellow chrysanthemums. Clara felt she completed the circle, and it was a pleasure to her. But she was rather afraid of the self-possession of the Morels, father and all. She took their tone; there was a feeling of balance. It was a cool, clear atmosphere, where everyone was himself, and in harmony. Clara enjoyed it, but there was a fear deep at the bottom of her.

Paul cleared the table whilst his mother and Clara talked. Clara was conscious of his quick, vigorous body as it came and went, seeming blown quickly by a wind at its work. It was almost like the hither and thither of a leaf that comes unexpected. Most of herself went with him. By the way she leaned forward, as if listening, Mrs. Morel could see she was possessed elsewhere as she talked, and again the elder woman was sorry for her.

Having finished, he strolled down the garden, leaving the two women to talk. It was a hazy, sunny afternoon, mild and soft. Clara glanced through the window after him as he loitered among the chrysanthemums. She felt as if something almost tangible fastened her to him; yet he seemed so easy in his graceful, indolent movement, so detached as he tied up the too-heavy flower branches to their stakes, that she wanted to shriek in her helplessness.

Mrs. Morel rose.

"You will let me help you wash up," said Clara.

"Eh, there are so few, it will only take me a minute," said the other.

Clara, however, dried the tea-things, and was glad to be on such good terms with his mother; but it was torture not to be able to follow him down the garden. At last she allowed herself to go; she felt as if a rope were taken off her ankle.

The afternoon was golden over the hills of Derbyshire. He stood across in the other garden, beside a bush of pale Michaelmas daisies, watching the last bees crawl into the hive. Hearing her coming, he turned to her with an easy motion, saying:

"It's the end of the run with these chaps."

Clara stood near him. Over the low red wall in front was the country and the far-off hills, all golden dim.

At that moment Miriam was entering through the garden door. She saw Clara go up to him, saw him turn, and saw them come to rest together. Something in their perfect isolation together made her know that it was accomplished between them, that they were, as she put it, married. She walked very slowly down the cinder track of the long garden.

Clara had pulled a button from a hollyhock spire, and was breaking it to get the seeds. Above her bowed head the pink flowers stared, as if defending her. The last bees were falling down to the hive.

"Count your money," laughed Paul, as she broke the flat seeds one by one from the roll of coin. She looked at him.

"I'm well off," she said, smiling.

"How much? Pf!" He snapped his fingers. "Can I turn them into gold?"

"I'm afraid not," she laughed.

They looked into each other's eyes, laughing. At that moment they became aware of Miriam. There was a click, and everything had altered.

"Hello, Miriam!" he exclaimed. "You said you'd come!"

"Yes. Had you forgotten?"

She shook hands with Clara, saying:

"It seems strange to see you here."

"Yes," replied the other; "it seems strange to be here."

There was a hesitation.

"It is pretty, isn't it?" said Miriam.

"I like it very much," replied Clara.

Then Miriam realized that Clara was accepted as she had never been.

"Have you come down alone?" asked Paul.

"Yes; I went to Agatha's to tea. We are going to chapel. I only called in for a moment to see Clara."

"You should have come in here to tea," he said.

Miriam laughed shortly, and Clara turned impatiently aside.

"Do you like the chrysanthemums?" he asked.

"Yes; they are very fine," replied Miriam.

"Which sort do you like best?" he asked.

"I don't know. The bronze, I think."

"I don't think you've seen all the sorts. Come and look. Come and see which are *your* favorites, Clara."

He led the two women back to his own garden, where the towzled bushes of flowers of all colors stood raggedly along the path down to the field. The situation did not embarrass him, to his knowledge.

"Look, Miriam; these are the white ones that came from your garden. They aren't so fine here, are they?"

"No," said Miriam.

"But they're harder. You're so sheltered; things grow big and tender, and then die. These little yellow ones I like. Will you have some?"

While they were out there the bells began to ring in the church, sounding loud across the town and the field. Miriam looked at the tower, proud among the clustering roofs, and remembered the sketches he had brought her. It had been different then, but he had not left her even yet. She asked him for a book to read. He ran indoors.

"What! is that Miriam?" asked his mother coldly.

"Yes; she said she'd call and see Clara."

"You told her, then?" came the sarcastic answer.

"Yes; why shouldn't I?"

"There's certainly no reason why you shouldn't," said Mrs. Morel, and she returned to her book. He winced from his mother's irony, frowned irritably, thinking: "Why can't I do as I like?"

"You've not seen Mrs. Morel before?" Miriam was saying to Clara.

"No; but she's *so* nice!"

"Yes," said Miriam, dropping her head; "in some ways she's very fine."

"I should think so."

"Had Paul told you much about her?"

"He had talked a good deal."

"Ha!"

There was silence until he returned with the book.

"When will you want it back?" Miriam asked.

"When you like," he answered.

Clara turned to go indoors, whilst he accompanied Miriam to the gate.

"When will you come up to Willey Farm?" the latter asked.

"I couldn't say," replied Clara.

"Mother asked me to say she'd be pleased to see you any time, if you cared to come."

"Thank you; I should like to, but I can't say when."

"Oh, very well!" exclaimed Miriam rather bitterly, turning away.

She went down the path with her mouth to the flowers he had given her.

"You're sure you won't come in?" he said.

"No, thanks."

"We are going to chapel."

"Ha, I shall see you then!" Miriam was very bitter.

"Yes."

They parted. He felt guilty towards her. She was bitter, and she scorned him. He still belonged to herself, she believed; yet he could have Clara, take her home, sit with her next his mother in chapel, give her the same hymnbook he had given herself years before. She heard him running quickly indoors.

But he did not go straight in. Halting on the plot of grass, he heard his mother's voice, then Clara's answer:

"What I hate is the bloodhound quality in Miriam."

"Yes," said his mother quickly, "yes; *doesn't* it make you hate her, now!"

His heart went hot, and he was angry with them for talking about the girl. What right had they to say that? Something in the speech itself stung him into a flame of hate against Miriam. Then his own heart rebelled furiously at Clara's taking the liberty of speaking so about Miriam. After all, the girl was the better woman of the two, he thought, if it came to goodness. He went indoors. His mother looked excited. She was beating with her hand rhythmically on the sofa-arm, as women do who are wearing out. He could never bear to see the movement. There was a silence; then he began to talk.

In chapel Miriam saw him find the place in the hymnbook for Clara, in exactly the same way as he used for herself. And during the sermon he could see the girl across the chapel, her hat throwing a dark shadow over her face. What did she think, seeing Clara with him? He did not stop to consider. He felt himself cruel towards Miriam.

After chapel he went over Pentrich with Clara. It was a dark autumn night. They had said good-bye to Miriam, and his heart had smitten him as he left the girl alone. "But it serves her right," he said inside himself, and it almost gave him pleasure to go off under her eyes with this other handsome woman.

There was a scent of damp leaves in the darkness. Clara's hand lay warm and inert in his own as they walked. He was full of conflict. The battle that raged inside him made him feel desperate.

Up Pentrich Hill Clara leaned against him as he went. He slid his arm round her waist. Feeling the strong motion of her body under his arm as she walked, the tightness in his chest because of Miriam relaxed, and the hot blood bathed him. He held her closer and closer.

Then: "You still keep on with Miriam," she said quietly.

"Only talk. There never *was* a great deal more than talk between us," he said bitterly.

"Your mother doesn't care for her," said Clara.

"No, or I might have married her. But it's all up, really!"

Suddenly his voice went passionate with hate.

"If I was with her now, we should be jawing about the 'Christian Mystery,' or some such tack. Thank God, I'm not!"

They walked on in silence for some time.

"But you can't really give her up," said Clara.

"I don't give her up, because there's nothing to give," he said.

"There is for her."

"I don't know why she and I shouldn't be friends as long as we live," he said. "But it'll only be friends."

Clara drew away from him, leaning away from contact with him.

"What are you drawing away for?" he asked.

Still there was no answer. She walked resentfully, hanging her head.

"Because I said I would be friends with Miriam!" he exclaimed.

She would not answer him anything.

"I tell you it's only words that go between us," he persisted, trying to take her again.

She resisted. Suddenly he strode across in front of her, barring her way.

"Damn it!" he said. "What do you want now?"

"You'd better run after Miriam," mocked Clara.

The blood flamed up in him. He stood showing his teeth. She drooped sulkily. The lane was dark, quite lonely. He suddenly caught her in his arms, stretched forward, and put his mouth on her face in a kiss of rage. She turned frantically to avoid him. He held her fast. Hard and relentless his mouth came for her. Her breasts hurt against the wall of his chest. Helpless, she went loose in his arms, and he kissed her, and kissed her.

He heard people coming down the hill.

"Stand up! stand up!" he said thickly, gripping her arm till it hurt. If he had let go, she would have sunk to the ground.

She sighed and walked dizzily beside him. They went on in silence.

"We will go over the fields," he said; and then she woke up.

But she let herself be helped over the stile, and she walked in silence with him over the first dark field. It was the way to Nottingham and to the station, she knew. He seemed to be looking about. They came out on a bare hilltop where stood the dark figure of the ruined windmill. There he halted. They stood together high up in the darkness, looking at the lights scattered on the night before them, handfuls of glittering points, villages lying high and low on the dark, here and there.

"Like treading among the stars," he said, with a quaky laugh.

Then he took her in his arms, and held her fast. She moved aside her mouth to ask, dogged and low:

"What time is it?"

"It doesn't matter," he pleaded thickly.

"Yes, it does—yes! I must go!"

"It's early yet," he said.

"What time is it?" she insisted.

All round lay the black night, speckled and spangled with lights.

"I don't know."

She put her hand on his chest, feeling for his watch. He felt his joints fuse into fire. She groped in his waistcoat pocket, while he stood panting. In the darkness she could see the round, pale face of the watch, but not the figures. She stooped over it. He was panting till he could take her in his arms again.

"I can't see," she said.

"Then don't bother."

"Yes; I'm going!" she said, turning away.

"Wait! I'll look!" But he could not see. "I'll strike a match."

He secretly hoped it was too late to catch the train. She saw the glowing lantern of his hands as he cradled the light; then his face lit up, his eyes fixed on the watch. Instantly all was dark again. All was black before her eyes; only a glowing match was red near her feet. Where was he?

"What is it?" she asked, afraid.

"You can't do it," his voice answered out of the darkness.

There was a pause. She felt in his power. She had heard the ring in his voice. It frightened her.

"What time is it?" she asked, quiet, definite, hopeless.

"Two minutes to nine," he replied, telling the truth with a struggle.

"And can I get from here to the station in fourteen minutes?"

"No. At any rate——"

She could distinguish his dark form again a yard or so away. She wanted to escape.

"But can't I do it?" she pleaded.

"If you hurry," he said brusquely. "But you could easily walk it, Clara; it's only seven miles to the tram. I'll come with you."

"No; I want to catch the train."

"But why?"

"I do—I want to catch the train."

Suddenly his voice altered.

"Very well," he said, dry and hard. "Come along, then."

And he plunged ahead into the darkness. She ran after him, wanting to cry. Now he was hard and cruel to her. She ran over the rough, dark fields behind him, out of breath, ready to drop. But the double row of lights at the station drew nearer. Suddenly:

"There she is!" he cried, breaking into a run.

There was a faint rattling noise. Away to the right the train, like a luminous caterpillar, was threading across the night. The rattling ceased.

"She's over the viaduct. You'll just do it."

Clara ran, quite out of breath, and fell at last into the train. The whistle blew. He was gone. Gone!—and she was in a carriage full of people. She felt the cruelty of it.

He turned round and plunged home. Before he knew where he was he was in the kitchen at home. He was very pale. His eyes were dark and dangerous-looking, as if he were drunk. His mother looked at him.

"Well, I must say your boots are in a nice state!" she said.

He looked at his feet. Then he took off his overcoat. His mother wondered if he were drunk.

"She caught the train, then?" she said.

"Yes."

"I hope *her* feet weren't so filthy. Where on earth you dragged her I don't know!"

He was silent and motionless for some time.

"Did you like her?" he asked grudgingly at last.

"Yes, I liked her. But you'll tire of her, my son; you know you will."

He did not answer. She noticed how he labored in his breathing.

"Have you been running?" she asked.

"We had to run for the train."

"You'll go and knock yourself up. You'd better drink hot milk."

It was as good a stimulant as he could have, but he refused and went to bed. There he lay face down on the counterpane, and shed tears of rage and pain. There was a physical pain that made him bite his lips till they bled, and the chaos inside him left him unable to think, almost to feel.

"This is how she serves me, is it?" he said in his heart over and over, pressing his face in the quilt. And he hated her. Again he went over the scene, and again he hated her.

The next day there was a new aloofness about him. Clara was very gentle, almost loving. But he treated her distantly, with a touch of contempt. She sighed, continuing to be gentle. He came round.

One evening of that week Sarah Bernhardt was at the Theatre Royal in Nottingham, giving *La Dame aux Camélias*. Paul wanted to see this old and famous actress, and he asked Clara to accompany him. He told his mother to leave the key in the window for him.

"Shall I book seats?" he asked of Clara.

"Yes. And put on an evening suit, will you? I've never seen you in it."

"But, good Lord, Clara! Think of *me* in evening suit at the theater!" he remonstrated.

"Would you rather not?" she asked.

"I will if you *want* me to; but I s'll feel a fool."

She laughed at him.

"Then feel a fool for my sake, once, won't you?"

The request made his blood flush up.

"I suppose I s'll have to."

"What are you taking a suitcase for?" his mother asked.

He blushed furiously.

"Clara asked me," he said.

"And what seats are you going in?"

"Circle—three-and-six each!"

"Well, I'm sure!" exclaimed his mother sarcastically.

"It's only once in the bluest of blue moons," he said.

He dressed at Jordan's, put on an overcoat and a cap, and met Clara in a café. She was with one of her suffragette friends. She wore an old long coat, which did not suit her, and had a little wrap over her head, which he hated. The three went to the theater together.

Clara took off her coat on the stairs, and he discovered she was in a sort of semi-evening dress, that left her arms and neck and part of her breast bare. Her hair was done fashionably. The dress, a simple thing of green crape, suited her. She looked quite grand, he thought. He could see her figure inside the frock, as if that were wrapped closely round her. The firmness and the softness of her upright body could almost be felt as he looked at her. He clenched his fists.

And he was to sit all the evening beside her beautiful naked arm, watching the strong throat rise from the strong chest, watching the breasts under the green stuff, the curve of her limbs in the tight dress. Something in him hated her again for submitting him to this torture of nearness. And he loved her as she balanced her head and stared straight in front of her, pouting, wistful, immobile, as if she yielded herself to her fate because it was too strong for her. She could not help herself; she was in the grip of something bigger than herself. A kind of eternal look about her, as if she were a wistful sphinx, made it necessary for him to kiss her. He dropped his programme, and crouched down on the floor to get it, so that he could kiss her hand and wrist. Her beauty was a torture to him. She sat immobile. Only, when the lights went down, she sank a little against him, and he caressed her hand and arm with his fingers. He could smell her faint perfume. All the time his blood kept sweeping up in great white-hot waves that killed his consciousness momentarily.

The drama continued. He saw it all in the distance, going on somewhere; he did not know where, but it seemed far away inside him. He was Clara's white heavy arms, her throat, her moving bosom. That seemed to be himself. Then away somewhere the play went on, and he was identified with that also. There was no himself. The gray and black eyes of Clara, her bosom coming down on him, her arm that he held gripped between his hands, were all that existed. Then he felt himself small and helpless, her towering in her force above him.

Only the intervals, when the lights came up, hurt him expressibly. He wanted to run anywhere, so long as it would be dark again. In a maze, he wandered out for a drink. Then the lights were out, and the strange, insane reality of Clara and the drama took hold of him again.

The play went on. But he was obsessed by the desire to kiss the tiny blue vein that nestled in the bend of her arm. He could feel it. His whole life seemed suspended till he had put his lips there. It must be done. And the other people! At last he bent quickly forward and touched it with his lips. His moustache brushed the sensitive flesh. Clara shivered, drew away her arm.

When all was over, the lights up, the people clapping, he came to himself and looked at his watch. His train was gone.

"I s'll have to walk home!" he said.

Clara looked at him.

"Is it too late?" she asked.

He nodded. Then he helped her on with her coat.

"I love you! You look beautiful in that dress," he murmured over her shoulder, among the throng of bustling people.

She remained quiet. Together they went out of the theater. He saw the cabs waiting, the people passing. It seemed he met a pair of brown eyes which hated him. But he did not know. He and Clara turned away, mechanically taking the direction to the station.

The train had gone. He would have to walk the ten miles home.

"It doesn't matter," he said. "I shall enjoy it."

"Won't you," she said, flushing, "come home for the night? I can sleep with mother."

He looked at her. Their eyes met.

"What will your mother say?" he asked.

"She won't mind."

"You're sure?"

"Quite!"

"*Shall* I come?"

"If you will."

"Very well."

And they turned away. At the first stopping-place they took the car. The wind blew fresh in their faces. The town was dark; the tram tipped in its haste. He sat with her hand fast in his.

"Will your mother be gone to bed?" he asked.

"She may be. I hope not."

They hurried along the silent, dark little street, the only people out of doors. Clara quickly entered the house. He hesitated.

"Come in," she said.

He leaped up the step and was in the room. Her mother appeared in the inner doorway, large and hostile.

"Who have you got there?" she asked.

"It's Mr. Morel; he has missed his train. I thought we might put him up for the night, and save him a ten-mile walk."

"H'm!" exclaimed Mrs. Radford. "That's *your* lookout! If you've invited him, he's very welcome as far as I'm concerned. *You* keep the house!"

"If you don't like me, I'll go away again," he said.

"Nay, nay, you needn't! Come along in! I dunno what you'll think of the supper I'd got her."

It was a little dish of chip potatoes and a piece of bacon. The table was roughly laid for one.

"You can have some more bacon," continued Mrs. Radford. "More chips you can't have."

"It's a shame to bother you," he said.

"Oh, don't you be apologetic! It doesn't *do* wi' me! You treated her to the theater, didn't you?" There was a sarcasm in the last question.

"Well?" laughed Paul uncomfortably.

"Well, and what's an inch of bacon! Take your coat off."

The big, straight-standing woman was trying to estimate the situation. She moved about the cupboard. Clara took his coat. The room was very warm and cozy in the lamplight.

"My sirs!" exclaimed Mrs. Radford; "but you two's a pair of bright beauties, I must say! What's all that get-up for?"

"I believe we don't know," he said, feeling a victim.

"There isn't room in *this* house for two such bobby-dazzlers, if you fly your kites *that* high!" she rallied them. It was a nasty thrust.

He in his dinner jacket, and Clara in her green dress and bare arms, were confused. They felt they must shelter each other in that little kitchen.

"And look at *that* blossom!" continued Mrs. Radford, pointing to Clara. "What does she reckon she did it for?"

Paul looked at Clara. She was rosy; her neck was warm with blushes. There was a moment of silence.

"You like to see it, don't you?" he asked.

The mother had them in her power. All the time his heart was beating hard, and he was tight with anxiety. But he would fight her.

"Me like to see it!" exclaimed the old woman. "What should I like to see her make a fool of herself for?"

"I've seen people look bigger fools," he said. Clara was under his protection now.

"Oh, ay! and when was that?" came the sarcastic rejoinder.

"When they made frights of themselves," he answered.

Mrs. Radford, large and threatening, stood suspended on the hearthrug, holding her fork.

"They're fools either road," she answered at length, turning to the Dutch oven.

"No," he said, fighting stoutly. "Folk ought to look as well as they can."

"And do you call *that* looking nice!" cried the mother, pointing a scornful fork at Clara. "That—that looks as if it wasn't properly dressed!"

"I believe you're jealous that you can't swank as well," he said, laughing.

"Me! I could have worn evening dress with anybody, if I'd wanted to!" came the scornful answer.

"And why didn't you want to?" he asked pertinently. "Or *did* you wear it?"

There was a long pause. Mrs. Radford readjusted the bacon in the Dutch oven. His heart beat fast, for fear he had offended her.

"Me!" she exclaimed at last. "No, I didn't! And when I was in service, I knew as soon as one of the maids came out in bare shoulders what sort *she* was, going to her sixpenny hop!"

"Were you too good to go to a sixpenny hop?" he said.

Clara sat with bowed head. His eyes were dark and glittering. Mrs. Radford took the Dutch oven from the fire, and stood near him, putting bits of bacon on his plate.

"*There's* a nice crozzly bit!" she said.

"Don't give me the best!" he said.

"*She's* got what *she* wants," was the answer.

There was a sort of scornful forbearance in the woman's tone that made Paul know she was mollified.

"But *do* have some!" he said to Clara.

She looked up at him with her gray eyes, humiliated and lonely.

"No, thanks!" she said.

"Why won't you?" he answered, caressively.

The blood was beating up like fire in his veins. Mrs. Radford sat down again, large and impressive and aloof. He left Clara altogether to attend to the mother.

"They say Sarah Bernhardt's fifty," he said.

"Fifty! She's turned sixty!" came the scornful answer.

"Well," he said, "you'd never think it! She made me want to howl even now."

"I should like to see myself howling at *that* bad old baggage!" said Mrs. Radford. "It's time she began to think herself a grandmother, not a shrieking catamaran——"

He laughed.

"A catamaran is a boat the Malays use," he said.

"And it's a word as *I* use," she retorted.

"My mother does sometimes, and it's no good my telling her," he said.

"I s'd think she boxes your ears," said Mrs. Radford, good-humoredly.

"She'd like to, and she says she will, so I give her a little stool to stand on."

"That's the worst of my mother," said Clara. "She never wants a stool for anything."

"But she often can't touch *that* lady with a long prop," retorted Mrs. Radford to Paul.

"I s'd think she doesn't want touching with a prop," he laughed. "*I* shouldn't."

"It might do the pair of you good to give you a crack on the head with one," said the mother, laughing suddenly.

"Why are you so vindictive towards me?" he said. "I've not stolen anything from you."

"No; I'll watch that," laughed the older woman.

Soon the supper was finished. Mrs. Radford sat guard in her chair. Paul lit a cigarette. Clara went upstairs, returning with a sleeping-suit, which she spread on the fender to air.

"Why, I'd forgot all about *them*!" said Mrs. Radford. "Where have they sprung from?"

"Out of my drawer."

"H'm! You bought 'em for Baxter, an' he wouldn't wear 'em, would he?"—laughing. "Said he reckoned to do wi'out trousers i' bed." she turned confidentially to Paul, saying: "He couldn't *bear*'em, them pyjama things."

The young man sat making rings of smoke.

"Well, it's everyone to his taste," he laughed.

Then followed a little discussion of the merits of pyjamas.

"My mother loves me in them," he said. "She says I'm a pierrot."

"I can imagine they'd suit you," said Mrs. Radford.

After a while he glanced at the little clock that was ticking on the mantelpiece. It was half-past twelve.

"It is funny," he said, "but it takes hours to settle down to sleep after the theater."

"It's about time you did," said Mrs. Radford, clearing the table.

"Are *you* tired?" he asked of Clara.

"Not the least bit," she answered, avoiding his eyes.

"Shall we have a game at cribbage?" he said.

"I've forgotten it."

"Well, I'll teach you again. May we play crib, Mrs. Radford?" he asked.

"You'll please yourselves," she said; "but it's pretty late."

"A game or so will make us sleepy," he answered.

Clara brought the cards, and sat spinning her wedding ring whilst he shuffled them. Mrs. Radford was washing up in the scullery. As it grew later Paul felt the situation getting more and more tense.

"Fifteen two, fifteen four, fifteen six, and two's eight——!"

The clock struck one. Still the game continued. Mrs. Radford had done all the little jobs preparatory to going to bed, had locked the door and filled the kettle. Still Paul went on dealing and counting. He was obsessed by Clara's arms and throat. He believed he could see where the division was just beginning for her breasts. He could not leave her. She watched his hands, and felt her joints melt as they moved quickly. She was so near; it was almost as if he touched her, and yet not quite. His mettle was roused. He hated Mrs. Radford. She sat on, nearly dropping asleep, but determined and obstinate in her chair. Paul glanced at her, then at Clara. She met his eyes, that were angry, mocking, and hard as steel. Her own answered him in shame. He knew *she*, at any rate, was of his mind. He played on.

At last Mrs. Radford roused herself stiffly, and said:

"Isn't it nigh on time you two was thinking o' bed?"

Paul played on without answering. He hated her sufficiently to murder her.

"Half a minute!" he said.

The elder woman rose and sailed stubbornly into the scullery, returning with his candle, which she put on the mantelpiece. Then she sat down again. The hatred of her went so hot down his veins, he dropped his cards.

"We'll stop, then," he said, but his voice was still a challenge.

Clara saw his mouth shut hard. Again he glanced at her. It seemed like an agreement. She bent over the cards, coughing, to clear her throat.

"Well, I'm glad you've finished," said Mrs. Radford. "Here, take your things"—she thrust the warm suit in his hand—"and this is your candle. Your room's over this; there's only two, so you can't go far wrong. Well, good-night. I hope you'll rest well."

"I'm sure I shall; I always do," he said.

"Yes; and so you ought at your age," she replied.

He bade good-night to Clara, and went. The twisting stairs of white, scrubbed wood creaked and clanged at every step. He went doggedly. The two doors faced each other. He went in his room, pushed the door to, without fastening the latch.

It was a small room with a large bed. Some of Clara's hairpins were on the dressing table—her hairbrush. Her clothes and some skirts hung under a cloth in a corner. There was actually a pair of stockings over a chair. He explored the room. Two books of his own were there on the shelf. He undressed, folded his suit, and sat on the bed, listening. Then he blew out the candle, lay down, and in two minutes was almost asleep. Then click!—he was wide awake and writhing in torment. It was as if, when he had nearly got to sleep, something had bitten him suddenly and sent him mad. He sat up and looked at the room in the darkness, his feet doubled under him, perfectly motionless, listening. He heard a cat somewhere away outside; then the heavy, poised tread of the mother; then Clara's distinct voice:

"Will you unfasten my dress?"

There was silence for some time. At last the mother said:

"Now then! aren't you coming up?"

"No, not yet," replied the daughter calmly.

"Oh, very well then! If it's not late enough, stop a bit longer. Only you needn't come waking me up when I've got to sleep."

"I shan't be long," said Clara.

Immediately afterwards Paul heard the mother slowly mounting the stairs. The candlelight flashed through the cracks in his door. Her dress brushed the door, and his heart jumped. Then it was dark, and he heard the chatter of her latch. She was very leisurely indeed in her preparations for sleep. After a long time it was quite still. He sat strung up on the bed, shivering slightly. His door was an inch open. As Clara came upstairs, he would intercept her. He waited. All was dead silence. The clock struck two. Then he heard a slight scrape of the fender downstairs. Now he could not help himself. His shivering was uncontrollable. He felt he must go or die.

He stepped off the bed, and stood a moment, shuddering. Then he went straight to the door. He tried to step lightly. The first stair cracked like a shot. He listened. The old woman stirred in her bed. The staircase was dark. There was a slit of light under the stair-foot door, which opened into the kitchen. He stood a moment. Then he went on, mechanically. Every step creaked, and his back was creeping, lest the old woman's door should open behind him up above. He fumbled with the door at the bottom. The latch opened with a loud clack. He went through into the kitchen, and shut the door noisily behind him. The old woman daren't come now.

Then he stood, arrested. Clara was kneeling on a pile of white underclothing on the hearthrug, her back towards him, warming herself. She did not look round, but sat crouching on her heels, and her rounded, beautiful back was towards him, and her face was hidden. She was warming her body at the fire for consolation. The glow was rosy on one side, the shadow was dark and warm on the other. Her arms hung slack.

He shuddered violently, clenching his teeth and fists hard to keep control. Then he went forward to her. He put one hand on her shoulder, the fingers of the other hand under her chin to raise her face. A convulsed shiver ran through her, once, twice, at his touch. She kept her head bent.

"Sorry!" he murmured, realizing that his hands were very cold.

Then she looked up at him, frightened, like a thing that is afraid of death.

"My hands are so cold," he murmured.

"I like it," she whispered, closing her eyes.

The breath of her words was on his mouth. Her arms clasped his knees. The cord of his sleeping-suit dangled against her and made her shiver. As the warmth went into him, his shuddering became less.

At length, unable to stand so any more, he raised her, and she buried her head on his shoulder. His hands went over her slowly with an infinite tenderness of caress. She clung close to him, trying to hide herself against him. He clasped her very fast. Then at last she looked at him, mute, imploring, looking to see if she must be ashamed.

His eyes were dark, very deep, and very quiet. It was as if her beauty and his taking it hurt him, made him sorrowful. He looked at her with a little pain, and was afraid. He was so humble before her. She kissed him fervently on the eyes, first one, then the other, and she folded herself to him. She gave herself. He held her fast. It was a moment intense almost to agony.

She stood letting him adore her and tremble with joy of her. It healed her hurt pride. It healed her; it made her glad. It made her feel erect and proud again. Her pride had been wounded inside her. She had been cheapened. Now she radiated with joy and pride again. It was her restoration and her recognition.

Then he looked at her, his face radiant. They laughed to each other, and he strained her to his chest. The seconds ticked off, the minutes passed, and still the two stood clasped rigid together, mouth to mouth, like a statue in one block.

But again his fingers went seeking over her, restless, wandering, dissatisfied. The hot blood came up wave upon wave. She laid her head on his shoulder.

"Come you to my room," he murmured.

She looked at him and shook her head, her mouth pouting disconsolately, her eyes heavy with passion. He watched her fixedly.

"Yes!" he said.

Again she shook her head.

"Why not?" he asked.

She looked at him still heavily, sorrowfully, and again she shook her head. His eyes hardened, and he gave way.

When, later on, he was back in bed, he wondered why she had refused to come to him openly, so that her mother would know. At any rate, then things would have been definite. And she could have stayed with him the night, without having to go, as she was, to her mother's bed. It was strange, and he could not understand it. And then almost immediately he fell asleep.

He awoke in the morning with someone speaking to him. Opening his eyes, he saw Mrs. Radford, big and stately, looking down on him. She held a cup of tea in her hand.

"Do you think you're going to sleep till Doomsday?" she said.

He laughed at once.

"It ought only to be about five o'clock," he said.

"Well," she answered, "it's half-past seven, whether or not. Here, I've brought you a cup of tea."

He rubbed his face, pushed the tumbled hair off his forehead, and roused himself.

"What's it so late for!" he grumbled.

He resented being awakened. It amused her. She saw his neck in the flannel sleeping-jacket, as white and round as a girl's. He rubbed his hair crossly.

"It's no good your scratching your head," she said. "It won't make it no earlier. Here, an' how long d'you think I'm going to stand waiting wi' this here cup?"

"Oh, dash the cup!" he said.

"You should go to bed earlier," said the woman.

He looked up at her, laughing with impudence.

"I went to bed before *you* did," he said.

"Yes, my Guyney, you did!" she exclaimed.

"Fancy," he said, stirring his tea, "having tea brought to bed to me! My mother'll think I'm ruined for life."

"Don't she never do it?" asked Mrs. Radford.

"She'd as leave think of flying."

"Ah, I always spoilt my lot! That's why they've turned out such bad uns," said the elderly woman.

"You'd only Clara," he said. "And Mr. Radford's in heaven. So I suppose there's only you left to be the bad un."

"I'm not bad; I'm only soft," she said, as she went out of the bedroom. "I'm only a fool, I am!"

Clara was very quiet at breakfast, but she had a sort of air of proprietorship over him that pleased him infinitely. Mrs. Radford was evidently fond of him. He began to talk of his painting.

"What's the good," exclaimed the mother, "of your whittling and worrying and twistin' and too-in' at that painting of yours? What *good* does it do you, I should like to know? You'd better be enjoyin' yourself."

"Oh, but," exclaimed Paul, "I made over thirty guineas last year."

"Did you! Well, that's a consideration, but it's nothing to the time you put in."

"And I've got four pounds owing. A man said he'd give me five pounds if I'd paint him and his missis and the dog and the cottage. And I went and put the fowls in instead of the dog, and he was waxy, so I had to knock a quid off. I was sick of it, and I didn't like the dog. I made a picture of it. What shall I do when he pays me the four pounds?"

"Nay! you know your own uses for your money," said Mrs. Radford.

"But I'm going to bust this four pounds. Should we go to the seaside for a day or two?"

"Who?"

"You and Clara and me."

"What, on your money!" she exclaimed, half wrathful.

"Why not?"

"*You* wouldn't be long in breaking your neck at a hurdle race!" she said.

"So long as I get a good run for my money! Will you?"

"Nay; you may settle that atween you."

"And you're willing?" he asked, amazed and rejoicing.

"You'll do as you like," said Mrs. Radford, "whether I'm willing or not."

❖ 13 ❖

BAXTER DAWES

Soon after Paul had been to the theater with Clara, he was drinking in the Punch Bowl with some friends of his when Dawes came in. Clara's husband was growing stout; his eyelids were getting slack over his brown eyes; he was losing his healthy firmness of flesh. He was very evidently on the downward track. Having quarreled with his sister he had gone into cheap lodgings. His mistress had left him for a man who would marry her. He had been in prison one night for fighting when he was drunk, and there was a shady betting episode in which he was concerned.

Paul and he were confirmed enemies, and yet there was between them that peculiar feeling of intimacy, as if they were secretly near to each other, which sometimes exists between two people, although they never speak to one another. Paul often thought of Baxter Dawes, often wanted to get at him and be friends with him. He knew that Dawes often thought about him, and that the man was drawn to him by some bond or other. And yet the two never looked at each other save in hostility.

Since he was a superior employee at Jordan's, it was the thing for Paul to offer Dawes a drink.

"What'll you have?" he asked of him.

"Nowt wi' a bleeder like you!" replied the man.

Paul turned away with a slight disdainful movement of the shoulders, very irritating.

"The aristocracy," he continued, "is really a military institution. Take Germany, now. She's got thousands of aristocrats whose only means of existence is the army. They're deadly poor, and life's deadly slow. So they hope for a war. They look for war as a chance of getting on. Till there's a war they are idle good-for-nothings. When there's a war, they are leaders and commanders. There you are, then—they *want* war!"

He was not a favorite debater in the public house, being too quick and overbearing. He irritated the older men by his assertive manner, and his cocksureness. They listened in silence, and were not sorry when he finished.

Dawes interrupted the young man's flow of eloquence by asking, in a loud sneer:

"Did you learn all that at th' theater th' other night?"

Paul looked at him; their eyes met. Then he knew Dawes had seen him coming out of the theater with Clara.

"Why, what about th' theater?" asked one of Paul's associates, glad to get a dig at the young fellow, and sniffing something tasty.

"Oh, him in a bobtailed evening suit, on the lardy-da!" sneered Dawes, jerking his head contemptuously at Paul.

"That's comin' it strong," said the mutual friend. "Tart an' all?"

"Tart, begod!" said Dawes.

"Go on; let's have it!" cried the mutual friend.

"You've got it," said Dawes, "an' I reckon Morelly had it an' all."

"Well, I'll be jiggered!" said the mutual friend. "An' was it a proper tart?"

"Tart, God blimey—yes!"

"How do you know?"

"Oh," said Dawes, "I reckon he spent th' night——"

There was a good deal of laughter at Paul's expense.

"But who was she? D'you know her?" asked the mutual friend.

"I should *shay sho*," said Dawes.

This brought another burst of laughter.

"Then spit it out," said the mutual friend.

Dawes shook his head, and took a gulp of beer.

"It's a wonder he hasn't let on himself," he said. "He'll be braggin' of it in a bit."

"Come on, Paul," said the friend; "it's no good. You might just as well own up."

"Own up what? That I happened to take a friend to the theater?"

"Oh well, if it was all right, tell us who she was, lad," said the friend.

"She *was* all right," said Dawes.

Paul was furious. Dawes wiped his golden moustache with his fingers, sneering.

"Strike me—! One o' that sort?" said the mutual friend. "Paul, boy, I'm surprised at you. And do you know her, Baxter?"

"Just a bit, like!"

He winked at the other men.

"Oh well," said Paul, "I'll be going!"

The mutual friend laid a detaining hand on his shoulder.

"Nay," he said, "you don't get off as easy as that, my lad. We've got to have a full account of this business."

"Then get it from Dawes!" he said.

"You shouldn't funk your own deeds, man," remonstrated the friend.

Then Dawes made a remark which caused Paul to throw half a glass of beer in his face.

"Oh, Mr. Morel!" cried the barmaid, and she rang the bell for the "chucker-out."

Dawes spat and rushed for the young man. At that minute a brawny fellow with his shirtsleeves rolled up and his trousers tight over his haunches intervened.

"Now, then!" he said, pushing his chest in front of Dawes.

"Come out!" cried Dawes.

Paul was leaning, white and quivering, against the brass rail of the bar. He hated Dawes, wished something could exterminate him at that minute; and at the same time, seeing the wet hair on the man's forehead, he thought he looked pathetic. He did not move.

"Come out, you—," said Dawes.

"That's enough, Dawes," cried the barmaid.

"Come on," said the "chucker-out," with kindly insistence, "you'd better be getting on."

And, by making Dawes edge away from his own close proximity, he worked him to the door.

"*That's* the little sod as started it!" cried Dawes, half cowed, pointing to Paul Morel.

"Why, what a story, Mr. Dawes!" said the barmaid. "You know it was you all the time."

Still the "chucker-out" kept thrusting his chest forward at him, still he kept edging back, until he was in the doorway and on the steps outside; then he turned round.

"All right," he said, nodding straight at his rival.

Paul had a curious sensation of pity, almost of affection, mingled with violent hate, for the man. The colored door swung to; there was silence in the bar.

"Serve him jolly well right!" said the barmaid.

"But it's a nasty thing to get a glass of beer in your eyes," said the mutual friend.

"I tell you *I* was glad he did," said the barmaid. "Will you have another, Mr. Morel?"

She held up Paul's glass questioningly. He nodded.

"He's a man as doesn't care for anything, is Baxter Dawes," said one.

"Pooh! is he?" said the barmaid. "He's a loudmouthed one, he is, and they're never much good. Give me a pleasant-spoken chap, if you want a devil!"

"Well, Paul, my lad," said the friend, "you'll have to take care of yourself now for a while."

"You won't have to give him a chance over you, that's all," said the barmaid.

"Can you box?" asked a friend.

"Not a bit," he answered, still very white.

"I might give you a turn or two," said the friend.

"Thanks, I haven't time."

And presently he took his departure.

"Go along with him, Mr. Jenkinson," whispered the barmaid, tipping Mr. Jenkinson the wink.

The man nodded, took his hat, said "Good-night all!" very heartily, and followed Paul, calling:

"Half a minute, old man. You an' me's going the same road, I believe."

"Mr. Morel doesn't like it," said the barmaid. "You'll see, we shan't have him in much more. I'm sorry; he's good company. And Baxter Dawes wants locking up, that's what he wants."

Paul would have died rather than his mother should get to know of this affair. He suffered tortures of humiliation and self-consciousness. There was now a good deal of his life of which necessarily he could not speak to his mother. He had a life apart from her—his sexual life. The rest she still kept. But he felt he had to conceal something from her, and it irked him. There was a certain silence between them, and he felt he had, in that silence, to defend himself against her; he felt condemned by her. Then sometimes he hated her, and pulled at her bondage. His life wanted to free itself of her. It was like a circle where life turned back on itself, and got no farther. She bore him, loved him, kept him, and his love turned back into her, so that he could not be free to go forward with his own life, really love another woman. At this period, unknowingly, he resisted his mother's influence. He did not tell her things; there was a distance between them.

Clara was happy, almost sure of him. She felt she had at last got him for herself; and then again came the uncertainty. He told her jestingly of the affair with her husband. Her color came up, her gray eyes flashed.

"That's him to a 'T' " she cried—"like a navvy! He's not fit for mixing with decent folk."

"Yet you married him," he said.

It made her furious that he reminded her.

"I did!" she cried. "But how was I to know!"

"I think he might have been rather nice," he said.

"You think *I* made him what he is!" she exclaimed.

"Oh no! he made himself. But there's something about him——"

Clara looked at her lover closely. There was something in him she hated, a sort of detached criticism of herself, a coldness which made her woman's soul harden against him.

"And what are you going to do?" she asked.

"How?"

"About Baxter."

"There's nothing to do, is there?" he replied.

"You can fight him if you have to, I suppose?" she said.

"No; I haven't the least sense of the 'fist.' It's funny. With most men there's the instinct to clench the fist and hit. It's not so with me. I should want a knife or a pistol or something to fight with."

"Then you'd better carry something," she said.

"Nay," he laughed; "I'm not daggeroso."

"But he'll do something to you. You don't know him."

"All right," he said, "we'll see."

"And you'll let him?"

"Perhaps, if I can't help it."

"And if he kills you?" she said.

"I should be sorry, for his sake and mine."

Clara was silent for a moment.

"You *do* make me angry!" she exclaimed.

"That's nothing afresh," he laughed.

"But why are you so silly? You don't know him."

"And don't want."

"Yes, but you're not going to let a man do as he likes with you?"

"What must I do?" he replied, laughing.

"*I* should carry a revolver," she said. "I'm sure he's dangerous."

"I might blow my fingers off," he said.

"No; but won't you?" she pleaded.

"No."

"Not anything?"

"No."

"And you'll leave him to——?"

"Yes."

"You are a fool!"

"Fact!"

She set her teeth with anger.

"I could *shake* you!" she cried, trembling with passion.

"Why?"

"Let a man like *him* do as he likes with you."

"You can go back to him if he triumphs," he said.

"Do you want me to hate you?" she asked.

"Well, I only tell you," he said.

"And *you* say you *love* me!" she exclaimed, low and indignant.

"Ought I to slay him to please you?" he said. "But if I did, see what a hold he'd have over me."

"Do you think I'm a fool?" she exclaimed.

"Not at all. But you don't understand me, my dear."

There was a pause between them.

"But you ought *not* to expose yourself," she pleaded.

He shrugged his shoulders.

> "The man in righteousness arrayed,
> The pure and blameless liver,
> Needs not the keen Toledo blade,
> Nor venom-freighted quiver,"

he quoted.

She looked at him searchingly.

"I wish I could understand you," she said.

"There's simply nothing to understand," he laughed.

She bowed her head, brooding.

He did not see Dawes for several days; then one morning as he ran upstairs from the spiral room he almost collided with the burly metalworker.

"What the—!" cried the smith.

"Sorry!" said Paul, and passed on.

"*Sorry!*" sneered Dawes.

Paul whistled lightly, "Put Me among the Girls."

"I'll stop your whistle, my jockey!" he said.

The other took no notice.

"You're goin' to answer for that job of the other night."

Paul went to his desk in his corner, and turned over the leaves of the ledger.

"Go and tell Fanny I want order 097, quick!" he said to his boy.

Dawes stood in the doorway, tall and threatening, looking at the top of the young man's head.

"Six and five's eleven and seven's one-and-six," Paul added aloud.

"An' you hear, do you!" said Dawes.

"*Five and ninepence!*" He wrote a figure. "What's that?" he said.

"I'm going to show you what it is," said the smith.

The other went on adding the figures aloud.

"Yer crawlin' little—yer daresn't face me proper!"

Paul quickly snatched the heavy ruler. Dawes started. The young man ruled some lines in his ledger. The elder man was infuriated.

"But wait till I light on you, no matter where it is, I'll settle your hash for a bit, yer little swine!"

"All right," said Paul.

At that the smith started heavily from the doorway. Just then a whistle piped shrilly. Paul went to the speaking-tube.

"Yes!" he said, and he listened. "Er—yes!" He listened, then he laughed. "I'll come down directly. I've got a visitor just now."

Dawes knew from his tone that he had been speaking to Clara. He stepped forward.

"Yer little devil!" he said. "I'll visitor you, inside of two minutes! Think I'm goin' ter have *you* whipperty-snappin' round?"

The other clerks in the warehouse looked up. Paul's office boy appeared, holding some white article.

"Fanny says you could have had it last night if you'd let her know," he said.

"All right," answered Paul, looking at the stocking. "Get it off."

Dawes stood frustrated, helpless with rage. Morel turned round.

"Excuse me a minute," he said to Dawes, and he would have run downstairs.

"By God, I'll stop your gallop!" shouted the smith, seizing him by the arm. He turned quickly.

"Hey! hey!" cried the office boy, alarmed.

Thomas Jordan started out of his little glass office, and came running down the room.

"What's a-matter, what's a-matter?" he said, in his old man's sharp voice.

"I'm just goin' ter settle this little—that's all," said Dawes desperately.

"What do you mean?" snapped Thomas Jordan.

"What I say," said Dawes, but he hung fire.

Morel was leaning against the counter, ashamed, half grinning.

"What's it all about?" snapped Thomas Jordan.

"Couldn't say," said Paul, shaking his head and shrugging his shoulders.

"Couldn't yer, couldn't yer!" cried Dawes, thrusting forward his handsome, furious face, and squaring his fist.

"Have you finished?" cried the old man, strutting. "Get off about your business, and don't come here tipsy in the morning."

Dawes turned his big frame slowly upon him.

"Tipsy!" he said. "Who's tipsy? I'm no more tipsy than *you* are!"

"We've heard that song before," snapped the old man. "Now you get off, and don't be long about it. Comin' *here* with your rowdying."

The smith looked down contemptuously on his employer. His hands, large and grimy, and yet well shaped for his labor, worked restlessly. Paul remembered they were the hands of Clara's husband, and a flash of hate went through him.

"Get out before you're turned out!" snapped Thomas Jordan.

"Why, who'll turn me out?" said Dawes, beginning to sneer.

Mr. Jordan started, marched up to the smith, waving him off, thrusting his stout little figure at the man, saying:

"Get off my premises—get off!"

He seized and twitched Dawes' arm.

"Come off!" said the smith, and with a jerk of the elbow he sent the little manufacturer staggering backwards.

Before anyone could help him, Thomas Jordan had collided with the flimsy spring-door. It had given way, and let him crash down the half-dozen steps into Fanny's room. There was a second of amazement; then men and girls were running. Dawes stood a moment looking bitterly on the scene, then he took his departure.

Thomas Jordan was shaken and bruised, not otherwise hurt. He was, however, beside himself with rage. He dismissed Dawes from his employment, and summoned him for assault.

At the trial Paul Morel had to give evidence. Asked how the trouble began, he said:

"Dawes took occasion to insult Mrs. Dawes and me because I accompanied her to the theater one evening; then I threw some beer at him, and he wanted his revenge."

"Cherchez la femme!" smiled the magistrate.

The case was dismissed after the magistrate had told Dawes he thought him a skunk.

"You gave the case away," snapped Mr. Jordan to Paul.

"I don't think I did," replied the latter. "Besides, you didn't really want a conviction, did you?"

"What do you think I took the case up for?"

"Well," said Paul, "I'm sorry if I said the wrong thing."

Clara was also very angry.

"Why need *my* name have been dragged in?" she said.

"Better speak it openly than leave it to be whispered."

"There was no need for anything at all," she declared.

"We are none the poorer," he said indifferently.

"*You* may not be," she said.

"And you?" he asked.

"I need never have been mentioned."

"I'm sorry," he said; but he did not sound sorry.

He told himself easily: "She will come round." And she did.

He told his mother about the fall of Mr. Jordan and the trial of Dawes. Mrs. Morel watched him closely.

"And what do you think of it all?" she asked him.

"I think he's a fool," he said.

But he was very uncomfortable, nevertheless.

"Have you ever considered where it will end?" his mother said.

"No," he answered; "things work out of themselves."

"They do, in a way one doesn't like, as a rule," said his mother.

"And then one has to put up with them," he said.

"You'll find you're not as good at 'putting up' as you imagine," she said.

He went on working rapidly at his design.

"Do you ever ask *her* opinion?" she said at length.

"What of?"

"Of you, and the whole thing."

"I don't care what her opinion of me is. She's fearfully in love with me, but it's not very deep."

"But quite as deep as your feeling for her."

He looked up at his mother curiously.

"Yes," he said. "You know, mother, I think there must be something the matter with me, that I *can't* love. When she's there, as a rule, I *do* love her. Sometimes, when I see her just as *the woman*, I love her, mother; but then, when she talks and criticizes, I often don't listen to her."

"Yet she's as much sense as Miriam."

"Perhaps; and I love her better than Miriam. But *why* don't they hold me?"

The last question was almost a lamentation. His mother turned away her face, sat looking across the room, very quiet, grave, with something of renunciation.

"But you wouldn't want to marry Clara?" she said.

"No; at first perhaps I would. But why—why don't I want to marry her or anybody? I feel sometimes as if I wronged my women, mother."

"How wronged them, my son?"

"I don't know."

He went on painting rather despairingly; he had touched the quick of the trouble.

"And as for wanting to marry," said his mother, "there's plenty of time yet."

"But no, mother. I even love Clara, and I did Miriam; but to *give* myself to them in marriage I couldn't. I couldn't belong to them. They seem to want *me*, and I can't ever give it them."

"You haven't met the right woman."

"And I never shall meet the right woman while you live," he said.

She was very quiet. Now she began to feel again tired, as if she were done.

"We'll see, my son," she answered.

The feeling that things were going in a circle made him mad.

Clara was, indeed, passionately in love with him, and he with her, as far as passion went. In the daytime he forgot her a good deal. She was working in the same building, but he was not aware of it. He was busy, and her existence was of no matter to him. But all the time she was in her spiral loom she had a sense that he was upstairs, a physical sense of his person in the same building. Every second she expected him to come through the door, and when he came it was a shock to her. But he was often short and offhand with her. He gave her his directions in an official manner, keeping her at bay. With what wits she had left she listened to him. She dared not misunderstand or fail to remember, but it was a cruelty to her. She wanted to touch his chest. She knew exactly how his breast was shapen under the waistcoat, and she wanted to touch it. It maddened her to hear his mechanical voice giving orders about the work. She wanted to break through the sham of it, smash the trivial coating of business which covered him with hardness, get at the man again; but she was afraid, and before she could feel one touch of his warmth he was gone, and she ached again.

He knew that she was dreary every evening she did not see him, so he gave her a good deal of his time. The days were often a misery to her, but the evenings and the nights were usually a bliss to them both. Then they were silent. For hours they sat together, or walked together in the dark, and talked only a few, almost meaningless words. But he had her hand in his, and her bosom left its warmth in his chest, making him feel whole.

One evening they were walking down by the canal, and something was troubling him. She knew she had not got him. All the time he whistled softly and persistently to himself. She listened, feeling she could learn more from his whistling than from his speech. It was a sad, dissatisfied tune—a tune that made her feel he would not stay with her. She walked on in silence. When they came to the swing bridge he sat down on the great pole, looking at the stars in the water. He was a long way from her. She had been thinking.

"Will you always stay at Jordan's?" she asked.

"No," he answered without reflecting. "No; I s'll leave Nottingham and go abroad—soon."

"Go abroad! What for?"

"I dunno! I feel restless."

"But what shall you do?"

"I shall have to get some steady designing work, and some sort of sale for my pictures first," he said. "I am gradually making my way. I know I am."

"And when do you think you'll go?"

"I don't know. I shall hardly go for long, while there's my mother."

"You couldn't leave her?"

"Not for long."

She looked at the stars in the black water. They lay very white and staring. It was an agony to know he would leave her, but it was almost an agony to have him near her.

"And if you made a nice lot of money, what would you do?" she asked.

"Go somewhere in a pretty house near London with my mother."

"I see."

There was a long pause.

"I could still come and see you," he said. "I don't know. Don't ask me what I should do; I don't know."

There was a silence. The stars shuddered and broke upon the water. There came a breath of wind. He went suddenly to her, and put his hand on her shoulder.

"Don't ask me anything about the future," he said miserably. "I don't know anything. Be with me now, will you, no matter what it is?"

And she took him in her arms. After all, she was a married woman, and she had no right even to what he gave her. He needed her badly. She had him in her arms, and he was miserable. With her warmth she folded him over, consoled him, loved him. She would let the moment stand for itself.

After a moment he lifted his head as if he wanted to speak.

"Clara," he said, struggling.

She caught him passionately to her, pressed his head down on her breast with her hand. She could not bear the suffering in his voice. She was afraid in her soul. He might have anything of her—anything; but she did not want to *know*. She felt she could not bear it. She wanted him to be soothed upon her—soothed. She stood clasping him and caressing him, and he was something unknown to her—something almost uncanny. She wanted to soothe him into forgetfulness.

And soon the struggle went down in his soul, and he forgot. But then Clara was not there for him, only a woman, warm, something he loved and almost worshipped, there in the dark. But it was not Clara, and she submitted to him. The naked hunger and inevitability of his loving her, something strong and blind and ruthless in its primitiveness, made the hour almost terrible to her. She knew how stark and alone he was, and she felt it was great that he came to her; and she took him simply because his need was bigger either than her or him, and her soul was still within her. She did this for him in his need, even if he left her, for she loved him.

All the while the peewits were screaming in the field. When he came to, he wondered what was near his eyes, curving and strong with life in the dark, and what voice it was speaking. Then he realized it was the grass, and the peewit was calling. The warmth was Clara's breathing heaving. He lifted his head, and looked into her eyes. They were dark and shining and strange, life wild at the source staring into his life, stranger to him, yet meeting him; and he put his face down on her throat, afraid. What was she? A strong, strange, wild life, that breathed with his in the darkness through this hour. It was all so much bigger than themselves that he was hushed. They had met, and included in their meeting the thrust of the manifold grass-stems, the cry of the peewit, the wheel of the stars.

When they stood up they saw other lovers stealing down the opposite hedge. It seemed natural they were there; the night contained them.

And after such an evening they both were very still, having known the immensity of passion. They felt small, half afraid, childish, and wondering, like Adam and Eve when they lost their innocence and realized the magnificence of the power which drove them out of Paradise and across the great night and the great day of humanity. It was for each of them an initiation and a satisfaction. To know their own nothingness, to know the tremendous living flood which carried them always, gave them rest within themselves. If so great a magnificent power could overwhelm them, identify them altogether with itself, so that they knew they were only grains in the tremendous heave that lifted every grass-blade its little height, and every tree, and living thing, then why fret about themselves? They could let themselves be carried by life, and they felt a sort of peace each in the other. There was a verification which they had had together. Nothing could nullify it, nothing could take it away; it was almost their belief in life.

But Clara was not satisfied. Something great was there, she knew; something great enveloped her. But it did not keep her. In the morning it was not the same. They had *known*, but she could not keep the moment. She wanted it again; she wanted something permanent. She had not realized fully. She thought it was he whom she wanted. He was not safe to her. This that had been between them might never be again; he might leave her. She had not got him; she was not satisfied. She had been there, but she had not gripped the—the something—she knew not what—which she was mad to have.

In the morning he had considerable peace, and was happy in himself. It seemed almost as if he had known the baptism of fire in passion, and it left him at rest. But it was not Clara. It was something that happened because of her, but it was not her. They were scarcely any nearer each other. It was as if they had been blind agents of a great force.

When she saw him that day at the factory her heart melted like a drop of fire. It was his body, his brows. The drop of fire grew more intense in her breast; she must hold him. But he, very quiet, very subdued this morning, went on giving his instructions. She followed him into the dark, ugly basement, and lifted her arms to him. He kissed her, and the intensity of passion began to burn him again. Somebody was at the door. He ran upstairs; she returned to her room, moving as if in a trance.

After that the fire slowly went down. He felt more and more that his experience had been impersonal, and not Clara. He loved her. There was a big tenderness, as after a strong emotion they had known together; but it was not she who could keep his soul steady. He had wanted her to be something she could not be.

And she was mad with desire of him. She could not see him without touching him. In the factory, as he talked to her about spiral hose, she ran her hand secretly along his side. She followed him out into the basement for a quick kiss; her eyes, always mute and yearning, full of unrestrained passion, she kept fixed on his. He was afraid of her, lest she should too flagrantly give herself away before the other girls. She invariably waited for him at dinner-time for him to embrace her before she went. He felt as if she were helpless, almost a burden to him, and it irritated him.

"But what do you always want to be kissing and embracing for?" he said. "Surely there's a time for everything."

She looked up at him, and the hate came into her eyes.

"*Do* I always want to be kissing you?" she said.

"Always, even if I come to ask you about the work. I don't want anything to do with love when I'm at work. Work's work——"

"And what is love?" she asked. "Has it to have special hours?"

"Yes; out of work hours."

"And you'll regulate it according to Mr. Jordan's closing time?"

"Yes; and according to the freedom from business of any sort."

"It is only to exist in spare time?"

"That's all, and not always then—not the kissing sort of love."

"And that's all you think of it?"

"It's quite enough."

"I'm glad you think so."

And she was cold to him for some time—she hated him; and while she was cold and contemptuous, he was uneasy till she had forgiven him again. But when they started afresh they were not any nearer. He kept her because he never satisfied her.

In the spring they went together to the seaside. They had rooms at a little cottage near Theddlethorpe, and lived as man and wife. Mrs. Radford sometimes went with them.

It was known in Nottingham that Paul Morel and Mrs. Dawes were going together, but as nothing was very obvious, and Clara was always a solitary person, and he seemed so simple and innocent, it did not make much difference.

He loved the Lincolnshire coast, and she loved the sea. In the early morning they often went out together to bathe. The gray of the dawn, the far, desolate reaches of the fenland smitten with winter, the sea-meadows rank with herbage, were stark enough to rejoice his soul. As they stepped on to the highroad from their plank bridge, and looked round at the endless monotony of levels, the land a little darker than the sky, the sea sounding small beyond the sandhills, his heart filled strong with the sweeping relentlessness of life. She loved him then. He was solitary and strong, and his eyes had a beautiful light.

They shuddered with cold; then he raced her down the road to the green turf bridge. She could run well. Her color soon came, her throat was bare, her eyes shone. He loved her for being so luxuriously heavy, and yet so quick. Himself was light; she went with a beautiful rush. They grew warm, and walked hand in hand.

A flush came into the sky; the wan moon, half-way down the west, sank into insignificance. On the shadowy land things began to take life, plants with great leaves became distinct. They came through a pass in the big, cold sand hills on to the beach. The long waste of foreshore lay moaning under the dawn and the sea; the ocean was a flat dark strip with a white edge. Over the gloomy sea the sky grew red. Quickly the fire spread among the clouds and scattered them. Crimson burned to orange, orange to dull gold, and in a golden glitter the sun came up, dribbling fierily over the waves in little splashes, as if someone had gone along and the light had spilled from her pail as she walked.

The breakers ran down the shore in long, hoarse strokes. Tiny seagulls, like specks of spray, wheeled above the line of surf. Their crying seemed larger than they. Far away the coast reached out, and melted into the morning, the tussocky sandhills seemed to sink to a level with the beach. Mablethorpe was tiny on their right. They had alone the space of all this level shore, the sea, and the upcoming sun, the faint noise of the waters, the sharp crying of the gulls.

They had a warm hollow in the sand hills where the wind did not come. He stood looking out to sea.

"It's very fine," he said.

"Now don't get sentimental," she said.

It irritated her to see him standing gazing at the sea, like a solitary and poetic person. He laughed. She quickly undressed.

"There are some fine waves this morning," she said triumphantly.

She was a better swimmer than he; he stood idly watching her.

"Aren't you coming?" she said.

"In a minute," he answered.

She was white and velvet skinned, with heavy shoulders. A little wind, coming from the sea, blew across her body and ruffled her hair.

The morning was of a lovely limpid gold color. Veils of shadow seemed to be drifting away on the north and the south. Clara stood shrinking slightly from the touch of the wind, twisting her hair. The sea-grass rose behind the white stripped woman. She glanced at the sea, then looked at him. He was watching her with dark eyes which she loved and could not understand. She hugged her breasts between her arms, cringing, laughing:

"Oo, it will be so cold!" she said.

He bent forward and kissed her, held her suddenly close, and kissed her again. She stood waiting. He looked into her eyes, then away at the pale sands.

"Go, then!" he said quietly.

She flung her arms round his neck, drew him against her, kissed him passionately, and went, saying:

"But you'll come in?"

"In a minute."

She went plodding heavily over the sand that was soft as velvet. He, on the sand hills, watched the great pale coast envelop her. She grew smaller, lost proportion, seemed only like a large white bird toiling forward.

"Not much more than a big white pebble on the beach, not much more than a clot of foam being blown and rolled over the sand," he said to himself.

She seemed to move very slowly across the vast sounding shore. As he watched, he lost her. She was dazzled out of sight by the sunshine. Again he saw her, the merest white speck moving against the white, muttering sea edge.

"Look how little she is!" he said to himself. "She's lost like a grain of sand in the beach—just a concentrated speck blown along, a tiny white foam-bubble, almost nothing among the morning. Why does she absorb me?"

The morning was altogether uninterrupted: she was gone in the water. Far and wide the beach, the sand hills with their blue marrain, the shining water, glowed together in immense, unbroken solitude.

"What is she, after all?" he said to himself. "Here's the seacoast morning, big and permanent and beautiful; there is she, fretting, always unsatisfied, and temporary as a bubble of foam. What does she mean to me, after all? She represents something, like a bubble of foam represents the sea. But what is *she*? It's not her I care for."

Then, startled by his own unconscious thoughts, that seemed to speak so distinctly that all the morning could hear, he undressed and ran quickly down the sands. She was watching for him. Her arm flashed up to him, she heaved on a wave, subsided, her shoulders in a pool of liquid silver. He jumped through the breakers, and in a moment her hand was on his shoulder.

He was a poor swimmer, and could not stay long in the water. She played round him in triumph, sporting with her superiority, which he begrudged her. The sunshine stood deep and fine on the water. They laughed in the sea for a minute or two, then raced each other back to the sand hills.

When they were drying themselves, panting heavily, he watched her laughing, breathless face, her bright shoulders, her breasts that swayed and made him frightened as she rubbed them, and he thought again:

"But she is magnificent, and even bigger than the morning and the sea. Is she—? is she—?"

She, seeing his dark eyes fixed on her, broke off from her drying with a laugh.

"What are you looking at?" she said.

"You," he answered, laughing.

Her eyes met his, and in a moment he was kissing her white "goose-fleshed" shoulder, and thinking:

"What is she? What is she?"

She loved him in the morning. There was something detached, hard, and elemental about his kisses then, as if he were only conscious of his own will, not in the least of her and her wanting him.

Later in the day he went out sketching.

"You," he said to her, "go with your mother to Sutton. I am so dull."

She stood and looked at him. He knew she wanted to come with him, but he preferred to be alone. She made him feel imprisoned when she was there, as if he could not get a free deep breath, as if there were something on top of him. She felt his desire to be free of her.

In the evening he came back to her. They walked down the shore in the darkness, then sat for awhile in the shelter of the sand hills.

"It seems," she said, as they stared over the darkness of the sea, where no light was to be seen—"it seemed as if you only loved me at night—as if you didn't love me in the daytime."

He ran the cold sand through his fingers, feeling guilty under the accusation.

"The night is free to you," he replied. "In the daytime I want to be by myself."

"But why?" she said. "Why, even now, when we are on this short holiday?"

"I don't know. Lovemaking stifles me in the daytime."

"But it needn't be always lovemaking," she said.

"It always is," he answered, "when you and I are together."

She sat feeling very bitter.

"Do you ever want to marry me?" he asked curiously.

"Do you me?" she replied.

"Yes, yes; I should like us to have children," he answered slowly.

She sat with her head bent, fingering the sand.

"But you don't really want a divorce from Baxter, do you?" he said.

It was some minutes before she replied.

"No," she said, very deliberately; "I don't think I do."

"Why?"

"I don't know."

"Do you feel as if you belonged to him?"

"No; I don't think so."

"What, then?"

"I think he belongs to me," she replied.

He was silent for some minutes, listening to the wind blowing over the hoarse, dark sea.

"And you never really intended to belong to *me*?" he said.

"Yes, I do belong to you," she answered.

"No," he said; "because you don't want to be divorced."

It was a knot they could not untie, so they left it, took what they could get, and what they could not attain they ignored.

"I consider you treated Baxter rottenly," he said another time.

He half expected Clara to answer him, as his mother would: "You consider your own affairs, and don't know so much about other people's." But she took him seriously, almost to his own surprise.

"Why?" she said.

"I suppose you thought he was a lily of the valley, and so you put him in an appropriate pot, and tended him according. You made up your mind he was a lily of the valley, and it was no good his being a cow parsnip. You wouldn't have it."

"I certainly never imagined him a lily of the valley."

"You imagined him something he wasn't. That's just what a woman is. She thinks she knows what's good for a man, and she's going to see he gets it; and no matter if he's starving, he may sit and whistle for what he needs, while she's got him, and is giving him what's good for him."

"And what are you doing?" she asked.

"I'm thinking what tune I shall whistle," he laughed.

And instead of boxing his ears, she considered him in earnest.

"You think I want to give you what's good for you?" she asked.

"I hope so; but love should give a sense of freedom, not of prison. Miriam made me feel tied up like a donkey to a stake. I must feed on her patch, and nowhere else. It's sickening!"

"And would *you* let a *woman* do as she likes?"

"Yes; I'll see that she *likes* to love me. If she doesn't—well, I don't hold her."

"If you were as wonderful as you say—," replied Clara.

"I should be the marvel I am," he laughed.

There was a silence in which they hated each other, though they laughed.

"Love's a dog in the manger," he said.

"And which of us is the dog?"

"Oh well, you, of course."

So there went on a battle between them. She knew she never fully had him. Some part, big and vital in him, she had no hold over; nor did she ever try to get it, or even to realize what it was. And he knew in some way that she held herself still as Mrs. Dawes. She did not love Dawes, never had loved him; but she believed he loved her, at least depended on her. She felt a certain surety about him that she never felt with Paul Morel. Her passion for the young man had filled her soul, given her a certain satisfaction, eased her of her self-mistrust, her doubt. Whatever else she was, she was inwardly assured. It was almost as if she had gained *herself*, and stood now distinct and complete. She had received her confirmation; but she never believed that her life belonged to Paul Morel, nor his to her. They would separate in the end, and the rest of her life would be an ache after him. But at any rate, she *knew* now, she was sure of herself. And the same could almost be said of him. Together they had received the baptism of life, each through the other; but now their missions were separate. Where he wanted to go she could not come with him. They would have to part sooner or later. Even if they married, and were faithful to each other, still he would have to leave her, go on alone, and she would only have to attend to him when he came home. But it was not possible. Each wanted a mate to go side by side with.

Clara had gone to live with her mother upon Mapperley Plains. One evening, as Paul and she were walking along Woodborough Road, they met Dawes. Morel knew something about the bearing of the man approaching, but he was absorbed in his thinking at the moment, so that only his artist's eye watched the form of the stranger. Then he suddenly turned to Clara with a laugh, and put his hand on her shoulder, saying, laughing:

"But we walk side by side, and yet I'm in London arguing with an imaginary Orpen; and where are you?"

At that instant Dawes passed, almost touching Morel. The young man glanced, saw the dark brown eyes burning, full of hate and yet tired.

"Who was that?" he asked of Clara.

"It was Baxter," she replied.

Paul took his hand from her shoulder and glanced round; then he saw again distinctly the man's form as it approached him. Dawes still walked erect, with his fine shoulders flung back, and his face lifted; but there was a furtive look in his eyes that gave one the impression he was trying to get unnoticed past every person he met, glancing suspiciously to see what they thought of him. And his hands seemed to be wanting to hide. He wore old clothes, the trousers were torn at the knee, and the handkerchief tied round his throat was dirty; but his cap was still defiantly over one eye. As she saw him, Clara felt guilty. There was a tiredness and despair on his face that made her hate him, because it hurt her.

"He looks shady," said Paul.

But the note of pity in his voice reproached her, and made her feel hard.

"His true commonness comes out," she answered.

"Do you hate him?" he asked.

"You talk," she said, "about the cruelty of women; I wish you knew the cruelty of men in their brute force. They simply don't know that the woman exists."

"Don't *I?*" he said.

"No," she answered.

"Don't I know you exist?"

"About *me* you know nothing," she said bitterly—"about *me!*"

"Not more than Baxter knew?" he asked.

"Perhaps not as much."

He felt puzzled, and helpless, and angry. There she walked, unknown to him, though they had been through such experience together.

"But you know *me* pretty well," he said.

She did not answer.

"Did you know Baxter as well as you know me?" he asked.

"He wouldn't let me," she said.

"And I have let you know me?"

"It's what men *won't* let you do. They won't let you get really near to them," she said.

"And haven't I let you?"

"Yes," she answered slowly; "but you've never come near to me. You can't come out of yourself, you can't. Baxter could do that better than you."

He walked on pondering. He was angry with her for preferring Baxter to him.

"You begin to value Baxter now you've not got him," he said.

"No; I can only see where he was different from you."

But he felt she had a grudge against him.

One evening, as they were coming home over the fields she startled him by asking:

"Do you think it's worth it—the—the sex part."

"The act of loving, itself?"

"Yes; is it worth anything to you?"

"But how can you separate it?" he said. "It's the culmination of everything. All our intimacy culminates then."

"Not for me," she said.

He was silent. A flash of hate for her came up. After all she was dissatisfied with him, even there, where he thought they fulfilled each other. But he believed her too implicitly.

"I feel," she continued slowly, "as if I hadn't got you, as if all of you weren't there, and as if it weren't *me* you were taking——"

"Who, then?"

"Something just for yourself. It has been fine, so that I daren't think of it. But is it *me* you want, or is it *It*?"

He again felt guilty. Did he leave Clara out of count, and take simply woman? But he thought that was splitting a hair.

"When I had Baxter, actually had him, then I *did* feel as if I had all of him," she said.

"And it was better?" he asked.

"Yes, yes; it was more whole. I don't say you haven't given me more than he ever gave me."

"Or could give you."

"Yes, perhaps; but you've never given me yourself."

He knitted his brows angrily.

"If I start to make love to you," he said, "I just go like a leaf down the wind."

"And leave me out of count," she said.

"And then is it nothing to you?" he asked, almost rigid with chagrin.

"It's something; and sometimes you have carried me away—right away—I know—and—I reverence you for it—but——"

"Don't 'but' me," he said, kissing her quickly, as a fire ran through him.

She submitted, and was silent.

It was true as he said. As a rule, when he started lovemaking, the emotion was strong enough to carry with it everything—reason, soul, blood—in a great sweep, like the Trent carries bodily its back-swirls and intertwinings, noiselessly. Gradually, the little criticisms, the little sensations, were lost, thought also went, everything borne along in one flood. He became, not a man with a mind, but a great instinct. His hands were like creatures, living; his limbs, his body, were all life and consciousness, subject to no will of his, but living in themselves. Just as he was, so it seemed the vigorous, wintry stars were strong also with life. He and they struck with the same pulse of fire, and the same joy of strength which held the bracken-frond stiff near his eyes held his own body firm. It was as if he, and the stars, and the dark herbage, and Clara were licked up in an immense tongue of flame, which tore onwards and upwards. Everything rushed along in living beside him; everything was still, perfect in itself, along with him. This wonderful stillness in each thing in itself, while it was being borne along in a very ecstasy of living, seemed the highest point of bliss.

And Clara knew this held him to her, so she trusted altogether to the passion. It, however, failed her very often. They did not often reach again the height of that once when the peewits had called. Gradually, some mechanical effort spoilt their loving, or, when they had splendid moments, they had them separately, and not so satisfactorily. So often he seemed merely to be running on alone; often they realized it had been a failure, not what they had wanted. He left her, knowing *that* evening had only made a little split between them. Their loving grew more mechanical, without the marvelous glamor. Gradually they began to introduce novelties, to get back some of the feeling of satisfaction. They would be very near, almost dangerously near to the river, so that the black water ran not far from his face, and it gave a little thrill; or they loved sometimes in a little hollow below the fence of the path where people were passing occasionally, on the edge of the town, and they heard footsteps coming, almost felt the vibration of the tread, and they heard what the passersby said—strange little things that were never intended to be heard. And afterwards each of them was rather ashamed, and these things caused a distance between the two of them. He began to despise her a little, as if she had merited it!

One night he left her to go to Daybrook Station over the fields. It was very dark, with an attempt at snow, although the spring was so far advanced. Morel had not much time; he plunged forward. The town ceases almost abruptly on the edge of a steep hollow; there the houses with their yellow lights stand up against the darkness. He went over the stile, and dropped quickly into the hollow of the fields. Under the orchard one warm window shone in Swineshead Farm. Paul glanced round. Behind, the houses stood on the brim of the dip, black against the sky, like wild beasts glaring curiously with yellow eyes down into the darkness. It was the town that seemed savage and uncouth, glaring on the clouds at the back of him. Some creature stirred under the willows of the farm pond. It was too dark to distinguish anything.

He was close up to the next stile before he saw a dark shape leaning against it. The man moved aside.

"Good-evening!" he said.

"Good-evening!" Morel answered, not noticing.

"Paul Morel?" said the man.

Then he knew it was Dawes. The man stopped his way.

"I've got yer, have I?" he said awkwardly.

"I shall miss my train," said Paul.

He could see nothing of Dawes' face. The man's teeth seemed to chatter as he talked.

"You're going to get it from me now," said Dawes.

Morel attempted to move forward; the other man stepped in front of him.

"Are yer goin' to take that topcoat off," he said, "or are you goin' to lie down to it?"

Paul was afraid the man was mad.

"But," he said, "I don't know how to fight."

"All right, then," answered Dawes, and before the younger man knew where he was he was staggering backwards from a blow across the face.

The whole night went black. He tore off his overcoat and coat, dodging a blow, and flung the garments over Dawes. The latter swore savagely. Morel, in his shirt sleeves, was now alert and furious. He felt his whole body unsheath itself like a claw. He could not fight, so he would use his wits. The other man became more distinct to him; he could see particularly the shirt-breast. Dawes stumbled over Paul's coats, then came rushing forward. The young man's mouth was bleeding. It was the other man's mouth he was dying to get at, and the desire was anguish in its strength. He stepped quickly through the stile, and as Dawes was coming through after him, like a flash he got a blow in over the other's mouth. He shivered with pleasure. Dawes advanced slowly, spitting. Paul was afraid; he moved round to get to the stile again. Suddenly, from out of nowhere, came a great blow against his ear, that sent him falling helpless backwards. He heard Dawes' heavy panting, like a wild beast's; then came a kick on his knee, giving him such agony that he got up and, quite blind leapt clean under his enemy's guard. He felt blows and kicks, but they did not hurt. He hung on to the bigger man like a wildcat, till at last Dawes fell with a crash, losing his presence of mind. Paul went down with him. Pure instinct brought his hands to the man's neck, and before Dawes, in frenzy and agony, could wrench him free, he had got his fists twisted in the scarf and his knuckles dug in the throat of the other man. He was a pure instinct, without reason or feeling. His body, hard and wonderful in itself, cleaved against the struggling body of the other man; not a muscle in him relaxed. He was quite unconscious, only his body had taken upon itself to kill this other man. For himself, he had neither feeling nor reason. He lay pressed hard against his adversary, his body adjusting itself to its one pure purpose of choking the other man, resisting exactly at the right moment, with exactly the right amount of strength, the struggles of the other, silent, intent, unchanging, gradually pressing its knuckles deeper, feeling the struggles of the other body become wilder and more frenzied. Tighter and tighter grew his body, like a screw that is gradually increasing in pressure, till something breaks.

Then suddenly he relaxed, full of wonder and misgiving. Dawes had been yielding. Morel felt his body flame with pain, as he realized what he was doing; he was all bewildered. Dawes' struggles suddenly renewed themselves in a furious spasm. Paul's hands were wrenched, torn out of the scarf in which they were knotted, and he was flung away, helpless. He heard the horrid sound of the other's gasping, but he lay stunned; then, still dazed, he felt the blows of the other's feet, and lost consciousness.

Dawes, grunting with pain like a beast, was kicking the prostrate body of his rival. Suddenly the whistle of the train shrieked two fields away. He turned round and glared suspiciously. What was coming? He saw the lights of the train draw across his vision. It seemed to him people were approaching. He made off across the field into Nottingham, and dimly in his consciousness as he went, he felt on his foot the place where his boot had knocked against one of the lad's bones. The knock seemed to re-echo inside him; he hurried to get away from it.

Morel gradually came to himself. He knew where he was and what had happened, but he did not want to move. He lay still, with tiny bits of snow tickling his face. It was pleasant to lie quite, quite still. The time passed. It was the bits of snow that kept rousing him when he did not want to be roused. At last his will clicked into action.

"I mustn't lie here," he said; "it's silly."

But still he did not move.

"I said I was going to get up," he repeated. "Why don't I?"

And still it was some time before he had sufficiently pulled himself together to stir; then gradually he got up. Pain made him sick and dazed, but his brain was clear. Reeling, he groped for his coats and got them on, buttoning his overcoat up to his ears. It was some time before he found his cap. He did not know whether his face was still bleeding. Walking blindly, every step making him sick with pain, he went back to the pond and washed his face and hands. The icy water hurt, but helped to bring him back to himself. He crawled back up the hill to the tram. He wanted to get to his mother—he must get to his mother—that was his blind intention. He covered his face as much as he could, and struggled sickly along. Continually the ground seemed to fall away from him as he walked, and he felt himself dropping with a sickening feeling into space; so, like a nightmare, he got through with the journey home.

Everybody was in bed. He looked at himself. His face was discolored and smeared with blood, almost like a dead man's face. He washed it, and went to bed. The night went by in delirium. In the morning he found his mother looking at him. Her blue eyes—they were all he wanted to see. She was there; he was in her hands.

"It's not much, mother," he said. "It was Baxter Dawes."

"Tell me where it hurts you," she said quietly.

"I don't know—my shoulder. Say it was a bicycle accident mother."

He could not move his arm. Presently Minnie, the little servant, came upstairs with some tea.

"Your mother's nearly frightened me out of my wits—fainted away," she said.

He felt he could not bear it. His mother nursed him; he told her about it.

"And now I should have done with them all," she said quietly.

"I will, mother."

She covered him up.

"And don't think about it," she said—"only try to go to sleep. The doctor won't be here till eleven."

He had a dislocated shoulder, and the second day acute bronchitis set in. His mother was pale as death now, and very thin. She would sit and look at him, then away into space. There was something between them that neither dared mention. Clara came to see him. Afterwards he said to his mother:

"She makes me tired, mother."

"Yes; I wish she wouldn't come," Mrs. Morel replied.

Another day Miriam came, but she seemed almost like a stranger to him.

"You know, I don't care about them, mother," he said.

"I'm afraid you don't, my son," she replied sadly.

It was given out everywhere that it was a bicycle accident. Soon he was able to go to work again, but now there was a constant sickness and gnawing at his heart. He went to Clara, but there seemed, as it were, nobody there. He could not work. He and his mother seemed almost to avoid each other. There was some secret between them which they could not bear. He was not aware of it. He only knew that his life seemed unbalanced, as if it were going to smash into pieces.

Clara did not know what was the matter with him. She realized that he seemed unaware of her. Even when he came to her he seemed unaware of her; also he was somewhere else. She felt she was clutching for him, and he was somewhere else. It tortured her, and so she tortured him. For a month at a time she kept him at arm's length. He almost hated her, and was driven to her in spite of himself. He went mostly into the company of men, was always at the George or the White Horse. His mother was ill, distant, quiet, shadowy. He was terrified of something; he dared not look at her. Her eyes seemed to grow darker, her face more waxen; still she dragged about at her work.

At Whitsuntide he said he would go to Blackpool for four days with his friend Newton. The latter was a big, jolly fellow, with a touch of the bounder about him. Paul said his mother must go to Sheffield to stay a week with Annie, who lived there. Perhaps the change would do her good. Mrs. Morel was attending a woman's doctor in Nottingham. He said her heart and her digestion were wrong. She consented to go to Sheffield, though she did not want to; but now she would do everything her son wished of her. Paul said he would come for her on the fifth day, and stay also in Sheffield till the holiday was up. It was agreed.

The two young men set off gaily for Blackpool. Mrs. Morel was quite lively as Paul kissed her and left her. Once at the station, he forgot everything. Four days were clear—not an anxiety, not a thought. The two young men simply enjoyed themselves. Paul was like another man. None of himself remained—no Clara, no Miriam, no mother that fretted him. He wrote to them all, and long letters to his mother; but they were jolly letters that made her laugh. He was having a good time, as young fellows will in a place like Blackpool. And underneath it all was a shadow for her.

Paul was very gay, excited at the thought of staying with his mother in Sheffield. Newton was to spend the day with them. Their train was late. Joking, laughing, with their pipes between their teeth, the young men swung their bags on to the tramcar. Paul had bought his mother a little collar of real lace that he wanted to see her wear, so that he could tease her about it.

Annie lived in a nice house, and had a little maid. Paul ran gaily up the steps. He expected his mother laughing in the hall, but it was Annie who opened to him. She seemed distant to him. He stood a second in dismay. Annie let him kiss her cheek.

"Is my mother ill?" he said.

"Yes; she's not very well. Don't upset her."

"Is she in bed?"

"Yes."

And then the queer feeling went over him, as if all the sunshine had gone out of him, and it was all shadow. He dropped the bag and ran upstairs. Hesitating, he opened the door. His mother sat up in bed, wearing a dressing gown of old rose color. She looked at him almost as if she were ashamed of herself, pleading to him, humble. He saw the ashy look about her.

"Mother!" he said.

"I thought you were never coming," she answered gaily.

But he only fell on his knees at the bedside, and buried his face in the bedclothes, crying in agony, and saying:

"Mother—mother—mother!"

She stroked his hair slowly with her thin hand.

"Don't cry," she said. "Don't cry—it's nothing."

But he felt as if his blood was melting into tears, and he cried in terror and pain.

"Don't—don't cry," his mother faltered.

Slowly she stroked his hair. Shocked out of himself, he cried, and the tears hurt in every fiber of his body. Suddenly he stopped, but he dared not lift his face out of the bedclothes.

"You *are* late. Where have you been?" his mother asked.

"The train was late," he replied, muffled in the sheet.

"Yes; that miserable Central! Is Newton come?"

"Yes."

"I'm sure you must be hungry, and they've kept dinner waiting."

With a wrench he looked up at her.

"What is it, mother?" he asked brutally.

She averted her eyes as she answered:

"Only a bit of a tumor, my boy. You needn't trouble. It's been there—the lump has—a long time."

Up came the tears again. His mind was clear and hard, but his body was crying.

"Where?" he said.

She put her hand on her side.

"Here. But you know they can sweal a tumor away."

He stood feeling dazed and helpless, like a child. He thought perhaps it was as she said. Yes; he reassured himself it was so. But all the while his blood and his body knew definitely what it was. He sat down on the bed, and took her hand. She had never had but the one ring—her wedding ring.

"When were you poorly?" he asked.

"It was yesterday it began," she answered submissively.

"Pains!"

"Yes; but not more than I've often had at home. I believe Dr. Ansell is an alarmist."

"You ought not to have traveled alone," he said, to himself more than to her.

"As if that had anything to do with it!" she answered quickly.

They were silent for a while.

"Now go and have your dinner," she said. "You *must* be hungry."

"Have you had yours?"

"Yes; a beautiful sole I had. Annie *is* good to me."

They talked a little while, then he went downstairs. He was very white and strained. Newton sat in miserable sympathy.

After dinner he went into the scullery to help Annie to wash up. The little maid had gone on an errand.

"Is it really a tumor?" he asked.

Annie began to cry again.

"The pain she had yesterday—I never saw anybody suffer like it!" she cried. "Leonard ran like a madman for Dr. Ansell, and when she'd got to bed she said to me: 'Annie, look at this lump on my side. I wonder what it is?' And there I looked, and I thought I should have dropped. Paul, as true as I'm here, it's a lump as big as my double fist. I said: 'Good gracious, mother, whenever did that come?' 'Why, child,' she said, 'it's been there a long time.' I thought I should have died, our Paul, I did. She's been having these pains for months at home, and nobody looking after her."

The tears came to his eyes, then dried suddenly.

"But she's been attending the doctor in Nottingham—and she never told me," he said.

"If I'd have been at home," said Annie, "I should have seen for myself."

He felt like a man walking in unrealities. In the afternoon he went to see the doctor. The latter was a shrewd, lovable man.

"But what is it?" he said.

The doctor looked at the young man, then knitted his fingers.

"It may be a large tumor which has formed in the membrane," he said slowly, "and which we *may* be able to make go away."

"Can't you operate?" asked Paul.

"Not there," replied the doctor.

"Are you sure?"

"*Quite*!"

Paul meditated a while.

"Are you sure it's a tumor?" he asked. "Why did Dr. Jameson in Nottingham never find out anything about it? She's been going to him for weeks, and he's treated her for heart and indigestion."

"Mrs. Morel never told Dr. Jameson about the lump," said the doctor.

"And do you *know* it's a tumor?"

"No, I am not sure."

"What else *might* it be? You asked my sister if there was cancer in the family. Might it be cancer?"

"I don't know."

"And what shall you do?"

"I should like an examination, with Dr. Jameson."

"Then have one."

"You must arrange about that. His fee wouldn't be less than ten guineas to come here from Nottingham."

"When would you like him to come?"

"I will call in this evening, and we will talk it over."

Paul went away, biting his lip.

His mother could come downstairs for tea, the doctor said. Her son went upstairs to help her. She wore the old rose dressing gown that Leonard had given Annie, and, with a little color in her face, was quite young again.

"But you look quite pretty in that," he said.

"Yes; they make me so fine, I hardly know myself," she answered.

But when she stood up to walk, the color went. Paul helped her, half carrying her. At the top of the stairs she was gone. He lifted her up and carried her quickly downstairs; laid her on the couch. She was light and frail. Her face looked as if she were dead, with the blue lips shut tight. Her eyes opened—her blue, unfailing eyes—and she looked at him pleadingly, almost wanting him to forgive her. He held brandy to her lips, but her mouth would not open. All the time she watched him lovingly. She was only sorry for him. The tears ran down his face without ceasing, but not a muscle moved. He was intent on getting a little brandy between her lips. Soon she was able to swallow a teaspoonful. She lay back, so tired. The tears continued to run down his face.

"But," she panted, "it'll go off. Don't cry!"

"I'm not doing," he said.

After a while she was better again. He was kneeling beside the couch. They looked into each other's eyes.

"I don't want you to make a trouble of it," she said.

"No, mother. You'll have to be quite still, and then you'll get better soon."

But he was white to the lips, and their eyes as they looked at each other understood. Her eyes were so blue—such a wonderful forget-me-not blue! He felt if only they had been of a different color he could have borne it better. His heart seemed to be ripping slowly in his breast. He kneeled there, holding her hand, and neither said anything. Then Annie came in.

"Are you all right?" she murmured timidly to her mother.

"Of course," said Mrs. Morel.

Paul sat down and told her about Blackpool. She was curious.

A day or two after, he went to see Dr. Jameson in Nottingham, to arrange for a consultation. Paul had practically no money in the world. But he could borrow.

His mother had been used to go to the public consultation on Saturday morning, when she could see the doctor for only a nominal sum. Her son went on the same day. The waiting room was full of poor women, who sat patiently on a bench around the wall. Paul thought of his mother, in her little black costume, sitting waiting likewise. The doctor was late. The women all looked rather frightened. Paul asked the nurse in attendance if he could see the doctor immediately he came. It was arranged so. The women sitting patiently round the walls of the room eyed the young man curiously.

At last the doctor came. He was about forty, good looking, brown-skinned. His wife had died, and he, who had loved her, had specialized on women's ailments. Paul told his name and his mother's. The doctor did not remember.

"Number forty-six M.," said the nurse; and the doctor looked up the case in his book.

"There is a big lump that may be a tumor," said Paul. "But Dr. Ansell was going to write you a letter."

"Ah, yes!" replied the doctor, drawing the letter from his pocket. He was very friendly, affable, busy, kind. He would come to Sheffield the next day.

"What is your father?" he asked.

"He is a coal miner," replied Paul.

"Not very well off, I suppose?"

"This—I see after this," said Paul.

"And you?" smiled the doctor.

"I am a clerk in Jordan's Appliance Factory."

The doctor smiled at him.

"Er—to go to Sheffield!" he said, putting the tips of his fingers together, and smiling with his eyes. "Eight guineas?"

"Thank you!" said Paul, flushing and rising. "And you'll come tomorrow?"

"Tomorrow—Sunday? Yes! Can you tell me about what time there is a train in the afternoon?"

"There is a Central gets in at four-fifteen."

"And will there be any way of getting up to the house? Shall I have to walk?" The doctor smiled.

"There is the tram," said Paul; "the Western Park tram."

The doctor made a note of it.

"Thank you!" he said, and shook hands.

Then Paul went on home to see his father, who was left in the charge of Minnie. Walter Morel was getting very gray now. Paul found him digging in the garden. He had written him a letter. He shook hands with his father.

"Hello, son! Tha has landed, then?" said the father.

"Yes," replied the son. "But I'm going back tonight."

"Are ter, beguy!" exclaimed the collier. "An' has ter eaten owt?"

"No."

"That's just like me," said Morel. "Come thy ways in."

The father was afraid of the mention of his wife. The two went indoors. Paul ate in silence; his father, with earthy hands, and sleeves rolled up, sat in the armchair opposite and looked at him.

"Well, an' how is she?" asked the miner at length, in a little voice.

"She can sit up; she can be carried down for tea," said Paul.

"That's a blessin'!" exclaimed Morel. "I hope we s'll soon be havin' her whoam, then. An' what's that Nottingham doctor say?"

"He's going tomorrow to have an examination of her."

"Is he, beguy! That's a tidy penny, I'm thinkin'!"

"Eight guineas."

"Eight guineas!" The miner spoke breathlessly. "Well, we mun find it from somewhere."

"I can pay that," said Paul.

There was a silence between them for some time.

"She says she hopes you're getting on all right with Minnie," Paul said.

"Yes, I'm all right, an' I wish as she was," answered Morel. "But Minnie's a good little wench, bless 'er heart!" He sat looking dismal.

"I s'll have to be going at half-past three," said Paul.

"It's a trapse for thee, lad! Eight guineas! An' when dost think she'll be able to get as far as this?"

"We must see what the doctors say tomorrow," Paul said.

Morel sighed deeply. The house seemed strangely empty and Paul thought his father looked lost, forlorn, and old.

"You'll have to go and see her next week, father," he said.

"I hope she'll be a-whoam by that time," said Morel.

"If she's not," said Paul, "then you must come."

"I dunno wheer I s'll find th' money," said Morel.

"And I'll write to you what the doctor says," said Paul.

"But tha writes i' such a fashion, I canna ma'e it out," said Morel.

"Well, I'll write plain."

It was no good asking Morel to answer, for he could scarcely do more than write his own name.

The doctor came. Leonard felt it his duty to meet him with a cab. The examination did not take long. Annie, Arthur, Paul, and Leonard were waiting in the parlor anxiously. The doctors came down. Paul glanced at them. He had never had any hope, except when he had deceived himself.

"It *may* be a tumor; we must wait and see," said Dr. Jameson.

"And if it is," said Annie, "can you sweal it away?"

"Probably," said the doctor.

Paul put eight sovereigns and a half sovereign on the table. The doctor counted them, took a florin out of his purse, and put that down.

"Thank you!" he said. "I'm sorry Mrs. Morel is so ill. But we must see what we can do."

"There can't be an operation?" said Paul.

The doctor shook his head.

"No," he said; "and even if there could, her heart wouldn't stand it."

"Is her heart risky?" asked Paul.

"Yes; you must be careful with her."

"Very risky?"

"No—er—no, no! Just take care."

And the doctor was gone.

Then Paul carried his mother downstairs. She lay simply, like a child. But when he was on the stairs, she put her arms round his neck, clinging.

"I'm so frightened of these beastly stairs," she said.

And he was frightened, too. He would let Leonard do it another time. He felt he could not carry her.

"He thinks it's only a tumor!" cried Annie to her mother. "And he can sweal it away."

"I *knew* he could," protested Mrs. Morel scornfully.

She pretended not to notice that Paul had gone out of the room. He sat in the kitchen, smoking. Then he tried to brush some gray ash off his coat. He looked again. It was one of his mother's gray hairs. It was so long! He held it up, and it drifted into the chimney. He let go. The long gray hair floated and was gone in the blackness of the chimney.

The next day he kissed her before going back to work. It was very early in the morning, and they were alone.

"You won't fret, my boy!" she said.

"No, mother."

"No; it would be silly. And take care of yourself."

"Yes," he answered. Then, after a while: "And I shall come next Saturday, and shall I bring my father?"

"I suppose he wants to come," she replied. "At any rate, if he does you'll have to let him."

He kissed her again, and stroked the hair from her temples gently, tenderly, as if she were a lover.

"Shan't you be late?" she murmured.

"I'm going," he said, very low.

Still he sat a few minutes, stroking the brown and gray hair from her temples.

"And you won't be any worse, mother?"

"No, my son."

"You promise me?"

"Yes; I won't be any worse."

He kissed her, held her in his arms for a moment, and was gone. In the early sunny morning he ran to the station, crying all the way; he did not know what for. And her blue eyes were wide and staring as she thought of him.

In the afternoon he went a walk with Clara. They sat in the little wood where bluebells were standing. He took her hand.

"You'll see," he said to Clara, "she'll never be better."

"Oh, you don't know!" replied the other.

"I do," he said.

She caught him impulsively to her breast.

"Try and forget it, dear," she said; "try and forget it."

"I will," he answered.

Her breast was there, warm for him; her hands were in his hair. It was comforting, and he held his arms round her. But he did not forget. He only talked to Clara of something else. And it was always so. When she felt it coming, the agony, she cried to him:

"Don't think of it, Paul! Don't think of it, my darling!"

And she pressed him to her breast, rocked him, soothed him like a child. So he put the trouble aside for her sake, to take it up again immediately he was alone. All the time, as he went about, he cried mechanically. His mind and hands were busy. He cried, he did not know why. It was his blood weeping. He was just as much alone whether he was with Clara or with the men in the White Horse. Just himself and this pressure inside him, that was all that existed. He read sometimes. He had to keep his mind occupied. And Clara was a way of occupying his mind.

On the Saturday Walter Morel went to Sheffield. He was a forlorn figure, looking rather as if nobody owned him. Paul ran upstairs.

"My father's come," he said, kissing his mother.

"Has he?" she answered weariedly.

The old collier came rather frightened into the bedroom.

"How dun I find thee, lass?" he said, going forward and kissing her in a hasty, timid fashion.

"Well, I'm middlin'," she replied.

"I see tha art," he said. He stood looking down on her. Then he wiped his eyes with his handkerchief. Helpless, and as if nobody owned him, he looked.

"Have you gone on all right?" asked the wife, rather wearily, as if it were an effort to talk to him.

"Yis," he answered. " 'Er's a bit behint-hand now and again, as yer might expect."

"Does she have your dinner ready?" asked Mrs. Morel.

"Well, I've 'ad to shout at 'er once or twice," he said.

"And you *must* shout at her if she's not ready. She *will* leave things to the last minute."

She gave him a few instructions. He sat looking at her as if she were almost a stranger to him, before whom he was awkward and humble, and also as if he had lost his presence of mind, and wanted to run. This feeling that he wanted to run away, that he was on thorns to be gone from so trying a situation, and yet must linger because it looked better, made his presence so trying. He put up his eyebrows for misery, and clenched his fists on his knees, feeling so awkward in presence of a big trouble.

Mrs. Morel did not change much. She stayed in Sheffield for two months. If anything, at the end she was rather worse. But she wanted to go home. Annie had her children. Mrs. Morel wanted to go home. So they got a motorcar from Nottingham—for she was too ill to go by train—and she was driven through the sunshine. It was just August; everything was bright and warm. Under the blue sky they could all see she was dying. Yet she was jollier than she had been for weeks. They all laughed and talked.

"Annie," she exclaimed, "I saw a lizard dart on that rock!"

Her eyes were so quick; she was still so full of life.

Morel knew she was coming. He had the front door open. Everybody was on tiptoe. Half the street turned out. They heard the sound of the great motor car. Mrs. Morel, smiling, drove home down the street.

"And just look at them all come out to see me!" she said. "But there, I suppose I should have done the same. How do you do, Mrs. Matthews? How are you, Mrs. Harrison?"

They none of them could hear, but they saw her smile and nod. And they all saw death on her face, they said. It was a great event in the street.

Morel wanted to carry her indoors, but he was too old. Arthur took her as if she were a child. They had set her a big, deep chair by the hearth where her rocking chair used to stand. When she was unwrapped and seated, and had drunk a little brandy, she looked round the room.

"Don't think I didn't like your house, Annie," she said; "but it's nice to be in my own home again."

And Morel answered huskily:

"It is, lass, it is."

And Minnie, the little quaint maid, said:

"An' we glad t' 'ave yer."

There was a lovely yellow ravel of sunflowers in the garden. She looked out of the window.

"There are my sunflowers!" she said.

❖ 14 ❖

The Release

"By the way," said Dr. Ansell one evening when Morel was in Sheffield, "we've got a man in the fever hospital here who comes from Nottingham—Dawes. He doesn't seem to have many belongings in this world."

"Baxter Dawes!" Paul exclaimed.

"That's the man—has been a fine fellow, physically, I should think. Been in a bit of a mess lately. You know him?"

"He used to work at the place where I am."

"Did he? Do you know anything about him? He's just sulking, or he'd be a lot better than he is by now."

"I don't know anything of his home circumstances, except that he's separated from his wife and has been a bit down, I believe. But tell him about me, will you? Tell him I'll come and see him."

The next time Morel saw the doctor he said:

"And what about Dawes?"

"I said to him," answered the other, " 'Do you know a man from Nottingham named Morel?' and he looked at me as if he'd jump at my throat. So I said, 'I see you know the name; it's Paul Morel.' Then I told him about your saying you would go and see him. 'What does he want?' he said, as if you were a policeman."

"And did he say he would see me?" asked Paul.

"He wouldn't say anything—good, bad, or indifferent," replied the doctor.

"Why not?"

"That's what I want to know. There he lies and sulks, day in, day out. Can't get a word of information out of him."

"Do you think I might go?" asked Paul.

"You might."

There was a feeling of connection between the rival men, more than ever since they had fought. In a way Morel felt guilty towards the other, and more or less responsible. And being in such a state of soul himself, he felt an almost painful nearness to Dawes, who was suffering and despairing, too. Besides, they had met in a naked extremity of hate, and it was a bond. At any rate, the elemental man in each had met.

He went down to the isolation hospital, with Dr. Ansell's card. The sister, a healthy young Irishwoman, led him down the ward.

"A visitor to see you, Jim Crow," she said.

Dawes turned over suddenly with a startled grunt.

"Eh?"

"Caw!" she mocked. "He can only say 'Caw!' I have brought you a gentleman to see you. Now say 'Thank you,' and show some manners."

Dawes looked swiftly with his dark, startled eyes beyond the sister at Paul. His look was full of fear, mistrust, hate, and misery. Morel met the swift, dark eyes, and hesitated. The two men were afraid of the naked selves they had been.

"Dr. Ansell told me you were here," said Morel, holding out his hand.

Dawes mechanically shook hands.

"So I thought I'd come in," continued Paul.

There was no answer. Dawes lay staring at the opposite wall.

"Say 'Caw!' " mocked the nurse. "Say 'Caw!' Jim Crow."

"He is getting on all right?" said Paul to her.

"Oh yes! He lies and imagines he's going to die," said the nurse, "and it frightens every word out of his mouth."

"And you *must* have somebody to talk to," laughed Morel.

"That's it!" laughed the nurse. "Only two old men and a boy who always cries. It *is* hard lines! Here am I dying to hear Jim Crow's voice, and nothing but an odd 'Caw!' will he give!"

"So rough on you!" said Morel.

"Isn't it?" said the nurse.

"I suppose I am a godsend," he laughed.

"Oh, dropped straight from heaven!" laughed the nurse.

Presently she left the two men alone. Dawes was thinner, and handsome again, but life seemed low in him. As the doctor said, he was lying sulking, and would not move forward towards convalescence. He seemed to grudge every beat of his heart.

"Have you had a bad time?" asked Paul.

Suddenly again Dawes looked at him.

"What are you doin' in Sheffield?" he asked.

"My mother was taken ill at my sister's in Thurston Street. What are you doing here?"

There was no answer.

"How long have you been in?" Morel asked.

"I couldn't say for sure," Dawes answered grudgingly.

He lay staring across at the wall opposite, as if trying to believe Morel was not there. Paul felt his heart go hard and angry.

"Dr. Ansell told me you were here," he said coldly.

The other man did not answer.

"Typhoid's pretty bad, I know," Morel persisted.

Suddenly Dawes said:

"What did you come for?"

"Because Dr. Ansell said you didn't know anybody here. Do you?"

"I know nobody nowhere," said Dawes.

"Well," said Paul, "it's because you don't choose to, then."

There was another silence.

"We s'll be taking my mother home as soon as we can," said Paul.

"What's a-matter with her?" asked Dawes, with a sick man's interest in illness.

"She's got a cancer."

There was another silence.

"But we want to get her home," said Paul. "We s'll have to get a motorcar."

Dawes lay thinking.

"Why don't you ask Thomas Jordan to lend you his?" said Dawes.

"It's not big enough," Morel answered.

Dawes blinked his dark eyes as he lay thinking.

"Then ask Jack Pilkington; he'd lend it you. You know him."

"I think I s'll hire one," said Paul.

"You're a fool if you do," said Dawes.

The sick man was gaunt and handsome again. Paul was sorry for him because his eyes looked so tired.

"Did you get a job here?" he asked.

"I was only here a day or two before I was taken bad," Dawes replied.

"You want to get in a convalescent home," said Paul.

The other's face clouded again.

"I'm goin' in no convalescent home," he said.

"My father's been in the one at Seathorpe, an' he liked it. Dr. Ansell would get you a recommend."

Dawes lay thinking. It was evident he dared not face the world again.

"The seaside would be all right just now," Morel said. "Sun on those sand hills, and the waves not far out."

The other did not answer.

"By Gad!" Paul concluded, too miserable to bother much, "it's all right when you know you're going to walk again, and swim!"

Dawes glanced at him quickly. The man's dark eyes were afraid to meet any other eyes in the world. But the real misery and helplessness in Paul's tone gave him a feeling of relief.

"Is she far gone?" he asked.

"She's going like wax," Paul answered; "but cheerful—lively!"

He bit his lip. After a minute he rose:

"Well, I'll be going," he said. "I'll leave you this half-crown."

"I don't want it," Dawes muttered.

Morel did not answer, but left the coin on the table.

"Well," he said, "I'll try and run in when I'm back in Sheffield. Happen you might like to see my brother-in-law? He works in Pyecrofts."

"I don't know him," said Dawes.

"He's all right. Should I tell him to come? He might bring you some papers to look at."

The other man did not answer. Paul went. The strong emotion that Dawes aroused in him, repressed, made him shiver.

He did not tell his mother, but next day he spoke to Clara about this interview. It was in the dinner-hour. The two did not often go out together now, but this day he asked her to go with him to the Castle grounds. There they sat while the scarlet geraniums and the yellow calceolarias blazed in the sunlight. She was now always rather protective, and rather resentful towards him.

"Did you know Baxter was in Sheffield Hospital with typhoid?" he asked.

She looked at him with startled gray eyes, and her face went pale.

"No," she said, frightened.

"He's getting better. I went to see him yesterday—the doctor told me."

Clara seemed stricken by the news.

"Is he very bad?" she asked guiltily.

"He has been. He's mending now."

"What did he say to you?"

"Oh, nothing! He seems to be sulking."

There was a distance between the two of them. He gave her more information.

She went about shut up and silent. The next time they took a walk together, she disengaged herself from his arm, and walked at a distance from him. He was wanting her comfort badly.

"Won't you be nice with me?" he asked.

She did not answer.

"What's the matter?" he said, putting his arm across her shoulder.

"Don't!" she said, disengaging herself.

He left her alone, and returned to his own brooding.

"Is it Baxter that upsets you?" he asked at length.

"I *have* been *vile* to him!" she said.

"I've said many a time you haven't treated him well," he replied.

And there was a hostility between them. Each pursued his own train of thought.

"I've treated him—no, I've treated him badly," she said. "And now you treat *me* badly. It serves me right."

"How do I treat you badly?" he said.

"It serves me right," she repeated. "I never considered him worth having, and now you don't consider *me*. But it serves me right. He loved me a thousand times better than you ever did."

"He didn't!" protested Paul.

"He did! At any rate, he did respect me, and that's what you don't do."

"It looked as if he respected you!" he said.

"He did! And I *made* him horrid—I know I did! You've taught me that. And he loved me a thousand times better than ever you do."

"All right," said Paul.

He only wanted to be left alone now. He had his own trouble, which was almost too much to bear. Clara only tormented him and made him tired. He was not sorry when he left her.

She went on the first opportunity to Sheffield to see her husband. The meeting was not a success. But she left him roses and fruit and money. She wanted to make restitution. It was not that she loved him. As she looked at him lying there her heart did not warm with love. Only she wanted to humble herself to him, to kneel before him. She wanted now to be self-sacrificial. After all, she had failed to make Morel really love her. She was morally frightened. She wanted to do penance. So she kneeled to Dawes, and it gave him a subtle pleasure. But the distance between them was still very great—too great. It frightened the man. It almost pleased the woman. She liked to feel she was serving him across an insuperable distance. She was proud now.

Morel went to see Dawes once or twice. There was a sort of friendship between the two men, who were all the while deadly rivals. But they never mentioned the woman who was between them.

Mrs. Morel got gradually worse. At first they used to carry her downstairs, sometimes even into the garden. She sat propped in her chair, smiling, and so pretty. The gold wedding ring shone on her white hand; her hair was carefully brushed. And she watched the tangled sunflowers, dying, the chrysanthemums coming out, and the dahlias.

Paul and she were afraid of each other. He knew, and she knew, that she was dying. But they kept up a pretense of cheerfulness. Every morning, when he got up, he went into her room in his pyjamas.

"Did you sleep, my dear?" he asked.

"Yes," she answered.

"Not very well?"

"Well, yes!"

Then he knew she had lain awake. He saw her hand under the bedclothes, pressing the place on her side where the pain was.

"Has it been bad?" he asked.

"No. It hurt a bit, but nothing to mention."

And she sniffed in her old scornful way. As she lay she looked like a girl. And all the while her blue eyes watched him. But there were the dark pain-circles beneath that made him ache again.

"It's a sunny day," he said.

"It's a beautiful day."

"Do you think you'll be carried down?"

"I shall see."

Then he went away to get her breakfast. All day long he was conscious of nothing but her. It was a long ache that made him feverish. Then, when he got home in the early evening, he glanced through the kitchen window. She was not there; she had not got up.

He ran straight upstairs and kissed her. He was almost afraid to ask:

"Didn't you get up, Pigeon?"

"No," she said. "It was that morphia; it made me tired."

"I think he gives you too much," he said.

"I think he does," she answered.

He sat down by the bed, miserably. She had a way of curling and lying on her side, like a child. The gray and brown hair was loose over her ear.

"Doesn't it tickle you?" he said, gently putting it back.

"It does," she replied.

His face was near hers. Her blue eyes smiled straight into his, like a girl's—warm, laughing with tender love. It made him pant with terror, agony, and love.

"You want your hair doing in a plait," he said. "Lie still."

And going behind her, he carefully loosened her hair, brushed it out. It was like fine long silk of brown and gray. Her head was snuggled between her shoulders. As he lightly brushed and plaited her hair, he bit his lip and felt dazed. It all seemed unreal, he could not understand it.

At night he often worked in her room, looking up from time to time. And so often he found her blue eyes fixed on him. And when their eyes met, she smiled. He worked away again, mechanically, producing good stuff without knowing what he was doing.

Sometimes he came in, very pale and still, with watchful, sudden eyes, like a man who is drunk almost to death. They were both afraid of the veils that were ripping between them.

Then she pretended to be better, chattered to him gaily, made a great fuss over some scraps of news. For they had both come to the condition when they had to make much of the trifles, lest they should give in to the big thing, and their human independence would go smash. They were afraid, so they made light of things and were gay.

Sometimes as she lay he knew she was thinking of the past. Her mouth gradually shut hard in a line. She was holding herself rigid, so that she might die without ever uttering the great cry that was tearing from her. He never forgot that hard, utterly lonely and stubborn clenching of her mouth, which persisted for weeks. Sometimes, when it was lighter, she talked about her husband. Now she hated him. She did not forgive him. She could not bear him to be in the room. And a few things, the things that had been most bitter to her, came up again so strongly that they broke from her, and she told her son.

He felt as if his life were being destroyed, piece by piece, within him. Often the tears came suddenly. He ran to the station, the teardrops falling on the pavement. Often he could not go on with his work. The pen stopped writing. He sat staring, quite unconscious. And when he came round again he felt sick, and trembled in his limbs. He never questioned what it was. His mind did not try to analyze or understand. He merely submitted, and kept his eyes shut; let the thing go over him.

His mother did the same. She thought of the pain, of the morphia, of the next day; hardly ever of the death. That was coming, she knew. She had to submit to it. But she would never entreat it or make friends with it. Blind, with her face shut hard and blind, she was pushed towards the door. The days passed, the weeks, the months.

Sometimes, in the sunny afternoons, she seemed almost happy.

"I try to think of the nice times—when we went to Mablethorpe, and Robin Hood's Bay, and Shanklin," she said. "After all, not everybody has seen those beautiful places. And wasn't it beautiful! I try to think of that, not of the other things."

Then, again, for a whole evening she spoke not a word; neither did he. They were together, rigid, stubborn, silent. He went into his room at last to go to bed, and leaned against the doorway as if paralyzed, unable to go any farther. His consciousness went. A furious storm, he knew not what, seemed to ravage inside him. He stood leaning there, submitting, never questioning.

In the morning they were both normal again, though her face was gray with the morphia, and her body felt like ash. But they were bright again, nevertheless. Often, especially if Annie or Arthur were at home, he neglected her. He did not see much of Clara. Usually he was with men. He was quick and active and lively; but when his friends saw him go white to the gills, his eyes dark and glittering, they had a certain mistrust of him. Sometimes he went with Clara, but she was almost cold to him.

"Take me!" he said simply.

Occasionally she would. But she was afraid. When he had her then, there was something in it that made her shrink away from him—something unnatural. She grew to dread him. He was so quiet, yet so strange. She was afraid of the man who was not there with her, whom she could feel behind this make-belief lover; somebody sinister, that filled her with horror. She began to have a kind of horror of him. It was almost as if he were a criminal. He wanted her—he had her—and it made her feel as if death itself had her in its grip. She lay in horror. There was no man there loving her. She almost hated him. Then came little bouts of tenderness. But she dared not pity him.

Dawes had come to Colonel Seely's Home near Nottingham. There Paul visited him sometimes, Clara very occasionally. Between the two men the friendship had developed peculiarly. Dawes, who mended very slowly and seemed very feeble, seemed to leave himself in the hands of Morel.

In the beginning of November Clara reminded Paul that it was her birthday.

"I'd nearly forgotten," he said.

"I thought quite," she replied.

"No. Shall we go to the seaside for the weekend?"

They went. It was cold and rather dismal. She waited for him to be warm and tender with her, instead of which he seemed hardly aware of her. He sat in the railway carriage, looking out, and was startled when she spoke to him. He was not definitely thinking. Things seemed as if they did not exist. She went across to him.

"What is it, dear?" she asked.

"Nothing!" he said. "Don't those windmill sails look monotonous?"

He sat holding her hand. He could not talk nor think. It was a comfort, however, to sit holding her hand. She was dissatisfied and miserable. He was not with her; she was nothing.

And in the evening they sat among the sand hills, looking at the black, heavy sea.

"She will never give in, " he said quietly.

Clara's heart sank.

"No," she replied.

"There are different ways of dying. My father's people are frightened, and have to be hauled out of life into death like cattle into a slaughterhouse, pulled by the neck; but my mother's people are pushed from behind, inch by inch. They are stubborn people, and won't die."

"Yes," said Clara.

"And she won't die. She can't. Mr. Renshaw, the parson, was in the other day. 'Think!' he said to her; 'you will have your mother and father, and your sisters, and your son, in the Other Land.' And she said: 'I have done without them for a long time, and *can* do without them now. It is the living I want, not the dead.' She wants to live even now."

"Oh, how horrible!" said Clara, too frightened to speak.

"And she looks at me, and she wants to stay with me," he went on monotonously. "She's got such a will, it seems as if she would never go—never!"

"Don't think of it!" cried Clara.

"And she was religious—she is religious now—but it is no good. She simply won't give in. And do you know, I said to her on Thursday, 'Mother, if I had to die, I'd die. I'd *will* to die.' And she said to me, sharp: 'Do you think I haven't? Do you think you can die when you like?' "

His voice ceased. He did not cry, only went on speaking monotonously. Clara wanted to run. She looked round. There was the black, re-echoing shore, the dark sky down on her. She got up terrified. She wanted to be where there was light, where there were other people. She wanted to be away from him. He sat with his head dropped, not moving a muscle.

"And I don't want her to eat," he said, "and she knows it. When I ask her, 'Shall you have anything?' she's almost afraid to say 'Yes' 'I'll have a cup of Benger's,' she says 'It'll only keep your strength up,' I said to her. 'Yes'—and she almost cried—'but there's such a gnawing when I eat nothing, I can't bear it.' So I went and made her the food. It's the cancer that gnaws like that at her. I wish she'd die!"

"Come!" said Clara roughly. "I'm going."

He followed her down the darkness of the sands. He did not come to her. He seemed scarcely aware of her existence. And she was afraid of him, and disliked him.

In the same acute daze they went back to Nottingham. He was always busy, always doing something, always going from one to the other of his friends.

On the Monday he went to see Baxter Dawes. Listless and pale, the man rose to greet the other, clinging to his chair as he held out his hand.

"You shouldn't get up," said Paul.

Dawes sat down heavily, eyeing Morel with a sort of suspicion.

"Don't you waste your time on me," he said, "if you've owt better to do."

"I wanted to come," said Paul. "Here! I brought you some sweets."

The invalid put them aside.

"It's not been much of a weekend," said Morel.

"How's your mother?" asked the other.

"Hardly any different."

"I thought she was perhaps worse, being as you didn't come on Sunday."

"I was at Skegness," said Paul. "I wanted a change."

The other looked at him with dark eyes. He seemed to be waiting, not quite daring to ask, trusting to be told.

"I went with Clara," said Paul.

"I knew as much," said Dawes quietly.

"It was an old promise," said Paul.

"You have it your own way," said Dawes.

This was the first time Clara had been definitely mentioned between them.

"Nay," said Morel slowly; "she's tired of me."

Again Dawes looked at him.

"Since August she's been getting tired of me," Morel repeated.

The two men were very quiet together. Paul suggested a game of draughts. They played in silence.

"I s'll go abroad when my mother's dead," said Paul.

"Abroad!" repeated Dawes.

"Yes; I don't care what I do."

They continued the game. Dawes was winning.

"I s'll have to begin a new start of some sort," said Paul; "and you as well, I suppose."

He took one of Dawes' pieces.

"I dunno where, " said the other.

"Things have to happen, " Morel said. "It's no good doing anything—at least—no, I don't know. Give me some toffee."

The two men ate sweets, and began another game of draughts.

"What made that scar on your mouth?" asked Dawes.

Paul put his hand hastily to his lips, and looked over the garden.

"I had a bicycle accident," he said.

Dawes' hand trembled as he moved the piece.

"You shouldn't ha' laughed at me," he said very low.

"When?"

"That night on Woodborough Road, when you and her passed me—you with your hand on her shoulder."

"I never laughed at you," said Paul.

Dawes kept his fingers on the draught piece.

"I never knew you were there till the very second when you passed," said Morel.

"It was that as did me," he said, very low.

Paul took another sweet.

"I never laughed," he said, "except as I'm always laughing."

They finished the game.

That night Morel walked home from Nottingham, in order to have something to do. The furnaces flared in a red blotch over Bulwell; the black clouds were like a low ceiling. As he went along the ten miles of highroad, he felt as if he were walking out of life, between the black levels of the sky and the earth. But at the end was only the sickroom. If he walked and walked for ever, there was only that place to come to.

He was not tired when he got near home, or he did not know it. Across the field he could see the red firelight leaping in her bedroom window.

"When she's dead," he said to himself, "that fire will go out."

He took off his boots quietly and crept upstairs. His mother's door was wide open, because she slept alone still. The red firelight dashed its glow on the landing. Soft as a shadow, he peeped in her doorway.

"Paul!" she murmured.

His heart seemed to break again. He went in and sat by the bed.

"How late you are!" she murmured.

"Not very," he said.

"Why, what time is it?" The murmur came plaintive and helpless.

"It's only just gone eleven."

That was not true; it was nearly one o'clock.

"Oh!" she said; "I thought it was later."

And he knew the unutterable misery of her nights that would not go.

"Can't you sleep, my pigeon?" he said.

"No, I can't," she wailed.

"Never mind, little!" he said crooning. "Never mind, my love. I'll stop with you half an hour, my pigeon; then perhaps it will be better."

And he sat by the bedside, slowly, rhythmically stroking her brows with his fingertips, stroking her eyes shut, soothing her, holding her fingers in his free hand. They could hear the sleepers' breathing in the other rooms.

"Now go to bed," she murmured, lying quite still under his fingers and his love.

"Will you sleep?" he asked.

"Yes, I think so."

"You feel better, my little, don't you?"

"Yes," she said, like a fretful, half-soothed child.

Still the days and the weeks went by. He hardly ever went to see Clara now. But he wandered restlessly from one person to another for some help, and there was none anywhere. Miriam had written to him tenderly. He went to see her. Her heart was very sore when she saw him, white, gaunt, with his eyes dark and bewildered. Her pity came up, hurting her till she could not bear it.

"How is she?" she asked.

"The same—the same!" he said. "The doctor says she can't last, but I know she will. She'll be here at Christmas."

Miriam shuddered. She drew him to her; she pressed him to her bosom; she kissed him and kissed him. He submitted, but it was torture. She could not kiss his agony. That remained alone and apart. She kissed his face, and roused his blood, while his soul was apart writhing with the agony of death. And she kissed him and fingered his body, till at last, feeling he would go mad, he got away from her. It was not that he wanted just then—not that. And she thought she had soothed him and done him good.

December came, and some snow. He stayed at home all the while now. They could not afford a nurse. Annie came to look after her mother; the parish nurse, whom they loved, came in morning and evening. Paul shared the nursing with Annie. Often, in the evenings, when friends were in the kitchen with them, they all laughed together and shook with laughter. It was reaction. Paul was so comical, Annie was so quaint. The whole party laughed till they cried, trying to subdue the sound. And Mrs. Morel, lying alone in the darkness, heard them, and among her bitterness was a feeling of relief.

Then Paul would go upstairs gingerly, guiltily, to see if she had heard.

"Shall I give you some milk?" he asked.

"A little," she replied plaintively.

And he would put some water with it, so that it should not nourish her. Yet he loved her more than his own life.

She had morphia every night, and her heart got fitful. Annie slept beside her. Paul would go in in the early morning, when his sister got up. His mother was wasted and almost ashen in the morning with the morphia. Darker and darker grew her eyes, all pupil, with the torture. In the mornings the weariness and ache were too much to bear. Yet she could not—would not—weep, or even complain much.

"You slept a bit later this morning, little one," he would say to her.

"Did I?" she answered, with fretful weariness.

"Yes; it's nearly eight o'clock."

He stood looking out of the window. The whole country was bleak and pallid under the snow. Then he felt her pulse. There was a strong stroke and a weak one, like a sound and its echo. That was supposed to betoken the end. She let him feel her wrist, knowing what he wanted.

Sometimes they looked in each other's eyes. Then they almost seemed to make an agreement. It was almost as if he were agreeing to die also. But she did not consent to die; she would not. Her body was wasted to a fragment of ash. Her eyes were dark and full of torture.

"Can't you give her something to put an end to it?" he asked the doctor at last.

But the doctor shook his head.

"She can't last many days now, Mr. Morel," he said.

Paul went indoors.

"I can't bear it much longer; we shall all go mad," said Annie.

The two sat down to breakfast.

"Go and sit with her while we have breakfast, Minnie," said Annie. But the girl was frightened.

Paul went through the country, through the woods, over the snow. He saw the marks of rabbits and birds in the white snow. He wandered miles and miles. A smoky red sunset came on slowly, painfully, lingering. He thought she would die that day. There was a donkey that came up to him over the snow by the, wood's edge, and put its head against him, and walked with him alongside. He put his arms round the donkey's neck, and stroked his cheeks against his ears.

His mother, silent, was still alive, with her hard mouth gripped grimly, her eyes of dark torture only living.

It was nearing Christmas; there was more snow. Annie and he felt as if they could go on no more. Still her dark eyes were alive. Morel, silent and frightened, obliterated himself. Sometimes he would go into the sickroom and look at her. Then he backed out, bewildered.

She kept her hold on life still. The miners had been out on strike, and returned a fortnight or so before Christmas. Minnie went upstairs with the feeding-cup. It was two days after the men had been in.

"Have the men been saying their hands are sore, Minnie?" she asked, in the faint, querulous voice that would not give in. Minnie stood surprised.

"Not as I know of, Mrs. Morel," she answered.

"But I'll bet they are sore," said the dying woman, as she moved her head with a sigh of weariness. "But, at any rate, there'll be something to buy in with this week."

Not a thing did she let slip.

"Your father's pit things will want well airing, Annie," she said, when the men were going back to work.

"Don't you bother about that, my dear," said Annie.

One night Annie and Paul were alone. Nurse was upstairs.

"She'll live over Christmas," said Annie. They were both full of horror.

"She won't," he replied grimly. "I s'll give her morphia."

"Which?" said Annie.

"All that came from Sheffield," said Paul.

"Ay—do!" said Annie.

The next day he was painting in the bedroom. She seemed to be asleep. He stepped softly backwards and forwards at his painting. Suddenly her small voice wailed:

"Don't walk about, Paul."

He looked round. Her eyes, like dark bubbles in her face, were looking at him.

"No, my dear," he said gently. Another fiber seemed to snap in his heart.

That evening he got all the morphia pills there were, and took them downstairs. Carefully he crushed them to powder.

"What are you doing?" said Annie.

"I s'll put 'en in her night milk."

Then they both laughed together like two conspiring children. On top of all their horror flickered this little sanity.

Nurse did not come that night to settle Mrs. Morel down. Paul went up with the hot milk in a feeding-cup. It was nine o'clock.

She was reared up in bed, and he put the feeding-cup between her lips that he would have died to save from any hurt. She took a sip, then put the spout of the cup away and looked at him with her dark, wondering eyes. He looked at her.

"Oh, it *is* bitter, Paul!" she said, making a little grimace.

"It's a new sleeping draught the doctor gave me for you," he said. "He thought it wouldn't leave you in such a state in the morning."

"And I hope it won't," she said, like a child.

She drank some more of the milk.

"But it *is* horrid!" she said.

He saw her frail fingers over the cup, her lips making little move.

"I know—I tasted it," he said. "But I'll give you some clean milk afterwards."

"I think so," she said, and she went on with the draught. She was obedient to him like a child. He wondered if she knew. He saw her poor wasted throat moving as she drank with difficulty. Then he ran downstairs for more milk. There were no grains in the bottom of the cup.

"Has she had it?" whispered Annie.

"Yes—and she said it was bitter."

"Oh!" laughed Annie, putting her under lip between her teeth.

"And I told her it was a new draught. Where's that milk?"

They both went upstairs.

"I wonder why nurse didn't come to settle me down?" complained the mother, like a child, wistfully.

"She said she was going to a concert, my love," replied Annie.

"Did she?"

They were silent a minute. Mrs. Morel gulped the little clean milk.

"Annie, that draught *was* horrid!" she said plaintively.

"Was it, my love? Well, never mind."

The mother sighed again with weariness. Her pulse was very irregular.

"Let *us* settle you down," said Annie. "Perhaps nurse will be so late."

"Ay," said the mother—"try."

They turned the clothes back. Paul saw his mother like a girl curled up in her flannel nightdress. Quickly they made one half the bed, moved her, made the other, straightened her nightgown over her small feet, and covered her up.

"There," said Paul, stroking her softly. "There!—now you'll sleep."

"Yes," she said. "I didn't think you could do the bed so nicely," she added, almost gaily. Then she curled up, with her cheek on her hand, her head snugged between her shoulder. Paul put the long thin plait of gray hair over her shoulder and kissed her.

"You'll sleep, my love," he said.

"Yes," she answered trustfully. "Good-night."

They put out the light, and it was still.

Morel was in bed. Nurse did not come. Annie and Paul came to look at her about eleven. She seemed to be sleeping as usual after her draught. Her mouth had come a bit open.

"Shall we sit up?" said Paul.

"I s'll lie with her as I always do," said Annie. "She might wake up."

"All right. And call me if you see any difference."

"Yes."

They lingered before the bedroom fire, feeling the night big and black and snowy outside, their two selves alone in the world. At last he went into the next room and went to bed.

He slept almost immediately, but kept waking every now and again. Then he went sound asleep. He started awake at Annie's whispered, "Paul, Paul!" He saw his sister in her white nightdress, with her long plait of hair down her back, standing in the darkness.

"Yes?" he whispered, sitting up.

"Come and look at her."

He slipped out of bed. A bud of gas was burning in the sick-chamber. His mother lay with her cheek on her hand, curled up as she had gone to sleep. But her mouth had fallen open, and she breathed with great, hoarse breaths, like snoring, and there were long intervals between.

"She's going!" he whispered.

"Yes," said Annie.

"How long has she been like it?"

"I only just woke up."

Annie huddled into the dressing gown, Paul wrapped himself in a brown blanket. It was three o'clock. He mended the fire. Then the two sat waiting. The great, snoring breath was taken—held awhile—then given back. There was a space—a long space. Then they started. The great, snoring breath was taken again. He bent close down and looked at her.

"Isn't it awful!" whispered Annie.

He nodded. They sat down again helplessly. Again came the great, snoring breath. Again they hung suspended. Again it was given back, long and harsh. The sound, so irregular, at such wide intervals, sounded through the house. Morel, in his room, slept on. Paul and Annie sat crouched, huddled motionless. The great, snoring sound began again—there was a painful pause while the breath was held—back came the rasping breath. Minute after minute passed. Paul looked at her again, bending low over her.

"She may last like this," he said.

They were both silent. He looked out of the window, and could faintly discern the snow on the garden.

"You go to my bed," he said to Annie. "I'll sit up."

"No," she said, "I'll stop with you."

"I'd rather you didn't," he said.

At last Annie crept out of the room, and he was alone. He hugged himself in his brown blanket, crouched in front of his mother, watching. She looked dreadful, with the bottom jaw fallen back. He watched. Sometimes he thought the great breath would never begin again. He could not bear it—the waiting. Then suddenly, startling him, came the great harsh sound. He mended the fire again, noiselessly. She must not be disturbed. The minutes went by. The night was going, breath by breath. Each time the sound came he felt it wring him, till at last he could not feel so much.

His father got up. Paul heard the miner drawing his stocking on, yawning. Then Morel, in shirt and stockings, entered.

"Hush!" said Paul.

Morel stood watching. Then he looked at his son, helplessly, and in horror.

"Had I better stop a-whoam?" he whispered.

"No. Go to work. She'll last through tomorrow."

"I don't think so."

"Yes. Go to work."

The miner looked at her again, in fear, and went obediently out of the room. Paul saw the tape of his garters swinging against his legs.

After another half-hour Paul went downstairs and drank a cup of tea, then returned. Morel, dressed for the pit, came upstairs again.

"Am I to go?" he said.

"Yes."

And in a few minutes Paul heard his father's heavy steps go thudding over the deadening snow. Miners called in the street as they tramped in gangs to work.

The terrible, long-drawn breaths continued—heave—heave—heave; then a long pause—then ah—ah-h-h-h! as it came back. Far away over the snow sounded the hooters of the ironworks. One after another they crowed and boomed, some small and far away, some near, the blowers of the collieries and the other works. Then there was silence. He mended the fire. The great breaths broke the silence—she looked just the same. He put back the blind and peered out. Still it was dark. Perhaps there was a lighter tinge. Perhaps the snow was bluer. He drew up the blind and got dressed. Then, shuddering, he drank brandy from the bottle on the washstand. The snow *was* growing blue. He heard a cart clanking down the street. Yes, it was seven o'clock, and it was coming a little bit light. He heard some people calling. The world was waking. A gray, deathly dawn crept over the snow. Yes, he could see the houses. He put out the gas. It seemed very dark. The breathing came still, but he was almost used to it. He could see her. She was just the same. He wondered if he piled heavy clothes on top of her it would make it heavier and the horrible breathing would stop. He looked at her. That was not her—not her a bit. If he piled the blanket and heavy coats on her—

Suddenly the door opened, and Annie entered. She looked at him questioningly.

"Just the same," he said calmly.

They whispered together a minute, then went downstairs to get breakfast. It was twenty to eight. Soon Annie came down.

"Isn't it awful! Doesn't she look awful!" she whispered, dazed with horror.

He nodded.

"If she looks like that!" said Annie.

"Drink some tea," he said.

They went upstairs again. Soon the neighbors came with their frightened question:

"How is she?"

It went on just the same. She lay with her cheek in her hand, her mouth fallen open, and the great, ghastly snores came and went.

At ten o'clock nurse came. She looked strange and woebegone.

"Nurse," cried Paul, "she'll last like this for days?"

"She can't, Mr. Morel," said nurse. "She can't."

There was a silence.

"Isn't it dreadful!" wailed the nurse. "Who would have thought she could stand it? Go down now, Mr. Morel, go down."

At last, at about eleven o'clock, he went downstairs and sat in the neighbor's house. Annie was downstairs also. Nurse and Arthur were upstairs. Paul sat with his head in his hands. Suddenly Annie came flying across the yard crying, half mad:

"Paul—Paul—she's gone!"

In a second he was back in his own house and upstairs. She lay curled up and still, with her face on her hand, and nurse was wiping her mouth. They all stood back. He kneeled down, and put his face to hers and his arms round her:

"My love—my love—oh, my love!" he whispered again and again. "My love—oh, my love!"

Then he heard the nurse behind him, crying, saying:

"She's better, Mr. Morel, she's better."

When he took his face up from his warm, dead mother he went straight downstairs and began blacking his boots.

There was a good deal to do, letters to write, and so on. The doctor came and glanced at her, and sighed.

"Ay—poor thing!" he said, then turned away. "Well, call at the surgery about six for the certificate."

The father came home from work at about four o'clock. He dragged silently into the house and sat down. Minnie bustled to give him his dinner. Tired, he laid his black arms on the table. There were swede turnips for his dinner, which he liked. Paul wondered if he knew. It was some time, and nobody had spoken. At last the son said:

"You noticed the blinds were down?"

Morel looked up.

"No," he said. "Why—has she gone?"

"Yes."

"When wor that?"

"About twelve this morning."

"H'm!"

The miner sat still for a moment, then began his dinner. It was as if nothing had happened. He ate his turnips in silence. Afterwards he washed and went upstairs to dress. The door of her room was shut.

"Have you seen her?" Annie asked of him when he came down.

"No," he said.

In a little while he went out. Annie went away, and Paul called on the undertaker, the clergyman, the doctor, the registrar. It was a long business. He got back at nearly eight o'clock. The undertaker was coming soon to measure for the coffin. The house was empty except for her. He took a candle and went upstairs.

The room was cold, that had been warm for so long. Flowers, bottles, plates, all sickroom litter was taken away; everything was harsh and austere. She lay raised on the bed, the sweep of the sheet from the raised feet was like a clean curve of snow, so silent. She lay like a maiden asleep. With his candle in his hand, he bent over her. She lay like a girl asleep and dreaming of her love. The mouth was a little open, as if wondering from the suffering, but her face was young, her brow clear and white as if life had never touched it. He looked again at the eyebrows, at the small, winsome nose a bit on one side. She was young again. Only the hair as it arched so beautifully from her temples was mixed with silver, and the two simple plaits that lay on her shoulders were filigree of silver and brown. She would wake up. She would lift her eyelids. She was with him still. He bent and kissed her passionately. But there was a coldness against his mouth. He bit his lip with horror. Looking at her, he felt he could never, never let her go. No! He stroked the hair from her temples. That, too, was cold. He saw the mouth so dumb and wondering at the hurt. Then he crouched on the floor, whispering to her:

"Mother, mother!"

He was still with her when the undertakers came, young men who had been to school with him. They touched her reverently, and in a quiet, businesslike fashion. They did not look at her. He watched jealously. He and Annie guarded her fiercely. They would not let anybody come to see her, and the neighbors were offended.

After a while Paul went out of the house, and played cards at a friend's. It was midnight when he got back. His father rose from the couch as he entered, saying in a plaintive way:

"I thought tha wor niver comin', lad."

"I didn't think you'd sit up," said Paul.

His father looked so forlorn. Morel had been a man without fear—simply nothing frightened him. Paul realized with a start that he had been afraid to go to bed, alone in the house with his dead. He was sorry.

"I forgot you'd be alone, father," he said.

"Dost want owt to eat?" asked Morel.

"No."

"Sithee—I made thee a drop o' hot milk. Get it down thee; it's cold enough for owt."

Paul drank it.

"I must go to Nottingham tomorrow," he said.

After a while Morel went to bed. He hurried past the closed door, and left his own door open. Soon the son came upstairs also. He went in to kiss her goodnight, as usual. It was cold and dark. He wished they had kept her fire burning. Still she dreamed her young dream. But she would be cold.

"My dear!" he whispered. "My dear!"

And he did not kiss her, for fear she should be cold and strange to him. It eased him she slept so beautifully. He shut her door softly, not to wake her, and went to bed.

In the morning Morel summoned his courage, hearing Annie downstairs and Paul coughing in the room across the landing. He opened her door, and went into the darkened room. He saw the white uplifted form in the twilight, but her he dared not see. Bewildered, too frightened to possess any of his faculties, he got out of the room again and left her. He never looked at her again. He had not seen her for months, because he had not dared to look. And she looked like his young wife again.

"Have you seen her?" Annie asked of him sharply after breakfast.

"Yes," he said.

"And don't you think she looks nice?"

"Yes."

He went out of the house soon after. And all the time he seemed to be creeping aside to avoid it.

Paul went about from place to place, doing the business of the death. He met Clara in Nottingham, and they had tea together in a café, when they were quite jolly again. She was infinitely relieved to find he did not take it tragically.

Later, when the relatives began to come for the funeral, the affair became public, and the children became social beings. They put themselves aside. They buried her in a furious storm of rain and wind. The wet clay glistened, all the white flowers were soaked. Annie gripped his arm and leaned forward. Down below she saw a dark corner of William's coffin. The oak box sank steadily. She was gone. The rain poured in the grave. The procession of black, with its umbrellas glistening, turned away. The cemetery was deserted under the drenching cold rain.

Paul went home and busied himself supplying the guests with drinks. His father sat in the kitchen with Mrs. Morel's relatives, "superior" people, and wept, and said what a good lass she'd been, and how he'd tried to do everything he could for her—everything. He had striven all his life to do what he could for her, and he'd nothing to reproach himself with. She was gone, but he'd done his best for her. He wiped his eyes with his white handkerchief. He'd nothing to reproach himself for, he repeated. All his life he'd done his best for her.

And that was how he tried to dismiss her. He never thought of her personally. Everything deep in him he denied. Paul hated his father for sitting sentimentalizing over her. He knew he would do it in the public houses. For the real tragedy went on in Morel in spite of himself. Sometimes, later, he came down from his afternoon sleep, white and cowering.

"I *have* been dreaming of thy mother," he said in a small voice.

"Have you, father? When I dream of her it's always just as she was when she was well. I dream of her often, but it seems quite nice and natural, as if nothing had altered."

But Morel crouched in front of the fire in terror.

The weeks passed half real, not much pain, not much of anything, perhaps a little relief, mostly a *nuit blanche*. Paul went restlessly from place to place. For some months, since his mother had been worse, he had not made love to Clara. She was, as it were, dumb to him, rather distant. Dawes saw her very occasionally, but the two could not get an inch across the great distance between them. The three of them were drifting forward.

Dawes mended very slowly. He was in the convalescent home at Skegness at Christmas, nearly well again. Paul went to the seaside for a few days. His father was with Annie in Sheffield. Dawes came to Paul's lodgings. His time in the home was up. The two men, between whom was such a big reserve, seemed faithful to each other. Dawes depended on Morel now. He knew Paul and Clara had practically separated.

Two days after Christmas Paul was to go back to Nottingham. The evening before he sat with Dawes smoking before the fire.

"You know Clara's coming down for the day tomorrow?" he said.

The other man glanced at him.

"Yes, you told me," he replied.

Paul drank the remainder of his glass of whisky.

"I told the landlady your wife was coming," he said.

"Did you?" said Dawes, shrinking, but almost leaving himself in the other's hands. He got up rather stiffly, and reached for Morel's glass.

"Let me fill you up," he said.

Paul jumped up.

"You sit still," he said.

But Dawes, with rather shaky hand, continued to mix the drink.

"Say when," he said.

"Thanks!" replied the other. "But you've no business to get up."

"It does me good, lad," replied Dawes. "I begin to think I'm right again, then."

"You are about right, you know."

"I am, certainly I am," said Dawes, nodding to him.

"And Len says he can get you on in Sheffield."

Dawes glanced at him again, with dark eyes that agreed with everything the other would say, perhaps a trifle dominated by him.

"It's funny," said Paul, "starting again. I feel in a lot bigger mess than you."

"In what way, lad?"

"I don't know. I don't know. It's as if I was in a tangled sort of hole, rather dark and dreary, and no road anywhere."

"I know—I understand it," Dawes said, nodding. "But you'll find it'll come all right."

He spoke caressingly.

"I suppose so," said Paul.

Dawes knocked his pipe in a hopeless fashion.

"You've not done for yourself like I have," he said.

Morel saw the wrist and the white hand of the other man gripping the stem of the pipe and knocking out the ash, as if he had given up.

"How old are you?" Paul asked.

"Thirty-nine," replied Dawes, glancing at him.

Those brown eyes, full of the consciousness of failure, almost pleading for reassurance, for someone to re-establish the man in himself, to warn him, to set him up firm again, troubled Paul.

"You'll just be in your prime," said Morel. "You don't look as if much life had gone out of you."

The brown eyes of the other flashed suddenly.

"It hasn't," he said. "The go is there."

Paul looked up and laughed.

"We've both got plenty of life in us yet to make things fly," he said.

The eyes of the two men met. They exchanged one look. Having recognized the stress of passion each in the other, they both drank their whisky.

"Yes, begod!" said Dawes, breathless.

There was a pause.

"And I don't see," said Paul, "why you shouldn't go on where you left off."

"What—" said Dawes, suggestively.

"Yes—fit your old home together again."

Dawes hid his face and shook his head.

"Couldn't be done," he said, and he looked up with an ironic smile.

"Why? Because you don't want?"

"Perhaps."

They smoked in silence. Dawes showed his teeth as he bit his pipe stem.

"You mean you don't want her?" asked Paul.

Dawes stared up at the picture with a caustic expression on his face.

"I hardly know," he said.

The smoke floated softly up.

"I believe she wants you," said Paul.

"Do you?" replied the other, soft, satirical, abstract.

"Yes. She never really hitched on to me—you were always there in the background. That's why she wouldn't get a divorce."

Dawes continued to stare in a satirical fashion at the picture over the mantelpiece.

"That's how women are with me," said Paul. "They want me like mad, but they don't want to belong to me. And she *belonged* to you all the time. I knew."

The triumphant male came up in Dawes. He showed his teeth more distinctly.

"Perhaps I was a fool," he said.

"You were a big fool," said Morel.

"But perhaps even *then* you were a bigger fool," said Dawes.

There was a touch of triumph and malice in it.

"Do you think so?" said Paul.

They were silent for some time.

"At any rate, I'm clearing out tomorrow," said Morel.

"I see," answered Dawes.

Then they did not talk any more. The instinct to murder each other had returned. They almost avoided each other.

They shared the same bedroom. When they retired Dawes seemed abstract, thinking of something. He sat on the side of the bed in his shirt, looking at his legs.

"Aren't you getting cold?" asked Morel.

"I was lookin' at these legs," replied the other.

"What's up with 'em? They look all right," replied Paul, from his bed.

"They look all right. But there's some water in 'em yet."

"And what about it?"

"Come and look."

Paul reluctantly got out of bed and went to look at the rather handsome legs of the other man that were covered with glistening, dark gold hair.

"Look here," said Dawes, pointing to his shin. "Look at the water under here."

"Where?" said Paul.

The man pressed in his fingertips. They left little dents that filled up slowly.

"It's nothing," said Paul.

"You feel," said Dawes.

Paul tried with his fingers. It made little dents.

"H'm!" he said.

"Rotten, isn't it?" said Dawes.

"Why! It's nothing much."

"You're not much of a man with water in your legs."

"I can't see as it makes any difference," said Morel. "I've got a weak chest."

He returned to his own bed.

"I suppose the rest of me's all right," said Dawes, and he put out the light.

In the morning it was raining. Morel packed his bag. The sea was gray and shaggy and dismal. He seemed to be cutting himself off from life more and more. It gave him a wicked pleasure to do it.

The two men were at the station. Clara stepped out of the train, and came along the platform, very erect and coldly composed. She wore a long coat and a tweed hat. Both men hated her for her composure. Paul shook hands with her at the barrier. Dawes was leaning against the bookstall, watching. His black overcoat was buttoned up to the chin because of the rain. He was pale, with almost a touch of nobility in his quietness. He came forward, limping slightly.

"You ought to look better than this," she said.

"Oh, I'm all right now."

The three stood at a loss. She kept the two men hesitating near her.

"Shall we go to the lodging straight off," said Paul, "or somewhere else?"

"We may as well go home," said Dawes.

Paul walked on the outside of the pavement, then Dawes, then Clara. They made polite conversation. The sitting room faced the sea, whose tide, gray and shaggy, hissed not far off.

Morel swung up the big armchair

"Sit down, Jack," he said.

"I don't want that chair," said Dawes.

"Sit down!" Morel repeated.

Clara took off her things and laid them on the couch. She had a slight air of resentment. Lifting her hair with her fingers, she sat down, rather aloof and composed. Paul ran downstairs to speak to the landlady.

"I should think you're cold," said Dawes to his wife. "Come nearer to the fire."

"Thank you, I'm quite warm," she answered.

She looked out of the window at the rain and at the sea.

"When are you going back?" she asked.

"Well, the rooms are taken until tomorrow, so he want me to stop. He's going back tonight."

"And then you're thinking of going to Sheffield?"

"Yes."

"Are you fit to start work?"

"I'm going to start."

"You've really got a place?"

"Yes—begin on Monday."

"You don't look fit."

"Why don't I?"

She looked again out of the window instead of answering.

"And have you got lodgings in Sheffield?"

"Yes."

Again she looked away out of the window. The panes were blurred with streaming rain.

"And can you manage all right?" she asked.

"I s'd think so. I s'll have to!"

They were silent when Morel returned.

"I shall go by the four-twenty," he said as he entered.

Nobody answered.

"I wish you'd take your boots off," he said to Clara. "There's a pair of slippers of mine."

"Thank you," she said. "They aren't wet."

He put the slippers near her feet. She felt them there.

Morel sat down. Both the men seemed helpless, and each of them had a rather hunted look. But Dawes now carried himself quietly, seemed to yield himself, while Paul seemed to screw himself up. Clara thought she had never seen him look so small and mean. He was as if trying to get himself into the smallest possible compass. And as he went about arranging, and as he sat talking, there seemed something false about him and out of tune. Watching him unknown, she said to herself there was no stability about him. He was fine in his way, passionate, and able to give her drinks of pure life when he was in one mood. And now he looked paltry and insignificant. There was nothing stable about him. Her husband had more manly dignity. At any rate *he* did not waft about with any wind. There was something evanescent about Morel, she thought, something shifting and false. He would never make sure ground for any woman to stand on. She despised him rather for his shrinking together, getting smaller. Her husband at least was manly, and when he was beaten gave in. But this other would never own to being beaten. He would shift round and round, prowl, get smaller. She despised him. And yet she watched him rather than Dawes, and it seemed as if their three fates lay in his hands. She hated him for it.

She seemed to understand better now about men, and what they could or would do. She was less afraid of them, more sure of herself. That they were not the small egoists she had imagined them made her more comfortable. She had learned a good deal—almost as much as she wanted to learn. Her cup had been full. It was still as full as she could carry. On the whole, she would not be sorry when he was gone.

They had dinner, and sat eating nuts and drinking by the fire. Not a serious word had been spoken. Yet Clara realized that Morel was withdrawing from the circle, leaving her the option to stay with her husband. It angered her. He was a mean fellow, after all, to take what he wanted and then give her back. She did not remember that she herself had had what she wanted, and really, at the bottom of her heart, wished to be given back.

Paul felt crumpled up and lonely. His mother had really supported his life. He had loved her; they two had, in fact, faced the world together. Now she was gone, and forever behind him was the gap in life, the tear in the veil, through which his life seemed to drift slowly, as if he were drawn towards death. He wanted someone of their own free initiative to help him. The lesser things he began to let go from him, for fear of this big thing, the lapse towards death, following in the wake of his beloved. Clara could not stand for him to hold on to. She wanted him, but not to understand him. He felt she wanted the man on top, not the real him that was in trouble. That would be too much trouble to her; he dared not give it her. She could not cope with him. It made him ashamed. So, secretly ashamed because he was in such a mess, because his own hold on life was so unsure, because nobody held him, feeling unsubstantial, shadowy, as if he did not count for much in this concrete world, he drew himself together smaller and smaller. He did not want to die; he would not give in. But he was not afraid of death. If nobody would help, he would go on alone.

Dawes had been driven to the extremity of life, until he was afraid. He could go to the brink of death, he could lie on the edge and look in. Then cowed, afraid, he had to crawl back, and like a beggar take what offered. There was a certain nobility in it. As Clara saw, he owned himself beaten, and he wanted to be taken back whether or not. That she could do for him.

It was three o'clock.

"I am going by the four-twenty," said Paul again to Clara. "Are you coming then or later?"

"I don't know," she said.

"I'm meeting my father in Nottingham at seven-fifteen," he said.

"Then," she answered, "I'll come later."

Dawes jerked suddenly, as if he had been held on a strain. He looked out over the sea, but he saw nothing.

"There are one or two books in the corner," said Morel. "I've done with 'em."

At about four o'clock he went.

"I shall see you both later," he said, as he shook hands.

"I suppose so," said Dawes. "An' perhaps—one day—I s'll be able to pay you back the money as——"

"I shall come for it, you'll see," laughed Paul. "I s'll be on the rocks before I'm very much older."

"Ay—well—" said Dawes.

"Good-bye," he said to Clara.

"Good-bye," she said, giving him her hand. Then she glanced at him for the last time, dumb and humble.

He was gone. Dawes and his wife sat down again.

"It's a nasty day for traveling," said the man.

"Yes," she answered.

They talked in a desultory fashion until it grew dark. The landlady brought in the tea. Dawes drew up his chair to the table without being invited, like a husband. Then he sat humbly waiting for his cup. She served him as she would, like a wife, not consulting his wish.

After tea, as it drew near to six o'clock, he went to the window. All was dark outside. The sea was roaring.

"It's raining yet," he said.

"Is it?" she answered.

"You won't go tonight, shall you?" he said, hesitating.

She did not answer. He waited.

"I shouldn't go in this rain," he said.

"Do you *want* me to stay?" she asked.

His hand as he held the dark curtain trembled.

"Yes," he said.

He remained with his back to her. She rose and went slowly to him. He let go the curtain, turned, hesitating, towards her. She stood with her hands behind her back, looking up at him in a heavy, inscrutable fashion.

"Do you want me, Baxter?" she asked.

His voice was hoarse as he answered:

"Do you want to come back to me?"

She made a moaning noise, lifted her arms, and put them round his neck, drawing him to her. He hid his face on her shoulder, holding her clasped.

"Take me back!" she whispered, ecstatic. "Take me back, take me back!" And she put her fingers through his fine, thin dark hair, as if she were only semi-conscious. He tightened his grasp on her.

"Do you want me again?" he murmured, broken.

❖ 15 ❖

DERELICT

Clara went with her husband to Sheffield, and Paul scarcely saw her again. Walter Morel seemed to have let all the trouble go over him, and there he was, crawling about on the mud of it, just the same. There was scarcely any bond between father and son, save that each felt he must not let the other go in any actual want. As there was no one to keep on the home, and as they could neither of them bear the emptiness of the house, Paul took lodgings in Nottingham, and Morel went to live with a friendly family in Bestwood.

Everything seemed to have gone smash for the young man. He could not paint. The picture he finished on the day of his mother's death—one that satisfied him—was the last thing he did. At work there was no Clara. When he came home he could not take up his brushes again. There was nothing left.

So he was always in the town at one place or another, drinking, knocking about with the men he knew. It really wearied him. He talked to barmaids, to almost any woman, but there was that dark, strained look in his eyes, as if he were hunting something.

Everything seemed so different, so unreal. There seemed no reason why people should go along the street, and houses pile up in the daylight. There seemed no reason why these things should occupy the space, instead of leaving it empty. His friends talked to him: he heard the sounds, and he answered. But why there should be the noise of speech he could not understand.

He was most himself when he was alone, or working hard and mechanically at the factory. In the latter case there was pure forgetfulness, when he lapsed from consciousness. But it had to come to an end. It hurt him so, that things had lost their reality. The first snowdrops came. He saw the tiny drop-pearls among the gray. They would have given him the liveliest emotion at one time. Now they were there, but they did not seem to mean anything. In a few moments they would cease to occupy that place, and just the space would be, where they had been. Tall, brilliant tramcars ran along the street at night. It seemed almost a wonder they should trouble to rustle backwards and forwards. "Why trouble to go tilting down to Trent Bridges?" he asked of the big trams. It seemed they just as well might *not* be as be.

The realest thing was the thick darkness at night. That seemed to him whole and comprehensible and restful. He could leave himself to it. Suddenly a piece of paper started near his feet and blew along down the pavement. He stood still, rigid, with clenched fists, a flame of agony going over him. And he saw again the sickroom, his mother, her eyes. Unconsciously he had been with her, in her company. The swift hop of the paper reminded him she was gone. But he had been with her. He wanted everything to stand still, so that he could be with her again.

The days passed, the weeks. But everything seemed to have fused, gone into a conglomerated mass. He could not tell one day from another, one week from another, hardly one place from another. Nothing was distinct or distinguishable. Often he lost himself for an hour at a time, could not remember what he had done.

One evening he came home late to his lodging. The fire was burning low; everybody was in bed. He threw on some more coal, glanced at the table, and decided he wanted no supper. Then he sat down in the armchair. It was perfectly still. He did not know anything, yet he saw the dim smoke wavering up the chimney. Presently two mice came out, cautiously, nibbling the fallen crumbs. He watched them as it were from a long way off. The church clock struck two. Far away he could hear the sharp clinking of the trucks on the railway. No, it was not they that were far away. They were there in their places. But where was he himself?

The time passed. The two mice, careering wildly, scampered cheekily over his slippers. He had not moved a muscle. He did not want to move. He was not thinking of anything. It was easier so. There was no wrench of knowing anything. Then from time to time, some other consciousness, working mechanically, flashed into sharp phrases.

"What am I doing?"

And out of the semi-intoxicated trance came the answer:

"Destroying myself."

Then a dull, live feeling, gone in an instant, told him that it was wrong. After a while, suddenly came the question:

"Why wrong?"

Again there was no answer, but a stroke of hot stubbornness inside his chest resisted his own annihilation.

There was a sound of a heavy cart clanking down the road. Suddenly the electric light went out; there was a bruising thud in the penny-in-the-slot meter. He did not stir, but sat gazing in front of him. Only the mice had scuttled, and the fire glowed red in the dark room.

Then, quite mechanically and more distinctly, the conversation began again inside him.

"She's dead. What was it all for—her struggle?"

That was his despair wanting to go after her.

"You're alive."

"She's not."

"She is—in you."

Suddenly he felt tired with the burden of it.

"You've got to keep alive for her sake," said his will in him.

Something felt sulky, as if it would not rouse.

"You've got to carry forward her living, and what she had done, go on with it."

But he did not want to. He wanted to give up.

"But you can go on with your painting," said the will in him. "Or else you can beget children. They both carry on her effort."

"Painting is not living."

"Then live."

"Marry whom?" came the sulky question.

"As best you can."

"Miriam?"

But he did not trust that.

He rose suddenly, went straight to bed. When he got inside his bedroom and closed the door, he stood with clenched fists.

"Mater, my dear—" he began, with the whole force of his soul. Then he stopped. He would not say it. He would not admit that he wanted to die, to have done. He would not own that life had beaten him, or that death had beaten him.

Going straight to bed, he slept at once, abandoning himself to the sleep.

So the weeks went on. Always alone, his soul oscillated, first on the side of death, then on the side of life, doggedly. The real agony was that he had nowhere to go, nothing to do, nothing to say, and *was* nothing himself. Sometimes he ran down the streets as if he were mad: sometimes he was mad; things weren't there, things were there. It made him pant. Sometimes he stood before the bar of the public house where he had called for a drink. Everything suddenly stood back away from him. He saw the face of the barmaid, the gabbling drinkers, his own glass on the slopped, mahogany board, in the distance. There was something between him and them. He could not get into touch. He did not want them; he did not want his drink. Turning abruptly, he went out. On the threshold he stood and looked at the lighted street. But he was not of it or in it. Something separated him. Everything went on there below those lamps, shut away from him. He could not get at them. He felt he couldn't touch the lampposts, not if he reached. Where could he go? There was nowhere to go, neither back into the inn, nor forward anywhere. He felt stifled. There was nowhere for him. The stress grew inside him; he felt he should smash.

"I mustn't," he said; and, turning blindly, he went in and drank. Sometimes the drink did him good; sometimes it made him worse. He ran down the road. Forever restless, he went here, there, everywhere. He determined to work. But when he had made six strokes, he loathed the pencil violently, got up, and went away, hurried off to a club where he could play cards or billiards, to a place where he could flirt with a barmaid who was no more to him than the brass pump handle she drew.

He was very thin and lantern-jawed. He dared not meet his own eyes in the mirror; he never looked at himself. He wanted to get away from himself, but there was nothing to get hold of. In despair he thought of Miriam. Perhaps—perhaps—?

Then, happening to go into the Unitarian Church one Sunday evening, when they stood up to sing the second hymn he saw her before him. The light glistened on her lower lip as she sang. She looked as if she had got something, at any rate: some hope in heaven, if not in earth. Her comfort and her life seemed in the afterworld. A warm, strong feeling for her came up. She seemed to yearn, as she sang, for the mystery and comfort. He put his hope in her. He longed for the sermon to be over, to speak to her.

The throng carried her out just before him. He could nearly touch her. She did not know he was there. He saw the brown, humble nape of her neck under its black curls. He would leave himself to her. She was better and bigger than he. He would depend on her.

She went wandering, in her blind way, through the little throngs of people outside the church. She always looked so lost and out of place among people. He went forward and put his hand on her arm. She started violently. Her great brown eyes dilated in fear, then went questioning at the sight of him. He shrank slightly from her.

"I didn't know—" she faltered.

"Nor I," he said.

He looked away. His sudden, flaring hope sank again.

"What are you doing in town?" he asked.

"I'm staying at Cousin Anne's."

"Ha! For long?"

"No; only till tomorrow."

"Must you go straight home?"

She looked at him, then hid her face under her hat brim.

"No," she said—"no; it's not necessary."

He turned away, and she went with him. They threaded through the throng of church people. The organ was still sounding in St. Mary's. Dark figures came through the lighted doors; people were coming down the steps. The large colored windows glowed up in the night. The church was like a great lantern suspended. They went down Hollow Stone, and he took the car for the Bridges.

"You will just have supper with me," he said; "then I'll bring you back."

"Very well," she replied, low and husky.

They scarcely spoke while they were on the car. The Trent ran dark and full under the bridge. Away towards Colwick all was black night. He lived down Holme Road, on the naked edge of the town, facing across the river meadows towards Sneinton Hermitage and the steep scarp of Colwick Wood. The floods were out. The silent water and the darkness spread away on their left. Almost afraid, they hurried along by the houses.

Supper was laid. He swung the curtain over the window. There was a bowl of freesias and scarlet anemones on the table. She bent to them. Still touching them with her fingertips, she looked up at him, saying:

"Aren't they beautiful?"

"Yes," he said. "What will you drink—coffee?"

"I should like it," she said.

"Then excuse me a moment."

He went out to the kitchen.

Miriam took off her things and looked round. It was a bare, severe room. Her photo, Clara's, Annie's, were on the wall. She looked on the drawing board to see what he was doing. There were only a few meaningless lines. She looked to see what books he was reading. Evidently just an ordinary novel. The letters in the rack she saw were from Annie, Arthur, and from some man or other she did not know. Everything he had touched, everything that was in the least personal to him, she examined with lingering absorption. He had been gone from her so long, she wanted to rediscover him, his position, what he was now. But there was not much in the room to help her. It only made her feel rather sad, it was so hard and comfortless.

She was curiously examining a sketchbook when he returned with the coffee.

"There's nothing new in it," he said, "and nothing very interesting."

He put down the tray, and went to look over her shoulder. She turned the pages slowly, intent on examining everything.

"H'm!" he said, as she paused at a sketch. "I'd forgotten that. It's not bad, is it?"

"No," she said. "I don't quite understand it."

He took the book from her and went through it. Again he made a curious sound of surprise and pleasure.

"There's some not bad stuff in there," he said.

"Not at all bad," she answered gravely.

He felt again her interest in his work. Or was it for himself? Why was she always most interested in him as he appeared in his work?

They sat down to supper.

"By the way," he said, "didn't I hear something about your earning your own living?"

"Yes," she replied, bowing her dark head over her cup.

"And what of it?"

"I'm merely going to the farming college at Broughton for three months, and I shall probably be kept on as a teacher there."

"I say—that sounds all right for you! You always wanted to be independent."

"Yes."

"Why didn't you tell me?"

"I only knew last week."

"But I heard a month ago," he said.

"Yes; but nothing was settled then."

"I should have thought," he said, "you'd have told me you were trying."

She ate her food in the deliberate, constrained way, almost as if she recoiled a little from doing anything so publicly, that he knew so well.

"I suppose you're glad," he said.

"Very glad."

"Yes—it will be something."

He was rather disappointed.

"I think it will be a great deal," she said, almost haughtily, resentfully.

He laughed shortly.

"Why do you think it won't?" she asked.

"Oh, I don't think it won't be a great deal. Only you'll find earning your own living isn't everything."

"No," she said, swallowing with difficulty; "I don't suppose it is."

"I suppose work *can* be nearly everything to a man," he said, "though it isn't to me. But a woman only works with a part of herself. The real and vital part is covered up."

"But a man can give *all* himself to a work?" she asked.

"Yes, practically."

"And a woman only the unimportant part of herself?"

"That's it."

She looked up at him, and her eyes dilated with anger.

"Then," she said, "if it's true, it's a great shame."

"It is. But I don't know everything," he answered.

After supper they drew up to the fire. He swung her a chair facing him, and they sat down. She was wearing a dress of dark claret color, that suited her dark complexion and her large features. Still, the curls were fine and free, but her face was much older, the brown throat much thinner. She seemed old to him, older than Clara. Her bloom of youth had quickly gone. A sort of stiffness, almost of woodenness, had come upon her. She meditated a little while, then looked at him.

"And how are things with you?" she asked.

"About all right," he answered.

She looked at him, waiting.

"Nay," she said, very low.

Her brown, nervous hands were clasped over her knee. They had still the lack of confidence or repose, the almost hysterical look. He winced as he saw them. Then he laughed mirthlessly. She put her fingers between her lips. His slim, black, tortured body lay quite still in the chair. She suddenly took her finger from her mouth and looked at him.

"And have you broken off with Clara?"

"Yes."

His body lay like an abandoned thing, strewn in the chair.

"You know," she said, "I think we ought to be married."

He opened his eyes for the first time since many months, and attended to her with respect.

"Why?" he said.

"See," she said, "how you waste yourself! You might be ill, you might die, and I never know—be no more then than if I had never known you."

"And if we married?" he asked.

"At any rate, I could prevent you wasting yourself and being a prey to other women—like—like Clara."

"A prey?" he repeated, smiling.

She bowed her head in silence. He lay feeling his despair come up again.

"I'm not sure," he said slowly, "that marriage would be much good."

"I only think of you," she replied.

"I know you do. But—you love me so much, you want to put me in your pocket. And I should die there smothered."

She bent her head, put her finger between her lips, while the bitterness surged up in her heart.

"And what will you do otherwise?" she asked.

"I don't know—go on, I suppose. Perhaps I shall soon go abroad."

The despairing doggedness in his tone made her go on her knees on the rug before the fire, very near to him. There she crouched as if she were crushed by something, and could not raise her head. His hands lay quite inert on the arms of his chair. She was aware of them. She felt that now he lay at her mercy. If she could rise, take him, put her arms round him, and say, "You are mine," then he would leave himself to her. But dare she? She could easily sacrifice herself. But dare she assert herself? She was aware of his dark-clothed, slender body, that seemed one stroke of life, sprawled in the chair close to her. But no; she dared not put her arms round it, take it up, and say, "It is mine, this body. Leave it to me." And she wanted to. It called to all her woman's instinct. But she crouched, and dared not. She was afraid he would not let her. She was afraid it was too much. It lay there, his body, abandoned. She knew she ought to take it up and claim it, and claim every right to it. But—could she do it? Her impotence before him, before the strong demand of some unknown thing in him, was her extremity. Her hands fluttered; she half lifted her head. Her eyes, shuddering, appealing, gone almost distracted, pleaded to him suddenly. His heart caught with pity. He took her hands, drew her to him, and comforted her.

"Will you have me, to marry me?" he said very low.

Oh, why did not he take her? Her very soul belonged to him. Why would he not take what was his? She had borne so long the cruelty of belonging to him and not being claimed by him. Now he was straining her again. It was too much for her. She drew back her head, held his face between her hands, and looked him in the eyes. No, he was hard. He wanted something else. She pleaded to him with all her love not to make it *her* choice. She could not cope with it, with him, she knew not with what. But it strained her till she felt she would break.

"Do you want it?" she asked, very gravely.

"Not much," he replied, with pain.

She turned her face aside; then, raising herself with dignity, she took his head to her bosom, and rocked him softly. She was not to have him, then! So she could comfort him. She put her fingers through his hair. For her, the anguished sweetness of self-sacrifice. For him, the hate and misery of another failure. He could not bear it—that breast which was warm and which cradled him without taking the burden of him. So much he wanted to rest on her that the feint of rest only tortured him. He drew away.

"And without marriage we can do nothing?" he asked.

His mouth was lifted from his teeth with pain. She put her little finger between her lips.

"No," she said, low and like the toll of a bell. "No, I think not."

It was the end then between them. She could not take him and relieve him of the responsibility of himself. She could only sacrifice herself to him—sacrifice herself every day, gladly. And that he did not want. He wanted her to hold him and say, with joy and authority: "Stop all this restlessness and beating against death. You are mine for a mate." She had not the strength. Or was it a mate she wanted? or did she want a Christ in him?

He felt, in leaving her, he was defrauding her of life. But he knew that, in staying, stifling the inner, desperate man, he was denying his own life. And he did not hope to give life to her by denying his own.

She sat very quiet. He lit a cigarette. The smoke went up from it, wavering. He was thinking of his mother, and had forgotten Miriam. She suddenly looked at him. Her bitterness came surging up. Her sacrifice, then, was useless. He lay there aloof, careless about her. Suddenly she saw again his lack of religion, his restless instability. He would destroy himself like a perverse child. Well, then, he would!

"I think I must go," she said softly.

By her tone he knew she was despising him. He rose quietly.

"I'll come along with you," he answered.

She stood before the mirror pinning on her hat. How bitter, how unutterably bitter, it made her that he rejected her sacrifice! Life ahead looked dead, as if the glow were gone out. She bowed her face over the flowers—the freesias so sweet and spring-like, the scarlet anemones, flaunting over the table. It was like him to have those flowers.

He moved about the room with a certain sureness of touch, swift and relentless and quiet. She knew she could not cope with him. He would escape like a weasel out of her hands. Yet without him her life would trail on lifeless. Brooding, she touched the flowers.

"Have them!" he said; and he took them out of the jar, dripping as they were, and went quickly into the kitchen. She waited for him, took the flowers, and they went out together, he talking, she feeling dead.

She was going from him now. In her misery she leaned against him as they sat on the car. He was unresponsive. Where would he go? What would be the end of him? She could not bear it, the vacant feeling where he should be. He was so foolish, so wasteful, never at peace with himself. And now where would he go? And what did he care that he wasted her? He had no religion; it was all for the moment's attraction that he cared, nothing else, nothing deeper. Well, she would wait and see how it turned out with him. When he had had enough he would give in and come to her.

He shook hands and left her at the door of her cousin's house. When he turned away he felt the last hold for him had gone. The town, as he sat upon the car, stretched away over the bay of railway, a level fume of lights. Beyond the town the country, little smoldering spots for more towns—the sea—the night—on and on! And he had no place in it! Whatever spot he stood on, there he stood alone. From his breast, from his mouth, sprang the endless space, and it was there behind him, everywhere. The people hurrying along the streets offered no obstruction to the void in which he found himself. They were small shadows whose footsteps and voices could be heard, but in each of them the same night, the same silence. He got off the car. In the country all was dead still. Little stars shone high up; little stars spread far away in the flood waters, a firmament below. Everywhere the vastness and terror of the immense night which is roused and stirred for a brief while by the day, but which returns, and will remain at last eternal, holding everything in its silence and its living gloom. There was no Time, only Space. Who could say his mother had lived and did not live? She had been in one place, and was in another; that was all. And his soul could not leave her, wherever she was. Now she was gone abroad into the night, and he was with her still. They were together. But yet there was his body, his chest, that leaned against the stile, his hands on the wooden bar. They seemed something. Where was he?—one tiny upright speck of flesh, less than an ear of wheat lost in the field. He could not bear it. On every side the immense dark silence seemed pressing him, so tiny a spark, into extinction, and yet, almost nothing, he could not be extinct. Night, in which everything was lost, went reaching out, beyond stars and sun. Stars and sun, a few bright grains, went spinning round for terror, and holding each other in embrace, there in a darkness that outpassed them all, and left them tiny and daunted. So much, and himself, infinitesimal, at the core a nothingness, and yet not nothing.

"Mother!" he whimpered—"mother!"

She was the only thing that held him up, himself, amid all this. And she was gone, intermingled herself. He wanted her to touch him, have him alongside with her.

But no, he would not give in. Turning sharply, he walked towards the city's gold phosphorescence. His fists were shut. his mouth set fast. He would not take that direction, to the darkness, to follow her. He walked towards the faintly humming, glowing town, quickly.

The Prussian Officer and Other Stories

Contents

THE PRUSSIAN OFFICER

I

They had marched more than thirty kilometers since dawn, along the white, hot road where occasional thickets of trees threw a moment of shade, then out into the glare again. On either hand, the valley, wide and shallow, glittered with heat; dark green patches of rye, pale young corn, fallow and meadow and black pine woods spread in a dull, hot diagram under a glistening sky. But right in front the mountains ranged across, pale blue and very still, snow gleaming gently out of the deep atmosphere. And towards the mountains, on and on, the regiment marched between the rye fields and the meadows, between the ruined fruit trees set regularly on either side the high road. The burnished, dark green rye threw off a suffocating heat, the mountains drew gradually nearer and more distinct. While the feet of the soldiers grew hotter, sweat ran through their hair under their helmets, and their knapsacks could burn no more in contact with their shoulders, but seemed instead to give off a cold, prickly sensation.

He could now walk almost without pain. At the start, he had determined not to limp. It had made him sick to take the first steps, and during the first mile or so, he had held his breath, and the cold drops of sweat had stood on his forehead. But he had walked it off. What were they after all but bruises! He had looked at them, as he was getting up: deep bruises on the backs of his thighs. And since he had made his first step in the morning, he had been conscious of them, till now he had a tight, hot place in his chest, with suppressing the pain, and holding himself in. There seemed no air when he breathed. But he walked almost lightly.

The Captain's hand had trembled at taking his coffee at dawn: his orderly saw it again. And he saw the fine figure of the Captain wheeling on horseback at the farmhouse ahead, a handsome figure in pale blue uniform with facings of scarlet, and the metal gleaming on the black helmet and the sword scabbard, and dark streaks of sweat coming on the silky bay horse. The orderly felt he was connected with that figure moving so suddenly on horseback: he followed it like a shadow, mute and inevitable and damned by it. And the officer was always aware of the tramp of the company behind, the march of his orderly among the men.

The Captain was a tall man of about forty, gray at the temples. He had a handsome, finely-knit figure, and was one of the best horsemen in the West. His orderly, having to rub him down, admired the amazing riding-muscles of his loins.

For the rest, the orderly scarcely noticed the officer any more than he noticed himself. It was rarely he saw his master's face: he did not look at it. The Captain had reddish-brown, stiff hair, that he wore short and well brushed. His moustache was also cut short and bristly over a full, brutal mouth. His face was rather rugged, the cheeks thin. Perhaps the man was the more handsome for the deep lines in his face, the irritable tension of his brow, which gave him the look of a man who fights with life. His fair eyebrows stood bushy over light blue eyes that were always flashing with cold fire. He was a Prussian aristocrat, haughty and overbearing. Having made too many gambling debts when he was young, he had ruined his prospects in the Army, and remained an infantry captain. He had never married: his position did not allow of it, and no woman had ever moved him to it. His time he spent riding—occasionally on one of his own horses at the races—and at the officers' club. Now and then he took himself a mistress. But after such an event, he returned to duty with his brow still more tense, his eyes still more hostile and irritable.

The orderly was a youth of about twenty-two, of medium height, and well built. He had strong, heavy limbs, was swarthy, with a soft, black, young moustache. There was something altogether warm and young about him. He had firmly-marked eyebrows over dark, expressionless eyes, that seemed never to have thought, only to have received life direct through his senses, as if he acted straight from instinct.

Gradually the officer had become aware of his servant's young, vigorous, unconscious presence about him. He could not get away from the sense of the youth's person, while he was in attendance. There was something so free and self-contained about him, and something in the young fellow's movement, that made the elder man glance at him. And this irritated the Prussian. To see the soldier's young, brown, shapely peasant's hand grasp the loaf or the wine bottle sent a flash of hate or of anger through the other man's blood. It was not that the youth was clumsy: it was rather the blind, instinctive sureness of movement of an unhampered young animal that irritated the officer to such a degree.

He had served the Captain for more than a year, and so knew his duty. This he performed easily, as if it were natural to him. The officer and his commands he took for granted, as he took the sun and the rain, and he served as a matter of course. It did not implicate him personally.

But in spite of himself, the Captain could not regain his neutrality of feeling towards his orderly. Nor could he leave the man alone. In spite of himself, he watched him, gave him sharp orders, tried to take up as much of his time as possible. Sometimes he flew into a rage with the young soldier, and bullied him. Then the orderly shut himself off, as it were out of earshot, and waited, with sullen, flushed face for the end of the noise. The words never pierced to his intelligence, and he made himself, protectively, impervious to the feelings of his master.

He had a scar on his left thumb, a deep seam going across the knuckle. The officer had long suffered from it, and wanted to do something to it. Still it was there, ugly and brutal on the young, brown hand. At last the Captain's reserve gave way. One day, as the orderly was smoothing out the tablecloth, the officer pinned down his thumb with a pencil, asking:

"How did you come by that?"

The young man winced and drew back at attention.

"A wood axe, Sir," he answered.

The officer waited for further explanation. None came. The orderly went about his duties. The elder man was sullenly angry. His servant avoided him. And the next day he had to use all his willpower to avoid seeing the scarred thumb. He wanted to get hold of it and——. A hot flame ran in his blood.

He knew his servant would soon be free, and would be glad. As yet, the soldier had held himself off from the elder man. The Captain grew madly irritable. He could not rest when the soldier was away, and when he was present, he glared at him with tormented eyes. He hated those fine, black brows over the reserved, dark eyes, he was infuriated by the free movement of the handsome limbs, which no military discipline could make stiff. And he became harsh and cruelly bullying, using contempt and satire. The young soldier only grew more mute and expressionless.

"What scum were you bred by, that you can't keep straight eyes? Look at me when I speak to you."

And the soldier turned his dark eyes to the other's face, but there was no sight in them: he stared with the slightest possible cast, holding back his sight, perceiving the blue of his master's eyes, but receiving no look from them. And the elder man went pale with fury, and his reddish eyebrows twitched. He gave his order, barrenly.

But there were only two months more. The youth tried to keep himself intact: he tried to serve the officer as if the latter were an abstract authority and not a man. All his instinct was to avoid personal contact, even definite hate. But in spite of himself the hate grew, responsive to the officer's passion. However, he would keep it in the background. When he had left the Army he could vent it in expression. By nature he was active, and had many friends. But there was always some part of himself that had been apart from his comrades, they had ranged themselves on their own side, left him alone on his. Now this solitariness was intensified. It would carry him through his term. But the officer seemed to be going irritably insane, and the youth was deeply frightened.

The soldier had a sweetheart, a girl from the mountains, independent and primitive. The two walked together, rather silently. He went with her, not to talk, but to have his arm round her, and for the physical contact. This eased him, made it easier for him to ignore the Captain; for he could rest with her held fast against his chest. And she, in some unbroken fashion, was there for him.

But the Captain perceived it, and was mad with mortification. He kept the young man engaged all the evenings long, and took pleasure in the dark look that came on his face. Occasionally, the eyes of the two men met, those of the younger sullen and reserved, waiting doggedly, those of the elder sneering with restless contempt.

The officer tried hard not to acknowledge the passion that had got hold of him. He would not admit that his feeling for his orderly was anything but that of a man incensed by a stupid, perverse servant. So, keeping quite justified and conventional in his consciousness, he let the other thing run on. His nerves, however, were suffering. At last he slung the end of a belt in his servant's face. When he saw the youth start back, the pain-tears in his eyes and the blood on his mouth, he had felt at once a thrill of deep pleasure and of shame.

But this, he acknowledged to himself, was a thing he had never done before. The fellow was too exasperating. But his own nerves must be going to pieces. He went away for some days with a woman.

It was a mockery of pleasure. He simply did not want the woman. But he hung on for his time. At the end of it, he came back in an agony of irritation, torment, and misery. He rode all the evening, then came straight in to supper. His orderly was out. The officer sat with his long, fine hands lying on the table, perfectly still, and all his blood seemed to be corroding.

At last his servant entered. He watched the strong, easy young figure, the fine eyebrows, the thick black hair. In a week's time the youth had got back his old well-being. The hands of the officer twitched and seemed to be full of mad flame. The young man stood at attention, unmoving, shut off.

The meal went in silence. But the orderly seemed eager. He made a clatter with the dishes.

"Are you in a hurry?" asked the officer, watching the intent, warm face of his servant. The other did not reply.

"Will you answer my question?" said the Captain.

"Yes, Sir," replied the orderly, standing with his pile of deep Army plates. The Captain waited, looked at him, then asked again:

"Are you in a hurry?"

"Yes, Sir," came the answer, that sent a flash through the listener.

"For what?"

"I was going out, Sir."

"I want you this evening."

There was a moment's hesitation. The officer had a curious stiffness of countenance.

"Yes, Sir," replied the servant, in his throat.

"I want you tomorrow evening also—in fact, you may consider your evenings occupied, unless I give you leave."

The mouth with the young moustache set close.

"Yes, Sir," answered the orderly, through shut teeth.

He again turned to the door.

"And why have you a piece of pencil in your ear?"

The orderly hesitated, then continued on his way without answering. He set the plates in a pile outside the door, took the stump of pencil from his ear, and put it in his pocket. Having had a sentimental impulse, he had been copying a verse for his sweetheart's birthday card. He returned to finish clearing the table. The officer's eyes were dancing, he had a little, eager smile.

"Why have you a piece of pencil in your ear?" he asked.

The orderly took his hands full of dishes. His master was standing near the great green stove, a little smile on his face, his chin thrust forward. When the young soldier saw him his heart suddenly ran hot. He felt blind. Instead of answering, he turned dazedly to the door. As he was crouching to set down the dishes, he was pitched forward by a kick from behind. The pots went in a stream down the stairs, he clung to the pillar of the bannisters. And as he was rising he was kicked heavily again, and again, so that he clung sickly to the post for some moments. His master had gone swiftly into the room and closed the door. The maidservant downstairs looked up the staircase and made a mocking face at the crockery disaster.

The officer's heart was plunging.

"Schöner!" he said.

The soldier was a little slower in coming to attention.

"Yes, Sir!"

The youth stood before him, with pathetic young moustache, and fine eyebrows very distinct on his forehead of dark marble.

"I asked you a question."

"Yes, Sir."

The officer's tone bit like acid.

"Why had you a pencil in your ear?"

Again the servant's heart ran hot, and he could not breathe. With dark, strained eyes, he looked at the officer as if fascinated. And he stood there sturdily planted, unconscious. The withering smile came into the Captain's eyes, and he lifted his foot.

"I—I forgot it—Sir," panted the soldier, his dark eyes fixed on the other man's dancing blue ones.

"What was it doing there?"

He saw the young man's breast heaving as he panted for words.

"I had been writing."

"Writing what?"

Again the soldier looked him up and down. The officer could hear him panting. The smile came into the blue eyes. The soldier worked his dry throat, but could not speak. Suddenly the smile lit like a flame on the officer's face, and a kick came heavily against the orderly's thigh. The youth moved a pace sideways. His face went dead, with two black, staring eyes.

"Well?" said the officer.

The orderly's mouth had gone dry, and his tongue rubbed in it as on dry brown paper. He worked his throat. The officer raised his foot. The servant went stiff.

"Some poetry, Sir," came the crackling, unrecognizable sound of his voice.

"Poetry, to whom?" asked the Captain, with a sickly smile.

Again there was the working in the throat. The Captain's heart had suddenly gone down heavily, and he stood sick and tired.

"My girl, Sir," he heard the dry, inhuman sound.

"Oh!" he said, turning away. "Clear the table."

"Click" went the soldier's throat; then again, "click!"; and then the half-articulate:

"Yes, Sir."

The young soldier was gone, looking old, and walking heavily.

The officer, left alone, held himself rigid, to prevent himself from thinking. His instinct warned him that he must not think. Deep inside him was the intense gratification of his passion, still working powerfully. Then there was a counteraction, a horrible breaking down of something inside him, a whole agony of reaction. He stood there for an hour motionless, a chaos of sensations, but rigid with a will to keep blank his consciousness, to prevent his mind grasping. And he held himself so until the worst of the stress had passed, when he began to drink, drank himself to an intoxication, till he slept obliterated.

The orderly had gone about in a stupor all the evening. He drank some beer because he was parched, but not much, the alcohol made his feeling come back, and he could not bear it. He was dulled, as if nine-tenths of the ordinary man in him were killed. He crawled about disfigured. Still, when he thought of the kicks, he went sick, and when he thought of the threat of more kicking, in the room afterwards, his heart went hot and faint, and he panted, remembering the one that had come. He had been forced to say, "To my girl." He was much too done even to want to cry.

In the morning were the maneuvers. But he woke even before the bugle sounded. The painful ache in his chest, the dryness of his throat, the awful steady feeling of misery made his eyes come awake and dreary at once. But he knew, without thinking, what had happened. And he knew that the day had come again, when he must go on with his round. The last bit of darkness was being pushed out of the room. He would have to drag up his inert body and go on. He was so young, and had known so little trouble, that he was bewildered. He only wished it would stay night, so that he could lie still, covered up by the darkness. And yet nothing would prevent the day from coming, nothing would save him from having to get up and saddle the Captain's horse, and make the Captain's coffee. It was there, inevitable. And then, he thought, it was impossible. Yet they would not leave him alone. He must go and take the coffee to the Captain. He was too stunned to understand it. He only knew it was inevitable—inevitable, however long he lay inert.

At last, after heaving at himself, for he seemed to be a mass of inertia, he got up. But he had to force every one of his movements from behind, with his will. He felt lost, and dazed, and helpless. Then he clutched hold of the bed, the pain was so keen. And looking at his thighs, he saw the darker bruises on his swarthy flesh and he knew that, if he pressed one of his fingers on one of the bruises, he should faint. But he did not want to faint—he did not want anybody to know. No one should ever know. It was between him and the Captain. There were only the two people in the world now—himself and the Captain.

Slowly, economically, he got dressed and forced himself to walk. Everything was obscure, except just what he had his hands on. But he managed to get through his work. The very pain revived his dull senses. The worst remained yet. He took the tray and went up to the Captain's room. The officer, pale and heavy, sat at the table. The orderly, as he saluted, felt himself put out of existence. He stood still for a moment submitting to his own nullification—then he gathered himself, on the rebound, and then the Captain seemed to grow vague, unreal, and the young soldier's heart beat up with pride. He clung to this sensation—that the Captain did not exist—so that he himself might live. But when he saw his officer's hand tremble as he took the coffee, he felt everything falling shattered. And he went away, feeling as if he himself were coming to pieces, disintegrated. And when the Captain was there on horseback, giving orders, while he himself stood, with rifle and knapsack, sick with pain, he felt as if he must shut his eyes and be gone—as if he must shut his eyes on his own existence. It was only the long agony of marching with a parched throat that filled him with one single, sleep-heavy intention: to get away, to save himself.

II

He was getting used even to his parched throat. That the snowy peaks were radiant among the sky, that the whitey-green glacier-river twisted through its pale shoals, in the valley below, seemed almost supernatural. But he was going mad with fever and thirst. He plodded on, uncomplaining. He did not want to complain, not to anybody. There were two gulls, like flakes of water and snow, over the river. The scent of green rye soaked in sunshine came like a sickness. And the march continued, monotonously, almost like a bad sleep.

At the next farmhouse, which stood low and broad near the high road, tubs of water had been put out. The soldiers clustered round to drink. They took off their helmets, and the steam mounted from their wet hair. The Captain sat on horseback, watching. He needed to see his orderly. His helmet threw a dark shadow over his light, fierce eyes, but his moustache and mouth and chin were distinct in the sunshine. The orderly could scarcely move in the presence of the figure of the horseman. It was not that he was afraid, or cowed. It was as if he was disemboweled, made empty, like an empty shell. He felt himself as nothing, a shadow creeping under the sunshine. And, thirsty as he was, he could scarcely drink, feeling the Captain near him. He would not take off his helmet to wipe his wet hair. He wanted to efface himself, not to be forced into consciousness. Starting, he saw the light heel of the officer prick the belly of the horse; the Captain cantered away, and he himself could relapse into vacancy.

Nothing, however, could give him back his living place in the hot, bright morning. He felt like a gap among it all. Whereas the Captain was prouder and fuller. A hot flash went through the young servant's body. The Captain was firmer and prouder with life, he himself was empty as a shadow. Again the flash went through him, dazing him out. But his heart ran a little firmer.

The company turned up the hill, to make a loop for the return. Below, from among the trees, the farm bell clanged. He saw the laborers, mowing barefoot at the thick grass, leave off their work and go down hill, their scythes hanging over their shoulders, like long, bright claws curving down behind them. They seemed like dream-people, as if they had no relation to himself. He felt as he felt in a blackish dream: as if all the other things were there and had form, but he himself was only a consciousness, a gap that could think and perceive.

At last there was the halt. They stacked rifles in a conical stack, put down their kit in a scattered circle around it, and dispersed a little, sitting on a small knoll high on the hillside. The chatter began. The soldiers were steaming with heat, but were lively. He sat still, seeing the blue mountains rising upon the land, twenty kilometers away.

Suddenly something moved into the colored mirage before his eyes. The Captain, a small, light-blue and scarlet figure, was trotting evenly between the strips of corn, along the level brow of the hill. And the man making flag-signals was coming on. Proud and sure moved the horseman's figure, the quick, bright thing, in which was concentrated all the light of this morning, which for the rest lay a fragile, shining shadow. Submissive, apathetic, the young soldier sat and stared. But as the horse slowed to a walk, coming up the last steep path, the great flash flared over the body and soul of the orderly. He sat waiting. The back of his head felt as if it were weighted with a heavy piece of fire. He did not want to eat. His hands trembled slightly as he moved them. Meanwhile the officer on horseback was approaching slowly and proudly. The tension grew in the orderly's soul. Then again, seeing the Captain ease himself on the saddle, the flash blazed through him.

The Captain looked at the patch of light-blue and scarlet, and dark heads, scattered closely on the hillside. It pleased him. The command pleased him. And he was feeling proud. His orderly was among them in common subjection. The officer rose a little on his stirrups to look. The young soldier sat with averted, dumb face. The Captain relaxed on to his seat. His slim-legged, beautiful horse, brown as a beechnut, walked proudly uphill. The Captain passed into the zone of the company's atmosphere: a hot smell of men, of sweat, of leather. He knew it very well. After a word with the lieutenant, he went a few paces higher, and sat there, a dominant figure, his sweat-marked horse swishing its tail, while he looked down on his men, on his orderly, a nonentity among the crowd.

The young soldier's heart was like fire in his chest, and he breathed with difficulty. The officer, looking downhill, saw three of the young soldiers, two pails of water between them, staggering across a sunny green field. A table had been set up under a tree, and there the slim lieutenant stood, importantly busy. Then the Captain summoned himself to an act of courage. He called his orderly.

The flame leapt into the young soldier's throat as he heard the command, and he rose blindly, stifled. He saluted, standing below the officer. He did not look up. But there was the flicker in the Captain's voice.

"Go to the inn and fetch me . . . ." the officer gave his commands. "Quick!" he added.

At the last word, the heart of the servant leapt with a flash, and he felt the strength come over his body. But he turned in mechanical obedience, and set off at a heavy run downhill, looking almost like a bear, his trousers bagging over his military boots. And the officer watched this blind, plunging run all the way.

But it was only the outside of the orderly's body that was obeying so humbly and mechanically. Inside had gradually accumulated a core into which all the energy of that young life was compact and concentrated. He executed his commission, and plodded quickly back uphill. There was a pain in his head, as he walked, that made him twist his features unknowingly. But hard there in the center of his chest was himself, himself, firm, and not to be plucked to pieces.

The Captain had gone up into the wood. The orderly plodded through the hot, powerfully-smelling zone of the company's atmosphere. He had a curious mass of energy inside him now. The Captain was less real than himself. He approached the green entrance to the wood. There, in the half-shade, he saw the horse standing, the sunshine and the flickering shadow of leaves dancing over his brown body. There was a clearing where timber had lately been felled. Here, in the gold-green shade beside the brilliant cup of sunshine, stood two figures, blue and pink, the bits of pink showing out plainly. The Captain was talking to his lieutenant.

The orderly stood on the edge of the bright clearing, where great trunks of trees, supple and glistening, lay stretched like naked, brown-skinned bodies. Chips of wood littered the trampled floor, and the bases of the felled trees rose here and there, with their raw, level tops. Beyond was the brilliant, sunlit green of a beech.

"Then I will ride forward," the orderly heard his Captain say. The lieutenant saluted and strode away. He himself went forward. A hot flash passed through his belly, as he tramped towards his officer.

The Captain watched the rather heavy figure of the young soldier stumble forward, and his veins, too, ran hot. This was to be another man to man encounter. He yielded before the solid, stumbling figure with bent head. The orderly stooped and put the food on a level-sawn tree base. The Captain watched the glistening sun-inflamed, naked hands. He wanted to speak to the young soldier, but could not. The servant propped a bottle against his thigh, pressed open the cork, and poured out the beer into the mug. He kept his head bent. The Captain accepted the mug.

"Hot!" he said, as if amiably.

The flame sprang out of the orderly's heart, nearly suffocating him.

"Yes, Sir," he replied, between shut teeth.

And he heard the sound of the Captain's drinking, and he clenched his fists, such a strong torment came into his wrists. Then came the faint clang of the closing of the pot lid. He looked up. The Captain was watching him. He glanced swiftly away. Then he saw the officer stoop and take a piece of bread from the tree base. Again the flash of flame went through the young soldier, seeing the proud body stoop beneath him, and his hands jerked. He looked away. He could feel the officer was nervous. The bread fell as it was being broken. The officer ate the other piece. The two men stood tense and still, the master laboriously chewing his bread, the servant staring with averted face, his fists clenched.

Then the young soldier started. The officer had pressed open the lid of the pot again. The orderly watched the lid of the mug, and the white hand that clenched the handle, as if he were fascinated. It was raised. The youth followed it with his eyes. And then he saw the thin, strong throat of the elder man moving up and down as he drank, the strong jaw working. And the instinct which had been jerking at the young man's wrists suddenly jerked free. He jumped, feeling as if he were rent in two by a strong flame. He had lost his normal consciousness.

The spur of the officer caught in a tree root, he went down backwards with a crash, the middle of his back thudding sickeningly against a sharp-edged tree base, the pot flying away. And in a second his orderly, with serious, earnest young face, and underlip between his teeth, had got his knee in his chest and was pressing the chin backward over the farther edge of the tree stump, pressing, with all his heart behind in a passion of relief, the tension of his wrists exquisite with relief. And with the base of his palms he shoved at the chin, with all his might. And it was pleasant, too, to have that chin, that hard jaw already slightly rough with beard, in his hands. He did not relax one hair's breadth, but, all the force of all his blood exulting in his thrust, he shoved back the head of the other man, till there was a little "cluck" and a crunching sensation. Then he felt as if his head went to vapor. Heavy convulsions shook the body of the officer, frightening and horrifying the young soldier. Yet it pleased him, too, to repress them. It pleased him to keep his hands pressing back the chin, to feel the chest of the other man yield in expiration to the weight of his strong, young knees, to feel the hard twitchings of the prostrate body jerking his own whole frame, which was pressed down on it.

But it went still. He could look into the nostrils of the other man, the eyes he could scarcely see. How curiously the mouth was pushed out, exaggerating the full lips, and the moustache bristling up from them. Then, with a start, he noticed the nostrils gradually filled with blood. The red brimmed, hesitated, ran over, and went in a thin trickle down the face to the eyes.

It shocked and distressed him. Slowly, he got up. The body twitched and sprawled there, inert. He stood and looked at it in silence. It was a pity *it* was broken. It represented more than the thing which had kicked and bullied him. He was afraid to look at the eyes. They were hideous now, only the whites showing, and the blood running to them. The face of the orderly was drawn with horror at the sight. Well, it was so. In his heart he was satisfied. He had hated the face of the Captain, It was extinguished now. There was a heavy relief in the orderly's soul. That was as it should be. But he could not bear to see the long, military body lying broken over the tree base, the fine fingers crisped. He wanted to hide it away.

Quickly, busily, he gathered it up and laid it under the felled tree trunks, which rested their beautiful, smooth length either end on logs. The face was horrible with blood. He covered it with the helmet. Then he put the limbs straight and decent, and brushed the dead leaves off the fine cloth of the uniform. So, it lay quite still in the shadow under there. A little strip of sunshine ran along the breast, from a chink between the logs. The orderly sat by it for a few moments. Here his own life also ended.

Then, through his daze, he heard the lieutenant, in a loud voice, explaining to the men outside the wood, that they were to suppose the bridge on the river below was held by the enemy. Now they were to march to the attack in such and such a manner. The lieutenant had no gift of expression. The orderly, listening from habit, got muddled. And when the lieutenant began it all again, he ceased to hear.

He knew he must go. He stood up. It surprised him that the leaves were glittering in the sun, and the chips of wood reflecting white from the ground. For him a change had come over the world. But for the rest it had not—all the world seemed the same. Only he had left it. And he could not go back. It was his duty to return with the beer-pot and the bottle. He could not. He had left all that. The lieutenant was still hoarsely explaining. He must go, or they would overtake him. And he could not bear contact with anyone now.

He drew his fingers over his eyes, trying to find out where he was. Then he turned away. He saw the horse standing in the path. He went up to it and mounted. It hurt him to sit in the saddle. The pain of keeping his seat occupied him as they cantered through the wood. He would not have minded anything, but he could not get away from the sense of being cut off from the others. The path led out of the trees. On the edge of the wood he pulled up and stood watching. There in the spacious sunshine of the valley soldiers were moving in a little swarm.

Every now and then, a man harrowing on a strip of fallow shouted to his oxen, at the turn. The village and the white-towered church was small in the sunshine. And he no longer belonged to it—he sat there, beyond, like a man outside in the dark. He had gone out from everyday life into the unknown, and he could not, he even did not want to go back.

Turning from the sun-blazing valley, he rode deep into the wood. Tree trunks, like people standing gray and still, took no notice as he went. A doe, herself a moving bit of sunshine and shadow, went running through the flecked shade. There were bright green rents in the foliage. Then it was all pinewood, dark and cool. And he was sick with pain, he had an intolerable great pulse in his head, and he was sick. He had never been ill in his life. He felt lost, quite dazed with all this.

Trying to get down from the horse, he fell, astonished at the pain and his lack of balance. The horse shifted uneasily. He jerked its bridle and sent it cantering jerkily away. It was his last connection with the rest of things.

But he only wanted to lie down and not be disturbed. Stumbling through the trees, he came on a quiet place where beeches and pine trees grew on a slope. Immediately he had lain down and closed his eyes, his consciousness went racing on without him. A big pulse of sickness beat in him as if it throbbed through the whole earth. He was burning with dry heat. But he was too busy, too tearingly active in the incoherent race of delirium to observe.

III

He came to with a start. His mouth was dry and hard, his heart beat heavily, but he had not the energy to get up. His heart beat heavily. Where was he?—the barracks—at home? There was something knocking. And, making an effort, he looked round—trees, and litter of greenery, and reddish, bright, still pieces of sunshine on the floor. He did not believe he was himself, he did not believe what he saw. Something was knocking. He made a struggle towards consciousness, but relapsed. Then he struggled again. And gradually his surroundings fell into relationship with himself. He knew, and a great pang of fear went through his heart. Somebody was knocking. He could see the heavy, black rags of a fir tree overhead. Then everything went black. Yet he did not believe he had closed his eyes. He had not. Out of the blackness sight slowly emerged again. And someone was knocking. Quickly, he saw the blood-disfigured face of his Captain, which he hated. And he held himself still with horror. Yet, deep inside him, he knew that it was so, the Captain should be dead. But the physical delirium got hold of him.

Someone was knocking. He lay perfectly still, as if dead, with fear. And he went unconscious.

When he opened his eyes again, he started, seeing something creeping swiftly up a tree trunk. It was a little bird. And a bird was whistling overhead. Tap-tap-tap—it was the small, quick bird rapping the tree trunk with its beak, as if its head were a little round hammer. He watched it curiously. It shifted sharply, in its creeping fashion. Then, like a mouse, it slid down the bare trunk. Its swift creeping sent a flash of revulsion through him. He raised his head. It felt a great weight. Then, the little bird ran out of the shadow across a still patch of sunshine, its little head bobbing swiftly, its white legs twinkling brightly for a moment. How neat it was, in its build, so compact, with pieces of white on its wings. There were several of them. They were so pretty—but they crept like swift, erratic mice, running here and there among the beechmast.

He lay down again, exhausted, and his consciousness lapsed. He had a horror of the little creeping birds. All his blood seemed to be darting and creeping.

Struggling to his feet, he lurched away. He went on walking, walking, looking for something—for a drink. His brain felt hot and inflamed for want of water. He stumbled on. Then he did not know anything. He went unconscious as he walked. Yet he stumbled on, his mouth open.

When, to his dumb wonder, he opened his eyes on the world again, he no longer tried to remember what it was. There was thick, golden light behind golden-green glitterings, and tall, gray-purple shafts, and darknesses further off, surrounding him, growing deeper. He was conscious of a sense of arrival. He was amid the truth. But there was the thirst burning a hole in his brain. He felt lighter, not so heavy. He supposed it was newness. The air was muttering with thunder. He thought he was walking wonderfully swiftly and was coming straight to relief—or to water to drink.

Suddenly he stood still with fear. There was a tremendous flare of deep gold, immense—just a few dark trunks like bars between him and it. All the young level wheat was burnished, gold glaring on its silky green. A woman, full-skirted, a black cloth on her head for headdress, was passing like a block of shadow through the glistening, green corn, into the full glare. There was a farm, too, pale blue in shadow, and the timber black. And there was a church spire, nearly fused away in the gold. The woman moved on, away from him. He had no language with which to speak to her. His connection with her was gone. She would make a noise of words that would confuse him, and her eyes would look at him without seeing him. She was crossing there to the other side. He stood leaning against a tree.

When at last he turned, looking down the long, bare groove whose flat bed was already filling dark, he saw the mountains in a wonder-light, not far away, and radiant. Behind the soft, gray ridge of the nearest range the further mountains stood golden and pale gray, the snow all radiant like pure, soft gold. So still, gleaming in the sky, fashioned pure out of the ore of the sky, they shone in their silence. He stood and looked at them, his face illuminated. And like the golden, lustrous gleaming of the snow he felt his own thirst bright in him. He stood and gazed, leaning against a tree. And then everything slid away into space.

During the night the lightning fluttered perpetually, making the whole sky white. He must have walked again. The world hung livid round him for moments, fields a level sheen of gray-green light, trees in dark bulk, and the range of clouds black across a white sky. Then the darkness fell like a shutter, and the night was whole. A faint flutter of a half-revealed world, that could not quite leap out of the darkness!—Then there again stood a sweep of pallor for the land, dark shapes looming, a range of clouds hanging overhead. The world was a ghostly shadow, thrown for a moment upon the pure darkness, which returned ever whole and complete.

And the mere delirium of sickness and fever went on inside him—his brain opening and shutting like the night—then sometimes convulsions of terror from something with great eyes that stared round a tree—then the long agony of the march, and the sun decomposing his blood—then the pang of hate for the Captain, followed by the pang of tenderness and ease. But everything was distorted, born of an ache and resolving into an ache.

In the morning he came definitely awake. Then his brain flamed with the sole horror of thirstiness! The sun was on his face, the dew was steaming from his wet clothes. Like one possessed, he got up. There, straight in front of him, blue and cool and tender, the mountains ranged across the pale edge of the morning sky. He wanted them—he wanted them alone—he wanted to leave himself, to be identified with them. They did not move, they were still and soft, with white, gentle markings of snow. He stood still, mad with suffering, his hands crisping and clutching. Then he was twisting in a paroxysm on the grass.

He lay still, in a kind of dream of anguish. His thirst seemed to have separated itself from him, and to stand apart, a single demand. Then the pain he felt was another single self. Then there was the clog of his body, another separate thing. He was divided among all kinds of separate beings. There was some strange, agonized connection between them, but they were drawing further apart. Then they would all split. The sun, drilling down on him, was drilling through the bond. Then they would all fall, fall through the everlasting lapse of space.

Then again, his consciousness reasserted itself. He roused on to his elbow and stared at the gleaming mountains. There they ranked, all still and wonderful between earth and heaven. He stared till his eyes went black, and the mountains, as they stood in their beauty, so clean and cool, seemed to have it, that which was lost in him.

IV

When the soldiers found him, three hours later, he was lying with his face over his arm, his black hair giving off heat under the sun. But he was still alive. Seeing the open, black mouth the young soldiers started from him in horror.

He died in the hospital at night without having seen again.

The doctors saw the bruises on his legs, behind, and were silent. On this account the affair was hushed up.

The bodies of the two men lay together, side by side, in the mortuary, the one white and slender, but laid rigidly at rest, the other looking as if every moment it must rouse into life again, so young and unused, from a slumber.

THE THORN IN THE FLESH

I

A wind was running, so that occasionally the poplars whitened as if a flame flew up them. The sky was broken and blue among moving clouds. Patches of sunshine lay on the level fields, and shadows on the rye and the vineyards. In the distance, very blue, the cathedral bristled against the sky, and the houses of the city of Metz clustered vaguely below, like a hill.

Among the fields by the lime trees stood the barracks, upon bare, dry ground, a collection of round-roofed huts of corrugated iron, where the soldiers' nasturtiums climbed brilliantly. There was a tract of vegetable garden at the side, with the soldiers' yellowish lettuces in rows, and at the back the big, hard drilling-yard surrounded by a wire fence.

At this time in the afternoon, the huts were deserted, all the beds pushed up, the soldiers were lounging about under the lime trees waiting for the call to drill. Bachmann sat on a bench in the shade that smelled sickly with blossom. Pale green, wrecked lime flowers were scattered on the ground. He was writing his weekly postcard to his mother. He was a fair, long, limber youth, good-looking. He sat very still indeed, trying to write his postcard. His blue uniform, sagging on him as he sat bent over the card, disfigured his youthful shape. His sunburnt hand waited motionless for the words to come. "Dear mother"— was all he had written. Then he scribbled mechanically: "Many thanks for your letter with what you sent. Everything is all right with me. We are just off to drill on the fortifications——" Here he broke off and sat suspended, oblivious of everything, held in some definite suspense. He looked again at the card. But he could write no more. Out of the knot of his consciousness no word would come. He signed himself, and looked up, as a man looks to see if any one has noticed him in his privacy.

There was a self-conscious strain in his blue eyes, and a pallor about his mouth, where the young, fair moustache glistened. He was almost girlish in his good looks and his grace. But he had something of military consciousness, as if he believed in the discipline for himself, and found satisfaction in delivering himself to his duty. There was also a trace of youthful swagger and daredevilry about his mouth and his limber body, but this was in suppression now.

He put the postcard in the pocket of his tunic, and went to join a group of his comrades who were lounging in the shade, laughing and talking grossly. Today he was out of it. He only stood near to them for the warmth of the association. In his own consciousness something held him down.

Presently they were summoned to ranks. The sergeant came out to take command. He was a strongly built, rather heavy man of forty. His head was thrust forward, sunk a little between his powerful shoulders, and the strong jaw was pushed out aggressively. But the eyes were smoldering, the face hung slack and sodden with drink.

He gave his orders in brutal, barking shouts, and the little company moved forward, out of the wire-fenced yard to the open road, marching rhythmically, raising the dust. Bachmann, one of the inner file of four deep, marched in the airless ranks, half suffocated with heat and dust and enclosure. Through the moving of his comrades' bodies, he could see the small vines dusty by the roadside, the poppies among the tares fluttering and blown to pieces, the distant spaces of sky and fields all free with air and sunshine. But he was bound in a very dark enclosure of anxiety within himself.

He marched with his usual ease, being healthy and well adjusted. But his body went on by itself. His spirit was clenched apart. And ever the few soldiers drew nearer and nearer to the town, ever the consciousness of the youth became more gripped and separate, his body worked by a kind of mechanical intelligence, a mere presence of mind.

They diverged from the high road and passed in single file down a path among trees. All was silent and green and mysterious, with shadow of foliage and long, green, undisturbed grass. Then they came out in the sunshine on a moat of water, which wound silently between the long, flowery grass, at the foot of the earthworks, that rose in front in terraces walled smooth on the face, but all soft with long grass at the top. Marguerite daisies and lady's-slipper glimmered white and gold in the lush grass, preserved here in the intense peace of the fortifications.

Thickets of trees stood round about. Occasionally a puff of mysterious wind made the flowers and the long grass that crested the earthworks above bow and shake as with signals of oncoming alarm.

The group of soldiers stood at the end of the moat, in their light blue and scarlet uniforms, very bright. The sergeant was giving them instructions, and his shout came sharp and alarming in the intense, untouched stillness of the place. They listened, finding it difficult to make the effort of understanding.

Then it was over, and the men were moving to make preparations. On the other side of the moat the ramparts rose smooth and clear in the sun, sloping slightly back. Along the summit grass grew and tall daisies stood ledged high, like magic, against the dark green of the treetops behind. The noise of the town, the running of tramcars, was heard distinctly, but it seemed not to penetrate this still place.

The water of the moat was motionless. In silence the practice began. One of the soldiers took a scaling ladder, and passing along the narrow ledge at the foot of the earthworks, with the water of the moat just behind him, tried to get a fixture on the slightly sloping wall-face. There he stood, small and isolated, at the foot of the wall, trying to get his ladder settled. At last it held, and the clumsy, groping figure in the baggy blue uniform began to clamber up. The rest of the soldiers stood and watched. Occasionally the sergeant barked a command. Slowly the clumsy blue figure clambered higher up the wall-face. Bachmann stood with his bowels turned to water. The figure of the climbing soldier scrambled out on to the terrace up above, and moved, blue and distinct, among the bright green grass. The officer shouted from below. The soldier tramped along, fixed the ladder in another spot, and carefully lowered himself on to the rungs. Bachmann watched the blind foot groping in space for the ladder, and he felt the world fall away beneath him. The figure of the soldier clung cringing against the face of the wall, cleaving, groping downwards like some unsure insect working its way lower and lower, fearing every movement. At last, sweating and with a strained face, the figure had landed safely and turned to the group of soldiers. But still it had a stiffness and a blank, mechanical look, was something less than human.

Bachmann stood there heavy and condemned, waiting for his own turn and betrayal. Some of the men went up easily enough, and without fear. That only showed it could be done lightly, and made Bachmann's case more bitter. If only he could do it lightly, like that.

His turn came. He knew intuitively that nobody knew his condition. The officer just saw him as a mechanical thing. He tried to keep it up, to carry it through on the face of things. His inside gripped tight, as yet under control, he took the ladder and went along under the wall. He placed his ladder with quick success, and wild, quivering hope possessed him. Then blindly he began to climb. But the ladder was not very firm; and at every hitch a great, sick, melting feeling took hold of him. He clung on fast. If only he could keep that grip on himself, he would get through. He knew this, in agony. What he could not understand was the blind gush of white-hot fear, that came with great force whenever the ladder swerved, and which almost melted his belly and all his joints, and left him powerless. If once it melted all his joints and his belly, he was done. He clung desperately to himself. He knew the fear, he knew what it did when it came, he knew he had only to keep a firm hold. He knew all this. Yet, when the ladder swerved and his foot missed, there was the great blast of fear blowing on his heart and bowels, and he was melting weaker and weaker, in a horror of fear and lack of control, melting to fall.

Yet he groped slowly higher and higher, always staring upwards with desperate face, and always conscious of the space below. But all of him, body and soul, was growing hot to fusion point. He would have to let go for very relief's sake. Suddenly his heart began to lurch. It gave a great, sickly swoop, rose, and again plunged in a swoop of horror. He lay against the wall inert as if dead, inert, at peace, save for one deep core of anxiety, which knew that it was *not* all over, that he was still high in space against the wall. But the chief effort of will was gone.

There came into his consciousness a small, foreign sensation. He woke up a little. What was it? Then slowly it penetrated him. His water had run down his leg. He lay there, clinging, still with shame, half conscious of the echo of the sergeant's voice thundering from below. He waited, in depths of shame beginning to recover himself. He had been shamed so deeply. Then he could go on, for his fear for himself was conquered. His shame was known and published. He must go on.

Slowly he began to grope for the rung above, when a great shock shook through him. His wrists were grasped from above, he was being hauled out of himself up, up to the safe ground. Like a sack he was dragged over the edge of the earthworks by the large hands, and landed there on his knees, groveling in the grass to recover command of himself, to rise up on his feet.

Shame, blind, deep shame and ignominy overthrew his spirit and left it writhing. He stood there shrunk over himself, trying to obliterate himself.

Then the presence of the officer who had hauled him up made itself felt upon him. He heard the panting of the elder man, and then the voice came down on his veins like a fierce whip. He shrank in tension of shame.

"Put up your head—eyes front," shouted the enraged sergeant, and mechanically the soldier obeyed the command, forced to look into the eyes of the sergeant. The brutal, hanging face of the officer violated the youth. He hardened himself with all his might from seeing it. The tearing noise of the sergeant's voice continued to lacerate his body.

Suddenly he set back his head, rigid, and his heart leapt to burst. The face had suddenly thrust itself close, all distorted and showing the teeth, the eyes smoldering into him. The breath of the barking words was on his nose and mouth. He stepped aside in revulsion. With a scream the face was upon him again. He raised his arm, involuntarily, in self-defense. A shock of horror went through him, as he felt his forearm hit the face of the officer a brutal blow. The latter staggered, swerved back, and with a curious cry, reeled backwards over the ramparts, his hands clutching the air. There was a second of silence, then a crash to water.

Bachmann, rigid, looked out of his inner silence upon the scene. Soldiers were running.

"You'd better clear," said one young, excited voice to him. And with immediate instinctive decision he started to walk away from the spot. He went down the tree-hidden path to the high road where the trams ran to and from the town. In his heart was a sense of vindication, of escape. He was leaving it all, the military world, the shame. He was walking away from it.

Officers on horseback rode sauntering down the street, soldiers passed along the pavement. Coming to the bridge, Bachmann crossed over to the town that heaped before him, rising from the flat, picturesque French houses down below at the water's edge, up a jumble of roofs and chasms of streets, to the lovely dark cathedral with its myriad pinnacles making points at the sky.

He felt for the moment quite at peace, relieved from a great strain. So he turned along by the river to the public gardens. Beautiful were the heaped, purple lilac trees upon the green grass, and wonderful the walls of the horse-chestnut trees, lighted like an altar with white flowers on every ledge. Officers went by, elegant and all colored, women and girls sauntered in the chequered shade. Beautiful it was, he walked in a vision, free.

II

But where was he going? He began to come out of his trance of delight and liberty. Deep within him he felt the steady burning of shame in the flesh. As yet he could not bear to think of it. But there it was, submerged beneath his attention, the raw, steady-burning shame.

It behooved him to be intelligent. As yet he dared not remember what he had done. He only knew the need to get away, away from everything he had been in contact with.

But how? A great pang of fear went through him. He could not bear his shamed flesh to be put again between the hands of authority. Already the hands had been laid upon him, brutally upon his nakedness, ripping open his shame and making him maimed, crippled in his own control.

Fear became an anguish. Almost blindly he was turning in the direction of the barracks. He could not take the responsibility of himself. He must give himself up to someone. Then his heart, obstinate in hope, became obsessed with the idea of his sweetheart. He would make himself her responsibility.

Blenching as he took courage, he mounted the small, quick-hurrying tram that ran out of the town in the direction of the barracks. He sat motionless and composed, static.

He got out at the terminus and went down the road. A wind was still running. He could hear the faint whisper of the rye, and the stronger swish as a sudden gust was upon it. No one was about. Feeling detached and impersonal, he went down a field-path between the low vines. Many little vine trees rose up in spires, holding out tender pink shoots, waving their tendrils. He saw them distinctly, and wondered over them. In a field a little way off, men and women were taking up the hay. The bullock-wagon stood by on the path, the men in their blue shirts, the women with white cloths over their heads carried hay in their arms to the cart, all brilliant and distinct upon the shorn, glowing green acres. He felt himself looking out of darkness on to the glamorous, brilliant beauty of the world around him, outside him.

The Baron's house, where Emilie was maidservant, stood square and mellow among trees and garden and fields. It was an old French grange. The barracks was quite near. Bachmann walked, drawn by a single purpose, towards the courtyard. He entered the spacious, shadowy, sun-swept place. The dog, seeing a soldier, only jumped and whined for greeting. The pump stood peacefully in a corner, under a lime tree, in the shade.

The kitchen door was open. He hesitated, then walked in, speaking shyly and smiling involuntarily. The two women started, but with pleasure. Emilie was preparing the tray for afternoon coffee. She stood beyond the table, drawn up, startled, and challenging, and glad. She had the proud, timid eyes of some wild animal, some proud animal. Her black hair was closely banded, her gray eyes watched steadily. She wore a peasant dress of blue cotton sprigged with little red roses, that buttoned tight over her strong maiden breasts.

At the table sat another young woman, the nursery governess, who was picking cherries from a huge heap, and dropping them into a bowl. She was young, pretty, freckled.

"Good day!" she said pleasantly. "The unexpected."

Emilie did not speak. The flush came in her dark cheek. She still stood watching, between fear and a desire to escape, and on the other hand joy that kept her in his presence.

"Yes," he said, bashful and strained, while the eyes of the two women were upon him. "I've got myself in a mess this time."

"What?" asked the nursery governess, dropping her hands in her lap. Emilie stood rigid.

Bachmann could not raise his head. He looked sideways at the glistening, ruddy cherries. He could not recover the normal world.

"I knocked Sergeant Huber over the fortifications down into the moat," he said. "It was an accident—but——"

And he grasped at the cherries, and began to eat them, unknowing, hearing only Emilie's little exclamation.

"You knocked him over the fortifications!" echoed Fräulein Hesse in horror. "How?"

Spitting the cherry-stones into his hand, mechanically, absorbedly, he told them.

"Ach!" exclaimed Emilie sharply.

"And how did you get here?" asked Fräulein Hesse.

"I ran off," he said.

There was a dead silence. He stood, putting himself at the mercy of the women. There came a hissing from the stove, and a stronger smell of coffee. Emilie turned swiftly away. He saw her flat, straight back and her strong loins, as she bent over the stove.

"But what are you going to do?" said Fräulein Hesse, aghast.

"I don't know," he said, grasping at more cherries. He had come to an end.

"You'd better go to the barracks," she said. "We'll get the Herr Baron to come and see about it."

Emilie was swiftly and quietly preparing the tray. She picked it up, and stood with the glittering china and silver before her, impassive, waiting for his reply. Bachmann remained with his head dropped, pale and obstinate. He could not bear to go back.

"I'm going to try to get into France," he said.

"Yes, but they'll catch you," said Fräulein Hesse.

Emilie watched with steady, watchful gray eyes.

"I can have a try, if I could hide till tonight," he said.

Both women knew what he wanted. And they all knew it was no good. Emilie picked up the tray, and went out. Bachmann stood with his head dropped. Within himself he felt the dross of shame and incapacity.

"You'd never get away," said the governess.

"I can try," he said.

Today he could not put himself between the hands of the military. Let them do as they liked with him tomorrow, if he escaped today.

They were silent. He ate cherries. The color flushed bright into the cheek of the young governess.

Emilie returned to prepare another tray.

"He could hide in your room," the governess said to her.

The girl drew herself away. She could not bear the intrusion.

"That is all I can think of that is safe from the children," said Fräulein Hesse.

Emilie gave no answer. Bachmann stood waiting for the two women. Emilie did not want the close contact with him.

"You could sleep with me," Fräulein Hesse said to her.

Emilie lifted her eyes and looked at the young man, direct, clear, reserving herself.

"Do you want that?" she asked, her strong virginity proof against him.

"Yes—yes——" he said uncertainly, destroyed by shame.

She put back her head.

"Yes," she murmured to herself.

Quickly she filled the tray, and went out.

"But you can't walk over the frontier in a night," said Fräulein Hesse.

"I can cycle," he said.

Emilie returned, a restraint, a neutrality in her bearing.

"I'll see if it's all right," said the governess.

In a moment or two Bachmann was following Emilie through the square hall, where hung large maps on the walls. He noticed a child's blue coat with brass buttons on the peg, and it reminded him of Emilie walking holding the hand of the youngest child, whilst he watched, sitting under the lime tree. Already this was a long way off. That was a sort of freedom he had lost, changed for a new, immediate anxiety.

They went quickly, fearfully up the stairs and down a long corridor. Emilie opened her door, and he entered, ashamed, into her room.

"I must go down," she murmured, and she departed, closing the door softly.

It was a small, bare, neat room. There was a little dish for holy water, a picture of the Sacred Heart, a crucifix, and a *prie-Dieu*. The small bed lay white and untouched, the wash-hand bowl of red earth stood on a bare table, there was a little mirror and a small chest of drawers. That was all.

Feeling safe, in sanctuary, he went to the window, looking over the courtyard at the shimmering, afternoon country. He was going to leave this land, this life. Already he was in the unknown.

He drew away into the room. The curious simplicity and severity of the little Roman Catholic bedroom was foreign but restoring to him. He looked at the crucifix. It was a long, lean, peasant Christ carved by a peasant in the Black Forest. For the first time in his life Bachmann saw the figure as a human thing. It represented a man hanging there in helpless torture. He stared at it, closely, as if for new knowledge.

Within his own flesh burned and smoldered the restless shame. He could not gather himself together. There was a gap in his soul. The shame within him seemed to displace his strength and his manhood.

He sat down on his chair. The shame, the roused feeling of exposure acted on his brain, made him heavy, unutterably heavy.

Mechanically, his wits all gone, he took off his boots, his belt, his tunic, put them aside, and lay down, heavy, and fell into a kind of drugged sleep.

Emilie came in a little while, and looked at him. But he was sunk in sleep. She saw him lying there inert, and terribly still, and she was afraid. His shirt was unfastened at the throat. She saw his pure white flesh, very clean and beautiful. And he slept inert. His legs, in the blue uniform trousers, his feet in the coarse stockings, lay foreign on her bed. She went away.

III

She was uneasy, perturbed to her last fiber. She wanted to remain clear, with no touch on her. A wild instinct made her shrink away from any hands which might be laid on her.

She was a foundling, probably of some gypsy race, brought up in a Roman Catholic Rescue Home. A naive, paganly religious being, she was attached to the Baroness, with whom she had served for seven years, since she was fourteen.

She came into contact with no one, unless it were with Ida Hesse, the governess. Ida was a calculating, good-natured, not very straightforward flirt. She was the daughter of a poor country doctor. Having gradually come into connection with Emilie, more an alliance than an attachment, she put no distinction of grade between the two of them. They worked together, sang together, walked together, and went together to the rooms of Franz Brand, Ida's sweetheart. There the three talked and laughed together, or the women listened to Franz, who was a forester, playing on his violin.

In all this alliance there was no personal intimacy between the young women. Emilie was naturally secluded in herself, of a reserved, native race. Ida used her as a kind of weight to balance her own flighty movement. But the quick, shifty governess, occupied always in her dealings with admirers, did all she could to move the violent nature of Emilie towards some connection with men.

But the dark girl, primitive yet sensitive to a high degree, was fiercely virgin. Her blood flamed with rage when the common soldiers made the long, sucking, kissing noise behind her as she passed. She hated them for their almost jeering offers. She was well protected by the Baroness.

And her contempt of the common men in general was ineffable. But she loved the Baroness, and she revered the Baron, and she was at her ease when she was doing something for the service of a gentleman. Her whole nature was at peace in the service of real masters or mistresses. For her, a gentleman had some mystic quality that left her free and proud in service. The common soldiers were brutes, merely nothing. Her desire was to serve.

She held herself aloof. When, on Sunday afternoon, she had looked through the windows of the Reichshalle in passing, and had seen the soldiers dancing with the common girls, a cold revulsion and anger had possessed her. She could not bear to see the soldiers taking off their belts and pulling open their tunics, dancing with their shirts showing through the open, sagging tunic, their movements gross, their faces transfigured and sweaty, their coarse hands holding their coarse girls under the armpits, drawing the female up to their breasts. She hated to see them clutched breast to breast, the legs of the men moving grossly in the dance.

At evening, when she had been in the garden, and heard on the other side of the hedge the sexual, inarticulate cries of the girls in the embraces of the soldiers, her anger had been too much for her, and she had cried, loud and cold:

"What are you doing there, in the hedge?"

She would have had them whipped.

But Bachmann was not quite a common soldier. Fräulein Hesse had found out about him, and had drawn him and Emilie together. For he was a handsome, blond youth, erect and walking with a kind of pride, unconscious yet clear. Moreover, he came of a rich farming stock, rich for many generations. His father was dead, his mother controlled the moneys for the time being. But if Bachmann wanted a hundred pounds at any moment, he could have them. By trade he, with one of his brothers, was a wagon-builder. The family had the farming, smithy, and wagon-building of their village. They worked because that was the form of life they knew. If they had chosen, they could have lived independent upon their means.

In this way, he was a gentleman in sensibility, though his intellect was not developed. He could afford to pay freely for things. He had, moreover, his native, fine breeding. Emilie wavered uncertainly before him. So he became her sweetheart, and she hungered after him. But she was virgin, and shy, and needed to be in subjection, because she was primitive and had no grasp on civilized forms of living, nor on civilized purposes.

IV

At six o'clock came the inquiry of the soldiers: Had anything been seen of Bachmann? Fräulein Hesse answered, pleased to be playing a role:

"No, I've not seen him since Sunday—have you, Emilie?"

"No, I haven't seen him," said Emilie, and her awkwardness was construed as bashfulness. Ida Hesse, stimulated, asked questions, and played her part.

"But it hasn't killed Sergeant Huber?" she cried in consternation.

"No. He fell into the water. But it gave him a bad shock, and smashed his foot on the side of the moat. He's in hospital. It's a bad lookout for Bachmann."

Emilie, implicated and captive, stood looking on. She was no longer free, working with all this regulated system which she could not understand and which was almost godlike to her. She was put out of her place. Bachmann was in her room, she was no longer the faithful in service serving with religious surety.

Her situation was intolerable to her. All evening long the burden was upon her, she could not live. The children must be fed and put to sleep. The Baron and Baroness were going out, she must give them light refreshment. The manservant was coming in to supper after returning with the carriage. And all the while she had the insupportable feeling of being out of the order, self-responsible, bewildered. The control of her life should come from those above her, and she should move within that control. But now she was out of it, uncontrolled and troubled. More than that, the man, the lover, Bachmann, who was he, what was he? He alone of all men contained for her the unknown quantity which terrified her beyond her service. Oh, she had wanted him as a distant sweetheart, not close, like this, casting her out of her world.

When the Baron and Baroness had departed, and the young manservant had gone out to enjoy himself, she went upstairs to Bachmann. He had wakened up, and sat dimly in the room. Out in the open he heard the soldiers, his comrades, singing the sentimental songs of the nightfall, the drone of the concertina rising in accompaniment.

> Wenn ich zu mei . . . nem Kinde geh' . . .
> In seinem Au . . . g die Mutter seh' . . . .

But he himself was removed from it now. Only the sentimental cry of young, unsatisfied desire in the soldiers' singing penetrated his blood and stirred him subtly. He let his head hang; he had become gradually roused: and he waited in concentration, in another world.

The moment she entered the room where the man sat alone, waiting intensely, the thrill passed through her, she died in terror, and after the death, a great flame gushed up, obliterating her. He sat in trousers and shirt on the side of the bed. He looked up as she came in, and she shrank from his face. She could not bear it. Yet she entered near to him.

"Do you want anything to eat?" she said.

"Yes," he answered, and as she stood in the twilight of the room with him, he could only hear his heart beat heavily. He saw her apron just level with his face. She stood silent, a little distance off, as if she would be there forever. He suffered.

As if in a spell she waited, standing motionless and looming there, he sat rather crouching on the side of the bed. A second will in him was powerful and dominating. She drew gradually nearer to him, coming up slowly, as if unconscious. His heart beat up swiftly. He was going to move.

As she came quite close, almost invisibly he lifted his arms and put them round her waist, drawing her with his will and desire. He buried his face into her apron, into the terrible softness of her belly. And he was a flame of passion intense about her. He had forgotten. Shame and memory were gone in a whole, furious flame of passion.

She was quite helpless. Her hands leapt, fluttered, and closed over his head, pressing it deeper into her belly, vibrating as she did so. And his arms tightened on her, his hands spread over her loins, warm as flame on her loveliness. It was intense anguish of bliss for her, and she lost consciousness.

When she recovered, she lay translated in the peace of satisfaction.

It was what she had had no inkling of, never known could be. She was strong with eternal gratitude. And he was there with her. Instinctively with an instinct of reverence and gratitude, her arms tightened in a little embrace upon him who held her thoroughly embraced.

And he was restored and completed, close to her. That little, twitching, momentary clasp of acknowledgment that she gave him in her satisfaction, roused his pride unconquerable. They loved each other, and all was whole. She loved him, he had taken her, she was given to him. It was right. He was given to her, and they were one, complete.

Warm, with a glow in their hearts and faces, they rose again, modest, but transfigured with happiness.

"I will get you something to eat," she said, and in joy and security of service again, she left him, making a curious little homage of departure. He sat on the side of the bed, escaped, liberated, wondering, and happy.

V

Soon she came again with the tray, followed by Fräulein Hesse. The two women watched him eat, watched the pride and wonder of his being, as he sat there blond and naive again. Emilie felt rich and complete. Ida was a lesser thing than herself.

"And what are you going to do?" asked Fräulein Hesse, jealous.

"I must get away," he said.

But words had no meaning for him. What did it matter? He had the inner satisfaction and liberty.

"But you'll want a bicycle," said Ida Hesse.

"Yes," he said.

Emilie sat silent, removed and yet with him, connected with him in passion. She looked from this talk of bicycles and escape.

They discussed plans. But in two of them was the one will, that Bachmann should stay with Emilie. Ida Hesse was an outsider.

It was arranged, however, that Ida's lover should put out his bicycle, leave it at the hut where he sometimes watched. Bachmann should fetch it in the night, and ride into France. The hearts of all three beat hot in suspense, driven to thought. They sat in a fire of agitation.

Then Bachmann would get away to America, and Emilie would come and join him. They would be in a fine land then. The tale burned up again.

Emilie and Ida had to go round to Franz Brand's lodging. They departed with slight leave-taking. Bachmann sat in the dark, hearing the bugle for retreat sound out of the night. Then he remembered his postcard to his mother. He slipped out after Emilie, gave it her to post. His manner was careless and victorious, hers shining and trustful. He slipped back to shelter.

There he sat on the side of the bed, thinking. Again he went over the events of the afternoon, remembering his own anguish of apprehension because he had known he could not climb the wall without fainting with fear. Still, a flush of shame came alight in him at the memory. But he said to himself: "What does it matter?—I can't help it, well then I can't. If I go up a height, I get absolutely weak, and can't help myself." Again memory came over him, and a gush of shame, like fire. But he sat and endured it. It had to be endured, admitted, and accepted. "I'm not a coward, for all that," he continued. "I'm not afraid of danger. If I'm made that way, that heights melt me and make me let go my water"—it was torture for him to pluck at this truth—"if I'm made like that, I shall have to abide by it, that's all. It isn't all of me." He thought of Emilie, and was satisfied. "What I am, I am; and let it be enough," he thought.

Having accepted his own defect, he sat thinking, waiting for Emilie, to tell her. She came at length, saying that Franz could not arrange about his bicycle this night. It was broken. Bachmann would have to stay over another day.

They were both happy. Emilie, confused before Ida, who was excited and prurient, came again to the young man. She was stiff and dignified with an agony of unusedness. But he took her between his hands, and uncovered her, and enjoyed almost like madness her helpless, virgin body that suffered so strongly, and that took its joy so deeply. While the moisture of torment and modesty was still in her eyes, she clasped him closer, and closer, to the victory and the deep satisfaction of both of them. And they slept together, he in repose still satisfied and peaceful, and she lying close in her static reality.

VI

In the morning, when the bugle sounded from the barracks they rose and looked out of the window. She loved his body that was proud and blond and able to take command. And he loved her body that was soft and eternal. They looked at the faint gray vapor of summer steaming off from the greenness and ripeness of the fields. There was no town anywhere, their look ended in the haze of the summer morning. Their bodies rested together, their minds tranquil. Then a little anxiety stirred in both of them from the sound of the bugle. She was called back to her old position, to realize the world of authority she did not understand but had wanted to serve. But this call died away again from her. She had all.

She went downstairs to her work, curiously changed. She was in a new world of her own, that she had never even imagined, and which was the land of promise for all that. In this she moved and had her being. And she extended it to her duties. She was curiously happy and absorbed. She had not to strive out of herself to do her work. The doing came from within her without call or command. It was a delicious outflow, like sunshine, the activity that flowed from her and put her tasks to rights.

Bachmann sat busily thinking. He would have to get all his plans ready. He must write to his mother, and she must send him money to Paris. He would go to Paris, and from thence, quickly, to America. It had to be done. He must make all preparations. The dangerous part was the getting into France. He thrilled in anticipation. During the day he would need a timetable of the trains going to Paris—he would need to think. It gave him delicious pleasure, using all his wits. It seemed such an adventure.

This one day, and he would escape then into freedom. What an agony of need he had for absolute, imperious freedom. He had won to his own being, in himself and Emilie, he had drawn the stigma from his shame, he was beginning to be himself. And now he wanted madly to be free to go on. A home, his work, and absolute freedom to move and to be, in her, with her, this was his passionate desire. He thought in a kind of ecstasy, living an hour of painful intensity.

Suddenly he heard voices, and a tramping of feet. His heart gave a great leap, then went still. He was taken. He had known all along. A complete silence filled his body and soul, a silence like death, a suspension of life and sound. He stood motionless in the bedroom, in perfect suspension.

Emilie was busy passing swiftly about the kitchen preparing the children's breakfasts when she heard the tramp of feet and the voice of the Baron. The latter had come in from the garden, and was wearing an old green linen suit. He was a man of middle stature, quick, finely made, and of whimsical charm. His right hand had been shot in the Franco-Prussian war, and now, as always when he was much agitated, he shook it down at his side, as if it hurt. He was talking rapidly to a young, stiff Ober-lieutenant. Two private soldiers stood bearishly in the doorway.

Emilie, shocked out of herself, stood pale and erect, recoiling.

"Yes, if you think so, we can look," the Baron was hastily and irascibly saying.

"Emilie," he said, turning to the girl, "did you put a postcard to the mother of this Bachmann in the box last evening?"

Emilie stood erect and did not answer.

"Yes?" said the Baron sharply.

"Yes, Herr Baron," replied Emilie, neutral.

The Baron's wounded hand shook rapidly in exasperation. The lieutenant drew himself up still more stiffly. He was right.

"And do you know anything of the fellow?" asked the Baron, looking at her with his blazing, grayish-golden eyes. The girl looked back at him steadily, dumb, but her whole soul naked before him. For two seconds he looked at her in silence. Then in silence, ashamed and furious, he turned away.

"Go up!" he said, with his fierce, peremptory command, to the young officer.

The lieutenant gave his order, in military cold confidence, to the soldiers. They all tramped across the hall. Emilie stood motionless, her life suspended.

The Baron marched swiftly upstairs and down the corridor, the lieutenant and the common soldiers followed. The Baron flung open the door of Emilie's room, and looked at Bachmann, who stood watching, standing in shirt and trousers beside the bed, fronting the door. He was perfectly still. His eyes met the furious, blazing look of the Baron. The latter shook his wounded hand, and then went still. He looked into the eyes of the soldier, steadily. He saw the same naked soul exposed, as if he looked really into the *man*. And the man was helpless, the more helpless for his singular nakedness.

"Ha!" he exclaimed impatiently, turning to the approaching lieutenant.

The latter appeared in the doorway. Quickly his eyes traveled over the barefooted youth. He recognized him as his object. He gave the brief command to dress.

Bachmann turned round for his clothes. He was very still, silent in himself. He was in an abstract, motionless world. That the two gentlemen and the two soldiers stood watching him, he scarcely realized. They could not see him.

Soon he was ready. He stood at attention. But only the shell of his body was at attention. A curious silence, a blankness, like something eternal, possessed him. He remained true to himself.

The lieutenant gave the order to march. The little procession went down the stairs with careful, respectful tread, and passed through the hall to the kitchen. There Emilie stood with her face uplifted, motionless and expressionless. Bachmann did not look at her. They knew each other. They were themselves. Then the little file of men passed out into the courtyard.

The Baron stood in the doorway watching the four figures in uniform pass through the checkered shadow under the lime trees. Bachmann was walking neutralized, as if he were not there. The lieutenant went brittle and long, the two soldiers lumbered beside. They passed out into the sunny morning, growing smaller, going towards the barracks.

The Baron turned into the kitchen. Emilie was cutting bread.

"So he stayed the night here?" he said.

The girl looked at him, scarcely seeing. She was too much herself. The Baron saw the dark, naked soul of her body in her unseeing eyes.

"What were you going to do?" he asked.

"He was going to America," she replied, in a still voice.

"Pah! You should have sent him straight back," fired the Baron.

Emilie stood at his bidding, untouched.

"He's done for now," he said.

But he could not bear the dark, deep nakedness of her eyes, that scarcely changed under this suffering.

"Nothing but a fool," he repeated, going away in agitation, and preparing himself for what he could do.

DAUGHTERS OF THE VICAR

I

Mr. Lindley was first vicar of Aldecross. The cottages of this tiny hamlet had nestled in peace since their beginning, and the country folk had crossed the lanes and farmlands, two or three miles, to the parish church at Greymeed, on the bright Sunday mornings.

But when the pits were sunk, blank rows of dwellings started up beside the high roads, and a new population, skimmed from the floating scum of workmen, was filled in, the cottages and the country people almost obliterated.

To suit the convenience of these new collier-inhabitants, a church must be built at Aldecross. There was not too much money. And so the little building crouched like a humped stone-and-mortar mouse, with two little turrets at the west corners for ears, in the fields near the cottages and the apple trees, as far as possible from the dwellings down the high road. It had an uncertain, timid look about it. And so they planted big-leaved ivy, to hide its shrinking newness. So that now the little church stands buried in its greenery, stranded and sleeping among the fields, while the brick houses elbow nearer and nearer, threatening to crush it down. It is already obsolete.

The Reverend Ernest Lindley, aged twenty-seven, and newly married, came from his curacy in Suffolk to take charge of his church. He was just an ordinary young man, who had been to Cambridge and taken orders. His wife was a self-assured young woman, daughter of a Cambridgeshire rector. Her father had spent the whole of his thousand a year, so that Mrs. Lindley had nothing of her own. Thus the young married people came to Aldecross to live on a stipend of about a hundred and twenty pounds, and to keep up a superior position.

They were not very well received by the new, raw, disaffected population of colliers. Being accustomed to farm laborers, Mr. Lindley had considered himself as belonging indisputably to the upper or ordering classes. He had to be humble to the country families, but still, he was of their kind, whilst the common people were something different. He had no doubts of himself.

He found, however, that the collier population refused to accept this arrangement. They had no use for him in their lives, and they told him so, callously. The women merely said, "they were throng," or else, "Oh, it's no good you coming here, we're Chapel." The men were quite good-humored so long as he did not touch them too nigh, they were cheerfully contemptuous of him, with a preconceived contempt he was powerless against.

At last, passing from indignation to silent resentment, even, if he dared have acknowledged it, to conscious hatred of the majority of his flock, and unconscious hatred of himself, he confined his activities to a narrow round of cottages, and he had to submit. He had no particular character, having always depended on his position in society to give him position among men. Now he was so poor, he had no social standing even among the common vulgar tradespeople of the district, and he had not the nature nor the wish to make his society agreeable to them, nor the strength to impose himself where he would have liked to be recognized. He dragged on, pale and miserable and neutral.

At first his wife raged with mortification. She took on airs and used a high hand. But her income was too small, the wrestling with tradesmen's bills was too pitiful, she only met with general, callous ridicule when she tried to be impressive.

Wounded to the quick of her pride, she found herself isolated in an indifferent, callous population. She raged indoors and out. But soon she learned that she must pay too heavily for her outdoor rages, and then she only raged within the walls of the rectory. There her feeling was so strong that she frightened herself. She saw herself hating her husband, and she knew that, unless she were careful, she would smash her form of life and bring catastrophe upon him and upon herself. So in very fear she went quiet. She hid, bitter and beaten by fear, behind the only shelter she had in the world, her gloomy, poor parsonage.

Children were born one every year; almost mechanically, she continued to perform her maternal duty, which was forced upon her. Gradually, broken by the suppressing of her violent anger and misery and disgust, she became an invalid and took to her couch.

The children grew up healthy, but unwarmed and rather rigid. Their father and mother educated them at home, made them very proud and very genteel, put them definitely and cruelly in the upper classes, apart from the vulgar around them. So they lived quite isolated. They were good-looking, and had that curiously clean, semi-transparent look of the genteel, isolated poor.

Gradually Mr. and Mrs. Lindley lost all hold on life, and spent their hours, weeks and years merely haggling to make ends meet, and bitterly repressing and pruning their children into gentility, urging them to ambition, weighting them with duty. On Sunday morning the whole family, except the mother, went down the lane to church, the long-legged girls in skimpy frocks, the boys in black coats and long, gray, unfitting trousers. They passed by their father's parishioners with mute, clear faces, childish mouths closed in pride that was like a doom to them, and childish eyes already unseeing. Miss Mary, the eldest, was the leader. She was a long, slim thing with a fine profile and a proud, pure look of submission to a high fate. Miss Louisa, the second, was short and plump and obstinate-looking. She had more enemies than ideals. She looked after the lesser children, Miss Mary after the elder. The collier children watched this pale, distinguished procession of the vicar's family pass mutely by, and they were impressed by the air of gentility and distance, they made mock of the trousers of the small sons, they felt inferior in themselves, and hate stirred their hearts.

In her time, Miss Mary received as governess a few little daughters of tradesmen; Miss Louisa managed the house and went among her father's churchgoers, giving lessons on the piano to the colliers' daughters at thirteen shillings for twenty-six lessons.

II

One winter morning, when his daughter Mary was about twenty years old, Mr. Lindley, a thin, unobtrusive figure in his black overcoat and his wideawake, went down into Aldecross with a packet of white papers under his arm. He was delivering the parish almanacs.

A rather pale, neutral man of middle age, he waited while the train thumped over the level-crossing, going up to the pit which rattled busily just along the line. A wooden-legged man hobbled to open the gate, Mr. Lindley passed on. Just at his left hand, below the road and the railway, was the red roof of a cottage, showing through the bare twigs of apple trees. Mr. Lindley passed round the low wall, and descended the worn steps that led from the highway down to the cottage which crouched darkly and quietly away below the rumble of passing trains and the clank of coal carts, in a quiet little underworld of its own. Snowdrops with tight-shut buds were hanging very still under the bare currant bushes.

The clergyman was just going to knock when he heard a clinking noise, and turning saw through the open door of a black shed just behind him an elderly woman in a black lace cap stooping among reddish big cans, pouring a very bright liquid into a tundish. There was a smell of paraffin. The woman put down her can, took the tundish and laid it on a shelf, then rose with a tin bottle. Her eyes met those of the clergyman.

"Oh, is it you, Mr. Lin'ley!" she said, in a complaining tone. "Go in."

The minister entered the house. In the hot kitchen sat a big, elderly man with a great gray beard, taking snuff. He grunted in a deep, muttering voice, telling the minister to sit down, and then took no more notice of him, but stared vacantly into the fire. Mr. Lindley waited.

The woman came in, the ribbons of her black lace cap, or bonnet, hanging on her shawl. She was of medium stature, everything about her was tidy. She went up a step out of the kitchen, carrying the paraffin tin. Feet were heard entering the room up the step. It was a little haberdashery shop, with parcels on the shelves of the walls, a big, old-fashioned sewing machine with tailor's work lying round it, in the open space. The woman went behind the counter, gave the child who had entered the paraffin bottle, and took from her a jug.

"My mother says shall yer put it down," said the child, and she was gone. The woman wrote in a book, then came into the kitchen with her jug. The husband, a very large man, rose and brought more coal to the already hot fire. He moved slowly and sluggishly. Already he was going dead; being a tailor, his large form had become an encumbrance to him. In his youth he had been a great dancer and boxer. Now he was taciturn, and inert. The minister had nothing to say, so he sought for his phrases. But John Durant took no notice, existing silent and dull.

Mrs. Durant spread the cloth. Her husband poured himself beer into a mug, and began to smoke and drink.

"Shall you have some?" he growled through his beard at the clergyman, looking slowly from the man to the jug, capable of this one idea.

"No, thank you," replied Mr. Lindley, though he would have liked some beer. He must set the example in a drinking parish.

"We need a drop to keep us going," said Mrs. Durant.

She had rather a complaining manner. The clergyman sat on uncomfortably while she laid the table for the half-past ten lunch. Her husband drew up to eat. She remained in her little round armchair by the fire.

She was a woman who would have liked to be easy in her life, but to whose lot had fallen a rough and turbulent family, and a slothful husband who did not care what became of himself or anybody. So, her rather good-looking square face was peevish, she had that air of having been compelled all her life to serve unwillingly, and to control where she did not want to control. There was about her, too, that masterful *aplomb* of a woman who has brought up and ruled her sons: but even them she had ruled unwillingly. She had enjoyed managing her little haberdashery shop, riding in the carrier's cart to Nottingham, going through the big warehouses to buy her goods. But the fret of managing her sons she did not like. Only she loved her youngest boy, because he was her last, and she saw herself free.

This was one of the houses the clergyman visited occasionally. Mrs. Durant, as part of her regulation, had brought up all her sons in the Church. Not that she had any religion. Only, it was what she was used to. Mr. Durant was without religion. He read the fervently evangelical *Life of John Wesley* with a curious pleasure, getting from it a satisfaction as from the warmth of the fire, or a glass of brandy. But he cared no more about John Wesley, in fact, than about John Milton, of whom he had never heard.

Mrs. Durant took her chair to the table.

"I don't feel like eating," she sighed.

"Why—aren't you well?" asked the clergyman, patronizing.

"It isn't that," she sighed. She sat with shut, straight mouth. "I don't know what's going to become of us."

But the clergyman had ground himself down so long that he could not easily sympathize.

"Have you any trouble?" he asked.

"Ay, have I any trouble!" cried the elderly woman. "I shall end my days in the workhouse."

The minister waited unmoved. What could she know of poverty, in her little house of plenty!

"I hope not," he said.

"And the one lad as I wanted to keep by me——" she lamented.

The minister listened without sympathy, quite neutral.

"And the lad as would have been a support to my old age! What is going to become of us?" she said.

The clergyman, justly, did not believe in the cry of poverty, but wondered what had become of the son.

"Has anything happened to Alfred?" he asked.

"We've got word he's gone for a Queen's sailor," she said sharply.

"He has joined the Navy!" exclaimed Mr. Lindley. "I think he could scarcely have done better—to serve his Queen and country on the sea . . . ."

"He is wanted to serve *me*," she cried. "And I wanted my lad at home."

Alfred was her baby, her last, whom she had allowed herself the luxury of spoiling.

"You will miss him," said Mr. Lindley, "that is certain. But this is no regrettable step for him to have taken—on the contrary."

"That's easy for you to say, Mr. Lindley," she replied tartly. "Do you think I want my lad climbing ropes at another man's bidding, like a monkey——?"

"There is no *dishonor*, surely, in serving in the Navy?"

"Dishonor this dishonor that," cried the angry old woman. "He goes and makes a slave of himself, and he'll rue it."

Her angry, scornful impatience nettled the clergyman, and silenced him for some moments.

"I do not see," he retorted at last, white at the gills and inadequate, "that the Queen's service is any more to be called slavery than working in a mine."

"At home he was at home, and his own master. *I* know he'll find a difference."

"It may be the making of him," said the clergyman. "It will take him away from bad companionship and drink."

Some of the Durants' sons were notorious drinkers, and Alfred was not quite steady.

"And why indeed shouldn't he have his glass?" cried the mother. "He picks no man's pocket to pay for it!"

The clergyman stiffened at what he thought was an allusion to his own profession, and his unpaid bills.

"With all due consideration, I am glad to hear he has joined the Navy," he said.

"Me with my old age coming on, and his father working very little! I'd thank you to be glad about something else besides that, Mr. Lindley."

The woman began to cry. Her husband, quite impassive, finished his lunch of meat-pie, and drank some beer. Then he turned to the fire, as if there were no one in the room but himself.

"I shall respect all men who serve God and their country on the sea, Mrs. Durant," said the clergyman stubbornly.

"That is very well, when they're not your sons who are doing the dirty work. It makes a difference," she replied tartly.

"I should be proud if one of my sons were to enter the Navy."

"Ay—well—we're not all of us made alike——"

The minister rose. He put down a large folded paper.

"I've brought the almanac," he said.

Mrs. Durant unfolded it.

"I do like a bit of color in things," she said, petulantly.

The clergyman did not reply.

"There's that envelope for the organist's fund——" said the old woman, and rising, she took the thing from the mantelpiece, went into the shop, and returned sealing it up.

"Which is all I can afford," she said.

Mr. Lindley took his departure, in his pocket the envelope containing Mrs. Durant's offering for Miss Louisa's services. He went from door to door delivering the almanacs, in dull routine. Jaded with the monotony of the business, and with the repeated effort of greeting half-known people, he felt barren and rather irritable. At last he returned home.

In the dining room was a small fire. Mrs. Lindley, growing very stout, lay on her couch. The vicar carved the cold mutton; Miss Louisa, short and plump and rather flushed, came in from the kitchen; Miss Mary, dark, with a beautiful white brow and gray eyes, served the vegetables; the children chattered a little, but not exuberantly. The very air seemed starved.

"I went to the Durants," said the vicar, as he served out small portions of mutton; "it appears Alfred has run away to join the Navy."

"Do him good," came the rough voice of the invalid.

Miss Louisa, attending to the youngest child, looked up in protest.

"Why has he done that?" asked Mary's low, musical voice.

"He wanted some excitement, I suppose," said the vicar. "Shall we say grace?"

The children were arranged, all bent their heads, grace was pronounced, at the last word every face was being raised to go on with the interesting subject.

"He's just done the right thing, for once," came the rather deep voice of the mother; "save him from becoming a drunken sot, like the rest of them."

"They're not *all* drunken, mama," said Miss Louisa, stubbornly.

"It's no fault of their upbringing if they're not. Walter Durant is a standing disgrace."

"As I told Mrs. Durant," said the vicar, eating hungrily, "it is the best thing he could have done. It will take him away from temptation during the most dangerous years of his life—how old is he—nineteen?"

"Twenty," said Miss Louisa.

"Twenty!" repeated the vicar. "It will give him wholesome discipline and set before him some sort of standard of duty and honor—nothing could have been better for him. But——"

"We shall miss him from the choir," said Miss Louisa, as if taking opposite sides to her parents.

"That is as it may be," said the vicar. "I prefer to know he is safe in the Navy than running the risk of getting into bad ways here."

"Was he getting into bad ways?" asked the stubborn Miss Louisa.

"You know, Louisa, he wasn't quite what he used to be," said Miss Mary gently and steadily. Miss Louisa shut her rather heavy jaw sulkily. She wanted to deny it, but she knew it was true.

For her he had been a laughing, warm lad, with something kindly and something rich about him. He had made her feel warm. It seemed the days would be colder since he had gone.

"Quite the best thing he could do," said the mother with emphasis.

"I think so," said the vicar. "But his mother was almost abusive because I suggested it."

He spoke in an injured tone.

"What does she care for her children's welfare?" said the invalid. "Their wages is all her concern."

"I suppose she wanted him at home with her," said Miss Louisa.

"Yes, she did—at the expense of his learning to be a drunkard like the rest of them," retorted her mother.

"George Durant doesn't drink," defended her daughter.

"Because he got burned so badly when he was nineteen—in the pit—and that frightened him. The Navy is a better remedy than that, at least."

"Certainly," said the vicar. "Certainly."

And to this Miss Louisa agreed. Yet she could not but feel angry that he had gone away for so many years. She herself was only nineteen.

III

It happened when Miss Mary was twenty-three years old that Mr. Lindley was very ill. The family was exceedingly poor at the time, such a lot of money was needed, so little was forthcoming. Neither Miss Mary nor Miss Louisa had suitors. What chance had they? They met no eligible young men in Aldecross. And what they earned was a mere drop in a void. The girls' hearts were chilled and hardened with fear of this perpetual, cold penury, this narrow struggle, this horrible nothingness of their lives.

A clergyman had to be found for the church work. It so happened the son of an old friend of Mr. Lindley's was waiting three months before taking up his duties. He would come and officiate, for nothing. The young clergyman was keenly expected. He was not more than twenty-seven, a Master of Arts of Oxford, had written his thesis on Roman Law. He came of an old Cambridgeshire family, had some private means, was going to take a church in Northamptonshire with a good stipend, and was not married. Mrs. Lindley incurred new debts, and scarcely regretted her husband's illness.

But when Mr. Massy came there was a shock of disappointment in the house. They had expected a young man with a pipe and a deep voice, but with better manners than Sidney, the eldest of the Lindleys. There arrived instead a small, chétif man, scarcely larger than a boy of twelve, spectacled, timid in the extreme, without a word to utter at first; yet with a certain inhuman self-sureness.

"What a little abortion!" was Mrs. Lindley's exclamation to herself on first seeing him, in his buttoned-up clerical coat. And for the first time for many days she was profoundly thankful to God that all her children were decent specimens.

He had not normal powers of perception. They soon saw that he lacked the full range of human feelings, but had rather a strong, philosophical mind, from which he lived. His body was almost unthinkable, in intellect he was something definite. The conversation at once took a balanced, abstract tone when he participated. There was no spontaneous exclamation, no violent assertion or expression of personal conviction, but all cold, reasonable assertion. This was very hard on Mrs. Lindley. The little man would look at her, after one of her pronouncements, and then give, in his thin voice, his own calculated version, so that she felt as if she were tumbling into thin air through a hole in the flimsy floor on which their conversation stood. It was she who felt a fool. Soon she was reduced to a hardy silence.

Still, at the back of her mind, she remembered that he was an unattached gentleman, who would shortly have an income altogether of six or seven hundred a year. What did the man matter, if there were pecuniary ease! The man was a trifle thrown in. After twenty-two years her sentimentality was ground away, and only the millstone of poverty mattered to her. So she supported the little man as a representative of a decent income.

His most irritating habit was that of a sneering little giggle, all on his own, which came when he perceived or related some illogical absurdity on the part of another person. It was the only form of humor he had. Stupidity in thinking seemed to him exquisitely funny. But any novel was unintelligibly meaningless and dull, and to an Irish sort of humor he listened curiously, examining it like mathematics, or else simply not hearing. In normal human relationship he was not there. Quite unable to take part in simple everyday talk, he padded silently round the house, or sat in the dining room looking nervously from side to side, always apart in a cold, rarefied little world of his own. Sometimes he made an ironic remark, that did not seem humanly relevant, or he gave his little laugh, like a sneer. He had to defend himself and his own insufficiency. And he answered questions grudgingly, with a yes or no, because he did not see their import and was nervous. It seemed to Miss Louisa he scarcely distinguished one person from another, but that he liked to be near to her, or to Miss Mary, for some sort of contact which stimulated him unknown.

Apart from all this, he was the most admirable workman. He was unremittingly shy, but perfect in his sense of duty: as far as he could conceive Christianity, he was a perfect Christian. Nothing that he realized he could do for anyone did he leave undone, although he was so incapable of coming into contact with another being that he could not proffer help. Now he attended assiduously to the sick man, investigated all the affairs of the parish or the church which Mr. Lindley had in control, straightened out accounts, made lists of the sick and needy, padded round with help and to see what he could do. He heard of Mrs. Lindley's anxiety about her sons, and began to investigate means of sending them to Cambridge. His kindness almost frightened Miss Mary. She honored it so, and yet she shrank from it. For, in it all Mr. Massy seemed to have no sense of any person, any human being whom he was helping: he only realized a kind of mathematical working out, solving of given situations, a calculated well-doing. And it was as if he had accepted the Christian tenets as axioms. His religion consisted in what his scrupulous, abstract mind approved of.

Seeing his acts, Miss Mary must respect and honor him. In consequence she must serve him. To this she had to force herself, shuddering and yet desirous, but he did not perceive it. She accompanied him on his visiting in the parish, and whilst she was cold with admiration for him, often she was touched with pity for the little padding figure with bent shoulders, buttoned up to the chin in his overcoat. She was a handsome, calm girl, tall, with a beautiful repose. Her clothes were poor, and she wore a black silk scarf, having no furs. But she was a lady. As the people saw her walking down Aldecross beside Mr. Massy they said:

"My word, Miss Mary's got a catch. Did ever you see such a sickly little shrimp!"

She knew they were talking so, and it made her heart grow hot against them, and she drew herself as it were protectively towards the little man beside her. At any rate, she could see and give honor to his genuine goodness.

He could not walk fast, or far.

"You have not been well?" she asked, in her dignified way.

"I have an internal trouble."

He was not aware of her slight shudder. There was silence, whilst she bowed to recover her composure, to resume her gentle manner towards him.

He was fond of Miss Mary. She had made it a rule of hospitality that he should always be escorted by herself or by her sister on his visits in the parish, which were not many. But some mornings she was engaged. Then Miss Louisa took her place. It was no good Miss Louisa's trying to adopt to Mr. Massy an attitude of queenly service. She was unable to regard him save with aversion. When she saw him from behind, thin and bent-shouldered, looking like a sickly lad of thirteen, she disliked him exceedingly, and felt a desire to put him out of existence.

And yet a deeper justice in Mary made Louisa humble before her sister.

They were going to see Mr. Durant, who was paralyzed and not expected to live. Miss Louisa was crudely ashamed at being admitted to the cottage in company with the little clergyman.

Mrs. Durant was, however, much quieter in the face of her real trouble.

"How is Mr. Durant?" asked Louisa.

"He is no different—and we don't expect him to be," was the reply. The little clergyman stood looking on.

They went upstairs. The three stood for some time looking at the bed, at the gray head of the old man on the pillow, the gray beard over the sheet. Miss Louisa was shocked and afraid.

"It is so dreadful," she said, with a shudder.

"It is how I always thought it would be," replied Mrs. Durant.

Then Miss Louisa was afraid of her. The two women were uneasy, waiting for Mr. Massy to say something. He stood, small and bent, too nervous to speak.

"Has he any understanding?" he asked at length.

"Maybe," said Mrs. Durant. "Can you hear, John?" she asked loudly. The dull blue eye of the inert man looked at her feebly.

"Yes, he understands," said Mrs. Durant to Mr. Massy. Except for the dull look in his eyes, the sick man lay as if dead. The three stood in silence. Miss Louisa was obstinate but heavy-hearted under the load of unlivingness. It was Mr. Massy who kept her there in discipline. His nonhuman will dominated them all.

Then they heard a sound below, a man's footsteps, and a man's voice called subduedly:

"Are you upstairs, mother?"

Mrs. Durant started and moved to the door. But already a quick, firm step was running up the stairs.

"I'm a bit early, mother," a troubled voice said, and on the landing they saw the form of the sailor. His mother came and clung to him. She was suddenly aware that she needed something to hold on to. He put his arms round her, and bent over her, kissing her.

"He's not gone, mother?" he asked anxiously, struggling to control his voice.

Miss Louisa looked away from the mother and son who stood together in the gloom on the landing. She could not bear it that she and Mr. Massy should be there. The latter stood nervously, as if ill at ease before the emotion that was running. He was a witness nervous, unwilling, but dispassionate. To Miss Louisa's hot heart it seemed all, all wrong that they should be there.

Mrs. Durant entered the bedroom, her face wet.

"There's Miss Louisa and the vicar," she said, out of voice and quavering.

Her son, red-faced and slender, drew himself up to salute. But Miss Louisa held out her hand. Then she saw his hazel eyes recognize her for a moment, and his small white teeth showed in a glimpse of the greeting she used to love. She was covered with confusion. He went round to the bed; his boots clicked on the plaster floor, he bowed his head with dignity.

"How are you, dad?" he said, laying his hand on the sheet, faltering. But the old man stared fixedly and unseeing. The son stood perfectly still for a few minutes, then slowly recoiled. Miss Louisa saw the fine outline of his breast, under the sailor's blue blouse, as his chest began to heave.

"He doesn't know me," he said, turning to his mother. He gradually went white.

"No, my boy!" cried the mother, pitiful, lifting her face. And suddenly she put her face against his shoulder, he was stooping down to her, holding her against him, and she cried aloud for a moment or two. Miss Louisa saw his sides heaving, and heard the sharp hiss of his breath. She turned away, tears streaming down her face. The father lay inert upon the white bed, Mr. Massy looked queer and obliterated, so little now that the sailor with his sunburned skin was in the room. He stood waiting. Miss Louisa wanted to die, she wanted to have done. She dared not turn round again to look.

"Shall I offer a prayer?" came the frail voice of the clergyman, and all kneeled down.

Miss Louisa was frightened of the inert man upon the bed. Then she felt a flash of fear of Mr. Massy, hearing his thin, detached voice. And then, calmed, she looked up. On the far side of the bed were the heads of the mother and son, the one in the black lace cap, with the small white nape of the neck beneath, the other, with brown, sun-scorched hair too close and wiry to allow of a parting, and neck tanned firm, bowed as if unwillingly. The great gray beard of the old man did not move, the prayer continued. Mr. Massy prayed with a pure lucidity that they all might conform to the higher Will. He was like something that dominated the bowed heads, something dispassionate that governed them inexorably. Miss Louisa was afraid of him. And she was bound, during the course of the prayer, to have a little reverence for him. It was like a foretaste of inexorable, cold death, a taste of pure justice.

That evening she talked to Mary of the visit. Her heart, her veins were possessed by the thought of Alfred Durant as he held his mother in his arms; then the break in his voice, as she remembered it again and again, was like a flame through her; and she wanted to see his face more distinctly in her mind, ruddy with the sun, and his golden-brown eyes, kind and careless, strained now with a natural fear, the fine nose tanned hard by the sun, the mouth that could not help smiling at her. And it went through her with pride, to think of his figure, a straight, fine jet of life.

"He is a handsome lad," said she to Miss Mary, as if he had not been a year older than herself. Underneath was the deeper dread, almost hatred, of the inhuman being of Mr. Massy. She felt she must protect herself and Alfred from him.

"When I felt Mr. Massy there," she said, "I almost hated him. What right had he to be there!"

"Surely he has all right," said Miss Mary after a pause. "He is *really* a Christian."

"He seems to me nearly an imbecile," said Miss Louisa.

Miss Mary, quiet and beautiful, was silent for a moment:

"Oh, no," she said. "Not *imbecile*——"

"Well then—he reminds me of a six months' child—or a five months' child—as if he didn't have time to get developed enough before he was born."

"Yes," said Miss Mary, slowly. "There is something lacking. But there is something wonderful in him: and he is really *good*——"

"Yes," said Miss Louisa, "it doesn't seem right that he should be. What right has *that* to be called goodness!"

"But it *is* goodness," persisted Mary. Then she added, with a laugh: "And come, you wouldn't deny that as well."

There was a doggedness in her voice. She went about very quietly. In her soul, she knew what was going to happen. She knew that Mr. Massy was stronger than she, and that she must submit to what he was. Her physical self was prouder, stronger than he, her physical self disliked and despised him. But she was in the grip of his moral, mental being. And she felt the days allotted out to her. And her family watched.

IV

A few days after, old Mr. Durant died. Miss Louisa saw Alfred once more, but he was stiff before her now, treating her not like a person, but as if she were some sort of will in command and he a separate, distinct will waiting in front of her. She had never felt such utter steel-plate separation from anyone. It puzzled her and frightened her. What had become of him? And she hated the military discipline—she was antagonistic to it. Now he was not himself. He was the will which obeys set over against the will which commands. She hesitated over accepting this. He had put himself out of her range. He had ranked himself inferior, subordinate to her. And that was how he would get away from her, that was how he would avoid all connection with her: by fronting her impersonally from the opposite camp, by taking up the abstract position of an inferior.

She went brooding steadily and sullenly over this, brooding and brooding. Her fierce, obstinate heart could not give way. It clung to its own rights. Sometimes she dismissed him. Why should he, her inferior, trouble her?

Then she relapsed to him, and almost hated him. It was his way of getting out of it. She felt the cowardice of it, his calmly placing her in a superior class, and placing himself inaccessibly apart, in an inferior, as if she, the sentient woman who was fond of him, did not count. But she was not going to submit. Dogged in her heart she held on to him.

V

In six month's time Miss Mary had married Mr. Massy. There had been no love-making, nobody had made any remark. But everybody was tense and callous with expectation. When one day Mr. Massy asked for Mary's hand, Mr. Lindley started and trembled from the thin, abstract voice of the little man. Mr. Massy was very nervous, but so curiously absolute.

"I shall be very glad," said the vicar, "but of course the decision lies with Mary herself." And his still feeble hand shook as he moved a Bible on his desk.

The small man, keeping fixedly to his idea, padded out of the room to find Miss Mary. He sat a long time by her, while she made some conversation, before he had readiness to speak. She was afraid of what was coming, and sat stiff in apprehension. She felt as if her body would rise and fling him aside. But her spirit quivered and waited. Almost in expectation she waited, almost wanting him. And then she knew he would speak.

"I have already asked Mr. Lindley," said the clergyman, while suddenly she looked with aversion at his little knees, "if he would consent to my proposal." He was aware of his own disadvantage, but his will was set.

She went cold as she sat, and impervious, almost as if she had become stone. He waited a moment nervously. He would not persuade her. He himself never even heard persuasion, but pursued his own course. He looked at her, sure of himself, unsure of her, and said:

"Will you become my wife, Mary?"

Still her heart was hard and cold. She sat proudly.

"I should like to speak to mama first," she said.

"Very well," replied Mr. Massy. And in a moment he padded away.

Mary went to her mother. She was cold and reserved.

"Mr. Massy has asked me to marry him, mama," she said. Mrs. Lindley went on staring at her book. She was cramped in her feeling.

"Well, and what did you say?"

They were both keeping calm and cold.

"I said I would speak to you before answering him."

This was equivalent to a question. Mrs. Lindley did not want to reply to it. She shifted her heavy form irritably on the couch. Miss Mary sat calm and straight, with closed mouth.

"Your father thinks it would not be a bad match," said the mother, as if casually.

Nothing more was said. Everybody remained cold and shut-off. Miss Mary did not speak to Miss Louisa, the Reverend Ernest Lindley kept out of sight.

At evening Miss Mary accepted Mr. Massy.

"Yes, I will marry you," she said, with even a little movement of tenderness towards him. He was embarrassed, but satisfied. She could see him making some movement towards her, could feel the male in him, something cold and triumphant, asserting itself. She sat rigid, and waited.

When Miss Louisa knew, she was silent with bitter anger against everybody, even against Mary. She felt her faith wounded. Did the real things to her not matter after all? She wanted to get away. She thought of Mr. Massy. He had some curious power, some unanswerable right. He was a will that they could not controvert. Suddenly a flush started in her. If he had come to her she would have flipped him out of the room. He was never going to touch *her*. And she was glad. She was glad that her blood would rise and exterminate the little man, if he came too near to her, no matter how her judgment was paralyzed by him, no matter how he moved in abstract goodness. She thought she was perverse to be glad, but glad she was. "I would just flip him out of the room," she said, and she derived great satisfaction from the open statement. Nevertheless, perhaps she ought still to feel that Mary, on her plane, was a higher being than herself. But then Mary was Mary, and she was Louisa, and that also was inalterable.

Mary, in marrying him, tried to become a pure reason such as he was, without feeling or impulse. She shut herself up, she shut herself rigid against the agonies of shame and the terror of violation which came at first. She *would* not feel, and she *would* not feel. She was a pure will acquiescing to him. She elected a certain kind of fate. She would be good and purely just, she would live in a higher freedom than she had ever known, she would be free of mundane care, she was a pure will towards right. She had sold herself, but she had a new freedom. She had got rid of her body. She had sold a lower thing, her body, for a higher thing, her freedom from material things. She considered that she paid for all she got from her husband. So, in a kind of independence, she moved proud and free. She had paid with her body: that was henceforward out of consideration. She was glad to be rid of it. She had bought her position in the world—that henceforth was taken for granted. There remained only the direction of her activity towards charity and high-minded living.

She could scarcely bear other people to be present with her and her husband. Her private life was her shame. But then, she could keep it hidden. She lived almost isolated in the rectory of the tiny village miles from the railway. She suffered as if it were an insult to her own flesh, seeing the repulsion which some people felt for her husband, or the special manner they had of treating him, as if he were a "case." But most people were uneasy before him, which restored her pride.

If she had let herself, she would have hated him, hated his padding round the house, his thin voice devoid of human understanding, his bent little shoulders and rather incomplete face that reminded her of an abortion. But rigorously she kept to her position. She took care of him and was just to him. There was also a deep, craven fear of him, something slave-like.

There was not much fault to be found with his behavior. He was scrupulously just and kind according to his lights. But the male in him was cold and self-complete, and utterly domineering. Weak, insufficient little thing as he was, she had not expected this of him. It was something in the bargain she had not understood. It made her hold her head, to keep still. She knew, vaguely, that she was murdering herself. After all, her body was not quite so easy to get rid of. And this manner of disposing of it—ah, sometimes she felt she must rise and bring about death, lift her hand for utter denial of everything, by a general destruction.

He was almost unaware of the conditions about him. He did not fuss in the domestic way, she did as she liked in the house. Indeed, she was a great deal free of him. He would sit obliterated for hours. He was kind, and almost anxiously considerate. But when he considered he was right, his will was just blindly male, like a cold machine. And on most points he was logically right, or he had with him the right of the creed they both accepted. It was so. There was nothing for her to go against.

Then she found herself with child, and felt for the first time horror, afraid before God and man. This also she had to go through—it was the right. When the child arrived, it was a bonny, healthy lad. Her heart hurt in her body, as she took the baby between her hands. The flesh that was trampled and silent in her must speak again in the boy. After all, she had to live—it was not so simple after all. Nothing was finished completely. She looked and looked at the baby, and almost hated it, and suffered an anguish of love for it. She hated it because it made her live again in the flesh, when she *could* not live in the flesh, she could not. She wanted to trample her flesh down, down, extinct, to live in the mind. And now there was this child. It was too cruel, too racking. For she must love the child. Her purpose was broken in two again. She had to become amorphous, purposeless, without real being. As a mother, she was a fragmentary, ignoble thing.

Mr. Massy, blind to everything else in the way of human feeling, became obsessed by the idea of his child. When it arrived, suddenly it filled the whole world of feeling for him. It was his obsession, his terror was for its safety and well-being. It was something new, as if he himself had been born a naked infant, conscious of his own exposure, and full of apprehension. He who had never been aware of anyone else, all his life, now was aware of nothing but the child. Not that he ever played with it, or kissed it, or tended it. He did nothing for it. But it dominated him, it filled, and at the same time emptied his mind. The world was all baby for him.

This his wife must also bear, his question: "What is the reason that he cries?"—his reminder, at the first sound: "Mary, that is the child"—his restlessness if the feeding time were five minutes past. She had bargained for this—now she must stand by her bargain.

VI

Miss Louisa, at home in the dingy vicarage, had suffered a great deal over her sister's wedding. Having once begun to cry out against it, during the engagement, she had been silenced by Mary's quiet: "I don't agree with you about him, Louisa, I *want* to marry him." Then Miss Louisa had been angry deep in her heart, and therefore silent. This dangerous state started the change in her. Her own revulsion made her recoil from the hitherto undoubted Mary.

"I'd beg the streets barefoot first," said Miss Louisa, thinking of Mr. Massy.

But evidently Mary could perform a different heroism. So she, Louisa the practical, suddenly felt that Mary, her ideal, was questionable after all. How could she be pure—one cannot be dirty in act and spiritual in being. Louisa distrusted Mary's high spirituality. It was no longer genuine for her. And if Mary were spiritual and misguided, why did not her father protect her? Because of the money. He disliked the whole affair, but he backed away, because of the money. And the mother frankly did not care: her daughters could do as they liked. Her mother's pronouncement:

"Whatever happens to *him*, Mary is safe for life"—so evidently and shallowly a calculation, incensed Louisa.

"I'd rather be safe in the workhouse," she cried.

"Your father will see to that," replied her mother brutally. This speech, in its indirectness, so injured Miss Louisa that she hated her mother deep, deep in her heart, and almost hated herself. It was a long time resolving itself out, this hate. But it worked and worked, and at last the young woman said:

"They are wrong—they are all wrong. They have ground out their souls for what isn't worth anything, and there isn't a grain of love in them anywhere. And I *will* have love. They want us to deny it. They've never found it, so they want to say it doesn't exist. But I *will* have it. I *will* love—it is my birthright. I will love the man I marry—that is all I care about."

So Miss Louisa stood isolated from everybody. She and Mary had parted over Mr. Massy. In Louisa's eyes, Mary was degraded, married to Mr. Massy. She could not bear to think of her lofty, spiritual sister degraded in the body like this. Mary was wrong, wrong, wrong: she was not superior, she was flawed, incomplete. The two sisters stood apart. They still loved each other, they would love each other as long as they lived. But they had parted ways. A new solitariness came over the obstinate Louisa, and her heavy jaw set stubbornly. She was going on her own way. But which way? She was quite alone, with a blank world before her. How could she be said to have any way? Yet she had her fixed will to love, to have the man she loved.

VII

When her boy was three years old, Mary had another baby, a girl. The three years had gone by monotonously. They might have been an eternity, they might have been brief as a sleep. She did not know. Only, there was always a weight on top of her, something that pressed down her life. The only thing that had happened was that Mr. Massy had had an operation. He was always exceedingly fragile. His wife had soon learned to attend to him mechanically, as part of her duty.

But this third year, after the baby girl had been born, Mary felt oppressed and depressed. Christmas drew near: the gloomy, unleavened Christmas of the rectory, where all the days were of the same dark fabric. And Mary was afraid. It was as if the darkness were coming upon her.

"Edward, I should like to go home for Christmas," she said, and a certain terror filled her as she spoke.

"But you can't leave baby," said her husband, blinking.

"We can all go."

He thought, and stared in his collective fashion.

"Why do you wish to go?" he asked.

"Because I need a change. A change would do me good, and it would be good for the milk."

He heard the will in his wife's voice, and was at a loss. Her language was unintelligible to him. But somehow he felt that Mary was set upon it. And while she was breeding, either about to have a child, or nursing, he regarded her as a special sort of being.

"Wouldn't it hurt baby to take her by the train?" he said.

"No," replied the mother, "why should it?"

They went. When they were in the train it began to snow. From the window of his first-class carriage the little clergyman watched the big flakes sweep by, like a blind drawn across the country. He was obsessed by thought of the baby, and afraid of the draughts of the carriage.

"Sit right in the corner," he said to his wife, "and hold baby close back."

She moved at his bidding, and stared out of the window. His eternal presence was like an iron weight on her brain. But she was going partially to escape for a few days.

"Sit on the other side, Jack," said the father. "It is less draughty. Come to this window."

He watched the boy in anxiety. But his children were the only beings in the world who took not the slightest notice of him.

"Look, mother, look!" cried the boy. "They fly right in my face"—he meant the snowflakes.

"Come into this corner," repeated his father, out of another world.

"He's jumped on this one's back, mother, an' they're riding to the bottom!" cried the boy, jumping with glee.

"Tell him to come on this side," the little man bade his wife.

"Jack, kneel on this cushion," said the mother, putting her white hand on the place.

The boy slid over in silence to the place she indicated, waited still for a moment, then almost deliberately, stridently cried:

"Look at all those in the corner, mother, making a heap," and he pointed to the cluster of snowflakes with finger pressed dramatically on the pane, and he turned to his mother a bit ostentatiously.

"All in a heap!" she said.

He had seen her face, and had her response, and he was somewhat assured. Vaguely uneasy, he was reassured if he could win her attention.

They arrived at the vicarage at half-past two, not having had lunch.

"How are you, Edward?" said Mr. Lindley, trying on his side to be fatherly. But he was always in a false position with his son-in-law, frustrated before him, therefore, as much as possible, he shut his eyes and ears to him. The vicar was looking thin and pale and ill-nourished. He had gone quite gray. He was, however, still haughty; but, since the growing-up of his children, it was a brittle haughtiness, that might break at any moment and leave the vicar only an impoverished, pitiable figure. Mrs. Lindley took all the notice of her daughter, and of the children. She ignored her son-in-law. Miss Louisa was clucking and laughing and rejoicing over the baby. Mr. Massy stood aside, a bent, persistent little figure.

"Oh a pretty!—a little pretty! oh a cold little pretty come in a railway train!" Miss Louisa was cooing to the infant, crouching on the hearthrug, opening the white woollen wraps and exposing the child to the fireglow.

"Mary," said the little clergyman, "I think it would be better to give baby a warm bath; she may take a cold."

"I think it is not necessary," said the mother, coming and closing her hand judiciously over the rosy feet and hands of the mite. "She is not chilly."

"Not a bit," cried Miss Louisa. "She's not caught cold."

"I'll go and bring her flannels," said Mr. Massy, with one idea.

"I can bath her in the kitchen then," said Mary, in an altered, cold tone.

"You can't, the girl is scrubbing there," said Miss Louisa. "Besides, she doesn't want a bath at this time of day."

"She'd better have one," said Mary, quietly, out of submission. Miss Louisa's gorge rose, and she was silent. When the little man padded down with the flannels on his arm, Mrs. Lindley asked:

"Hadn't *you* better take a hot bath, Edward?"

But the sarcasm was lost on the little clergyman. He was absorbed in the preparations round the baby.

The room was dull and threadbare, and the snow outside seemed fairy-like by comparison, so white on the lawn and tufted on the bushes. Indoors the heavy pictures hung obscurely on the walls, everything was dingy with gloom.

Except in the fireglow, where they had laid the bath on the hearth. Mrs. Massy, her black hair always smoothly coiled and queenly, kneeled by the bath, wearing a rubber apron, and holding the kicking child. Her husband stood holding the towels and the flannels to warm. Louisa, too cross to share in the joy of the baby's bath, was laying the table. The boy was hanging on the doorknob, wrestling with it to get out. His father looked round.

"Come away from the door, Jack," he said ineffectually. Jack tugged harder at the knob as if he did not hear. Mr. Massy blinked at him.

"He must come away from the door, Mary," he said. "There will be a draught if it is opened."

"Jack, come away from the door, dear," said the mother, dexterously turning the shiny wet baby on to her toweled knee, then glancing round: "Go and tell Auntie Louisa about the train."

Louisa, also afraid to open the door, was watching the scene on the hearth. Mr. Massy stood holding the baby's flannel, as if assisting at some ceremonial.

If everybody had not been subduedly angry, it would have been ridiculous.

"I want to see out of the window," Jack said. His father turned hastily.

"Do *you* mind lifting him on to a chair, Louisa," said Mary hastily. The father was too delicate.

When the baby was flanneled, Mr. Massy went upstairs and returned with four pillows, which he set in the fender to warm. Then he stood watching the mother feed her child, obsessed by the idea of his infant.

Louisa went on with her preparations for the meal. She could not have told why she was so sullenly angry. Mrs. Lindley, as usual, lay silently watching.

Mary carried her child upstairs, followed by her husband with the pillows. After a while he came down again.

"What is Mary doing? Why doesn't she come down to eat?" asked Mrs. Lindley.

"She is staying with baby. The room is rather cold. I will ask the girl to put in a fire." He was going absorbedly to the door.

"But Mary has had nothing to eat. It is *she* who will catch cold," said the mother, exasperated.

Mr. Massy seemed as if he did not hear. Yet he looked at his mother-in-law, and answered:

"I will take her something."

He went out. Mrs. Lindley shifted on her couch with anger. Miss Louisa glowered. But no one said anything, because of the money that came to the vicarage from Mr. Massy.

Louisa went upstairs. Her sister was sitting by the bed, reading a scrap of paper.

"Won't you come down and eat?" the younger asked.

"In a moment or two," Mary replied, in a quiet, reserved voice, that forbade anyone to approach her.

It was this that made Miss Louisa most furious. She went downstairs, and announced to her mother:

"I am going out. I may not be home to tea."

VIII

No one remarked on her exit. She put on her fur hat, that the village people knew so well, and the old Norfolk jacket. Louisa was short and plump and plain. She had her mother's heavy jaw, her father's proud brow, and her own gray, brooding eyes that were very beautiful when she smiled. It was true, as the people said, that she looked sulky. Her chief attraction was her glistening, heavy, deep-blonde hair, which shone and gleamed with a richness that was not entirely foreign to her

"Where am I going?" she said to herself, when she got outside in the snow. She did not hesitate, however, but by mechanical walking found herself descending the hill towards Old Aldecross. In the valley that was black with trees, the colliery breathed in stertorous pants, sending out high conical columns of steam that remained upright, whiter than the snow on the hills, yet shadowy, in the dead air. Louisa would not acknowledge to herself whither she was making her way, till she came to the railway crossing. Then the bunches of snow in the twigs of the apple tree that leaned towards the fence told her she must go and see Mrs. Durant. The tree was in Mrs. Durant's garden.

Alfred was now at home again, living with his mother in the cottage below the road. From the highway hedge, by the railway crossing, the snowy garden sheered down steeply, like the side of a hole, then dropped straight in a wall. In this depth the house was snug, its chimney just level with the road. Miss Louisa descended the stone stairs, and stood below in the little backyard, in the dimness and the semisecrecy. A big tree leaned overhead, above the paraffin hut. Louisa felt secure from all the world down there. She knocked at the open door, then looked round. The tongue of garden narrowing in from the quarry bed was white with snow: she thought of the thick fringes of snowdrops it would show beneath the currant bushes in a month's time. The ragged fringe of pinks hanging over the garden brim behind her was whitened now with snowflakes, that in summer held white blossom to Louisa's face. It was pleasant, she thought, to gather flowers that stooped to one's face from above.

She knocked again. Peeping in, she saw the scarlet glow of the kitchen, red firelight falling on the brick floor and on the bright chintz cushions. It was alive and bright as a peep show. She crossed the scullery, where still an almanac hung. There was no one about. "Mrs. Durant," called Louisa softly, "Mrs. Durant."

She went up the brick step into the front room, that still had its little shop counter and its bundles of goods, and she called from the stair-foot. Then she knew Mrs. Durant was out.

She went into the yard, to follow the old woman's footsteps up the garden path.

She emerged from the bushes and raspberry canes. There was the whole quarry bed, a wide garden white and dimmed, brindled with dark bushes, lying half submerged. On the left, overhead, the little colliery train rumbled by. Right away at the back was a mass of trees.

Louisa followed the open path, looking from right to left, and then she gave a cry of concern. The old woman was sitting rocking slightly among the ragged snowy cabbages. Louisa ran to her, found her whimpering with little, involuntary cries.

"Whatever have you done?" cried Louisa, kneeling in the snow.

"I've—I've—I was pulling a brussel-sprout stalk—and—oh-h!—something tore inside me. I've had a pain," the old woman wept from shock and suffering, gasping between her whimpers—"I've had a pain there—a long time—and now—oh—oh!" She panted, pressed her hand on her side, leaned as if she would faint, looking yellow against the snow. Louisa supported her.

"Do you think you could walk now?" she asked.

"Yes," gasped the old woman.

Louisa helped her to her feet.

"Get the cabbage—I want it for Alfred's dinner," panted Mrs. Durant. Louisa picked up the stalk of brussel sprouts, and with difficulty got the old woman indoors. She gave her brandy, laid her on the couch, saying:

"I'm going to send for a doctor—wait just a minute."

The young woman ran up the steps to the public house a few yards away. The landlady was astonished to see Miss Louisa.

"Will you send for a doctor at once to Mrs. Durant," she said, with some of her father in her commanding tone.

"Is something the matter?" fluttered the landlady in concern.

Louisa, glancing out up the road, saw the grocer's cart driving to Eastwood. She ran and stopped the man, and told him.

Mrs. Durant lay on the sofa, her face turned away, when the young woman came back.

"Let me put you to bed," Louisa said. Mrs. Durant did not resist.

Louisa knew the ways of the working people. In the bottom drawer of the dresser she found dusters and flannels. With the old pit-flannel she snatched out the oven shelves, wrapped them up, and put them in the bed. From the son's bed she took a blanket, and, running down, set it before the fire. Having undressed the little old woman, Louisa carried her upstairs.

"You'll drop me, you'll drop me!" cried Mrs. Durant.

Louisa did not answer, but bore her burden quickly. She could not light a fire, because there was no fireplace in the bedroom. And the floor was plaster. So she fetched the lamp, and stood it lighted in one corner.

"It will air the room," she said.

"Yes," moaned the old woman.

Louisa ran with more hot flannels, replacing those from the oven shelves. Then she made a bran-bag and laid it on the woman's side. There was a big lump on the side of the abdomen.

"I've felt it coming a long time," moaned the old lady, when the pain was easier, "but I've not said anything; I didn't want to upset our Alfred."

Louisa did not see why "our Alfred" should be spared.

"What time is it?" came the plaintive voice.

"A quarter to four."

"Oh!" wailed the old lady, "he'll be here in half an hour, and no dinner ready for him."

"Let me do it?" said Louisa, gently.

"There's that cabbage—and you'll find the meat in the pantry—and there's an apple pie you can hot up. But *don't you* do it——!"

"Who will, then?" asked Louisa.

"I don't know," moaned the sick woman, unable to consider.

Louisa did it. The doctor came and gave serious examination. He looked very grave.

"What is it, doctor?" asked the old lady, looking up at him with old, pathetic eyes in which already hope was dead.

"I think you've torn the skin in which a tumor hangs," he replied.

"Ay!" she murmured, and she turned away.

"You see, she may die any minute—and it *may* be swaled away," said the old doctor to Louisa.

The young woman went upstairs again.

"He says the lump may be swaled away, and you may get quite well again," she said.

"Ay!" murmured the old lady. It did not deceive her. Presently she asked:

"Is there a good fire?"

"I think so," answered Louisa.

"He'll want a good fire," the mother said. Louisa attended to it.

Since the death of Durant, the widow had come to church occasionally, and Louisa had been friendly to her. In the girl's heart the purpose was fixed. No man had affected her as Alfred Durant had done, and to that she kept. In her heart, she adhered to him. A natural sympathy existed between her and his rather hard, materialistic mother.

Alfred was the most lovable of the old woman's sons. He had grown up like the rest, however, headstrong and blind to everything but his own will. Like the other boys, he had insisted on going into the pit as soon as he left school, because that was the only way speedily to become a man, level with all the other men. This was a great chagrin to his mother, who would have liked to have this last of her sons a gentleman.

But still he remained constant to her. His feeling for her was deep and unexpressed. He noticed when she was tired, or when she had a new cap. And he bought little things for her occasionally. She was not wise enough to see how much he lived by her.

At the bottom he did not satisfy her, he did not seem manly enough. He liked to read books occasionally, and better still he liked to play the piccolo. It amused her to see his head nod over the instrument as he made an effort to get the right note. It made her fond of him, with tenderness, almost pity, but not with respect. She wanted a man to be fixed, going his own way without knowledge of women. Whereas she knew Alfred depended on her. He sang in the choir because he liked singing. In the summer he worked in the garden, attended to the fowls and pigs. He kept pigeons. He played on Saturday in the cricket or football team. But to her he did not seem the man, the independent man her other boys had been. He was her baby—and whilst she loved him for it, she was a little bit contemptuous of him.

There grew up a little hostility between them. Then he began to drink, as the others had done; but not in their blind, oblivious way. He was a little self-conscious over it. She saw this, and she pitied it in him. She loved him most, but she was not satisfied with him because he was not free of her. He could not quite go his own way.

Then at twenty he ran away and served his time in the Navy. This had made a man of him. He had hated it bitterly, the service, the subordination. For years he fought with himself under the military discipline, for his own self-respect, struggling through blind anger and shame and a cramping sense of inferiority. Out of humiliation and self-hatred he rose into a sort of inner freedom. And his love for his mother, whom he idealized, remained the fact of hope and of belief.

He came home again, nearly thirty years old, but naïve and inexperienced as a boy, only with a silence about him that was new: a sort of dumb humility before life, a fear of living. He was almost quite chaste. A strong sensitiveness had kept him from women. Sexual talk was all very well among men, but somehow it had no application to living women. There were two things for him, the *idea* of women, with which he sometimes debauched himself, and real women, before whom he felt a deep uneasiness, and a need to draw away. He shrank and defended himself from the approach of any woman. And then he felt ashamed. In his innermost soul he felt he was not a man, he was less than the normal man. In Genoa he went with an under-officer to a drinking house where the cheaper sort of girl came in to look for lovers. He sat there with his glass, the girls looked at him, but they never came to him. He knew that if they did come he could only pay for food and drink for them, because he felt a pity for them, and was anxious lest they lacked good necessities. He could not have gone with one of them; he knew it, and was ashamed, looking with curious envy at the swaggering, easy-passionate Italian whose body went to a woman by instinctive impersonal attraction. They were men, he was not a man. He sat feeling short, feeling like a leper. And he went away imagining sexual scenes between himself and a woman, walking rapt in this indulgence. But when the ready woman presented herself, the very fact that she was a palpable woman made it impossible for him to touch her. And this incapacity was like a core of rottenness in him.

So several times he went, drunk, with his companions, to the licensed prostitute houses abroad. But the sordid insignificance of the experience appalled him. It had not been anything really: it meant nothing. He felt as if he were, not physically, but spiritually impotent: not actually impotent, but intrinsically so.

He came home with this secret, never-changing burden of his unknown, unbestowed self torturing him. His Navy training left him in perfect physical condition. He was sensible of, and proud of his body. He bathed and used dumb-bells, and kept himself fit. He played cricket and football. He read books and began to hold fixed ideas which he got from the Fabians. He played his piccolo, and was considered an expert. But at the bottom of his soul was always this canker of shame and incompleteness: he was miserable beneath all his healthy cheerfulness, he was uneasy and felt despicable among all his confidence and superiority of ideas. He would have changed with any mere brute, just to be free of himself, to be free of this shame of self-consciousness. He saw some collier lurching straight forward without misgiving, pursuing his own satisfactions, and he envied him. Anything, he would have given anything for this spontaneity and this blind stupidity which went to its own satisfaction direct.

IX

He was not unhappy in the pit. He was admired by the men, and well enough liked. It was only he himself who felt the difference between himself and the others. He seemed to hide his own stigma. But he was never sure that the others did not really despise him for a ninny, as being less a man than they were. Only he pretended to be more manly, and was surprised by the ease with which they were deceived. And, being naturally cheerful, he was happy at work. He was sure of himself there. Naked to the waist, hot and grimy with labor, they squatted on their heels for a few minutes and talked, seeing each other dimly by the light of the safety lamps, while the black coal rose jutting round them, and the props of wood stood like little pillars in the low, black, very dark temple. Then the pony came and the gang-lad with a message from Number 7, or with a bottle of water from the horse trough or some news of the world above. The day passed pleasantly enough. There was an ease, a go-as-you-please about the day underground, a delightful camaraderie of men shut off alone from the rest of the world, in a dangerous place, and a variety of labor, holing, loading, timbering, and a glamor of mystery and adventure in the atmosphere, that made the pit not unattractive to him when he had again got over his anguish of desire for the open air and the sea.

This day there was much to do and Durant was not in humor to talk. He went on working in silence through the afternoon.

"Loose-all" came, and they tramped to the bottom. The whitewashed underground office shone brightly. Men were putting out their lamps. They sat in dozens round the bottom of the shaft, down which black, heavy drops of water fell continuously into the sump. The electric lights shone away down the main underground road.

"Is it raining?" asked Durant.

"Snowing," said an old man, and the younger was pleased. He liked to go up when it was snowing.

"It'll just come right for Christmas?" said the old man.

"Ay," replied Durant.

"A green Christmas, a fat churchyard," said the other sententiously.

Durant laughed, showing his small, rather pointed teeth.

The cage came down, a dozen men lined on. Durant noticed tufts of snow on the perforated, arched roof of the chain, and he was pleased. He wondered how it liked its excursion underground. But already it was getting soppy with black water.

He liked things about him. There was a little smile on his face. But underlying it was the curious consciousness he felt in himself.

The upper world came almost with a flash, because of the glimmer of snow. Hurrying along the bank, giving up his lamp at the office, he smiled to feel the open about him again, all glimmering round him with snow. The hills on either hand were pale blue in the dusk, and the hedges looked savage and dark. The snow was trampled between the railway lines. But far ahead, beyond the black figures of miners moving home, it became smooth again, spreading right up to the dark wall of the coppice.

To the west there was a pinkness, and a big star hovered half-revealed. Below, the lights of the pit came out crisp and yellow among the darkness of the buildings, and the lights of Old Aldecross twinkled in rows down the bluish twilight.

Durant walked glad with life among the miners, who were all talking animatedly because of the snow. He liked their company, he liked the white dusky world. It gave him a little thrill to stop at the garden gate and see the light of home down below, shining on the silent blue snow.

X

By the big gate of the railway, in the fence, was a little gate, that he kept locked. As he unfastened it, he watched the kitchen light that shone on to the bushes and the snow outside. It was a candle burning till night set in, he thought to himself. He slid down the steep path to the level below. He liked making the first marks in the smooth snow. Then he came through the bushes to the house. The two women heard his heavy boots ring outside on the scraper, and his voice as he opened the door:

"How much worth of oil do you reckon to save by that candle, mother?" He liked a good light from the lamp.

He had just put down his bottle and snap-bag and was hanging his coat behind the scullery door, when Miss Louisa came upon him. He was startled, but he smiled.

His eyes began to laugh—then his face went suddenly straight, and he was afraid.

"Your mother's had an accident," she said.

"How?" he exclaimed.

"In the garden," she answered. He hesitated with his coat in his hands. Then he hung it up and turned to the kitchen.

"Is she in bed?" he asked.

"Yes," said Miss Louisa, who found it hard to deceive him. He was silent. He went into the kitchen, sat down heavily in his father's old chair, and began to pull off his boots. His head was small, rather finely shapen. His brown hair, close and crisp, would look jolly whatever happened. He wore heavy, moleskin trousers that gave off the stale, exhausted scent of the pit. Having put on his slippers, he carried his boots into the scullery.

"What is it?" he asked, afraid.

"Something internal," she replied.

He went upstairs. His mother kept herself calm for his coming. Louisa felt his tread shake the plaster floor of the bedroom above.

"What have you done?" he asked.

"It's nothing, my lad," said the old woman, rather hard. "It's nothing. You needn't fret, my boy, it's nothing more the matter with me than I had yesterday, or last week. The doctor said I'd done nothing serious."

"What were you doing?" asked her son.

"I was pulling up a cabbage, and I suppose I pulled too hard; for, oh—there was such a pain—"

Her son looked at her quickly. She hardened herself.

"But who doesn't have a sudden pain sometimes, my boy? We all do."

"And what's it done?"

"I don't know," she said, "but I don't suppose it's anything."

The big lamp in the corner was screened with a dark green screen, so that he could scarcely see her face. He was strung tight with apprehension and many emotions. Then his brow knitted.

"What did you go pulling your inside out at cabbages for," he asked, "and the ground frozen? You'd go on dragging and dragging, if you killed yourself."

"Somebody's got to get them," she said.

"You needn't do yourself harm."

But they had reached futility.

Miss Louisa could hear plainly downstairs. Her heart sank. It seemed so hopeless between them.

"Are you sure it's nothing much, mother?" he asked, appealing, after a little silence.

"Ay, it's nothing," said the old woman, rather bitter.

"I don't want you to—to—to be badly—you know."

"Go an' get your dinner," she said. She knew she was going to die: moreover, the pain was torture just then. "They're only cosseting me up a bit because I'm an old woman. Miss Louisa's *very* good—and she'll have got your dinner ready, so you'd better go and eat it."

He felt stupid and ashamed. His mother put him off. He had to turn away. The pain burned in his bowels. He went downstairs. The mother was glad he was gone, so that she could moan with pain.

He had resumed the old habit of eating before he washed himself. Miss Louisa served his dinner. It was strange and exciting to her. She was strung up tense, trying to understand him and his mother. She watched him as he sat. He was turned away from his food, looking in the fire. Her soul watched him, trying to see what he was. His black face and arms were uncouth, he was foreign. His face was masked black with coal-dust. She could not see him, she could not know him. The brown eyebrows, the steady eyes, the coarse, small moustache above the closed mouth—these were the only familiar indications. What was he, as he sat there in his pit-dirt? She could not see him, and it hurt her.

She ran upstairs, presently coming down with the flannels and the bran-bag, to heat them, because the pain was on again.

He was half-way through his dinner. He put down the fork, suddenly nauseated.

"They will soothe the wrench," she said. He watched, useless and left out.

"Is she bad?" he asked.

"I think she is," she answered.

It was useless for him to stir or comment. Louisa was busy. She went upstairs. The poor old woman was in a white, cold sweat of pain. Louisa's face was sullen with suffering as she went about to relieve her. Then she sat and waited. The pain passed gradually, the old woman sank into a state of coma. Louisa still sat silent by the bed. She heard the sound of water downstairs. Then came the voice of the old mother, faint but unrelaxing:

"Alfred's washing himself—he'll want his back washing——"

Louisa listened anxiously, wondering what the sick woman wanted.

"He can't bear if his back isn't washed——" the old woman persisted, in a cruel attention to his needs. Louisa rose and wiped the sweat from the yellowish brow.

"I will go down," she said soothingly.

"If you would," murmured the sick woman.

Louisa waited a moment. Mrs. Durant closed her eyes, having discharged her duty. The young woman went downstairs. Herself, or the man, what did they matter? Only the suffering woman must be considered.

Alfred was kneeling on the hearthrug, stripped to the waist, washing himself in a large panchion of earthenware. He did so every evening, when he had eaten his dinner; his brothers had done so before him. But Miss Louisa was strange in the house.

He was mechanically rubbing the white lather on his head, with a repeated, unconscious movement, his hand every now and then passing over his neck. Louisa watched. She had to brace herself to this also. He bent his head into the water, washed it free of soap, and pressed the water out of his eyes.

"Your mother said you would want your back washing," she said.

Curious how it hurt her to take part in their fixed routine of life! Louisa felt the almost repulsive intimacy being forced upon her. It was all so common, so like herding. She lost her own distinctness.

He ducked his face round, looking up at her in what was a very comical way. She had to harden herself.

"How funny he looks with his face upside down," she thought. After all, there was a difference between her and the common people. The water in which his arms were plunged was quite black, the soap-froth was darkish. She could scarcely conceive him as human. Mechanically, under the influence of habit, he groped in the black water, fished out soap and flannel, and handed them backward to Louisa. Then he remained rigid and submissive, his two arms thrust straight in the panchion, supporting the weight of his shoulders. His skin was beautifully white and unblemished, of an opaque, solid whiteness. Gradually Louisa saw it: this also was what he was. It fascinated her. Her feeling of separateness passed away: she ceased to draw back from contact with him and his mother. There was this living center. Her heart ran hot. She had reached some goal in this beautiful, clear, male body. She loved him in a white, impersonal heat. But the sunburnt, reddish neck and ears: they were more personal, more curious. A tenderness rose in her, she loved even his queer ears. A person—an intimate being he was to her. She put down the towel and went upstairs again, troubled in her heart. She had only seen one human being in her life—and that was Mary. All the rest were strangers. Now her soul was going to open, she was going to see another. She felt strange and pregnant.

"He'll be more comfortable," murmured the sick woman abstractedly, as Louisa entered the room. The latter did not answer. Her own heart was heavy with its own responsibility. Mrs. Durant lay silent awhile, then she murmured plaintively:

"You mustn't mind, Miss Louisa."

"Why should I?" replied Louisa, deeply moved.

"It's what we're used to," said the old woman.

And Louisa felt herself excluded again from their life. She sat in pain, with the tears of disappointment distilling in her heart. Was that all?

Alfred came upstairs. He was clean, and in his shirt-sleeves. He looked a workman now. Louisa felt that she and he were foreigners, moving in different lives. It dulled her again. Oh, if she could only find some fixed relations, something sure and abiding.

"How do you feel?" he said to his mother.

"It's a bit better," she replied wearily, impersonally. This strange putting herself aside, this abstracting herself and answering him only what she thought good for him to hear, made the relations between mother and son poignant and cramping to Miss Louisa. It made the man so ineffectual, so nothing. Louisa groped as if she had lost him. The mother was real and positive—he was not very actual. It puzzled and chilled the young woman.

"I'd better fetch Mrs. Harrison?" he said, waiting for his mother to decide.

"I suppose we shall have to have somebody," she replied.

Miss Louisa stood by, afraid to interfere in their business. They did not include her in their lives, they felt she had nothing to do with them, except as a help from outside. She was quite external to them. She felt hurt and powerless against this unconscious difference. But something patient and unyielding in her made her say:

"I will stay and do the nursing: you can't be left."

The other two were shy, and at a loss for an answer.

"We s'll manage to get somebody," said the old woman wearily. She did not care very much what happened, now.

"I will stay until tomorrow, in any case," said Louisa. "Then we can see."

"I'm sure you've no right to trouble yourself," moaned the old woman. But she must leave herself in any hands.

Miss Louisa felt glad that she was admitted, even in an official capacity. She wanted to share their lives. At home they would need her, now Mary had come. But they must manage without her.

"I must write a note to the vicarage," she said.

Alfred Durant looked at her inquiringly, for her service. He had always that intelligent readiness to serve, since he had been in the Navy. But there was a simple independence in his willingness, which she loved. She felt nevertheless it was hard to get at him. He was so deferential, quick to take the slightest suggestion of an order from her, implicitly, that she could not get at the man in him.

He looked at her very keenly. She noticed his eyes were golden brown, with a very small pupil, the kind of eyes that can see a long way off. He stood alert, at military attention. His face was still rather weather-reddened.

"Do you want pen and paper?" he asked, with deferential suggestion to a superior, which was more difficult for her than reserve.

"Yes, please," she said.

He turned and went downstairs. He seemed to her so self-contained, so utterly sure in his movement. How was she to approach him? For he would take not one step towards her. He would only put himself entirely and impersonally at her service, glad to serve her, but keeping himself quite removed from her. She could see he felt real joy in doing anything for her, but any recognition would confuse him and hurt him. Strange it was to her, to have a man going about the house in his shirt-sleeves, his waistcoat unbuttoned, his throat bare, waiting on her. He moved well, as if he had plenty of life to spare. She was attracted by his completeness. And yet, when all was ready, and there was nothing more for him to do, she quivered, meeting his questioning look.

As she sat writing, he placed another candle near her. The rather dense light fell in two places on the overfoldings of her hair till it glistened heavy and bright, like a dense golden plumage folded up. Then the nape of her neck was very white, with fine down and pointed wisps of gold. He watched it as if it were a vision, losing himself. She was all that was beyond him, of revelation and exquisiteness. All that was ideal and beyond him, she was that—and he was lost to himself in looking at her. She had no connection with him. He did not approach her. She was there like a wonderful distance. But it was a treat, having her in the house. Even with this anguish for his mother tightening about him, he was sensible of the wonder of living this evening. The candles glistened on her hair, and seemed to fascinate him. He felt a little awe of her, and a sense of uplifting, that he and she and his mother should be together for a time, in the strange, unknown atmosphere. And, when he got out of the house, he was afraid. He saw the stars above ringing with fine brightness, the snow beneath just visible, and a new night was gathering round him. He was afraid almost with obliteration. What was this new night ringing about him, and what was he? He could not recognize himself nor any of his surroundings. He was afraid to think of his mother. And yet his chest was conscious of her, and of what was happening to her. He could not escape from her, she carried him with her into an unformed, unknown chaos.

XI

He went up the road in an agony, not knowing what it was all about, but feeling as if a red-hot iron were gripped round his chest. Without thinking, he shook two or three tears onto the snow. Yet in his mind he did not believe his mother would die. He was in the grip of some greater consciousness. As he sat in the hall of the vicarage, waiting whilst Mary put things for Louisa into a bag, he wondered why he had been so upset. He felt abashed and humbled by the big house, he felt again as if he were one of the rank and file. When Miss Mary spoke to him, he almost saluted.

"An honest man," thought Mary. And the patronage was applied as salve to her own sickness. She had station, so she could patronize: it was almost all that was left to her. But she could not have lived without having a certain position. She could never have trusted herself outside a definite place, nor respected herself except as a woman of superior class.

As Alfred came to the latch-gate, he felt the grief at his heart again, and saw the new heavens. He stood a moment looking northward to the Plough climbing up the night, and at the far glimmer of snow in distant fields. Then his grief came on like physical pain. He held tight to the gate, biting his mouth, whispering "Mother!" It was a fierce, cutting, physical pain of grief, that came on in bouts, as his mother's pain came on in bouts, and was so acute he could scarcely keep erect. He did not know where it came from, the pain, nor why. It had nothing to do with his thoughts. Almost it had nothing to do with him. Only it gripped him and he must submit. The whole tide of his soul, gathering in its unknown towards this expansion into death, carried him with it helplessly, all the fritter of his thought and consciousness caught up as nothing, the heave passing on towards its breaking, taking him further than he had ever been. When the young man had regained himself, he went indoors, and there he was almost gay. It seemed to excite him. He felt in high spirits: he made whimsical fun of things.

He sat on one side of his mother's bed, Louisa on the other, and a certain gaiety seized them all. But the night and the dread was coming on.

Alfred kissed his mother and went to bed. When he was half-undressed the knowledge of his mother came upon him, and the suffering seized him in its grip like two hands, in agony. He lay on the bed screwed up tight. It lasted so long, and exhausted him so much, that he fell asleep, without having the energy to get up and finish undressing. He awoke after midnight to find himself stone cold. He undressed and got into bed, and was soon asleep again.

At a quarter to six he woke, and instantly remembered. Having pulled on his trousers and lighted a candle, he went into his mother's room. He put his hand before the candle flame so that no light fell on the bed.

"Mother!" he whispered.

"Yes," was the reply.

There was a hesitation.

"Should I go to work?"

He waited, his heart was beating heavily.

"I think I'd go, my lad."

His heart went down in a kind of despair.

"You want me to?"

He let his hand down from the candle flame. The light fell on the bed. There he saw Louisa lying looking up at him. Her eyes were upon him. She quickly shut her eyes and half-buried her face in the pillow, her back turned to him. He saw the rough hair like bright vapor about her round head, and the two plaits flung coiled among the bedclothes. It gave him a shock. He stood almost himself, determined. Louisa cowered down. He looked, and met his mother's eyes. Then he gave way again, and ceased to be sure, ceased to be himself.

"Yes, go to work, my boy," said the mother.

"All right," replied he, kissing her. His heart was down at despair, and bitter. He went away.

"Alfred!" cried his mother faintly.

He came back with beating heart.

"What, mother?"

"You'll always do what's right, Alfred?" the mother asked, beside herself in terror now he was leaving her. He was too terrified and bewildered to know what she meant.

"Yes," he said.

She turned her cheek to him. He kissed her, then went away, in bitter despair. He went to work.

XII

By midday his mother was dead. The word met him at the pit-mouth. As he had known, inwardly, it was not a shock to him, and yet he trembled. He went home quite calmly, feeling only heavy in his breathing.

Miss Louisa was still at the house. She had seen to everything possible. Very succinctly, she informed him of what he needed to know. But there was one point of anxiety for her.

"You *did* half expect it—it's not come as a blow to you?" she asked, looking up at him. Her eyes were dark and calm and searching. She too felt lost. He was so dark and inchoate.

"I suppose—yes," he said stupidly. He looked aside, unable to endure her eyes on him.

"I could not bear to think you might not have guessed," she said.

He did not answer.

He felt it a great strain to have her near him at this time. He wanted to be alone. As soon as the relatives began to arrive, Louisa departed and came no more. While everything was arranging, and a crowd was in the house, whilst he had business to settle, he went well enough, with only those uncontrollable paroxysms of grief. For the rest, he was superficial. By himself, he endured the fierce, almost insane bursts of grief which passed again and left him calm, almost clear, just wondering. He had not known before that everything could break down, that he himself could break down, and all be a great chaos, very vast and wonderful. It seemed as if life in him had burst its bounds, and he was lost in a great, bewildering flood, immense and unpeopled. He himself was broken and spilled out amid it all. He could only breathe panting in silence. Then the anguish came on again.

When all the people had gone from the Quarry Cottage, leaving the young man alone with an elderly housekeeper, then the long trial began. The snow had thawed and frozen, a fresh fall had whitened the gray, this then began to thaw. The world was a place of loose gray slosh. Alfred had nothing to do in the evenings. He was a man whose life had been filled up with small activities. Without knowing it, he had been centralized, polarized in his mother. It was she who had kept him. Even now, when the old housekeeper had left him, he might still have gone on in his old way. But the force and balance of his life was lacking. He sat pretending to read, all the time holding his fists clenched, and holding himself in, enduring he did not know what. He walked the black and sodden miles of field-paths, till he was tired out: but all this was only running away from whence he must return. At work he was all right. If it had been summer he might have escaped by working in the garden till bedtime. But now, there was no escape, no relief, no help. He, perhaps, was made for action rather than for understanding; for doing than for being. He was shocked out of his activities, like a swimmer who forgets to swim.

For a week, he had the force to endure this suffocation and struggle, then he began to get exhausted, and knew it must come out. The instinct of self-preservation became strongest. But there was the question: Where was he to go? The public house really meant nothing to him, it was no good going there. He began to think of emigration. In another country he would be all right. He wrote to the emigration offices.

On the Sunday after the funeral, when all the Durant people had attended church, Alfred had seen Miss Louisa, impassive and reserved, sitting with Miss Mary, who was proud and very distant, and with the other Lindleys, who were people removed. Alfred saw them as people remote. He did not think about it. They had nothing to do with his life. After service Louisa had come to him and shaken hands.

"My sister would like you to come to supper one evening, if you would be so good."

He looked at Miss Mary, who bowed. Out of kindness, Mary had proposed this to Louisa, disapproving of herself even as she did so. But she did not examine herself closely.

"Yes," said Durant awkwardly, "I'll come if you want me." But he vaguely felt that it was misplaced.

"You'll come tomorrow evening, then, about half-past six."

He went. Miss Louisa was very kind to him. There could be no music, because of the babies. He sat with his fists clenched on his thighs, very quiet and unmoved, lapsing, among all those people, into a kind of muse or daze. There was nothing between him and them. They knew it as well as he. But he remained very steady in himself, and the evening passed slowly. Mrs. Lindley called him "young man."

"Will you sit here, young man?"

He sat there. One name was as good as another. What had they to do with him?

Mr. Lindley kept a special tone for him, kind, indulgent, but patronizing. Durant took it all without criticism or offense, just submitting. But he did not want to eat—that troubled him, to have to eat in their presence. He knew he was out of place. But it was his duty to stay yet awhile. He answered precisely, in monosyllables.

When he left he winced with confusion. He was glad it was finished. He got away as quickly as possible. And he wanted still more intensely to go right away, to Canada.

Miss Louisa suffered in her soul, indignant with all of them, with him too, but quite unable to say why she was indignant.

XIII

Two evenings after, Louisa tapped at the door of the Quarry Cottage, at half-past six. He had finished dinner, the woman had washed up and gone away, but still he sat in his pit dirt. He was going later to the New Inn. He had begun to go there because he must go somewhere. The mere contact with other men was necessary to him, the noise, the warmth, the forgetful flight of the hours. But still he did not move. He sat alone in the empty house till it began to grow on him like something unnatural.

He was in his pit dirt when he opened the door.

"I have been wanting to call—I thought I would," she said, and she went to the sofa. He wondered why she wouldn't use his mother's round armchair. Yet something stirred in him, like anger, when the housekeeper placed herself in it.

"I ought to have been washed by now," he said, glancing at the clock, which was adorned with butterflies and cherries, and the name of "T. Brooks, Mansfield." He laid his black hands along his mottled dirty arms. Louisa looked at him. There was the reserve, and the simple neutrality towards her, which she dreaded in him. It made it impossible for her to approach him.

"I am afraid," she said, "that I wasn't kind in asking you to supper."

"I'm not used to it," he said, smiling with his mouth, showing the interspaced white teeth. His eyes, however, were steady and unseeing.

"It's not *that*," she said hastily. Her repose was exquisite and her dark gray eyes rich with understanding. He felt afraid of her as she sat there, as he began to grow conscious of her.

"How do you get on alone?" she asked.

He glanced away to the fire.

"Oh——" he answered, shifting uneasily, not finishing his answer.

Her face settled heavily.

"How close it is in this room. You have such immense fires. I will take off my coat," she said.

He watched her take off her hat and coat. She wore a cream cashmere blouse embroidered with gold silk. It seemed to him a very fine garment, fitting her throat and wrists close. It gave him a feeling of pleasure and cleanness and relief from himself.

"What were you thinking about, that you didn't get washed?" she asked, half intimately. He laughed, turning aside his head. The whites of his eyes showed very distinct in his black face.

"Oh," he said, "I couldn't tell you."

There was a pause.

"Are you going to keep this house on?" she asked.

He stirred in his chair, under the question.

"I hardly know," he said. "I'm very likely going to Canada."

Her spirit became very quiet and attentive.

"What for?" she asked.

Again he shifted restlessly on his seat.

"Well"—he said slowly—"to try the life."

"But which life?"

"There's various things—farming or lumbering or mining. I don't mind much what it is."

"And is that what you want?"

He did not think in these times, so he could not answer.

"I don't know," he said, "till I've tried."

She saw him drawing away from her forever.

"Aren't you sorry to leave this house and garden?" she asked.

"I don't know," he answered reluctantly. "I suppose our Fred would come in—that's what he's wanting."

"You don't want to settle down?" she asked.

He was leaning forward on the arms of his chair. He turned to her. Her face was pale and set. It looked heavy and impassive, her hair shone richer as she grew white. She was to him something steady and immovable and eternal presented to him. His heart was hot in an anguish of suspense. Sharp twitches of fear and pain were in his limbs. He turned his whole body away from her. The silence was unendurable. He could not bear her to sit there any more. It made his heart go hot and stifled in his breast.

"Were you going out tonight?" she asked.

"Only to the New Inn," he said.

Again there was silence.

She reached for her hat. Nothing else was suggested to her. She *had* to go. He sat waiting for her to be gone, for relief. And she knew that if she went out of that house as she was, she went out a failure. Yet she continued to pin on her hat; in a moment she would have to go. Something was carrying her.

Then suddenly a sharp pang, like lightning, seared her from head to foot, and she was beyond herself.

"Do you want me to go?" she asked, controlled, yet speaking out of a fiery anguish, as if the words were spoken from her without her intervention.

He went white under his dirt.

"Why?" he asked, turning to her in fear, compelled.

"Do you want me to go?" she repeated.

"Why?" he asked again.

"Because I wanted to stay with you," she said, suffocated, with her lungs full of fire.

His face worked, he hung forward a little, suspended, staring straight into her eyes, in torment, in an agony of chaos, unable to collect himself. And as if turned to stone, she looked back into his eyes. Their souls were exposed bare for a few moments. It was agony. They could not bear it. He dropped his head, whilst his body jerked with little sharp twitchings.

She turned away for her coat. Her soul had gone dead in her. Her hands trembled, but she could not feel anymore. She drew on her coat. There was a cruel suspense in the room. The moment had come for her to go. He lifted his head. His eyes were like agate, expressionless, save for the black points of torture. They held her, she had no will, no life anymore. She felt broken.

"Don't you want me?" she said helplessly.

A spasm of torture crossed his eyes, which held her fixed.

"I—I——" he began, but he could not speak. Something drew him from his chair to her. She stood motionless, spellbound, like a creature given up as prey. He put his hand tentatively, uncertainly, on her arm. The expression of his face was strange and inhuman. She stood utterly motionless. Then clumsily he put his arms round her, and took her, cruelly, blindly, straining her till she nearly lost consciousness, till he himself had almost fallen.

Then, gradually, as he held her gripped, and his brain reeled round, and he felt himself falling, falling from himself, and whilst she, yielded up, swooned to a kind of death of herself, a moment of utter darkness came over him, and they began to wake up again as if from a long sleep. He was himself.

After a while his arms slackened, she loosened herself a little, and put her arms round him, as he held her. So they held each other close, and hid each against the other for assurance, helpless in speech. And it was ever her hands that trembled more closely upon him, drawing him nearer into her, with love.

And at last she drew back her face and looked up at him, her eyes wet, and shining with light. His heart, which saw, was silent with fear. He was with her. She saw his face all somber and inscrutable, and he seemed eternal to her. And all the echo of pain came back into the rarity of bliss, and all her tears came up.

"I love you," she said, her lips drawn to sobbing. He put down his head against her, unable to hear her, unable to bear the sudden coming of the peace and passion that almost broke his heart. They stood together in silence whilst the thing moved away a little.

At last she wanted to see him. She looked up. His eyes were strange and glowing, with a tiny black pupil. Strange, they were, and powerful over her. And his mouth came to hers, and slowly her eyelids closed, as his mouth sought hers closer and closer, and took possession of her.

They were silent for a long time, too much mixed up with passion and grief and death to do anything but hold each other in pain and kiss with long, hurting kisses wherein fear was transfused into desire. At last she disengaged herself. He felt as if his heart were hurt, but glad, and he scarcely dared look at her.

"I'm glad," she said also.

He held her hands in passionate gratitude and desire. He had not yet the presence of mind to say anything. He was dazed with relief.

"I ought to go," she said.

He looked at her. He could not grasp the thought of her going, he knew he could never be separated from her anymore. Yet he dared not assert himself. He held her hands tight.

"Your face is black," she said.

He laughed.

"Yours is a bit smudged," he said.

They were afraid of each other, afraid to talk. He could only keep her near to him. After a while she wanted to wash her face. He brought her some warm water, standing by and watching her. There was something he wanted to say, that he dared not. He watched her wiping her face, and making tidy her hair.

"They'll see your blouse is dirty," he said.

She looked at her sleeves and laughed for joy.

He was sharp with pride.

"What shall you do?" he asked.

"How?" she said.

He was awkward at a reply.

"About me," he said.

"What do you want me to do?" she laughed.

He put his hand out slowly to her. What did it matter!

"But make yourself clean," she said.

XIV

As they went up the hill, the night seemed dense with the unknown. They kept close together, feeling as if the darkness were alive and full of knowledge, all around them. In silence they walked up the hill. At first the street lamps went their way. Several people passed them. He was more shy than she, and would have let her go had she loosened in the least. But she held firm.

Then they came into the true darkness, between the fields. They did not want to speak, feeling closer together in silence. So they arrived at the vicarage gate. They stood under the naked horse chestnut tree.

"I wish you didn't have to go," he said.

She laughed a quick little laugh.

"Come tomorrow," she said, in a low tone, "and ask father."

She felt his hand close on hers.

She gave the same sorrowful little laugh of sympathy. Then she kissed him, sending him home.

At home, the old grief came on in another paroxysm, obliterating Louisa, obliterating even his mother for whom the stress was raging like a burst of fever in a wound. But something was sound in his heart.

XV

The next evening he dressed to go to the vicarage, feeling it was to be done, not imagining what it would be like. He would not take this seriously. He was sure of Louisa, and this marriage was like fate to him. It filled him also with a blessed feeling of fatality. He was not responsible, neither had her people anything really to do with it.

They ushered him into the little study, which was fireless. By and by the vicar came in. His voice was cold and hostile as he said:

"What can I do for you, young man?"

He knew already, without asking.

Durant looked up at him, again like a sailor before a superior. He had the subordinate manner. Yet his spirit was clear.

"I wanted, Mr. Lindley——" he began respectfully, then all the color suddenly left his face. It seemed now a violation to say what he had to say. What was he doing there? But he stood on, because it had to be done. He held firmly to his own independence and self-respect. He must not be indecisive. He must put himself aside: the matter was bigger than just his personal self. He must not feel. This was his highest duty.

"You wanted——" said the vicar.

Durant's mouth was dry, but he answered with steadiness:

"Miss Louisa—Louisa—promised to marry me——"

"You asked Miss Louisa if she would marry you—yes——" corrected the vicar. Durant reflected he had not asked her this:

"If she would marry me, sir. I hope you—don't mind."

He smiled. He was a good-looking man, and the vicar could not help seeing it.

"And my daughter was willing to marry you?" said Mr. Lindley.

"Yes," said Durant seriously. It was pain to him, nevertheless. He felt the natural hostility between himself and the elder man.

"Will you come this way?" said the vicar. He led into the dining room, where were Mary, Louisa, and Mrs. Lindley. Mr. Massy sat in a corner with a lamp.

"This young man has come on your account, Louisa?" said Mr. Lindley.

"Yes," said Louisa, her eyes on Durant, who stood erect, in discipline. He dared not look at her, but he was aware of her.

"You don't want to marry a collier, you little fool," cried Mrs. Lindley harshly. She lay obese and helpless upon the couch, swathed in a loose dove-gray gown.

"Oh, hush, mother," cried Mary, with quiet intensity and pride.

"What means have you to support a wife?" demanded the vicar's wife roughly.

"I!" Durant replied, starting. "I think I can earn enough."

"Well, and how much?" came the rough voice.

"Seven and six a day," replied the young man.

"And will it get to be any more?"

"I hope so."

"And are you going to live in that poky little house?"

"I think so," said Durant, "if it's all right."

He took small offense, only was upset, because they would not think him good enough. He knew that, in their sense, he was not.

"Then she's a fool, I tell you, if she marries you," cried the mother roughly, casting her decision.

"After all, mama, it is Louisa's affair," said Mary distinctly, "and we must remember——"

"As she makes her bed, she must lie—but she'll repent it," interrupted Mrs. Lindley.

"And after all," said Mr. Lindley, "Louisa cannot quite hold herself free to act entirely without consideration for her family."

"What do you want, papa?" asked Louisa sharply.

"I mean that if you marry this man, it will make my position very difficult for me, particularly if you stay in this parish. If you were moving quite away, it would be simpler. But living here in a collier's cottage, under my nose, as it were—it would be almost unseemly. I have my position to maintain, and a position which may not be taken lightly."

"Come over here, young man," cried the mother, in her rough voice, "and let us look at you."

Durant, flushing, went over and stood—not quite at attention, so that he did not know what to do with his hands. Miss Louisa was angry to see him standing there, obedient and acquiescent. He ought to show himself a man.

"Can't you take her away and live out of sight?" said the mother. "You'd both of you be better off."

"Yes, we can go away," he said.

"Do you want to?" asked Miss Mary clearly.

He faced round. Mary looked very stately and impressive. He flushed.

"I do if it's going to be a trouble to anybody," he said.

"For yourself, you would rather stay?" said Mary.

"It's my home," he said, "and that's the house I was born in."

"Then"—Mary turned clearly to her parents, "I really don't see how you can make the conditions, papa. He has his own rights, and if Louisa wants to marry him——"

"Louisa, Louisa!" cried the father impatiently. "I cannot understand why Louisa should not behave in the normal way. I cannot see why she should only think of herself, and leave her family out of count. The thing is enough in itself, and she ought to try to ameliorate it as much as possible. And if——"

"But I love the man, papa," said Louisa.

"And I hope you love your parents, and I hope you want to spare them as much of the—the loss of prestige, as possible."

"We *can* go away to live," said Louisa, her face breaking to tears. At last she was really hurt.

"Oh, yes, easily," Durant replied hastily, pale, distressed.

There was dead silence in the room.

"I think it would really be better," murmured the vicar, mollified.

"Very likely it would," said the rough-voiced invalid.

"Though I think we ought to apologize for asking such a thing," said Mary haughtily.

"No," said Durant. "It will be best all round." He was glad there was no more bother.

"And shall we put up the banns here or go to the registrar?" he asked clearly, like a challenge.

"We will go to the registrar," replied Louisa decidedly.

Again there was a dead silence in the room.

"Well, if you will have your own way, you must go your own way," said the mother emphatically.

All the time Mr. Massy had sat obscure and unnoticed in a corner of the room. At this juncture he got up, saying:

"There is baby, Mary."

Mary rose and went out of the room, stately; her little husband padded after her. Durant watched the fragile, small man go, wondering.

"And where," asked the vicar, almost genial, "do you think you will go when you are married?"

Durant started.

"I was thinking of emigrating," he said.

"To Canada? Or where?"

"I think to Canada."

"Yes, that would be very good."

Again there was a pause.

"We shan't see much of you then, as a son-in-law," said the mother, roughly but amicably.

"Not much," he said.

Then he took his leave. Louisa went with him to the gate. She stood before him in distress.

"You won't mind them, will you?" she said humbly.

"I don't mind them, if they don't mind me!" he said. Then he stooped and kissed her.

"Let us be married soon," she murmured, in tears.

"All right," he said. "I'll go tomorrow to Barford."

A FRAGMENT OF STAINED GLASS

Beauvale is, or was, the largest parish in England. It is thinly populated, only just netting the stragglers from shoals of houses in three large mining villages. For the rest, it holds a great tract of woodland, fragment of old Sherwood, a few hills of pasture and arable land, three collieries, and, finally, the ruins of a Cistercian abbey. These ruins lie in a still rich meadow at the foot of the last fall of woodland, through whose oaks shines a blue of hyacinths, like water, in Maytime. Of the abbey, there remains only the east wall of the chancel standing, a wild thick mass of ivy weighting one shoulder, while pigeons perch in the tracery of the lofty window. This is the window in question.

The vicar of Beauvale is a bachelor of forty-two years. Quite early in life some illness caused a slight paralysis of his right side, so that he drags a little, and so that the right corner of his mouth is twisted up into his cheek with a constant grimace, unhidden by a heavy moustache. There is something pathetic about this twist on the vicar's countenance: his eyes are so shrewd and sad. It would be hard to get near to Mr. Colbran. Indeed, now, his soul has some of the twist of his face, so that, when he is not ironical, he is satiric. Yet a man of more complete tolerance and generosity scarcely exists. Let the boors mock him, he merely smiles on the other side, and there is no malice in his eyes, only a quiet expression of waiting till they have finished. His people do not like him, yet none could bring forth an accusation against him, save that "You never can tell when he's having you."

I dined the other evening with the vicar in his study. The room scandalizes the neighborhood because of the statuary which adorns it: a Laocoön and other classic copies, with bronze and silver Italian Renaissance works. For the rest, it is all dark and tawny.

Mr. Colbran is an archaeologist. He does not take himself seriously, however, in his hobby, so that nobody knows the worth of his opinions on the subject.

"Here you are," he said to me after dinner, "I've found another paragraph for my great work."

"What's that?" I asked.

"Haven't I told you I was compiling a Bible of the English people—the Bible of their hearts—their exclamations in presence of the unknown? I've found a fragment at home, a jump at God from Beauvale."

"Where?" I asked, startled.

The vicar closed his eyes whilst looking at me.

"Only on parchment," he said.

Then, slowly, he reached for a yellow book, and read, translating as he went:

"Then, while we chanted, came a crackling at the window, at the great east window, where hung our Lord on the Cross. It was a malicious coveitous Devil wrathed by us, rended the lovely image of the glass. We saw the iron clutches of the fiend pick the window, and a face flaming red like fire in a basket did glower down on us. Our hearts melted away, our legs broke, we thought to die. The breath of the wretch filled the chapel.

"But our dear Saint, etc., etc., came hastening down heaven to defend us. The fiend began to groan and bray—he was daunted and beat off.

"When the sun uprose, and it was morning, some went out in dread upon the thin snow. There the figure of our Saint was broken and thrown down, whilst in the window was a wicked hole as from the Holy Wounds the Blessed Blood was run out at the touch of the Fiend, and on the snow was the Blood, sparkling like gold. Some gathered it up for the joy of this House. . . ."

"Interesting," I said. "Where's it from?"

"Beauvale records—fifteenth century."

"Beauvale Abbey," I said; "they were only very few, the monks. What frightened them, I wonder."

"I wonder," he repeated.

"Somebody climbed up," I supposed, "and attempted to get in."

"What?" he exclaimed, smiling.

"Well, what do you think?"

"Pretty much the same," he replied. "I glossed it out for my book."

"Your great work? Tell me."

He put a shade over the lamp so that the room was almost in darkness.

"Am I more than a voice?" he asked.

"I can see your hand," I replied. He moved entirely from the circle of light. Then his voice began, sing-song, sardonic:

"I was a serf at Rollestoun's, Newthorpe Manor, master of the stables I was. One day a horse bit me as I was grooming him. He was an old enemy of mine. I fetched him a blow across the nose. Then, when he got a chance, he lashed out at me and caught me a gash over the mouth. I snatched at a hatchet and cut his head. He yelled, fiend as he was, and strained for me with all his teeth bare. I brought him down.

"For killing him they flogged me till they thought I was dead. I was sturdy, because we horse-serfs got plenty to eat. I was sturdy, but they flogged me till I did not move. The next night I set fire to the stables, and the stables set fire to the house. I watched and saw the red flame rise and look out of the window, I saw the folk running, each for himself, master no more than one of a frightened party. It was freezing, but the heat made me sweat. I saw them all turn again to watch, all rimmed with red. They cried, all of them when the roof went in, when the sparks splashed up at rebound. They cried then like dogs at the bagpipes howling. Master cursed me, till I laughed as I lay under a bush quite near.

"As the fire went down I got frightened. I ran for the woods with fire blazing in my eyes and crackling in my ears. For hours I was all fire. Then I went to sleep under the bracken. When I woke it was evening. I had no mantle, was frozen stiff. I was afraid to move, lest all the sores of my back should be broken like thin ice. I lay still until I could bear my hunger no longer. I moved then to get used to the pain of movement, when I began to hunt for food. There was nothing to be found but hips.

"After wandering about till I was faint I dropped again in the bracken. The boughs above me creaked with frost. I started and looked round. The branches were like hair among the starlight. My heart stood still. Again there was a creak, creak, and suddenly a whoop, that whistled in fading. I fell down in the bracken like dead wood. Yet, by the peculiar whistling sound at the end, I knew it was only the ice bending or tightening in the frost. I was in the woods above the lake, only two miles from the Manor. And yet, when the lake whooped hollowly again, I clutched the frozen soil, every one of my muscles as stiff as the stiff earth. So all the night long I dare not move my face, but pressed it flat down, and taut I lay as if pegged down and braced.

"When morning came still I did not move, I lay still in a dream. By afternoon my ache was such it enlivened me. I cried, rocking my breath in the ache of moving. Then again I became fierce. I beat my hands on the rough bark to hurt them, so that I should not ache so much. In such a rage I was I swung my limbs to torture till I fell sick with pain. Yet I fought the hurt, fought it and fought by twisting and flinging myself, until it was overcome. Then the evening began to draw on. All day the sun had not loosened the frost. I felt the sky chill again towards afternoon. Then I knew the night was coming, and, remembering the great space I had just come through, horrible so that it seemed to have made me another man, I fled across the wood.

"But in my running I came upon the oak where hanged five bodies. There they must hang, bar-stiff, night after night. It was a terror worse than any. Turning, blundering through the forest, I came out where the trees thinned, where only hawthorns, ragged and shaggy, went down to the lake's edge.

"The sky across was red, the ice on the water glistened as if it were warm. A few wild geese sat out like stones on the sheet of ice. I thought of Martha. She was the daughter of the miller at the upper end of the lake. Her hair was red like beech leaves in a wind. When I had gone often to the mill with the horses she had brought me food.

" 'I thought,' said I to her, ' 'twas a squirrel sat on your shoulder. 'Tis your hair fallen loose.'

" 'They call me the fox,' she said.

" 'Would I were your dog,' said I. She would bring me bacon and good bread, when I called at the mill with the horses. The thought of cakes of bread and of bacon made me reel as if drunk. I had torn at the rabbit holes, I had chewed wood all day. In such a dimness was my head that I felt neither the soreness of my wounds nor the cuts of thorns on my knees, but stumbled towards the mill, almost past fear of man and death, panting with fear of the darkness that crept behind me from trunk to trunk.

"Coming to the gap in the wood, below which lay the pond, I heard no sound. Always I knew the place filled with the buzz of water, but now it was silent. In fear of this stillness I ran forward, forgetting myself, forgetting the frost. The wood seemed to pursue me. I fell, just in time, down by a shed wherein were housed the few wintry pigs. The miller came riding in on his horse, and the barking of dogs was for him. I heard him curse the day, curse his servant, curse me, whom he had been out to hunt, in his rage of wasted labor, curse all. As I lay I heard inside the shed a sucking. Then I knew that the sow was there, and that the most of her sucking pigs would be already killed for tomorrow's Christmas. The miller, from forethought to have young at that time, made profit by his sucking pigs that were sold for the midwinter feast.

"When in a moment all was silent in the dusk, I broke the bar and came into the shed. The sow grunted, but did not come forth to discover me. By and by I crept in towards her warmth. She had but three young left, which now angered her, she being too full of milk. Every now and again she slashed at them and they squealed. Busy as she was with them, I in the darkness advanced towards her. I trembled so that scarce dared I trust myself near her, for long dared not put my naked face towards her. Shuddering with hunger and fear; I at last fed of her, guarding my face with my arm. Her own full young tumbled squealing against me, but she, feeling her ease, lay grunting. At last, I, too, lay drunk, swooning.

"I was roused by the shouting of the miller. He, angered by his daughter who wept, abused her, driving her from the house to feed the swine. She came, bowing under a yoke, to the door of the shed. Finding the pin broken she stood afraid, then, as the sow grunted, she came cautiously in. I took her with my arm, my hand over her mouth. As she struggled against my breast my heart began to beat loudly. At last she knew it was I. I clasped her. She hung in my arms, turning away her face, so that I kissed her throat. The tears blinded my eyes, I know not why, unless it were the hurt of my mouth, wounded by the horse, was keen.

" 'They will kill you,' she whispered.

" 'No,' I answered.

"And she wept softly. She took my head in her arms and kissed me, wetting me with her tears, brushing me with her keen hair, warming me through.

" 'I will not go away from here,' I said. 'Bring me a knife, and I will defend myself.'

" 'No,' she wept. 'Ah, no!'

"When she went I lay down, pressing my chest where she had rested on the earth, lest being alone were worse emptiness than hunger.

"Later she came again. I saw her bend in the doorway, a lanthorn hanging in front. As she peered under the redness of her falling hair, I was afraid of her. But she came with food. We sat together in the dull light. Sometimes still I shivered and my throat would not swallow.

" 'If,' said I, 'I eat all this you have brought me, I shall sleep till somebody finds me.'

"Then she took away the rest of the meat.

" 'Why,' said I, 'should I not eat?' She looked at me in tears of fear.

" 'What?' I said, but still she had no answer. I kissed her, and the hurt of my wounded mouth angered me.

" 'Now there is my blood,' said I, 'on your mouth.' Wiping her smooth hand over her lips, she looked thereat, then at me.

" 'Leave me,' I said, 'I am tired.' She rose to leave me.

" 'But bring a knife,' I said. Then she held the lanthorn near my face, looking as at a picture.

" 'You look to me,' she said, 'like a stirk that is roped for the axe. Your eyes are dark, but they are wide open.'

" 'Then I will sleep,' said I, 'but will not wake too late.'

" 'Do not stay here,' she said.

" 'I will not sleep in the wood,' I answered, and it was my heart that spoke, 'for I am afraid. I had better be afraid of the voice of man and dogs, than the sounds in the woods. Bring me a knife, and in the morning I will go. Alone will I not go now.'

" 'The searchers will take you,' she said.

" 'Bring me a knife,' I answered.

" 'Ah, go,' she wept.

" 'Not now—I will not——'

"With that she lifted the lanthorn, lit up her own face and mine. Her blue eyes dried of tears. Then I took her to myself, knowing she was mine.

" 'I will come again,' she said.

"She went, and I folded my arms, lay down and slept.

"When I woke, she was rocking me wildly to rouse me.

" 'I dreamed,' said I, 'that a great heap, as if it were a hill, lay on me and above me.'

"She put a cloak over me, gave me a hunting knife and a wallet of food, and other things I did not note. Then under her own cloak she hid the lanthorn.

" 'Let us go,' she said, and blindly I followed her.

"When I came out into the cold someone touched my face and my hair.

" 'Ha!' I cried, 'who now—?' Then she swiftly clung to me, hushed me.

" 'Someone has touched me,' I said aloud, still dazed with sleep.

" 'Oh hush!' she wept. ' 'Tis snowing.' The dogs within the house began to bark. She fled forward, I after her. Coming to the ford of the stream she ran swiftly over, but I broke through the ice. Then I knew where I was. Snowflakes, fine and rapid, were biting at my face. In the wood there was no wind nor snow.

" 'Listen,' said I to her, 'listen, for I am locked up with sleep.'

" 'I hear roaring overhead,' she answered. 'I hear in the trees like great bats squeaking.'

" 'Give me your hand,' said I.

"We heard many noises as we passed. Once as there uprose a whiteness before us, she cried aloud.

" 'Nay,' said I, 'do not untie thy hand from mine,' and soon we were crossing fallen snow. But ever and again she started back from fear.

" 'When you draw back my arm,' I said, angry, 'you loosen a weal on my shoulder.'

"Thereafter she ran by my side like a fawn beside its mother.

" 'We will cross the valley and gain the stream,' I said. 'That will lead us on its ice as on a path deep into the forest. There we can join the outlaws. The wolves are driven from this part. They have followed the driven deer.'

"We came directly on a large gleam that shaped itself up among flying grains of snow.

" 'Ah!' she cried, and she stood amazed.

"Then I thought we had gone through the bounds into fairy realm, and I was no more a man. How did I know what eyes were gleaming at me between the snow, what cunning spirits in the draughts of air? So I waited for what would happen, and I forgot her, that she was there. Only I could feel the spirits whirling and blowing about me.

"Whereupon she clung upon me, kissing me lavishly, and, were dogs or men or demons come upon us at that moment, she had let us be stricken down, nor heeded not. So we moved forward to the shadow that shone in colors upon the passing snow. We found ourselves under a door of light which shed its colors mixed with snow. This Martha had never seen, nor I, this door open for a red and brave issuing like fires. We wondered.

" 'It is fairy,' she said, and after a while, 'Could one catch such——Ah, no!'

"Through the snow shone bunches of red and blue.

" 'Could one have such a little light like a red flower—only a little, like a rose-berry scarlet on one's breast!—then one were singled out as Our Lady.'

"I flung off my cloak and my burden to climb up the face of the shadow. Standing on rims of stone, then in pockets of snow, I reached upward. My hand was red and blue, but I could not take the stuff. Like color of a moth's wing it was on my hand, it flew on the increasing snow. I stood higher on the head of a frozen man, reached higher my hand. Then I felt the bright stuff cold. I could not pluck it off. Down below she cried to me to come again to her. I felt a rib that yielded, I struck at it with my knife. There came a gap in the redness. Looking through, I saw below as it were white stunted angels, with sad faces lifted in fear. Two faces they had each, and round rings of hair. I was afraid. I grasped the shining red, I pulled. Then the cold man under me sank, so I fell as if broken onto the snow.

"Soon I was risen again, and we were running downwards towards the stream. We felt ourselves eased when the smooth road of ice was beneath us. For a while it was resting, to travel thus evenly. But the wind blew round us, the snow hung upon us, we leaned us this way and that, towards the storm. I drew her along, for she came as a bird that stems lifting and swaying against the wind. By and by the snow came smaller, there was no wind in the wood. Then I felt nor labor, nor cold. Only I knew the darkness drifted by on either side, that overhead was a lane of paleness where a moon fled us before. Still, I can feel the moon fleeing from me, can feel the trees passing round me in slow dizzy reel, can feel the hurt of my shoulder and my straight arm torn with holding her. I was following the moon and the stream, for I knew where the water peeped from its burrow in the ground there were shelters of the outlaw. But she fell, without sound or sign.

"I gathered her up and climbed the bank. There all round me hissed the larchwood, dry beneath, and laced with its dry-fretted cords. For a little way I carried her into the trees. Then I laid her down till I cut flat hairy boughs. I put her in my bosom on this dry bed, so we swooned together through the night. I laced her round and covered her with myself, so she lay like a nut within its shell.

"Again, when morning came, it was pain of cold that woke me. I groaned, but my heart was warm as I saw the heap of red hair in my arms. As I looked at her, her eyes opened into mine. She smiled—from out of her smile came fear. As if in a trap she pressed back her head.

" 'We have no flint,' said I.

" 'Yes—in the wallet, flint and steel and tinder box,' she answered.

" 'God yield you blessing,' I said.

"In a place a little open I kindled a fire of larch boughs. She was afraid of me, hovering near, yet never crossing a space.

" 'Come,' said I, 'let us eat this food.'

" 'Your face,' she said, 'is smeared with blood.'

"I opened out my cloak.

" 'But come,' said I, 'you are frosted with cold.'

"I took a handful of snow in my hand, wiping my face with it, which then I dried on my cloak.

" 'My face is no longer painted with blood, you are no longer afraid of me. Come here then, sit by me while we eat.'

"But as I cut the cold bread for her, she clasped me suddenly, kissing me. She fell before me, clasped my knees to her breast, weeping. She laid her face down to my feet, so that her hair spread like a fire before me. I wondered at the woman. 'Nay,' I cried. At that she lifted her face to me from below. 'Nay,' I cried, feeling my tears fall. With her head on my breast, my own tears rose from their source, wetting my cheek and her hair, which was wet with the rain of my eyes.

"Then I remembered and took from my bosom the colored light of that night before. I saw it was black and rough.

" 'Ah,' said I, 'this is magic.'

" 'The black stone!' she wondered.

" 'It is the red light of the night before,' I said.

" 'It is magic,' she answered.

" 'Shall I throw it?' said I, lifting the stone, 'shall I throw it away, for fear?'

" 'It shines!' she cried, looking up, 'it shines like the eye of a creature at night, the eye of a wolf in the doorway.'

" ' 'Tis magic,' I said, 'let me throw it from us.' But nay, she held my arm.

" 'It is red and shining,' she cried.

" 'It is a bloodstone,' I answered. 'It will hurt us, we shall die in blood.'

" 'But give it to me,' she answered.

" 'It is red of blood,' I said.

" 'Ah, give it to me,' she called.

" 'It is my blood,' I said.

" 'Give it,' she commanded, low.

" 'It is my life-stone,' I said.

" 'Give it me,' she pleaded.

" 'I gave it her. She held it up, she smiled, she smiled in my face, lifting her arms to me. I took her with my mouth, her mouth, her white throat. Nor she ever shrank, but trembled with happiness.

"What woke us, when the woods were filling again with shadow, when the fire was out, when we opened our eyes and looked up as if drowned, into the light which stood bright and thick on the treetops, what woke us was the sound of wolves. . . ."

* * *

"Nay," said the vicar, suddenly rising, "they lived happily ever after."

"No," I said.

THE SHADES OF SPRING

I

It was a mile nearer through the wood. Mechanically, Syson turned up by the forge and lifted the field-gate. The blacksmith and his mate stood still, watching the trespasser. But Syson looked too much a gentleman to be accosted. They let him go in silence across the small field to the wood.

There was not the least difference between this morning and those of the bright springs, six or eight years back. White and sandy-gold fowls still scratched round the gate, littering the earth and the field with feathers and scratched-up rubbish. Between the two thick holly bushes in the wood-hedge was the hidden gap, whose fence one climbed to get into the wood; the bars were scored just the same by the keeper's boots. He was back in the eternal.

Syson was extraordinarily glad. Like an uneasy spirit he had returned to the country of his past, and he found it waiting for him, unaltered. The hazel still spread glad little hands downwards, the bluebells here were still wan and few, among the lush grass and in shade of the bushes.

The path through the wood, on the very brow of a slope, ran winding easily for a time. All around were twiggy oaks, just issuing their gold, and floor spaces diapered with woodruff, with patches of dog-mercury and tufts of hyacinth. Two fallen trees still lay across the track. Syson jolted down a steep, rough slope, and came again upon the open land, this time looking north as through a great window in the wood. He stayed to gaze over the level fields of the hilltop, at the village which strewed the bare upland as if it had tumbled off the passing waggons of industry, and been forsaken. There was a stiff, modern, gray little church, and blocks and rows of red dwellings lying at random; at the back, the twinkling headstocks of the pit, and the looming pit-hill. All was naked and out-of-doors, not a tree! It was quite unaltered.

Syson turned, satisfied, to follow the path that sheered downhill into the wood. He was curiously elated, feeling himself back in an enduring vision. He started. A keeper was standing a few yards in front, barring the way.

"Where might you be going this road, sir?" asked the man. The tone of his question had a challenging twang. Syson looked at the fellow with an impersonal, observant gaze. It was a young man of four or five-and-twenty, ruddy and well favored. His dark blue eyes now stared aggressively at the intruder. His black moustache, very thick, was cropped short over a small, rather soft mouth. In every other respect the fellow was manly and good-looking. He stood just above middle height; the strong forward thrust of his chest, and the perfect ease of his erect, self-sufficient body, gave one the feeling that he was taut with animal life, like the thick jet of a fountain balanced in itself. He stood with the butt of his gun on the ground, looking uncertainly and questioningly at Syson. The dark, restless eyes of the trespasser, examining the man and penetrating into him without heeding his office, troubled the keeper and made him flush.

"Where is Naylor? Have you got his job?" Syson asked.

"You're not from the House, are you?" inquired the keeper. It could not be, since everyone was away.

"No, I'm not from the House," the other replied. It seemed to amuse him.

"Then might I ask where you were making for?" said the keeper, nettled.

"Where I am making for?" Syson repeated. "I am going to Willey-Water Farm."

"This isn't the road."

"I think so. Down this path, past the well, and out by the white gate."

"But that's not the public road."

"I suppose not. I used to come so often, in Naylor's time, I had forgotten. Where is he, by the way?"

"Crippled with rheumatism," the keeper answered reluctantly.

"Is he?" Syson exclaimed in pain.

"And who might you be?" asked the keeper, with a new intonation.

"John Adderley Syson; I used to live in Cordy Lane."

"Used to court Hilda Millership?"

Syson's eyes opened with a pained smile. He nodded. There was an awkward silence.

"And you—who are you?" asked Syson.

"Arthur Pilbeam—Naylor's my uncle," said the other.

"You live here in Nuttall?"

"I'm lodgin' at my uncle's—at Naylor's."

"I see!"

"Did you say you was goin' down to Willey-Water?" asked the keeper.

"Yes."

There was a pause of some moments, before the keeper blurted:

"*I'm* courtin' Hilda Millership."

The young fellow looked at the intruder with a stubborn defiance, almost pathetic. Syson opened new eyes.

"Are you?" he said, astonished. The keeper flushed dark.

"She and me are keeping company," he said.

"I didn't know!" said Syson. The other man waited uncomfortably.

"What, is the thing settled?" asked the intruder.

"How, settled?" retorted the other sulkily.

"Are you going to get married soon, and all that?"

The keeper stared in silence for some moments, impotent.

"I suppose so," he said, full of resentment.

"Ah!" Syson watched closely.

"I'm married myself," he added, after a time.

"You are?" said the other incredulously.

Syson laughed in his brilliant, unhappy way.

"This last fifteen months," he said.

The keeper gazed at him with wide, wondering eyes, apparently thinking back, and trying to make things out.

"Why, didn't you know?" asked Syson.

"No, I didn't," said the other sulkily.

There was silence for a moment.

"Ah well!" said Syson. "I will go on. I suppose I may." The keeper stood in silent opposition. The two men hesitated in the open, grassy space, set round with small sheaves of sturdy bluebells; a little open platform on the brow of the hill. Syson took a few indecisive steps forward, then stopped.

"I say, how beautiful!" he cried.

He had come in full view of the downslope. The wide path ran from his feet like a river, and it was full of bluebells, save for a green winding thread down the center, where the keeper walked. Like a stream the path opened into azure shallows at the levels, and there were pools of bluebells, with still the green thread winding through, like a thin current of ice water through blue lakes. And from under the twig-purple of the bushes swam the shadowed blue, as if the flowers lay in flood water over the woodland.

"Ah, isn't it lovely!" Syson exclaimed; this was his past, the country he had abandoned, and it hurt him to see it so beautiful. Wood pigeons cooed overhead, and the air was full of the brightness of birds singing.

"If you're married, what do you keep writing to her for, and sending her poetry books and things?" asked the keeper. Syson stared at him, taken aback and humiliated. Then he began to smile.

"Well," he said, "I did not know about you . . ."

Again the keeper flushed darkly.

"But if you are married——" he charged.

"I am," answered the other cynically.

Then, looking down the blue, beautiful path, Syson felt his own humiliation. "What right *have* I to hang on to her?" he thought, bitterly self-contemptuous.

"She knows I'm married and all that," he said.

"But you keep sending her books," challenged the keeper.

Syson, silenced, looked at the other man quizzically, half pitying. Then he turned.

"Good day," he said, and was gone. Now, everything irritated him: the two sallows, one all gold and perfume and murmur, one silver-green and bristly, reminded him that here he had taught her about pollination. What a fool he was! What godforsaken folly it all was!

"Ah well," he said to himself; "the poor devil seems to have a grudge against me. I'll do my best for him." He grinned to himself, in a very bad temper.

II

The farm was less than a hundred yards from the wood's edge. The wall of trees formed the fourth side to the open quadrangle. The house faced the wood. With tangled emotions, Syson noted the plum blossom falling on the profuse, colored primroses, which he himself had brought here and set. How they had increased! There were thick tufts of scarlet, and pink, and pale purple primroses under the plum trees. He saw somebody glance at him through the kitchen window, heard men's voices.

The door opened suddenly: very womanly she had grown! He felt himself going pale.

"You?—Addy!" she exclaimed, and stood motionless.

"Who?" called the farmer's voice. Men's low voices answered. Those low voices, curious and almost jeering, roused the tormented spirit in the visitor. Smiling brilliantly at her, he waited.

"Myself—why not?" he said.

The flush burned very deep on her cheek and throat.

"We are just finishing dinner," she said.

"Then I will stay outside." He made a motion to show that he would sit on the red earthenware pipkin that stood near the door among the daffodils, and contained the drinking water.

"Oh no, come in," she said hurriedly. He followed her. In the doorway, he glanced swiftly over the family, and bowed. Everyone was confused. The farmer, his wife, and the four sons sat at the coarsely laid dinner table, the men with arms bare to the elbows.

"I am sorry I come at lunchtime," said Syson.

"Hello, Addy!" said the farmer, assuming the old form of address, but his tone cold. "How are you?"

And he shook hands.

"Shall you have a bit?" he invited the young visitor, but taking for granted the offer would be refused. He assumed that Syson was become too refined to eat so roughly. The young man winced at the imputation.

"Have you had any dinner?" asked the daughter.

"No," replied Syson. "It is too early. I shall be back at half-past one."

"You call it lunch, don't you?" asked the eldest son, almost ironical. He had once been an intimate friend of this young man.

"We'll give Addy something when we've finished," said the mother, an invalid, deprecating.

"No—don't trouble. I don't want to give you any trouble," said Syson.

"You could allus live on fresh air an' scenery," laughed the youngest son, a lad of nineteen.

Syson went round the buildings, and into the orchard at the back of the house, where daffodils all along the hedgerow swung like yellow, ruffled birds on their perches. He loved the place extraordinarily, the hills ranging round, with bear-skin woods covering their giant shoulders, and small red farms like brooches clasping their garments; the blue streak of water in the valley, the bareness of the home pasture, the sound of myriad-threaded bird-singing, which went mostly unheard. To his last day, he would dream of this place, when he felt the sun on his face, or saw the small handfuls of snow between the winter twigs, or smelt the coming of spring.

Hilda was very womanly. In her presence he felt constrained. She was twenty-nine, as he was, but she seemed to him much older. He felt foolish, almost unreal, beside her. She was so static. As he was fingering some shed plum blossom on a low bough, she came to the back door to shake the tablecloth. Fowls raced from the stackyard, birds rustled from the trees. Her dark hair was gathered up in a coil like a crown on her head. She was very straight, distant in her bearing. As she folded the cloth, she looked away over the hills.

Presently Syson returned indoors. She had prepared eggs and curd cheese, stewed gooseberries and cream.

"Since you will dine tonight," she said, "I have only given you a light lunch."

"It is awfully nice," he said. "You keep a real idyllic atmosphere—your belt of straw and ivy buds."

Still they hurt each other.

He was uneasy before her. Her brief, sure speech, her distant bearing, were unfamiliar to him. He admired again her gray-black eyebrows, and her lashes. Their eyes met. He saw, in the beautiful gray and black of her glance, tears and a strange light, and at the back of all, calm acceptance of herself, and triumph over him.

He felt himself shrinking. With an effort he kept up the ironic manner.

She sent him into the parlor while she washed the dishes. The long low room was refurnished from the Abbey sale, with chairs upholstered in claret-colored rep, many years old, and an oval table of polished walnut, and another piano, handsome, though still antique. In spite of the strangeness, he was pleased. Opening a high cupboard let into the thickness of the wall, he found it full of his books, his old lesson-books, and volumes of verse he had sent her, English and German. The daffodils in the white window-bottoms shone across the room, he could almost feel their rays. The old glamour caught him again. His youthful watercolors on the wall no longer made him grin; he remembered how fervently he had tried to paint for her, twelve years before.

She entered, wiping a dish, and he saw again the bright, kernel-white beauty of her arms.

"You are quite splendid here," he said, and their eyes met.

"Do you like it?" she asked. It was the old, low, husky tone of intimacy. He felt a quick change beginning in his blood. It was the old, delicious sublimation, the thinning, almost the vaporizing of himself, as if his spirit were to be liberated.

"Aye," he nodded, smiling at her like a boy again. She bowed her head.

"This was the countess's chair," she said in low tones. "I found her scissors down here between the padding."

"Did you? Where are they?"

Quickly, with a lilt in her movement, she fetched her workbasket, and together they examined the long-shanked old scissors.

"What a ballad of dead ladies!" he said, laughing, as he fitted his fingers into the round loops of the countess's scissors.

"I knew you could use them," she said, with certainty. He looked at his fingers, and at the scissors. She meant his fingers were fine enough for the small-looped scissors.

"That is something to be said for me," he laughed, putting the scissors aside. She turned to the window. He noticed the fine, fair down on her cheek and her upper lip, and her soft, white neck, like the throat of a nettle flower, and her forearms, bright as newly blanched kernels. He was looking at her with new eyes, and she was a different person to him. He did not know her. But he could regard her objectively now.

"Shall we go out awhile?" she asked.

"Yes!" he answered. But the predominant emotion, that troubled the excitement and perplexity of his heart, was fear, fear of that which he saw. There was about her the same manner, the same intonation in her voice, now as then, but she was not what he had known her to be. He knew quite well what she had been for him. And gradually he was realizing that she was something quite other, and always had been.

She put no covering on her head, merely took off her apron, saying, "We will go by the larches." As they passed the old orchard, she called him in to show him a blue-tit's nest in one of the apple trees, and a sycock's in the hedge. He rather wondered at her surety, at a certain hardness like arrogance hidden under her humility.

"Look at the apple buds," she said, and he then perceived myriads of little scarlet balls among the drooping boughs. Watching his face, her eyes went hard. She saw the scales were fallen from him, and at last he was going to see her as she was. It was the thing she had most dreaded in the past, and most needed, for her soul's sake. Now he was going to see her as she was. He would not love her, and he would know he never could have loved her. The old illusion gone, they were strangers, crude and entire. But he would give her her due—she would have her due from him.

She was brilliant as he had not known her. She showed him nests: a jenny wren's in a low bush.

"See this jinty's!" she exclaimed.

He was surprised to hear her use the local name. She reached carefully through the thorns, and put her finger in the nest's round door.

"Five!" she said. "Tiny little things."

She showed him nests of robins, and chaffinches, and linnets, and buntings; of a wagtail beside the water.

"And if we go down, nearer the lake, I will show you a kingfisher's. . . ."

"Among the young fir trees," she said, "there's a throstle's or a blackie's on nearly every bough, every ledge. The first day, when I had seen them all, I felt as if I mustn't go in the wood. It seemed a city of birds: and in the morning, hearing them all, I thought of the noisy early markets. I was afraid to go in my own wood."

She was using the language they had both of them invented. Now it was all her own. He had done with it. She did not mind his silence, but was always dominant, letting him see her wood. As they came along a marshy path where forget-me-nots were opening in a rich blue drift: "We know all the birds, but there are many flowers we can't find out," she said. It was half an appeal to him, who had known the names of things.

She looked dreamily across to the open fields that slept in the sun.

"I have a lover as well, you know," she said, with assurance, yet dropping again almost into the intimate tone.

This woke in him the spirit to fight her.

"I think I met him. He is good-looking—also in Arcady."

Without answering, she turned into a dark path that led uphill, where the trees and undergrowth were very thick.

"They did well," she said at length, "to have various altars to various gods, in old days."

"Ah yes!" he agreed. "To whom is the new one?"

"There are no old ones," she said. "I was always looking for this."

"And whose is it?" he asked.

"I don't know," she said, looking full at him.

"I'm very glad, for your sake," he said, "that you are satisfied."

"Aye—but the man doesn't matter so much," she said. There was a pause.

"No!" he exclaimed, astonished, yet recognizing her as her real self.

"It is one's self that matters," she said. "Whether one is being one's own self and serving one's own God."

There was silence, during which he pondered. The path was almost flowerless, gloomy. At the side, his heels sank into soft clay.

III

"I," she said, very slowly, "I was married the same night as you."

He looked at her.

"Not legally, of course," she replied. "But—actually."

"To the keeper?" he said, not knowing what else to say.

She turned to him.

"You thought I could not?" she said. But the flush was deep in her cheek and throat, for all her assurance.

Still he would not say anything.

"You see"—she was making an effort to explain—"*I* had to understand also."

"And what does it amount to, this *understanding*?" he asked.

"A very great deal—does it not to you?" she replied. "One is free."

"And you are not disappointed?"

"Far from it!" Her tone was deep and sincere.

"You love him?"

"Yes, I love him."

"Good!" he said.

This silenced her for a while.

"Here, among his things, I love him," she said.

His conceit would not let him be silent.

"It needs this setting?" he asked.

"It does," she cried. "You were always making me to be not myself."

He laughed shortly.

"But is it a matter of surroundings?" he said. He had considered her all spirit.

"I am like a plant," she replied. "I can only grow in my own soil."

They came to a place where the undergrowth shrank away, leaving a bare, brown space, pillared with the brick-red and purplish trunks of pine trees. On the fringe, hung the somber green of elder trees, with flat flowers in bud, and below were bright, unfurling pennons of fern. In the midst of the bare space stood a keeper's log hut. Pheasant coops were lying about, some occupied by a clucking hen, some empty.

Hilda walked over the brown pine needles to the hut, took a key from among the eaves, and opened the door. It was a bare wooden place with a carpenter's bench and form, carpenter's tools, an axe, snares, traps, some skins pegged down, everything in order. Hilda closed the door. Syson examined the weird flat coats of wild animals, that were pegged down to be cured. She turned some notch in the side wall, and disclosed a second, small apartment.

"How romantic!" said Syson.

"Yes. He is very curious—he has some of a wild animal's cunning—in a nice sense—and he is inventive, and thoughtful—but not beyond a certain point."

She pulled back a dark green curtain. The apartment was occupied almost entirely by a large couch of heather and bracken, on which was spread an ample rabbit-skin rug. On the floor were patchwork rugs of cat-skin, and a red calfskin, while hanging from the wall were other furs. Hilda took down one, which she put on. It was a cloak of rabbit-skin and of white fur, with a hood, apparently of the skins of stoats. She laughed at Syson from out of this barbaric mantle, saying:

"What do you think of it?"

"Ah——! I congratulate you on your man," he replied.

"And look!" she said.

In a little jar on a shelf were some sprays, frail and white, of the first honeysuckle.

"They will scent the place at night," she said.

He looked round curiously.

"Where does he come short, then?" he asked. She gazed at him for a few moments. Then, turning aside:

"The stars aren't the same with him," she said. "You could make them flash and quiver, and the forget-me-nots come up at me like phosphorescence. You could make things *wonderful*. I have found it out—it is true. But I have them all for myself, now."

He laughed, saying:

"After all, stars and forget-me-nots are only luxuries. You ought to make poetry."

"Aye," she assented. "But I have them all now."

Again he laughed bitterly at her.

She turned swiftly. He was leaning against the small window of the tiny, obscure room, and was watching her, who stood in the doorway, still cloaked in her mantle. His cap was removed, so she saw his face and head distinctly in the dim room. His black, straight, glossy hair was brushed clean back from his brow. His black eyes were watching her, and his face, that was clear and cream, and perfectly smooth, was flickering.

"We are very different," she said bitterly.

Again he laughed.

"I see you disapprove of me," he said.

"I disapprove of what you have become," she said.

"You think we might"—he glanced at the hut—"have been like this—you and I?"

She shook her head.

"You! No; never! You plucked a thing and looked at it till you had found out all you wanted to know about it, then you threw it away," she said.

"Did I?" he asked. "And could your way never have been my way? I suppose not."

"Why should it?" she said. "I am a separate being."

"But surely two people sometimes go the same way," he said.

"You took me away from myself," she said.

He knew he had mistaken her, had taken her for something she was not. That was his fault, not hers.

"And did you always know?" he asked.

"No—you never let me know. You bullied me. I couldn't help myself. I was glad when you left me, really."

"I know you were," he said. But his face went paler, almost deathly luminous.

"Yet," he said, "it was you who sent me the way I have gone."

"I!" she exclaimed, in pride.

"You *would* have me take the Grammar School scholarship—and you would have me foster poor little Botell's fervent attachment to me, till he couldn't live without me—and because Botell was rich and influential. You triumphed in the wine-merchant's offer to send me to Cambridge, to befriend his only child. You wanted me to rise in the world. And all the time you were sending me away from you—every new success of mine put a separation between us, and more for you than for me. You never wanted to come with me: you wanted just to send me to see what it was like. I believe you even wanted me to marry a lady. You wanted to triumph over society in me."

"And I am responsible," she said, with sarcasm.

"I distinguished myself to satisfy you," he replied.

"Ah!" she cried, "you always wanted change, change, like a child."

"Very well! And I am a success, and I know it, and I do some good work. But—I thought you were different. What right have you to a man?"

"What do you want?" she said, looking at him with wide, fearful eyes.

He looked back at her, his eyes pointed, like weapons.

"Why, nothing," he laughed shortly.

There was a rattling at the outer latch, and the keeper entered. The woman glanced round, but remained standing, fur-cloaked, in the inner doorway. Syson did not move.

The other man entered, saw, and turned away without speaking. The two also were silent.

Pilbeam attended to his skins.

"I must go," said Syson.

"Yes," she replied.

"Then I give you 'To our vast and varying fortunes.'" He lifted his hand in pledge.

"'To our vast and varying fortunes,'" she answered gravely, and speaking in cold tones.

"Arthur!" she said.

The keeper pretended not to hear. Syson, watching keenly, began to smile. The woman drew herself up.

"Arthur!" she said again, with a curious upward inflection, which warned the two men that her soul was trembling on a dangerous crisis.

The keeper slowly put down his tool and came to her.

"Yes," he said.

"I wanted to introduce you," she said, trembling.

"I've met him a'ready," said the keeper.

"Have you? It is Addy, Mr. Syson, whom you know about—This is Arthur, Mr. Pilbeam," she added, turning to Syson. The latter held out his hand to the keeper, and they shook hands in silence.

"I'm glad to have met you," said Syson. "We drop our correspondence, Hilda?"

"Why need we?" she asked.

The two men stood at a loss.

"*Is* there no need?" said Syson.

Still she was silent.

"It is as you will," she said.

They went all three together down the gloomy path.

" 'Qu'il était bleu, le ciel, et grand l'espoir,' " quoted Syson, not knowing what to say.

"What do you mean?" she said. "Besides, *we* can't walk in *our* wild oats—we never sowed any."

Syson looked at her. He was startled to see his young love, his nun, his Botticelli angel, so revealed. It was he who had been the fool. He and she were more separate than any two strangers could be. She only wanted to keep up a correspondence with him—and he, of course, wanted it kept up, so that he could write to her, like Dante to some Beatrice who had never existed save in the man's own brain.

At the bottom of the path she left him. He went along with the keeper, towards the open, towards the gate that closed on the wood. The two men walked almost like friends. They did not broach the subject of their thoughts.

Instead of going straight to the highroad gate, Syson went along the wood's edge, where the brook spread out in a little bog, and under the alder trees, among the reeds, great yellow stools and bosses of marigolds shone. Threads of brown water trickled by, touched with gold from the flowers. Suddenly there was a blue flash in the air, as a kingfisher passed.

Syson was extraordinarily moved. He climbed the bank to the gorse bushes, whose sparks of blossom had not yet gathered into a flame. Lying on the dry brown turf, he discovered sprigs of tiny purple milkwort and pink spots of lousewort. What a wonderful world it was—marvelous, forever new. He felt as if it were underground, like the fields of monotone hell, notwithstanding. Inside his breast was a pain like a wound. He remembered the poem of William Morris, where in the Chapel of Lyonesse a knight lay wounded, with the truncheon of a spear deep in his breast, lying always as dead, yet did not die, while day after day the colored sunlight dipped from the painted window across the chancel, and passed away. He knew now it never had been true, that which was between him and her, not for a moment. The truth had stood apart all the time.

Syson turned over. The air was full of the sound of larks, as if the sunshine above were condensing and falling in a shower. Amid this bright sound, voices sounded small and distinct.

"But if he's married, an' quite willing to drop it off, what has ter against it?" said the man's voice.

"I don't want to talk about it now. I want to be alone."

Syson looked through the bushes. Hilda was standing in the wood, near the gate. The man was in the field, loitering by the hedge, and playing with the bees as they settled on the white bramble flowers.

There was silence for a while, in which Syson imagined her will among the brightness of the larks. Suddenly the keeper exclaimed "Ah!" and swore. He was gripping at the sleeve of his coat, near the shoulder. Then he pulled off his jacket, threw it on the ground, and absorbedly rolled up his shirt-sleeve right to the shoulder.

"Ah!" he said vindictively, as he picked out the bee and flung it away. He twisted his fine, bright arm, peering awkwardly over his shoulder.

"What is it?" asked Hilda.

"A bee—crawled up my sleeve," he answered.

"Come here to me," she said.

The keeper went to her, like a sulky boy. She took his arm in her hands.

"Here it is—and the sting left in—poor bee!"

She picked out the sting, put her mouth to his arm, and sucked away the drop of poison. As she looked at the red mark her mouth had made, and at his arm, she said, laughing:

"That is the reddest kiss you will ever have."

When Syson next looked up, at the sound of voices, he saw in the shadow the keeper with his mouth on the throat of his beloved, whose head was thrown back, and whose hair had fallen, so that one rough rope of dark brown hair hung across his bare arm.

"No," the woman answered. "I am not upset because he's gone. You won't understand. . . ."

Syson could not distinguish what the man said. Hilda replied, clear and distinct:

"You know I love you. He has gone quite out of my life—don't trouble about him. . . ." He kissed her, murmuring. She laughed hollowly.

"Yes," she said, indulgent. "We will be married, we will be married. But not just yet." He spoke to her again. Syson heard nothing for a time. Then she said:

"You must go home, now, dear—you will get no sleep."

Again was heard the murmur of the keeper's voice, troubled by fear and passion.

"But why should we be married at once?" she said. "What more would you have, by being married? It is most beautiful as it is."

At last he pulled on his coat and departed. She stood at the gate, not watching him, but looking over the sunny country.

When at last she had gone, Syson also departed, going back to town.

SECOND BEST

Oh, I'm tired!" Frances exclaimed petulantly, and in the same instant she dropped down on the turf, near the hedge-bottom. Anne stood a moment surprised, then, accustomed to the vagaries of her beloved Frances, said:

"Well, and aren't you always likely to be tired, after traveling that blessed long way from Liverpool yesterday?" and she plumped down beside her sister. Anne was a wise young body of fourteen, very buxom, brimming with common sense. Frances was much older, about twenty-three, and whimsical, spasmodic. She was the beauty and the clever child of the family. She plucked the goose-grass buttons from her dress in a nervous, desperate fashion. Her beautiful profile, looped above with black hair, warm with the dusky-and-scarlet complexion of a pear, was calm as a mask, her thin brown hand plucked nervously.

"It's not the journey," she said, objecting to Anne's obtuseness. Anne looked inquiringly at her darling. The young girl, in her self-confident, practical way, proceeded to reckon up this whimsical creature. But suddenly she found herself full in the eyes of Frances; felt two dark, hectic eyes flaring challenge at her, and she shrank away. Frances was peculiar for these great, exposed looks, which disconcerted people by their violence and their suddenness.

"What's a matter, poor old duck?" asked Anne, as she folded the slight, willful form of her sister in her arms. Frances laughed shakily, and nestled down for comfort on the budding breasts of the strong girl.

"Oh, I'm only a bit tired," she murmured, on the point of tears.

"Well, of course you are, what do you expect?" soothed Anne. It was a joke to Frances that Anne should play elder, almost mother to her. But then, Anne was in her unvexed teens; men were like big dogs to her: while Frances, at twenty-three, suffered a good deal.

The country was intensely morning-still. On the common everything shone beside its shadow, and the hillside gave off heat in silence. The brown turf seemed in a low state of combustion, the leaves of the oaks were scorched brown. Among the blackish foliage in the distance shone the small red and orange of the village.

The willows in the brook-course at the foot of the common suddenly shook with a dazzling effect like diamonds. It was a puff of wind. Anne resumed her normal position. She spread her knees, and put in her lap a handful of hazel nuts, whity-green leafy things, whose one cheek was tanned between brown and pink. These she began to crack and eat. Frances, with bowed head, mused bitterly.

"Eh, you know Tom Smedley?" began the young girl, as she pulled a tight kernel out of its shell.

"I suppose so," replied Frances sarcastically.

"Well, he gave me a wild rabbit what he'd caught, to keep with my tame one—and it's living."

"That's a good thing," said Frances, very detached and ironic.

"Well, it *is*! He reckoned he'd take me to Ollerton Feast, but he never did. Look here, he took a servant from the rectory; I saw him."

"So he ought," said Frances.

"No, he oughtn't! And I told him so. And I told him I should tell you—an' I have done."

Click and snap went a nut between her teeth. She sorted out the kernel, and chewed complacently.

"It doesn't make much difference," said Frances.

"Well,'appen it doesn't; but I was mad with him all the same."

"Why?"

"Because I was; he's no right to go with a servant."

"He's a perfect right," persisted Frances, very just and cold.

"No, he hasn't, when he'd said he'd take me."

Frances burst into a laugh of amusement and relief.

"Oh, no; I'd forgot that," she said, adding, "and what did he say when you promised to tell me?"

"He laughed and said, 'She won't fret her fat over that.' "

"And she won't," sniffed Frances.

There was silence. The common, with its sere, blonde-headed thistles, its heaps of silent bramble, its brown-husked gorse in the glare of sunshine, seemed visionary. Across the brook began the immense pattern of agriculture, white checkering of barley stubble, brown squares of wheat, khaki patches of pasture, red stripes of fallow, with the woodland and the tiny village dark like ornaments, leading away to the distance, right to the hills, where the check-pattern grew smaller and smaller, till, in the blackish haze of heat, far off, only the tiny white squares of barley stubble showed distinct.

"Eh, I say, here's a rabbit hole!" cried Anne suddenly. "Should we watch if one comes out? You won't have to fidget, you know."

The two girls sat perfectly still. Frances watched certain objects in her surroundings: they had a peculiar, unfriendly look about them: the weight of greenish elderberries on their purpling stalks; the twinkling of the yellowing crab apples that clustered high up in the hedge, against the sky: the exhausted, limp leaves of the primroses lying flat in the hedge-bottom: all looked strange to her. Then her eyes caught a movement. A mole was moving silently over the warm, red soil, nosing, shuffling hither and thither, flat, and dark as a shadow, shifting about, and as suddenly brisk, and as silent, like a very ghost of *joie de vivre*. Frances started, from habit was about to call on Anne to kill the little pest. But, today her lethargy of unhappiness was too much for her. She watched the little brute paddling, snuffing, touching things to discover them, running in blindness, delighted to ecstasy by the sunlight and the hot, strange things that caressed its belly and its nose. She felt a keen pity for the little creature.

"Eh, our Fran, look there! It's a mole."

Anne was on her feet, standing watching the dark, unconscious beast. Frances frowned with anxiety.

"It doesn't run off, does it?" said the young girl softly. Then she stealthily approached the creature. The mole paddled fumblingly away. In an instant Anne put her foot upon it, not too heavily. Frances could see the struggling, swimming movement of the little pink hands of the brute, the twisting and twitching of its pointed nose, as it wrestled under the sole of the boot.

"It *does* wriggle!" said the bonny girl, knitting her brows in a frown at the eerie sensation. Then she bent down to look at her trap. Frances could now see, beyond the edge of the boot-sole, the heaving of the velvet shoulders, the pitiful turning of the sightless face, the frantic rowing of the flat, pink hands.

"Kill the thing," she said, turning away her face.

"Oh—I'm not," laughed Anne, shrinking. "You can, if you like."

"I *don't* like," said Frances, with quiet intensity.

After several dabbing attempts, Anne succeeded in picking up the little animal by the scruff of its neck. It threw back its head, flung its long blind snout from side to side, the mouth open in a peculiar oblong, with tiny pinkish teeth at the edge. The blind, frantic mouth gaped and writhed. The body, heavy and clumsy, hung scarcely moving.

"Isn't it a snappy little thing," observed Anne, twisting to avoid the teeth.

"What are you going to do with it?" asked Frances sharply.

"It's got to be killed—look at the damage they do. I s'll take it home and let dadda or somebody kill it. I'm not going to let it go."

She swaddled the creature clumsily in her pocket-handkerchief and sat down beside her sister. There was an interval of silence, during which Anne combated the efforts of the mole.

"You've not had much to say about Jimmy this time. Did you see him often in Liverpool?" Anne asked suddenly.

"Once or twice," replied Frances, giving no sign of how the question troubled her.

"And aren't you sweet on him anymore, then?"

"I should think I'm not, seeing that he's engaged."

"Engaged? Jimmy Barrass! Well, of all things! I never thought *he'd* get engaged."

"Why not, he's as much right as anybody else?" snapped Frances.

Anne was fumbling with the mole.

" 'Appen so," she said at length; "but I never thought Jimmy would, though."

"Why not?" snapped Frances.

"*I* don't know—this blessed mole, it'll not keep still!—who's he got engaged to?"

"How should I know?"

"I thought you'd ask him; you've known him long enough. I s'd think he thought he'd get engaged now he's a Doctor of Chemistry."

Frances laughed in spite of herself.

"What's that got to do with it?" she asked.

"I'm sure it's got a lot. He'll want to feel *somebody* now, so he's got engaged. Hey, stop it; go in!"

But at this juncture the mole almost succeeded in wriggling clear. It wrestled and twisted frantically, waved its pointed blind head, its mouth standing open like a little shaft, its big, wrinkled hands spread out.

"Go in with you!" urged Anne, poking the little creature with her forefinger, trying to get it back into the handkerchief. Suddenly the mouth turned like a spark on her finger.

"Oh!" she cried, "he's bit me."

She dropped him to the floor. Dazed, the blind creature fumbled round. Frances felt like shrieking. She expected him to dart away in a flash, like a mouse, and there he remained groping; she wanted to cry to him to be gone. Anne, in a sudden decision of wrath, caught up her sister's walking-cane. With one blow the mole was dead. Frances was startled and shocked. One moment the little wretch was fussing in the heat, and the next it lay like a little bag, inert and black—not a struggle, scarce a quiver.

"It is dead!" Frances said breathlessly. Anne took her finger from her mouth, looked at the tiny pinpricks, and said:

"Yes, he is, and I'm glad. They're vicious little nuisances, moles are."

With which her wrath vanished. She picked up the dead animal.

"Hasn't it got a beautiful skin," she mused, stroking the fur with her forefinger, then with her cheek.

"Mind," said Frances sharply. "You'll have the blood on your skirt!"

One ruby drop of blood hung on the small snout, ready to fall. Anne shook it off on to some harebells. Frances suddenly became calm; in that moment, grown-up.

"I suppose they have to be killed," she said, and a certain rather dreary indifference succeeded to her grief. The twinkling crab apples, the glitter of brilliant willows now seemed to her trifling, scarcely worth the notice. Something had died in her, so that things lost their poignancy. She was calm, indifference overlying her quiet sadness. Rising, she walked down to the brook course.

"Here, wait for me," cried Anne, coming tumbling after.

Frances stood on the bridge, looking at the red mud trodden into pockets by the feet of cattle. There was not a drain of water left, but everything smelled green, succulent. Why did she care so little for Anne, who was so fond of her? she asked herself. Why did she care so little for anyone? She did not know, but she felt a rather stubborn pride in her isolation and indifference.

They entered a field where stooks of barley stood in rows, the straight, blonde tresses of the corn streaming onto the ground. The stubble was bleached by the intense summer, so that the expanse glared white. The next field was sweet and soft with a second crop of seeds; thin, straggling clover whose little pink knobs rested prettily in the dark green. The scent was faint and sickly. The girls came up in single file, Frances leading.

Near the gate a young man was mowing with the scythe some fodder for the afternoon feed of the cattle. As he saw the girls he left off working and waited in an aimless kind of way. Frances was dressed in white muslin, and she walked with dignity, detached and forgetful. Her lack of agitation, her simple, unheeding advance made him nervous. She had loved the far-off Jimmy for five years, having had in return his half-measures. This man only affected her slightly.

Tom was of medium stature, energetic in build. His smooth, fair-skinned face was burned red, not brown, by the sun, and this ruddiness enhanced his appearance of good humor and easiness. Being a year older than Frances, he would have courted her long ago had she been so inclined. As it was, he had gone his uneventful way amiably, chatting with many a girl, but remaining unattached, free of trouble for the most part. Only he knew he wanted a woman. He hitched his trousers just a trifle self-consciously as the girls approached. Frances was a rare, delicate kind of being, whom he realized with a queer and delicious stimulation in his veins. She gave him a slight sense of suffocation. Somehow, this morning, she affected him more than usual. She was dressed in white. He, however, being matter-of-fact in his mind, did not realize. His feeling had never become conscious, purposive.

Frances knew what she was about. Tom was ready to love her as soon as she would show him. Now that she could not have Jimmy, she did not poignantly care. Still, she would have something. If she could not have the best—Jimmy, whom she knew to be something of a snob—she would have the second best, Tom. She advanced rather indifferently.

"You are back, then!" said Tom. She marked the touch of uncertainty in his voice.

"No," she laughed, "I'm still in Liverpool," and the undertone of intimacy made him burn.

"This isn't you, then?" he asked.

Her heart leapt up in approval. She looked in his eyes, and for a second was with him.

"Why, what do you think?" she laughed.

He lifted his hat from his head with a distracted little gesture. She liked him, his quaint ways, his humour, his ignorance, and his slow masculinity.

"Here, look here, Tom Smedley," broke in Anne.

"A moudiwarp! Did you find it dead?" he asked.

"No, it bit me," said Anne.

"Oh, aye! An' that got your rag out, did it?"

"No, it didn't!" Anne scolded sharply. "Such language!"

"Oh, what's up wi' it?"

"I can't bear you to talk broad."

"Can't you?"

He glanced at Frances.

"It isn't nice," Frances said. She did not care, really. The vulgar speech jarred on her as a rule; Jimmy was a gentleman. But Tom's manner of speech did not matter to her.

"I like you to talk *nicely*," she added.

"Do you," he replied, tilting his hat, stirred.

"And generally you *do*, you know," she smiled.

"I s'll have to have a try," he said, rather tensely gallant.

"What?" she asked brightly.

"To talk nice to you," he said. Frances colored furiously bent her head for a moment, then laughed gaily, as if she liked this clumsy hint.

"Eh now, you mind what you're saying," cried Anne, giving the young man an admonitory pat.

"You wouldn't have to give yon mole many knocks like that," he teased, relieved to get on safe ground, rubbing his arm.

"No indeed, it died in one blow," said Frances, with a flippancy that was hateful to her.

"You're not so good at knockin' 'em?" he said, turning to her.

"I don't know, if I'm cross," she said decisively.

"No?" he replied, with alert attentiveness.

"I could," she added, harder, "if it was necessary."

He was slow to feel her difference.

"And don't you consider it *is* necessary?" he asked, with misgiving.

"W—ell—is it?" she said, looking at him steadily, coldly.

"I reckon it is," he replied, looking away, but standing stubborn.

She laughed quickly.

"But it isn't necessary for *me*," she said, with slight contempt.

"Yes, that's quite true," he answered.

She laughed in a shaky fashion.

"*I know it is*," she said; and there was an awkward pause.

"Why, would you *like* me to kill moles then?" she asked tentatively, after a while.

"They do us a lot of damage," he said, standing firm on his own ground, angered.

"Well, I'll see the next time I come across one," she promised, defiantly. Their eyes met, and she sank before him, her pride troubled. He felt uneasy and triumphant and baffled, as if fate had gripped him. She smiled as she departed.

"Well," said Anne, as the sisters went through the wheat stubble; "I don't know what you two's been jawing about, I'm sure."

"Don't you?" laughed Frances significantly.

"No, I don't. But, at any rate, Tom Smedley's a good deal better to my thinking than Jimmy, so there—and nicer."

"Perhaps he is," said Frances coldly.

And the next day, after a secret, persistent hunt, she found another mole playing in the heat. She killed it, and in the evening, when Tom came to the gate to smoke his pipe after supper, she took him the dead creature.

"Here you are then!" she said.

"Did you catch it?" he replied, taking the velvet corpse into his fingers and examining it minutely. This was to hide his trepidation.

"Did you think I couldn't?" she asked, her face very near his.

"Nay, I didn't know."

She laughed in his face, a strange little laugh that caught her breath, all agitation, and tears, and recklessness of desire. He looked frightened and upset. She put her hand to his arm.

"Shall you go out wi' me?" he asked, in a difficult, troubled tone.

She turned her face away, with a shaky laugh. The blood came up in him, strong, overmastering. He resisted it. But it drove him down, and he was carried away. Seeing the winsome, frail nape of her neck, fierce love came upon him for her, and tenderness.

"We s'll 'ave to tell your mother," he said. And he stood, suffering, resisting his passion for her.

"Yes," she replied, in a dead voice. But there was a thrill of pleasure in this death.

THE SHADOW IN THE ROSE GARDEN

A rather small young man sat by the window of a pretty seaside cottage trying to persuade himself that he was reading the newspaper. It was about half-past eight in the morning. Outside, the glory roses hung in the morning sunshine like little bowls of fire tipped up. The young man looked at the table, then at the clock, then at his own big silver watch. An expression of stiff endurance came on to his face. Then he rose and reflected on the oil paintings that hung on the walls of the room, giving careful but hostile attention to "The Stag at Bay." He tried the lid of the piano, and found it locked. He caught sight of his own face in a little mirror, pulled his brown moustache, and an alert interest sprang into his eyes. He was not ill-favored. He twisted his moustache. His figure was rather small, but alert and vigorous. As he turned from the mirror a look of self-commiseration mingled with his appreciation of his own physiognomy.

In a state of self-suppression, he went through into the garden. His jacket, however, did not look dejected. It was new, and had a smart and self-confident air, sitting upon a confident body. He contemplated the Tree of Heaven that flourished by the lawn, then sauntered on to the next plant. There was more promise in a crooked apple tree covered with brown-red fruit. Glancing round, he broke off an apple and, with his back to the house, took a clean, sharp bite. To his surprise the fruit was sweet. He took another. Then again he turned to survey the bedroom windows overlooking the garden. He started, seeing a woman's figure;

but it was only his wife. She was gazing across to the sea, apparently ignorant of him.

For a moment or two he looked at her, watching her. She was a good-looking woman, who seemed older than he, rather pale, but healthy, her face yearning. Her rich auburn hair was heaped in folds on her forehead. She looked apart from him and his world, gazing away to the sea. It irked her husband that she should continue abstracted and in ignorance of him; he pulled poppy fruits and threw them at the window. She started, glanced at him with a wild smile, and looked away again. Then almost immediately she left the window. He went indoors to meet her. She had a fine carriage, very proud, and wore a dress of soft white muslin.

"I've been waiting long enough," he said.

"For me or for breakfast?" she said lightly. "You know we said nine o'clock. I should have thought you could have slept after the journey."

"You know I'm always up at five, and I couldn't stop in bed after six. You might as well be in pit as in bed, on a morning like this."

"I shouldn't have thought the pit would occur to you, here."

She moved about examining the room, looking at the ornaments under glass covers. He, planted on the hearthrug, watched her rather uneasily, and grudgingly indulgent. She shrugged her shoulders at the apartment.

"Come," she said, taking his arm, "let us go into the garden till Mrs. Coates brings the tray."

"I hope she'll be quick," he said, pulling his moustache. She gave a short laugh, and leaned on his arm as they went. He had lighted a pipe.

Mrs. Coates entered the room as they went down the steps. The delightful, erect old lady hastened to the window for a good view of her visitors. Her china-blue eyes were bright as she watched the young couple go down the path, he walking in an easy, confident fashion, with his wife on his arm. The landlady began talking to herself in a soft, Yorkshire accent.

"Just of a height they are. She wouldn't ha' married a man less than herself in stature, I think, though he's not her equal otherwise." Here her granddaughter came in, setting a tray on the table. The girl went to the old woman's side.

"He's been eating the apples, gran'," she said.

"Has he, my pet? Well, if he's happy, why not?"

Outside, the young, well-favored man listened with impatience to the chink of the teacups. At last, with a sigh of relief, the couple came in to breakfast. After he had eaten for some time, he rested a moment and said:

"Do you think it's any better place than Bridlington?"

"I do," she said, "infinitely! Besides, I am at home here—it's not like a strange seaside place to me."

"How long were you here?"

"Two years."

He ate reflectively.

"I should ha' thought you'd rather go to a fresh place," he said at length.

She sat very silent, and then, delicately, put out a feeler.

"Why?" she said. "Do you think I shan't enjoy myself?"

He laughed comfortably, putting the marmalade thick on his bread.

"I hope so," he said.

She again took no notice of him.

"But don't say anything about it in the village, Frank," she said casually. "Don't say who I am, or that I used to live here. There's nobody I want to meet, particularly, and we should never feel free if they knew me again."

"Why did you come, then?"

" 'Why?' Can't you understand why?"

"Not if you don't want to know anybody."

"I came to see the place, not the people."

He did not say anymore.

"Women," she said, "are different from men. I don't know why I wanted to come—but I did."

She helped him to another cup of coffee, solicitously.

"Only," she resumed, "don't talk about me in the village."

She laughed shakily. "I don't want my past brought up against me, you know." And she moved the crumbs on the cloth with her fingertip.

He looked at her as he drank his coffee; he sucked his moustache, and putting down his cup, said phlegmatically:

"I'll bet you've had a lot of past."

She looked with a little guiltiness, that flattered him, down at the tablecloth.

"Well," she said, caressive, "you won't give me away, who I am, will you?"

"No," he said, comforting, laughing, "I won't give you away."

He was pleased.

She remained silent. After a moment or two she lifted her head, saying:

"I've got to arrange with Mrs. Coates, and do various things. So you'd better go out by yourself this morning—and we'll be in to dinner at one."

"But you can't be arranging with Mrs. Coates all morning," he said.

"Oh, well—then I've some letters to write, and I must get that mark out of my skirt. I've got plenty of little things to do this morning. You'd better go out by yourself."

He perceived that she wanted to be rid of him, so that when she went upstairs, he took his hat and lounged out on to the cliffs, suppressedly angry.

Presently she too came out. She wore a hat with roses, and a long lace scarf hung over her white dress. Rather nervously, she put up her sunshade, and her face was half-hidden in its colored shadow. She went along the narrow track of flagstones that were worn hollow by the feet of the fishermen. She seemed to be avoiding her surroundings, as if she remained safe in the little obscurity of her parasol.

She passed the church, and went down the lane till she came to a high wall by the wayside. Under this she went slowly, stopping at length by an open doorway, which shone like a picture of light in the dark wall. There in the magic beyond the doorway, patterns of shadow lay on the sunny court, on the blue and white sea-pebbles of its paving, while a green lawn glowed beyond, where a bay tree glittered at the edges. She tiptoed nervously into the courtyard, glancing at the house that stood in shadow. The uncurtained windows looked black and soulless, the kitchen door stood open. Irresolutely she took a step forward, and again forward, leaning, yearning, towards the garden beyond.

She had almost gained the corner of the house when a heavy step came crunching through the trees. A gardener appeared before her. He held a wicker tray on which were rolling great, dark red gooseberries, overripe. He moved slowly.

"The garden isn't open today," he said quietly to the attractive woman, who was poised for retreat.

For a moment she was silent with surprise. How should it be public at all?

"When is it open?" she asked, quick-witted.

"The rector lets visitors in on Fridays and Tuesdays."

She stood still, reflecting. How strange to think of the rector opening his garden to the public!

"But everybody will be at church," she said coaxingly to the man. "There'll be nobody here, will there?"

He moved, and the big gooseberries rolled.

"The rector lives at the new rectory," he said.

The two stood still. He did not like to ask her to go. At last she turned to him with a winning smile.

"Might I have *one* peep at the roses?" she coaxed, with pretty willfulness.

"I don't suppose it would matter," he said, moving aside; "you won't stop long——"

She went forward, forgetting the gardener in a moment. Her face became strained, her movements eager. Glancing round, she saw all the windows giving on to the lawn were curtainless and dark. The house had a sterile appearance, as if it were still used, but not inhabited. A shadow seemed to go over her. She went across the lawn towards the garden, through an arch of crimson ramblers, a gate of color. There beyond lay the soft blue sea within the bay, misty with morning, and the furthest headland of black rock jutting dimly out between blue and blue of the sky and water. Her face began to shine, transfigured with pain and joy. At her feet the garden fell steeply, all a confusion of flowers, and away below was the darkness of treetops covering the beck.

She turned to the garden that shone with sunny flowers around her. She knew the little corner where was the seat beneath the yew tree. Then there was the terrace where a great host of flowers shone, and from this, two paths went down, one at each side of the garden. She closed her sunshade and walked slowly among the many flowers. All round were rosebushes, big banks of roses, then roses hanging and tumbling from pillars, or roses balanced on the standard bushes. By the open earth were many other flowers. If she lifted her head, the sea was upraised beyond, and the Cape.

Slowly she went down one path, lingering, like one who has gone back into the past. Suddenly she was touching some heavy crimson roses that were soft as velvet, touching them thoughtfully, without knowing, as a mother sometimes fondles the hand of her child. She leaned slightly forward to catch the scent. Then she wandered on in abstraction. Sometimes a flame-colored, scentless rose would hold her arrested. She stood gazing at it as if she could not understand it. Again the same softness of intimacy came over her, as she stood before a tumbling heap of pink petals. Then she wondered over the white rose, that was greenish, like ice, in the center. So, slowly, like a white, pathetic butterfly, she drifted down the path, coming at last to a tiny terrace all full of roses. They seemed to fill the place, a sunny, gay throng. She was shy of them, they were so many and so bright. They seemed to be conversing and laughing. She felt herself in a strange crowd. It exhilarated her, carried her out of herself. She flushed with excitement. The air was pure scent.

Hastily, she went to a little seat among the white roses, and sat down. Her scarlet sunshade made a hard blot of color. She sat quite still, feeling her own existence lapse. She was no more than a rose, a rose that could not quite come into blossom, but remained tense. A little fly dropped on her knee, on her white dress. She watched it, as if it had fallen on a rose. She was not herself.

Then she started cruelly as a shadow crossed her and a figure moved into her sight. It was a man who had come in slippers, unheard. He wore a linen coat. The morning was shattered, the spell vanished away. She was only afraid of being questioned. He came forward. She rose. Then, seeing him, the strength went from her and she sank on the seat again.

He was a young man, military in appearance, growing slightly stout. His black hair was brushed smooth and bright, his moustache was waxed. But there was something rambling in his gait. She looked up, blanched to the lips, and saw his eyes. They were black, and stared without seeing. They were not a man's eyes. He was coming towards her.

He stared at her fixedly, made an unconscious salute, and sat down beside her on the seat. He moved on the bench, shifted his feet, saying, in a gentlemanly, military voice:

"I don't disturb you—do I?"

She was mute and helpless. He was scrupulously dressed in dark clothes and a linen coat. She could not move. Seeing his hands, with the ring she knew so well upon the little finger, she felt as if she were going dazed. The whole world was deranged. She sat unavailing. For his hands, her symbols of passionate love, filled her with horror as they rested now on his strong thighs.

"May I smoke?" he asked intimately, almost secretly, his hand going to his pocket.

She could not answer, but it did not matter, he was in another world. She wondered, craving, if he recognized her—if he could recognize her. She sat pale with anguish. But she had to go through it.

"I haven't got any tobacco," he said thoughtfully.

But she paid no heed to his words, only she attended to him.

Could he recognize her, or was it all gone? She sat still in a frozen kind of suspense.

"I smoke John Cotton," he said, "and I must economize with it, it is expensive. You know, I'm not very well-off while these lawsuits are going on."

"No," she said, and her heart was cold, her soul kept rigid.

He moved, made a loose salute, rose, and went away. She sat motionless. She could see his shape, the shape she had loved with all her passion: his compact, soldier's head, his fine figure now slackened. And it was not he. It only filled her with horror too difficult to know.

Suddenly he came again, his hand in his jacket pocket.

"Do you mind if I smoke?" he said. "Perhaps I shall be able to see things more clearly."

He sat down beside her again, filling a pipe. She watched his hands with the fine strong fingers. They had always inclined to tremble slightly. It had surprised her, long ago, in such a healthy man. Now they moved inaccurately, and the tobacco hung raggedly out of the pipe.

"I have legal business to attend to. Legal affairs are always so uncertain. I tell my solicitor exactly, precisely what I want, but I can never get it done."

She sat and heard him talking. But it was not he. Yet those were the hands she had kissed, there were the glistening, strange black eyes that she had loved. Yet it was not he. She sat motionless with horror and silence. He dropped his tobacco pouch, and groped for it on the ground. Yet she must wait to see if he would recognize her. Why could she not go! In a moment he rose.

"I must go at once," he said. "The owl is coming." Then he added confidentially: "His name isn't really the owl, but I call him that. I must go and see if he has come."

She rose too. He stood before her, uncertain. He was a handsome, soldierly fellow, and a lunatic. Her eyes searched him, and searched him, to see if he would recognize her, if she could discover him.

"You don't know me?" she asked, from the terror of her soul, standing alone.

He looked back at her quizzically. She had to bear his eyes. They gleamed on her, but with no intelligence. He was drawing nearer to her.

"Yes, I do know you," he said, fixed, intent, but mad, drawing his face nearer hers. Her horror was too great. The powerful lunatic was coming too near to her.

A man approached, hastening.

"The garden isn't open this morning," he said.

The deranged man stopped and looked at him. The keeper went to the seat and picked up the tobacco pouch left lying there.

"Don't leave your tobacco, sir," he said, taking it to the gentleman in the linen coat.

"I was just asking this lady to stay to lunch," the latter said politely. "She is a friend of mine."

The woman turned and walked swiftly, blindly, between the sunny roses, out from the garden, past the house with the blank, dark windows, through the sea-pebbled courtyard to the street. Hastening and blind, she went forward without hesitating, not knowing whither. Directly she came to the house she went upstairs, took off her hat, and sat down on the bed. It was as if some membrane had been torn in two in her, so that she was not an entity that could think and feel. She sat staring across at the window, where an ivy spray waved slowly up and down in the sea wind. There was some of the uncanny luminousness of the sunlit sea in the air. She sat perfectly still, without any being. She only felt she might be sick, and it might be blood that was loose in her torn entrails. She sat perfectly still and passive.

After a time she heard the hard tread of her husband on the floor below, and, without herself changing, she registered his movement. She heard his rather disconsolate footsteps go out again, then his voice speaking, answering, growing cheery, and his solid tread drawing near.

He entered, ruddy, rather pleased, an air of complacency about his alert, sturdy figure. She moved stiffly. He faltered in his approach.

"What's the matter?" he asked, a tinge of impatience in his voice. "Aren't you feeling well?"

This was torture to her.

"Quite," she replied.

His brown eyes became puzzled and angry.

"What is the matter?" he said.

"Nothing."

He took a few strides, and stood obstinately, looking out of the window.

"Have you run up against anybody?" he asked.

"Nobody who knows me," she said.

His hands began to twitch. It exasperated him, that she was no more sensible of him than if he did not exist. Turning on her at length, driven, he asked:

"Something has upset you, hasn't it?"

"No, why?" she said, neutral. He did not exist for her, except as an irritant.

His anger rose, filling the veins in his throat.

"It seems like it," he said, making an effort not to show his anger, because there seemed no reason for it. He went away downstairs. She sat still on the bed, and with the residue of feeling left to her, she disliked him because he tormented her. The time went by. She could smell the dinner being served, the smoke of her husband's pipe from the garden. But she could not move. She had no being. There was a tinkle of the bell. She heard him come indoors. And then he mounted the stairs again. At every step her heart grew tight in her. He opened the door.

"Dinner is on the table," he said.

It was difficult for her to endure his presence, for he would interfere with her. She could not recover her life. She rose stiffly and went down. She could neither eat nor talk during the meal. She sat absent, torn, without any being of her own. He tried to go on as if nothing were the matter. But at last he became silent with fury. As soon as it was possible, she went upstairs again, and locked the bedroom door. She must be alone. He went with his pipe into the garden. All his suppressed anger against her who held herself superior to him filled and blackened his heart. Though he had not known it, yet he had never really won her, she had never loved him. She had taken him on sufferance. This had foiled him. He was only a laboring electrician in the mine, she was superior to him. He had always given way to her. But all the while, the injury and ignominy had been working in his soul because she did not hold him seriously. And now all his rage came up against her.

He turned and went indoors. The third time, she heard him mounting the stairs. Her heart stood still. He turned the catch and pushed the door—it was locked. He tried it again, harder. Her heart was standing still.

"Have you fastened the door?" he asked quietly, because of the landlady.

"Yes. Wait a minute."

She rose and turned the lock, afraid he would burst it. She felt hatred towards him, because he did not leave her free. He entered, his pipe between his teeth, and she returned to her old position on the bed. He closed the door and stood with his back to it.

"What's the matter?" he asked determinedly.

She was sick with him. She could not look at him.

"Can't you leave me alone?" she replied, averting her face from him.

He looked at her quickly, fully, wincing with ignominy. Then he seemed to consider for a moment.

"There's something up with you, isn't there?" he asked definitely.

"Yes," she said, "but that's no reason why you should torment me."

"I don't torment you. What's the matter?"

"Why should you know?" she cried, in hate and desperation.

Something snapped. He started and caught his pipe as it fell from his mouth. Then he pushed forward the bitten-off mouthpiece with his tongue, took it from off his lips, and looked at it. Then he put out his pipe, and brushed the ash from his waistcoat. After which he raised his head.

"I want to know," he said. His face was grayish pale, and set uglily.

Neither looked at the other. She knew he was fired now. His heart was pounding heavily. She hated him, but she could not withstand him. Suddenly she lifted her head and turned on him.

"What right have you to know?" she asked.

He looked at her. She felt a pang of surprise for his tortured eyes and his fixed face. But her heart hardened swiftly. She had never loved him. She did not love him now.

But suddenly she lifted her head again swiftly, like a thing that tries to get free. She wanted to be free of it. It was not him so much, but it, something she had put on herself, that bound her so horribly. And having put the bond on herself, it was hardest to take it off. But now she hated everything and felt destructive. He stood with his back to the door, fixed, as if he would oppose her eternally, till she was extinguished. She looked at him. Her eyes were cold and hostile. His workman's hands spread on the panels of the door behind him.

"You know I used to live here?" she began, in a hard voice, as if willfully to wound him. He braced himself against her, and nodded.

"Well, I was companion to Miss Birch of Torril Hall—she and the rector were friends, and Archie was the rector's son." There was a pause. He listened without knowing what was happening. He stared at his wife. She was squatted in her white dress on the bed, carefully folding and refolding the hem of her skirt. Her voice was full of hostility.

"He was an officer—a sub-lieutenant—then he quarreled with his colonel and came out of the army. At any rate"—she plucked at her skirt hem, her husband stood motionless, watching her movements which filled his veins with madness—"he was awfully fond of me, and I was of him—awfully."

"How old was he?" asked the husband.

"When—when I first knew him? Or when he went away?——"

"When you first knew him."

"When I first knew him, he was twenty-six—now—he's thirty-one—nearly thirty-two—because I'm twenty-nine, and he is nearly three years older——"

She lifted her head and looked at the opposite wall.

"And what then?" said her husband.

She hardened herself, and said callously:

"We were as good as engaged for nearly a year, though nobody knew—at least—they talked—but—it wasn't open. Then he went away——"

"He chucked you?" said the husband brutally, wanting to hurt her into contact with himself. Her heart rose wildly with rage. Then "Yes," she said, to anger him. He shifted from one foot to the other, giving a "Ph!" of rage. There was silence for a time.

"Then," she resumed, her pain giving a mocking note to her words, "he suddenly went out to fight in Africa, and almost the very day I first met you, I heard from Miss Birch he'd got sunstroke—and two months after, that he was dead——"

"That was before you took on with me?" said the husband.

There was no answer. Neither spoke for a time. He had not understood. His eyes were contracted uglily.

"So you've been looking at your old courting places!" he said. "That was what you wanted to go out by yourself for this morning."

Still she did not answer him anything. He went away from the door to the window. He stood with his hands behind him, his back to her. She looked at him. His hands seemed gross to her, the back of his head paltry.

At length, almost against his will, he turned round, asking:

"How long were you carrying on with him?"

"What do you mean?" she replied coldly.

"I mean how long were you carrying on with him?"

She lifted her head, averting her face from him. She refused to answer. Then she said:

"I don't know what you mean, by carrying on. I loved him from the first days I met him—two months after I went to stay with Miss Birch."

"And do you reckon he loved you?" he jeered.

"I know he did."

"How do you know, if he'd have no more to do with you?"

There was a long silence of hate and suffering.

"And how far did it go between you?" he asked at length, in a frightened, stiff voice.

"I hate your not-straightforward questions," she cried, beside herself with his baiting. "We loved each other, and we *were* lovers—we were. I don't care what *you* think: what have you got to do with it? We were lovers before ever I knew you——"

"Lovers—lovers," he said, white with fury. "You mean you had your fling with an army man; and then came to me to marry you when you'd done——"

She sat swallowing her bitterness. There was a long pause.

"Do you mean to say you used to go—the whole hogger?" he asked, still incredulous.

"Why, what else do you think I mean?" she cried brutally.

He shrank, and became white, impersonal. There was a long, paralyzed silence. He seemed to have gone small.

"You never thought to tell me all this before I married you," he said, with bitter irony, at last.

"You never asked me," she replied.

"I never thought there was any need."

"Well, then, you *should* think."

He stood with expressionless, almost childlike set face, revolving many thoughts, whilst his heart was mad with anguish.

Suddenly she added:

"And I saw him today," she said. "He is not dead, he's mad."

Her husband looked at her, startled.

"Mad!" he said involuntarily.

"A lunatic," she said. It almost cost her her reason to utter the word. There was a pause.

"Did he know you?" asked the husband, in a small voice.

"No," she said.

He stood and looked at her. At last he had learned the width of the breach between them. She still squatted on the bed. He could not go near her. It would be violation to each of them to be brought into contact with the other. The thing must work itself out. They were both shocked so much, they were impersonal, and no longer hated each other. After some minutes he left her and went out.

GOOSE FAIR

I

Through the gloom of evening, and the flare of torches of the night before the fair, through the still fogs of the succeeding dawn came paddling the weary geese, lifting their poor feet that had been dipped in tar for shoes, and trailing them along the cobblestones into the town. Last of all, in the afternoon, a country girl drove in her dozen birds, disconsolate because she was so late. She was a heavily built girl, fair, with regular features, and yet unprepossessing. She needed chiseling down, her contours were brutal. Perhaps it was weariness that hung her eyelids a little lower than was pleasant. When she spoke to her clumsily lagging birds it was in a snarling nasal tone. One of the silly things sat down in the gutter and refused to move. It looked very ridiculous, but also rather pitiful, squat there with its head up, refusing to be urged on by the ungentle toe of the girl. The latter swore heavily, then picked up the great complaining bird, and fronting her road stubbornly, drove on the lamentable eleven.

No one had noticed her. This afternoon the women were not sitting chatting on their doorsteps, seaming up the cotton hose, or swiftly passing through their fingers the piled white lace; and in the high dark houses the song of the hosiery frames was hushed: "Shackety-boom, Shackety-shackety-boom, Z—zzz!" As she dragged up Hollow Stone, people returning from the fair chaffed her and asked her what o'clock it was. She did not reply, her look was sullen. The Lace Market was quiet as the Sabbath: even the great brass plates on the doors were dull with neglect. There seemed an afternoon atmosphere of raw discontent. The girl stopped a moment before the dismal prospect of one of the great warehouses that had been gutted with fire. She looked at the lean, threatening walls, and watched her white flock waddling in reckless misery below, and she would have laughed out loud had the wall fallen flat upon them and relieved her of them. But the wall did not fall, so she crossed the road, and walking on the safe side, hurried after her charge. Her look was even more sullen. She remembered the state of trade—Trade, the invidious enemy; Trade, which thrust out its hand and shut the factory doors, and pulled the stockingers off their seats, and left the web half-finished on the frame; Trade, which mysteriously choked up the sources of the rivulets of wealth, and blacker and more secret than a pestilence, starved the town. Through this morose atmosphere of bad trade, in the afternoon of the first day of the fair, the girl strode down to the Poultry with eleven sound geese and one lame one to sell.

The Frenchmen were at the bottom of it! So everybody said, though nobody quite knew how. At any rate, they had gone to war with the Prussians and got beaten, and trade was ruined in Nottingham!

A little fog rose up, and the twilight gathered around. Then they flared abroad their torches in the fair, insulting the night. The girl still sat in the Poultry, and her weary geese unsold on the stones, illuminated by the hissing lamp of a man who sold rabbits and pigeons and such-like assorted livestock.

II

In another part of the town, near Sneinton Church, another girl came to the door to look at the night. She was tall and slender, dressed with the severe accuracy which marks the girl of superior culture. Her hair was arranged with simplicity about the long, pale, cleanly cut face. She leaned forward very slightly to glance down the street, listening. She very carefully preserved the appearance of having come quite casually to the door, yet she lingered and lingered and stood very still to listen when she heard a footstep, but when it proved to be only a common man, she drew herself up proudly and looked with a small smile over his head. He hesitated to glance into the open hall, lighted so spaciously with a scarlet-shaded lamp, and at the slim girl in brown silk lifted up before the light. But she, she looked over his head. He passed on.

Presently she started and hung in suspense. Somebody was crossing the road. She ran down the steps in a pretty welcome, not effuse, saying in quick but accurately articulated words: "Will! I began to think you'd gone to the fair. I came out to listen to it. I felt almost sure you'd gone. You're coming in, aren't you?" She waited a moment anxiously. "We expect you to dinner, you know," she added wistfully.

The man, who had a short face and spoke with his lip curling up on one side, in a drawling speech with ironically exaggerated intonation, replied after a short hesitation:

"I'm awfully sorry, I am, straight, Lois. It's a shame. I've got to go round to the biz. Man proposes—the devil disposes." He turned aside with irony in the darkness.

"But surely, Will!" remonstrated the girl, keenly disappointed.

"Fact, Lois!—I feel wild about it myself. But I've got to go down to the works. They may be getting a bit warm down there, you know"—he jerked his head in the direction of the fair. "If the Lambs get frisky!—they're a bit off about the work, and they'd just be in their element if they could set a lighted match to something——"

"Will, you don't think——!" exclaimed the girl, laying her hand on his arm in the true fashion of romance, and looking up at him earnestly.

"Dad's not sure," he replied, looking down at her with gravity. They remained in this attitude for a moment, then he said:

"I might stop a bit. It's all right for an hour, I should think."

She looked at him earnestly, then said in tones of deep disappointment and of fortitude: "No, Will, you must go. You'd better go——"

"It's a shame!" he murmured, standing a moment at a loose end. Then, glancing down the street to see he was alone, he put his arm round her waist and said in a difficult voice: "How goes it?"

She let him keep her for a moment, then he kissed her as if afraid of what he was doing. They were both uncomfortable.

"Well——!" he said at length.

"Good night!" she said, setting him free to go.

He hung a moment near her, as if ashamed. Then "Good night," he answered, and he broke away. She listened to his footsteps in the night, before composing herself to turn indoors.

"Helloa!" said her father, glancing over his paper as she entered the dining room. "What's up, then?"

"Oh, nothing," she replied, in her calm tones. "Will won't be here to dinner tonight."

"What, gone to the fair?"

"No."

"Oh! What's got him then?"

Lois looked at her father, and answered:

"He's gone down to the factory. They are afraid of the hands."

Her father looked at her closely.

"Oh, aye!" he answered, undecided, and they sat down to dinner.

III

Lois retired very early. She had a fire in her bedroom. She drew the curtains and stood holding aside a heavy fold, looking out at the night. She could see only the nothingness of the fog; not even the glare of the fair was evident, though the noise clamored small in the distance. In front of everything she could see her own faint image. She crossed to the dressing table, and there leaned her face to the mirror, and looked at herself. She looked a long time, then she rose, changed her dress for a dressing jacket, and took up *Sesame and Lilies*.

Late in the night she was roused from sleep by a bustle in the house. She sat up and heard a hurrying to and fro and the sound of anxious voices. She put on her dressing gown and went out to her mother's room. Seeing her mother at the head of the stairs, she said in her quick, clean voice:

"Mother, what is it?"

"Oh, child, don't ask me! Go to bed, dear, do! I shall surely be worried out of my life."

"Mother, what is it?" Lois was sharp and emphatic.

"I hope your father won't go. Now I do hope your father won't go. He's got a cold as it is."

"Mother, tell me what it is?" Lois took her mother's arm.

"It's Selby's. I should have thought you would have heard the fire engine, and Jack isn't in yet. I hope we're safe!" Lois returned to her bedroom and dressed. She coiled her plaited hair, and having put on a cloak, left the house.

She hurried along under the fog-dripping trees towards the meaner part of the town. When she got near, she saw a glare in the fog, and closed her lips tight. She hastened on till she was in the crowd. With peaked, noble face she watched the fire. Then she looked a little wildly over the fire-reddened faces in the crowd, and catching sight of her father, hurried to him.

"Oh, Dadda—is he safe? Is Will safe——?"

"Safe, aye, why not? You've no business here. Here, here's Sampson, he'll take you home. I've enough to bother me; there's my own place to watch. Go home now, I can't do with you here."

"Have you seen Will?" she asked.

"Go home—Sampson, just take Miss Lois home—now!"

"You don't really know where he is—father?"

"Go home now—I don't want you here——" her father ordered peremptorily.

The tears sprang to Lois's eyes. She looked at the fire and the tears were quickly dried by fear. The flames roared and struggled upward. The great wonder of the fire made her forget even her indignation at her father's light treatment of herself and of her lover. There was a crashing and bursting of timber, as the first floor fell in a mass into the blazing gulf, splashing the fire in all directions, to the terror of the crowd. She saw the steel of the machines growing white-hot and twisting like flaming letters. Piece after piece of the flooring gave way, and the machines dropped in red ruin as the wooden framework burned out. The air became unbreathable; the fog was swallowed up; sparks went rushing up as if they would burn the dark heavens; sometimes cards of lace went whirling into the gulf of the sky, waving with wings of fire. It was dangerous to stand near this great cup of roaring destruction.

Sampson, the gray old manager of Buxton and Co.'s, led her away as soon as she would turn her face to listen to him. He was a stout, irritable man. He elbowed his way roughly through the crowd, and Lois followed him, her head high, her lips closed. He led her for some distance without speaking, then at last, unable to contain his garrulous irritability, he broke out:

"What do they expect? What can they expect? They can't expect to stand a bad time. They spring up like mushrooms as big as a house-side, but there's no stability in 'em. I remember William Selby when he'd run on my errands. Yes, there's some as can make much out of little, and there's some as can make much out of nothing, but they find it won't last. William Selby's sprung up in a day, and he'll vanish in a night. You can't trust to luck alone. Maybe he thinks it's a lucky thing this fire has come when things are looking black. But you can't get out of it as easy as that. There's been a few too many of 'em. No, indeed, a fire's the last thing I should hope to come to—the very last!"

Lois hurried and hurried, so that she brought the old manager panting in distress up the steps of her home. She could not bear to hear him talking so. They could get no one to open the door for some time. When at last Lois ran upstairs, she found her mother dressed, but all unbuttoned again, lying back in the chair in her daughter's room, suffering from palpitation of the heart, with *Sesame and Lilies* crushed beneath her. Lois administered brandy, and her decisive words and movements helped largely to bring the good lady to a state of recovery sufficient to allow of her returning to her own bedroom.

Then Lois locked the door. She glanced at her fire-darkened face, and taking the flattened Ruskin out of the chair, sat down and wept. After a while she calmed herself, rose, and sponged her face. Then once more on that fatal night she prepared for rest. Instead, however, of retiring, she pulled a silk quilt from her disordered bed and, wrapping it round her, sat miserably to think. It was two o'clock in the morning.

IV

The fire was sunk to cold ashes in the grate, and the gray morning was creeping through the half-opened curtains like a thing ashamed, when Lois awoke. It was painful to move her head: her neck was cramped. The girl awoke in full recollection. She sighed, roused herself and pulled the quilt closer about her. For a little while she sat and mused. A pale, tragic resignation fixed her face like a mask. She remembered her father's irritable answer to her question concerning her lover's safety—"Safe, aye—why not?" She knew that he suspected the factory of having been purposely set on fire. But then, he had never liked Will. And yet—and yet—Lois' heart was heavy as lead. She felt her lover was guilty. And she felt she must hide her secret of his last communication to her. She saw herself being cross-examined—"When did you last see this man?" But she would hide what he had said about watching at the works. How dreary it was—and how dreadful. Her life was ruined now, and nothing mattered anymore. She must only behave with dignity, and submit to her own obliteration. For even if Will were never accused, she knew in her heart he was guilty. She knew it was over between them.

It was dawn among the yellow fog outside, and Lois, as she moved mechanically about her toilet, vaguely felt that all her days would arrive slowly struggling through a bleak fog. She felt an intense longing at this uncanny hour to slough the body's trammeled weariness and to issue at once into the new bright warmth of the far Dawn where a lover waited transfigured; is it so easy and pleasant in imagination to step out of the chill gray dampness of another terrestrial daybreak, straight into the sunshine of the eternal morning? And who can escape his hour? So Lois performed the meaningless routine of her toilet, which at last she made meaningful when she took her black dress, and fastened a black jet brooch at her throat.

Then she went downstairs and found her father eating a mutton chop. She quickly approached and kissed him on the forehead. Then she retreated to the other end of the table. Her father looked tired, even haggard.

"You are early," he said, after a while. Lois did not reply. Her father continued to eat for a few moments, then he said:

"Have a chop—here's one! Ring for a hot plate. Eh, what? Why not?"

Lois was insulted, but she gave no sign. She sat down and took a cup of coffee, making no pretence to eat. Her father was absorbed, and had forgotten her.

"Our Jack's not come home yet," he said at last.

Lois stirred faintly. "Hasn't he?" she said.

"No." There was silence for a time. Lois was frightened. Had something happened also to her brother? This fear was closer and more irksome.

"Selby's was cleaned out, gutted. We had a near shave of it——"

"You have no loss, Dadda?"

"Nothing to mention." After another silence, her father said:

"I'd rather be myself than William Selby. Of course it may merely be bad luck—you don't know. But whatever it was, I wouldn't like to add one to the list of fires just now. Selby was at the 'George' when it broke out—I don't know where the lad was——!"

"Father," broke in Lois, "why do you talk like that? Why do you talk as if Will had done it?" She ended suddenly. Her father looked at her pale, mute face.

"I don't talk as if Will had done it," he said. "I don't even think it."

Feeling she was going to cry, Lois rose and left the room. Her father sighed, and leaning his elbows on his knees, whistled faintly into the fire. He was not thinking about her.

Lois went down to the kitchen and asked Lucy, the parlormaid, to go out with her. She somehow shrank from going alone, lest people should stare at her overmuch: and she felt an overpowering impulse to go to the scene of the tragedy, to judge for herself.

The churches were chiming half-past eight when the young lady and the maid set off down the street. Nearer the fair, swarthy, thin-legged men were pushing barrels of water towards the marketplace, and the gypsy women, with hard brows, and dressed in tight velvet bodices, hurried along the pavement with jugs of milk, and great brass water ewers and loaves and breakfast parcels. People were just getting up, and in the poorer streets was a continual splash of tea-leaves, flung out onto the cobblestones. A teapot came crashing down from an upper story just behind Lois, and she, starting round and looking up, thought that the trembling, drink-bleared man at the upper window, who was stupidly staring after his pot, had had designs on her life; and she went on her way shuddering at the grim tragedy of life.

In the dull October morning the ruined factory was black and ghastly. The window frames were all jagged, and the walls stood gaunt. Inside was a tangle of twisted debris, the iron, in parts red with bright rust, looking still hot; the charred wood was black and satiny; from disheveled heaps, sodden with water, a faint smoke rose dimly. Lois stood and looked. If he had done that! He might even be dead there, burned to ash and lost forever. It was almost soothing to feel so. He would be safe in the eternity which now she must hope in.

At her side the pretty, sympathetic maid chatted plaintively. Suddenly, from one of her lapses into silence, she exclaimed:

"Why if there isn't Mr. Jack!"

Lois turned suddenly and saw her brother and her lover approaching her. Both looked soiled, untidy and wan. Will had a black eye, some ten hours old, well colored. Lois turned very pale as they approached. They were looking gloomily at the factory, and for a moment did not notice the girls.

"I'll be jiggered if there ain't our Lois!" exclaimed Jack, the reprobate, swearing under his breath.

"Oh, God!" exclaimed the other in disgust.

"Jack, where have you been?" said Lois sharply, in keen pain, not looking at her lover. Her sharp tone of suffering drove her lover to defend himself with an affectation of comic recklessness.

"In quod," replied her brother, smiling sicklily.

"Jack!" cried his sister very sharply.

"Fact."

Will Selby shuffled on his feet and smiled, trying to turn away his face so that she should not see his black eye. She glanced at him. He felt her boundless anger and contempt, and with great courage he looked straight at her, smiling ironically. Unfortunately his smile would not go over his swollen eye, which remained grave and lurid.

"Do I look pretty?" he inquired with a hateful twist of his lip.

"Very!" she replied.

"I thought I did," he replied. And he turned to look at his father's ruined works, and he felt miserable and stubborn. The girl standing there so clean and out of it all! Oh, God, he felt sick. He turned to go home.

The three went together, Lois silent in anger and resentment. Her brother was tired and overstrung, but not suppressed. He chattered on, blindly.

"It was a lark we had! We met Bob Osborne and Freddy Mansell coming down Poultry. There was a girl with some geese. She looked a tanger sitting there, all like statues, her and the geese. It was Will who began it. He offered her threepence and asked her to begin the show. She called him a—she called him something, and then somebody poked an old gander to stir him up, and somebody squirted him in the eye. He upped and squawked and started off with his neck out. Laugh! We nearly killed ourselves, keeping back those old birds with squirts and teasers. Oh, Lum! Those old geese, oh, scrimmy, they didn't know where to turn, they fairly went off their dots, coming at us right an' left, and such a row—it was fun, you never knew? Then the girl she got up and knocked somebody over the jaw, and we were right in for it. Well, in the end, Billy here got hold of her round the waist——"

"Oh, dry it up!" exclaimed Will bitterly.

Jack looked at him, laughed mirthlessly, and continued: "An' we said we'd buy her birds. So we got hold of one goose apiece—an' they took some holding, I can tell you—and off we set round the fair, Billy leading with the girl. The bloomin' geese squawked an' pecked. Laugh—I thought I should a' died. Well, then we wanted the girl to have her birds back—and then she fired up. She got some other chaps on her side, and there was a proper old row. The girl went tooth and nail for Will there—she was dead set against him. She gave him a black eye, by gum, and we went at it, I can tell you. It was a free fight, a beauty, an' we got run in. I don't know what became of the girl."

Lois surveyed the two men. There was no glimmer of a smile on her face, though the maid behind her was sniggering. Will was very bitter. He glanced at his sweetheart and at the ruined factory.

"How's dad taken it?" he asked, in a biting, almost humble tone.

"I don't know," she replied coldly. "Father's in an awful way. I believe everybody thinks you set the place on fire."

Lois drew herself up. She had delivered her blow. She drew herself up in cold condemnation and for a moment enjoyed her complete revenge. He was despicable, abject in his disheveled, disfigured, unwashed condition.

"Aye, well, they made a mistake for once," he replied, with a curl of the lip.

Curiously enough, they walked side by side as if they belonged to each other. She was his conscience-keeper. She was far from forgiving him, but she was still further from letting him go. And he walked at her side like a boy who has to be punished before he can be exonerated. He submitted. But there was a genuine bitter contempt in the curl of his lip.

THE WHITE STOCKING

I

"I'm getting up, Teddilinks," said Mrs. Whiston, and she sprang out of bed briskly.

"What the Hanover's got you?" asked Whiston.

"Nothing. Can't I get up?" she replied animatedly.

It was about seven o'clock, scarcely light yet in the cold bedroom. Whiston lay still and looked at his wife. She was a pretty little thing, with her fleecy, short black hair all tousled. He watched her as she dressed quickly, flicking her small, delightful limbs, throwing her clothes about her. Her slovenliness and untidiness did not trouble him. When she picked up the edge of her petticoat, ripped off a torn string of white lace, and flung it on the dressing table, her careless abandon made his spirit glow. She stood before the mirror and roughly scrambled together her profuse little mane of hair. He watched the quickness and softness of her young shoulders, calmly, like a husband, and appreciatively.

"Rise up," she cried, turning to him with a quick wave of her arm—"and shine forth."

They had been married two years. But still, when she had gone out of the room, he felt as if all his light and warmth were taken away, he became aware of the raw, cold morning. So he rose himself, wondering casually what had roused her so early. Usually she lay in bed as late as she could.

Whiston fastened a belt round his loins and went downstairs in shirt and trousers. He heard her singing in her snatchy fashion. The stairs creaked under his weight. He passed down the narrow little passage, which she called a hall, of the seven and sixpenny house which was his first home.

He was a shapely young fellow of about twenty-eight, sleepy now and easy with well-being. He heard the water drumming into the kettle, and she began to whistle. He loved the quick way she dodged the supper cups under the tap to wash them for breakfast. She looked an untidy minx, but she was quick and handy enough.

"Teddilinks," she cried.

"What?"

"Light a fire, quick."

She wore an old, sack-like dressing jacket of black silk pinned across her breast. But one of the sleeves, coming unfastened, showed some delightful pink upper-arm.

"Why don't you sew your sleeve up?" he said, suffering from the sight of the exposed soft flesh.

"Where?" she cried, peering round. "Nuisance," she said, seeing the gap, then with light fingers went on drying the cups.

The kitchen was of fair size, but gloomy. Whiston poked out the dead ashes.

Suddenly a thud was heard at the door down the passage.

"I'll go," cried Mrs. Whiston, and she was gone down the hall. The postman was a ruddy-faced man who had been a soldier. He smiled broadly, handing her some packages.

"They've not forgot you," he said impudently.

"No—lucky for them," she said, with a toss of the head. But she was interested only in her envelopes this morning. The postman waited inquisitively, smiling in an ingratiating fashion. She slowly, abstractedly, as if she did not know anyone was there, closed the door in his face, continuing to look at the addresses on her letters.

She tore open the thin envelope. There was a long, hideous, cartoon valentine. She smiled briefly and dropped it on the floor. Struggling with the string of a packet, she opened a white cardboard box, and there lay a white silk handkerchief packed neatly under the paper lace of the box, and her initial, worked in heliotrope, fully displayed. She smiled pleasantly, and gently put the box aside. The third envelope contained another white packet—apparently a cotton handkerchief neatly folded. She shook it out. It was a long white stocking, but there was a little weight in the toe. Quickly, she thrust down her arm, wriggling her fingers into the toe of the stocking, and brought out a small box. She peeped inside the box, then hastily opened a door on her left hand, and went into the little, cold sitting room. She had her lower lip caught earnestly between her teeth.

With a little flash of triumph, she lifted a pair of pearl earrings from the small box, and she went to the mirror. There, earnestly, she began to hook them through her ears, looking at herself sideways in the glass. Curiously concentrated and intent she seemed as she fingered the lobes of her ears, her head bent on one side.

Then the pearl earrings dangled under her rosy, small ears. She shook her head sharply, to see the swing of the drops. They went chill against her neck, in little, sharp touches. Then she stood still to look at herself, bridling her head in the dignified fashion. Then she simpered at herself. Catching her own eye, she could not help winking at herself and laughing.

She turned to look at the box. There was a scrap of paper with this posy:

Pearls may be fair, but thou are fairer.
Wear these for me, and I'll love the wearer.

She made a grimace and a grin. But she was drawn to the mirror again, to look at her earrings.

Whiston had made the fire burn, so he came to look for her. When she heard him, she started round quickly, guiltily. She was watching him with intent blue eyes when he appeared.

He did not see much, in his morning-drowsy warmth. He gave her, as ever, a feeling of warmth and slowness. His eyes were very blue, very kind, his manner simple.

"What ha' you got?" he asked.

"Valentines," she said briskly, ostentatiously turning to show him the silk handkerchief. She thrust it under his nose. "Smell how good," she said.

"Who's that from?" he replied, without smelling.

"It's a valentine," she cried. "How do I know who it's from?"

"I'll bet you know," he said.

"Ted!—I don't!" she cried, beginning to shake her head, then stopping because of the earrings.

He stood still a moment, displeased.

"They've no right to send you valentines, now," he said.

"Ted!—Why not? You're not jealous, are you? I haven't the least idea who it's from. Look—there's my initial"—she pointed with an emphatic finger at the heliotrope embroidery—

E for Elsie,
Nice little gelsie,

she sang.

"Get out," he said. "You know who it's from."

"Truth, I don't," she cried.

He looked round, and saw the white stocking lying on a chair.

"Is this another?" he said.

"No, that's a sample," she said. "There's only a comic." And she fetched in the long cartoon.

He stretched it out and looked at it solemnly.

"Fools!" he said, and went out of the room.

She flew upstairs and took off the earrings. When she returned, he was crouched before the fire blowing the coals. The skin of his face was flushed, and slightly pitted, as if he had had smallpox. But his neck was white and smooth and goodly. She hung her arms round his neck as he crouched there, and clung to him. He balanced on his toes.

"This fire's a slow-coach," he said.

"And who else is a slow-coach?" she said.

"One of us two, I know," he said, and he rose carefully. She remained clinging round his neck, so that she was lifted off her feet. "Ha!—swing me," she cried.

He lowered his head, and she hung in the air, swinging from his neck, laughing. Then she slipped off.

"The kettle is singing," she sang, flying for the teapot. He bent down again to blow the fire. The veins in his neck stood out, his shirt collar seemed too tight.

Doctor Wyer,
Blow the fire,
Puff! puff! puff!

she sang, laughing.

He smiled at her.

She was so glad because of her pearl earrings.

Over the breakfast she grew serious. He did not notice. She became portentous in her gravity. Almost it penetrated through his steady good-humor to irritate him.

"Teddy!" she said at last.

"What?" he asked.

"I told you a lie," she said, humbly tragic.

His soul stirred uneasily.

"Oh aye?" he said casually.

She was not satisfied. He ought to be more moved.

"Yes," she said.

He cut a piece of bread.

"Was it a good one?" he asked.

She was piqued. Then she considered—*was* it a good one? Then she laughed.

"No," she said, "it wasn't up to much."

"Ah!" he said easily, but with a steady strength of fondness for her in his tone. "Get it out then."

It became a little more difficult.

"You know that white stocking," she said earnestly. "I told you a lie. It wasn't a sample. It was a valentine."

A little frown came on his brow.

"Then what did you invent it as a sample for?" he said. But he knew this weakness of hers. The touch of anger in his voice frightened her.

"I was afraid you'd be cross," she said pathetically.

"I'll bet you were vastly afraid," he said.

"I *was*, Teddy."

There was a pause. He was resolving one or two things in his mind.

"And who sent it?" he asked.

"I can guess," she said, "though there wasn't a word with it—except——"

She ran to the sitting room and returned with a slip of paper.

Pearls may be fair, but thou art fairer
Wear these for me, and I'll love the wearer.

He read it twice, then a dull red flush came on his face.

"And *who* do you guess it is?" he asked, with a ringing of anger in his voice.

"I suspect it's Sam Adams," she said, with a little virtuous indignation.

Whiston was silent for a moment.

"Fool!" he said. "An' what's it got to do with pearls?—and how can he say 'wear these for me' when there's only one? He hasn't got the brain to invent a proper verse."

He screwed the slip of paper into a ball and flung it into the fire.

"I suppose he thinks it'll make a pair with the one last year," she said.

"Why, did he send one then?"

"Yes. I thought you'd be wild if you knew."

His jaw set rather sullenly.

Presently he rose, and went to wash himself, rolling back his sleeves and pulling open his shirt at the breast. It was as if his fine, clear-cut temples and steady eyes were degraded by the lower, rather brutal part of his face. But she loved it. As she whisked about, clearing the table, she loved the way in which he stood washing himself. He was such a man. She liked to see his neck glistening with water as he swilled it. It amused her and pleased her and thrilled her. He was so sure, so permanent, he had her so utterly in his power. It gave her a delightful, mischievous sense of liberty. Within his grasp, she could dart about excitingly.

He turned round to her, his face red from the cold water, his eyes fresh and very blue.

"You haven't been seeing anything of him, have you?" he asked roughly.

"Yes," she answered, after a moment, as if caught guilty. "He got into the tram with me, and he asked me to drink a coffee and a Benedictine in the Royal."

"You've got it off fine and glib," he said sullenly. "And did you?"

"Yes," she replied, with the air of a traitor before the rack.

The blood came up into his neck and face, he stood motionless, dangerous.

"It was cold, and it was such fun to go into the Royal," she said.

"You'd go off with a nigger for a packet of chocolate," he said, in anger and contempt, and some bitterness. Queer how he drew away from her, cut her off from him.

"Ted—how beastly!" she cried. "You know quite well——" She caught her lip, flushed, and the tears came to her eyes.

He turned away, to put on his necktie. She went about her work, making a queer pathetic little mouth, down which occasionally dripped a tear.

He was ready to go. With his hat jammed down on his head, and his overcoat buttoned up to his chin, he came to kiss her. He would be miserable all the day if he went without. She allowed herself to be kissed. Her cheek was wet under his lips, and his heart burned. She hurt him so deeply. And she felt aggrieved, and did not quite forgive him.

In a moment she went upstairs to her earrings. Sweet they looked nestling in the little drawer—sweet! She examined them with voluptuous pleasure, she threaded them in her ears, she looked at herself, she posed and postured and smiled and looked sad and tragic and winning and appealing, all in turn before the mirror. And she was happy, and very pretty.

She wore her earrings all morning, in the house. She was self-conscious, and quite brilliantly winsome, when the baker came, wondering if he would notice. All the tradesmen left her door with a glow in them, feeling elated, and unconsciously favoring the delightful little creature, though there had been nothing to notice in her behavior.

She was stimulated all the day. She did not think about her husband. He was the permanent basis from which she took these giddy little flights into nowhere. At night, like chickens and curses, she would come home to him, to roost.

Meanwhile Whiston, a traveler and confidential support of a small firm, hastened about his work, his heart all the while anxious for her, yearning for surety, and kept tense by not getting it.

II

She had been a warehouse girl in Adams's lace factory before she was married. Sam Adams was her employer. He was a bachelor of forty, growing stout, a man well dressed and florid, with a large brown moustache and thin hair. From the rest of his well-groomed, showy appearance, it was evident his baldness was a chagrin to him. He had a good presence, and some Irish blood in his veins.

His fondness for the girls, or the fondness of the girls for him, was notorious. And Elsie, quick, pretty, almost witty little thing—she *seemed* witty, although, when her sayings were repeated, they were entirely trivial—she had a great attraction for him. He would come into the warehouse dressed in a rather sporting reefer coat, of fawn color, and trousers of fine black-and-white check, a cap with a big peak and scarlet carnation in his buttonhole, to impress her. She was only half impressed. He was too loud for her good taste. Instinctively perceiving this, he sobered down to navy blue. Then a well-built man, florid, with large brown whiskers, smart navy blue suit, fashionable boots, and manly hat, he was the irreproachable. Elsie was impressed.

But meanwhile Whiston was courting her, and she made splendid little gestures, before her bedroom mirror, of the constant-and-true sort.

True, true till death——

That was her song. Whiston was made that way, so there was no need to take thought for him.

Every Christmas Sam Adams gave a party at his house, to which he invited his superior workpeople—not factory hands and laborers but those above. He was a generous man in his way, with a real warm feeling for giving pleasure.

Two years ago Elsie had attended this Christmas party for the last time. Whiston had accompanied her. At that time he worked for Sam Adams.

She had been very proud of herself, in her closefitting, full-skirted dress of blue silk. Whiston called for her. Then she tripped beside him, holding her large cashmere shawl across her breast. He strode with long strides, his trousers handsomely strapped under his boots, and her silk shoes bulging the pockets of his full-skirted overcoat.

They passed through the park gates, and her spirits rose. Above them the Castle Rock loomed grandly in the night, the naked trees stood still and dark in the frost, along the boulevard.

They were rather late. Agitated with anticipation, in the cloakroom she gave up her shawl, donned her silk shoes, and looked at herself in the mirror. The loose bunches of curls on either side her face danced prettily, her mouth smiled.

She hung a moment in the door of the brilliantly lighted room. Many people were moving within the blaze of lamps, under the crystal chandeliers, the full skirts of the women balancing and floating, the side whiskers and white cravats of the men bowing above. Then she entered the light.

In an instant Sam Adams was coming forward, lifting both his arms in boisterous welcome. There was a constant red laugh on his face.

"Come late, would you," he shouted, "like royalty."

He seized her hands and led her forward. He opened his mouth wide when he spoke, and the effect of the warm, dark opening behind the brown whiskers was disturbing. But she was floating into the throng on his arm. He was very gallant.

"Now then," he said, taking her card to write down the dances, "I've got carte blanche, haven't I?"

"Mr. Whiston doesn't dance," she said.

"I am a lucky man!" he said, scribbling his initials. "I was born with an *amourette* in my mouth."

He wrote on, quietly. She blushed and laughed, not knowing what it meant.

"Why, what is that?" she said.

"It's you, even littler than you are, dressed in little wings," he said.

"I should have to be pretty small to get in your mouth," she said.

"You think you're too big, do you!" he said easily.

He handed her her card, with a bow.

"Now I'm set up, my darling, for this evening," he said.

Then, quick, always at his ease, he looked over the room. She waited in front of him. He was ready. Catching the eye of the band, he nodded. In a moment, the music began. He seemed to relax, giving himself up. "Now then, Elsie," he said, with a curious caress in his voice that seemed to lap the outside of her body in a warm glow, delicious. She gave herself to it. She liked it.

He was an excellent dancer. He seemed to draw her close into him by some male warmth of attraction, so that she became all soft and pliant to him, flowing to his form, whilst he united her with him and they lapsed along in one movement. She was just carried in a kind of strong, warm flood, her feet moved of themselves, and only the music threw her away from him, threw her back to him, to his clasp, in his strong form moving against her, rhythmically, deliciously.

When it was over, he was pleased and his eyes had a curious gleam which thrilled her and yet had nothing to do with her. Yet it held her. He did not speak to her. He only looked straight into her eyes with a curious, gleaming look that disturbed her fearfully and deliciously. But also there was in his look some of the automatic irony of the *roué*. It left her partly cold. She was not carried away.

She went, driven by an opposite, heavier impulse, to Whiston. He stood looking gloomy, trying to admit that she had a perfect right to enjoy herself apart from him. He received her with rather grudging kindliness.

"Aren't you going to play whist?" she asked.

"Aye," he said. "Directly."

"I do wish you could dance."

"Well, I can't," he said. "So you enjoy yourself."

"But I should enjoy it better if I could dance with you."

"Nay, you're all right," he said. "I'm not made that way."

"Then you ought to be!" she cried.

"Well, it's my fault, not yours. You enjoy yourself," he bade her. Which she proceeded to do, a little bit irked.

She went with anticipation to the arms of Sam Adams, when the time came to dance with him. It *was* so gratifying, irrespective of the man. And she felt a little grudge against Whiston, soon forgotten when her host was holding her near to him, in a delicious embrace. And she watched his eyes, to meet the gleam in them, which gratified her.

She was getting warmed right through, the glow was penetrating into her, driving away everything else. Only in her heart was a little tightness, like conscience.

When she got a chance, she escaped from the dancing room to the card room. There, in a cloud of smoke, she found Whiston playing cribbage. Radiant, roused, animated, she came up to him and greeted him. She was too strong, too vibrant a note in the quiet room. He lifted his head, and a frown knitted his gloomy forehead.

"Are you playing cribbage? Is it exciting? How are you getting on?" she chattered.

He looked at her. None of these questions needed answering, and he did not feel in touch with her. She turned to the cribbage board.

"Are you white or red?" she asked.

"He's red," replied the partner.

"Then you're losing," she said, still to Whiston. And she lifted the red peg from the board. "One—two—three—four—five—six—seven—eight——Right up there you ought to jump——"

"Now put it back in its right place," said Whiston.

"Where was it?" she asked gaily, knowing her transgression. He took the little red peg away from her and stuck it in its hole.

The cards were shuffled.

"What a shame you're losing!" said Elsie.

"You'd better cut for him," said the partner.

She did so, hastily. The cards were dealt. She put her hand on his shoulder, looking at his cards.

"It's good," she cried, "isn't it?"

He did not answer, but threw down two cards. It moved him more strongly than was comfortable, to have her hand on his shoulder, her curls dangling and touching his ears, whilst she was roused to another man. It made the blood flame over him.

At that moment Sam Adams appeared, florid and boisterous, intoxicated more with himself, with the dancing, than with wine. In his eye the curious, impersonal light gleamed.

"I thought I should find you here, Elsie," he cried boisterously, a disturbing, high note in his voice.

"What made you think so?" she replied, the mischief rousing in her.

The florid, well-built man narrowed his eyes to a smile.

"I should never look for you among the ladies," he said, with a kind of intimate, animal call to her. He laughed, bowed, and offered her his arm.

"Madam, the music waits."

She went almost helplessly, carried along with him, unwilling, yet delighted.

That dance was an intoxication to her. After the first few steps, she felt herself slipping away from herself. She almost knew she was going, she did not even want to go. Yet she must have chosen to go. She lay in the arm of the steady, close man with whom she was dancing, and she seemed to swim away out of contact with the room, into him. She had passed into another, denser element of him, an essential privacy. The room was all vague around her, like an atmosphere, like under sea, with a flow of ghostly, dumb movements. But she herself was held real against her partner, and it seemed she was connected with him, as if the movements of his body and limbs were her own movements, yet not her own movements—and oh, delicious! He also was given up, oblivious, concentrated, into the dance. His eye was unseeing. Only his large, voluptuous body gave off a subtle activity. His fingers seemed to search into her flesh. Every moment, and every moment, she felt she would give way utterly, and sink molten: the fusion point was coming when she would fuse down into perfect unconsciousness at his feet and knees. But he bore her round the room in the dance, and he seemed to sustain all her body with his limbs, his body, and his warmth seemed to come closer into her, nearer, till it would fuse right through her, and she would be as liquid to him, as an intoxication only.

It was exquisite. When it was over, she was dazed, and was scarcely breathing. She stood with him in the middle of the room as if she were alone in a remote place. He bent over her. She expected his lips on her bare shoulder, and waited. Yet they were not alone, they were not alone. It was cruel.

" 'Twas good, wasn't it, my darling?" he said to her, low and delighted. There was a strange impersonality about his low, exultant call that appealed to her irresistibly. Yet why was she aware of some part shut off in her? She pressed his arm, and he led her towards the door.

She was not aware of what she was doing, only a little grain of resistant trouble was in her. The man, possessed, yet with a superficial presence of mind, made way to the dining room, as if to give her refreshment, cunningly working to his own escape with her. He was molten hot, filmed over with presence of mind, and bottomed with cold disbelief. In the dining room was Whiston, carrying coffee to the plain, neglected ladies. Elsie saw him, but felt as if he could not see her. She was beyond his reach and ken. A sort of fusion existed between her and the large man at her side. She ate her custard, but an incomplete fusion all the while sustained and contained within the being of her employer.

But she was growing cooler. Whiston came up. She looked at him, and saw him with different eyes. She saw his slim, young man's figure real and enduring before her. That was he. But she was in the spell with the other man, fused with him, and she could not be taken away.

"Have you finished your cribbage?" she asked, with hasty evasion of him.

"Yes," he replied. "Aren't you getting tired of dancing?"

"Not a bit," she said.

"Not she," said Adams heartily. "No girl with any spirit gets tired of dancing. Have something else, Elsie. Come—sherry. Have a glass of sherry with us, Whiston."

Whilst they sipped the wine, Adams watched Whiston almost cunningly, to find his advantage.

"We'd better be getting back—there's the music," he said. "See the women get something to eat, Whiston, will you, there's a good chap."

And he began to draw away. Elsie was drifting helplessly with him. But Whiston put himself beside them, and went along with them. In silence they passed through to the dancing room. There Adams hesitated, and looked round the room. It was as if he could not see.

A man came hurrying forward, claiming Elsie, and Adams went to his other partner. Whiston stood watching during the dance. She was conscious of him standing there observant of her, like a ghost, or a judgment, or a guardian angel. She was also conscious, much more intimately and impersonally, of the body of the other man moving somewhere in the room. She still belonged to him, but a feeling of distraction possessed her, and helplessness. Adams danced on, adhering to Elsie, waiting his time, with the persistence of cynicism.

The dance was over. Adams was detained. Elsie found herself beside Whiston. There was something shapely about him as he sat, about his knees and his distinct figure, that she clung to. It was as if he had enduring form. She put her hand on his knee.

"Are you enjoying yourself?" he asked.

"*Ever* so," she replied, with a fervent, yet detached tone.

"It's going on for one o'clock," he said.

"Is it?" she answered. It meant nothing to her.

"Should we be going?" he said.

She was silent. For the first time for an hour or more an inkling of her normal consciousness returned. She resented it.

"What for?" she said.

"I thought you might have had enough," he said.

A slight soberness came over her, an irritation at being frustrated of her illusion.

"Why?" she said.

"We've been here since nine," he said.

That was no answer, no reason. It conveyed nothing to her. She sat detached from him. Across the room Sam Adams glanced at her. She sat there exposed for him.

"You don't want to be too free with Sam Adams," said Whiston cautiously, suffering. "You know what he is."

"How, free?" she asked.

"Why—you don't want to have too much to do with him."

She sat silent. He was forcing her into consciousness of her position. But he could not get hold of her feelings, to change them. She had a curious, perverse desire that he should not.

"I like him," she said.

"What do you find to like in him?" he said, with a hot heart.

"I don't know—but I like him," she said.

She was immutable. He sat feeling heavy and dulled with rage. He was not clear as to what he felt. He sat there unliving whilst she danced. And she, distracted, lost to herself between the opposing forces of the two men, drifted. Between the dances, Whiston kept near to her. She was scarcely conscious. She glanced repeatedly at her card, to see when she would dance again with Adams, half in desire, half in dread. Sometimes she met his steady, glaucous eye as she passed him in the dance. Sometimes she saw the steadiness of his flank as he danced. And it was always as if she rested on his arm, were borne along, upborne by him, away from herself. And always there was present the other's antagonism. She was divided.

The time came for her to dance with Adams. Oh, the delicious closing of contact with him, of his limbs touching her limbs, his arm supporting her. She seemed to resolve. Whiston had not made himself real to her. He was only a heavy place in her consciousness.

But she breathed heavily, beginning to suffer from the closeness of strain. She was nervous. Adams also was constrained. A tightness, a tension was coming over them all. And he was exasperated, feeling something counteracting physical magnetism, feeling a will stronger with her than his own, intervening in what was becoming a vital necessity to him.

Elsie was almost lost to her own control. As she went forward with him to take her place at the dance, she stooped for her pocket handkerchief. The music sounded for quadrilles. Everybody was ready. Adams stood with his body near her, exerting his attraction over her. He was tense and fighting. She stooped for her pocket handkerchief, and shook it as she rose. It shook out and fell from her hand. With agony, she saw she had taken a white stocking instead of a handkerchief. For a second it lay on the floor, a twist of white stocking. Then, in an instant, Adams picked it up, with a little, surprised laugh of triumph.

"That'll do for me," he whispered—seeming to take possession of her. And he stuffed the stocking in his trousers pocket, and quickly offered her his handkerchief.

The dance began. She felt weak and faint, as if her will were turned to water. A heavy sense of loss came over her. She could not help herself anymore. But it was peace.

When the dance was over, Adams yielded her up. Whiston came to her.

"What was it as you dropped?" Whiston asked.

"I thought it was my handkerchief—I'd taken a stocking by mistake," she said, detached and muted.

"And he's got it?"

"Yes."

"What does he mean by that?"

She lifted her shoulders.

"Are you going to let him keep it?" he asked.

"I don't let him."

There was a long pause.

"Am I to go and have it out with him?" he asked, his face flushed, his blue eyes going hard with opposition.

"No," she said, pale.

"Why?"

"No—I don't want you to say anything about it."

He sat exasperated and nonplussed.

"You'll let him keep it, then?" he asked.

She sat silent and made no form of answer.

"What do you mean by it?" he said, dark with fury. And he started up.

"No!" she cried. "Ted!" And she caught hold of him, sharply detaining him.

It made him black with rage.

"Why?" he said.

The something about her mouth was pitiful to him. He did not understand, but he felt she must have her reasons.

"Then I'm not stopping here," he said. "Are you coming with me?"

She rose mutely, and they went out of the room. Adams had not noticed.

In a few moments they were in the street.

"What the hell do you mean?" he said, in a black fury.

She went at his side, in silence, neutral.

"That great hog, an' all," he added.

Then they went a long time in silence through the frozen, deserted darkness of the town. She felt she could not go indoors. They were drawing near her house.

"I don't want to go home," she suddenly cried in distress and anguish. "I don't want to go home."

He looked at her.

"Why don't you?" he said.

"I don't want to go home," was all she could sob.

He heard somebody coming.

"Well, we can walk a bit farther," he said.

She was silent again. They passed out of the town into the fields. He held her by the arm—they could not speak.

"What's a-matter?" he asked at length, puzzled.

She began to cry again.

At last he took her in his arms, to soothe her. She sobbed by herself, almost unaware of him.

"Tell me what's a-matter, Elsie," he said. "Tell me what's a-matter—my dear—tell me, then——"

He kissed her wet face, and caressed her. She made no response. He was puzzled and tender and miserable.

At length she became quiet. Then he kissed her, and she put her arms round him, and clung to him very tight, as if for fear and anguish. He held her in his arms, wondering.

"Ted!" she whispered, frantic. "Ted!"

"What, my love?" he answered, becoming also afraid.

"Be good to me," she cried. "Don't be cruel to me."

"No, my pet," he said, amazed and grieved. "Why?"

"Oh, be good to me," she sobbed.

And he held her very safe, and his heart was white-hot with love for her. His mind was amazed. He could only hold her against his chest that was white-hot with love and belief in her. So she was restored at last.

III

She refused to go to her work at Adams's anymore. Her father had to submit and she sent in her notice—she was not well. Sam Adams was ironical. But he had a curious patience. He did not fight.

In a few weeks, she and Whiston were married. She loved him with passion and worship, a fierce little abandon of love that moved him to the depths of his being, and gave him a permanent surety and sense of realness in himself. He did not trouble about himself anymore: he felt he was fulfilled and now he had only the many things in the world to busy himself about. Whatever troubled him, at the bottom was surety. He had found himself in this love.

They spoke once or twice of the white stocking.

"Ah!" Whiston exclaimed. "What does it matter?"

He was impatient and angry, and could not bear to consider the matter. So it was left unresolved.

She was quite happy at first, carried away by her adoration of her husband. Then gradually she got used to him. He always was the ground of her happiness, but she got used to him, as to the air she breathed. He never got used to her in the same way.

Inside of marriage she found her liberty. She was rid of the responsibility of herself. Her husband must look after that. She was free to get what she could out of her time.

So that, when, after some months, she met Sam Adams, she was not quite as unkind to him as she might have been. With a young wife's new and exciting knowledge of men, she perceived he was in love with her, she knew he had always kept an unsatisfied desire for her. And, sportive, she could not help playing a little with this, though she cared not one jot for the man himself.

When Valentine's day came, which was near the first anniversary of her wedding day, there arrived a white stocking with a little amethyst brooch. Luckily Whiston did not see it, so she said nothing of it to him. She had not the faintest intention of having anything to do with Sam Adams, but once a little brooch was in her possession, it was hers, and she did not trouble her head for a moment how she had come by it. She kept it.

Now she had the pearl earrings. They were a more valuable and a more conspicuous present. She would have to ask her mother to give them to her, to explain their presence. She made a little plan in her head. And she was extraordinarily pleased. As for Sam Adams, even if he saw her wearing them, he would not give her away. What fun, if he saw her wearing his earrings! She would pretend she had inherited them from her grandmother, her mother's mother. She laughed to herself as she went downtown in the afternoon, the pretty drops dangling in front of her curls. But she saw no one of importance.

Whiston came home tired and depressed. All day the male in him had been uneasy, and this had fatigued him. She was curiously against him, inclined, as she sometimes was nowadays, to make mock of him and jeer at him and cut him off. He did not understand this, and it angered him deeply. She was uneasy before him.

She knew he was in a state of suppressed irritation. The veins stood out on the backs of his hands, his brow was drawn stiffly. Yet she could not help goading him.

"What did you do wi' that white stocking?" he asked, out of a gloomy silence, his voice strong and brutal.

"I put it in a drawer—why?" she replied flippantly.

"Why didn't you put it on the fireback?" he said harshly. "What are you hoarding it up for?"

"I'm not hoarding it up," she said. "I've got a pair."

He relapsed into gloomy silence. She, unable to move him, ran away upstairs, leaving him smoking by the fire. Again she tried on the earrings. Then another little inspiration came to her. She drew on the white stockings, both of them.

Presently she came down in them. Her husband still sat immovable and glowering by the fire.

"Look!" she said. "They'll do beautifully."

And she picked up her skirts to her knees, and twisted round, looking at her pretty legs in the neat stockings.

He filled with unreasonable rage, and took the pipe from his mouth.

"Don't they look nice?" she said. "One from last year and one from this, they just do. Save you buying a pair."

And she looked over her shoulders at her pretty calves, and at the dangling frills of her knickers.

"Put your skirts down and don't make a fool of yourself," he said.

"Why a fool of myself?" she asked.

And she began to dance slowly round the room, kicking up her feet half reckless, half jeering, in a ballet dancer's fashion. Almost fearfully, yet in defiance, she kicked up her legs at him, singing as she did so. She resented him.

"You little fool, ha' done with it," he said. "And you'll backfire them stockings, I'm telling you." He was angry. His face flushed dark, he kept his head bent. She ceased to dance.

"I shan't," she said. "They'll come in very useful."

He lifted his head and watched her, with lighted, dangerous eyes.

"You'll put 'em on the fireback, I tell you," he said.

It was a war now. She bent forward, in a ballet dancer's fashion, and put her tongue between her teeth.

"I shan't backfire them stockings," she sang, repeating his words, "I shan't, I shan't, I shan't."

And she danced round the room doing a high kick to the tune of her words. There was a real biting indifference in her behavior.

"We'll see whether you will or not," he said, "trollops! You'd like Sam Adams to know you was wearing 'em, wouldn't you? That's what would please you."

"Yes, I'd like him to see how nicely they fit me, he might give me some more then."

And she looked down at her pretty legs.

He knew somehow that she *would* like Sam Adams to see how pretty her legs looked in the white stockings. It made his anger go deep, almost to hatred.

"Yer nasty trolley," he cried. "Put yer petticoats down, and stop being so foul-minded."

"I'm not foul-minded," she said. "My legs are my own. And why shouldn't Sam Adams think they're nice?"

There was a pause. He watched her with eyes glittering to a point.

"Have you been havin' owt to do with him?" he asked.

"I've just spoken to him when I've seen him," she said. "He's not as bad as you would make out."

"Isn't he?" he cried, a certain wakefulness in his voice. "Them who has anything to do wi' him is too bad for me, I tell you."

"Why, what are you frightened of him for?" she mocked.

She was rousing all his uncontrollable anger. He sat glowering. Every one of her sentences stirred him up like a red-hot iron. Soon it would be too much. And she was afraid herself; but she was neither conquered nor convinced.

A curious little grin of hate came on his face. He had a long score against her.

"What am I frightened of him for?" he repeated automatically. "What am I frightened of him for? Why, for you, you stray-running little bitch."

She flushed. The insult went deep into her, right home.

"Well, if you're so dull——" she said, lowering her eyelids, and speaking coldly, haughtily.

"If I'm so dull I'll break your neck the first word you speak to him," he said, tense.

"Pf!" she sneered. "Do you think I'm frightened of you?" She spoke coldly, detached.

She was frightened, for all that, white round the mouth.

His heart was getting hotter.

"You *will* be frightened of me, the next time you have anything to do with him," he said.

"Do you think *you'd* ever be told—ha!"

Her jeering scorn made him go white-hot, molten. He knew he was incoherent, scarcely responsible for what he might do. Slowly, unseeing, he rose and went out of doors, stifled, moved to kill her.

He stood leaning against the garden fence, unable either to see or hear. Below him, far off, fumed the lights of the town. He stood still, unconscious with a black storm of rage, his face lifted to the night.

Presently, still unconscious of what he was doing, he went indoors again. She stood, a small, stubborn figure with tight-pressed lips and big, sullen, childish eyes, watching him, white with fear. He went heavily across the floor and dropped into his chair.

There was a silence.

"*You're* not going to tell me everything I shall do, and everything I shan't," she broke out at last.

He lifted his head.

"I tell you *this*," he said, low and intense. "Have anything to do with Sam Adams, and I'll break your neck."

She laughed, shrill and false.

"How I hate your word 'break your neck,' " she said, with a grimace of the mouth. "It sounds so common and beastly. Can't you say something else——"

There was a dead silence.

"And besides," she said, with a queer chirrup of mocking laughter, "what do you know about anything? He sent me an amethyst brooch and a pair of pearl earrings."

"He what?" said Whiston, in a suddenly normal voice. His eyes were fixed on her.

"Sent me a pair of pearl earrings, and an amethyst brooch," she repeated, mechanically, pale to the lips.

And her big, black, childish eyes watched him, fascinated, held in her spell.

He seemed to thrust his face and his eyes forward at her, as he rose slowly and came to her. She watched transfixed in terror. Her throat made a small sound, as she tried to scream.

Then, quick as lightning, the back of his hand struck her with a crash across the mouth, and she was flung black blinded against the wall. The shock shook a queer sound out of her. And then she saw him still coming on, his eyes holding her, his fist drawn back, advancing slowly. At any instant the blow might crash into her.

Mad with terror, she raised her hands with a queer clawing movement to cover her eyes and her temples, opening her mouth in a dumb shriek. There was no sound. But the sight of her slowly arrested him. He hung before her, looking at her fixedly, as she stood crouched against the wall with open, bleeding mouth, and wide-staring eyes, and two hands clawing over her temples. And his lust to see her bleed, to break her and destroy her, rose from an old source against her. It carried him. He wanted satisfaction.

But he had seen her standing there, a piteous, horrified thing, and he turned his face aside in shame and nausea. He went and sat heavily in his chair, and a curious ease, almost like sleep, came over his brain.

She walked away from the wall towards the fire, dizzy, white to the lips, mechanically wiping her small, bleeding mouth. He sat motionless. Then, gradually, her breath began to hiss, she shook, and was sobbing silently, in grief for herself. Without looking, he saw. It made his mad desire to destroy her come back.

At length he lifted his head. His eyes were glowing again, fixed on her.

"And what did he give them you for?" he asked, in a steady, unyielding voice.

Her crying dried up in a second. She also was tense.

"They came as valentines," she replied, still not subjugated, even if beaten.

"When, today?"

"The pearl earrings today—the amethyst brooch last year."

"You've had it a year?"

"Yes."

She felt that now nothing would prevent him if he rose to kill her. She could not prevent him anymore. She was yielded up to him. They both trembled in the balance, unconscious.

"What have you had to do with him?" he asked, in a barren voice.

"I've not had anything to do with him," she quavered.

"You just kept 'em because they were jewelry?" he said.

A weariness came over him. What was the worth of speaking anymore of it? He did not care anymore. He was dreary and sick.

She began to cry again, but he took no notice. She kept wiping her mouth on her handkerchief. He could see it, the blood-mark. It made him only more sick and tired of the responsibility of it, the violence, the shame.

When she began to move about again, he raised his head once more from his dead, motionless position.

"Where are the things?" he said.

"They are upstairs," she quavered. She knew the passion had gone down in him.

"Bring them down," he said.

"I won't," she wept, with rage. "You're not going to bully me and hit me like that on the mouth."

And she sobbed again. He looked at her in contempt and compassion and in rising anger.

"Where are they?" he said.

"They're in the little drawer under the looking glass," she sobbed.

He went slowly upstairs, struck a match, and found the trinkets. He brought them downstairs in his hand.

"These?" he said, looking at them as they lay in his palm.

She looked at them without answering. She was not interested in them anymore.

He looked at the little jewels. They were pretty.

"It's none of their fault," he said to himself.

And he searched round slowly, persistently, for a box. He tied the things up and addressed them to Sam Adams. Then he went out in his slippers to post the little package.

When he came back she was still sitting crying.

"You'd better go to bed," he said.

She paid no attention. He sat by the fire. She still cried.

"I'm sleeping down here," he said. "Go you to bed."

In a few moments she lifted her tearstained, swollen face and looked at him with eyes all forlorn and pathetic. A great flash of anguish went over his body. He went over, slowly, and very gently took her in his hands. She let herself be taken. Then as she lay against his shoulder, she sobbed aloud:

"I never meant——"

"My love—my little love——" he cried, in anguish of spirit, holding her in his arms.

A SICK COLLIER

She was too good for him, everybody said. Yet still she did not regret marrying him. He had come courting her when he was only nineteen, and she twenty. He was in build what they call a tight little fellow; short, dark, with a warm color, and that upright set of the head and chest, that flaunting way in movement recalling a mating bird, which denotes a body taut and compact with life. Being a good worker he had earned decent money in the mine, and having a good home had saved a little.

She was a cook at "Uplands," a tall, fair girl, very quiet. Having seen her walk down the street, Horsepool had followed her from a distance. He was taken with her, he did not drink, and he was not lazy. So, although he seemed a bit simple, without much intelligence, but having a sort of physical brightness, she considered, and accepted him.

When they were married they went to live in Scargill Street, in a highly respectable six-roomed house which they had furnished between them. The street was built up the side of a long, steep hill. It was narrow and rather tunnel-like. Nevertheless, the back looked out over the adjoining pasture, across a wide valley of fields and woods, in the bottom of which the mine lay snugly.

He made himself gaffer in his own house. She was unacquainted with a collier's mode of life. They were married on a Saturday. On the Sunday night he said:

"Set th' table for my breakfast, an' put my pit-things afront o' th' fire. I s'll be gettin' up at ha'ef pas' five. Tha nedna shift thysen not till when ter likes."

He showed her how to put a newspaper on the table for a cloth. When she demurred:

"I want none o' your white cloths i' th' mornin'. I like ter be able to slobber if I feel like it," he said.

He put before the fire his moleskin trousers, a clean singlet, or sleeveless vest of thick flannel, a pair of stockings and his pit boots, arranging them all to be warm and ready for morning.

"Now tha sees. That wants doin' ivery night."

Punctually at half-past five he left her, without any form of leave-taking, going downstairs in his shirt.

When he arrived home at four o'clock in the afternoon his dinner was ready to be dished up. She was startled when he came in, a short, sturdy figure, with a face indescribably black and streaked. She stood before the fire in her white blouse and white apron, a fair girl, the picture of beautiful cleanliness. He "clommaxed" in, in his heavy boots.

"Well, how 'as ter gone on?" he asked.

"I was ready for you to come home," she replied tenderly. In his black face the whites of his brown eyes flashed at her.

"An' I wor ready for comin'," he said. He planked his tin bottle and snap-bag on the dresser, took off his coat and scarf and waistcoat, dragged his armchair nearer the fire and sat down.

"Let's ha'e a bit o' dinner, then—I'm about clammed," he said.

"Aren't you goin' to wash yourself first?"

"What am I to wesh mysen for?"

"Well, you can't eat your dinner——"

"Oh, strike a daisy, Missis! Dunna I eat my snap i' th' pit wi'out weshin'?—forced to."

She served the dinner and sat opposite him. His small bullet head was quite black, save for the whites of his eyes and his scarlet lips. It gave her a queer sensation to see him open his red mouth and bare his white teeth as he ate. His arms and hands were mottled black; his bare, strong neck got a little fairer as it settled towards his shoulders, reassuring her. There was the faint indescribable odor of the pit in the room, an odor of damp, exhausted air.

"Why is your vest so black on the shoulders?" she asked.

"My singlet? That's wi' th' watter droppin' on us from th' roof. This is a dry un as I put on afore I come up. They ha'e gre't clothes-'osses, an' as we change us things, we put 'em on theer ter dry."

When he washed himself, kneeling on the hearth-rug stripped to the waist, she felt afraid of him again. He was so muscular, he seemed so intent on what he was doing, so intensely himself, like a vigorous animal. And as he stood wiping himself, with his naked breast towards her, she felt rather sick, seeing his thick arms bulge their muscles.

They were nevertheless very happy. He was at a great pitch of pride because of her. The men in the pit might chaff him, they might try to entice him away, but nothing could reduce his self-assured pride because of her, nothing could unsettle his almost infantile satisfaction. In the evening he sat in his armchair chattering to her, or listening as she read the newspaper to him. When it was fine, he would go into the street, squat on his heels as colliers do, with his back against the wall of his parlor, and call to the passersby, in greeting, one after another. If no one were passing, he was content just to squat and smoke, having such a fund of sufficiency and satisfaction in his heart. He was well married.

They had not been wed a year when all Brent and Wellwood's men came out on strike. Willy was in the Union, so with a pinch they scrambled through. The furniture was not all paid for, and other debts were incurred. She worried and contrived, he left it to her. But he was a good husband; he gave her all he had.

The men were out fifteen weeks. They had been back just over a year when Willy had an accident in the mine, tearing his bladder. At the pit head the doctor talked of the hospital. Losing his head entirely, the young collier raved like a madman, what with pain and fear of hospital.

"Tha s'lt go whoam, Willy, tha s'lt go whoam," the deputy said.

A lad warned the wife to have the bed ready. Without speaking or hesitating she prepared. But when the ambulance came, and she heard him shout with pain at being moved, she was afraid lest she should sink down. They carried him in.

"Yo' should 'a' had a bed i' th' parlor, Missis," said the deputy, "then we shouldna' ha' had to hawkse 'im upstairs, an' it 'ud 'a' saved your legs."

But it was too late now. They got him upstairs.

"They let me lie, Lucy," he was crying, "they let me lie two mortal hours on th' sleck afore they took me outer th' stall. Th' peen, Lucy, th' peen; oh, Lucy, th' peen, th' peen!"

"I know th' pain's bad, Willy, I know. But you must try an' bear it a bit."

"Tha manna carry on in that form, lad, thy missis'll niver be able ter stan' it," said the deputy.

"I canna 'elp it, it's th' peen, it's th' peen," he cried again. He had never been ill in his life. When he had smashed a finger he could look at the wound. But this pain came from inside, and terrified him. At last he was soothed and exhausted.

It was some time before she could undress him and wash him. He would let no other woman do for him, having that savage modesty usual in such men.

For six weeks he was in bed, suffering much pain. The doctors were not quite sure what was the matter with him, and scarcely knew what to do. He could eat, he did not lose flesh, nor strength, yet the pain continued, and he could hardly walk at all.

In the sixth week the men came out in the national strike. He would get up quite early in the morning and sit by the window. On Wednesday, the second week of the strike, he sat gazing out on the street as usual, a bullet-headed young man, still vigorous-looking, but with a peculiar expression of hunted fear in his face.

"Lucy," he called, "Lucy!"

She, pale and worn, ran upstairs at his bidding.

"Gi'e me a han'kercher," he said.

"Why, you've got one," she replied, coming near.

"Tha nedna touch me," he cried. Feeling his pocket, he produced a white handkerchief.

"I non want a white un, gi'e me a red un," he said.

"An' if anybody comes to see you," she answered, giving him a red handkerchief.

"Besides," she continued, "you needn't ha' brought me upstairs for that."

"I b'lieve th' peen's commin' on again," he said, with a little horror in his voice.

"It isn't, you know it isn't," she replied. "The doctor says you imagine it's there when it isn't."

"Canna I feel what's inside me?" he shouted.

"There's a traction-engine coming downhill," she said. "That'll scatter them—I'll just go an' finish your pudding."

She left him. The traction-engine went by, shaking the houses. Then the street was quiet, save for the men. A gang of youths from fifteen to twenty-five years old were playing marbles in the middle of the road. Other little groups of men were playing on the pavement. The street was gloomy. Willy could hear the endless calling and shouting of men's voices.

"Tha'rt skinchin'!"

"I arena!"

"Come 'ere with that blood-alley."

"Swop us four for't."

"Shonna, gie's hold on't."

He wanted to be out, he wanted to be playing marbles. The pain had weakened his mind, so that he hardly knew any self-control.

Presently another gang of men lounged up the street. It was pay morning. The Union was paying the men in the Primitive Chapel. They were returning with their half-sovereigns.

"Sorry!" bawled a voice. "Sorry!"

The word is a form of address, corruption probably of "Sirrah." Willy started almost out of his chair.

"Sorry!" again bawled a great voice. "Art goin' wi' me to see Notts play Villa?"

Many of the marble players started up.

"What time is it? There's no treens, we s'll ha'e ter walk."

The street was alive with men.

"Who's goin' ter Nottingham ter see th' match?" shouted the same big voice. A very large, tipsy man, with his cap over his eye, was calling.

"Com' on—aye, com' on!" came many voices. The street was full of the shouting of men. They split up in excited cliques and groups.

"Play up, Notts!" the big man shouted.

"Plee up, Notts!" shouted the youths and men. They were at kindling pitch. It only needed a shout to rouse them. Of this the careful authorities were aware.

"I'm goin', I'm goin'!" shouted the sick man at his window.

Lucy came running upstairs.

"I'm goin' ter see Notts play Villa on th' Meadows ground," he declared.

"You—*you* can't go. There are no trains. You can't walk nine miles."

"I'm goin' ter see th' match," he declared, rising.

"You know you can't. Sit down now an' be quiet."

She put her hand on him. He shook it off.

"Leave me alone, leave me alone. It's thee as ma'es th' peen come, it's thee. I'm goin' ter Nottingham to see th' football match."

"Sit down—folks'll hear you, and what will they think?"

"Come off'n me. Com' off. It's her, it's her as does it. Com' off."

He seized hold of her. His little head was bristling with madness, and he was strong as a lion.

"Oh, Willy!" she cried.

"It's 'er, it's 'er. Kill her!" he shouted, "kill her."

"Willy, folks'll hear you."

"Th' peen's commin' on again, I tell yer. I'll kill her for it."

He was completely out of his mind. She struggled with him to prevent his going to the stairs. When she escaped from him, who was shouting and raving, she beckoned to her neighbor, a girl of twenty-four, who was cleaning the window across the road.

Ethel Mellor was the daughter of a well-to-do check-weighman. She ran across in fear to Mrs. Horsepool. Hearing the man raving, people were running out in the street and listening. Ethel hurried upstairs. Everything was clean and pretty in the young home.

Willy was staggering round the room, after the slowly retreating Lucy, shouting:

"Kill her! Kill her!"

"Mr. Horsepool!" cried Ethel, leaning against the bed, white as the sheets, and trembling. "Whatever are you saying?"

"I tell yer it's 'er fault as th' pain comes on—I tell yer it is! Kill 'er—kill 'er!"

"Kill Mrs. Horsepool!" cried the trembling girl. "Why, you're ever so fond of her, you know you are."

"The peen—I ha'e such a lot o' peen—I want to kill 'er."

He was subsiding. When he sat down his wife collapsed in a chair, weeping noiselessly. The tears ran down Ethel's face. He sat staring out of the window; then the old, hurt look came on his face.

"What 'ave I been sayin'?" he asked, looking piteously at his wife.

"Why!" said Ethel, "you've been carrying on something awful, saying, 'Kill her, kill her!' "

"Have I, Lucy?" he faltered.

"You didn't know what you was saying," said his young wife gently but coldly.

His face puckered up. He bit his lip, then broke into tears, sobbing uncontrollably, with his face to the window.

There was no sound in the room but of three people crying bitterly, breath caught in sobs. Suddenly Lucy put away her tears and went over to him.

"You didn't know what you was sayin', Willy, I know you didn't. I knew you didn't, all the time. It doesn't matter, Willy. Only don't do it again."

In a little while, when they were calmer, she went downstairs with Ethel.

"See if anybody is looking in the street," she said.

Ethel went into the parlor and peeped through the curtains.

"Aye!" she said. "You may back your life Lena an' Mrs. Severn'll be out gorping, and that clat-fartin' Mrs. Allsop."

"Oh, I hope they haven't heard anything! If it gets about as he's out of his mind, they'll stop his compensation, I know they will."

"They'd never stop his compensation for *that*," protested Ethel.

"Well, they *have* been stopping some—"

"It'll not get about. I s'll tell nobody."

"Oh, but if it does, whatever shall we do? . . ."

THE CHRISTENING

The mistress of the British School stepped down from her school gate, and instead of turning to the left as usual, she turned to the right. Two women who were hastening home to scramble their husbands' dinners together—it was five minutes to four—stopped to look at her. They stood gazing after her for a moment; then they glanced at each other with a woman's little grimace.

To be sure, the retreating figure was ridiculous: small and thin, with a black straw hat, and a rusty cashmere dress hanging full all round the skirt. For so small and frail and rusty a creature to sail with slow, deliberate stride was also absurd. Hilda Rowbotham was less than thirty, so it was not years that set the measure of her pace; she had heart disease. Keeping her face, that was small with sickness, but not uncomely, firmly lifted and fronting ahead, the young woman sailed on past the marketplace, like a black swan of mournful, disreputable plumage.

She turned into Berryman's, the baker's. The shop displayed bread and cakes, sacks of flour and oatmeal, flitches of bacon, hams, lard and sausages. The combination of scents was not unpleasing. Hilda Rowbotham stood for some minutes nervously tapping and pushing a large knife that lay on the counter, and looking at the tall, glittering brass scales. At last a morose man with sandy whiskers came down the step from the house-place.

"What is it?" he asked, not apologizing for his delay.

"Will you give me six-pennyworth of assorted cakes and pastries—and put in some macaroons, please?" she asked, in remarkably rapid and nervous speech. Her lips fluttered like two leaves in a wind, and her words crowded and rushed like a flock of sheep at a gate.

"We've got no macaroons," said the man churlishly.

He had evidently caught that word. He stood waiting.

"Then I can't have any, Mr. Berryman. Now I do feel disappointed. I like those macaroons, you know, and it's not often I treat myself. One gets so tired of trying to spoil oneself, don't you think? It's less profitable even than trying to spoil somebody else." She laughed a quick little nervous laugh, putting her hand to her face.

"Then what'll you have?" asked the man, without the ghost of an answering smile. He evidently had not followed, so he looked more glum than ever.

"Oh, anything you've got," replied the schoolmistress, flushing slightly. The man moved slowly about, dropping the cakes from various dishes one by one into a paper bag.

"How's that sister o' yours getting on?" he asked, as if he were talking to the flour scoop.

"Whom do you mean?" snapped the schoolmistress.

"The youngest," answered the stooping, pale-faced man, with a note of sarcasm.

"Emma! Oh, she's very well, thank you!" The schoolmistress was very red, but she spoke with sharp, ironical defiance. The man grunted. Then he handed her the bag, and watched her out of the shop without bidding her "Good afternoon."

She had the whole length of the main street to traverse, a half-mile of slow-stepping torture, with shame flushing over her neck. But she carried her white bag with an appearance of steadfast unconcern. When she turned into the field she seemed to droop a little. The wide valley opened out from her, with the far woods withdrawing into twilight, and away in the center the great pit streaming its white smoke and chuffing as the men were being turned up. A full, rose-colored moon, like a flamingo flying low under the far, dusky east, drew out of the mist. It was beautiful, and it made her irritable sadness soften, diffuse.

Across the field, and she was at home. It was a new, substantial cottage, built with unstinted hand, such a house as an old miner could build himself out of his savings. In the rather small kitchen a woman of dark, saturnine complexion sat nursing a baby in a long white gown; a young woman of heavy, brutal cast stood at the table, cutting bread and butter. She had a downcast, humble mien that sat unnaturally on her, and was strangely irritating. She did not look round when her sister entered. Hilda put down the bag of cakes and left the room, not having spoken to Emma, nor to the baby, nor to Mrs. Carlin, who had come in to help for the afternoon.

Almost immediately the father entered from the yard with a dustpan full of coals. He was a large man, but he was going to pieces. As he passed through, he gripped the door with his free hand to steady himself, but turning, he lurched and swayed. He began putting the coals on the fire, piece by piece. One lump fell from his hand and smashed on the white hearth. Emma Rowbotham looked round, and began in a rough, loud voice of anger: "Look at you!" Then she consciously moderated her tones. "I'll sweep it up in a minute—don't you bother; you'll only be going head first into the fire."

Her father bent down nevertheless to clear up the mess he had made, saying, articulating his words loosely and slavering in his speech:

"The lousy bit of a thing, it slipped between my fingers like a fish." As he spoke he went tilting toward the fire. The dark-browed woman cried out; he put his hand on the hot stove to save himself; Emma swung round and dragged him off.

"Didn't I tell you!" she cried roughly. "Now, have you burnt yourself?"

She held tight hold of the big man, and pushed him into his chair.

"What's the matter?" cried a sharp voice from the other room. The speaker appeared, a hard, well-favored woman of twenty-eight.

"Emma, don't speak like that to father." Then, in a tone not so cold, but just as sharp: "Now, father, what have you been doing?"

Emma withdrew to her table sullenly.

"It's nöwt," said the old man, vainly protesting. "It's nöwt at a'. Get on wi' what you're doin'."

"I'm afraid 'e's burnt 'is 'and," said the black-browed woman, speaking of him with a kind of hard pity, as if he were a cumbersome child. Bertha took the old man's hand and looked at it, making a quick tut-tutting noise of impatience.

"Emma, get that zinc ointment—and some white rag," she commanded sharply. The younger sister put down her loaf with the knife in it, and went. To a sensitive observer, this obedience was more intolerable than the most hateful discord. The dark woman bent over the baby and made silent, gentle movements of motherliness to it. The little one smiled and moved on her lap. It continued to move and twist.

"I believe this child's hungry," she said. "How long is it since he had anything?"

"Just afore dinner," said Emma dully.

"Good gracious!" exclaimed Bertha. "You needn't starve the child now you've got it. Once every two hours it ought to be fed, as I've told you; and now it's three. Take him, poor little mite—I'll cut the bread." She bent and looked at the bonny baby. She could not help herself: she smiled, and pressed its cheek with her finger, and nodded to it, making little noises. Then she turned and took the loaf from her sister. The woman rose and gave the child to its mother. Emma bent over the little sucking mite. She hated it when she looked at it, and saw it as a symbol, but when she felt it, her love was like fire in her blood.

"I should think 'e canna be comin'," said the father uneasily, looking up at the clock.

"Nonsense, father—the clock's fast! It's but half-past four! Don't fidget!" Bertha continued to cut the bread and butter.

"Open a tin of pears," she said to the woman, in a much milder tone. Then she went into the next room. As soon as she was gone, the old man said again: "I should ha'e thought he'd 'a' been 'ere by now, if he means comin'."

Emma, engrossed, did not answer. The father had ceased to consider her, since she had become humbled.

" 'E'll come—'e'll come!" assured the stranger.

A few minutes later Bertha hurried into the kitchen, taking off her apron. The dog barked furiously. She opened the door, commanded the dog to silence, and said: "He will be quiet now, Mr. Kendal."

"Thank you," said a sonorous voice, and there was the sound of a bicycle being propped against a wall. A clergyman entered, a big-boned, thin, ugly man of nervous manner. He went straight to the father.

"Ah—how are you?" he asked musically, peering down on the great frame of the miner, ruined by locomotor ataxy.

His voice was full of gentleness, but he seemed as if he could not see distinctly, could not get things clear.

"Have you hurt your hand?" he said comfortingly, seeing the white rag.

"It wor nöwt but a pestered bit o' coal as dropped, an' I put my hand on th' hub. I thought tha worna commin'."

The familiar "tha," and the reproach, were unconscious retaliation on the old man's part. The minister smiled, half wistfully, half indulgently. He was full of vague tenderness. Then he turned to the young mother, who flushed sullenly because her dishonored breast was uncovered.

"How are *you?*" he asked, very softly and gently, as if she were ill and he were mindful of her.

"I'm all right," she replied, awkwardly taking his hand without rising, hiding her face and the anger that rose in her.

"Yes—yes"—he peered down at the baby, which sucked with distended mouth upon the firm breast. "Yes, yes." He seemed lost in a dim musing.

Coming to, he shook hands unseeingly with the woman.

Presently they all went into the next room, the minister hesitating to help his crippled old deacon.

"I can go by myself, thank yer," testily replied the father.

Soon all were seated. Everybody was separated in feeling and isolated at table. High tea was spread in the middle kitchen, a large, ugly room kept for special occasions.

Hilda appeared last, and the clumsy, rawboned clergyman rose to meet her. He was afraid of this family, the well-to-do old collier, and the brutal, self-willed children. But Hilda was queen among them. She was the clever one, and had been to college. She felt responsible for the keeping up of a high standard of conduct in all the members of the family. There *was* a difference between the Rowbothams and the common collier folk. Woodbine Cottage was a superior house to most—and was built in pride by the old man. She, Hilda, was a college-trained schoolmistress; she meant to keep up the prestige of her house in spite of blows.

She had put on a dress of green voile for this special occasion. But she was very thin; her neck protruded painfully. The clergyman, however, greeted her almost with reverence, and, with some assumption of dignity, she sat down before the tray. At the far end of the table sat the broken, massive frame of her father. Next to him was the youngest daughter, nursing the restless baby. The minister sat between Hilda and Bertha, hulking his bony frame uncomfortably.

There was a great spread on the table, of tinned fruits and tinned salmon, ham and cakes. Miss Rowbotham kept a keen eye on everything: she felt the importance of the occasion. The young mother who had given rise to all this solemnity ate in sulky discomfort, snatching sullen little smiles at her child, smiles which came, in spite of her, when she felt its little limbs stirring vigorously on her lap. Bertha, sharp and abrupt, was chiefly concerned with the baby. She scorned her sister, and treated her like dirt. But the infant was a streak of light to her. Miss Rowbotham concerned herself with the function and the conversation. Her hands fluttered; she talked in little volleys, exceedingly nervous. Toward the end of the meal, there came a pause. The old man wiped his mouth with his red handkerchief, then, his blue eyes going fixed and staring, he began to speak, in a loose, slobbering fashion, charging his words to the clergyman.

"Well, mester—we'n axed you to come here ter christen this childt, an' you'n come, an' I'm sure we're very thankful. I can't see lettin' the poor blessed childt miss baptizing, an' they aren't for goin' to church wi't——" He seemed to lapse into a muse. "So," he resumed, "we'n axed you to come here to do the job. I'm not sayin' as it's not 'ard on us, it is. I'm breakin' up, an' mother's gone. I don't like leavin' a girl o' mine in a situation like 'ers is, but what the Lord's done, He's done, an' it's no matter murmuring. . . . There's one thing to be thankful for, an' we *are* thankful for it: they never need know the want of bread."

Miss Rowbotham, the lady of the family, sat very stiff and pained during this discourse. She was sensitive to so many things that she was bewildered. She felt her young sister's shame, then a kind of swift protecting love for the baby, a feeling that included the mother; she was at a loss before her father's religious sentiment, and she felt and resented bitterly the mark upon the family, against which the common folk could lift their fingers. Still she winced from the sound of her father's words. It was a painful ordeal.

"It is hard for you," began the clergyman in his soft, lingering, unworldly voice. "It is hard for you today, but the Lord gives comfort in His time. A man child is born unto us, therefore let us rejoice and be glad. If sin has entered in among us, let us purify our hearts before the Lord. . . ."

He went on with his discourse. The young mother lifted the whimpering infant, till its face was hid in her loose hair. She was hurt, and a little glowering anger shone in her face. But nevertheless her fingers clasped the body of the child beautifully. She was stupefied with anger against this emotion let loose on her account.

Miss Bertha rose and went to the little kitchen, returning with water in a china bowl. She placed it there among the tea things.

"Well, we're all ready," said the old man, and the clergyman began to read the service. Miss Bertha was godmother, the two men godfathers. The old man sat with bent head. The scene became impressive. At last Miss Bertha took the child and put it in the arms of the clergyman. He, big and ugly, shone with a kind of unreal love. He had never mixed with life, and women were all unliving, Biblical things to him. When he asked for the name, the old man lifted his head fiercely. "Joseph William, after me," he said, almost out of breath.

"Joseph William, I baptize thee . . ." resounded the strange, full, chanting voice of the clergyman. The baby was quite still.

"Let us pray!" It came with relief to them all. They knelt before their chairs, all but the young mother, who bent and hid herself over her baby. The clergyman began his hesitating, struggling prayer.

Just then heavy footsteps were heard coming up the path, ceasing at the window. The young mother, glancing up, saw her brother, black in his pit-dirt, grinning in through the panes. His red mouth curved in a sneer; his fair hair shone above his blackened skin. He caught the eye of his sister and grinned. Then his black face disappeared. He had gone on into the kitchen. The girl with the child sat still and anger filled her heart. She herself hated now the praying clergyman and the whole emotional business; she hated her brother bitterly. In anger and bondage she sat and listened.

Suddenly her father began to pray. His familiar, loud, rambling voice made her shut herself up and become even insentient. Folks said his mind was weakening.

She believed it to be true, and kept herself always disconnected from him.

"We ask Thee, Lord," the old man cried, "to look after this childt. Fatherless he is. But what does the earthly father matter before Thee? The childt is Thine, he is Thy childt. Lord, what father has a man but Thee? Lord, when a man says he is a father, he is wrong from the first word. For Thou art the Father, Lord. Lord, take away from us the conceit that our children are ours. Lord, Thou art Father of this childt as is fatherless here. O God, Thou bring him up. For I have stood between Thee and my children; I've had *my* way with them, Lord; I've stood between Thee and my children; I've cut 'em off from Thee because they were mine. And they've grown twisted, because of me. Who is their father, Lord, but Thee? But I put myself in the way, they've been plants under a stone, because of me. Lord, if it hadn't been for me, they might ha' been trees in the sunshine. Let me own it, Lord, I've done 'em mischief. It would ha' been better if they'd never known no father. No man is a father, Lord: only Thou art. They can never grow beyond Thee, but I hampered them. Lift 'em up again, and undo what I've done to my children. And let this young childt be like a willow tree beside the waters, with no father but Thee, O God. Aye, an' I wish it had been so with my children, that they'd had no father but Thee. For I've been like a stone upon them, and they rise up and curse me in their wickedness. But let me go, an' lift Thou them up, Lord . . ."

The minister, unaware of the feelings of a father, knelt in trouble, hearing without understanding the special language of fatherhood. Miss Rowbotham alone felt and understood a little. Her heart began to flutter; she was in pain. The two younger daughters kneeled unhearing, stiffened and impervious. Bertha was thinking of the baby; and the young mother thought of the father of her child, whom she hated. There was a clatter outside in the scullery. There the youngest son made as much noise as he could, pouring out the water for his wash, muttering in deep anger:

"Blortin', slaverin' old fool!"

And while the praying of his father continued, his heart was burning with rage. On the table was a paper bag. He picked it up and read, "John Berryman—Bread, Pastries, etc." Then he grinned with a grimace. The father of the baby was baker's man at Berryman's. The prayer went on in the middle kitchen. Laurie Rowbotham gathered together the mouth of the bag, inflated it, and burst it with his fist. There was a loud report. He grinned to himself. But he writhed at the same time with shame and fear of his father.

The father broke off from his prayer; the party shuffled to their feet. The young mother went into the scullery.

"What art doin', fool?" she said.

The collier youth tipped the baby under the chin, singing:

Pat-a-cake, pat-a-cake, baker's man,
Bake me a cake as fast as you can....

The mother snatched the child away. "Shut thy mouth," she said, the color coming into her cheek.

Prick it and stick it and mark it with P,
And put it i' th' oven for baby an' me....

He grinned, showing a grimy, and jeering and unpleasant red mouth and white teeth.

"I s'll gi'e thee a dab ower th' mouth," said the mother of the baby grimly. He began to sing again, and she struck out at him.

"Now what's to do?" said the father, staggering in.

The youth began to sing again. His sister stood sullen and furious.

"Why does *that* upset you?" asked the eldest Miss Rowbotham, sharply, of Emma the mother. "Good gracious, it hasn't improved your temper."

Miss Bertha came in, and took the bonny baby.

The father sat big and unheeding in his chair, his eyes vacant, his physique wrecked. He let them do as they would, he fell to pieces. And yet some power, involuntary, like a curse, remained in him. The very ruin of him was like a lodestone that held them in its control. The wreck of him still dominated the house, in his dissolution even he compelled their being. They had never lived; his life, his will had always been upon them and contained them. They were only half-individuals.

The day after the christening he staggered in at the doorway declaring, in a loud voice, with joy in life still: "The daisies light up the earth, they clap their hands in multitudes, in praise of the morning." And his daughters shrank, sullen.

ODOR OF CHRYSANTHEMUMS

I

The small locomotive engine, Number 4, came clanking, stumbling down from Selston with seven full wagons. It appeared round the corner with loud threats of speed, but the colt that it startled from among the gorse, which still flickered indistinctly in the raw afternoon, outdistanced it at a canter. A woman, walking up the railway line to Underwood, drew back into the hedge, held her basket aside, and watched the footplate of the engine advancing. The trucks thumped heavily past, one by one, with slow inevitable movement, as she stood insignificantly trapped between the jolting black wagons and the hedge; then they curved away towards the coppice where the withered oak leaves dropped noiselessly, while the birds, pulling at the scarlet hips beside the track, made off into the dusk that had already crept into the spinney. In the open, the smoke from the engine sank and cleaved to the rough grass. The fields were dreary and forsaken, and in the marshy strip that led to the whimsey, a reedy pit-pond, the fowls had already abandoned their run among the alders, to roost in the tarred fowl-house. The pit-bank loomed up beyond the pond, flames like red sores licking its ashy sides, in the afternoon's stagnant light. Just beyond rose the tapering chimneys and the clumsy black headstocks of Brinsley Colliery. The two wheels were spinning fast up against the sky, and the winding-engine rapped out its little spasms. The miners were being turned up.

The engine whistled as it came into the wide bay of railway lines beside the colliery, where rows of trucks stood in harbor.

Miners, single, trailing and in groups, passed like shadows diverging home. At the edge of the ribbed level of sidings squat a low cottage, three steps down from the cinder track. A large bony vine clutched at the house, as if to claw down the tiled roof. Round the bricked yard grew a few wintry primroses. Beyond, the long garden sloped down to a bush-covered brook course. There were some twiggy apple trees, winter-crack trees, and ragged cabbages. Beside the path hung disheveled pink chrysanthemums, like pink cloths hung on bushes. A woman came stooping out of the felt-covered fowl-house, halfway down the garden. She closed and padlocked the door, then drew herself erect, having brushed some bits from her white apron.

She was a tall woman of imperious mien, handsome, with definite black eyebrows. Her smooth black hair was parted exactly. For a few moments she stood steadily watching the miners as they passed along the railway: then she turned towards the brook course. Her face was calm and set, her mouth was closed with disillusionment. After a moment she called:

"John!" There was no answer. She waited, and then said distinctly:

"Where are you?"

"Here!" replied a child's sulky voice from among the bushes. The woman looked piercingly through the dusk.

"Are you at that brook?" she asked sternly.

For answer the child showed himself before the raspberry-canes that rose like whips. He was a small, sturdy boy of five. He stood quite still, defiantly.

"Oh!" said the mother, conciliated. "I thought you were down at that wet brook—and you remember what I told you——"

The boy did not move or answer.

"Come, come on in," she said more gently, "it's getting dark. There's your grandfather's engine coming down the line!"

The lad advanced slowly, with resentful, taciturn movement. He was dressed in trousers and waistcoat of cloth that was too thick and hard for the size of the garments. They were evidently cut down from a man's clothes.

As they went slowly towards the house he tore at the ragged wisps of chrysanthemums and dropped the petals in handfuls along the path.

"Don't do that—it does look nasty," said his mother. He refrained, and she, suddenly pitiful, broke off a twig with three or four wan flowers and held them against her face. When mother and son reached the yard her hand hesitated, and instead of laying the flower aside, she pushed it in her apron-band. The mother and son stood at the foot of the three steps looking across the bay of lines at the passing home of the miners. The trundle of the small train was imminent. Suddenly the engine loomed past the house and came to a stop opposite the gate.

The engine driver, a short man with round gray beard, leaned out of the cab high above the woman.

"Have you got a cup of tea?" he said in a cheery, hearty fashion.

It was her father. She went in, saying she would mash. Directly, she returned.

"I didn't come to see you on Sunday," began the little gray-bearded man.

"I didn't expect you," said his daughter.

The engine driver winced; then, reassuming his cheery, airy manner, he said:

"Oh, have you heard then? Well, and what do you think——?"

"I think it is soon enough," she replied.

At her brief censure the little man made an impatient gesture, and said coaxingly, yet with dangerous coldness:

"Well, what's a man to do? It's no sort of life for a man of my years, to sit at my own hearth like a stranger. And if I'm going to marry again it may as well be soon as late—what does it matter to anybody?"

The woman did not reply, but turned and went into the house. The man in the engine cab stood assertive, till she returned with a cup of tea and a piece of bread and butter on a plate. She went up the steps and stood near the footplate of the hissing engine.

"You needn't 'a' brought me bread an' butter," said her father. "But a cup of tea"—he sipped appreciatively—"it's very nice." He sipped for a moment or two, then: "I hear as Walter's got another bout on," he said.

"When hasn't he?" said the woman bitterly.

"I heered tell of him in the 'Lord Nelson' braggin' as he was going to spend that b——afore he went: half a sovereign that was."

"When?" asked the woman.

"A' Sat'day night—I know that's true."

"Very likely," she laughed bitterly. "He gives me twenty-three shillings."

"Aye, it's a nice thing, when a man can do nothing with his money but make a beast of himself!" said the gray-whiskered man. The woman turned her head away. Her father swallowed the last of his tea and handed her the cup.

"Aye," he sighed, wiping his mouth. "It's a settler, it is——"

He put his hand on the lever. The little engine strained and groaned, and the train rumbled towards the crossing. The woman again looked across the metals. Darkness was settling over the spaces of the railway and trucks: the miners, in gray somber groups, were still passing home. The winding-engine pulsed hurriedly, with brief pauses. Elizabeth Bates looked at the dreary flow of men, then she went indoors. Her husband did not come.

The kitchen was small and full of firelight; red coals piled glowing up the chimney mouth. All the life of the room seemed in the white, warm hearth and the steel fender reflecting the red fire. The cloth was laid for tea; cups glinted in the shadows. At the back, where the lowest stairs protruded into the room, the boy sat struggling with a knife and a piece of whitewood. He was almost hidden in the shadow. It was half-past four. They had but to await the father's coming to begin tea. As the mother watched her son's sullen little struggle with the wood, she saw herself in his silence and pertinacity; she saw the father in her child's indifference to all but himself. She seemed to be occupied by her husband. He had probably gone past his home, slung past his own door, to drink before he came in, while his dinner spoiled and wasted in waiting. She glanced at the clock, then took the potatoes to strain them in the yard. The garden and fields beyond the brook were closed in uncertain darkness. When she rose with the saucepan, leaving the drain steaming into the night behind her, she saw the yellow lamps were lit along the high road that went up the hill away beyond the space of the railway lines and the field.

Then again she watched the men trooping home, fewer now and fewer.

Indoors the fire was sinking and the room was dark red. The woman put her saucepan on the hob, and set a batter pudding near the mouth of the oven. Then she stood unmoving. Directly, gratefully, came quick young steps to the door. Someone hung on the latch a moment, then a little girl entered and began pulling off her outdoor things, dragging a mass of curls, just ripening from gold to brown, over her eyes with her hat.

Her mother chid her for coming late from school, and said she would have to keep her at home the dark winter days.

"Why, mother, it's hardly a bit dark yet. The lamp's not lighted, and my father's not home."

"No, he isn't. But it's a quarter to five! Did you see anything of him?"

The child became serious. She looked at her mother with large, wistful blue eyes.

"No, mother, I've never seen him. Why? Has he come up an' gone past, to Old Brinsley? He hasn't, mother, 'cos I never saw him."

"He'd watch that," said the mother bitterly, "he'd take care as you didn't see him. But you may depend upon it, he's seated in the 'Prince o' Wales.' He wouldn't be this late."

The girl looked at her mother piteously.

"Let's have our teas, mother, should we?" said she.

The mother called John to table. She opened the door once more and looked out across the darkness of the lines. All was deserted: she could not hear the winding-engines.

"Perhaps," she said to herself, "he's stopped to get some ripping done."

They sat down to tea. John, at the end of the table near the door, was almost lost in the darkness. Their faces were hidden from each other. The girl crouched against the fender slowly moving a thick piece of bread before the fire. The lad, his face a dusky mark on the shadow, sat watching her who was transfigured in the red glow.

"I do think it's beautiful to look in the fire," said the child.

"Do you?" said her mother. "Why?"

"It's so red, and full of little caves—and it feels so nice, and you can fair smell it."

"It'll want mending directly," replied her mother, "and then if your father comes he'll carry on and say there never is a fire when a man comes home sweating from the pit. A public house is always warm enough."

There was silence till the boy said complainingly: "Make haste, our Annie."

"Well, I am doing! I can't make the fire do it no faster, can I?"

"She keeps wafflin' it about so's to make 'er slow," grumbled the boy.

"Don't have such an evil imagination, child," replied the mother.

Soon the room was busy in the darkness with the crisp sound of crunching. The mother ate very little. She drank her tea determinedly, and sat thinking. When she rose her anger was evident in the stern unbending of her head. She looked at the pudding in the fender, and broke out:

"It is a scandalous thing as a man can't even come home to his dinner! If it's crozzled up to a cinder I don't see why I should care. Past his very door he goes to get to a public house, and here I sit with his dinner waiting for him——"

She went out. As she dropped piece after piece of coal on the red fire, the shadows fell on the walls, till the room was almost in total darkness.

"I canna see," grumbled the invisible John. In spite of herself, the mother laughed.

"You know the way to your mouth," she said. She set the dustpan outside the door. When she came again like a shadow on the hearth, the lad repeated, complaining sulkily:

"I canna see."

"Good gracious!" cried the mother irritably, "you're as bad as your father if it's a bit dusk!"

Nevertheless she took a paper spill from a sheaf on the mantelpiece and proceeded to light the lamp that hung from the ceiling in the middle of the room. As she reached up, her figure displayed itself just rounding with maternity.

"Oh, mother——!" exclaimed the girl.

"What?" said the woman, suspended in the act of putting the lamp glass over the flame. The copper reflector shone handsomely on her, as she stood with uplifted arm, turning to face her daughter.

"You've got a flower in your apron!" said the child, in a little rapture at this unusual event.

"Goodness me!" exclaimed the woman, relieved. "One would think the house was afire." She replaced the glass and waited a moment before turning up the wick. A pale shadow was seen floating vaguely on the floor.

"Let me smell!" said the child, still rapturously, coming forward and putting her face to her mother's waist.

"Go along, silly!" said the mother, turning up the lamp. The light revealed their suspense so that the woman felt it almost unbearable. Annie was still bending at her waist. Irritably, the mother took the flowers out from her apron-band.

"Oh, mother—don't take them out!" Annie cried, catching her hand and trying to replace the sprig.

"Such nonsense!" said the mother, turning away. The child put the pale chrysanthemums to her lips, murmuring:

"Don't they smell beautiful!"

Her mother gave a short laugh.

"No," she said, "not to me. It was chrysanthemums when I married him, and chrysanthemums when you were born, and the first time they ever brought him home drunk, he'd got brown chrysanthemums in his buttonhole."

She looked at the children. Their eyes and their parted lips were wondering. The mother sat rocking in silence for some time. Then she looked at the clock.

"Twenty minutes to six!" In a tone of fine bitter carelessness she continued: "Eh, he'll not come now till they bring him. There he'll stick! But he needn't come rolling in here in his pit-dirt, for *I* won't wash him. He can lie on the floor—— Eh, what a fool I've been, what a fool! And this is what I came here for, to this dirty hole, rats and all, for him to slink past his very door. Twice last week—he's begun now——"

She silenced herself, and rose to clear the table.

While for an hour or more the children played, subduedly intent, fertile of imagination, united in fear of the mother's wrath, and in dread of their father's homecoming, Mrs. Bates sat in her rocking chair making a "singlet" of thick cream-colored flannel, which gave a dull wounded sound as she tore off the gray edge. She worked at her sewing with energy, listening to the children, and her anger wearied itself, lay down to rest, opening its eyes from time to time and steadily watching, its ears raised to listen. Sometimes even her anger quailed and shrank, and the mother suspended her sewing, tracing the footsteps that thudded along the sleepers outside; she would lift her head sharply to bid the children "hush," but she recovered herself in time, and the footsteps went past the gate, and the children were not flung out of their play-world.

But at last Annie sighed, and gave in. She glanced at her wagon of slippers, and loathed the game. She turned plaintively to her mother.

"Mother!"—but she was inarticulate.

John crept out like a frog from under the sofa. His mother glanced up.

"Yes," she said, "just look at those shirt-sleeves!"

The boy held them out to survey them, saying nothing. Then somebody called in a hoarse voice away down the line, and suspense bristled in the room, till two people had gone by outside, talking.

"It is time for bed," said the mother.

"My father hasn't come," wailed Annie plaintively. But her mother was primed with courage.

"Never mind. They'll bring him when he does come—like a log." She meant there would be no scene. "And he may sleep on the floor till he wakes himself. I know he'll not go to work tomorrow after this!"

The children had their hands and faces wiped with a flannel. They were very quiet. When they had put on their nightdresses, they said their prayers, the boy mumbling. The mother looked down at them, at the brown silken bush of intertwining curls in the nape of the girl's neck, at the little black head of the lad, and her heart burst with anger at their father who caused all three such distress. The children hid their faces in her skirts for comfort.

When Mrs. Bates came down, the room was strangely empty, with a tension of expectancy. She took up her sewing and stitched for some time without raising her head. Meantime her anger was tinged with fear.

II

The clock struck eight and she rose suddenly, dropping her sewing on her chair. She went to the stairfoot door, opened it, listening. Then she went out, locking the door behind her.

Something scuffled in the yard, and she started, though she knew it was only the rats with which the place was overrun. The night was very dark. In the great bay of railway lines, bulked with trucks, there was no trace of light, only away back she could see a few yellow lamps at the pit-top, and the red smear of the burning pit-bank on the night. She hurried along the edge of the track, then, crossing the converging lines, came to the stile by the white gates, whence she emerged on the road. Then the fear which had led her shrank. People were walking up to New Brinsley; she saw the lights in the houses; twenty yards further on were the broad windows of the "Prince of Wales," very warm and bright, and the loud voices of men could be heard distinctly. What a fool she had been to imagine that anything had happened to him! He was merely drinking over there at the "Prince of Wales." She faltered. She had never yet been to fetch him, and she never would go. So she continued her walk towards the long straggling line of houses, standing blank on the highway. She entered a passage between the dwellings.

"Mr. Rigley?—Yes! Did you want him? No, he's not in at this minute."

The rawboned woman leaned forward from her dark scullery and peered at the other, upon whom fell a dim light through the blind of the kitchen window.

"Is it Mrs. Bates?" she asked in a tone tinged with respect.

"Yes. I wondered if your Master was at home. Mine hasn't come yet."

" 'Asn't 'e! Oh, Jack's been 'ome an' 'ad 'is dinner an' gone out. 'E's just gone for 'alf an hour afore bedtime. Did you call at the 'Prince of Wales'?"

"No——"

"No, you didn't like——! It's not very nice." The other woman was indulgent. There was an awkward pause. "Jack never said nothink about—about your Mester," she said.

"No!—I expect he's stuck in there!"

Elizabeth Bates said this bitterly, and with recklessness. She knew that the woman across the yard was standing at her door listening, but she did not care. As she turned:

"Stop a minute! I'll just go an' ask Jack if'e knows anythink," said Mrs. Rigley.

"Oh, no—I wouldn't like to put——!"

"Yes, I will, if you'll just step inside an' see as th' childer doesn't come downstairs and set theirselves afire."

Elizabeth Bates, murmuring a remonstrance, stepped inside. The other woman apologized for the state of the room.

The kitchen needed apology. There were little frocks and trousers and childish undergarments on the squab and on the floor, and a litter of playthings everywhere. On the black American cloth of the table were pieces of bread and cake, crusts, slops, and a teapot with cold tea.

"Eh, ours is just as bad," said Elizabeth Bates, looking at the woman, not at the house. Mrs. Rigley put a shawl over her head and hurried out, saying:

"I shanna be a minute."

The other sat, noting with faint disapproval the general untidiness of the room. Then she fell to counting the shoes of various sizes scattered over the floor. There were twelve. She sighed and said to herself, "No wonder!"—glancing at the litter. There came the scratching of two pairs of feet on the yard, and the Rigleys entered. Elizabeth Bates rose. Rigley was a big man, with very large bones. His head looked particularly bony. Across his temple was a blue scar, caused by a wound got in the pit, a wound in which the coal dust remained blue like tattooing.

" 'Asna 'e come whoam yit?" asked the man, without any form of greeting, but with deference and sympathy. "I couldna say wheer he is—'e's non ower theer!"—he jerked his head to signify the "Prince of Wales."

" 'E's 'appen gone up to th' 'Yew,' " said Mrs. Rigley.

There was another pause. Rigley had evidently something to get off his mind:

"Ah left 'im finishin' a stint," he began. "Loose-all 'ad bin gone about ten minutes when we com'n away, an' I shouted, 'Are ter comin', Walt?' an' 'e said, 'Go on, Ah shanna be but a'ef a minnit,' so we com'n ter th' bottom, me an' Bowers, thinkin' as 'e wor just behint, an' 'ud come up i' th' next bantle——"

He stood perplexed, as if answering a charge of deserting his mate. Elizabeth Bates, now again certain of disaster, hastened to reassure him:

"I expect 'e's gone up to th' 'Yew Tree,' as you say. It's not the first time. I've fretted myself into a fever before now. He'll come home when they carry him."

"Ay, isn't it too bad!" deplored the other woman.

"I'll just step up to Dick's an' see if 'e *is* theer," offered the man, afraid of appearing alarmed, afraid of taking liberties.

"Oh, I wouldn't think of bothering you that far," said Elizabeth Bates, with emphasis, but he knew she was glad of his offer.

As they stumbled up the entry, Elizabeth Bates heard Rigley's wife run across the yard and open her neighbour's door. At this, suddenly all the blood in her body seemed to switch away from her heart.

"Mind!" warned Rigley. "Ah've said many a time as Ah'd fill up them ruts in this entry, sumb'dy 'll be breakin' their legs yit." She recovered herself and walked quickly along with the miner. "I don't like leaving the children in bed, and nobody in the house," she said.

"No, you dunna!" he replied courteously. They were soon at the gate of the cottage.

"Well, I shanna be many minnits. Dunna you be frettin' now, 'e'll be all right," said the butty.

"Thank you very much, Mr. Rigley," she replied.

"You're welcome!" he stammered, moving away. "I shanna be many minnits."

The house was quiet. Elizabeth Bates took off her hat and shawl, and rolled back the rug. When she had finished, she sat down. It was a few minutes past nine. She was startled by the rapid chuff of the winding-engine at the pit, and the sharp whirr of the brakes on the rope as it descended. Again she felt the painful sweep of her blood, and she put her hand to her side, saying aloud, "Good gracious!—it's only the nine o'clock deputy going down," rebuking herself.

She sat still, listening. Half an hour of this, and she was wearied out.

"What am I working myself up like this for?" she said pitiably to herself, "I s'll only be doing myself some damage."

She took out her sewing again.

At a quarter to ten there were footsteps. One person! She watched for the door to open. It was an elderly woman, in a black bonnet and a black woolen shawl—his mother. She was about sixty years old, pale, with blue eyes, and her face all wrinkled and lamentable. She shut the door and turned to her daughter-in-law peevishly.

"Eh, Lizzie, whatever shall we do, whatever shall we do!" she cried.

Elizabeth drew back a little, sharply.

"What is it, mother?" she said.

The elder woman seated herself on the sofa.

"I don't know, child, I can't tell you!"—she shook her head slowly. Elizabeth sat watching her, anxious and vexed.

"I don't know," replied the grandmother, sighing very deeply. "There's no end to my troubles, there isn't. The things I've gone through, I'm sure it's enough——!" She wept without wiping her eyes, the tears running.

"But, mother," interrupted Elizabeth, "what do you mean? What is it?"

The grandmother slowly wiped her eyes. The fountains of her tears were stopped by Elizabeth's directness. She wiped her eyes slowly.

"Poor child! Eh, you poor thing!" she moaned. "I don't know what we're going to do, I don't—and you as you are—it's a thing, it is indeed!"

Elizabeth waited.

"Is he dead?" she asked, and at the words her heart swung violently, though she felt a slight flush of shame at the ultimate extravagance of the question. Her words sufficiently frightened the old lady, almost brought her to herself.

"Don't say so, Elizabeth! We'll hope it's not as bad as that; no, may the Lord spare us that, Elizabeth. Jack Rigley came just as I was sittin' down to a glass afore going to bed, an' 'e said, "Appen you'll go down th'line, Mrs. Bates. Walt's had an accident. 'Appen you'll go an' sit wi' 'er till we can get him home.' I hadn't time to ask him a word afore he was gone. An' I put my bonnet on an' come straight down, Lizzie. I thought to myself, 'Eh, that poor blessed child, if anybody should come an' tell her of a sudden, there's no knowin' what'll 'appen to 'er.' You mustn't let it upset you, Lizzie—or you know what to expect. How long is it, six months—or is it five, Lizzie? Ay!"—the old woman shook her head—"time slips on, it slips on! Ay!"

Elizabeth's thoughts were busy elsewhere. If he was killed—would she be able to manage on the little pension and what she could earn?—she counted up rapidly. If he was hurt—they wouldn't take him to the hospital—how tiresome he would be to nurse!—but perhaps she'd be able to get him away from the drink and his hateful ways. She would—while he was ill. The tears offered to come to her eyes at the picture. But what sentimental luxury was this she was beginning?

She turned to consider the children. At any rate she was absolutely necessary for them. They were her business.

"Ay!" repeated the old woman, "it seems but a week or two since he brought me his first wages. Ay—he was a good lad, Elizabeth, he was, in his way. I don't know why he got to be such a trouble, I don't. He was a happy lad at home, only full of spirits. But there's no mistake he's been a handful of trouble, he has! I hope the Lord'll spare him to mend his ways. I hope so, I hope so. You've had a sight o' trouble with him, Elizabeth, you have indeed. But he was a jolly enough lad wi' me, he was, I can assure you I don't know how it is. . . ."

The old woman continued to muse aloud, a monotonous irritating sound, while Elizabeth thought concentratedly, startled once, when she heard the winding-engine chuff quickly, and the brakes skirr with a shriek. Then she heard the engine more slowly, and the brakes made no sound. The old woman did not notice. Elizabeth waited in suspense. The mother-in-law talked, with lapses into silence.

"But he wasn't your son, Lizzie, an' it makes a difference. Whatever he was, I remember him when he was little, an' I learned to understand him and to make allowances. You've got to make allowances for them——"

It was half-past ten, and the old woman was saying: "But it's trouble from beginning to end; you're never too old for trouble, never too old for that——" when the gate banged back, and there were heavy feet on the steps.

"I'll go, Lizzie, let me go," cried the old woman, rising. But Elizabeth was at the door. It was a man in pit-clothes.

"They're bringin' 'im, Missis," he said. Elizabeth's heart halted a moment. Then it surged on again, almost suffocating her.

"Is he—is it bad?" she asked.

The man turned away, looking at the darkness:

"The doctor says 'e'd been dead hours. 'E saw im i' th' lamp-cabin."

The old woman, who stood just behind Elizabeth, dropped into a chair, and folded her hands, crying: "Oh, my boy, my boy!"

"Hush!" said Elizabeth, with a sharp twitch of a frown. "Be still, mother, don't waken th' children: I wouldn't have them down for anything!"

The old woman moaned softly, rocking herself. The man was drawing away. Elizabeth took a step forward.

"How was it?" she asked.

"Well, I couldn't say for sure," the man replied, very ill at ease. " 'E wor finishin' a stint an' th' butties 'ad gone, an' a lot o' stuff come down atop 'n 'im."

"And crushed him?" cried the widow, with a shudder.

"No," said the man, "it fell at th' back of 'im. 'E wor under th' face, an' it niver touched 'im. It shut 'im in. It seems 'e wor smothered."

Elizabeth shrank back. She heard the old woman behind her cry:

"What?—what did e' say it was?"

The man replied, more loudly: " 'E wor smothered!"

Then the old woman wailed aloud, and this relieved Elizabeth.

"Oh, mother," she said, putting her hand on the old woman, "don't waken th' children, don't waken th' children."

She wept a little, unknowing, while the old mother rocked herself and moaned. Elizabeth remembered that they were bringing him home, and she must be ready. "They'll lay him in the parlor," she said to herself, standing a moment pale and perplexed.

Then she lighted a candle and went into the tiny room. The air was cold and damp, but she could not make a fire, there was no fireplace. She set down the candle and looked round. The candlelight glittered on the luster-glasses, on the two vases that held some of the pink chrysanthemums, and on the dark mahogany. There was a cold, deathly smell of chrysanthemums in the room. Elizabeth stood looking at the flowers. She turned away, and calculated whether there would be room to lay him on the floor, between the couch and the chiffonier. She pushed the chairs aside. There would be room to lay him down and step round him. Then she fetched the old red tablecloth, and another old cloth, spreading them down to save her bit of carpet. She shivered on leaving the parlor; so, from the dresser drawer she took a clean shirt and put it at the fire to air. All the time her mother-in-law was rocking herself in the chair and moaning.

"You'll have to move from there, mother," said Elizabeth. "They'll be bringing him in. Come in the rocker."

The old mother rose mechanically, and seated herself by the fire, continuing to lament. Elizabeth went into the pantry for another candle, and there, in the little penthouse under the naked tiles, she heard them coming. She stood still in the pantry doorway, listening. She heard them pass the end of the house, and come awkwardly down the three steps, a jumble of shuffling footsteps and muttering voices. The old woman was silent. The men were in the yard.

Then Elizabeth heard Matthews, the manager of the pit, say: "You go in first, Jim. Mind!"

The door came open, and the two women saw a collier backing into the room, holding one end of a stretcher, on which they could see the nailed pit-boots of the dead man. The two carriers halted, the man at the head stooping to the lintel of the door.

"Wheer will you have him?" asked the manager, a short, white-bearded man.

Elizabeth roused herself and came from the pantry carrying the unlighted candle.

"In the parlor," she said.

"In there, Jim!" pointed the manager, and the carriers backed round into the tiny room. The coat with which they had covered the body fell off as they awkwardly turned through the two doorways, and the women saw their man, naked to the waist, lying stripped for work. The old woman began to moan in a low voice of horror.

"Lay th' stretcher at th' side," snapped the manager, "an' put 'im on th' cloths. Mind now, mind! Look you now——!"

One of the men had knocked off a vase of chrysanthemums. He stared awkwardly, then they set down the stretcher. Elizabeth did not look at her husband. As soon as she could get in the room, she went and picked up the broken vase and the flowers.

"Wait a minute!" she said.

The three men waited in silence while she mopped up the water with a duster.

"Eh, what a job, what a job, to be sure!" the manager was saying, rubbing his brow with trouble and perplexity. "Never knew such a thing in my life, never! He'd no business to ha' been left. I never knew such a thing in my life! Fell over him clean as a whistle, an' shut him in. Not four foot of space, there wasn't—yet it scarce bruised him."

He looked down at the dead man, lying prone, half-naked, all grimed with coal-dust.

" ' 'Sphyxiated,' the doctor said. It *is* the most terrible job I've ever known. Seems as if it was done o' purpose. Clean over him, an' shut 'im in, like a mouse-trap"—he made a sharp, descending gesture with his hand.

The colliers standing by jerked aside their heads in hopeless comment.

The horror of the thing bristled upon them all.

Then they heard the girl's voice upstairs calling shrilly: "Mother, mother—who is it? Mother, who is it?"

Elizabeth hurried to the foot of the stairs and opened the door:

"Go to sleep!" she commanded sharply. "What are you shouting about? Go to sleep at once—there's nothing——"

Then she began to mount the stairs. They could hear her on the boards, and on the plaster floor of the little bedroom. They could hear her distinctly:

"What's the matter now?—what's the matter with you, silly thing?"—her voice was much agitated, with an unreal gentleness. "I thought it was some men come," said the plaintive voice of the child. "Has he come?"

"Yes, they've brought him. There's nothing to make a fuss about. Go to sleep now, like a good child."

They could hear her voice in the bedroom, they waited whilst she covered the children under the bedclothes.

"Is he drunk?" asked the girl, timidly, faintly.

"No! No—he's not! He—he's asleep."

"Is he asleep downstairs?"

"Yes—and don't make a noise."

There was silence for a moment, then the men heard the frightened child again: "What's that noise?"

"It's nothing, I tell you, what are you bothering for?"

The noise was the grandmother moaning. She was oblivious of everything, sitting on her chair rocking and moaning. The manager put his hand on her arm and bade her "Sh—sh!"

The old woman opened her eyes and looked at him. She was shocked by this interruption, and seemed to wonder.

"What time is it?"—the plaintive thin voice of the child, sinking back unhappily into sleep, asked this last question.

"Ten o'clock," answered the mother more softly. Then she must have bent down and kissed the children.

Matthews beckoned to the men to come away. They put on their caps and took up the stretcher. Stepping over the body, they tiptoed out of the house. None of them spoke till they were far from the wakeful children.

When Elizabeth came down she found her mother alone on the parlor floor, leaning over the dead man, the tears dropping on him.

"We must lay him out," the wife said. She put on the kettle, then returning knelt at the feet, and began to unfasten the knotted leather laces. The room was clammy and dim with only one candle, so that she had to bend her face almost to the floor. At last she got off the heavy boots and put them away.

"You must help me now," she whispered to the old woman. Together they stripped the man.

When they arose, saw him lying in the naïve dignity of death, the women stood arrested in fear and respect. For a few moments they remained still, looking down, the old mother whimpering. Elizabeth felt countermanded. She saw him, how utterly inviolable he lay in himself. She had nothing to do with him. She could not accept it. Stooping, she laid her hand on him, in claim. He was still warm, for the mine was hot where he had died. His mother had his face between her hands, and was murmuring incoherently. The old tears fell in succession as drops from wet leaves; the mother was not weeping, merely her tears flowed. Elizabeth embraced the body of her husband, with cheek and lips. She seemed to be listening, inquiring, trying to get some connection. But she could not. She was driven away. He was impregnable.

She rose, went into the kitchen, where she poured warm water into a bowl, brought soap and flannel and a soft towel.

"I must wash him," she said.

Then the old mother rose stiffly, and watched Elizabeth as she carefully washed his face, carefully brushing the big blond moustache from his mouth with the flannel. She was afraid with a bottomless fear, so she ministered to him. The old woman, jealous, said:

"Let me wipe him!"—and she kneeled on the other side drying slowly as Elizabeth washed, her big black bonnet sometimes brushing the dark head of her daughter-in-law. They worked thus in silence for a long time. They never forgot it was death, and the touch of the man's dead body gave them strange emotions, different in each of the women; a great dread possessed them both, the mother felt the lie was given to her womb, she was denied; the wife felt the utter isolation of the human soul, the child within her was a weight apart from her.

At last it was finished. He was a man of handsome body, and his face showed no traces of drink. He was blond, full-fleshed, with fine limbs. But he was dead.

"Bless him," whispered his mother, looking always at his face, and speaking out of sheer terror. "Dear lad—bless him!" She spoke in a faint, sibilant ecstasy of fear and mother love.

Elizabeth sank down again to the floor, and put her face against his neck, and trembled and shuddered. But she had to draw away again. He was dead, and her living flesh had no place against his. A great dread and weariness held her: she was so unavailing. Her life was gone like this.

"White as milk he is, clear as a twelve-month baby, bless him, the darling!" the old mother murmured to herself. "Not a mark on him, clear and clean and white, beautiful as ever a child was made," she murmured with pride. Elizabeth kept her face hidden.

"He went peaceful, Lizzie—peaceful as sleep. Isn't he beautiful, the lamb? Ay—he must ha' made his peace, Lizzie. 'Appen he made it all right, Lizzie, shut in there. He'd have time. He wouldn't look like this if he hadn't made his peace. The lamb, the dear lamb. Eh, but he had a hearty laugh. I loved to hear it. He had the heartiest laugh, Lizzie, as a lad——"

Elizabeth looked up. The man's mouth was fallen back, slightly open under the cover of the moustache. The eyes, half-shut, did not show glazed in the obscurity. Life with its smoky burning gone from him, had left him apart and utterly alien to her. And she knew what a stranger he was to her. In her womb was ice of fear, because of this separate stranger with whom she had been living as one flesh. Was this what it all meant—utter, intact separateness, obscured by heat of living? In dread she turned her face away. The fact was too deadly. There had been nothing between them, and yet they had come together, exchanging their nakedness repeatedly. Each time he had taken her, they had been two isolated beings, far apart as now. He was no more responsible than she. The child was like ice in her womb. For as she looked at the dead man, her mind, cold and detached, said clearly: "Who am I? What have I been doing? I have been fighting a husband who did not exist. *He* existed all the time. What wrong have I done? What was that I have been living with? There lies the reality, this man." And her soul died in her for fear: she knew she had never seen him, he had never seen her, they had met in the dark and had fought in the dark, not knowing whom they met nor whom they fought. And now she saw, and turned silent in seeing. For she had been wrong. She had said he was something he was not; she had felt familiar with him. Whereas he was apart all the while, living as she never lived, feeling as she never felt.

In fear and shame she looked at his naked body, that she had known falsely. And he was the father of her children. Her soul was torn from her body and stood apart. She looked at his naked body and was ashamed, as if she had denied it. After all, it was itself. It seemed awful to her. She looked at his face, and she turned her own face to the wall. For his look was other than hers, his way was not her way. She had denied him what he was—she saw it now. She had refused him as himself. And this had been her life, and his life. She was grateful to death, which restored the truth. And she knew she was not dead.

And all the while her heart was bursting with grief and pity for him. What had he suffered? What stretch of horror for this helpless man! She was rigid with agony. She had not been able to help him. He had been cruelly injured, this naked man, this other being, and she could make no reparation. There were the children—but the children belonged to life. This dead man had nothing to do with them. He and she were only channels through which life had flowed to issue in the children. She was a mother—but how awful she knew it now to have been a wife. And he, dead now, how awful he must have felt it to be a husband. She felt that in the next world he would be a stranger to her. If they met there, in the beyond, they would only be ashamed of what had been before. The children had come, for some mysterious reason, out of both of them. But the children did not unite them. Now he was dead, she knew how eternally he was apart from her, how eternally he had nothing more to do with her. She saw this episode of her life closed. They had denied each other in life. Now he had withdrawn. An anguish came over her. It was finished then: it had become hopeless between them long before he died. Yet he had been her husband. But how little!

"Have you got his shirt, 'Lizabeth?"

Elizabeth turned without answering, though she strove to weep and behave as her mother-in-law expected. But she could not, she was silenced. She went into the kitchen and returned with the garment.

"It is aired," she said, grasping the cotton shirt here and there to try. She was almost ashamed to handle him; what right had she or any one to lay hands on him; but her touch was humble on his body. It was hard work to clothe him. He was so heavy and inert. A terrible dread gripped her all the while: that he could be so heavy and utterly inert, unresponsive, apart. The horror of the distance between them was almost too much for her—it was so infinite a gap she must look across.

At last it was finished. They covered him with a sheet and left him lying, with his face bound. And she fastened the door of the little parlor, lest the children should see what was lying there. Then, with peace sunk heavy on her heart, she went about making tidy the kitchen. She knew she submitted to life, which was her immediate master. But from death, her ultimate master, she winced with fear and shame.

Lady Chatterley's Lover

❖ 1 ❖

Ours is essentially a tragic age, so we refuse to take it tragically. The cataclysm has happened, we are among the ruins, we start to build up new little habits, to have new little hopes. It is rather hard work: there is now no smooth road into the future: but we go round, or scramble over the obstacles. We've got to live, no matter how many skies have fallen.

This was more or less Constance Chatterley's position. The war had brought the roof down over her head. And she had realized that one must live and learn.

She married Clifford Chatterley in 1917, when he was home for a month on leave. They had a month's honeymoon. Then he went back to Flanders: to be shipped over to England again six months later, more or less in bits. Constance, his wife, was then twenty-three years old, and he was twenty-nine.

His hold on life was marvelous. He didn't die, and the bits seemed to grow together again. For two years he remained in the doctor's hands. Then he was pronounced a cure, and could return to life again, with the lower half of his body, from the hips down, paralyzed forever.

This was in 1920. They returned, Clifford and Constance, to his home, Wragby Hall, the family "seat." His father had died, Clifford was now a baronet, Sir Clifford, and Constance was Lady Chatterley. They came to start housekeeping and married life in the rather forlorn home of the Chatterleys on a rather inadequate income. Clifford had a sister, but she had departed. Otherwise there were no near relatives. The elder brother was dead in the war. Crippled forever, knowing he could never have any children, Clifford came home to the smoky Midlands to keep the Chatterley name alive while he could.

He was not really downcast. He could wheel himself about in a wheeled chair, and he had a bath-chair with a small motor attachment, so he could drive himself slowly round the garden and into the fine melancholy park, of which he was really so proud, though he pretended to be flippant about it.

Having suffered so much, the capacity for suffering had to some extent left him. He remained strange and bright and cheerful, almost, one might say, chirpy, with his ruddy, healthy-looking face, and his pale-blue, challenging bright eyes. His shoulders were broad and strong, his hands were very strong.

He was expensively dressed, and wore handsome neckties from Bond Street. Yet still in his face one saw the watchful look, the slight vacancy of a cripple.

He had so very nearly lost his life, that what remained was wonderfully precious to him. It was obvious in the anxious brightness of his eyes, how proud he was, after the great shock, of being alive. But he had been so much hurt that something inside him had perished, some of his feelings had gone. There was a blank of insentience.

Constance, his wife, was a ruddy, country-looking girl with soft brown hair and sturdy body, and slow movements, full of unusual energy. She had big, wondering eyes, and a soft mild voice, and seemed just to have come from her native village. It was not so at all. Her father was the once well-known R.A., old Sir Malcolm Reid. Her mother had been one of the cultivated Fabians in the palmy, rather pre-Raphaelite days. Between artists and cultured socialists, Constance and her sister Hilda had had what might be called an aesthetically unconventional upbringing. They had been taken to Paris and Florence and Rome to breathe in art, and they had been taken also in the other direction, to the Hague and Berlin, to great Socialist conventions, where the speakers spoke in every civilized tongue, and no one was abashed.

The two girls, therefore, were from an early age not the least daunted by either art or ideal politics. It was their natural atmosphere. They were at once cosmopolitan and provincial, with the cosmopolitan provincialism of art that goes with pure social ideals.

They had been sent to Dresden at the age of fifteen, for music among other things. And they had had a good time there. They lived freely among the students, they argued with the men over philosophical, sociological and artistic matters, they were just as good as the men themselves: only better, since they were women. And they tramped off to the forests with sturdy youths bearing guitars, twang-twang! They sang the Wandervogel songs, and they were free. Free! That was the great word. Out in the open world, out in the forests of the morning, with lusty and splendid-throated young fellows, free to do as they liked, and—above all—to say what they liked. It was the talk that mattered supremely: the impassioned interchange of talk. Love was only a minor accompaniment.

Both Hilda and Constance had had their tentative love affairs by the time they were eighteen. The young men with whom they talked so passionately and sang so lustily and camped under the trees in such freedom wanted, of course, the love connection. The girls were doubtful, but then the thing was so much talked about, it was supposed to be so important. And the men were so humble and craving. Why couldn't a girl be queenly, and give the gift of herself?

So they had given the gift of themselves, each to the youth with whom she had the most subtle and intimate arguments. The arguments, the discussions were the great thing: the lovemaking and connection were only a sort of primitive reversion and a bit of an anticlimax. One was less in love with the boy afterwards, and a little inclined to hate him, as if he had trespassed on one's privacy and inner freedom. For, of course, being a girl, one's whole dignity and meaning in life consisted in the achievement of an absolute, a perfect, a pure and noble freedom. What else did a girl's life mean? To shake off the old and sordid connections and subjections.

And however one might sentimentalize it, this sex business was one of the most ancient, sordid connections and subjections. Poets who glorified it were mostly men. Women had always known there was something better, something higher. And now they knew it more definitely than ever. The beautiful pure freedom of a woman was infinitely more wonderful than any sexual love. The only unfortunate thing was that men lagged so far behind women in the matter. They insisted on the sex thing like dogs.

And a woman had to yield. A man was like a child with his appetites. A woman had to yield him what he wanted, or like a child he would probably turn nasty and flounce away and spoil what was a very pleasant connection. But a woman could yield to a man without yielding her inner, free self. That the poets and talkers about sex did not seem to have taken sufficiently into account. A woman could take a man without really giving herself away. Certainly she could take him without giving herself into his power. Rather she could use this sex thing to have power over him. For she only had to hold herself back in sexual intercourse, and let him finish and expend himself without herself coming to the crisis: and then she could prolong the connection and achieve her orgasm and her crisis while he was merely her tool.

Both sisters had had their love experience by the time the war came, and they were hurried home. Neither was ever in love with a young man unless he and she were verbally very near: that is unless they were profoundly interested, TALKING to one another. The amazing, the profound, the unbelievable thrill there was in passionately talking to some really clever young man by the hour, resuming day after day for months . . . this they had never realized till it happened! The paradisal promise: Thou shalt have men to talk to!—had never been uttered. It was fulfilled before they knew what a promise it was.

And if after the roused intimacy of these vivid and soul-enlightened discussions the sex thing became more or less inevitable, then let it. It marked the end of a chapter. It had a thrill of its own too: a queer vibrating thrill inside the body, a final spasm of self-assertion, like the last word, exciting, and very like the row of asterisks that can be put to show the end of a paragraph, and a break in the theme.

When the girls came home for the summer holidays of 1913, when Hilda was twenty and Connie eighteen, their father could see plainly that they had had the love experience.

L'amour avait passé par là as somebody puts it. But he was a man of experience himself, and let life take its course. As for the mother, a nervous invalid in the last few months of her life, she only wanted her girls to be "free," and to "fulfill themselves." She herself had never been able to be altogether herself: it had been denied her. Heaven knows why, for she was a woman who had her own income and her own way. She blamed her husband. But as a matter of fact, it was some old impression of authority on her own mind or soul that she could not get rid of. It had nothing to do with Sir Malcolm, who left his nervously hostile, high-spirited wife to rule her own roost, while he went his own way.

So the girls were "free," and went back to Dresden, and their music, and the university and the young men. They loved their respective young men, and the respective young men loved them with all the passion of mental attraction. All the wonderful things the young men thought and expressed and wrote, they thought and expressed and wrote for the young women. Connie's young man was musical, Hilda's was technical. But they simply lived for their young women. In their minds and their mental excitements, that is. Somewhere else they were a little rebuffed, though they did not know it.

It was obvious in them too that love had gone through them: that is, the physical experience. It is curious what a subtle but unmistakable transmutation it makes, both in the body of men and women: the women more blooming, more subtly rounded, her young angularities softened, and her expression either anxious or triumphant: the man much quieter, more inward, the very shapes of his shoulders and his buttocks less assertive, more hesitant.

In the actual sex-thrill within the body, the sisters nearly succumbed to the strange male power. But quickly they recovered themselves, took the sex-thrill as a sensation, and remained free. Whereas the men, in gratitude to the women for the sex experience, let their souls go out to her. And afterwards looked rather as if they had lost a shilling and found sixpence. Connie's man could be a bit sulky, and Hilda's a bit jeering. But that is how men are! Ungrateful and never satisfied. When you don't have them they hate you because you won't; and when you do have them they hate you again, for some other reason. Or for no reason at all, except that they are discontented children, and can't be satisfied whatever they get, let a woman do what she may.

However, came the war, Hilda and Connie were rushed home again after having been home already in May, to their mother's funeral. Before Christmas of 1914 both their German young men were dead: whereupon the sisters wept, and loved the young men passionately, but underneath forgot them. They didn't exist any more.

Both sisters lived in their father's, really their mother's, Kensington house, and mixed with the young Cambridge group, the group that stood for "freedom" and flannel trousers, and flannel shirts open at the neck, and a well-bred sort of emotional anarchy, and a whispering, murmuring sort of voice, and an ultra-sensitive sort of manner. Hilda, however, suddenly married a man ten years older than herself, an elder member of the same Cambridge group, a man with a fair amount of money, and a comfortable family job in the government: he also wrote philosophical essays. She lived with him in a smallish house in Westminster, and moved in that good sort of society of people in the government who are not tip-toppers, but who are, or would be, the real intelligent power in the nation: people who know what they're talking about, or talk as if they did.

Connie did a mild form of war-work, and consorted with the flannel-trousered Cambridge intransigents, who gently mocked at everything, so far. Her "friend" was a Clifford Chatterley, a young man of twenty-two, who had hurried home from Bonn, where he was studying the technicalities of coal mining. He had previously spent two years at Cambridge. Now he had become a first lieutenant in a smart regiment, so he could mock at everything more becomingly in uniform.

Clifford Chatterley was more upper class than Connie. Connie was well-to-do intelligentsia, but he was aristocracy. Not the big sort, but still *it*. His father was a baronet, and his mother had been a viscount's daughter.

But Clifford, while he was better bred than Connie, and more "society," was in his own way more provincial and more timid. He was at his ease in the narrow "great world," that is, landed aristocracy society, but he was shy and nervous of all that other big world which consists of the vast hordes of the middle and lower classes, and foreigners. If the truth must be told, he was a little bit frightened of middle and lower class humanity, and of foreigners not of his own class. He was, in some paralyzing way, conscious of his own defenselessness, though he had all the defense of privilege. Which is curious, but a phenomenon of our day.

Therefore the peculiar soft assurance of a girl like Constance Reid fascinated him. She was so much more mistress of herself in that outer world of chaos than he was master of himself.

Nevertheless he too was a rebel: rebelling even against his class. Or perhaps rebel is too strong a word; far too strong. He was only caught in the general, popular recoil of the young against convention and against any sort of real authority. Fathers were ridiculous: his own obstinate one supremely so. And governments were ridiculous: our own wait-and-see sort especially so. And armies were ridiculous, and old buffers of generals altogether, the red-faced

Kitchener supremely. Even the war was ridiculous, though it did kill rather a lot of people.

In fact everything was a little ridiculous, or very ridiculous: certainly everything connected with authority, whether it were in the army or the government or the universities, was ridiculous to a degree. And as far as the governing class made any pretensions to govern, they were ridiculous too. Sir Geoffrey, Clifford's father, was intensely ridiculous, chopping down his trees, and weeding men out of his colliery to shove them into the war: and himself being so safe and patriotic; but, also, spending more money on his country than he'd got.

When Miss Chatterley—Emma—came down to London from the Midlands to do some nursing work, she was very witty in a quiet way about Sir Geoffrey and his determined patriotism. Herbert, the elder brother and heir, laughed outright, though it was his trees that were falling for trench props. But Clifford only smiled a little uneasily. Everything was ridiculous, quite true. But when it came too close and oneself became ridiculous too . . . ? At least people of a different class, like Connie, were earnest about something. They believed in something.

They were rather earnest about the Tommies, and the threat of conscription, and the shortage of sugar and toffee for the children. In all these things, of course, the authorities were ridiculously at fault. But Clifford could not take it to heart. To him the authorities were ridiculous *ab ovo*, not because of toffee or Tommies.

And the authorities felt ridiculous, and behaved in a rather ridiculous fashion, and it was all a mad hatter's tea party for a while. Till things developed over there, and Lloyd George came to save the situation over here. And this surpassed even ridicule, the flippant young laughed no more.

In 1916 Herbert Chatterley was killed, so Clifford became heir. He was terrified even of this. His importance as son of Sir Geoffrey and child of Wragby was so ingrained in him, he could never escape it. And yet he knew that this too, in the eyes of the vast seething world, was ridiculous. Now he was heir and responsible for Wragby. Was that not terrible? And also splendid and at the same time, perhaps, purely absurd?

Sir Geoffrey would have none of the absurdity. He was pale and tense, withdrawn into himself, and obstinately determined to save his country and his own position, let it be Lloyd George or who it might. So cut off he was, so divorced from the England that was really England, so utterly incapable, that he even thought well of Horatio Bottomley. Sir Geoffrey stood for England and Lloyd George as his forebears had stood for England and St. George: and he never knew there was a difference. So Sir Geoffrey felled timber and stood for Lloyd George and England, England and Lloyd George.

And he wanted Clifford to marry and produce an heir. Clifford felt his father was a hopeless anachronism. But wherein was he himself any further ahead, except in a wincing sense of the ridiculousness of everything, and the paramount ridiculousness of his own position? For willy-nilly he took his baronetcy and Wragby with the last seriousness.

The gay excitement had gone out of the war . . . dead. Too much death and horror. A man needed support and comfort. A man needed to have an anchor in the safe world. A man needed a wife.

The Chatterleys, two brothers and a sister, had lived curiously isolated, shut in with one another at Wragby, in spite of all their connections. A sense of isolation intensified the family tie, a sense of the weakness of their position, a sense of defenselessness, in spite of, or because of the title and the land. They were cut off from those industrial Midlands in which they passed their lives. And they were cut off from their own class by the brooding, obstinate, shut-up nature of Sir Geoffrey, their father, whom they ridiculed but whom they were so sensitive about.

The three had said they would all live together always. But now Herbert was dead, and Sir Geoffrey wanted Clifford to marry. Sir Geoffrey barely mentioned it: he spoke very little. But his silent, brooding insistence that it should be so was hard for Clifford to bear up against.

But Emma said No! She was ten years older than Clifford, and she felt his marrying would be a desertion and a betrayal of what the young ones of the family had stood for.

Clifford married Connie, nevertheless, and had his month's honeymoon with her. It was the terrible year 1917, and they were intimate as two people who stand together on a sinking ship. He had been virgin when he married: and the sex part did not mean much to him. They were so close, he and she, apart from that. And Connie exulted a little in this intimacy which was beyond sex, and beyond a man's "satisfaction." Clifford anyhow was not just keen on his "satisfaction," as so many men seemed to be. No, the intimacy was deeper, more personal than that. And sex was merely an accident, or an adjunct, one of the curious obsolete, organic processes which persisted in its own clumsiness, but was not really necessary. Though Connie did want children: if only to fortify her against her sister-in-law Emma.

But early in 1918 Clifford was shipped home smashed, and there was no child. And Sir Geoffrey died of chagrin.

❖ 2 ❖

Connie and Clifford came home to Wragby in the autumn of 1920. Miss Chatterley, still disgusted at her brother's defection, had departed and was living in a little flat in London.

Wragby was a long low old house in brown stone, begun about the middle of the eighteenth century, and added on to, till it was a warren of a place without much distinction. It stood on an eminence in a rather fine old park of oak trees, but alas, one could see in the near distance the chimney of Tevershall pit, with its clouds of stream and smoke, and on the damp, hazy distance of the hill the raw straggle of Tevershall village, a village which began almost at the park gates, and trailed in utter hopeless ugliness for a long and gruesome mile: houses, rows of wretched, small, begrimed, brick houses, with black slate roofs for lids, sharp angles and willful, blank dreariness.

Connie was accustomed to Kensington or the Scottish hills or the Sussex downs: that was her England. With the stoicism of the young she took in the utter, soulless ugliness of the coal-and-iron Midlands at a glance, and left it at what it was: unbelievable and not to be thought about. From the rather dismal rooms at Wragby she heard the rattle-rattle of the screens at the pit, the puff of the winding-engine, the clink-clink of shunting trucks, and the hoarse little whistle of the colliery locomotives. Tevershall pit-bank was burning, had been burning for years, and it would cost thousands to put it out. So it had to burn. And when the wind was that way, which was often, the house was full of the stench of this sulphurous combustion of the earth's excrement. But even on windless days the air always smelled of something under-earth: sulphur, iron, coal, or acid. And even on the Christmas roses the smuts settled persistently, incredible, like black manna from skies of doom.

Well, there it was: fated like the rest of things! It was rather awful, but why kick? You couldn't kick it away. It just went on. Life, like all the rest! On the low dark ceiling of cloud at night red blotches burned and quavered, dappling and swelling and contracting, like burns that give pain. It was the furnaces. At first they fascinated Connie with a sort of horror; she felt she was living underground. Then she got used to them. And in the morning it rained.

Clifford professed to like Wragby better than London. This country had a grim will of its own, and the people had guts. Connie wondered what else they had: certainly neither eyes nor minds. The people were as haggard, shapeless, and dreary as the countryside, and as unfriendly. Only there was something in their deep-mouthed slurring of the dialect, and the thresh-thresh of their hobnailed pit-boots as they trailed home in gangs on the asphalt from work, that was terrible and a bit mysterious.

There had been no welcome home for the young squire, no festivities, no deputation, not even a single flower. Only a dank ride in a motorcar up a dark, damp drive, burrowing through gloomy trees, out to the slope of the park where grey damp sheep were feeding, to the knoll where the house spread its dark brown façade, and the housekeeper and her husband were hovering, like unsure tenants on the face of the earth, ready to stammer a welcome.

There was no communication between Wragby Hall and Tevershall village, none. No caps were touched, no curtseys bobbed. The colliers merely stared; the tradesmen lifted their caps to Connie as to an acquaintance, and nodded awkwardly to Clifford; that was all. Gulf impassable, and a quiet sort of resentment on either side. At first Connie suffered from the steady drizzle of resentment that came from the village. Then she hardened herself to it, and it became a sort of tonic, something to live up to. It was not that she and Clifford were unpopular, they merely belonged to another species altogether from the colliers. Gulf impassable, breach indescribable, such as is perhaps nonexistent south of the Trent. But in the Midlands and the industrial North gulf impassable, across which no communication could take place. You stick to your side, I'll stick to mine! A strange denial of the common pulse of humanity.

Yet the village sympathized with Clifford and Connie in the abstract. In the flesh it was—You leave me alone!—on either side.

The rector was a nice man of about sixty, full of his duty, and reduced, personally, almost to a nonentity by the silent—You leave me alone!—of the village. The miners' wives were nearly all Methodists. The miners were nothing. But even so much official uniform as the clergyman wore was enough to obscure entirely the fact that he was a man like any other man. No, he was Mester Ashby, a sort of automatic preaching and praying concern.

This stubborn, instinctive—We think ourselves as good as you, if you *are* Lady Chatterley!—puzzled and baffled Connie at first extremely. The curious, suspicious, false amiability with which the miners' wives met her overtures; the curiously offensive tinge of—Oh dear me! I *am* somebody now, with Lady Chatterley talking to me! But she needn't think I'm not as good as her for all that!—which she always heard twanging in the women's half-fawning voices, was impossible. There was no getting past it. It was hopelessly and offensively nonconformist.

Clifford left them alone, and she learnt to do the same: she just went by without looking at them, and they stared as if she were a walking wax figure. When he had to deal with them, Clifford was rather haughty and contemptuous; one could no longer afford to be friendly. In fact he was altogether rather supercilious and contemptuous of anyone not in his own class. He stood his ground, without any attempt at conciliation. And he was neither liked nor disliked by the people; he was just part of things, like the pit-bank and Wragby itself.

But Clifford was really extremely shy and self-conscious now he was lamed. He hated seeing anyone except just the personal servants. For he had to sit in a wheeled chair or a sort of bath-chair. Nevertheless he was just as carefully dressed as ever, by his expensive tailors, and he wore the careful Bond Street neckties just as before, and from the top he looked just as smart and impressive as ever. He had never been one of the modern ladylike young men: rather bucolic even, with his ruddy face and broad shoulders. But his very quiet, hesitating voice, and his eyes, at the same time bold and frightened, assured and uncertain, revealed his nature. His manner was often offensively supercilious, and then again modest and self-effacing, almost tremulous.

Connie and he were attached to one another, in the aloof modern way. He was much too hurt in himself, the great shock of his maiming, to be easy and flippant. He was a hurt thing. And as such Connie stuck to him passionately.

But she could not help feeling how little connection he really had with people. The miners were, in a sense, his own men; but he saw them as objects rather than men, parts of the pit rather than parts of life, crude raw phenomena rather than human beings along with him. He was in some way afraid of them, he could not bear to have them look at him now he was lame. And their queer, crude life seemed as unnatural as that of hedgehogs.

He was remotely interested; but like a man looking down a microscope, or up a telescope. He was not in touch. He was not in actual touch with anybody, save, traditionally, with Wragby, and, through the close bond of family defense, with Emma. Beyond this nothing really touched him. Connie felt that she herself didn't really, not really touch him; perhaps there was nothing to get at ultimately; just a negation of human contact.

Yet he was absolutely dependent on her, he needed her every moment. Big and strong as he was, he was helpless. He could wheel himself about in a wheeled chair, and he had a sort of bath-chair with a motor attachment, in which he could puff slowly round the park. But alone he was like a lost thing. He needed Connie to be there, to assure him he existed at all.

Still he was ambitious. He had taken to writing stories; curious, very personal stories about people he had known. Clever, rather spiteful, and yet, in some mysterious way, meaningless. The observation was extraordinary and peculiar.

But there was no touch, no actual contact. It was as if the whole thing took place in a vacuum. And since the field of life is largely an artificially-lighted stage today, the stories were curiously true to modern life, to the modern psychology, that is.

Clifford was almost morbidly sensitive about these stories. He wanted everyone to think them good, of the best, *ne plus ultra*. They appeared in the most modern magazines, and were praised and blamed as usual. But to Clifford the blame was torture, like knives goading him. It was as if the whole of his being were in his stories.

Connie helped him as much as she could. At first she was thrilled. He talked everything over with her monotonously, insistently, persistently, and she had to respond with all her might. It was as if her whole soul and body and sex had to rouse up and pass into these stories of his. This thrilled her and absorbed her.

Of physical life they lived very little. She had to superintend the house. But the housekeeper had served Sir Geoffrey for many years, and the dried-up, elderly, superlatively correct female . . . you could hardly call her a parlormaid, or even a woman . . . who waited at table, had been in the house for forty years. Even the very housemaids were no longer young. It was awful! What could you do with such a place, but leave it alone! All these endless rooms that nobody used, all the Midlands routine, the mechanical cleanliness and the mechanical order! Clifford had insisted on a new cook, an experienced woman who had served him in his rooms in London. For the rest the place seemed run by mechanical anarchy. Everything went on in pretty good order, strict cleanliness, and strict punctuality; even pretty strict honesty. And yet, to Connie, it was a methodical anarchy. No warmth of feeling united it organically. The house seemed as dreary as a disused street.

What could she do but leave it alone . . . ? So she left it alone. Miss Chatterley came sometimes, with her aristocratic thin face, and triumphed, finding nothing altered. She would never forgive Connie for ousting her from her union in consciousness with her brother. It was she, Emma, who should be bringing forth the stories, these books, with him; the Chatterley stories, something new in the world, that *they*, the Chatterleys, had put there. There was no other standard. There was no organic connection with the thought and expression that had gone before. Only something new in the world: the Chatterley books, entirely personal.

Connie's father, when he paid a flying visit to Wragby, said in private to his daughter: As for Clifford's writing, it's smart, but there's nothing in it. It won't last! . . . Connie looked at the burly Scottish knight who had done himself well all his life, and her eyes, her big, still-wondering blue eyes became vague.

Nothing in it! What did he mean by *nothing in it?* If the critics praised it, and Clifford's name was almost famous, and it even brought in money . . . what did her father mean by saying there was nothing in Clifford's writing? What else could there be?

For Connie had adopted the standard of the young: what there was in the moment was everything. And moments followed one another without necessarily belonging to one another.

It was in her second winter at Wragby her father said to her: "I hope, Connie, you won't let circumstances force you into being a *demi-vierge.*"

"A *demi-vierge*!" replied Connie vaguely. "Why? Why not?"

"Unless you like it, of course!" said her father hastily. To Clifford he said the same, when the two men were alone: "I'm afraid it doesn't quite suit Connie to be a *demi-vierge.*"

"A half-virgin!" replied Clifford, translating the phrase to be sure of it.

He thought for a moment, then flushed very red. He was angry and offended.

"In what way doesn't it suit her?" he asked stiffly.

"She's getting thin . . . angular. It's not her style. She's not the pilchard sort of little slip of a girl, she's a bonny Scotch trout."

"Without the spots, of course!" said Clifford.

He wanted to say something later to Connie about the demi-vierge business . . . the half-virgin state of her affairs. But he could not bring himself to do it. He was at once too intimate with her and not intimate enough. He was so very much at one with her, in his mind and hers, but bodily they were nonexistent to one another, and neither could bear to drag in the corpus delicti. They were so intimate, and utterly out of touch.

Connie guessed, however, that her father had said something, and that something was in Clifford's mind. She knew that he didn't mind whether she were demi-vierge or demi-monde, so long as he didn't absolutely know, and wasn't made to see. What the eye doesn't see and the mind doesn't know, doesn't exist.

Connie and Clifford had now been nearly two years at Wragby, living their vague life of absorption in Clifford and his work. Their interests had never ceased to flow together over his work. They talked and wrestled in the throes of composition, and felt as if something were happening, really happening, really in the void.

And thus far it was a life: in the void. For the rest it was nonexistence. Wragby was there, the servants . . . but spectral, not really existing. Connie went for walks in the park, and in the woods that joined the park, and enjoyed the solitude and the mystery, kicked the brown leaves of autumn, and picked the primroses of spring. But it was all a dream; or rather it was like the simulacrum of reality. The oak leaves were to her like oak-leaves seen ruffling in a mirror, she herself was a figure somebody had read about, picking primroses that were only shadows or memories, or words. No substance to her or anything . . . no touch, no contact! Only this life with Clifford, this endless spinning of webs of yarn, of the minutiae of consciousness, these stories Sir Malcolm said there was nothing in, and they wouldn't last. Why should there be anything in them, why should they last? Sufficient unto the day is the evil thereof. Sufficient unto the moment is the *appearance* of reality.

Clifford had quite a number of friends, acquaintances really, and he invited them to Wragby. He invited all sorts of people, critics and writers, people who would help to praise his books. And they were flattered at being asked to Wragby, and they praised. Connie understood it all perfectly. But why not? This was one of the fleeting patterns in the mirror. What was wrong with it?

She was hostess to these people . . . mostly men. She was hostess also to Clifford's occasional aristocratic relations. Being a soft, ruddy, country-looking girl, inclined to freckles, with big blue eyes, and curling, brown hair, and a soft voice and rather strong, female loins she was considered a little old-fashioned and "womanly." She was not a "little pilchard sort of fish," like a boy. She was too feminine to be quite smart.

So the men, especially those no longer young, were very nice to her indeed. But, knowing what torture poor Clifford would feel at the slightest sign of flirting on her part, she gave them no encouragement at all. She was quiet and vague, she had no contact with them and intended to have none. Clifford was extraordinarily proud of himself.

His relatives treated her quite kindly. She knew that the kindliness indicated a lack of fear, and that these people had no respect for you unless you could frighten them a little. But again she had no contact. She let them be kindly and disdainful, she let them feel they had no need to draw their steel in readiness. She had no real connection with them.

Time went on. Whatever happened, nothing happened, because she was so beautifully out of contact. She and Clifford lived in their ideas and his books. She entertained . . . there were always people in the house. Time went on as the clock does, half-past eight instead of half-past seven.

❖ 3 ❖

Connie was aware, however, of a growing restlessness. Out of her disconnection, a restlessness was taking possession of her like madness. It twitched her limbs when she didn't want to twitch them, it jerked her spine when she didn't want to jerk upright but preferred to rest comfortably. It thrilled inside her body, in her womb, somewhere, till she felt she must jump into water and swim to get away from it; a mad restlessness. It made her heart beat violently for no reason. And she was getting thinner.

It was just restlessness. She would rush off across the park, and abandon Clifford, and lie prone in the bracken. To get away from the house . . . she must get away from the house and everybody. The wood was her one refuge, her sanctuary.

But it was not really a refuge, a sanctuary, because she had no connection with it. It was only a place where she could get away from the rest. She never really touched the spirit of the wood itself . . . if it had any such nonsensical thing.

Vaguely she knew herself that she was going to pieces in some way. Vaguely she knew she was out of connection: she had lost touch with the substantial and vital world. Only Clifford and his books, which did not exist . . . which had nothing in them! Void to void. Vaguely she knew. But it was like beating her head against a stone.

Her father warned her again: "Why don't you get yourself a beau, Connie? Do you all the good in the world."

That winter Michaelis came for a few days. He was a young Irishman who had already made a large fortune by his plays in America. He had been taken up quite enthusiastically for a time by smart society in London, for he wrote smart society plays. Then gradually smart society realized that it had been made ridiculous at the hands of a down-at-heel Dublin street rat, and revulsion came. Michaelis was the last word in what was caddish and bounderish. He was discovered to be anti-English, and to the class that made this discovery this was worse than the dirtiest crime. He was cut dead, and his corpse thrown into the refuse-can.

Nevertheless Michaelis had his apartment in Mayfair, and walked down Bond

Street the image of a gentleman, for you cannot get even the best tailors to cut their lowdown customers, when the customers pay.

Clifford was inviting the young man of thirty at an inauspicious moment in that young man's career. Yet Clifford did not hesitate. Michaelis had the ear of a few million people, probably; and, being a hopeless outsider, he would no doubt be grateful to be asked down to Wragby at this juncture, when the rest of the smart world was cutting him. Being grateful, he would no doubt do Clifford "good" over there in America. Kudos! A man gets a lot of kudos, whatever that may be, by being talked about in the right way, especially "over there." Clifford was a coming man; and it was remarkable what a sound publicity instinct he had. In the end Michaelis did him most nobly in a play, and Clifford was a sort of popular hero. Till the reaction, when he found he had been made ridiculous.

Connie wondered a little over Clifford's blind, imperious instinct to become known: known, that is, to the vast amorphous world he did not himself know, and of which he was uneasily afraid; known as a writer, as a first-class modern writer. Connie was aware from successful, old, hearty, bluffing Sir Malcolm, that artists did advertise themselves, and exert themselves to put their goods over. But her father used channels ready-made, used by all the other R.A.'s who sold their pictures. Whereas Clifford discovered new channels of publicity, all kinds. He had all kinds of people at Wragby, without exactly lowering himself. But, determined to build himself a monument of a reputation quickly, he used any handy rubble in the making.

Michaelis arrived duly, in a very neat car, with a chauffeur and a manservant. He was absolutely Bond Street! But at sight of him something in Clifford's country soul recoiled. He wan't exactly . . . not exactly . . . in fact, he wasn't at all, well, what his appearance intended to imply. To Clifford this was final and enough. Yet he was very polite to the man; to the amazing success in him. The bitch-goddess, as she is called, of Success, roamed, snarling and protective, round the half-humble, half-defiant Michaelis' heels, and intimidated Clifford completely: for he wanted to prostitute himself to the bitch-goddess Success also, if only she would have him.

Michaelis obviously wasn't an Englishman, in spite of all the tailors, hatters, barbers, booters of the very best quarter of London. No, no, he obviously wasn't an Englishman: the wrong sort of flattish, pale face and bearing; and the wrong sort of grievance. He had a grudge and a grievance: that was obvious to any trueborn English gentleman, who would scorn to let such a thing appear blatant in his own demeanor. Poor Michaelis had been much kicked, so that he had a slightly tail-between-the-legs look even now. He had pushed his way by sheer instinct and sheerer effrontery onto the stage and to the front of it, with his plays. He had caught the public. And he had thought the kicking days were over. Alas, they weren't. . . . They never would be. For he, in a sense, asked to be kicked. He pined to be where he didn't belong . . . among the English upper classes. And how they enjoyed the various kicks they got at him! And how he hated them!

Nevertheless he traveled with his manservant and his very neat car, this Dublin mongrel.

There was something about him that Connie liked. He didn't put on airs to himself; he had no illusions about himself. He talked to Clifford sensibly, briefly, practically about all the things Clifford wanted to know. He didn't expand or let himself go. He knew he had been asked down to Wragby to be made use of, and like an old, shrewd, almost indifferent businessman, or big-businessman, he let himself be asked questions, and he answered with as little waste of feeling as possible.

"Money!" he said. "Money is a sort of instinct. It's a sort of property of nature in a man to make money. It's nothing you do. It's no trick you play. It's a sort of permanent accident of your own nature; once you start, you make money, and you go on; up to a point, I suppose."

"But you've got to begin," said Clifford.

"Oh, quite! You've got to get in. You can do nothing if you are kept outside. You've got to beat your way in. Once you've done that, you can't help it!"

"But could you have made money except by plays?" asked Clifford.

"Oh, probably not! I may be a good writer or I may be a bad one, but a writer and a writer of plays is what I am, and I've got to be. There's no question of that."

"And you think it's a writer of popular plays that you've got to be?" asked Connie.

"There, exactly!" he said, turning to her in a sudden flash. "There's nothing in it! There's nothing in popularity. There's nothing in the public, if it comes to that. There's nothing really in my plays to *make* them popular. It's not that. They just are, like the weather . . . the sort that will *have* to be . . . for the time being."

He turned his slow, rather full eyes, that had been drowned in such fathomless disillusion, on Connie, and she trembled a little. He seemed so old . . . endlessly old, built up of layers of disillusion, going down in him generation after generation, like geological strata; and at the same time he was forlorn like a child. An outcast, in a certain sense; but with the desperate bravery of his rat-like existence.

"At least it's wonderful what you've done at your time of life," said Clifford contemplatively.

"I'm thirty . . . yes, I'm thirty!" said Michaelis, sharply and suddenly, with a curious laugh; hollow, triumphant, and bitter.

"And are you alone?" asked Connie.

"How do you mean? Do I live alone? I've got my servant. He's a Greek, so he says, and quite incompetent. But I keep him. And I'm going to marry. Oh, yes, I must marry."

"It sounds like going to have your tonsils cut," laughed Connie. "Will it be an effort?"

He looked at her admiringly. "Well, Lady Chatterley, somehow it will! I find . . . excuse me . . . I find I can't marry an Englishwoman, not even an Irishwoman. . . ."

"Try an American," said Clifford.

"Oh, American!" he laughed a hollow laugh. "No, I've asked my man if he will find me a Turk or something . . . something nearer to the Oriental."

Connie really wondered at this queer, melancholy specimen of extraordinary success; it was said he had an income of fifty thousand dollars from America alone. Sometimes he was handsome: sometimes as he looked sideways, downwards, and the light fell on him, he had the silent, enduring beauty of a carved ivory negro mask, with his rather full eyes, and the strong queerly-arched brows, the immobile compressed mouth; that momentary but revealed immobility, an immobility, a timelessness which the Buddha aims at, and which negroes express sometimes without even aiming at it; something old, old, and acquiescent in the race! Aeons of acquiescence in race destiny, instead of our individual resistance. And then a swimming through, like rats in a dark river. Connie felt a sudden, strange leap of sympathy for him, a leap mingled with compassion, and tinged with repulsion, amounting almost to love. The outsider! The outsider! And they called him a bounder! How much more bounderish and assertive Clifford looked! How much stupider!

Michaelis knew at once he had made an impression on her. He turned his full, hazel, slightly prominent eyes on her in a look of pure detachment. He was estimating her, and the extent of the impression he had made. With the English nothing could save him from being the eternal outsider, not even love. Yet women sometimes fell for him. . . . Englishwomen too.

He knew just where he was with Clifford. They were two alien dogs which would have liked to snarl at one another, but which smiled instead, perforce. But with the woman he was not quite so sure.

Breakfast was served in the bedrooms; Clifford never appeared before lunch, and the dining room was a little dreary. After coffee Michaelis, restless and illsitting soul, wondered what he should do. It was a fine November day . . . fine for Wragby. He looked over the melancholy park. My God! What a place!

He sent a servant to ask, could he be of any service to Lady Chatterley: he thought of driving into Sheffield. The answer came, would he care to go up to Lady Chatterley's sitting room?

Connie had a sitting room on the third floor, the top floor of the central portion of the house. Clifford's rooms were on the ground floor, of course. Michaelis was flattered by being asked up to Lady Chatterley's own parlor. He followed blindly after the servant . . . he never noticed things, or had contact with his surroundings. In her room he did glance vaguely round at the fine German reproductions of Renoir and Cézanne.

"It's very pleasant up here," he said, with his queer smile, as if it hurt him to smile, showing his teeth. "You are wise to get up to the top."

"Yes, I think so," she said.

Her room was the only gay, modern one in the house, the only spot in Wragby where her personality was at all revealed. Clifford had never seen it, and she asked very few people up.

Now she and Michaelis sat on opposite sides of the fire and talked. She asked him about himself, his mother and father, his brothers . . . other people were always something of a wonder to her, and when her sympathy was awakened she was quite devoid of class feeling. Michaelis talked frankly about himself, quite frankly, without affectation, simply revealing his bitter, indifferent, stray dog's soul, then showing a gleam of revengeful pride in his success.

"But why are you such a lonely bird?" Connie asked him; and again he looked at her, with his full, searching, hazel look.

"Some birds *are* that way," he replied. Then, with a touch of familiar irony: "But, look here, what about yourself? Aren't you by way of being a lonely bird yourself?" Connie, a little startled, thought about it for a few moments, and then she said: "Only in a way! Not altogether, like you!"

"Am I altogether a lonely bird?" he asked, with his queer grin of a smile, as if he had toothache; it was so wry, and his eyes were so perfectly unchangingly melancholy, or stoical, or disillusioned, or afraid.

"Why?" she said, a little breathless, as she looked at him. "You are, aren't you?"

She felt a terrible appeal coming to her from him, that made her almost lose her balance.

"Oh, you're quite right!" he said, turning his head away, and looking sideways, downwards, with that strange immobility of an old race that is hardly here in our present day. It was that that really made Connie lose her power to see him detached from herself.

He looked up at her with the full glance that saw everything, registered everything. At the same time, the infant crying in the night was crying out of his breast to her, in a way that affected her very womb.

"It's awfully nice of you to think of me," he said laconically.

"Why shouldn't I think of you?" she exclaimed, with hardly breath to utter it.

He gave the wry, quick hiss of a laugh.

"Oh, in that way! . . . May I hold your hand for a minute?" he asked suddenly, fixing his eyes on her with almost hypnotic power, and sending out an appeal that affected her direct in the womb.

She stared at him, dazed and transfixed, and he went over and kneeled beside her, and took her two feet close in his two hands, and buried his face in her lap, remaining motionless. She was perfectly dim and dazed, looking down in a sort of amazement at the rather tender nape of his neck, feeling his face pressing against her. In all her burning dismay, she could not help putting her hand, with tenderness and compassion, on the defenseless nape of his neck, and he trembled, with a deep shudder.

Then he looked up at her with that awful appeal in his full, glowing eyes. She was utterly incapable of resisting it. From her breast flowed the answering, immense yearning over him; she must give him anything, anything.

He was a curious and very gentle lover, very gentle with the woman, trembling uncontrollably, and yet at the same time detached, aware, aware of every sound outside.

To her it meant nothing except that she gave herself to him. And at length he ceased to quiver anymore, and lay quite still, quite still. Then, with dim, compassionate fingers, she stroked his head, that lay on her breast.

When he rose, he kissed both her hands, then both her feet, in their suede slippers, and in silence went away to the end of the room, where he stood with his back to her. There was silence for some minutes. Then he turned and came to her again as she sat in her old place by the fire.

"And now, I suppose you'll hate me!" he said in a quiet, inevitable way. She looked up at him quickly.

"Why should I?" she asked.

"They mostly do," he said; then he caught himself up. "I mean . . . a woman is supposed to."

"This is the last moment when I ought to hate you," she said resentfully.

"I know! I know! It should be so! You're *frightfully* good to me . . ." he cried miserably.

She wondered why he should be miserable. "Won't you sit down again?" she said. He glanced at the door.

"Sir Clifford!" he said, "won't he . . . won't he be . . . ?"

She paused a moment to consider. "Perhaps!" she said. And she looked up at him. "I don't want Clifford to know . . . not even to suspect. It would hurt him so much. But I don't think it's wrong, do you?"

"Wrong! Good God, no! You're only too infinitely good to me. . . . I can hardly bear it."

He turned aside, and she saw that in another moment he would be sobbing.

"But we needn't let Clifford know, need we?" she pleaded. "It *would* hurt him so. And if he never knows, never suspects, it hurts nobody."

"Me!" he said, almost fiercely; "he'll know nothing from me! You see if he does. Me give myself away! Ha! Ha!" he laughed hollowly, cynically at such an idea. She watched him in wonder. He said to her: "May I kiss your hand and go? I'll run into Sheffield I think, and lunch there, if I may, and be back to tea. May I do anything for you? May I be sure you don't hate me—and that you won't?"—he ended with a desperate note of cynicism.

"No, I don't hate you," she said. "I think you're nice."

"Ah!" he said to her fiercely, "I'd rather you said that to me than that you love me! It means such a lot more. . . . Till afternoon then. I've plenty to think about till then." He kissed her hands humbly and was gone.

"I don't think I can stand that young man," said Clifford at lunch.

"Why?" asked Connie.

"He's such a bounder underneath his veneer . . . just waiting to bounce us."

"I think people have been so unkind to him," said Connie.

"Do you wonder? And do you think he employs his shining hours doing deeds of kindness?"

"I think he has a certain sort of generosity."

"Towards whom?"

"I don't quite know."

"Naturally you don't. I'm afraid you mistake unscrupulousness for generosity."

Connie paused. Did she? It was just possible. Yet the unscrupulousness of Michaelis had a certain fascination for her. He went whole lengths where Clifford only crept a few timid paces. In his way he had conquered the world, which was what Clifford wanted to do. Ways and means . . . ? Were those of Michaelis more despicable than those of Clifford? Was the way the poor outsider had shoved and bounced himself forward in person, and by the back doors, any worse than Clifford's way of advertising himself into prominence? The bitch-goddess, Success, was trailed by thousands of gasping dogs with lolling tongues. The one that got her first was the real dog among dogs, if you go by success! So Michaelis could keep his tail up.

The queer thing was, he didn't. He came back towards teatime with a large handful of violets and lilies, and the same hangdog expression. Connie wondered sometimes if it were a sort of mask to disarm opposition, because it was almost too fixed. Was he really such a sad dog?

His sad dog sort of extinguished self persisted all the evening, though through it Clifford felt the inner effrontery. Connie didn't feel it, perhaps because it was not directed against woman; only against men, and their presumptions and assumptions. That indestructible, inward effrontery in the meager fellow was what made men so down on Michaelis. His very presence was an affront to a man of society, cloak it as he might in an assumed good manner.

Connie was in love with him, but she managed to sit with her embroidery and let the men talk, and not give herself away. As for Michaelis, he was perfect; exactly the same melancholic, attentive, aloof young fellow of the previous evening, millions of degrees remote from his hosts, but laconically playing up to them to the required amount, and never coming forth to them for a moment. Connie felt he must have forgotten the morning. He had not forgotten. But he knew where he was . . . in the same old place outside, where the born outsiders are. He didn't take the lovemaking altogether personally. He knew it would not change him from an ownerless dog, whom everybody begrudges its golden collar, into a comfortable society dog.

The final fact being that at the very bottom of his soul he *was* an outsider, and antisocial, and he accepted the fact inwardly, no matter how Bond-Streety he was on the outside. His isolation was a necessity to him; just as the appearance of conformity and mixing-in with the smart people was also a necessity.

But occasional love, as a comfort and soothing, was also a good thing, and he was not ungrateful. On the contrary, he was burningly, poignantly grateful for a piece of natural, spontaneous kindness: almost to tears. Beneath his pale, immobile, disillusioned face, his child's soul was sobbing with gratitude to the woman, and burning to come to her again; just as his outcast soul was knowing he would keep really clear of her.

He found an opportunity to say to her, as they were lighting the candles in the hall:

"May I come?"

"I'll come to you," she said.

"Oh, good!"

He waited for her a long time . . . but she came.

He was the trembling excited sort of lover, whose crisis soon came, and was finished. There was something curiously childlike and defenseless about him. His defenses were all in his wits and cunning, his very instincts of cunning, and when these were in abeyance he seemed doubly naked and like a child, of unfinished, tender flesh, and somehow struggling helplessly.

He aroused in the woman a wild sort of compassion and yearning, and a wild, craving physical desire. The physical desire he did not satisfy in her; he was always come and finished so quickly, then shrinking down on her breast, and recovering somewhat his effrontery while she lay dazed, disappointed, lost.

But then she soon learnt to hold him, to keep him there inside her when his crisis was over. And there he was generous and curiously potent; he stayed firm inside her, given to her, while she was active . . . wildly, passionately active, coming to her own crisis. And as he felt the frenzy of her achieving her own orgasmic satisfaction from his hard, erect passivity, he had a curious sense of pride and satisfaction.

"Ah, how good!" she whispered tremulously, and she became quite still, clinging to him. And he lay there in his own isolation, but somehow proud.

He stayed that time only the three days, and to Clifford was exactly the same as on the first evening; to Connie also. There was no breaking down his external man.

He wrote to Connie with the same plaintive melancholy note as ever, sometimes witty, and touched with a queer, sexless affection. A kind of hopeless affection he seemed to feel for her, and the essential remoteness remained the same. He was hopeless at the very core of him, and he wanted to be hopeless. He rather hated hope. "*Une immense espérance an traversé la terre*," he read somewhere, and his comment was: "—and it's darned-well drowned everything worth having."

Connie never really understood him, but in her way, she loved him. And all the time she felt the reflection of his hopelessness in her. She couldn't quite, quite love in hopelessness. And he, being hopeless, couldn't ever quite love at all.

So they went on for quite a time, writing, and meeting occasionally in London. She still wanted the physical, sexual thrill she could get with him by her own activity, his little orgasm being over. And he still wanted to give it her. Which was enough to keep them connected.

And enough to give her a subtle sort of self-assurance, something blind and a little arrogant. It was an almost mechanical confidence in her own powers, and went with a great cheerfulness.

She was terrifically cheerful at Wragby. And she used all her aroused cheerfulness and satisfaction to stimulate Clifford, so that he wrote his best at this time, and was almost happy in his strange blind way. He really reaped the fruits of the sensual satisfaction she got out of Michaelis' male passivity erect inside her. But of course he never knew it, and, if he had, he wouldn't have said thank you!

Yet when those days of her grand joyful cheerfulness and stimulus were gone, quite gone, and she was depressed and irritable, how Clifford longed for them again! Perhaps if he'd known he might even have wished to get her and Michaelis together again.

4

Connie always had a foreboding of the hopelessness of her affair with Mick, as people called him. Yet other men seemed to mean nothing to her. She was attached to Clifford. He wanted a good deal of her life and she gave it to him. But she wanted a good deal from the life of a man, and this Clifford did not give her, could not. There were occasional spasms of Michaelis. But, as she knew by foreboding, that would come to an end. Mick *couldn't* keep anything up. It was part of his very being that he must break off any connection, and be loose, isolated, absolutely lone dog again. It was his major necessity, even though he always said: She turned me down!

The world is supposed to be full of possibilities, but they narrow down to pretty few in most personal experience. There's lots of good fish in the sea . . . maybe . . . but the vast masses seem to be mackerel or herring, and if you're not mackerel or herring yourself, you are likely to find very few good fish in the sea.

Clifford was making strides into fame, and even money. People came to see him. Connie nearly always had somebody at Wragby. But if they weren't mackerel they were herring, with an occasional catfish, or conger eel.

There were a few regular men, constants; men who had been at Cambridge with Clifford. There was Tommy Dukes, who had remained in the army, and was a Brigadier General. "The army leaves me time to think, and saves me from having to face the battle of life," he said.

There was Charles May, an Irishman, who wrote scientifically about stars. There was Hammond, another writer. All were about the same age as Clifford; the young intellectuals of the day. They all believed in the life of the mind. What you did apart from that was your private affair, and didn't much matter. No one thinks of inquiring of another person at what hour he retires to the privy. It isn't interesting to anyone but the person concerned.

And so with most of the matters of ordinary life . . . how you make your money, or whether you love your wife, or if you have "affairs." All these matters concern only the person concerned, and, like going to the privy, have no interest for anyone else.

"The whole point about the sexual problem," said Hammond, who was a tall thin fellow with a wife and two children, but much more closely connected with a typewriter, "is that there is no point to it. Strictly there is no problem. We don't want to follow a man into the W.C., so why should we want to follow him into bed with a woman? And therein lies the problem. If we took no more notice of the one thing than the other, there'd be no problem. It's all utterly senseless and pointless; a matter of misplaced curiosity."

"Quite, Hammond, quite! But if someone starts making love to Julia, you begin to simmer; and if he goes on, you are soon at boiling point." . . . Julia was Hammond's wife.

"Why, exactly! So I should be if he began to urinate in a corner of my drawing room. There's a place for all these things."

"You mean you wouldn't mind if he made love to Julia in some discreet alcove?"

Charlie May was slightly satirical, for he had flirted a very little with Julia, and Hammond had cut up very roughly.

"Of course I should mind. Sex is a private thing between me and Julia; and of course I should mind anyone else trying to mix in."

"As a matter of fact," said the lean and freckled Tommy Dukes, who looked much more Irish than May, who was pale and rather fat: "as a matter of fact, Hammond, you have a strong property instinct, and a strong will to self-assertion, and you want success. Since I've been in the army definitely, I've got out of the way of the world, and now I see how inordinately strong the craving for self-assertion and success is in men. It is enormously overdeveloped. All our individuality has run that way. And of course men like you think you'll get through better with a woman's backing. That's why you're so jealous. That's what sex is to you . . . a vital little dynamo between you and Julia to bring success. If you began to be unsuccessful you'd begin to flirt, like Charlie, who isn't successful. Married people like you and Julia have labels on you, like travelers' trunks. Julia is labeled *Mrs. Arnold B. Hammond* . . . just like a trunk on the railway that belongs to somebody. And you are labeled Arnold B. Hammond, *c/o Mrs. Arnold B. Hammond.* Oh, you're quite right, you're quite right! The life of the mind needs a comfortable house and decent cooking. You're quite right. It even needs posterity. But it all hinges on the instinct for success. That is the pivot on which all things turn."

Hammond looked rather piqued. He was rather proud of the integrity of his mind, and of his *not* being a timeserver. None the less, he did want success.

"It's quite true, you can't live without cash," said May. "You've got to have a certain amount of it to be able to live and get along . . . even to be free to *think* you must have a certain amount of money, or your stomach stops you. But it seems to me you might leave the labels off sex. We're free to talk to anybody; so why shouldn't we be free to make love to any woman who inclines us that way?"

"There speaks the lascivious Celt," said Clifford.

"Lascivious! Well, why not? I can't see I do a woman any more harm by sleeping with her than by dancing with her . . . or even talking to her about the weather. It's just an interchange of sensations instead of ideas, so why not?"

"Be as promiscuous as the rabbits!" said Hammond.

"Why not? What's wrong with rabbits? Are they any worse than a neurotic, revolutionary humanity, full of nervous hate?"

"But we're not rabbits, even so," said Hammond.

"Precisely! I have my mind: I have certain calculations to make in certain astronomical matters that concern me almost more than life or death. Sometimes indigestion interferes with me. Hunger would interfere with me disastrously. In the same way starved sex interferes with me. What then?"

"I should have thought sexual indigestion from surfeit would have interfered with you more seriously," said Hammond satirically.

"Not it! I don't overeat myself, and I don't overfuck myself. One has a choice about eating too much. But you would absolutely starve me."

"Not at all. You can marry."

"How do you know I can? It may not suit the process of my mind. Marriage might . . . and would . . . stultify my mental processes. I'm not properly pivoted that way . . . and so must I be chained in a kennel like a monk? All rot and funk, my boy. I must live and do my calculations. I need women sometimes. I refuse to make a mountain of it, and I refuse anybody's moral condemnation or prohibition. I'd be ashamed to see a woman walking around with my name-label on her, address and railway station, like a wardrobe trunk."

These two men had not forgiven each other about the Julia flirtation.

"It's an amusing idea, Charlie," said Dukes, "that sex is just another form of talk, where you act the words instead of saying them. I suppose it's quite true. I suppose we might exchange as many sensations and emotions with women as we do ideas about the weather, and so on. Sex might be a sort of normal, physical conversation between a man and a woman. You don't talk to a woman unless you have ideas in common: that is you don't talk with any interest. And in the same way, unless you had some emotion or sympathy in common with a woman you wouldn't sleep with her. But if you had. . . ."

"If you *have* the proper sort of emotion or sympathy with a woman, you *ought* to sleep with her," said May. "It's the only decent thing to do with her. Just as, when you are interested talking to someone, the only decent thing is to have the talk out. You don't prudishly put your tongue between your teeth and bite it. You just say out your say. And the same the other way."

"No," said Hammond. "It's wrong. You, for example, May, you squander half your force with women. You'll never really do what you should do, with a fine mind such as yours. Too much of you goes the other way."

"Maybe it does. . . . and too little of you goes that way, Hammond, my boy, married or not. You can keep the purity and integrity of your mind, but it's going damned dry. Your pure mind is going as dry as fiddlesticks, from what I see of it. You're simply talking it down."

Tommy Dukes burst into a laugh.

"Go it, you two minds!" he said. "Look at me . . . I don't do any high and pure mental work, nothing but jot down a few ideas. And yet I neither marry nor run after women. I think Charlie's quite right; if he wants to run after the women, he's quite free not to run too often. But I wouldn't prohibit him from running. As for Hammond, he's got a property instinct, so naturally the straight road and the narrow gate are right for him. You'll see he'll be an English Man of Letters before he's done, A. B. C. from top to toe. Then there's me. I'm nothing. Just a squib. And what about you, Clifford? Do you think sex is a dynamo to help a man on to success in the world?"

Clifford rarely talked much at these times. He never held forth; his ideas were really not vital enough for it, he was too confused and emotional. Now he blushed and looked uncomfortable.

"Well!" he said, "being myself *hors de combat*, I don't see I've anything to say on the matter."

"Not at all," said Dukes; "the top of you's by no means *hors de combat*. You've got the life of the mind sound and intact. So let us hear your ideas."

"Well," stammered Clifford, "even then I don't suppose I have much idea. . . . I suppose marry-and-have-done-with-it would pretty well stand for what I think. Though of course between a man and woman who care for one another, it is a great thing."

"What sort of great thing?" said Tommy.

"Oh, . . . it perfects the intimacy," said Clifford, uneasy as a woman in such talk.

"Well, Charlie and I believe that sex is a sort of communication like speech. Let any woman start a sex conversation with me, and it's natural for me to go to bed with her to finish it, all in due season. Unfortunately no woman makes any particular start with me, so I go to bed by myself; and am none the worse for it. . . . I hope so anyway, for how should I know? Anyhow I've no starry calculations to be interfered with, and no immortal works to write. I'm merely a fellow skulking in the army. . . ."

Silence fell. The four men smoked. And Connie sat there and put another stitch in her sewing. . . . Yes, she sat there! She had to sit mum. She had to be quiet as a mouse, not to interfere with the immensely important speculations of these highly-mental gentlemen. But she had to be there. They didn't get on so well without her; their ideas didn't flow so freely. Clifford was much more edgy and nervous, he got cold feet much quicker in Connie's absence, and the talk didn't run. Tommy Dukes came off best; he was a little inspired by her presence. Hammond she didn't really like; he seemed so selfish in a mental way. And Charles May, though she liked something about him, seemed a little distasteful and messy, in spite of his stars.

How many evenings had Connie sat and listened to the manifestations of these four men! these, and one or two others. That they never seemed to get anywhere didn't trouble her deeply. She liked to hear what they had to say, especially when Tommy was there. It was fun. Instead of men kissing you, and touching you, they revealed their minds to you. It was great fun! But what cold minds!

And also it was a little irritating. She had more respect for Michaelis, on whose name they all poured such withering contempt, as a little mongrel arriviste, and uneducated bounder of the worst sort. Mongrel and bounder or not, he jumped to his own conclusions. He didn't merely walk round them with millions of words, in the parade of the life of the mind.

Connie quite liked the life of the mind, and got a great thrill out of it. But she did think it overdid itself a little. She loved being there, amidst the tobacco smoke of those famous evenings of the cronies, as she called them privately to herself. She was infinitely amused, and proud too, that even their talking they could not do without her silent presence. She had an immense respect for thought . . . and these men, at least, tried to think honestly. But somehow there was a cat, and it wouldn't jump. They all alike talked at something, though what it was, for the life of her she couldn't say. It was something that Mick didn't clear, either.

But then Mick wasn't trying to do anything, but just get through his life, and put as much across other people as they tried to put across him. He was really antisocial, which was what Clifford and his cronies had against him. Clifford and his cronies were not antisocial; they were more or less bent on saving mankind, or on instructing it, to say the least.

There was a gorgeous talk on Sunday evening, when the conversation drifted again to love.

> Blest be the tie that binds
> Our hearts in kindred something-or-other—

said Tommy Dukes. "I'd like to know what the tie is. . . . The tie that binds *us* just now is mental friction on one another. And, apart from that, there's damned little tie between us. We bust apart, and say spiteful things about one another, like all the other damned intellectuals in the world. Damned everybodies, as far as that goes, for they all do it. Else we bust apart, and cover up the spiteful things we feel against one another by saying false sugaries. It's a curious thing that the mental life seems to flourish with its roots in spite, ineffable and fathomless spite. Always has been so! Look at Socrates, in Plato, and his bunch round him! The sheer spite of it all, just sheer joy in pulling somebody else to bits. . . . Protagoras, or whoever it was! And Alcibiades, and all the other little disciple dogs joining in the fray! I must say it makes one prefer Buddha, quietly sitting under a bo tree, or Jesus, telling his disciples little Sunday stories, peacefully, and without any mental fireworks. No, there's something wrong with the mental life, radically. It's rooted in spite and envy, envy and spite. Ye shall know the tree by its fruit."

"I don't think we're altogether so spiteful," protested Clifford.

"My dear Clifford, think of the way we talk each other over, all of us. I'm rather worse than anybody else, myself. Because I infinitely prefer the spontaneous spite to the concocted sugaries; now they *are* poison; when I begin saying what a fine fellow Clifford is, etc., etc., then poor Clifford is to be pitied. For God's sake, all of you, say spiteful things about me, then I shall know I mean something to you. Don't say sugaries, or I'm done."

"Oh, but I do think we honestly like one another," said Hammond.

"I tell you we must . . . we say such spiteful things to one another, about one another, behind our backs! I'm the worst."

"And I do think you confuse the mental life with the critical activity. I agree with you, Socrates gave the critical activity a grand start, but he did more than that," said Charlie May, rather magisterially. The cronies had such a curious pomposity under their assumed modesty. It was all so *ex cathedra*, and it all pretended to be so humble.

Dukes refused to be drawn out about Socrates.

"That's quite true, criticism and knowledge are not the same thing," said Hammond.

"They aren't, of course," chimed in Berry, a brown, shy young man, who had called to see Dukes, and was staying the night.

They all looked at him as if the ass had spoken.

"I wasn't talking about knowledge. . . . I was talking about the mental life," laughed Dukes. "Real knowledge comes out of the whole corpus of the consciousness; out of your belly and your penis as much as out of your brain and mind. The mind can only analyze and rationalize. Set the mind and the reason to cock it over the rest, and all they can do is criticize, and make a deadness. I say *all* they can do. It is vastly important. My God, the world needs criticizing to death.

Therefore let's live the mental life, and glory in our spite, and strip the rotten old show. But, mind you, it's like this; while you *live* your life, you are in some way an organic whole with all life. But once you start the mental life you pluck the apple. You've severed the connection between the apple and the tree: the organic connection. And if you've got nothing in your life *but* the mental life, then you yourself are a plucked apple . . . you've fallen off the tree. And then it is a logical necessity to be spiteful, just as it's a natural necessity for a plucked apple to go bad."

Clifford made big eyes: it was all stuff to him. Connie secretly laughed to herself.

"Well then, we're all plucked apples," said Hammond, rather acidly and petulantly.

"So let's make cider of ourselves," said Charlie.

"But what do you think of Bolshevism?" put in the brown Berry, as if everything had led up to it.

"Bravo!" roared Charlie. "What do you think of Bolshevism?"

"Come on! Let's make hay of Bolshevism!" said Dukes.

"I'm afraid Bolshevism is a large question," said Hammond, shaking his head seriously.

"Bolshevism, it seems to me," said Charlie, "is just a superlative hatred of the thing they call the bourgeois; and what the bourgeois is, isn't quite defined. It is Capitalism, among other things. Feelings and emotions are also so decidedly bourgeois that you have to invent a man without them.

"Then the individual, especially the *personal* man, is bourgeois: so he must be suppressed. You must submerge yourselves in the great thing, the Soviet-social thing. Even an organism is bourgeois: so the ideal must be mechanical. The only thing that is a unit, nonorganic, composed of many different, and equally essential parts, is the machine. Each man a machine part, and the driving power of the machine, hate . . . hate of the bourgeois. That, to me, is Bolshevism."

"Absolutely!" said Tommy. "But also, it seems to me a perfect description of the whole of the industrial ideal. It's the factory owner's ideal in a nutshell; except that he would deny that the driving power was hate. Hate it is, all the same: hate of life itself. Just look at these Midlands, if it isn't plainly written up . . . but it's all part of the life of the mind, it's a logical development."

"I deny that Bolshevism is logical, it rejects the major part of the premises," said Hammond.

"My dear man, it allows the material premise; so does the pure mind . . . exclusively."

"At least Bolshevism has got down to rock bottom," said Charlie.

"Rock bottom! The bottom that has no bottom! The Bolshevists will have the finest army in the world in a very short time, with the finest mechanical equipment."

"But this thing can't go on . . . this hate business. There must be a reaction . . ." said Hammond.

"Well, we've been waiting for years . . . we wait longer. Hate's a growing thing like anything else. It's the inevitable outcome of forcing ideas on to life, of forcing one's deepest instincts; our deepest feelings we force according to certain ideas. We drive ourselves with a formula, like a machine. The logical mind pretends to rule the roost, and the roost turns into pure hate. We're all Bolshevists, only we are hypocrites. The Russians are Bolshevists without hypocrisy."

"But there are many other ways," said Hammond, "than the Soviet way. The Bolshevists aren't really intelligent."

"Of course not. But sometimes it's intelligent to be half-witted: if you want to make your end. Personally, I consider Bolshevism half-witted; but so do I consider our social life in the west half-witted. So I even consider our far-famed mental life half-witted. We're all as cold as crétins, we're all as passionless as idiots. We're all of us Bolshevists, only we give it another name. We think we're gods . . . men like gods! It's just the same as Bolshevism. One has to be human, and have a heart and a penis, if one is going to escape being either a god or a bolshevist . . . for they are the same thing: they're both too good to be true."

Out of the disapproving silence came Berry's anxious question:

"You do believe in love then, Tommy, don't you?"

"You lovely lad!" said Tommy. "No, my cherub, nine times out of ten, no! Love's another of those half-witted performances today. Fellows with swaying waists fucking little jazz girls with small-boy buttocks, like two collar studs! Do you mean that sort of love? Or the joint-property, make-a-success-of-it, my-husband-my-wife sort of love? No, my fine fellow, I don't believe in it at all!"

"But you do believe in something?"

"Me? Oh, intellectually I believe in having a good heart, a chirpy penis, a lively intelligence, and the courage to say 'shit!' in front of a lady."

"Well, you've got them all," said Berry.

Tommy Dukes roared with laughter. "You angel boy! If only I had! If only I had! No; my heart's as numb as a potato, my penis droops and never lifts its head up, I dare rather cut him clean off than say 'shit!' in front of my mother or my aunt . . . they are real ladies, mind you; and I'm not really intelligent, I'm only a 'mental-lifer.' It would be wonderful to be intelligent: then one would be alive in all the parts mentioned and unmentionable. The penis rouses his head and says: How do you do? to any really intelligent person. Renoir said he painted his pictures with his penis . . . he did too, lovely pictures! I wish I did something with mine. God! when one can only talk! Another torture added to Hades! And Socrates started it."

"There are nice women in the world," said Connie, lifting her head up and speaking at last.

The men resented it . . . she should have pretended to hear nothing. They hated her admitting she had attended so closely to such talk.

"My God!—*'If they be not nice to me*
What care I how nice they be?'—

No, it's hopeless! I just simply can't vibrate in unison with a woman. There's no woman I can really want when I'm faced with her, and I'm not going to start forcing myself to it . . . My God, no! I'll remain as I am, and lead the mental life. It's the only honest thing I can do. I can be quite happy *talking* to women; but it's all pure, hopelessly pure. Hopelessly pure! What do you say, Hildebrand, my chicken?"

"It's much less complicated if one stays pure," said Berry.

"Yes, life is all too simple!"

❖ 5 ❖

On a frosty morning with a little February sun, Clifford and Connie went for a walk across the park to the wood. That is, Clifford chuffed in his motorchair, and Connie walked beside him.

The hard air was still sulphurous, but they were both used to it. Round the near horizon went the haze, opalescent with frost and smoke, and on the top lay the small blue sky; so that it was like being inside an enclosure, always inside. Life always a dream or a frenzy, inside an enclosure.

The sheep coughed in the rough, sere grass of the park, where frost lay bluish in the sockets of the tufts. Across the park ran a path to the wood-gate, a fine ribbon of pink. Clifford had had it newly graveled with sifted gravel from the pit-bank. When the rock and refuse of the underworld had burned and given off its sulphur, it turned bright pink, shrimp-colored on dry days, darker, crab-colored on wet. Now it was pale shrimp-color, with a bluish-white hoar of frost. It always pleased Connie, this underfoot of sifted, bright pink. It's an ill-wind that brings nobody good.

Clifford steered cautiously down the slope of the knoll from the hall, and

Connie kept her hand on the chair. In front lay the wood, the hazel thicket nearest, the purplish density of oaks beyond. From the wood's edge rabbits bobbed and nibbled. Rooks suddenly rose in a black train, and went trailing off over the little slope.

Connie opened the wood-gate, and Clifford puffed slowly through into the broad riding that ran up an incline between the clean-whipped thickets of the hazel. The wood was a remnant of the great forest where Robin Hood hunted, and this riding was an old, old thoroughfare coming across country. But now, of course, it was only a riding through the private wood. The road from Mansfield swerved round to the north.

In the wood everything was motionless, the old leaves on the ground keeping the frost on their underside. A jay called harshly, many little birds fluttered. But there was no game; no pheasants. They had been killed off during the war, and the wood had been left unprotected, till now Clifford had got his gamekeeper again.

Clifford loved the wood; he loved the old oak trees. He felt they were his own through generations. He wanted to protect them. He wanted this place inviolate, shut off from the world.

The chair chuffed slowly up the incline, rocking and jolting on the frozen clods. And suddenly, on the left, came a clearing where there was nothing but a ravel of dead bracken, a thin and spindling sappling leaning here and there, big sawn stumps showing their tops and their grasping roots, lifeless. And patches of blackness where the woodmen had burned the brushwood and rubbish.

This was one of the places that Sir Geoffrey had cut during the war for trench timber. The whole knoll, which rose softly on the right of the riding, was denuded and strangely forlorn. On the crown of the knoll where the oaks had stood, now was bareness; and from there you could look out over the trees to the colliery railway, and the new works at Stacks Gate. Connie had stood and looked, it was a breach in the pure seclusion of the wood. It let in the world. But she didn't tell Clifford.

This denuded place always made Clifford curiously angry. He had been through the war, had seen what it meant. But he didn't get really angry till he saw this bare hill. He was having it replanted. But it made him hate Sir Geoffrey.

Clifford sat with a fixed face as the chair slowly mounted. When they came to the top of the rise he stopped; he would not risk the long and very jolty downslope. He sat looking at the greenish sweep of the riding downwards, a clear way through the bracken and oaks. It swerved at the bottom of the hill and disappeared; but it had such a lovely easy curve, of knights riding and ladies on palfreys.

"I consider this is really the heart of England," said Clifford to Connie, as he sat there in the dim February sunshine.

"Do you?" she said, seating herself, in her blue knitted dress, on a stump by the path.

"I do! This is the old England, the heart of it; and I intend to keep it intact."

"Oh, yes!" said Connie. But, as she said it she heard the eleven-o'clock hooters at Stacks Gate colliery. Clifford was too used to the sound to notice.

"I want this wood perfect . . . untouched. I want nobody to trespass in it," said Clifford.

There was a certain pathos. The wood still had some of the mystery of wild, old England; but Sir Geoffrey's cuttings during the war had given it a blow. How still the trees were, with their crinkly, innumerable twigs against the sky, and their grey, obstinate trunks rising from the brown bracken! How safely the birds flitted among them! And once there had been deer, and archers, and monks paddling along on asses. The place remembered, still remembered.

Clifford sat in the pale sun, with the light on his smooth, rather blond hair, his reddish full face inscrutable.

"I mind more, not having a son, when I come here, than any other time," he said.

"But the wood is older than your family," said Connie gently.

"Quite!" said Clifford. "But we've preserved it. Except for us it would go . . . it would be gone already, like the rest of the forest. One must preserve some of the Old England!"

"Must one?" said Connie. "If it has to be preserved, and preserved against the new England? It's sad, I know."

"If some of the old England isn't preserved, there'll be no England at all," said Clifford. "And we who have this kind of property, and the feeling for it, *must* preserve it."

There was a sad pause.

"Yes, for a little while," said Connie.

"For a little while! It's all we can do. We can only do our bit. I feel every man of my family has done his bit here, since we've had the place. One may go against convention, but one must keep up tradition." Again there was a pause.

"What tradition?" asked Connie.

"The tradition of England! of this!"

"Yes," she said slowly.

"That's why having a son helps; one is only a link in a chain," he said.

Connie was not keen on chains, but she said nothing. She was thinking of the curious impersonality of his desire for a son.

"I'm sorry we can't have a son," she said.

He looked at her steadily, with his full, pale-blue eyes.

"It would almost be a good thing if you had a child by another man," he said. "If we brought it up at Wragby, it would belong to us and to the place. I don't believe very intensely in fatherhood. If we had the child to rear, it would be our own, and it would carry on. Don't you think it's worth considering?"

Connie looked up at him at last. The child, her child, was just an "it" to him. It . . . it . . . it!

"But what about the other man?" she asked.

"Does it matter very much? Do these things really affect us very deeply? . . . You had that lover in Germany . . . what is it now? Nothing almost. It seems to me that it isn't these little acts and little connections we make in our lives that matter so very much. They pass away, and where are they? Where . . . Where are the snows of yesteryear? . . . It's what endures through one's life that matters; my own life matters to me, in its long continuance and development. But what do the occasional connections matter? And the occasional sexual connections specially. If people don't exaggerate them ridiculously, they pass like the mating of birds. And so they should. What does it matter? It's the lifelong companionship that matters. It's the living together from day to day, not the sleeping together once or twice. You and I are married, no matter what happens to us. We have the habit of each other. And habit, to my thinking, is more vital than any occasional excitement. The long, slow, enduring thing . . . that's what we live by . . . not the occasional spasm of any sort. Little by little, living together, two people fall into a sort of unison, they vibrate so intricately to one another. That's the real secret of marriage, not sex; at least not the simple function of sex. You and I are interwoven in a marriage. If we stick to that we ought to be able to arrange this sex thing, as we arrange going to the dentist; since fate has given us a checkmate physically there."

Connie sat and listened in a sort of wonder, and a sort of fear. She did not know if he was right or not. There was Michaelis, whom she loved; so she said to herself. But her love was somehow only an excursion from her marriage with Clifford; the long, slow habit of intimacy, formed through years of suffering and patience. Perhaps the human soul needs excursions, and must not be denied them. But the point of an excursion is that you come home again.

"And wouldn't you mind *what* man's child I got?" she asked.

"Why, Connie, I should trust your natural instinct of decency and selection. You just wouldn't let the wrong sort of fellow touch you."

She thought of Michaelis! He was absolutely Clifford's idea of the wrong sort of fellow.

"But men and women may have different feelings about the wrong sort of fellow," she said.

"No," he replied. "You cared for me. I don't believe you would ever care for a man who was purely antipathetic to me. Your rhythm wouldn't let you."

She was silent. Logic might be unanswerable because it was so absolutely wrong.

"And should you expect me to tell you?" she asked, glancing up at him almost furtively.

"Not at all. I'd better not know.... But you do agree with me, don't you, that the casual sex thing is nothing, compared to the long life lived together? Don't you think one can just subordinate the sex thing to the necessities of a long life? Just use it, since that's what we're driven to? After all, *do* these temporary excitements matter? Isn't the whole problem of life the slow building up of an integral personality, through the years? living an integrated life? There's no point in a disintegrated life. If lack of sex is going to disintegrate you, then go out and have a love affair. If lack of a child is going to disintegrate you, then have a child if you possibly can. But only do these things so that you have an integrated life, that makes a long harmonious thing. And you and I can do that together.... don't you think?... if we adapt ourselves to the necessities, and at the same time weave the adaptation together into a piece with our steadily lived life. Don't you agree?"

Connie was a little overwhelmed by his words. She knew he was right theoretically. But when she actually touched her steadily-lived life with him she hesitated.... Was it actually her destiny to go on weaving herself into his life all the rest of her life? Nothing else?

Was it just that? She was to be content to weave a steady life with him, all one fabric, but perhaps brocaded with the occasional flower of an adventure. But how could she know what she would feel next year? How could one ever know? How could one say Yes? for years and years? The little yes, gone on a breath! Why should one be pinned down by that butterfly word? Of course it had to flutter away and be gone, to be followed by other yes's and no's! Like the straying of butterflies.

"I think you're right, Clifford. And as far as I can see I agree with you. Only life may turn quite a new face on it all."

"But until life turns a new face on it all, you do agree?"

"Oh, yes! I think I do, really."

She was watching a brown spaniel that had run out of a side-path, and was looking toward them with lifted nose, making a soft, fluffy bark. A man with a gun strode swiftly, softly out after the dog, facing their way as if about to attack them; then stopped instead, saluted, and was turning downhill. It was only the new gamekeeper, but he had frightened Connie, he seemed to emerge with such a swift menace. That was how she had seen him, like a sudden rush of a threat out of nowhere.

He was a man in dark green velveteens and gaiters . . . the old style, with a red face and red moustache and distant eyes. He was going quickly downhill.

"Mellors!" called Clifford.

The man faced lightly round, and saluted with a quick little gesture, a soldier!

"Will you turn the chair round and get it started? That makes it easier," said Clifford.

The man at once slung his gun over his shoulder, and came forward with the same curious swift, yet soft movements, as if keeping invisible. He was moderately tall and lean, and was silent. He did not look at Connie at all, only at the chair.

"Connie, this is the new gamekeeper, Mellors. You haven't spoken to her ladyship yet, Mellors?"

"No, Sir!" came the ready, neutral words.

The man lifted his hat as he stood, showing his thick, almost fair hair. He stared straight into Connie's eyes, with a perfect, fearless, impersonal look, as if he wanted to see what she was like. He made her feel shy. She bent her head to him shyly, and he changed his hat to his left hand and made her a slight bow, like a gentleman; but he said nothing at all. He remained for a moment still, with his hat in his hand.

"But you've been here some time, haven't you?" Connie said to him.

"Eight months, Madam . . . your Ladyship!" he corrected himself calmly.

"And do you like it?"

She looked him in the eyes. His eyes narrowed a little, with irony, perhaps with impudence.

"Why, yes, thank you, your Ladyship! I was reared here. . . ." He gave another slight bow, turned, put his hat on, and strode to take hold of the chair. His voice on the last words had fallen into the heavy broad drag of the dialect . . . perhaps also in mockery, because there had been no trace of dialect before. He might almost be a gentleman. Anyhow, he was a curious, quick, separate fellow, alone, but sure of himself.

Clifford started the little engine, the man carefully turned the chair, and set it nose-forwards to the incline that curved gently to the dark hazel thicket.

"Is that all then, Sir Clifford?" asked the man.

"No, you'd better come along in case she sticks. The engine isn't really strong enough for the uphill work." The man glanced round for his dog . . . a thoughtful glance. The spaniel looked at him and faintly moved its tail. A little smile, mocking or teasing her, yet gentle, came into his eyes for a moment, then faded away, and his face was expressionless. They went fairly quickly down the slope, the man with his hand on the rail of the chair, steadying it. He looked like a free soldier rather than a servant. And something about him reminded Connie of Tommy Dukes.

When they came to the hazel grove, Connie suddenly ran forward and opened the gate into the park. As she stood holding it, the two men looked at her in passing. Clifford critically, the other man with a curious, cool wonder; impersonally wanting to see what she looked like. And she saw in his blue, impersonal eyes a look of suffering and detachment, yet a certain warmth. But why was he aloof, apart?

Clifford stopped the chair, once through the gate, and the man came quickly, courteously to close it.

"Why did you run to open?" asked Clifford in his quiet, calm voice, that showed he was displeased. "Mellors would have done it."

"I thought you would go straight ahead," said Connie.

"And leave you to run after us?" said Clifford.

"Oh, well, I like to run sometimes!"

Mellors took the chair again, looking perfectly unheeding, yet Connie felt he noted everything. As he pushed the chair up the steepish rise of the knoll in the park, he breathed rather quickly, through parted lips. He was rather frail, really. Curiously full of vitality, but a little frail and quenched. Her woman's instinct sensed it.

Connie fell back, let the chair go on. The day had grayed over: the small blue sky that had poised low on its circular rims of haze was closed in again, the lid was down, there was a raw coldness. It was going to snow. All gray, all gray! the world looked worn out.

The chair waited at the top of the pink path. Clifford looked around for Connie.

"Not tired, are you?" he asked.

"Oh, no!" she said.

But she was. A strange, weary yearning, a dissatisfaction had started in her. Clifford did not notice: those were not things he was aware of. But the stranger knew. To Connie, everything in her world and life seemed worn out, and her dissatisfaction was older than the hills.

They came to the house, and round to the back, where there were no steps. Clifford managed to swing himself over onto the low, wheeled house-chair; he was very strong and agile with his arms. Then Connie lifted the burden of his dead legs after him.

The keeper, waiting at attention to be dismissed, watched everything narrowly, missing nothing. He went pale, with a sort of fear, when he saw Connie lifting the inert legs of the man in her arms, into the other chair, Clifford pivoting round as she did so. He was frightened.

"Thanks, then, for the help, Mellors," said Clifford casually, as he began to wheel down the passage to the servants' quarters.

"Nothing else, Sir?" came the neutral voice, like one in a dream.

"Nothing. Good-morning!"

"Good-morning, Sir."

"Good-morning! It was kind of you to push the chair up that hill. . . . I hope it wasn't too heavy for you," said Connie, looking back at the keeper outside the door.

His eyes came to her in an instant, as if wakened up. He was aware of her.

"Oh, no, not heavy!" he said quickly. Then his voice dropped again into the broad sound of the vernacular: "Good-mornin' to your ladyship!"

"Who is your gamekeeper?" Connie asked at lunch.

"Mellors! You saw him," said Clifford.

"Yes, but where did he come from?"

"Nowhere! He was a Tevershall boy . . . son of a collier, I believe."

"And was he a collier himself?"

"Blacksmith on the pit-bank, I believe: overhead smith. But he was keeper here for two years before the war . . . before he joined up. My father always had a good opinion of him, so when he came back, and went to the pit for a blacksmith's job, I just took him back here as keeper. I was really very glad to get him . . . it's almost impossible to find a good man round here, for a game-keeper . . . and it needs a man who knows the people."

"And isn't he married?"

"He was. But his wife went off with . . . with various men . . . but finally with a collier at Stacks Gate, and I believe she's living there still."

"So this man is alone?"

"More or less! He has a mother in the village . . . and a child, I believe."

Clifford looked at Connie, with his pale, slightly prominent blue eyes, in which a certain vagueness was coming. He seemed alert in the foreground, but the background was like the Midlands atmosphere, haze, smoky mist. And the haze seemed to be creeping forward. So when he stared at Connie in his peculiar way, giving her his peculiar, precise information, she felt all the background of his mind filling up with mist, with nothingness. And it frightened her. It made him seem impersonal, almost to idiocy.

And dimly she realized one of the great laws of the human soul: that when the emotional soul receives a wounding shock, which does not kill the body, the soul seems to recover as the body recovers. But this is only appearance. It is really only the mechanism of the reassumed habit. Slowly, slowly the wound to the soul begins to make itself felt, like a bruise, which only slowly deepens its terrible ache, till it fills all the psyche. And when we think we have recovered and forgotten, it is then that the terrible aftereffects have to be encountered at their worst.

So it was with Clifford. Once he was "well," once he was back at Wragby, and writing his stories, and feeling sure of life, in spite of all, he seemed to forget, and to have recovered all his equanimity. But now, as the years went by, slowly, slowly, Connie felt the bruise of fear and horror coming up, and spreading in him. For a time it had been so deep as to be numb, as it were nonexistent. Now slowly it began to assert itself in a spread of fear, almost paralysis. Mentally he still was alert. But the paralysis, the bruise of the too great shock was gradually spreading in his affective self.

And as it spread in him, Connie felt it spread in her. An inward dread, an emptiness, an indifference to everything gradually spread in her soul. When Clifford was aroused, he could still talk brilliantly, and, as it were, command the future: as when, in the wood, he talked about her having a child, and giving an heir to Wragby. But the day after, all the brilliant words seemed like dead leaves, crumpling up and turning to powder, meaning really nothing, blown away on any gust of wind. They were not the leafy words of an effective life, young with energy and belonging to the tree. They were the hosts of fallen leaves of a life that is ineffectual.

So it seemed to her everywhere. The colliers at Tevershall were talking again of a strike, and it seemed to Connie there again it was not a manifestation of energy, it was the bruise of the war that had been in abeyance, slowly rising to the surface and creating the great ache of unrest, and stupor of discontent. The bruise was deep, deep, deep . . . the bruise of the false inhuman war. It would take many years for the living blood of the generations to dissolve the vast black clot of bruised blood, deep inside their souls and bodies. And it would need a new hope.

Poor Connie! As the years drew on it was the fear of nothingness in her life that affected her. Clifford's mental life and hers gradually began to feel like nothingness. Their marriage, their integrated life based on a habit of intimacy, that he talked about: there were days when it all became utterly blank and nothing. It was words, just so many words. The only reality was nothingness, and over it a hypocrisy of words.

There was Clifford's success: the bitch-goddess! It was true he was almost famous, and his books brought him in a thousand pounds. His photograph appeared everywhere. There was a bust of him in one of the galleries, and a portrait of him in two galleries. He seemed the most modern of modern voices.

With his uncanny lame instinct for publicity, he had become in four or five years one of the best known of the young "intellectuals." Where the intellect came in, Connie did not quite see. Clifford was really clever at that slightly humorous analysis of people and motives which leaves everything in bits at the end. But it was rather like puppies tearing the sofa cushions to bits; except that it was not young and playful, but curiously old, and rather obstinately conceited. It was weird and it was nothing. This was the feeling that echoed and reechoed at the bottom of Connie's soul: it was all nothing, a wonderful display of nothingness. At the same time a display. A display! a display! a display!

Michaelis had seized upon Clifford as the central figure for a play; already he had sketched in the plot, and written the first act. For Michaelis was even better than Clifford at making a display of nothingness. It was the last bit of passion left in these men: the passion for making a display. Sexually they were passionless, even dead. And now it was not money that Michaelis was after. Clifford had never been primarily out for money, though he made it where he could, for money is the seal and stamp of success. And success was what they wanted. They wanted, both of them, to make a real display . . . a man's own very display of himself, that should capture for a time the vast populace.

It was strange . . . the prostitution to the bitch-goddess. To Connie, since she was really outside of it, and since she had grown numb to the thrill of it, it was again nothingness. Even the prostitution to the bitch-goddess was nothingness, though the men prostituted themselves innumerable times. Nothingness even that.

Michaelis wrote to Clifford about the play. Of course she knew about it long ago. And Clifford was again thrilled. He was going to be displayed again, this time somebody was going to display him, and to advantage. He invited Michaelis down to Wragby with Act I.

Michaelis came: in summer, in pale-colored suit and white suede gloves, with mauve orchids for Connie, very lovely, and Act I was a great success. Even Connie was thrilled . . . thrilled to what bit of marrow she had left. And Michaelis, thrilled by his power to thrill, was really wonderful . . . and quite beautiful, in Connie's eyes. She saw in him that ancient motionlessness of a race that can't be disillusioned anymore, an extreme, perhaps, of impurity that is pure. On the far side of his supreme prostitution to the bitch-goddess he seemed pure, pure as an African ivory mask that dreams impurity into purity, in its ivory curves and planes.

His moment of sheer thrill with the two Chatterleys, when he simply carried Connie and Clifford away, was one of the supreme moments of Michaelis' life. He had succeeded: he had carried them away. Even Clifford was temporarily in love with him . . . if that is the way one can put it.

So next morning Mick was more uneasy than ever: restless, devoured, with his hands restless in his trouser pockets. Connie had not visited him the night . . . and he had not known where to find her. Coquetry! . . . at his moment of triumph.

He went up to her sitting room in the morning. She knew he would come. And his restlessness was evident. He asked her about his play . . . did she think it good? He *had* to hear it praised. That affected him with the last thin thrill of passion beyond any sexual orgasm. And she praised it rapturously. Yet all the while, at the bottom of her soul, she knew it was nothing.

"Look here!" he said suddenly at last. "Why don't you and I make a clean thing of it? Why don't we marry?"

"But I am married," she said amazed, and yet feeling nothing.

"Oh, that! . . . he'll divorce you all right. . . . Why don't you and I marry? I want to marry. I know it would be the best thing for me . . . marry and lead a regular life. I lead the deuce of a life, simply tearing myself to pieces. Look here, you and I, we're made for one another . . . hand and glove. Why don't we marry? Do you see any reason why we shouldn't?"

Connie looked at him amazed: and yet she felt nothing. These men, they were all alike, they left everything out. They just went off from the top of their heads as if they were squibs, and expected you to be carried heavenwards along with their own thin sticks.

"But I am married already," she said. "I can't leave Clifford, you know."

"Why not? But why not?" he cried. "He'll hardly know you've gone, after six months. He doesn't know that anybody exists, except himself. Why, the man has no use for you at all, as far as I can see; he's entirely wrapped up in himself."

Connie felt there was truth in this. But she also felt that Mick was hardly making a display of selflessness.

"Aren't all men wrapped up in themselves?" she asked.

"Oh, more or less, I allow. A man's got to be, to get through. But that's not the point. The point is, what sort of a time can a man give a woman? Can he give her a damn good time, or can't he? If he can't he's no right to the woman. . . ." He paused and gazed at her with his full, hazel eyes, almost hypnotic. "Now, I consider," he added, "I can give a woman the darndest good time she can ask for. I think I can guarantee myself."

"And what sort of a good time?" asked Connie, gazing on him still with a sort of amazement, that looked like thrill; and underneath feeling nothing at all.

"Every sort of a good time, damn it, every sort! Dress, jewels up to a point, any nightclub you like, know anybody you want to know, live the pace . . . travel and be somebody wherever you go. . . . Darn it, every sort of good time."

He spoke it almost in a brilliancy of triumph, and Connie looked at him as if dazzled, and really feeling nothing at all. Hardly even the surface of her mind was tickled at the glowing prospects he offered her. Hardly even her most outside self responded, that at any other time would have been thrilled. She just got no feeling from it all, she couldn't "go off." She just sat and stared and looked dazzled, and felt nothing, only somewhere she smelled the extraordinary unpleasant smell of the bitch-goddess.

Mick sat on tenterhooks, leaning forward in his chair, glaring at her almost hysterically: and whether he was more anxious out of vanity for her to say Yes! or whether he was more panic-stricken for fear she *should* say Yes—who can tell?

"I should have to think about it," she said. "I couldn't say now. It may seem to you Clifford doesn't count, but he does. When you think how disabled he is. . . ."

"Oh, damn it all! if a fellow's going to trade on his disabilities, I might begin to say how lonely I am, and always have been, and all the rest of the my-eye-Betty-Martin sob-stuff! Damn it all, if a fellow's got nothing but disabilities to recommend him. . . ."

He turned aside, working his hands furiously in his trouser pockets. That evening he said to her:

"You're coming round to my room tonight, aren't you? I don't darned know where your room is."

"All right!" she said.

He was a more excited lover that night, with his strange, small boy's frail nakedness. Connie found it impossible to come to her crisis before he had really finished his. And he roused a certain craving passion in her, with his little boy's nakedness and softness; she had to go on after he had finished, in the wild tumult and heaving of her loins, while he heroically kept himself up, and present in her, with all his will and self-offering, till she brought about her own crisis, with weird little cries.

When at last he drew away from her, he said, in a bitter, almost sneering little voice:

"You couldn't go off at the same time as a man, could you? You'd have to bring yourself off! You'd have to run the show!"

This little speech, at the moment, was one of the shocks of her life. Because that passive sort of giving himself was so obviously his only real mode of intercourse.

"What do you mean?" she said.

"You know what I mean. You keep on for hours after I've gone off . . . and I have to hang on with my teeth till you bring yourself off by your own exertions."

She was stunned by this unexpected piece of brutality, at the moment when she was glowing with a sort of pleasure beyond words, and a sort of love for him. Because after all, like so many modern men, he was finished almost before he had begun. And that forced the woman to be active.

"But you want me to go on, to get my own satisfaction?" she said.

He laughed grimly: "I want it!" he said. "That's good! I want to hang on with my teeth clenched, while you go for me!"

"But don't you?" she insisted.

He avoided the question. "All the darned women are like that," he said. "Either they don't go off at all, as if they were dead in there . . . or else they wait till a chap's really done, and then they start in to bring themselves off, and a chap's got to hang on. I never had a woman yet who went off just at the same moment as I did."

Connie only half heard this piece of novel, masculine information. She was only stunned by his feeling against her . . . his incomprehensible brutality. She felt so innocent.

"But you want me to have my satisfaction too, don't you?" she repeated.

"Oh, all right! I'm quite willing. But I'm darned if hanging on waiting for a woman to go off is much of a game for a man. . . ."

This speech was one of the crucial blows of Connie's life. It killed something in her. She had not been so very keen on Michaelis; till he started it, she did not want him. It was as if she never positively wanted him. But once he had started her, it seemed only natural for her to come to her own crisis with him. Almost she had loved him for it . . . almost that night she loved him, and wanted to marry him.

Perhaps instinctively he knew it, and that was why he had to bring down the whole show with a smash; the house of cards. Her whole sexual feeling for him, or for any man, collapsed that night. Her life fell apart from his as completely as if he had never existed.

And she went through the days drearily. There was nothing now but this empty treadmill of what Clifford called the integrated life, the long living together of two people, who are in the habit of being in the same house with one another.

Nothingness! To accept the great nothingness of life seemed to be the one end of living. All the many busy and important little things that make up the grand sum total of nothingness!

❖ 6 ❖

"Why don't men and women really like one another nowadays?" Connie asked Tommy Dukes, who was more or less her oracle.

"Oh, but they do! I don't think since the human species was invented, there has ever been a time when men and women have liked one another as much as they do today. Genuine liking! Take myself. . . . I really *like* women better than men; they are braver, one can be more frank with them."

Connie pondered this.

"Ah, yes, but you never have anything to do with them!" she said.

"I? What am I doing but talking perfectly sincerely to a woman at this moment?"

"Yes, talking. . . ."

"And what more could I do if you were a man, than talk perfectly sincerely to you?"

"Nothing perhaps. But a woman. . . ."

"A woman wants you to like her and talk to her, and at the same time love her and desire her; and it seems to me the two things are mutually exclusive."

"But they shouldn't be!"

"No doubt water ought not to be so wet as it is; it overdoes it in wetness. But there it is! I like women and talk to them, and therefore I don't love them and desire them. The two things don't happen at the same time in me."

"I think they ought to."

"All right. The fact that things ought to be something else than what they are is not my department."

Connie considered this. "It isn't true," she said. "Men can love women and talk to them. I don't see how they can love them *without* talking, and being friendly and intimate. How can they?"

"Well," he said, "I don't know. What's the use of my generalizing? I only know my own case. I like women, but I don't desire them. I like talking to them; but talking to them, though it makes me intimate in one direction, sets me poles apart from them as far as kissing is concerned. So there you are! But don't take me as a general example, probably I'm just a special case: one of the men who like women, but don't love women, and even hate them if they force me into a pretense of love, or an entangled appearance."

"But doesn't it make you sad?"

"Why should it? Not a bit! I look at Charlie May, and the rest of the men who have affairs. . . . No, I don't envy them a bit! If fate sent me a woman I wanted, well and good. Since I don't know any woman I want, and never see one . . . why, I presume I'm cold, and really *like* some women very much."

"Do you like me?"

"Very much! And you see there's no question of kissing between us, is there?"

"None at all!" said Connie. "But oughtn't there to be?"

"*Why*, in God's name? I like Clifford, but what would you say if I went and kissed him?"

"But isn't there a difference?"

"Where does it lie, as far as we're concerned? We're all intelligent human beings, and the male and female business is in abeyance. Just in abeyance. How would you like me to start acting up like a continental male at this moment, and parading the sex thing?"

"I should hate it."

"Well then! I tell you, if I'm really a male thing at all, I never run across the female of my species. And I don't miss her, I just *like* women. Who's going to force me into loving, or pretending to love them, working up the sex game?"

"No, I'm not. But isn't something wrong?"

"You may feel it, I don't."

"Yes, I feel something is wrong between men and women. A woman has no glamor for a man anymore."

"Has a man for a woman?"

She pondered the other side of the question.

"Not much," she said truthfully.

"Then let's leave it alone, and just be decent and simple, like proper human beings with one another. Be damned to the artificial sex-compulsion! I refuse it!"

Connie knew he was right, really. Yet it left her feeling so forlorn, so forlorn and stray. Like a chip on a dreary pond, she felt. What was the point, of her or anything?

It was her youth which rebelled. These men seemed so old and cold. Everything seemed old and cold. And Michaelis let one down so; he was no good. The men didn't want one; they just didn't really want a woman, even Michaelis didn't.

And the bounders who pretended they did, and started working the sex game, they were worse than ever.

It was just dismal, and one had to put up with it. It was quite true, men had no real glamor for a woman: if you could fool yourself into thinking they had, even as she had fooled herself over Michaelis, that was the best you could do. Meanwhile you just lived on and there was nothing to it. She understood perfectly well why people had cocktail parties, and jazzed, and Charlestoned till they were ready to drop. You had to take it out some way or other, your youth, or it ate you up. But what a ghastly thing, this youth! you felt as old as Methuselah, and yet the thing fizzed somehow, and didn't let you be comfortable. A mean sort of life! And no prospect! She almost wished she had gone off with Mick, and made her life one long cocktail party, and jazz evening. Anyhow that was better than just mooning yourself into the grave.

On one of her bad days she went out alone to walk in the wood, ponderously, heeding nothing, not even noticing where she was. The report of a gun not far off startled and angered her.

Then, as she went, she heard voices, and recoiled. People! She didn't want people. But her quick ear caught another sound, and she roused; it was a child sobbing. At once she attended; someone was ill-treating a child. She strode swinging down the wet drive, her sullen resentment uppermost. She felt prepared to make a scene.

Turning the corner, she saw two figures in the drive beyond her: the keeper, and a little girl in a purple coat and moleskin cap, crying.

"Ah, shut it up, tha false little bitch!" came the man's angry voice, and the child sobbed louder.

Constance strode nearer, with blazing eyes. The man turned and looked at her, saluting coolly, but he was pale with anger.

"What's the matter? Why is she crying?" demanded Constance, peremptory but a little breathless.

A faint smile like a sneer came on the man's face. "Nay, yo' mun ax 'er," he replied callously, in broad vernacular.

Connie felt as if he had hit her in the face, and she changed color. Then she gathered her defiance, and looked at him, her dark blue eyes blazing rather vaguely.

"I asked *you*," she panted.

He gave a queer little bow, lifting his hat. "You did, your Ladyship," he said; then, with a return to the vernacular: "but I canna tell yer." And he became a soldier, inscrutable, only pale with annoyance.

Connie turned to the child, a ruddy, black-haired thing of nine or ten. "What is it, dear? Tell me why you're crying!" she said, with the conventionalized sweetness suitable. More violent sobs, self-conscious. Still more sweetness on Connie's part.

"There, there, don't you cry! Tell me what they've done to you!" . . . an intense tenderness of tone. At the same time she felt in the pocket of her knitted jacket, and luckily found a sixpence.

"Don't you cry then!" she said, bending in front of the child. "See what I've got for you!"

Sobs, snuffles, a fist taken from a blubbered face, and a black shrewd eye cast for a second on the sixpence. Then more sobs, but subduing. "There, tell me what's the matter, tell me!" said Connie, putting the coin into the child's chubby hand, which closed over it.

"It's the . . . it's the . . . pussy!"

Shudders of subsiding sobs.

"What pussy, dear?"

After a silence the shy fist, clenching on sixpence, pointed into a bramble brake.

"There!"

Connie looked, and there, sure enough, was a big black cat, stretched out grimly, with a bit of blood on it.

"Oh!" she said in repulsion.

"A poacher, your Ladyship," said the man satirically.

She glanced at him angrily. "No wonder the child cried," she said, "if you shot it when she was there. No wonder she cried!"

He looked into Connie's eyes, laconic, contemptuous, not hiding his feelings. And again Connie flushed; she felt she had been making a scene, the man did not respect her.

"What is your name?" she said playfully to the child. "Won't you tell me your name?"

Sniffs; then very affectedly in a piping voice: "Connie Mellors!"

"Connie Mellors! Well, that's a nice name! And did you come out with your Daddy, and he shot a pussy? But it was a bad pussy!"

The child looked at her, with bold, dark eyes of scrutiny, sizing her up, and her condolence.

"I wanted to stop with my Gran," said the little girl.

"Did you? But where is your Gran?"

The child lifted an arm, pointing down the drive. "At th' cottidge."

"At the cottage! And would you like to go back to her?"

Sudden, shuddering quivers of reminiscent sobs. "Yes!"

"Come then, shall I take you? Shall I take you to your Gran? Then your Daddy can do what he has to do." She turned to the man. "It is your little girl, isn't it?"

He saluted, and made a slight movement of the head in affirmation.

"I suppose I can take her to the cottage?"

"If your Ladyship wishes."

Again he looked into her eyes, with that calm, searching detached glance. A man very much alone, and on his own.

"Would you like to come with me to the cottage, to your Gran, dear?"

The child peeped up again. "Yes!" she simpered.

Connie disliked her; the spoilt, false little female. Nevertheless she wiped her face, and took her hand. The keeper saluted in silence.

"Good morning!" said Connie.

It was nearly a mile to the cottage, and Connie senior was well bored by Connie junior by the time the gamekeeper's picturesque little home was in sight. The child was already as full to the brim with tricks as a little monkey, and so self-assured.

At the cottage the door stood open, and there was a rattling heard inside. Connie lingered, the child slipped her hand, and ran indoors.

"Gran! Gran!"

"Why, are yer back a'ready!"

The grandmother had been blackleading the stove, it was Saturday morning. She came to the door in her sacking apron, a blacklead-brush in her hand, and a black smudge on her nose. She was a little, rather dry woman.

"Why, whatever?" she said, hastily wiping her arm across her face as she saw Connie standing outside.

"Good morning!" said Connie. "She was crying, so I just brought her home."

The grandmother looked round swiftly at the child:

"Why, wheer was yer Dad?"

The little girl clung to her grandmother's skirts and simpered.

"He was there," said Connie, "but he'd shot a poaching cat, and the child was upset."

"Oh, you'd no right t'ave bothered, Lady Chatterley, I'm sure! I'm sure it was very good of you, but you shouldn't 'ave bothered. Why, did ever you see!"—and the old woman turned to the child. "Fancy Lady Chatterley takin' all that trouble over yer! Why, she shouldn't 'ave bothered!"

"It was no bother, just a walk," said Connie, smiling.

"Why, I'm sure 'twas very kind of you, I must say! So she was crying! I knew there'd be something afore they got far. She's frightened of 'im, that's wheer it is. Seems 'e's almost a stranger to 'er, fair a stranger, and I don't think they're two as'd hit it off very easy. He's got funny ways."

Connie didn't know what to say.

"Look, Gran!" simpered the child.

The old woman looked down at the sixpence in the little girl's hand.

"An' sixpence an' all! Or, your Ladyship, you shouldn't, you shouldn't. Why, isn't Lady Chatterley good to yer! My word, you're a lucky girl this morning!"

She pronounced the name, as all the people did: Chat'ley. "Isn't Lady Chat'ley *good* to you!" Connie couldn't help looking at the old woman's nose, and the latter again vaguely wiped her face with the back of her wrist, but missed the smudge.

Connie was moving away. "Well, thank you ever so much, Lady Chat'ley, I'm sure. Say thank you to Lady Chat'ley!"—this last to the child.

"Thank you," piped the child.

"There's a dear!" laughed Connie, and she moved away, saying "Good morning," heartily relieved to get away from the contact. Curious, she thought, that that thin, proud man should have that little, sharp woman for a mother!

And the old woman, as soon as Connie was gone, rushed to the bit of mirror in the scullery, and looked at her face. Seeing it, she stamped her foot with impatience. "Of *course*, she had to catch me in my coarse apron, and a dirty face! Nice idea she'd get of me!"

Connie went slowly home to Wragby. "Home!" . . . it was a warm word to use for that great, weary warren. But then it was a word that had had its day. It was somehow canceled. All the great words, it seemed to Connie, were canceled for her generation: love, joy, happiness, home, mother, father, husband, all these great dynamic words were half dead now, and dying from day to day. Home was a place you lived in, love was a thing you didn't fool yourself about, joy was a word you applied to a good Charleston, happiness was a term of hypocrisy used to bluff other people, a father was an individual who enjoyed his own existence, a husband was a man you lived with and kept going in spirits. As for sex, the last of the great words, it was just a cocktail term for an excitement that bucked you up for a while, then left you more raggy than ever. Frayed! It was as if the very material you were made of was cheap stuff, and was fraying out to nothing.

All that really remained was a stubborn stoicism: and in that there was a certain pleasure. In the very experience of the nothingness of life, phase after phase, *étape* after *étape*, there was a certain grisly satisfaction. So that's *that!* Always this was the last utterance: home, love, marriage, Michaelis: So that's *that!*—And when one died, the last words to life would be: So that's *that!*—

Money? Perhaps one couldn't say the same there. Money one always wanted. Money, success, the bitch-goddess, as Tommy Dukes persisted in calling it, after Henry James, that was a permanent necessity. You couldn't spend your last sou, and say finally: So that's *that!*—No, if you lived even another ten minutes, you wanted a few more sous for something or other. Just to keep the business mechanically going, you needed money. You had to have it. Money you *have* to have. You needn't really have anything else. So that's *that!*—

Since, of course, it's not your own fault you are alive. Once you are alive, money is a necessity, and the only absolute necessity. All the rest you can get along without, at a pinch. But not money. Emphatically, that's *that!*—

She thought of Michaelis, and the money she might have had with him; and even that she didn't want. She preferred the lesser amount which she helped Clifford to make by his writing. That she actually helped to make—"Clifford and I together, we make twelve hundred a year out of writing"; so she put it to herself. Make money! Make it! Out of nowhere! Wring it out of the thin air! The last feat to be humanly proud of! The rest all-my-eye-Betty-Martin.

So she plodded home to Clifford, to join forces with him again, to make another story out of nothingness: and a story meant money. Clifford seemed to care very much whether his stories were considered first-class literature or not. Strictly, she didn't care. Nothing in it! said her father. Twelve hundred pounds last year! was the retort simple and final.

If you were young, you just set your teeth, and bit on and held on, till the money began to flow from the invisible; it was a question of power. It was a question of will; a subtle, subtle, powerful emanation of will out of yourself brought back to you the mysterious nothingness of money: a word on a bit of paper. It was a sort of magic, certainly it was triumph. The bitch-goddess! Well, if one had to prostitute oneself, let it be to a bitch-goddess! One could always despise her even while one prostituted oneself to her, which was good.

Clifford, of course, had still many childish taboos and fetishes. He wanted to be thought "really good," which was all cock-a-hoopy nonsense. What was really good was what actually caught on. It was no good being really good and getting left with it. It seemed as if most of the "really good" men just missed the bus. After all you only lived one life, and if you missed the bus, you were just left on the pavement, along with the rest of the failures.

Connie was contemplating a winter in London with Clifford, next winter. He and she had caught the bus all right, so they might as well ride on top for a bit, and show it.

The worst of it was, Clifford tended to become vague, absent, and to fall into fits of vacant depression. It was the wound to his psyche coming out. But it made Connie want to scream. Oh, God, if the mechanism of the consciousness itself was going to go wrong, then what was one to do? Hang it all, one did one's bit! Was one to be let down *absolutely?*

Sometimes she wept bitterly, but even as she wept she was saying to herself: Silly fool, wetting hankies! As if that would get you anywhere!

Since Michaelis, she had made up her mind she wanted nothing. That seemed the simplest solution of the otherwise insoluble. She wanted nothing more than what she'd got; only she wanted to get ahead with what she'd got: Clifford, the stories, Wragby, the Lady Chatterley business, money and fame, such as it was... she wanted to go ahead with it all. Love, sex, all that sort of stuff, just water-ices! Lick it up and forget it. If you don't hang on to it in your mind, it's nothing. Sex especially... nothing! Make up your mind to it, and you've solved the problem. Sex and a cocktail: they both lasted about as long, had the same effect, and amounted to about the same thing.

But a child, a baby! that was still one of the sensations. She would venture very gingerly on that experiment. There was the man to consider, and it was curious, there wasn't a man in the world whose children you wanted. Mick's children! Repulsive thought! As lief have a child to a rabbit! Tommy Dukes?... he was very nice, but somehow you couldn't associate him with a baby, another generation. He ended in himself. And out of all the rest of Clifford's pretty wide acquaintance, there was not a man who did not rouse her contempt, when she thought of having a child by him. There were several who would have been quite possible as lovers, even Mick. But as people to have children with! Ugh! Humiliation and abomination.

So that was that!

Nevertheless, Connie had the child at the back of her mind. Wait! Wait! She would sift the generations of men through her sieve, and see if she couldn't find one who would do—"Go ye into the streets and byways of Jerusalem, and see if ye can find *a man*." It had been impossible to find a man in the Jerusalem of the prophet, though there were thousands of male humans. But *a man!* C'est une autre chose!

She had an idea that he would have to be a foreigner: not an Englishman, still less an Irishman. A real foreigner.

But wait! wait! Next winter she would get Clifford to London; the following winter she would get him abroad to the south of France, Italy. Wait! She was in no hurry about the child. That was her own private affair, and the one point on which, in her own queer, female way, she was serious to the bottom of her soul. She was not going to risk any chance comer, not she! One might take a lover almost at any moment, but a man who should beget a child on one... wait! wait! it's a very different matter—"Go ye into the streets and byways of Jerusalem...." It was not a question of love; it was a question of *a man*. Why, one might even rather hate him, personally. Yet if he was the man, what would one's personal hate matter? This business concerned another part of oneself.

It had rained as usual, and the paths were too sodden for Clifford's chair, but Connie would go out. She went out alone every day now, mostly in the wood, where she was really alone. She saw nobody there.

This day, however, Clifford wanted to send a message to the keeper, and as the boy was laid up with influenza—somebody always seemed to have influenza at Wragby—Connie said she would call at the cottage.

The air was soft and dead, as if all the world were slowly dying. Gray and clammy and silent, even from the shuffling of the collieries, for the pits were working short time, and today they were stopped altogether. The end of all things!

In the wood all was utterly inert and motionless, only great drops fell from the bare boughs, with a hollow little crash. For the rest, among the old trees was depth within depth of gray, hopeless inertia, nothingness.

Connie walked dimly on. From the old wood came an ancient melancholy, somehow soothing to her, better than the harsh insentience of the outer world. She liked the *inwardness* of the remnant of forest, the unspeaking reticence of the old trees. They seemed a very power of silence, and yet a vital presence. They, too, were waiting: obstinately, stoically waiting, and giving off a potency of silence. Perhaps they were only waiting for the end; to be cut down, cleared away, the end of the forest, for them the end of all things. But perhaps their strong and aristocratic silence, the silence of strong trees, meant something else.

As she came out of the wood on the north side, the keeper's cottage, a rather dark, brown stone cottage, with gables and a handsome chimney, looked uninhabited, it was so silent and alone. But a thread of smoke rose from the chimney, and the little railed-in garden in the front of the house was dug and kept very tidy. The door was shut.

Now she was here she felt a little shy of the man, with his curious farseeing eyes. She did not like bringing him orders, and felt like going away again. She knocked softly, no one came. She knocked again, but still not loudly. There was no answer. She peeped through the window, and saw the dark little room, with its almost sinister privacy, not wanting to be invaded.

She stood and listened, and it seemed to her she heard sounds from the back of the cottage. Having failed to make herself heard, her mettle was roused, she would not be defeated.

So she went around the side of the house. At the back of the cottage the land rose steeply, so the back yard was sunken, and enclosed by a low stone wall. She turned the corner of the house and stopped. In the little yard two paces beyond her, the man was washing himself, utterly unaware. He was naked to the hips, his velveteen breeches slipping down over his slender loins. And his white slim back was curved over a big bowl of soapy water, in which he ducked his head, shaking his head with a queer, quick little motion, lifting his slender white arms, and pressing the soapy water from his ears, quick, subtle as a weasel playing with water, and utterly alone. Connie backed away round the corner of the house, and hurried away to the wood. In spite of herself, she had had a shock. After all, merely a man washing himself; commonplace enough, Heaven knows!

Yet in some curious way it was a visionary experience: it had hit her in the middle of the body. She saw the clumsy breeches slipping down over the pure, delicate, white loins, the bones showing a little, and the sense of aloneness, of a creature purely alone, overwhelmed her. Perfect, white, solitary nudity of a creature that lives alone, and inwardly alone. And beyond that, a certain beauty of a pure creature. Not the stuff of beauty, not even the body of beauty, but a lambency, the warm, white flame of a single life, revealing itself in contours that one might touch: a body!

Connie had received the shock of vision in her womb, and she knew it; it lay inside her. But with her mind she was inclined to ridicule. A man washing himself in a backyard! No doubt with evil-smelling yellow soap!—She was rather annoyed; why should she be made to stumble on these vulgar privacies?

So she walked away from herself, but after a while she sat down on a stump. She was too confused to think. But in the coil of her confusion, she was determined to deliver her message to the fellow. She would not be balked. She must give him time to dress himself, but not time to go out. He was probably preparing to go out somewhere.

So she sauntered slowly back, listening. As she came near, the cottage looked just the same. A dog barked, and she knocked at the door, her heart beating in spite of herself.

She heard the man coming lightly downstairs. He opened the door quickly, and startled her. He looked uneasy himself, but instantly a laugh came on his face.

"Lady Chatterley!" he said. "Will you come in?"

His manner was so perfectly easy and good, she stepped over the threshold into the rather dreary little room.

"I only called with a message from Sir Clifford," she said in her soft, rather breathless voice.

The man was looking at her with those blue, all-seeing eyes of his, which made her turn her face aside a little. He thought her comely, almost beautiful, in her shyness, and he took command of the situation himself at once.

"Would you care to sit down?" he asked, presuming she would not. The door stood open.

"No thanks! Sir Clifford wondered if you would . . ." and she delivered her message, looking unconsciously into his eyes again. And now his eyes looked warm and kind, particularly to a woman, wonderfully warm, and kind, and at ease.

"Very good, your Ladyship. I will see to it at once."

Taking an order, his whole self had changed, glazed over with a sort of hardness and distance. Connie hesitated, she ought to go. But she looked round the clean, tidy, rather dreary little sitting-room with something like dismay.

"Do you live here quite alone?" she asked.

"Quite alone, your Ladyship."

"But your mother . . . ?"

"She lives in her own cottage in the village."

"With the child?" asked Connie.

"With the child!"

And his plain, rather worn face took on an indefinable look of derision. It was a face that changed all the time, baffling.

"No," he said, seeing Connie stand at a loss, "my mother comes and cleans up for me on Saturdays; I do the rest myself."

Again Connie looked at him. His eyes were smiling again, a little mockingly, but warm and blue, and somehow kind. She wondered at him. He was in trousers and flannel shirt and a gray tie, his hair soft and damp, his face rather pale and worn-looking. When the eyes ceased to laugh they looked as if they had suffered a great deal, still without losing their warmth. But a pallor of isolation came over him, she was not really there for him.

She wanted to say so many things, and she said nothing. Only she looked up at him again, and remarked:

"I hope I didn't disturb you?"

The faint smile of mockery narrowed his eyes.

"Only combing my hair, if you don't mind. I'm sorry I hadn't a coat on, but then I had no idea who was knocking. Nobody knocks here, and the unexpected sounds ominous."

He went in front of her down the garden path to hold the gate. In his shirt, without the clumsy velveteen coat, she saw again how slender he was, thin, stooping a little. Yet, as she passed him, there was something young and bright in his fair hair, and his quick eyes. He would be a man about thirty-seven or eight.

She plodded on into the wood, knowing he was looking after her; he upset her so much, in spite of herself.

And he, as he went indoors, was thinking: "She's nice, she's real! she's nicer than she knows."

She wondered very much about him; he seemed so unlike a gamekeeper, so unlike a workingman anyhow; although he had something in common with the local people. But also something very uncommon.

"The gamekeeper, Mellors, is a curious kind of person," she said to Clifford: "he might almost be a gentleman."

"Might he?" said Clifford. "I hadn't noticed."

"But isn't there something special about him?" Connie insisted.

"I think he's quite a nice fellow, but I know very little about him. He only came out of the army last year, less than a year ago. From India, I rather think. He may have picked up certain tricks out there; perhaps he was an officer's servant, and improved on his position. Some of the men were like that. But it does them no good, they have to fall back into their old places when they get home again."

Connie gazed at Clifford contemplatively. She saw in him the peculiar tight rebuff against anyone of the lower classes who might be really climbing up, which she knew was characteristic of his breed.

"But don't you think there is something special about him?" she asked.

"Frankly, no! Nothing I had noticed."

He looked at her curiously, uneasily, half-suspiciously. And she felt he wasn't telling her the real truth; he wasn't telling himself the real truth, that was it. He disliked any suggestion of a really exceptional human being. People must be more or less at his level, or below it.

Connie felt again the tightness, niggardliness of the men of her generation. They were so tight, so scared of life!

7

When Connie went up to her bedroom she did what she had not done for a long time: took off all her clothes, and looked at herself naked in the huge mirror. She did not know what she was looking for, or at, very definitely, yet she moved the lamp till it shone full on her.

And she thought, as she had thought so often, . . . what a frail, easily hurt, rather pathetic thing a human body is, naked; somehow a little unfinished, incomplete!

She had been supposed to have a rather good figure, but now she was out of fashion: a little too female, not enough like an adolescent boy. She was not very tall, a bit Scottish and short; but she had a certain fluent, down-slipping grace that might have been beauty. Her skin was faintly tawny, her limbs had a certain stillness, her body should have had a full, down-slipping richness; but it lacked something.

Instead of ripening its firm, down-running curves, her body was flattening and going a little harsh. It was as if it had not had enough sun and warmth; it was a little grayish and sapless.

Disappointed of its real womanhood, it had not succeeded in becoming boyish, and unsubstantial, and transparent; instead it had gone opaque.

Her breasts were rather small, and dropping pear-shaped. But they were unripe, a little bitter, without meaning hanging there. And her belly had lost the fresh, round gleam it had had when she was young, in the days of her German boy, who had really loved her physically. Then it was young and expectant, with a real look of its own. Now it was going slack, and a little flat, thinner, but with a slack thinness. Her thighs, too, that used to look so quick and glimpsey in their female roundness, somehow they too were going flat, slack, meaningless.

Her body was going meaningless, going full and opaque, so much insignificant substance. It made her feel immensely depressed and hopeless. What hope was there? She was old, old at twenty-seven, with no gleam and sparkle in the flesh. Old through neglect and denial, yes denial. Fashionable women kept their bodies bright like delicate porcelain, by external attention. There was nothing inside the porcelain; but she was not even as bright as that. The mental life! Suddenly she hated it with a rushing fury, the swindle!

She looked in the other mirror's reflection at her back, her waist, her loins. She was getting thinner, but to her it was not becoming. The crumple of her waist at the back, as she bent back to look, was a little weary; and it used to be so gay-looking. And the longish slope of her haunches and her buttocks had lost its gleam and its sense of richness. Gone! Only the German boy had loved it, and he was ten years dead, very nearly. How time went by! Ten years dead, and she was only twenty-seven. That healthy boy with his fresh, clumsy sensuality that she had then been so scornful of! Where would she find it now? It was gone out of men. They had their pathetic, two-seconds spasms like Michaelis; but no healthy human sensuality, that warms the blood and freshens the whole being.

Still she thought the most beautiful part of her was the long-sloping fall of the haunches from the socket of the back, and the slumberous, round stillness of the buttocks. Like hillocks of sand the Arabs say, soft and downward-slipping with a long slope. Here the life still lingered hoping. But here too she was thinner, and going unripe, astringent.

But the front of her body made her miserable. It was already beginning to slacken, with a slack sort of thinness, almost withered, going old before it had ever really lived. She thought of the child she might somehow bear. Was she fit, anyhow?

She slipped into her nightdress, and went to bed, where she sobbed bitterly. And in her bitterness burned a cold indignation against Clifford, and his writings and his talk: against all the men of his sort who defrauded a woman even of her own body.

Unjust! Unjust! The sense of deep physical injustice burned to her very soul.

But in the morning, all the same, she was up at seven, and going downstairs to Clifford. She had to help him in all the intimate things, for he had no man, and refused a womanservant. The housekeeper's husband, who had known him as a boy, helped him, and did any heavy lifting; but Connie did the personal things, and she did them willingly. It was a demand on her, but she had wanted to do what she could.

So she hardly ever went away from Wragby, and never for more than a day or two; when Mrs. Betts, the housekeeper, attended to Clifford. He, as was inevitable in the course of time, took all the service for granted. It was natural he should.

And yet, deep inside herself, a sense of injustice, of being defrauded, began to burn in Connie. The physical sense of injustice is a dangerous feeling, once it is awakened. It must have outlet, or it eats away the one in whom it is aroused. Poor Clifford, he was not to blame. His was the greater misfortune. It was all part of the general catastrophe.

And yet was he not in a way to blame? The lack of warmth, this lack of the simple, warm, physical contact, was he not to blame for that? He was never really warm, nor even kind, only thoughtful, considerate, in a well-bred, cold sort of way! But never warm as a man can be warm to a woman, as even Connie's father could be warm to her, with the warmth of a man who did himself well, and intended to, but who still could comfort a woman with a bit of his masculine glow.

But Clifford was not like that. His whole race was not like that. They were all inwardly hard and separate, and warmth to them was just bad taste. You had to get on without it, and hold your own; which was all very well if you were of the same class and race. Then you could keep yourself cold and be very estimable, and hold your own, and enjoy the satisfaction of holding it. But if you were of another class and another race it wouldn't do; there was no fun merely holding your own, and feeling you belonged to the ruling class. What was the point, when even the smartest aristocrats had really nothing positive of their own to hold, and their rule was really a farce, not rule at all? What was the point? It was all cold nonsense.

A sense of rebellion smoldered in Connie. What was the good of it all? What was the good of her sacrifice, her devoting her life to Clifford? What was she serving, after all? A cold spirit of vanity, that had no warm human contacts, and that was as corrupt as any low-born Jew, in craving for prostitution to the bitch-goddess, Success. Even Clifford's cool and contactless assurance that he belonged to the ruling class didn't prevent his tongue lolling out of his mouth, as he panted after the bitch-goddess. After all, Michaelis was really more dignified in the matter, and far, far more successful. Really, if you looked closely at Clifford, he was a buffoon, and a buffoon is more humiliating than a bounder.

As between the two men, Michaelis really had far more use for her than Clifford had. He had even more need of her. Any good nurse can attend to crippled legs! And as for the heroic effort, Michaelis was a heroic rat, and Clifford was very much of a poodle showing off.

There were people staying in the house, among them Clifford's Aunt Eva, Lady Bennerley. She was a thin woman of sixty, with a red nose, a widow, and still something of a "grande dame." She belonged to one of the best families, and had the character to carry it off. Connie liked her, she was so perfectly simple and frank, as far as she intended to be frank, and superficially kind. Inside herself she was a past-mistress in holding her own, and holding other people a little lower. She was not at all a snob: far too sure of herself. She was perfect at the social sport of coolly holding her own, and making other people defer to her.

She was kind to Connie, and tried to worm into her woman's soul with the sharp gimlet of her well-born observations.

"You're quite wonderful, in my opinion," she said to Connie. "You've done wonders for Clifford. I never saw any budding genius myself, and there he is all the rage"—Aunt Eva was quite complacently proud of Clifford's success. Another feather in the family cap. She didn't care a straw about his books, but why should she?

"Oh, I don't think it's my doing," said Connie.

"It must be! Can't be anybody else's. And it seems to me you don't get enough out of it."

"How?"

"Look at the way you are shut up here. I said to Clifford: 'If that child rebels one day, you'll have yourself to thank!' "

"But Clifford never denies me anything," said Connie.

"Look here, my dear child"—and Lady Bennerley laid her thin hand on Connie's arm. "A woman has to live her life, or live to repent not having lived it. Believe me!" And she took another sip of brandy, which maybe was her form of repentance.

"But I do live my life, don't I?"

"Not in my idea! Clifford should bring you to London and let you go about. His sort of friends are all right for him, but what are they for you? If I were you I should think it wasn't good enough. You'll let your youth slip by, and you'll spend your old age, and your middle age too, repenting it."

Her ladyship lapsed into contemplative silence, soothed by the brandy.

But Connie was not keen on going to London, and being steered into the smart world by Lady Bennerley. She didn't feel really smart, it wasn't interesting. And she did feel the peculiar, withering coldness under it all; like the soil of Labrador, which has gay little flowers on its surface, and a foot down is frozen.

Tommy Dukes was at Wragby, and another man, Harry Winterslow, and Jack Strangeways with his wife Olive. The talk was much more desultory than when only the cronies were there, and everybody was a bit bored, for the weather was bad and there was only billiards, and the pianola to dance to.

Olive was reading a book about the future, when babies would be bred in bottles, and women would be "immunized."

"Jolly good thing too!" she said. "Then a woman can live her own life." Strangeways wanted children, and she didn't.

"How'd you like to be immunized?" Winterslow asked her with an ugly smile.

"I hope I am; naturally," she said. "Anyhow the future's going to have more sense, and a woman needn't be dragged down by her *functions*."

"Perhaps she'll float off into space altogether," said Dukes.

"I do think sufficient civilization ought to eliminate a lot of the physical disabilities," said Clifford. "All the love business, for example; it might just as well go. I suppose it would if we could breed babies in bottles."

"No!" cried Olive. "That might leave all the more room for fun."

"I suppose," said Lady Bennerley, contemplatively, "if the love business went, something else would take its place. Morphia, perhaps. A little morphine in all the air. It would be wonderfully refreshing for everybody."

"The government releasing ether into the air on Saturdays, for a cheerful weekend!" said Jack. "Sounds all right, but where should we be by Wednesday?"

"So long as you can forget your body you are happy," said Lady Bennerley. "And the moment you begin to be aware of your body, you are wretched. So, if civilization is any good, it has to help us forget our bodies, and then time passes happily without our knowing it."

"Help us to get rid of our bodies altogether," said Winterslow. "It's quite time man began to improve on his own nature, especially the physical side of it."

"Imagine if we floated like tobacco smoke," said Connie.

"It won't happen," said Dukes. "Our old show will come flop; our civilization is going to fall. It's going down the bottomless pit, down the chasm. And, believe me, the only bridge across the chasm will be the phallus!"

"Oh! do, *do* be impossible, General!" cried Olive.

"I believe our civilization is going to collapse," said Aunt Eva.

"And what will come after it?" asked Clifford.

"I haven't the faintest idea; but something, I suppose," said the elderly lady.

"Connie says people like wisps of smoke, and Olive says immunized women and babies in bottles, and Dukes says the phallus is the bridge to what comes next. I wonder what it will really be?" said Clifford.

"Oh, don't bother! Let's get on with today," said Olive. "Only hurry up with the breeding bottle, and let us poor women off."

"There might even be real men, in the next phase," said Tommy. "Real, intelligent, wholesome men, and wholesome nice women! Wouldn't that be a change, an enormous change from us? *We're* not men, and the women aren't women. We're only cerebrating makeshifts, mechanical and intellectual experiments. There may even come a civilization of genuine men and women, instead of our little lot of cleverjacks, all at the intelligence-age of seven. It would be even more amazing than men of smoke or babies in bottles."

"Oh, when people begin to talk about real women, I give up," said Olive.

"Certainly nothing but the spirit in us is worth having," said Winterslow.

"Spirits!" said Jack, drinking his whiskey-and-soda.

"Think so? Give me the resurrection of the body!" said Dukes. "But it'll come, in time, when we've shoved the cerebral stone away a bit, the money and the rest. Then we'll get a democracy of touch, instead of a democracy of pocket."

Something echoed inside Connie: "Give me the democracy of touch, the resurrection of the body!" She didn't at all know what it meant, but it comforted her, as meaningless things may do.

Anyhow everything was terribly silly, and she was exasperatedly bored by it all, by Clifford, by Aunt Eva, by Olive and Jack, and Winterslow, and even by Dukes. Talk, talk, talk! What hell it was, the continual rattle of it!

Then, when all the people went, it was no better. She continued plodding on, but exasperation and irritation had got hold of her body, she couldn't escape. The days seemed to grind by, with curious painfulness, yet nothing happened. Only she was getting thinner; even the housekeeper noticed it, and asked her about herself. Even Tommy Dukes insisted she was not well, though she said she was all right. Only she began to be afraid of the ghastly white tombstones, that peculiar loathsome whiteness of Carrara marble, detestable as false teeth, which stuck up on the hillside, under Tevershall Church, and which she saw with such grim plainness from the park. The bristling of the hideous false teeth of tombstones on the hill affected her with a grisly kind of horror. She felt the time not far off when she would be buried there, added to the ghastly host under the tombstones and the monuments, in these filthy Midlands.

She needed help, and she knew it; so she wrote a little *cri de coeur* to her sister, Hilda. "I'm not well lately, and I don't know what's the matter with me."

Down posted Hilda from Scotland, where she had taken up her abode. She came in March, alone, driving herself in a nimble two-seater. Up the drive she came, tooting up the incline, then sweeping round the oval of grass, where the two great wild beech trees stood, on the flat in front of the house.

Connie had run out to the steps. Hilda pulled up her car, got out, and kissed her sister.

"But, Connie!" she cried. "Whatever is the matter?"

"Nothing!" said Connie, rather shamefacedly; but she knew how she had suffered in contrast to Hilda. Both sisters had the same rather golden, glowing skin, and soft brown hair, and naturally strong, warm physique. But now Connie was thin and earthy-looking, with a scraggy, yellowish neck, that stuck out of her jumper.

"But you're ill, child!" said Hilda, in the soft, rather breathless voice, that both sisters had alike. Hilda was nearly, but not quite, two years older than Connie.

"No, not ill. Perhaps I'm bored," said Connie a little pathetically.

The light of battle glowed in Hilda's face: she was a woman, soft and still as she seemed, of the old amazon sort, not made to fit with men.

"This wretched place!" she said softly, looking at poor old, lumbering Wragby with real hate. She looked soft and warm herself, as a ripe pear, and she was an amazon of the real old breed.

She went quietly in to Clifford. He thought how handsome she looked, but also he shrank from her. His wife's family did not have his sort of manners, or his sort of etiquette. He considered them rather outsiders, but once they got inside they made him jump through the hoop.

He sat square and well-groomed in his chair, his hair sleek and blond, and his face fresh, his blue eyes pale, and a little prominent, his expression inscrutable, but well-bred. Hilda thought it sulky and stupid, and he waited. He had an air of aplomb, but Hilda didn't care what he had an air of; she was up in arms, and if he'd been Pope or Emperor it would have been just the same.

"Connie's looking awfully unwell," she said in her soft voice, fixing him with her beautiful, glowering gray eyes. She looked so maidenly, so did Connie; but he well knew the stone of Scottish obstinacy underneath.

"She's a little thinner," he said.

"Haven't you done anything about it?"

"Do you think it necessary?" he asked, with his suavest English stiffness, for the two things often go together.

Hilda only glowered at him without replying; repartee was not her forte, nor Connie's; so she glowered, and he was much more uncomfortable than if she had said things.

"I'll take her to a doctor," said Hilda at length. "Can you suggest a good one round here?"

"I'm afraid I can't."

"Then I'll take her to London, where we have a doctor we trust."

Though boiling with rage, Clifford said nothing.

"I suppose I may as well stay the night," said Hilda, pulling off her gloves, "and I'll drive her to town tomorrow."

Clifford was yellow at the gills with anger, and at evening the whites of his eyes were a little yellow too. He ran to liver. But Hilda was consistently modest and maidenly.

"You must have a nurse or somebody to look after you personally. You should really have a manservant," said Hilda as they sat, with apparent calmness, at coffee after dinner. She spoke in her soft, seemingly gentle way, but Clifford felt she was hitting him on the head with a bludgeon.

"You think so?" he said coldly.

"I'm sure! It's necessary. Either that, or father and I must take Connie away for some months. This can't go on."

"What can't go on?"

"Haven't you looked at the child?" asked Hilda, gazing at him full stare. He looked rather like a huge, boiled crayfish, at the moment; or so she thought.

"Connie and I will discuss it," he said.

"I've already discussed it with her," said Hilda.

Clifford had been long enough in the hands of nurses; he hated them, because they left him no real privacy. And a manservant! . . . he couldn't stand a man hanging round him. Almost better any woman. But why not Connie?

The two sisters drove off in the morning, Connie looking rather like an Easter lamb, rather small beside Hilda, who held the wheel. Sir Malcolm was away, but the Kensington house was open.

The doctor examined Connie carefully, and asked her all about her life. "I see your photograph, and Sir Clifford's, in the illustrated papers sometimes. Almost notorieties, aren't you? That's how the quiet little girls grow up, though you're only a quiet little girl even now, in spite of the illustrated papers. No, no! There's nothing organically wrong, but it won't do! It won't do! Tell Sir Clifford he's got to bring you to town, to take you abroad, and amuse you. You've got to be amused, got to! Your vitality is much too low; no reserves, no reserves. The nerves of the heart a bit queer already: oh, yes. Nothing but nerves; I'd put you right in a month at Cannes or Biarritz. But it mustn't go on, *mustn't,*

I tell you, or I won't be answerable for consequences. You're spending your life without renewing it. You've got to be amused, properly, healthily amused. You're spending your vitality without making any. Can't go on, you know. Depression! avoid depression!"

Hilda set her jaw, and that meant something.

Michaelis heard they were in town, and came running with roses. "Why, whatever's wrong?" he cried. "You're a shadow of yourself. Why, I never saw such a change! Why ever didn't you let me know? Come to Nice with me! Come down to Sicily! Go on, come to Sicily with me, it's lovely there just now. You want sun! You want life! Why, you're wasting away! Come away with me! Come to Africa! Oh, hang Sir Clifford! Chuck him, and come along with me. I'll marry you the minute he divorces you. Come along and try a life! God's love! That place Wragby would kill anybody. Beastly place! Foul place! Kill anybody! Come away with me into the sun! It's the sun you want, of course, and a bit of normal life."

But Connie's heart simply stood still at the thought of abandoning Clifford there and then. She couldn't do it. No . . . no! She just couldn't. She had to go back to Wragby.

Michaelis was disgusted. Hilda didn't like Michaelis, but she *almost* preferred him to Clifford. Back went the sisters to the Midlands.

Hilda talked to Clifford, who still had yellow eyeballs when they got back. He, too, in his way was overwrought; but he had to listen to all Hilda said, to all the doctor had said, not to what Michaelis had said, of course, and he sat mum through the ultimatum.

"Here is the address of a good manservant, who was with an invalid patient of the doctor's till he died last month. He is really a good man, and fairly sure to come."

"But I'm *not* an invalid, and I will *not* have a manservant," said Clifford, poor devil.

"And here are the addresses of two women; I saw one of them, she would do very well; a woman of about fifty, quiet, strong, kind, and in her way cultured. . . ."

Clifford only sulked, and would not answer.

"Very well, Clifford. If we don't settle something by tomorrow, I shall telegraph to father, and we shall take Connie away."

"Will Connie go?" asked Clifford.

"She doesn't want to, but she knows she must. Mother died of cancer, brought on by fretting. We're not running any risks."

So next day Clifford suggested Mrs. Bolton, the Tevershall parish nurse. Apparently Mrs. Betts had thought of her. Mrs. Bolton was just retiring from her parish duties to take up private nursing jobs. Clifford had a queer dread of delivering himself into the hands of a stranger, but this Mrs. Bolton had once nursed him through scarlet fever, and he knew her.

The two sisters at once called on Mrs. Bolton, in a newish house in a row, quite select for Tevershall. They found a rather good-looking woman of forty-odd, in a nurse's uniform, with a white collar and apron, just making herself tea, in a small, crowded sitting room.

Mrs. Bolton was most attentive and polite, seemed quite nice, spoke with a bit of a broad slur, but in heavily correct English, and from having bossed the sick colliers for a good many years, had a very good opinion of herself, and a fair amount of assurance. In short, in her tiny way, one of the governing class in the village, very much respected.

"Yes, Lady Chatterley's not looking at all well! Why she used to be that bonny, didn't she now? But she's been failing all winter! Oh, it's hard, it is. Poor Sir Clifford! Eh, that war, it's a lot to answer for."

And Mrs. Bolton would come to Wragby at once, if Dr. Shardlow would let her off. She had another fortnight's parish nursing to do, by rights, but they might get a substitute, you know.

Hilda posted off to Dr. Shardlow, and on the following Sunday Mrs. Bolton drove up in Leiver's cab to Wragby, with two trunks. Hilda had talks with her; Mrs. Bolton was ready at any moment to talk. And she seemed so young! the way the passion would flush in her rather pale cheek. She was forty-seven.

Her husband, Ted Bolton, had been killed in the pit, twenty-two years ago, twenty-two years last Christmas, just at Christmas time, leaving her with two children, one a baby in arms. Oh, the baby was married now—Edith—to a young man in Boots Cash Chemists in Sheffield. The other one was a schoolteacher in Chesterfield, she came home weekends, when she wasn't asked out anywhere. Young folks enjoyed themselves nowadays; not like when she, Ivy Bolton, was young.

Ted Bolton was twenty-eight when he was killed in an explosion down th' pit. The butty in front shouted to them all to lie down quick; there were four of them. And they all lay down in time, only Ted, and it killed him. Then at the inquiry, on the masters' side they said Ted had been frightened, and trying to run away, and not obeying orders, so it was like his fault really. So the compensation was only three hundred pounds, and they made out as if it was more of a gift than legal compensation, because it was really the man's own fault. And they wouldn't let her have the money down; she wanted to have a little shop. But they said she'd no doubt squander it, perhaps in drink! So she had to draw it thirty shillings a week. Yes, she had to go every Monday morning down to the offices, and stand there a couple of hours waiting her turn; yes, for almost four years she went every Monday. And what could she do with two little children on her hands? But Ted's mother was very good to her. When the baby could toddle she'd keep both the children for the day, while she, Ivy Bolton, went to Sheffield, and attended classes in ambulance, and then the fourth year she even took a nursing course and got qualified. She was determined to be independent and keep her children. So she was assistant at Uthwaite hospital, just a little place, for a while. But when the Company, the Tevershall Colliery Company, really Sir Geoffrey, saw that she could get on by herself, they were very good to her, gave her the parish nursing, and stood by her, she would say that for them. And she'd done it ever since, till now it was getting a bit too much for her, she needed something a bit lighter, there was such a lot of traipsing round if you were a district nurse.

"Yes, the Company's been very good to *me*, I always say it. But I should never forget what they said about Ted, for he was as steady and fearless a chap as ever set foot on the cage, and it was as good as branding him a coward. But there, he was dead, and could say nothing to none of 'em."

It was a queer mixture of feelings the woman showed as she talked. She liked the colliers, whom she had nursed for so long; but she felt very superior to them. She felt almost upper class; and at the same time a resentment against the ruling class smoldered in her. The masters! In a dispute between masters and men, she was always for the men. But when there was no question of contest, she was pining to be superior, to be one of the upper class. The upper classes fascinated her, appealing to her peculiar English passion for superiority. She was thrilled to come to Wragby, thrilled to talk to Lady Chatterley; my word, different from the common colliers' wives! She said so in so many words. Yet one could see a grudge against the Chatterleys peep out in her; the grudge against the masters.

"Why, yes, of course, it would wear Lady Chatterley out! It's a mercy she has a sister to come and help her. Men don't think; high and low alike, they take what a woman does for them for granted. Oh, I've told the colliers off about it many a time. But it's very hard for Sir Clifford, you know, crippled like that. They were always a haughty family, standoffish in a way, as they've a right to be. But then, to be brought down like that! And it's very hard on Lady Chatterley, perhaps harder on her. What she misses! I only had Ted three years, but my word, while I had him I had a husband I could never forget. He was one in a thousand, and jolly as the day. Who'd ever have thought he'd get killed? I don't believe it to this day, somehow; I've never believed it, though I washed him with my own hands. But he was never dead for me, he never was. I never took it in."

This was a new voice in Wragby, very new for Connie to hear; it roused a new ear in her.

For the first week or so, Mrs. Bolton, however, was very quiet at Wragby; her assured, bossy manner left her, and she was nervous. With Clifford she was shy, almost frightened and silent. He liked that, and soon recovered his self-possession, letting her do things for him without even noticing her.

"She's a useful nonentity!" he said. Connie opened her eyes in wonder, but did not contradict him. So different are impressions on two different people!

And he soon became rather superb, somewhat lordly with the nurse. She had rather expected it, and he played up without knowing. So susceptible we are to what is expected of us! The colliers had been so like children, talking to her, and telling her what hurt them, while she bandaged them, or nursed them. They had always made her feel so grand, almost superhuman in her administrations. Now Clifford made her feel small, and like a servant, and she accepted it without a word, adjusting herself to the upper classes.

She came very mute, with her long, handsome face, and downcast eyes, to administer to him. And she said very humbly: "Shall I do this now, Sir Clifford? Shall I do that?"

"No, leave it for a time, I'll have it done later."

"Very well, Sir Clifford."

"Come in again in half-an-hour."

"Very well, Sir Clifford."

"And just take those old papers out, will you?"

"Very well, Sir Clifford."

She went softly, and in half-an-hour she came softly again. She was bullied, but she didn't mind. She was experiencing the upper classes. She neither resented nor disliked Clifford; he was just part of a phenomenon, the phenomenon of the high-class folks, so far unknown to her, but now to be known. She felt more at home with Lady Chatterley, and after all it's the mistress of the house matters most.

Mrs. Bolton helped Clifford to bed at night, and slept across the passage from his room, and came if he rang for her in the night. She also helped him in the morning, and soon valeted him completely, even shaving him, in her soft, tentative woman's way. She was very good and competent, and she soon knew how to have him in her power. He wasn't so very different from the colliers after all, when you lathered his chin, and softly rubbed the bristles. The standoffishness and the lack of frankness didn't bother her, she was having a new experience.

Clifford, however, inside himself, never quite forgave Connie for giving up her personal care of him to a strange hired woman. It killed, he said to himself, the real flower of the intimacy between him and her. But Connie didn't mind that. The fine flower of their intimacy was to her rather like an orchid, a bulb stuck parasitic on her tree of life, and producing, to her eyes, a rather shabby flower.

Now she had more time to herself she could softly play the piano, up in her room, and sing: "Touch not the nettle . . . for the bonds of love are ill to loose."

She had not realized till lately how ill to loose they were, these bonds of love. But thank heaven she had loosened them! She was so glad to be alone, not always to have to talk to him. When he was alone he tapped-tapped-tapped on a typewriter, to infinity. But when he was not "working," and she was there, he talked, always talked; infinite small analysis of people and motives, and results, characters and personalities, till now she had had enough. For years she had loved it, until she had had enough, and then suddenly it was too much. She was thankful to be alone.

It was as if thousands and thousands of little roots and threads of consciousness in him and her had grown together into a tangled mass, till they could crowd no more, and the plant was dying. Now quietly, subtly she was unraveling the tangle of his consciousness and hers, breaking the threads gently, one by one, with patience and impatience to get clear. But the bonds of such love are more ill to loose even than most bonds; though Mrs. Bolton's coming had been a great help.

But he still wanted the old intimate evenings of talk with Connie: talk or reading aloud. But now she could arrange that Mrs. Bolton should come at ten to disturb them. At ten o'clock Connie could go upstairs and be alone. Clifford was in good hands with Mrs. Bolton.

Mrs. Bolton ate with Mrs. Betts in the housekeeper's room, since they were all agreeable. And it was curious how much closer the servants' quarters seemed to have come; right up to the doors of Clifford's study, when before they were so remote. For Mrs. Betts would sometimes sit in Mrs. Bolton's room, and Connie heard their lowered voices, and felt somehow the strong, outer vibration of the working people almost invading the sitting rooms, when she and Clifford were alone. So changed was Wragby merely by Mrs. Bolton's coming.

And Connie felt herself released, in another world; she felt she breathed differently. But still she was afraid of how many of her roots, perhaps mortal ones, were tangled with Clifford's. Yet still, she breathed freer, a new phase was going to begin in her life.

❖ 8 ❖

Mrs. Bolton also kept a cherishing eye on Connie, feeling she must extend to her her female and professional protection. She was always urging her ladyship to walk out, to drive to Uthwaite, to be in the air. For Connie had got into the habit of sitting still by the fire, pretending to read, or to sew feebly, and hardly going out at all.

It was a blowy day soon after Hilda had gone, that Mrs. Bolton said: "Now, why don't you go for a walk through the wood, and look at the daffs behind the keeper's cottage? They're the prettiest sight you'd see in a day's march. And you could put some in your room, wild daffs are always so cheerful-looking, aren't they?"

Connie took it in good part, even daffs for daffodils. Wild daffodils! After all, one should not stew in one's own juice. The spring came back.... "Seasons return, but not to me returns Day, or the sweet approach of Ev'n or Morn."

And the keeper, his thin, white body, like a lonely pistil of an invisible flower! She had forgotten him in her unspeakable depression. But now something roused... "Pale beyond porch and portal"... the thing to do was to pass the porches and the portals.

She was stronger, she could walk better, and in the wood the wind would not be so tiring as it was across the park, flattening against her. She wanted to forget, to forget the world, and all the dreadful carrion-bodied people. "Ye must be born again! I believe in the resurrection of the body! Except a grain of wheat fall into the earth and die, it shall by no means bring forth. When the crocus cometh forth I too will emerge and see the sun!" In the wind of March endless phrases swept through her consciousness.

Little gusts of sunshine blew, strangely bright, and lit up the celandines at the wood's edge, under the hazel-rods, they spangled out bright and yellow. And the wood was still, stiller, but yet gusty with crossing sun. The first windflowers were out, and all the wood seemed pale with the pallor of endless little anemones, sprinkling the shaken floor. "The world has grown pale with thy breath." But it was the breath of Persephone, this time; she was out of hell on a cold morning. Cold breaths of wind came, and overhead there was an anger of entangled wind caught among the twigs. It, too, was caught and trying to tear itself free, the wind, like Absalom. How cold the anemones looked, bobbing their naked white shoulders over crinoline skirts of green. But they stood it. A few first bleached little primroses, too, by the path, and yellow buds unfolding themselves.

The roaring and swaying was overhead, only cold currents came down below. Connie was strangely excited in the wood, and the color flew in her cheeks, and burned blue in her eyes. She walked ploddingly, picking a few primroses and the first violets, that smelled sweet and cold, sweet and cold. And she drifted on without knowing where she was.

Till she came to the clearing, at the far end of the wood, and saw the green-stained stone cottage, looking almost rosy, like the flesh underneath a mushroom, its stone warmed in a burst of sun. And there was a sparkle of yellow jasmine by the door; the closed door. But no sound; no smoke from the chimney; no dog barking.

She went quietly round to the back, where the bank rose up; she had an excuse, to see the daffodils.

And they were there, the short-stemmed flowers, rustling and fluttering and shivering, so bright and alive, but with nowhere to hide their faces, as they turned them away from the wind.

They shook their bright, sunny little rags in bouts of distress. But perhaps they liked it really; perhaps they really liked the tossing.

Constance sat down with her back to a young pine tree, that swayed against her with curious life, elastic and powerful, rising up. The erect, alive thing, with its top in the sun! And she watched the daffodils turn golden, in a burst of sun that was warm on her hands and lap. Even she caught the faint, tarry scent of the flowers. And then, being so still and alone, she seemed to get into the current of her own proper destiny. She had been fastened by a rope, and jagging and snarring like a boat at its moorings; now she was loose and adrift.

The sunshine gave way to chill; the daffodils were in shadow, dipping silently. So they would dip through the day and the long cold night. So strong in their frailty!

She rose, a little stiff, took a few daffodils, and went down. She hated breaking the flowers, but she wanted just one or two to go with her. She would have to go back to Wragby and its walls, and now she hated it, especially its thick walls. Walls! Always walls! Yet one needed them in this wind.

When she got home Clifford asked her:

"Where did you go?"

"Right across the wood! Look, aren't the little daffodils adorable? To think they should come out of the earth!"

"Just as much out of the air and sunshine," he said.

"But modeled in the earth," she retorted, with a prompt contradiction, that surprised her a little.

The next afternoon she went to the wood again. She followed the broad riding that swerved round and up through the larches to a spring called John's Well. It was cold on this hillside, and not a flower in the darkness of larches. But the icy little spring softly pressed upwards from its tiny well-bed of pure, reddish-white pebbles. How icy and clear it was! brilliant! The new keeper had no doubt put in fresh pebbles. She heard the faint tinkle of water, as the tiny overflow trickled over and downhill. Even above the hissing boom of the larch-wood, that spread its bristling, leafless, wolfish darkness on the downslope, she heard the tinkle as of tiny water-bells.

This place was a little sinister, cold, damp, Yet the well must have been a drinking-place for hundreds of years. Now no more. Its tiny cleared space was lush and cold and dismal.

She rose and went slowly towards home. As she went she heard a faint tapping away on the right, and stood still to listen. Was it hammering, or a woodpecker? It was surely hammering.

She walked on, listening. And then she noticed a narrow track between young fir trees, a track that seemed to lead nowhere. But she felt it had been used. She turned down it adventurously, between the thick young firs, which gave way soon to the old oak wood. She followed the track, and the hammering drew nearer, in the silence of the windy wood, for trees make a silence even in their noise of wind.

She saw a secret little clearing, and a secret little hut made of rustic poles. And she had never been here before! She realized it was the quiet place where the growing pheasants were reared; the keeper in his shirt-sleeves was kneeling, hammering. The dog trotted forward with a short, sharp bark, and the keeper lifted his face suddenly and saw her. He had a startled look in his eyes.

He straightened himself and saluted, watching her in silence, as she came forward with weakening limbs. He resented the intrusion, he cherished his solitude as his only and last freedom in life.

"I wondered what the hammering was," she said, feeling weak and breathless, and a little afraid of him, as he looked so straight at her.

"Ah'm gettin' th' coops ready for th' young bods," he said, in broad vernacular.

She did not know what to say, and she felt weak.

"I should like to sit down a bit," she said.

"Come and sit 'ere i' th' 'ut," he said, going in front of her to the hut, pushing aside more timber and stuff, and drawing out a rustic chair, made of hazel sticks.

"Am Ah t'light yer a little fire?" he asked, with the curious naiveté of the dialect.

"Oh, don't bother," she replied.

But she looked at her hands: they were rather blue. So he quickly took some larch twigs to the little brick fireplace in the corner, and in a moment the yellow flame was running up the chimney. He made a place by the brick hearth.

"Sit 'ere then a bit, and warm yer," he said.

She obeyed him. He had that curious kind of protective authority she obeyed at once. So she sat and warmed her hands at the blaze, and dropped logs on the fire, whilst outside he was hammering again. She did not really want to sit, poked in a corner by the fire; she would rather have watched from the door, but she was being looked after, so she had to submit.

The hut was quite cozy, paneled with unvarnished deal, having a little rustic table and stool besides her chair, and a carpenter's bench, then a big box, tools, new boards, nails; and many things hung from pegs: axe, hatchet, traps, things in sacks, his coat. It had no window, the light came in through the open door. It was a jumble, but also it was a sort of little sanctuary.

She listened to the tapping of the man's hammer; it was not so happy. He was oppressed. Here was a trespass on his privacy, and a dangerous one! A woman! He had reached the point where all he wanted on earth was to be alone. And yet he was powerless to preserve his privacy; he was a hired man, and these people were his masters.

Especially he did not want to come into contact with a woman again. He feared it; for he had a big wound from old contacts. He felt if he could not be alone, and if he could not be left alone, he would die. His recoil away from the outer world was complete; his last refuge was this wood; to hide himself there!

Connie grew warm by the fire, which she had made too big: then she grew hot. She went and sat on the stool in the doorway, watching the man at work. He seemed not to notice her, but he knew. Yet he worked on, as if absorbedly, and his brown dog sat on her tail near him, and surveyed the untrustworthy world.

Slender, quiet and quick, the man finished the coop he was making, turned it over, tried the sliding door, then set it aside. Then he rose, went for an old coop, and took it to the chopping-log where he was working. Crouching, he tried the bars; some broke in his hands; he began to draw the nails. Then he turned the coop over and deliberated, and he gave absolutely no sign of awareness of the woman's presence.

So Connie watched him fixedly. And the same solitary aloneness she had seen in him naked, she now saw in him clothed: solitary, and intent, like an animal that works alone, but also brooding, like a soul that recoils away, away from all human contact. Silently, patiently, he was recoiling away from her even now. It was the stillness, and the timeless sort of patience, in a man impatient and passionate, that touched Connie's womb. She saw it in his bent head, the quick, quiet hands, the crouching of his slender, sensitive loins; something patient and withdrawn. She felt his experience had been deeper and wider than her own; much deeper and wider, and perhaps more deadly. And this relieved her of herself; she felt almost irresponsible.

So she sat in the doorway of the hut in a dream, utterly unaware of time and of particular circumstances. She was so drifted away that he glanced up at her quickly, and saw the utterly still, waiting look on her face. To him it was a look of waiting. And a little thin tongue of fire suddenly flickered in his loins, at the root of his back, and he groaned in spirit. He dreaded, with a repulsion almost of death, any further close human contact. He wished above all things she would go away, and leave him to his own privacy. He dreaded her will, her female will, and her modern female insistency. And above all he dreaded her cool, upper-class impudence of having her own way. For after all he was only a hired man. He hated her presence there.

Connie came to herself with sudden uneasiness. She rose. The afternoon was turning to evening, yet she could not go away. She went over to the man, who stood up at attention, his worn face stiff and blank, his eyes watching her.

"It is so nice here, so restful," she said. "I have never been here before."

"No?"

"I think I shall come and sit here sometimes."

"Yes!"

"Do you lock the hut when you're not here?"

"Yes, your Ladyship."

"Do you think I could have a key too, so that I could sit here sometimes? Are there two keys?"

"Not as Ah know on, ther' isna."

He had lapsed into the vernacular. Connie hesitated; he was putting up an opposition. Was it his hut, after all?

"Couldn't we get another key?" she asked in her soft voice, that underneath had the ring of a woman determined to get her way.

"Another!" he said, glancing at her with a flash of anger, touched with derision.

"Yes, a duplicate," she said, flushing.

" 'Appen Sir Clifford 'ud know," he said, putting her off.

"Yes!" she said, "he might have another. Otherwise we could have one made from the one you have. It would only take a day or so, I suppose. You could spare your key for so long."

"Ah canna tell yer, m'lady! Ah know nob'dy as ma'es keys round 'ere."

Connie suddenly flushed with anger.

"Very well!" she said. "I'll see to it."

"All right, your Ladyship."

Their eyes met. His had a cold, ugly look of dislike and contempt, and indifference to what would happen. Hers were hot with rebuff.

But her heart sank, she saw how utterly he disliked her, when she went against him. And she saw him in a sort of desperation.

"Good afternoon!"

"Afternoon, my Lady!" He saluted and turned abruptly away. She had wakened the sleeping dogs of old voracious anger in him, anger against the self-willed female. And he was powerless, powerless. He knew it!

And she was angry against the self-willed male. A servant too! She walked sullenly home.

She found Mrs. Bolton under the great beech tree on the knoll, looking for her.

"I just wondered if you'd be coming, my Lady," the woman said brightly.

"Am I late?" asked Connie.

"Oh . . . only Sir Clifford was waiting for his tea."

"Why didn't *you* make it then?"

"Oh, I don't think it's hardly my place. I don't think Sir Clifford would like it at all, my Lady."

"I don't see why not," said Connie.

She went indoors to Clifford's study, where the old brass kettle was simmering on the tray.

"Am I late, Clifford?" she said, putting down the few flowers and taking up the tea-caddy, as she stood before the tray in her hat and scarf. "I'm sorry! Why didn't you let Mrs. Bolton make the tea?"

"I didn't think of it," he said ironically. "I don't quite see her presiding at the tea table."

"Oh, there's nothing sacrosanct about a silver teapot," said Connie.

He glanced up at her curiously.

"What did you do all afternoon?" he said.

"Walked and sat in a sheltered place. Do you know there are still berries on the big holly tree?"

She took off her scarf, but not her hat, and sat down to make tea. The toast would certainly be leathery. She put the tea-cosy over the teapot, and rose to get a little glass for her violets. The poor flowers hung over, limp on their stalks.

"They'll revive again!" she said, putting them before him in their glass for him to smell.

"Sweeter than the lids of Juno's eyes," he quoted.

"I don't see a bit of connection with the actual violets," she said. "The Elizabethans are rather upholstered."

She poured him his tea.

"Do you think there is a second key to that little hut not far from John's Well, where the pheasants are reared?" she said.

"There may be. Why?"

"I happened to find it today—and I'd never seen it before. I think it's a darling place. I could sit there sometimes, couldn't I?"

"Was Mellors there?"

"Yes! That's how I found it; his hammering. He didn't seem to like my intruding at all. In fact he was almost rude when I asked about a second key."

"What did he say?"

"Oh, nothing: just his manner; and he said he knew nothing about keys."

"There may be one in father's study. Betts knows them all; they're all there. I'll get him to look."

"Oh, do!" she said.

"So Mellors was almost rude?"

"Oh, nothing, really! But I don't think he wanted me to have the freedom of the castle, quite."

"I don't suppose he did."

"Still, I don't see why he should mind. It's not his home, after all! It's not his private abode. I don't see why I shouldn't sit there if I want to."

"Quite!" said Clifford. "He thinks too much of himself, that man."

"Do you think he does?"

"Oh, decidedly! He thinks he's something exceptional. You know he had a wife he didn't get on with, so he joined up in 1915 and was sent out to India, I believe. Anyhow he was blacksmith to the cavalry in Egypt for a time; always was connected with horses, a clever fellow that way. Then some Indian colonel took a fancy to him, and he was made a lieutenant. Yes, they gave him a commission. I believe he went back to India with his colonel, and up to the northwest frontier. He was ill; he has a pension. He didn't come out of the army till last year, I believe, and then, naturally, it isn't easy for a man like that to get back to his own level. He's bound to flounder. But he does his duty all right, as far as I'm concerned. Only, I'm not having any of the Lieutenant Mellors touch."

"How could they make him an officer when he speaks broad Derbyshire?"

"He doesn't . . . except by fits and starts. He can speak perfectly well, for him. I suppose he has an idea if he's come down to the ranks again, he'd better speak as the ranks speak."

"Why didn't you tell me about him before?"

"Oh, I've no patience with these romances. They're the ruin of all order. It's a thousand pities they ever happened."

Connie was inclined to agree. What was the good of discontented people who fitted in nowhere?

In the spell of fine weather Clifford, too, decided to go to the wood. The wind was cold, but not so tiresome, and the sunshine was like life itself, warm and full.

"It's amazing," said Connie, "how different one feels when there's a really fresh fine day. Usually one feels the very air is half dead. People are killing the very air."

"Do you think people are doing it?" he asked.

"I do. The steam of so much boredom, and discontent and anger out of all the people, just kills the vitality in the air. I'm sure of it."

"Perhaps some condition of the atmosphere lowers the vitality of the people?" he said.

"No, it's man that poisons the universe," she asserted.

"Fouls his own nest," remarked Clifford.

The chair puffed on. In the hazel copse catkins were hanging pale gold, and in sunny places the wood anemones were wide open, as if exclaiming with the joy of life, just as good as in past days, when people could exclaim along with them. They had a faint scent of apple blossom. Connie gathered a few for Clifford.

He took them and looked at them curiously.

"Thou still unravished bride of quietness," he quoted. "It seems to fit flowers so much better than Greek vases."

"Ravished is such a horrid word!" she said. "It's only people who ravish things."

"Oh, I don't know . . . snails and things," he said.

"Even snails only eat them, and bees don't ravish."

She was angry with him, turning everything into words. Violets were Juno's eyelids, and windflowers were unravished brides. How she hated words, always coming between her and life: they did the ravishing, if anything did: ready-made words and phrases, sucking all the life-sap out of living things.

The walk with Clifford was not quite a success. Between him and Connie there was a tension that each pretended not to notice, but there it was. Suddenly, with all the force of her female instinct, she was shoving him off. She wanted to be clear of him, and especially of his consciousness, his words, his obsession with himself, his endless treadmill obsession with himself, and his own words.

The weather came rainy again. But after a day or two she went out in the rain, and she went to the wood. And once there, she went towards the hut. It was raining, but not so cold, and the wood felt so silent and remote, inaccessible in the dusk of rain.

She came to the clearing. No one there! The hut was locked. But she sat on the log doorstep, under the rustic porch, and snuggled into her own warmth. So she sat, looking at the rain, listening to the many noiseless noises of it, and to the strange soughings of wind in upper branches, when there seemed to be no wind. Old oak trees stood around, grey, powerful trunks, rain-blackened, round and vital, throwing off reckless limbs. The ground was fairly free of undergrowth, the anemones sprinkled, there was a bush or two, elder, or guelderrose, and a purplish tangle of bramble; the old russet of bracken almost vanished under green anemone ruffs. Perhaps this was one of the unravished places. Unravished! The whole world was ravished.

Some things can't be ravished. You can't ravish a tin of sardines. And so many women are like that; and men. But the earth . . . !

The rain was abating. It was hardly making darkness among the oaks anymore. Connie wanted to go; yet she sat on. But she was getting cold; yet the overwhelming inertia of her inner resentment kept her there as if paralyzed.

Ravished! How ravished one could be without ever being touched. Ravished by dead words become obscene, and dead ideas become obsessions.

A wet brown dog came running and did not bark, lifting a wet feather of a tail. The man followed in a wet black oilskin jacket, like a chauffeur, and face flushed a little. She felt him recoil in his quick walk, when he saw her. She stood up in the handbreath of dryness under the rustic porch. He saluted without speaking, coming slowly near. She began to withdraw.

"I'm just going," she said.

"Was yer waitin' to get in?" he asked, looking at the hut, not at her.

"No, I only sat a few minutes in the shelter," she said, with quiet dignity.

He looked at her. She looked cold.

"Sir Clifford 'adn't got no other key then?" he asked.

"No, but it doesn't matter. I can sit perfectly dry under this porch. Good afternoon!" She hated the excess of vernacular in his speech.

He watched her closely, as she was moving away. Then he hitched up his jacket, and put his hand in his breeches pocket, taking out the key of the hut.

" 'Appen yer'd better 'ave this key, an' mun fend for t'bods some other road."

"What do you mean?" she asked.

"I mean as 'appen Ah can find anuther pleece as'll du for rearin' th' pheasants. If yer want ter be 'ere, yo'll non want me messin' abaht a' th' time."

She looked at him, getting his meaning through the fog of the dialect.

"Why don't you speak ordinary English?" she said coldly.

"Me! Ah thowt it *wor*' ordinary."

She was silent for a few moments in anger.

"So if yer want t' key, yer'd better ta'e it. Or 'appen Ah'd better gi'e 't yer termorrer, an' clear all t' stuff aht fust. Would that du for yer?"

She became more angry.

"I didn't want your key," she said. "I don't want you to clear anything out at all. I don't in the least want to turn you out of your hut, thank you! I only wanted to be able to sit here sometimes, like today. But I can sit perfectly well under the porch, so please say no more about it."

He looked at her again with his wicked blue eyes.

"Why," he began, in the broad slow dialect, "your Ladyship's as welcome as

Christmas ter th' hut an' th' key an' iverythink as it. On'y this time o' th' year ther's bods ter set, an' Ah've got ter be potterin' abaht a good bit, seein' after 'em, an' a'. Winter time Ah need 'ardly come nigh th' pleece. But what wi' spring, an' Sir Clifford wantin' ter start th' pheasants. . . . An' your Ladyship'd non want me tinkerin' around an' about when she was 'ere, all th' time."

She listened with a dim kind of amazement.

"Why should I mind your being here?" she asked.

He looked at her curiously.

"T' nuisance on me!" he said briefly, but significantly.

She flushed. "Very well!" she said finally. "I won't trouble you. But I don't think I should have minded at all sitting and seeing you look after the birds. I should have liked it. But since you think it interferes with you, I won't disturb you, don't be afraid. You are Sir Clifford's keeper, not mine."

The phrase sounded queer, she didn't know why. But she let it pass.

"Nay, your Ladyship. It's your Ladyship's own 'ut. It's as your Ladyship likes an' pleases, every time. Yer can turn me off at a wik's notice. It wor only . . ."

"Only what?" she asked, baffled.

He pushed back his hat in an odd comic way.

"On'y as 'appen yo'd like the place ter yersen, when yer did come, an' not me messin' abaht."

"But why?" she said, angry. "Aren't you a civilized human being? Do you think I ought to be afraid of you? Why should I take any notice of you and your being here or not? Why is it important?"

He looked at her, all his face glimmering with wicked laughter.

"It's not, your Ladyship. Not in the very least," he said.

"Well, why then?" she asked.

"Shall I get your Ladyship another key then?"

"No, thank you! I don't want it."

"Ah'll get it anyhow. We'd best 'ave two keys ter th' place."

"And I consider you are insolent," said Connie, with her color up, panting a little.

"Nay, nay!" he said quickly. "Dunna yer say that! Nay, nay! I niver meant nuthink. Ah on'y thought as if yo' come 'ere, Ah s'd 'ave ter clear out, an' it'd mean a lot o' work, settin' up somewheres else. But if your Ladyship isn't going ter take no notice o' me, then . . . it's Sir Clifford's 'ut, an' everythink is as your Ladyship likes, everythink is as your Ladyship likes an' pleases, barrin' yer take no notice o' me, doin' the bits of jobs as Ah've got ter do."

Connie went away completely bewildered. She was not sure whether she had been insulted and mortally offended, or not. Perhaps the man really only meant what he said; that he thought she would expect him to keep away. As if she would dream of it! And as if he could possibly be so important, he and his stupid presence.

She went home in confusion, not knowing what she thought or felt.

❖ 9 ❖

Connie was surprised at her own feeling of aversion for Clifford. What is more, she felt she had always really disliked him. Not hate: there was no passion in it. But a profound physical dislike. Almost it seemed to her, she had married him because she disliked him, in a secret, physical sort of way. But of course, she had married him really because in a mental way he attracted her and excited her. He had seemed, in some way, her master, beyond her.

Now the mental excitement had worn itself out and collapsed, and she was aware only of the physical aversion. It rose up in her from her depths: and she realized how it had been eating her life away.

She felt weak and utterly forlorn. She wished some help would come from outside. But in the whole world there was no help. Society was terrible because it was insane. Civilized society is insane. Money and so-called love are its two great manias; money a long way first. The individual asserts himself in his disconnected insanity in these two modes: money and love. Look at Michaelis! His life and activity were just insanity. His love was a sort of insanity.

And Clifford the same. All that talk! All that writing! All that wild struggling to push himself forward! It was just insanity. And it was getting worse, really maniacal.

Connie felt washed out with fear. But at least, Clifford was shifting his grip from her onto Mrs. Bolton. He did not know it. Like many insane people, his insanity might be measured by the things he was *not* aware of; the great desert tracts in his consciousness.

Mrs. Bolton was admirable in many ways. But she had that queer sort of bossiness, endless assertion of her own will, which is one of the signs of insanity in modern woman. She *thought* she was utterly subservient and living for others. Clifford fascinated her because he always, or so often, frustrated her will, as if by a finer instinct. He had a finer, subtler will of self-assertion than herself. This was his charm for her.

Perhaps that had been his charm, too, for Connie.

"It's a lovely day, today!" Mrs. Bolton would say in her caressive, persuasive voice. "I should think you'd enjoy a little run in your chair today, the sun's just lovely."

"Yes? Will you give me that book—there, that yellow one. And I think I'll have those hyacinths taken out."

"Why, they're so beautiful!" She pronounced it with the "y" sound: be-yutiful!—"And the scent is simply gorgeous."

"The scent is what I object to," he said. "It's a little funereal."

"Do you think so!" she exclaimed in surprise, just a little offended, but impressed. And she carried the hyacinths out of the room, impressed by his higher fastidiousness.

"Shall I shave you this morning, or would you rather do it yourself?" Always the same soft, caressive, subservient, yet managing voice.

"I don't know. Do you mind waiting a while. I'll ring when I'm ready."

"Very good, Sir Clifford!" she replied, so soft and submissive, withdrawing quietly. But every rebuff stored up new energy of will in her.

When he rang, after a time, she would appear at once. And then he would say:

"I think I'd rather you shaved me this morning."

Her heart gave a little thrill, and she replied with extra softness:

"Very good, Sir Clifford!"

She was very deft, with a soft, lingering touch, a little slow. At first he had resented the infinitely soft touch of her fingers on his face. But now he liked it, with a growing voluptuousness. He let her shave him nearly every day: her face near his, her eyes so very concentrated, watching that she did it right. And gradually her fingertips knew his cheeks and lips, his jaw and chin and throat perfectly. He was well fed and well groomed, his face and throat were handsome enough, and he was a gentleman.

She was handsome, too, pale, her face rather long and absolutely still, her eyes bright, but revealing nothing. Gradually, with infinite softness, almost with love, she was getting him by the throat, and he was yielding to her.

She now did almost everything for him, and he felt more at home with her, less ashamed of accepting her menial offices, than with Connie. She liked handling him. She loved having his body in her charge, absolutely, to the last menial offices. She said to Connie one day: "All men are babies, when you come to the bottom of them. Why, I've handled some of the toughest customers as ever went down Tevershall pit. But let anything ail them so that you have to do for them, and they're babies, just big babies. Oh, there's not much difference in men!"

At first Mrs. Bolton had thought there really was something different in a gentleman, a *real* gentleman, like Sir Clifford. So Clifford had got a good start of her. But gradually, as she came to the bottom of him, to use her own term, she found he was like the rest, a baby grown to man's proportions: but a baby with a queer temper and a fine manner and power in its control, and all sorts of odd knowledge that she had never dreamed of, with which he could still bully her.

Connie was sometimes tempted to say to him:

"For God's sake, don't sink so horribly into the hands of that woman!" But she found she didn't care for him enough to say it, in the long run.

It was still their habit to spend the evening together, till ten o'clock. Then they would talk, or read together, or go over his manuscript. But the thrill had gone out of it. She was bored by his manuscripts. But she still dutifully typed them out for him. But in time Mrs. Bolton would do even that.

For Connie had suggested to Mrs. Bolton that she should learn to use a typewriter. And Mrs. Bolton, always ready, had begun at once, and practiced assiduously. So now Clifford would sometimes dictate a letter to her, and she would take it down rather slowly, but correctly. And he was very patient, spelling for her the difficult words, or the occasional phrases in French. She was so thrilled, it was almost a pleasure to instruct her.

Now Connie would sometimes plead a headache as an excuse for going up to her room after dinner.

"Perhaps Mrs. Bolton will play piquet with you," she said to Clifford.

"Oh, I shall be perfectly all right. You go to your own room and rest, darling."

But no sooner had she gone, than he rang for Mrs. Bolton, and asked her to take a hand at piquet or bezique, or even chess. He had taught her all these games. And Connie found it curiously objectionable to see Mrs. Bolton, flushed and tremulous like a little girl, touching her queen or her knight with uncertain fingers, then drawing away again. And Clifford, faintly smiling with a half-teasing superiority, saying to her:

"You must say *j'adoube*!"

She looked up at him with bright, startled eyes, then murmured shyly, obediently:

"*J'adoube*"!

Yes, he was educating her. And he enjoyed it, it gave him a sense of power. And she was thrilled. She was coming bit by bit into possession of all that the gentry knew, all that made them upper class: apart from the money. That thrilled her. And at the same time, she was making him want to have her there with him. It was a subtle deep flattery to him, her genuine thrill.

To Connie, Clifford seemed to be coming out in his true colors: a little vulgar, a little common, and uninspired; rather fat. Ivy Bolton's tricks and humble bossiness were also only too transparent. But Connie did wonder at the genuine thrill which the woman got out of Clifford. To say she was in love with him would be putting it wrongly. She was thrilled by her contact with a man of the upper class, this titled gentleman, this author who could write books and poems, and whose photograph appeared in the illustrated newspapers. She was thrilled to a weird passion. And his "educating" her roused in her a passion of excitement and response much deeper than any love affair could have done. In truth, the very fact that there could *be* no love affair left her free to thrill to her very marrow with this other passion, the peculiar passion of *knowing*, knowing as he knew.

There was no mistake that the woman was in some way in love with him: whatever force we give to the word love. She looked so handsome and so young, and her gray eyes were sometimes marvelous. At the same time, there was a lurking soft satisfaction about her, even of triumph, and private satisfaction. Ugh, that private satisfaction! How Connie loathed it!

But no wonder Clifford was caught by the woman! She absolutely adored him, in her persistent fashion, and put herself absolutely at his service, for him to use as he liked. No wonder he was flattered!

Connie heard long conversations going on between the two. Or rather, it was mostly Mrs. Bolton talking. She had unloosed to him the stream of gossip about Tevershall village. It was more than gossip. It was Mrs. Gaskell and George Eliot and Miss Mitford all rolled in one, with a great deal more, that these women left out. Once started, Mrs. Bolton was better than any book, about the lives of the people. She knew them all so intimately, and had such a peculiar, flamey zest in all their affairs, it was wonderful, if just a *trifle* humiliating to listen to her. At first she had not ventured to "talk Tevershall," as she called it, to Clifford. But once started, it went. Clifford was listening for "material," and he found it in plenty. Connie realized that his so-called genius was just this: a perspicuous talent for personal gossip, clever and apparently detached. Mrs. Bolton, of course, was very warm when she "talked Tevershall." Carried away, in fact. And it was marvelous, the things that happened and that she knew about. She would have run to dozens of volumes.

Connie was fascinated, listening to her. But afterwards always a little ashamed. She ought not to listen with this queer rabid curiosity. After all, one may hear the most private affairs of other people, but only in a spirit of respect for the struggling, battered thing which any human soul is, and in a spirit of fine, discriminative sympathy. For even satire is a form of sympathy. It is the way our sympathy flows and recoils that really determines our lives. And here lies the vast importance of the novel, properly handled. It can inform and lead into new places the flow of our sympathetic consciousness, and it can lead our sympathy away in recoil from things gone dead. Therefore, the novel, properly handled, can reveal the most secret places of life: for it is in the *passional* secret places of life, above all, that the tide of sensitive awareness needs to ebb and flow, cleansing and freshening.

But the novel, like gossip, can also excite spurious sympathies and recoils, mechanical and deadening to the psyche. The novel can glorify the most corrupt feelings, so long as they are *conventionally* "pure." Then the novel, like gossip, becomes at last vicious, and, like gossip, all the more vicious because it is always ostensibly on the side of the angels. Mrs. Bolton's gossip was always on the side of the angels. "And he was such a *bad* fellow, and she was such a *nice* woman." Whereas, as Connie could see even from Mrs. Bolton's gossip, the woman had been merely a mealy-mouthed sort, and the man angrily honest. But angry honesty made a "bad man" of him, and mealy-mouthedness made a "nice woman" of her, in the vicious, conventional channeling of sympathy by Mrs. Bolton.

For this reason, the gossip was humiliating. And for the same reason, most novels, especially popular ones, are humiliating too. The public responds now only to an appeal to its vices.

Nevertheless, one got a new vision of Tevershall village from Mrs. Bolton's talk. A terrible, seething welter of ugly life it seemed: not at all the flat drabness it looked from outside. Clifford of course knew by sight most of the people mentioned; Connie knew only one or two. But it sounded really more like a Central African jungle than an English village.

"I suppose you heard as Miss Allsopp was married last week! Would you ever! Miss Allsopp, old James's daughter, the boot-and-shoe Allsopp. You know, they built a house up at Pye Croft. The old man died last year from a fall: eighty-three, he was, an' nimble as a lad. An' then he slipped on Bestwood Hill, on a slide as the lad's 'ad made last winter, an' broke his thigh, and that finished him, poor old man, it did seem a shame. Well, he left all his money to Tattie: didn't leave the boys a penny. An' Tattie, I know, is five years . . . yes, she's fifty-three last autumn. And you know they were such Chapel people, my word! She taught Sunday School for thirty years, till her father died. And then she started carrying on with a fellow from Kinbrook, I don't know if you know him, an oldish fellow with a red nose, rather dandified, Willcock, as works in Harrison's woodyard. Well, he's sixty-five if he's a day, yet you'd have thought they were a pair of young turtledoves, to see them, arm-in-arm, and kissing at the gate: yes, an' she sitting on his knee right in the bay window on Pye Croft Road, for anybody to see. And he's got sons over forty: only lost his wife two years ago. If old James Allsopp hasn't risen from his grave, it's because there is no rising: for he kept her that strict! Now they're married and gone to live down at Kinbrook, and they say she goes round in a dressing gown from morning to night, a veritable sight.

I'm sure it's awful, the way the old ones go on! Why, they're a lot worse than the young, and a sight more disgusting. I lay it down to the pictures, myself. But you can't keep them away. I was always saying: go to a good instructive film, but do for goodness sake keep away from these melodramas and love films. Anyhow keep the children away! But there you are, the grown-ups are worse than the children: and the old ones beat the band. Talk about morality; nobody cares a thing. Folks does as they like, and much better off they are for it, I must say. But they're having to draw their horns in nowadays, now th' pits are working so bad, and they haven't got the money. And the grumbling they do, it's awful, especially the women. The men are so good and patient! What can they do, poor chaps! But the women, oh, they do carry on! They go and show off, giving contributions for a wedding present for Princess Mary, and then when they see all the grand things that's been given, they simply rave: who's she, any better than anybody else! Why doesn't Swan & Edgar give me *one* fur coat, instead of giving her six? I wish I'd kept my ten shillings! What's she going to give *me,* I should like to know? Here I can't get a new spring coat, my dad's working that bad, and she gets van-loads. It's time as poor folks had some money to spend, rich ones 'as 'ad it long enough. I want a new spring coat, I do, an' wheer am I going to get it?—I say to them, be thankful you're well fed and well clothed, without all the new finery you want!—And they fly back at me: 'Why isn't Princess Mary thankful to go about in her old rags, then, an' have nothing? Folks like *her* get van-loads, an' I can't have a new spring coat. It's a damned shame. Princess! bloomin' rot about Princess! It's munney as matters, an' cos she's got lots, they give her more! Nobody's givin' me any, an' I've as much right as anybody else. Don't talk to me about education. It's munney as matters. I want a new spring coat, I do, an' I shan't get it, cos there's no munney'—That's all they care about, clothes. They think nothing of giving seven or eight guineas for a winter coat—collier's daughters, mind you—and two guineas for a child's summer hat. And then they go to the Primitive Chapel in their two-guinea hat, girls as would have been proud of a three-and-sixpenny one in my day. I heard that at the Primitive Methodist anniversary this year, when they have a built-up platform for the Sunday School children, like a grandstand going almost up to th' ceiling, I heard Miss Thompson, who has the first class of girls in the Sunday School, say there'd be over a thousand pounds in new Sunday clothes sitting on that platform! And times are what they are! But you can't stop them. They're mad for clothes. And boys the same. The lads spend every penny on themselves, clothes, smoking, drinking in the Miner's Welfare, jaunting off to Sheffield two or three times a week. Why, it's another world. And they fear nothing, and they respect nothing, the young don't. The older men are that patient and good, really, they let the women take everything. And this is what it leads to. The women are positive demons. But the lads aren't like their dads. They're sacrificing nothing, they aren't: they're all for self. If you tell them they ought to be putting a bit by, for a home, they say: That'll keep, that will, I'm goin' t' enjoy mysen while I can. Owt else'll keep!—Oh, they're rough an' selfish, if you like. Everything falls on the older men, an' it's a bad lookout all round."

Clifford began to get a new idea of his own village. The place had always frightened him, but he had thought it more or less stable. Now—?

"Is there much socialism, Bolshevism, among the people?" he asked.

"Oh!" said Mrs. Bolton, "You hear a few loudmouthed ones. But they're mostly women who've got into debt. The men take no notice. I don't believe you'll ever turn our Tevershall men into reds. They're too decent for that. But the young ones blether sometimes. Not that they care for it really. They only want a bit of money in their pocket, to spend at the Welfare, or go gadding to Sheffield. That's all they care. When they've got no money, they'll listen to the reds spouting. But nobody believes in it, really."

"So you think there's no danger?"

"Oh, no! Not if trade was good, there wouldn't be. But if things were bad for a long spell, the young ones might go funny. I tell you, they're a selfish, spoilt lot. But I don't see how they'd ever do anything. They aren't ever serious about anything, except showing off on motorbikes and dancing at the Palais-de-danse in Sheffield. You can't *make* them serious. The serious ones dress up in evening clothes and go off to the Pally to show off before a lot of girls and dance these new Charlestons and what not. I'm sure sometimes the bus'll be full of young fellows in evening suits, collier lads, off to the Pally: let alone those that have gone with their girls in motors or on motorbikes. They don't give a serious thought to a thing—save Doncaster races, and the Derby: for they all of them bet on every race. And football! But even football's not what it was, not by a long chalk. It's too much like hard work, they say. No, they'd rather be off on motorbikes to Sheffield or Nottingham, Saturday afternoons."

"But what do they do when they get there?"

"Oh, hang round—and have tea in some fine tea-place like the Mikado—and go to the Pally or the Pictures or the Empire, with some girl. The girls are as free as the lads. They do just what they like."

"And what do they do when they haven't the money for these things?"

"They seem to get it, somehow. And they begin talking nasty then. But I don't see how you're going to get Bolshevism, when all the lads want is just money to enjoy themselves, and the girls the same, with fine clothes: and they don't care about another thing. They haven't the brains to be socialists. They haven't enough seriousness to take anything really serious, and they never will have."

Connie thought, how extremely like all the rest of the classes the lower classes sounded. Just the same thing over again, Tevershall or Mayfair or Kensington. There was only one class nowadays: moneyboys. The moneyboy and the moneygirl, the only difference was how much you'd got, and how much you wanted.

Under Mrs. Bolton's influence, Clifford began to take a new interest in the mines. He began to feel he belonged. A new sort of self-assertion came into him. After all, he was the real boss in Tevershall, he was really the pits. It was a new sense of power, something he had till now shrunk from with dread.

Tevershall pits were running thin. There were only two collieries: Tevershall itself, and New London. Tevershall had once been a famous mine, and had made famous money. But its best days were over. New London was never very rich, and in ordinary times just got along decently. But now times were bad, and it was pits like New London that got left.

"There's a lot of Tevershall men left and gone to Stacks Gate and Whiteover," said Mrs. Bolton. "You've not seen the new works at Stacks Gate, opened after the war, have you, Sir Clifford? Oh, you must go one day, they're something quite new: great big chemical works at the pit-head, doesn't look a bit like a colliery. They say they get more money out of the chemical byproducts than out of the coal—I forget what it is. And the grand new houses for the men, fair mansions! But a lot of Tevershall men got on there, and doin' well, a lot better than our own men. They say Tevershall's done, finished: only a question of a few more years, and it'll have to shut down. And New London'll go first. My word, won't it be funny, when there's no Tevershall pit working. It's bad enough during a strike, but my word, if it closes for good, it'll be like the end of the world. Even when I was a girl it was the best pit in the country, and a man counted himself lucky if he could work here. Oh, there's been some money made in Tevershall. And now the men say it's a sinking ship, and it's time they all got out. Doesn't it sound awful! But of course there's a lot as'll never go till they have to. They don't like these new-fangled mines, such a depth, and all machinery to work them. Some of them simply dreads those iron men, as they call them, those machines for hewing the coal, where men always did it before. And they say it's wasteful as well. But what goes in waste is saved in wages, and a lot more. It seems soon there'll be no use for men on the face of the earth, it'll be all machines. But they say that's what folks said when they had to give up the old stocking frames. I can remember one or two. But my word, the more machines the more people, that's what it looks like. They say you can't get the same chemicals out of Tevershall coal as you can out of Stacks Gate, and that's funny, they're not three miles apart. But they say so. But everybody says it's a shame something can't be started, to keep the men going a bit better, and employ the girls. All the girls traipsing off to Sheffield every day! My word, it would be something to talk about if Tevershall Collieries took a new lease on life, after everybody saying they're finished, and a sinking ship, and the men ought to leave them like rats leave a sinking ship. But folks talk so much. Of course there was a boom during the war. When Sir Geoffrey made a trust of himself and got the money safe forever, somehow. So they say! But they say even the masters and the owners don't get much out of it now. You can hardly believe it, can you! Why, I always thought the Pits would go on forever and ever. Who'd have thought, when I was a girl! But New England's shut down, so is Colwick Wood: yes, it's fair haunting to go through that coppy and see Colwick Wood standing there deserted among the trees, and bushes growing up all over the pit-head, and the lines red rusty. It's like death itself, a dead colliery. Why, whatever we should do if Tevershall shut down—? it doesn't bear thinking of. Always that throng it's been, except at strikes, and even then the fan-wheels didn't stand, except when they fetched the ponies up. I'm sure it's a funny world, you don't know where you are from year to year, you really don't."

It was Mrs. Bolton's talk that really put a new fight into Clifford. His income, as she pointed out to him, was secure, from his father's trust, even though it was not large. The pits did not really concern him. It was the other world he wanted to capture, the world of literature and fame; the popular world, not the working world.

Now he realized the distinction between popular success and working success: the populace of pleasure and the populace of work. He, as a private individual, had been catering with his stories for the populace of pleasure. And he had caught on. But beneath the populace of pleasure lay the populace of work, grim, grimey, and rather terrible. They, too, had to have their providers. And it was a much grimmer business, providing for the populace of work, than for the populace of pleasure. While he was doing his stories, and "getting on" in the world, Tevershall was going to the wall.

He realized now that the bitch-goddess of success had two main appetites: one for flattery, adulation, stroking and tickling, such as writers and artists gave her; but the other a grimmer appetite for meat and bones. And the meat and bones for the bitch-goddess were provided by the men who made money in industry.

Yes, there were two great groups of dogs wrangling for the bitch-goddess: the group of the flatterers, those who offered her amusement, stories, films, plays: and the other, much less showy, much more savage breed, those who gave her meat, the real substance of money. The well-groomed showy dogs of amusement wrangled and snarled among themselves for the favors of the bitch-goddess. But it was nothing to the silent fight-to-the-death that went on among the indispensables, the bone-bringers.

But under Mrs. Bolton's influence, Clifford was tempted to enter this other fight, to capture the bitch-goddess by brute means of industrial production. Somehow he got his pecker up. In one way, Mrs. Bolton made a man of him, as Connie never did. Connie kept him apart, and made him sensitive and conscious of himself and his own states. Mrs. Bolton made him aware only of outside things. Inwardly he began to go soft as pulp. But outwardly he began to be effective.

He even roused himself to go to the mines once more: and when he was there, he went down in a tub, and in a tub he was hauled out into the workings. Things he had learned before the war, and seemed utterly to have forgotten, now came back to him. He sat there, crippled, in a tub, with the underground manager showing him the seam with a powerful torch. And he said little. But his mind began to work.

He began to read again his technical works on the coal-mining industry, he studied the Government reports, and he read with care the latest things on mining and the chemistry of coal and of shale which were written in German. Of course the most valuable discoveries were kept secret as far as possible. But once you started a sort of research in the field of coal-mining, a study of methods and means, a study of byproducts and the chemical possibilities of coal, it was astounding the ingenuity and the almost uncanny cleverness of the modern technical mind, as if really the devil himself had lent fiend's wits to the technical scientists of industry. It was far more interesting than art, than literature, poor emotional half-witted stuff, was this technical science of industry. In this field, men were like gods, or demons, inspired to discoveries, and fighting to carry them out. In this activity, men were beyond any mental age calculable. But Clifford knew that when it did come to the emotional and human life, these self-made men were of a mental age of about thirteen, feeble boys. The discrepancy was enormous and appalling.

But let that be. Let man slide down to general idiocy in the emotional and "human" mind, Clifford did not care. Let all that go hang. He was interested in the technicalities of modern coal-mining, and in pulling Tevershall out of the hole.

He went down to the pit day after day, he studied, he put the general manager, and the overhead manager, and the underground manager, and the engineers through a mill they had never dreamed of. Power! He felt a new sense of power flowing through him: power over all these men, over the hundreds and hundreds of colliers. He was finding out: and he was getting things into his grip.

And he seemed verily to be re-born. *Now* life came into him! He had been gradually dying, with Connie, in the isolated private life of the artist and the conscious being. Now let all that go. Let it sleep. He simply felt life rush into him out of the coal, out of the pit. The very stale air of the colliery was better than oxygen to him. It gave him a sense of power, power. He was doing something: and he was *going* to do something. He was going to win, to win: not as he had won with his stories, mere publicity, amid a whole sapping of energy and malice. But a man's victory.

At first he thought the solution lay in electricity: convert the coal into electric power. Then a new idea came. The Germans invented a new locomotive engine with a self-feeder, that did not need a fireman. And it was to be fed with a new fuel, that burnt in small quantities at a great heat, under peculiar conditions.

The idea of a new concentrated fuel that burnt with a hard slowness at a fierce heat was what first attracted Clifford. There must be some sort of external stimulus to the burning of such fuel, not merely air supply. He began to experiment, and got a clever young fellow who had proved brilliant in chemistry, to help him.

And he felt triumphant. He had at last got out of himself. He had fulfilled his life-long secret yearning to get out of himself. Art had not done it for him. Art had only made it worse. But now, now he had done it.

He was not aware how much Mrs. Bolton was behind him. He did not know how much he depended on her. But for all that, it was evident that when he was with her his voice dropped to an easy rhythm of intimacy, almost a trifle vulgar.

With Connie, he was a little stiff. He felt he owed her everything, everything, and he showed her the utmost respect and consideration, so long as she gave him mere outward respect. But it was obvious he had a secret dread of her. The new Achilles in him had a heel, and in this heel the woman, the woman like Connie his wife, could lame him fatally. He went in a certain half-subservient dread of her, and was extremely nice to her. But his voice was a little tense when he spoke to her, and he began to be silent whenever she was present.

Only when he was alone with Mrs. Bolton did he really feel a lord and a master, and his voice ran on with her almost as easily and garrulously as her own could run. And he let her shave him or sponge all his body as if he were a child, really as if he were a child.

10

Connie was a good deal alone now, fewer people came to Wragby. Clifford no longer wanted them. He had turned against even the cronies. He was queer. He preferred the radio, which he had installed at some expense, with a good deal of success at last. He could sometimes get Madrid or Frankfort, even there in the uneasy Midlands.

And he would sit alone for hours listening to the loudspeaker bellowing forth. It amazed and stunned Connie. But there he would sit, with a blank entranced expression on his face, like a person losing his mind, and listen, or seem to listen, to the unspeakable thing.

Was he really listening? Or was it a sort of soporific he took, whilst something else worked on underneath in him? Connie did not know. She fled up to her room, or out of doors to the wood. A kind of terror filled her sometimes, a terror of the incipient insanity of the whole civilized species.

But now that Clifford was drifting off to his other weirdness of industrial activity, becoming almost a *creature*, with a hard, efficient shell of an exterior and a pulpy interior, one of the amazing crabs and lobsters of the modern, industrial and financial world, invertebrates of the crustacean order, with shells of steel, like machines, and inner bodies of soft pulp, Connie herself was really completely stranded.

She was not even free, for Clifford must have her there, he seemed to have a nervous terror that she should leave him. The curious pulpy part of him, the emotional and humanly individual part, depended on her with terror, like a child, almost like an idiot. She must be there, there at Wragby, a Lady Chatterley, his wife. Otherwise he would be lost like an idiot on a moor.

This amazing dependence Connie realized with a sort of horror. She heard him with his pit managers, with the members of his board, with young scientists, and she was amazed at his shrewd insight into things, his power, his uncanny material power over what is called practical men. He had become a practical man himself, and an amazingly astute and powerful one, a master. Connie attributed it to Mrs. Bolton's influence upon him, just at the crisis in his life.

But this astute and practical man was almost an idiot when left alone to his own emotional life. He worshipped Connie, she was his wife, a higher being, and he worshipped her with a queer, craven idolatry, like a savage, a worship based on enormous fear, and even hate of the power of the idol, the dread idol. All he wanted was for Connie to swear, to swear not to leave him, not to give him away.

"Clifford," she said to him—but this was after she had the key to the hut—"would you really like me to have a child one day?"

He looked at her with a furtive apprehension in his rather prominent pale eyes.

"I shouldn't mind, if it made no difference between us," he said.

"No difference to what?" she asked.

"To you and me; to our love for one another. If it's going to affect that, then I'm all against it. Why, I might even one day have a child of my own!"

She looked at him in amazement.

"I mean, it might come back to me one of these days."

She still stared in amazement, and he was uncomfortable.

"So you would not like it if I had a child?" she said.

"I tell you," he replied quickly, like a cornered dog. "I am quite willing, provided it doesn't touch your love for me. If it would touch that, I am dead against it."

Connie could only be silent in cold fear and contempt. Such talk was really the gabbling of an idiot. He no longer knew what he was talking about.

"Oh, it wouldn't make any difference to my feeling for you," she said, with a certain sarcasm.

"There!" he said. "That is the point. In that case I don't mind in the least. I mean it would be awfully nice to have a child running about the house, and feel one was building up a future for it. I should have something to strive for then, and I should know it was your child, shouldn't I, dear? And it would seem just the same as my own. Because it is you who count in these matters. You know that, don't you, dear? I don't enter, I am a cipher. You are the great I-am, as far as life goes. You know that, don't you? I mean, as far as I am concerned. I mean, but for you I am absolutely nothing. I live for your sake and your future. I am nothing to myself."

Connie heard it all with deepening dismay and repulsion. It was one of the ghastly half-truths that poison human existence. What man in his senses would say such things to a woman! But men aren't in their senses. What man with a spark of honor would put this ghastly burden of life responsibility upon a woman, and leave her there, in the void?

Moreover, in half-an-hour's time, Connie heard Clifford talking to Mrs. Bolton, in a hot, impulsive voice, revealing himself in a sort of passionless passion to the woman, as if she were half mistress, half foster-mother to him. And Mrs. Bolton was carefully dressing him in evening clothes, for there were important business guests in the house.

Connie really sometimes felt she would die at this time. She felt she was being crushed to death by weird lies, and by the amazing cruelty of idiocy. Clifford's strange business efficiency in a way overawed her, and his declaration of private worship put her into a panic. There was nothing between them. She never even touched him nowadays, and he never touched her. He never even took her hand and held it kindly. No, and because they were so utterly out of touch, he tortured her with his declaration of idolatry. It was the cruelty of utter impotence. And she felt her reason would give way, or she would die.

She fled as much as possible to the wood. One afternoon, as she sat brooding, watching the water bubbling coldly in John's Well, the keeper had strode up to her.

"I got you a key made, my Lady!" he said, saluting, and he offered her the key.

"Thank you so much!" she said, startled.

"The hut's not very tidy, if you don't mind," he said. "I cleared it of what I could."

"But I didn't want you to trouble!" she said.

"Oh, it wasn't any trouble. I am setting the hens in about a week. But they won't be scared of you. I s'll have to see to them morning and night, but I shan't bother you any more than I can help."

"But you wouldn't bother me," she pleaded. "I'd rather not go to the hut at all, if I am going to be in the way."

He looked at her with his keen blue eyes. He seemed kindly, but distant. But at least he was sane, and wholesome, if even he looked thin and ill. A cough troubled him.

"You have a cough," she said.

"Nothing—a cold! The last pneumonia left me with a cough, but it's nothing."

He kept distant from her, and would not come any nearer.

She went fairly often to the hut, in the morning or in the afternoon, but he was never there. No doubt he avoided her on purpose. He wanted to keep his own privacy.

He had made the hut tidy, put the little table and chair near the fireplace, left a little pile of kindling and small logs, and put the tools and traps away as far as possible, effacing himself. Outside, by the clearing, he had built a low little roof of boughs and straw, a shelter for the birds, and under it stood the five coops. And, one day when she came, she found two brown hens sitting alert and fierce in the coops, sitting on pheasants' eggs, and fluffed out so proud and deep in all the heat of the pondering female blood. This almost broke Connie's heart. She, herself, was so forlorn and unused, not a female at all, just a mere thing of terrors.

Then all the five coops were occupied by hens, three brown and a gray and a black. All alike, they clustered themselves down on the eggs in the soft nestling ponderosity of the female urge, the female nature, fluffing out their feathers. And with brilliant eyes they watched Connie, as she crouched before them, and they gave short sharp clucks of anger and alarm, but chiefly of female anger at being approached.

Connie found corn in the corn-bin in the hut. She offered it to the hens in her hand. They would not eat it. Only one hen pecked at her hand with a fierce little jab, so Connie was frightened. But she was pining to give them something, the brooding mothers who neither fed themselves nor drank. She brought water in a little tin, and was delighted when one of the hens drank.

Now she came every day to the hens, they were the only things in the world that warmed her heart. Clifford's protestations made her go cold from head to foot. Mrs. Bolton's voice made her go cold, and the sound of the businessmen who came. An occasional letter from Michaelis affected her with the same sense of chill. She felt she would surely die if it lasted much longer.

Yet it was spring, and the bluebells were coming in the wood, and the leaf-buds on the hazels were opening like the spatter of green rain. How terrible it was that it should be spring, and everything cold-hearted, cold-hearted. Only the hens, fluffed so wonderfully on the eggs, were warm with their hot, brooding female bodies! Connie felt herself living on the brink of fainting all the time.

Then, one day, a lovely sunny day with great tufts of primroses under the hazels, and many violets dotting the paths, she came in the afternoon to the coops and there was one tiny, tiny perky chicken tinily prancing round in front of a coop, and the mother hen clucking in terror. The slim little chick was grayish-brown with dark markings, and it was the most alive little spark of a creature in seven kingdoms at that moment. Connie crouched to watch in a sort of ecstasy. Life, life! Pure, sparky, fearless new life! New life! So tiny and so utterly without fear! Even when it scampered a little scramblingly into the coop again, and disappeared under the hen's feathers in answer to the mother hen's wild alarm-cries, it was not really frightened; it took it as a game, the game of living. For in a moment a tiny sharp head was poking through the gold-brown feathers of the hen, and eyeing the Cosmos.

Connie was fascinated. And at the same time never had she felt so acutely the agony of her own female forlornness. It was becoming unbearable.

She had only one desire now, to go to the clearing in the wood. The rest was a kind of painful dream. But sometimes she was kept all day at Wragby, by her duties as hostess. And then she felt as if she, too, were going blank, just blank and insane.

One evening, guests or no guests, she escaped after tea. It was late, and she fled across the park like one who fears to be called back. The sun was setting rosy as she entered the wood, but she pressed on among the flowers. The light would last long overhead.

She arrived at the clearing, flushed and semiconscious. The keeper was there, in his shirt-sleeves, just closing up the coops for the night, so the little occupants would be safe. But still one little trio was pattering about on tiny feet, alert drab mites, under the straw shelter, refusing to be called in by the anxious mother.

"I had to come and see the chickens!" she said, panting, glancing shyly at the keeper, almost unaware of him. "Are there any more?"

"Thirty-six so far!" he said. "Not bad!"

He, too, took a curious pleasure in watching the young things come out.

Connie crouched in front of the last coop. The three chicks had run in. But still their cheeky heads came poking sharply through the yellow feathers, then withdrawing, then only one beady little head eyeing forth from the vast mother-body.

"I'd love to touch them," she said, putting her fingers gingerly through the bars of the coop. But the mother-hen pecked at her hand fiercely, and Connie drew back startled and frightened.

"How she pecks at me! She hates me!" she said in a wondering voice. "But I wouldn't hurt them!"

The man standing above her laughed, and crouched down beside her, knees apart, and put his hand with quiet confidence slowly into the coop. The old hen pecked at him, but not so savagely. And slowly, softly, with sure gentle fingers, he felt among the old bird's feathers and drew out a faintly peeping chick in his closed hand.

"There!" he said, holding out his hand to her. She took the little drab thing between her hands, and there it stood, on its impossible little stalks of legs, its atom of balancing life trembling through its almost weightless feet into Connie's hands. But it lifted its handsome, clean-shaped little head boldly, and looked sharply round, and gave a little "peep."

"So adorable! So cheeky!" she said softly.

The keeper, squatting beside her, was also watching with an amused face the bold little bird in her hands. Suddenly he saw a tear fall onto her wrist.

And he stood up, and stood away, moving to the other coop. For suddenly he was aware of the old flame shooting and leaping up in his loins, that he had hoped was quiescent forever. He fought against it, turning his back to her. But it leapt, and leapt downward, circling in his knees.

He turned again to look at her. She was kneeling and holding her two hands slowly forward, blindly, so that the chicken should run in to the mother hen again. And there was something so mute and forlorn in her, compassion flamed in his bowels for her.

Without knowing, he came quickly towards her and crouched beside her again, taking the chick from her hands, because she was afraid of the hen, and putting it back in the coop. At the back of his loins the fire suddenly darted stronger.

He glanced apprehensively at her. Her face was averted, and she was crying blindly, in all the anguish of her generation's forlornness. His heart melted suddenly, like a drop of fire, and he put out his hand and laid his fingers on her knee.

"You shouldn't cry," he said softly.

But then she put her hands over her face and felt that really her heart was broken and nothing mattered anymore.

He laid his hand on her shoulder, and softly, gently, it began to travel down the curve of her back, blindly, with a blind stroking motion, to the curve of her crouching loins. And there his hand softly, softly, stroked the curve of her flank, in the blind instinctive caress.

She had found her scrap of handkerchief and was blindly trying to dry her face.

"Shall you come to the hut?" he said, in a quiet, neutral voice.

And closing his hand softly on her upper arm, he drew her up and led her slowly to the hut, not letting go of her till she was inside. Then he cleared aside the chair and table, and took a brown soldier's blanket from the tool chest, spreading it slowly. She glanced at his face, as she stood motionless.

His face was pale and without expression, like that of a man submitting to fate.

"You lie there," he said softly, and he shut the door, so that it was dark, quite dark.

With a queer obedience, she lay down on the blanket. Then she felt the soft, groping, helplessly desirous hand touching her body, feeling for her face. The hand stroked her face softly, softly, with infinite soothing and assurance, and at last there was the soft touch of a kiss on her cheek.

She lay quite still, in a sort of sleep, in a sort of dream. Then she quivered as she felt his hand groping softly, yet with queer thwarted clumsiness among her clothing. Yet the hand knew, too, how to unclothe her where it wanted. He drew down the thin silk sheath, slowly, carefully, right down and over her feet. Then with a quiver of exquisite pleasure he touched the warm soft body, and touched her navel for a moment in a kiss. And he had to come into her at once, to enter the peace on earth of her soft, quiescent body. It was the moment of pure peace for him, the entry into the body of a woman.

She lay still, in a kind of sleep, always in a kind of sleep. The activity, the orgasm was his, all his; she could strive for herself no more. Even the tightness of his arms round her, even the intense movement of his body, and the springing seed in her, was a kind of sleep, from which she did not begin to rouse till he had finished and lay softly panting against her breast.

Then she wondered, just dimly wondered, why? Why was this necessary? Why had it lifted a great cloud from her and given her peace? Was it real? Was it real?

Her tormented modern-woman's brain still had no rest. Was it real? And she knew, if she gave herself to the man, it was real. But if she kept herself for herself, it was nothing. She was old; millions of years old, she felt. And at last, she could bear the burden of herself no more. She was to be had for the taking. To be had for the taking.

The man lay in a mysterious stillness. What was he feeling? What was he thinking? She did not know. He was a strange man to her, she did not know him. She must only wait, for she did not dare to break his mysterious stillness. He lay there with his arms round her, his body on hers, his wet body touching hers, so close. And completely unknown. Yet not unpeaceful. His very silence was peaceful.

She knew that, when at last he roused and drew away from her. It was like an abandonment. He drew her dress in the darkness down over her knees and stood for a few moments, apparently adjusting his own clothing. Then he quietly opened the door and went out.

She saw a very brilliant little moon shining above the afterglow over the oaks. Quickly she got up and arranged herself; she was tidy. Then she went to the door of the hut.

All the lower wood was in shadow, almost darkness. Yet the sky overhead was crystal. But it shed hardly any light. He came through the lower shadow towards her, his face lifted like a pale blotch.

"Shall we go, then?" he said.

"Where?"

"I'll go with you to the gate."

He arranged things his own way. He locked the door of the hut and came after her.

"You aren't sorry, are you?" he asked, as he went at her side.

"No! No! Are you?" she said.

"For that! No!" he said. Then after a while he added: "But there's the rest of things."

"What rest of things?" she said.

"Sir Clifford. Other folks. All the complications."

"Why complications?" she said, disappointed.

"It's always so. For you as well as for me. There's always complications." He walked on steadily in the dark.

"And are you sorry?" she said.

"In a way!" he replied, looking up at the sky. "I thought I'd done with it all. Now I've begun again."

"Begun what?"

"Life."

"Life!" she reechoed, with a queer thrill.

"It's life," he said. "There's no keeping clear. And if you do keep clear you might almost as well die. So if I've got to be broken open again, I have."

She did not quite see it that way, but still . . .

"It's just love," she said cheerfully.

"Whatever that may be," he replied.

They went on through the darkening wood in silence, till they were almost at the gate.

"But you don't hate me, do you?" she said wistfully.

"Nay, nay," he replied. And suddenly he held her fast against his breast again, with the old connecting passion. "Nay, for me it was good, it was good. Was it for you?"

"Yes, for me too," she answered, a little untruthfully, for she had not been conscious of much.

He kissed her softly, softly, with the kisses of warmth.

"If only there weren't so many other people in the world," he said lugubriously.

She laughed. They were at the gate to the park. He opened it for her.

"I won't come any farther," he said.

"No!" And she held out her hand, as if to shake hands. But he took it in both his.

"Shall I come again?" she asked wistfully.

"Yes! Yes!"

She left him and went across the park.

He stood back and watched her going into the dark, against the pallor of the horizon. Almost with bitterness he watched her go. She had connected him up again, when he had wanted to be alone. She had cost him that bitter privacy of a man who at last wants only to be alone.

He turned into the dark of the wood. All was still, the moon had set. But he was aware of the noises of the night, the engines at Stacks Gate, the traffic on the main road. Slowly he climbed the denuded knoll. And from the top he could see the country, bright rows of lights at Stacks Gate, smaller lights at Tevershall pit, the yellow lights of Tevershall and lights everywhere, here and there, on the dark country, with the distant blush of furnaces, faint and rosy, since the night was clear, the rosiness of the outpouring of white-hot metal. Sharp, wicked electric lights at Stacks Gate! An undefinable quick of evil in them! And all the unease, the ever-shifting dread of the industrial night in the Midlands. He could hear the winding-engines at Stacks Gate turning down the seven-o'clock miners. The pit worked three shifts.

He went down again into the darkness and seclusion of the wood. But he knew that the seclusion of the wood was illusory. The industrial noises broke the solitude, the sharp lights, though unseen, mocked it. A man could no longer be private and withdrawn. The world allows no hermits. And now he had taken the woman, and brought on himself a new cycle of pain and doom. For he knew by experience what it meant.

It was not woman's fault, nor even love's fault, nor the fault of sex. The fault lay there, out there, in those evil electric lights and diabolical rattlings of engines. There, in the world of the mechanical greedy, greedy mechanism and mechanized greed, sparkling with lights and gushing hot metal and roaring with traffic, there lay the vast evil thing, ready to destroy whatever did not conform. Soon it would destroy the wood, and the bluebells would spring no more. All vulnerable things must perish under the rolling and running of iron.

He thought with infinite tenderness of the woman. Poor forlorn thing, she was nicer than she knew, and oh! so much too nice for the tough lot she was in contact with. Poor thing, she too had some of the vulnerability of the wild hyacinths, she wasn't all tough rubber-goods and platinum, like the modern girl. And they would do her in! As sure as life, they would do her in, as they do in all naturally tender life. Tender! Somewhere she was tender, tender with a tenderness of the growing hyacinths, something that has gone out of the celluloid women of today. But he would protect her with his heart for a little while. For a little while, before the insentient iron world and the Mammon of mechanized greed did them both in, her as well as him.

He went home with his gun and his dog, to the dark cottage, lit the lamp, started the fire, and ate his supper of bread and cheese, young onions and beer. He was alone, in a silence he loved. His room was clean and tidy, but rather stark. Yet the fire was bright, the hearth white, the petroleum lamp hung right over the table, with its white, oilcloth. He tried to read a book about India, but tonight he could not read. He sat by the fire in his shirt-sleeves, not smoking, but with a mug of beer in reach. And he thought about Connie.

To tell the truth, he was sorry for what had happened, perhaps most for her sake. He had a sense of foreboding. No sense of wrong or sin; he was troubled by no conscience in that respect. He knew that conscience was chiefly fear of society, or fear of oneself. He was not afraid of himself. But he was quite consciously afraid of society, which he knew by instinct to be a malevolent, partly insane beast.

The woman! If she could be there with him, and there were nobody else in the world! The desire rose again, his penis began to stir like a live bird. At the same time an oppression, a dread of exposing himself and her to that outside Thing that sparkled viciously in the electric lights, weighed down his shoulders. She, poor thing, was just a young female creature to him; but a young female creature whom he had gone into and whom he desired again.

Stretching with the curious yawn of desire, for he had been alone and apart from man or woman for four years, he rose and took his coat again, and his gun, lowered the lamp and went out into the starry night, with the dog. Driven by desire and by dread of the malevolent Thing outside, he made his round in the wood, slowly, softly. He loved the darkness and folded himself into it. It fitted the turgidity of his desire which, in spite of all, was like a riches; the stirring restlessness of his penis, the stirring fire in his loins! Oh, if only there were other men to be with, to fight that sparkling electric Thing outside there, to preserve the tenderness of life, the tenderness of women, and the natural riches of desire. If only there were men to fight side by side with! But the men were all outside there, glorying in the Thing, triumphing or being trodden down in the rush of mechanized greed or of greedy mechanism.

Constance, for her part, had hurried across the park, home, almost without thinking. As yet she had no afterthought. She would be in time for dinner.

She was annoyed to find the doors fastened, however, so that she had to ring. Mrs. Bolton opened.

"Why, there you are, your Ladyship! I was beginning to wonder if you'd gone lost!" she said a little roguishly. "Sir Clifford hasn't asked for you, though; he's got Mr. Linley in with him, talking over something. It looks as if he'd stay to dinner, doesn't it, my Lady?"

"It does rather," said Connie.

"Shall I put dinner back a quarter of an hour? That would give you time to dress in comfort."

"Perhaps you'd better."

Mr. Linley was the general manager of the collieries, an elderly man from the north, with not quite enough punch to suit Clifford; not up to postwar conditions, nor postwar colliers either, with their "ca' canny" creed. But Connie liked Mr. Linley, though she was glad to be spared the toadying of his wife.

Linley stayed to dinner, and Connie was the hostess men liked so much, so modest, yet so attentive and aware, with big, wide blue eyes and a soft repose that sufficiently hid what she was really thinking. Connie had played this woman so much, it was almost second nature to her, but still, decidedly second. Yet it was curious how everything disappeared from her consciousness while she played it.

She waited patiently till she could go upstairs and think her own thoughts. She was always waiting, it seemed to be her *forte*.

Once in her room, however, she felt still vague and confused. She didn't know what to think. What sort of a man was he, really? Did he really like her? Not much, she felt. Yet he was kind. There was something, a sort of warm naïve kindness, curious and sudden, that almost opened her womb to him. But she felt he might be kind like that to any woman. Though even so, it was curiously soothing, comforting. And he was a passionate man, wholesome and passionate. But perhaps he wasn't quite individual enough; he might be the same with any woman as he had been with her. It really wasn't personal. She was only really a female to him.

But perhaps that was better. And after all, he was kind to the female in her, which no man had ever been. Men were very kind to the *person* she was, but rather cruel to the female, despising her or ignoring her altogether. Men were awfully kind to Constance Reid or to Lady Chatterley; but not to her womb they weren't kind. And he took no notice of Constance or of Lady Chatterley; he just softly stroked her loins or her breasts.

She went to the wood next day. It was a gray, still afternoon, with the dark-green dogs'-mercury spreading under the hazel copse, and all the trees making a silent effort to open their buds. Today she could almost feel it in her own body, the huge heave of the sap in the massive trees, upwards, up, up to the bud-tips, there to push into little flamey oak leaves, bronze as blood. It was like a tide running turgid upward, and spreading on the sky.

She came to the clearing, but he was not there. She had only half expected him. The pheasant chicks were running lightly abroad, light as insects, from the coops where the yellow hens clucked anxiously. Connie sat and watched them, and waited. She only waited. Even the chicks she hardly saw. She waited.

The time passed with dream like slowness, and he did not come. She had only half expected him. He never came in the afternoon. She must go home to tea. But she had to force herself to leave.

As she went home, a fine drizzle of rain fell.

"Is it raining again?" said Clifford, seeing her shake her hat.

"Just drizzle."

She poured tea in silence, absorbed in a sort of obstinacy. She did want to see the keeper today, to see if it were really real. If it were really real.

"Shall I read a little to you afterwards?" said Clifford.

She looked at him. Had he sensed something?

"The spring makes me feel queer—I thought I might rest a little," she said.

"Just as you like. Not feeling really unwell, are you?"

"No! Only rather tired—with the spring. Will you have Mrs. Bolton to play something with you?"

"No! I think I'll listen in."

She heard the curious satisfaction in his voice. She went upstairs to her bedroom. There she heard the loudspeaker begin to bellow, in an idiotically velveteen, genteel sort of voice, something about a series of street-cries, the very cream of genteel affectation imitating old criers. She pulled on her old violet colored mackintosh, and slipped out of the house at the side door.

The drizzle of rain was like a veil over the world, mysterious, hushed, not cold. She got very warm as she hurried across the park. She had to open her light waterproof.

The wood was silent, still and secret in the evening drizzle of rain, full of the mystery of eggs and half-open buds, half-unsheathed flowers. In the dimness of it all trees glistened naked and dark as if they had unclothed themselves, and the green things on earth seemed to hum with greenness.

There was still no one at the clearing. The chicks had nearly all gone under the mother hens, only one or two lost adventurous ones still dibbed about in the dryness under the straw roof-shelter. And they were doubtful of themselves.

So! He still had not been. He was staying away on purpose. Or perhaps something was wrong. Perhaps she should go to the cottage and see.

But she was born to wait. She opened the hut with her key. It was all tidy, the corn put in the bin, the blankets folded on the shelf, the straw neat in a corner; a new bundle of straw. The hurricane lamp hung on a nail. The table and chair had been put back where she had lain.

She sat down on a stool in the doorway. How still everything was! The fine rain blew very softly, filmily, but the wind made no noise. Nothing made any sound. The trees stood like powerful beings, dim, twilit, silent and alive. How alive everything was!

Night was drawing near again; she would have to go. He was avoiding her.

But suddenly he came striding into the clearing, in his black oilskin jacket like a chauffeur, shining with wet. He glanced quickly at the hut, half-saluted, then veered aside and went on to the coops. There he crouched in silence, looking carefully at everything, then carefully shutting the hens and chicks up safe against the night.

At last he came slowly towards her. She still sat on her stool. He stood before her under the porch.

"You came then," he said, using the intonation of the dialect.

"Yes," she replied, looking up at him. "You're late!"

"Ay!" he replied, looking away into the wood.

She rose slowly, drawing aside her stool.

"Did you want to come in?" she asked.

He looked down at her shrewdly.

"Won't folks be thinkin' somethink, you comin' here every night?" he said.

"Why?" She looked up at him, at a loss. "I said I'd come. Nobody knows."

"They soon will, though," he replied. "An' what then?"

She was at a loss for an answer.

"Why should they know?" she said.

"Folks always does," he said fatally.

Her lip quivered a little.

"Well, I can't help it," she faltered.

"Nay," he said. "You can help it by not comin'—if yer want to," he added, in a lower tone.

"But I don't want to," she murmured.

He looked away into the wood, and was silent.

"But what when folks finds out?" he asked at last. "Think about it! Think how lowered you'll feel, one of your husband's servants."

She looked up at his averted face.

"Is it," she stammered, "is it that you don't want me?"

"Think!" he said. "Think what if folks finds out—Sir Clifford an' a'—an' everybody talkin'—"

"Well, I can go away."

"Where to?"

"Anywhere! I've got money of my own. My mother left me twenty thousand pounds in trust, and I know Clifford can't touch it. I can go away."

"But 'appen you don't want to go away."

"Yes, yes! I don't care what happens to me."

"Ah, you think that! But you'll care! You'll have to care, everybody has. You've got to remember your ladyship is carrying on with a gamekeeper. It's not as if I was a gentleman. Yes, you'd care. You'd care."

"I shouldn't. What do I care about my ladyship! I hate it, really. I feel people are jeering every time they say it. And they are, they are! Even you jeer when you say it."

"Me!"

For the first time he looked straight at her, and into her eyes.

"I don't jeer at you," he said.

As he looked into her eyes she saw his own eyes go dark, quite dark, the pupils dilating.

"Don't you care about a' the risk?" he asked in a husky voice. "You should care. Don't care when it's too late!"

There was a curious warning pleading in his voice.

"But I've nothing to lose," she said fretfully. "If you knew what it is, you'd think I'd be glad to lose it. But are you afraid for yourself?"

"Ay!" he said briefly. "I am. I'm afraid. I'm afraid. I'm afraid o' things."

"What things?" she asked.

He gave a curious backward jerk of his head, indicating the outer world.

"Things! Everybody! The lot of 'em."

Then he bent down and suddenly kissed her unhappy face.

"Nay, I don't care," he said. "Let's have it, an' damn the rest. But if you was to feel sorry you'd ever done it—!"

"Don't put me off," she pleaded.

He put his fingers to her cheek and kissed her again suddenly.

"Let me come in then," he said softly. "An' take off your mackintosh."

He hung up his gun, slipped out of his wet leather jacket, and reached for the blankets.

"I brought another blanket," he said, "so we can put one over us if we like."

"I can't stay long," she said. "Dinner is half-past seven."

He looked at her swiftly, then at his watch.

"All right," he said.

He shut the door, and lit a tiny light in the hanging hurricane lamp.

"One time we'll have a long time," he said.

He put the blankets down carefully, one folded for her head. Then he sat down for a moment on the stool, and drew her to him, holding her close with one arm, feeling for her body with his free hand. She heard the catch of his intaken breath as he found her. Under her frail petticoat she was naked.

"Eh! what it is to touch thee!" he said, as his finger caressed the delicate, warm secret skin of her waist and hips. He put his face down and rubbed his cheek against her belly and against her thighs again and again. And again she wondered a little over the sort of rapture it was to him. She did not understand the beauty he found in her, through touch upon her living secret body, almost the ecstasy of beauty. For passion alone is awake to it. And when passion is dead, or absent, then the magnificent throb of beauty is incomprehensible and even a little despicable; warm, live beauty of contact, so much deeper than the beauty of vision. She felt the glide of his cheek on her thighs and belly and buttocks, and the close brushing of his moustache and his soft thick hair, and her knees began to quiver. Far down in her she felt a new stirring, a new nakedness emerging. And she was half afraid. Half she wished he would not caress her so. He was encompassing her somehow. Yet she was waiting, waiting.

And when he came into her, with an intensification of relief and consummation that was pure peace to him, still she was waiting. She felt herself a little left out. And she knew, partly it was her own fault. She willed herself into this separateness. Now perhaps she was condemned to it. She lay still, feeling his motion within her, his deep-sunk intentness, the sudden quiver of him at the springing of his seed, then slow-subsiding thrust. That thrust of the buttocks, surely it was a little ridiculous. If you were a woman, and apart in all the business, surely that thrusting of the man's buttocks was supremely ridiculous. Surely the man was intensely ridiculous in this posture and this act!

But she lay still, without recoil. Even, when he had finished, she did not rouse herself to get a grip on her own satisfaction, as she had done with Michaelis; she lay still, and the tears slowly filled and ran from her eyes.

He lay still, too. But he held her close and tried to cover her poor naked legs with his legs, to keep them warm. He lay on her with a close, undoubting warmth.

"Are ter cold?" he asked, in a soft, small voice, as if she were close, so close. Whereas she was left out, distant.

"No! But I must go," she said gently.

He sighed, held her closer, then relaxed to rest again.

He had not guessed her tears. He thought she was there with him.

"I must go," she repeated.

He lifted himself, kneeled beside her a moment, kissed the inner side of her thighs, then drew down her skirts, buttoning his own clothes unthinking, not even turning aside, in the faint, faint light from the lantern.

"Tha mun come ter th' cottage one time," he said, looking down at her with a warm, sure, easy face.

But she lay there inert, and was gazing up at him thinking. Stranger! Stranger! She even resented him a little.

He put on his coat and looked for his hat, which had fallen, then he slung on his gun.

"Come then!" he said, looking down at her with those warm, peaceful sort of eyes.

She rose slowly. She didn't want to go. She also rather resented staying. He helped her with her thin waterproof, and saw she was tidy.

Then he opened the door. The outside was quite dark. The faithful dog under the porch stood up with pleasure seeing him. The drizzle of rain drifted grayly past upon the darkness. It was quite dark.

"Ah mun ta'e th' lantern," he said. "The'll be nob'dy."

He walked just before her in the narrow path, swinging the hurricane lamp low, revealing the wet grass, the black shiny tree roots like snakes, wan flowers. For the rest, all was gray rain-mist and complete darkness.

"Tha mun come to the cottage one time," he said, "shall ta? We might as well be hung for a sheep as for a lamb."

It puzzled her, his queer, persistent wanting her, when there was nothing between them, when he never really spoke to her, and in spite of herself she resented the dialect. His "tha mun come" seemed not addressed to her, but some common woman. She recognized the foxglove leaves of the riding and knew, more or less, where they were.

"It's quarter past seven," he said, "you'll do it." He had changed his voice, seemed to feel her distance. As they turned the last bend in the riding towards the hazel wall and the gate, he blew out the light. "We'll see from here," he said, taking her gently by the arm.

But it was difficult, the earth under their feet was a mystery, but he felt his way by tread: he was used to it. At the gate he gave her his electric torch. "It's a bit lighter in the park," he said; "but take it for fear you get off th' path."

It was true, there seemed a ghost-glimmer of grayness in the open space of the park. He suddenly drew her to him and whipped his hand under her dress again, feeling her warm body with his wet, chill hand.

"I could die for the touch of a woman like thee," he said in his throat. "If tha would stop another minute."

She felt the sudden force of his wanting her again.

"No, I must run," she said, a little wildly.

"Ay," he replied, suddenly changed, letting her go.

She turned away, and on the instant she turned back to him saying: "Kiss me."

He bent over her indistinguishable and kissed her on the left eye. She held her mouth and he softly kissed it, but at once drew away. He hated mouth kisses.

"I'll come tomorrow," she said, drawing away; "if I can," she added.

"Ay! not so late," he replied out of the darkness. Already she could not see him at all. "Good night," she said.

"Good night, your Ladyship," his voice.

She stopped and looked back into the wet dark. She could just see the bulk of him. "Why did you say that?" she said.

"Nay," he replied. "Good night then, run!"

She plunged on in the dark-gray tangible night. She found the side door open, and slipped into her room unseen. As she closed the door the gong sounded, but she would take her bath all the same—she must take her bath. "But I won't be late anymore," she said to herself; "it's too annoying."

The next day she did not go to the wood. She went instead with Clifford to Uthwaite. He could occasionally go out now in the car, and had got a strong young man as chauffeur, who could help him out of the car if need be. He particularly wanted to see his godfather, Leslie Winter, who lived at Shipley Hall, not far from Uthwaite. Winter was an elderly gentleman now, wealthy, one of the wealthy coal-owners who had had their heyday in King Edward's time. King Edward had stayed more than once at Shipley, for the shooting. It was a handsome old stucco hall, very elegantly appointed, for Winter was a bachelor and prided himself on his style; but the place was beset by collieries. Leslie Winter was attached to Clifford, but personally did not entertain a great respect for him, because of the photographs in illustrated papers and the literature. The old man was a buck of the King Edward school, who thought life and the scribbling fellows were something else. Towards Connie the Squire was always rather gallant; he thought her an attractive demure maiden and rather wasted on Clifford, and it was a thousand pities she stood no chance of bringing forth an heir to Wragby. He himself had no heir.

Connie wondered what he would say if he knew that Clifford's gamekeeper had been having intercourse with her, and saying to her "tha mun come to th' cottage one time." He would detest and despise her, for he had come almost to hate the shoving forward of the working classes. A man of her own class he would not mind, for Connie was gifted from nature with this appearance of demure, submissive maidenliness, and perhaps it was part of her nature. Winter called her "dear child" and gave her a rather lovely miniature of an eighteenth-century lady, rather against her will.

But Connie was preoccupied with her affair with the keeper. After all Mr. Winter, who was really a gentleman and a man of the world, treated her as a person and a discriminating individual; he did not lump her together with all the rest of his female womanhood in his "thee" and "tha."

She did not go to the wood that day nor the next, nor the day following. She did not go so long as she felt, or imagined she felt, the man waiting for her, wanting her. But the fourth day she was terribly unsettled and uneasy. She still refused to go to the wood and open her thighs once more to the man. She thought of all the things she might do—drive to Sheffield, pay visits, and the thought of all these things was repellent. At last she decided to take a walk, not towards the wood, but in the opposite direction; she would go to Marehay, through the little iron gate in the other side of the park fence. It was a quiet gray day of spring, almost warm. She walked on unheeding, absorbed in thoughts she was not even conscious of. She was not really aware of anything outside her, till she was startled by the loud barking of the dog at Marehay Farm. Marehay Farm! Its pastures ran up to Wragby park fence, so they were neighbors, but it was some time since Connie had called.

"Bell!" she said to the big white bull terrier. "Bell! have you forgotten me? Don't you know me?"—She was afraid of dogs, and Bell stood back and bellowed, and she wanted to pass through the farmyard on to the warren path.

Mrs. Flint appeared. She was a woman of Constance's own age, had been a schoolteacher, but Connie suspected her of being rather a false little thing.

"Why, it's Lady Chatterley! Why!" And Mrs. Flint's eyes glowed again, and she flushed like a young girl. "Bell, Bell. Why! barking at Lady Chatterley! Bell! Be quiet!" She darted forward and slashed at the dog with a white cloth she held in her hand, then came forward to Connie.

"She used to know me," said Connie, shaking hands. The Flints were Chatterley tenants.

"Of course she knows your ladyship! She's just showing off," said Mrs. Flint, glowing and looking up with a sort of flushed confusion, "but it's so long since she's seen you. I do hope you are better."

"Yes, thanks, I'm all right."

"We've hardly seen you all winter. Will you come in and look at the baby?"

"Well!" Connie hesitated. "Just for a minute."

Mrs. Flint flew wildly in to tidy up, and Connie came slowly after her, hesitating in the rather dark kitchen where the kettle was boiling by the fire. Back came Mrs. Flint.

"I do hope you'll excuse me," she said. "Will you come in here."

They went into the living room, where a baby was sitting on the rag hearthrug, and the table was roughly set for tea. A young servant-girl backed down the passage, shy and awkward.

The baby was a perky little thing of about a year, with red hair like its father, and cheeky pale-blue eyes. It was a girl, and not to be daunted. It sat among cushions and was surrounded with rag dolls and other toys in modern excess.

"Why, what a dear she is!" said Connie, "and how she's grown! A big girl! A big girl."

She had given it a shawl when it was born, and celluloid ducks for Christmas.

"There, Josephine! Who's that come to see you? Who's this, Josephine? Lady Chatterley—you know Lady Chatterley, don't you?"

The queer pert little mite gazed cheekily at Connie. Ladyships were still all the same to her.

"Come! Will you come to me?" said Connie to the baby.

The baby didn't care one way or another, so Connie picked her up and held her in her lap. How warm and lovely it was to hold a child in one's lap, and the soft little arms, the unconscious cheeky little legs.

"I was just having a rough cup of tea all by myself. Luke's gone to market, so I can have it when I like. Would you care for a cup, Lady Chatterley? I don't suppose it's what you're used to, but if you would . . ."

Connie would, though she didn't want to be reminded of what she was used to. There was a great relaying of the table, and the best cups brought and the best teapot.

"If only you wouldn't take any trouble," said Connie.

But if Mrs. Flint took no trouble, where was the fun! So Connie played with the child and was amused by its little female dauntlessness, and got a deep voluptuous pleasure out of its soft young warmth. Young life. And so fearless! So fearless, because so defenseless. All the older people, so narrow with fear.

She had a cup of tea, which was rather strong, and very good bread and butter, and bottled damsons. Mrs. Flint flushed and glowed and bridled with excitement, as if Connie were some gallant knight. And they had a real female chat, and both of them enjoyed it.

"It's a poor little tea, though," said Mrs. Flint.

"It's much nicer than at home," said Connie truthfully.

"Oh-h!" said Mrs. Flint, not believing, of course.

But at last Connie rose.

"I must go," she said. "My husband has no idea where I am. He'll be wondering all kinds of things."

"He'll never think you're here," laughed Mrs. Flint excitedly. "He'll be sending the crier round."

"Good-bye, Josephine," said Connie, kissing the baby and ruffling its red, wispy hair.

Mrs. Flint insisted on opening the locked and barred front door. Connie emerged in the farm's little front garden, shut in by a privet hedge. There were two rows of auriculas by the path, very velvety and rich.

"Lovely auriculas," said Connie.

"Recklesses, as Luke calls them," laughed Mrs. Flint. "Have some."

And eagerly she picked the velvet and primrose flowers.

"Enough! Enough!" said Connie.

They came to the little garden gate.

"Which way were you going?" asked Mrs. Flint.

"By the warren."

"Let me see! Oh, yes, the cows are in the gin close. But they're not up yet. But the gate's locked, you'll have to climb."

"I can climb," said Connie.

"Perhaps I can just go down the close with you."

They went down the poor, rabbit-bitten pasture. Birds were whistling in wild evening triumph in the wood. A man was calling up the last cows, which trailed slowly over the path-worn pasture.

"They're late, milking, tonight," said Mrs. Flint severely. "They know Luke won't be back till after dark."

They came to the fence, beyond which the young firwood bristled dense. There was a little gate, but it was locked. In the grass on the inside stood a bottle, empty.

"There's the keeper's empty bottle for his milk," explained Mrs. Flint. "We bring it as far as here for him, and then he fetches it himself."

"When?" said Connie.

"Oh, any time he's around. Often in the morning. Well, good-bye, Lady Chatterley! And do come again. It was so lovely having you."

Connie climbed the fence into the narrow path between the dense, bristling young firs. Mrs. Flint went running back across the pasture, in a sunbonnet, because she was really a schoolteacher. Constance didn't like this dense new part of the wood; it seemed grotesque and choking. She hurried on with her head down, thinking of the Flint's baby. It was a dear little thing, but it would be a bit bowlegged like its father. It showed already, but perhaps it would grow out of it. How warm and fulfilling somehow to have a baby, and how Mrs. Flint showed it off! She had something anyhow that Connie hadn't got, and apparently couldn't have. Yes, Mrs. Flint had flaunted her motherhood. And Connie had been just a bit, just a little bit jealous. She couldn't help it.

She started out of her muse, and gave a little cry of fear. A man was there.

It was the keeper; he stood in the path like Balaam's ass, barring her way.

"How's this?" he said in surprise.

"How did you come?" she panted.

"How did you? Have you been to the hut?"

"No! No! I went to Marehay."

He looked at her curiously, searchingly, and she hung her head a little guiltily.

"And were you going to the hut now?" he asked rather sternly.

"No! I mustn't. I stayed at Marehay. No one knows where I am. I'm late. I've got to run."

"Giving me the slip, like?" he said, with a faint ironic smile.

"No! No, not that. Only—"

"Why, what else?" he said. And he stepped up to her, and put his arm around her. She felt the front of his body terribly near to her, and alive.

"Oh, not now, not now," she cried, trying to push him away.

"Why not? It's only six o'clock. You've got half-an-hour. Nay! Nay! I want you."

He held her fast and she felt his urgency. Her old instinct was to fight for her freedom. But something else in her was strange and inert and heavy. His body was urgent against her, and she hadn't the heart anymore to fight.

He looked around.

"Come—come here! Through here," he said, looking penetratingly into the dense fir trees, that were young and not more than half-grown.

He looked back at her. She saw his eyes, tense and brilliant, fierce, not loving. But her will had left her. A strange weight was on her limbs. She was giving way. She was giving up.

He led her through the wall of prickly trees, that were difficult to come through, to a place where was a little space and a pile of dead boughs. He threw one or two dry ones down, put his coat and waistcoat over them, and she had to lie down there under the boughs of the tree, like an animal, while he waited, standing there in his shirt and breeches, watching her with haunted eyes. But still he was provident—he made her lie properly, properly. Yet he broke the band of her underclothes, for she did not help him, only lay inert.

He too had bared the front part of his body and she felt his naked flesh against her as he came into her. For a moment he was still inside her, turgid there and quivering. Then as he began to move, in the sudden helpless orgasm, there awoke in her new strange thrills rippling inside her. Rippling, rippling, rippling, like a flapping overlapping of soft flames, soft as feathers, running to points of brilliance, exquisite, exquisite and melting her all molten inside. It was like bells rippling up and up to a culmination. She lay unconscious of the wild little cries she uttered at the last. But it was over too soon, too soon, and she could no longer force her own conclusion with her own activity. This was different, different. She could do nothing. She could no longer harden and grip for her own satisfaction upon him. She could only wait, wait and moan in spirit as she felt him withdrawing, withdrawing and contracting, coming to the terrible moment when he would slip out of her and be gone. Whilst all her womb was open and soft, and softly clamoring, like a sea-anemone under the tide, clamoring for him to come in again and make a fulfillment for her. She clung to him unconscious in passion, and he never quite slipped from her, and she felt the soft bud of him within her stirring, and strange rhythms flushing up into her with a strange rhythmic growing motion, swelling and swelling till it filled all her cleaving consciousness, and then began again the unspeakable motion that was not really motion, but pure deepening whirlpools of sensation swirling deeper and deeper through all her tissue and consciousness, till she was one perfect concentric fluid of feeling, and she lay there crying in unconscious inarticulate cries. The voice out of the uttermost night, the life! The man heard it beneath him with a kind of awe, as his life sprang out into her. And as it subsided, he subsided too and lay utterly still, unknowing, while her grip on him slowly relaxed, and she lay inert. And they lay and knew nothing, not even of each other, both lost. Till at last he began to rouse and become aware of his defenseless nakedness, and she was aware that his body was loosening its clasp on her. He was coming apart; but in her breast she felt she could not bear him to leave her uncovered. He must cover her now forever.

But he drew away at last, and kissed her and covered her over, and began to cover himself. She lay looking up to the boughs of the tree, unable as yet to move. He stood and fastened up his breeches, looking round. All was dense and silent, save for the awed dog that lay with its paws against its nose. He sat down again on the brushwood and took Connie's hand in silence.

She turned and looked at him. "We came off together that time," he said.

She did not answer.

"It's good when it's like that. Most folks live their lives through and they never know it," he said, speaking rather dreamily.

She looked into his brooding face.

"Do they?" she said. "Are you glad?"

He looked back into her eyes. "Glad," he said. "Ay, but never mind." He did not want her to talk. And he bent over her and kissed her, and she felt, so he must kiss her forever.

At last she sat up.

"Don't people often come off together?" she asked with naïve curiosity.

"A good many of them never. You can see by the raw look of them." He spoke unwittingly, regretting he had begun.

"Have you come off like that with other women?"

He looked at her amused.

"I don't know," he said, "I don't know."

And she knew he would never tell her anything he didn't want to tell her. She watched his face, and the passion for him moved in her bowels. She resisted it as far as she could, for it was the loss of herself to herself.

He put on his waistcoat and his coat, and pushed a way through to the path again.

The last level rays of the sun touched the wood. "I won't come with you," he said; "better not."

She looked at him wistfully before she turned. His dog was waiting so anxiously for him to go, and he seemed to have nothing whatever to say. Nothing left.

Connie went slowly home, realizing the depth of the other thing in her. Another self was alive in her, burning molten and soft in her womb and bowels, and with this self she adored him. She adored him till her knees were weak as she walked. In her womb and bowels she was flowing and alive now and vulnerable, and helpless in adoration of him as the most naive woman—It feels like a child, she said to herself; it feels like a child in me—And so it did, as if her womb, that had always been shut, had opened and filled with new life, almost a burden, yet lovely.

"If I had a child!" she thought to herself; "if I had him inside me as a child!"—and her limbs turned molten at the thought, and she realized the immense difference between having a child to oneself, and having a child to a man whom one's bowels yearned towards. The former seemed in a sense ordinary: but to have a child to a man whom one adored in one's bowels and one's womb, it made her feel she was very different from her old self, and as if she was sinking deep, deep to the center of all womanhood and the sleep of creation.

It was not the passion that was new to her, it was the yearning adoration. She knew she had always feared it, for it left her helpless; she feared it still, lest if she adored him too much, then she would lose herself, become effaced, and she did not want to be effaced, a slave, like a savage woman. She must not become a slave. She feared her adoration, yet she would not at once fight against it. She knew she could fight it. She had a devil of self-will in her breast that could have fought the full soft heaving adoration of her womb and crushed it. She could even now do it, or she thought so, and she could then take up her passion with her own will.

Ah! yes, to be passionate like a Bacchante, like a Bacchanal fleeing through the woods, to call on Iacchos, the bright phallus that had no independent personality behind it, but was pure god-servant to the woman! The man, the individual, let him not dare intrude. He was but a temple-servant, the bearer and keeper of the bright phallus, her own.

So, in the flux of a new awakening, the old hard passion flamed in her for a time, and the man dwindled to a contemptible object, the mere phallus-bearer, to be torn to pieces when his service was performed. She felt the force of the Bacchae in her limbs and her body, the woman gleaming and rapid, beating down the male; but while she felt this, her heart was heavy. She did not want it, it was known and barren, birthless; the adoration was her treasure. It was so fathomless, so soft, so deep and so unknown. No, no, she would give up her hard bright female power; she was weary of it, stiffened with it; she would sink in the new bath of life, in the depths of her womb and her bowels that sang the voiceless song of adoration. It was early yet to begin to fear the man.

"I walked over by Marehay, and I had tea with Mrs. Flint," she said to Clifford. "I wanted to see the baby. It's so adorable, with hair like red cobwebs. Such a dear! Mr. Flint had gone to market, so she and I and the baby had tea together. Did you wonder where I was?"

"Well, I wondered, but I guessed you had dropped in somewhere to tea," said Clifford jealously. With a sort of second sight he sensed something new in her, something to him quite incomprehensible, but he ascribed it to the baby. He thought that all that ailed Connie was that she did not have a baby; automatically bring one forth, so to speak.

"I saw you go across the park to the iron gate, my Lady," said Mrs. Bolton; "so I thought perhaps you'd called at the Rectory."

"I nearly did, then I turned towards Marehay instead."

The eyes of the two women met: Mrs. Bolton's gray and bright and searching; Connie's blue and veiled and strangely beautiful. Mrs. Bolton was almost sure she had a lover, yet how could it be, and who could it be? Where was there a man?

"Oh, it's so good for you, if you go out and see a bit of company sometimes," said Mrs. Bolton. "I was saying to Sir Clifford, it would do her ladyship a world of good if she'd go out among people more."

"Yes, I'm glad I went, and such a quaint dear cheeky baby, Clifford," said Connie. "It's got hair just like spiderwebs, and bright orange, and the oddest, cheekiest, pale-blue china eyes. Of course, it's a girl, or it wouldn't be so bold, bolder than any little Sir Francis Drake."

"You're right, my Lady—a regular little Flint. They were always a forward, sandy-headed family," said Mrs. Bolton.

"Wouldn't you like to see it, Clifford? I've asked them to tea for you to see it."

"Who?" he asked, looking at Connie in great uneasiness.

"Mrs. Flint and the baby, next Monday."

"You can have them to tea in your room," he said.

"Why, don't you want to see the baby?" she cried.

"Oh, I'll see it, but I don't want to sit through a teatime with them."

"Oh," said Connie, looking at him with wide veiled eyes.

She did not really see him, he was somebody else.

"You can have a nice cozy tea up in your room, my Lady, and Mrs. Flint will be more comfortable than if Sir Clifford was there," said Mrs. Bolton.

She was sure Connie had a lover, and something in her soul exulted. But who was he? Who was he? Perhaps Mrs. Flint would provide a clue.

Clifford was very uneasy. He would not let her go after dinner, and she had wanted so much to be alone. She looked at him, but was curiously submissive.

"Shall we play a game, or shall I read to you, or what shall it be?" he asked uneasily.

"You read to me," said Connie.

"What shall I read—verse or prose? Or drama?"

"Read Racine," she said.

It had been one of his stunts in the past, to read Racine in the real French grand manner, but he was rusty now, and a little self-conscious; he really preferred the loudspeaker. But Connie was sewing, sewing a little silk frock of primrose silk, cut out of one of her dresses, for Mrs. Flint's baby. Between coming home and dinner she had cut it out, and she sat in the soft quiescent rapture of herself, sewing, while the noise of the reading went on.

Inside herself she could feel the humming of passion, like the after-humming of deep bells.

Clifford said something to her about the Racine. She caught the sense after the words had gone.

"Yes! Yes!" she said, looking up at him. "It is splendid."

Again he was frightened at the deep blue haze of her eyes, and of her soft stillness, sitting there. She had never been so utterly soft and still. She fascinated him helplessly, as if some perfume about her intoxicated him. So he went on helplessly with his reading, and the throaty sound of the French was like the wind in the chimneys to her. Of the Racine she heard not one syllable.

She was gone in her own soft rapture, like a forest soughing with the dim, glad moan of spring, moving into bud. She could feel in the same world with her the man, the nameless man, moving on beautiful feet, beautiful in the phallic mystery. And in herself, in all her veins, she felt him and his child. His child was in all her veins, like a twilight.

"For hands she hath none, nor eyes, nor feet, nor golden Treasure of hair . . ."

She was like a forest, like the dark interlacing of the oak-wood, humming inaudibly with myriad unfolding buds. Meanwhile the birds of desire were asleep in the vast interlaced intricacy of her body.

But Clifford's voice went on, clapping and gurgling with unusual sounds. How extraordinary it was! How extraordinary he was, bent there over the book, queer and rapacious and civilized, with broad shoulders and no real legs! What a strange creature, with the sharp, cold, inflexible will of some bird, and no warmth, no warmth at all! One of those creatures of the afterwards, that have no soul, but an extra-alert will, cold will. She shuddered a little, afraid of him. But then, the soft warm flame of life was stronger than he, and the real things were hidden from him.

The reading finished. She was startled. She looked up, and was more startled still to see Clifford watching her with pale, uncanny eyes, like hate.

"Thank you *so* much! You do read Racine beautifully!" she said softly.

"Almost as beautifully as you listen to him," he said cruelly.

"What are you making?" he asked.

"I'm making a child's dress, for Mrs. Flint's baby."

He turned away. A child! A child! That was all her obsession.

"After all," he said, in a declamatory voice, "one gets all one wants out of Racine. Emotions that are ordered and given shape are more important than disorderly emotions."

She watched him with wide, vague, veiled eyes.

"Yes, I'm sure they are," she said.

"The modern world has only vulgarized emotion by letting it loose. What we need is classic control."

"Yes," she said slowly, thinking of him listening with vacant face to the emotional idiocy of the radio. "People pretend to have emotions, and they really feel nothing. I suppose that is being romantic."

"Exactly!" he said.

As a matter of fact, he was tired. This evening had tired him. He would rather have been with his technical books, or his pit-manager, or listening-in to the radio.

Mrs. Bolton came in with two glasses of malted milk: for Clifford, to make him sleep, and for Connie to fatten her again. It was a regular nightcap she had introduced.

Connie was glad to go, when she had drunk her glass, and thankful she needn't help Clifford to bed. She took his glass and put it on the tray, then took the tray, to leave it outside.

"Good night, Clifford! *Do* sleep well! The Racine gets into one like a dream. Good night!"

She had drifted to the door. She was going without kissing him good night. He watched her with sharp, cold eyes. So! She did not even kiss him good night, after he had spent an evening reading to her. Such depths of callousness in her! Even if the kiss was but a formality, it was on such formalities that life depends. She was a Bolshevik, really. Her instincts were bolshevistic. He gazed coldly and angrily at the door whence she had gone. Anger!

And again the dread of the night came on him. He was a networks of nerves, and when he was not braced up to work, and so full of energy: or when he was not listening-in, and so utterly neuter: then he was haunted by anxiety and a sense of dangerous impending void. He was afraid. And Connie could keep the fear off him, if she would. But it was obvious she wouldn't, she wouldn't. She was callous, cold and callous to all that he did for her. He gave up his life for her, and she was callous to him. She only wanted her own way. "The lady loves her will."

Now it was a baby she was obsessed by. Just so that it should be her own, all her own, and not his!

Clifford was so healthy, considering. He looked so well and ruddy, in the face, his shoulders were broad and strong, his chest deep, he had put on flesh. And yet, at the same time, he was afraid of death. A terrible hollow seemed to menace him somewhere, somehow, a void, and into this void his energy would collapse. Energyless, he felt at times he was dead, really dead.

So his rather prominent pale eyes had a queer look, furtive, and yet a little cruel, so cold: and at the same time, almost impudent. It was a very odd look, this look of impudence: as if he were triumphing over life in spite of life. "Who knoweth the mysteries of the will—for it can triumph even against the angels—"

But his dread was the nights when he could not sleep. Then it was awful indeed, when annihilation pressed in on him on every side. Then it was ghastly, to exist without having any life: lifeless, in the night, to exist.

But now he could ring for Mrs. Bolton. And she would always come. That was a great comfort. She would come in her dressing gown, with her hair in a plait down her back, curiously girlish and dim, though the brown plait was streaked with gray. And she would make him coffee or chamomile tea, and she would play chess or piquet with him. She had a woman's queer faculty of playing even chess well enough, when she was three parts asleep, well enough to make her worth beating. So, in the silent intimacy of the night, they sat, or she sat and he lay on the bed, with the reading lamp shedding its solitary light on them, she almost gone in sleep, he almost gone in a sort of fear, and they played, played together—then they had a cup of coffee and a biscuit together, hardly speaking, in the silence of night, but being a reassurance to one another.

And this night she was wondering who Lady Chatterley's lover was. And she was thinking of her own Ted, so long dead, yet for her never quite dead. And when she thought of him, the old, old grudge against the world rose up, but especially against the masters, that they had killed him. They had not really killed him. Yet, to her, emotionally, they had. And somewhere deep in herself, because of it, she was a nihilist, and really anarchic.

In her half-sleep, thoughts of her Ted and thoughts of Lady Chatterley's unknown lover commingled, and then she felt she shared with the other woman a great grudge against Sir Clifford and all he stood for. At the same time she was playing piquet with him, and they were gambling sixpences. And it was a source of satisfaction to be playing piquet with a baronet, and even losing sixpences to him.

When they played cards, they always gambled. It made him forget himself. And he usually won. Tonight, too, he was winning. So he would not go to sleep till the first dawn appeared. Luckily it began to appear at half-past four or thereabouts.

Connie was in bed, and fast asleep all this time. But the keeper, too, could not rest. He had closed the coops and made his round of the wood, then gone home and eaten supper. But he did not go to bed. Instead he sat by the fire and thought.

He thought of his boyhood in Tevershall, and of his five or six years of married life. He thought of his wife, and always bitterly. She had seemed so brutal. But he had not seen her now since 1915, in the spring when he joined up. Yet there she was, not three miles away, and more brutal than ever. He hoped never to see her again while he lived.

He thought of his life abroad, as a soldier. India, Egypt, then India again: the blind, thoughtless life with the horses: the colonel who had loved him and whom he had loved: the several years that he had been an officer, a lieutenant with a very fair chance of being a captain. Then the death of the colonel from pneumonia, and his own narrow escape from death: his damaged health: his deep restlessness: his leaving the army and coming back to England to be a working man again.

He was temporizing with life. He had thought he would be safe, at least for a time, in this wood. There was no shooting as yet: he had to rear the pheasants. He would have no guns to serve. He would be alone, and apart from life, which was all he wanted. He had to have some sort of a background. And this was his native place. There was even his mother, though she had never meant very much to him. And he could go on in life, existing from day to day, without connection and without hope. For he did not know what to do with himself.

He did not know what to do with himself. Since he had been an officer for some years, and had mixed among the other officers and civil servants, with their wives and families, he had lost all ambition to "get on." There was a toughness, a curious rubbernecked toughness and unlivingness about the middle and upper classes, as he had known them, which just left him feeling cold and different from them.

So, he had come back to his own class. To find there, what he had forgotten during his absence of years, a pettiness and a vulgarity of manner extremely distasteful. He admitted now at last, how important manner was. He admitted, also, how important it was even *to pretend* not to care about the halfpence and the small things of life. But among the common people there was no pretense. A penny more or less on the bacon was worse than a change in the Gospel. He could not stand it.

And again, there was the wage-squabble. Having lived among the owning classes, he knew the utter futility of expecting any solution of the wage-squabble. There was no solution, short of death. The only thing was not to care, not to care about the wages.

Yet, if you were poor and wretched you *had* to care. Anyhow, it was becoming the only thing they did care about. The *care* about money was like a great cancer, eating away individuals of all classes. He refused to care about money.

And what then? What did life offer apart from the care of money? Nothing.

Yet he could live alone, in the wan satisfaction of being alone, and raise pheasants to be shot ultimately by fat men after breakfast. It was futility, futility to the *n*th power.

But why care, why bother? And he had not cared nor bothered till now, when this woman had come into his life. He was nearly ten years older than she. And he was a thousand years older in experience, starting from the bottom. The connection between them was growing closer. He could see the day when it would clinch up and they would have to make a life together. "For the bonds of love are ill to loose!"

And what then? What then? Must he start again, with nothing to start on? Must he entangle this woman? Must he have the horrible broil with her lame husband? And also some sort of horrible broil with his own brutal wife, who hated him? Misery! lots of misery! And he was no longer young and merely buoyant. Neither was he the insouciant sort. Every bitterness and every ugliness would hurt him: and the woman!

But even if they got clear of Sir Clifford and of his own wife, even if they got clear, what were they going to do? What was he, himself, going to do? What was he going to do with his life? For he must do something. He couldn't be a mere hanger-on, on her money and his own very small pension.

It was insoluble. He could only think of going to America, to try a new air. He disbelieved in the dollar utterly. But perhaps, perhaps there was something else.

He could not rest nor even go to bed. After sitting in a stupor of bitter thoughts until midnight, he got suddenly from his chair and reached for his coat and gun.

"Come on, lass," he said to the dog. "We're best outside."

It was a starry night, but moonless. He went on a slow, scrupulous, soft-stepping and stealthy round. The only thing he had to contend with was the colliers setting snares for rabbits, particularly the Stacks Gate colliers, on the Marehay side. But it was breeding season, and even colliers respected it a little. Nevertheless the stealthy beating of the round in search of poachers soothed his nerves and took his mind off his thoughts.

But when he had done his slow, cautious beating of his bounds—it was nearly a five-mile walk—he was tired. He went to the top of the knoll and looked out. There was no sound save the noise, the faint shuffling noise from Stacks Gate colliery, that never ceased working: and there were hardly any lights, save the brilliant electric rows at the works. The world lay darkly and fumily sleeping.

It was half-past two. But even in its sleep it was an uneasy, cruel world, stirring with the noise of a train or some great lorry on the road, and flashing with some rosy lightning-flash from the furnaces. It was a world of iron and coal, the cruelty of iron and the smoke of coal, and the endless, endless greed that drove it all. Only greed, greed stirring in its sleep.

It was cold, and he was coughing. A fine cold draught blew over the knoll. He thought of the woman. Now he would have given all he had or even might have to hold her warm in his arms, both of them wrapped in one blanket, and sleep. All hopes of eternity and all gain from the past he would have given to have her there, to be wrapped warm with him in one blanket, and sleep, only sleep. It seemed the sleep with the woman in his arms was the only necessity.

He went to the hut, and wrapped himself in the blanket and lay on the floor to sleep. But he could not, he was cold. And besides, he felt cruelly his own unfinished nature. He felt his own unfinished condition of aloneness cruelly. He wanted her, to touch her, to hold her fast against him in one moment of completeness and rest.

He got up again and went out, towards the park gates this time: then slowly along the path towards the house. It was nearly four o'clock, still clear and cold, but no sign of dawn. He was so used to the dark, he could see well.

Slowly, slowly the great house drew him, as a magnet. He wanted to be near her. It was not desire, not that. It was the cruel sense of unfinished aloneness, that needed a silent woman folded in his arms. Perhaps he could find her. Perhaps he could even call her out to him: or find some way in to her. For the need was imperious.

He slowly, silently climbed the incline to the hall. Then he came round the great trees at the top of the knoll, on to the drive, which made a grand sweep round a lozenge of grass in front of the entrance. He could already see the two magnificent beeches which stood in this big level lozenge in front of the house, detaching themselves darkly in the dark air.

There was the house, low and long and obscure, with one light burning downstairs, in Sir Clifford's room. But which room she was in, the woman who held the other end of the frail thread which drew him so mercilessly, that he did not know.

He went a little nearer, gun in hand, and stood motionless on the drive, watching the house. Perhaps even now he could find her, come at her in some way. The house was not impregnable: he was as clever as burglars are. Why not come to her?

He stood motionless, waiting, while the dawn faintly and imperceptibly paled behind him. He saw the light in the house go out. But he did not see Mrs. Bolton come to the window and draw back the old curtain of dark-blue silk, and stand herself in the dark room, looking out on the half-dark of the approaching day, looking for the longed-for dawn, waiting for Clifford to be really reassured that it was daybreak. For when he was sure of daybreak, he would sleep almost at once.

She stood blind with sleep at the window, waiting. And as she stood, she started, and almost cried out. For there was a man out there on the drive, a black figure in the twilight. She woke up grayly, and watched, but without making a sound to disturb Sir Clifford.

The daylight began to rustle into the world, and the dark figure seemed to go smaller and more defined. She made out the gun and gaiters and baggy jacket—it would be Oliver Mellors, the keeper. Yes, there was the dog nosing around like a shadow, and waiting for him!

And what did the man want? Did he want to rouse the house? What was he standing there for, transfixed, looking up at the house like a lovesick male dog outside the house where the bitch is!

Goodness! The knowledge went through Mrs. Bolton like a shot. He was Lady Chatterley's lover. He! He!

To think of it! Why, she, Ivy Bolton, had once been a tiny bit in love with him herself! When he was a lad of sixteen and she a woman of twenty-six. It was when she was studying, and he had helped her a lot with the anatomy and things she had had to learn. He'd been a clever boy, had a scholarship for Sheffield Grammar School, and learned French and things: and then after all had become an overhead blacksmith shoeing horses, because he was fond of horses, he said: but really because he was frightened to go out and face the world, only he'd never admit it.

But he'd been a nice lad, a nice lad, had helped her a lot, so clever at making things clear to you. He was quite as clever as Sir Clifford: and always one for the women. More with women than men, they said.

Till he'd gone and married that Bertha Coutts, as if to spite himself. Some people do marry to spite themselves, because they're disappointed or something. And no wonder it had been a failure—For years he was gone, all the time of the war: and a lieutenant and all: quite the gentleman, really quite the gentleman!—Then to come back to Tevershall and go as a gamekeeper! Really, some people can't take their chances when they've got them! And talking broad Derbyshire again like the worst, when she, Ivy Bolton, knew he spoke like any gentleman, *really*.

Well, well! So her ladyship had fallen for him! Well, her ladyship wasn't the first: there was something about him. But fancy! A Tevershall lad born and bred, and she her ladyship in Wragby Hall! My word, that was a slap back at the high-and-mighty Chatterleys!

But he, the keeper, as the day grew, had realized: it's no good! It's no good trying to get rid of your own aloneness. You've got to stick to it all your life. Only at times, at times, the gap will be filled in. At times! But you have to wait for the times. Accept your own aloneness and stick to it, all your life. And then accept the times when the gap is filled in, when they come. But they've got to come. You can't force them.

With a sudden snap the bleeding desire that had drawn him after her broke. He had broken it, because it must be so. There must be a coming together on both sides. And if she wasn't coming to him, he wouldn't track her down. He mustn't. He must go away, till she came.

He turned slowly, ponderingly, accepting again the isolation. He knew it was better so. She must come to him: it was no use trailing after her. No use!

Mrs. Bolton saw him disappear, saw his dog run after him.

"Well, well!" she said. "He's the one man I never thought of; and the one man I might have thought of. He was nice to me when he was a lad, after I lost Ted. Well, well! Whatever would *he* say if he knew!"

And she glanced triumphantly at the already sleeping Clifford, as she stepped softly from the room.

❖ 11 ❖

Connie was sorting out one of the Wragby lumber rooms. There were several: the house was a warren, and the family never sold anything. Sir Geoffrey's father had liked pictures and Sir Geoffrey's mother had liked cinquecento furniture. Sir Geoffrey himself had liked old carved oak chests, vestry chests. So it went on through the generations. Clifford collected very modern pictures, at very moderate prices.

So in the lumber room there were bad Sir Edwin Landseers and pathetic William Henry Hunt birds' nests: and other Academy stuff, enough to frighten the daughter of an R.A. She determined to look through it one day, and clear it all. And the grotesque furniture interested her.

Wrapped up carefully to preserve it from damage and dry-rot was the old family cradle, of rosewood. She had to unwrap it, to look at it. It had a certain charm: she looked at it a long time.

"It's a thousand pities it won't be called for," sighed Mrs. Bolton, who was helping. "Though cradles like that are out-of-date nowadays."

"It might be called for. I might have a child," said Connie casually, as if saying she might have a new hat.

"You mean, if anything happened to Sir Clifford!" stammered Mrs. Bolton.

"No! I mean as things are. It's only muscular paralysis with Sir Clifford—it doesn't affect *him*," said Connie, lying as naturally as breathing.

Clifford had put the idea into her head. He had said: "Of course, *I* may have a child yet. I'm not really mutilated at all. The potency may easily come back even if the muscles of the hips and legs are paralyzed. And then the seed may be transferred."

He really felt, when he had his periods of energy and worked so hard at the question of the mines, as if his sexual potency were returning. Connie had looked at him in terror. But she was quite quick-witted enough to use his suggestion for her own preservation. For she would have a child if she could: but not his.

Mrs. Bolton was for a moment breathless, flabbergasted. Then she didn't believe it: she saw in it a ruse. Yet doctors could do such things nowadays. They might sort of graft seed.

"Well, my Lady, I only hope and pray you may. It would be lovely for you: and for everybody. My word, a child in Wragby, what a difference it would make!"

"Wouldn't it!" said Connie.

And she chose three R.A. pictures of sixty years ago, to send to the Duchess of Shortlands for that lady's next charitable bazaar. She was called "the bazaar duchess," and she would be delighted with the three framed R.A.'s. She might even call, on the strength of them. How furious Clifford was when she called!

But oh, my dear! Mrs. Bolton was thinking to herself. Is it Oliver Mellors's child you're preparing us for? Oh, my dear, that *would* be a Tevershall baby in the Wragby cradle, my word! Wouldn't shame it, neither!

Among other monstrosities in this lumber room was a largish black japanned box, excellently and ingeniously made some sixty or seventy years ago, and fitted with every imaginable object. On top was a concentrated toilet set: brushes, bottles, mirrors, combs, boxes, even three beautiful little razors in safety sheaths, shaving-bowl and all. Underneath came a sort of escritoire outfit: blotters, pens, ink-bottles, paper, envelopes, memorandum books: and then a perfect sewing outfit, with three different sized scissors, thimbles, needles, silks, and cottons, darning egg, all of the very best quality and perfectly finished. Then there was a little medicine store, with bottles labeled Laudanum, Tincture of Myrrh, Ess. Cloves, and so on: but empty. Everything was perfectly new, and the whole thing, when shut up, was as big as a small, but fat weekend bag. And inside, it fitted together like a puzzle. The bottles could not possibly have spilled: there wasn't room.

The thing was wonderfully made and contrived, excellent craftsmanship of the Victorian order. But somehow it was monstrous. Some Chatterley must even have felt it, for the thing had never been used. It had a peculiar soullessness.

Yet Mrs. Bolton was thrilled.

"Look what beautiful brushes, so expensive, even the shaving brushes, three perfect ones! No! and those scissors! They're the best that money could buy. Oh, I call it lovely!"

"Do you?" said Connie. "Then you have it."

"Oh, no, my Lady!"

"Of course! It will only lie here till Doomsday. If you won't have it, I'll send it to the Duchess as well as the pictures, and she doesn't deserve so much. Do have it!"

"Oh, your Ladyship! Why, I shall never be able to thank you."

"You needn't try," laughed Connie.

And Mrs. Bolton sailed down with the huge and very black box in her arms, flushing bright pink in her excitement.

Mr. Betts drove her in the trap to her house in the village, with the box. And she *had* to have a few friends in, to show it: the schoolmistress, the chemist's wife, Mrs. Weedon the under-cashier's wife. They thought it marvelous. And then started the whisper of Lady Chatterley's child.

"Wonders'll never cease!" said Mrs. Weedon.

But Mrs. Bolton was *convinced*, if it did come, it would be Sir Clifford's child. So there!

Not long after, the rector said gently to Clifford:

"And may we really hope for an heir to Wragby? Ah, that would be the hand of God in mercy, indeed!"

"Well! We may *hope*," said Clifford, with a faint irony, and, at the same time, a certain conviction. He had begun to believe it really possible it might even be *his* child.

Then one afternoon came Leslie Winter, Squire Winter, as everybody called him: lean, immaculate, and seventy: and every inch a gentleman, as Mrs. Bolton said to Mrs. Betts. Every millimeter, indeed! And with his old-fashioned, rather haw-haw! manner of speaking, he seemed more out-of-date than bag-wigs. Time, in her flight, drops these fine old feathers.

They discussed the collieries. Clifford's idea was, that his coal, even the poor sort, could be made into hard concentrated fuel that would burn at great heat if fed with certain damp, acidulated air at a fairly strong pressure. It had long been observed that in a particularly strong, wet wind the pit-bank burned very vivid, gave off hardly any fumes, and left a fine powder of ash, instead of the slow pink gravel.

"But where will you find the proper engines for burning your fuel?" asked Winter.

"I'll make them myself. And I'll use my fuel myself. And I'll sell electric power. I'm certain I could do it."

"If you can do it, then splendid, splendid, my dear boy. Haw! Splendid! If I can be of any help, I shall be delighted. I'm afraid I am a little out-of-date, and my collieries are like me. But who knows, when I'm gone, there may be men like you. Splendid! It will employ all the men again, and you won't have to sell your coal, or fail to sell it. A splendid idea, and I hope it will be a success. If I had sons of my own, no doubt they would have up-to-date ideas for Shipley: no doubt! By the way, dear boy, is there any foundation to the rumor that we may entertain hopes of an heir to Wragby?"

"Is there a rumor?" asked Clifford.

"Well, my dear boy, Marshall from Fillingwood asked *me*, that's all I can say about a rumor. Of course, I wouldn't repeat it for the world, if there were no foundation."

"Well, Sir," said Clifford uneasily, but with strange bright eyes. "There is a hope. There is a hope."

Winter came across the room and wrung Clifford's hand.

"My dear boy, my dear lad, can you believe what it means to me, to hear that! And to hear you are working in the hopes of a son: and that you may again employ every man at Tevershall. Ah my boy! to keep up the level of the race, and to have work waiting for any man who cares to work!—"

The old man was really moved.

Next day Connie was arranging tall yellow tulips in a glass vase.

"Connie," said Clifford, "did you know there was a rumor that you are going to supply Wragby with a son and heir?"

Connie felt dim with terror, yet she stood quite still, touching the flowers.

"No!" she said. "Is it a joke? Or malice?"

He paused before he answered:

"Neither, I hope. I hope it may be a prophecy."

Connie went on with her flowers.

"I had a letter from father this morning," she said. "He wants to know if I am aware he has accepted Sir Alexander Cooper's invitation for me for July and August, to the Villa Esmeralda in Venice."

"July *and* August?" said Clifford.

"Oh, I wouldn't stay all that time. Are you sure you wouldn't come?"

"I won't travel abroad," said Clifford, promptly.

She took her flowers to the window.

"Do you mind if I go?" she said. "You know it was promised, for this summer."

"For how long would you go?"

"Perhaps three weeks."

There was a silence for a time.

"Well," said Clifford slowly, and a little gloomily: "I suppose I could stand it for three weeks: if I were absolutely sure you'd want to come back."

"I should want to come back," she said, with a quiet simplicity, heavy with conviction. She was thinking of the other man.

Clifford felt her conviction, and somehow he believed her, he believed it was for him. He felt immensely relieved, joyful at once.

"In that case," he said, "I think it would be all right. Don't you?"

"I think so," she said.

"You'd enjoy the change?"

She looked up at him with strange blue eyes.

"I should like to see Venice again," she said, "and to bathe from one of the shingle islands across the lagoon. But you know I loathe Lido! And I don't fancy I shall like Sir Alexander Cooper and Lady Cooper. But if Hilda is there, and we have a gondola of our own: yes, it will be rather lovely. I *do* wish you'd come."

She said it sincerely. She would so love to make him happy, in these ways.

"Ah, but think of me, though, at the Gare du Nord: at Calais quay!"

"But why not? I see other men carried in litter-chairs, who have been wounded in the war. Besides, we'd motor all the way."

"We should need to take two men."

"Oh, no! We'd manage with Field. There would always be another man there."

But Clifford shook his head.

"Not this year, dear! Not this year! Next year, probably, I'll try."

She went away gloomily. Next year! What would next year bring? She herself did not really want to go to Venice: not now, now there was the other man. But she was going as a sort of discipline: and also because, if she had a child, Clifford would think she had a lover in Venice.

It was already May, and in June they were supposed to start. Always these arrangements! Always one's life arranged for one! Wheels that worked one and drove one, and over which one had no real control!

It was May, but cold and wet again. A cold wet May, good for corn and hay! Much the corn and hay matter nowadays! Connie had to go into Uthwaite, which was their little town, where the Chatterleys were still *the* Chatterleys. She went alone, Field driving her.

In spite of May and a new greenness, the country was dismal. It was rather chilly, and there was smoke in the rain, and a certain sense of exhaust vapor in the air. One just had to live from one's resistance. No wonder these people were ugly and tough.

The car plowed uphill through the long squalid straggle of Tevershall, the blackened brick dwellings, the black slate roofs glistening their sharp edges, the mud black with coal-dust, the pavements wet and black. It was as if dismalness had soaked through and through everything. The utter negation of natural beauty, the utter negation of the gladness of life, the utter absence of the instinct for shapely beauty which every bird and beast has, the utter death of the human intuitive faculty was appalling. The stacks of soap in the grocers' shops, the rhubarb and lemons in the green-grocers'! the awful hats in the milliners'! all went by ugly, ugly, ugly, followed by the plaster-and-gilt horror of the cinema with its wet picture announcements, "A Woman's Love!", and the new big Primitive chapel, primitive enough in its stark brick and big panes of greenish and raspberry glass in the windows. The Wesleyan chapel, higher up, was of blackened brick and stood behind iron railings and blackened shrubs. The Congregational chapel, which thought itself superior, was built of rusticated sandstone and had a steeple, but not a very high one. Just beyond were the new school buildings, expensive pink brick, and graveled playground inside iron railings, all very imposing, and mixing the suggestion of a chapel and a prison. Standard Five girls were having a singing lesson, just finishing the la-me-do-la exercises and beginning a "sweet children's song." Anything more unlike song, spontaneous song, would be impossible to imagine: a strange bawling yell that followed the outlines of a tune. It was not like savages: savages have subtle rhythms. It was not like animals: animals *mean* something when they yell. It was like nothing on earth, and it was called singing. Connie sat and listened with her heart in her boots, as Field was filling petrol. What could possibly become of such a people, a people in whom the living intuitive faculty was dead as nails, and only queer mechanical yells and uncanny will power remained?

A coal-cart was coming downhill, clanking in the rain. Field started upwards, past the big but weary looking drapers' and clothing shops, the post office, into the little marketplace of forlorn space, where Sam Black was peering out of the door of the "Sun," that called itself an inn, not a pub, and where the commercial travelers stayed, and was bowing to Lady Chatterley's car.

The church was away to the left among black trees. The car slid on downhill, past the Miners Arms. It had already passed the Wellington, the Nelson, the Three Tunns and the Sun, now it passed the Miners Arms, then the Mechanics Hall, then the new and almost gaudy Miners Welfare and so, past a few new "villas," out into the blackened road between dark hedges and dark green fields, towards Stacks Gate.

Tevershall! That was Tevershall! Merrie England! Shakespeare's England! No, but the England of today, as Connie had realized since she had come to live in it. It was producing a new race of mankind, over-conscious in the money and social and political side, on the spontaneous, intuitive side dead—but dead! Half-corpses, all of them: but with a terrible insistent consciousness in the other half. There was something uncanny and underground about it all. It was an underworld. And quite incalcuable. How shall we understand the reactions in half-corpses? When Connie saw the great lorries full of steelworkers from Sheffield, weird, distorted, smallish beings like men, off for an excursion to Matlock, her bowels fainted and she thought: Ah, God, what has man done to man? What have the leaders of men been doing to their fellowmen? They have reduced them to less than humanness; and now there can be no fellowship any more! It is just a nightmare.

She felt again in a wave of terror the gray, gritty hopelessness of it all. With such creatures for the industrial masses, and the upper classes as she knew them, there was no hope, no hope anymore. Yet she was wanting a baby, and an heir to Wragby! An heir to Wragby! She shuddered with dread.

Yet Mellors had come out of all this!—Yes, but he was as apart from it all as she was. Even in him there was no fellowship left. It was dead. The fellowship was dead. There was only apartness and hopelessness, as far as all this was concerned. And this was England, the vast bulk of England: as Connie knew, since she had motored from the center of it.

The car was rising towards Stacks Gate. The rain was holding off, and in the air came a queer pellucid gleam of May. The country rolled away in long undulations, south towards the Peak, east towards Mansfield and Nottingham. Connie was traveling south.

As she rose on to the high country, she could see on her left, on a height above the rolling land the shadowy, powerful bulk of Warsop Castle, dark gray, with below it the reddish plastering of miners' dwellings, newish, and below those the plumes of dark smoke and white steam from the great colliery which put so many thousand pounds per annum into the pockets of the Duke and the other shareholders. The powerful old castle was a ruin, yet still it hung its bulk on the low skyline, over the black plumes and the white that waved on the damp air below.

A turn, and they ran on the high level to Stacks Gate. Stacks Gate, as seen from the highroad, was just a huge and gorgeous new hotel, the Coningsby Arms, standing red and white and gilt in barbarous isolation off the road. But if you looked, you saw on the left rows of handsome "modern" dwellings, set down like a game of dominoes, with spaces and gardens: a queer game of dominoes that some weird 'masters' were playing on the surprised earth. And beyond these blocks of dwellings, at the back, rose all the astonishing and frightening overhead erections of a really modern mine, chemical works and long galleries, enormous, and of shapes not before known to man. The headstocks and pit-bank of the mine itself were insignificant among the huge new installations. And in front of this, the game of dominoes stood forever in a sort of surprise, waiting to be played.

This was Stacks Gate, new on the face of the earth, since the war. But as a matter of fact, though even Connie did not know it, downhill half a mile below the "hotel" was old Stacks Gate, with a little old colliery and blackish old brick dwellings, and a chapel or two and a shop or two and a little pub or two.

But that didn't count anymore. The vast plumes of smoke and vapor rose from the new works up above, and this was now Stacks Gate: no chapel, no pubs, even no shops. Only the great "works," which are the modern Olympia with temples to all the gods: then the model dwellings: then the hotel. The hotel in actuality was nothing but a miners' pub, though it looked first-classy.

Even since Connie's arrival at Wragby this new place had arisen on the face of the earth, and the model dwellings had filled with riff-raff drifting in from anywhere, to poach Clifford's rabbits among other occupations.

The car ran on along the uplands, seeing the rolling county spread out. The county; it had once been a proud and lordly county. In front, looming again and hanging on the brow of the skyline, was the huge and splendid bulk of Chadwick Hall, more window than wall, one of the most famous Elizabethan houses. Noble it stood alone above a great park, but out of date, passed over. It was still kept up, but as a showplace. "Look how our ancestors lorded it!"

That was the past. The present lay below. God alone knows where the future lies. The car was already turning, between little old blackened miners' cottages, to descend to Uthwaite. And Uthwaite, on a damp day, was sending up a whole array of smoke plumes and steam, to whatever gods there be. Uthwaite down in the valley, with all the steel threads of the railways to Sheffield drawn through it, and the coalmines and the steelworks sending up smoke and glare from long tubes, and the pathetic little corkscrew spire of the church, that is going to tumble down, still pricking the fumes, always affected Connie strangely. It was an old market town, center of the dales. One of the chief inns was the Chatterley Arms. There, in Uthwaite, Wragby was known as Wragby, as if it were a whole place, not just a house, as it was to outsiders: Wragby Hall, near Tevershall: Wragby, a "seat."

The miners' cottages, blackened, stood flush on the pavement, with that intimacy and smallness of colliers' dwellings over a hundred years old. They lined all the way. The road had become a street, and as you sank, you forgot instantly the open, rolling country where the castles and big houses still dominated, but like ghosts. Now you were just above the tangle of naked railway lines, and foundries and other "works" rose about you, so big you were only aware of walls. And iron clanked with a huge reverberating clank, and huge lorries shook the earth, and whistles screamed.

Yet again, once you had got right down and into the twisted and crooked heart of the town, behind the church, you were in the world of two centuries ago, in the crooked streets where the Chatterley Arms stood, and the old pharmacy, streets which used to lead out to the wild open world of the castles and stately couchant houses.

But at the corner a policeman held up his hand as three lorries loaded with iron rolled past, shaking the poor old church. And not till the lorries were past could he salute her ladyship.

So it was. Upon the old crooked burgess streets hordes of oldish, blackened miners' dwellings crowded, lining the roads out. And immediately after these came the newer, pinker rows of rather larger houses, plastering the valley: the homes of more modern workmen. And beyond that again, in the wide rolling regions of the castles, smoke waved against steam, and patch after patch of raw reddish brick showed the newer mining settlements, sometimes in the hollows, sometimes gruesomely ugly along the skyline of the slopes. And between, in between, were the tattered remnants of the old coaching and cottage England, even the England of Robin Hood, where the miners prowled with the dismalness of suppressed sporting instincts, when they were not at work.

England, my England! But which is *my* England? The stately homes of England make good photographs, and create the illusion of a connection with the Elizabethans. The handsome old halls are here, from the days of Good Queen Anne and Tom Jones. But smuts fall and blacken on the drab stucco, that has long ceased to be golden. And one by one, like the stately homes, they are abandoned. Now they are being pulled down. As for the cottages of England—there they are—great plasterings of brick dwellings on the hopeless countryside.

Now they are pulling down the stately homes, the Georgian halls are going. Fritchley, a perfect old Georgian mansion, was even now, as Connie passed in the car, being demolished. It was in perfect repair: till the war the Weatherleys had lived in style there. But now it was too big, too expensive, and the country had become too uncongenial. The gentry were departing to pleasanter places, where they could spend their money without having to see how it was made.

This is history. One England blots out another. The mines had made the halls wealthy. Now they were blotting them out, as they had already blotted out the cottages. The industrial England blots out the agricultural England. One meaning blots out another. The new England blots out the old England. And the continuity is not organic, but mechanical.

Connie, belonging to the leisured classes, had clung to the remnants of the old England. It had taken her years to realize that it was really blotted out by this terrifying new and gruesome England, and that the blotting out would go on till it was complete. Fritchley was gone, Eastwood was gone, Shipley was going: Squire Winter's beloved Shipley.

Connie called for a moment at Shipley. The park gates, at the back, opened just near the level crossing of the colliery railway; the Shipley colliery itself stood just beyond the trees. The gates stood open, because through the park was a right-of-way that the colliers used. They hung around the park.

The car passed the ornamental ponds, in which the colliers threw their newspapers, and took the private drive to the house. It stood above, aside, a very pleasant stucco building from the middle of the eighteenth century. It had a beautiful alley of yew trees, that had approached an older house, and the hall stood serenely spread out, winking its Georgian panes as if cheerfully. Behind, there were really beautiful gardens.

Connie liked the interior much better than Wragby. It was much lighter, more alive, shapen and elegant. The rooms were paneled with creamy-painted paneling, the ceilings were touched with gilt, and everything was kept in exquisite order, all the appointments were perfect, regardless of expense. Even the corridors managed to be ample and lovely, softly curved and full of life.

Leslie Winter was alone. He had adored his house. But his park was bordered by three of his own collieries. He had been a generous man in his ideas. He had almost welcomed the colliers in his park. Had the miners not made him rich! So, when he saw the gangs of unshapely men lounging by his ornamental waters—not on the *private* part of the park; no, he drew the line there—he would say: "The miners are perhaps not so ornamental as deer, but they are far more profitable."

But that was in the golden—monetarily—latter half of Queen Victoria's reign. Miners were then "good working men."

Winter had made this speech, half apologetic, to his guest, the then Prince of Wales. And the Prince had replied, in his rather guttural English:

"You are quite right. If there were coal under Sandringham, I would open a mine on the lawns, and think it first-rate landscape gardening. Oh, I am quite willing to exchange roe deer for colliers, at the price. Your men are good men, too, I hear."

But then, the Prince had perhaps an exaggerated idea of the beauty of money, and the blessings of industrialism.

However, the Prince had been a King, and the King had died, and now there was another King, whose chief function seemed to be to open soup kitchens.

And the good working men were somehow hemming Shipley in. New mining villages crowded on the park, and the squire felt somehow that the population was alien. He used to feel, in a good-natured but quite grand way, lord of his own domain and of his own colliers. Now, by a subtle pervasion of the new spirit, he had somehow been pushed out. It was he who did not belong anymore. There was no mistaking it. The mines, the industry had a will of its own, and this will was against the gentleman-owner. All the colliers took part in the will, and it was hard to live up against it. It either shoved you out of the place, or out of life altogether.

Squire Winter, a soldier, had stood it out. But he no longer cared to walk in the park after dinner. He almost hid, indoors. Once he had walked, bareheaded, and in his patent-leather shoes and purple silk socks, with Connie down to the gate, talking to her in his well-bred rather haw-haw fashion. But when it came to passing the little gangs of colliers who stood and stared without either salute or anything else, Connie felt how the lean, well-bred old man winced, winced as an elegant antelope stag in a cage winces from the vulgar stare. The colliers were not *personally* hostile: not at all. But their spirit was cold, and shoving him out. And deep down, there was a profound grudge. They "worked for him." And in their ugliness, they resented his elegant, well-groomed, well-bred existence. "Who's he!" It was the *difference* they resented.

And somewhere, in his secret English heart, being a good deal of a soldier, he believed they were right to resent the difference. He felt himself a little in the wrong, for having all the advantages. Nevertheless he represented a system, and he would not be shoved out.

Except by death. Which came on him soon after Connie's call, suddenly. And he remembered Clifford handsomely in his will.

The heirs at once gave out the order for the demolishing of Shipley. It cost too much to keep up. No one would live there. So it was broken up. The avenue of yews was cut down. The park was denuded of its timber, and divided into lots. It was near enough to Uthwaite. In the strange, bald desert of this still-one-more no-man's-land, new little streets of semidetacheds were run up, very desirable! The Shipley Hall Estate!

Within a year of Connie's last call, it had happened. There stood Shipley Hall

Estate, an array of red-brick semidetached 'villas' in new streets. No one would have dreamed that the stucco hall had stood there twelve months before.

But this is a later stage of King Edward's landscape gardening, the sort that has an ornamental coal-mine on the lawn.

One England blots out another. The England of the Squire Winters and the Wragby Halls was gone, dead. The blotting out was only not yet complete.

What would come after? Connie could not imagine. She could only see the new brick streets spreading into the fields, the new erections rising at the collieries, the new girls in their silk stockings, the new collier lads lounging into the Pally or the Welfare. The younger generation were utterly unconscious of the Old England. There was a gap in the continuity of consciousness, almost American: but industrial really. What next?

Connie always felt there was no next. She wanted to hide her head in the sand: or at least, in the bosom of a living man.

The world was so complicated and weird and gruesome! The common people were so many, and really, so terrible. So she thought as she was going home, and saw the colliers trailing from the pits, gray-black, distorted, one shoulder higher than the other, slurring their heavy iron-shod boots. Underground gray faces, whites of eyes rolling, necks cringing from the pit roof, shoulders out of shape. Men! Men! Alas, in some way patient and good men. In other ways, nonexistent. Something that men *should* have was bred and killed out of them. Yet they were men. They begot children. One might bear a child to them. Terrible, terrible thought! They were good and kindly. But they were only half, only the gray half of a human being. As yet, they were "good." But even that was the goodness of their halfness. Supposing the dead in them ever rose up! But no, it was too terrible to think of. Connie was absolutely afraid of the industrial masses. They seemed so *weird* to her. A life with utterly no beauty in it, no intuition, always "in the pit."

Children from such men. Oh, God! Oh, God!

Yet Mellors had come from such a father. Not quite. Forty years had made a difference, an appalling difference in manhood. The iron and the coal had eaten deep into the bodies and souls of the men.

Incarnate ugliness, and alive! What would become of them all? Perhaps with the passing of the coal they would disappear again, off the face of the earth. They had appeared out of nowhere in their thousands, when the coal had called for them. Perhaps they were only weird fauna of the coal-seams. Creatures of another reality, they were elementals, serving the elements of coal, as the metalworkers were elementals, serving the element of iron. Men not men, but animals of coal and iron and clay. Fauna of the elements, carbon, iron, silicon:

elementals. They had perhaps some of the weird, inhuman beauty of minerals, the luster of coal, the weight and blueness and resistance of iron, the transparency of glass. Elemental creatures, weird and distorted, of the mineral world! They belonged to the coal, the iron, the clay, as fish belong to the sea and worms to dead wood. The animal of mineral disintegration!

Connie was glad to be home, to bury her head in the sand. She was glad even to babble to Clifford. For her fear of the mining and iron Midlands affected her with a queer feeling that went all over her, like influenza.

"Of course, I had to have tea in Miss Bentley's shop," she said.

"Really! Winter would have given you tea."

"Oh, yes, but I daren't disappoint Miss Bentley."

Miss Bentley was a sallow old maid with a rather large nose and romantic disposition, who served tea with a careful intensity worthy of a sacrament.

"Did she ask after me?" said Clifford.

"Of course!—*May* I ask your Ladyship how Sir Clifford is?—I believe she ranks you even higher than Nurse Cavell!"

"And I suppose you said I was blooming."

"Yes! And she looked as rapt as if I had said the heavens had opened to you. I said if she ever came to Tevershall she was to come to see you."

"Me! Whatever for! See me!"

"Why, yes, Clifford. You can't be so adored without making some slight return. Saint George of Cappadocia was nothing to you, in her eyes."

"And do you think she'll come?"

"Oh, she blushed! and looked quite beautiful for a moment, poor thing! Why don't men marry the women who would really adore them?"

"The women start adoring too late. But did she say she'd come?"

"Oh!" Connie imitated the breathless Miss Bentley, "your Ladyship, if ever I should dare to presume!"

"Dare to presume! how absurd! But I hope to God she won't turn up. And how was her tea?"

"Oh, Lipton's and *very* strong! But, Clifford, do you realize you are the *Roman de la rose* of Miss Bentley and lots like her?"

"I'm not flattered, even then."

"They treasure up every one of your pictures in the illustrated papers, and probably pray for you every night. It's rather wonderful."

She went upstairs to change.

That evening he said to her:

"You do think, don't you, that there is something eternal in marriage?"

She looked at him.

"But Clifford, you make eternity sound like a lid or a long, long chain that trailed after one, no matter how far one went."

He looked at her, annoyed.

"What I mean," he said, "is that if you go to Venice, you won't go in the hopes of some love affair that you can take *au grand sérieux*, will you?"

"A love affair in Venice *au grand sérieux?* No, I assure you! No, I'd never take a love affair in Venice more than *au très petit sérieux.*"

She spoke with a queer kind of contempt. He knitted his brows, looking at her.

Coming downstairs in the morning, she found the keeper's dog Flossie sitting in the corridor outside Clifford's room, and whimpering very faintly.

"Why, Flossie!" she said softly. "What are you doing here?"

And she quietly opened Clifford's door. Clifford was sitting up in bed, with the bed-table and typewriter pushed aside, and the keeper was standing attention at the foot of the bed. Flossie ran in. With a faint gesture of head and eyes, Mellors ordered her to the door again, and she slunk out.

"Oh, good morning, Clifford!" Connie said. "I didn't know you were so busy." Then she looked at the keeper, saying good morning to him. He murmured his reply, looking at her as if vaguely. But she felt a whiff of passion touch her, from his mere presence.

"Did I interrupt you, Clifford? I'm sorry."

"No, it's nothing of any importance."

She slipped out of the room again, and up to the blue boudoir on the first floor. She sat in the window, and saw him go down the drive, with his curious, silent motion, effaced. He had a natural sort of quiet distinction, an aloof pride, and also a certain look of frailty. A hireling! One of Clifford's hirelings! "The fault, dear Brutus, is not in our stars, but in ourselves, that we are underlings."

Was he an underling? Was he? What did he think of *her*?

It was a sunny day, and Connie was working in the garden, and Mrs. Bolton was helping her. For some reason, the two women had drawn together, in one of the unaccountable flows and ebbs of sympathy that exist between people. They were pegging down carnations, and putting in small plants for the summer. It was work they both liked. Connie especially felt a delight in putting the soft roots of young plants into a soft black puddle, and cradling them down. On this spring morning she felt a quiver in her womb, too, as if the sunshine had touched it and made it happy.

"It is many years since you lost your husband?" she said to Mrs. Bolton, as she took up another little plant and laid it in its hole.

"Twenty-three!" said Mrs. Bolton, as she carefully separated the young columbines into single plants. "Twenty-three years since they brought him home."

Connie's heart gave a lurch, at the terrible finality of it. "Brought him home!"

"Why did he get killed, do you think?" she asked. "He was happy with you?"

It was a woman's question to a woman. Mrs. Bolton put aside a strand of hair from her face, with the back of her hand.

"I don't know, my Lady! He sort of wouldn't give in to things: he wouldn't really go with the rest. And then he hated ducking his head for anything on earth. A sort of obstinacy, that *gets* itself killed. You see, he didn't really care. I lay it down to the pit. He ought never to have been down the pit. But his dad made him go down, as a lad; and then, when you're over twenty, it's not very easy to come out."

"Did he say he hated it?"

"Oh, no! Never! He never said he hated anything. He just made a funny face. He was one of those who wouldn't take care: like some of the first lads as went off so blithe to the war and got killed right away. He wasn't really wezzle-brained. But he wouldn't care. I used to say to him: 'You care for nought nor nobody!' But he did! The way he sat when my first baby was born, motionless, and the sort of fatal eyes he looked at me with, when it was over! I had a bad time, but I had to comfort *him*. 'It's all right, lad, it's all right!' I said to him. And he gave me a look, and that funny sort of smile. He never said anything. But I don't believe he had any right pleasure with me at nights after; he'd never really let himself go. I used to say to him: 'Oh, let thysen go, lad!'—I'd talk broad to him sometimes. And he said nothing. But he wouldn't let himself go, or he couldn't. He didn't want me to have any more children. I always blamed his mother, for letting him in th' room. He'd no right t'ave been there. Men makes so much more of things than they should, once they start brooding."

"Did he mind so much?" said Connie in wonder.

"Yes, he sort of couldn't take it for natural, all that pain. And it spoilt his pleasure in his bit of married love. I said to him: If I don't care, why should you? It's my lookout!—But all he'd ever say was: It's not right!"

"Perhaps he was too sensitive," said Connie.

"That's it! When you come to know men, that's how they are: too sensitive in the wrong place. And I believe, unbeknown to himself, he hated the pit, just hated it. He looked so quiet when he was dead, as if he'd got free. He was such a nice-looking lad. It just broke my heart to see him, so still and pure looking, as if he'd *wanted* to die. Oh, it broke my heart, that did. But it was the pit."

She wept a few bitter tears, and Connie wept more. It was a warm spring day, with a perfume of earth and of yellow flowers, many things rising to bud, and the garden still with the very sap of sunshine.

"It must have been terrible for you!" said Connie.

"Oh, my Lady! I never realized at first. I could only say: Oh, my lad, what did you want to leave me for!—That was all my cry. But somehow I felt he'd come back."

"But he *didn't* want to leave you," said Connie.

"Oh, no, my Lady! That was only my silly cry. And I kept expecting him back. Especially at nights. I kept waking up, thinking: Why, he's not here with me!—It was as if my *feelings* wouldn't believe he'd gone. I just felt he'd *have* to come back and talk to me, so I could feel him with me. That was all I wanted, to feel him there with me, warm. And it took me a thousand shocks before I knew

"The touch of him," said Connie.

"That's it, my Lady, the touch of him! I've never got over it to this day, and never shall. And if there's a heaven above, he'll be there, and warm up against me so I can sleep."

Connie glanced at the handsome, brooding face in fear. Another passionate one out of Tevershall! The touch of him! For the bonds of love are ill to loose!

"It's terrible, once you've got a man into your blood." she said.

"Oh, my Lady! And that's what makes you feel so bitter. You feel folks *wanted* him killed. You feel the pit fair *wanted* to kill him. Oh, I felt, if it hadn't been for the pit, an' them as runs the pit, there'd have been no leaving me. But they all *want* to separate a woman and a man, if they're together."

"If they're physically together," said Connie.

"That's right, my Lady! There's a lot of hardhearted folks in the world. And every morning when he got up and went to th' pit, I felt it was wrong, wrong. But what else could he do? What can a man do?"

A queer hate flared in the woman.

"But can a touch last so long?" Connie asked suddenly. "That you could feel him so long?"

"Oh, my Lady, what else is there to last? Children grows away from you. But the man, well—! But even *that* they'd like to kill in you, the very thought of the touch of him. Even your own children! Ah, well! We might have drifted apart, who knows. But the feeling's something different. It's 'appen better never to care. But there, when I look at women who's never really been warmed through by a man, well, they seem to me poor dool-owls after all, no matter how they may dress up and gad. No, I'll abide by my own. I've not much respect for people."

❖ 12 ❖

Connie went to the wood directly after lunch. It was really a lovely day, the first dandelions making suns, the first daisies so white. The hazel thicket was a lacework of half-open leaves, and the last dusty perpendicular of the catkins. Yellow celandines now were in crowds, flat open, pressed back in urgency, and the yellow glitter of themselves. It was the yellow, the powerful yellow of early summer. And primroses were broad, and full of pale abandon, thick-clustered primroses no longer shy. The lush, dark green of hyacinths was a sea, with buds rising like pale corn, while in the riding the forget-me-nots were fluffing up, and columbines were unfolding their ink-purple riches, and there were bits of bluebird's eggshell under a bush. Everywhere the bud-knots and the leap of life!

The keeper was not at the hut. Everything was serene, brown chickens running lustily. Connie walked on towards the cottage, because she wanted to find him.

The cottage stood in the sun, off the wood's edge. In the little garden the double daffodils rose in tufts, near the wide-open door, and red double daisies made a border to the path. There was the bark of a dog, and Flossie came running.

The wide-open door! so he was at home. And the sunlight falling on the red-brick floor! As she went up the path, she saw him through the window, sitting at the table in his shirt-sleeves, eating. The dog wuffed softly, slowly wagging her tail.

He rose, and came to the door, wiping his mouth with a red handkerchief, still chewing.

"May I come in?" she said.

"Come in!"

The sun shone into the bare room, which still smelled of a mutton chop, done in a dutch oven before the fire, because the dutch oven still stood on the fender, with the black potato-saucepan on a piece of paper beside it on the white hearth. The fire was red, rather low, the bar dropped, the kettle singing.

On the table was his plate, with potatoes and the remains of the chop; also bread in a basket, salt, and a blue mug with beer. The tablecloth was white oilcloth. He stood in the shade.

"You are very late," she said. "Do go on eating!"

She sat down on a wooden chair, in the sunlight by the door.

"I had to go to Uthwaite," he said, sitting down at the table but not eating.

"Do eat," she said.

But he did not touch the food.

"Shall y'ave something?" he asked her. "Shall y'ave a cup of tea? t'kettle's on t' boil." He half rose again from his chair.

"If you'll let me make it myself," she said, rising. He seemed sad, and she felt she was bothering him.

"Well, teapot's in there"—he pointed to a little, drab corner cupboard; "an' cups. An' tea's on th' mantel over yer 'ead."

She got the black teapot, and the tin of tea from the mantelshelf. She rinsed the teapot with hot water, and stood a moment wondering where to empty it.

"Throw it out," he said, aware of her. "It's clean."

She went to the door and threw the drop of water down the path. How lovely it was here, so still, so really woodland. The oaks were putting out ocher yellow leaves; in the garden the red daisies were like red plush buttons. She glanced at the big, hollow sandstone slab of the threshold, now crossed by so few feet.

"But it's lovely here," she said. "Such a beautiful stillness, everything alive and still."

He was eating again, rather slowly and unwillingly, and she could feel he was discouraged. She made the tea in silence, and set the teapot on the hob, as she knew the people did. He pushed his plate aside and went to the back place; she heard a latch click, then he came back with cheese on a plate, and butter.

She set the two cups on the table: there were only two.

"Will you have a cup of tea?" she said.

"If you like. Sugar's in th' cupboard, and there's a little cream jug. Milk's in a jug in th' pantry."

"Shall I take your plate away?" she asked him. He looked up at her with a faint ironical smile.

"Why . . . if you like," he said, slowly eating bread and cheese. She went to the back, into the penthouse scullery, where the pump was. On the left was a door, no doubt the pantry door. She unlatched it, and almost smiled at the place he called a pantry; a long narrow whitewashed slip of a cupboard. But it managed to contain a little barrel of beer, as well as a few dishes and bits of food. She took a little milk from the yellow jug.

"How do you get your milk?" she asked him, when she came back to the table.

"Flints! They leave me a bottle at the warren end. You know, where I met you!"

But he was discouraged.

She poured out the tea, poising the cream jug.

"No milk," he said; then he seemed to hear a noise, and looked keenly through the doorway.

" 'Appen we'd better shut," he said.

"It seems a pity," she replied. "Nobody will come, will they?"

"Not unless it's one time in a thousand, but you never know."

"And even then it's no matter," she said. "It's only a cup of tea. Where are the spoons?"

He reached over, and pulled open the table drawer. Connie sat at table in the sunshine of the doorway.

"Flossie!" he said to the dog, who was lying on a little mat at the stair foot. "Go an' hark, hark!"

He lifted his finger, and his "hark!" was very vivid. The dog trotted out to reconnoiter.

"Are you sad today?" she asked him.

He turned his blue eyes quickly and gazed direct on her.

"Sad! No, bored! I had to go getting summonses for two poachers I caught, and oh, well I don't like people."

He spoke cold, good English, and there was anger in his voice.

"Do you hate being a gamekeeper?" she asked.

"Being a gamekeeper, no! So long as I'm left alone. But when I have to go messing around at the police station, and various other places, and waiting for a lot of fools to attend to me . . . oh, well, I get mad . . ." and he smiled, with a certain faint humor.

"Couldn't you be really independent?" she asked.

"Me? I suppose I could, if you mean manage to exist on my pension. I could! But I've got to work, or I should die. That is, I've got to have something that keeps me occupied. And I'm not in a good enough temper to work for myself. It's got to be a sort of job for somebody else, or I should throw it up in a month, out of bad temper. So altogether I'm very well off here, especially lately. . . ."

He laughed at her again, with mocking humor.

"But why are you in a bad temper?" she asked. "Do you mean you are *always* in a bad temper?"

"Pretty well," he said, laughing. "I don't quite digest my bile."

"But what bile?" she said.

"Bile!" he said. "Don't you know what that is?" She was silent, and disappointed. He was taking no notice of her.

"I'm going away for a while next month," she said.

"You are! Where to?"

"Venice."

"Venice! With Sir Clifford? For how long?"

"For a month or so," she replied. "Clifford won't go."

"He'll stay here?" he asked.

"Yes! He hates to travel as he is."

"Ay, poor devil!" he said, with sympathy.

There was a pause.

"You won't forget me when I'm gone, will you?" she asked. Again he lifted his eyes and looked full at her.

"Forget?" he said. "You know nobody forgets. It's not a question of memory."

She wanted to say: "What, then?" but she didn't. Instead, she said in a mute kind of voice: "I told Clifford I might have a child."

Now he really looked at her, intense and searching.

"You did?" he said at last. "And what did he say?"

"Oh, he wouldn't mind. He'd be glad, really, so long as it seemed to be his." She dared not look up at him.

He was silent a long time, then he gazed again on her face.

"No mention of *me*, of course?" he said.

"No. No mention of you," she said.

"No, he'd hardly swallow me as a substitute breeder—Then where are you supposed to be getting the child?"

"I might have a love affair in Venice," she said.

"You might," he replied slowly. "So that's why you're going?"

"Not to have the love affair," she said, looking up at him, pleading.

"Just the appearance of one," he said.

There was silence. He was staring out of the window, with a faint grin, half mockery, half bitterness, on his face. She hated his grin.

"You've not taken any precautions against having a child then?" he asked her suddenly. "Because I haven't."

"No," she said faintly. "I should hate that."

He looked at her, then again with the peculiar subtle grin out of the window. There was a tense silence.

At last he turned to her and said satirically:

"That was why you wanted me, then, to get a child?"

She hung her head.

"No. Not really," she said.

"What then, *really?*" he asked, rather bitingly.

She looked up at him reproachfully, saying: "I don't know." He broke into a laugh.

"Then I'm damned if I do," he said.

There was a long pause of silence, a cold silence.

"Well," he said at last. "It's as your Ladyship likes. If you get the baby, Sir Clifford's welcome to it. I shan't have lost anything. On the contrary, I've had a very nice experience; very nice, indeed!" And he stretched in a half-suppressed sort of yawn. "If you've made use of me," he said, "it's not the first time I've been made use of; and I don't suppose it's ever been as pleasant as this time; though, of course, one can't feel tremendously dignified about it." He stretched again, curiously, his muscles quivering and his jaw oddly set.

"But I didn't make use of you," she said, pleading.

"At your Ladyship's service," he replied.

"No," she said. "I liked your body."

"Did you?" he replied, and he laughed. "Well then, we're quits, because I liked yours."

He looked at her with queer darkened eyes.

"Would you like to go upstairs now?" he asked her, in a strangled sort of voice.

"No, not here. Not now!" she said heavily, though if he had used any power over her, she would have gone, for she had no strength against him.

He turned his face away again, and seemed to forget her.

"I want to touch you like you touch me," she said. "I've never really touched you."

He looked at her, and smiled again. "Now?" he said.

"No! No! Not here! At the hut. Would you mind?"

"How do I touch you?" he asked.

"When you feel me."

He looked at her, and met her heavy, anxious eyes.

"And do you like it when I touch you?" he asked, laughing at her still.

"Yes, do you?" she said.

"Oh, me!" Then he changed his tone. "Yes," he said. "You know without asking." Which was true.

She rose and picked up her hat. "I must go," she said.

"Will you go?" he replied politely.

She wanted him to touch her, to say something to her, but he said nothing, only waited politely.

"Thank you for the tea," she said.

"I haven't thanked your Ladyship for doing me the honors of my teapot," he said.

She went down the path; and he stood in the doorway, faintly grinning. Flossie came running with her tail lifted. And Connie had to plod dumbly across into the wood, knowing he was standing there watching her, with that incomprehensible grin on his face.

She walked home very much downcast and annoyed. She didn't at all like his saying he had been made use of; because, in a sense, it was true. But he oughtn't to have said it. Therefore, again, she was divided between two feelings; resentment against him, and a desire to make it up with him.

She passed a very uneasy and irritated teatime, and at once went to her room. But when she was there it was no good; she could neither sit nor stand. She would have to do something about it. She would have to go back to the hut; if he was not there, well and good.

She slipped out of the side door, and took her way direct and a little sullen. When she came to the clearing she was terribly uneasy. But there he was again, in his shirt-sleeves, stooping, letting the hens out of the coops, among the chicks that were now growing a little gawky, but were much more trim than hen-chickens.

She went straight across to him.

"You see, I've come!" she said.

"Ay, I see it!" he said, straightening his back, and looking at her with a faint amusement.

"Do you let the hens out now?" she asked.

"Yes, they've sat themselves to skin and bone," he said. "An' now they're not all that anxious to come out an' feed. There's no self in a sitting hen; she's all in the eggs or the chicks."

The poor mother hens; such blind devotion; even to eggs not their own! Connie looked at them in compassion. A helpless silence fell between the man and the woman.

"Shall us go i' th' 'ut?" he asked.

"Do you want me?" she asked, in a sort of mistrust.

"Ay, if you want to come."

She was silent.

"Come then!" he said.

And she went with him to the hut. It was quite dark when he had shut the door, so he made a small light in the lantern, as before.

"Have you left your underthings off?" he asked her.

"Yes!"

"Ay, well, then I'll take my things off too."

He spread the blankets, putting one at the side for a coverlet. She took off her hat, and shook her hair. He sat down, taking off his shoes and gaiters, and undoing his cord breeches.

"Lie down then!" he said, when he stood in his shirt. She obeyed in silence, and he lay beside her, and pulled the blanket over them both.

"There!" he said.

And he lifted her dress right back, till he came even to her breasts. He kissed them softly, taking the nipples in his lips in tiny caresses.

"Eh, but tha'rt nice, tha'rt nice!" he said, suddenly rubbing his face with a snuggling movement against her warm belly.

And she put her arms round him under his shirt, but she was afraid, afraid of his thin, smooth, naked body, that seemed so powerful, afraid of the violent muscles. She shrank, afraid.

And when he said, with a sort of little sigh: "Eh, tha'rt nice!" something in her quivered, and something in her spirit stiffened in resistance: stiffened from the terribly physical intimacy, and from the peculiar haste of his possession. And this time the sharp ecstasy of her own passion did not overcome her; she lay with her hands inert on his striving body, and do what she might, her spirit seemed to look on from the top of her head, and the butting of his haunches seemed ridiculous to her, and the sort of anxiety of his penis to come to its little evacuating crisis seemed farcical. Yes, this was love, this ridiculous bouncing of the buttocks, and the wilting of the poor insignificant, moist little penis. This was the divine love! After all, the moderns were right when they felt contempt for the performance; for it was a performance. It was quite true, as some poets said, that the God who created man must have had a sinister sense of humor, creating him a reasonable being, yet forcing him to take this ridiculous posture, and driving him with blind craving for this ridiculous performance. Even a Maupassant found it a humiliating anticlimax. Men despised the intercourse act, and yet did it.

Cold and derisive her queer female mind stood apart, and though she lay perfectly still, her impulse was to heave her loins, and throw the man out, escape his ugly grip, and the butting overriding of his absurd haunches. His body was a foolish, impudent, imperfect thing, a little disgusting in its unfinished clumsiness. For surely a complete evolution would eliminate this performance, this "function."

And yet when he had finished, soon over, and lay very still, receding into silence, and a strange, motionless distance, far, farther than the horizon of her awareness, her heart began to weep. She could feel him ebbing away, ebbing away, leaving her there like a stone on the shore. He was withdrawing, his spirit was leaving her. He knew.

And in real grief, tormented by her own double consciousness and reaction, she began to weep. He took no notice, or did not even know. The storm of weeping swelled and shook her, and shook him.

"Ay!" he said. "It was no good that time. You wasn't there"—So he knew! Her sobs became violent.

"But what's amiss?" he said. "It's once in a while that way."

"I . . . I can't love you," she sobbed, suddenly feeling her heart breaking.

"Canna ter? Well, dunna fret! There's no law says tha's got to. Ta'e it for what it is."

He still lay with his hand on her breast. But she had drawn both her hands from him.

His words were small comfort. She sobbed aloud.

"Nay, nay!" he said. "Ta'e the thick wi' th' thin. This wor' a bit o' thin for once."

She wept bitterly, sobbing: "But I want to love you, and I can't. It only seems horrid."

He laughed a little, half bitter, half amused.

"It isna horrid," he said, "even if tha thinks it is. An' tha canna ma'e it horrid. Dunna fret thysen about lovin' me. Tha'lt niver force thysen to 't. There's sure to be a bad nut in a basketful. Tha mun ta'e th' rough wi' th' smooth."

He took his hand away from her breast, not touching her. And now she was untouched she took an almost perverse satisfaction in it. She hated the dialect: the *thee* and the *tha* and the *thysen*. He could get up if he liked, and stand there above her buttoning down those absurd corduroy breeches, straight in front of her. After all, Michaelis had had the decency to turn away. This man was so assured in himself he didn't know what a clown other people found him, a half-bred fellow.

Yet, as he was drawing away, to rise silently and leave her, she clung to him in terror.

"Don't! Don't go! Don't leave me! Don't be cross with me! Hold me! Hold me fast!" she whispered in blind frenzy, not even knowing what she said, and clinging to him with uncanny force. It was from herself she wanted to be saved, from her own inward anger and resistance. Yet how powerful was that inward resistance that possessed her!

He took her in his arms again and drew her to him, and suddenly she became small in his arms, small and nestling. It was gone, and she began to melt in marvelous peace. And as she melted small and wonderful in his arms, she became infinitely desirable to him, all his blood vessels seemed to scald with intense yet tender desire, for her, for her softness, for the penetrating beauty of her in his arms, passing into his blood. And softly, with that marvelous swoon-like caress of his hand in pure soft desire, softly he stroked the silky slope of her loins, down, down between her soft warm buttocks, coming nearer and nearer to the very quick of her. And she felt him like a flame of desire, yet tender, and she felt herself melting in the flame. She let herself go. She felt his penis risen against her with silent amazing force and assertion, and she let herself go to him. She yielded with a quiver that was like death, she went all open to him. And oh, if he were not tender to her now, how cruel, for she was all open to him and helpless!

She quivered again at the potent inexorable entry inside her, so strange and terrible. It might come with the thrust of a sword in her softly-opened body, and that would be death. She clung in a sudden anguish of terror. But it came with a strange slow thrust of peace, the dark thrust of peace and a ponderous, primordial tenderness, such as made the world in the beginning. And her terror subsided in her breast, her breast dared to be gone in peace, she held nothing. She dared to let go everything, all herself, and be gone in the flood.

And it seemed she was like the sea, nothing but dark waves rising and heaving, heaving with a great swell, so that slowly her whole darkness was in motion, and she was ocean rolling its dark, dumb mass. Oh, and far down inside her the deeps parted and rolled asunder, in long, far-traveling billows, and ever, at the quick of her, the depths parted and rolled asunder, from the center of soft plunging, as the plunger went deeper and deeper, touching lower, and she was deeper and deeper and deeper disclosed, and heavier the billows of her rolled away to some shore, uncovering her, and closer and closer plunged the palpable unknown, and further and further rolled the waves of herself away from herself, leaving her, till suddenly, in a soft, shuddering convulsion, the quick of all her plasm was touched, she knew herself touched, the consummation was upon her, and she was gone. She was gone, she was not, and she was born: a woman.

Ah, too lovely, too lovely! In the ebbing she realized all the loveliness. Now all her body clung with tender love to the unknown man, and blindly to the wilting penis, as it so tenderly, frailly, unknowingly withdrew, after the fierce thrust of its potency. As it drew out and left her body, the secret, sensitive thing, she gave an unconscious cry of pure loss, and she tried to put it back. It had been so perfect! And she loved it so!

And only now she became aware of the small, bud-like reticence and tenderness of the penis, and a little cry of wonder and poignancy escaped her again, her woman's heart crying out over the tender frailty of that which had been the power.

"It was so lovely!" she moaned. "It was so lovely!" But he said nothing, only softly kissed her, lying still above her. And she moaned with a sort of bliss, as a sacrifice, and a newborn thing.

And now in her heart the queer wonder of him was awakened. A man! the strange potency of manhood upon her! Her hands strayed over him, still a little afraid. Afraid of that strange, hostile, slightly repulsive thing that he had been to her, a man. And now she touched him, and it was the sons of god with the daughters of men. How beautiful he felt, how pure in tissue! How lovely, how lovely, strong, and yet pure and delicate, such stillness of the sensitive body! Such utter stillness of potency and delicate flesh! How beautiful! How beautiful! Her hands came timorously down his back to the soft, smallish globes of the buttocks. Beauty! What beauty! a sudden little flame of new awareness went through her. How was it possible this beauty here, where she had previously been repelled? The unspeakable beauty to the touch, of the warm, living buttocks! The life within life, the sheer warm, potent loveliness. And the strange weight of the balls between his legs! What a mystery! What a strange heavy weight of mystery, that could lie soft and heavy in one's hand! The roots, root of all that is lovely, the primeval root of all full beauty.

She clung to him, with a hiss of wonder that was almost awe, terror. He held her close, but he said nothing. He would never say anything. She crept nearer to him, nearer, only to be near the sensual wonder of him. And out of his utter, incomprehensible stillness, she felt again the slow, momentous, surging rise of the phallus again, the other power. And her heart melted out with a kind of awe.

And this time his being within her was all soft and iridescent, purely soft and iridescent, such as no consciousness could seize. Her whole self quivered unconscious and alive, like plasm. She could not know what it was. She could not remember what it had been. Only that it had been more lovely than anything ever could be. Only that. And afterwards she was utterly still, utterly unknowing, she was not aware for how long. And he was still with her, in an unfathomable silence along with her. And of this, they would never speak.

When awareness of the outside began to come back, she clung to his breast, murmuring: "My love! my love!" And he held her silently. And she curled on his breast, perfect.

But his silence was fathomless. His hands held her like flowers, so still and strange. "Where are you?" she whispered to him. "Where are you? Speak to me! Say something to me!"

He kissed her softly, murmuring: "Ay, my lass!"

But she did not know what he meant, she did not know where he was. In his silence he seemed lost to her.

"You love me, don't you?" she murmured.

"Ay, tha knows!" he said.

"But tell me!" she pleaded.

"Ay! Ay! 'asn't ter felt it?" he said dimly, but softly and surely. And she clung close to him, closer. He was so much more peaceful in love than she was, and she wanted him to reassure her.

"You do love me!" she whispered, assertive. And his hands stroked her softly, as if she were a flower, without the quiver of desire, but with delicate nearness. And still there haunted her a restless necessity to get a grip on love.

"Say you'll always love me!" she pleaded.

"Ay!" he said, abstractedly. And she felt her questions driving him away from her.

"Mustn't we get up?" he said at last.

"No!" she said.

But she could feel his consciousness straying, listening to the noises outside.

"It'll be nearly dark," he said. And she heard the pressure of circumstance in his voice. She kissed him, with a woman's grief at yielding up her hour.

He rose, and turned up the lantern, then began to pull on his clothes, quickly disappearing inside them. Then he stood there, above her, fastening his breeches and looking down at her with dark, wide eyes, his face a little flushed and his hair ruffled, curiously warm and still and beautiful in the dim light of the lantern, so beautiful, she would never tell him how beautiful. It made her want to cling fast to him, to hold him, for there was a warm, half-sleepy remoteness in his beauty that made her want to cry out and clutch him, to have him. She would never have him. So she lay on the blanket with curved, soft naked haunches, and he had no idea what she was thinking, but to him she too was beautiful, the soft, marvelous thing he could go into, beyond everything.

"I love thee that I can go into thee," he said.

"Do you like me?" she said, her heart beating.

"It heals it all up, that I can go into thee. I love thee that tha opened to me. I love thee that I came into thee like that."

He bent down and kissed her soft flank, rubbed his cheek against it, then covered it up.

"And will you never leave me?" she said.

"Dunna ask them things," he said.

"But you do believe I love you?" she said.

"Tha loved me just now, wider than iver tha thout tha would. But who knows what'll 'appen, once tha starts thinkin' about it!"

"No, don't say those things!—And you don't really think that I wanted to make use of you, do you?"

"How?"

"To have a child—?"

"Now anybody can 'ave any childt i' th' world," he said, as he sat down fastening on his leggings.

"Ah no!" she cried. "You don't mean it?"

"Eh well!" he said, looking at her under his brows. "This wor t' best."

She lay still. He softly opened the door. The sky was dark blue, with crystalline, turquoise rim. He went out, to shut up the hens, speaking softly to his dog. And she lay and wondered at the wonder of life, and of being.

When he came back she was still lying there, glowing like a gypsy. He sat on the stool by her.

"Tha mun come one naight ter th' cottage, afore tha goos; sholl ter?" he asked, lifting his eyebrows as he looked at her, his hands dangling between his knees.

"Sholl ter?" she echoed, teasing.

He smiled.

"Ay, sholl ter?" he repeated.

"Ay!" she said, imitating the dialect sound.

"Yi!" he said.

"Yi!" she repeated.

"An' slaip wi' me," he said. "It needs that. When sholt come?"

"When sholl I?" she said.

"Nay," he said, "tha canna do't. When sholt come then?"

" 'Appen Sunday," she said.

" 'Appen a' Sunday! Ay!"

He laughed at her quickly.

"Nay, tha canna," he protested.

"Why canna I?" she said.

He laughed. Her attempts at the dialect were so ludicrous, somehow.

"Coom then, tha mun goo!" he said.

"Mun I?" she said.

"Maun Ah!" he corrected.

"Why should I say *maun* when you say *mun*," she protested. "You're not playing fair."

"Arena Ah!" he said, leaning forward and softly stroking her face.

"Th'art good cunt, though, are'nt ter? Best bit o' cunt left on earth. When ter likes! When tha'rt willin'!"

"What is cunt?" she said.

"An' doesn't ter know? Cunt! It's thee down theer; an' what I get when I'm i'side thee; it's a' as it is, all on't."

"All on't," she teased. "Cunt! It's like fuck then."

"Nay, nay! Fuck's only what you do. Animals fuck. But cunt's a lot more than that. It's thee, dost see: an' tha'rt a lot besides an animal, aren't ter? even ter fuck! Cunt! Eh, that's the beauty o' thee, lass."

She got up and kissed him between the eyes that looked at her so dark and soft and unspeakably warm, so unbearably beautiful.

"Is it?" she said. "And do you care for me?"

He kissed her without answering.

"Tha mun goo, let me dust thee," he said.

His hand passed over the curves of her body, firmly, without desire, but with soft, intimate knowledge.

As she ran home in the twilight the world seemed a dream; the trees in the park seemed bulging and surging at anchor on a tide, and the heave of the slope to the house was alive.

❖ 13 ❖

On Sunday Clifford wanted to go into the wood. It was a lovely morning, the pear blossom and plum had suddenly appeared in the world in a wonder of white here and there.

It was cruel for Clifford, while the world bloomed, to have to be helped from chair to bath-chair. But he had forgotten, and even seemed to have a certain conceit of himself in his lameness. Connie still suffered, having to lift his inert legs into place. Mrs. Bolton did it now, or Field.

She waited for him at the top of the drive, at the edge of the screen of beeches. His chair came puffing along with a sort of valetudinarian slow importance. As he joined his wife he said:

"Sir Clifford on his foaming steed!"

"Snorting, at least!" she laughed.

He stopped and looked around at the facade of the long, low old brown house.

"Wragby doesn't wink an eyelid!" he said. "But then why should it? I ride upon the achievements of the mind of man, and that beats a horse."

"I suppose it does. And the souls in Plato riding up to heaven in a two-horse chariot would go in a Ford car now," she said.

"Or a Rolls-Royce: Plato was an aristocrat!"

"Quite! No more black horse to thrash and maltreat. Plato never thought we'd go one better than his black steed and his white steed, and have no steeds at all, only an engine!"

"Only an engine and gas!" said Clifford.

"I hope I can have some repairs done to the old place next year. I think I shall have about a thousand to spare for that: but work costs so much!" he added.

"Oh, good!" said Connie. "If only there aren't more strikes!"

"What would be the use of their striking again! Merely ruin the industry, what's left of it: and surely the owls are beginning to see it!"

"Perhaps they don't mind ruining the industry," said Connie.

"Ah, don't talk like a woman! The industry fills their bellies, even if it can't keep their pockets quite so flush," he said, using terms of speech that oddly had a twang of Mrs. Bolton.

"But didn't you say the other day that you were a conservative-anarchist?" she asked innocently.

"And did you understand what I meant?" he retorted. "All I meant is, people can be what they like and feel what they like and do what they like, strictly privately, so long as they keep the *form* of life intact, and the apparatus."

Connie walked on in silence a few paces. Then she said, obstinately:

"It sounds like saying an egg may go as addled as it likes, so long as it keeps its shell on whole. But addled eggs do break of themselves."

"I don't think people are eggs," he said. "Not even angels' eggs, my dear little evangelist."

He was in rather high feather this bright morning. The larks were trilling away over the park, the distant pit in the hollow was fuming silent steam. It was almost like old days, before the war. Connie didn't really want to argue. But then she did not really want to go to the wood with Clifford either. So she walked beside his chair in a certain obstinacy of spirit.

"No," he said. "There will be no more strikes, if the thing is properly managed."

"Why not?"

"Because strikes will be made as good as impossible."

"But will the men let you?" she asked.

"We shan't ask them. We shall do it while they aren't looking: for their own good, to save the industry."

"For your own good, too," she said.

"Naturally! For the good of everybody. But for their good even more than mine. I can live without the pits. They can't. They'll starve if there are no pits. I've got other provision."

They looked up the shallow valley at the mine, and beyond it, at the black-lidded houses of Tevershall crawling like some serpent up the hill. From the old brown church the bells were ringing: Sunday, Sunday, Sunday!

"But will the men let you dictate terms?" she said.

"My dear, they will have to: if one does it gently."

"But mightn't there be a mutual understanding?"

"Absolutely: when they realize that the industry comes before the individual."

"But must you own the industry?" she said.

"I don't. But to the extent I do own it, yes, most decidedly. The ownership of property has now become a religious question: as it has been since Jesus and St. Francis. The point is *not*: take all thou hast and give to the poor, but use all thou hast to encourage the industry and give work to the poor. It's the only way to feed all the mouths and clothe all the bodies. Giving away all we have to the poor spells starvation for the poor just as much as for us. And universal starvation is no high aim. Even general poverty is no lovely thing. Poverty is ugly."

"But the disparity?"

"That is fate. Why is the star Jupiter bigger than the star Neptune? You can't start altering the make-up of things!"

"But when this envy and jealousy and discontent has once started," she began.

"Do your best to stop it. Somebody's *got* to be boss of the show."

"But who is the boss of the show?" she asked.

"The men who own and run the industries."

There was a long silence.

"It seems to me they're a bad boss," she said.

"Then you suggest what they should do."

"They don't take their boss-ship seriously enough," she said.

"They take it far more seriously than you take your ladyship," he said.

"That's thrust upon me. I don't really want it," she blurted out. He stopped the chair and looked at her.

"Who's shirking their responsibility now!" he said. "Who is trying to get away *now* from the responsibility of their own boss-ship, as you call it?"

"But I don't want any boss-ship," she protested.

"Ah! But that is funk. You've got it: fated to it. And you should live up to it. Who has given the colliers all they have that's worth having; all their political liberty, and their education, such as it is; their sanitation, their health conditions, their books, their music, everything? Who has given it to them? Have colliers given it to the colliers? No! All the Wragbys and Shipleys in England have given their part, and must go on giving. There's your responsibility."

Connie listened, and flushed very red.

"I'd like to give something," she said. "But I'm not allowed. Everything is to be sold and paid for now; and all the things you mention now, Wragby and Shipley *sell* them to the people, at a good profit. Everything is sold. You don't give one heartbeat of real sympathy. And besides, who has taken away from the people their natural life and manhood, and given them this industrial horror? Who has done that?"

"And what must I do?" he asked, green. "Ask them to come and pillage me?"

"Why is Tevershall so ugly, so hideous? Why are their lives so hopeless?"

"They built their own Tevershall. That's part of their display of freedom. They built themselves their pretty Tevershall, and they live their own pretty lives. I can't live their lives for them. Every beetle must live its own life."

"But you make them work for you. They live the life of your coal mine."

"Not at all. Every beetle finds its own food. Not one man is forced to work for me."

"Their lives are industrialized and hopeless, and so are ours," she cried.

"I don't think they are. That's just a romantic figure of speech, a relic of the swooning and die-away romanticism. You don't look at all a hopeless figure standing there, Connie, my dear."

Which was true. For her dark blue eyes were flashing, color was hot in her cheeks, she looked full of a rebellious passion far from the dejection of hopelessness. She noticed, in the tussocky places of the grass, cottony young cowslips standing up still bleared in their down. And she wondered with rage, why it was she felt Clifford was so *wrong*, yet she couldn't say it to him, she could not say exactly *where* he was wrong.

"No wonder the men hate you," she said.

"They don't!" he replied. "And don't fall into errors: in your sense of the word, they are *not* men. They are animals you don't understand and never could. Don't thrust your illusions on other people. The masses were always the same, and will always be the same. Nero's slaves were extremely little different from our colliers or the Ford motorcar workmen. I mean Nero's mine slaves and his field slaves. It is the masses: they are the unchangeable. An individual may emerge from the masses. But the emergence doesn't alter the mass. The masses are unalterable. It is one of the most momentous facts of social science. *Panem et circenses!* Only today education is one of the bad substitutes for a circus. What is wrong today is that we've made a profound hash of the circuses part of the program, and poisoned our masses with a little education."

When Clifford became really aroused in his feelings about the common people, Connie was frightened. There was something devastatingly true in what he said. But it was a truth that killed.

Seeing her pale and silent, Clifford started the chair again, and no more was said till he halted again at the wood gate, which she opened.

"And what we need to take up now," he said, "is whips, not swords. The masses have been ruled since time began, and, till time ends, ruled they will have to be. It is sheer hypocrisy and farce to say they can rule themselves."

"But can you rule them?" she asked.

"I? Oh, yes! Neither my mind nor my will is crippled, and I don't rule with my legs. I can do my share of ruling: absolutely, my share; and give me a son, and he will be able to rule his portion after me."

"But he wouldn't be your own son, of your own ruling class; or, perhaps not," she stammered.

"I don't care who his father may be, so long as he is a healthy man not below normal intelligence. Give me the child of any healthy, normally intelligent man, and I will make a perfectly competent Chatterley of him. It is not who begets us that matters, but where fate places us. Place any child among the ruling classes, and he will grow up, to his own extent, a ruler. Put kings' and dukes' children among the masses, and they'll be little plebians, mass products. It is the overwhelming pressure of environment."

"Then the common people aren't a race, and the aristocrats aren't blood," she said.

"No, my child! All that is romantic illusion. Aristocracy is a function, a part of fate. And the masses are a functioning of another part of fate. The individual hardly matters. It is a question of which function you are brought up to and adapted to. It is not the individuals that make an aristocracy: it is the functioning of the aristocratic whole. And it is the functioning of the whole mass that makes the common man what he is."

"Then there is no common humanity between us all!"

"Just as you like. We all need to fill our bellies. But when it comes to expressive or executive functioning, I believe there is a gulf and an absolute one, between the ruling and the serving classes. The two functions are opposed. And the function determines the individual."

Connie looked at him with dazed eyes.

"Won't you come on?" she said.

And he started his chair. He had said his say. Now he lapsed into his peculiar and rather vacant apathy, that Connie found so trying. In the wood, anyhow, she was determined not to argue.

In front of them ran the open cleft of the riding, between the hazel walls and the gray trees. The chair puffed slowly on, slowly surging into the forget-me-nots that rose up in the drive like milk froth, beyond the hazel shadows. Clifford steered the middle course, where feet passing had kept a channel through the flowers. But Connie, walking behind, had watched the wheels jolt over the woodruff and the bugle, and squash the little yellow cups of the creeping-jenny. Now they made a wake through the forget-me-nots.

All the flowers were there, the first bluebells in blue pools, like standing water.

"You are quite right about its being beautiful," said Clifford. "It is so amazingly. What is *quite* so lovely as an English spring!"

Connie thought it sounded as if even the spring bloomed by Act of Parliament. An English spring! Why not an Irish one? or Jewish? The chair moved slowly ahead, past tufts of sturdy bluebells that stood up like wheat and over gray burdock leaves. Then they came to the open place where the trees had been felled, the light flooded in rather stark. And the bluebells made sheets of bright blue color, here and there, sheering off into lilac and purple. And between, the bracken was lifting its brown curled heads, like legions of young snakes with a new secret to whisper to Eve.

Clifford kept the chair going till he came to the brow of the hill; Connie followed slowly behind. The oak buds were opening soft and brown. Everything came tenderly out of the old hardness. Even the snaggy craggy oak trees put out the softest leaves, spreading thin, brown little wings like young bat wings in the light. Why had men never any newness in them, any freshness to come forth with? Stale men!

Clifford stopped the chair at the top of the rise and looked down. The bluebells washed blue like floodwater over the broad riding, and lit up the downhill with a warm blueness.

"It's a very fine color in itself," said Clifford, "but useless for making a painting."

"Quite!" said Connie, completely uninterested.

"Shall I venture as far as the spring?" said Clifford.

"Will the chair get up again?" she said.

"We'll try; nothing venture, nothing win!"

And the chair began to advance slowly, joltingly down the beautiful broad riding washed over with blue encroaching hyacinths. Oh last of all ships, through the hyacinthian shallows! Oh pinnace on the last wild waters, sailing on the last voyage of our civilization! Whither, Oh weird wheeled ship, your slow course steering! Quiet and complacent, Clifford sat at the wheel of adventure: in his old black hat and tweed jacket, motionless and cautious. Oh captain, my Captain, our splendid trip is done! Not yet though! Downhill in the wake, came Constance in her gray dress, watching the chair jolt downwards.

They passed the narrow track to the hut. Thank heaven it was not wide enough for the chair: hardly wide enough for one person. The chair reached the bottom of the slope, and swerved round, to disappear. And Connie heard a low whistle behind her. She glanced sharply round: the keeper was striding downhill towards her, his dog keeping behind him.

"Is Sir Clifford going to the cottage?" he asked, looking into her eyes.

"No, only to the well."

"Ah! Good! Then I can keep out of sight. But I shall see you tonight. I shall wait for you at the park gate about ten."

He looked again direct into her eyes.

"Yes," she faltered.

They heard the Papp! Papp! of Clifford's horn, tooting for Connie. She "Cooeed!" in reply. The keeper's face flickered with a little grimace, and with his hand he softly brushed her breast upwards, from underneath. She looked at him, frightened, and started running down the hill, calling Coo-ee! again to Clifford. The man above watched her, then turned, grinning faintly, back into his path.

She found Clifford slowly mounting to the spring, which was halfway up the slope of the dark larch-wood. He was there by the time she caught him up. "She did that all right," he said, referring to the chair.

Connie looked at the great gray leaves of burdock that grew out ghostly from the edge of the larch-wood. The people call it Robin Hood's Rhubarb. How silent and gloomy it seemed by the well! Yet the water bubbled so bright, wonderful! And there were bits of eye-bright and strong blue bugle. And there, under the bank, the yellow earth was moving. A mole! It emerged, rowing its pink hands, and waving its blind gimlet of a face, with the tiny nose-tip uplifted.

"It seems to see with the end of its nose," said Connie.

"Better than with its eyes!" he said. "Will you drink?"

"Will you?"

She took an enamel mug from a twig on a tree, and stooped to fill it for him.

He drank in sips. Then she stooped again, and drank a little herself.

"So icy!" she said, gasping.

"Good, isn't it! Did you wish?"

"Did you?"

"Yes, I wished. But I won't tell."

She was aware of the rapping of a woodpecker, then of the wind, soft and eerie through the larches. She looked up. White clouds were crossing the blue.

"Clouds!" she said.

"White lambs only," he replied.

A shadow crossed the little clearing. The mole had swum out onto the soft yellow earth.

"Unpleasant little beast, we ought to kill him," said Clifford.

"Look! he's like a parson in a pulpit," said she.

She gathered some sprigs of woodruff and brought them to him.

"New-mown hay!" he said. "Doesn't it smell like the romantic ladies of the last century, who had their heads screwed on the right way after all!"

She was looking at the white clouds.

"I wonder if it will rain," she said.

"Rain! Why! Do you want it to?"

They started on the return journey, Clifford jolting cautiously downhill. They came to the dark bottom of the hollow, turned to the right, and after a hundred yards swerved up the foot of the long slope, where bluebells stood in the light.

"Now, old girl!" said Clifford, putting the chair to it.

It was a steep and jolty climb. The chair plugged slowly, in a struggling unwilling fashion. Still, she nosed her way up unevenly, till she came to where the hyacinths were all around her, then she balked, struggled, jerked a little way out of the flowers, then stopped.

"We'd better sound the horn and see if the keeper will come," said Connie. "He could push her a bit. For that matter, I will push. It helps."

"We'll let her breathe," said Clifford. "Do you mind putting a scotch under the wheel?"

Connie found a stone, and they waited. After a while Clifford started his motor again, then set the chair in motion. It struggled and faltered like a sick thing, with curious noises.

"Let me push!" said Connie, coming up behind.

"No! Don't push!" he said angrily. "What's the good of the damned thing, if it has to be pushed! Put the stone under!"

There was another pause, then another start; but more ineffectual than before.

"You *must* let me push," she said. "Or sound the horn for the keeper."

"Wait!"

She waited; and he had another try, doing more harm than good.

"Sound the horn, then, if you won't let me push," she said.

"Hell! Be quiet a moment!"

She was quiet a moment: he made shattering efforts with the little motor.

"You'll only break the thing down altogether, Clifford," she remonstrated: "besides wasting your nervous energy."

"If I could only get out and look at the damned thing!" he said, exasperated. And he sounded the horn stridently. "Perhaps Mellors can see what's wrong."

They waited, among the mashed flowers under a sky softly curdling with clouds. In the silence a wood pigeon began to coo, roo-hoo hoo! roo-hoo hoo! Clifford shut her up with a blast on the horn.

The keeper appeared directly, striding inquiringly round the corner. He saluted.

"Do you know anything about motors?" asked Clifford sharply.

"I'm afraid I don't. Has she gone wrong?"

"Apparently!" snapped Clifford.

The man crouched solicitously by the wheel, and peered at the little engine.

"I'm afraid I know nothing at all about these mechanical things, Sir Clifford," he said calmly. "If she has enough petrol and oil—"

"Just look carefully and see if you can see anything broken," snapped Clifford.

The man laid his gun against a tree, took off his coat and threw it beside it. The brown dog sat guard. Then he sat down on his heels and peered under the chair, poking with his finger at the greasy little engine, and resenting the grease-marks on his clean Sunday shirt.

"Doesn't seem anything broken," he said. And he stood up, pushing back his hat from his forehead, rubbing his brow and apparently studying.

"Have you looked at the rods underneath?" asked Clifford. "See if they are all right!"

The man lay flat on his stomach on the floor, his neck pressed back, wriggling under the engine and poking with his finger. Connie thought what a pathetic sort of thing a man was, feeble and small looking, when he was lying on his belly on the big earth.

"Seems all right as far as I can see," came his muffled voice.

"I don't suppose you can do anything," said Clifford.

"Seems as if I can't!" And he scrambled up and sat on his heels, collier fashion. "There's certainly nothing obviously broken."

Clifford started his engine, then put her in gear. She would not move.

"Run her a bit hard, like," suggested the keeper.

Clifford resented the interference: but he made his engine buzz like a bluebottle. Then she coughed and snarled and seemed to go better.

"Sounds as if she'd come clear," said Mellors.

But Clifford had already jerked her into gear. She gave a sick lurch and ebbed weakly forwards.

"If I give her a push, she'll do it," said the keeper, going behind.

"Keep off!" snapped Clifford. "She'll do it by herself."

"But Clifford!" put in Connie from the bank, "you know it's too much for her. Why are you so obstinate!"

Clifford was pale with anger. He jabbed at his levers. The chair gave a sort of scurry, reeled on a few more yards, and came to her end amid a particularly promising patch of bluebells.

"She's done!" said the keeper. "Not power enough."

"She's been up here before," said Clifford coldly.

"She won't do it this time," said the keeper.

Clifford did not reply. He began doing things with his engine, running her fast and slow as if to get some sort of tune out of her. The wood reechoed with weird noises. Then he put her in gear with a jerk, having jerked off his brake.

"You'll rip her inside out," murmured the keeper.

The chair charged in a sick lurch sideways at the ditch.

"Clifford!" cried Connie, rushing forward.

But the keeper had got the chair by the rail. Clifford, however, putting on all his pressure, managed to steer into the riding, and with a strange noise the chair was fighting the hill. Mellors pushed steadily behind, and up she went, as if to retrieve herself.

"You see, she's doing it!" said Clifford victorious, glancing over his shoulder. There he saw the keeper's face.

"Are you pushing her?"

"She won't do it without."

"Leave her alone. I asked you not."

"She won't do it."

"*Let her try!*" snarled Clifford, with all his emphasis.

The keeper stood back: then turned to fetch his coat and gun. The chair seemed to strangle immediately. She stood inert. Clifford, seated a prisoner, was white with vexation. He jerked at the levers with his hand, his feet were no good. He got queer noises out of her. In savage impatience he moved little handles and got more noises out of her. But she would not budge. No, she would not budge. He stopped the engine and sat rigid with anger.

Constance sat on the bank and looked at the wretched and trampled bluebells. "Nothing quite so lovely as an English spring." "I can do my share of ruling." "What we need to take up now is whips, not swords." "The ruling classes!"

The keeper strode up with his coat and gun, Flossie cautiously at his heels. Clifford asked the man to do something or other to the engine. Connie, who understood nothing at all of the technicalities of motors, and who had had experience of breakdowns, sat patiently on the bank as if she were a cipher. The keeper lay on his stomach again. The ruling classes and the serving classes!

He got to his feet and said patiently:

"Try her again, then."

He spoke in a quiet voice, almost as if to a child.

Clifford tried her, and Mellors stepped quickly behind and began to push. She was going, the engine doing about half the work, the man the rest.

Clifford glanced round yellow with anger.

"Will you get off there!"

The keeper dropped his hold at once, and Clifford added: "How shall I know what she is doing!"

The man put his gun down and began to pull on his coat. He'd done.

The chair began slowly to run backwards.

"Clifford, your brake!" cried Connie.

She, Mellors, and Clifford moved at once, Connie and the keeper jostling lightly. The chair stood. There was a moment of dead silence.

"It's obvious I'm at everybody's mercy!" said Clifford. He was yellow with anger.

No one answered. Mellors was slinging his gun over his shoulder, his face queer and expressionless, save for an abstracted look of patience. The dog Flossie, standing on guard almost between her master's legs, moved uneasily, eyeing the chair with great suspicion and dislike, and very much perplexed between the three human beings. The *tableau vivant* remained set among the squashed bluebells, nobody proffering a word.

"I expect she'll have to be pushed," said Clifford at last, with an affectation of *sang froid*.

No answer. Mellors's abstracted face looked as if he had heard nothing. Connie glanced anxiously at him. Clifford, too, glanced round.

"Do you mind pushing her home, Mellors!" he said in a cold, superior tone. "I hope I have said nothing to offend you," he added, in a tone of dislike.

"Nothing at all, Sir Clifford! Do you want me to push that chair?"

"If you please."

The man stepped up to it: but this time it was without effect. The brake was jammed. They poked and pulled, and the keeper took off his gun and his coat once more. And now Clifford said never a word. At last the keeper heaved the back of the chair off the ground, and with an instantaneous push of his foot, tried to loosen the wheels. He failed, the chair sank. Clifford was clutching the sides. The man gasped with the weight.

"Don't do it!" cried Connie to him.

"If you'll pull the wheel that way, so!" he said to her, showing her how.

"No! You mustn't lift it! You'll strain yourself," she said, flushed now with anger.

But he looked into her eyes and nodded. And she had to go and take hold of the wheel, ready. He heaved and she tugged, and the chair reeled.

"For God's sake!" cried Clifford in terror.

But it was all right, and the brake was off. The keeper put a stone under the wheel, and went to sit on the bank, his heart beating and his face white with the effort, semiconscious. Connie looked at him, and almost cried with anger. There was a pause and a dead silence. She saw his hands trembling on his thighs.

"Have you hurt yourself?" she asked, going to him.

"No. No!" he turned away almost angrily.

There was dead silence. The back of Clifford's fair head did not move. Even the dog stood motionless. The sky had clouded over.

At last he sighed, and blew his nose on his red handkerchief.

"That pneumonia took a lot out of me," he said.

No one answered. Connie calculated the amount of strength it must have taken to heave up that chair and the bulky Clifford: too much, far too much! If it hadn't killed him!

He rose, and again picked up his coat, slinging it through the handle of the chair.

"Are you ready, then, Sir Clifford?"

"When you are!"

He stooped and took out the scotch, then put his weight against the chair. He was paler than Connie had ever seen him: and more absent. Clifford was a heavy man: and the hill was steep. Connie stepped to the keeper's side.

"I'm going to push too!" she said.

And she began to shove with a woman's turbulent energy of anger. The chair went faster. Clifford looked round.

"Is that necessary?" he said.

"Very! Do you want to kill the man! If you'd let the motor work while it would—"

But she did not finish. She was already panting. She slackened off a little, for it was surprisingly hard work.

"Ay! slower!" said the man at her side, with a faint smile of the eyes.

"Are you sure you've not hurt yourself?" she said fiercely.

He shook his head. She looked at his smallish, short, alive hand, browned by the weather. It was the hand that caressed her. She had never even looked at it before. It seemed so still, like him, with a curious inward stillness that made her want to clutch it, as if she could not reach it. All her soul suddenly swept towards him: he was so silent, and out of reach! And he felt his limbs revive. Shoving with his left hand, he laid his right on her round white wrist, softly enfolding her wrist, with caress. And the flame of strength went down his back and his loins, reviving him. And she bent suddenly and kissed his hand. Meanwhile the back of Clifford's head was held sleek and motionless, just in front of them.

At the top of the hill they rested, and Connie was glad to let go. She had had fugitive dreams of friendship between these two men: one her husband, the other the father of her child. Now she saw the screaming absurdity of her dreams. The two males were as hostile as fire and water. They mutually exterminated one another. And she realized for the first time, what a queer subtle thing hate is. For the first time, she had consciously and definitely hated Clifford, with vivid hate: as if he ought to be obliterated from the face of the earth. And it was strange, how free and full of life it made her feel, to hate him and to admit it fully to herself—"Now, I've hated him, I shall never be able to go on living with him," came the thought into her mind.

On the level the keeper could push the chair alone. Clifford made a little conversation with her, to show his complete composure: about Aunt Eva, who was at Dieppe, and about Sir Malcolm, who had written to ask would Connie drive with him in his small car, to Venice, or would she and Hilda go by train.

"I'd much rather go by train," said Connie. "I don't like long motor drives, especially when there's dust. But I shall see what Hilda wants."

"She will want to drive her own car, and take you with her," he said.

"Probably!—I must help up here. You've no idea how heavy this chair is."

She went to the back of his chair, and plodded side by side with the keeper, shoving up the pink path. She did not care who saw.

"Why not let me wait, and fetch Field. He is strong enough for the job," said Clifford.

"It's so near," she panted.

But both she and Mellors wiped the sweat from their faces when they came to the top. It was curious, but this bit of work together had brought them much closer than they had been before.

"Thanks so much, Mellors," said Clifford, when they were at the house door. "I must get a different sort of motor, that's all. Won't you go to the kitchen and have a meal? it must be about time."

"Thank you, Sir Clifford. I was going to my mother for dinner today, Sunday."

"As you like."

Mellors slung into his coat, looked at Connie, saluted, and was gone. Connie, furious, went upstairs.

At lunch she could not contain her feelings.

"Why are you so abominably inconsiderate, Clifford?" she said to him.

"Of whom?"

"Of the keeper! If that is what you call the ruling classes, I'm sorry for you."

"Why?"

"A man who's been ill, and isn't strong! My word, if I were the serving classes, I'd let you wait for service. I'd let you whistle."

"I quite believe it."

"If he'd been sitting in a chair with paralyzed legs, and behaved as you behaved, what would you have done for *him?*"

"My dear evangelist, this confusing of persons and personalities is in bad taste."

"And your nasty, sterile want of common sympathy is in the worst taste imaginable. *Noblesse oblige!* You and your ruling class!"

"And to what should it oblige me? To have a lot of unnecessary emotions about my gamekeeper? I refuse. I leave it all to my evangelist."

"As if he weren't a man as much as you are, my word!"

"My gamekeeper to boot, and I pay him two pounds a week and give him a house."

"Pay him! What do you think you pay him for, with two pounds a week and a house?"

"His services."

"Bah! I would tell you to keep your two pounds a week and your house."

"Probably he would like to; but can't afford the luxury!"

"You and *rule!*" she said. "You don't rule, don't flatter yourself. You have only got more than your share of the money, and make people work for you for two pounds a week, or threaten them with starvation. Rule! What do you give forth of rule? Why, you're dried up! You only bully with your money, like any Jew or any Schieber!"

"You are very elegant in your speech, Lady Chatterley!"

"I assure you, you were very elegant altogether out there in the wood. I was utterly ashamed of you. Why, my father is ten times the human being you are: you *gentleman!*"

He reached and rang the bell for Mrs. Bolton. But he was yellow at the gills.

She went up to her room, furious, saying to herself: "Him and buying people! Well, he doesn't buy me, and therefore there's no need for me to stay with him. Dead fish of a gentleman, with his celluloid soul! And how they take one in, with their manners and their mock wistfulness and gentleness. They've got about as much feeling as celluloid has."

She made her plans for the night, and determined to get Clifford off her mind. She didn't want to hate him. She didn't want to be mixed up very intimately with him in any sort of feeling. She wanted him not to know anything at all about herself: and especially, not to know anything about her feeling for the keeper. This squabble of her attitude to the servants was an old one. He found her too familiar, she found him stupidly insentient, tough and india rubbery where other people were concerned.

She went downstairs calmly, with her old demure bearing, at dinner time. He was still yellow at the gills: in for one of his liver bouts, when he was really very queer—He was reading a French book.

"Have you ever read Proust?" he asked her.

"I've tried, but he bores me."

"He's really very extraordinary."

"Possibly! But he bores me: all that sophistication! He doesn't have feelings, he only has streams of words about feelings. I'm tired of self-important mentalities."

"Would you prefer self-important animalities?"

"Perhaps! But one might possibly get something that wasn't self-important."

"Well, I like Proust's subtlety and his well-bred anarchy."

"It makes you very dead, really."

"There speaks my evangelical little wife."

They were at it again, at it again! But she couldn't help fighting him. He seemed to sit there like a skeleton, sending out a skeleton's cold grizzly *will* against her. Almost she could feel the skeleton clutching her and pressing her to its cage of ribs. He, too, was really up in arms: and she was a little afraid of him.

She went upstairs as soon as possible, and went to bed quite early. But at half-past nine she got up, and went outside to listen. There was no sound. She slipped on a dressing gown and went downstairs. Clifford and Mrs. Bolton were playing cards, gambling. They would probably go on until midnight.

Connie returned to her room, threw her pajamas on the tossed bed, put on a thin tennis dress and over that a woolen day-dress, put on rubber tennis shoes, and then a light coat. And she was ready. If she met anybody, she was just going out for a few minutes. And in the morning, when she came in again, she would just have been for a little walk in the dew, as she fairly often did before breakfast. For the rest, the only danger was that someone should go into her room during the night. But that was most unlikely: not one chance in a hundred.

Betts had not yet locked up. He fastened up the house at ten o'clock, and unfastened it again at seven in the morning. She slipped out silently and unseen. There was a half-moon shining, enough to make a little light in the world, not enough to show her up in her dark gray coat. She walked quickly across the park, not really in the thrill of the assignation, but with a certain anger and rebellion burning in her heart. It was not the right sort of heart to take to a love-meeting. But *à la guerre comme à la guerre!*

❖ 14 ❖

When she got near the park gate, she heard the click of the latch. He was there, then, in the darkness of the wood, and had seen her!

"You are good and early," he said out of the dark. "Was everything all right?"

"Perfectly easy."

He shut the gate quietly after her, and made a spot of light on the dark ground, showing the pallid flowers still standing there open in the night. They went on apart, in silence.

"Are you sure you didn't hurt yourself this morning with that chair?" she asked.

"No, no!"

"When you had that pneumonia, what did it do to you?"

"Oh nothing! It left my heart not so strong and the lungs not so elastic. But it always does that."

"And you ought not to make violent physical efforts?"

"Not often."

She plodded on in an angry silence.

"Did you hate Clifford?" she said at last.

"Hate him, no! I've met too many like him to upset myself hating him. I know beforehand I don't care for his sort, and I let it go at that."

"What is his sort?"

"Nay, you know better than I do. The sort of youngish gentleman, a bit like a lady, and no balls."

"What balls?"

"Balls! A man's balls!"

She pondered this.

"But is it a question of that?" she said, a little annoyed.

"You say a man's got no brain, when he's a fool: and no heart, when he's mean; and no stomach when he's a funker. And when he's got none of that spunky wild bit of a man in him, you say he's got no balls. When he's sort of tame."

She pondered this.

"And is Clifford tame?" she asked.

"Tame, and nasty with it: like most such fellows, when you come up against 'em."

"And do you think you're not tame?"

"Maybe not quite!"

At length she saw in the distance a yellow light.

She stood still.

"There is a light!" she said.

"I always leave a light in the house," he said.

She went on again at his side, but not touching him, wondering why she was going with him at all.

He unlocked, and they went in, he bolting the door behind them. As if it were a prison, she thought! The kettle was singing by the red fire, there were cups on the table.

She sat in the wooden armchair by the fire. It was warm after the chill outside.

"I'll take off my shoes, they are wet," she said.

She sat with her stockinged feet on the bright steel fender. He went to the pantry, bringing food: bread and butter and pressed tongue. She was warm: she took off her coat. He hung it on the door.

"Shall you have cocoa or tea or coffee to drink?" he asked.

"I don't think I want anything," she said, looking at the table. "But you eat."

"Nay, I don't care about it. I'll just feed the dog."

He tramped with a quiet inevitability over the brick floor, putting food for the dog in a brown bowl. The spaniel looked up at him anxiously.

"Ay, this thy supper, tha nedna look as if tha wouldna get it!" he said.

He set the bowl on the stairfoot mat, and sat himself on a chair by the wall, to take off his leggings and boots. The dog, instead of eating, came to him again, and sat looking up at him, troubled.

He slowly unbuckled his leggings. The dog edged a little nearer.

"What's amiss wi' thee then? Art upset because there's somebody else here? Tha'rt a female, tha art! Go an' eat thy supper."

He put his hand on her head, and the bitch leaned her head sideways against him. He slowly, softly pulled the long silky ear.

"There!" he said. "There! Go an' eat thy supper! Go!"

He tilted his chair towards the pot on the mat, and the dog meekly went, and fell to eating.

"Do you like dogs?" Connie asked him.

"No, not really. They're too tame and clinging."

He had taken off his leggings and was unlacing his heavy boots. Connie had turned from the fire. How bare the little room was! Yet over his head on the wall hung a hideous enlarged photograph of a young married couple, apparently him and a bold-faced young woman, no doubt his wife.

"Is that you?" Connie asked him.

He twisted and looked at the enlargement above his head.

"Ay! Taken just afore we was married, when I was twenty-one." He looked at it impassively.

"Do you like it?" Connie asked him.

"Like it? No! I never liked the thing. But she fixed it all up to have it done, like."

He returned to pulling off his boots.

"If you don't like it, why do you keep it hanging there? Perhaps your wife would like to have it," she said.

He looked up at her with a sudden grin.

"She carted off iverything as was worth taking from th'ouse," he said. "But she left *that!*"

"Then why do you keep it? For sentimental reasons?"

"Nay, I niver look at it. I hardly knowed it wor theer. It's been theer sin' we come to this place."

"Why don't you burn it?" she said.

He twisted round again and looked at the enlarged photograph. It was framed in a brown-and-gilt frame, hideous. It showed a clean shaven, alert, very young looking man in a rather high collar, and a somewhat plump, bold young woman with hair fluffed out and crimped, and wearing a dark satin blouse.

"It wouldn't be a bad idea, would it?" he said.

He pulled off his boots, and put on a pair of slippers. He stood up on the chair, and lifted down the photograph. It left a big pale place on the greenish wallpaper.

"No use dusting it now," he said, setting the thing against the wall.

He went to the scullery, and returned with hammer and pincers. Sitting where he had sat before, he started to tear off the back-paper from the big frame and to pull out the sprigs that held the backboard in position, working with the immediate quiet absorption that was characteristic of him.

He soon had the nails out: then he pulled out the backboards, then the enlargement itself, in its solid white mount. He looked at the photograph with amusement.

"Shows me for what I was, a young curate, and her for what she was, a bully," he said. "The prig and the bully!"

"Let me look!" said Connie.

He did look indeed very clean-shaven and very clean altogether, one of the clean young men of twenty years ago. But even in the photograph his eyes were alert, and dauntless. And the woman was not altogether a bully, though her jowl was heavy. There was a touch of appeal in her.

"One never should keep these things," said Connie.

"That one shouldn't! One should never have them made!"

He broke the cardboard photograph and mount over his knee, and when it was small enough, put it on the fire.

"It'll spoil the fire, though," he said.

The glass and the backboards he carefully took upstairs.

The frame he knocked asunder with a few blows of the hammer, making the stucco fly. Then he took the pieces into the scullery.

"We'll burn that tomorrow," he said. "There's too much plaster molding on it."

Having cleared away, he sat down.

"Did you love your wife?" she asked him.

"Love?" he said. "Did you love Sir Clifford?"

But she was not going to be put off.

"But you cared for her?" she insisted.

"Cared?" he grinned.

"Perhaps you care for her now," she said.

"Me!" His eyes widened. "Ah, no, I can't think of her," he said quietly.

"Why?"

But he shook his head.

"Then why don't you get a divorce? She'll come back to you one day," said Connie.

He looked up at her sharply.

"She wouldn't come within a mile of me. She hates me a lot worse than I hate her."

"You'll see, she'll come back to you."

"That she never shall. That's done. It would make me sick to see her."

"You will see her. And you're not even legally separated, are you?"

"No."

"Ah, well, then she'll come back, and you'll have to take her in."

He gazed at Connie fixedly. Then he gave the queer toss of his head.

"You may be right. I was a fool ever to come back here. But I felt stranded and had to go somewhere. A man's a poor bit of a wastrel, blown about. But you're right. I'll get a divorce and get clear. I hate those things like death, officials and courts and judges. But I've got to get through with it. I'll get a divorce."

And she saw his jaw set. Inwardly she exulted.

"I think I will have a cup of tea now," she said.

He rose to make it. But his face was set.

As they sat at the table she asked him:

"Why did you marry her? She was commoner than yourself. Mrs. Bolton told me about her. She could never understand why you married her."

He looked at her fixedly.

"I'll tell you," he said. "The first girl I had, I began with when I was sixteen. She was a schoolmaster's daughter over at Ollerton, pretty, beautiful really. I was supposed to be a clever sort of young fellow from Sheffield Grammar School, with a bit of French and German, very much up aloft. She was the romantic sort that hated commonness. She egged me on to poetry and reading: in a way, she made a man of me. I read and I thought like a house on fire, for her. And I was a clerk in Butterley Offices, a thin, white-faced fellow fuming with all the things I read. And about *everything* I talked to her: but everything. We talked ourselves into Persepolis and Timbuctoo. We were the most literary-cultured couple in ten counties. I held forth with rapture to her, positively with rapture. I simply went up in smoke. And she adored me. The serpent in the grass was sex. She somehow didn't have any; at least where it's supposed to be. I got thinner and crazier. Then I said we'd got to be lovers. I talked her into it, as usual. So she let me. I was excited, and she never wanted it. She just didn't want it. She adored me, she loved me to talk to her and kiss her: in that way she had a passion for me. But the other, she just didn't want it. And there are lots of women like her. And it was just the other that I *did* want. So there we split. I was cruel, and left her. Then I took on with another girl, a teacher, who had made a scandal by carrying on with a married man and driving him nearly out of his mind. She was a soft, white-skinned, soft sort of a woman, older than me, and played the fiddle. And she was a demon. She loved everything about love, except the sex. Clinging, caressing, creeping into you in every way: but if you forced her to sex itself, she just ground her teeth and sent out hate. I forced her to it, and she could simply numb me with hate because of it. So I was balked again. I loathed all that. I wanted a woman who wanted me, and wanted *it*.

"Then came Bertha Coutts. They'd lived next door to us when I was a little lad, so I knew 'em all right. And they were common. Well, Bertha went away to some place or other in Birmingham; she said, as a lady's companion; everybody else said, as a waitress or something in an hotel. Anyhow, just when I was more than fed up with that other girl, when I was twenty-one, back comes Bertha, with airs and grace and smart clothes and a sort of bloom on her: a sort of sensual bloom that you'd see sometimes on a woman, or on a trolly. Well I was in a state of murder. I chucked up my job at Butterley because I thought I was a weed, clerking there: and I got on as overhead blacksmith at Tevershall:

shoeing horses mostly. It had been my dad's job, and I'd always been with him. It was a job I liked: handling horses: and it came natural to me. So I stopped talking "fine," as they call it, talking proper English, and went back to talking broad. I still read books, at home, but I blacksmithed and had a pony-trap of my own, and was My Lord Duckfoot. My dad left me three hundred pounds when he died. So I took on with Bertha, and I was glad she was common. I wanted her to be common. I wanted to be common myself. Well, I married her, and she wasn't bad. Those other 'pure' women had nearly taken all the balls out of me, but she was all right that way. She wanted me, and made no bones about it. And I was as pleased as punch. That was what I wanted: a woman who *wanted* me to fuck her. So I fucked her like a good un. And I think she despised me a bit, for being so pleased about it, and bringin' her her breakfast in bed sometimes. She sort of let things go, didn't get me a proper dinner when I came home from work, and if I said anything, flew out at me. And I flew back, hammer and tongs. She flung a cup at me, and I took her by the scruff of the neck and squeezed the life out of her. That sort of thing! But she treated me with insolence. And she got so's she'd never see me when I wanted her; never. Always put me off, brutal as you like. And then when she'd put me right off, and I didn't want her, she'd come all lovey-dovey, and get me. And I always went. But when I had her, she'd never come off when I did. Never! She'd just wait. If I kept back for half an hour, she'd keep back longer. And when I'd come and really finished then she'd start on her own account, and I had to stop inside her till she brought herself off, wriggling and shouting, she'd clutch clutch with herself down there, an' then she'd come off, fair in ecstasy. And then she'd say: That was lovely! Gradually, I got sick of it: and she got worse. She sort of got harder and harder to bring off, and she'd sort of tear at me down there, as if it was a beak tearing me. By God, you think a woman's soft down there, like a fig. But I tell you the old rampers have beaks between their legs, and they tear at you with it till you're sick. Self! Self! Self! all self! tearing and shouting! They talk about men's selfishness, but I doubt if it can ever touch a woman's blind beakishness, once she's gone that way. Like an old trull! And she couldn't help it. I told her about it, I told her how I hated it. And she'd even try. She'd try to lie still and let *me* work the business. She'd try. But it was no good. She got no feeling off it, from my working. She had to work the thing herself, grind her own coffee. And it came back on her like a raving necessity; she had to let herself go, and tear, tear, tear, as if she had no sensation in her except in the top of her beak, the very outside top tip, that rubbed and tore. That's how old whores used to be, so men used to say. It was a low kind of self-will in her, a raving sort of self-will: like in a woman who drinks. Well, in the end I couldn't stand it. We slept apart. She herself had started it, in her bouts, when she wanted to be clear of me, when she said I bossed her. She had started having a room for herself. But the time came when I wouldn't have her coming to my room. I wouldn't.

"I hated her. And she hated me. My God, how she hated me before that child was born! I often think that she conceived it out of hate. Anyhow, after the child was born I left her alone. And then came the war, and I joined up. And I didn't come back till I knew she was with that fellow at Stacks Gate."

He broke off, pale in the face.

"And what is the man at Stacks Gate like?" asked Connie.

"A big baby sort of fellow, very low-mouthed. She bullies him, and they both drink."

"My word, if she came back!"

"My God, yes! I should just go, disappear again."

There was a silence. The pasteboard in the fire had turned to gray ash.

"So when you did get a woman who wanted you," said Connie, "you got a bit too much of a good thing."

"Ay! Seems so! Yet even then I'd rather have her than the never-never ones: the white love of my youth, and that other poison-smelling lily, and the rest."

"What about the rest?" said Connie.

"The rest? There is no rest. Only to my experience the mass of women are like this: most of them want a man, but don't want the sex, but they put up with it, as part of the bargain. The more old-fashioned sort just lie there like nothing and let you go ahead. They don't mind afterwards: then they like you. But the actual thing itself is nothing to them, a bit distasteful. And most men like it that way. I hate it. But the sly sort of women who are like that pretend they're not. They pretend they're passionate and have thrills. But it's all cockaloopy. They make it up—Then there's the ones that love everything, every kind of feeling and cuddling and going off, every kind except the natural one. They always make you go off when you're *not* in the only place you should be, when you go off—Then there's the hard sort, that are the devil to bring off at all, and bring themselves off, like my wife. They want to be the active party—Then there's the sort that's just dead inside: but dead: and they know it. Then there's the sort that puts you out before you really 'come,' and go on writhing their loins till they bring themselves off against your thighs. But they're mostly the Lesbian sort. It's astonishing how Lesbian women are, consciously or unconsciously. Seems to me they're nearly all Lesbian."

"And do you mind?" asked Connie.

"I could kill them. When I'm with a woman who's really Lesbian, I fairly howl in my soul, wanting to kill her."

"And what do you do?"

"Just get away as fast as I can."

"But do you think Lesbian women any worse than homosexual men?"

"*I* do! Because I've suffered more from them. In the abstract, I've no idea. When I get with a Lesbian woman, whether she knows she's one or not, I see red. No, no! But I wanted to have nothing to do with any woman anymore. I wanted to keep to myself: keep my privacy and my decency."

He looked pale, and his brows were somber.

"And were you sorry when I came along?" she said.

"I was sorry and I was glad."

"And what are you now?"

"I'm sorry, from the outside: all the complications and the ugliness and recrimination that's bound to come, sooner or later. That's when my blood sinks, and I'm low. But when my blood comes up, I'm glad. I'm even triumphant. I was really getting bitter. I thought there was no real sex left: never a woman who'd really 'come' naturally with a man: except black women, and somehow, well, we're white men: and they're a bit like mud."

"And now, are you glad of me?" she asked.

"Yes. When I can forget the rest. When I can't forget the rest, I want to get under the table and die."

"Why under the table?"

"Why?" he laughed. "Hide, I suppose. Baby!"

"You do seem to have had awful experiences of women," she said.

"You see, I couldn't fool myself. That's where most men manage. They take an attitude, and accept a lie. I could never fool myself I knew what I wanted with a woman, and I could never say I'd got it when I hadn't."

"But have you got it now?"

"Looks as if I might have."

"Then why are you so pale and gloomy?"

"Bellyfull of remembering: and perhaps afraid of myself."

She sat in silence. It was growing late.

"And you do think it's important, a man and a woman?" she asked him.

"For me it is. For me it's the core of my life: if I have a right relation with a woman."

"And if you didn't get it?"

"Then I'd have to do without."

Again she pondered, before she asked:

"And do you think you've always been right with women?"

"God, no! I let my wife get to what she was: my fault a good deal. I spoilt her. And I'm very mistrustful. You'll have to expect it. It takes a lot to make me trust anybody, inwardly. So perhaps I'm a fraud too. I mistrust. And tenderness is not to be mistaken."

She looked at him.

"You don't mistrust with your body, when your blood comes up," she said. "You don't mistrust then, do you?"

"No, alas! That's how I've got into all the trouble. And that's why my mind mistrusts so thoroughly."

"Let your mind mistrust. What does it matter!"

The dog sighed with discomfort on the mat. The ash-clogged fire sank.

"We *are* a couple of battered warriors," said Connie.

"Are you battered too?" he laughed. "And here we are returning to the fray!"

"Yes! I feel really frightened."

"Ay!"

He got up, and put her shoes to dry, and wiped his own and set them near the fire. In the morning he would grease them. He poked the ash of pasteboard as much as possible out of the fire. "Even burnt, it's filthy," he said. Then he brought sticks and put them on the hob for the morning. Then he went out awhile with the dog.

When he came back Connie said: "I want to go out, too, for a minute."

She went alone into the darkness. There were stars overhead. She could smell flowers on the night air. And she could feel her shoes getting wetter again. But she felt like going away, right away from him and everybody.

It was chilly. She shuddered, and returned to the house. He was sitting in front of the low fire.

"Ugh! Cold!" she shuddered.

He put the sticks on the fire, and fetched more, till they had a good crackling chimneyful of blaze. The rippling running yellow flame made them both happy, warmed their faces and their souls.

"Never mind!" she said, taking his hand as he sat silent and remote. "One does one's best."

"Ay"—He sighed, with a twist of a smile.

She slipped over to him, and into his arms, as he sat there before the fire.

"Forget then!" she whispered. "Forget!"

He held her close, in the running warmth of the fire. The flame itself was like a forgetting. And her soft, warm, ripe weight! Slowly his blood turned, and began to ebb back into strength and reckless vigor again.

"And perhaps the women *really* wanted to be there and love you properly, only perhaps they couldn't. Perhaps it wasn't all their fault," she said.

"I know it. Do you think I don't know what a broken-backed snake that's been trodden on I was myself!"

She clung to him suddenly. She had not wanted to start all this again. Yet some perversity had made her.

"But you're not now," she said. "You're not that now: a broken-backed snake that's been trodden on."

"I don't know what I am. There's black days ahead," he repeated with a prophetic gloom.

"No! You're not to say it!"

He was silent. But she could feel the black void of despair inside him. That was the death of all desire, the death of all love: this despair that was like the dark cave inside the men, in which their spirit was lost.

"And you talk so coldly about sex," she said. "You talk as if you had only wanted your own pleasure and satisfaction."

She was protesting nervously against him.

"Nay!" he said. "I wanted to have my pleasure and satisfaction of a woman, and I never got it: because I could never get my pleasure and satisfaction of *her* unless she got hers of me at the same time. And it never happened. It takes two."

"But you never believed in your women. You don't even believe really in me," she said.

"I don't know what believing in a woman means."

"That's it, you see!"

She still was curled on his lap. But his spirit was gray and absent, he was not there for her. And everything she said drove him further.

"But what *do* you believe in?" she insisted.

"I don't know."

"Nothing, like all the men I've ever known," she said.

They were both silent. Then he roused himself and said:

"Yes, I do believe in something. I believe in being warmhearted. I believe especially in being warmhearted in love, in fucking with a warm heart. I believe if men could fuck with warm hearts, and the women take it warmheartedly, everything would come all right. It's all this coldhearted fucking that is death and idiocy."

"But you don't fuck me coldheartedly," she protested.

"I don't want to fuck you at all. My heart's as cold as cold potatoes just now."

"Oh!" she said, kissing him mockingly. "Let's have them *sautées*." He laughed, and sat erect.

"It's a fact!" he said. "Anything for a bit of warmheartedness. But the women don't like it. Even you don't really like it. You like good, sharp, piercing coldhearted fucking, and then pretending it's all sugar. Where's your tenderness for me? You're as suspicious of me as a cat is of a dog. I tell you it takes two even to be tender and warmhearted. You love fucking all right: but you want it to be called something grand and mysterious, just to flatter your own self-importance. Your own self-importance is more to you, fifty times more, than any man, or being together with a man."

"But that's what I'd say of you. Your own self-importance is everything to you."

"Ay! Very well then!" he said, moving as if he wanted to rise. "Let's keep apart then. I'd rather die than do any more coldhearted fucking."

She slid away from him, and he stood up.

"And do you think *I* want it?" she said.

"I hope you don't," he replied. "But anyhow, you go to bed an' I'll sleep down here."

She looked at him. He was pale, his brows were sullen, he was as distant in recoil as the cold pole. Men were all alike.

"I can't go home till morning," she said.

"No! Go to bed. It's a quarter to one."

"I certainly won't," she said.

He went across and picked up his boots.

"Then I'll go out!" he said.

He began to put on his boots. She stared at him.

"Wait!" she faltered. "Wait! What's come between us?"

He was bent over, lacing his boot, and did not reply. The moments passed. A dimness came over her, like a swoon. All her consciousness died, and she stood there wide-eyed, looking at him from the unknown, knowing nothing any more.

He looked up, because of the silence, and saw her wide-eyed and lost. And as if a wind tossed him he got up and hobbled over to her, one shoe off and one shoe on, and took her in his arms, pressing her against his body, which somehow felt hurt right through. And there he held her, and there she remained.

Till his hands reached blindly down and felt for her, and felt under the clothing to where she was smooth and warm.

"Ma lass!" he murmured. "Ma little lass! Dunna let's fight! Dunna let's niver fight! I love thee an' th' touch on thee. Dunna argue wi' me! Dunna! Dunna! Dunna! Let's be together."

She lifted her face and looked at him.

"Don't be upset," she said steadily. "It's no good being upset. Do you really want to be together with me?"

She looked with wide, steady eyes into his face. He stopped, and went suddenly still, turning his face aside. All his body went perfectly still, but did not withdraw.

Then he lifted his head and looked into her eyes, with his odd, faintly mocking grin, saying: "Ay-ay! Let's be together on oath."

"But really?" she said, her eyes filling with tears.

"Ay really! Heart an' belly an' cock."

He still smiled faintly down at her, with the flicker of irony in his eyes, and a touch of bitterness.

She was silently weeping, and he lay with her and went into her there on the hearthrug, and so they gained a measure of equanimity. And then they went quickly to bed, for it was growing chill, and they had tired each other out. And she nestled up to him, feeling small and enfolded, and they both went to sleep at once, fast in one sleep. And so they lay and never moved, till the sun rose over the wood and day was beginning.

Then he woke up and looked at the light. The curtains were drawn. He listened to the loud wild calling of blackbirds and thrushes in the wood. It would be a brilliant morning, about half-past five, his hour for rising. He had slept so fast! It was such a new day! The woman was still curled asleep and tender. His hand moved on her, and she opened her blue wondering eyes, smiling unconsciously into his face.

"Are you awake?" she said to him.

He was looking into her eyes. He smiled, and kissed her. And suddenly she roused and sat up.

"Fancy that I am here!" she said.

She looked round the whitewashed little bedroom with its sloping ceiling and gable window where the white curtains were closed. The room was bare save for a little yellow-painted chest of drawers, and a chair. and the smallish white bed in which she lay.

"Fancy that we are here!" she said, looking down at him. He was lying watching her, stroking her breasts with his fingers, under the thin nightdress. When he was warm and smoothed out, he looked young and handsome. His eyes could look so warm. And she was fresh and young like a flower.

"I want to take this off!" he said, gathering the thin batiste nightdress and pulling it over her head. She sat there with bare shoulders and longish breasts faintly golden. He loved to make her breasts swing softly, like bells.

"You must take off your pyjamas too," she said.

"Eh nay!"

"Yes! Yes!" she commanded.

And he took off his old cotton pyjama jacket and pushed down the trousers. Save for his hands and wrists and face and neck he was white as milk, with fine slender muscular flesh. To Connie he was suddenly piercingly beautiful again, as when she had seen him that afternoon washing himself.

Gold of sunshine touched the closed white curtains. She felt it wanted to come in.

"Oh! do let's draw the curtains! The birds are singing so! Do let the sun in," she said.

He slipped out of bed with his back to her, naked and white and thin, and went to the window, stooping a little, drawing the curtains and looking out for a moment. The back was white and fine, the small buttocks beautiful with exquisite, delicate manliness, the back of the neck ruddy and delicate and yet strong.

There was an inward, not an outward strength in the delicate and yet strong body.

"But you are beautiful!" she said. "So pure and fine! Come!" She held her arms out.

He was ashamed to turn to her, because of his aroused nakedness.

He caught his shirt off the floor, and held it to him, coming to her.

"No!" she said, still holding out her beautiful slim arms from her drooping breasts. "Let me see you!"

He dropped the shirt and stood still, looking towards her. The sun through the low window sent a beam that lit up his thighs and slim belly, and the erect phallus rising darkish and hot looking from the little cloud of vivid gold-red hair. She was startled and afraid.

"How strange!" she said slowly. "How strange he stands there! So big! and so dark and cocksure! Is he like that?"

The man looked down the front of his slender white body, and laughed. Between the slim breasts the hair was dark, almost black. But at the root of the belly, where the phallus rose thick and arching, it was gold-red, vivid in a little cloud.

"So proud!" she murmured, uneasy. "And so lordly! Now I know why men are so overbearing. But he's lovely, *really*. Like another being! A bit terrifying! But lovely really! And he comes to *me*!—" She caught her lower lip between her teeth, in fear and excitement.

The man looked down in silence at his tense phallus, that did not change—"Ay!" he said at last, in a little voice. "Ay ma lad! Tha'rt theer right enough. Yi, tha mun rear thy head! Theer on thy own, eh? an ta'es no count o' nob'dy! Tha ma'es nowt o' me, John Thomas. Art boss? of me? Eh well, tha'rt more cocky than me, an' tha says less. John Thomas! Dost want *her*? Dost want my lady Jane? Tha's dipped me in again, tha hast. Ay, an' tha comes up smilin'—Ax 'er than! Ax lady Jane! Say: Lift up you heads o' ye gates, that the king of glory may come in. Ay, th' cheek on thee! Cunt, that's what tha'rt after. Tell lady Jane tha wants cunt. John Thomas, an' th' cunt o'lady Jane!—"

"Oh, don't tease him" said Connie, crawling on her knees on the bed towards him and putting her arms round his white slender loins, and drawing him to her so that her hanging, swinging breasts touched the tip of the stirring, erect phallus, and caught the drop of moisture. She held the man fast.

"Lie down!" he said. "Lie down! Let me come!"

He was in a hurry now.

And afterwards, when they had been quite still, the woman had to uncover the man again, to look at the mystery of the phallus.

"And now he's tiny, and soft like a little bud of life!" she said, taking the soft small penis in her hand. "Isn't he somehow lovely! so on his own, so strange! And *so* innocent! And he comes so far into me! You must *never* insult him, you know. He's mine too. He's not only yours. He's mine! And so lovely and innocent!" And she held the penis soft in her hand.

He laughed.

"Blest be the tie that binds our hearts in kindred love," he said.

"Of course!" she said. "Even when he's soft and little I feel my heart simply tied to him. And how lovely your hair is here! quite quite different!"

"That's John Thomas's hair, not mine!" he said.

"John Thomas! John Thomas!" and she quickly kissed the soft penis, that was beginning to stir again.

"Ay!" said the man, stretching his body almost painfully. "He's got his root in my soul, has that gentleman! An' sometimes I don't know what ter do wi' him. Ay, he's got a will of his own, an' it's hard to suit him. Yet I wouldn't have him killed."

"No wonder men have always been afraid of him!" she said. "He's rather terrible."

The quiver was going through the man's body, as the stream of consciousness again changed its direction, turning downwards. And he was helpless, as the penis in slow soft undulations filled and surged and rose up, and grew hard, standing there hard and overweening, in its curious towering fashion. The woman too trembled a little as she watched.

"There! Take him then! He's thine," said the man.

And she quivered, and her own mind melted out. Sharp soft waves of unspeakable pleasure washed over her as he entered her, and started the curious molten thrilling that spread and spread till she was carried away with the last, blind flush of extremity.

He heard the distant hooters of Stacks Gate for seven o'clock. It was Monday morning. He shivered a little, and with his face between her breasts pressed her soft breasts up over his ears, to deafen him.

She had not even heard the hooters. She lay perfectly still, her soul washed transparent.

"You must get up, mustn't you?" he muttered.

"What time?" came her colorless voice.

"Seven o'clock blowers a bit sin'."

"I suppose I must."

She was resenting, as she always did, the compulsion from outside.

He sat up and looked blankly out of the window.

"You do love me, don't you?" she asked calmly.

He looked down at her.

"Tha knows what tha knows. What dost ax for!" he said, a little fretfully.

"I want you to keep me, not to let me go," she said.

His eyes seemed full of a warm, soft darkness that could not think.

"When? Now?"

"Now, in your heart. Then I want to come and live with you always, soon."

He sat on the bed, with his head dropped, unable to think.

"Don't you want it?" she asked.

"Ay!" he said.

Then with the same eyes darkened with another flame of consciousness, almost like sleep, he looked at her.

"Dunna ax me nowt now," he said. "Let me be. I like thee. I luv thee when tha lies theer. A woman's a lovely thing when 'er's deep ter fuck, and cunt's good. Ah luv thee, thy legs, an' th' shape on thee, an' th' womanness on thee. Ah luv th' womanness on thee. Ah luv thee wi' my ba's an' wi' my heart. But dunna ax me nowt. Dunna ma'e me say nowt. Let me stop as I am while I can. Tha can ax me ivrything after. Now let me be, let me be!"

And softly, he laid his hand over her mound of Venus, on the soft brown maiden-hair, and himself sat still and naked on the bed, his face motionless in physical abstraction, almost like the face of Buddha. Motionless, and in the invisible flame of another consciousness, he sat with his hand on her, and waited for the turn.

After a while, he reached for his shirt and put it on, dressed himself swiftly in silence, looked at her once as she still lay naked and faintly golden like a Gloire de Dijon rose on the bed, and was gone. She heard him downstairs opening the door.

And she still lay musing, musing. It was very hard to go: to go out of his house. He called from the foot of the stairs: "Half-past seven!" She sighed, and got out of bed. The bare little room! Nothing in it at all but the small chest of drawers and the smallish bed. But the board floor was scrubbed clean. And in the corner by the window gable was a shelf with some books, and some from a circulating library. She looked. There were books about Bolshevist Russia, books of travel, a volume about the atom and the electron, another about the composition of the earth's core, and the causes of earthquakes: then a few novels: then three books on India. So! He was a reader after all.

The sun fell on her naked limbs through the gable window. Outside she saw the dog Flossie roaming round. The hazel-brake was misted with green, and dark green dogs'-mercury under. It was a clear clean morning with birds flying and triumphantly singing. If only she could stay! If only there weren't the other ghastly world of smoke and iron! If only *he* would make her a world.

She came downstairs, down the steep, narrow wooden stairs. Still, she would be content with this little house, if only it were in a world of its own.

He was washed and fresh, and the fire was burning.

"Will you eat anything?" he said.

"No! Only lend me a comb."

She followed him into the scullery, and combed her hair before the handbreath of mirror by the back door. Then she was ready to go.

She stood in the little front garden, looking at the dewy flowers, the gray bed of pinks in bud already.

"I would like to have all the rest of the world disappear," she said, "and live with you here."

"It won't disappear," he said.

They went almost in silence through the lovely dewy wood. But they were together in a world of their own.

It was bitter to her to go on to Wragby.

"I want soon to come and live with you altogether," she said as she left him.

He smiled unanswering.

She got home quietly and unremarked, and went up to her room.

❖ 15 ❖

There was a letter from Hilda on the breakfast tray. "Father is going to London this week, and I shall call for you on Thursday week, June 17. You must be ready so that we can go at once. I don't want to waste time at Wragby, it's an awful place. I shall probably stay the night at Retford with the Colemans, so I should be with you for lunch Thursday. Then we could start at teatime, and sleep perhaps in Grantham. It is no use our spending an evening with Clifford. If he hates your going, it would be no pleasure to him."

So! She was being pushed around on the chessboard again.

Clifford hated her going, but it was only because he didn't feel *safe* in her absence. Her presence, for some reason, made him feel safe, and free to do the things he was occupied with. He was a great deal at the pits, and wrestling in spirit with the almost hopeless problems of getting out his coal in the most economical fashion, and then selling it when he'd got it out. He knew he ought to find some way of *using* it, or converting it, so that he needn't sell it, or needn't have the chagrin of failing to sell it. But if he made electric power, could he sell that or use it? And to convert into oil was as yet too costly and elaborate. To keep industry alive there must be more industry, like a madness.

It was a madness, and it required a madman to succeed in it. Well, he was a little mad. Connie thought so. His very intensity and acumen in the affairs of the pits seemed like a manifestation of madness to her, his very inspirations were the inspirations of insanity.

He talked to her of all his serious schemes, and she listened in a kind of wonder, and let him talk. Then his flow ceased, and he turned on the loudspeaker, and became a blank, while apparently his schemes coiled on inside him like a kind of dream.

And every night now he played pontoon, that game of the Tommies, with Mrs. Bolton, gambling with sixpences. And again, in the gambling he was gone in a kind of unconscious, or blank intoxication, or intoxication of blankness, whatever it was. Connie could not bear to see him. But when she had gone to bed, he and Mrs. Bolton would gamble on till two and three in the morning, safely, and with strange lust. Mrs. Bolton was caught in the lust as much as Clifford: the more so, as she nearly always lost.

She told Connie one day: "I lost twenty-three shillings to Sir Clifford last night."

"And did he take the money from you?" asked Connie aghast.

"Why, of course, my Lady! Debt of honor!"

Connie expostulated roundly and was angry with both of them. The upshot was, Sir Clifford raised Mrs. Bolton's wages a hundred a year, and she could gamble on that. Meanwhile it seemed to Connie, Clifford was really going deader.

She told him at length she was leaving on the seventeenth.

"Seventeenth!" he said. "And when will you be back?"

"By the twentieth of July at the latest."

"Yes! the twentieth of July."

Strangely and blankly he looked at her, with the vagueness of a child, but with the queer blank cunning of an old man.

"You won't let me down, will you?" he said.

"How?"

"While you're away. I mean, you're sure to come back?"

"I'm as sure as I can be of anything, that I shall come back."

"Yes! Well! Twentieth of July."

Yet he really wanted her to go. That was so curious. He wanted her to go, positively, to have her little adventures and perhaps become pregnant, and all that. At the same time, he was afraid of her going.

She was quivering, watching her real opportunity for leaving him altogether, waiting till the time, herself, himself, should be ripe.

She sat and talked to the keeper of her going abroad.

"And then when I come back," she said, "I can tell Clifford I must leave him. And you and I can go away. They never need even know it is you. We can go to another country. Shall we? To Africa or Australia. Shall we?"

She was quite thrilled by her plan.

"You've never been to the colonies, have you?" he asked her.

"No! Have you?"

"I've been in India, and South Africa, and Egypt."

"Why shouldn't we go to South Africa?"

"We might!" he said slowly.

"Or don't you want to?" she asked.

"I don't care. I don't much care what I do."

"Doesn't it make you happy? Why not? We shan't be poor. I have about six hundred a year. I wrote and asked. It's not much, but it's enough, isn't it?"

"It's riches to me."

"Oh, how lovely it will be!"

"But I ought to get divorced, and so ought you, unless we're going to have complications."

There was plenty to think about.

Another day she asked him about himself. They were in the hut, and there was a thunderstorm.

"And weren't you happy, when you were a lieutenant and an officer and a gentleman?"

"Happy? All right. I liked my Colonel."

"Did you love him?"

"Yes! I loved him."

"And did he love you?"

"Yes! In a way, he loved me."

"Tell me about him."

"What is there to tell? He had risen from the ranks. He loved the army. And he had never married. He was twenty years older than me. He was a very intelligent man: and alone in the army, as such a man is: a passionate man in his way: and a very clever officer. I lived under his spell while I was with him. I sort of let him run my life. And I never regret it."

"And did you mind very much when he died?"

"I was as near death myself. But when I came to, I knew another part of me was finished. But then I had always known it would finish in death. All things do, as far as that goes."

She sat and ruminated. The thunder crashed outside. It was like being in a little ark in the Flood.

"You seem to have such a lot *behind* you," she said.

"Do I? It seems to me I've died once or twice already. Yet here I am, pegging on, and in for more trouble."

She was thinking hard, yet listening to the storm.

"And weren't you happy as an officer and a gentleman, when your Colonel was dead?"

"No! They were a mingy lot." He laughed suddenly. "The Colonel used to say: Lad, the English middle classes have to chew every mouthful thirty times because their guts are so narrow, a bit as big as a pea would give them a stoppage. They're the mingiest set of ladylike snipe ever invented: full of conceit of themselves, frightened even if their bootlaces aren't correct, rotten as high game, and always in the right. That's what finishes me up. Kow-tow, kow-tow, arse-licking till their tongues are tough: yet they're always in the right. Prigs on top of everything. Prigs! A generation of ladylike prigs with half a ball each—"

Connie laughed. The rain was rushing down.

"He hated them!"

"No," said he. "He didn't bother. He just disliked them. There's a difference. Because, as he said, the Tommies are getting just as priggish and half-balled and narrow-gutted. It's the fate of mankind, to go that way."

"The common people, too, the working people?"

"All the lot. Their spunk is gone dead. Motorcars and cinemas and aeroplanes suck that last bit out of them. I tell you, every generation breeds a more rabbity generation, with india rubber tubing for guts and tin legs and tin faces. Tin people! It's all a steady sort of Bolshevism just killing off the human thing, and worshipping the mechanical thing. Money, money, money! All the modern lot get their real kick out of killing the old human feeling out of man, making mincemeat of the old Adam and the old Eve. They're all alike. The world is all alike: kill off the human reality, a quid for every foreskin, two quid for each pair of balls. What is cunt but machine-fucking!—It's all alike. Pay 'em money to cut off the world's cock. Pay money, money, money to them that will take spunk out of mankind, and leave 'em all little twiddling machines."

He sat there in the hut, his face pulled to mocking irony. Yet even then, he had one ear set backwards, listening to the storm over the wood. It made him feel so alone.

"But won't it ever come to an end?" she said.

"Ay, it will. It'll achieve its own salvation. When the last real man is killed, and they're *all* tame: white, black, yellow, all colors of tame ones: then they'll *all* be insane. Because the root of sanity is in the balls. Then they'll all be *insane*, and they'll make their grand *auto de fé*. You know *auto da fé* means act of faith? Ay, well, they'll make their own grand little act of faith. They'll offer one another up."

"You mean kill one another?"

"I do, duckie! If we go on at our present rate then in a hundred years' time there won't be ten thousand people in this island: there may not be ten. They'll have lovingly wiped each other out." The thunder was rolling further away.

"How nice!" she said.

"Quite nice! To contemplate the extermination of the human species and the long pause that follows before some other species crops up, it calms you more than anything else. And if we go on in that way, with everybody, intellectuals, artists, government, industrialists and workers all frantically killing off the last human feeling, the last bit of their intuition, the last healthy instinct; if it goes on in algebraical progression, as it is going on: then ta-tah! to the human species! Good-bye! darling! the serpent swallows itself and leaves a void, considerably messed up, but not hopeless. Very nice! When savage wild dogs bark in Wragby, and savage wild pit-ponies stamp on Tevershall pit-bank! *te deum laudamus!*"

Connie laughed, but not very happily.

"Then you ought to be pleased that they are all Bolshevists," she said. "You ought to be pleased that they hurry on towards the end."

"So I am. I don't stop 'em. Because I couldn't if I would."

"Then why are you so bitter?"

"I'm not! If my cock gives its last crow, I don't mind."

"But if you have a child?" she said.

He dropped his head.

"Why," he said at last. "It seems to me a wrong and bitter thing to do, to bring a child into this world."

"No! Don't say it! Don't say it!" she pleaded. "I think I'm going to have one. Say you'll be pleased." She laid her hand on his.

"I'm pleased for you to be pleased," he said. "But for me it seems a ghastly treachery to the unborn creature."

"Ah, no!" she said, shocked. "Then you can't ever really want me! You *can't* want me, if you feel that!"

Again he was silent, his face sullen. Outside there was only the threshing of the rain.

"It's not quite true!" she whispered. "It's not quite true! There's another truth." She felt he was bitter now partly because she was leaving him, deliberately going away to Venice. And this half pleased her.

She pulled open his clothing and uncovered his belly, and kissed his navel. Then she laid her cheek on his belly, and pressed her arm around his warm, silent, loins. They were alone in the flood.

"Tell me you want a child, in hope!" she murmured, pressing her face against his belly. "Tell me you do!"

"Why!" he said at last: and she felt the curious quiver of changing consciousness and relaxation going through his body. "Why, I've thought sometimes if one but tried, here among th' colliers even! They workin' bad now, an' not earnin' much. If a man could say to 'em: Dunna think o' nowt but th' money. When it comes ter *wants*, we want but little. Let's not live for money—"

She softly rubbed her cheek on his belly, and gathered his balls in her hand. The penis stirred softly, with strange life, but did not rise up. The rain beat bruisingly outside.

"Let's live for summat else. Let's not live ter make money, neither for usselves nor for anybody else. Now we're forced to. We're forced to make a bit for usselves, an' a fair lot for th' bosses. Let's stop it! Bit by bit, let's stop it. We needn't rant an' rave. Bit by bit, let's drop the whole industrial life, an' go back. The least little bit o' money'll do. For everybody, me an' you, bosses an' masters, even th' king. The least little bit o' money'll really do. Just make up your mind to it, an' you've got out o' th' mess." He paused, then went on:

"An' I'd tell 'em: Look! Look at Joe! He moves lovely! Look how he moves, alive and aware. He's beautiful! An' look at Jonah! He's clumsy, he's ugly, because he's niver willin' to rouse himself. I'd tell 'em: Look! look at yourselves! one shoulder higher than t'other, legs twisted, feet all lumps! What have yer done ter yerselves, wi' the blasted work? Spoilt yerselves. No need to work that much. Take yer clothes off an' look at yourselves. Yer ought ter be alive an' beautiful, an' yer ugly an' half dead. So I'd tell 'em. An' I'd get my men to wear different clothes: 'appen close red trousers, bright red, an' little short white jackets. Why, if men had red, fine legs, that alone would change them in a month. They'd begin to be men again, to be men! An' the women could dress as they liked. Because if once the men walked with legs close bright scarlet, and buttocks nice and showing scarlet under a little white jacket: then the women 'ud begin to be women. It's because th' men *aren't* men, that th' women have to be—An' in time pull down Tevershall and build a few beautiful buildings, that would hold us all. An' clean the country up again. An' not have many children, because the world is overcrowded.

"But I wouldn't preach to the men: only strip 'em an' say: Look at yourselves! That's workin' for money!—Hark at yourselves! That's working for money. You've been working for money! Look at Tevershall! It's horrible. That's because it was built while you was working for money. Look at your girls! They don't care about you, you don't care about them. It's because you've spent your time working an' caring for money. You can't talk nor move nor live, you can't properly be with a woman. You're not alive. Look at yourselves!"

There fell a complete silence. Connie was half listening, and threading in the hair at the root of his belly a few forget-me-nots that she had gathered on the way to the hut. Outside the world had gone still, and a little icy.

"You've got four kinds of hair," she said to him. "On your chest it's nearly black, and your hair isn't dark on your head: but your moustache is hard and dark red, and your hair here, your love-hair, is like a little bush of bright red-gold mistletoe. It's the loveliest of all!"

He looked down and saw the milky bits of forget-me-nots in the hair on his groin.

"Ay! That's where to put forget-me-nots, in the man-hair, or the maiden-hair. But don't you care about the future?"

She looked up at him.

"Oh, I do, terribly!" she said.

"Because when I feel the human world is doomed, has doomed itself by its own mingy beastliness, then I feel the colonies aren't far enough. The moon wouldn't be far enough, because even there you could look back and see the earth, dirty, beastly, unsavory among all the stars: made foul by men. Then I feel I've swallowed gall, and it's eating my inside out, and nowhere's far enough away to get away. But when I get a turn, I forget it all again. Though it's a shame, what's been done to people these last hundred years: men turned into nothing but labor-insects, and all their manhood taken away, and all their real life. I'd wipe the machines off the face of the earth again, and end the industrial epoch absolutely, like a black mistake. But since I can't, an' nobody can, I'd better hold my peace, an' try an' live my own life: if I've got one to live, which I rather doubt."

The thunder had ceased outside, but the rain which had abated, suddenly came striking down, with a last blench of lightning and mutter of departing storm. Connie was uneasy. He had talked so long now, and he was really talking to himself, not to her. Despair seemed to come down on him completely, and she was feeling happy, she hated despair. She knew her leaving him, which he had only just realized inside himself, had plunged him back into this mood. And she triumphed a little.

She opened the door and looked at the straight, heavy rain, like a steel curtain, and had a sudden desire to rush out into it, to rush away. She got up, and began swiftly pulling off her stockings, then her dress and underclothing, and he held his breath. Her pointed keen animal breasts tipped and stirred as she moved. She was ivory-colored in the greenish light. She slipped on her rubber shoes again and ran out with a wild little laugh, holding up her breasts to the heavy rain and spreading her arms, and running blurred in the rain with the eurythmic dance movements she had learned so long ago in Dresden. It was a strange pallid figure lifting and falling, bending so the rain beat and glistened on the full haunches, swaying up again and coming belly-forward through the rain, then stooping again so that only the full loins and buttocks were offered in a kind of homage towards him, repeating a wild obeisance.

He laughed wryly, and threw off his clothes. It was too much. He jumped out, naked and white, with a little shiver, into the hard slanting rain. Flossie sprang before him with a frantic little bark. Connie, her hair all wet and sticking to her head, turned her hot face and saw him. Her blue eyes blazed with excitement as she turned and ran fast, with a strange charging movement, out of the clearing and down the path, the wet boughs whipping her. She ran, and he saw nothing but the round wet head, the wet back leaning forward in flight, the round buttocks twinkling: a wonderful cowering female nakedness in flight.

She was nearly at the wide riding when he came up and flung his naked arm round her soft naked-wet middle. She gave a shriek and straightened herself, and the heap of her soft, chill flesh came up against his body. He pressed it all up against him, madly, the heap of soft, chilled female flesh that became quickly warm as flame, in contact. The rain streamed on them till they smoked.

He gathered her lovely, heavy posteriors one in each hand and pressed them in towards him in a frenzy, quivering motionless in the rain. Then suddenly he tipped her up and fell with her on the path, in the roaring silence of the rain, and short and sharp, he took her, short and sharp and finished, like an animal.

He got up in an instant, wiping the rain from his eyes.

"Come in," he said, and they started running back to the hut. He ran straight and swift: he didn't like the rain. But she came slower, gathering forget-me-nots and campion and bluebells, running a few steps and watching him fleeting away from her.

When she came with her flowers, panting to the hut, he had already started a fire, and the twigs were crackling. Her sharp breasts rose and fell, her hair was plastered down with rain, her face was flushed ruddy and her body glistened and trickled. Wide-eyed and breathless, with a small wet head and full, trickling, naive haunches, she looked another creature.

He took the old sheet and rubbed her down, she standing like a child. Then he rubbed himself, having shut the door of the hut. The fire was blazing up. She ducked her head in the other end of the sheet, and rubbed her wet hair.

"We're drying ourselves together on the same towel, we shall quarrel!" he said.

She looked up for a moment, her hair all odds and ends.

"No!" she said, her eyes wide. "It's not a towel, it's a sheet."

And she went on busily rubbing her head, while he busily rubbed his.

Still panting with their exertions, each wrapped in an army blanket, but the front of the body open to the fire, they sat on a log side by side before the blaze, to get quiet. Connie hated the feel of the blanket against her skin. But now the sheet was all wet.

She dropped her blanket and kneeled on the clay hearth, holding her head to the fire, and shaking her hair to dry it. He watched the beautiful curving drop of her haunches. That fascinated him today. How it sloped with a rich downslope to the heavy roundness of her buttocks! And in between, folded in the secret warmth, the secret entrances!

He stroked her tail with his hand, long and subtly taking in the curves and the globefulness.

"Tha's got such a nice tail on thee," he said, in the throaty caressive dialect. "Tha's got the nicest arse of anybody. It's the nicest, nicest woman's arse as is! An' ivry bit of it is woman, woman sure as nuts. Tha'rt not one o' them button-arsed lasses as should be lads, are ter! Tha's got a real soft sloping bottom on thee, as a man loves in 'is guts. It's a bottom as could hold the world up, it is."

All the while he spoke he exquisitely stroked the rounded tail, till it seemed as if a slippery sort of fire came from it into his hands. And his fingertips touched the two secret openings to her body, time after time, with a soft little brush of fire.

"An' if tha shits an' if tha pisses, I'm glad. I don't want a woman as couldna shit nor piss."

Connie couldn't help a sudden snort of astonished laughter, but he went on unmoved.

"Tha'rt real, tha art! Tha'rt real, even a bit of a bitch. Here tha shits an' here tha pisses: an' I lay my hand on 'em both an' like thee for it. I like thee for it. Tha's got a proper, woman's arse, proud of itself. It's none ashamed of itself, this isna."

He laid his hand close and firm over her secret places, in a kind of close greeting.

"I like it," he said. "I like it! An' if I only lived ten minutes, an' stroked thy arse an' got to know it, I should reckon I'd lived *one* life, sees ter! Industrial system or not! Here's one o' my lifetimes."

She turned round and climbed into his lap, clinging to him. "Kiss me!" she whispered.

And she knew the thought of their separation was latent in both their minds, and at last she was sad.

She sat on his thighs, her head against his breast, and her ivory-gleaming legs loosely apart, the fire glowing unequally upon them. Sitting with his head dropped, he looked at the folds of her body in the fireglow, and at the fleece of soft brown hair that hung down to a point between her open thighs. He reached to the table behind, and took up a bunch of flowers, still so wet that drops of rain fell on the floor.

"Flowers stops out of doors all weathers," he said. "They have no houses."

"Not even a hut!" she murmured.

With quiet fingers he threaded a few forget-me-not flowers in the fine brown fleece of the mount of Venus.

"There!" he said. "There's forget-me-nots in the right place!"

She looked down at the milky odd little flowers among the brown maiden-hair at the lower tip of her body.

"Doesn't it look pretty!" she said.

"Pretty as life," he replied.

And he stuck a pink campion-bud among the hair.

"There! That's me where you won't forget me! That's Moses in the bulrushes."

"You don't mind, do you, that I'm going away?" she asked wistfully, looking up into his face.

But his face was inscrutable, under the heavy brows. He kept it quite blank.

"You do as you wish," he said.

And he spoke in good English.

"But I won't go if you don't wish it," she said, clinging to him.

There was silence. He leaned and put another piece of wood on the fire. The flame glowed on his silent, abstracted face. She waited, but he said nothing.

"Only I thought it would be a good way to begin a break with Clifford. I do want a child. And it would give me a chance to, to—" she resumed.

"To let them think a few lies," he said.

"Yes, that among other things. Do you want them to think the truth?"

"I don't care what they think."

"I do! I don't want them handling me with their unpleasant cold minds, not while I'm still at Wragby. They can think what they like when I'm finally gone."

He was silent.

"But Sir Clifford expects you to come back to him?"

"Oh, I must come back," she said: and there was silence.

"And would you have a child in Wragby?" he asked.

She closed her arm round his neck.

"If you wouldn't take me away, I should have to," she said.

"Take you where to?"

"Anywhere! away! But right away from Wragby."

"When?"

"Why, when I come back."

"But what's the good of coming back, doing the thing twice, if you're once gone?" he said.

"Oh, I must come back. I've promised! I've promised so faithfully. Besides, I come back to you, really."

"To your husband's gamekeeper?"

"I don't see that that matters," she said.

"No?" He mused a while. "And when would you think of going away again, then; finally? When exactly?"

"Oh, I don't know. I'd come back from Venice. And then we'd prepare everything."

"How prepare?"

"Oh, I'd tell Clifford. I'd have to tell him."

"Would you!"

He remained silent. She put her arms fast round his neck.

"Don't make it difficult for me," she pleaded.

"Make what difficult?"

"For me to go to Venice and arrange things."

A little smile, half a grin, flickered on his face.

"I don't make it difficult," he said. "I only want to find out just what you are after. But you don't really know yourself. You want to take time: get away and look at it. I don't blame you. I think you're wise. You may prefer to stay mistress of Wragby. I don't blame you. I've no Wragbys to offer. In fact, you know what you'll get out of me. No, no, I think you're right! I really do! And I'm not keen on coming to live on you, being kept by you. There's that too."

She felt, somehow, as if he were giving her tit for tat.

"But you want me, don't you?" she asked.

"Do you want me?"

"You know I do. *That's* evident."

"Quite! And *when* do you want me?"

"You know we can arrange it all when I come back. Now I'm out of breath with you. I must get calm and clear."

"Quite! Get calm and clear!"

She was a little offended.

"But you trust me, don't you?" she said.

"Oh, absolutely!"

She heard the mockery in his tone.

"Tell me, then," she said flatly, "do you think it would be better if I *don't* go to Venice?"

"I'm sure it's better if you *do* go to Venice," he replied in the cool, slightly mocking voice.

"You know it's next Thursday?" she said.

"Yes!"

She now began to muse. At last she said:

"And we *shall* know better where we are when I come back, shan't we?"

"Oh, surely!"

The curious gulf of silence between them!

"I've been to the lawyer about my divorce," he said, a little constrainedly.

She gave a slight shudder.

"Have you!" she said. "And what did he say?"

"He said I ought to have done it before; that may be a difficulty. But since I was in the army, he thinks it will go through all right. If only it doesn't bring *her* down on my head!"

"Will she have to know?"

"Yes! she is served with a notice: so is the man she lives with, the co-respondent."

"Isn't it hateful, all the performances! I suppose I'd have to go through it with Clifford."

There was a silence.

"And of course," he said, "I have to live an exemplary life for the next six or eight months. So if you go to Venice, there's temptation removed for a week or two, at least."

"Am I temptation!" she said, stroking his face. "I'm so glad I'm temptation to you! Don't let's think about it! You frighten me when you start thinking: you roll me out flat. Don't let's think about it. We can think so much when we are apart. That's the whole point! I've been thinking, I *must* come to you for another night before I go. I must come once more to the cottage. Shall I come on Thursday night?"

"Isn't that when your sister will be there?"

"Yes! But she said we would start at teatime. So we could start at teatime. But she could sleep somewhere else and I could sleep with you."

"But then she'd have to know."

"Oh, I shall tell her. I've more or less told her already. I must talk it all over with Hilda. She's a great help, so sensible."

He was thinking of her plan.

"So you'd start off from Wragby at teatime, as if you were going to London? Which way were you going?"

"By Nottingham and Grantham."

"And then your sister would drop you somewhere and you'd walk or drive back here? Sounds very risky, to me."

"Does it? Well then, Hilda could bring me back. She could sleep at Mansfield, and bring me back here in the evening, and fetch me again in the morning. It's quite easy."

"And the people who see you?"

"I'll wear goggles and a veil."

He pondered for some time.

"Well," he said. "You please yourself, as usual."

"But wouldn't it please you?"

"Oh, yes! It'd please me all right," he said a little grimly. "I might as well smite while the iron's hot."

"Do you know what I thought?" she said suddenly. "It suddenly came to me. You are the 'Knight of the Burning Pestle!' "

"Ay! And you? Are you the Lady of the Red-Hot Mortar?"

"Yes!" she said. "Yes! You're Sir Pestle and I'm Lady Mortar."

"All right, then I'm knighted. John Thomas is Sir John, to your Lady Jane."

"Yes! John Thomas is knighted! I'm my-lady-maiden-hair, and you must have flowers too. Yes!"

She threaded two pink campions in the bush of red-gold hair above his penis.

"There!" she said. "Charming! Charming! Sir John!"

And she pushed a bit of forget-me-not in the dark hair of his breast.

"And you won't forget me *there*, will you?" she kissed him on the breast, and made two bits of forget-me-not lodge one over each nipple, kissing him again.

"Make a calendar of me!" he said. He laughed and the flowers shook from his breast.

"Wait a bit!" he said.

He rose, and opened the door of the hut. Flossie, lying in the porch, got up and looked at him.

"Ay, it's me!" he said.

The rain had ceased. There was a wet, heavy perfumed stillness. Evening was approaching.

He went out and down the little path in the opposite direction from the riding. Connie watched his thin, white figure, and it looked to her like a ghost, an apparition moving away from her.

When she could see it no more, her heart sank. She stood in the door of the hut, with a blanket round her, looking into the drenched motionless silence.

But he was coming back, trotting strangely, and carrying flowers. She was a little afraid of him, as if he were not quite human. And when he came near, his eyes looked into hers, but she could not understand the meaning.

He had brought columbines and campions, and new-mown hay, and oak-tufts and honeysuckle in small bud. He fastened fluffy young oak sprays round her breasts, sticking in tufts of bluebells and campion: and in her navel he poised a pink campion flower, and in her maiden-hair were forget-me-nots and woodruff.

"That's you in all your glory!" he said. "Lady Jane, at her wedding with John Thomas."

And he stuck flowers in the hair of his own body, and wound a bit of creeping-jenny round his penis, and stuck a single bell of a hyacinth in his navel. She watched him with amusement, his odd intentness. And she pushed a campion flower in his moustache, where it stuck dangling under his nose.

"This is John Thomas marryin' Lady Jane," he said. "An' we mun let Constance an' Oliver go their ways. Maybe—"

He spread out his hand with a gesture, and then he sneezed, sneezing away the flowers from his nose and his navel. He sneezed again.

"Maybe what?" she said, waiting for him to go on.

"Eh?" he said.

"Maybe what? Go on with what you were going to say," she insisted.

"Ay, what *was* I going to say?"

He had forgotten. And it was one of the disappointments of her life, that he never finished.

A yellow ray of sun shone over the trees.

"Sun!" he said. "And time you went. Time, my lady, time! What's that as flies without wings, your ladyship? Time! Time!"

He reached for his shirt.

"Say good night! to John Thomas," he said, looking down at his penis. "He's safe in the arms of creeping-jenny! Not much burning pestle about him just now."

And he put his flannel shirt over his head.

"A man's most dangerous moment," he said, when his head emerged, "is when he's getting into his shirt. Then he puts his head in a bag. That's why I prefer those American shirts, that you put on like a jacket." She still stood watching him. He stepped into his short drawers, and buttoned them round his waist.

"Look at Jane!" he said. "In all her blossoms! Who'll put blossoms on you next year, Jinny? Me, or somebody else? 'Good-bye my bluebell, farewell to you!' I hate that song, it's early war days." He had sat down, and was pulling on his stockings. She still stood unmoving. He laid his hand on the slope of her buttocks. "Pretty little lady Jane!" he said. "Perhaps in Venice you'll find a man who'll put jasmine in your maiden-hair, and a pomegranate flower in your navel. Poor little lady Jane!"

"Don't say those things!" she said. "You only say them to hurt me."

He dropped his head. Then he said, in dialect:

"Ay, maybe I do, maybe I do! Well then, I'll say nowt, an' ha' done wi't. But tha mun dress thysen, an' go back to thy stately homes of England, how beautiful they stand. Time's up. Time's up for Sir John, an' for little lady Jane! Put thy shimmy on, Lady Chatterley! Tha might be anybody, standin' there be-out even a shimmy, an' a few rags o' flowers. There then, there then, I'll undress thee, tha bob-tailed young throstle." And he took the leaves from her hair, kissing her damp hair, and the flowers from her breasts, and kissed her breasts, and kissed her navel, and kissed her maiden-hair, where he left the flowers threaded. "They mun stop while they will," he said. "So! There th'art bare again, nowt but a bare-arsed lass an' a bit of a lady Jane! Now put thy shimmy on, for tha mun go, or else Lady Chatterley's goin' to be late for dinner, an' where 'ave yer been to my pretty maid!"

She never knew how to answer him when he was in this condition of the vernacular. So she dressed herself and prepared to go a little ignominiously home to Wragby. Or so she felt it: a little ignominiously home.

He would accompany her to the broad riding. His young pheasants were all right under the shelter.

When he and she came out onto the riding, there was Mrs. Bolton faltering palely towards them.

"Oh, my Lady, we wondered if anything had happened!"

"No! Nothing has happened."

Mrs. Bolton looked into the man's face, that was smooth and new-looking with love. She met his half-laughing, half-mocking eyes. He always laughed at mischance. But he looked at her kindly.

"Evening, Mrs. Bolton! Your Ladyship will be all right now, so I can leave you. Good night to your Ladyship! Good night, Mrs. Bolton!"

He saluted and turned away.

❖ 16 ❖

Connie arrived home to an ordeal of cross-questioning. Clifford had been out at teatime, had come in just before the storm, and where was her ladyship? Nobody knew, only Mrs. Bolton suggested she had gone for a walk into the wood. Into the wood, in such a storm!—Clifford for once let himself get into a state of nervous frenzy. He started at every flash of lightning, and blenched at every roll of thunder. He looked at the icy thunder-rain as if it were the end of the world. He got more and more worked up.

Mrs. Bolton tried to soothe him.

"She'll be sheltering in the hut, till it's over. Don't worry, her ladyship is all right."

"I don't like her being in the wood in a storm like this! I don't like her being in the wood at all! She's been gone now more than two hours. When did she go out?"

"A little while before you came in."

"I didn't see her in the park. God knows where she is and what has happened to her."

"Oh, nothing's happened to her. You'll see, she'll be home directly after the rain stops. It's just the rain that's keeping her."

But her ladyship did not come home directly the rain stopped. In fact time went by, the sun came out for his last yellow glimpse, and there was still no sign of her. The sun was set, it was growing dark, and the first dinner-gong had rung.

"It's no good!" said Clifford in a frenzy. "I'm going to send out Field and Betts to find her."

"Oh, don't do that!" cried Mrs. Bolton. "They'll think there's a suicide or something. Oh, don't start a lot of talk going—Let me slip over to the hut and see if she's not there. I'll find her all right."

So, after some persuasion, Clifford allowed her to go.

And so Connie had come upon her in the drive, alone and palely loitering.

"You mustn't mind me coming to look for you, my Lady! But Sir Clifford worked himself up into such a state. He made sure you were struck by lightning, or killed by a falling tree. And he was determined to send Field and Betts to the wood to find the body. So I thought I'd better come, rather than set all the servants agog."

She spoke nervously. She could still see on Connie's face the smoothness and the half-dream of passion, and she could feel the irritation against herself.

"Quite!" said Connie. And she could say no more.

The two women plodded on through the wet world, in silence, while great drops splashed like explosions in the wood. When they came to the park, Connie strode ahead, and Mrs. Bolton panted a little. She was getting plumper.

"How foolish of Clifford to make a fuss!" said Connie at length, angrily, really speaking to herself.

"Oh, you know what men are! They like working themselves up. But he'll be all right as soon as he sees your ladyship."

Connie was very angry that Mrs. Bolton knew her secret: for certainly she knew it.

Suddenly Constance stood still on the path.

"It's monstrous that I should have to be followed!" she said, her eyes flashing.

"Oh, your Ladyship, don't say that! He'd certainly have sent the two men, and they'd have come straight to the hut. I didn't know where it was, really."

Connie flushed darker with rage, at the suggestion. Yet, while her passion was on her, she could not lie. She could not even pretend there was nothing between herself and the keeper. She looked at the other woman, who stood so sly, with her head dropped: yet somehow, in her femaleness, an ally.

"Oh well!" she said. "If it is so, it is so. I don't mind!"

"Why, you're all right, my Lady! You've only been sheltering in the hut. It's absolutely nothing."

They went on to the house. Connie marched into Clifford's room, furious with him, furious with his pale, overwrought face and prominent eyes.

"I must say, I don't think you need send the servants after me!" she burst out.

"My God!" he exploded. "Where have you been, woman? You've been gone hours, hours, and in a storm like this! What the hell do you go to that bloody wood for? What have you been up to? It's hours even since the rain stopped, hours! Do you know what time it is? You're enough to drive anybody mad. Where have you been? What in the name of hell have you been doing?"

"And what if I don't choose to tell you?" She pulled her hat from her head and shook her hair.

He looked at her with his eyes bulging, and yellow coming into the whites. It was very bad for him to get into these rages: Mrs. Bolton had a weary time with him, for days after. Connie felt a sudden qualm.

"But, really!" she said, milder. "Anyone would think I'd been I don't know where! I just sat in the hut during all the storm, and made myself a little fire, and was happy."

She spoke now easily. After all, why work him up any more! He looked at her suspiciously.

"And look at your hair!" he said; "look at yourself!"

"Yes!" she replied calmly. "I ran out into the rain with no clothes on."

He stared at her speechless.

"You must be mad!" he said.

"Why? To like a shower bath from the rain?"

"And how did you dry yourself?"

"On an old towel and at the fire."

He still stared at her in a dumbfounded way.

"And supposing anybody came," he said.

"Who would come?"

"Who? Why, anybody! And Mellors. Does he come? He must come in the evenings."

"Yes, he came later, when it had cleared up, to feed the pheasants with corn."

She spoke with amazing nonchalance. Mrs. Bolton, who was listening in the next room, heard in sheer admiration. To think a woman would carry it off so naturally!

"And suppose he'd come while you were running about in the rain with nothing on, like a maniac?"

"I suppose he'd have had the fright of his life, and cleared out as fast as he could."

Clifford still stared at her transfixed. What he thought in his under-consciousness he would never know. And he was too much taken aback to form one clear thought in his upper consciousness. He just simply accepted what she said, in a sort of blank. And he admired her. He could not help admiring her. She looked flushed and handsome and smooth: love-smooth.

"At least," he said, subsiding, "you'll be lucky if you've got off without a severe cold."

"Oh, I haven't got a cold," she replied. She was thinking to herself of the other man's words: Tha's got the nicest woman's arse of anybody! She wished, she dearly wished she could tell Clifford that this had been said to her, during the famous thunderstorm. However! She bore herself rather like an offended queen and went upstairs to change.

That evening, Clifford wanted to be nice to her. He was reading one of the latest scientific-religious books: he had a streak of a spurious sort of religion in him, and was egocentrically concerned with the future of his own ego. It was like his habit to make conversation to Connie about some book, since the conversation between them had to be made, almost chemically. They had almost chemically to concoct it in their heads.

"What do you think of this, by the way?" he said, reaching for his book. "You'd have no need to cool your ardent body by running out in the rain, if only we had a few more aeons of evolution behind us. Ah, here it is!—'The universe shows us two aspects: on one side it is physically wasting, on the other it is spiritually ascending.' "

Connie listened, expecting more. But Clifford was waiting. She looked at him in surprise.

"And if it spiritually ascends," she said, "what does it leave down below, in the place where its tail used to be?"

"Ah!" he said. "Take the man for what he means. *Ascending* is the opposite of his *wasting*, I presume."

"Spiritually blown out, so to speak!"

"No. But seriously, without joking: do you think there is anything in it?"

She looked at him again.

"Physically wasting?" she said. "I see you getting fatter, and I'm not wasting myself. Do you think the sun is smaller than he used to be? He's not, to me. And I suppose the apple Adam offered Eve wasn't really much bigger, if any, than one of our orange pippins. Do you think it was?"

"Well, hear how he goes on: 'It is thus slowly passing, with a slowness inconceivable in our measures of time, to new creative conditions, amid which the physical world, as we at present know it, will be represented by a ripple barely to be distinguished from nonentity.' "

She listened with a glisten of amusement. All sorts of improper things suggested themselves. But she only said:

"What silly hocus-pocus! As if his little conceited consciousness could know what was happening as slowly as all that! It only means *he's* a physical failure on earth, so he wants to make the whole universe a physical failure. Priggish little impertinence!"

"Oh, but listen! Don't interrupt the great man's solemn words!—The present type of order in the world has risen from an unimaginable past, and will find its grave in an unimaginable future. There remains the inexhaustive realm of abstract forms, and creativity with its shifting character ever determined afresh by its own creatures, and God, upon whose wisdom all forms of order depend—There, that's how he winds up!"

Connie sat listening contemptuously.

"He's spiritually blown out," she said. "What a lot of stuff! Unimaginables, and types of order in graves, and realms of abstract forms, and creativity with a shifty character, and God mixed up with forms of order! Why, it's idiotic!"

"I must say, it is a little vaguely conglomerate, a mixture of gases, so to speak," said Clifford. "Still, I think there is something in the idea that the universe is physically wasting and spiritually ascending."

"Do you? Then let it ascend, so long as it leaves me safely and solidly physically here below."

"Do you like your physique?" he asked.

"I love it!" And through her mind went the words: It's the nicest, nicest woman's arse as is!

"But that is really rather extraordinary, because there's no denying it's an encumbrance. But then, I suppose a woman doesn't take a supreme pleasure in the life of the mind."

"Supreme pleasure?" she said, looking up at him. "Is that sort of idiocy the supreme pleasure of the life of the mind? No, thank you! Give me the body. I believe the life of the body is a greater reality than the life of the mind: when the body is really awakened to life. But so many people, like your famous wind-machine, have only got minds tacked onto their physical corpses."

He looked at her in wonder.

"The life of the body," he said, "is just the life of the animals."

"And that's better than the life of professional corpses. But it's not true! The human body is only just coming to real life. With the Greeks it gave a lovely flicker, then Plato and Aristotle killed it, and Jesus finished it off. But now the body is coming really to life, it is really rising from the tomb. And it will be a lovely, lovely life in the lovely universe, the life of the human body."

"My dear, you speak as if you were ushering it all in! True, you are going away on a holiday: but don't please be quite so indecently elated about it. Believe me, whatever God there is is slowly eliminating the guts and alimentary system from the human being, to evolve a higher, more spiritual being."

"Why should I believe you, Clifford, when I feel that whatever God there is has at last wakened up in my guts, as you call them, and is rippling so happily there, like dawn? Why should I believe you, when I feel so very much the contrary?"

"Oh, exactly! And what has caused this extraordinary change in you? running out stark naked in the rain, and playing Bacchante? Desire for sensation, or the anticipation of going to Venice?"

"Both! Do you think it is horrid of me to be so thrilled at going off?" she said.

"Rather horrid to show it so plainly."

"Then I'll hide it."

"Oh, don't trouble! You almost communicate a thrill to me. I almost feel that it is *I* who am going off."

"Well, why don't you come?"

"We've gone over all that. And, as a matter of fact, I suppose your greatest thrill comes from being able to say a temporary farewell to all this. Nothing so thrilling, for the moment, as Good-bye-to-it-all!—But every parting means a meeting elsewhere. And every meeting is a new bondage."

"I am not going to enter any new bondages."

"Don't boast, while the gods are listening," he said.

She pulled up short.

"No! I won't boast!" she said.

But she was thrilled, none the less, to be going off; to feel bonds snap. She couldn't help it.

Clifford, who couldn't sleep, gambled all night with Mrs. Bolton, till she was too sleepy almost to live.

And the day came around for Hilda to arrive. Connie had arranged with Mellors that if everything promised well for their night together, she would hang a green shawl out of the window. If there were frustration, a red one.

Mrs. Bolton helped Connie to pack.

"It will be so good for your ladyship to have a change."

"I think it will. You don't mind having Sir Clifford on your hands alone for a time, do you?"

"Oh, no! I can manage him quite all right. I mean, I can do all he needs me to do. Don't you think he's better than he used to be?"

"Oh, much! You do wonders with him."

"Do I though! But men are all alike: just babies and you have to flatter them and wheedle them and let them think they're having their own way. Don't you find it so, my Lady?"

"I'm afraid I haven't much experience."

Connie paused in her occupation.

"Even your husband, did you have to manage him, and wheedle him like a baby?" she asked, looking at the other woman.

Mrs. Bolton paused too.

"Well!" she said. "I had to do a good bit of coaxing with him too. But he always knew what I was after, I must say that. But he generally gave in to me."

"He was never the lord and master thing?"

"No! At least, there'd be a look in his eyes sometimes, and then I knew *I'd* got to give in. But usually he gave in to me. No, he was never lord and master. But neither was I. I knew when I could go no further with him, and then I gave in: though it cost me a good bit, sometimes."

"And what if you had held out against him?"

"Oh, I don't know. I never did. Even when he was in the wrong, if he was fixed, I gave in. You see, I never wanted to break what was between us. And if you really set your will against a man, that finishes it. If you care for a man, you have to give in to him once he's really determined; whether you're in the right or not, you have to give in. Else you break something. But I must say, Ted 'ud give in to me sometimes, when I was set on a thing, and in the wrong. So I suppose it cuts both ways."

"And that's how you are with all your patients?" asked Connie.

"Oh, that's different. I don't care at all, in the same way. I know what's good for them, or I try to, and then I just contrive to manage them for their own good. It's not like anybody as you're really fond of. It's quite different. Once you've been really fond of a man, you can be affectionate to almost any man, if he needs you at all. But it's not the same thing. You don't really *care*. I doubt, once you've *really* cared, if you can ever really care again."

These words frightened Connie.

"Do you think one can only care once?" she asked.

"Or never. Most women never care, never begin to. They don't know what it means. Nor men either. But when I see a woman as cares, my heart stands still for her."

"And do you think men easily take offense?"

"Yes! If you wound them on their pride. But aren't women the same? Only, our two prides are a bit different."

Connie pondered this. She began again to have some misgiving about her going away. After all, was she not giving her man the go-by, if only for a short time? And he knew it. That's why he was so queer and sarcastic.

Still! the human existence is a good deal controlled by the machine of external circumstance. She was in the power of this machine. She couldn't extricate herself all in five minutes. She didn't even want to.

Hilda arrived in good time on Thursday morning, in a nimble two-seater car, with her suitcase strapped firmly behind. She looked as demure and maidenly as ever, but she had the same will of her own. She had the very hell of a will of her own, as her husband had found out. But her husband was now divorcing her. Yes, she even made it easy for him to do that, though she had no lover. For the time being, she was "off" men. She was very well content to be quite her own mistress: and mistress of her two children, whom she was going to bring up "properly," whatever that may mean.

Connie was only allowed a suitcase, also. But she had sent on a trunk to her father, who was going by train. No use taking a car to Venice. And Italy was much too hot to motor in, in July. He was going comfortably by train. He had just come down from Scotland.

So, like a demure arcadian field marshal, Hilda arranged the material part of the journey. She and Connie sat in the upstairs room, chatting.

"But, Hilda!" said Connie, a little frightened. "I want to stay near here tonight. Not here: near here!"

Hilda fixed her sister with gray, inscrutable eyes. She seemed so calm: and she was so often furious.

"Where, near here?" she asked softly.

"Well, you know I love somebody, don't you?"

"I gathered there was something."

"Well, he lives near here, and I want to spend this last night with him. I must! I've promised."

Connie became insistent.

Hilda bent her Minerva-like head in silence. Then she looked up.

"Do you want to tell me who he is," she said.

"He's our gamekeeper," faltered Connie, and she flushed vividly, like a shamed child.

"Connie!" said Hilda, lifting her nose slightly with disgust: a motion she had from her mother.

"I know: but he's lovely, really. He really understands tenderness," said Connie, trying to apologize for him.

Hilda, like a ruddy, rich-colored Athena, bowed her head and pondered. She was really violently angry. But she dared not show it, because Connie, taking after her father, would straightway become obstreperous and unmanageable.

It was true, Hilda did not like Clifford: his cool assurance that he was somebody! She thought he made use of Connie shamefully and impudently. She had hoped her sister *would* leave him. But, being solid Scotch middle class, she loathed any "lowering" of oneself, or the family. She looked up at last.

"You'll regret it," she said.

"I shan't," cried Connie, flushing red. "He's quite the exception. I *really* love him. He's lovely as a lover."

Hilda still pondered.

"You'll get over him quite soon," she said, "and live to be ashamed of yourself because of him."

"I shan't! I hope I'm going to have a child of his."

"*Connie*!" said Hilda, hard as a hammer-stroke, and pale with anger.

"I shall, if I possibly can. I should be fearfully proud if I had a child by him."

It was no use talking to her. Hilda pondered.

"And doesn't Clifford suspect?" she said.

"Oh, no! Why should he?"

"I've no doubt you've given him plenty of occasion for suspicion," said Hilda.

"Not at all."

"And tonight's business seems quite gratuitous folly. Where does the man live?"

"In the cottage at the other end of the wood."

"Is he a bachelor?"

"No! His wife left him."

"How old?"

"I don't know. Older than me."

Hilda became more angry at every reply, angry as her mother used to be, in a kind of paroxysm. But she still hid it.

"I would give up tonight's escapade if I were you," she advised calmly.

"I can't! I *must* stay with him tonight, or I can't go to Venice at all. I just can't."

Hilda heard her father over again, and she gave way, out of mere diplomacy. And she consented to drive to Mansfield, both of them, to dinner, to bring Connie back to the lane-end after dark, and to fetch her from the lane-end the next morning, herself sleeping in Mansfield, only half-an-hour away, good going. But she was furious. She stored it up against her sister, this balk in her plans.

Connie flung an emerald-green shawl over her windowsill.

On the strength of her anger, Hilda warmed towards Clifford. After all, he had a mind. And if he had no sex, functionally, all the better; so much the less to quarrel about. Hilda wanted no more of that sex business, where men became nasty, selfish little horrors. Connie really had less to put up with than many women, if she did but know it.

And Clifford decided that Hilda, after all, was a decidedly intelligent woman, and would make a man a first-rate helpmeet, if he were going in for politics, for example. Yes, she had none of Connie's silliness, Connie was more a child: you had to make excuses for her, because she was not altogether dependable.

There was an early cup of tea in the hall, where doors were open to let in the sun. Everybody seemed to be panting a little.

"Goodbye, Connie girl! Come back to me safely."

"Goodbye, Clifford! Yes, I shan't be long." Connie was almost tender.

"Goodbye, Hilda! You will keep an eye on her, won't you?"

"I'll even keep two!" said Hilda. "She shan't go very far astray."

"It's a promise!"

"Goodbye, Mrs. Bolton. I know you'll look after Sir Clifford nobly."

"I'll do what I can, your Ladyship."

"And write to me if there is any news, and tell me about Sir Clifford, how he is."

"Very good, your Ladyship, I will. And have a good time, and come back and cheer us up."

Everybody waved. The car went off. Connie looked back and saw Clifford sitting at the top of the steps in his house-chair. After all, he was her husband: Wragby was her home: circumstance had done it.

Mrs. Chambers held the gate and wished her ladyship a happy holiday. The car slipped out of the dark spinney that masked the park, onto the highroad where the colliers were trailing home. Hilda turned to the Crosshill Road, that was not a main road, but ran to Mansfield. Connie put on goggles. They ran beside the railway, which was in a cutting below them. Then they crossed the cutting on a bridge.

"That's the lane to the cottage!" said Connie.

Hilda glanced at it impatiently.

"It's a frightful pity we can't go straight off!" she said. "We could have been in Pall Mall by nine o'clock."

"I'm sorry for your sake," said Connie, from behind her goggles.

They were soon at Mansfield, that once-romantic, now utterly disheartening colliery town. Hilda stopped at the hotel named in the motorcar book, and took a room. The whole thing was utterly uninteresting, and she was almost too angry to talk. However, Connie *had* to tell her something of the man's history.

"*He*! *He*! What name do you call him by? You only say *he*," said Hilda.

"I've never called him by any name: nor he me: which is curious, when you come to think of it. Unless we say Lady Jane and John Thomas. But his name is Oliver Mellors."

"And how would you like to be Mrs. Oliver Mellors, instead of Lady Chatterley?"

"I'd love it."

There was nothing to be done with Connie. And anyhow, if the man had been a lieutenant in the army in India for four or five years, he must be more or less presentable. Apparently he had character. Hilda began to relent a little.

"But you'll be through with him in a while," she said, "and then you'll be ashamed of having been connected with him. One *can't* mix up with the working people."

"But you are such a socialist! you're always on the side of the working classes."

"I may be on their side in a political crisis, but being on their side makes me know how impossible it is to mix one's life with theirs. Not out of snobbery, but just because the whole rhythm is different."

Hilda had lived among the real political intellectuals, so she was disastrously unanswerable.

The nondescript evening in the hotel dragged out, and at last they had a nondescript dinner. Then Connie slipped a few things into a little silk bag, and combed her hair once more.

"After all, Hilda," she said, "love can be wonderful; when you feel you *live*, and are in the very middle of creation." It was almost like bragging on her part.

"I suppose every mosquito feels the same," said Hilda.

"Do you think it does? How nice for it!"

The evening was wonderfully clear and long-lingering even in the small town. It would be half-light all night. With a face like a mask, from resentment, Hilda started her car again, and the two sped back on their tracks, taking the other road, through Bolsover.

Connie wore her goggles and disguising cap, and she sat in silence. Because of Hilda's opposition, she was fiercely on the side of the man, she would stand by him through thick and thin.

They had their headlights on, by the time they passed Crosshill, and the small lit-up train that chuffed past in the cutting made it seem like real night. Hilda had calculated the turn into the lane at the bridge-end. She slowed up rather suddenly and swerved off the road, the lights glaring white into the grassy, overgrown lane. Connie looked out. She saw a shadowy figure, and she opened the door.

"Here we are!" she said softly.

But Hilda had switched off the lights, and was absorbed backing, making the turn.

"Nothing on the bridge?" she asked shortly.

"You're all right," said the man's voice.

She backed on to the bridge, reversed, let the car run forward a few yards along the road, then backed into the lane, under a wych-elm tree, crushing the grass and bracken. Then all the lights went out. Connie stepped down. The man stood under the trees.

"Did you wait long?" Connie asked.

"Not so very," he replied.

They both waited for Hilda to get out. But Hilda shut the door of the car and sat tight.

"This is my sister Hilda. Won't you come and speak to her? Hilda! This is Mr. Mellors."

The keeper lifted his hat, but went no nearer.

"Do walk down to the cottage with us, Hilda," Connie pleaded. "It's not far."

"What about the car?"

"People do leave them in the lanes. You have the key."

Hilda was silent, deliberating. Then she looked backwards down the lane.

"Can I back round that bush?" she said.

"Oh, yes!" said the keeper.

She backed slowly round the curve, out of sight of the road, locked the car, and got down. It was night, but luminous dark. The hedges rose high and wild, by the unused lane, and very dark seeming. There was a fresh sweet scent on the air. The keeper went ahead, then came Connie, then Hilda, and in silence. He lit up the difficult places with a flashlight torch, and they went on again, while an owl softly hooted over the oaks, and Flossie padded silently around. Nobody could speak. There was nothing to say.

At length Connie saw the yellow light of the house, and her heart beat fast. She was a little frightened. They trailed on, still in Indian file.

He unlocked the door and preceded them into the warm but bare little room. The fire burned low and red in the grate. The table was set with two plates and two glasses, on a proper white tablecloth for once. Hilda shook her hair and looked round the bare, cheerless room. Then she summoned her courage and looked at the man.

He was moderately tall, and thin, and she thought him good-looking. He kept a quiet distance of his own, and seemed absolutely unwilling to speak.

"Do sit down, Hilda," said Connie.

"Do!" he said. "Can I make you tea or anything, or will you drink a glass of beer? It's moderately cool."

"Beer!" said Connie.

"Beer for me, please!" said Hilda, with a mock sort of shyness. He looked at her and blinked.

He took a blue jug and tramped to the scullery. When he came back with the beer, his face had changed again.

Connie sat down by the door, and Hilda sat in his seat, with the back to the wall, against the window corner.

"That is his chair," said Connie softly. And Hilda rose as if it had burnt her.

"Sit yer still, sit yer still! Ta'e ony cheer as yo'n a mind to, none of us is th' big bear," he said, with complete equanimity.

And he brought Hilda a glass, and poured her beer first from the blue jug.

"As for cigarettes," he said, "I've got none, but 'appen you've got your own. I dunna smoke, mysen. Shall y' eat summat?"—He turned direct to Connie: "Shall t'eat a smite o' summat, if I bring it thee? Tha can usually do wi' a bite." He spoke the vernacular with a curious calm assurance, as if he were the landlord of the inn.

"What is there?" asked Connie, flushing.

"Boiled ham, cheese, pickled wa'nuts, if yer like—Nowt much."

"Yes," said Connie. "Won't you, Hilda?"

Hilda looked up at him.

"Why do you speak Yorkshire?" she said softly.

"That! That's non Yorkshire, that's Derby."

He looked back at her with that faint, distant grin.

"Derby, then! Why do you speak Derby? You spoke natural English at first."

"Did Ah though? An' canna Ah change if Ah'n a mind to it? Nay, nay, let me talk Derby if it suits me. If yo'n nowt against it."

"It sounds a little affected," said Hilda.

"Ay, 'appen so! An' up i' Tevershall yo'd sound affected." He looked again at her, with a queer calculating distance, along his cheekbones, as if to say: Yi, an' who are you?

He tramped away to the pantry for the food.

The sisters sat in silence. He brought another plate, and knife and fork. Then he said:

"An' if it's the same to you, I s'll ta'e my coat off, like I allers do."

And he took off his coat, and hung it on the peg, then sat down to the table, in his shirtsleeves: a shirt of thin, cream-colored flannel.

" 'Elp yerselves!" he said. " 'Elp yerselves! Dunna wait f'r axin'!"

He cut the bread, then sat motionless. Hilda felt, as Connie once used to, his power of silence and distance. She saw his smallish, sensitive, loose hand on the table. He was no simple working man, not he: he was acting! Acting!

"Still!" she said, as she took a little cheese. "It would be more natural if you spoke to us in normal English, not in vernacular."

He looked at her, feeling her devil of a will.

"Would it?" he said in the normal English. "Would it? Would anything that was said between you and me be quite natural, unless you said you wished me to hell before your sister ever saw me again: and unless I said something almost as unpleasant back again? Would anything else be natural?"

"Oh, yes!" said Hilda. "Just good manners would be quite natural."

"Second nature, so to speak!" he said: then he began to laugh. "Nay," he said. "I'm weary o' manners. Let me be!"

Hilda was frankly baffled and furiously annoyed. After all, he might show that he realized he was being honored. Instead of which, with his playacting and lordly airs, he seemed to think it was he who was conferring the honor. Just impudence! Poor misguided Connie, in the man's clutches!

The three ate in silence. Hilda looked to see what his table manners were like. She could not help realizing that he was instinctively much more delicate and well-bred than herself. She had a certain Scottish clumsiness. And moreover, he had all the quiet self-contained assurance of the English, no loose edges. It would be very difficult to get the better of him.

"And do you really think," she said, a little more humanly, "it's worth the risk?"

"Is what worth what risk?"

"This escapade with my sister."

He flickered his irritating grin.

"Yo' maun ax 'er!"

Then he looked at Connie.

"Tha comes o' thine own accord, lass, doesn't yer? It's non me as forces thee?"

Connie looked at Hilda.

"I wish you wouldn't cavil, Hilda."

"Naturally, I don't want to. But someone has to think about things. You've got to have some continuity in your life. You can't just go making a mess."

There was a moment's pause.

"Eh, continuity!" he said. "An' what by that? What continuity 'ave yer got i' *your* life? I thought you was gettin' divorced. What continuity's that? Continuity o' yer own stubbornness. I can see that much. An' what good's it goin' to do yer? Yo'll be sick o' yer continuity afore yer a fat sight older. A stubborn woman an' 'er own self-will: ay, they make a fast continuity, they do. Thank heaven, it isn't me as 'as got th' 'andlin' of yer!"

"What right have you to speak like that to me?" said Hilda.

"Right! What right ha' yo' ter start harnessin' other folks i' your Continuity? Leave folks to their own continuities."

"My dear man, do you think I am concerned with you?" said Hilda softly.

"Ay," he said. "Yo' are. For it's a force-put. Yo' more or less my sister-in-law."

"Still far from it, I assure you."

"Not a' that far, I assure *you*. I've got my own sort o' continuity, back your life! Good as yours, any day. An' if your sister there comes ter me for a bit o' cunt an' tenderness, she knows what she's after. She's been in my bed afore: which you 'aven't, thank the Lord, with your continuity." There was a dead pause, before he added: "—Eh, I don't wear me breeches arse-forrards. An' if I get a windfall, I thank my stars. A man gets a lot of enjoyment out o' that lass theer, which is more than anybody gets out o' th' likes o' you. Which is a pity, for you might 'appen a' bin a good apple, 'stead of a handsome crab. Women like you needs proper graftin'."

He was looking at her with an odd, flickering smile, faintly sensual and appreciative.

"And men like you," she said, "ought to be segregated: justifying their own vulgarity and selfish lust."

"Ay, ma'am. It's a mercy there's a few men left like me. But you deserve what you get: to be left severely alone."

Hilda had risen and gone to the door. He rose and took his coat from the peg.

"I can find my way quite well alone," she said.

"I doubt you can't," he replied easily.

They tramped in ridiculous file down the lane again, in silence. An owl still hooted. He knew he ought to shoot it.

The car stood untouched, a little dewy. Hilda got in and started the engine. The other two waited.

"All I mean," she said from her entrenchment, "is that I doubt if you'll find it's been worth it, either of you!"

"One man's meat is another man's poison," he said, out of the darkness. "But it's meat an' drink to me."

The lights flared out.

"Don't make me wait in the morning, Connie."

"No, I won't. Good night!"

The car rose slowly on to the highroad, then slid swiftly away, leaving the night silent.

Connie timidly took his arm, and they went down the lane. He did not speak. At length she drew him to a standstill.

"Kiss me!" she murmured.

"Nay, wait a bit! Let me simmer down," he said.

That amused her. She still kept hold of his arm, and they went quickly down the lane, in silence. She was so glad to be with him, just now. She shivered, knowing that Hilda might have snatched her away. He was inscrutably silent.

When they were in the cottage again, she almost jumped with pleasure, that she should be free of her sister.

"But you were horrid to Hilda," she said to him.

"She should ha' been slapped in time."

"But why? and she's *so* nice."

He didn't answer, went round doing the evening chores, with a quiet, inevitable sort of motion. He was outwardly angry, but not with her. So Connie felt. And his anger gave him a peculiar handsomeness, an inwardness and glisten that thrilled her and made her limbs go molten.

Still he took no notice of her.

Till he sat down and began to unlace his boots. Then he looked up at her from under his brows, on which the anger still sat firm.

"Shan't you go up?" he said. "There's a candle!"

He jerked his head swiftly to indicate the candle burning on the table. She took it obediently, and he watched the full curve of her hips as she went up the first stairs.

It was a night of sensual passion, in which she was a little startled and almost unwilling: yet pierced again with piercing thrills of sensuality, different, sharper, more terrible than the thrills of tenderness, but, at the moment, more desirable. Though a little frightened, she let him have his way, and the reckless, shameless sensuality shook her to her foundations, stripped her to the very last, and made a different woman of her. It was not really love. It was not voluptuousness. It was sensuality sharp and searing as fire, burning the soul to tinder.

Burning out the shames, the deepest, oldest shames, in the most secret places. It cost her an effort to let him have his way and his will of her. She had to be a passive, consenting thing, like a slave, a physical slave. Yet the passion licked round her, consuming, and when the sensual flame of it pressed through her bowels and breast, she really thought she was dying: yet a poignant, marvelous death.

She had often wondered what Abélard meant, when he said that in their year of love he and Heloïse had passed through all the stages and refinements of passion. The same thing, a thousand years ago: ten thousand years ago! The same on the Greek vases, everywhere! The refinements of passion, the extravagances of sensuality! And necessary, forever necessary, to burn out false shames and smelt out the heaviest ore of the body into purity. With the fire of sheer sensuality.

In the short summer night she learnt so much. She would have thought a woman would have died of shame. Instead of which, the shame died. Shame, which is fear: the deep organic shame, the old, old physical fear which crouches in the bodily roots of us, and can only be chased away by the sensual fire, at last it was roused up and routed by the phallic hunt of the man, and she came to the very heart of the jungle of herself. She felt, now, she had come to the real bedrock of her nature, and was essentially shameless. She was her sensual self, naked and unashamed. She felt a triumph, almost a vainglory. So! That was how it was! That was life! That was how oneself really was! There was nothing left to disguise or be ashamed of. She shared her ultimate nakedness with a man, another being.

And what a reckless devil the man was! really like a devil! One had to be strong to bear him. But it took some getting at, the core of the physical jungle, the last and deepest recess of organic shame. The phallus alone could explore it. And how he had pressed in on her!

And how, in fear, she had hated it. But how she had really wanted it! She knew now. At the bottom of her soul, fundamentally, she had needed this phallic hunting out, she had secretly wanted it, and she had believed that she would never get it. Now suddenly there it was, and a man was sharing her last and final nakedness, she was shameless.

What liars poets and everybody were! They made one think one wanted sentiment. When what one supremely wanted was this piercing, consuming, rather awful sensuality. To find a man who dared do it, without shame or sin or final misgiving! If he had been ashamed afterwards, and made one feel ashamed, how awful! What a pity most men are so doggy, a bit shameful, like Clifford! Like Michaelis even! Both sensually a bit doggy and humiliating. The supreme pleasure of the mind! And what is that to a woman? What is it, really, to the man either? He becomes merely messy and doggy, even in his mind. It needs sheer sensuality even to purify and quicken the mind. Sheer fiery sensuality, not messiness.

Ah God, how rare a thing a man is! They are all dogs that trot and sniff and copulate. To have found a man who was not afraid and not ashamed! She looked at him now, sleeping so like a wild animal asleep, gone, gone in the remoteness of it. She nestled down, not to be away from him.

Till his rousing waked her completely. He was sitting up in bed, looking down at her. She saw her own nakedness in his eyes, immediate knowledge of her.

And the fluid, male knowledge of herself seemed to flow to her from his eyes and wrap her voluptuously. Oh, how voluptuous and lovely it was to have limbs and body half-asleep, heavy and suffused with passion!

"Is it time to wake up?" she said.

"Half-past six."

She had to be at the lane-end at eight. Always, always, always this compulsion on one!

"I might make the breakfast and bring it up here: should I?" he said.

"Oh, yes!"

Flossie whimpered gently below. He got up and threw off his pyjamas, and rubbed himself with a towel. When the human being is full of courage and full of life, how beautiful it is! So she thought, as she watched him in silence.

"Draw the curtain, will you?"

The sun was shining already on the tender green leaves of morning, and the wood stood bluey-fresh, in the nearness. She sat up in bed, looking dreamily out through the dormer window, her naked arms pushing her naked breasts together. He was dressing himself. She was half-dreaming of life, a life together with him: just a life.

He was going, fleeing from her dangerous, crouching nakedness.

"Have I lost my nightie altogether?" she said.

He pushed his hand down in the bed, and pulled out the bit of flimsy silk.

"I knowed I felt silk at my ankles," he said.

But the nightdress was slit almost in two.

"Never mind!" she said. "It belongs here, really. I'll leave it."

"Ay, leave it, I can put it between my legs at night, for company. There's no name or mark on it, is there?"

She slipped on the torn thing, and sat dreamily looking out of the window. The window was open, the air of morning drifted in, and the sound of birds. Birds flew continuously past. Then she saw Flossie roaming out. It was morning.

Downstairs she heard him making the fire, pumping water, going out at the back door. By and by came the smell of bacon, and at length he came upstairs with a huge black tray that would only just go through the door. He set the tray on the bed, and poured out the tea. Connie squatted in her nightdress, and fell on her food hungrily. He sat on the one chair, with his plate on his knees.

"How good it is!" she said. "How nice to have breakfast together."

He ate in silence, his mind on the time that was quickly passing. That made her remember.

"Oh, how I wish I could stay here with you, and Wragby were a million miles away! It's Wragby I'm going away from really. You know that, don't you?"

"Ay!"

"And you promise we will live together and have a life together, you and me! You promise me, don't you?"

"Ay! When we can."

"Yes! And we *will*! We *will*, won't we?" She leaned over, making the tea spill, catching his wrist.

"Ay!" he said, tidying up the tea.

"We can't possibly *not* live together now, can we?" she said appealingly.

He looked up at her with his flickering grin.

"No!" he said. "Only, you've got to start in twenty-five minutes."

"Have I?" she cried. Suddenly he held up a warning finger, and rose to his feet.

Flossie had given a short bark, then three loud sharp yaps of warning.

Silent, he put his plate on the tray and went downstairs. Constance heard him go down the garden path. A bicycle bell tinkled outside there.

"Morning, Mr. Mellors! Registered letter!"

"Oh, ay! Got a pencil?"

"Here y'are!"

There was a pause.

"Canada!" said the stranger's voice.

"Ay! That's a mate o' mine out there in British Columbia. Dunno what he's got to register."

" 'Appen sent y'a fortune, like."

"More like wants summat."

Pause.

"Well! Lovely day again!"

"Ay!"

"Morning!"

"Morning!"

After a time he came upstairs again, looking a little angry.

"Postman," he said.

"Very early!" she replied.

"Rural round; he's mostly here by seven, when he does come."

"Did your mate send you a fortune?"

"No! Only some photographs and papers about a place out there in British Columbia."

"Would you go there?"

"I thought perhaps we might."

"Oh, yes! I believe it's lovely!"

But he was put out by the postman's coming.

"Them damned bikes, they're on you afore you know where you are. I hope he twigged nothing."

"After all, what could he twig?"

"You must get up now, and get ready. I'm just goin' ter look round outside."

She saw him go reconnoitering into the lane, with dog and gun. She went downstairs and washed, and was ready by the time he came back, with the few things in the little silk bag.

He locked up, and they set off, but through the wood, not down the lane. He was being wary.

"Don't you think one lives for times like last night?" she said to him.

"Ay! But there's the rest o' times to think on," he replied, rather short.

They plodded on down the overgrown path, he in front, in silence.

"And we *will* live together and make a life together, won't we?" she pleaded.

"Ay!" he replied, striding on without looking round. "When t' time comes! Just now you're off to Venice or somewhere."

She followed him dumbly, with sinking heart. Oh, now she *was* to go!

At last he stopped.

"I'll just strike across here," he said, pointing to the right.

But she flung her arms round his neck, and clung to him.

"But you'll keep the tenderness for me, won't you?" she whispered. "I loved last night. But you'll keep the tenderness for me, won't you?"

He kissed her and held her close for a moment. Then he sighed, and kissed her again.

"I must go an' look if th' car's there."

He strode over the low brambles and bracken, leaving a trail through the fern. For a minute or two he was gone. Then he came striding back.

"Car's not there yet," he said. "But there's the baker's cart on t' road."

He seemed anxious and troubled.

"Hark!"

They heard a car softly hoot as it came nearer. It slowed up on the bridge.

She plunged with utter mournfulness in his track through the fern, and came to a huge holly hedge. He was just behind her.

"Here! Go through there!" he said, pointing to a gap. "I shan't come out."

She looked at him in despair. But he kissed her and made her go. She crept in sheer misery through the holly and through the wooden fence, stumbled down the little ditch and up into the lane, where Hilda was just getting out of the car in vexation.

"Why, you're there!" said Hilda. "Where's *he?*"

"He's not coming."

Connie's face was running with tears as she got into the car with her little bag. Hilda snatched up the motoring helmet with the disfiguring goggles.

"Put it on!" she said. And Connie pulled on the disguise, then the long motoring coat, and she sat down, a goggling, inhuman, unrecognizable creature. Hilda started the car with a businesslike motion. They heaved out of the lane, and were away down the road. Connie had looked round, but there was no sight of him. Away! Away! She sat in bitter tears. The parting had come so suddenly, so unexpectedly. It was like death.

"Thank goodness you'll be away from him for some time!" said Hilda, turning to avoid Crosshill village.

❖ 17 ❖

"You see, Hilda," said Connie after lunch, when they were nearing London, "you have never known either real tenderness or real sensuality: and if you do know them, with the same person, it makes a great difference."

"For mercy's sake, don't brag about your experiences!" said Hilda. "I've never met the man yet who was capable of intimacy with a woman, giving himself up to her. That was what I wanted. I'm not keen on their self-satisfied tenderness, and their sensuality. I'm not content to be any man's little petsywetsy, nor his *chair à plaisir* either. I wanted a complete intimacy, and I didn't get it. That's enough for me."

Connie pondered this. Complete intimacy! She supposed that meant revealing everything concerning yourself to the other person, and his revealing everything concerning himself. But that was a bore. And all that weary self-consciousness between a man and a woman! a disease!

"I think you're too conscious of yourself all the time, with everybody," she said to her sister.

"I hope at least I haven't a slave nature," said Hilda.

"But perhaps you have! Perhaps you are a slave to your own idea of yourself."

Hilda drove in silence for some time after this piece of unheard-of insolence from that chit Connie.

"At least I'm not a slave to somebody else's idea of me: and the somebody else a servant of my husband's," she retorted at last, in crude anger.

"You see, it's not so," said Connie calmly.

She had always let herself be dominated by her elder sister. Now, though somewhere inside herself she was weeping, she was free of the dominion of *other women*. Ah! that in itself was a relief, like being given another life: to be free of the strange dominion and obsession of *other women*. How awful they were, women!

She was glad to be with her father, whose favorite she had always been. She and Hilda stayed in a little hotel off Pall Mall, and Sir Malcolm was in his club. But he took his daughters out in the evening, and they liked going with him.

He was still handsome and robust, though just a little afraid of the new world that had sprung up around him. He had got a second wife in Scotland, younger than himself, and richer. But he had as many holidays away from her as possible: just as with his first wife.

Connie sat next to him at the opera. He was moderately stout, and had stout thighs, but they were still strong and well-knit, the thighs of a healthy man who had taken his pleasure in life. His good-humored selfishness, his dogged sort of independence, his unrepenting sensuality, it seemed to Connie she could see them all in his well-knit, straight thighs. Just a man! And now becoming an old man, which is sad. Because in his strong, thick male legs there was none of the alert sensitiveness and power of tenderness which is the very essence of youth, that which never dies, once it is there.

Connie woke up to the existence of legs. They became more important to her than faces, which are no longer very real. How few people had live, alert legs. She looked at the men in the stalls. Great puddingy thighs in black pudding-cloth, or lean wooden sticks in black funeral stuff, or well-shaped young legs without any meaning whatever, either sensuality or tenderness or sensitiveness, just mere leggy ordinariness that pranced around. Not even any sensuality like her father's. They were all daunted, daunted out of existence.

But the women were not daunted. The awful mill-posts of most females! really shocking, really enough to justify murder! Or the poor thin legs! or the trim neat things in silk stockings, without the slightest look of life! Awful, the millions of meaningless legs prancing meaninglessly around!

But she was not happy in London. The people seemed so spectral and blank. They had no alive happiness, no matter how brisk and good-looking they were. It was all barren. And Connie had a woman's blind craving for happiness, to be assured of happiness.

In Paris at any rate she felt a bit of sensuality still. But what a weary, tired worn-out sensuality. Worn-out for lack of tenderness. Oh! Paris was sad. One of the saddest towns: weary of its now-mechanical sensuality, weary of the tension of money, money, money, weary even of resentment and conceit, just weary to death, and still not sufficiently Americanized or Londonized to hide the weariness under a mechanical jig-jig-jig! Ah, these manly he-men, these flaneurs, these oglers, these eaters of good dinners! How weary they were! Weary, worn-out for lack of a little tenderness given and taken. The efficient, sometimes charming women knew a thing or two about the sensual realities: they had that pull over their jigging English sisters. But they knew even less of tenderness. Dry, with the endless dry tension of will, they too were wearing out. The human world was just getting worn out. Perhaps it would turn fiercely destructive. A sort of anarchy! Clifford and his conservative anarchy! Perhaps it wouldn't be conservative much longer. Perhaps it would develop into a very radical anarchy.

Connie found herself shrinking and afraid of the world. Sometimes she was happy for a little while in the boulevards or in the bois or the Luxembourg Gardens. But already Paris was full of Americans and English, strange Americans in the oddest uniforms, and the usual dreary English that are so hopeless abroad.

She was glad to drive on. It was suddenly hot weather, so Hilda was going through Switzerland and over the Brenner, then through the Dolomites down to Venice. Hilda loved all the managing and the driving and being mistress of the show. Connie was quite content to keep quiet.

And the trip was really quite nice. Only, Connie kept saying to herself: Why don't I really care? Why am I never really thrilled? How awful, that I don't really care about the landscape anymore! But I don't. It's rather awful. I'm like Saint Bernard, who could sail down the lake of Lucerne without ever noticing that there were even mountains and green water. I just don't care for landscape anymore. Why should one stare at it? Why should one? I refuse to.

No, she found nothing vital in France or Switzerland or the Tyrol or Italy. She just was carted through it all. And it was all less real than Wragby. Less real than the awful Wragby! She felt she didn't care if she never saw France or Switzerland or Italy again. They'd keep. Wragby was more real.

As for people! people were all alike, with very little differences. They all wanted to get money out of you: or, if they were travelers, they wanted to get enjoyment, perforce, like squeezing blood out of a stone. Poor mountains! poor landscape! it all had to be squeezed and squeezed and squeezed again, to provide a thrill, to provide enjoyment. What did people mean, with their simply *determined* enjoying of themselves?

No! said Connie to herself. I'd rather be at Wragby, where I can go about and be still, and not stare at anything or do any performing of any sort. This tourist performance of enjoying oneself is too hopelessly humiliating: it's such a failure.

She wanted to go back to Wragby, even to Clifford, even to poor crippled Clifford. He wasn't such a fool as this swarming holiday lot, anyhow.

But in her inner consciousness she was keeping touch with the other man. She mustn't let her connection with him go: oh, she mustn't let it go, or she was lost, lost utterly in this world of riff-raffy expensive people and joy-hogs. Oh, the joy-hogs! Oh, "enjoying oneself!" Another modern form of sickness.

They left the car in Mestre, in a garage, and took the regular steamer over to Venice. It was a lovely summer afternoon, the shallow lagoon rippled, the full sunshine made Venice, turning its back to them across the water, look dim.

At the station quay they changed to a gondola, giving the man the address. He was a regular gondolier in white-and-blue blouse, not very good-looking, not at all impressive.

"Yes! The Villa Esmeralda! Yes! I know it! I have been the gondolier for a gentleman there. But a fair distance out!"

He seemed a rather childish, impetuous fellow. He rowed with a certain exaggerated impetuosity, through the dark side-canals with the horrible, slimy green walls, the canals that go through the poorer quarters, where the washing hangs high up on ropes, and there is a slight, or strong odor of sewage.

But at last he came to one of the open canals with pavement on either side, and looping bridges, that run straight, at right angles to the Grand Canal. The two women stayed under a little awning, the man was perched above, behind them.

"Are the signorine staying long at the Villa Esmeralda?" he asked, rowing easy, and wiping his perspiring face with a white-and-blue handkerchief.

"Some twenty days: we are both married ladies," said Hilda, in her curious hushed voice, that made her Italian sound so foreign.

"Ah! Twenty days!" said the man. There was a pause. After which he asked: "Do the signore want a gondolier for the twenty days or so that they will stay at the Villa Esmeralda? Or by the day, or by the week?"

Connie and Hilda considered. In Venice, it is always preferable to have one's own gondola, as it is preferable to have one's own car on land.

"What is there at the Villa? what boats?"

"There is a motor launch, also a gondola. But—" The *but* meant: they won't be your property.

"How much do you charge?"

It was about thirty shillings a day, or ten pounds a week.

"Is that the regular price?" asked Hilda.

"Less, Signora, less. The regular price—"

The sisters considered.

"Well," said Hilda, "come tomorrow morning, and we will arrange it. What is your name?"

His name was Giovanni, and he wanted to know at what time he should come, and then for whom should he say he was waiting. Hilda had no card.

Connie gave him one of hers. He glanced at it swiftly, with his hot, southern blue eyes, then glanced again.

"Ah!" he said, lighting up, "Milady! Milady! isn't it?"

"Milady Constanza!" said Connie.

He nodded, repeating: "Milady Constanza!" and putting the card carefully away in his blouse.

The Villa Esmeralda was quite a long way out, on the edge of the lagoon looking towards Chioggia. It was not a very old house, and pleasant, with the terraces looking seawards, and below, quite a big garden with dark trees, walled in from the lagoon.

Their host was a heavy, rather coarse Scotchman who had made a good fortune in Italy before the war, and had been knighted for his ultrapatriotism during the war. His wife was a thin, pale, sharp kind of person with no fortune of her own, and the misfortune of having to regulate her husband's rather sordid amorous exploits. He was terribly tiresome with the servants. But having had a slight stroke during the winter, he was now more manageable.

The house was pretty full. Besides Sir Malcolm and his two daughters, there were seven more people, a Scotch couple, again with two daughters; a young Italian Contessa, a widow; a young Georgian prince, and a youngish English clergyman who had had pneumonia and was being chaplain to Sir Alexander for his health's sake. The prince was penniless, good-looking, would make an excellent chauffeur, with the necessary impudence, and basta! The contessa was a quiet little puss with a game on somewhere. The clergyman was a raw simple fellow from a Bucks vicarage: luckily he had left his wife and two children at home. And the Guthries, the family of four, were good solid Edinburgh middle-class, enjoying everything in a solid fashion, and daring everything while risking nothing.

Connie and Hilda ruled out the prince at once. The Guthries were more or less their own sort, substantial, but boring: and the girls wanted husbands. The chaplain was not a bad fellow, but too deferential. Sir Alexander, after his slight stroke, had a terrible heaviness in his joviality, but he was still thrilled at the presence of so many handsome young women. Lady Cooper was a quiet, catty person who had a thin time of it, poor thing, and who watched every other woman with a cold watchfulness that had become her second nature, and who said cold, nasty little things which showed what an utterly low opinion she had of all human nature. She was also quite venomously overbearing with the servants, Connie found: but in a quiet way. And she skillfully behaved so that Sir Alexander should think that *he* was lord and monarch of the whole caboosh, with his stout, would-be-genial paunch, and his utterly boring jokes, his humorosity, as Hilda called it.

Sir Malcolm was painting. Yes, he still would do a Venetian lagoonscape, now and then, in contrast to his Scottish landscapes. So in the morning he was rowed off with a huge canvas, to his "site." A little later, Lady Cooper would be rowed off into the heart of the city, with sketching-block and colors. She was an inveterate watercolor painter, and the house was full of rose-colored palaces, dark canals, swaying bridges, medieval façades, and so on. A little later the Guthries, the prince, the countess, Sir Alexander and sometimes Mr. Lind, the chaplain, would go off to the Lido where they would bathe; coming home to a late lunch at half-past one.

The house party, as a house party, was distinctly boring. But this did not trouble the sisters. They were out all the time. Their father took them to the exhibition, miles and miles of weary paintings. He took them to all the cronies of his in the Villa Lucchese, he sat with them on warm evenings in Piazza, having got a table at Florian's: he took them to the theater, to the Goldoni plays. There were illuminated water-fetes, there were dances. This was a holiday place of all holiday places. The Lido with its acres of sun-pinked or pyjamaed bodies, was like a strand with an endless heap of seals come up for mating. Too many people in Piazza, too many limbs and trunks of humanity on the Lido, too many gondolas, too many motor launches, too many steamers, too many pigeons, too many ices, too many cocktails, too many men servants wanting tips, too many languages rattling, too much, too much sun, too much smell of Venice, too many cargoes of strawberries, too many silk shawls, too many huge, raw-beef slices of watermelon on stalls: too much enjoyment, altogether far too much enjoyment!

Connie and Hilda went around in their sunny frocks. There were dozens of people they knew, dozens of people knew them. Michaelis turned up like a bad penny. "Hullo! Where you staying? Come and have an ice cream or something! Come with me somewhere in my gondola." Even Michaelis *almost* sunburned: though sun-cooked is more appropriate to the look of the mass of human flesh.

It was pleasant in a way. It was *almost* enjoyment. But anyhow, with all the cocktails, all the lying in warmish water and sunbathing on hot sand in hot sun, jazzing with your stomach up against some fellow in the warm nights, cooling off with ices, it was a complete narcotic. And that was what they all wanted, a drug: the slow water, a drug; the sun, a drug; jazz, a drug; cigarettes, cocktails, ices, vermouth. To be drugged! Enjoyment! Enjoyment!

Hilda half liked being drugged. She liked looking at all the women, speculating about them. The women were absorbingly interested in the women. How does she look? What man has she captured? What fun is she getting out of it?— The men were like great dogs in white flannel trousers, waiting to be patted, waiting to wallow, waiting to plaster some woman's stomach against their own, in jazz.

Hilda liked jazz, because she could plaster her stomach against the stomach of some so-called man, and let him control her movements from the visceral center, here and there across the floor, and then she could break loose and ignore "the creature." He had been merely made use of. Poor Connie was rather unhappy. She wouldn't jazz, because she simply couldn't plaster her stomach against some "creature's" stomach. She hated the conglomerate mass of nearly nude flesh on the Lido: there was hardly enough water to wet them all. She disliked Sir Alexander and Lady Cooper. She did not want Michaelis or anybody else trailing her.

The happiest times were when she got Hilda to go with her away across the Lagoon, far across to some lonely shingle-bank, where they could bathe quite alone, the gondola remaining on the inner side of the reef.

Then Giovanni got another gondolier to help him, because it was a long way and he sweated terrifically in the sun. Giovanni was very nice: affectionate, as the Italians are, and quite passionless. The Italians are not passionate: passion has deep reserves. They are easily moved, and often affectionate, but they rarely have any abiding passion of any sort.

So Giovanni was already devoted to his ladies, as he had been devoted to cargoes of ladies in the past. He was perfectly ready to prostitute himself to them, if they wanted him: he secretly hoped they would want him. They would give him a handsome present, and it would come in very handy, as he was just going to be married. He told them about his marriage, and they were suitably interested.

He thought this trip to some lonely bank across the lagoon probably meant business: business being *l'amore* love. So he got a mate to help him, for it *was* a long way; and after all, they were two ladies. Two ladies, two mackerels! Good arithmetic! Beautiful ladies too! He was justly proud of them. And though it was the Signora who paid him and gave him orders, he rather hoped it would be the young milady who would select him for *l'amore*. She would give more money too.

The mate he brought was called Daniele. He was not a regular gondolier, so he had none of the cadger and prostitute about him. He was a sandola man, a sandola being a big boat that brings in fruit and produce from the islands.

Daniele was beautiful, tall and well-shapen, with a light round head of little, close, pale-blond curls, and a good-looking man's face, a little like a lion, and long-distance blue eyes. He was not effusive, loquacious, and bibulous like Giovanni. He was silent and he rowed with a strength and ease as if he were alone on the water. The ladies were ladies, remote from him. He did not even look at them. He looked ahead.

He was a real man, a little angry when Giovanni drank too much wine and rowed awkwardly, with effusive shoves of the great oar. He was a man as Mellors was a man, unprostituted. Connie pitied the wife of the easily-overflowing Giovanni. But Daniele's wife could be one of those sweet Venetian women of the people whom one still sees, modest and flowerlike, in the back of that labyrinth of a town.

Ah, how sad that man first prostitutes woman, then woman prostitutes man. Giovanni was pining to prostitute himself, dribbling like a dog, wanting to give himself to a woman. And for money!

Connie looked at Venice far off, low and rose-colored upon the water. Built of money, blossomed of money, and dead with money. The money-deadness! Money, money, money, prostitution and deadness.

Yet Daniele was still a man capable of a man's free allegiance. He did not wear the gondolier's blouse: only the knitted blue jersey. He was a little wild, uncouth and proud. So he was hireling to the rather doggy Giovanni, who was hireling again of two women. So it is! When Jesus refused the devil's money, he left the devil like a Jewish banker, master of the whole situation.

Connie would come home from the blazing light of the lagoon in a kind of stupor, to find letters from home. Clifford wrote regularly. He wrote very good letters: they might all have been printed in a book. And for this reason Connie found them not very interesting.

She lived in the stupor of the light of the lagoon, the lapping saltiness of the water, the space, the emptiness, the nothingness: but health, health, complete stupor of health. It was gratifying, and she was lulled away in it, not caring for anything. Besides, she was pregnant. She knew now. So the stupor of sunlight and the lagoon salt and sea-bathing and lying on shingle and finding shells and drifting away, away in a gondola was completed by the pregnancy inside her, another fullness of health, satisfying and stupefying.

She had been at Venice a fortnight, and she was to stay another ten days or a fortnight. The sunshine blazed over any count of time, and the fullness of physical health made forgetfulness complete. She was in a sort of stupor of well-being.

From which a letter of Clifford roused her.

"We, too, have had our mild local excitement. It appears the truant wife of Mellors, the keeper, turned up at the cottage, and found herself unwelcome. He packed her off and locked the door. Report has it, however, that when he returned from the wood he found the no longer fair lady firmly established in his bed, in *puris naturalibus;* or one should say, in *impuris naturalibus*. She had broken a window and got in that way. Unable to evict the somewhat manhandled Venus from his couch, he beat a retreat and retired, it is said, to his mother's house in Tevershall. Meanwhile, the Venus of Stacks Gate is established in the cottage, which she claims is her home, and Apollo, apparently, is domiciled in Tevershall.

"I repeat this from hearsay, as Mellors has not come to me personally. I had the particular bit of local garbage from our garbage bird, our ibis, our scavenging turkey-buzzard, Mrs. Bolton. I would not have repeated it had she not exclaimed: her Ladyship will go no more to the wood if *that* woman's going to be about!

"I like your picture of Sir Malcolm striding into the sea with white hair blowing and pink flesh glowing. I envy you that sun. Here it rains. But I don't envy Sir Malcolm his inveterate mortal carnality. However, it suits his age. Apparently one grows more carnal and more mortal as one grows older. Only youth has a taste of immortality—"

This news affected Connie in her state of semistupified well-being with vexation amounting to exasperation. Now she had got to be bothered by that beast of a woman! Now she must start and fret! She had no letter from Mellors. They had agreed not to write at all, but now she wanted to hear from him personally. After all, he was the father of the child that was coming. Let him write!

But how hateful! How everything was messed up. How foul those low people were! How nice it was here, in the sunshine and the indolence, compared to that dismal mess of that English midlands! After all, a clear sky was almost the most important thing in life.

She did not mention the fact of her pregnancy, even to Hilda. She wrote to Mrs. Bolton for exact information.

Duncan Forbes, an artist, friend of theirs, had arrived at the Villa Esmeralda, coming north from Rome. Now he made a third in the gondola, and he bathed with them across the lagoon, and was their escort: a quiet, almost taciturn young man, very advanced in his art.

She had a letter from Mrs. Bolton: "You will be pleased, I am sure, my Lady, when you see Sir Clifford. He's looking quite blooming and working very hard, and very hopeful. Of course, he is looking forward to seeing you among us again. It is a dull house without my Lady, and we shall all welcome her presence among us once more.

"About Mr. Mellors, I don't know how much Sir Clifford told you. It seems his wife came back all of a sudden one afternoon, and he found her sitting on the doorstep when he came in from the wood. She said she was come back to him and wanted to live with him again, as she was his legal wife, and he wasn't going to divorce her. Because it seems Mr. Mellors was trying for a divorce. But he wouldn't have anything to do with her, and wouldn't let her in the house, and did not go in himself; he went back into the wood without even opening the door.

"But when he came back after dark, he found the house broken into, so he went upstairs to see what she'd done, and he found her in bed without a rag on her. He offered her money, but she said she was his wife and he must take her back. I don't know what sort of a scene they had. His mother told me about it, she's terribly upset. Well, he told her he'd rot rather than ever live with her again, so he took his things and went straight to his mother's on Tevershall hill. He stopped the night and went to the wood next day through the park, never going near the cottage. It seems he never saw his wife that day. But the day after she was at her brother Dan's at Beggarlee, swearing and carrying on, saying she was his legal wife, and that he'd been having women at the cottage, because she'd found a scent-bottle in his drawer, and gold-tipped cigarette ends on the ashheap, and I don't know what all. Then it seems the postman, Fred Kirk, says he heard somebody talking in Mr. Mellors's bedroom early one morning, and a motorcar had been in the lane.

"Mr. Mellors stayed on with his mother, and went to the wood through the park, and it seems she stayed on at the cottage. Well, there was no end of talk. So at last Mr. Mellors and Tom Phillips went to the cottage and fetched away most of the furniture and bedding, and unscrewed the handle of the pump, so she was forced to go. But instead of going back to Stacks Gate she went and lodged with that Mrs. Swain at Beggarlee, because her brother Dan's wife wouldn't have her. And she kept going to old Mrs. Mellors's house, to catch him, and she began swearing he'd got in bed with her in the cottage, and she went to a lawyer to make him pay her an allowance. She's grown heavy, and more common than ever, and as strong as a bull. And she goes about saying the most awful things about him, how he has women at the cottage, and how he behaved to her when they were married, the low, beastly things he did to her, and I don't know what all. I'm sure it's awful, the mischief a woman can do, once she starts talking. And no matter how low she may be, there'll be some as will believe her, and some of the dirt will stick. I'm sure the way she makes out that Mr. Mellors was one of those low, beastly men with women, is simply shocking. And people are only too ready to believe things against anybody, especially things like that. She declares she'll never leave him alone while he lives. Though what I say is, if he was so beastly to her, why is she so anxious to go back to him? But, of course, she's coming near her change of life, for she's years older than he is. And these common, violent women always go partly insane when the change of life comes upon them."

This was a nasty blow to Connie. Here she was, sure as life, coming in for her share of the lowness and dirt. She felt angry with him for not having got clear of a Bertha Coutts: nay, for ever having married her. Perhaps he had a certain hankering after lowness. Connie remembered the last night she had spent with him, and shivered. He had known all that sensuality, even with a Bertha Coutts! It was really rather disgusting. It would be well to be rid of him, clear of him altogether. He was perhaps really common, really low.

She had a revulsion against the whole affair, and almost envied the Guthrie girls their gawky inexperience and crude maidenliness. And she now dreaded the thought that anybody would know about herself and the keeper. How unspeakably humiliating! She was weary, afraid, and felt a craving for utter respectability, even for the vulgar and deadening respectability of the Guthrie girls. If Clifford knew about her affair, how unspeakably humiliating! She was afraid, terrified of society and its unclean bite. She almost wished she could get rid of the child again, and be quite clear. In short, she fell into a state of funk.

As for the scent-bottle, that was her own folly. She had not been able to refrain from perfuming his one or two handkerchiefs and his shirts in the drawer, just out of childishness, and she had left a little bottle of Coty's Wood Violet perfume, half empty, among his things. She wanted him to remember her in the perfume. As for the cigarette ends, they were Hilda's.

She could not help confiding a little in Duncan Forbes. She didn't say she had been the keeper's lover, she only said she liked him, and told Forbes the history of the man.

"Oh," said Forbes, "you'll see, they'll never rest till they've pulled the man down and done him in. If he has refused to creep up into the middle classes, when he had a chance; and if he's a man who stands up for his own sex, then they'll do him in. It's the one thing they won't let you be, straight and open in your sex. You can be as dirty as you like. In fact the more dirt you do on sex, the better they like it. But if you believe in your own sex, and won't have it done dirt to: they'll down you. It's the one insane taboo left: sex as a natural and vital thing. They won't have it, and they'll kill you before they'll let you have it. You'll see, they'll hound that man down. And what's he done, after all? If he's made love to his wife all ends on, hasn't he a right to? She ought to be proud of it. But you see, even a low bitch like that turns on him, and uses the hyena instinct of the mob against sex, to pull him down. You have to snivel and feel sinful or awful about your sex, before you're allowed to have any. Oh, they'll hound the poor devil down."

Connie had a revulsion in the opposite direction now. What had he done, after all? What had he done to herself, Connie, but give her an exquisite pleasure, and a sense of freedom and life? He had released her warm, natural sexual flow. And for that they would hound him down.

No, no, it should not be. She saw the image of him, naked white with tanned face and hands, looking down and addressing his erect penis as if it were another being, the odd grin flickering on his face. And she heard his voice again: Tha's got the nicest woman's arse of anybody! And she felt his hand warmly and softly closing over her tail again, over her secret places, like a benediction. And the warmth ran through her womb, and the little flames flickered in her knees, and she said: Oh no! I mustn't go back on it! I must not go back on him. I must stick to him and to what I had of him, through everything. I had no warm, flamy life till he gave it me. And I won't go back on it.

She did a rash thing. She sent a letter to Ivy Bolton, enclosing a note to the keeper, and asking Mrs. Bolton to give it to him. And she wrote to him: "I am very much distressed to hear of all the trouble your wife is making for you, but don't mind it, it is only a sort of hysteria. It will all blow over as suddenly as it came. But I'm awfully sorry about it, and I do hope you are not minding very much. After all, it isn't worth it. She is only a hysterical woman who wants to hurt you. I shall be home in ten days' time, and I hope everything will be all right."

A few days later came a letter from Clifford. He was evidently upset.

"I am delighted to hear you are prepared to leave Venice on the sixteenth. But if you are enjoying it, don't hurry home. We miss you, Wragby misses you. But it is essential that you should get your full amount of sunshine, sunshine and pyjamas, as the advertisements of the Lido say. So please do stay on a little longer, if it is cheering you up and preparing you for our sufficiently awful winter. Even today, it rains.

"I am assiduously, admirably looked after by Mrs. Bolton. She is a queer specimen. The more I live, the more I realize what strange creatures human beings are. Some of them might just as well have a hundred legs, like a centipede, or six, like a lobster. The human consistency and dignity one has been led to expect from one's fellowmen seem actually nonexistent. One doubts if they exist to any startling degree even in oneself.

"The scandal of the keeper continues and gets bigger like a snowball. Mrs. Bolton keeps me informed. She reminds me of a fish which, though dumb, seems to be breathing silent gossip through its gills, while ever it lives. All goes through the sieve of her gills, and nothing surprises her. It is as if the events of other people's lives were the necessary oxygen of her own.

"She is preoccupied with the Mellors scandal, and if I will let her begin, she takes me down to the depths. Her great indignation, which even then is like the indignation of an actress playing a role, is against the wife of Mellors, whom she persists in calling Bertha Coutts. I have been to the depths of the muddy lives of the Bertha Couttses of this world, and when, released from the current of gossip, I slowly rise to the surface again, I look at the daylight in wonder that it ever should be.

"It seems to me absolutely true, that our world, which appears to us the surface of all things, is really the *bottom* of a deep ocean: all our trees are submarine growths, and we are weird, scaly-clad submarine fauna, feeding ourselves on offal like shrimps. Only occasionally the soul rises gasping through the fathomless fathoms under which we live, far up to the surface of the ether, where there is true air. I am convinced that the air we normally breathe is a kind of water, and men and women are a species of fish.

"But sometimes the soul does come up, shoots like a kittiwake into the light, with ecstasy, after having preyed on the submarine depths. It is our mortal destiny, I suppose, to prey upon the ghastly subaqueous life of our fellow men, in the submarine jungle of mankind. But our immortal destiny is to escape, once we have swallowed our swimmy catch, up again into the bright ether, bursting out from the surface of Old Ocean into real light. Then one realizes one's eternal nature.

"When I hear Mrs. Bolton talk, I feel myself plunging down, down, to the depths where the fish of human secrets wriggle and swim. Carnal appetite makes one seize a beakful of prey: then up, up again, out of the dense into the ethereal, from the wet into the dry. To you I can tell the whole process. But with Mrs. Bolton I only feel the downward plunge, down, horribly, among the seaweeds and the pallid monsters of the very bottom.

"I am afraid we are going to lose our gamekeeper. The scandal of the truant wife, instead of dying down, has reverberated to greater and greater dimensions. He is accused of all unspeakable things, and curiously enough, the woman has managed to get the bulk of the colliers' wives behind her, gruesome fish, and the village is putrescent with talk.

"I hear this Bertha Coutts besieges Mellors in his mother's house, having ransacked the cottage and the hut. She seized one day upon her own daughter, as that chip of the female block was returning from school; but the little one, instead of kissing the loving mother's hand, bit it firmly, and so received from the other hand a smack in the face which sent her reeling into the gutter: whence she was rescued by an indignant and harassed grandmother.

"The woman has blown off an amazing quantity of poison gas. She has aired in detail all those incidents of her conjugal life which are usually buried down in the deepest grave of matrimonial silence, between married couples. Having chosen to exhume them, after ten years of burial, she has a weird array. I hear these details from Linley and the doctor: the latter being amused. Of course, there is really nothing in it. Humanity has always had a strange avidity for unusual sexual postures, and if a man likes to use his wife, as Benvenuto Cellini says, "in the Italian way," well that is a matter of taste. But I had hardly expected our gamekeeper to be up to so many tricks. No doubt Bertha

Coutts herself first put him up to them. In any case, it is a matter of their own personal squalor, and nothing to do with anybody else.

"However, everybody listens: as I do myself. A dozen years ago, common decency would have hushed the thing. But common decency no longer exists, and the colliers' wives are all up in arms and unabashed in voice. One would think every child in Tevershall, for the past fifty years, had been an immaculate conception, and every one of our nonconformist females was a shining Joan of Arc. That our estimable gamekeeper should have about him a touch of Rabelais seems to make him more monstrous and shocking than a murderer like Crippen. Yet these people in Tevershall are a loose lot, if one is to believe all accounts.

"The trouble is, however, the execrable Bertha Coutts has not confined herself to her own experiences and sufferings. She has discovered, at the top of her voice, that her husband has been "keeping" women down at the cottage, and has made a few random shots at naming the women. This has brought a few decent names trailing through the mud, and the thing has gone quite considerably too far. An injunction has been taken out against the woman.

"I have had to interview Mellors about the business, as it was impossible to keep the woman away from the wood. He goes about as usual, with his Miller-of-the-Dee air, I care for nobody, no, not I, if nobody care for me! Nevertheless, I shrewdly suspect he feels like a dog with a tin can tied to its tail: though he makes a very good show of pretending the tin can isn't there. But I hear that in the village the women call away their children if he is passing, as if he were the Marquis de Sade in person. He goes on with a certain impudence, but I am afraid the tin can is firmly tied to his tail, and that inwardly he repeats, like Don Rodrigo in the Spanish ballad: 'Ah, now it bites me where I most have sinned!'

"I asked him if he thought he would be able to attend to his duty in the wood, and he said he did not think he had neglected it. I told him it was a nuisance to have the woman trespassing: to which he replied that he had no power to arrest her. Then I hinted at the scandal and its unpleasant course. 'Ay,' he said. 'Folks should do their own fuckin', then they wouldn't want to listen to a lot of clatfart about another man's.'

"He said it with some bitterness, and no doubt it contains the real germ of truth. The mode of putting it, however, is neither delicate nor respectful. I hinted as much, and then I heard the tin can rattle again. 'It's not for a man i' the shape you're in, Sir Clifford, to twit me for havin' a cod atween my legs.'

"These things, said indiscriminately to all and sundry, of course do not help him at all, and the rector, and Linley, and Burroughs all think it would be as well if the man left the place.

"I asked him if it was true that he entertained ladies down at the cottage, and all he said was: 'Why what's that to you, Sir Clifford?' I told him I intended to have decency observed on my estate, to which he replied: 'Then you mun button the mouths o' a' th' women'—When I pressed him about his manner of life at the cottage, he said: 'Surely you might ma'e a scandal out o' me an' my bitch Flossie. You've missed summat there.' As a matter of fact, for an example of impertinence he'd be hard to beat.

"I asked him if it would be easy for him to find another job. He said: 'If you're hintin' that you'd like to shunt me out of this job, it'd be as easy as wink.' So he made no trouble at all about leaving at the end of next week, and apparently is willing to initiate a young fellow, Joe Chambers, into as many mysteries of the craft as possible. I told him I would give him a month's wages extra, when he left. He said he'd rather I kept my money, as I'd no occasion to ease my conscience. I asked him what he meant, and he said: 'You don't owe me nothing extra, Sir Clifford, so don't pay me nothing extra. If you think you see my shirt hanging out, just tell me.'

"Well, there is the end of it for the time being. The woman has gone away: we don't know where to: but she is liable to arrest if she shows her face in Tevershall. And I hear she is mortally afraid of jail, because she merits it so well. Mellors will depart on Saturday week, and the place will soon become normal again.

"Meanwhile, my dear Connie, if you would enjoy the stay in Venice or in Switzerland till the beginning of August, I should be glad to think you were out of all this buzz of nastiness, which will have died quite away by the end of the month.

"So you see, we are deep-sea monsters, and when the lobster walks on mud, he stirs it up for everybody. We must perforce take it philosophically."—The irritation, and the lack of any sympathy in any direction, of Clifford's letter, had a bad effect on Connie. But she understood it better when she received the following from Mellors: "The cat is out of the bag, along with various other pussies. You have heard that my wife Bertha came back to my unloving arms, and took up her abode in the cottage: where, to speak disrespectfully, she smelled a rat in the shape of a little bottle of Coty. Other evidence she did not find, at least for some days, when she began to howl about the burnt photograph. She noticed the glass and the backboard in the spare bedroom. Unfortunately, on the backboard somebody had scribbled little sketches, and the initials, several times repeated: C. S. R. This, however, afforded no clue until she broke into the hut, and found one of your books, an autobiography of the actress Judith, with your name, Constance Stewart Reid, on the front page. After this, for some days she went round loudly saying that my paramour was no less a person than Lady

Chatterley herself. The news came at last to the rector, Mr. Burroughs, and to Sir Clifford. They then proceeded to take legal steps against my liege lady, who for her part disappeared, having always had a mortal fear of the police.

"Sir Clifford asked to see me, so I went to him. He talked around things and seemed annoyed with me. Then he asked if I knew that even her ladyship's name had been mentioned. I said I never listened to scandal, and was surprised to hear this bit from Sir Clifford himself. He said, of course, it was a great insult, and I told him there was Queen Mary on a calendar in the scullery, no doubt because Her Majesty formed part of my harem. But he didn't appreciate the sarcasm. He as good as told me I was a disreputable character who walked about with all of my breeches' buttons undone, and I as good as told him he'd nothing to unbutton anyhow, so he gave me the sack, and I leave on Saturday week, and the place thereof shall know me no more.

"I shall go to London, and my old landlady, Mrs. Inger, 17 Coburg Square, will either give me a room or will find one for me.

"Be sure your sins will find you out, especially if you're married and her name's Bertha—"

There was not a word about herself, or to her. Connie resented this. He might have said some few words of consolation or reassurance. But she knew he was leaving her free, free to go back to Wragby and to Clifford. She resented that too. He need not be so falsely chivalrous. She wished he had said to Clifford: "Yes, she is my lover and mistress and I am proud of it!" But his courage wouldn't carry him so far.

So her name was coupled with his in Tevershall! It was a mess. But that would soon die down.

She was angry, with the complicated and confused anger that made her inert. She did not know what to do nor what to say, so she said and did nothing. She went on at Venice just the same, rowing out in the gondola with Duncan Forbes, bathing, letting the days slip by. Duncan, who had been rather depressingly in love with her ten years ago, was in love with her again. But she said to him: "I only want one thing of men, and that is, that they should leave me alone."

So Duncan left her alone: really quite pleased to be able to. All the same, he offered her a soft stream of a queer, inverted sort of love. He wanted to be *with* her.

"Have you ever thought," he said to her one day, "how very little people are connected with one another. Look at Daniele! He is handsome as a son of the sun. But see how alone he looks in his handsomeness. Yet I bet he has a wife and family, and couldn't possibly go away from them."

"Ask him," said Connie.

Duncan did so. Daniele said he was married, and had two children, both male, aged seven and nine. But he betrayed no emotion over the fact.

"Perhaps only people who are capable of real togetherness have that look of being alone in the universe," said Connie. "The others have a certain stickiness, they stick to the mass, like Giovanni"—"And," she thought to herself, "like you, Duncan."

❖ 18 ❖

She had to make up her mind what to do. She would leave Venice on the Saturday that he was leaving Wragby: in six days' time. This would bring her to London on the Monday following, and she would then see him. She wrote to him to the London address, asking him to send her a letter to Hartland's hotel, and to call for her on the Monday evening at seven.

Inside herself, she was curiously and complicatedly angry, and all her responses were numb. She refused to confide even in Hilda, and Hilda, offended by her steady silence, had become rather intimate with a Dutch woman. Connie hated those rather stifling intimacies between women, intimacies into which Hilda always entered ponderously.

Sir Malcolm decided to travel with Connie, and Duncan could come on with Hilda. The old artist always did himself well: he took berths on the Orient Express, in spite of Connie's dislike of *trains de luxe*, the atmosphere of vulgar depravity there is aboard them nowadays. However, it would make the journey to Paris shorter.

Sir Malcolm was always uneasy going back to his wife. It was a habit carried over from the first wife. But there would be a house party for the grouse, and he wanted to be well ahead. Connie, sunburnt and handsome, sat in silence, forgetting all about the landscape.

"A little dull for you, going back to Wragby," said her father, noticing her glumness.

"I'm not sure I shall go back to Wragby," she said, with startling abruptness, looking into his eyes with her big blue eyes. His big blue eyes took on the frightened look of a man whose social conscience is not quite clear.

"You mean you'll stay on in Paris a while?"

"No! I mean never go back to Wragby."

He was bothered by his own little problems, and sincerely hoped he was getting none of hers to shoulder.

"How's that, all at once?" he asked.

"I'm going to have a child."

It was the first time she had uttered the words to any living soul, and it seemed to mark a cleavage in her life.

"How do you know?" said her father.

She smiled.

"How *should* I know?"

"But not Clifford's child, of course?"

"No! Another man's."

She rather enjoyed tormenting him.

"Do I know the man?" asked Sir Malcolm.

"No! You've never seen him."

There was a long pause.

"And what are your plans?"

"I don't know. That's the point."

"No patching it up with Clifford?"

"I suppose Clifford would take it," said Connie. "He told me, after last time you talked to him, he wouldn't mind if I had a child, so long as I went about it discreetly."

"Only sensible thing he could say, under the circumstances. Then I suppose it'll be all right."

"In what way?" said Connie, looking into her father's eyes. They were big blue eyes rather like her own, but with a certain uneasiness in them, a look sometimes of an uneasy little boy, sometimes a look of sullen selfishness, usually goodhumored and wary.

"You can present Clifford with an heir to all the Chatterleys, and put another baronet in Wragby."

Sir Malcolm's face smiled with a half-sensual smile.

"But I don't think I want to," she said.

"Why not? Feeling entangled with the other man? Well! If you want the truth from me, my child, it's this. The world goes on. Wragby stands and will go on standing. The world is more or less a fixed thing, and, externally, we have to adapt ourselves to it. Privately, in my private opinion, we can please ourselves. Emotions change. You may like one man this year and another next. But Wragby still stands. Stick to Wragby as far as Wragby sticks to you. Then please yourself. But you'll get very little out of making a break. You can make a break if you wish. You have an independent income, the only thing that never lets you down. But you won't get much out of it. Put a little baronet in Wragby. It's an amusing thing to do."

And Sir Malcolm sat back and smiled again. Connie did not answer.

"I hope you had a real man at last," he said to her after a while, sensually alert.

"I did. That's the trouble. There aren't many of them about," she said.

"No, by God!" he mused. "There aren't! Well, my dear, to look at you, he was a lucky man. Surely he wouldn't make trouble for you?"

"Oh, no! He leaves me my own mistress entirely."

"Quite! Quite! A genuine man would."

Sir Malcolm was pleased. Connie was his favorite daughter, he had always liked the female in her. Not so much of her mother in her as in Hilda. And he had always disliked Clifford. So he was pleased, and very tender with his daughter, as if the unborn child were his child.

He drove with her to Hartland's hotel, and saw her installed: then went round to his club. She had refused his company for the evening.

She found a letter from Mellors. "I won't come round to your hotel, but I'll wait for you outside the Golden Cock in Adam Street at seven."

There he stood, tall and slender, and so different, in a formal suit of thin dark cloth. He had a natural distinction, but he had not the cut-to-pattern look of her class. Yet, she saw at once, he could go anywhere. He had a native breeding which was really much nicer than the cut-to-pattern class thing.

"Ah, there you are! How well you look!"

"Yes! But not you."

She looked in his face anxiously. It was thin, and the cheekbones showed. But his eyes smiled at her, and she felt at home with him. There it was: suddenly, the tension of keeping up her appearances fell from her. Something flowed out of him physically, that made her feel inwardly at ease and happy, at home. With a woman's now alert instinct for happiness, she registered it at once. "I'm happy when he's there!" Not all the sunshine of Venice had given her this inward expansion and warmth.

"Was it horrid for you?" she asked as she sat opposite him at table. He was too thin; she saw it now. His hand lay as she knew it, with that curious loose forgottenness of a sleeping animal. She wanted so much to take it and kiss it. But she did not quite dare.

"People are always horrid," he said.

"And did you mind very much?"

"I minded, as I always shall mind. And I knew I was a fool to mind."

"Did you feel like a dog with a tin can tied to its tail? Clifford said you felt like that."

He looked at her. It was cruel of her at that moment: for his pride had suffered bitterly.

"I suppose I did," he said.

She never knew the fierce bitterness with which he resented insult.

There was a long pause.

"And did you miss me?" she asked.

"I was glad you were out of it."

Again there was a pause.

"But did people *believe* about you and me?" she asked.

"No! I don't think so for a moment."

"Did Clifford?"

"I should say not. He put it off without thinking about it. But naturally it made him want to see the last of me."

"I'm going to have a child."

The expression died utterly out of his face, out of his whole body. He looked at her with darkened eyes, whose look she could not understand at all: like some dark-flamed spirit looking at her.

"Say you're glad!" she pleaded, groping for his hand. And she saw a certain exultance spring up in him. But it was netted down by things she could not understand.

"It's the future," he said.

"But aren't you glad?" she persisted.

"I have such a terrible mistrust of the future."

"But you needn't be troubled by any responsibility. Clifford would have it as his own, he'd be glad."

She saw him go pale, and recoil under this. He did not answer.

"Shall I go back to Clifford and put a little baronet into Wragby?" she asked.

He looked at her, pale and very remote. The ugly little grin flickered on his face.

"You wouldn't have to tell him who the father was."

"Oh!" she said; "he'd take it even then, if I wanted him to."

He thought for a time.

"Ay!" he said at last, to himself. "I suppose he would."

There was silence. A big gulf was between them.

"But you don't want me to go back to Clifford, do you?" she asked him.

"What do you want yourself?" he replied.

"I want to live with you," she said simply.

In spite of himself, little flames ran over his belly as he heard her say it, and he dropped his head. Then he looked up at her again, with those haunted eyes.

"If it's worth it to you," he said. "I've got nothing."

"You've got more than most men. Come, you know it," she said.

"In one way, I know it." He was silent for a time, thinking. Then he resumed: "They used to say I had too much of the woman in me. But it's not that. I'm not a woman because I don't want to shoot birds, neither because I don't want to make money, or get on. I could have got on in the army, easily, but I didn't like the army. Though I could manage the men all right: they liked me and they had a bit of a holy fear of me when I got mad. No, it was stupid, dead-handed higher authority that made the army dead: absolutely fool-dead. I like men, and men like me. But I can't stand the twaddling bossy impudence of the people who run this world. That's why I can't get on. I hate the impudence of money, and I hate the impudence of class. So in the world as it is, what have I to offer a woman?"

"But why offer anything? It's not a bargain. It's just that we love one another," she said.

"Nay, nay! It's more than that. Living is moving and moving on. My life won't get down the proper gutters, it just won't. So I'm a bit of a waste ticket by myself. And I've no business to take a woman into my life, unless my life does something and gets somewhere, inwardly at least, to keep us both fresh. A man must offer a woman *some* meaning in his life, if it's going to be an isolated life, and if she's a genuine woman. I can't be just your male concubine."

"Why not?" she said.

"Why, because I can't. And you would soon hate it."

"As if you couldn't trust me," she said.

The grin flickered on his face.

"The money is yours, the position is yours, the decisions will lie with you. I'm not just my lady's fucker, after all."

"What else are you?"

"You may well ask. It no doubt is invisible. Yet I'm something to myself at least. I can see the point of my own existence, though I can quite understand nobody else's seeing it."

"And will your existence have less point, if you live with me?"

He paused a long time before replying:

"It might."

She, too, stayed to think about it.

"And what is the point of your existence?"

"I tell you, it's invisible. I don't believe in the world, not in money, nor in advancement, nor in the future of our civilization. If there's got to be a future for humanity, there'll have to be a very big change from what now is."

"And what will the real future have to be like?"

"God knows! I can feel something inside me, all mixed up with a lot of rage. But what it really amounts to, I don't know."

"Shall I tell you?" she said, looking into his face. "Shall I tell you what you have that other men don't have, and that will make the future? Shall I tell you?"

"Tell me, then," he replied.

"It's the courage of your own tenderness, that's what it is, like when you put your hand on my tail and say I've got a pretty tail."

The grin came flickering on his face.

"That!" he said.

Then he sat thinking.

"Ay!" he said. "You're right. It's that really. It's that all the way through. I knew it with the men. I had to be in touch with them, physically, and not go back on it. I had to be bodily aware of them and a bit tender to them, even if I put 'em through hell. It's a question of awareness, as Buddha said. But even he fought shy of the bodily awareness, and that natural physical tenderness which is the best, even between men; in a proper manly way. Makes 'em really manly, not so monkeyish. Ay! it's tenderness, really; it's cunt-awareness. Sex is really only touch, the closest of all touch. And it's touch we're afraid of. We're only half-conscious, and half alive. We've got to come alive and aware. Especially the English have got to get into touch with one another, a bit delicate and a bit tender. It's our crying need."

She looked at him.

"Then why are you afraid of me?" she said.

He looked at her a long time before he answered.

"It's the money, really, and the position. It's the world in you."

"But isn't there tenderness in me?" she said wistfully.

He looked down at her, with darkened, abstract eyes.

"Ay! It come an' goes, like in me."

"But can't you trust it between you and me?" she asked, gazing anxiously at him.

She saw his face all softening down, losing its armor.

"Maybe!" he said.

They were both silent.

"I want you to hold me in your arms," she said. "I want you to tell me you are glad we are having a child."

She looked so lovely and warm and wistful, his bowels stirred towards her.

"I suppose we can go to my room," he said. "Though it's scandalous again."

But she saw the forgetfulness of the world coming over him again, his face taking the soft, pure look of tender passion.

They walked by the remoter streets to Coburg Square, where he had a room at the top of the house, an attic room where he cooked for himself on a gas range. It was small, but decent and tidy.

She took off her things, and made him do the same. She was lovely in the soft first flush of her pregnancy.

"I ought to leave you alone," he said.

"No!" she said. "Love me! Love me, and say you'll keep me. Say you'll keep me! Say you'll never let me go, to the world nor to anybody!"

She crept close against him, clinging fast to his thin, strong naked body, the only home she had ever known.

"Then I'll keep thee," he said. "If tha wants it, then I'll keep thee."

He held her round and fast.

"And say you're glad about the child," she repeated. "Kiss it! Kiss my womb and say you're glad it's there."

But that was more difficult for him.

"I've a dread of puttin' children i' th' world," he said. "I've such a dread o' th' future for 'em."

"But you've put it into me. Be tender to it, and that will be its future already. Kiss it!"

He quivered, because it was true. "Be tender to it, and that will be its future"—At that moment he felt a sheer love for the woman. He kissed her belly and her mount of Venus, to kiss close to the womb and the fetus within the womb.

"Oh, you love me! You love me!" she said, in a little cry like one of her blind, inarticulate love cries. And he went in to her softly, feeling the stream of tenderness flowing in release from his bowels to hers, the bowels of compassion kindled between them.

And he realized as he went in to her that this was the thing he had to do, to come into tender touch, without losing his pride or his dignity or his integrity as a man. After all, if she had money and means, and he had none, he should be too proud and honorable to hold back his tenderness from her on that account. "I stand for the touch of bodily awareness between human beings," he said to himself, "and the touch of tenderness. And she is my mate. And it is a battle against the money, and the machine, and the insentient ideal monkeyishness of the world. And she will stand behind me there. Thank God I've got a woman! Thank God I've got a woman who is with me, and tender and aware of me. Thank God she's not a bully, nor a fool. Thank God she's a tender, aware woman." And as his seed sprang in her, his soul sprang towards her too, in the creative act that is far more than procreative.

She was quite determined now that there should be no parting between him and her. But the ways and means were still to settle.

"Did you hate Bertha Coutts?" she asked him.

"Don't talk to me about her."

"Yes! You must let me. Because once you liked her. And once you were as intimate with her as you are with me. So you have to tell me. Isn't it rather terrible, when you've been intimate with her, to hate her so? Why is it?"

"I don't know. She sort of kept her will ready against me, always, always: her ghastly female will: her freedom! A woman's ghastly freedom that ends in the most beastly bullying! Oh, she always kept her freedom against me, like vitriol in my face."

"But she's not free of you even now. Does she still love you?"

"No, no! If she's not free of me, it's because she's got that mad rage, she must try to bully me."

"But she must have loved you."

"No! Well, in specks, she did. She was drawn to me. And I think even that she hated. She loved me in moments. But she always took it back, and started bullying. Her deepest desire was to bully me, and there was no altering her. Her *will* was wrong, from the first."

"But perhaps she felt you didn't really love her, and she wanted to make you."

"My God, it was bloody making."

"But you didn't really love her, did you? You did her that wrong."

"How could I? I began to. I began to love her. But somehow, she always ripped me up. No, don't let's talk of it. It was a doom, that was. And she was a doomed woman. This last time, I'd have shot her like I shoot a stoat, if I'd but been allowed: a raving, doomed thing in the shape of a woman! If only I could have shot her, and ended the whole misery! It ought to be allowed. When a woman gets absolutely possessed by her own will, her own will set against everything, then it's fearful, and she should be shot at last."

"And shouldn't men be shot at last, if they get possessed by their own will?"

"Ay!—the same! But I must get free of her, or she'll be at me again. I wanted to tell you. I must get a divorce if I possibly can. So we must be careful. We mustn't really be seen together, you and I. I never, *never* could stand it if she came down on me and you."

Connie pondered this.

"Then we can't be together?" she said.

"Not for six months or so. But I think my divorce will go through in September, then till March."

"But the baby will probably be born at the end of February," she said.

He was silent.

"I could wish the Cliffords and Berthas all dead," he said.

"It's not being very tender to them," she said.

"Tender to them? Yea, even then the tenderest thing you could do for them, perhaps, would be to give them death. They can't live. They only frustrate life. Their souls are awful inside them. Death ought to be sweet to them. And I ought to be allowed to shoot them."

"But you wouldn't do it," she said.

"I would though! and with less qualms than I shoot a weasel. It anyhow has a prettiness and a loneliness. But they are legion. Oh, I'd shoot them."

"Then perhaps it is just as well you daren't."

"Well."

Connie had now plenty to think of. It was evident he wanted absolutely to be free of Bertha Coutts. And she felt he was right. The last attack had been too grim—This meant her living alone, till spring. Perhaps she could get divorced from Clifford. But how? If Mellors were named, then there was an end to *his* divorce. How loathsome! Couldn't one go right away, to the far ends of the earth, and be free from it all?

One could not. The far ends of the world are not five minutes from Charing Cross, nowadays. While the wireless is active, there are no far ends of the earth. Kings of Dahomey and Lamas of Tibet listen in to London and New York.

Patience! Patience! The world is a vast and ghastly intricacy of mechanism, and one has to be very wary, not to get mangled by it.

Connie confided in her father.

"You see, father, he was Clifford's gamekeeper: but he was an officer in the army in India. Only he is like Colonel C. E. Florence, who preferred to become a private soldier again."

Sir Malcolm, however, had no sympathy with the unsatisfactory mysticism of the famous C. E. Florence. He saw too much advertisement behind all the humility. It looked just the sort of conceit the knight most loathed, the conceit of self-abasement.

"Where did your gamekeeper spring from?" asked Sir Malcolm irritably.

"He was a collier's son in Tevershall. But he's absolutely presentable."

The knight artist became more angry.

"Looks to me like a gold digger," he said. "And you're a pretty easy gold mine, apparently."

"No, father, it's not like that. You'd know if you saw him. He's a man. Clifford always detested him for not being humble."

"Apparently he had a good instinct, for once."

What Sir Malcolm could not bear, was the scandal of his daughter's having an intrigue with a gamekeeper. He did not mind the intrigue: he minded the scandal.

"I care nothing about the fellow. He's evidently been able to get around you all right. But by God, think of all the talk. Think of your stepmother, how she'll take it!"

"I know," said Connie. "Talk is beastly: especially if you live in society. And he wants so much to get his own divorce. I thought we might perhaps say it was another man's child, and not mention Mellors's name at all."

"Another man's! What other man's?"

"Perhaps Duncan Forbes. He has been our friend all his life. And he's a fairly well-known artist. And he's fond of me."

"Well I'm damned! Poor Duncan. And what's he going to get out of it?"

"I don't know. But he might rather like it, even."

"He might, might he? Well, he's a funny man, if he does. Why, you've never had an affair with him, have you?"

"No! But he doesn't really want it. He only loves me to be near him, but not to touch him."

"My God, what a generation!"

"He would like me most of all to be a model for him to paint from. Only I never wanted to."

"God help him! But he looks downtrodden enough for anything."

"Still, you wouldn't mind so much the talk about him?"

"My God, Connie, all the bloody contriving!"

"I know! It's sickening! But what can I do?"

"Contriving, conniving; conniving, contriving! Makes a man think he's lived too long."

"Come, father, if you haven't done a good deal of contriving and conniving in your time, you may talk."

"But it was different, I assure you."

"It's *always* different."

Hilda arrived, also furious when she heard of the new developments. And she also simply could not stand the thought of a public scandal about her sister and a gamekeeper. Too, too humiliating!

"Why should we not just disappear, separately, to British Columbia, and have no scandal?" said Connie.

But that was no good. The scandal would come out just the same. And if Connie was going with the man, she'd better be able to marry him. This was Hilda's opinion. Sir Malcolm wasn't sure. The affair might still blow over.

"But will you see him, father?"

Poor Sir Malcolm! he was by no means keen on it. And poor Mellors, he was still less keen. Yet the meeting took place: lunch in a private room at the club, the two men alone, looking one another up and down.

Sir Malcolm drank a fair amount of whiskey, Mellors also drank. And they talked all the while about India, on which the younger man was well informed.

This lasted during the meal. Only when coffee was served, and the waiter had gone, Sir Malcolm lit a cigar and said, heartily:

"Well, young man, and what about my daughter?"

The grin flickered on Mellors's face.

"Well, Sir, and what about her?"

"She's to have a child of yours, I understand."

"I have that honor!" grinned Mellors.

"Honor by God!" Sir Malcolm gave a little squirting laugh, and became Scotch and lewd. "Honor! How was the going, eh? Good, my boy, what?"

"Good!"

"I'll bet it was! Ha-ha! My daughter, chip of the old block, what! I never went back on a good bit of fucking, myself. Though her mother, oh, holy saints!" he rolled his eyes to heaven. "But you warmed her up, oh, you warmed her up, I can see that. Ha-ha! My blood in her! You set fire to her haystack all right. Ha-ha-ha! I was jolly glad of it, I can tell you. She needed it. Oh, she's a nice girl, she's a nice girl, and I knew she'd be good going, if only some damned man would set her stack on fire! Ha-ha-ha! A gamekeeper, oh, my boy! Bloody good poacher, if you ask me. Ha-ha! But now, look here, speaking seriously, what are we going to do about it? Speaking seriously, you know!"

Speaking seriously, they didn't get very far. Mellors, though a little tipsy, was much the soberer of the two. He kept the conversation as intelligent as possible: which isn't saying much.

"So you're a gamekeeper! Oh, you're quite right! That sort of game is worth a man's while, eh, what? The test of a woman is when you pinch her bottom. You can tell just by the feel of her bottom if she's going to come up all right. Ha-ha! I envy you, my boy. How old are you?"

"Thirty-nine."

The knight lifted his eyebrows.

"As much as that! Well, you've another good twenty years, by the look of you. Oh, gamekeeper or not, you're a good cock. I can see that with one eye shut. Not like that blasted Clifford! A lily-livered hound with never a fuck in him, never had. I like you, my boy. I'll bet you've a good cod on you: oh, you're a bantam, I can see that. You're a fighter. Gamekeeper! ha-ha, by crickey, I wouldn't trust my game to you! But look here, seriously, what are we going to do about it? The world's full of blasted old women."

Seriously, they didn't do anything about it, except establish the old freemasonry of male sensuality between them.

"And look here, my boy, if ever I can do anything for you, you can rely on me. Gamekeeper? Christ, but it's rich! I like it! Oh, I like it! Shows the girl's got spunk. What? After all, you know, she has her own income: moderate, moderate, but above starvation. And I'll leave her what I've got. By God, I will. She deserves it, for showing spunk, in a world of old women. I've been struggling to get myself clear of the skirts of old women for seventy years, and haven't managed it yet. But you're the man, I can see that."

"I'm glad you think so. They usually tell me, in a sideways fashion, that I'm the monkey."

"Oh, they would! My dear fellow, what could you be but a monkey, to all the old women?"

They parted most genially, and Mellors laughed inwardly all the time for the rest of the day.

The following day he had lunch with Connie and Hilda at some discreet place.

"It's a very great pity it's such an ugly situation all round," said Hilda.

"I had a lot o' fun out of it," said he.

"I think you might have avoided putting children into the world until you were both free to marry and have children."

"The Lord blew a bit too soon on the spark," said he.

"I think the Lord had nothing to do with it. Of course, Connie has enough money to keep you both, but the situation is unbearable."

"But then, you don't have to bear more than a small corner of it, do you?" said he.

"If you'd been in her own class."

"Or if I'd been in a cage at the zoo."

There was silence.

"I think," said Hilda, "it will be best if she names quite another man as corespondent, and you stay out of it altogether."

"But I thought I'd put my foot right in."

"I mean, in the divorce proceedings."

He gazed at her in wonder. Connie had not dared mention the Duncan scheme to him.

"I don't follow," he said.

"We have a friend who would probably agree to be named as corespondent, so that your name need not appear," said Hilda.

"You mean a man?"

"Of course!"

"But she's got no other?"

He looked in wonder at Connie.

"No, no!" she said hastily. "Only that old friendship, quite simple, no love."

"Then why should the fellow take the blame? If he's had nothing out of you?"

"Some men are chivalrous and don't only count what they get out of a woman," said Hilda.

"One for me, eh? But who's the johnny?"

"A friend whom we've known since we were children in Scotland, an artist."

"Duncan Forbes!" he said at once, for Connie had talked of him. "And how would you shift the blame on to him?"

"They could stay together in some hotel, or she could even stay in his apartment."

"Seems to me like a lot of fuss for nothing," he said.

"What else do you suggest?" said Hilda. "If your name appears, you will get no divorce from your wife, who is apparently quite an impossible person to be mixed up with."

"All that!" he said grimly.

There was a long silence.

"We could go right away," he said.

"There is no right away for Connie," said Hilda. "Clifford is too well known."

Again the silence of pure frustration.

"The world is what it is. If you want to live together without being persecuted, you will have to marry. To marry, you both have to be divorced. So how are you both going about it?"

He was silent for a long time.

"How are *you* going about it for us?" he said.

"We will see if Duncan will consent to figure as corespondent: then we must get Clifford to divorce Connie: and you must go on with your divorce, and you must both keep apart till you are free."

"Sounds like a lunatic asylum."

"Possibly! And the world would look on you as lunatics: or worse."

"What is worse?"

"Criminals, I suppose."

"Hope I can plunge in the dagger a few more times yet," he said grinning. Then he was silent and angry.

"Well!" he said at last. "I agree to anything. The world is a raving idiot, and no man can kill it: though I'll do my best. But you're right. We must rescue ourselves as best we can."

He looked in humiliation, anger, wariness and misery at Connie.

"Ma lass!" he said. "The world's goin' to put salt on thy tail."

"Not if we don't let it," she said.

She minded this conniving against the world less than he did.

Duncan, when approached, also insisted on seeing the delinquent gamekeeper, so there was a dinner, this time in his flat: the four of them. Duncan was a rather short, broad, dark-skinned, taciturn Hamlet of a fellow with straight black hair and a weird Celtic conceit of himself. His art was all tubes and valves and spirals and strange colors, ultra modern, yet with a certain power, even a certain purity of form and tone: only Mellors thought it cruel and repellent. He did not venture to say so, for Duncan was almost insane on the point of his art; it was a personal cult, a personal religion with him.

They were looking at the pictures in the studio, and Duncan kept his smallish brown eyes on the other man. He wanted to hear what the gamekeeper would say. He knew already Connie's and Hilda's opinions.

"It is like a pure bit of murder," said Mellors at last; a speech Duncan by no means expected from a gamekeeper.

"And who is murdered?" asked Hilda, rather coldly and sneeringly.

"Me! It murders all the bowels of compassion in a man."

A wave of pure hate came out of the artist. He heard the note of dislike in the other man's voice, and the note of contempt. And he himself loathed the mention of bowels of compassion. Sickly sentiment!

Mellors stood rather tall and thin, worn-looking, gazing with flickering detachment that was something like the dancing of a moth on the wing, at the pictures.

"Perhaps stupidity is murdered; sentimental stupidity," sneered the artist.

"Do you think so? I think all these tubes and corrugated vibrations are stupid enough for anything and pretty sentimental. They show a lot of self-pity and an awful lot of nervous self-opinion, seems to me."

In another wave of hate, the artist's face looked yellow. But with a sort of silent hauteur he turned the pictures to the wall.

"I think we may go to the dining room," he said.

And they trailed off, dismally.

After coffee, Duncan said:

"I don't at all mind posing as the father of Connie's child. But only on the condition that she'll come and pose as a model for me. I've wanted her for years, and she's always refused." He uttered it with the dark finality of an inquisitor announcing an *auto da fé*.

"Ah!" said Mellors. "You only do it on condition, then?"

"Quite! I only do it on that condition." The artist tried to put the utmost contempt of the other person into his speech. He put a little too much.

"Better have me as a model at the same time," said Mellors. "Better do us in a group, Vulcan and Venus under the net of art. I used to be a blacksmith, before I was a gamekeeper."

"Thank you," said the artist. "I don't think Vulcan has a figure that interests me."

"Not even if it was tubified and tittivated up?"

There was no answer. The artist was too haughty for further words.

It was a dismal party, in which the artist henceforth steadily ignored the presence of the other man, and talked only briefly, as if the words were wrung out of the depths of his gloomy portentousness, to the women.

"You didn't like him, but he's better than that, really. He's really kind," Connie explained as they left.

"He's a little black pup with a corrugated distemper," said Mellors.

"No, he wasn't nice today."

"And will you go and be a model to him?"

"Oh, I don't really mind anymore. He won't touch me. And I don't mind anything, if it paves the way to a life together for you and me."

"But he'll only shit on you on canvas."

"I don't care. He'll only be painting his own feelings for me, and I don't mind if he does that. I wouldn't have him touch me, not for anything. But if he thinks he can do anything with his owlish arty staring, let him stare. He can make as many empty tubes and corrugations out of me as he likes. It's his funeral. He hated you for what you said: that his tubified art is sentimental and self-important. But of course it's true."

❖ 19 ❖

Dear Clifford, I am afraid what you foresaw has happened. I am really in love with another man, and I do hope you will divorce me. I am staying at present with Duncan in his flat. I told you he was at Venice with us. I'm awfully unhappy for your sake: but do try to take it quietly. You don't really need me anymore, and I can't bear to come back to Wragby. I'm most awfully sorry. But do try to forgive me, and divorce me and find someone better. I'm not really the right person for you, I am too impatient and selfish, I suppose. But I can't ever come back to live with you again. And I feel so frightfully sorry about it all, for your sake. But if you don't let yourself get worked up, you'll see you won't mind so frightfully. You didn't really care about me personally. So do forgive me and get rid of me."

Clifford was not *inwardly* surprised to get this letter. Inwardly, he had known for a long time she was leaving him. But he had absolutely refused any outward admission of it. Therefore, outwardly, it came as the most terrible blow and shock to him. He had kept the surface of his confidence in her quite serene.

And that is how we are. By strength of will we cut off our inner intuitive knowledge from admitted consciousness. This causes a state of dread, or apprehension, which makes the blow ten times worse when it does fall.

Clifford was like a hysterical child. He gave Mrs. Bolton a terrible shock, sitting up in bed ghastly and blank.

"Why, Sir Clifford, whatever's the matter?"

No answer! She was terrified lest he had had a stroke. She hurried and felt his face, took his pulse.

"Is there a pain? Do try and tell me where it hurts you. Do tell me!"

No answer!

"Oh, dear! Oh, dear! Then I'll telephone to Sheffield for Dr. Carrington, and Dr. Lecky may as well run round straight away."

She was moving to the door, when he said in a hollow tone:

"No!"

She stopped and gazed at him. His face was yellow, blank, and like the face of an idiot.

"Do you mean you'd rather I didn't fetch the doctor?"

"Yes! I don't want him," came the sepulchral voice.

"Oh, but, Sir Clifford, you're ill, and I daren't take the responsibility. I *must* send for the doctor, or *I* shall be blamed."

A pause; then the hollow voice said:

"I'm not ill. My wife isn't coming back."—It was as if an image spoke.

"Not coming back? You mean her ladyship?" Mrs. Bolton moved a little nearer to the bed. "Oh, don't you believe it. You can trust her ladyship to come back."

The image in the bed did not change, but it pushed a letter over the counterpane.

"Read it!" said the sepulchral voice.

"Why, if it's a letter from her ladyship, I'm sure her ladyship wouldn't want me to read her letter to you, Sir Clifford. You can tell me what she says, if you wish."

But the face with the fixed blue eyes sticking out did not change.

"Read it!" repeated the voice.

"Why, if I must, I do it to obey you, Sir Clifford," she said.

And she read the letter.

"Well I *am* surprised at her ladyship," she said. "She promised so faithfully she'd come back!"

The face in the bed seemed to deepen its expression of wild, but motionless distraction. Mrs. Bolton looked at it and was worried. She knew what she was up against: male hysteria. She had not nursed soldiers without learning something about that very unpleasant disease.

She was a little impatient of Sir Clifford. Any man in his senses must have *known* his wife was in love with somebody else, and was going to leave him. Even, she was sure, Sir Clifford was inwardly absolutely aware of it, only he wouldn't admit it to himself. If he would have admitted it, and prepared himself for it! or if he would have admitted it, and actively struggled with his wife against it: that would have been acting like a man. But no! he knew it, and all the time tried to kid himself it wasn't so. He felt the devil twisting his tail, and pretended it was the angels smiling on him. This state of falsity had now brought on that crisis of falsity and dislocation, hysteria, which is a form of insanity. "It comes," she thought to herself, hating him a little, "because he always thinks of himself. He's so wrapped up in his own immortal self, that when he does get a shock he's like a mummy tangled in its own bandages. Look at him!"

But hysteria is dangerous: and she was a nurse, it was her duty to pull him out. Any attempt to rouse his manhood and his pride would only make him worse: for his manhood was dead, temporarily if not finally. He would only squirm softer and softer, like a worm, and become more dislocated.

The only thing was to release his self-pity. Like the lady in Tennyson, he must weep or he must die.

So Mrs. Bolton began to weep first. She covered her face with her hands and burst into little wild sobs. "I would never have believed it of her ladyship, I wouldn't!" She wept, suddenly summoning up all her old grief and sense of woe, and weeping the tears of her own bitter chagrin. Once she started her weeping was genuine enough, for she had had something to weep for.

Clifford thought of the way he had been betrayed by the woman Connie, and in a contagion of grief, tears filled his eyes and began to run down his cheeks. He was weeping for himself. Mrs. Bolton, as soon as she saw the tears running over his blank face, hastily wiped her own wet cheeks on her little handkerchief, and leaned towards him.

"Now don't you fret, Sir Clifford!" she said, in a luxury of emotion. "Now, don't you fret; don't, you'll only do yourself an injury!"

His body shivered suddenly in an indrawn breath of silent sobbing, and the tears ran quicker down his face. She laid her hand on his arm, and her own tears fell again. Again the shiver went through him, like a convulsion, and she laid her arm round his shoulder. "There, there! There, there! Don't you fret, then, don't you! Don't you fret!" she moaned to him, while her own tears fell. And she drew him to her, and held her arms round his great shoulders, while he laid his face on her bosom and sobbed, shaking and hulking his huge shoulders, whilst she softly stroked his dusky-blond hair and said: "There! There! There! There, then! There, then! Never you mind! Never you mind, then!"

And he put his arms round her and clung to her like a child, wetting the bib of her starched white apron, and the bosom of her pale-blue cotton dress, with his tears. He had let himself go altogether, at last.

So at length she kissed him, and rocked him on her bosom, and in her heart she said to herself: "Oh, Sir Clifford! Oh, high and mighty Chatterleys! Is this what you've come down to!" And finally he even went to sleep, like a child. And she felt worn out, and went to her own room, where she laughed and cried at once with a hysteria of her own. It was so ridiculous! It was so awful! such a come down! so shameful! And it *was* so upsetting as well.

After this, Clifford became like a child with Mrs. Bolton. He would hold her hand, and rest his head on her breast, and when she once lightly kissed him, he said: "Yes! Do kiss me! Do kiss me!" And when she sponged his great blond body, he would say the same: "Do kiss me!" and she would lightly kiss his body, anywhere, half in mockery.

And he lay with a queer, blank face like a child, with a bit of the wonderment of a child. And he would gaze on her with wide, childish eyes, in a relaxation of madonna-worship. It was sheer relaxation on his part, letting go all his manhood, and sinking back to a childish position that was really perverse. And then he would put his hand into her bosom and feel her breasts, and kiss them in exaltation, the exaltation of perversity, of being a child when he was a man.

Mrs. Bolton was both thrilled and ashamed, she both loved and hated it. Yet she never rebuffed nor rebuked him. And they drew into a closer physical intimacy, an intimacy of perversity, when he was a child stricken with an apparent candor and an apparent wonderment, that looked almost like a religious exaltation: the perverse and literal rendering of "except ye become again as a little child."—While she was the Magna Mater, full of power and potency, having the great blond child-man under her will and her stroke entirely.

The curious thing was that when this child-man, which Clifford was now and which he had been becoming for years, emerged into the world, he was much sharper and keener than the real man he used to be. This perverted child-man was now a *real* businessman; when it was a question of affairs, he was an absolute he-man, sharp as a needle, and impervious as a bit of steel. When he was out among men, seeking his own ends, and "making good" his colliery workings, he had an almost uncanny shrewdness, hardness, and a straight sharp punch. It was as if his very passivity and prostitution to the Magna Mater gave him insight into material business affairs, and lent him a certain remarkable inhuman force. The wallowing in private emotion, the utter abasement of his manly self, seemed to lend him a second nature, cold, almost visionary, business clever. In business he was quite inhuman.

And in this Mrs. Bolton triumphed. "How he's getting on!" she would say to herself in pride. "And that's my doing! My word, he'd never have got on like this with Lady Chatterley. She was not the one to put a man forward. She wanted too much for herself."

At the same time, in some corner of her weird female soul, how she despised him and hated him! He was to her the fallen beast, the squirming monster. And while she aided and abetted him all she could, away in the remotest corner of her ancient healthy womanhood she despised him with a savage contempt that knew no bounds. The merest tramp was better than he.

His behavior with regard to Connie was curious. He insisted on seeing her again. He insisted, moreover, on her coming to Wragby. On this point he was finally and absolutely fixed. Connie had promised to come back to Wragby, faithfully.

"But is it any use?" said Mrs. Bolton. "Can't you let her go, and be rid of her?"

"No! She said she was coming back, and she's got to come."

Mrs. Bolton opposed him no more. She knew what she was dealing with.

"I needn't tell you what effect your letter has had on me," he wrote to Connie to London. "Perhaps you can imagine it if you try, though no doubt you won't trouble to use your imagination on my behalf.

"I can only say one thing in answer: I must see you personally, here at Wragby, before I can do anything. You promised faithfully to come back to Wragby, and I hold you to the promise. I don't believe anything nor understand anything until I see you personally, here under normal circumstances. I needn't tell you that nobody here suspects anything, so your return would be quite normal. Then if you feel, after we have talked things over, that you still remain in the same mind, no doubt we can come to terms."

Connie showed this letter to Mellors.

"He wants to begin his revenge on you," said he, handing the letter back.

Connie was silent. She was somewhat surprised to find that she was afraid of Clifford. She was afraid to go near him. She was afraid of him as if he were evil and dangerous.

"What shall I do?" she said.

"Nothing, if you don't want to do anything."

She replied, trying to put Clifford off. He answered: "If you don't come back to Wragby now, I shall consider that you are coming back one day, and act accordingly. I shall just go on the same, and wait for you here, if I wait for fifty years."

She was frightened. This was bullying of an insidious sort. She had no doubt he meant what he said. He would not divorce her, and the child would be his, unless she could find some means of establishing its illegitimacy.

After a time of worry and harassment, she decided to go to Wragby. Hilda would go with her. She wrote this to Clifford. He replied: "I shall not welcome your sister, but I shall not deny her the door. I have no doubt she has connived at your desertion of your duties and responsibilities, so do not expect me to show pleasure in seeing her."

They went to Wragby. Clifford was away when they arrived. Mrs. Bolton received them.

"Oh, your Ladyship, it isn't the happy homecoming we hoped for, is it?" she said.

"Isn't it!" said Connie.

So this woman knew! How much did the rest of the servants know or suspect?

She entered the house which now she hated with every fiber in her body. The great, rambling mass of a place seemed evil to her, just a menace over her. She was no longer its mistress, she was its victim.

"I can't stay long here," she whispered to Hilda, terrified.

And she suffered going into her own bedroom, reentering into possession as if nothing had happened. She hated every minute inside the Wragby walls.

They did not meet Clifford till they went down to dinner. He was dressed, and with a black tie: rather reserved, and very much the superior gentleman. He behaved perfectly politely during the meal, and kept a polite sort of conversation going: but it seemed all touched with insanity.

"How much do the servants know?" asked Connie when the woman was out of the room.

"Of your intentions? Nothing whatsoever."

"Mrs. Bolton knows."

He changed color.

"Mrs. Bolton is not exactly one of the servants," he said.

"Oh, I don't mind."

There was tension till after coffee, when Hilda said she would go up to her room.

Clifford and Connie sat in silence when she had gone. Neither would begin to speak. Connie was so glad that he wasn't taking the pathetic line, she kept him up to as much haughtiness as possible. She just sat silent and looked down at her hands.

"I suppose you don't at all mind having gone back on your word?" he said at last.

"I can't help it," she murmured.

"But if you can't, who can?"

"I suppose nobody."

He looked at her with curious cold rage. He was used to her. She was as it were embedded in his will. How dared she now go back on him, and destroy the fabric of his daily existence? How dared she try to cause this derangement of his personality!

"And for *what* do you want to go back on everything?" he insisted.

"Love!" she said. It was best to be hackneyed.

"Love of Duncan Forbes? But you didn't think that worth having, when you met me. Do you mean to say you now love him better than anything else in life?"

"One changes," she said.

"Possibly! Possibly you may have whims. But you still have to convince me of the importance of the change. I merely don't believe in your love of Duncan Forbes."

"But why *should* you believe in it? You have only to divorce me, not to believe in my feelings."

"And why should I divorce you?"

"Because I don't want to live here anymore. And you really don't want me."

"Pardon me! I don't change. For my part, since you are my wife, I should prefer that you should stay under my roof in dignity and quiet. Leaving aside personal feelings, and I assure you, on my part it is leaving aside a great deal, it is bitter as death to me to have this order of life broken up, here in Wragby, and the decent round of daily life smashed, just for some whim of yours."

After a time of silence she said:

"I can't help it. I've got to go. I expect I shall have a child." He, too, was silent for a time.

"And is it for the child's sake you must go?" he asked at length.

She nodded.

"And why? Is Duncan Forbes so keen on his spawn?"

"Surely keener than you would be," she said.

"But really? I want my wife, and I see no reason for letting her go. If she likes to bear a child under my roof, she is welcome, and the child is welcome, provided that the decency and order of life is preserved. Do you mean to tell me that Duncan Forbes has a greater hold over you? I don't believe it."

There was a pause.

"But don't you see," said Connie. "I *must* go away from you, and I *must* live with the man I love."

"No, I don't see it! I don't give tuppence for your love, nor for the man you love. I don't believe in that sort of cant."

"But, you see, I do."

"Do you? My dear Madam, you are too intelligent, I assure you, to believe in your own love for Duncan Forbes. Believe me, even now you really care more for me. So why should I give in to such nonsense!"

She felt he was right there. And she felt she could keep silent no longer.

"Because it isn't Duncan that I *do* love," she said, looking up at him. "We only said it was Duncan, to spare your feelings."

"To spare my feelings?"

"Yes! Because who I really love, and it'll make you hate me, is Mr. Mellors, who was our gamekeeper here."

If he could have sprung out of his chair, he would have done so. His face went yellow, and his eyes bulged with disaster as he glared at her.

Then he dropped back in the chair, gasping and looking up at the ceiling.

At length he sat up.

"Do you mean to say you're telling me the truth?" he asked, looking gruesome.

"Yes! You know I am."

"And when did you begin with him?"

"In the spring."

He was silent like some beast in a trap.

"And it *was* you, then, in the bedroom at the cottage?"

So he had really inwardly known all the time.

"Yes!"

He still leaned forward in his chair, gazing at her like a cornered beast.

"My God, you ought to be wiped off the face of the earth!"

"Why?" she ejaculated faintly.

But he seemed not to hear her.

"That scum! That bumptious lout! That miserable cad! And carrying on with him all the time, while you were here and he was one of my servants! My God, my God, is there any limit to the beastly lowness of women!"

He was beside himself with rage, as she knew he would be.

"And you mean to say you want to have a child to a cad like that?"

"Yes! I'm going to."

"You're going to! You mean you're sure! How long have you been sure?"

"Since June."

He was speechless, and the queer blank look of a child came over him again.

"You'd wonder," he said at last, "that such beings were ever allowed to be born."

"What beings?" she asked.

He looked at her weirdly, without an answer. It was obvious he couldn't even accept the fact of the existence of Mellors, in any connection with his own life. It was sheer, unspeakable, impotent hate.

"And do you mean to say you'd marry him?—and bear his foul name?" he asked at length.

"Yes, that's what I want."

He was again as if dumbfounded.

"Yes!" he said at last. "That proves what I've always thought about you is correct: you're not normal, you're not in your right senses. You're one of those half-insane, perverted women who must run after depravity, the *nostalgie de la boue*."

Suddenly he had become almost wistfully moral, seeing himself the incarnation of good, and people like Mellors and Connie the incarnation of mud, of evil. He seemed to be growing vague, inside a nimbus.

"So don't you think you'd better divorce me and have done with it?" she said.

"No! You can go where you like, but I shan't divorce you," he said idiotically.

"Why not?"

He was silent, in the silence of imbecile obstinacy.

"Would you even let the child be legally yours, and your heir?" she said.

"I care nothing about the child."

"But if it's a boy it will be legally your son, and it will inherit your title, and have Wragby."

"I care nothing about that," he said.

"But you *must*! I shall prevent the child from being legally yours, if I can. I'd so much rather it were illegitimate and mine: if it can't be Mellors's."

"Do as you like about that."

He was immovable.

"And won't you divorce me?" she said. "You can use Duncan as a pretext! There'd be no need to bring in the real name. Duncan doesn't mind."

"*I* shall never divorce you," he said, as if a nail had been driven in.

"But why? Because I want you to?"

"Because I follow my own inclination, and I'm not inclined to."

It was useless. She went upstairs, and told Hilda the upshot.

"Better get away tomorrow," said Hilda, "and let him come to his senses."

So Connie spent half the night packing her really private and personal effects. In the morning she had her trunks sent to the station, without telling Clifford. She decided to see him only to say good-bye, before lunch.

But she spoke to Mrs. Bolton.

"I must say good-bye to you, Mrs. Bolton. You know why, but I can trust you not to talk."

"Oh, you can trust me, your Ladyship, though it's a sad blow for us here, indeed. But I hope you'll be happy with the other gentleman."

"The other gentleman! It's Mr. Mellors, and I care for him. Sir Clifford knows. But don't say anything to anybody. And if one day you think Sir Clifford may be willing to divorce me, let me know, will you? I should like to be properly married to the man I care for."

"I'm sure you would, my Lady. Oh, you can trust me. I'll be faithful to Sir Clifford, and I'll be faithful to you, for I can see you're both right in your own ways."

"Thank you! And look! I want to give you this—may I?—" So Connie left Wragby once more, and went on with Hilda to Scotland. Mellors went into the country and got work on a farm. The idea was, he should get his divorce, if possible, whether Connie got hers or not. And for six months he should work at farming, so that eventually he and Connie could have some small farm of their own, into which he could put his energy. For he would have to have some work, even hard work, to do, and he would have to make his own living, even if her capital started him.

So they would have to wait till spring was in, till the baby was born, till the early summer came round again.

The Grange Farm,
Old Heanor, 29 September.

"I got on here with a bit of contriving, because I knew Richards, the company engineer, in the army. It is a farm belonging to Butler & Smitham Colliery Company, they use it for raising hay and oats for the pit-ponies; not a private concern. But they've got cows and pigs and all the rest of it, and I get thirty shillings a week as laborer. Rowley, the farmer, puts me on to as many jobs as he can, so that I can learn as much as possible between now and next Easter. I've not heard a thing about Bertha. I've no idea why she didn't show up at the divorce, nor where she is nor what she's up to. But if I keep quiet till March I suppose I shall be free. And don't you bother about Sir Clifford. He'll want to get rid of you one of these days. If he leaves you alone, it's a lot.

"I've got lodgings in a bit of an old cottage in Engine Row, very decent. The man is engine-driver at High Park, tall, with a beard, and very chapel. The woman is a birdy bit of a thing who loves anything superior, King's English and allow-me! all the time. But they lost their only son in the war, and it's sort of knocked a hole in them. There's a long gawky lass of a daughter training for a schoolteacher, and I help her with her lessons sometimes, so we're quite the family. But they're very decent people, and only too kind to me. I expect I'm more coddled than you are.

"I like farming all right. It's not inspiring, but then I don't ask to be inspired. I'm used to horses, and cows, though they are very female, have a soothing effect on me. When I sit with my head in her side, milking, I feel very solaced. They have six rather fine Herefords. Oat harvest is just over and I enjoyed it, in spite of sore hands and a lot of rain. I don't take much notice of people, but get on with them all right. Most things one just ignores.

"The pits are working badly; this is a colliery district like Tevershall, only prettier. I sometimes sit in the Wellington and talk to the men. They grumble a lot, but they're not going to alter anything. As everybody says, the Notts-Derby miners have got their hearts in the right place. But the rest of their anatomy must be in the wrong place, in a world that has no use for them. I like them, but they don't cheer me much: not enough of the old fighting-cock in them. They talk a lot about nationalism, nationalization of royalties, nationalization of the whole industry. But you can't nationalize coal and leave all the other industries as they are. They talk about putting coal to new uses, like Sir Clifford is trying to do. It may work here and there, but not as a general thing, I doubt. Whatever you make you've got to sell it. The men are very apathetic. They feel the whole damned thing is doomed, and I believe it is. And they are doomed along with it. Some of the young ones spout about a Soviet, but there's not much conviction in them. There's no sort of conviction about anything, except that it's all a muddle and a hole. Even under a Soviet you've still got to sell coal: and that's the difficulty.

"We've got this great industrial population, and they've got to be fed, so the damn show has to be kept going somehow. The women talk a lot more than the men nowadays, and they are a sight more cocksure. The men are limp, they feel a doom somewhere, and they go about as if there was nothing to be done. Anyhow nobody knows what should be done, in spite of all the talk. The young ones get mad because they've no money to spend. Their whole life depends on spending money, and now they've got none to spend. That's our civilization and our education: bring up the masses to depend entirely on spending money, and then the money gives out. The pits are working two days, two-and-a-half days a week, and there's no sign of betterment even for the winter. It means a man bringing up a family on twenty-five and thirty shillings. The women are the maddest of all. But then they're the maddest for spending, nowadays.

"If you could only tell them that living and spending isn't the same thing! But it's no good. If only they were educated to *live* instead of earn and spend, they could manage very happily on twenty-five shillings. If the men wore scarlet trousers, as I said, they wouldn't think so much of money: if they could dance and hop and skip, and sing and swagger and be handsome, they could do with very little cash. And amuse the women themselves, and be amused by the women. They ought to learn to be naked and handsome, and to sing in a mass and dance the old group dances, and carve the stools they sit on, and embroider their own emblems. Then they wouldn't need money. And that's the only way to solve the industrial problem: train the people to be able to live, and live in handsomeness, without needing to spend. But you can't do it. They're all one-track minds nowadays. Whereas the mass of people oughtn't even to try to think, because they *can't*! They should be alive and frisky, and acknowledge the great god Pan. He's the only god for the masses, forever. The few can go in for higher cults if they like. But let the mass be forever pagan.

"But the colliers aren't pagan, far from it. They're a sad lot, a deadened lot of men: dead to their women, dead to life. The young ones scoot about on motor-bikes with girls, and jazz when they get a chance. But they're very dead. And it needs money. Money poisons you when you've got it, and starves you when you haven't.

"I'm sure you're sick of all this. But I don't want to harp on myself, and I've nothing happening to me. I don't like to think too much about you, in my head, that only makes a mess of us both. But of course what I live for now is for you and me to live together. I'm frightened, really. I feel the devil in the air, and he'll try to get us. Or not the devil, Mammon: which I think, after all, is only the mass-will of people, wanting money and hating life. Anyhow I feel great grasping white hands in the air, wanting to get hold of the throat of anybody who tries to live, to live beyond money, and squeeze the life out. There's a bad time coming. There's a bad time coming, boys, there's a bad time coming! If things go on as they are, there's nothing lies in the future but death and destruction, for these industrial masses. I feel my inside turn to water sometimes, and there you are, going to have a child by me. But never mind. All the bad times that ever have been, haven't been able to blow the crocus out: not even the love of women. So they won't be able to blow out my wanting you, nor the little glow there is between you and me. We'll be together next year. And though I'm frightened, I believe in your being with me. A man has to fend and fettle for the best, and then trust in something beyond himself. You can't insure against the future, except by really believing in the best bit of you, and in the power beyond it. So I believe in the little flame between us. For me now, it's the only thing in the world. I've got no friends, not inward friends. Only you. And now the little flame is all I care about in my life. There's the baby, but that is a side issue. It's my Pentecost, the forked flame between me and you. The old Pentecost isn't quite right. Me and God is a bit uppish, somehow. But the little forked flame between me and you: there you are! That's what I abide by, and will abide by, Cliffords and Berthas, colliery companies and governments and the money-mass of people all notwithstanding.

"That's why I don't like to start thinking about you actually. It only tortures me, and does you no good. I don't want you to be away from me. But if I start fretting it wastes something. Patience, always patience. This is my fortieth winter. And I can't help all the winters that have been. But this winter I'll stick to my little pentecost flame, and have some peace. And I won't let the breath of people blow it out. I believe in a higher mystery, that doesn't let even the crocus be blown out. And if you're in Scotland and I'm in the Midlands, and I can't put my arms round you, and wrap my legs round you, yet I've got something of you. My soul softly flaps in the little pentecost flame with you, like the peace of fucking. We fucked a flame into being. Even the flowers are fucked into being between the sun and the earth. But it's a delicate thing, and takes patience and the long pause.

"So I love chastity now, because it is the peace that comes of fucking. I love being chaste now. I love it as snowdrops love the snow. I love this chastity, which is the pause of peace of our fucking, between us now like a snowdrop of forked white fire. And when the real spring comes, when the drawing together comes, then we can fuck the little flame brilliant and yellow, brilliant. But not now, not yet! Now is the time to be chaste, it is so good to be chaste, like a river of cool water in my soul. I love the chastity now that it flows between us. It is like fresh water and rain. How can men want wearisomely to philander! What a misery to be like Don Juan, and impotent ever to fuck oneself into peace, and the little flame alight, impotent and unable to be chaste in the cool between-whiles, as by a river.

"Well, so many words, because I can't touch you. If I could sleep with my arms round you, the ink could stay in the bottle. We could be chaste together just as we can fuck together. But we have to be separate for a while, and I suppose it is really the wiser way. If only one were sure.

"Never mind, never mind, we won't get worked up. We really trust in the little flame, in the unnamed god that shields it from being blown out. There's so much of you here with me, really, that it's a pity you aren't all here.

"Never mind about Sir Clifford. If you don't hear anything from him, never mind. He can't really do anything to you. Wait, he will want to get rid of you at last, to cast you out. And if he doesn't, we'll manage to keep clear of him. But he will. In the end he will want to spew you out as the abominable thing.

"Now I can't even leave off writing to you.

"But a great deal of us is together, and we can but abide by it, and steer our courses to meet soon. John Thomas says good night to lady Jane, a little droopingly, but with a hopeful heart."

A PROPOS OF *LADY CHATTERLEY'S LOVER*

Owing to the existence of various pirated editions of *Lady Chatterley's Lover*, I brought out in 1929 a cheap popular edition, produced in France and offered to the public at sixty francs, hoping at least to meet the European demand. The pirates, in the United States certainly, were prompt and busy. The first stolen edition was being sold in New York almost within a month of the arrival in America of the first genuine copies from Florence. It was a facsimile of the original, produced by the photographic method, and was sold, even by reliable booksellers, to the unsuspecting public as if it were the original first edition. The price was usually fifteen dollars, whereas the price of the original was ten dollars: and the purchaser was left in fond ignorance of the fraud.

This gallant attempt was followed by others. I am told there was still another facsimile edition produced in New York or Philadelphia: and I myself possess a filthy looking book bound in a dull orange cloth, with green label, smearily produced by photography, and containing my signature forged by the little boy of the piratical family. It was when this edition appeared in London, from New York, towards the end of 1928, and was offered to the public at thirty shillings, that I put out from Florence my little second edition of two hundred copies, which I offered at a guinea. I had wanted to save it for a year or more, but had to launch it against the dirty orange pirate. But the number was too small. The orange pirate persisted.

Then I have had in my hand a very funereal volume, bound in black and elongated to look like a bible or long hymn-book, gloomy. This time the pirate was not only sober, but earnest. He has not one, but two title pages, and on each is a vignette representing the American Eagle, with six stars round his head and lightning splashing from his paw, all surrounded by a laurel wreath in honor of his latest exploit in literary robbery. Altogether it is a sinister volume—like Captain Kidd with his face blackened, reading a sermon to those about to walk the plank. Why the pirate should have elongated the page, by adding a false page-heading, I don't know. The effect is peculiarly depressing, sinisterly high-brow. For of course this book also was produced by the photographic process. The signature anyhow is omitted. And I am told this lugubrious tome sells for ten, twenty, thirty, and fifty dollars, according to the whim of the bookseller and the gullibility of the purchaser.

That makes three pirated editions in the United States for certain. I have heard mentioned the report of a fourth, another facsimile of the original. But since I haven't seen it, I want not to believe in it.

There is, however, the European pirated edition of fifteen hundred, produced by a Paris firm of booksellers, and stamped *Imprimé en Allemagne:* Printed in Germany. Whether printed in Germany or not, it was certainly printed, not photographed, for some of the spelling errors of the original are corrected. And it is a very respectable volume, a very close replica of the original, but lacking the signature and it gives itself away also by the green-and-yellow silk edge of the back-binding. This edition is sold to the trade at one hundred francs, and offered to the public at three hundred, four hundred, five hundred francs. Very unscrupulous booksellers are said to have forged the signature and offered the book as the original signed edition. Let us hope it is not true. But it all sounds very black against the "trade." Still there is some relief. Certain booksellers will not handle the pirated edition at all. Both sentimental and business scruples prevent them. Others handle it, but not very warmly. And apparently they would all rather handle the authorized edition. So that sentiment does genuinely enter in, against the pirates, even if not strong enough to keep them out altogether.

None of these pirated editions has received any sort of authorization from me, and from none of them have I received a penny. A semirepentant bookseller of New York did, however, send me some dollars which were, he said my 10% royalty on all copies sold in his shop. "I know," he wrote, "it is but a drop in the bucket." He meant of course, a drop out of the bucket. And since, for a drop, it was quite a nice little sum, what a beautiful bucketful there must have been for the pirates!

I received a belated offer from the European Pirates, who found the booksellers stiff-necked, offering me a royalty on all copies sold in the past as well as the future, if I would authorize their edition. Well, I thought to myself, in a world of: Do him or you will be done by him—why not?—When it came to the point, however, pride rebelled. It is understood that Judas is always ready with a kiss. But that I should have to kiss him back—!

So I managed to get published the little cheap French edition, photographed down from the original, and offered at sixty francs. English publishers urge me to make an expurgated edition, promising large returns, perhaps even a little bucket, one of those children's seaside pails!—and insisting that I should show the public that here is a fine novel, apart from all "purple" and all "words." So I begin to be tempted and start in to expurgate. But impossible! I might as well try to clip my own nose into shape with scissors. The book bleeds.

And in spite of all antagonism, I put forth this novel as an honest, healthy book, necessary for us today. The words that shock so much at first don't shock at all after a while. Is this because the mind is depraved by habit? Not a bit. It is that the words merely shocked the eye, they never shocked the mind at all. People without minds may go on being shocked, but they don't matter. People with minds realize that they aren't shocked, and never really were: and they experience a sense of relief.

And that is the whole point. We are today, as human beings, evolved and cultured far beyond the taboos which are inherent in our culture. This is a very important fact to realize. Probably, to the Crusaders, mere words were potent and evocative to a degree we can't realize. The evocative power of the so-called obscene words must have been very dangerous to the dim-minded, obscure, violent natures of the Middle Ages, and perhaps are still too strong for slow-minded, half-evoked lower natures today. But real culture makes us give to a word only those mental and imaginative reactions which belong to the mind, and saves us from violent and indiscriminate physical reactions which may wreck social decency. In the past, man was too weak-minded, or crude-minded, to contemplate his own physical body and physical functions, without getting all messed up with physical reactions that overpowered him. It is no longer so. Culture and civilization have taught us to separate the reactions. We now know the act does not necessarily follow on the thought. In fact, thought and action, word and deed, are two separate forms of consciousness, two separate lives which we lead. We need, very sincerely, to keep a connection. But while we think, we do not act, and while we act we do not think. The great necessity is that we should act according to our thoughts, and think according to our acts. But while we are in thought we cannot really act, and while we are in action we cannot really think. The two conditions, of thought and action, are mutually exclusive. Yet they should be related in harmony.

And this is the real point of this book. I want men and women to be able to think sex, fully, completely, honestly and cleanly.

Even if we can't act sexually to our complete satisfaction, let us at least think sexually, complete and clear. All this talk of young girls and virginity, like a blank white sheet on which nothing is written, is pure nonsense. A young girl and a young boy is a tormented tangle, a seething confusion of sexual feelings and sexual thoughts which only the years will disentangle. Years of honest thoughts of sex, and years of struggling action in sex will bring us at last where we want to get, to our real and accomplished chastity, our completeness, when our sexual act and our sexual thought are in harmony, and the one does not interfere with the other.

Far be it from me to suggest that all women should go running after gamekeepers for lovers. Far be it from me to suggest that they should be running after anybody. A great many men and women today are happiest when they abstain and stay sexually apart, quite clean: and at the same time, when they understand and realize sex more fully. Ours is the day of realization rather than action. There has been so much action in the past, especially sexual action, a wearying repetition over and over, without a corresponding thought, a corresponding realization. Now our business is to realize sex. Today the full conscious realization of sex is even more important than the act itself. After centuries of obfuscation, the mind demands to know and know fully. The body is a good deal in abeyance, really. When people act in sex, nowadays, they are half the time acting up. They do it because they think it is expected of them. Whereas as a matter of fact it is the mind which is interested, and the body has to be provoked. The reason being that our ancestors have so assiduously acted sex without ever thinking it or realizing it, that now the act tends to be mechanical, dull and disappointing, and only fresh mental realization will freshen up the experience.

The mind has to catch up, in sex: indeed, in all the physical acts. Mentally, we lag behind in our sexual thought, in a dimness, a lurking, groveling fear which belongs to our raw, somewhat bestial ancestors. In this one respect, sexual and physical, we have left the mind unevolved. Now we have to catch up, and make a balance between the consciousness of the body's sensations and experiences, and these sensations and experiences themselves. Balance up the consciousness of the act, and the act itself. Get the two in harmony. It means having a proper reverence for sex, and a proper awe of the body's strange experience. It means being able to use the so-called obscene words, because these are a natural part of the mind's consciousness of the body. Obscenity only comes in when the mind despises and fears the body, and the body hates and resists the mind.

When we read of the case of Colonel Barker, we see what is the matter. Colonel Barker was a woman who masqueraded as a man. The "Colonel" married a wife, and lived five years with her in "conjugal happiness." And the poor wife thought all the time she was married normally and happily to a real husband.

The revelation at the end is beyond all thought cruel for the poor woman. The situation is monstrous. Yet there are thousands of women today who might be so deceived, and go on being deceived. Why? Because they know nothing, they can't think sexually at all; they are morons in this respect. It is better to give all girls this book, at the age of seventeen.

The same with the case of the venerable schoolmaster and clergyman, for years utterly "holy and good": and at the age of sixty-five, tried in the police courts for assaulting little girls. This happens at the moment when the Home Secretary, himself growing elderly, is most loudly demanding and enforcing a mealy-mouthed silence about sexual matters. Doesn't the experience of that other elderly, most righteous and "pure" gentleman, make him pause at all?

But so it is. The mind has an old groveling fear of the body and the body's potencies. It is the mind we have to liberate, to civilize on these points. The mind's terror of the body has probably driven more men mad than ever could be counted. The insanity of a great mind like Swift's is at least partly traceable to this cause. In the poem to his mistress Celia, which has the maddened refrain "But—Celia, Celia, Celia s***s," (the word rhymes with spits), we see what can happen to a great mind when it falls into panic. A great wit like Swift could not see how ridiculous he made himself. Of course Celia s***s! Who doesn't? And how much worse if she didn't. It is hopeless. And then think of poor Celia, made to feel iniquitous about her proper natural function, by her "lover." It is monstrous. And it comes from having taboo words, and from not keeping the mind sufficiently developed in physical and sexual consciousness.

In contrast to the puritan hush! hush!, which produces the sexual moron, we have the modern young jazzy and highbrow person who has gone one better, and won't be hushed in any respect, and just "does as she likes." From fearing the body, and denying its existence, the advanced young go to the other extreme and treat it as a sort of toy to be played with, a slightly nasty toy, but still you can get some fun out of it, before it lets you down. These young people scoff at the importance of sex, take it like a cocktail, and flout their elders with it. These young ones are advanced and superior. They despise a book like *Lady Chatterley's Lover*. It is much too simple and ordinary for them. The naughty words they care nothing about, and the attitude to love they find old-fashioned. Why make a fuss about it? Take it like a cocktail! The book, they say, shows the mentality of a boy of fourteen. But perhaps the mentality of a boy of fourteen, who still has a little natural awe and proper fear in fact of sex, is more wholesome than the mentality of the young cocktaily person who has no respect for anything and whose mind has nothing to do but play with the toys of life, sex being one of the chief toys, and who loses his mind in the process. Heliogabulus, indeed!

So, between the stale gray puritan who is likely to fall into sexual indecency in advanced age, and the smart jazzy person of the young world, who says: "We can do anything. If we can think a thing we can do it," and then the low uncultured person with a dirty mind, who looks for dirt—this book has hardly a space to turn in. But to them all I say the same: Keep your perversions if you like them—your perversion of puritanism, your perversion of smart licentiousness, your perversion of a dirty mind. But I stick to my book and my position: Life is only bearable when the mind and the body are in harmony, and there is a natural balance between them, and each has a natural respect for the other.

And it is obvious, there is no balance and no harmony now. The body is at the best the tool of the mind, at the worst, the toy. The businessman keeps himself "fit," that is, keeps his body in good working order, for the sake of his business, and the usual young person who spends much time on keeping fit does so as a rule out of self-conscious self-absorption, narcissism. The mind has a stereotyped set of ideas and "feelings," and the body is made to act up, like a trained dog: to beg for sugar, whether it wants sugar or whether it doesn't, to shake hands when it would dearly like to snap the hand it has to shake. The body of men and women today is just a trained dog. And of no one is this more true than of the free and emancipated young. Above all, their bodies are the bodies of trained dogs. And because the dog is trained to do things the old-fashioned dog never did, they call themselves free, full of real life, the real thing.

But they know perfectly well it is false. Just as the businessman knows, somewhere, that he's all wrong. Men and women aren't really dogs: they only look like it and behave like it. Somewhere inside there is a great chagrin and a gnawing discontent. The body is, in its spontaneous natural self, dead or paralyzed. It has only the secondary life of a circus dog, acting up and showing off: and then collapsing.

What life could it have, of itself? The body's life is the life of sensations and emotions. The body feels real hunger, real thirst, real joy in the sun or the snow, real pleasure in the smell of roses or the look of a lilac bush; real anger, real sorrow, real love, real tenderness, real warmth, real passion, real hate, real grief. All the emotions belong to the body, and are only recognized by the mind. We may hear the most sorrowful piece of news, and only feel a mental excitement. Then, hours after, perhaps in sleep, the awareness may reach the bodily centers, and true grief wrings the heart.

How different they are, mental feelings and real feelings. Today, many people live and die without having had any real feelings—though they have had a "rich emotional life" apparently, having showed strong mental feeling. But it is all counterfeit. In magic, one of the so-called "occult" pictures represents a man standing, apparently, before a flat table mirror, which reflects him from the waist to the head, so that you have the man from head to waist, then his reflection downwards from waist to head again. And whatever it may mean in magic, it means what we are today, creatures whose active emotional self has no real existence, but is all reflected downwards from the mind. Our education from the start has *taught* us a certain range of emotions, what to feel and what not to feel, and how to feel the feelings we allow ourselves to feel. All the rest is just nonexistent. The vulgar criticism of any new good book is: Of course nobody ever felt like that!—People allow themselves to feel a certain number of finished feelings. So it was in the last century. This feeling only what you allow yourselves to feel at last kills all capacity for feeling, and in the higher emotional range you feel nothing at all: This has come to pass in our present century. The higher emotions are strictly dead. They have to be faked.

And by higher emotions we mean love in all its manifestations, from genuine desire to tender love, love of our fellowmen, and love of God: we mean love, joy, delight, hope, true indignant anger, passionate sense of justice and injustice, truth and untruth, honor and dishonor, and real belief in *anything*: for belief is a profound emotion that has the mind's connivance. All these things, today, are more or less dead. We have in their place the loud and sentimental counterfeit of all such emotion.

Never was an age more sentimental, more devoid of real feeling, more exaggerated in false feeling, than our own. Sentimentality and counterfeit feeling have become a sort of game, everybody trying to outdo his neighbor. The radio and the film are mere counterfeit emotion all the time, the current press and literature the same. People wallow in emotion: counterfeit emotion. They lap it up: they live in it and on it. They ooze with it.

And at times, they seem to get on very well with it all. And then, more and more, they break down. They go to pieces. You can fool yourself for a long time about your own feelings. But not forever. The body itself hits back at you, and hits back remorselessy in the end.

As for other people—you can fool most people all the time, and all people most of the time, but not all people all the time, with false feelings. A young couple fall in counterfeit love, and fool themselves and each other completely. But, alas, counterfeit love is good cake but bad bread. It produces a fearful emotional indigestion. Then you get a modern marriage, and a still more modern separation.

The trouble with counterfeit emotion is that nobody is really happy, nobody is really contented, nobody has any peace. Everybody keeps on rushing to get away from the counterfeit emotion which is in themselves worst of all. They rush from the false feelings of Peter to the false feelings of Adrian, from the counterfeit emotions of Margaret to those of Virginia, from film to radio, from Eastbourne to Brighton, and the more it changes the more it is the same thing.

Above all things love is a counterfeit feeling today. Here, above all things, the young will tell you, is the greatest swindle. That is, if you take it seriously. Love is all right if you take it lightly, as an amusement. But if you begin taking it seriously you are let down with a crash.

There are, the young women say, no *real* men to love. And there are, the young men say, no *real* girls to fall in love with. So they go on falling in love with unreal ones, on either side; which means, if you can't have real feelings, you've got to have counterfeit ones: since some feelings you've *got* to have: like falling in love. There are still some young people who would *like* to have real feelings, and they are bewildered to death to know why they can't. Especially in love.

But especially in love, only counterfeit emotions exist nowadays. We have all been taught to mistrust everybody emotionally, from parents downwards, or upwards. Don't trust *anybody* with your real emotions: if you've got any: that is the slogan of today. Trust them with your money, even, but *never* with your feelings. They are bound to trample on them.

I believe there has never been an age of greater mistrust between persons than ours today: under a superficial but quite genuine social trust. Very few of my friends would pick my pocket, or let me sit on a chair where I might hurt myself. But practically all my friends would turn my real emotions to ridicule. They can't help it; it's the spirit of the day. So there goes love, and there goes friendship: for each implies a fundamental emotional sympathy. And hence, counterfeit love, which there is no escaping.

And with counterfeit emotions there is no real sex at all. Sex is the one thing you cannot really swindle; and it is the center of the worst swindling of all, emotional swindling. Once come down to sex, and the emotional swindle must collapse. But in all the approaches to sex, the emotional swindle intensifies more and more. Till you get there. Then collapse.

Sex lashes out against counterfeit emotion, and is ruthless, devastating against false love. The peculiar hatred of people who have not loved one another, but who have pretended to, even perhaps have imagined they really did love, is one of the phenomena of our time. The phenomenon, of course, belongs to all time. But today it is almost universal. People who thought they loved one another dearly, dearly, and went on for years, ideal: lo! suddenly the most profound and vivid hatred appears. If it doesn't come out fairly young, it saves itself till the happy couple are nearing fifty, the time of the great sexual change—and then—cataclysm!

Nothing is more startling. Nothing is more staggering, in our age, than the intensity of the hatred people, men and women, feel for one another when they have once "loved" one another. It breaks out in the most extraordinary ways. And when you know people intimately, it is almost universal. It is the charwoman as much as the mistress, and the duchess as much as the policeman's wife.

And it would be too horrible, if one did not remember that in all of them, men and women alike, it is the organic reaction against counterfeit love. All love today is counterfeit. It is a stereotyped thing. All the young know just how they ought to feel and how they ought to behave, in love. And they feel and they behave like that. And it is counterfeit love. So that revenge will come back at them, tenfold. The sex, the very sexual organism in man and woman alike accumulates a deadly and desperate rage, after a certain amount of counterfeit love has been palmed off on it, even if itself has given nothing but counterfeit love. The element of counterfeit in love at last maddens, or else kills, sex, the deepest sex in the individual. But perhaps it would be safe to say that it *always* enrages the inner sex, even if at last it kills it. There is always the period of rage. And the strange thing is, the worst offenders in the counterfeit-love game fall into the greatest rage. Those whose love has been a bit sincere are always gentler, even though they have been most swindled.

Now the real tragedy is here: that we are none of us all of a piece, none of us *all* counterfeit, or *all* true love. And in many a marriage, in among the counterfeit there flickers a little flame of the true thing, on both sides. The tragedy is, that in an age peculiarly conscious of counterfeit, peculiarly suspicious of substitute and swindle in emotion, particularly sexual emotion, the rage and mistrust against the counterfeit element is likely to overwhelm and extinguish the small, true flame of real loving communion, which might have made two lives happy. Herein lies the danger of harping only on the counterfeit and the swindle of emotion, as most "advanced" writers do. Though they do it, of course, to counterbalance the hugely greater swindle of the sentimental "sweet" writers.

Perhaps I shall have given some notion of my feeling about sex, for which I have been so monotonously abused. When a "serious" young man said to me the other day: "I can't believe in the regeneration of England by sex, you know," I could only say, "I'm sure you can't." He had no sex, anyhow poor, self-conscious, uneasy, narcissus-monk as he was. And he didn't know what it meant, to have any. To him, people only had minds, or no minds, mostly no minds, so they were only there to be gibed at, and he wandered round ineffectively seeking for gibes or for truth, tight shut in inside his own ego.

Now when brilliant young people like this talk to me about sex: or scorn to: I say nothing. There is nothing to say. But I feel a terrible weariness. To them, sex means just plainly and simply, a lady's underclothing, and the fumbling therewith. They have read all the love literature, *Anna Karenina*, all the rest, and looked at statues and pictures of Aphrodite, all very laudable. Yet when it comes to actuality, to today, sex means to them meaningless young women and expensive underthings. Whether they are young men from Oxford, or working men, it is the same. The story from the modish summer resort, where city ladies take up with young mountaineer "dancing partners" for a season—or less—is typical. It was end of September, the summer visitors had almost all gone. Young John, the young mountain farmer, had said goodbye to his "lady" from the capital, and was lounging about alone. "Ho, John! you'll be missing your lady!" "Nay!" he said. "Only she had such nice underclothes."

That is all sex means to them: just the trimmings. The regeneration of England with that? Good God! Poor England, she will have to regenerate the sex in her young people, before they do any regenerating of her. It isn't England that needs regeneration, it is her young.

They accuse me of barbarism. I want to drag England down to the level of savages. But it is this crude stupidity, deadness, about sex which I find barbaric and savage. The man who finds a woman's underclothing the most exciting part about her is a savage. Savages are like that. We read of the woman-savage who wore three overcoats on top of one another to excite her man: and did it. That ghastly crudity of seeing in sex nothing but a functional act and a certain fumbling with clothes is, in my opinion, a low degree of barbarism, savagery. And as far as sex goes, our white civilization is crude, barbaric, and uglily savage: especially England and America.

Witness Bernard Shaw, one of the greatest exponents of our civilization. He says clothes arouse sex and lack of clothes tends to kill sex—speaking of muffled up women or our present bare-armed and barelegged sisters: and scoffs at the Pope for wanting to cover women up; saying that the last person in the world to know anything about sex is the Chief Priest of Europe: and that the one person to ask about it would be the chief Prostitute of Europe, if there were such a person.

Here we see the flippancy and vulgarity of our chief thinkers, at least. The half-naked women of today certainly do not rouse much sexual feeling in the muffled-up men of today—who don't rouse much sexual feeling in the women, either—But why? Why does the bare woman of today rouse so much less sexual feeling than the muffled-up woman of Mr. Shaw's muffled-up eighties? It would be silly to make it a question of mere muffling.

When a woman's sex is in itself dynamic and alive, then it is a power in itself, beyond her reason. And of itself it emits its peculiar spell, drawing men in the first delight of desire. And the woman has to protect herself, hide herself as much as possible. She veils herself in timidity and modesty, because her sex is a power in itself, exposing her to the desire of men. If a woman in whom sex was alive and positive were to expose her naked flesh as women do today, then men would go mad for her. As David was mad for Bathsheba.

But when a woman's sex has lost its dynamic call, and is in a sense dead or static, then the woman *wants* to attract men, for the simple reason that she finds she no longer does attract them. So all the activity that used to be unconscious and delightful becomes conscious and repellant. The woman exposes her flesh more and more, and the more she exposes, the more men are sexually repelled by her. But let us not forget that the men are *socially* thrilled, while sexually repelled. The two things are opposites, today. Socially, men like the gesture of the half-naked woman, half-naked in the street. It is *chic*, it is a declaration of defiance and independence, it is modern, it is free, it is popular because it is strictly asexual, or antisexual. Neither men nor women *want* to feel real desire, today. They want the counterfeit, mental substitute.

But we are very mixed, all of us, and creatures of many diverse and often opposing desires. The very men who encourage women to be most daring and sexless complain most bitterly of the sexlessness of women. The same with women. The women who adore men so tremendously for their social smartness and sexlessness as males, hate them most bitterly for not being "men." In public, *en masse*, and socially, everybody today wants counterfeit sex. But at certain hours in their lives, all individuals hate counterfeit sex with deadly and maddened hate, and those who have dealt it out most perhaps have the wildest hate of it, in the other person—or persons.

The girls of today could muffle themselves up to the eyes, wear crinolines and chignons and all the rest, and though they would not, perhaps, have the peculiar hardening effect on the hearts of men that our half-naked women truly have, neither would they exert any more real sexual attraction. If there is no sex to muffle up, it's no good muffling. Or not much good. Man is often willing to be deceived—for a time—even by muffled-up nothingness.

The point is, when women are sexually alive and quivering and helplessly attractive, beyond their will, then they always cover themselves, and drape themselves with clothes, gracefully. The extravagance of 1880 bustles and such things was only a forewarning of approaching sexlessness.

While sex is a power in itself, women try all kinds of fascinating disguise, and men flaunt. When the Pope insists that women shall cover their naked flesh in church, it is not sex he is opposing, but the sexless tricks of female immodesty. The Pope, and the priests, conclude that the flaunting of naked women's flesh in street and church produces a bad, "unholy" state of mind both in men and women. And they are right. But not because the exposure arouses sexual desire: it doesn't, or very rarely: even Mr. Shaw knows that. But when women's flesh arouses no sort of desire, something is specially wrong! Something is sadly wrong. For the naked arms of women today arouse a feeling of flippancy, cynicism and vulgarity which is indeed the very last feeling to go to church with, if you have any respect for the Church. The bare arms of women in an Italian church are really a mark of disrespect, given the tradition.

The Catholic Church, especially in the south, is neither antisexual, like the northern churches, nor asexual, like Mr. Shaw and such social thinkers. The Catholic Church recognizes sex, and makes of marriage a sacrament based on the sexual communion, for the purpose of procreation. But procreation in the south, is not the bare and scientific fact, and act, that it is in the north. The act of procreation is still charged with all the sensual mystery and importance of the old past. The man is potential creator, and in this has his splendor. All of which has been stripped away by the northern churches and the Shavian logical triviality.

But all this which has gone in the north, the Church has tried to keep in the south, knowing that it is of basic importance in life. The sense of being a potential creator and lawgiver, as father and husband, is perhaps essential to the day-by-day life of a man, if he is to live full and satisfied. The sense of the eternality of marriage is perhaps necessary to the inward peace, both of men and women. Even if it carry a sense of doom, it is necessary. The Catholic Church does not spend its time reminding the people that in heaven there is no marrying nor giving in marriage. It insists: if you marry, you marry forever! And the people accept the decree, the doom, and the dignity of it. To the priest, sex is the clue to marriage and marriage is the clue to the daily life of the people and the Church is the clue to the greater life.

So that sexual lure in itself is not deadly to the Church. Much more deadly is the antisexual defiance of bare arms and flippancy, "freedom," cynicism, irreverence. Sex may be obscene in church, or blasphemous, but never cynical and atheist. Potentially, the bare arms of women today are cynical, atheist, in the dangerous, vulgar form of atheism. Naturally the Church is against it. The Chief Priest of Europe knows more about sex than Mr. Shaw does, anyhow, because he knows more about the essential nature of the human being. Traditionally, he has a thousand years' experience. Mr. Shaw jumped up in a day. And Mr. Shaw, as a dramatist, has jumped up to play tricks with the counterfeit sex of the modern public. No doubt he can do it. So can the cheapest film. But it is equally obvious that he *cannot* touch the deeper sex of the real individual, whose existence he hardly seems to suspect.

And, as a parallel to himself, Mr. Shaw suggests that the Chief Prostitute of Europe would be the one to consult about sex, not the Chief Priest. The parallel is just. The Chief Prostitute of Europe would know truly as much about sex as Mr. Shaw himself does. Which is, not much. Just like Mr. Shaw, the Chief

Prostitute of Europe would know an immense amount about the counterfeit sex of men, the shoddy thing that is worked by tricks. And just like him, she would know nothing at all about the real sex in a man, that has the rhythm of the seasons and the years, the crisis of the winter solstice and the passion of Easter. This the Chief Prostitute would know nothing about, positively, because to be a prostitute she would have to have lost it. But even then, she would know more than Mr. Shaw. She would know that the profound, rhythmic sex of a man's inward life *existed*. She would know, because time and again she would have been up against it. All the literature of the world shows the prostitute's ultimate impotence in sex, her inability to keep a man, her rage against the profound instinct of fidelity in a man, which is, as shown by world history, just a little deeper and more powerful than his instinct of faithless sexual promiscuity. All the literature of the world shows how profound is the instinct of fidelity in both man and woman, how men and women both hanker restlessly after the satisfaction of this instinct, and fret at their own inability to find the real mode of fidelity. The instinct of fidelity is perhaps the deepest instinct in the great complex we call sex. Where there is real sex there is the underlying passion for fidelity. And the prostitute knows this, because she is up against it. She can only keep men who have no real sex, the counterfeits: and these she despises. The men with real sex leave her inevitably, as unable to satisfy their real desire.

The Chief Prostitute knows so much. So does the Pope, if he troubles to think of it, for it is all in the traditional consciousness of the Church. But the Chief Dramatist knows nothing of it. He has a curious blank in his makeup. To him, all sex is infidelity and only infidelity is sex. Marriage is sexless, null. Sex is only manifested in infidelity, and the queen of sex is the chief prostitute. If sex crops up in marriage, it is because one party falls in love with somebody else, and wants to be unfaithful. Infidelity is sex, and prostitutes know all about it. Wives know nothing and are nothing in that respect.

This is the teaching of the Chief Dramatists and Chief Thinkers of our generation. And the vulgar public agrees with them entirely. Sex is a thing you don't have except to be naughty with. Apart from naughtiness, that is, apart from infidelity and fornication, sex doesn't exist. Our chief thinkers, ending in the flippantly cocksure Mr. Shaw, have taught this trash so thoroughly, that it has almost become a fact. Sex is almost nonexistent, apart from the counterfeit forms of prostitution and shallow fornication. And marriage is empty, hollow.

Now this question of sex and marriage is of paramount importance. Our social life is established on marriage, and marriage, the sociologists say, is established upon property. Marriage has been found the best method of conserving property and stimulating production. Which is all there is to it.

But is it? We are just in the throes of a great revolt against marriage, a passionate revolt against its ties and restrictions. In fact, at least three-quarters of the unhappiness of modern life could be laid at the door of marriage. There are few married people today, and few unmarried, who have not felt an intense and vivid hatred against marriage itself, marriage as an institution and an imposition upon human life. Far greater than the revolt against governments is this revolt against marriage.

And everybody, pretty well, takes it for granted that as soon as we can find a possible way out of it, marriage will be abolished. The Soviet abolishes marriage: or did. If new "modern" states spring up, they will almost certainly follow suit. They will try to find some social substitute for marriage, and abolish the hated yoke of conjugality. State support of motherhood, state support of children, and independence of women. It is on the programme of every great scheme of reform. And it means, of course, the abolition of marriage.

The only question to ask ourselves is, do we really want it? Do we want the absolute independence of women, state support of motherhood and of children, and consequent doing away with the necessity of marriage? Do we want it? Because all that matters is that men and women shall do what they *really* want to do. Though here, as everywhere, we must remember that man has a double set of desires, the shallow and the profound, the personal, superficial, temporary desires, and the inner, impersonal, great desires that are fulfilled in long periods of time. The desires of the moment are easy to recognize, but the others, the deeper ones, are difficult. It is the business of our Chief Thinkers to tell us of our deeper desires, not to keep shrilling our little desires in our ears.

Now the Church is established upon a recognition of some, at least, of the greatest and deepest desires in man, desires that take years, or a lifetime, or even centuries to fulfill. And the Church, celibate as its priesthood may be, built as it may be upon the lonely rock of Peter, or of Paul, really rests upon the indissolubility of marriage. Make marriage in any serious degree unstable, dissoluble, destroy the permanency of marriage, and the Church falls. Witness the enormous decline of the Church of England.

The reason being that the Church is established upon the element of *union* in mankind. And the first element of union in the Christian world is the marriage tie. The marriage tie, the marriage bond, take it which way you like, is the fundamental connecting link in Christian society. Break it, and you will have to go back to the overwhelming dominance of the State, which existed before the Christian era. The Roman State was all-powerful, the Roman Fathers represented the State, the Roman family was the father's estate, held more or less in fee for the State itself. It was the same in Greece, with not so much feeling for the *permanence* of property, but rather a dazzling splash of the moment's possessions. The family was much more insecure in Greece than in Rome.

But, in either case, the family was the man, as representing the State. There are States where the family is the woman: or there have been. There are States where the family hardly exists, priest States where the priestly control is everything, even functioning as family control. Then there is the Soviet State, where again family is not supposed to exist, and the State controls every individual direct, mechanically, as the great religious States, such as early Egypt, may have controlled every individual direct, through priestly surveillance and ritual.

Now the question is, do we want to go back, or forward, to any of these forms of State control? Do we want to be like the Romans under the Empire, or even under the Republic? Do we want to be, as far as our family and our freedom is concerned, like the Greek citizens of a City State in Hellas? Do we want to imagine ourselves in the strange priest-controlled, ritual-fulfilled condition of the earlier Egyptians? Do we want to be bullied by a Soviet?

For my part, I have to say NO! every time. And having said it, we have to come back and consider the famous saying, that perhaps the greatest contribution to the social life of man made by Christianity is—marriage. Christianity brought marriage into the world: marriage as we know it. Christianity established the little autonomy of the family within the greater rule of the State. Christianity made marriage in some respects inviolate, not to be violated by the State. It is marriage, perhaps, which had given man the best of his freedom, given him his little kingdom of his own within the big kingdom of the State, given him his foothold of independence on which to stand and resist an unjust State. Man and wife, a king and queen with one or two subjects, and a few square yards of territory of their own: this, really, is marriage. It is a true freedom because it is a true fulfillment, for man, woman, and children.

Do we, then, want to break marriage? If we do break it, it means we all fall to a far greater extent under the direct sway of the State. Do we want to fall under the direct sway of the State, any State? For my part, I don't.

And the Church created marriage by making it a sacrament, a sacrament of man and woman united in the sex communion, and never to be separated, except by death. And even when separated by death, still not freed from the marriage. Marriage, as far as the individual went, eternal. Marriage, making one complete body out of two incomplete ones, and providing for the complex development of the man's soul and the woman's soul in unison, throughout a lifetime. Marriage sacred and inviolable, the great way of earthly fulfillment for man and woman, in unison, under the spiritual rule of the Church.

This is Christianity's great contribution to the life of man, and it is only too easily overlooked. Is it, or is it not, a great step in the direction of life fulfillment, for men and women? Is it, or is it not? Is marriage a great help to the fulfillment of man and woman, or is it a frustration? It is a very important question indeed, and every man and woman must answer it.

If we are to take the Nonconformist, protestant idea of ourselves: that we are all isolated individual souls, and our supreme business is to save our own souls; then marriage surely is a hindrance. If I am only out to save my own soul, I'd better leave marriage alone. As the monks and hermits knew. But also, if I am only out to save other people's souls, I had also best leave marriage alone, as the apostles knew, and the preaching saints.

But supposing I am neither bent on saving my own soul nor other people's souls? Supposing Salvation seems incomprehensible to me, as I confess it does. "Being saved" seems to me just jargon, the jargon of self-conceit. Supposing, then, that I cannot see this Savior and Salvation stuff, supposing that I see the soul as something which must be developed and fulfilled throughout a lifetime, sustained and nourished, developed and further fulfilled, to the very end; what then?

Then I realize that marriage, or something like it, is essential, and that the old Church knew best the enduring needs of man, beyond the spasmodic needs of today and yesterday. The Church established marriage for life, for the fulfillment of the soul's living life, not postponing it till the after-death.

The old Church knew that life is here our portion, to be lived, to be lived in fulfillment. The stern rule of Benedict, the wild flights of Francis of Assisi, these were coruscations in the steady heaven of the Church. The rhythm of life itself was preserved by the Church hour by hour, day by day, season by season, year by year, epoch by epoch, down among the people, and the wild coruscations were accommodated to this permanent rhythm. We feel it, in the south, in the country, when we hear the jangle of the bells at dawn, at noon, at sunset, marking the hours with the sound of mass or prayers. It is the rhythm of the daily sun. We feel it in the festivals, the processions, Christmas, the Three Kings, Easter, Pentecost, St. John's Day, All Saints, All Souls. This is the wheeling of the year, the movement of the sun through solstice and equinox, the coming of the seasons, the going of the seasons. And it is the inward rhythm of man and woman, too, the sadness of Lent, the delight of Easter, the wonder of Pentecost, the fires of St. John, the candles on the graves of All Souls, the lit-up tree of Christmas, all representing kindled rhythmic emotions in the souls of men and women. And men experience the great rhythm of emotion man-wise, women experience it woman-wise, and in the unison of men and women it is complete.

Augustine said that God created the universe new every day: and to the living, emotional soul, this is true. Every dawn dawns upon an entirely new universe, every Easter lights up an entirely new glory of a new world opening in utterly new flower. And the soul of man and the soul of woman is new in the same way, with the infinite delight of life and the ever-newness of life. So a man and a woman are new to one another throughout a lifetime, in the rhythm of marriage that matches the rhythm of the year.

Sex is the balance of male and female in the universe, the attraction, the repulsion, the transit of neutrality, the new attraction, the new repulsion, always different, always new. The long neuter spell of Lent, when the blood is low, and the delight of the Easter kiss, the sexual revel of spring, the passion of midsummer, the slow recoil, revolt, and grief of autumn, grayness again, then the sharp stimulus of winter of the long nights. Sex goes through the rhythm of the year, in man and woman, ceaselessly changing: the rhythm of the sun in his relation to the earth. Oh, what a catastrophe for man when he cut himself off from the rhythm of the year, from his unison with the sun and the earth. Oh, what a catastrophe, what a maiming of love when it was made a personal, merely personal feeling, taken away from the rising and the setting of the sun, and cut off from the magic connection of the solstice and the equinox! This is what is the matter with us. We are bleeding at the roots, because we are cut off from the earth and sun and stars, and love is a grinning mockery, because, poor blossom, we plucked it from its stem on the tree of Life, and expected it to keep on blooming in our civilized vase on the table.

Marriage is the clue to human life, but there is no marriage apart from the wheeling sun and the nodding earth, from the straying of the planets and the magnificence of the fixed stars. Is not a man different, utterly different, at dawn from what he is at sunset? and a woman too? And does not the changing harmony and discord of their variation make the secret music of life?

And is it not so throughout life? A man is different at thirty, at forty, at fifty, at sixty, at seventy: and the woman at his side is different. But is there not some strange conjunction in their differences? Is there not some peculiar harmony, through youth, the period of childbirth, the period of florescence and young children, the period of the woman's change of life, painful yet also a renewal, the period of waning passion but mellowing delight of affection, the dim, unequal period of the approach of death, when the man and woman look at one another with the dim apprehension of separation that is not really a separation: is there not, throughout it all, some unseen, unknown interplay of balance, harmony, completion, like some soundless symphony which moves with a rhythm from phase to phase, so different, so very different in the various movements, and yet one symphony, made out of the soundless singing of two strange and incompatible lives, a man's and a woman's?

This is marriage, the mystery of marriage, marriage which fulfills itself here, in this life. We may well believe that in heaven there is no marrying or giving in marriage. All this has to be fulfilled here, and if it is not fulfilled here, it will never be fulfilled. The great saints only live, even Jesus only lives to add a new fulfillment and a new beauty to the permanent sacrament of marriage.

But—and this *but* crashes through our heart like a bullet—marriage is no marriage that is not basically and permanently phallic, and that is not linked up with the sun and the earth, the moon and the fixed stars and the planets, in the rhythm of days, in the rhythm of months, in the rhythm of quarters, of years, of decades and of centuries. Marriage is no marriage that is not a correspondence of blood. For the blood is the substance of the soul, and of the deepest consciousness. It is by blood that we are: and it is by the heart and the liver that we live and move and have our being. In the blood, knowing and being, or feeling, are one and undivided: no serpent and no apple has caused a split. So that only when the conjunction is of the blood, is marriage truly marriage. The blood of man and the blood of woman are two eternally different streams, that can never be mingled. Even scientifically we know it. But therefore they are the two rivers that encircle the whole of life, and in marriage the circle is complete, and in sex the two rivers touch and renew one another, without ever commingling or confusing. We know it. The phallus is a column of blood that fills the valley of blood of a woman. The great river of male blood touches to its depths the great river of female blood—yet neither breaks its bounds. It is the deepest of all communions, as all the religions, in practice, know. And it is one of the greatest mysteries, in fact, the greatest, as almost every initiation shows, showing the supreme achievement of the mystic marriage.

And this is the meaning of the sexual act: this Communion, this touching on one another of the two rivers, Euphrates and Tigris—to use old jargon—and the enclosing of the land of Mesopotamia, where Paradise was, or the Park of Eden, where man had his beginning. This is marriage, this circuit of the two rivers, this communion of the two bloodstreams, this, and nothing else: as all the religions know.

Two rivers of blood, are man and wife, two distinct eternal streams, that have the power of touching and communing and so renewing, making new one another, without any breaking of the subtle confines, any confusing or commingling. And the phallus is the connecting link between the two rivers, that establishes the two streams in a oneness, and gives out of their duality a single circuit, forever. And this, this oneness gradually accomplished throughout a lifetime in twoness, is the highest achievement of time or eternity. From it all things human spring, children and beauty and well-made things; all the true creations of humanity. And all we know of the will of God is that He wishes this, this oneness, to take place, fulfilled over a lifetime, this oneness within the great dual bloodstream of humanity.

Man dies, and woman dies, and perhaps separate the souls go back to the Creator. Who knows? But we know that the oneness of the bloodstream of man and woman in marriage completes the universe, as far as humanity is concerned, completes the streaming of the sun and the flowing of the stars.

There is, of course, the counterpart to all this, the counterfeit. There is counterfeit marriage, like nearly all marriage today. Modern people are just personalities, and modern marriage takes place when two people are "thrilled" by each other's personality: when they have the same tastes in furniture or books or sport or amusement, when they love "talking" to one another, when they admire one another's "minds." Now this, this affinity of mind and personality is an excellent basis of friendship between the sexes, but a disastrous basis for marriage. Because marriage inevitably starts the sex-activity, and the sex-activity is, and always was and will be, in some way hostile to the mental, *personal* relationship between man and woman. It is almost an axiom that the marriage of two *personalities* will end in a startling physical hatred. People who are personally devoted to one another at first end by hating one another with a hate which they cannot account for, which they try to hide, for it makes them ashamed, and which is none the less only too painfully obvious, especially to one another. In people of strong individual feeling the irritation that accumulates in marriage increases only too often to a point of rage that is close akin to madness. And, apparently, all without reason.

But the real reason is, that the exclusive sympathy of nerves and mind and personal interest is, alas, hostile to blood-sympathy, in the sexes. The modern cult of personality is excellent for friendship between the sexes, and fatal for marriage. On the whole, it would be better if modern people didn't marry. They could remain so much more true to what they are, to their own personality.

But marriage or no marriage, the fatal thing happens. If you have only known personal sympathy and personal love, then rage and hatred will sooner or later take possession of the soul, because of the frustration and denial of bloodsympathy, blood-contact. In celibacy, the denial is withering and souring, but in marriage, the denial produces a sort of rage. And we can no more avoid this, nowadays, than we can avoid thunderstorms. It is part of the phenomenon of the psyche. The important point is that sex itself comes to subserve the personality and the personal "love" entirely, without ever giving sexual satisfaction or fulfillment. In fact, there is probably far more sexual activity in a "personal" marriage than in a blood-marriage. Woman sighs for a perpetual lover: and in the personal marriage, relatively, she gets him. And how she comes to hate him, with his never-ending desire, which never gets anywhere or fulfills anything!

It is a mistake I have made, talking of sex I have always inferred that sex meant blood-sympathy and blood-contact. Technically this is so. But as a matter of fact, nearly all modern sex is a pure matter of nerves, cold and bloodless. This is personal sex. And this white, cold, nervous, "poetic" personal sex, which is practically all the sex that moderns know, has a very peculiar physiological effect, as well as psychological. The two blood-streams are brought into contact, in man and woman, just the same as in the urge of blood-passion and blood-desire. But whereas the contact in the urge of blood-desire is positive, making a newness in the blood, in the insistence of this nervous, personal desire the blood-contact becomes frictional and destructive, there is a resultant whitening and impoverishment of the blood. Personal or nervous or spiritual sex is destructive to the blood, has a katabolistic activity, whereas coition in warm blood-desire is an activity of metabolism. The katabolism of "nervous" sex-activity may produce for a time a sort of ecstasy and a heightening of consciousness. But this, like the effect of alcohol or drugs, is the result of the decomposition of certain corpuscles in the blood, and is a process of impoverishment. This is one of the many reasons for the failure of energy in modern people; sexual activity, which ought to be refreshing and renewing, becomes exhaustive and debilitating. So that when the young man fails to believe in the regeneration of England by sex, I am constrained to agree with him. Since modern sex is practically all personal and nervous, and, in effect, exhaustive, disintegrative. The disintegrative effect of modern sex activity is undeniable. It is only less fatal than the disintegrative effect of masturbation, which is more deadly still.

So that at last I begin to see the point of my critics' abuse of my exalting of sex. They only know one form of sex: in fact, to them there *is* only one form of sex: the nervous, personal, disintegrative sort, the "white" sex. And this, of course, is something to be flowery and false about, but nothing to be very hopeful about. I quite agree. And I quite agree, we can have no hope of the regeneration of England from such sort of sex.

At the same time, I cannot see any hope of regeneration for a sexless England. An England that has lost its sex seems to me nothing to feel very hopeful about. And nobody feels very hopeful about it. Though I may have been a fool for insisting on sex where the current sort of sex is just what I *don't* mean and *don't* want, still I can't go back on it all and believe in the regeneration of England by pure sexlessness. A sexless England!—it doesn't ring very hopeful, to me.

And the other, the warm blood-sex that establishes the living and revitalizing connection between man and woman, how are we to get that back? I don't know. Yet get it back we must: or the younger ones must, or we are all lost. For the bridge to the future is the phallus, and there's the end of it. But not the poor, nervous counterfeit phallus of modern "nervous" love. Not that.

For the new impulse to life will never come without blood-contact; the true, positive blood-contact, not the nervous negative reaction. And the essential blood-contact is between man and woman, always has been so, always will be. The contact of positive sex. The homosexual contacts are secondary, even if not merely substitutes of exasperated reaction from the utterly unsatisfactory nervous sex between men and women.

If England is to be regenerated—to use the phrase of the young man who seemed to think there was need of *regeneration*—the very word is his—then it will be by the arising of a new blood-contact, a new touch, and a new marriage. It will be a phallic rather than a sexual regeneration. For the phallus is only the great old symbol of godly vitality in a man, and of immediate contact.

It will also be a renewal of marriage: the true phallic marriage. And, still further, it will be marriage set again in relationship to the rhythmic cosmos. The rhythm of the cosmos is something we cannot get away from, without bitterly impoverishing our lives. The Early Christians tried to kill the old pagan rhythm of cosmic ritual, and to some extent succeeded. They killed the planets and the zodiac, perhaps because astrology had already become debased to fortune telling. They wanted to kill the festivals of the year. But the Church, which knows that man doth not live by man alone, but by the sun and moon and earth in their revolutions, restored the sacred days and feasts almost as the pagans had them, and the Christian peasants went on very much as the pagan peasants had gone, with the sunrise pause for worship, and the sunset, and noon, the three great daily moments of the sun: then the new holy-day, one in the ancient seven-cycle: then Easter and the dying and rising of God, Pentecost, Midsummer Fire, the November dead and the spirits of the grave, then Christmas, then Three Kings. For centuries the mass of people lived in this rhythm, under the Church. And it is down in the mass that the roots of religion are eternal. When the mass of a people loses the religious rhythm, that people is dead, without hope. But Protestantism came and gave a great blow to the religious and ritualistic rhythm of the year, in human life. Nonconformity *almost* finished the deed. Now you have a poor, blind, disconnected people with nothing but politics and bank holidays to satisfy the eternal human need of living in ritual adjustment to the cosmos in its revolutions, in eternal submission to the greater laws. And marriage, being one of the greater necessities, has suffered the same from the loss of the sway of the greater laws, the cosmic rhythms which should sway life always. Mankind has got to get back to the rhythm of the cosmos, and the permanence of marriage.

All this is postscript, or afterthought, to my novel, *Lady Chatterley's Lover*. Man has little needs and deeper needs. We have fallen into the mistake of living from our little needs till we have almost lost our deeper needs in a sort of madness. There is a little morality, which concerns persons and the little needs of man: and this, alas, is the morality we live by. But there is a deeper morality, which concerns all womanhood, all manhood, and nations, and races, and classes of men. This greater morality affects the destiny of mankind over long stretches of time, applies to man's greater needs, and is often in conflict with the little morality of the little needs. The tragic consciousness has taught us, even, that one of the greater needs of man is a knowledge and experience of death; every man needs to know death in his own body. But the greater consciousness of the pre-tragic and post-tragic epochs teaches us—though we have not yet reached the post-tragic epoch—that the greatest need of man is the renewal forever of the complete rhythm of life and death, the rhythm of the sun's year, the body's year of a lifetime, and the greater year of the stars, the soul's year of immortality. This is our need, our imperative need. It is a need of the mind and soul, body, spirit and sex: all. It is no use asking for a Word to fulfill such a need. No Word, no Logos, no Utterance will ever do it. The Word is uttered, most of it: we need only pay true attention. But who will call us to the Deed, the great Deed of the Seasons and the year, the Deed of the soul's cycle, the Deed of a woman's life at one with a man's, the little Deed of the moon's wandering, the bigger Deed of the sun's, and the biggest, of the great still stars? It is the *Deed* of life we have now to learn: we are supposed to have learnt the Word, but, alas, look at us. Word-perfect we may be, but Deed-demented. Let us prepare now for the death of our present "little" life, and the reemergence in a bigger life, in touch with the moving cosmos.

It is a question, practically, of relationship. We *must* get back into relation, vivid and nourishing relation to the cosmos and the universe. The way is through daily ritual, and the reawakening. We *must* once more practise the ritual of dawn and noon and sunset, the ritual of the kindling fire and pouring water, the ritual of the first breath, and the last. This is an affair of the individual and the household, a ritual of day. The ritual of the moon in her phases, of the morning star and the evening star is for men and women separate. Then the ritual of the seasons, with the Drama and the Passion of the soul embodied in procession and dance, this is for the community, an act of men and women, a whole community, in togetherness. And the ritual of the great events in the year of stars is for nations and whole peoples. To these rituals we must return: or we must evolve them to suit our needs. For the truth is, we are perishing for lack of fulfillment of our greater needs, we are cut off from the great sources of our inward nourishment and renewal, sources which flow eternally in the universe. Vitally, the human race is dying. It is like a great uprooted tree, with its roots in the air. We must plant ourselves again in the universe.

It means a return to ancient forms. But we shall have to create these forms again, and it is more difficult than the preaching of an evangel. The Gospel came to tell us we were all saved. We look at the world today and realize that humanity, alas, instead of being saved from sin, whatever that may be, is almost completely lost, lost to life, and near to nullity and extermination. We have to go back, a long way, before the idealist conceptions began, before Plato, before the tragic idea of life arose, to get onto our feet again. For the gospel of salvation through the Ideals and escape from the body coincided with the tragic conception of human life. Salvation and tragedy are the same thing, and they are now both beside the point.

Back, before the idealist religions and philosophies arose and started man on the great excursion of tragedy. The last three thousand years of mankind have been an excursion into ideals, bodilessness, and tragedy, and now the excursion is over. And it is like the end of a tragedy in the theater. The stage is strewn with dead bodies, worse still, with meaningless bodies, and the curtain comes down.

But in life, the curtain never comes down on the scene. There the dead bodies lie, and the inert ones, and somebody has to clear them away, somebody has to carry on. It is the day after. Today is already the day after the end of the tragic and idealist epoch. Utmost inertia falls on the remaining protagonists. Yet we have to carry on.

Now we have to reestablish the great relationships which the grand idealists, with their underlying pessimism, their belief that life is nothing but futile conflict, to be avoided even unto death, destroyed for us. Buddha, Plato, Jesus, they were all three utter pessimists as regards life, teaching that the only happiness lay in abstracting oneself from life, the daily, yearly, seasonal life of birth and death and fruition, and in living in the "immutable" or eternal spirit. But now, after almost three thousand years, now that we are almost abstracted entirely from the rhythmic life of the seasons, birth and death and fruition, now we realize that such abstraction is neither bliss nor liberation, but nullity. It brings null inertia. And the great saviors and teachers only cut us off from life. It was the tragic *excursus*.

The universe is dead for us, and how is it to come to life again? "Knowledge" has killed the sun, making it a ball of gas, with spots; "knowledge" has killed the moon, it is a dead little earth fretted with extinct craters as with smallpox; the machine has killed the earth for us, making it a surface, more or less bumpy, that you travel over. How, out of all this, are we to get back the grand orbs of the soul's heavens, that fill us with unspeakable joy? How are we to get back Apollo, and Attis, Demeter, Persephone, and the halls of Dis? How even see the star Hesperus, or Betelguese?

We've got to get them back, for they are the world our soul, our greater consciousness, lives in. The world of reason and science, the moon, a dead lump of earth, the sun, so much gas with spots: this is the dry and sterile little world the abstracted mind inhabits. The world of our little consciousness, which we know in our pettifogging *apartness*. This is how we know the world when we know it apart from ourselves, in the mean separateness of everything. When we know the world in togetherness with ourselves, we know the earth hyacinthine or Plutonic, we know the moon gives us our body as delight upon us, or steals it away, we know the purring of the great gold lion of the sun, who licks us like a lioness her cubs, making us bold, or else, like the red, angry lion, dashes at us with open claws. There are many ways of knowing, there are many sorts of knowledge. But the two ways of knowing, for man, are knowing in terms of apartness, which is mental, rational, scientific, and knowing in terms of togetherness, which is religious and poetic. The Christian religion lost, in Protestantism finally, the togetherness with the universe, the togetherness of the body, the sex, the emotions, the passions, with the earth and sun and stars.

But relationship is threefold. First, there is the relation to the living universe. Then comes the relation of man to woman. Then comes the relation of man to man. And each is a blood-relationship, not mere spirit or mind. We have abstracted the universe into Matter and Force, we have abstracted men and women into separate personalities—personalities being isolated units, incapable of togetherness—so that all three great relationships are bodiless, dead.

None, however, is quite so dead as the man-to-man relationship. I think, if we came to analyze to the last what men feel about one another today, we should find that every man feels every other man as a menace. It is a curious thing, but the more mental and ideal men are, the more they seem to feel the bodily presence of any other man a menace, a menace, as it were, to their very being. Every man that comes near me threatens my very existence: nay, more, my very being.

This is the ugly fact which underlies our civilization. As the advertisement of one of the war novels said, it is an epic of "friendship and hope, mud and blood," which means, of course, that the friendship and hope must end in mud and blood.

When the great crusade against sex and the body started in full blast with Plato, it was a crusade for "ideals," and for this "spiritual" knowledge in apartness. Sex is the great unifier. In its big, slower vibration it is the warmth of heart which makes people happy together, in togetherness. The idealist philosophies and religions set out deliberately to kill this. And they did it. Now they have done it. The last great ebullition of friendship and hope was squashed out in mud and blood. Now men are all separate little entities. While "kindness" is the glib order of the day—everybody *must* be "kind"—underneath this "kindness" we find a coldness of heart, a lack of heart, a callousness, that is very dreary. Every man *is* a menace to every other man.

Men only know one another in menace. Individualism has triumphed. If I am a sheer individual, then every other being, every other man especially, is over against me as a menace to me. This is the peculiarity of our society today. We are all extremely sweet and "nice" to one another, because we merely fear one another.

The sense of isolation, followed by the sense of menace and of fear, is bound to arise as the feeling of oneness and community with our fellowmen declines, and the feeling of individualism and personality, which is existence in isolation, increases. The so-called "cultured" classes are the first to develop "personality" and individualism, and the first to fall into this state of unconscious menace and fear. The working classes retain the old blood-warmth of oneness and togetherness some decades longer. Then they lose it too. And then class-consciousness becomes rampant, and class-hate. Class-hate and class-consciousness are only a sign that the old togetherness, the old blood-warmth has collapsed, and every man is really aware of himself in apartness. Then we have these hostile groupings of men for the sake of opposition, strife. Civil strife becomes a necessary condition of self-assertion.

This, again, is the tragedy of social life today. In the old England, the curious blood-connection held the classes together. The squires might be arrogant, violent, bullying and unjust, yet in some ways they were *at one* with the people, part of the same blood-stream. We feel it in Defoe or Fielding. And then, in the mean Jane Austen, it is gone. Already this old maid typifies "personality" instead of character, the sharp knowing in apartness instead of knowing in togetherness, and she is, to my feeling, thoroughly unpleasant, English in the bad, mean, snobbish sense of the word, just as Fielding is English in the good, generous sense.

So, in *Lady Chatterley's Lover* we have a man, Sir Clifford, who is purely a personality, having lost entirely all connection with his fellowmen and women, except those of usage. All warmth is gone entirely, the hearth is cold, the heart does not humanly exist. He is a pure product of our civilization, but he is the death of the great humanity of the world. He is kind by rule, but he does not know what warm sympathy means. He is what he is. And he loses the woman of his choice.

The other man still has the warmth of a man, but he is being hunted down, destroyed. Even it is a question if the woman who turns to him will really stand by him and his vital meaning.

I have been asked many times if I intentionally made Clifford paralyzed, if it is symbolic. And literary friends say, it would have been better to have left him whole and potent, and to have made the woman leave him nevertheless.

As to whether the "symbolism" is intentional—I don't know. Certainly not in the beginning, when Clifford was created. When I created Clifford and Connie, I had no idea what they were or why they were. They just came, pretty much as they are. But the novel was written, from start to finish, three times. And when I read the first version, I recognized that the lameness of Clifford was symbolic of the paralysis, the deeper emotional or passional paralysis, of most men of his sort and class today. I realized that it was perhaps taking an unfair advantage of Connie, to paralyze him technically. It made it so much more vulgar of her to leave him. Yet the story came as it did, by itself, so I left it alone. Whether we call it symbolism or not, it is, in the sense of its happening, inevitable.

And these notes, which I write now almost two years after the novel was finished, are not intended to explain or expound anything: only to give the emotional beliefs which perhaps are necessary as a background to the book. It is so obviously a book written in defiance of convention that perhaps some reason should be offered for the attitude of defiance: since the silly desire to *épater le bourgeois*, to bewilder the commonplace person, is not worth entertaining. If I use the taboo words, there is a reason. We shall never free the phallic reality from the "uplift" taint till we give it its own phallic language, and use the obscene words. The greatest blasphemy of all against the phallic reality is this "lifting it to a higher plane." Likewise, if the lady marries the gamekeeper—she hasn't done it yet—it is not class-spite, but in spite of class.

Finally, there are the correspondents who complain that I describe the pirated editions—some of them—but not the original. The original first edition, issued in Florence, is bound in hard covers, dullish mulberry-red paper with my phoenix (symbol of immortality, the bird rising new from the nest of flames) printed in black on the cover, and a white paper label on the back. The paper is good, creamy hand-rolled Italian paper, but the print, though nice, is ordinary, and the binding is just the usual binding of a little Florentine shop. There is no expert bookmaking in it: yet it is a pleasant volume, much more so than many far "superior" books.

And if there are many spelling errors—there are—it is because the book was set up in a little Italian printing shop, such a family affair, in which nobody knew one word of English. They none of them knew any English at all, so they were spared all blushes: and the proofs were terrible. The printer would do fairly well for a few pages, then he would go drunk, or something. And then the words danced weird and *macabre*, but not English. So that if still some of the hosts of errors exist, it is a mercy they are not more.

Then one paper wrote pitying the poor printer who was deceived into printing the book. Not deceived at all. A white-moustached little man who has just married a second wife, he was told: Now the book contains such-and-such words, in English, and it describes certain things. Don't you print it if you think it will get you into trouble!—What does it describe?" he asked. And when told, he said, with the short indifference of a Florentine: "O! *ma*! but we do it every day!"—And it seemed, to him, to settle the matter entirely. Since it was nothing political or out of the way, there was nothing to think about. Everyday concerns, commonplace.

But it was a struggle, and the wonder is the book came out as well as it did. There was just enough type to set up a half of it: so the half was set up, the thousand copies were printed and, as a measure of caution, the two hundred on ordinary paper, the little second edition, as well: then the type was distributed, and the second half set up.

Then came the struggle of delivery. The book was stopped by the American customs almost at once. Fortunately in England there was a delay. So that practically the whole edition—at least eight hundred copies, surely—must have gone to England.

Then came the storms of vulgar vituperation. But they were inevitable. "But we do it every day," says a little Italian printer. "Monstrous and horrible!" shrieks a section of the British press. "Thank you for a really sexual book about sex, at last. I am so tired of asexual books," says one of the most distinguished citizens of Florence to me—an Italian. "I don't know—I don't know—if it's not a bit too strong," says a timid Florentine critic—an Italian. "Listen, Signor Lawrence, you find it really necessary to *say* it?" I told him I did, and he pondered—"Well, one of them was a brainy vamp, and the other was a sexual moron," said an American woman, referring to the two men in the book—"so I'm afraid Connie had a poor choice—*as usual*!"